BY KATHLEEN DOHERTY

ILLUSTRATED BY
CHIP WASS

DON'T FEED THE BEAR

STERLING CHILDREN'S BOOKS
New York

Bear loved when campers left him grub.

Mac and cheese . . .
carrot cake . . . meatball stew!

Early one morning, Bear heard

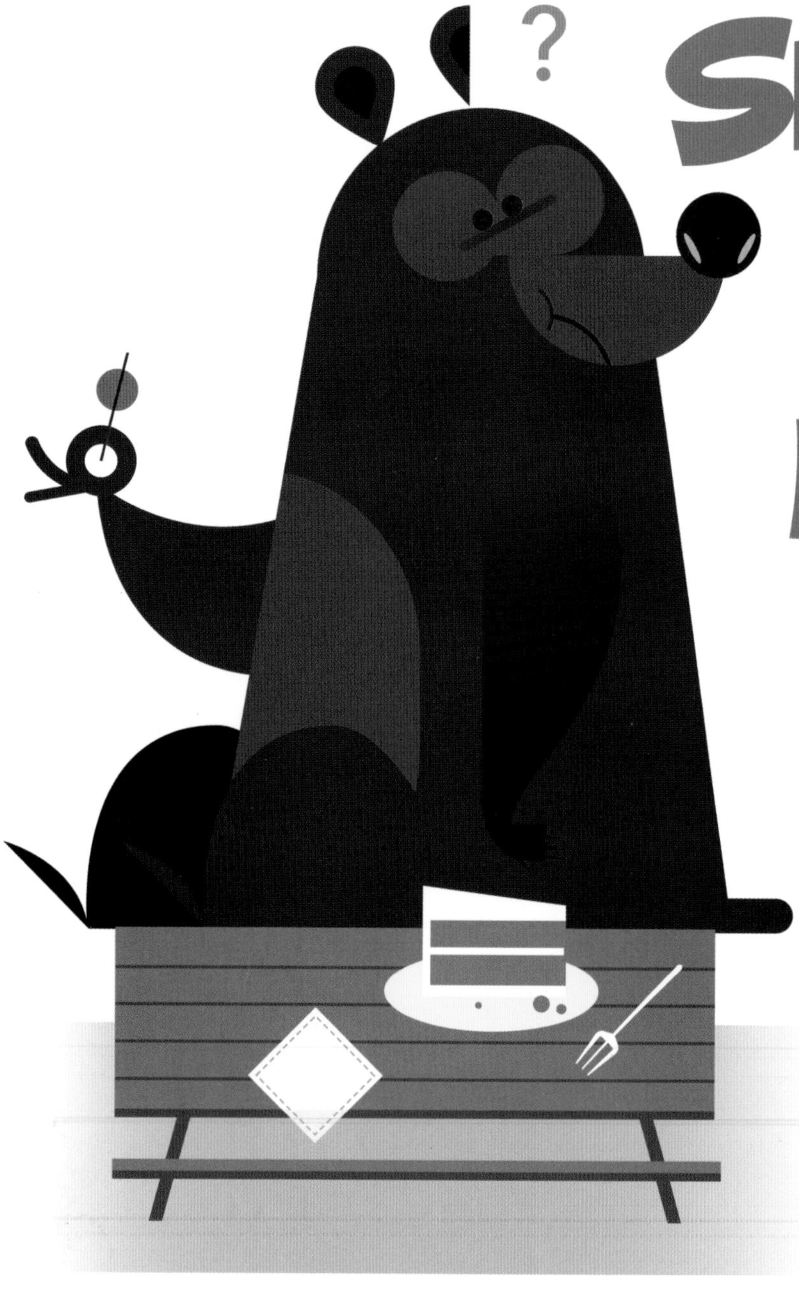

SMACKiTY! SMACK! WHOMP!

**He clomped off
to investigate.**

The ranger was pounding
a sign into the ground.

DON'T FEED
THE BEAR

INFORMATION, ASYMMETRIC

INFORMATION, ECONOMICS OF

INFORMED CONSENT

INGRATIATION

INHERITANCE

INHERITANCE TAX

INIKORI, JOSEPH

INITIAL PUBLIC OFFERING (IPO)

INITIATIVE

INPUT-OUTPUT MATRIX

INSTITUTIONAL REVIEW BOARD

INSTITUTIONALISM

INSTRUMENTAL VARIABLES
  REGRESSION

INSURANCE

INSURANCE INDUSTRY

INTEGRATED PUBLIC USE
  MICRODATA SERIES

INTEGRATION

INTELLECTUALISM, ANTI-

INTELLECTUALS, ORGANIC

INTELLECTUALS, PUBLIC

INTELLECTUALS, VERNACULAR

INTELLIGENCE

INTELLIGENCE, SOCIAL

INTERACTIONISM, SYMBOLIC

INTEREST, NATURAL RATE OF

INTEREST, NEUTRAL RATE OF

INTEREST, OWN RATE OF

INTEREST, REAL RATE OF

INTEREST GROUPS AND INTERESTS

INTEREST RATES

INTEREST RATES, NOMINAL

INTERGENERATIONAL
  TRANSMISSION

INTERGROUP RELATIONS

INTERNATIONAL ECONOMIC
  ORDER

INTERNATIONAL MONETARY FUND

INTERNATIONAL
  NONGOVERNMENTAL
  ORGANIZATIONS (INGOs)

INTERNATIONAL RELATIONS

INTERNATIONALISM

INTERNET

INTERNET, IMPACT ON POLITICS

INTERNET BUBBLE

INTERROGATION

INTERSECTIONALITY

INTERSUBJECTIVITY

INTERVENTIONS, SOCIAL POLICY

INTERVENTIONS, SOCIAL SKILLS

INTERWAR YEARS

INTIFADA, THE

INUIT

INVENTORIES

INVERSE MATRIX

INVESTMENT

INVESTORS

INVESTORS, INSTITUTIONAL

INVOLUNTARY UNEMPLOYMENT

IQ CONTROVERSY

IRAN-CONTRA AFFAIR

IRAN-IRAQ WAR

IRANIAN REVOLUTION

IRAQ-U.S. WAR

IRISH REPUBLICAN ARMY

IRON CURTAIN

IROQUOIS

IRRIGATION

ISLAM, SHIA AND SUNNI

IS-LM MODEL

ISOLATIONISM

J

JACOBIAN MATRIX

JACOBINISM

JACOBS, JANE

JAINISM

JAJMANI MATRIX

JAMES, C. L. R.

JAMES, WILLIAM

JANATA PARTY

JANOWITZ, MORRIS

JAPANESE AMERICANS

JAZZ

J-CURVE

JEFFERSON, THOMAS

JENCKS, CHRISTOPHER

JERVIS, ROBERT

JESUS CHRIST

JEWISH DIASPORA

JEWS

JIHAD

JIM CROW

JINGOISM

JINNAH, MOHAMMED ALI

JOB GUARANTEE

JOHANSON, DONALD

JOHN HENRYISM

JOHNSON, LYNDON B.

JONES, EDWARD ELLSWORTH

JOURNALISM

JOURNALS, PROFESSIONAL

JUÁREZ, BENITO

JUDAISM

JUDICIAL REVIEW

JUDICIARY

JUNG, CARL

JURISPRUDENCE

JURORS, DEATH-QUALIFIED

JURY SELECTION

JUST WAR

JUSTICE

JUSTICE, DISTRIBUTIVE

JUSTICE, SOCIAL

K

KAHN, RICHARD F.

KALECKI, MICHAL

KANT, IMMANUEL

KARIEL, HENRY S.

KAUNDA, KENNETH

KEFAUVER, ESTES

KELLEY, HAROLD

KENNEDY, JOHN F.

KENYATTA, JOMO

KEOHANE, ROBERT

KERNER COMMISSION REPORT

KEY, V. O., JR.

KEYNES, JOHN MAYNARD

KHMER ROUGE

KHOMEINI, AYATOLLAH RUHOLLAH

KHRUSHCHEV, NIKITA

KILLING FIELDS

KIMATHI, DEDAN

KINDLEBERGER, CHARLES POOR

KING, MARTIN LUTHER, JR.

KINSEY, ALFRED

KINSHIP

KINSHIP, EVOLUTIONARY THEORY OF

KISSINGER, HENRY

KLEIN, LAWRENCE

KNESSET, THE

KNOWLEDGE

KNOWLEDGE, DIFFUSION OF

KNOWLEDGE SOCIETY

KOHLBERG, LAWRENCE

KOOPMANS, TJALLING

KOREAN WAR

KROEBER, ALFRED LOUIS

KSHATRIYAS

KUHN, THOMAS

KU KLUX KLAN

KUZNETS HYPOTHESIS

L

LABELING THEORY

LABOR

LABOR, MARGINAL PRODUCT OF

LABOR, SURPLUS: CONVENTIONAL ECONOMICS

LABOR, SURPLUS: MARXIST AND RADICAL ECONOMICS

LABOR DEMAND

LABOR FORCE PARTICIPATION

LABOR LAW

LABOR MARKET

LABOR MARKET SEGMENTATION

LABOR SUPPLY

LABOR THEORY OF VALUE

LABOR UNION

LABOUR PARTY (BRITAIN)

LADEJINSKY, WOLF

LAFARGUE, PAUL

LAGGING, LEADING, AND COINCIDENT INDICATORS

LAGRANGE MULTIPLIER

LAGS, DISTRIBUTED

LAISSEZ-FAIRE

LAKATOS, IMRE

LAND CLAIMS

LAND REFORM

LANDLORDS

LANDLORDS, ABSENTEE

LARGE SAMPLE PROPERTIES

LASSWELL, HAROLD

LATIFUNDIA

LATINO NATIONAL POLITICAL SURVEY

LATINO/A STUDIES

LATINOS

LAUSANNE, SCHOOL OF

LAW

LAW, JOHN

LAW AND ECONOMICS

LAW AND ORDER

LAW OF LARGE NUMBERS

LAY THEORIES

LAZARSFELD, PAUL FELIX

LEADERS

LEADERSHIP

LEADERSHIP, CONTINGENCY MODELS OF

LEAGUE OF NATIONS

LEAKEY, RICHARD

LEARNED HELPLESSNESS

LEARY, TIMOTHY

LEAST SQUARES, ORDINARY

LEAST SQUARES, THREE-STAGE

LEAST SQUARES, TWO-STAGE

LEBANESE CIVIL WAR

LE DUC THO

LEE, ROBERT E.

LEFEBVRE, HENRI

LEFT AND RIGHT

LEFT WING

LEGACY EFFECTS

LEGAL SYSTEMS

LE GUIN, URSULA K.

LEISURE

LENDER OF LAST RESORT

LENIN, VLADIMIR ILITCH

LENINISM

LEONTIEF, WASSILY

LEVELLERS

LEVERAGE

LÉVI-STRAUSS, CLAUDE

LEWIN, KURT

LEWIS, OSCAR

LEWIS, W. ARTHUR

LEXICOGRAPHIC PREFERENCES

LIBERAL PARTY (BRITAIN)

LIBERALISM

LIBERALIZATION, TRADE

LIBERATION

LIBERATION MOVEMENTS

LIBERATION THEOLOGY

LIBERTARIANISM

LIBERTY

LIFE-CYCLE HYPOTHESIS

LIFE EVENTS, STRESS

LIFESTYLES

LIKERT SCALE

LIMITS OF GROWTH

LINCOLN, ABRAHAM

LINDBLOM, CHARLES EDWARD

LINEAR REGRESSION

LINEAR SYSTEMS

LINGUISTIC TURN

LIQUIDITY

LIQUIDITY PREMIUM

LIQUIDITY TRAP

LITERATURE

LITIGATION, SOCIAL SCIENCE ROLE IN

LITTLE RED BOOK

LIVERPOOL SLAVE TRADE

LOAN PUSHING

LOANS

LOBBYING

LOBOTOMY

LOCKE, JOHN

LOCUS OF CONTROL

LOGIC

LOGIC, SYMBOLIC

LOGISTIC REGRESSION

LOG-LINEAR MODELS

LOMBARD STREET (BAGEHOT)

LONELINESS

LONELY CROWD, THE

LONG PERIOD ANALYSIS

LONG RUN

LONG WAVES

LOOKING-GLASS EFFECT

LOSS FUNCTIONS

LOTTERIES

LOVE CANAL

LOWI, THEODORE J.

LOWIE, ROBERT

LOYALISTS

LUCAS, ROBERT E., JR.

LUCAS CRITIQUE

LUCK

LUDDITES

LUKACS, GEORG

LUMPENPROLETARIAT

LUMUMBA, PATRICE

LUNDBERG, ERIK

LUXEMBOURG INCOME STUDY

LUXEMBURG, ROSA

LYING

LYNCHINGS

LYND, ROBERT AND HELEN

LYND, STAUGHTON

M

MACCOBY, ELEANOR

MACHEL, SAMORA

MACHIAVELLI, NICCOLÒ

MACHINERY

MACHINERY QUESTION, THE

MACMILLAN, HAROLD

MACROECONOMICS

MACROECONOMICS, STRUCTURALIST

MACROFOUNDATIONS

MADISON, JAMES

MADNESS

MAFIA, THE

MAGIC

MAGNA CARTA

MAHATHIR MOHAMAD

MAJORITARIANISM

MAJORITIES

MAJORITY RULE

MAJORITY VOTING

MALCOLM X

MALINCHISTAS

MALINOWSKI, BRONISLAW

MALNUTRITION

MALTHUS, THOMAS ROBERT

MALTHUSIAN TRAP

MANAGEMENT

MANAGEMENT SCIENCE

MANAGERIAL CLASS

MANDEL, ERNEST

MANDELA, NELSON

MANDELA, WINNIE

MANIAS

MANIC DEPRESSION

MANIFOLDS

MANKILLER, WILMA

MANNHEIM, KARL

MAO ZEDONG

MAOISM

MAQUILADORAS

MARCUSE, HERBERT

MARGINAL PRODUCTIVITY

MARGINALISM

MARGINALIZATION

MARITAL CONFLICT

MARKET CLEARING

MARKET CLEARINGHOUSE

MARKET CORRECTION

MARKET ECONOMY

MARKET FUNDAMENTALS

MARKETS

MARKOWITZ, HARRY M.

MARKUP PRICING

MARRIAGE

MARRIAGE, INTERRACIAL

MARRIAGE, SAME-SEX

MARS

MARSHALL, ALFRED

MARSHALL, THURGOOD

MARTYRDOM

MARX, KARL

MARX, KARL: IMPACT ON ANTHROPOLOGY

MARX, KARL: IMPACT ON ECONOMICS

MARX, KARL: IMPACT ON SOCIOLOGY

MARXISM

MARXISM, BLACK

MASCULINITY

MASCULINITY STUDIES

MASLOW, ABRAHAM

MATERIAL CULTURE

MATERIALISM

MATERIALISM, DIALECTICAL

MATHEMATICAL ECONOMICS

MATHEMATICS IN THE SOCIAL SCIENCES

MATRIARCHY

MATRIX, THE

MATRIX ALGEBRA

MATURATION

MAU MAU

MAXIMIN PRINCIPLE

MAXIMIZATION

MAXIMUM LIKELIHOOD REGRESSION

McCARTHYISM

McFADDEN, DANIEL L.

McLUHAN, MARSHALL

MEAD, GEORGE HERBERT

MEAD, MARGARET

MEADE, JAMES

MEAN, THE

MEANING

MEANS, RUSSELL

MEASUREMENT

MEASUREMENT ERROR

MECCA

MECHANISM DESIGN

MEDIA

MEDICAID

MEDICARE

MEDICINE

MEDICINE, SOCIALIZED

MEDICIS, THE

MEDIUM IS THE MESSAGE

MEIJI RESTORATION

MEIR, GOLDA

MELTING POT

MEMÍN PINGUÍN

MEMORY

MEMORY IN PSYCHOLOGY

MEN

MENDEL'S LAW

MENTAL HEALTH

MENTAL ILLNESS

MENTAL RETARDATION

MENTORING

MERCANTILISM

MERIT

MERIT GOODS

MERITOCRACY

MERITOCRACY, MULTIRACIAL

MERRIAM, CHARLES EDWARD, JR.

MERTON, ROBERT K.

META-ANALYSIS

METHOD OF MOMENTS

METHODOLOGY

METHODS, QUALITATIVE

METHODS, QUANTITATIVE

METHODS, RESEARCH (IN SOCIOLOGY)

METHODS, SURVEY

METROPOLIS

MEXICAN AMERICANS

MEXICAN-AMERICAN WAR

MEXICAN REVOLUTION (1910–1920)

MICHELS, ROBERT

MICROANALYSIS

MICROECONOMICS

MICROELECTRONICS INDUSTRY

MICROFINANCE

MICROFOUNDATIONS

MICROSOFT

MIDDLE CLASS

MIDDLE WAY

MIDDLEMAN MINORITIES

MIDLIFE CRISIS

MIDWIFERY

MIGRANT LABOR

MIGRATION

MIGRATION, RURAL TO URBAN

MILGRAM, STANLEY

MILITANTS

MILITARISM

MILITARY

MILITARY-INDUSTRIAL COMPLEX

MILITARY REGIMES

MILL, JAMES

MILL, JOHN STUART

MILLER, WARREN

MILLS, C. WRIGHT

MILLS, EDWIN

MILOSEVIC, SLOBODAN

MINIMIZATION

MINIMUM WAGE

MINING INDUSTRY

MINORITIES

MINSKY, HYMAN

MINSTRELSY

MINTZ, SIDNEY W.

MIRACLES

MISANTHROPY

MISCEGENATION

MISERY INDEX

MISES, LUDWIG EDLER VON

MISOGYNY

MISSIONARIES

MITCHELL, WESLEY CLAIR

MIXED STRATEGY

MOBILITY

MOBILITY, LATERAL

MOBILIZATION

MOBUTU, JOSEPH

MODE, THE

MODE OF PRODUCTION

MODEL MINORITY

MODEL SELECTION TESTS

MODELS AND MODELING

MODERATES

MODERNISM

MODERNITY

MODERNIZATION

MODIGLIANI, FRANCO

MODIGLIANI-MILLER THEOREMS

MOMENT GENERATING FUNCTION

MONARCHISM

MONARCHY

MONARCHY, CONSTITUTIONAL

MONETARISM

MONETARY BASE

MONETARY THEORY

MONEY

MONEY, DEMAND FOR

MONEY, ENDOGENOUS

MONEY, EXOGENOUS

MONEY, SUPPLY OF

MONEY ILLUSION

MONEY LAUNDERING

MONOPOLY

MONOPOLY CAPITALISM

MONOPSONY

MONOTHEISM

MONROE DOCTRINE

MONT PELERIN SOCIETY

MONTAGU, ASHLEY

MONTE CARLO EXPERIMENTS

MOOD

MOOD CONGRUENT RECALL

MOORE, BARRINGTON

MORAL DOMAIN THEORY

MORAL HAZARD

MORAL SENTIMENTS

MORAL SUASION

MORALITY

MORALITY AND INEQUALITY

MORBIDITY AND MORTALITY

MORENO/A

MORGENTHAU, HANS

MOSES, ROBERT

MOSSADEGH, MOHAMMAD

MOTHERHOOD

MOTIVATION

MOVING TO OPPORTUNITY

MOYNIHAN, DANIEL PATRICK

MOYNIHAN REPORT

MUGABE, ROBERT

MUHAMMAD

MUHAMMAD, ELIJAH

MULATTO ESCAPE HATCH

MULATTOS

MULTI-CITY STUDY OF URBAN INEQUALITY

MULTICOLLINEARITY

MULTICULTURALISM

MULTIDIMENSIONAL INVENTORY OF BLACK IDENTITY

MULTIFINALITY

MULTILATERALISM

MULTIPARTY SYSTEMS

MULTIPLE BIRTHS

MULTIPLE EQUILIBRIA

MULTIPLE INTELLIGENCES THEORY

MULTIPLE PERSONALITIES

MULTIPLIER, THE

MULTIRACIAL MOVEMENT

MULTIRACIALS IN THE UNITED STATES

MULTISECTOR MODELS

MUNDELL-FLEMING MODEL

MÜNSTERBERG, HUGO

MURDER

MUSEVENI, YOWERI

MUSIC

MUSIC, PSYCHOLOGY OF

MUSLIMS

MUSSOLINI, BENITO

MYRDAL, GUNNAR

MYSTICISM

MYSTIFICATION

MYTH AND MYTHOLOGY

N

NADER, RALPH

NADER'S RAIDERS

NANOTECHNOLOGY

NAPOLÉON BONAPARTE

NAPOLEON COMPLEX

NAPOLEONIC WARS

NARCISSISM

NARRATIVES

NASH, JOHN

NASH EQUILIBRIUM

NASSER, GAMAL ABDEL

NAST, THOMAS

NATION

NATION OF ISLAM

NATIONAL ASSESSMENT OF EDUCATIONAL PROGRESS

NATIONAL ASSOCIATION FOR THE ADVANCEMENT OF COLORED PEOPLE (NAACP)

NATIONAL DEBT

NATIONAL ECONOMIC ASSOCIATION

NATIONAL EDUCATION LONGITUDINAL STUDY

NATIONAL FAMILY HEALTH SURVEYS

NATIONAL GEOGRAPHIC

NATIONAL HEALTH INSURANCE

NATIONAL INCOME ACCOUNTS

NATIONAL LONGITUDINAL STUDY OF ADOLESCENT HEALTH

NATIONAL LONGITUDINAL SURVEY OF YOUTH

NATIONAL ORGANIZATION FOR WOMEN

NATIONAL SAMPLE SURVEY (INDIA)

NATIONAL SECURITY

NATIONAL SERVICE PROGRAMS

NATIONAL SURVEY OF BLACK AMERICANS

NATIONALISM AND NATIONALITY

NATIONALIZATION

NATION-STATE

NATIVE AMERICANS

NATIVES

NATIVISM

NATURAL CHILDBIRTH

NATURAL DISASTERS

NATURAL EXPERIMENTS

NATURAL RATE OF UNEMPLOYMENT

NATURAL RESOURCES, NONRENEWABLE

NATURAL RIGHTS

NATURAL SELECTION

NATURALISM

NATURALIZATION

NATURE VS. NURTURE

NAVAJOS

NAZISM

NECESSITIES

NEED FOR COGNITION

NEEDS

NEEDS, BASIC

NEGATIVE INCOME TAX

NEGOTIATION

NEGRO

NEHRU, JAWAHARLAL

NEIGHBORHOOD EFFECTS

NEIGHBORHOODS

NEOCLASSICAL GROWTH MODEL

NEOCOLONIALISM

NEOCONSERVATISM

NEOIMPERIALISM

NEOINSTITUTIONALISM

NEOLIBERALISM

NETWORK ANALYSIS

NETWORKS

NETWORKS, COMMUNICATION

NEUMANN, FRANZ

NEUROECONOMICS

NEUROSCIENCE

NEUROSCIENCE, SOCIAL

NEUROTICISM

NEUTRAL STATES

NEUTRALITY, POLITICAL

NEUTRALITY OF MONEY

NEW CLASS, THE

NEW DEAL, THE

NEW IMMIGRANT SURVEY

NEW SCHOOL FOR SOCIAL RESEARCH

NIETZSCHE, FRIEDRICH

NIRVĀNA

NIXON, RICHARD M.

NKRUMAH, KWAME

NOBEL PEACE PRIZE

NODE, STABLE

NOMINAL INCOME

NOMINAL WAGES

NON-ALIGNMENT

NONBLACKS

NONCOMPETING GROUPS

NONCOOPERATIVE GAMES

NONDECISION-MAKING

NON-EXPECTED UTILITY THEORY

NONGOVERNMENTAL ORGANIZATIONS (NGOs)

NONLINEAR REGRESSION

NONLINEAR SYSTEMS

NONPARAMETRIC ESTIMATION

NONPARAMETRIC REGRESSION

NONVERBAL COMMUNICATION

NONWHITES

NONZERO-SUM GAME

NORMALIZATION

NORMATIVE SOCIAL SCIENCE

NORMS

NORTH, DOUGLASS

NORTH AMERICAN FREE TRADE AGREEMENT

NORTH AND SOUTH, THE (GLOBAL)

NORTH ATLANTIC TREATY ORGANIZATION

NORTH-SOUTH MODELS

NOUVEAUX RICHES

NURSERY RHYMES

NUTRITION

NUYORICANS

NYERERE, JULIUS

O

OAXACA, RONALD

OBEDIENCE, DESTRUCTIVE

OBESE EXTERNALITY

OBESITY

OBJECTIVE FUNCTION

OBJECTIVISM

OBJECTIVITY

OBOTE, APOLLO MILTON

OBSCENITY

OBSERVATION, PARTICIPANT

OBSESSION

OBSESSIVE-COMPULSIVE DISORDER

OCCAM'S RAZOR

OCCULT, THE

OCCUPATIONAL HAZARDS

OCCUPATIONAL REGULATION

OCCUPATIONAL SAFETY

OCCUPATIONAL SCORE INDEX (OCCSCORE)

OCCUPATIONAL STATUS

OEDIPUS COMPLEX

OFFSHORE BANKING

OGBU, JOHN U.

OKUN'S LAW

OLIGARCHY

OLIGARCHY, IRON LAW OF

OLMECS

OLYMPIC GAMES

ONE-PARTY STATES

OPEN MARKET OPERATIONS

OPERANT CONDITIONING

OPERATION BOOTSTRAP

OPIUM WARS

OPPORTUNITY COST

OPPOSITIONALITY

OPPOSITIONALITY, SCHOOLING

OPTIMAL GROWTH

OPTIMISM/PESSIMISM

OPTIMIZING BEHAVIOR

ORDINALITY

ORDINARY LEAST SQUARES
  REGRESSION

ORGANIZATION MAN

ORGANIZATION OF AFRICAN UNITY
  (OAU)

ORGANIZATION OF PETROLEUM
  EXPORTING COUNTRIES (OPEC)

ORGANIZATION THEORY

ORGANIZATIONS

ORGANIZATIONS, PEASANT

ORIENTALISM

O-RING THEORY

ORTHODOXY

ORTIZ, FERNANDO

OSCEOLA

OTHER, THE

OTTOMAN EMPIRE

OUGHT SELF

OUTSOURCING

OVERACHIEVERS

OVER-ATTRIBUTION BIAS

OVEREATING

OVEREMPLOYMENT

OVERFISHING

OVERLAPPING GENERATIONS
  MODEL

OVERLENDING

OVERPOPULATION

OVERPRODUCTION

OVERSHOOTING

OVERTIME

P

PACIFISM

PALESTINE LIBERATION
  ORGANIZATION (PLO)

PALESTINIAN AUTHORITY

PALESTINIAN DIASPORA

PALESTINIANS

PAN-AFRICAN CONGRESSES

PAN-AFRICANISM

PAN-ARABISM

PAN-CARIBBEANISM

PANEL STUDIES

PANEL STUDY OF INCOME
  DYNAMICS

PANIC

PANICS

PARADIGM

PARADOX OF VOTING

PARANOIA

PARDO

PARENT-CHILD RELATIONSHIPS

PARENTHOOD, TRANSITION TO

PARENTING STYLES

PARETO, VILFREDO

PARETO OPTIMUM

PARK, ROBERT E.

PARK SCHOOL, THE

PARLIAMENT, UNITED KINGDOM

PARLIAMENTS AND PARLIAMENTARY
  SYSTEMS

PARNES, HERBERT

PARODY

PARSONS, TALCOTT

PARTIAL EQUILIBRIUM

PARTICIPATION, POLITICAL

PARTICULARISM

PARTIDO REVOLUCIONARIO
  INSTITUCIONAL

PARTITION

PARTY SYSTEMS, COMPETITIVE

PASINETTI, LUIGI

PASINETTI PARADOX

PASSING

PASSIVE RESISTANCE

PATH ANALYSIS

PATHOLOGY, SOCIAL

PATINKIN, DON

PATRIARCHY

PATRICIANS

PATRIOTISM

PATRONAGE

PAVLOV, IVAN

PAX BRITANNICA

PEACE

PEACE MOVEMENTS

PEACE PROCESS

PEACEFUL COEXISTENCE

PEANUT INDUSTRY

PEARL HARBOR

PEARSON, KARL

PEASANTRY

PEDAGOGY

PEER CLIQUES

PEER EFFECTS

PEER INFLUENCE

PEER RELATIONS RESEARCH

PENN WORLD TABLE

PERCEPTION, PERSON

PERFORMANCE

PERIOD EFFECTS

PERIODIZATION

PERMANENT INCOME HYPOTHESIS

PERONISM

PERSON MEMORY

PERSONAL CONSTRUCTS

PERSONALITY

PERSONALITY, AUTHORITARIAN

PERSONALITY, CULT OF

PERSONALITY, TYPE A/TYPE B

PERSON-SITUATION DEBATE

PERSPECTIVE-TAKING

PERSUASION

PERSUASION, MESSAGE-BASED

PETROLEUM INDUSTRY

PETTIGREW, THOMAS F.

PHALANGISTS

PHARMACEUTICAL INDUSTRY

PHASE DIAGRAMS

PHENOMENOLOGY

PHENOTYPE

PHILANTHROPY

PHILLIPS, A. W. H.

PHILLIPS CURVE

PHILOSOPHY

PHILOSOPHY, MORAL

PHILOSOPHY, POLITICAL

PHILOSOPHY OF SCIENCE

PHOBIA

PHYSICAL CAPITAL

PHYSICAL QUALITY OF LIFE INDEX

PHYSIOCRACY

PIAGET, JEAN

PIMPS

PITKIN, HANNA

PLANNING

PLANTATION

PLANTATION ECONOMY MODEL

PLATO

PLUMBING

PLURALISM

PLURALITY

POGROMS

POL POT

POLICING, BIASED

POLICY, FISCAL

POLICY, MONETARY

POLICY ANALYSIS

POLITICAL CONVENTIONS

POLITICAL CORRECTNESS

POLITICAL CULTURE

POLITICAL ECONOMY

POLITICAL INSTABILITY, INDICES
OF

POLITICAL PARTIES

POLITICAL PSYCHOLOGY

POLITICAL SCIENCE

POLITICAL SCIENCE, BEHAVIORAL

POLITICAL SYSTEM

POLITICAL THEORY

POLITICS

POLITICS, ASIAN AMERICAN

POLITICS, BLACK

POLITICS, COMPARATIVE

POLITICS: GAY, LESBIAN,
TRANSGENDER, AND BISEXUAL

POLITICS, GENDER

POLITICS, IDENTITY

POLITICS, LATINO

POLITICS, SOUTHERN

POLITICS, URBAN

POLL TAX

POLLING

POLLS, OPINION

POLLSTERS

POLLUTION

POLLUTION, AIR

POLLUTION, NOISE

POLLUTION, WATER

POLYARCHY

POLYTHEISM

PONZI SCHEME

POOLED TIME SERIES AND CROSS-
SECTIONAL DATA

POPPER, KARL

POPULAR CULTURE

POPULAR MUSIC

POPULATION CONTROL

POPULATION GROWTH

POPULATION STUDIES

POPULISM

POSITIVE PSYCHOLOGY

POSITIVE SOCIAL SCIENCE

POSITIVISM

POSTCOLONIALISM

POSTLETHWAYT, MALACHY

POSTMODERNISM

POSTNATIONALISM

POSTSTRUCTURALISM

POST-TRAUMATIC STRESS

POTRON, MAURICE

POULANTZAS, NICOS

POVERTY

POVERTY, INDICES OF

POVERTY, URBAN

POWER

POWER, POLITICAL

POWER ELITE

PRACTICE THEORY

PRAGMATISM

PRAXIS

PREBISCH, RAÚL

PREBISCH-SINGER HYPOTHESIS

PRE-COLUMBIAN PEOPLES

PREDATORY PRICING

PREDICTION

PREEMPTIVE STRIKE

PREFERENCE, COLOR

PREFERENCE, GENDER

PREFERENCES

PREFERENCES, INTERDEPENDENT

PREJUDICE

PRESIDENCY, THE

PRESSURE GROUPS

PRESTIGE

PREVENTION SCIENCE

PRICE INDICES

PRICE SETTING AND PRICE TAKING

PRICE VS. QUANTITY ADJUSTMENT

PRICES

PRIMACY/RECENCY EFFECTS

PRIMARIES

PRIMATES

PRIMING

PRIMITIVE ACCUMULATION

PRIMITIVISM

PRINCIPAL COMPONENTS

PRINCIPAL-AGENT MODELS

PRISON INDUSTRY

PRISON PSYCHOLOGY

PRISONER'S DILEMMA
(ECONOMICS)

PRISONER'S DILEMMA
(PSYCHOLOGY)

PRISONS

PRIVACY

PRIVATE INTERESTS

PRIVATE SECTOR

PRIVATIZATION

PROBABILISTIC REGRESSION

PROBABILITY

PROBABILITY, LIMITS IN

PROBABILITY, SUBJECTIVE

PROBABILITY DISTRIBUTIONS

PROBABILITY THEORY

PRO-CHOICE/PRO-LIFE

PRODUCER SURPLUS

PRODUCTION

PRODUCTION FRONTIER

PRODUCTION FUNCTION

PRODUCTIVITY

PROFANITY

PROFESSIONALIZATION

PROFESSORIATE

PROFITABILITY

PROFITS

PROGRAMMED RETARDATION

PROGRAMMING, LINEAR AND
  NONLINEAR

PROGRESS

PROGRESSIVE MOVEMENT

PROGRESSIVES

PROLETARIAT

PROLIFERATION, NUCLEAR

PROPAGANDA

PROPENSITY TO CONSUME,
  MARGINAL

PROPENSITY TO IMPORT, MARGINAL

PROPENSITY TO SAVE, MARGINAL

PROPERTIES OF ESTIMATORS
  (ASYMPTOTIC AND EXACT)

PROPERTY

PROPERTY, PRIVATE

PROPERTY RIGHTS

PROPERTY RIGHTS, INTELLECTUAL

PROSPECT THEORY

PROSTITUTION

PROTECTED MARKETS

PROTECTIONISM

PROTEST

PROTESTANT ETHIC, THE

PROTESTANTISM

PROTOTYPES

PSYCHIATRIC DISORDERS

PSYCHOANALYTIC THEORY

PSYCHOLINGUISTICS

PSYCHOLOGICAL CAPITAL

PSYCHOLOGY

PSYCHOLOGY, AGENCY IN

PSYCHOMETRICS

PSYCHONEUROENDOCRINOLOGY

PSYCHONEUROIMMUNOLOGY

PSYCHOPATHOLOGY

PSYCHOSOMATICS

PSYCHOSOMATICS, SOCIAL

PSYCHOTHERAPY

PSYCHOTROPIC DRUGS

PUBLIC ADMINISTRATION

PUBLIC ASSISTANCE

PUBLIC CHOICE THEORY

PUBLIC GOODS

PUBLIC HEALTH

PUBLIC INTEREST

PUBLIC INTEREST ADVOCACY

PUBLIC OPINION

PUBLIC POLICY

PUBLIC RIGHTS

PUBLIC SECTOR

PUBLIC SPHERE

PUBLIC UTILITIES

PUBLIC WELFARE

PULLMAN PORTERS

PUNCTUATED EQUILIBRIUM

PUNISHMENT

PURCHASING POWER PARITY

PURGATORY

PURIFICATION

PUTIN, VLADIMIR

PUTNAM, ROBERT

PUTTING-OUT SYSTEM

PYGMALION EFFECTS

Q

QADHAFI, MUAMMAR AL

QUALIFICATIONS

QUALITY, PRODUCT

QUALITY CONTROLS

QUANTIFICATION

QUANTITY INDEX

QUANTITY THEORY OF MONEY

QUEBECOIS MOVEMENT

QUEER STUDIES

QUESNAY, FRANCOIS

QUOTA SYSTEM, FARM

QUOTA SYSTEMS

QUOTAS

QUOTAS, TRADE

R

RABIN, YITZHAK

RACE

RACE AND ANTHROPOLOGY

RACE AND ECONOMICS

RACE AND EDUCATION

RACE AND POLITICAL SCIENCE

RACE AND PSYCHOLOGY

RACE AND RELIGION

RACE MIXING

RACE RELATIONS

RACE RELATIONS CYCLE

RACE RIOTS, UNITED STATES

RACE-BLIND POLICIES

RACE-CONSCIOUS POLICIES

RACIAL CLASSIFICATION

RACIAL SLURS

RACIALIZATION

RACISM

RADCLIFFE-BROWN, A. R.

RADICALISM

RADIO TALK SHOWS

RAILWAY INDUSTRY

RAJ, THE

RANDOM EFFECTS REGRESSION

RANDOM SAMPLES

RANDOM WALK

RANDOMNESS

RAPE

RASTAFARI

RATE OF EXPLOITATION

RATE OF PROFIT

RATIONAL CHOICE THEORY

RATIONALISM

RATIONALITY

RAWLS, JOHN

REACTANCE THEORY

READINESS, SCHOOL

REAGAN, RONALD

REAL INCOME

REALISM

REALISM, EXPERIMENTAL

REALISM, MORAL

REALISM, POLITICAL

REALIST THEORY

REALITY

RECALL

RECESSION

RECIPROCITY

RECIPROCITY, NORM OF

RECOGNITION

RECONCILIATION

RECONSTRUCTION ERA (U.S.)

RECORDING INDUSTRY

RECURSIVE MODELS

REDUCTIONISM

REFERENDUM

REFLECTION PROBLEM

REFLEXIVITY

REFUGEE CAMPS

REFUGEES

REGGAE

REGIONS

REGIONS, METROPOLITAN

REGRESSION

REGRESSION ANALYSIS

REGRESSION TOWARDS THE MEAN

REGULATION

REINCARNATION

REINFORCEMENT THEORIES

REJECTION/ACCEPTANCE

RELATIONSHIP SATISFACTION

RELATIVE DEPRIVATION

RELATIVE INCOME HYPOTHESIS

RELATIVE SURPLUS VALUE

RELATIVISM

RELIABILITY, STATISTICAL

RELIGION

RELIGIOSITY

RENT

RENT CONTROL

REPARATIONS

REPATRIATION

REPLICATOR DYNAMICS

REPRESENTATION

REPRESENTATION IN
    POSTCOLONIAL ANALYSIS

REPRESENTATIVE AGENT

REPRESSION

REPRESSIVE TOLERANCE

REPRODUCTION

REPRODUCTIVE POLITICS

REPRODUCTIVE RIGHTS

REPUBLIC

REPUBLICAN PARTY

REPUBLICANISM

RESEARCH, CROSS-SECTIONAL

RESEARCH, DEMOCRACY

RESEARCH, ETHNOGRAPHIC

RESEARCH, LONGITUDINAL

RESEARCH, SURVEY

RESEARCH, TRANS-DISCIPLINARY

RESEARCH AND DEVELOPMENT

RESEGREGATION OF SCHOOLS

RESERVES, FOREIGN

RESIDUALS

RESILIENCY

RESISTANCE

RESOURCE ECONOMICS

RESOURCES

RESTITUTION PRINCIPLE

RETALIATION

RETURNS

RETURNS, DIMINISHING

RETURNS, INCREASING

RETURNS TO A FIXED FACTOR

RETURNS TO SCALE

RETURNS TO SCALE, ASYMMETRIC

REVEALED PREFERENCE

REVENUE

REVENUE, MARGINAL

REVOLUTION

REVOLUTION OF RISING
    EXPECTATIONS

REVOLUTIONS, LATIN AMERICAN

REVOLUTIONS, SCIENTIFIC

RHETORIC

RHODES, CECIL

RICARDIAN EQUIVALENCE

RICARDIAN VICE

RICARDO, DAVID

RIGHT WING

RIKER, WILLIAM

RIOTS

RISK

RISK NEUTRALITY

RISK TAKERS

RISK-RETURN TRADEOFF

RITES OF PASSAGE

RITUALS

ROBESON, PAUL

ROBINSON, JOAN

ROCK 'N' ROLL

RODNEY, WALTER

ROE V. WADE

ROLE CONFLICT

ROLE MODELS

ROLE THEORY

ROLL CALLS

ROMA, THE

ROMAN CATHOLIC CHURCH

ROMANCE

ROOSEVELT, FRANKLIN D.

RORSCHACH TEST

RORTY, RICHARD

ROSCAs

ROSENBERG'S SELF-ESTEEM SCALE

ROTHSCHILDS, THE

ROTTER'S INTERNAL-EXTERNAL LOCUS OF CONTROL SCALE

ROUSSEAU, JEAN-JACQUES

ROYAL COMMISSIONS

RULE OF LAW

RULES VERSUS DISCRETION

RUMORS

RUSSIAN ECONOMICS

RUSSIAN FEDERATION

RUSSIAN REVOLUTION

RYBCZYNSKI THEOREM

S

SADAT, ANWAR

SAHLINS, MARSHALL

SAID, EDWARD

SALIENCE, MORTALITY

SAMBO

SAMPLE ATTRITION

SAMPLING

SAMUELSON, PAUL A.

SANDINISTAS

SANITATION

SANSKRITIZATION

SANTERÍA

SARGENT, THOMAS

SARTRE, JEAN-PAUL

SATIATION

SATIRE

SATISFICING BEHAVIOR

SAVING RATE

SAY'S LAW

SCALES

SCARCITY

SCARR, SANDRA WOOD

SCHACHTER, STANLEY

SCHATTSCHNEIDER, E. E.

SCHEMAS

SCHIZOPHRENIA

SCHLIEMANN, HEINRICH

SCHOOL VOUCHERS

SCHOOLING

SCHOOLING IN THE USA

SCHUMPETER, JOSEPH ALOIS

SCIENCE

SCIENCE FICTION

SCIENTIFIC METHOD

SCIENTISM

SCOPES TRIAL

SCOTTISH MORALISTS

SCREENING AND SIGNALING GAMES

SCRIPT MODELS

SECESSION

SECRECY

SECULAR, SECULARISM, SECULARIZATION

SEEMINGLY UNRELATED REGRESSIONS

SEGREGATION

SEGREGATION, RESIDENTIAL

SEGREGATION, SCHOOL

SELECTION BIAS

SELECTIVE ATTENTION

SELECTIVE SERVICE

SELF DISCREPANCY THEORY

SELF-ACTUALIZATION

SELF-AFFIRMATION THEORY

SELF-AWARENESS THEORY

SELF-CLASSIFICATION

SELF-CONCEPT

SELF-CONSCIOUSNESS, PRIVATE VS. PUBLIC

SELF-CONTROL

SELF-DEFEATING BEHAVIOR

SELF-DETERMINATION

SELF-DETERMINATION THEORY

SELF-DISCLOSURE

SELF-EFFICACY

SELF-EMPLOYMENT

SELF-ENHANCEMENT

SELF-ESTEEM

SELF-FULFILLING PROPHECIES

SELF-GUIDES

SELF-HATRED

SELF-IDENTITY

SELF-JUSTIFICATION

SELF-MONITORING

SELF-PERCEPTION THEORY

SELF-PRESENTATION

SELF-REPORT METHOD

SELF-REPRESENTATION

SELF-SCHEMATA

SELF-SERVING BIAS

SELF-SYSTEM

SELF-VERIFICATION

SELIGMAN, MARTIN

SELLING LONG AND SELLING SHORT

SELLOUTS

SEMANTIC MEMORY

SEMIOTICS

SEMIPARAMETRIC ESTIMATION

SEN, AMARTYA KUMAR

SENECA

SENSATIONALISM

SEPARABILITY

SEPARATE-BUT-EQUAL

SEPARATION ANXIETY

SEPARATION OF POWERS

SEPARATISM

SEPTEMBER 11, 2001

SEQUOYAH

SERBS

SERIAL CORRELATION

SEROTONIN

SERVITUDE

SETTLEMENT

SETTLEMENT, NEGOTIATED

SETTLEMENT, TOBACCO

SEX, INTERRACIAL

SEX AND MATING

SEXISM

SEXUAL HARASSMENT

SEXUAL ORIENTATION,
    DETERMINANTS OF

SEXUAL ORIENTATION, SOCIAL AND
    ECONOMIC CONSEQUENCES

SEXUAL SELECTION THEORY

SEXUALITY

SHADOW PRICES

SHAMANS

SHAME

SHARECROPPING

SHARON, ARIEL

SHARP, GRANVILLE

SHERIF, MUZAFER

SHINTO

SHIPPING INDUSTRY

SHKLAR, JUDITH

SHOCKS

SHORT PERIOD

SHORT RUN

SHTETL

SHYNESS

SIBLING RELATIONSHIPS

SIGNALS

SIKHISM

SILICON VALLEY

SILK ROAD

SILVER INDUSTRY

SIMILARITY/ATTRACTION THEORY

SIMON, HERBERT A.

SIMULTANEOUS EQUATION BIAS

SIN

SINGER, HANS

SINGH, V. P.

SITTING BULL

SKILL

SKINNER, B. F.

SKINNER BOX

SKOCPOL, THEDA

SLAVE LIVES, ARCHAEOLOGY OF

SLAVE MODE OF PRODUCTION

SLAVE RESISTANCE

SLAVE TRADE

SLAVE-GUN CYCLE

SLAVERY

SLAVERY HYPERTENSION
    HYPOTHESIS

SLAVERY INDUSTRY

SLEEPER EFFECTS

SLUMS

SMITH, ADAM

SMITH, VERNON L.

SMOKING

SOCIAL ACCOUNTING MATRIX

SOCIAL ANXIETY

SOCIAL CAPITAL

SOCIAL CATEGORIZATION

SOCIAL CHANGE

SOCIAL COGNITION

SOCIAL COGNITIVE MAP

SOCIAL COMPARISON

SOCIAL CONSTRUCTIONISM

SOCIAL CONSTRUCTS

SOCIAL CONTRACT

SOCIAL COST

SOCIAL DOMINANCE ORIENTATION

SOCIAL ECONOMY

SOCIAL EXCHANGE THEORY

SOCIAL EXCLUSION

SOCIAL EXPERIMENT

SOCIAL FACILITATION

SOCIAL IDENTIFICATION

SOCIAL INFLUENCE

SOCIAL INFORMATION PROCESSING

SOCIAL ISOLATION

SOCIAL JUDGMENT THEORY

SOCIAL LEARNING PERSPECTIVE

SOCIAL MOVEMENTS

SOCIAL PSYCHOLOGY

SOCIAL RELATIONS

SOCIAL SCIENCE

SOCIAL SCIENCE, VALUE FREE

SOCIAL STATICS

SOCIAL STATUS

SOCIAL STRUCTURE

SOCIAL SYSTEM

SOCIAL THEORY

SOCIAL WELFARE FUNCTIONS

SOCIAL WELFARE SYSTEM

SOCIAL WORK

SOCIALISM

SOCIALISM, AFRICAN

SOCIALISM, CHRISTIAN

SOCIALISM, ISLAMIC

SOCIALISM, MARKET

SOCIALIZATION

SOCIALIZATION OF INVESTMENT

SOCIETY

SOCIOBIOLOGY

SOCIOECONOMIC STATUS

SOCIOLOGY

SOCIOLOGY, AFRICAN

SOCIOLOGY, AMERICAN

SOCIOLOGY, ECONOMIC

SOCIOLOGY, EUROPEAN

SOCIOLOGY, FEMINIST

SOCIOLOGY, INSTITUTIONAL
    ANALYSIS IN

SOCIOLOGY, KNOWLEDGE IN

SOCIOLOGY, LATIN AMERICAN

SOCIOLOGY, MACRO-

SOCIOLOGY, MICRO-

SOCIOLOGY, PARSONIAN

SOCIOLOGY, POLITICAL

SOCIOLOGY, POST-PARSONIAN
AMERICAN

SOCIOLOGY, RURAL

SOCIOLOGY, SCHOOLS IN

SOCIOLOGY, THIRD WORLD

SOCIOLOGY, URBAN

SOCIOLOGY, VOLUNTARISTIC VS.
STRUCTURALIST

SOCIOMETRY

SOFT SKILLS

SOLAR ENERGY

SOLIDARITY

SOLIDARNOŚĆ

SOLOW, ROBERT M.

SOLOW RESIDUAL, THE

SOLZHENITSYN, ALEKSANDR

SOMBART, WERNER

SOROS, GEORGE

SOUTH, THE (USA)

SOUTH SEA BUBBLE

SOUTHERN BLOC

SOUTHERN STRATEGY

SOVEREIGNTY

SPACE EXPLORATION

SPANISH CIVIL WAR

SPATIAL THEORY

SPEARMAN RANK CORRELATION
COEFFICIENT

SPECIFICATION

SPECIFICATION ERROR

SPECIFICATION TESTS

SPECULATION

SPEECH ACT THEORY

SPENCER, HERBERT

SPIRITUALITY

SPOCK, BENJAMIN

SPORTS

SPORTS INDUSTRY

SPOT MARKET

SPREADS

SPREADS, BID-ASK

SRAFFA, PIERO

STABILITY, POLITICAL

STABILITY, PSYCHOLOGICAL

STABILITY IN ECONOMICS

STAGES OF DEVELOPMENT

STAGES OF ECONOMIC GROWTH

STAGFLATION

STAGNATION

STAKEHOLDERS

STALIN, JOSEPH

STALINISM

STANDARD CROSS-CULTURAL
SAMPLE

STANDARD DEVIATION

STANDARDIZED TESTS

STAR TREK

STAR WARS

STARE, THE

STATE, THE

STATE ENTERPRISE

STATE OF NATURE

STATE-DEPENDENT RETRIEVAL

STATELESSNESS

STATIONARY PROCESS

STATIONARY STATE

STATISM

STATISTICAL NOISE

STATISTICS

STATISTICS IN THE SOCIAL
SCIENCES

STEADY STATE

STEEL INDUSTRY

STEELE, CLAUDE M.

STEINEM, GLORIA

STEM CELLS

STEPFORD WIVES

STEREOTYPE THREAT

STEREOTYPES

STERILIZATION, ECONOMIC

STERILIZATION, HUMAN

STEROIDS

STICKY PRICES

STIGLER, GEORGE JOSEPH

STIGLITZ, JOSEPH E.

STIGMA

STOCHASTIC FRONTIER ANALYSIS

STOCK EXCHANGES

STOCK EXCHANGES IN DEVELOPING
COUNTRIES

STOCK OPTIONS

STOCKHOLM SCHOOL

STOCKS

STOCKS, RESTRICTED AND
UNRESTRICTED

STOCKS AND FLOWS

STOLEN GENERATIONS (AUSTRALIA)

STOLPER-SAMUELSON THEOREM

STORYTELLING

STOWE, HARRIET BEECHER

STRATEGIC BEHAVIOR

STRATEGIC GAMES

STRATEGIES, SELF-HANDICAPPING

STRATEGY AND VOTING GAMES

STRATIFICATION

STRATIFICATION, POLITICAL

STREAM OF CONSCIOUSNESS

STREET CULTURE

STRESS

STRESS-BUFFERING MODEL

STRUCTURAL ADJUSTMENT

STRUCTURAL EQUATION MODELS

STRUCTURAL TRANSFORMATION

STRUCTURALISM

STUDENT NONVIOLENT
COORDINATING COMMITTEE

STUDENT'S T-STATISTIC

STUNTED GROWTH

STYLIZED FACT

SUBALTERN

SUBGAME PERFECTION

SUBJECT/SELF

SUBJECTIVITY: AN OVERVIEW

SUBJECTIVITY: ANALYSIS

SUBLIMATE

SUBLIMINAL SUGGESTION

SUBSIDIES

SUBSIDIES, FARM

SUBSISTENCE AGRICULTURE

SUBSTITUTABILITY

SUBURBAN SPRAWL

SUBURBS

SUDRAS

SUEZ CRISIS

SUFFRAGE, WOMEN'S

SUGAR INDUSTRY

SUICIDE

SUICIDE BOMBERS

SUN YAT-SEN

SUPERORDINATE GOALS

SUPPLY

SUPREME BEING

SUPREME COURT, U.S.

SURPLUS

SURPLUS POPULATION

SURPLUS VALUE

SURVEY

SURVEY OF INCOME AND PROGRAM
   PARTICIPATION

SURVEYS, SAMPLE

SURVIVAL ANALYSIS REGRESSION

SWEATSHOPS

SYMBOLS

SYMPATHY

SYNDICALISM

SYSTEM ANALYSIS

SYSTEMS THEORY

T

TABOOS

TAINO

TALENT

TALIBAN

TALLY'S CORNER

TARIFFS

TASTES

TÂTONNEMENT

TAWNEY, R. H.

TAX CREDITS

TAX EVASION AND TAX AVOIDANCE

TAX INCIDENCE

TAX RELIEF

TAX REVOLTS

TAXATION

TAXES

TAXES, PROGRESSIVE

TAXES, REGRESSIVE

TAYLOR, LANCE

TAYLOR RULE

TAYLORISM

TEA INDUSTRY

TEACHER EXPECTATIONS

TEACHER-CHILD RELATIONSHIPS

TEACHERS

TECHNOCRACY

TECHNOCRAT

TECHNOLOGICAL PROGRESS,
   ECONOMIC GROWTH

TECHNOLOGICAL PROGRESS, SKILL
   BIAS

TECHNOLOGY

TECHNOLOGY, ADOPTION OF

TECHNOLOGY, CELLULAR

TECHNOLOGY, TRANSFER OF

TECHNOLOGY, VIDEO

TECHNOPHOBIA

TECHNOTOPIA

TELECOMMUNICATIONS INDUSTRY

TELEOLOGY

TELEVISION

TEMPERAMENT

TERM LIMITS

TERMS OF TRADE

TERROR

TERROR MANAGEMENT THEORY

TERRORISM

TERRORISTS

TEST STATISTICS

TEXTILE INDUSTRY

THANT, U.

THATCHER, MARGARET

THEATER

THEIL INDEX

THEISM

THEOCRACY

THEORY

THEORY OF MIND

THEORY OF SECOND BEST

THIRD WORLD

THOMPSON, EDWARD P.

THOREAU, HENRY DAVID

THORNDIKE, EDWARD

THRESHOLD EFFECTS

THURMOND, STROM

TIME

TIME ALLOCATION

TIME AND MOTION STUDY

TIME ON THE CROSS

TIME ORIENTATION

TIME PREFERENCE

TIME SERIES REGRESSION

TIME TRENDS

TIME-AND-A-HALF

TINBERGEN, JAN

TITO (JOSIP BROZ)

TOBACCO INDUSTRY

TOBIN, JAMES

TOBIN'S Q

TOBIT

TOCQUEVILLE, ALEXIS DE

TOILETS

TOLERANCE, DRUG

TOLERANCE, POLITICAL

TOLMAN, EDWARD

TOOLS

TOPOGRAPHY

TOPOLOGY

TORTURE

TOTALITARIANISM

TOTEMISM

TOURISM

TOURISM INDUSTRY

TOUSSAINT LOUVERTURE

TOWNS

TOWNSHIPS

TOXIC WASTE

TRACKING IN SCHOOLS

TRADE

TRADE, ANGLO-PORTUGUESE

TRADE, BILATERAL

TRADE DEFICIT

TRADE SURPLUS

TRADE-OFFS

TRADITION

TRAGEDY OF THE COMMONS

TRAIL OF TEARS

TRAIT INFERENCE

TRAIT THEORY

TRANSACTION COST

TRANSACTION TAXES

TRANSFER PRICING

TRANSFORMATION PROBLEM

TRANSGENDER

TRANSNATIONALISM

TRANSPARENCY

TRANSPORTATION INDUSTRY

TRAUMA

TRAUMATIC BONDING

TRAVEL AND TRAVEL WRITING

TREASURY VIEW, THE

TREATY FEDERALISM

TRENDS

TRIBALISM

TRIBE

TRIGUEÑO

TRILATERAL COMMISSION

TRILATERALISM

TRIUMPHALISM

TROTSKY, LEON

TROUILLOT, MICHEL-ROLPH

TRUMAN, HARRY S.

TRUST

TRUTH, SOJOURNER

TRUTH AND RECONCILIATION
COMMISSIONS

TUBMAN, HARRIET

TULSA RIOT

TURGOT, JACQUES

TURNER, NAT

TURNER, VICTOR

TUSKEGEE SYPHILIS STUDY

TWIN STUDIES

TWO-SECTOR MODELS

TWO-STATE SOLUTION

TYRANNY OF THE MAJORITY

U

UNCERTAINTY

UNCLE TOM

UNDERACHIEVERS

UNDERCLASS

UNDERCONSUMPTION

UNDERDEVELOPMENT

UNDEREATING

UNDEREMPLOYMENT

UNDEREMPLOYMENT RATE

UNDERREPRESENTATION

UNEMPLOYABLE

UNEMPLOYMENT

UNEMPLOYMENT RATE

UNEQUAL EXCHANGE

UNIDENTIFIED FLYING OBJECTS

UNILATERALISM

UNION OF SOVIET SOCIALIST
REPUBLICS

UNIONS

UNIT ROOT AND COINTEGRATION
REGRESSION

UNITED ARAB REPUBLIC

UNITED NATIONS

UNIVERSALISM

UNIVERSITY OF OXFORD

UNIVERSITY OF TEXAS INEQUALITY
PROJECT

UNIVERSITY, THE

UPWARD MOBILITY

URBAN RENEWAL

URBAN RIOTS

URBAN SPRAWL

URBAN STUDIES

URBANITY

URBANIZATION

URUGUAY ROUND

U.S. CIVIL WAR

USER COST

UTILITARIANISM

UTILITY FUNCTION

UTILITY, OBJECTIVE

UTILITY, SUBJECTIVE

UTILITY, VON NEUMANN-
MORGENSTERN

UTOPIANISM

UZAWA, HIROFUMI

V

VACATIONS

VAGABONDS

VAISYAS

VAJPAYEE, ATAL BIHARI

VALIDATION

VALIDITY, STATISTICAL

VALUE

VALUE, OBJECTIVE

VALUE, SUBJECTIVE

VALUES

VANILLA INDUSTRY

VARIABILITY

VARIABLES, LATENT

VARIABLES, PREDETERMINED

VARIABLES, RANDOM

VARIANCE

VARIANCE-COVARIANCE MATRIX

VARIATION

VATICAN, THE

VEBLEN, THORSTEIN

VECTOR AUTOREGRESSION

VECTORS

VEIL, IN AFRICAN AMERICAN
   CULTURE

VEIL, IN MIDDLE EASTERN AND
   NORTH AFRICAN CULTURES

VENTURE CAPITAL

VERBA, SIDNEY

VERDOORN'S LAW

VESEY, DENMARK

VETO

VIDEO GAMES

VIETNAM WAR

VILLA, FRANCISCO (PANCHO)

VINDICATION

VINTAGE MODELS

VINYL RECORDINGS

VIOLENCE

VIOLENCE, FRANTZ FANON ON

VIOLENCE, ROLE IN RESOURCE
   ALLOCATION

VIOLENCE IN TERRORISM

VIRGINS

VISUAL ARTS

VODOU

VOLTAIRE

VOLUNTARY UNEMPLOYMENT

VOLUNTEER PROGRAMS

VOLUNTEERISM

VON NEUMANN, JOHN

VOTE, ALTERNATIVE

VOTING

VOTING PATTERNS

VOTING RIGHTS ACT

VOTING SCHEMES

VULNERABILITY

W

WAGE AND PRICE CONTROLS

WAGES

WAGES, COMPENSATING

WALL STREET

WALLERSTEIN, IMMANUEL

WALRAS, LÉON

WALRAS' LAW

WALTZ, KENNETH

WANT CREATION

WANTS

WAR

WAR AND PEACE

WAR CRIMES

WAR OF 1898

WAR ON POVERTY

WARFARE, NUCLEAR

WARREN, EARL

WARREN REPORT

WARSAW PACT

WASHINGTON, GEORGE

WASHINGTON CONSENSUS

WATER RESOURCES

WATERGATE

WEALTH

WEAPONRY, NUCLEAR

WEAPONS INDUSTRY

WEAPONS OF MASS DESTRUCTION

WEAVER, ROBERT C.

WEBER, MAX

WEIGHT

WELFARE

WELFARE ANALYSIS

WELFARE ECONOMICS

WELFARE STATE

WELLS-BARNETT, IDA B.

WELTANSCHAUUNG

WHISTLE-BLOWERS

WHITE, WALTER

WHITE NOISE

WHITE PRIMARY

WHITE SUPREMACY

WHITENESS

WHITENING

WHITES

WHOLESALE PRICE INDEX

WICKSELL EFFECTS

WIDOW'S CRUSE

WILLIAMS, ERIC

WILMINGTON RIOT OF 1898

WILSON, WILLIAM JULIUS

WILSON, WOODROW

WINNER-TAKE-ALL SOCIETY

WINNER'S CURSE

WIZARD OF OZ

WOLF, ERIC

WOMANISM

WOMEN

WOMEN AND POLITICS

WOMEN'S LIBERATION

WOMEN'S MOVEMENT

WOMEN'S STUDIES

WOODSTOCK

WORK

WORK AND WOMEN

WORK DAY

WORK WEEK

WORKING CLASS

WORKING DAY, LENGTH OF

WORKPLACE RELATIONS

WORLD BANK, THE

WORLD HEALTH ORGANIZATION

WORLD MUSIC

WORLD TRADE ORGANIZATION

WORLD WAR I

WORLD WAR II

WORLD-SYSTEM

WORSHIP

X

X-CRISE

XENOPHOBIA

Y

YELTSIN, BORIS

YIELD

YIELD CURVE

YOUTH CULTURE

YUGOSLAVIAN CIVIL WAR

Z

ZAPATA, EMILIANO

Z-D MODEL

ZERO POPULATION GROWTH

ZERO-SUM GAME

ZIMBARDO, PHILIP

ZIONISM

ZOMBIES

Z-TEST

Contributors

Philip Abbott
Distinguished Professor, Department
of Political Science
Wayne State University
POPULISM

Khaled I. Abdel-Kader
Assistant Professor of Economics
Institute of National Planning, Egypt
MACROECONOMICS

Thomas S. Abler
Professor, Department of
Anthropology
University of Waterloo, Canada
IROQUOIS

W. Todd Abraham
Doctoral Candidate, Department of
Psychology and the Institute for Social
and Behavioral Research
Iowa State University
LONELINESS

Gilbert Abraham-Frois
Emeritus Professor, EconomiX
University Paris–X–Nanterre
   AVERAGE AND MARGINAL COST
   EIGEN-VALUES AND EIGEN-
      VECTORS, PERRON-
      FROBENIUS THEOREM:
      ECONOMIC APPLICATIONS
   POTRON, MAURICE
   PRICE SETTING AND PRICE
      TAKING
   VECTORS

As'ad Abu Khalil
Professor, Department of Politics
California State University, Stanislaus
PHALANGISTS

Rikki Abzug
Associate Professor of Management,
Anisfield School of Business
Ramapo College of New Jersey
QUALIFICATIONS

Thomas M. Achenbach
Professor of Psychiatry and
Psychology, Department of Psychiatry
University of Vermont
CHILD BEHAVIOR CHECKLIST

Jeffrey Ackerman
Assistant Professor, Department of
Sociology
Texas A&M University
VARIABILITY

Takanori Adachi
Department of Economics
University of Pennsylvania
DISCRIMINATION, PRICE

Kathleen M. Adams
Professor, Department of
Anthropology
Loyola University Chicago
CULTURAL TOURISM

Paul S. Adams
Assistant Professor of Political Science
University of Pittsburgh at Greensburg
FEUDALISM

Robert Adams
Professor, School of Health and
Social Care
University of Teesside, United
Kingdom
NEEDS, BASIC

Tunde Adeleke
Professor, Department of History, and
Director, African-American Studies
Iowa State University
UNCLE TOM

Jìmí O. Adésínà
Professor of Sociology
Rhodes University, South Africa
SOCIOLOGY, AFRICAN

Olutayo Charles Adesina
Senior Lecturer and Head,
Department of History
University of Ibadan, Nigeria
KIMATHI, DEDAN

Mohamed Adhikari
History Department
University of Cape Town
COLOREDS (SOUTH AFRICA)

Ari Adut
University of Texas at Austin
SOCIOLOGY, POST-PARSONIAN
AMERICAN

Joseph Agassi
Department of Philosophy
Tel–Aviv University and York
University, Toronto
  COMMUNALISM
  DISCRIMINATION, STATISTICAL
  INFORMATION, ECONOMICS
  OF
  POPPER, KARL
  PROBABILITY
  RATIONALISM
  SCIENCE
  SCIENTIFIC METHOD

Judith Buber Agassi
Retired university instructor;
comparative historical sociologist
Herzliya, Israel
  GENDER STUDIES

Opoku Agyeman
Professor of Political Science
Montclair State University
  NKRUMAH, KWAME

Akbar S. Ahmed
Ibn Khaldūn Chair of Islamic Studies
American University, Washington,
D.C.
  JINNAH, MOHAMMED ALI

Michael G. Ainette
Associate Researcher, Department of
Epidemiology and Population Health
Albert Einstein College of Medicine
  DIATHESIS-STRESS MODEL

James W. Ainsworth
Associate Professor, Department of
Sociology
Georgia State University
  MORALITY AND INEQUALITY

Richard Alba
Distinguished Professor of Race and
Ethnicity, Department of Sociology
State University of New York, Albany
  MELTING POT

Carol Mulford Albrecht
Senior Lecturer, Department of
Sociology
Texas A&M University
  FAMILY STRUCTURE

Don E. Albrecht
Professor, Department of Recreation,
Park, and Tourism Sciences
Texas A&M University
  AGRICULTURAL INDUSTRY

  FAMILY STRUCTURE
  SPORTS

Delores P. Aldridge
Department of Sociology
Emory University
  SOCIOLOGY, FEMINIST

José A. Alemán
Assistant Professor, Political Science
Fordham University
  DIRECT ACTION
  STABILITY, POLITICAL

Claire Alexander
Department of Sociology
London School of Economics
  CULTURAL STUDIES

David E. Alexander
Professor
University of Florence, Italy
  NATURAL DISASTERS

Elizabeth Alexander
Loyola University Chicago
  GENERAL MOTORS

Klint W. Alexander
Attorney and Senior Lecturer of
Political Science
Vanderbilt University
  LABOR LAW
  LEGAL SYSTEMS
  MONARCHISM
  SETTLEMENT, NEGOTIATED

Susan G. Alexander
Executive Director and Research
Scientist
Duke University Transdisciplinary
Prevention Research Center
  RESEARCH, TRANS-
  DISCIPLINARY

Mikhail A. Alexseev
Associate Professor, Department of
Political Science
San Diego State University
  SEPARATISM

Leslie D. Alldritt
A. D. Mary Elizabeth Andersen
Hulings Distinguished Chair in the
Humanities
Northland College, Ashland,
Wisconsin
  BURAKU OR BURAKUMIN

Kieran Allen
School of Sociology
University College Dublin
  INDUSTRIALIZATION
  INDUSTRY

Walter R. Allen
Professor of Sociology, Allan Murray
Cartter Professor of Higher Education,
Graduate School of Education and
Information Studies
University of California, Los Angeles
  AMERICAN DILEMMA

Mark DaCosta Alleyne
Associate Professor of Communication
Georgia State University
  MEMÍN PINGUÍN
  NON-ALIGNMENT
  WHITE SUPREMACY

Scott T. Allison
Professor of Psychology
University of Richmond
  PERCEPTION, PERSON
  PROTOTYPES

Paul Almeida
Assistant Professor, Sociology
Texas A&M University
  SOCIAL MOVEMENTS

Bradley A. Almond
Boston College
  ORGANIZATION THEORY

Scott L. Althaus
Associate Professor, Department of
Political Science and Department of
Speech Communication
University of Illinois
Urbana–Champaign
  POLLS, OPINION

Morris Altman
Department of Economics
University of Saskatchewan
  ECONOMICS, BEHAVIORAL

Donald Altschiller
Librarian, Mugar Memorial Library
Boston University
  HATE CRIMES

Milagros Alvarez-Verdugo
Associate Professor, Department of
International Law and Economy
Facultat de Dret, Universitat de
Barcelona
  DISARMAMENT

J. David Alvis
University of West Florida
PROGRESSIVE MOVEMENT

Richard F. America
Professor of the Practice, School of
Business
Georgetown University
CAPITALISM, BLACK
REPARATIONS
RESTITUTION PRINCIPLE

Frimpomaa Ampaw
Graduate Student, Department of
Economics
University of North Carolina at
Chapel Hill
KUZNETS HYPOTHESIS

Jeffrey S. Anastasi
Assistant Professor, Department of
Psychology
Sam Houston State University
COGNITION

David R. Andersen
Assistant Professor, Department of
Government
California State
University–Sacramento
NOBEL PEACE PRIZE
WARFARE, NUCLEAR
WEAPONRY, NUCLEAR

Bernard E. Anderson
Professor
University of Pennsylvania
NATIONAL ECONOMIC
ASSOCIATION

Elizabeth J. Anderson
University Teacher, Bradford
Dementia Group
University of Bradford, United
Kingdom
DEMENTIA

James E. Anderson
William B. Neenan S. J. Millennium
Professor of Economics
Boston College
BARRIERS TO TRADE
QUOTAS, TRADE
TARIFFS
TRADE

Richard G. Anderson
Federal Reserve Bank of St. Louis
MONETARY BASE

Shannon Latkin Anderson
Visiting Postdoctoral Fellow, Institute
for Advanced Studies in Culture
University of Virginia
HOLOCAUST, THE

Simon P. Anderson
Commonwealth Professor of
Economics
University of Virginia
CONSUMER SURPLUS
PRODUCER SURPLUS

Siwan Anderson
Assistant Professor, Department of
Economics
University of British Columbia
ROSCAs

Linda C. Andrist
Professor, Graduate Program in
Nursing, MGH Institute of Health
Professions, Boston, MA
Visiting Research Associate, Women's
Studies Research Center, Brandeis
University, Waltham, MA
CONTRACEPTION

Gil Anidjar
Associate Professor, Department of
Middle East and Asian Languages and
Cultures
Columbia University
ANTI-SEMITISM

Dennis R. Appleyard
James B. Duke Professor of
International Studies and Professor of
Economics
Davidson College
DORNBUSCH-FISCHER-
SAMUELSON MODEL
HECKSCHER-OHLIN-
SAMUELSON MODEL

Andrew Apter
Professor, Departments of History and
Anthropology; Director, James S.
Coleman African Studies Center
University of California, Los Angeles
SOCIALISM, AFRICAN

Sally L. Archer
Professor, Department of Psychology
The College of New Jersey
ERIKSON, ERIK
IDENTITY CRISIS

Doreen Arcus
University of Massachusetts Lowell
AINSWORTH, MARY

William Arens
Professor of Anthropology and Dean,
International Academic Programs
Stony Brook University
CANNIBALISM

Robert M. Arkin
Professor of Psychology
The Ohio State University
OVERACHIEVERS
STRATEGIES, SELF-
HANDICAPPING

Ralph Armbruster-Sandoval
Associate Professor, Department of
Chicana and Chicano Studies
University of California, Santa Barbara
BONACICH, EDNA

Roy Armes
Emeritus Professor of Film
Middlesex University
BATTLE OF ALGIERS, THE

Fred Arnold
Vice President, Demographic and
Health Research Division
Macro International
NATIONAL FAMILY HEALTH
SURVEYS

Joshua Aronson
Associate Professor
New York University
STEELE, CLAUDE M.

Vivek Arora
International Monetary Fund
INCOME TAX, CORPORATE

Monica Arruda de Almeida
Faculty Fellow, Department of
Political Science
University of California, Los Angeles
IMPORT SUBSTITUTION

Bala G. Arshanapalli
School of Business and Economics
Indiana University Northwest
LAGS, DISTRIBUTED

Jeffery S. Ashby
Professor
Georgia State University
INFERIORITY COMPLEX

Mark Ashley
PhD Candidate, Department of
Political Science
University of Chicago
NATION

Claire E. Ashton-James
University of British Columbia
SUBLIMINAL SUGGESTION

Lonna Rae Atkeson
Professor, Department of Political
Science
University of New Mexico
PRIMARIES

David C. Atkins
Associate Professor, Department of
Clinical Psychology
Fuller Theological Seminary
INFIDELITY
LEARY, TIMOTHY
REGRESSION

Scott E. Atkinson
Department of Economics
University of Georgia
SHADOW PRICES

Boaz Atzili
Research Fellow, Belfer Center for
Science and International Affairs
Kennedy School of Government,
Harvard University
PEACE PROCESS

Ralph A. Austen
Professor Emeritus, Department of
History
University of Chicago
INDIRECT RULE

Javier Auyero
Associate Professor, Department of
Sociology
SUNY–Stony Brook, New York
PERONISM

Patricia G. Avery
Professor, College of Education and
Human Development
University of Minnesota
TOLERANCE, POLITICAL

Joseph R. Avitable
PhD Candidate
University of Rochester
INIKORI, JOSEPH

Mark Axelrod
Department of Political Science
Duke University
CONSTITUTIONALISM
GRUTTER DECISION

María Isabel Ayala
Doctoral Student, Department of
Sociology
Texas A&M University
FREQUENCY DISTRIBUTIONS
MIGRATION

Ozlem Ayduk
Assistant Professor, Department of
Psychology
University of California, Berkeley
RELATIONSHIP SATISFACTION

Fakhreddin Azimi
Department of History
University of Connecticut
MOSSADEGH, MOHAMMAD

Lawrence A. Babb
Professor, Department of
Anthropology, Sociology; Department
of Asian Languages and Civilizations
Amherst College
JAINISM

Christopher Baber
University of Birmingham
TOOLS

Jörg Baberowski
Professor of East European History
Institut für Geschichtswissenschaften
STALINISM

Roger E. Backhouse
University of Birmingham
BARRO-GROSSMAN MODEL

Edwin T. Bacon
Reader in Comparative Politics,
Birkbeck College
University of London
GULAGS

Rachel E. Baden
Duke University Medical Center,
University of Alabama
ATTENTION-DEFICIT/
HYPERACTIVITY DISORDER

M. V. Lee Badgett
Associate Professor of Economics,
University of Massachusetts, Amherst
Research Director, Williams Institute,
University of California, Los Angeles
SEXUAL ORIENTATION, SOCIAL
AND ECONOMIC
CONSEQUENCES

John Baffes
Senior Economist
The World Bank
COFFEE INDUSTRY
COTTON INDUSTRY
SUBSIDIES, FARM
TEA INDUSTRY

Mohsen Bahmani-Oskooee
Patricia and Harvey Wilmeth Professor
of Economics
University of Wisconsin–Milwaukee
J-CURVE

DeeVon Bailey
Professor, Department of Economics
Utah State University
CATTLE INDUSTRY

Ronald W. Bailey
Professor, Department of African
American Studies/History,
Northeastern University
Visiting Distinguished Professor,
Africana Studies, Savannah State
University
SLAVE TRADE
SLAVERY INDUSTRY

Stanley R. Bailey
Assistant Professor, Department of
Sociology
University of California, Irvine
DEMOCRACY, RACIAL
MULATTO ESCAPE HATCH

William Sims Bainbridge
Independent Scholar
Virginia
CLASSICAL MUSIC
COMPUTERS: SCIENCE AND
SOCIETY
FUTUROLOGY
SPACE EXPLORATION

Anne Baker
PhD Student
University of Notre Dame
CONGRESS, U.S.

John R. Baker
Professor of Anthropology, Life
Sciences Department
Moorpark College
HALLUCINOGENS

Lee D. Baker
Department of Cultural Anthropology
Duke University
BOAS, FRANZ

Falu Bakrania
Ethnic Studies Program
San Francisco State University
HYBRIDITY

Diana E. Baldermann
PhD Student, Department of
Sociology
SUNY–Stony Brook, New York
PERONISM

John D. Baldwin
Department of Sociology
University of California at Santa
Barbara
MEAD, GEORGE HERBERT

Laura C. Ball
Department of Psychology
York University
TWIN STUDIES

Terence Ball
Professor, Department of Political
Science
Arizona State University
CIVIL DISOBEDIENCE

Mohammed A. Bamyeh
Hubert H. Humphrey Professor of
International Studies
Macalester College
AL JAZEERA
ARAB LEAGUE, THE
ARABS
BEN-GURION, DAVID
GRAMSCI, ANTONIO
MUHAMMAD

Taradas Bandyopadhyay
Department of Economics
University of California, Riverside
REVEALED PREFERENCE

Geoffrey Banks
Department of Sociology
University of Illinois at Chicago
OPPOSITIONALITY

Sergey S. Barabanov
Assistant Professor, Department of
Finance, Opus College of Business
University of Saint Thomas
INVESTORS, INSTITUTIONAL

Maryann Barakso
American University
NATIONAL ORGANIZATION FOR
WOMEN

Amatzia Baram
Faculty of Humanities, Department of
Middle East History
University of Haifa, Israel
HUSSEIN, SADDAM

Roberto Baranzini
Professor, Centre Walras-Pareto
University of Lausanne, Switzerland
LAUSANNE, SCHOOL OF
WALRAS, LÉON

Benjamin R. Barber
Walt Whitman Professor Emeritus,
Rutgers University
Distinguished Senior Fellow, Demos
in New York
DEMOCRACY, REPRESENTATIVE
AND PARTICIPATORY
HARTZ, LOUIS

Nelson H. Barbosa-Filho
Professor, Institute of Economics
Federal University of Rio de Janeiro
VERDOORN'S LAW

Franco Barchiesi
Assistant Professor, Department of
African-American and African Studies
Ohio State University
ASIATIC MODE OF
PRODUCTION
CAPITALIST MODE OF
PRODUCTION
CLASS CONSCIOUSNESS
FEUDAL MODE OF
PRODUCTION

David L. Barkley
Professor, Department of Applied
Economics and Statistics
Clemson University
BACKWASH EFFECTS

Crystal L. Barksdale
Duke University Medical Center
HOMELESSNESS

Alan Barnard
Professor, School of Social and
Political Studies
University of Edinburgh, United
Kingdom
ANTHROPOLOGY, BRITISH
STRUCTURALISM

William T. Barndt
Department of Politics
Princeton University
CORPORATISM

Sandra L. Barnes
Associate Professor, Department of
Sociology and Anthropology and the
African American Studies Research
Center
Purdue University
GHETTO

Vincent Barnett
Independent researcher
London
KEYNES, JOHN MAYNARD
RUSSIAN ECONOMICS

William A. Barnett
Oswald Distinguished Professor of
Macroeconomics
University of Kansas
DIVISIA MONETARY INDEX
MONEY, SUPPLY OF

John Barnshaw
Disaster Research Center
University of Delaware
RIOTS

Michael D. Barr
Lecturer, International Relations
School of Political and International
Studies, Flinders University, Adelaide
MERITOCRACY, MULTIRACIAL

Humberto Barreto
Department of Economics
Wabash College
SIMULTANEOUS EQUATION
BIAS

Lowell W. Barrington
Associate Professor, Department of
Political Science
Marquette University
AUTHORITARIANISM

Alexandre Rands Barros
Professor, Department of Economics
Federal University of Pernambuco,
Brazil
PERIODIZATION

Clyde Barrow
Department of Policy Studies
University of Massachusetts at
Dartmouth
POLITICAL SCIENCE
STATE, THE

Adam Etheridge Barry
Instructor, Department of Health and
Kinesiology
Texas A&M University
ALCOHOLISM

Diane Barthel-Bouchier
Professor, Department of Sociology
Stony Brook University
LONELY CROWD, THE

Frances Bartkowski
Associate Professor, English and
Women's Studies
Rutgers University, Newark
UTOPIANISM

Ira Bashkow
Associate Professor, Department of
Anthropology
University of Virginia
SAHLINS, MARSHALL

Robert H. Bates
Eaton Professor of the Science of
Government, Department of
Government
Harvard University
DEVELOPMENT AND ETHNIC
DIVERSITY

Juan Battle
Professor
City University of New York Graduate
Center
ATTITUDES, BEHAVIORAL

Whitney L. Battle-Baptiste
Assistant Professor, Department of
Anthropology
University of Massachusetts–Amherst
SLAVE LIVES, ARCHAEOLOGY
OF

Harald Bauder
Associate Professor, Department of
Geography
University of Guelph, Canada
NEIGHBORHOODS

Reşat Bayer
Assistant Professor, Department of
International Relations
Koç University, Istanbul
PEACE

Annemarie Bean
Visiting Associate Professor, African
American Studies Program
Wesleyan University
MINSTRELSY

Geraldine Cannon Becker
Assistant Professor of English and
Creative Writing
University of Maine at Fort Kent
STORYTELLING

Marc Becker
Associate Professor of Latin American
History
Truman State University
INDIGENISMO
MEXICAN REVOLUTION
(1910–1920)
REVOLUTIONS, LATIN
AMERICAN
ZAPATA, EMILIANO

William E. Becker
Professor of Economics
Indiana University, Bloomington
LAW OF LARGE NUMBERS
SAMPLING

Jason Beckfield
Assistant Professor, Department of
Sociology
Harvard University
GLOBALIZATION, SOCIAL AND
ECONOMIC ASPECTS OF

Peter R. Bedford
John and Jane Wold Professor
Union College, Schenectady, NY
RETALIATION

Jamie D. Bedics
Department of Clinical Psychology
Fuller Theological Seminary
LEARY, TIMOTHY

Leonard Beeghley
Professor of Sociology
University of Florida
WEBER, MAX

James K. Beggan
Associate Professor of Sociology
University of Louisville
PROTOTYPES

A. L. Beier
Professor, Department of History
Illinois State University
VAGABONDS

Bernard C. Beins
Professor, Department of Psychology
Ithaca College
EQUILIBRIUM IN PSYCHOLOGY
GESTALT THERAPY

PERIOD EFFECTS
SELIGMAN, MARTIN
STATISTICS IN THE SOCIAL
SCIENCES
TEACHERS

René Bekkers
Department of Sociology, Utrecht
University, Netherlands
Department of Philanthropic Studies,
Vrije Universiteit Amsterdam,
Netherlands
VOLUNTEERISM

Marc F. Bellemare
Assistant Professor of Public Policy
and Economics
Duke University
SHARECROPPING
TOBIT

Riccardo Bellofiore
Professor of Political Economy,
Department of Economics
University of Bergamo, Italy
LUXEMBURG, ROSA

Todd L. Belt
Assistant Professor, Department of
Political Science
University of Hawai'i at Hilo
PEARL HARBOR

Stephen Benard
Department of Sociology
Cornell University
NORMS

Hichem Ben-El-Mechaiekh
Professor and Chair, Department of
Mathematics
Brock University, St. Catharines,
Ontario, Canada
MATHEMATICAL ECONOMICS

Joann P. Benigno
Assistant Professor, School of Hearing,
Speech and Language Sciences
Ohio University
CHILDREN
SCARR, SANDRA WOOD

Ludy T. Benjamin, Jr.
Professor, Department of Psychology
Texas A&M University
MÜNSTERBERG, HUGO

Gary G. Bennett
Assistant Professor, Harvard School of
Public Health

Dana–Farber Cancer Institute
JOHN HENRYISM

Gerren J. Bennett
University of California, Los Angeles
AMERICAN DILEMMA

Paul Benneworth
Academic Fellow
Newcastle University, United
Kingdom
FACTORIES
GEOGRAPHY

John F. Berdell
DePaul University
TRADE, ANGLO-PORTUGUESE

Manfred Berg
University of Heidelberg, Germany
LYND, STAUGHTON

Manfred Max Bergman
Professor, Department of Sociology
University of Basel, Switzerland
STRATIFICATION, POLITICAL

Villy Bergström
Retired Associate Professor of
Economics, Uppsala University
Former Deputy Governor of the
Riksbank (Swedish Centry Bank)
LUNDBERG, ERIK

Dagmar Bergs-Winkels
Professor for Educational Studies and
Early Education
Hochschule für angewandte
Wissenschaften, Germany
DEVELOPMENT,
INSTITUTIONAL

Lisa J. Berlin
Research Scientist, Center for Child
and Family Policy
Duke University
ATTACHMENT THEORY

Walter Berns
Professor Emeritus, Georgetown
University
Resident Scholar, American Enterprise
Institute
PATRIOTISM

Irwin S. Bernstein
Department of Psychology
University of Georgia
ALPHA-MALE

Jared Bernstein
Senior Economist
Economic Policy Institute
GREENSPAN, ALAN
HARD-CORE UNEMPLOYED

R. B. Bernstein
Distinguished Adjunct Professor of
Law
New York Law School
JEFFERSON, THOMAS

Gary G. Berntson
Professor of Psychology, Psychiatry,
and Pediatrics
Ohio State University
DETERMINISM, NONADDITIVE
NEUROSCIENCE, SOCIAL

Daniele Besomi
Independent Researcher
BUSINESS CYCLES, THEORIES
COBWEB CYCLES
OVERPRODUCTION

William J. G. Bewick
PhD Candidate, Department of
Political Science
Michigan State University
DIVINE RIGHT

Vivek Bhandari
Associate Professor of History and
South Asian Studies
Hampshire College
GANDHI, INDIRA

Muhammad Ishaq Bhatti
Department of Economics and
Finance, La Trobe University,
Melbourne, Australia
International Centre for Education in
Islamic Finance, Malaysia
ECONOMICS, ISLAMIC

Alexandr Bialsky
School of Political Science
University of Haifa
AL-QAEDA
SUICIDE BOMBERS
VIOLENCE IN TERRORISM

Ana Maria Bianchi
Professor, Department of Economics
Universidade de São Paulo
ECONOMIC RHETORIC

Thomas K. Bias
Assistant Editor, The West Virginia
Public Affairs Reporter

The Institute for Public Affairs at West
Virginia University
MICHELS, ROBERT

Douglas Bicket
Assistant Professor of
Communication/Journalism
St. John Fisher College, Rochester,
New York
DETERMINISM,
TECHNOLOGICAL

John Bickle
Professor, Department of Philosophy
and Neuroscience Graduate Program
University of Cincinnati
REDUCTIONISM

Laada Bilaniuk
Associate Professor, Department of
Anthropology
University of Washington
ANTHROPOLOGY, LINGUISTIC

Sherrilyn M. Billger
Assistant Professor, Department of
Economics
Illinois State University
BLUE COLLAR AND WHITE
COLLAR
WORK WEEK

Anne Binderkrantz
Assistant Professor, Department of
Political Science
University of Aarhus, Denmark
INTEREST GROUPS AND
INTERESTS

Kevin Binfield
Professor of English and Humanities
Murray State University
LUDDITES

Sharon R. Bird
Associate Professor, Department of
Sociology
Iowa State University
MASCULINITY STUDIES

Michael A. Bishop
Department of Philosophy
Florida State University
DECISION-MAKING

Aristidis Bitzenis
Assistant Professor, Department of
International and European Economic
and Political Studies

University of Macedonia,
Thessaloniki, Greece
  BUSINESS
  ECONOMIES, TRANSITIONAL
  ENTERPRISE
  EXCHANGE RATES
  INTERNATIONAL MONETARY
    FUND
  MARKET ECONOMY
  MONEY LAUNDERING
  PRIVATE SECTOR
  TRADE, BILATERAL

Ulf Ingvar Bjereld
Professor and Head of Department of
Political Science
Göteborg University
  DESTABILIZATION

Maureen M. Black
John A. Scholl Professor, Department
of Pediatrics
University of Maryland School of
Medicine
  STUNTED GROWTH

Bethany E. Blalock
Department of Sociology
University of Virginia
  LIFESTYLES

Stephen J. Blank
Professor, Strategic Studies Institute
U.S. Army War College
  CIVIL-MILITARY RELATION
  DEFENSE, NATIONAL

Thomas Blass
Professor, Department of Psychology
University of Maryland, Baltimore
County
  MILGRAM, STANLEY
  OBEDIENCE, DESTRUCTIVE

Judith Blau
Professor, Department of Sociology
University of North Carolina, Chapel
Hill
  BLAU, PETER M.
  HUMAN RIGHTS

Reva Blau
Wellfleet, Massachusetts
  BLAU, PETER M.

Michael Blim
Professor of Anthropology, Graduate
Center
City University of New York
  JUSTICE, DISTRIBUTIVE

TRIUMPHALISM
TRUST

Ray Block, Jr.
Assistant Professor, Department of
Political Science
Florida State University
  POLITICS, URBAN

S. Brock Blomberg
Claremont McKenna College
  BUSINESS CYCLES, POLITICAL

Joel David Bloom
University at Albany, State University
of New York
  DIXIECRATS

Scott C. Blum
Department of Psychology and Social
Behavior
University of California, Irvine
  COPING

Stephan Boehm
Department of Economics
University of Graz, Austria
  HAYEK, FRIEDRICH AUGUST
    VON
  SCHUMPETER, JOSEPH ALOIS

Klaus Boehnke
Full Professor of Social Science
Methodology, School of Humanities
and Social Sciences
Jacobs University Bremen, Germany
  DEVELOPMENT,
    INSTITUTIONAL

Johanna Boers
PhD Student, Department of
Sociology
Georgia State University
  MORALITY AND INEQUALITY

Peter J. Boettke
University Professor, Economics
Department
George Mason University
  DIRIGISTE
  LAISSEZ-FAIRE

Vicki L. Bogan
Assistant Professor, Department of
Applied Economics and Management
Cornell University
  MARKOWITZ, HARRY M.

Barrymore Anthony Bogues
Harmon Family Professor of Africana
Studies and Political Science; Chair,

Africana Studies; Honorary Professor
in Humanities, Brown University;
Center of African Studies, University
of Cape Town
  REGGAE

Mauro Boianovsky
Professor, Department of Economics
Universidade de Brasilia
  FRIEDMAN, MILTON
  PATINKIN, DON

Lawrence A. Boland
Professor, Department of Economics
Simon Fraser University
  ECONOMICS, NEOCLASSICAL
  EQUILIBRIUM IN ECONOMICS

Ronald Keith Bolender
Professor of Organizational Leadership
Mount Vernon Nazarene University
  SOCIAL STATICS

John Boli
Professor, Department of Sociology
Emory University
  INTERNATIONAL
    NONGOVERNMENTAL
    ORGANIZATIONS (INGOs)

O. Nigel Bolland
Professor Emeritus, Department of
Sociology and Anthropology
Colgate University
  CREOLIZATION

David Bollier
Editor, OntheCommons.org
Amherst, Massachusetts
  COMMON LAND

Julio Boltvinik
El Colegio de México
  NEEDS

Idrissa A. Boly
Associate in Research
Duke University
  HESSIAN MATRIX
  JACOBIAN MATRIX
  NODE, STABLE

Charles F. Bond, Jr.
Professor of Psychology
Texas Christian University
  LYING
  SOCIAL FACILITATION

Patrick Bond
Professor, School of Development
Studies

University of KwaZulu–Natal, Durban, South Africa
TOWNSHIPS

Michael E. Bonine
Professor, Departments of Geography and Near Eastern Studies
University of Arizona
FERTILE CRESCENT

Alan Booth
Professor of History
University of Exeter, Cornwall Campus
TREASURY VIEW, THE

Joel Bordeaux
Teaching Fellow, Department of Religion
Columbia University
KSHATRIYAS

Lea Bornstein
Department of Biology, University of Pennsylvania
National Institute of Mental Health
PARENTHOOD, TRANSITION TO STABILITY, PSYCHOLOGICAL

Marc H. Bornstein
Senior Scientist, Child and Family Research
National Institute of Child Health and Human Development
PARENTHOOD, TRANSITION TO STABILITY, PSYCHOLOGICAL

Robert F. Bornstein
Professor, Department of Psychology
Adelphi University
DEPENDENCY

David A. Boruchoff
Associate Professor, Department of Hispanic Studies
McGill University
CORTÉS, HERNÁN

Julie-Anne Boudreau
Canada Research Chair on the City and Issues of Insecurity, National Institute for Scientific Research
University of Quebec
URBANITY

Hassan Bougrine
Professor, Department of Economics
Laurentian University, Canada
WEALTH

Vasilios T. Bournas
Graduate Student, Department of Sociology
Boston College
MANKILLER, WILMA

Natasha K. Bowen
Assistant Professor, School of Social Work
University of North Carolina at Chapel Hill
VALIDATION

Roger Bowles
Professor, Centre for Criminal Justice Economics and Psychology
University of York
CONFISCATION

Simon W. Bowmaker
Visiting Lecturer in Economics
New York University
RECORDING INDUSTRY

Jonathan Boyarin
Distinguished Professor of Modern Jewish Thought
University of North Carolina at Chapel Hill
JEWS
ZIONISM

Jay Boyer
Professor
Arizona State University
COMEDY
MODERNISM
STEPFORD WIVES

Glenn E. Bracey, II
Research Assistant
Texas A&M University
RACIAL SLURS

Richard Bradley
History/Honors
Central Methodist University
HAYMARKET SQUARE RIOT

York W. Bradshaw
Dean, College of Arts and Sciences and Professor of Sociology
University of South Carolina Upstate
SOCIOLOGY, THIRD WORLD

David Brady
Associate Professor, Department of Sociology
Duke University

GLOBALIZATION, SOCIAL AND ECONOMIC ASPECTS OF STRATIFICATION

Steven J. Brams
Professor of Politics
New York University
GAME THEORY

Jennie E. Brand
Assistant Professor
University of California, Los Angeles
INTERVENTIONS, SOCIAL POLICY
POPULATION STUDIES

John Brandenburg
Florida Space Institute, University of Central Florida
Kennedy Space Center Florida
MARS

Peter Bratsis
Lecturer in Political Theory
University of Salford
NEOINSTITUTIONALISM
POULANTZAS, NICOS

William E. Breen
George Mason University
SOCIAL ANXIETY

David M. Brennan
Assistant Professor, Department of Economics
Franklin and Marshall College
STAKEHOLDERS

Adam Briggle
Department of Philosophy
University of Twente, The Netherlands
MODERNITY

Thomas A. Brigham
Professor and Scientist, Department of Psychology
Washington State University
AIDS

Klaus E. Brinkmann
Associate Professor, Department of Philosophy
Boston University
IDEALISM

Thomas M. Brinthaupt
Professor, Department of Psychology
Middle Tennessee State University, Murfreesboro, Tennessee
IDENTITY
NATURAL SELECTION

PERSONALITY, TYPE A/TYPE B
ROTTER'S INTERNAL-
    EXTERNAL LOCUS OF
    CONTROL SCALE
SELF-DISCLOSURE
SELF-MONITORING

William A. Brock
Vilas Research Professor of Economics,
Department of Economics
University of Wisconsin–Madison
EXCHANGEABILITY
MICROECONOMICS
OPTIMIZING BEHAVIOR
PRINCIPAL-AGENT MODELS
PRISONER'S DILEMMA
    (ECONOMICS)

Simon J. Bronner
Distinguished Professor of American
Studies and Folklore
The Pennsylvania State University,
Harrisburg
ETHNOLOGY AND FOLKLORE
TRADITION

Alfred L. Brophy
University of Alabama
SLAVERY
TULSA RIOT

Curtis Brown
Professor, Department of Philosophy
Trinity University
FUNCTIONALISM

Judith K. Brown
Professor of Anthropology,
Department of Sociology and
Anthropology
Oakland University, Michigan
WOMEN

Leslie Brown
Assistant Professor of History and
African and African American Studies
Washington University
JIM CROW

Pete Brown
Associate Professor of Anthropology,
Department of Religious Studies and
Anthropology
University of Wisconsin Oshkosh
CHIAPAS

Seyom Brown
Department of Politics
Brandeis University
PAX BRITANNICA

Thomas F. Brown
Assistant Professor of Sociology
Northeast Lakeview College
BLOOD AND BLOODLINE
PASSING
VINDICATION

Khalilah L. Brown-Dean
Yale University
MARSHALL, THURGOOD

Jeffrey L. Brudney
Albert A. Levin Chair of Urban
Studies and Public Service, Maxine
Goodman Levin College of Urban
Affairs
Cleveland State University
NATIONAL SERVICE PROGRAMS
VOLUNTEER PROGRAMS

Michael J. Brun
Visiting Instructor
Illinois State University
CAPITALISM
VIOLENCE, ROLE IN RESOURCE
    ALLOCATION

David L. Brunsma
Associate Professor of Sociology and
Black Studies
University of Missouri–Columbia
COLONIALISM

Kevin Bruyneel
Assistant Professor of Politics
Babson College
VIOLENCE, FRANTZ FANON ON

Anne Buchanan
Senior Research Scientist, Department
of Anthropology
Pennsylvania State University,
University Park
ANTHROPOLOGY, BIOLOGICAL

Julie A. Buck
Assistant Professor of Criminal Justice
Weber State University
HEARSAY

Stephen Buckles
Senior Lecturer in Economics
Vanderbilt University
NATIONAL ASSESSMENT OF
    EDUCATIONAL PROGRESS

Peter Buckroyd
English Department
University of Washington
SATIRE

Barbara Bucur
Center for the Study of Aging and
Human Development
Duke University Medical Center
SELECTIVE ATTENTION

Eloise A. Buker
Retired Professor of Political Science
and Director of Women's Studies
Saint Louis University
WOMEN'S LIBERATION

Peter Edward Bull
Department of Psychology
University of York
MICROANALYSIS

Ashley A. Buller
Doctoral Student, Department of
Psychology
Iowa State University
SELF-FULFILLING PROPHECIES

Sarah A. Burgard
Assistant Professor, Department of
Sociology
University of Michigan
OCCUPATIONAL STATUS

John D. Burger
Associate Professor of Economics
Loyola College in Maryland
FIELDS' INDEX OF ECONOMIC
    INEQUALITY

Heidi Burgess
Codirector, Conflict Research
Consortium
University of Colorado
CONFLICT

Robert G. Burgess
Vice Chancellor
University of Leicester
OBSERVATION, PARTICIPANT

Raymonda Burgman
DePauw University
MILL, JOHN STUART

Meghan A. Burke
PhD Candidate
Loyola University Chicago
COLORISM
DETERMINISM, BIOLOGICAL
FACTORY SYSTEM

Andrew E. Busch
Professor, Department of Government

Claremont McKenna College
CONSERVATISM

Joan Busfield
Professor, Department of Sociology
University of Essex
MENTAL HEALTH

Roderick Bush
Associate Professor
St. John's University, New York
COLONY, INTERNAL

Colin D. Butler
School of Health and Social
Development
Deakin University, Australia
DEFORESTATION
NORTH AND SOUTH, THE
(GLOBAL)

Kenneth J. Button
University Professor, School of Public
Policy
George Mason University
LEGACY EFFECTS
SHIPPING INDUSTRY

William Byne
Associate Professor, Department of
Psychiatry
Mount Sinai School of Medicine
SEXUAL ORIENTATION,
DETERMINANTS OF

Goldie S. Byrd
Professor, Department of Biology
North Carolina A&T State University
HEREDITY
MIDLIFE CRISIS

Malcolm Byrne
Director of Research, The National
Security Archive
The George Washington University
HUNGARIAN REVOLUTION

Chonghyun Byun
Visiting Assistant Professor, Rose-
Hulman Institute of Technology
Terre Haute, IN
UTILITY FUNCTION

Rachel Bzostek
Assistant Professor, Department of
Political Science
California State University, Bakersfield
ARAFAT, YASIR
KNESSET, THE

PREEMPTIVE STRIKE
SUEZ CRISIS

Luís M.B. Cabral
W. R. Berkley Professor of Economics
and Business
New York University
PREDATORY PRICING

John T. Cacioppo
Tiffany and Margaret Blake
Distinguished Service Professor
University of Chicago
DETERMINISM, NONADDITIVE
NEUROSCIENCE, SOCIAL

Carlo Caduff
Research Associate
Anthropology of the Contemporary
Research Collaboratory
GENOMICS

Christopher J. Caes
Assistant Professor, Center for
European Studies and Department of
Germanic and Slavic Studies
University of Florida
SOLIDARNOŚĆ

C. George Caffentzis
Professor, Department of Philosophy
University of Southern Maine
HUME, DAVID

Ryan Ashley Caldwell
Texas A&M University
CLASS, LEISURE
EMPIRICISM
NATURAL RIGHTS
PARSONS, TALCOTT
SUICIDE
VEBLEN, THORSTEIN

Brian Calfano
Assistant Professor, Political Science
Chatham University
CUBAN MISSILE CRISIS
SURVEYS, SAMPLE

Craig Calhoun
President
Social Science Research Council
MERTON, ROBERT K.

Peter L. Callero
Professor, Department of Sociology
Western Oregon University
ROLE THEORY

Lynn Clark Callister
Professor, College of Nursing

Brigham Young University
HOPE

Ernesto F. Calvo
University of Houston
PATRONAGE

Gavin Cameron
Reader in Macroeconomics,
Department of Economics
Oxford University
PRODUCTIVITY

Kevin Cameron
Department of Government and Law
Lafayette College
TOTALITARIANISM

Maxwell A. Cameron
Professor, Department of Political
Science
The University of British Columbia
SEPARATION OF POWERS

Horace G. Campbell
Syracuse University
AMIN, IDI

Lorne Campbell
Associate Professor, Department of
Psychology
University of Western Ontario
MARITAL CONFLICT
SOCIOBIOLOGY

W. Keith Campbell
Associate Professor of Psychology
University of Georgia
NARCISSISM

Margo A. Candelaria
Postdoctoral Fellow, Department of
Pediatrics
University of Maryland School of
Medicine
STUNTED GROWTH

Nergis Canefe
Associate Professor, Department of
Political Science
York University, Toronto, Canada
XENOPHOBIA

Shi Larry Cao
Morningstar, Inc.
LIFE-CYCLE HYPOTHESIS
MODIGLIANI-MILLER
THEOREMS
SOROS, GEORGE

Arthur L. Caplan
Director, Center for Bioethics, School of Medicine
University of Pennsylvania
BIOETHICS

Richard K. Caputo
Professor and Doctoral Program Director, Wurzweiler School of Social Work
Yeshiva University
DEVELOPMENT IN SOCIOLOGY
HEAD START

Art A. Carden
Assistant Professor
Rhodes College
NORTH, DOUGLASS

Bernardo J. Carducci
Professor, Department of Psychology and Director, Shyness Research Institute
Indiana University Southeast
JUNG, CARL
SHYNESS

Henry F. Carey
Department of Political Science
Georgia State University
POSITIVISM

Michael C. Carhart
Assistant Professor, History Department
Old Dominion University
ENLIGHTENMENT

Kenneth I. Carlaw
Associate Professor, Economics
University of British Columbia, Kelowna, Canada
RETURNS, DIMINISHING
RETURNS TO SCALE
RETURNS TO SCALE, ASYMMETRIC

Donal E. Carlston
Professor of Psychology
Purdue University
PERSON MEMORY

Charles V. Carnegie
Professor, Department of Anthropology
Bates College
MINTZ, SIDNEY W.

Marine Carrasco
Professor, Department of Economics
University of Montreal, Quebec, Canada
METHOD OF MOMENTS

Patrick J. Carroll
Assistant Professor, Department of Psychology
The Ohio State University–Lima
MULTIFINALITY
OVERACHIEVERS
SELF-PERCEPTION THEORY

Jamie L. Carson
Assistant Professor, Department of Political Science
The University of Georgia
VETO

Niambi M. Carter
Visiting Assistant Professor
Duke University
CHISHOLM, SHIRLEY

Rosalind D. Cartwright
Professor, Department of Behavioral Sciences
Rush University Medical Center
DREAMING

Andrés Carvajal
Assistant Professor, Department of Economics
University of Warwick
DEMAND
MANIFOLDS
PREFERENCES

Graham Cassano
Assistant Professor, Department of Sociology and Anthropology
Oakland University, Michigan
SUBJECT/SELF
UNIONS

Felipe González Castro
Professor, Department of Psychology
Arizona State University
PREVENTION SCIENCE

A. Charles Catania
University of Maryland, Baltimore County (UMBC)
PAVLOV, IVAN
SKINNER, B. F.

Brian J. Caterino
Independent Scholar
Rochester, New York
CRITICAL THEORY
FREEDOM

POSTSTRUCTURALISM
POWER ELITE

Peter P. Catterall
Queen Mary, University of London
NATIONALIZATION
SOCIALISM, CHRISTIAN

Stephen G. Cecchetti
Barbara and Richard M. Rosenberg Professor of Global Finance, International Business School, Brandeis University
Research Associate, National Bureau of Economic Research
POLICY, MONETARY

Aydin A. Cecen
Professor of Economics; Director, Center for International Trade and Economic Research
Central Michigan University
CHAOS THEORY

Zeynep Cemalcilar
Department of Psychology
Koç University, Istanbul, Turkey
TIME ORIENTATION

Antonio Cepeda-Benito
Professor of Psychology and Associate Dean of Faculties
Texas A&M University
TOLERANCE, DRUG

Cécile Cézanne
Assistant Lecturer, Department of Economics
University of Nice Sophia Antipolis, France
CAPITALISM, MANAGERIAL

Bhaskar Chakravorti
Partner
McKinsey and Company
PARADOX OF VOTING

Stephen Chan
Professor of International Relations, University of London
Foundation Dean of Law and Social Sciences, School of Oriental and African Studies
MUGABE, ROBERT

Seth J. Chandler
Foundation Professor of Law
University of Houston Law Center
INSURANCE INDUSTRY

Chiung-Fang Chang
Department of Sociology, Social
Work, and Criminal Justice
Lamar University
LINEAR REGRESSION

Hua-Hua Chang
University of Illinois at
Urbana–Champaign
PSYCHOMETRICS

Tanya L. Chartrand
Duke University
SUBLIMINAL SUGGESTION

Lydia Chávez
Professor, Graduate School of
Journalism
University of California, Berkeley
CALIFORNIA CIVIL RIGHTS
INITIATIVE

Larry W. Chavis
University of North Carolina–Chapel
Hill
BRIBERY

Xi Chen
Research Fellow, Department of
Sociology, Texas A&M University
Lecturer in the Department of
Sociology, Quinnipiac University
MEASUREMENT

Yuelan Chen
Department of Economics
The University of Melbourne
STRATEGY AND VOTING GAMES

Victor Chernozhukov
Massachusetts Institute of Technology
BAYESIAN ECONOMETRICS

Frances Cherry
Professor, Department of Psychology
Carleton University, Ottawa
PETTIGREW, THOMAS F.

Jorge L. Chinea
Associate Professor of History and
Director, Center for Chicano-Boricua
Studies
Wayne State University
BORICUA

Ngina Chiteji
Associate Professor, Department of
Economics

Skidmore College, Saratoga Springs,
New York
INHERITANCE
INHERITANCE TAX

Jamsheed K. Choksy
Professor of Central Eurasian Studies;
Professor of History; Adjunct Professor
of Religious Studies
Indiana University, Bloomington
PURIFICATION
SUBALTERN

Dennis Chong
John D. and Catherine T. MacArthur
Professor, Department of Political
Science
Northwestern University
COLLECTIVE ACTION

Rosalind S. Chou
Department of Sociology
Texas A&M University
WHITENING

Mark Christian
Department of Sociology and Black
World Studies Program
Miami University
RACE-BLIND POLICIES

Yvette Christiansë
Associate Professor, English and
Literary Studies
Fordham University
GOBINEAU, COMTE DE
NARRATIVES

Charlene Christie
Assistant Professor, Department of
Psychology
SUNY College at Oneonta
REALISM, EXPERIMENTAL

Costas Christou
Senior Economist
International Monetary Fund,
Washington, DC
BALANCE OF PAYMENTS
EXPORTS

Hyejin Iris Chu
Senior Researcher, Department of
Women's Policy
Daejeon Development Institute
SOCIAL CONSTRUCTIONISM
SOCIAL IDENTIFICATION

Ken Chujo
Professor of History, College of Liberal
Arts
J. F. Oberlin University
DAUGHTERS OF THE
AMERICAN REVOLUTION

Constance F. Citro
Director, Committee on National
Statistics
National Research Council of the
National Academies
SURVEY OF INCOME AND
PROGRAM PARTICIPATION

Donald H. Clairmont
Professor Emeritus and Director,
Atlantic Institute of Criminology
Dalhousie University
AFRICVILLE (CANADA)

Margaret S. Clark
Professor, Department of Psychology
Yale University
FRIENDSHIP

Terry Nichols Clark
Professor of Sociology
University of Chicago
SOCIAL THEORY
SOCIOLOGY, URBAN

Harold D. Clarke
Ashbel Smith Professor, School of
Economic, Political and Policy
Sciences
University of Texas at Dallas
CONSERVATIVE PARTY
(BRITAIN)

Andrew Clarkwest
Research Associate, Mathematica
Policy Research
Washington DC
JENCKS, CHRISTOPHER

William M. Clements
Professor, Department of English and
Philosophy
Arkansas State University
RELIGION

David Coates
Worrell Professor of Anglo-American
Studies
Wake Forest University
BLAIR, TONY

Rodney D. Coates
Department of Sociology and
Gerontology
Miami University of Ohio
DESEGREGATION
ETHNIC ENTERPRISES
MULTICULTURALISM

James Cobbe
Professor, Department of Economics
Florida State University
MAHATHIR MOHAMAD

W. Paul Cockshott
Department of Computing Science
University of Glasgow
CLASS, RENTIER
RELATIVE SURPLUS VALUE

Peter A. Coclanis
Albert R. Newsome Professor of
History
University of North Carolina–Chapel
Hill
TIME ON THE CROSS

Andrew I. Cohen
Associate Director, Jean Beer
Blumenfeld Center for Ethics
Georgia State University
SOCIAL CONTRACT

David Cohen
Director, Berkeley War Crimes Studies
Center; Sidney and Margaret Ancker
Distinguished Professor of the
Humanities
University of California, Berkeley
WAR CRIMES

Deborah Cohen
Assistant Professor
University of Missouri–St. Louis
BRACERO PROGRAM

Erik Cohen
George S. Wise Professor Emeritus of
Sociology, Department of Sociology
and Social Anthropology
The Hebrew University of Jerusalem
TOURISM

Giorgio Colacchio
Associate Professor of Economics,
Department of Juridical Studies
University of Salento, Lecce, Italy
LABOR, MARGINAL PRODUCT
OF

Damon Coletta
Associate Professor, Department of
Political Science
U.S. Air Force Academy
DEFENSE
FRANCO, FRANCISCO

Randall Collins
Professor of Sociology
University of Pennsylvania
GOFFMAN, ERVING

Josep M. Colomer
Higher Council of Scientific Research
(CSIC) and Pompeu Fabra University
Barcelona, Cat., Spain
ELECTORAL SYSTEMS
MAJORITY RULE
MULTIPARTY SYSTEMS

Scott Coltrane
Professor, Department of Sociology;
Associate Dean, College of
Humanities, Arts & Social Sciences
University of California, Riverside
MEN

Pasquale Commendatore
Professor, Department of Economic
Theory and Applications
University of Naples "Federico II"
ECONOMICS, NEO-RICARDIAN

Pedro Conceição
Director, Office of Development
Studies
United Nations Development
Programme
INCOME DISTRIBUTION
UNIVERSITY OF TEXAS
INEQUALITY PROJECT

James H. Cone
Charles Augustus Briggs Distinguished
Professor of Systematic Theology
Union Theological Seminary
MALCOLM X

Katherine Jewsbury Conger
Family Research Group, Department
of Human and Community
Development
University of California, Davis
HUMAN ECOLOGY
SIBLING RELATIONSHIPS

David B. Conklin
Chelsea School
HYPOTHESIS, NESTED

INTERNET, IMPACT ON
POLITICS
SYSTEMS THEORY

Tamlin S. Conner
Postdoctoral Fellow, Department of
Psychiatry
University of Connecticut Health
Center
PERSONALITY

Cecilia Conrad
Vice President and Dean of the
Faculty
Scripps College
WEAVER, ROBERT C.

Philip E. Converse
Professor Emeritus
University of Michigan
CAMPBELL, ANGUS

Cita Cook
Associate Professor, History
Department
University of West Georgia
GENTILITY

Philip J. Cook
ITT/Sanford Professor of Public Policy
Duke University
ACTING WHITE
WINNER-TAKE-ALL SOCIETY

Alexandra Cooper
Associate Director for Education and
Training, Social Science Research
Institute
Duke University
NADER'S RAIDERS

David E. Cooper
Professor of Philosophy
University of Durham, United
Kingdom
AESTHETICS

François Cooren
Professor
Université de Montréal
SPEECH ACT THEORY

J. Angelo Corlett
Professor of Philosophy and Ethics
San Diego State University
PUNISHMENT

Rachel Traut Cortes
Doctoral Student in Sociology

Texas A&M University
IMMIGRANTS TO NORTH
AMERICA

Kelli Ann Costa
Programme Director, Achill
Archaeological Field School
Dooagh, Achill Island, Co. Mayo,
Ireland
AUTOCRACY
IRISH REPUBLICAN ARMY
POSTCOLONIALISM

Paul T. Costa
National Institute on Aging
NEUROTICISM

Matthew C. Costello
Research Associate, Department of
Psychiatry and Behavioral Sciences
Duke University Medical Center
SEMANTIC MEMORY

Ronald W. Cotterill
Editor, *Agribusiness: An International
Journal*
Professor of Agricultural and Resource
Economics and Economics; Director,
Food Marketing Policy Center,
University of Connecticut
AGRIBUSINESS

Richard W. Cottle
Professor Emeritus
Stanford University
DETERMINANTS
INVERSE MATRIX
MULTIPLE EQUILIBRIA
OBJECTIVE FUNCTION
PROGRAMMING, LINEAR AND
NONLINEAR

Allin F. Cottrell
Professor, Department of Economics
Wake Forest University
CHOLESKY DECOMPOSITION
RANDOM EFFECTS REGRESSION

Edward Countryman
University Distinguished Professor,
Clements Department of History
Southern Methodist University
AMERICAN REVOLUTION

Dennis D. Cox
Professor of Statistics
Rice University
INFERENCE, BAYESIAN

Edward L. Cox
Associate Professor, Department of
History
Rice University
GRENADIAN REVOLUTION

Margaret Coyle
Professor in Theatre
University of Maryland at College
Park
THEATER

Russell Craig
Professor, National Graduate School of
Management
Australian National University
POSTLETHWAYT, MALACHY

Kellina M. Craig-Henderson
Professor, Social Psychology Program,
National Science Foundation
Associate Professor of Psychology,
Howard University
BIGOTRY
INTERGROUP RELATIONS

Roger Craine
Professor of Economics
University of California at Berkeley
MARKET CLEARINGHOUSE

Charles B. Crawford
Emeritus Professor of Psychology
Simon Fraser University
DARWIN, CHARLES
KINSHIP, EVOLUTIONARY
THEORY OF

Timothy W. Crawford
Assistant Professor, Department of
Political Science
Boston College
ALLIANCES
ARMS CONTROL AND ARMS
RACE

Tim Cresswell
Professor of Human Geography, Royal
Holloway
University of London
HOBOS

Michaeline A. Crichlow
Associate Professor, African and
African American Studies
Duke University
PLANTATION

Jennifer L. Croissant
Associate Professor, Women's Studies

University of Arizona
TECHNOLOGY, ADOPTION OF
VALUES
VANILLA INDUSTRY

Mai'a K. Davis Cross
Assistant Professor of Political Science
Colgate University
DIPLOMACY
EUROPEAN UNION

William E. Cross, Jr.
Professor of Psychology and African
American Studies
Graduate Center–City University of
New York
OGBU, JOHN U.

Nick Crossley
School of Social Sciences
University of Manchester, United
Kingdom
SOCIAL CHANGE

Phillip C. F. Crowson
Centre for Energy, Petroleum and
Mineral Law and Policy
University of Dundee
COPPER INDUSTRY
MINING INDUSTRY

Anthony Crubaugh
Associate Professor, Department of
History
Illinois State University
BURKE, EDMUND
FRENCH REVOLUTION

Mario J. Crucini
Associate Professor
Vanderbilt University
PURCHASING POWER PARITY

Carole L. Crumley
Professor, Department of
Anthropology
University of North Carolina, Chapel
Hill
HETERARCHY

Robert D. Crutchfield
Professor
University of Washington
IMPRISONMENT

Jonathan Crystal
Associate Professor of Political Science
Fordham University
MULTILATERALISM
UNILATERALISM

Lauren Renee Cummings
MA Criminal Justice & MA
Certificate in Terrorism Studies, John
Jay College
Hunter College, City University of
New York
BIN LADEN, OSAMA

Hugh Cunningham
Emeritus Professor of Social History,
School of History
University of Kent
JINGOISM

Gregory Currie
Professor, Department of Philosophy
University of Nottingham
FICTION

Rebecca C. Curtis
Professor, Derner Institute of
Advanced Psychological Studies
Adelphi University
SELF-DEFEATING BEHAVIOR

William M. Curtis
Visiting Assistant Professor of
Government
University of Alabama, Birmingham
MARCUSE, HERBERT

Anthony P. D'Costa
Professor of Comparative International
Development
University of Washington
STEEL INDUSTRY

Claudia Dahlerus
Visiting Assistant Professor of Political
Science
Albion College
MOBILIZATION
REPRESSION

John G. Dale
Department of Sociology and
Anthropology
George Mason University
INTERWAR YEARS

Violetta Dalla
Lecturer, Department of Economics
Royal Holloway, University of London
STATIONARY PROCESS

Amy N. Dalton
Fuqua School of Business
Duke University
PRIMING

Damian S. Damianov
Assistant Professor of Economics,
Department of Economics and
Finance
College of Business Administration,
University of Texas–Pan American
ANTITRUST REGULATION
AUCTIONS

Anita Dancs
Research Director, National Priorities
Project
Northampton, MA
OPPORTUNITY COST

Marcel Danesi
Coordinator of the University of
Toronto Undergraduate Program
University of Toronto
YOUTH CULTURE

E. Valentine Daniel
Columbia University
OBJECTIVITY
SEMIOTICS

Aden L. M. Darity
Cornell College
BAMBOOZLED

Regna Darnell
Distinguished University Professor,
Anthropology and First Nations
Studies
University of Western Ontario
AMERICAN ANTHROPOLOGICAL
ASSOCIATION

Masako N. Darrough
Professor, Stan Ross Department of
Accountancy
Baruch College–City University of
New York
INITIAL PUBLIC OFFERING
(IPO)

Mitali Das
Associate Professor
Columbia University
LEAST SQUARES, THREE-STAGE
SAMPLE ATTRITION

Monica Das
Assistant Professor, Economics
Department
Skidmore College, New York
ABSOLUTE AND COMPARATIVE
ADVANTAGE
COMPARATIVE STATICS

MATRIX ALGEBRA
NONPARAMETRIC ESTIMATION
POOLED TIME SERIES AND
CROSS-SECTIONAL DATA

Shakuntala Das
Research Assistant, Center for Full
Employment and Price Stability,
Department of Economics
University of Missouri–Kansas City
BLUES

Swapan Dasgupta
Professor, Department of Economics
Dalhousie University
OPTIMAL GROWTH

Christian Davenport
Professor
University of Maryland, College Park
BLACK PANTHERS

Steven R. David
Professor
Johns Hopkins University
THIRD WORLD

James Davidson
Professor of Econometrics
University of Exeter, United Kingdom
ERROR-CORRECTION
MECHANISMS

Paul Davidson
Editor of the *Journal of Post Keynesian
Economics* and Visiting Scholar
New School for Social Research
AGGREGATE DEMAND AND
SUPPLY PRICE
ECONOMICS, POST KEYNESIAN

Russell Davidson
Canada Research Chair in Economics,
McGill University
Groupement de Recherche en
Economie Quantitative d'Aix
Marseille
CHOW TEST

Antony Davies
Associate Professor of Economics
Duquesne University
PROPERTY RIGHTS
SHOCKS
SPOT MARKET
SUPPLY
UTILITY, SUBJECTIVE

Angelique M. Davis
Visiting Assistant Professor, Political
Science Department
Seattle University
ADMINISTRATIVE LAW

John B. Davis
Professor of History and Philosophy of
Economics, University of Amsterdam
Professor of Economics, Marquette
University
ECONOMIC MODEL
IDENTITIES, DEADLY
IDENTITY, SOCIAL
SOCIAL ECONOMY

Lewis S. Davis
Assistant Professor, Department of
Economics
Union College, Schenectady, New
York
DEVELOPMENT ECONOMICS
TECHNOLOGICAL PROGRESS,
ECONOMIC GROWTH

Mark Davis
Lecturer in Sociology
University of Leeds
ETHNOMETHODOLOGY
GANS, HERBERT J.
SOCIOLOGY, MACRO-

Mary Ann Davis
Assistant Professor of Sociology
Sam Houston State University
CENTRAL TENDENCIES,
MEASURES OF
METHODS, RESEARCH (IN
SOCIOLOGY)
MORBIDITY AND MORTALITY

Robbie E. Davis-Floyd
Senior Research Fellow, Department
of Anthropology
University of Texas–Austin
MIDWIFERY
REPRODUCTION
RITES OF PASSAGE
RITUALS

Rene V. Dawis
Professor Emeritus
University of Minnesota
LIKERT SCALE

Malathi de Alwis
Senior Research Fellow, International
Centre for Ethnic Studies
Colombo, Sri Lanka
ALTHUSSER, LOUIS

Massimo De Angelis
Reader
University of East London
PRIMITIVE ACCUMULATION

Olivier de La Grandville
Professor of Economics
University of Geneva, Switzerland
ECONOMIC GROWTH

Evelyne de Leeuw
Faculty of Health, Medicine, Nursing,
and Behavioural Sciences
Chair of Health and Social
Development, School of Health and
Social Development
Deakin University, Victoria, Australia
PUBLIC HEALTH

Cedric de Leon
Assistant Professor of Sociology
Providence College
CLASS

Tom De Luca
Professor of Political Science
Fordham University
RESEARCH, DEMOCRACY

Michel De Vroey
Professor of Economics
Université Catholique de Louvain
IS-LM MODEL

James J. Dean
Assistant Professor of Sociology
Sonoma State University
QUEER STUDIES

Edward L. Deci
Professor of Psychology and Gowen
Professor in the Social Sciences
University of Rochester
SELF-DETERMINATION THEORY

Rich DeJordy
Boston College
ORGANIZATION THEORY

Stefanie DeLuca
Assistant Professor, Department of
Sociology
Johns Hopkins University
GAUTREAUX RESIDENTIAL
MOBILITY PROGRAM

Chares Demetriou
Boston University
SOCIOLOGY, POLITICAL

Amy P. Demorest
Professor, Department of Psychology
Amherst College
SCRIPT MODELS

Milagros Denis
Visiting Assistant Professor,
Department of Africana and Puerto
Rican/Latino Studies, Hunter College
(CUNY)
Part-time Lecturer, Department of
Latino and Hispanic Caribbean
Studies, Rutgers University
PAN-CARIBBEANISM

Anil B. Deolalikar
Professor of Economics
University of California, Riverside
NATIONAL SAMPLE SURVEY
(INDIA)

Jeffrey L. Derevensky
Professor, School/Applied Child
Psychology
McGill University
GAMBLING

Melissa E. DeRosier
Director
3–C Institute for Social Development
INTERVENTIONS, SOCIAL
SKILLS
PEER RELATIONS RESEARCH

Alan D. DeSantis
Associate Professor, Department of
Communication
University of Kentucky
CHICAGO *DEFENDER*

Ashwini Deshpande
Department of Economics, Delhi
School of Economics
University of Delhi, India
CREAMY LAYER, THE
THEIL INDEX

Kathleen Musante DeWalt
Professor of Anthropology and Public
Health
University of Pittsburgh
ANTHROPOLOGY, MEDICAL

Boris DeWiel
Associate Professor, Department of
Political Science
University of Northern British
Columbia
EGALITARIANISM

Mustafah Dhada
Dean, Division of Extended
Education, and Professor, Pan-African
Studies
California State University, Los
Angeles
CABRAL, AMÍLCAR

Spencer M. Di Scala
Professor of History and Graduate
Program Director
University of Massachusetts–Boston
MUSSOLINI, BENITO

John B. Diamond
Assistant Professor of Education
Harvard Graduate School of
Education
ACHIEVEMENT GAP, RACIAL

Augusto Diana
Division of Epidemiology, Services
and Prevention Research
National Institute on Drug Abuse
BEHAVIOR, SELF-CONSTRAINED

Miguel Díaz-Barriga
Professor of Anthropology
Swarthmore College
LEWIS, OSCAR
NEIGHBORHOOD EFFECTS

Alberto Diaz-Cayeros
Stanford University
DEMOCRATIC CENTRALISM

Niki T. Dickerson
Assistant Professor, School of
Management and Labor Relations
Rutgers University
MOBILITY

Wendy L. Dickinson
Counseling Psychologist
Georgia State University
INFERIORITY COMPLEX
INFERTILITY DRUGS,
PSYCHOSOCIAL ISSUES

Lisa M. Dickson
Economics Department
University of Maryland, Baltimore
County
NATIONAL EDUCATION
LONGITUDINAL STUDY

David R. Dietrich
Duke University
CULTURE OF POVERTY
TRACKING IN SCHOOLS

Jason Dietrich
Fair Lending Lead Expert
Office of the Comptroller of the
Currency
OCCUPATIONAL SCORE INDEX
(OCCSCORE)

Nicholas DiFonzo
Professor of Psychology
Rochester Institute of Technology
RUMORS

Gerald M. DiGiusto
Postdoctoral Research Fellow, Niehaus
Center for Globalization and
Governance
Princeton University
WALTZ, KENNETH

Robert W. Dimand
Professor, Department of Economics
Brock University
EFFICIENT MARKET
HYPOTHESIS
FISHER, IRVING
KOOPMANS, TJALLING
MATHEMATICAL ECONOMICS
MULTIPLIER, THE
NEOCLASSICAL GROWTH
MODEL
NONCOOPERATIVE GAMES
PROBABILITY, SUBJECTIVE

Martin Dimitrov
Assistant Professor
Dartmouth College
PROPERTY RIGHTS,
INTELLECTUAL

Gniesha Yvonne Dinwiddie
Post Doctoral Fellow, Office of
Population Research
Princeton University
EDUCATION, USA

Jeffrey C. Dixon
Assistant Professor, Department of
Sociology
Koç University, Istanbul
CIVILIZATIONS, CLASH OF

Martin J. Dixon
Reader in the Law of Real Property
Cambridge University
LANDLORDS, ABSENTEE

Robert Dixon
Department of Economics
University of Melbourne, Australia

RECURSIVE MODELS
WALRAS' LAW

Göran Djurfeldt
Professor, Department of Sociology
Lund University, Sweden
FOOD CRISIS

Ashley ("Woody") Doane
Professor, Department of Social
Sciences
University of Hartford
WHITENESS

John L. Dobra
Director, Natural Resource Industry
Institute
Associate Professor of Economics,
University of Nevada, Reno
GOLD INDUSTRY
SILVER INDUSTRY

Laurent Dobuzinskis
Associate Professor of Political Science
Simon Fraser University, Canada
GOLD STANDARD

Peter B. Doeringer
Professor, Department of Economics
Boston University
FISHING INDUSTRY
NONCOMPETING GROUPS

Stefan P. Dolgert
Doctoral Candidate
Duke University
ANARCHISM
RORTY, RICHARD

Seán Patrick Donlan
Lecturer, School of Law
University of Limerick
MAGNA CARTA

Renske Doorenspleet
Assistant Professor, Department of
Politics and International Studies
University of Warwick, United
Kingdom
DEMOCRATIZATION

David Dorward
Director, African Research Institute
LaTrobe University, Australia
LUMUMBA, PATRICE

William G. Doty
Professor and Chair Emeritus, College
of Arts and Sciences

The University of Alabama, Tuscaloosa
MYTH AND MYTHOLOGY

Karen Manges Douglas
Department of Sociology
Sam Houston State University
MIDDLEMAN MINORITIES

Sheila C. Dow
Professor, Department of Economics
University of Stirling
ECONOMIC METHODOLOGY

Robert A. Dowd
Assistant Professor of Political Science
University of Notre Dame
DEMOCRACY, CHRISTIAN

Jason Downer
Senior Research Scientist, Center for
Advanced Study of Teaching and
Learning
University of Virginia
TEACHER-CHILD
RELATIONSHIPS

Stephen M. Downes
Professor, Department of Philosophy
University of Utah
EVOLUTIONARY PSYCHOLOGY

Jocelyn Downie
Canada Research Chair in Health Law
and Policy, Professor, Faculties of Law
and Medicine
Dalhousie University
ASSISTED DEATH

Marymay Downing
Institute of Women's Studies,
University of Ottawa
Pauline Jewett Institute of Women's
Studies, Carleton University
FEMININITY

William M. Downs
Associate Professor and Chair,
Department of Political Science
Georgia State University
COALITION
COALITION THEORY
GOVERNMENT, COALITION

David M. Doyle
PhD Candidate, Centre for Irish
Studies
National University of Ireland, Galway
OLYMPIC GAMES

Thomas E. Drabek
John Evans Professor Emeritus
University of Denver
DISASTER MANAGEMENT

Norman R. Draper
Professor Emeritus, Department of
Statistics
University of Wisconsin, Madison
DEGREES OF FREEDOM

Michael C. Dreiling
Associate Professor, Department of
Sociology
University of Oregon
NORTH AMERICAN FREE TRADE
AGREEMENT

Steven Curtis Dreyer
Lecturer in Sociology
University of Wisconsin–Milwaukee
ACCIDENTS, INDUSTRIAL

Daniel W. Drezner
Associate Professor of International
Politics, Fletcher School of Law and
Diplomacy
Tufts University
INTERNATIONAL ECONOMIC
ORDER

Noah D. Drezner
Research Associate, Graduate School
of Education
University of Pennsylvania
PHILANTHROPY

Kate Driscoll
Postdoctoral fellow, Yale Child Study
Center
Yale University
TEACHER-CHILD
RELATIONSHIPS

Daniel Druckman
George Mason University, Fairfax,
Virginia
University of Queensland, Brisbane,
Australia
NONVERBAL COMMUNICATION

Amaresh Dubey
Senior Fellow
National Council of Applied
Economic Research, New Delhi
NATIONAL SAMPLE SURVEY
(INDIA)

Melvyn Dubofsky
Distinguished Professor of History and
Sociology Emeritus
Binghamton University, State
University of New York
SYNDICALISM

Faye Duchin
Professor, Department of Economics
Rensselaer Polytechnic Institute
ENERGY SECTOR

John Duckitt
Professor
University of Auckland, New Zealand
PERSONALITY, AUTHORITARIAN
SOCIAL DOMINANCE
ORIENTATION

Mary L. Dudziak
Judge Edward J. and Ruey L. Guirado
Professor of Law, History, and Political
Science
University of Southern California Law
School
CIVIL RIGHTS, COLD WAR

Alistair S. Duff
Senior Lecturer, School of Creative
Industries
Napier University
TAWNEY, R. H.

William M. Dugger
Department of Economics
The University of Tulsa
WANT CREATION

Dustin T. Duncan
Research Assistant, Harvard School of
Public Health
Dana–Farber Cancer Institute
JOHN HENRYISM

Starkey Duncan, Jr.
Professor, Department of Psychology
University of Chicago
MACCOBY, ELEANOR

Stephen Duncombe
Associate Professor, Gallatin School
New York University
RESISTANCE

William N. Dunn
Professor of Public Policy
University of Pittsburgh
CAMPBELL, DONALD

David Dunning
Professor of Psychology
Cornell University
SOCIAL COGNITION

Julie C. Dunsmore
Assistant Professor, Department of
Psychology
Virginia Polytechnic Institute and
State University
BAUMRIND, DIANA
PARENTING STYLES
SELF-REPRESENTATION

Joshua Duntley
Assistant Professor, Criminal Justice
and Psychology
The Richard Stockton College of New
Jersey
MURDER

Deborah Vakas Duong
Senior Computational Social Scientist
Science Applications International
Corporation
DISTRIBUTION, UNIFORM

Davido Dupree
Graduate School of Education
University of Pennsylvania
CHILD DEVELOPMENT

Kristina M. Durante
Department of Psychology
University of Texas at Austin
SEX AND MATING

Ramesh Durbarry
University of Technology, Maurtius
TOURISM INDUSTRY

Steven N. Durlauf
Arrow Professor of Economics,
Department of Economics
University of Wisconsin–Madison
EXCHANGEABILITY
MICROECONOMICS
OPTIMIZING BEHAVIOR
PRINCIPAL-AGENT MODELS
PRISONER'S DILEMMA
(ECONOMICS)

Amitava Krishna Dutt
Professor, Department of Economics
and Policy Studies
University of Notre Dame
AGGREGATE SUPPLY
CONSUMER
CONSUMERISM
ECONOMICS, KEYNESIAN

MYRDAL, GUNNAR
NORTH-SOUTH MODELS
STAGNATION
TAYLOR, LANCE

Manoranjan Dutta
Professor of Economics
Rutgers University
EURO, THE

Kelly Dye
Assistant Professor, F. C. Manning
School of Business
Acadia University
MASLOW, ABRAHAM

Gary A. Dymski
Director, University of California
Center Sacramento
Professor of Economics, University of
California, Riverside
BANKING
MICROFINANCE
PONZI SCHEME
STIGLITZ, JOSEPH E.

Stephen Benedict Dyson
Assistant Professor of Political Science
University of Connecticut
FALKLAND ISLANDS WAR

Jonathan Eacott
PhD Candidate
University of Michigan
ROTHSCHILDS, THE

Alice H. Eagly
Professor of Psychology, James Padilla
Chair of Arts and Sciences, and
Faculty Fellow of Institute for Policy
Northwestern University
ATTITUDES

Gerald Easter
Boston College
TAXATION
TAXES, PROGRESSIVE
TAXES, REGRESSIVE

Charles C. Ebere
Sociologist
University of the Gambia
GREEN BOOK, THE (LIBYA)
TALIBAN

Stefan Ecks
Lecturer
University of Edinburgh
EVANS-PRITCHARD, E. E.
MALINOWSKI, BRONISLAW
RADCLIFFE-BROWN, A. R.

Marc Edelman
Professor of Anthropology
Hunter College and the Graduate
Center, City University of New York
ORGANIZATIONS, PEASANT

Ennis B. Edmonds
Assistant Professor, Department of
Religious Studies
Kenyon College
RASTAFARI

Christopher L. Edwards
Director of Chronic Pain Management
Program
Duke University Medical Center
DISCRIMINATION, RACIAL
HARASSMENT
HEREDITY
HOMELESSNESS
MENTORING
MIDLIFE CRISIS
PSYCHONEUROENDOCRINOLOGY
PSYCHOSOMATICS

Patrick J. Egan
Assistant Professor of Politics
New York University
FREEDOM OF INFORMATION
ACT

Douglas R. Egerton
Professor of History
Le Moyne College
GABRIEL (PROSSER)
SLAVE RESISTANCE
TURNER, NAT
VESEY, DENMARK

Thráinn Eggertsson
Professor of Economics, University of
Iceland, Reykjavík
Global Distinguished Professor of
Politics, New York University
PROPERTY

Daina S. Eglitis
Assistant Professor of Sociology and
International Affairs
George Washington University
CONSUMPTION

Isaac Ehrlich
SUNY and UB Distinguished
Professor of Economics and Melvin H.
Baker Professor of American
Enterprise, Department of Economics
and School of Management

State University of New York at
Buffalo
   BECKER, GARY S.

Wolfgang Eichert
Research Assistant, Department of
Economics
University of Graz, Austria
   LONG RUN
   SOFT SKILLS

Nancy Eisenberg
Regents' Professor of Psychology
Arizona State University
   EMPATHY

Bill Ellis
Professor, English and American
Studies
Penn State University, Hazleton
   CULTS
   MAGIC
   OCCULT, THE
   TABOOS

Stephen Ellis
Department of Philosophy
University of Oklahoma
   THEORY

Julian Ellison
Independent Scholar
Formerly Treasury Department
   GINZBERG, ELI
   HURWICZ, LEONID
   LAFARGUE, PAUL
   PAN-AFRICAN CONGRESSES
   PETROLEUM INDUSTRY
   STATE ENTERPRISE
   UZAWA, HIROFUMI
   WAR ON POVERTY

Frank W. Elwell
Dean and Professor of Sociology,
School of Liberal Arts
Rogers State University
   BOSERUP, ESTER
   CLUB OF ROME
   MILLS, C. WRIGHT

David Geronimo Embrick
Assistant Professor, Department of
Sociology
Loyola University Chicago
   ACTIVISM
   ASSIMILATION
   CHINESE AMERICANS
   COLORISM
   DETERMINISM, BIOLOGICAL
   FACTORY SYSTEM
   GENERAL MOTORS

   INEQUALITY, RACIAL
   MUSLIMS
   POLICING, BIASED
   PULLMAN PORTERS
   TALLY'S CORNER

Patrick M. Emerson
Assistant Professor, Department of
Economics
Oregon State University
   RENT CONTROL

Ross B. Emmett
Associate Professor, James Madison
College
Michigan State University
   CHICAGO SCHOOL

Walter Enders
Bidgood Professor of Economics and
Finance, Department of Economics
and Finance
University of Alabama
   FUNCTIONAL FORM

Maxim P. Engers
Professor, Department of Economics
University of Virginia
   CONSUMER SURPLUS
   PRODUCER SURPLUS

Elaine E. Englehardt
Distinguished Professor of Ethics and
Special Assistant to the President
Utah Valley State College
   COMMUNITARIANISM

Richard L. Engstrom
Consultant, Center for Civil Rights
University of North Carolina, Chapel
Hill
   ELECTORAL COLLEGE

Terrence W. Epperson
Social Sciences Librarian
The College of New Jersey
   BURIAL GROUNDS, AFRICAN
   GAZE, PANOPTIC

Jeffery N. Epstein
Associate Professor, Department of
Pediatrics
Cincinnati Children's Hospital
Medical Center
   HYPERACTIVITY

Narges Erami
Department of Anthropology
Columbia University
   ISLAM, SHIA AND SUNNI

David F. Ericson
Associate Professor, Department of
Political Science
Wichita State University
   DAVIS, JEFFERSON
   GOVERNMENT, FEDERAL

Neil R. Ericsson
Section Chief, Division of
International Finance
Federal Reserve Board
   COINTEGRATION

Zachary Ernst
Assistant Professor, Department of
Philosophy
University of Missouri–Columbia
   EVOLUTIONARY GAMES

Pavel Erochkine
Head of Research
Centre for Global Studies, London
   GLASNOST

Matthew Eshbaugh-Soha
Assistant Professor, Department of
Political Science
University of North Texas
   CARTER, JIMMY
   NIXON, RICHARD M.
   REFERENDUM

Kenneth N. Eslinger
Associate Professor of Sociology
John Carroll University
   RANDOMNESS
   REGIONS, METROPOLITAN
   REGIONS
   SOCIOECONOMIC STATUS

Eli N. Evans
Author, *Judah P. Benjamin: The Jewish
Confederate*
   BENJAMIN, JUDAH P.

George W. Evans
Professor of Economics
University of Oregon
   SARGENT, THOMAS

R. Gregory Evans
Director, Institute for Biosecurity
Saint Louis University School of
Public Health
   BIOTERRORISM

Richard J. Evans
Professor of Modern History
University of Cambridge
   NAZISM

Robert E. Evenson
Professor, Department of Economics
Yale University
GREEN REVOLUTION

Emmanuel Chukwudi Eze
Department of Philosophy
DePaul University
SCOTTISH MORALISTS

Yanqin Fan
Professor of Economics, Department
of Economics
Vanderbilt University
TEST STATISTICS

Ying Fang
PhD Candidate
Rice University
AVIATION INDUSTRY

João Ricardo Faria
Professor of Economics, Nottingham
Business School
Nottingham Trent University
CITATIONS
JOURNALS, PROFESSIONAL
O-RING THEORY

Raymond A. Farkouh
Associate Director, Health Economics
Research Triangle Institute Health
Solutions
SHORT RUN

Stephen J. Farnsworth
Associate Professor, Department of
Political Science
University of Mary Washington
BUSH, GEORGE H. W.

Grant Farred
Associate Professor in the Program in
Literature
Duke University
INTELLECTUALS, VERNACULAR

Martin M. G. Fase
Former Executive Deputy Director,
De Nederlandsche Bank
Professor Emeritus, University of
Amsterdam
MONEY ILLUSION

Robert Fastiggi
Professor of Systematic Theology
Sacred Heart Major Seminary
CHURCH, THE
HELL
MONOTHEISM

PURGATORY
ROMAN CATHOLIC CHURCH

James D. Faubion
Professor of Anthropology
Rice University
DETERMINISM
DISCOURSE
EPISTEMOLOGY

Clare Faulhaber
Menomonie, WI
SCARR, SANDRA WOOD

Michael Faure
Professor of Comparative and
International Environmental Law
Maastricht University
CONFISCATION

David R. Faust
Ames Library of South Asia
University of Minnesota
NONGOVERNMENTAL
    ORGANIZATIONS (NGOS)

Kristen Fay
Tufts University
ADOLESCENT PSYCHOLOGY

Ansar Fayyazuddin
Department of Natural Sciences
Baruch College–City University of
New York
GOULD, STEPHEN JAY
LAGRANGE MULTIPLIER

Joe R. Feagin
Ella C. McFadden Professor of
Sociology
Texas A&M University
RACIAL SLURS
SEGREGATION
SEGREGATION, SCHOOL

Giulio Federico
CRA International, London
CONDITIONALITY

Suzanne G. Fegley
Graduate School of Education
University of Pennsylvania
CHILD DEVELOPMENT

Vanda Felbab-Brown
Nonresident Fellow, Foreign Policy
Studies, The Brookings Institution
Assistant Professor, School of Foreign
Service, Georgetown University
GUERRILLA WARFARE

Jesus Felipe
Principal Economist, Economics and
Research Department
Asian Development Bank, Manila
PRODUCTION FUNCTION

Gary Feng
Assistant Professor, Department of
Psychology and Neuroscience
Duke University
THEORY OF MIND

Lisa L. Ferrari
Associate Professor, Department of
Politics and Government
University of Puget Sound
QUEBECOIS MOVEMENT
WORLD WAR I

Marko Ferst
Independent Scholar
Berlin, Germany
BAHRO, RUDOLF

Ed J. Feulner
President
The Heritage Foundation
MONT PELERIN SOCIETY

David P. Fidler
James Louis Calamaras Professor of
Law
Indiana University School of Law
WORLD HEALTH
    ORGANIZATION

Alfred J. Field, Jr.
Department of Economics
University of North Carolina at
Chapel Hill
CUSTOMS UNION

John Field
University of Reading, United
Kingdom
PSYCHOLINGUISTICS

Gary S. Fields
Professor
Cornell University
DUAL ECONOMY
HARRIS-TODARO MODEL
LABOR MARKET

Autumn Fiester
Center for Bioethics, School of
Medicine
University of Pennsylvania
BIOETHICS

Deborah M. Figart
Dean of Graduate Studies and
Professor of Economics
Richard Stockton College of New
Jersey
DISCRIMINATION, TASTE FOR

Jay Courtney Fikes
Professor, Department of
Anthropology
Yeditepe University, Istanbul, Turkey
CASTANEDA, CARLOS
SENSATIONALISM

Bernard J. Firestone
Professor of Political Science, Dean of
College of Liberal Arts
Hofstra University
THANT, U.

Michael R. Fischbach
Professor of History
Randolph–Macon College
HUSSEIN, KING OF JORDAN

Markus Fischer
Associate Professor
California State University Fullerton
MACHIAVELLI, NICCOLÒ
REALISM, POLITICAL

Marianne Fischman
Paris, France
X-CRISE

Jonathan S. Fish
Leverhulme Trust Research Fellow
Department of Sociology, University
of Birmingham, UK
DURKHEIM, ÉMILE
SOCIOLOGY, PARSONIAN

Jeanette Fisher
Lake Elsinore, CA
PREFERENCE, COLOR

Susan T. Fiske
Eugene Higgins Professor of
Psychology
Princeton University
PREJUDICE
STEREOTYPES

Terence D. Fitzgerald
Independent Researcher
Champaign, Illinois
FEAGIN, JOSEPH
SCHOOLING IN THE USA

William J. FitzPatrick
Associate Professor, Department of
Philosophy
Virginia Tech
TELEOLOGY

Diane Flaherty
Professor and Chair, Economics
Department
University of Massachusetts, Amherst
SWEATSHOPS

Richard M. Flanagan
Associate Professor of Political Science
College of Staten Island, City
University of New York
NADER, RALPH

Patrick Flavin
PhD Student
University of Notre Dame
CONGRESS, U.S.

Cynthia Griggs Fleming
Full Professor of History
University of Tennessee
STUDENT NONVIOLENT
COORDINATING COMMITTEE

Marc Fleurbaey
Senior Researcher
Centre National de la Recherche
Scientifique, Paris
FUNCTIONINGS
SOCIAL WELFARE FUNCTIONS

Juan Flores
Professor
Hunter College of the City of New
York, and New York University
NUYORICANS

Nadia Y. Flores
Assistant Professor, Department of
Sociology
Texas A&M University
DEMOGRAPHY
NETWORKS

Nilda Flores-Gonzalez
Department of Sociology and Latin
American and Latino Studies Program
University of Illinois at Chicago
OPPOSITIONALITY, SCHOOLING

Luciano Floridi
Fellow of St. Cross College, University
of Oxford

Professor of Logic and Epistemology,
Università degli Studi di Bari, Italy
DATA

James R. Flynn
Emeritus Professor
University of Otago, Dunedin, New
Zealand
IQ CONTROVERSY

Elżbieta M. Foeller-Pituch
Associate Director, Alice Kaplan
Institute for the Humanities
Northwestern University
LITERATURE

Fred Foldvary
Department of Economics
Santa Clara University
INVESTMENT
LANDLORDS
PUBLIC SECTOR
UNIVERSALISM

Erin Foley-Reynolds
Doctoral Candidate, Department of
Communication
University of Colorado, Boulder
GENDER

Martin H. Folly
Brunel University, England
NORTH ATLANTIC TREATY
ORGANIZATION

Franz Foltz
Associate Professor, Science,
Technology, and Society/Public Policy
Department
Rochester Institute of Technology
ENVIRONMENTAL IMPACT
ASSESSMENT

Charlotte Elisheva Fonrobert
Associate Professor of Religious
Studies
Stanford University
ORTHODOXY

Gonçalo L. Fonseca
Graduate Program in International
Affairs
The New School
NEW SCHOOL FOR SOCIAL
RESEARCH

H. D. Forbes
Professor, Department of Political
Science

University of Toronto
CONTACT HYPOTHESIS

Donna Y. Ford
Professor, Betts Chair of Education
and Human Development,
Department of Special Education
Peabody College of Education,
Vanderbilt University
GIFTED AND TALENTED

Mathew Forstater
University of Missouri–Kansas City
AFRICAN STUDIES
BEAUTY CONTEST METAPHOR
ECONOMICS OF CONTROL
HEILBRONER, ROBERT
LABOR, SURPLUS:
   CONVENTIONAL ECONOMICS
MORAL SENTIMENTS
PAN-AFRICANISM
POLLUTION, AIR
POLLUTION, NOISE
RETURNS
STATIONARY STATE

Donelson R. Forsyth
Professor, Jepson School of Leadership
Studies
University of Richmond, Virginia
AUTOKINETIC EFFECT
ETHICS IN EXPERIMENTATION
SELF-SERVING BIAS

Maximilian C. Forte
Assistant Professor, Department of
Sociology and Anthropology
Concordia University, Montreal
ETHNOGRAPHY

Mark Fossett
Professor of Sociology
Texas A&M University, College
Station
SEGREGATION, RESIDENTIAL

Norman Fost
Professor, Pediatrics and Bioethics
University of Wisconsin–Madison
STEM CELLS

Angela K. Fournier
Assistant Professor, Department of
Psychology
Virginia Wesleyan College
SURVEY

Aaron A. Fox
The Center for Ethnomusicology
Columbia University
MUSIC

Richard A. Fox
Department of Anthropology
The University of South Dakota
BATTLE OF THE LITTLE BIG
   HORN

Robin Fox
University Professor of Social Theory
Rutgers University
MONTAGU, ASHLEY

Luis Ricardo Fraga
Associate Vice Provost for Faculty
Advancement, Director of the
Diversity Research Institute, Russell F.
Stark University Professor, Professor of
Political Science
University of Washington
BLOC VOTE

Jana E. Frances-Fischer
Postdoctoral Psychology Resident,
University Counseling Services
Virginia Commonwealth University,
Richmond, Virginia
INFERTILITY DRUGS,
   PSYCHOSOCIAL ISSUES

Neville Francis
Assistant Professor, Department of
Economics
University of North Carolina, Chapel
Hill
BUSINESS CYCLES, EMPIRICAL
   LITERATURE
BUSINESS CYCLES, REAL

Robert H. Frank
Johnson Graduate School of
Management
Cornell University
WINNER-TAKE-ALL SOCIETY

Alexis T. Franzese
Department of Sociology and
Department of Psychology
Duke University
ADDICTION
SELF-PRESENTATION

Elio Frattaroli
Faculty
Psychoanalytic Center of Philadelphia
BETTELHEIM, BRUNO

Craig Freedman
Director, Centre for Japanese
Economic Studies

Macquarie University, Sydney,
Australia
STIGLER, GEORGE JOSEPH

Damon Freeman
Assistant Professor, School of Social
Policy and Practice
University of Pennsylvania
CLARK, KENNETH B.

James Freeman
Professor, Political Science
City University of New York, Bronx
Community College
IRAN-CONTRA AFFAIR
LAZARSFELD, PAUL FELIX
MILOSEVIC, SLOBODAN
SEPTEMBER 11, 2001
WATERGATE

Sally French
Professor of Disability and Inclusion,
School of Health, Community and
Education Studies
Northumbria University
DISABILITY

Steven M. Frenk
Graduate Student, Department of
Sociology
Duke University
MANKILLER, WILMA

Lars Frers
Lecturer, Department of Sociology
Darmstadt University of Technology,
Germany
IBN KHALDŪN

Kelli Friedman
Department of Psychiatry and
Behavioral Sciences
Duke University Medical Center
BODY IMAGE
BODY MASS INDEX
WEIGHT

Luke M. Froeb
William Oehmig Associate Professor
of Free Enterprise
Vanderbilt University
ANTITRUST
CONSUMER PROTECTION

Manuel Frondel
Rheinisch-Westfälisches Institut für
Wirtschaftsforschung (RWI)
Essen
SEPARABILITY

Bernard F. Fuemmeler
Assistant Professor, Department of
Community and Family Medicine
Duke University Medical Center
DISEASE
PANEL STUDIES

Steve Fuller
Professor, Department of Sociology
University of Warwick
LUKACS, GEORG
MANNHEIM, KARL
REVOLUTIONS, SCIENTIFIC

Andrew S. Fullerton
Department of Sociology
Oklahoma State University
UPWARD MOBILITY

Jayson J. Funke
PhD Candidate, Graduate School of
Geography
Clark University
STOCK OPTIONS
STOCKS, RESTRICTED AND
UNRESTRICTED

R. Michael Furr
Assistant Professor, Department of
Psychology
Wake Forest University
PERSON-SITUATION DEBATE

Nadav Gabay
PhD Candidate, Department of
Sociology
University of California, San Diego
SHARON, ARIEL

Satyananda J. Gabriel
Professor, Department of Economics
Mount Holyoke College
CONJUNCTURES,
TRANSITIONAL

Vivian L. Gadsden
William T. Carter Professor of
Education and Child Development,
Graduate School of Education and
Director, National Center on Fathers
and Families
University of Pennsylvania
FATHERHOOD

Brian J. Gaines
Associate Professor, Department of
Political Science, Institute of
Government and Public Affairs
University of Illinois at
Urbana–Champaign

BALLOTS
VOTE, ALTERNATIVE

Sarah Gamble
Reader in English with Gender
Swansea University
WOMANISM

Adam Gamoran
Director, Wisconsin Center for
Education Research
University of Wisconsin–Madison
CREAMING

Jennifer Gandhi
Assistant Professor, Department of
Political Science
Emory University
DICTATORSHIP

Giancarlo Gandolfo
Professor, Faculty of Economics
Sapienza University of Rome, and
Accademia Nazionale dei Lincei,
Rome
COMPARATIVE DYNAMICS

Giovanni Ganelli
Economist
International Monetary Fund
MUNDELL-FLEMING MODEL
PROPENSITY TO IMPORT,
MARGINAL

Joshua Samuel Gans
Professor, Melbourne Business School
University of Melbourne, Parkville,
Australia
COMPETITION, MONOPOLISTIC

Judy Garber
Professor
Vanderbilt University
DEPRESSION, PSYCHOLOGICAL

Ginny E. Garcia
Doctoral Student in Sociology
Texas A&M University
METHODOLOGY

Jerry Garcia
Assistant Professor of History and
Chicano/Latino Studies
Michigan State University
MEXICAN AMERICANS

Jesus A. Garcia
PhD Student
Texas A&M University
LATINOS

Fernando García-Belenguer
Department of Economics
Universidad Autónoma de Madrid
SOLOW RESIDUAL, THE
TWO-SECTOR MODELS

Nuno Garoupa
Professor of Law
University of Illinois College of Law
CONFISCATION

Roger W. Garrison
Auburn University
AUSTRIAN ECONOMICS

G. David Garson
Professor, Department of Public
Administration
North Carolina State University
VALIDITY, STATISTICAL

Marybeth Gasman
Assistant Professor, Graduate School of
Education
University of Pennsylvania
PHILANTHROPY

Philip Gasper
Professor, Department of Philosophy
Notre Dame de Namur University,
Belmont, CA
LENINISM
PROLETARIAT

Sarah N. Gatson
Associate Professor, Department of
Sociology
Texas A&M University
HABITUS
LABELING THEORY
MATRIARCHY
NATURALIZATION

Charles Geisst
Department of Economics and
Finance
Manhattan College
AMERICAN DREAM

Shamira M. Gelbman
Assistant Professor
Illinois State University
JOHNSON, LYNDON B.

Susan A. Gelman
Frederick G. L. Huetwell Professor of
Psychology
University of Michigan
ESSENTIALISM

Glen Gendzel
Assistant Professor, Department of History
San José State University
LE DUC THO

Russell J. Geoffrey
University Correctional Health Care
University of Medicine and Dentistry of New Jersey
PRISON PSYCHOLOGY

Stephen A. Germic
Assistant Professor of English and Comparative Literature
American University in Cairo
CHIEF JOSEPH
FREE TRADE
NATIVISM
ORIENTALISM

Scott D. Gest
Associate Professor of Human Development and Family Studies
Pennsylvania State University
SOCIAL COGNITIVE MAP

Malcolm Getz
Associate Professor, Department of Economics
Vanderbilt University
EDUCATIONAL QUALITY

B. N. Ghosh
Professor of Economics
Eastern Mediterranean University, North Cyprus
UNEQUAL EXCHANGE

Michael T. Gibbons
Department of Government and International Affairs
University of South Florida
EASTON, DAVID
HERMENEUTICS

James L. Gibson
Sidney W. Souers Professor of Government, Washington University in St. Louis
Fellow, Centre for Comparative and International Politics, Stellenbosch University, South Africa
TRUTH AND RECONCILIATION COMMISSIONS

Karen J. Gibson
Associate Professor, Nohad A. Toulan School of Urban Studies and Planning

Portland State University, Portland, Oregon
CROWDING HYPOTHESIS

Daniel Gilbert
Department of Psychology
Harvard University
JONES, EDWARD ELLSWORTH

Shelby Gilbert
Department of Curriculum and Instruction
Florida International University
CURRICULUM
SCHOOLING

Jennie K. Gill
University of Victoria
LEARNED HELPLESSNESS

George Peter Gilligan
Senior Research Fellow, Department of Business Law and Taxation
Monash University, Melbourne, Australia
ROYAL COMMISSIONS

David D Gilmore
Professor of Anthropology, Department of Anthropology
Stony Brook University
MISOGYNY

Martha E Gimenez
Professor, Department of Sociology
University of Colorado at Boulder
CLASS CONFLICT
FORMATION, SOCIAL
LABOR, SURPLUS: MARXIST AND RADICAL ECONOMICS
MIDDLE CLASS
SURPLUS POPULATION
WORKING CLASS

A. G. G. Gingyera-Pinycwa
Dean, Faculty of Social Sciences
Kampala International University, Uganda
OBOTE, APOLLO MILTON

Mwangi wa Gīthīnji
University of Massachusetts–Amherst
BRAIN DRAIN
GINI COEFFICIENT

Michael Givel
Associate Professor, Department of Political Science
University of Oklahoma
SETTLEMENT, TOBACCO

Kristian Skrede Gleditsch
Department of Government
University of Essex
YUGOSLAVIAN CIVIL WAR

Harvey Glickman
Professor Emeritus, Political Science
Haverford College
KAUNDA, KENNETH

Isar P. Godreau
Researcher, Institute of Interdisciplinary Research
University of Puerto Rico at Cayey
TRIGUEÑO

Rajeev K. Goel
Professor, Department of Economics
Illinois State University
CHANGE, TECHNOLOGICAL
MONOPOLY
PUBLIC UTILITIES
REGULATION
TECHNOLOGY
TOBACCO INDUSTRY

Tanya Maria Golash-Boza
Department of Sociology and Program in American Studies
University of Kansas, Lawrence
IDENTIFICATION, RACIAL

Lonnie M. Golden
Professor of Economics and Labor Studies, Division of Social Sciences, Abington College
Pennsylvania State University
OVEREMPLOYMENT
OVERTIME

Phyllis Goldfarb
Jacob Burns Professor of Law and Associate Dean for Clinical Affairs
George Washington University Law School
RAPE

Johnny Goldfinger
Assistant Professor, Department of Political Science
Indiana University–Purdue University Indianapolis
CITY-STATE
COMMON GOOD, THE
LIBERTY
MAJORITIES
RECALL
STATE OF NATURE
TOCQUEVILLE, ALEXIS DE

Joshua L. Golding
Associate Professor of Philosophy
Bellarmine University
THEISM

Arthur H. Goldsmith
Professor, Department of Economics
Washington and Lee University
PSYCHOLOGICAL CAPITAL
WORKPLACE RELATIONS

Jack A. Goldstone
Hazel Professor of Public Policy
George Mason University
REVOLUTION

Douglas Gomery
Resident Scholar, Library of American
Broadcasting
College Park, Maryland
FILM INDUSTRY
PUBLIC POLICY

Richard A. Gonce
Professor Emeritus of Economics
Grand Valley State University
MISES, LUDWIG EDLER VON

Halit Gonenc
Assistant Professor, Faculty of
Economics and Business
University of Groningen, The
Netherlands
VENTURE CAPITAL

Gloria González-Rivera
Professor of Economics
University of California, Riverside
IDENTITY MATRIX
MAXIMUM LIKELIHOOD
REGRESSION
SERIAL CORRELATION
TRENDS
VECTOR AUTOREGRESSION

Judith Goode
Professor of Anthropology and Urban
Studies
Temple University
PATHOLOGY, SOCIAL

Jeff Goodwin
Professor of Sociology
New York University
LIBERATION MOVEMENTS

Eda Gorbis
Assistant Clinical Professor,
Department of Psychiatry and
Biobehavioral Sciences

University of California, Los Angeles
OBSESSIVE-COMPULSIVE
DISORDER

Andrew Gordon
Associate Professor, Department of
English
University of Florida
MATRIX, THE

Leonard A. Gordon
Professor Emeritus
City University of New York
BOSE, SUBHAS CHANDRA AND
SARAT CHANDRA
INDIAN NATIONAL ARMY

Lewis R. Gordon
Laura H. Carnell University Professor
of Philosophy and Director of the
Institute for the Study of Race and
Social Thought and the Center for
Afro-Jewish Studies
Temple University
SARTRE, JEAN-PAUL

Jessica Gordon Nembhard
Assistant Professor, African American
Studies Department
University of Maryland, College Park
CAPITAL CONTROLS
COMMUNITY ECONOMIC
DEVELOPMENT
COOPERATIVES

Janet C. Gornick
Director, Luxembourg Income Study;
Professor of Political Science and
Sociology, The Graduate Center;
Professor of Political Science, Baruch
College
City University of New York
LUXEMBOURG INCOME STUDY

Dennis S. Gouran
Professor of the Communication Arts
and Sciences and Labor Studies and
Employment Relations
Pennsylvania State University
COLLECTIVE WISDOM

Peter A. Gourevitch
Professor of Political Science, School
of International Relations and Pacific
Studies
University of California, San Diego
KEOHANE, ROBERT

Stathis Gourgouris
Professor of Comparative Literature

University of California, Los Angeles
INTELLECTUALISM, ANTI-
INTELLECTUALS, PUBLIC

John M. Gowdy
Rittenhouse Teaching Professor of
Humanities and Social Science,
Department of Economics
Rensselaer Polytechnic Institute
ENERGY

Alexander Grab
Department of History
University of Maine
NAPOLÉON BONAPARTE

Benjamin Graber
Independent Scholar
PREFERENCE, GENDER

Melissa D. Grady
Clinical Assistant Professor, School of
Social Work
University of North Carolina at
Chapel Hill
BOWLBY, JOHN
POST-TRAUMATIC STRESS

R. Quentin Grafton
Professor of Economics
The Australian National University
RETURNS TO A FIXED FACTOR

Carol Graham
Senior Fellow, Economics Studies
Program, The Brookings Institution
Professor, School of Public Policy,
University of Maryland
HAPPINESS

Steven M. Graham
Visiting Assistant Professor, Division
of Social Sciences
New College of Florida
FRIENDSHIP

Donald Granberg
Emeritus Professor of Sociology
University of Missouri
SHERIF, MUZAFER

Tarek C. Grantham
Associate Professor and Gifted and
Creative Education Program
Coordinator, Department of
Educational Psychology and
Instructional Technology
College of Education, University of
Georgia
GIFTED AND TALENTED

Laura Grattan
Doctoral Candidate, Department of
Political Science
Duke University
CONSENSUS

Virginia Gray
Robert Watson Winston Distinguished
Professor of Political Science
University of North Carolina at
Chapel Hill
LOBBYING

Clara H. Greed
Professor of Inclusive Urban Planning,
School of Planning and Architecture
University of the West of England
Bristol
PLUMBING
TOILETS
URBAN SPRAWL

Rodney D. Green
Professor, Economics Department
Howard University
BRIMMER, ANDREW
HARRIS, ABRAM L., JR.
URBAN STUDIES

Jeff Greenberg
Professor of Psychology
University of Arizona
SALIENCE, MORTALITY

Paul D. Greene
Associate Professor, Ethnomusicology
and Integrative Arts
Pennsylvania State University
WORLD MUSIC

William Greene
Toyota Motor Corp. Professor of
Economics, Stern School of Business
New York University
CENSORING, SAMPLE

Alfred Greiner
Professor, Department of Business
Administration and Economics
Bielefeld University, Germany
INADA CONDITIONS

Jeremy A. Grey
Educational Policy and Administration
University of Minnesota
IDENTITY CRISIS

John D. Griffin
Assistant Professor

University of Notre Dame
CONGRESS, U.S.

Elena L. Grigorenko
Child Study Center, Department of
Psychology, and Department of
Epidemiology and Public Health
Yale University
INTELLIGENCE
INTELLIGENCE, SOCIAL
MULTIPLE INTELLIGENCES
THEORY

Alexandru Grigorescu
Assistant Professor
Loyola University Chicago
TRANSPARENCY

Paul W. Grimes
Professor of Economics
Mississippi State University
EXPERIMENTS, HUMAN
INSTITUTIONAL REVIEW
BOARD

Peter D. Groenewegen
Emeritus Professor in Economics
University of Sydney, Australia
MARSHALL, ALFRED

Patrick Groff
Professor of Education Emeritus
San Diego State University
READINESS, SCHOOL

Kimmo Grönlund
Director of Research, Social Science
Research Institute
Åbo Akademi University, Finland
COMPULSORY VOTING

Anke Grosskopf
Assistant Professor, Department of
Political Science
Long Island University, C. W. Post
Campus
CONSTITUTIONAL COURTS

James Grossman
Vice President for Research and
Education
The Newberry Library
WELLS-BARNETT, IDA B.

Siba Grovogui
Johns Hopkins University
OTHER, THE

Caren Grown
Economist-in-Residence, Department
of Economics

American University, Washington, DC
GENDER AND DEVELOPMENT

June Gruber
Psychology Department
University of California, Berkeley
EMOTION REGULATION

Jeffrey Grynaviski
Assistant Professor
University of Chicago
APPROPRIATIONS
RIKER, WILLIAM

Christine E. Guarneri
PhD Candidate in Sociology
Texas A&M University
PATRIARCHY

Gabriela Guazzo
Doctoral Student, Department of
Sociology
Texas A&M University
AUTHORITY
METHODS, QUALITATIVE

David W. Guillet
Professor, Department of
Anthropology
Catholic University of America
IRRIGATION

Craig Gundersen
Associate Professor, Department of
Human Development and Family
Studies
Iowa State University
CURRENT POPULATION SURVEY

Frank R. Gunter
Associate Professor, Economics
Department
Lehigh University, Bethlehem,
Pennsylvania
CAPITAL FLIGHT

Alexander J. Gunz
University of Missouri–Columbia
SOCIAL PSYCHOLOGY

Baogang Guo
Dalton State College, Georgia
LITTLE RED BOOK
MAOISM

Gábor Gyáni
Senior Research Fellow
Institute of History, Hungary
Academy of Sciences
METROPOLIS

Anett Gyurak
Graduate Student, Department of
Psychology
University of California, Berkeley
RELATIONSHIP SATISFACTION

Karl A. Hack
Open University
DECOLONIZATION

Tay Hack
Purdue University
PERSON MEMORY

Axel Hadenius
Lund University
DEMOCRACY, INDICES OF

Christian W. Haerpfer
Reader, Head of Department of
Politics and International Relations;
Director of Research, School of Social
Science
King's College, University of
Aberdeen, UK
FIRST-PAST-THE-POST
IRON CURTAIN
ONE-PARTY STATES
RUSSIAN FEDERATION

Harald Hagemann
Department of Economics
University of Hohenheim, Germany
INTEREST, OWN RATE OF

David Hakken
Professor of Social Informatics, School
of Informatics
Indiana University
CYBERSPACE
TECHNOCRACY

Oded Haklai
Assistant Professor, Department of
Political Studies
Queen's University, Kingston, Ontario
UNITED ARAB REPUBLIC

Galina Borisova Hale
Economist
Federal Reserve Bank of San Francisco
BEGGAR-THY-NEIGHBOR
CURRENCY
CURRENCY APPRECIATION AND
    DEPRECIATION
CURRENCY DEVALUATION AND
    REVALUATION
DIRTY FLOAT
DISCOUNTED PRESENT VALUE
ELASTICITY
EXPECTATIONS, STATIC

OVERSHOOTING
RESERVES, FOREIGN
STERILIZATION, ECONOMIC
STOCKS AND FLOWS

J. Travis Hale
Researcher, University of Texas
Inequality Project, LBJ School of
Public Affairs
University of Texas at Austin
VARIATION

Bronwyn H. Hall
Professor of the Graduate School,
University of California at Berkeley
Professor of Technology and the
Economy, Maastricht University
RESEARCH AND DEVELOPMENT

Juliane Hammer
Assistant Professor for Islamic Studies,
Department of Religious Studies
University of North Carolina at
Charlotte
PALESTINIAN DIASPORA

Shigeyuki Hamori
Professor, Graduate School of
Economics
Kobe University
IMPORT PENETRATION

Omar Hamouda
Associate Professor of Economics
York University
ROBINSON, JOAN

Michael Hanagan
Adjunct Associate Professor, History
Department
Vassar College
CRONY CAPITALISM
MARGINALIZATION
SOCIAL RELATIONS

Ange-Marie Hancock
Assistant Professor, African American
Studies and Political Science
Yale University
PUBLIC WELFARE
QUOTAS
WELFARE

Richard Handler
Professor, Department of
Anthropology
University of Virginia
BENEDICT, RUTH

Ian F. Haney López
Professor, Boalt Hall School of Law
University of California, Berkeley
HERNANDEZ V. TEXAS

Steven J. Hanley
Candidate, Michigan Psychoanalytic
Institute
PSYCHOANALYTIC THEORY
PSYCHOTHERAPY

Robert Hanneman
Professor of Sociology
University of California, Riverside
COVARIANCE
ERRORS, STANDARD

Karl Hanson
Senior Lecturer and Researcher,
Children's Rights Unit
University Institute Kurt Bösch,
Switzerland
CHILDREN'S RIGHTS

Sirène Harb
Assistant Professor, Department of
English
American University of Beirut
FANON, FRANTZ

Jacalyn D. Harden
Professor, Department of
Anthropology
Wayne State University
JAPANESE AMERICANS

Russell Hardin
Professor, Wilf Family Department of
Politics
New York University
INEGALITARIANISM

David J. Harding
Assistant Professor, Department of
Sociology; Assistant Research Scientist,
Population Studies Center
University of Michigan
JENCKS, CHRISTOPHER

Shaun P. Hargreaves Heap
Professor of Economics
University of East Anglia
COMMON KNOWLEDGE
RATIONALITY GAMES

Kathleen Mullan Harris
Gillian T. Cell Distinguished Professor
of Sociology
University of North Carolina at
Chapel Hill

NATIONAL LONGITUDINAL
STUDY OF ADOLESCENT
HEALTH

Lasana T. Harris
Postdoctoral Research Scientist,
Department of Psychology
New York University
PREJUDICE

Monica J. Harris
Associate Professor, Department of
Psychology
University of Kentucky
PYGMALION EFFECTS

Faye V. Harrison
Professor of African American Studies
and Anthropology
University of Florida
DRAKE, ST. CLAIR
DU BOIS, W. E. B.
ORTIZ, FERNANDO
RACE AND ANTHROPOLOGY

Glenn W. Harrison
Department of Economics, College of
Business Administration
University of Central Florida
VALUE, SUBJECTIVE

Nathan W. Harter
Associate Professor, Department of
Organizational Leadership
Purdue University
BUREAUCRACY
BUREAUCRAT

James E. Hartley
Professor, Department of Economics
Mount Holyoke College
REPRESENTATIVE AGENT

Victoria K. Haskins
Lecturer in History, School of
Humanities and Social Sciences
University of Newcastle, Australia
STOLEN GENERATIONS
(AUSTRALIA)

Elaine Hatfield
Professor of Psychology
University of Hawaii
ROMANCE

Angela J. Hattery
Zachary T. Smith Reynolds Associate
Professor of Sociology and Women's &
Gender Studies; Adjunct Associate
Professor, Public Health Sciences

Wake Forest University
DRED SCOTT V. SANFORD

Dirk Haubrich
Department of Politics and
International Relations
University of Oxford
COST-BENEFIT ANALYSIS
DEREGULATION
EQUALITY
PHILOSOPHY, POLITICAL
PRIVATIZATION

Jerry A. Hausman
John and Jennie S. MacDonald
Professor
Massachusetts Institute of Technology
HAUSMAN TESTS

Dorothy L. Hawkins
Graduate Teaching Assistant, Center
for Full Employment and Price
Stability, Department of Economics
University of Missouri at Kansas City
BLUES

Takashi Hayashi
Assistant Professor, Department of
Economics
University of Texas at Austin
EXPECTED UTILITY THEORY

Ron Hayduk
Associate Professor of Political Science,
Department of Social Science
Borough of Manhattan Community
College, City University of New York
PROGRESSIVES
SUBURBAN SPRAWL

Calvin Hayes
Brock University
DE SOTO, HERNANDO
KANT, IMMANUEL
NIETZSCHE, FRIEDRICH
PREDICTION

Floyd W. Hayes III
Senior Lecturer, Department of
Political Science
Coordinator of Programs and
Undergraduate Studies, Center for
Africana Studies, Johns Hopkins
University
PROGRAMMED RETARDATION

Alvin E. Headen
Department of Economics
North Carolina State University
HEALTH ECONOMICS

Joseph F. Healey
Department of Sociology and
Anthropology
Christopher Newport University,
Newport News, VA
RACE RELATIONS CYCLE

Michael T. Heaney
Department of Political Science
University of Florida
GOSNELL, HAROLD
INITIATIVE
PUBLIC INTEREST ADVOCACY

Todd F. Heatherton
Department of Psychological and
Brain Sciences
Dartmouth College
NEUROSCIENCE

Charles Heckscher
Center for Workplace Transformation
Rutgers School of Management and
Labor Relations
EMPLOYMENT, WHITE COLLAR

Krista Hegburg
PhD Candidate, Department of
Anthropology
Columbia University
FOUCAULT, MICHEL
HABERMAS, JÜRGEN

Aviad Heifetz
The Economics and Management
Department
The Open University of Israel
TOPOLOGY

Samuel C. Heilman
Distinguished Professor of Sociology,
Queens College and Graduate Center
City University of New York
FUNERALS

Jeremy Hein
Professor, Department of Sociology
University of Wisconsin–Eau Claire
REFUGEES

Caroline Heldman
Assistant Professor, Politics
Department
Occidental College
CAMPAIGNING

Raymond G. Helmick, S.J.
Instructor in Conflict Resolution,
Department of Theology

Boston College
RECONCILIATION

David F. Hendry
Economics Department
Oxford University
COINTEGRATION

Peter Hennen
Assistant Professor of Sociology
Ohio State University at Newark
CASE METHOD, EXTENDED

Karl H. Hennig
Department of Psychology
University of Guelph
KOHLBERG, LAWRENCE

Martha L. Henning
Professor, Department of English and
World Languages
Portland Community College
STOWE, HARRIET BEECHER

Makada Henry
Doctoral Student, Economics
Department
Howard University
SPATIAL THEORY

Steven E. Henson
Associate Professor, Department of
Economics
Western Washington University
SOLAR ENERGY

Pa Her
Graduate Student, Department of
Psychology
Virginia Polytechnic Institute and
State University
EMOTION AND AFFECT
PARENTING STYLES
PEER CLIQUES
SELF-REPRESENTATION

Gilbert Herdt
Professor and Chair, Sexuality Studies,
San Francisco State University
Director, National Sexuality Resource
Center
KINSEY, ALFRED

C. Peter Herman
Professor, Department of Psychology
University of Toronto
OBESE EXTERNALITY
SCHACHTER, STANLEY

Mark A. Hernández
Assistant Professor of Latin American
and U.S. Latino Literatures and
Cultures, Department of Romance
Languages
Tufts University
MALINCHISTAS

Ronald J. Herring
Professor
Cornell University
LADEJINSKY, WOLF

Stefanie M. Herrmann
Postdoctoral Fellow
National Center for Atmospheric
Research (NCAR)
DROUGHT

Marjorie Randon Hershey
Professor, Department of Political
Science
Indiana University, Bloomington
CONSTITUENCY
POLLUTION

Alan Heston
Professor, Department of Economics
University of Pennsylvania
PENN WORLD TABLE

Gabriel Hetland
Doctoral Student, Sociology
Department
University of California, Berkeley
LIBERATION MOVEMENTS

Donald R. Hill
Professor of Africana/Latino Studies
and Anthropology
State University of New York–College
at Oneonta
ETHNOMUSICOLOGY

Eric Hirsch
Reader in Social Anthropology, School
of Social Sciences
Brunel University, United Kingdom
CULTURAL LANDSCAPE

Philip Hiscock
Associate Professor, Department of
Folklore
Memorial University of
Newfoundland
NURSERY RHYMES

Sara D. Hodges
Associate Professor, Department of
Psychology

University of Oregon
PERSPECTIVE-TAKING

James B. Hoelzle
Doctoral Candidate, Department of
Psychology
University of Toledo
RORSCHACH TEST

Derek S. Hoff
Department of History
Kansas State University
ZERO POPULATION GROWTH

Mathias Hoffmann
Economic Researcher
Deutsche Bundesbank, Germany
TRADE SURPLUS

Boris Hofmann
Economics Department
Deutsche Bundesbank, Germany
TRADE SURPLUS

Mirya Rose Holman
Doctoral Student
Claremont Graduate University
FENNO, RICHARD F.

Ric Holt
Southern Oregon University
BANANA PARABLE

Rolf Holtz
Department of Psychological Science
Ball State University
GROUPTHINK

Thomas T. Holyoke
Assistant Professor of Political Science
California State University, Fresno
POLITICAL SYSTEM
PRESSURE GROUPS

Seppo Honkapohja
Professor of International
Macroeconomics
University of Cambridge
SARGENT, THOMAS

Marc Hooghe
Associate Professor of Political Science
Catholic University of Leuven,
Belgium
ETHNOCENTRISM

Renée C. Hoogland
Professor, Institute for Gender Studies
Radboud University Nijmegen,
Netherlands

LE GUIN, URSULA K.
REPRESENTATION
SUBJECTIVITY: ANALYSIS

Gregory Hooks
Department of Sociology
Washington State University
PRISON INDUSTRY
WEAPONS INDUSTRY

B. D. Hopkins
Fellow, Corpus Christi College
University of Cambridge
RAJ, THE

Mark R. Hopkins
Assistant Professor, Department of
Economics
Gettysburg College
PUBLIC GOODS

W. Wat Hopkins
Virginia Tech
CENSORSHIP

William C. Horrace
Associate Professor of Economics
Syracuse University
STOCHASTIC FRONTIER
ANALYSIS

Allan V. Horwitz
Professor, Department of Sociology
and Institute for Health, Health Care
Policy, and Aging Research
Rutgers University
MADNESS

David W. Hosmer, Jr.
Professor Emeritus, Department of
Public Health
University of Massachusetts at
Amherst
SURVIVAL ANALYSIS
REGRESSION

Gert-Jan Hospers
Assistant Professor, Department of
Economics
University of Twente, The Netherlands
INFANT INDUSTRY
JACOBS, JANE
SOMBART, WERNER
TEXTILE INDUSTRY

Jerry F. Hough
Professor of Political Science
Duke University
BOLSHEVISM
LENIN, VLADIMIR ILITCH
MOORE, BARRINGTON

Donna Houston
Urban and Environmental Planning
Program, Griffith School of
Environment
Griffith University, Australia
FREIRE, PAULO

Daniel H. Hovelson
Research Assistant, Harvard Program
in Refugee Trauma
Massachusetts General Hospital
TORTURE

Mary Hovsepian
Department of Sociology
Duke University
INTIFADA, THE
PALESTINIANS

Cheryl Howard
Associate Professor, Department of
Sociology and Anthropology
University of Texas at El Paso
MODE, THE

Michael C. Howard
Professor, Department of Economics
University of Waterloo, Canada
VALUE

Lindsay M. Howden
Doctoral Student in Sociology
Texas A&M University
DEPOPULATION

Stephen Howe
Professor, Department of Historical
Studies
University of Bristol
EMPIRE

William G. Howell
Associate Professor, Harris School of
Public Policy
University of Chicago
SCHOOL VOUCHERS

Dustin Ells Howes
St. Mary's College of Maryland
HOBBES, THOMAS
POLITICAL THEORY

E. Philip Howrey
Professor Emeritus, Department of
Economics; Professor Emeritus,
Department of Statistics
University of Michigan
MOMENT GENERATING
FUNCTION

Susan Howson
Professor of Economics
University of Toronto
MEADE, JAMES

Melanie B. Hoy
Department of Psychology and
Neuroscience
Duke University
SELF-CONCEPT
SOCIALIZATION

Timothy Hoye
Professor of Government
Texas Woman's University
AMERICAN POLITICAL SCIENCE
ASSOCIATION
ARISTOTLE
CHECKS AND BALANCES
MEDICIS, THE
PLATO

Rick H. Hoyle
Research Professor, Department of
Psychology and Neuroscience
Duke University
EXPERIMENTS, CONTROLLED
FORMULAS
SELF-CONSCIOUSNESS, PRIVATE
VS. PUBLIC
SELF-ESTEEM
SELF-SYSTEM

Cheng Hsiao
Department of Economics
University of Southern California and
City University of Hong Kong
UNIT ROOT AND
COINTEGRATION
REGRESSION

Mai Noguchi Hubbard
Department of Economics
University of North Carolina at
Chapel Hill
AKERLOF, GEORGE A.
STICKY PRICES
WAGES

Michael Hudson
Distinguished Professor of Economics
University of Missouri–Kansas City
HOT MONEY

William G. Huitt
Professor
Valdosta State University, Georgia
SKINNER BOX
SOCIAL LEARNING
PERSPECTIVE

John H. Hummel
Professor, Department of Psychology
and Counseling
Valdosta State University
SKINNER BOX

Benjamin Kline Hunnicutt
University of Iowa
LEISURE
WORK DAY

Kaye G. Husbands Fealing
William Brough Professor of
Economics
Williams College
AUTOMOBILE INDUSTRY

Philo A. Hutcheson
Associate Professor
Georgia State University
DAVIS, ANGELA
DE GAULLE, CHARLES
FRIEDAN, BETTY

Vincent L. Hutchings
Associate Professor, Department of
Political Science
University of Michigan
ATTITUDES, POLITICAL
RACE AND POLITICAL SCIENCE

George Hutchinson
Booth Tarkington Professor of Literary
Studies, Chair of the Department of
English
Indiana University, Bloomington
HARLEM RENAISSANCE

Patrick H. Hutton
Professor Emeritus, Department of
History
University of Vermont
MEMORY

Shelley Hymel
Professor, Department of Educational
and Counselling Psychology and
Special Education
University of British Columbia
PEER EFFECTS

Keith R. Ihlanfeldt
Professor, Department of Economics
Florida State University
MILLS, EDWIN

Sanford Ikeda
Associate Professor of Economics

Purchase College, The State University
of New York
MOSES, ROBERT

Tom Ikeda
Executive Director
Densho: The Japanese American
Legacy Project
INCARCERATION, JAPANESE
AMERICAN

Indridi H. Indridason
Associate Professor, Department of
Political Science, University of Iceland;
CD Fellow in Formal Analysis,
Department of Politics and
International Relations, University of
Oxford
OLIGARCHY

Daniel W. Ingersoll, Jr.
Professor of Anthropology
St. Mary's College of Maryland
MATERIAL CULTURE

Joseph E. Inikori
Professor
University of Rochester
SLAVE-GUN CYCLE

Chester A. Insko
Professor, Department of Psychology
University of North Carolina at
Chapel Hill
PRISONER'S DILEMMA
(PSYCHOLOGY)
SOCIAL INFLUENCE

Timothy Insoll
Chair of Archaeology
University of Manchester, United
Kingdom
TOTEMISM

Miguel A. Iraola
Department of Business
Administration
Universidad Carlos III de Madrid,
Spain
MARKET FUNDAMENTALS

Robert Mark Isaac
John and Hallie Quinn Eminent
Scholar and Professor, Department of
Economics
Florida State University
ECONOMICS, EXPERIMENTAL
SMITH, VERNON L.

Judy L. Isaksen
Associate Professor, Department of
English and Communications
High Point University
GENERATION X
VEIL, IN AFRICAN AMERICAN
CULTURE

Guy-Erik Isaksson
Associate Professor, Department of
Political Science
Åbo Akademi University, Finland
BICAMERALISM

Carmen R. Isasi
Assistant Professor, Department of
Epidemiology and Population Health
Albert Einstein College of Medicine of
Yeshiva University, Bronx, New York
NUTRITION
RESEARCH, CROSS-SECTIONAL

Richard Iton
Associate Professor, Department of
African American Studies
Northwestern University
HIP HOP

Duncan Ivison
Professor, School of Philosophical and
Historical Inquiry
University of Sydney
INDIGENOUS RIGHTS

Ira Jacknis
Research Anthropologist, Phoebe A.
Hearst Museum of Anthropology
University of California, Berkeley
LOWIE, ROBERT

Craig C. Jackson
Assistant Professor, Department of
Psychology
Virginia Wesleyan College
LOBOTOMY

James S. Jackson
Director and Research Professor,
Daniel Katz Distinguished University
Professor of Psychology
Institute for Social Research,
University of Michigan
NATIONAL SURVEY OF BLACK
AMERICANS

Regine O. Jackson
Assistant Professor of American
Studies
Emory University
IMMIGRANTS, BLACK

Sarita D. Jackson
Adjunct Assistant Professor,
Department of Global Business and
Public Policy
University of Maryland University
College
   CHÁVEZ, HUGO
   ORGANIZATION OF
     PETROLEUM EXPORTING
     COUNTRIES (OPEC)
   PARTIDO REVOLUCIONARIO
     INSTITUCIONAL
   RABIN, YITZHAK
   VILLA, FRANCISCO (PANCHO)

Susan A. Jackson
Senior Research Fellow, School of
Human Movement Studies
University of Queensland
   FLOW

Jonathan Jacobs
Professor of History
Barry University
   HUNTINGTON, SAMUEL P.
   MEXICAN-AMERICAN WAR
   VIDEO GAMES
   WAR OF 1898

Arvind K. Jain
Associate Professor, Department of
Finance
Concordia University
   CORPORATE SOCIAL
     RESPONSIBILITY
   CORRUPTION
   HERD BEHAVIOR

Nicholas Jakobson
Research Assistant
Iran Policy Committee
   PARTITION

Vanus James
School for Graduate Studies and
Research
University of the West Indies, Mona,
Jamaica
   LEWIS, W. ARTHUR

Ji-Hyang Jang
Research Fellow, Brain Korea 21
Program, Department of Political
Science
Seoul National University
   FUNDAMENTALISM, ISLAMIC

Kenneth R. Janken
Professor, Department of African and
Afro-American Studies, and Adjunct
Professor, Department of History
University of North Carolina at
Chapel Hill
   WHITE, WALTER

David R. Jansson
Visiting Assistant Professor,
Department of Geology and
Geography
Vassar College
   NATIONAL GEOGRAPHIC

Patricia A. Jaramillo
Assistant Professor, Department of
Political Science and Geography
University of Texas at San Antonio
   PRIMARIES

Konrad H. Jarausch
Lurcy Professor of European
Civilization
University of North Carolina, Chapel
Hill
   BERLIN WALL

Charles Jaret
Professor, Department of Sociology
Georgia State University
   CITIES
   SEPARATE-BUT-EQUAL
   SLUMS

Guillermina Jasso
Professor of Sociology
New York University
   NEW IMMIGRANT SURVEY
   PROBABILITY DISTRIBUTIONS

Timothy B. Jay
Professor, Department of Psychology
Massachusetts College of Liberal Arts
   PROFANITY

Arjun Jayadev
Assistant Professor
University of Massachusetts, Boston
   SEN, AMARTYA KUMAR

Philip N. Jefferson
Professor of Economics, Department
of Economics
Swarthmore College
   POLICY, FISCAL

Judson L. Jeffries
Professor of African American Studies,
Department of African American and

African Studies, Community
Extension Center
Ohio State University
   BLACK POWER

Tony James Jeffs
Department of Applied Social Sciences
Durham University, England
   EDUCATION, INFORMAL

Ted G. Jelen
Professor of Political Science
University of Nevada, Las Vegas
   CHURCH AND STATE

Gwynne L. Jenkins
American Association for the
Advancement of Science Fellow in
Science & Technology Policy
National Institutes of Health
   MIDWIFERY

J. Craig Jenkins
Professor and Chair of Sociology
Ohio State University
   PROTEST

Richard Jenkins
Professor, Department of Sociological
Studies
University of Sheffield
   SOCIAL CATEGORIZATION

Robert Jensen
School of Journalism
University of Texas at Austin
   OBSCENITY

Jennifer Jensen Wallach
Assistant Professor, Department of
History, Geography, and Philosophy
Georgia College & State University
   KING, MARTIN LUTHER, JR.

Victor Jew
Honorary Associate/Fellow,
Department of History
University of Wisconsin, Madison
   IMMIGRANTS, ASIAN

Joseph O. Jewell
Associate Professor, Department of
Sociology and Interim Director, Race
& Ethnic Studies Institute
Texas A&M University
   EDUCATION, UNEQUAL

Sheridan Johns
Professor Emeritus of Political Science
Duke University

APARTHEID
MANDELA, NELSON

Kimberley S. Johnson
Assistant Professor, Barnard College
Columbia University
POLL TAX

Loch K. Johnson
Regents Professor of Public and
International Affairs
University of Georgia
CENTRAL INTELLIGENCE
AGENCY, U.S.

Sheri L. Johnson
Professor, Department of Psychology
University of Miami
MANIAS
MANIC DEPRESSION

Stephanie R. Johnson
Director of Applied Psychological
Science
American Psychological Association
MENTORING

Willene A. Johnson
President
Komaza, Inc.
OVERLENDING

Yolanda Y. Johnson
Department of Sociology
University of Nebraska–Lincoln
PARK SCHOOL, THE
WILSON, WILLIAM JULIUS

Hank Johnston
Associate Professor of Sociology
San Diego State University
REVOLUTION OF RISING
EXPECTATIONS

Seth Jolly
Lecturer & Postdoctoral Fellow,
Committee on International Relations
University of Chicago
CLEAVAGES
CODETERMINATION

Barry Jones
Associate Professor, Department of
Economics
Binghamton University
PRICE INDICES
QUANTITY INDEX

Kim Jones
Research Assistant

University of California, San Francisco
OBESITY

Nikki Jones
Department of Sociology
University of California, Santa Barbara
CASE METHOD

Susanna Jones
Assistant Professor, Department of
Social Work
Long Island University
SOCIAL WORK

Òscar Jordà
Associate Professor, Department of
Economics
University of California, Davis
OPEN MARKET OPERATIONS

David L. Jordan
Professor and Extension Specialist,
Department of Crop Science
North Carolina State University,
Raleigh
PEANUT INDUSTRY

Kurt A. Jordan
Assistant Professor, Department of
Anthropology and American Indian
Program
Cornell University
SENECA

Julia S. Jordan-Zachery
Assistant Professor, Department of
Political Science
Howard University
NONDECISION-MAKING
POLICY ANALYSIS

John T. Jost
Associate Professor
New York University
FAHRENHEIT 9/11

David Judge
Professor, Department of Government
University of Strathclyde, United
Kingdom
ARISTOCRACY
PARLIAMENT, UNITED
KINGDOM
PARLIAMENTS AND
PARLIAMENTARY SYSTEMS
THATCHER, MARGARET

P. N. Junankar
Professor, School of Economics and
Finance, University of Western
Sydney, Australia
IZA, Institute for the Study of Labor,
Bonn, Germany
ECONOMICS, LABOR
LABOR DEMAND
LABOR FORCE PARTICIPATION
LABOR SUPPLY

Meheroo Jussawalla
Emerita Research Fellow, Economist
East–West Center, Honolulu, Hawaii
MICROELECTRONICS INDUSTRY

Fadhel Kaboub
Assistant Professor of Economics
Drew University
CENTRAL BANKS
PRICE VS. QUANTITY
ADJUSTMENT
SOCIALIZATION OF
INVESTMENT

Padma Kadiyala
Associate Professor, Lubin School of
Business
Pace University
MARKET CORRECTION

John Kadvany
Principal, Policy and Decision Science
Menlo Park, California
LAKATOS, IMRE

Michael Kagan
Senior Fellow in Human Rights Law,
Department of Law
American University in Cairo
DARFUR

John H. Kagel
Department of Economics
The Ohio State University
WINNER'S CURSE

Erin B. Kaheny
Assistant Professor, Department of
Political Science
University of Wisconsin–Milwaukee
ROE V. WADE

Shulamit Kahn
Associate Professor, Department of
Finance and Economics
Boston University School of
Management
NOMINAL WAGES
TIME-AND-A-HALF

Stephen Kalberg
Associate Professor, Department of
Sociology
Boston University
PROTESTANT ETHIC, THE

Madhavi Kale
Department of History
Bryn Mawr College
EAST INDIAN DIASPORA

Devorah Kalekin-Fishman
Senior Researcher, Faculty of
Education
University of Haifa
ALIENATION-ANOMIE

Arne L. Kalleberg
Kenan Distinguished Professor of
Sociology
University of North Carolina at
Chapel Hill
BERG, IVAR E.

Jill Kamil
Independent Researcher, Coptic
Studies
Cairo, Egypt
COPTIC CHRISTIAN CHURCH

Gen Kanayama
Instructor in Psychiatry, Harvard
Medical School
Member, Biological Psychiatry
Laboratory, McLean Hospital
STEROIDS

Edward J. Kane
James F. Cleary Professor in Finance
Boston College, Chestnut Hill, MA
KINDLEBERGER, CHARLES
POOR

Jae Ho Kang
Assistant Professor, Department of
Sociology, Department of Media
Studies and Film
The New School, New York
FRANKFURT SCHOOL
MEDIA
MEDIUM IS THE MESSAGE

Kristin Kanthak
Assistant Professor of Political Science
University of Pittsburgh
MAJORITY VOTING
VOTING SCHEMES

Marshall B. Kapp
Garwin Distinguished Professor of
Law and Medicine
Southern Illinois University Schools of
Law and Medicine
INFORMED CONSENT

Mustafa C. Karakus
Senior Economist
WESTAT, Rockville, Maryland
PHARMACEUTICAL INDUSTRY

Lynn A. Karoly
Senior Economist
RAND Corporation
HEAD START EXPERIMENTS

Peter Karsten
University of Pittsburgh
MILITARY

Todd B. Kashdan
George Mason University
SOCIAL ANXIETY

Mika Kato
Assistant Professor
Howard University
MARKUP PRICING

Mark Katz
Assistant Professor, Department of
Music
University of North Carolina at
Chapel Hill
VINYL RECORDINGS

Andrew D. Kaufman
Teaching and Research Fellow, Office
of the Vice President and Provost
University of Virginia
WAR AND PEACE

Jay S. Kaufman
Associate Professor, Department of
Epidemiology
University of North Carolina School
of Public Health
SLAVERY HYPERTENSION
HYPOTHESIS

Eric P. Kaufmann
Reader, School of Politics and
Sociology
Birkbeck College, University of
London
LOYALISTS

Yunus Kaya
University of North Carolina
Wilmington
STRATIFICATION

Michael Keane
PhD Student
University of Notre Dame
CONGRESS, U.S.

Michael C. Kearl
Professor, Department of Sociology
and Anthropology
Trinity University
DEATH AND DYING
TIME

Michael Kearney
Professor, Department of
Anthropology
University of California, Riverside
PEASANTRY

Robert O. Keel
Teaching Professor, Department of
Sociology
University of Missouri–St. Louis
RATIONAL CHOICE THEORY

Steve L. Keen
School of Economics & Finance
University of Western Sydney
DEPRESSION, ECONOMIC
FINANCIAL INSTABILITY
HYPOTHESIS
LABOR THEORY OF VALUE
LIMITS OF GROWTH
MONEY, ENDOGENOUS
NONLINEAR SYSTEMS

Louis G. Keith
Emeritus Professor of Obstetrics and
Gynecology and Former Head,
Section of Undergraduate Education
and Medical Student Affairs, Feinberg
School of Medicine
Northwestern University
MULTIPLE BIRTHS

Verna M. Keith
Professor, Department of Sociology,
Center for Demography and
Population Health
Florida State University
PHENOTYPE

Michal Kejak
Associate Professor
Center for Economic Research and
Graduate Education, Charles

University, and the Economics Institute of the Academy of Sciences of the Czech Republic
STAGES OF ECONOMIC GROWTH

Donald R. Kelley
Professor Emeritus, Department of History
Rutgers University
LINGUISTIC TURN

Douglas Kellner
George F. Kneller Philosophy of Education Chair
University of California, Los Angeles
FROMM, ERICH

John D. Kelly
Professor, Department of Anthropology
University of Chicago
CULTURAL RELATIVISM
NEOIMPERIALISM

John Kelsay
Distinguished Research Professor and Richard L. Rubenstein Professor of Religion
Florida State University
JIHAD

Christopher M. Kelty
Assistant Professor, Department of Anthropology
Rice University, Houston, TX
INTERNET

Pamela M. Kenealy
Reader in Psychology, School of Human and Life Sciences
Roehampton University, London
STATE-DEPENDENT RETRIEVAL

Charles D. Kenney
Associate Professor, Department of Political Science
University of Oklahoma
POLYARCHY

Keith Kerr
Assistant Professor of Sociology
Quinnipiac University
SOCIAL SCIENCE

J. R. Kerr-Ritchie
History Department
Howard University
ROBESON, PAUL
SLAVE MODE OF PRODUCTION

Ken I. Kersch
Assistant Professor of Political Science and Law
Boston College
REPRESSIVE TOLERANCE
SCOPES TRIAL

Michael Kessler
Assistant Director and Visiting Assistant Professor of Government, Berkley Center for Religion, Peace, and World Affairs
Georgetown University
MORALITY

Paul Ketchum
Professor
University of Oklahoma
PULLMAN PORTERS
SUBURBS

David Kettler
Professor Emeritus, Political Studies, Trent University
Research Professor, Social Sciences Division, Bard College
NEUMANN, FRANZ

Elias L. Khalil
Associate Professor, Department of Economics
Monash University
TASTES

M. Ali Khan
Abram Hutzler Professor of Political Economy
Johns Hopkins University
FORESIGHT, PERFECT
MINIMIZATION
PROBABILITY THEORY
SATIATION

Paulette Kidder
Associate Professor of Philosophy
Seattle University
ABORTION RIGHTS
JUSTICE
UTILITARIANISM

Nicholas J. Kiersey
Teaching Fellow, Department of Social Sciences
University of Virginia, Wise
TRILATERAL COMMISSION

John F. Kihlstrom
Professor, Department of Psychology
University of California, Berkeley
TOLMAN, EDWARD

Melanie Killen
Professor, Department of Human Development
University of Maryland, College Park
MORAL DOMAIN THEORY

JongHan Kim
Professor of Psychology
University of Richmond
PERCEPTION, PERSON

Michael S. Kimmel
State University of New York at Stony Brook
MASCULINITY

John Kincaid
Robert B. and Helen S. Meyner Professor of Government and Public Service; Director, the Meyner Center for the Study of the State
Lafayette College
CONFEDERATIONS

J. E. King
Department of Economics and Finance
La Trobe University
UNDERCONSUMPTION
VALUE

Jonathan T. King
Music Department
Columbia University
BLUEGRASS

Stewart Royce King
Associate Professor of History
Mount Angel Seminary
DUVALIERS, THE
GARVEY, MARCUS
HAITIAN REVOLUTION
NEOCOLONIALISM
SERVITUDE
SEX, INTERRACIAL
TOUSSAINT LOUVERTURE
TRUTH, SOJOURNER

Barbara Sgouraki Kinsey
Assistant Professor, Department of Political Science
University of Central Florida
FRANCHISE

Simon Kirchin
Lecturer, Philosophy
University of Kent
PARTICULARISM

John M. Kirk
Professor of Latin American Studies
Dalhousie University
CUBAN REVOLUTION

Richard F. Kitchener
Department of Philosophy
Colorado State University
BEHAVIORISM
PHILOSOPHY, MORAL

Ran Kivetz
Professor of Business
Columbia University
FARSIGHTEDNESS

Peter Kivisto
Richard Swanson Professor of Social
Thought
Augustana College
CITIZENSHIP
MODE OF PRODUCTION
PUBLIC SPHERE

Daniel B. Klein
Professor of Economics
George Mason University
LIBERTARIANISM

Lawrence R. Klein
Benjamin Franklin Professor of
Economics (emeritus)
University of Pennsylvania
FRISCH, RAGNAR
TINBERGEN, JAN

Martin Klein
Professor Emeritus, Department of
History
University of Toronto
AFRICAN DIASPORA

Morris M. Kleiner
Professor of Public Policy, Humphrey
Institute and Industrial Relations
Center, University of Minnesota
Research Associate, National Bureau of
Economic Research
OCCUPATIONAL REGULATION

Ronald A. Kleinknecht
Professor of Psychology and Dean
College of Humanities and Social
Sciences, Western Washington
University, Bellingham
ANXIETY
PHOBIA
PSYCHOPATHOLOGY

N. Anders Klevmarken
Professor, Department of Economics
Uppsala University, Sweden
TIME ALLOCATION

Alexis Klimoff
Professor of Russian Studies
Vassar College
SOLZHENITSYN, ALEKSANDR

Klaus Konrad Klostermaier
University Distinguished Professor
Emeritus
University of Manitoba
ARYANS
HINDUISM

Robert J. Klotz
Associate Professor, Department of
Political Science
University of Southern Maine
INTERNET BUBBLE

Christa Knellwolf
Adjunct Associate Professor
The Australian National University
EXOTICISM

Michael W. Knox
University of California, Los Angeles
AMERICAN DILEMMA

Tarja Knuuttila
Department of Philosophy
University of Helsinki
MODELS AND MODELING

Becky Kochenderfer-Ladd
Associate Professor, School of Social
and Family Dynamics
Arizona State University
SEPARATION ANXIETY

Levent Koçkesen
Assistant Professor, Department of
Economics
Koç University, Turkey
RELATIVE INCOME
HYPOTHESIS

Gregory Koger
University of Miami
FILIBUSTER

Andrew I. Kohen
Professor of Economics
James Madison University
PARNES, HERBERT

Ivar Kolstad
Senior Researcher

Chr. Michelsen Institute
POLITICAL INSTABILITY,
INDICES OF

Sokratis M. Koniordos
Associate Professor, Department of
Sociology
University of Crete, Greece
SOCIAL CAPITAL
SOCIOLOGY, ECONOMIC

Daniel Y. Kono
Assistant Professor, Department of
Political Science
University of California, Davis
GENERAL AGREEMENT ON
TARIFFS AND TRADE

Rex Koontz
Associate Professor
University of Houston
OLMECS

Samuel Kotz
Department of Engineering
Management and Systems Engineering
George Washington University
PROBABILITY DISTRIBUTIONS

Marie-José Kouassi
Professor, Economics Department
Howard University
HARRIS, ABRAM L., JR.

Thad Kousser
Assistant Professor, Department of
Political Science
University of California, San Diego
TERM LIMITS

Jackie Krafft
Groupe de Recherche en Droit,
Economie, et Gestion
Université de Nice Sophia Antipolis,
Centre National de la Recherche
Scientifique
FIRM

Mark Kramer
Director of Cold War Studies
Harvard University
DEININGER AND SQUIRE
WORLD BANK INEQUALITY
DATABASE

Michael I. Krauss
Professor of Law
George Mason University
RULE OF LAW

Brian V. Krauth
Associate Professor, Department of Economics
Simon Fraser University, Canada
SOCIAL ISOLATION

Daniel Kreiss
Department of Communication
Stanford University
FUTURE SHOCK

Anne C. Krendl
Department of Psychological and Brain Sciences
Dartmouth College
NEUROSCIENCE

Ben Kriechel
Maastricht University
LABOR

Peter Kriesler
University of New South Wales
EXCHANGE VALUE
PARTIAL EQUILIBRIUM

Dennis Kristensen
Department of Economics
Columbia University
CENTRAL LIMIT THEOREM
DESCRIPTIVE STATISTICS

Charles A. Kromkowski
Department of Politics
University of Virginia
SUFFRAGE, WOMEN'S

Mona Lena Krook
Assistant Professor
Washington University in St. Louis
POLITICS, GENDER
WOMEN'S MOVEMENT

Joachim I. Krueger
Professor of Psychology
Brown University
BAYESIAN STATISTICS
DAWES, ROBYN
OVER-ATTRIBUTION BIAS
SELF-ENHANCEMENT

Douglas L. Kuck
Associate Professor of Sociology
University of South Carolina Aiken
PRISONS

Kathy J. Kuipers
Assistant Professor, Sociology
University of Montana
SOCIOLOGY

Vikram Kumar
Professor of Economics
Davidson College
BALANCE OF TRADE

G. Tarcan Kumkale
Department of Psychology
Koç University, Istanbul, Turkey
GUTTMAN SCALE
SLEEPER EFFECTS
TIME ORIENTATION

Alan J. Kuperman
Assistant Professor, Lyndon Baines Johnson School of Public Affairs
University of Texas at Austin
RELATIVE DEPRIVATION

Haydar Kurban
Assistant Professor, Economics Department
Howard University
REGRESSION ANALYSIS
SPATIAL THEORY
URBAN STUDIES

Heinz D. Kurz
Professor of Economics
University of Graz, Austria
CAPITAL
ECONOMICS, CLASSICAL
PHYSIOCRACY
QUESNAY, FRANCOIS
RICARDIAN VICE
RICARDO, DAVID
SRAFFA, PIERO
TURGOT, JACQUES
WICKSELL EFFECTS

Charles Kurzman
Associate Professor, Department of Sociology
University of North Carolina at Chapel Hill
SOCIOLOGY, VOLUNTARISTIC VS. STRUCTURALIST

Richard Lachmann
Professor, Department of Sociology
State University of New York, Albany
ANDERSON, PERRY

Brian Ladd
Research Associate, Department of History
University at Albany, State University of New York
TOWNS

Anthony Laden
Associate Professor of Philosophy
University of Illinois at Chicago
MAXIMIN PRINCIPLE

Joanna N. Lahey
Assistant Professor, Bush School of Government and Public Service
Texas A&M University, College Station
DISCRIMINATION, WAGE, BY AGE

Bidisha Lahiri
Assistant Professor, Department of Economics
Oklahoma State University, Stillwater
ENVIRONMENTAL KUZNETS CURVES

Sajal Lahiri
Vandeveer Professor of Economics
Southern Illinois University–Carbondale
LEONTIEF, WASSILY
SOCIAL ACCOUNTING MATRIX

Dejian Lai
Professor of Biostatistics
The University of Texas School of Public Health
STUDENT'S *T*-STATISTIC
WHITE NOISE
Z-TEST

David A. Lake
Professor, Department of Political Science
University of California, San Diego
HIERARCHY

Sharon Lamb
Professor of Psychology
Saint Michael's College
GILLIGAN, CAROL

Alexander P. Lamis
Associate Professor, Department of Political Science
Case Western Reserve University
KEY, V. O., JR.

Christopher J. Lamping
Department of Anthropology
Columbia University
HISTORY, SOCIAL
LEVELLERS
THOMPSON, EDWARD P.

Peter M. Lance
Research Associate, Carolina
Population Center
University of North Carolina at
Chapel Hill
CONSTRAINED CHOICE
HECKMAN SELECTION
    CORRECTION PROCEDURE
MEASUREMENT ERROR

Bruce Landesman
Associate Professor, Philosophy
University of Utah
POLITICAL ECONOMY

Kristin E. Landfield
Department of Psychology
Emory University
PSYCHIATRIC DISORDERS

Anthony Landreth
University of Cincinnati
MOTIVATION

Larry M. Lane
Lecturer in Political Science
University of Tennessee, Knoxville
MERIT

Anthony F. Lang, Jr.
Senior Lecturer, School of
International Relations
University of St. Andrews, St.
Andrews, Scotland, U.K.
APPEASEMENT
INTERNATIONALISM

Graeme Lang
Associate Professor, Department of
Asian and International Studies
City University of Hong Kong
MECCA

Kevin Lang
Professor, Department of Economics,
Boston University
Research Associate, National Bureau of
Economic Research
DISCRIMINATION, WAGE
LABOR MARKET
    SEGMENTATION

Lauren Langman
Department of Sociology
Loyola University Chicago
ALIENATION-ANOMIE
OEDIPUS COMPLEX

Jennifer E. Lansford
Research Scientist, Center for Child
and Family Policy
Duke University
CORPORAL PUNISHMENT
PEER INFLUENCE
SOCIAL INFORMATION
    PROCESSING

Kevin T. Larkin
Professor, Department of Psychology
West Virginia University
HYPERTENSION

Kate Clifford Larson
Lecturer, Department of History
Simmons College, Boston
TUBMAN, HARRIET

Pierre Lasserre
Professor of Economics
Université du Québec à Montréal
TRAGEDY OF THE COMMONS

G. Daniel Lassiter
Professor, Department of Psychology
Ohio University
NEED FOR COGNITION
SELF-JUSTIFICATION

William D. Lastrapes
Professor, Department of Economics
University of Georgia, Athens
AUTOREGRESSIVE MODELS
ECONOMICS, NEW CLASSICAL
TIME SERIES REGRESSION

Michael E. Latham
Associate Professor, Department of
History
Fordham University
MODERNIZATION

Maureen Lauder
Michigan State University
VIRGINS

Pat Lauderdale
Professor, School of Justice
Arizona State University, Tempe
JUSTICE, SOCIAL

Robert Launay
Professor, Department of
Anthropology
Northwestern University
POLYTHEISM

Kristen Lavelle
Department of Sociology

Texas A&M University
ATTITUDES, RACIAL
FORMATION, RACIAL

Marc Lavoie
University of Ottawa
WIDOW'S CRUSE

Ian Law
Reader, School of Sociology and Social
Policy
University of Leeds
ETHNICITY

Michael S. Lawlor
Professor of Economics
Wake Forest University
CARRYING COST
Z-D MODEL

Janet H. Lawrence
Associate Professor, Center for the
Study of Higher and Postsecondary
Education, School of Education
University of Michigan
PROFESSORIATE

Vicheka Lay
LL.M Candidate and DFDL Mekong
Law Group
Cambodia
POL POT

Keith Laybourn
Professor of History
University of Huddersfield
LABOUR PARTY (BRITAIN)
LIBERAL PARTY (BRITAIN)

Thomas Leahey
Professor of Psychology
Virginia Commonwealth University
THORNDIKE, EDWARD

Angela D. Ledford
Assistant Professor of Political Science,
Department of History and Political
Science
The College of Saint Rose
UNDERREPRESENTATION

Francis Graham Lee
Professor, Department of Political
Science
Saint Joseph's University
IMPEACHMENT

Hedwig Lee
Graduate Student, Department of
Sociology

University of North Carolina at
Chapel Hill
NATIONAL LONGITUDINAL
STUDY OF ADOLESCENT
HEALTH

Jeffrey K. Lee
PhD Student
School of Business, Harvard
University
INTERGENERATIONAL
TRANSMISSION
NEUROECONOMICS

Martha F. Lee
Associate Professor, Department of
Political Science
The University of Windsor
ILLUMINATI, THE

Richard E. Lee
Professor of Sociology; Director,
Fernand Braudel Center
Binghamton University
HUMANISM

Tae-Hwy Lee
Department of Economics
University of California, Riverside
LOSS FUNCTIONS

Taeku Lee
Associate Professor, Department of
Political Science
University of California, Berkeley
POLITICS, ASIAN AMERICAN

Tiane L. Lee
Graduate Student, Department of
Psychology
Princeton University
STEREOTYPES

Young-joo Lee
Doctoral Student, School of Public
and International Affairs
University of Georgia
NATIONAL SERVICE PROGRAMS
VOLUNTEER PROGRAMS

Elisabeth S. Leedham-Green
Fellow and Archivist, Darwin College
Cambridge University
CAMBRIDGE UNIVERSITY

Harriet P. Lefley
Professor, Department of Psychiatry
and Behavioral Sciences
University of Miami Miller School of
Medicine

MENTAL ILLNESS
SCHIZOPHRENIA

Helena Legido-Quigley
Research Fellow
HEALTH IN DEVELOPING
COUNTRIES

Jeffrey W. Legro
Professor, Department of Politics
University of Virginia
BILATERALISM

Justin Leiber
Department of Philosophy
Florida State University
CHOMSKY, NOAM
SCIENCE FICTION

J. Paul Leigh
Professor of Health Economics, Center
for Healthcare Policy and Research,
Medical School
University of California, Davis
WAGES, COMPENSATING

Jonathan E. Leightner
Professor of Economics
Augusta State University
BUBBLES
TECHNOLOGY, TRANSFER OF

Anthony J. Lemelle
Professor, Department of Sociology,
John Jay College
City University of New York
COX, OLIVER C.

Thomas Lemke
Senior Researcher
Institute for Social Research
Frankfurt/Main
GOVERNMENTALITY

Emeric Lendjel
Associate Professor, Centre d'économie
de la Sorbonne
University of Paris I, Panthéon
Sorbonne
POTRON, MAURICE
X-CRISE

Susan Lepselter
Assistant Professor of Communication
and Culture, and American Studies
Indiana University
UNIDENTIFIED FLYING
OBJECTS

Richard M. Lerner
Bergstrom Chair in Applied
Developmental Science
Tufts University
ADOLESCENT PSYCHOLOGY

Tera D. Letzring
Assistant Professor, Department of
Psychology
Idaho State University
SELF-REPORT METHOD

Constance Lever-Tracy
Flinders University of South Australia
CHINESE DIASPORA
GLOBAL WARMING

Geoffrey Brahm Levey
Senior Lecturer, School of Social
Sciences and International Studies
University of New South Wales
CULTURAL RIGHTS

Jerome M. Levi
Associate Professor of Anthropology,
Department of Sociology and
Anthropology
Carleton College
SYMBOLS

Dan Levin
Department of Economics
The Ohio State University
WINNER'S CURSE

Paul T. Levin
PhD Candidate, School of
International Relations
University of Southern California, Los
Angeles, California
NATION-STATE

Brett Levinson
State University of New York
INTELLECTUALS, ORGANIC

Daniel J. Levitin
Professor of Psychology and Music
McGill University, Montreal, Québec,
Canada
MUSIC, PSYCHOLOGY OF

Heidi M. Levitt
Associate Professor, Department of
Psychology
University of Memphis
TRANSGENDER

David M. Levy
Professor, Center for the Study of
Public Choice
George Mason University
CREATIVE DESTRUCTION
GALTON, FRANCIS

Sheri R. Levy
Associate Professor, Department of
Psychology
State University of New York at Stony
Brook
LAY THEORIES

Noemi Levy-Orlik
Professor
National Autonomous University of
Mexico
MACROECONOMICS,
STRUCTURALIST

David Lewin
Neil H. Jacoby Professor of
Management, Human Resources, and
Organizational Behavior
University of California, Los Angeles,
Anderson School of Management
MANAGEMENT

Leif Lewin
Johan Skytte Professor of Eloquence
and Government
Uppsala University, Sweden
VERBA, SIDNEY

Amanda E. Lewis
Associate Professor, Departments of
Sociology and African American
Studies
University of Illinois at Chicago
OPPOSITIONALITY

Frank D. Lewis
Professor, Department of Economics
Queen's University, Kingston, Canada
ENGERMAN, STANLEY

Patsy P. Lewis
Senior Fellow, Sir Arthur Lewis
Institute for Social and Economic
Studies
University of the West Indies, Mona
BANANA INDUSTRY

Rupert C. Lewis
Professor of Political Thought
University of the West Indies,
Kingston, Jamaica
RODNEY, WALTER

Dong Li
Associate Professor, Department of
Economics
Kansas State University
TRANSACTION TAXES

Norman P. Li
Assistant Professor, Department of
Psychology
University of Texas at Austin
SEX AND MATING

Yibing Li
Tufts University
ADOLESCENT PSYCHOLOGY

Kan Liang
Associate Professor of History
Seattle University
CHIANG KAI-SHEK

Victor Lidz
Department of Psychiatry
Drexel University College of Medicine
SOCIAL SYSTEM

Donald Lien
Richard S. Liu Distinguished Chair in
Business,
University of Texas at San Antonio
ARBITRAGE AND
ARBITRAGEURS
CONTANGO
FINANCIAL MARKETS
HEDGING

Scott O. Lilienfeld
Department of Psychology
Emory University
PSYCHIATRIC DISORDERS

Gregory A. Lilly
Associate Professor, Department of
Economics
Elon University, North Carolina
MAXIMIZATION

Cheng-Hsien Lin
Department of Psychology and
Sociology
Texas A&M University–Kingsville;
System Center–San Antonio
DATA, LONGITUDINAL
DATA, PSEUDOPANEL
FACTOR ANALYSIS
VARIABLES, LATENT

James Lin
Research Assistant

Economic Policy Institute
HARD-CORE UNEMPLOYED

Tony Tian-Ren Lin
Graduate Instructor
University of Virginia, Charlottesville
RELIGIOSITY

Dana F. Lindemann
Assistant Professor of Psychology,
Department of Psychology
Western Illinois University
AIDS

Darwyn E. Linder
Professor Emeritus, Department of
Psychology
Arizona State University, Tempe
ARONSON, ELLIOT
FESTINGER, LEON
LEWIN, KURT

Evelin G. Lindner
Founding Manager of Human Dignity
and Humiliation Studies
Senior Lecturer, Department of
Psychology, Norwegian University of
Science and Technology in Trondheim
HUMILIATION

Derick H. Lindquist
Research Associate, Departments of
Psychology and Molecular Biosciences
The University of Kansas
CLASSICAL CONDITIONING

Godfrey Linge
Emeritus Professor, Contemporary
China Centre
The Australian National University
AIDS/HIV IN DEVELOPING
COUNTRIES, IMPACT OF

Richard G. Lipsey
Professor Emeritus, Economics
Simon Fraser University, Vancouver,
Canada
RETURNS, DIMINISHING
RETURNS TO SCALE
RETURNS TO SCALE,
ASYMMETRIC

David A. Lishner
Assistant Professor, Department of
Psychology
University of Wisconsin, Oshkosh
ALTRUISM
ALTRUISM AND PROSOCIAL
BEHAVIOR

EXPERIMENTS
SCALES

Daniel Little
Professor of Philosophy and
Chancellor
University of Michigan–Dearborn
DEVELOPMENT
FALSE CONSCIOUSNESS
MARXISM

Elena Llaudet
Research Associate, Program on
Education Policy and Governance
Harvard University
SCHOOL VOUCHERS

Kim M. Lloyd
Assistant Professor, Department of
Sociology
Washington State University
MARRIAGE

Peter J. Lloyd
Professor Emeritus
University of Melbourne
STOLPER-SAMUELSON
THEOREM

Stephen R. Lloyd-Moffett
Assistant Professor, Religious Studies
Program, Philosophy Department
California Polytechnic University, San
Luis Obispo
GREEK ORTHODOX CHURCH

Clarence Y. H. Lo
Associate Professor, Department of
Sociology
University of Missouri at Columbia
CAPITALISM, STATE

Craig A. Lockard
Professor, Department of Social
Change and Development
University of Wisconsin–Green Bay
GOLD, GOD, AND GLORY
ROCK 'N' ROLL

Corinna E. Löckenhoff
Research Fellow
National Institute on Aging
NEUROTICISM

Zachary Lockman
Professor, Department of Middle
Eastern and Islamic Studies
New York University
PAN-ARABISM

John Lodewijks
School of Economics and Finance
University of Western Sydney,
Australia
LIBERALIZATION, TRADE
OKUN'S LAW
STRUCTURAL ADJUSTMENT

Hein F. M. Lodewijkx
Associate Professor, Faculty of
Psychology
The Netherlands Open University
RECIPROCITY, NORM OF

Tom Lodge
Department of Politics
University of Limerick
AFRICAN NATIONAL CONGRESS

Chung-Ping Albert Loh
Assistant Professor, Department of
Economics and Geography, Coggin
College of Business
University of North Florida
ARROW-DEBREU MODEL

Paul A. Lombardo
Professor, College of Law
Georgia State University
STERILIZATION, HUMAN

Tehama M. Lopez
PhD Student, Department of Political
Science
University of Chicago
BLACK SEPTEMBER

C. A. Knox Lovell
Emeritus Professor, Department of
Economics
University of Georgia
PRODUCTION FRONTIER

Michael C. Lovell
Chester D. Hubbard Professor of
Economics and Social Sciences,
Emeritus
Wesleyan University
EXPECTATIONS, IMPLICIT
MISERY INDEX

Scott Loveridge
Associate Chairperson, Department of
Agricultural Economics
Michigan State University
DEVELOPMENT, RURAL

David Lowery
Professor, Department of Public
Administration

University of Leiden, The Netherlands
EXIT, VOICE, AND LOYALTY
INCREMENTALISM
TAX REVOLTS

Sherry R. Lowrance
Assistant Professor, Department of
International Affairs
University of Georgia
TWO-STATE SOLUTION

Riccardo "Jack" Lucchetti
Dipartimento di Economia
Università Politecnica delle Marche
(Ancona, Italy)
RANDOM EFFECTS REGRESSION

Jacquelyne Marie Luce
Research Fellow, Karl-Mannheim
Chair for Cultural Studies
Zeppelin University, Germany
GENETIC TESTING

Paul Luif
Austrian Institute for International
Affairs, Vienna, Austria
NEUTRAL STATES

Ritty A. Lukose
Graduate School of Education
University of Pennsylvania
GLOBALIZATION,
ANTHROPOLOGICAL ASPECTS
OF

Mark R. Lukowitsky
Doctoral Student
Pennsylvania State University
TRAIT THEORY

Tukumbi Lumumba-Kasongo
Professor of Political Science and
Chair of the Division of Social
Sciences, Wells College; Visiting
Scholar, Department of City and
Regional Planning, Cornell University
Adjunct Professor of Government,
Department of Government, Suffolk
University; Research Associate at the
Institute d'Ethnosociologie, Université
de Cocody
DIOP, CHEIKH ANTA

Adam Lupel
Editor
International Peace Academy
GOVERNMENT, WORLD
POSTNATIONALISM

Arthur Lupia
Hal R. Varian Collegiate Professor of
Political Science
University of Michigan
AMERICAN NATIONAL
ELECTION STUDIES (ANES)

Nancy Lutkehaus
Associate Professor, Department of
Anthropology
University of Southern California
MEAD, MARGARET

Monique L. Lyle
PhD Candidate, Political Science
Duke University
CIVIL LIBERTIES
ZERO-SUM GAME

Peter Lyon
Senior Research Fellow, Institute of
Commonwealth Studies
University of London, England
COMMONWEALTH, THE

Katerina C. Lyroudi
Assistant Professor
University of Macedonia,
Thessaloniki, Greece
INVENTORIES
SELLING LONG AND SELLING
SHORT
SEROTONIN
SIGNALS
SPEARMAN RANK
CORRELATION COEFFICIENT
TAX CREDITS

Debin Ma
Lecturer, Department of Economic
History
London School of Economics
SILK ROAD

Sheng-mei Ma
Professor of English
Michigan State University
DISNEY, WALT
SUN YAT-SEN

David Macarthur
Senior Lecturer, Department of
Philosophy
University of Sydney
NATURALISM

Alan Macfarlane
Professor, Department of Social
Anthropology

University of Cambridge
MALTHUSIAN TRAP

Karen E. MacGregor
The Ohio State University
STRATEGIES, SELF-
HANDICAPPING

Mark J. Machina
Professor of Economics
University of California, San Diego
NON-EXPECTED UTILITY
THEORY

Joseph A. Maciariello
Horton Professor of Management,
Peter F. Drucker and Masatoshi Ito
Graduate School of Management
Claremont Graduate University
DRUCKER, PETER

Christopher S. Mackay
Department of History and Classics
University of Alberta
PATRICIANS

D. W. MacKenzie
Department of Economics and
Finance
State University of New York at
Plattsburgh
STOCK EXCHANGES
STOCK EXCHANGES IN
DEVELOPING COUNTRIES
STOCKS

Robert Sean Mackin
Assistant Professor of Sociology
Texas A&M University
ALLENDE, SALVADOR
SOCIAL WELFARE SYSTEM
SOCIOLOGY, LATIN AMERICAN

Alison G. Mackinnon
Professor Emeritus, Hawke Research
Institute
University of South Australia
DEMOGRAPHIC TRANSITION

James G. MacKinnon
Sir Edward Peacock Professor of
Econometrics, Department of
Economics
Queen's University
SPECIFICATION ERROR

David J. Madden
Professor of Medical Psychology,
Department of Psychiatry and
Behavioral Sciences

Duke University Medical Center
MEMORY IN PSYCHOLOGY
SELECTIVE ATTENTION
SEMANTIC MEMORY

Stephanie Madon
Associate Professor, Department of
Psychology
Iowa State University
SELF-FULFILLING PROPHECIES

Nuno Luís Madureira
Professor, Department of History
University of Lisbon, ISCTE
DECISIVE EVENTS
WHOLESALE PRICE INDEX
WORKING DAY, LENGTH OF

Otto Maduro
Professor of World Christianity
Drew University
LIBERATION THEOLOGY

Abdel-Fattah Mady
Assistant Professor of Political Science
Alexandria University, Egypt
GOVERNMENT
MEIR, GOLDA

Frederick R. Magdoff
Professor Emeritus, Department of
Plant and Soil Science
University of Vermont
FERTILITY, LAND

M. Eileen Magnello
Research Associate
University College London
PEARSON, KARL

Lars Magnusson
Professor and chair in Economic
History
Uppsala University
MERCANTILISM

Cheleen Ann-Catherine Mahar
Professor, Department of Sociology
and Anthropology
Pacific University
PRACTICE THEORY

Srabani Maitra
Department of Adult Education and
Counseling Psychology
Ontario Institute for Studies in
Education, University of Toronto
HEGEMONY
WORK AND WOMEN

Sudeshna Maitra
Assistant Professor, Department of
Economics
York University
DOWRY AND BRIDE PRICE

Solomon Major
University of California—Santa
Barbara
DIVESTITURE
DOMINO THEORY
PUBLIC CHOICE THEORY

Sumon Majumdar
Associate Professor
Queen's University
STRATEGIC BEHAVIOR

Edmund J. Malesky
Graduate School of International
Relations and Pacific Studies
University of California–San Diego
VIETNAM WAR

Burton G. Malkiel
Chemical Bank Chairman's Professor
of Economics
Princeton University
RANDOM WALK
YIELD CURVE

Seth W. Mallios
Chair and Professor, Department of
Anthropology
San Diego State University
BURIAL GROUNDS
RECIPROCITY

Helge Malmgren
Professor, Department of Philosophy
Göteborg University
CONSCIOUSNESS

W. O. Maloba
University of Delaware
MAU MAU

Patrick S. Malone
Department of Psychology
University of South Carolina
GROWTH CURVE ANALYSIS
PATH ANALYSIS
STRUCTURAL EQUATION
  MODELS

William A. Maloney
Professor of Politics
University of Newcastle
FREE RIDER

Michael A. Malpass
Professor, Department of
Anthropology
Ithaca College
INCAS

Jelani Mandara
Program in Human Development and
Social Policy
Northwestern University
PARENT-CHILD RELATIONSHIPS

Anandi Mani
Associate Professor, Department of
Economics
University of Warwick, UK
POVERTY

Catherine L. Mann
Professor of International Economics
and Finance
Brandeis University
TRADE DEFICIT

Bruce Mannheim
University of Michigan
ESSENTIALISM

Philip D. Manning
Professor of Sociology
Cleveland State University
INTERACTIONISM, SYMBOLIC

Jeffrey W. Mantz
Assistant Professor, Department of
Anthropology
George Mason University
MARX, KARL: IMPACT ON
  ANTHROPOLOGY
MATERIALISM
MYSTIFICATION

John Marangos
Associate Professor, Department of
Economics
Colorado State University
BUSINESS
ECONOMIES, TRANSITIONAL
ENTERPRISE
EXCHANGE RATES
INTERNATIONAL MONETARY
  FUND
MARKET ECONOMY
MONEY LAUNDERING
PRIVATE SECTOR
TRADE, BILATERAL

Patricia Cronin Marcello
Independent Scholar and Author
Bradenton, FL

FEMINISM, SECOND WAVE
GANDHI, MOHANDAS K.
HUMAN SACRIFICE
PRE-COLUMBIAN PEOPLES
STEINEM, GLORIA

Paul R. Marchant
Chartered Statistician
Leeds Metropolitan University
REGRESSION TOWARDS THE
  MEAN

Maria Cristina Marcuzzo
Professor of Political Economy
Università di Roma, La Sapienza
KAHN, RICHARD F.

Robert A. Margo
Professor of Economics and African-
American Studies
Boston University
URBAN RIOTS

Amy R. Mariaskin
Graduate Student, Department of
Psychology and Neuroscience
Duke University
OBSESSION

Rebeca A. Marin
Doctoral Student, Department of
Clinical Psychology
Fuller Theological Seminary
INFIDELITY

Ian S. Markham
Dean and President
Virginia Theological Seminary
SUPREME BEING

Lawrence P. Markowitz
Visiting Assistant Professor
Oberlin College
ELITES

Jonathan H. Marks
Associate Professor of Bioethics,
Humanities, and Law, Pennsylvania
State University
Barrister and Founding Member,
Matrix Chambers, London
INTERROGATION

William Marling
Professor
Case Western Reserve University
TECHNOLOGY, CELLULAR

Douglas B. Marlowe
Director, Law and Ethics Research,
Treatment Research Institute
University of Pennsylvania
DRUGS OF ABUSE

Diane T. Marsh
Professor, Department of Psychology
University of Pittsburgh at Greensburg
SCHIZOPHRENIA

Kris Marsh
Postdoctoral Scholar, Carolina
Population Center
University of North Carolina at
Chapel Hill
BLACK MIDDLE CLASS

Joan Morgan Martin
Assistant Professor, Educational
Psychology
University of Victoria
LEARNED HELPLESSNESS
MATURATION

Michel Louis Martin
Professor, Political Science
Université Toulouse 1 Sciences
Sociales
JANOWITZ, MORRIS

Nathan D. Martin
Department of Sociology
Duke University
NOUVEAUX RICHES

Tony Martin
Professor Emeritus of Africana Studies
Wellesley College
WILLIAMS, ERIC

Linda S. Martín Alcoff
Professor of Philosophy and Women's
Studies
Syracuse University
POLITICS, IDENTITY

Erin E. Martinez
Duke University Medical Center
BODY IMAGE
BODY MASS INDEX

Martin E. Marty
Fairfax M. Cone Distinguished Service
Professor Emeritus
University of Chicago
CHRISTIANITY
FUNDAMENTALISM, CHRISTIAN
HEAVEN

JESUS CHRIST
SIN

Akbar Marvasti
Associate Professor
University of Southern Mississippi
NONLINEAR REGRESSION
PROTECTIONISM

Jeff Maskovsky
Queens College and the Graduate
Center
City University of New York
POVERTY, URBAN

Michael Atwood Mason
Anthropologist and Exhibit Developer
Smithsonian National Museum of
Natural History
SANTERÍA

Paul M. Mason
Professor and Chair, Department of
Economics and Geography
University of North Florida
LOTTERIES

T. David Mason
Johnie Christian Family Professor of
Peace Studies, Department of Political
Science
University of North Texas
CIVIL WARS

Scott E. Masten
Professor of Business Economics and
Public Policy, Stephen M. Ross School
of Business
University of Michigan
TRANSACTION COST

David Mastro
Department of Political Science
West Virginia University
MILITARY REGIMES
UNION OF SOVIET SOCIALIST
REPUBLICS

James I. Matray
Professor and Chair, Department of
History
California State University, Chico
KOREAN WAR

Noritada Matsuda
Associate Professor, Faculty of Law
University of Kitakyushu, Japan
DIET, THE

David Matsumoto
San Francisco State University
CONTEMPT

Shannon Mattern
Assistant Professor, Department of
Media Studies and Film
The New School
MEDIA

Joseph A. Maxwell
College of Education and Human
Development
George Mason University
SCIENTISM

Matthew May
Historian/Archivist
Detroit, MI
KARIEL, HENRY S.
POLITICAL CONVENTIONS
SELECTIVE SERVICE

Susanne May
Assistant Professor, Division of
Biostatistics and Bioinformatics
University of California San Diego
SURVIVAL ANALYSIS
REGRESSION

Thomas Mayer
Emeritus Professor of Economics
University of California, Davis
RECESSION

William L. McBride
Arthur G. Hansen Distinguished
Professor of Philosophy
Purdue University
IDEOLOGY

Roger A. McCain
Department of Economics and
International Business
Drexel University
NONZERO-SUM GAME
WELFARE ECONOMICS

Paul T. McCartney
Towson University
NATIONALISM AND
NATIONALITY

Clark McCauley
Professor, Psychology Department
Bryn Mawr College
ASCH, SOLOMON

Irma McClaurin
Program Officer, Education, Sexuality and Religion Unit of Knowledge, Creativity Program
Ford Foundation
ANTHROPOLOGY, U.S.
DIASPORA
GARIFUNA
HURSTON, ZORA NEALE

Thomas V. McClendon
Professor of History
Southwestern University
RHODES, CECIL

Rowena McClinton
Associate Professor, Department of Historical Studies
Southern Illinois University Edwardsville
SEQUOYAH

Aminah Beverly McCloud
Professor
DePaul University
MUHAMMAD, ELIJAH

James P. McCoy
Distinguished Professor, Department of Economics and Finance
Murray State University
BAUXITE INDUSTRY

Rachel McCulloch
Rosen Family Professor of International Finance
Department of Economics and International Business School,
Brandeis University
IMPORT PROMOTION
RYBCZYNSKI THEOREM

Gael M. McDonald
Professor of Business Ethics
Unitec, New Zealand
ETHICS, BUSINESS

W. Wesley McDonald
Professor, Department of Political Science
Elizabethtown College, Pennsylvania
JACOBINISM
KERNER COMMISSION REPORT
LEFT WING
MODERATES
POLITICAL PARTIES
RIGHT WING

Camela S. McDougald
Duke University Medical Center
PSYCHOSOMATICS

Patricia McDougall
Associate Professor, Department of Psychology
St. Thomas More College, University of Saskatchewan
PEER EFFECTS

Andrew S. McFarland
Professor of Political Science
University of Illinois at Chicago
DAHL, ROBERT ALAN
LOWI, THEODORE J.

Deborah R. McFarlane
Professor
University of New Mexico
ABORTION
REPRODUCTIVE POLITICS

John McGarry
Department of Political Studies
Queen's University, Canada
SECESSION

Patrick J. McGowan
Professor Emeritus, Department of Political Science, Arizona State University
Extraordinary Professor, Department of Political Science, Stellenbosch University, South Africa
COUP D'ETAT

Charlton D. McIlwain
Assistant Professor, Department of Culture, Media, and Communication
New York University
OSCEOLA
POLITICS, BLACK

Wm. Alex McIntosh
Professor, Department of Sociology
Texas A&M University
METHODS, SURVEY

Lee C. McIntyre
Research Fellow, Center for Philosophy and History of Science
Boston University
LOGIC

David W. McIvor
Duke University
PITKIN, HANNA
WELTANSCHAUUNG

Mary M. McKenzie
Adjunct Faculty, Department of Political Science
University of San Diego
GUANTÁNAMO BAY

David McLellan
Professor of Political Theory, Goldsmiths College
University of London
LUMPENPROLETARIAT

Eric McLuhan
The Harris Institute for the Arts
Toronto, Canada
McLUHAN, MARSHALL

Peter McNamara
Associate Professor, Department of Political Science
Utah State University
BURR, AARON
HAMILTON, ALEXANDER

Stephen J. McNamee
Associate Dean and Professor, Department of Sociology and Criminal Justice
University of North Carolina at Wilmington
MERITOCRACY

Susan J. McWilliams
Assistant Professor, Department of Politics
Pomona College
SHKLAR, JUDITH

Ferdinando Meacci
Professor of Economics
University of Padova, Italy
MACHINERY QUESTION, THE

Jay Mechling
Professor of American Studies
University of California, Davis
POPULAR CULTURE

Craig Allan Medlen
Professor of Economics, Menlo College
Atherton, California
TOBIN'S Q

Gaminie Meepagala
Associate Professor, Department of Economics
Howard University
REGRESSION ANALYSIS

Aashish Mehta
Economics and Research Department
Asian Development Bank, Manila
PRODUCTION FUNCTION

Brinda J. Mehta
Professor of French and Francophone
Studies
Mills College
EAST INDIES

Brian P. Meier
Professor
Gettysburg College
EXPERIMENTS, SHOCK
ZIMBARDO, PHILIP

Lars Meier
Institute of Sociology
Darmstadt University of Technology,
Germany
RACISM

Stephan Meier
Economist, Center for Behavioral
Economics and Decision-Making
Federal Reserve Bank of Boston
NATURAL EXPERIMENTS

Allan H. Meltzer
The American Enterprise Institute
Carnegie Mellon University
FEDERAL RESERVE SYSTEM,
U.S.: ANALYSIS

Kim S. Ménard
Senior Lecturer, Crime, Law, and
Justice Program, Department of
Sociology
Pennsylvania State University
FEMINISM

Josephine Méndez-Negrete
Associate Professor
University of Texas, San Antonio
CHÁVEZ, CÉSAR

Don Mendoza
Research Associate, Department of
Epidemiology and Population Health
Albert Einstein College of Medicine,
Bronx, NY
STRESS-BUFFERING MODEL

Rodolfo Mendoza-Denton
Department of Psychology
University of California, Berkeley
STIGMA

Xiao-Li Meng
Whipple V.N. Jones Professor and
Chair of Statistics
Harvard University
INFERENCE, STATISTICAL

Nivedita Menon
Reader, Department of Political
Science
Delhi University
SECULAR, SECULARISM,
SECULARIZATION

Gordon Douglas Menzies
Senior Lecturer in Economics, School
of Finance and Economics, University
of Technology, Sydney
Research Affiliate, Australian National
University
EXPECTATIONS, RATIONAL

Jennifer L. Merolla
Assistant Professor
Claremont Graduate University
AGENDA SETTING
PARTICIPATION, POLITICAL

Ellen Messer
Friedman School of Nutrition Science
and Policy, Tufts University
Sustainable International
Development, The Heller School,
Brandeis University
MALNUTRITION

Adam Messinger
Graduate Student, Department of
Sociology
University of California, Riverside
MEN

Gilbert E. Metcalf
Professor, Department of Economics
Tufts University
DISTORTIONS

Andrew Metrick
Department of Finance
The Wharton School of the University
of Pennsylvania
TOBIN, JAMES

Gregory J. Meyer
Associate Professor of Psychology
University of Toledo
RORSCHACH TEST

Charles Michalopoulos
Senior Fellow, MDRC

New York, NY
NEGATIVE INCOME TAX

John L. Michela
Associate Professor, Department of
Psychology
University of Waterloo, Ontario
KELLEY, HAROLD

Stephan Michelson
President
Longbranch Research Associates
LITIGATION, SOCIAL SCIENCE
ROLE IN

Thomas R. Michl
Professor of Economics
Colgate University
PASINETTI PARADOX

Marci M. Middleton
Doctoral Candidate, College of
Education, Department of
Educational Policy Studies
Georgia State University
SOCIAL STATUS

Eric Mielants
Assistant Professor, Department of
Sociology
Fairfield University
FRANK, ANDRE GUNDER
WALLERSTEIN, IMMANUEL

Joni L. Mihura
Associate Professor of Psychology
University of Toledo
RORSCHACH TEST

Lydia Miljan
Associate Professor, Political Science
Department
University of Windsor, Ontario,
Canada
G8 COUNTRIES
JOURNALISM
TELEVISION

Barbara D. Miller
Professor, Department of
Anthropology and Elliott School of
International Affairs
George Washington University
ANTHROPOLOGY

Christopher J. Miller
Graduate Student Assistant,
Department of Psychology
University of Miami

MANIAS
MANIC DEPRESSION

David Reed Miller
Indigenous Studies
First Nations University of Canada
NATIVES

Fiona Miller
Visiting Assistant Professor
Department of Political Science,
Colgate University
ROUSSEAU, JEAN-JACQUES

Joshua D. Miller
Assistant Professor of Psychology
University of Georgia
NARCISSISM

Paul J. Miranti
Professor
Rutgers–The State University of New
Jersey
QUALITY CONTROLS

Kiran Mirchandani
Associate Professor, Department of
Adult Education and Counselling
Psychology, Ontario Institute for
Studies in Education
University of Toronto
WORK

Frederic S. Mishkin
Graduate School of Business,
Columbia University
Research Associate, National Bureau of
Economic Research
FEDERAL RESERVE SYSTEM,
U.S.

Vinod Mishra
Director of Research, Demographic
and Health Research Division
Macro International
NATIONAL FAMILY HEALTH
SURVEYS

Kamal K. Misra
Professor, Department of
Anthropology
University of Hyderabad, India
TRIBALISM
TRIBE

David Mitch
Professor, Department of Economics
University of Maryland, Baltimore
County
FOGEL, ROBERT

Daniel J. B. Mitchell
Ho-su Wu Professor of Management
and Public Policy
University of California, Los Angeles
WAGE AND PRICE CONTROLS

William F. Mitchell
Centre of Full Employment and
Equity
University of Newcastle, Australia
UNEMPLOYMENT RATE

Ronald L. Mize
Assistant Professor of Development
Sociology and Latino Studies
Cornell University
CRITICAL RACE THEORY
SAMBO

Robert A. Moffitt
Krieger-Eisenhower Professor of
Economics
Johns Hopkins University
INCOME MAINTENANCE
EXPERIMENTS

Valentine M. Moghadam
Professor of Sociology and Women's
Studies, Purdue University, West
Lafayette, Indiana
Director of the Women's Studies
Program, UNESCO
VEIL, IN MIDDLE EASTERN
AND NORTH AFRICAN
CULTURES

A. Rafik Mohamed
Associate Professor of Sociology
University of San Diego
CRIME AND CRIMINOLOGY
DESEGREGATION, SCHOOL
DEVIANCE
DRUG TRAFFIC

Satya P. Mohanty
Professor of English
Cornell University
REALIST THEORY

Edwin E. Moise
Professor, Department of History
Clemson University
IRAQ-U.S. WAR

Stephanie Moller
Assistant Professor of Sociology
University of North Carolina at
Charlotte
STANDARDIZED TESTS

Richard F. Mollica
Director, Harvard Program in Refugee
Trauma, Massachusetts General
Hospital
Professor of Psychiatry, Harvard
Medical School
TORTURE

Andre V. Mollick
Associate Professor, Department of
Economics and Finance
University of Texas–Pan American
ADAPTIVE EXPECTATIONS
LUCAS CRITIQUE

David Michael Monetti
Department of Psychology and
Counseling
Valdosta State University
SOCIAL LEARNING
PERSPECTIVE

Gary Mongiovi
St. John's University
LONG PERIOD ANALYSIS

Benoît Monin
Assistant Professor, Department of
Psychology
Stanford University
COGNITIVE DISSONANCE

Catia Montagna
Reader, Economic Studies, School of
Social Sciences
University of Dundee
CUMULATIVE CAUSATION

Alexander Moon
Assistant Professor, Politics
Department
Ithaca College
DIFFERENCE PRINCIPLE

Jerry D. Moore
Professor of Anthropology
California State University,
Dominguez Hills
GEERTZ, CLIFFORD

Anthony P. Mora
Assistant Professor
University of Michigan
COLUMBUS, CHRISTOPHER
COOK, JAMES

M. Cristina Morales
Department of Sociology and
Anthropology
University of Texas at El Paso

ETHNIC ENCLAVE
MODE, THE

Bryon J. Moraski
Assistant Professor, Department of
Political Science
University of Florida
ELECTIONS

Carlo Morelli
School of Social Sciences
University of Dundee
GENERAL ELECTRIC
MICROSOFT

S. Philip Morgan
Professor of Sociology
Duke University
CHILDLESSNESS

David Morley
Professor of Media and
Communications
Goldsmiths College, London
HALL, STUART

Fiorenzo Mornati
Assistant Professor, Department of
Economics
University of Turin
PARETO, VILFREDO
PARETO OPTIMUM

Thomas J. Morrione
Charles A. Dana Professor of
Sociology
Colby College, Waterville, Maine
BLUMER, HERBERT

Lorenzo Morris
Professor, Department of Political
Science
Howard University
BUNCHE, RALPH JOHNSON

Matthew C. Morris
Vanderbilt University
DEPRESSION, PSYCHOLOGICAL

Rosalind C. Morris
Professor, Department of
Anthropology
Columbia University
AUTONOMY
BOURGEOISIE
BOURGEOISIE, PETTY
GAZE, THE
SECRECY
TRAUMA

Catherine J. Morrison Paul
Professor, Department of Agricultural
and Resource Economics
University of California, Davis
GROWTH ACCOUNTING
OVERFISHING

Robert A. Mortimer
Professor of Political Science
Haverford College
ANTICOLONIAL MOVEMENTS

Fred Moseley
Professor of Economics
Mount Holyoke College
TRANSFORMATION PROBLEM

Charles Moser
Chair and Professor, Department of
Sexual Medicine
Institute for Advanced Study of
Human Sexuality
EROTICISM

Paul K. Moser
Professor and Chairperson,
Department of Philosophy
Loyola University Chicago
AGNOSTICISM
ATHEISM
RELATIVISM

Clayton Mosher
Department of Sociology
Washington State University
Vancouver
PRISON INDUSTRY

Charles B. Moss
Professor, Food and Resource
Economics Department
University of Florida
SUGAR INDUSTRY

Jamee K. Moudud
Economics Faculty
Sarah Lawrence College
COMPETITION
SURPLUS

Anne Mozena
Graduate Student, Department of
Political Science
Marquette University
AUTHORITARIANISM

Jennifer C. Mueller
Department of Sociology
Texas A&M University

SEGREGATION, SCHOOL
WHITENING

James P. Muldoon, Jr.
Senior Fellow, Center for Global
Change and Governance
Rutgers University
FOOD DIPLOMACY
NEGOTIATION

John P. Muller
Director of Training
Austen Riggs Center, Stockbridge,
Massachusetts
SUBLIMATE

Michael C. Munger
Department of Political Science and
Department of Economics
Duke University
LEADERS
LEFT AND RIGHT
MAJORITARIANISM
PUBLIC INTEREST

Anne Murcott
Professor Emerita, Sociology
London South Bank University
FOOD

Aurelia Lorena Murga
Department of Sociology
Texas A&M University
LATINO/A STUDIES
LATINOS
MORENO/A

Antoin E. Murphy
Professor, Department of Economics
Trinity College, Dublin
LAW, JOHN

Pat Murphy
Associate Professor of Sociology
SUNY Geneseo
DIVORCE AND SEPARATION

Carolyn B. Murray
Professor, Department of Psychology
University of California, Riverside
NYERERE, JULIUS
SELF-HATRED
SUPERORDINATE GOALS
UNDERACHIEVERS

Desiree W. Murray
Assistant Professor, Department of
Psychiatry
Duke University Medical Center
ATTENTION-DEFICIT/
HYPERACTIVITY DISORDER

Ellen Mutari
Associate Professor of Economics and
Women's Studies Coordinator
Richard Stockton College of New
Jersey
  DISCRIMINATION, TASTE FOR

Daniel J. Myers
Professor, Department of Sociology
University of Notre Dame
  RACE RIOTS, UNITED STATES

David G. Myers
Hope College
  SOCIAL PSYCHOLOGY

Samuel L. Myers, Jr.
Roy Wilkins Professor of Human
Relations and Social Justice
University of Minnesota
  MULTIRACIALS IN THE UNITED
    STATES
  UNDERCLASS

Roger B. Myerson
Professor, Department of Economics
University of Chicago
  NASH, JOHN

Carol Nackenoff
Department of Political Science
Swarthmore College
  ALGER, HORATIO

Richa Nagar
Department of Gender, Women, and
Sexuality Studies
University of Minnesota
  NONGOVERNMENTAL
    ORGANIZATIONS (NGOS)

Leonard I. Nakamura
Assistant Vice President and
Economist
Federal Reserve Bank of Philadelphia
  NATIONAL INCOME ACCOUNTS

Gino J. Naldi
Senior Lecturer, School of Law
University of East Anglia
  ORGANIZATION OF AFRICAN
    UNITY (OAU)

Jaime L. Napier
New York University
  FAHRENHEIT 9/11

Nauman Naqvi
Department of Anthropology

Columbia University
  CIVILIZATION

Jack Nation
Department of Psychology
Texas A&M University
  DOPAMINE

Thomas Natsoulas
Professor of Psychology, Emeritus
University of California, Davis
  STREAM OF CONSCIOUSNESS

Pramod K. Nayar
Department of English
University of Hyderabad, India
  PRAXIS

David T. Neal
Research Fellow, Department of
Psychology and Neuroscience
Duke University
  HABITS

Edward M. Neal
Director of Faculty Development
University of North Carolina at
Chapel Hill
  PEDAGOGY

Brigitte U. Neary
Associate Professor of Sociology
University of South Carolina Upstate
  ETHNIC CONFLICT
  IRANIAN REVOLUTION
  TAYLORISM

Raúl Antonio Necochea López
Doctoral Candidate, Department of
History
McGill University
  BIRTH CONTROL

Victor Nee
Goldwin Smith Professor, Department
of Sociology
Cornell University
  MELTING POT

Zvika Neeman
Department of Economics, Boston
University
The Eitan Berglas School of
Economics, Tel–Aviv University
  MECHANISM DESIGN

Gabriel L. Negretto
Research Professor, Division of
Political Studies

Centro de Investigación y Docencia
Económica (C.I.D.E), Mexico
  CONSTITUTIONS

Jacob Neusner
Distinguished Service Professor of the
History and Theology of Judaism,
Institute of Advanced Theology
Bard College
  JUDAISM

J. W. Nevile
Emeritus Professor, School of
Economics
University of New South Wales
  INTEREST, REAL RATE OF
  INTEREST RATES
  INTEREST RATES, NOMINAL

Paul R. Newcomb
Associate Professor of Social Work
Indiana University
  COHABITATION
  MYSTICISM

Elana Newman
Associate Professor of Clinical
Psychology
University of Tulsa
  MULTIPLE PERSONALITIES

Leonard S. Newman
Associate Professor of Psychology
Syracuse University
  TRAIT INFERENCE

Saul Newman
Senior Lecturer, Politics Department
Goldsmiths College, University of
London
  POWER

Julie M. Newton
Associate Professor, Department of
International and Comparative
Politics, American University of Paris
Visiting Fellow, St. Antony's College,
University of Oxford, U.K.
  BREZHNEV, LEONID
  GORBACHEV, MIKHAIL

Liwa Rachel Ngai
Department of Economics
London School of Economics
  MULTISECTOR MODELS

Zolani Ngwane
Assistant Professor, Department of
Anthropology

Haverford College
PROGRESS

Tarique Niazi
University of Wisconsin, Eau Claire
TOXIC WASTE
WATER RESOURCES

Isak Niehaus
School of Social Sciences
Brunel University
ZOMBIES

Ingemar Nilsson
Department of History of Ideas and
Theory of Science
Göteborg University
CONSCIOUSNESS

Donna J. Nincic
Associate Professor and Chair,
Department of Global and Maritime
Studies, California Maritime Academy
California State University
WEAPONS OF MASS
DESTRUCTION

Elizabeth Nisbet
Doctoral student, Bloustein School of
Planning and Public Policy
Rutgers University
OAXACA, RONALD

Cajetan Nnaocha
Lecturer, Department of Humanities
University of the Gambia
TAX RELIEF
WANTS

Diana C. Noone
Assistant Professor, Criminal Justice
Department
Fairmont State University
ACTIVISM, JUDICIAL

Andrew Norris
Department of Political Science
University of California at Santa
Barbara
HEGELIANS

Julie Novkov
Associate Professor of Political Science
and Women's Studies
University at Albany, SUNY
MISCEGENATION
RACE MIXING

J. Kevin Nugent
Professor of Child and Family Studies,
University of Massachusetts at
Amherst;
Director, the Brazelton Institute at
Children's Hospital and Lecturer in
Pediatrics at Harvard Medical School
BRAZELTON, T. BERRY

Shayla C. Nunnally
Assistant Professor, Department of
Political Science and Institute for
African American Studies
University of Connecticut, Storrs
ASSOCIATIONS, VOLUNTARY
NATIONAL ASSOCIATION FOR
THE ADVANCEMENT OF
COLORED PEOPLE (NAACP)
THURMOND, STROM

Stephen A. Nuño
PhD Candidate
University of California, Irvine
POLITICS, LATINO

Luca Nunziata
Professor, Department of Economics
University of Padua
BEVERIDGE CURVE
COMPENSATION,
UNEMPLOYMENT
FIXED EFFECTS REGRESSION
FLEXIBILITY
LABOR UNION
MONTE CARLO EXPERIMENTS
RESIDUALS
VOLUNTARY UNEMPLOYMENT

John V. C. Nye
Professor of Economics and Frederic
Bastiat Chair in Political Economy at
the Mercatus Center, George Mason
University
Professor of Economics, Washington
University
CORN LAWS

Brendan Nyhan
PhD Candidate
Duke University
BUSH, GEORGE W.
MILLER, WARREN

Eileen O'Brien
Assistant Professor of Sociology
University of Richmond
RACE

Cara O'Connell
Assistant Clinical Professor

University of North Carolina at
Chapel Hill
WEIGHT

Phillip Anthony O'Hara
Professor of Global Political Economy
and Governance, Global Political
Economy Research Unit
Curtin University, Australia
CULTURAL CAPITAL
ECONOMIC CRISES
MONOPOLY CAPITALISM

Paul A. O'Keefe
Department of Psychology and
Neuroscience
Duke University
SOCIAL JUDGMENT THEORY

Brendan O'Leary
Lauder Professor of Political Science
University of Pennsylvania
DEMOCRACY,
CONSOCIATIONAL

Dennis P. O'Neil
Major, U.S. Army
Assistant Professor, Department of
Behavioral Sciences and Leadership,
U.S. Military Academy, West Point
LEADERSHIP

Gananath Obeyesekere
Emeritus Professor, Department of
Anthropology
Princeton University
REINCARNATION

Misael Obregón
Graduate Student, Department of
Sociology
Texas A&M University
LATINO NATIONAL POLITICAL
SURVEY

Gina Ogden
Independent Researcher
Cambridge, MA
SEXUALITY

Tomson Ogwang
Professor, Department of Economics
Brock University
INEQUALITY, INCOME
NOMINAL INCOME
PUBLIC ASSISTANCE
REAL INCOME

Albert A. Okunade
Holder of First Tennessee University
Professorship and Professor of
Economics
The University of Memphis, Tennessee
PHARMACEUTICAL INDUSTRY

Jeffrey K. Olick
Professor of Sociology and History
University of Virginia
COLLECTIVE MEMORY
HOLOCAUST, THE
POLITICAL CULTURE
SOCIOLOGY, POLITICAL

Paul Omach
Department of Political Science and
Public Administration
Makerere University, Uganda
AFRICAN CRISIS RESPONSE
INITIATIVE

Sarah Holland Omar
Graduate student, Department of
Psychology
Virginia Polytechnic Institute and
State University
BANDURA, ALBERT
BAUMRIND, DIANA

Tatiana Omeltchenko
University of Virginia
POLITICAL CULTURE

Maggie Opondo
Senior Lecturer, Department of
Geography and Environmental Studies
University of Nairobi
FLOWER INDUSTRY

Amy J. Orr
Associate Professor of Sociology,
Department of Sociology and
Anthropology
Linfield College
CULTURE, LOW AND HIGH

Scott D. Orr
Visiting Assistant Professor
Emory and Henry College
VOTING

Joan K. Orrell-Valente
Assistant Professor of Pediatrics
University of California, San Francisco
OBESITY
OVEREATING
UNDEREATING

Maryjane Osa
Visiting Professor, Department of
Sociology
Northwestern University
SOLIDARITY

Kenneth Osgood
Associate Professor of History
Florida Atlantic University
PROPAGANDA

Lucius T. Outlaw, Jr.
Professor, Department of Philosophy,
Program in African American and
Diaspora Studies
Vanderbilt University
AFROCENTRISM

Frederick Ugwu Ozor
Department of Social Sciences
University of the Gambia
PLANNING
QUALITY, PRODUCT
SOCIAL CONSTRUCTS

Jouni Paavola
Sustainability Research Institute
School of Earth and Environment,
University of Leeds
MERIT GOODS
POLLUTION, WATER
RESOURCE ECONOMICS
RESOURCES

Allen Packwood
Director, Churchill Archives Centre
University of Cambridge, United
Kingdom
CHURCHILL, WINSTON

Adrian Pagan
Professor of Economics
Queensland University of Technology
PHILLIPS, A. W. H.

Poornima Paidipaty
Department of Anthropology
Columbia University
GAZE, COLONIAL

Frank Pajares
Professor
Emory University
DETERMINISM, RECIPROCAL
POSITIVE PSYCHOLOGY
PSYCHOLOGY, AGENCY IN
SELF-EFFICACY

Jan Pakulski
Professor of Sociology

University of Tasmania
ELITE THEORY

Ronen Palan
Department of Political and
International Studies
University of Birmingham, United
Kingdom
OFFSHORE BANKING

Thomas I. Palley
Economist
Washington, D.C.
NATURAL RATE OF
UNEMPLOYMENT

Frank Palmeri
Professor, Department of English
University of Miami
PARODY

Ryne A. Palombit
Associate Professor, Department of
Anthropology
Rutgers University
PRIMATES

Arvind Panagariya
Professor of Economics and
International and Public Affairs
Columbia University
BHAGWATI, JAGDISH

Erika Pani
Research Professor, History Division
Centro de Investigación y Docencia
Económicas
JUÁREZ, BENITO

Neni Panourgiá
Associate Professor, Department of
Anthropology
Columbia University
ALIENATION
CULTURE
LEVI-STRAUSS, CLAUDE

Dennis A. Pantin
Professor of Economics, Department
of Economics
University of the West Indies, St.
Augustine Campus, Trinidad and
Tobago
PLANTATION ECONOMY
MODEL

Paul Paolucci
Associate Professor, Department of
Anthropology, Sociology, and Social
Work

Eastern Kentucky University
MARX, KARL: IMPACT ON
SOCIOLOGY

Dimitri B. Papadimitriou
Professor and President
The Levy Economics Institute of Bard
College
MINSKY, HYMAN

Lisa Sun-Hee Park
Associate Professor, Department of
Ethnic Studies
University of California, San Diego
SILICON VALLEY

Thomas K. Park
Department of Anthropology
University of Arizona, Tucson
AMIN, SAMIR

Jay M. Parker
Senior Fellow, Center for the Study of
the Presidency
Visiting Associate Professor,
Georgetown University
EISENHOWER, DWIGHT D.

Erika A. Patall
Department of Psychology and
Neuroscience
Duke University
CHOICE IN PSYCHOLOGY

Nicholas S. Patapis
Research Scientist, Treatment Research
Institute
University of Pennsylvania
DRUGS OF ABUSE

Marc W. Patry
Department of Psychology
Saint Mary's University Halifax, Nova
Scotia
JURORS, DEATH-QUALIFIED

Eric Patterson
Assistant Director, Berkley Center for
Religion, Peace, and World Affairs
Georgetown University
PRAGMATISM

Thomas C. Patterson
Distinguished Professor of
Anthropology
University of California, Riverside
COOPERATION

Tiffany Ruby Patterson
Program in African American and
Diaspora Studies
Vanderbilt University
BLACKNESS
NEGRO

Paul A. Pautler
Deputy Director for Consumer
Protection, Bureau of Economics
U.S. Federal Trade Commission
CONSUMER PROTECTION

Heather Anne Paxson
Assistant Professor, Anthropology
Program
Massachusetts Institute of Technology
PRO-CHOICE/PRO-LIFE

James E. Payne
Professor and Chair, Department of
Economics
Illinois State University
MONETARISM

Stanley G. Payne
Professor Emeritus
University of Wisconsin–Madison
SPANISH CIVIL WAR

Fay Cobb Payton
Associate Professor of Information
Systems, College of Management
North Carolina State University
DIGITAL DIVIDE

James L. Peacock
Professor, Department of
Anthropology
University of North Carolina at
Chapel Hill
ANTHROPOLOGY, PUBLIC

Douglas K. Pearce
Professor, Department of Economics
North Carolina State University
STAGFLATION

Frederic S. Pearson
Professor of Political Science; Director,
Center for Peace and Conflict Studies
Wayne State University
DETERRENCE, MUTUAL

Sidney A. Pearson, Jr.
Professor Emeritus
Radford University, Virginia
SCHATTSCHNEIDER, E. E.

Sandra J. Peart
Dean and Professor, Jepson School of
Leadership Studies
University of Richmond
CREATIVE DESTRUCTION
GALTON, FRANCIS

Ami Pedahzur
Department of Government
University of Texas at Austin
AL-QAEDA
SUICIDE BOMBERS
VIOLENCE IN TERRORISM

Cory L. Pedersen
Department of Psychology
Kwantlen University College, Surrey,
British Columbia
DEVELOPMENTAL PSYCHOLOGY

Gustav Peebles
Assistant Professor of Anthropology
and Associate Director of the
Bachelor's Program
New School for General Studies
BOURDIEU, PIERRE

David N. Pellow
Department of Ethnic Studies
University of California, San Diego
SILICON VALLEY

Peter Pels
Professor
University of Leiden
ETHICS

Alan R. Pence
Professor, School of Child and Youth
Care
University of Victoria, BC
DAY CARE

James H. Peoples
Professor, Department of Economics
University of Wisconsin–Milwaukee
TELECOMMUNICATIONS
INDUSTRY
TRANSPORTATION INDUSTRY

Tracey A. Pepper
Lecturer, Department of History
Seattle University
ANNEXATION
FASCISM
HITLER, ADOLF
SOCIALISM

Anthony Daniel Perez
University of Washington
SELF-CLASSIFICATION

Héctor Perla, Jr.
Assistant Professor, Department of
Political Science
Ohio University
SANDINISTAS

Richard M. Perloff
Professor and Director, School of
Communication
Cleveland State University
PERSUASION, MESSAGE-BASED

Michael Perman
Department of History
University of Illinois at Chicago
RECONSTRUCTION ERA (U.S.)

Geoffrey Peterson
Associate Professor of Political Science
and American Indian Studies
University of Wisconsin–Eau Claire
PRESIDENCY, THE

J. E. Peterson
Center for Middle Eastern Studies
University of Arizona
GULF STATES

Joseph A. Petrick
Professor, Department of Management
Wright State University
MANAGEMENT SCIENCE

Larissa Petrillo
Instructor
University of British Columbia
CRAZY HORSE

Marta Petrusewicz
Professor of History, City University
of New York
Università della Calabria; Institute for
Advanced Study, Wissenschaftskolleg
zu Berlin
LATIFUNDIA

Thomas F. Pettigrew
University of California, Santa Cruz
ALLPORT, GORDON
RACE AND EDUCATION

Bryan Pfaffenberger
Associate Professor of Science,
Technology, and Society
University of Virginia
MEANING

SOCIETY
TECHNOTOPIA

Michael J. Pfeifer
Associate Professor of History, John
Jay College of Criminal Justice
City University of New York
LYNCHINGS

Peter C. Phan
Ignacio Ellacuria Professor of Catholic
Social Thought
Georgetown University
WORSHIP

Daniel J. Phaneuf
Associate Professor of Agricultural and
Resource Economics
North Carolina State University,
Raleigh, NC
WELFARE ANALYSIS

Liz Philipose
Department of Women's Studies
California State University, Long
Beach
WOMEN'S STUDIES

Ronnie J. Phillips
Professor, Department of Economics
Colorado State University, Fort
Collins
INSTITUTIONALISM

Ann Phoenix
Professor and Co-Director Thomas
Coram research unit, Institute of
Education
University of London
MOTHERHOOD

Robert Pianta
Novartis Professor of Education and
Professor of Psychology; Director,
Center for Advanced Study of
Teaching and Learning
Dean, Curry School of Education,
University of Virginia
TEACHER-CHILD
RELATIONSHIPS

Bruce Pietrykowski
Professor of Economics, Department
of Social Sciences
University of Michigan–Dearborn
FORD MOTOR COMPANY

Paul R. Pillar
Professor, Security Studies

Georgetown University
COUNTERTERRORISM

Devan Pillay
Associate Professor, Sociology
University of the Witwatersrand
UNDERDEVELOPMENT

Suren Pillay
Senior Lecturer, Department of
Political Studies, University of the
Western Cape, Cape Town, South
Africa
Senior Researcher Specialist, Human
Sciences Research Council of South
Africa
LIBERATION

Roger Pilon
Director, Center for Constitutional
Studies
Cato Institute
DECLARATION OF
INDEPENDENCE, U.S.

Aaron L. Pincus
Associate Professor of Psychology
Pennsylvania State University
TRAIT THEORY

Fred L. Pincus
Professor, Department of Sociology
and Anthropology
University of Maryland, Baltimore
County
DIVERSITY

Katy M. Pinto
Assistant Professor, Department of
Sociology
California State University Dominguez
Hills
MIGRANT LABOR

Thane S. Pittman
Department of Psychology
Colby College
ACHIEVEMENT

David W. Pitts
Assistant Professor, Andrew Young
School of Policy Studies
Georgia State University
LASSWELL, HAROLD

Nancy Plankey Videla
Assistant Professor
Texas A&M University
MAQUILADORAS

Geoffrey Poitras
Professor of Finance, Faculty of
Business Administration
Simon Fraser University, Vancouver,
BC, Canada
FORWARD AND FUTURES
MARKETS
RISK

Attila Pók
Institute of History
Hungarian Academy of Sciences
FABIANISM

Melvin Pollner
Department of Sociology
University of California, Los Angeles
REFLEXIVITY

James J. Ponzetti, Jr.
Associate Professor of Family Studies
The University of British Columbia
FAMILY, EXTENDED
FAMILY, NUCLEAR
FAMILY FUNCTIONING

Harrison G. Pope
Professor of Psychiatry, Harvard
Medical School
Director, Biological Psychiatry
Laboratory, McLean Hospital
STEROIDS

Susan J. Popkin
Principal Research Associate
The Urban Institute, Washington,
D.C.
MOVING TO OPPORTUNITY

Pier Luigi Porta
Professor of Economics
University of Milano–Bicocca, Milan,
Italy
PASINETTI, LUIGI

Stephen G. Post
Professor, Department of Bioethics,
School of Medicine
Case Western Reserve University
GENEROSITY/SELFISHNESS

Dudley L. Poston, Jr.
Professor of Sociology
Texas A&M University
CENTRAL TENDENCIES,
MEASURES OF
DEMOGRAPHY
DEPOPULATION
FERTILITY, HUMAN

IMMIGRANTS TO NORTH
AMERICA
METHODOLOGY
METHODS, RESEARCH (IN
SOCIOLOGY)
ORDINARY LEAST SQUARES
REGRESSION
OVERPOPULATION
PATRIARCHY
POPULATION GROWTH

Tim Poston
Sir Ashertosh Mukherjee Professor
National Institute of Advanced
Studies, Banglore, India
CATASTROPHE THEORY

Stephanie Potochnick
Doctoral Candidate, Department of
Public Policy
University of North Carolina at
Chapel Hill
STANDARDIZED TESTS

Marilyn Power
Professor of Economics
Sarah Lawrence College
MOBILITY, LATERAL

Basanta Kumar Pradhan
Chief Economist, National Council of
Applied Economic Research
New Delhi, India
MONEY, DEMAND FOR

Adrian Praetzellis
Professor, Department of
Anthropology
Sonoma State University, California
CULTURAL RESOURCE
MANAGEMENT

Vijay Prashad
George and Martha Kellner Chair of
South Asian History
Trinity College
MODEL MINORITY

Giuliana B. Prato
Co-Chair, Commission on Urban
Anthropology, International Union of
Anthropological and Ethnological
Sciences
Department of Anthropology,
University of Kent, United Kingdom
ANTHROPOLOGY, URBAN

Beverly Pratt
Master's degree student, Department
of Sociology

Texas A&M University
LATINO NATIONAL POLITICAL
SURVEY

Kristopher J. Preacher
Assistant Professor, Department of
Psychology
University of Kansas
CHI-SQUARE

Harland Prechel
Professor, Department of Sociology
Texas A&M University
ORGANIZATIONS

Deborah A. Prentice
Professor, Department of Psychology
Princeton University
IGNORANCE, PLURALISTIC

David H. Price
Associate Professor of Anthropology
Saint Martin's University
McCARTHYISM

Valeria Procupez
PhD Candidate, Department of
Anthropology
Johns Hopkins University
PRIVACY

Roy L. Prosterman
Chairman Emeritus, Rural
Development Institute
Professor Emeritus, School of Law,
University of Washington, Seattle
LAND REFORM

Thomas A. Pugel
Professor, Department of Economics
New York University, Stern School of
Business
DUMPING, PRODUCT

Steven Puro
St. Louis University
EXIT POLL
MERRIAM, CHARLES EDWARD,
JR.

Samuel P. Putnam
Associate Professor, Department of
Psychology
Bowdoin College
TEMPERAMENT

Louis Putterman
Professor of Economics
Brown University
PRICES

Tom Pyszczynski
Professor of Psychology
University of Colorado at Colorado
Springs
  TERROR

Zhenchao Qian
Professor, Department of Sociology
Ohio State University
  MARRIAGE, INTERRACIAL

Enrico L. Quarantelli
Emeritus Professor, Disaster Research
Center
University of Delaware
  PANIC

Donald Quataert
Binghamton University, State
University of New York
  OTTOMAN EMPIRE

Munir Quddus
Professor of Economics and Dean,
College of Business
Prairie View A&M University
  GRAMEEN BANK

Marian Radetzki
Professor of Economics
Lulea University of Technology, Lulea,
Sweden
  NATURAL RESOURCES,
    NONRENEWABLE

Dagmar Radin
Assistant Professor, Department of
Political Science and Public
Administration
Mississippi State University
  CROATS
  SERBS
  TITO (JOSIP BROZ)
  WARSAW PACT

Mridu Rai
Associate Professor of History
Yale University
  NEHRU, JAWAHARLAL

Lall Ramrattan
Instructor, Department of Business
and Management
University of California, Berkeley
Extension
  COMMUNISM, PRIMITIVE
  CONSUMPTION FUNCTION
  DEBREU, GERARD
  DIAMOND INDUSTRY

  DISCRIMINATION, WAGE, BY
    RACE
  DRAVIDIANS
  ECONOMETRICS
  EXPECTATIONS
  HAMILTON'S RULE
  HICKS, JOHN R.
  HILFERDING, RUDOLF
  IDENTIFICATION PROBLEM
  MATHEMATICS IN THE SOCIAL
    SCIENCES
  MINIMUM WAGE
  MODIGLIANI, FRANCO
  REFLECTION PROBLEM
  RULES VERSUS DISCRETION
  SHORT PERIOD
  TÂTONNEMENT
  TAYLOR RULE

G. N. Ramu
Professor of Sociology
University of Manitoba
  CASTE

Wimal Rankaduwa
Associate Professor, Department of
Economics
University of Prince Edward Island
  EXPORT PENETRATION

J. Mohan Rao
Professor, Department of Economics
University of Massachusetts, Amherst
  AGRICULTURAL ECONOMICS

Rayna Rapp
Professor of Anthropology
New York University
  WOLF, ERIC

Richard L. Rapson
Professor of History
University of Hawaii
  ROMANCE

Deborah L. Rapuano
Assistant Professor, Department of
Sociology and Anthropology
Gettysburg College
  IDEAL TYPE

Salim Rashid
Professor of Economics
University of Illinois, Champaign
Urbana
  DIVISION OF LABOR
  GRAMEEN BANK
  HUME PROCESS
  SMITH, ADAM

Jonathan D. Raskin
Professor, Department of Psychology
State University of New York at New
Paltz
  PERSONAL CONSTRUCTS

Dennis C. Rasmussen
Postdoctoral Research Associate,
Political Theory Project
Brown University
  COMTE, AUGUSTE
  LOCKE, JOHN

Anne Warfield Rawls
Department of Sociology
Bentley College
  CONVERSATIONAL ANALYSIS

Indrajit Ray
Professor, Department of Economics
University of Birmingham
  SUBGAME PERFECTION

David Rayside
Professor of Political Science and
Sexual Diversity Studies
University of Toronto
  POLITICS: GAY, LESBIAN,
    TRANSGENDER, AND
    BISEXUAL

Malia Reddick
Director of Research & Programs
American Judicature Society
  BILL OF RIGHTS, U.S.
  CONGRESS OF RACIAL
    EQUALITY
  EQUAL PROTECTION
  HOUSTON, CHARLES
    HAMILTON
  WARREN, EARL

Kent Redding
Associate Professor, Department of
Sociology
University of Wisconsin–Milwaukee
  STRUCTURAL
    TRANSFORMATION

Adolph Reed
Professor, Department of Political
Science
University of Pennsylvania
  BIRTH OF A NATION

Thomas J. Reese, S.J.
Senior Fellow, Woodstock Theological
Center
Georgetown University
  VATICAN, THE

Andrea Reeves
Department of Psychiatry and
Behavioral Sciences
Duke University Medical Center
HARASSMENT

Douglas B. Reeves
Chairman
The Leadership and Learning Center
ACCOUNTABILITY

Charlene Regester
Assistant Professor
University of North Carolina–Chapel
Hill
GONE WITH THE WIND

Thomas Ehrlich Reifer
Assistant Professor, Department of
Sociology, University of San Diego
Associate Fellow, Transnational
Institute, Amsterdam
CORPORATIONS

Michael A. Rembis
Coordinator, Disability Studies;
Affiliated Faculty, Department of
History
University of Arizona
EUGENICS

Rory Remer
Centre of Creative Chaos
SOCIOMETRY

B. Jeffrey Reno
Assistant Professor, Department of
Political Science
College of the Holy Cross
REPUBLIC

Greg Restall
Associate Professor, School of
Philosophy
University of Melbourne, Australia
LOGIC, SYMBOLIC

Terry Rey
Associate Professor, Department of
Religion
Temple University
VODOU

Gilbert Reyes
Associate Dean, School of Psychology
Fielding Graduate University
TRAUMATIC BONDING

David A. Rezvani
Postdoctoral Research Fellow

Belfer Center for Science and
International Affairs, Harvard
University
ISOLATIONISM

Peter A. Riach
Research Fellow
Institute for the Study of Labor (IZA)
CORRESPONDENCE TESTS

Joseph Ricciardi
Babson College
WALL STREET

Judith Rich
Institute for the Study of Labor (IZA)
University of Portsmouth
CORRESPONDENCE TESTS

Nicole Richardt
Assistant Professor, Department of
Political Science
University of Utah
EQUAL OPPORTUNITY
GENDER GAP

Laura S. Richman
Assistant Research Professor,
Department of Psychology and
Neuroscience
Duke University
LIFE EVENTS, STRESS
SELF-AFFIRMATION THEORY

Jessica Richmond
The University of Akron, Ohio
EUTHANASIA AND ASSISTED
SUICIDE

Larry R. Ridener
Professor and Chair, Department of
Sociology and Criminal Justice
Pfeiffer University
PARK, ROBERT E.

Mark Rider
Associate Professor of Economics
Georgia State University
BEQUESTS
EXCESS SUPPLY
IN VIVO TRANSFERS
INCOME

Edward J. Rielly
Professor, Department of English
Saint Joseph's College, Maine
SITTING BULL

Alberto Rigoni
Partner, GLR Advisory

Milan, Italy
EXCESS DEMAND

John G. Riley
Distinguished Professor, Department
of Economics
UCLA, Los Angeles
SCREENING AND SIGNALING
GAMES

Ingrid H. Rima
Professor of Economics
Temple University
MARKET CLEARING
MARKETS
RETURNS, INCREASING

Maggie Rivas-Rodriguez
Associate Professor
University of Texas at Austin
IMMIGRANTS, LATIN
AMERICAN

Lauren A. Rivera
PhD Candidate, Department of
Sociology
Harvard University
DISTINCTIONS, SOCIAL AND
CULTURAL

Francisco L. Rivera-Batiz
Professor of Economics and
Education, Teachers College
Columbia University
IMMIGRANTS, NEW YORK CITY

Larry Eugene Rivers
President
Fort Valley State University
TRAIL OF TEARS

Abbey R. Roach
Department of Psychology
University of Kentucky
OPTIMISM/PESSIMISM

Nathaniel P. Roberts
ESRC Postdoctoral Fellow,
Department of Anthropology
London School of Economics and
Political Science
CASTE, ANTHROPOLOGY OF

Sally I. Roberts
Associate Dean, School of Education
University of Kansas
MENTAL RETARDATION

David Brian Robertson
Professor, Department of Political
Science
University of Missouri–St. Louis
CROSS OF GOLD

Philip K. Robins
Professor of Economics
University of Miami
SOCIAL EXPERIMENT

Dean E. Robinson
Associate Professor, Department of
Political Science
University of Massachusetts at
Amherst
BLACK NATIONALISM

Jorgianne Civey Robinson
Doctoral Candidate, Department of
Psychology and Neuroscience
Duke University
LOOKING-GLASS EFFECT
MOOD
REJECTION/ACCEPTANCE
ROSENBERG'S SELF-ESTEEM
SCALE
SIMILARITY/ATTRACTION
THEORY

Scott E. Robinson
Associate Professor of Government
and Public Service, Bush School
Texas A&M University
HYPOTHESIS AND HYPOTHESIS
TESTING

Louis-Philippe Rochon
Associate Professor of Economics
Laurentian University
INFLATION
MACROECONOMICS,
STRUCTURALIST
PROFITS
UNCERTAINTY

Thomas R. Rochon
Executive Vice President and Chief
Academic Officer
University of St. Thomas in
Minnesota
PUTNAM, ROBERT

Samuel K. Rock
Lecturer in Psychology
Texas A&M University–Kingsville:
San Antonio
MEAN, THE
STANDARD DEVIATION
VARIANCE

Hugh Rockoff
Professor, Department of Economics
Rutgers University, New Brunswick,
NJ, and National Bureau of Economic
Research
GREAT DEPRESSION

William M. Rodgers, III
Professor, Edward J. Bloustein School
of Planning and Public Policy, Rutgers
University Graduate Faculty, School of
Management and Labor Relations
Chief Economist, John J. Heldrich
Center for Workforce Development
ECONOMETRIC
DECOMPOSITION
OAXACA, RONALD

Lúcia Lima Rodrigues
Associate Professor, School of
Economics and Management
University of Minho, Portugal
POSTLETHWAYT, MALACHY

David J. Roelfs
SUNY–Stony Brook
PROBABILISTIC REGRESSION

Melvin L. Rogers
Assistant Professor, Woodrow Wilson
Department of Politics
University of Virginia
REPUBLICANISM

Malcolm J. Rohrbough
Professor, Department of History
University of Iowa
GOLD

Judith Roof
Professor of English and Film Studies
Michigan State University
JAZZ

Wade Clark Roof
Professor of Religion and Society
University of California at Santa
Barbara
SPIRITUALITY

Steve C. Ropp
Professor of Political Science
University of Wyoming
CLIENTELISM

Jaime Ros
Professor of Economics, Department
of Economics and Policy Studies;
Faculty Fellow, Kellogg Institute for
International Studies

University of Notre Dame
DUTCH DISEASE

Steven Rosefielde
Professor, Department of Economics
The University of North Carolina at
Chapel Hill
CONVERGENCE THEORY

Lawrence Rosen
Professor, Department of
Anthropology
Princeton University
BURIAL GROUNDS, NATIVE
AMERICAN

James E. Rosenbaum
Professor of Sociology, Education and
Social Policy
Northwestern University
GAUTREAUX RESIDENTIAL
MOBILITY PROGRAM

Alex Rosenberg
R. Taylor Cole Professor of Philosophy
Duke University
KUHN, THOMAS

Beth A. Rosenson
Assistant Professor, Department of
Political Science
University of Florida
ELITISM

Jalil Roshandel
Associate Professor of Political Science
East Carolina University
VAJPAYEE, ATAL BIHARI

David A. Rossiter
Assistant Professor, Department of
Environmental Studies
Western Washington University
LAND CLAIMS
TOPOGRAPHY

Leland M. Roth
Marion Dean Ross Professor of
Architectural History, School of
Architecture and Allied Arts
University of Oregon
ARCHITECTURE

Sheldon Rothblatt
Professor Emeritus of History
University of California at Berkeley
UNIVERSITY OF OXFORD
UNIVERSITY, THE

Roy J. Rotheim
Quadracci Professor in Social
Responsibility; Professor in Economics
Skidmore College
SAY'S LAW

Daniel Rothenberg
Executive Director, International
Human Rights Law Institute
DePaul University College of Law
GENOCIDE

Joyce Rothschild
Professor of Sociology, School of
Public and International Affairs
Virginia Tech, Blacksburg, Virginia
WHISTLE-BLOWERS

Victor Roudometof
Department of Social and Political
Sciences
University of Cyprus
COSMOPOLITANISM

Carolyn M. Rouse
Associate Professor, Department of
Anthropology
Princeton University
NATION OF ISLAM

Stephen R. Routh
Associate Professor, Department of
Politics and Public Administration
California State University, Stanislaus
REAGAN, RONALD

Stephanie Johnson Rowley
Associate Professor
University of Michigan
MULTIDIMENSIONAL
    INVENTORY OF BLACK
    IDENTITY

Anya Peterson Royce
Chancellor's Professor of
Anthropology
Indiana University
DANCE

Stephen Rubb
John F. Welch College of Business
Sacred Heart University
UNDEREMPLOYMENT RATE

James H. Rubin
Professor of Art History, Department
of Art, Stony Brook, State University
of New York

Faculty of Humanities and Social
Sciences, The Cooper Union, New
York
REALISM

Michael Rubin
Resident Scholar
The American Enterprise Institute,
Washington, D.C.
KHOMEINI, AYATOLLAH
    RUHOLLAH

Joshua B. Rubongoya
Professor, Department of Public
Affairs
Roanoke College
MUSEVENI, YOWERI

Christopher S. Ruebeck
Assistant Professor, Lafayette College,
Easton, Pennsylvania
COMPETITION, IMPERFECT
CORPORATE STRATEGIES
INFORMATION, ASYMMETRIC
INSTRUMENTAL VARIABLES
    REGRESSION
REVENUE

Steven Ruggles
Distinguished McKnight University
Professor
University of Minnesota
INTEGRATED PUBLIC USE
    MICRODATA SERIES

Mark A. Runco
Professor, California State University
Fullerton
The Norwegian School of Economics
and Business Administration
BUTTERFLY EFFECT
CREATIVITY
NATURE VS. NURTURE
OPERANT CONDITIONING
PARADIGM
STAGES OF DEVELOPMENT
TALENT

Michael Ruse
Lucyle T. Werkmeister Professor of
Philosophy
Florida State University
CREATIONISM
DARWINISM, SOCIAL

Mark Rush
Robert G. Brown Professor of Politics
and Law; Head, Department of
Politics
Washington and Lee University

GERRYMANDERING
VOTING RIGHTS ACT

Chris Nicole Russell
Doctoral Student in Sociology
Texas A&M University
OVERPOPULATION

Daniel W. Russell
Professor, Human Development and
Family Studies, Institute for Social and
Behavioral Research
Iowa State University
LONELINESS

James W. Russell
University Professor, Department of
Sociology, Anthropology, and Social
Work
Eastern Connecticut State University
OPERATION BOOTSTRAP

Peter H. Russell
Professor Emeritus, Department of
Political Science
University of Toronto
MONARCHY, CONSTITUTIONAL

Malcolm Rutherford
Professor, Department of Economics
University of Victoria, Canada
MITCHELL, WESLEY CLAIR

Paul A. Ruud
Professor, Department of Economics
University of California, Berkeley
GENERALIZED LEAST SQUARES

Richard M. Ryan
Professor of Psychology, Psychiatry,
and Education
University of Rochester
SELF-DETERMINATION THEORY

Jens Rydgren
Associate Professor, Department of
Sociology
Stockholm University
CONFORMITY

Steven Rytina
Associate Professor of Sociology
McGill University
SOCIAL STRUCTURE

Rogelio Saenz
Department of Sociology
Texas A&M University
ETHNIC ENCLAVE

LATINO NATIONAL POLITICAL
   SURVEY
LATINOS
MIDDLEMAN MINORITIES
MIGRATION
MIGRATION, RURAL TO URBAN

Eirik J. Saethre
Postdoctoral Fellow
University of Pretoria, South Africa
   MEDICINE

Emile Sahliyeh
Professor of Middle East Studies and
Director of International Studies
University of North Texas
   NASSER, GAMAL ABDEL
   QADHAFI, MUAMMAR AL

Anandi P. Sahu
School of Business Administration
Oakland University, Michigan
   INVESTORS

Sunil K. Sahu
Frank L. Hall Professor of Political
Science
DePauw University
   INDIAN NATIONAL CONGRESS

Richard Sakwa
Professor of Russian and European
Politics
University of Kent at Canterbury
   YELTSIN, BORIS

Noel B. Salazar
PhD Candidate, Department of
Anthropology
University of Pennsylvania
   REPRESENTATION IN
     POSTCOLONIAL ANALYSIS
   VACATIONS

Jeffrey J. Sallaz
Professor, Department of Sociology
University of Arizona
   OUTSOURCING

Maurice Salles
CREM and Institute for SCW,
University of Caen
CPNSS, London School of Economics
   ARROW POSSIBILITY THEOREM
   CHOICE IN ECONOMICS

Warren J. Samuels
Professor Emeritus, Department of
Economics
Michigan State University

ECONOMICS
ECONOMICS, INSTITUTIONAL
ENTREPRENEURSHIP
MARGINAL PRODUCTIVITY
MARGINALISM
PROPERTY, PRIVATE
RENT
SUBSIDIES

Paul A. Samuelson
Institute Professor Emeritus
Massachusetts Institute of Technology
   SOLOW, ROBERT M.

Kijua Sanders-McMurtry
Instructor, Honors Program
Georgia State University
   KENYATTA, JOMO
   LEAKEY, RICHARD
   MANDELA, WINNIE

Günther Sandner
Independent Scholar, Lecturer
University of Vienna
   AUSTRO-MARXISM

Barry Sandywell
Senior Lecturer, Department of
Sociology
University of York
   CONSTRUCTIVISM
   DERRIDA, JACQUES
   SOCIOLOGY, EUROPEAN
   STARE, THE
   SUBJECTIVITY: OVERVIEW

Manuel S. Santos
Department of Economics
University of Miami
   MARKET FUNDAMENTALS
   SOLOW RESIDUAL, THE
   TWO-SECTOR MODELS

Prabirjit Sarkar
Professor of Economics
Jadavpur University, Calcutta
(Kolkata), India
   PREBISCH-SINGER HYPOTHESIS
   SINGER, HANS
   TERMS OF TRADE

Camilo Sarmiento
Senior Economist
Fannie Mae
   TIME TRENDS

Lisa Saunders
Associate Professor, Department of
Economics
University of Massachusetts, Amherst

DISCRIMINATION, WAGE, BY
   GENDER

Sean J. Savage
Professor of Political Science
Saint Mary's College
   CIVIL RIGHTS MOVEMENT, U.S.
   CLINTON, BILL
   DEMOCRATIC PARTY, U.S.
   KISSINGER, HENRY
   MACMILLAN, HAROLD
   MILITARY-INDUSTRIAL
     COMPLEX
   MONROE DOCTRINE
   PUBLIC ADMINISTRATION
   REPUBLICAN PARTY
   ROOSEVELT, FRANKLIN D.
   TRUMAN, HARRY S.
   URBAN RENEWAL
   WARREN REPORT
   WASHINGTON, GEORGE
   WILSON, WOODROW

Malcolm C. Sawyer
Professor of Economics
University of Leeds
   KALECKI, MICHAL
   PHILLIPS CURVE

Mark Q. Sawyer
Associate Professor, Department of
Political Science and Ralph J. Bunche
Center for African American Studies,
and Director, Center for the Study of
Race, Ethnicity and Politics
University of California, Los Angeles
   CONCENTRATION CAMPS

Elizabeth A. Say
Dean, College of Humanities
California State University, Northridge
   FAMILY VALUES

Serdar Sayan
Professor, Department of Economics
TOBB University of Economics and
Technology, Ankara
   OVERLAPPING GENERATIONS
     MODEL

W. George Scarlett
Assistant Professor, Eliot-Pearson
Department of Child Development
Tufts University
   FUNDAMENTALISM

Dominik J. Schaller
Karman Center for Advanced Studies
in the Humanities

University of Berne, Switzerland, and
University of Heidelberg
POGROMS

Richard L. Scheaffer
Professor Emeritus
University of Florida
RANDOM SAMPLES

Thomas J. Scheff
Professor Emeritus
University of California, Santa Barbara
SHAME

Philip W. Scher
Department of Anthropology
University of Oregon
CALYPSO
CREOLE

Kyle Scherr
Doctoral Candidate, Department of
Psychology
Iowa State University
SELF-FULFILLING PROPHECIES

Lucas D. Schipper
Psychology Graduate Student
Florida Atlantic University
DETERMINISM, GENETIC

Andrew J. Schlewitz
Professor, Political Science
Albion College
MILITARISM

Kay Lehman Schlozman
J. Joseph Moakley Professor,
Department of Political Science
Boston College
INEQUALITY, POLITICAL

H. E. Schmeisser
Department of Political Science
University of Florida
ELITISM

A. Allan Schmid
University Distinguished Professor,
Emeritus, Department of Agricultural
Economics
Michigan State University
EXTERNALITY
GALBRAITH, JOHN KENNETH
LEXICOGRAPHIC PREFERENCES
PHYSICAL CAPITAL
SATISFICING BEHAVIOR

Christoph M. Schmidt
Professor, Rheinisch-Westfälisches
Institut für Wirtschaftsforschung,
Essen
Fellow, Centre for Economic Policy
Research, London
SEPARABILITY

Frederick C. Schneid
Professor of History
High Point University
NAPOLEONIC WARS

Jane Schneider
PhD Program in Anthropology
Graduate Center, City University of
New York
MAFIA, THE

Robert F. Schoeni
Research Professor, Institute for Social
Research; Professor of Public Policy
and Economics
University of Michigan
PANEL STUDY OF INCOME
DYNAMICS

James L. Schoff
Associate Director of Asia-Pacific
Studies
Institute for Foreign Policy Analysis,
Cambridge, MA
TRILATERALISM

Philip Schofield
Professor
University College London
BENTHAM, JEREMY

Christa Scholtz
Assistant Professor, Department of
Political Science
McGill University
TREATY FEDERALISM

Kimberly A. Schonert-Reichl
Department of Educational and
Counselling Psychology, and Special
Education
University of British Columbia,
Vancouver
DEVELOPMENTAL PSYCHOLOGY

Anja Schüler
Instructor, Department of Foreign
Languages
Heidelberg College of Education,
Germany
SETTLEMENT
SEXISM

Gerhard Schutte
Professor, Department of Sociology
and Anthropology
University of Wisconsin–Parkside
PHENOMENOLOGY

Abraham P. Schwab
Assistant Professor, Department of
Philosophy
Brooklyn College, City University of
New York
TUSKEGEE SYPHILIS STUDY

Joseph M. Schwartz
Department of Political Science
Temple University
POSTMODERNISM

Bill Schwarz
Reader, School of English and Drama
Queen Mary, University of London
HALL, STUART

Maureen Trudelle Schwarz
Associate Professor, Department of
Anthropology
Maxwell School of Citizenship and
Public Affairs, Syracuse University
NAVAJO

Stefan Schwarzkopf
Lecturer, School of Business and
Management
Queen Mary College, University of
London
HIDDEN PERSUADERS

Loren Schweninger
Elizabeth Rosenthal Excellence
Professor of History
University of North Carolina at
Greensboro
KU KLUX KLAN

Chris Matthew Sciabarra
Visiting Scholar, Department of
Politics
New York University
OBJECTIVISM

Kim Scipes
Assistant Professor of Sociology
Purdue University North Central
DEVELOPING COUNTRIES

Elliott D. Sclar
Director, Center for Sustainable Urban
Development, Earth Institute,
Columbia University

Professor of Urban Planning and International Affairs, Graduate School of Architecture, Planning, and Preservation, and School of International and Public Affairs, Columbia University
URBANIZATION

Stanley L. Sclove
Professor, Department of Information and Decision Sciences
University of Illinois at Chicago
CLUSTER ANALYSIS
PRINCIPAL COMPONENTS

John Scott
Professor of Sociology
University of Essex
NETWORK ANALYSIS

Rebecca J. Scott
Professor of History and Law
University of Michigan
PUBLIC RIGHTS

W. Richard Scott
Professor Emeritus, Department of Sociology
Stanford University
SOCIOLOGY, INSTITUTIONAL ANALYSIS IN

Thomas J. Scotto
Lecturer, Department of Government
University of Essex
APPORTIONMENT

James G. Scoville
Professor of Human Resources and Industrial Relations
University of Minnesota
JAJMANI MATRIX

Matthew H. Scullin
Assistant Professor, Department of Psychology
University of Texas at El Paso
FLYNN EFFECT

David O. Sears
Professor of Psychology and Political Science
University of California, Los Angeles
RACE-CONSCIOUS POLICIES

Ronald E. Seavoy
Professor Emeritus, History
Bowling Green State University
FAMINE
SUBSISTENCE AGRICULTURE

Jason Seawright
Department of Political Science
University of California at Berkeley
PARTY SYSTEMS, COMPETITIVE

Mario Seccareccia
Professor, Department of Economics
University of Ottawa
AGGREGATE DEMAND
INVOLUNTARY UNEMPLOYMENT

Erika Seeler
PhD Candidate, Department of Political Science
Duke University
NATIONAL SECURITY

Robert Self
Professor, Department of Law, Governance and International Relations
London Metropolitan University, United Kingdom
CHAMBERLAIN, NEVILLE

Sayida L. Self
Anthropology Department
The Graduate Center of the City University of New York
MARXISM, BLACK

Jane Sell
Professor, Sociology
Texas A&M University
GROUPS
SOCIAL EXCHANGE THEORY
SOCIOLOGY
SOCIOLOGY, MICRO-

Mike Sell
Associate Professor of English
Indiana University of Pennsylvania
BLACK ARTS MOVEMENT

Saher Selod
Department of Sociology
Loyola University Chicago
CHINESE AMERICANS
INEQUALITY, RACIAL
MUSLIMS

Willi Semmler
Professor
New School for Social Research
MARKUP PRICING

Atreyee Sen
Research Council United Kingdom (RCUK) Fellow

University of Manchester
MILITANTS

Sudipta Sen
Professor, Department of History
University of California, Davis
IMPERIALISM

Esther-Mirjam Sent
Professor of Economic Theory and Policy
University of Nijmegen, The Netherlands
ARROW, KENNETH J.
LUCAS, ROBERT E., JR.
SIMON, HERBERT A.

Susan Sered
Department of Sociology
Suffolk University, Boston
BIRTHS, OUT-OF-WEDLOCK
OCCUPATIONAL HAZARDS

Apostolos Serletis
University Professor and Professor of Economics and Finance
University of Calgary
LIQUIDITY
NEUTRALITY OF MONEY
SPREADS
SUBSTITUTABILITY
TECHNOLOGICAL PROGRESS, SKILL BIAS
YIELD

Rajiv Sethi
Associate Professor of Economics
Barnard College, Columbia University
COLLECTIVE ACTION GAMES
MIXED STRATEGY
NASH EQUILIBRIUM

Mark Setterfield
Professor of Economics, Department of Economics, Trinity College, Hartford
Associate Member, Cambridge Centre for Economic and Public Policy, Cambridge University
MACROFOUNDATIONS
STABILITY IN ECONOMICS
UNEMPLOYABLE
UNEMPLOYMENT

Todd K. Shackelford
Associate Professor of Psychology
Florida Atlantic University
DETERMINISM, GENETIC

Russ S. Shafer-Landau
Professor of Philosophy

University of Wisconsin–Madison
REALISM, MORAL

Hongxia Shan
Doctoral Candidate, Department of
Adult Education and Counseling
Psychology
Ontario Institute for Studies in
Education of the University of
Toronto
IMMIGRATION

Jeffrey Shandler
Associate Professor, Department of
Jewish Studies
Rutgers University
SHTETL

Torrey J. Shanks
Postdoctoral Fellow, Department of
Political Science
University of British Columbia
EQUAL OPPORTUNITY

Andrew Sharpe
Executive Director
International Association for Research
in Income and Wealth, Ottawa,
Canada
GROSS DOMESTIC PRODUCT

Rhonda V. Sharpe
Assistant Professor of Economics,
Department of Economics
University of Vermont
HESSIAN MATRIX
JACOBIAN MATRIX
NODE, STABLE

Steven Shavell
Samuel R. Rosenthal Professor of Law
and Economics
Harvard University
LAW AND ECONOMICS

Gabriel (Gabi) Sheffer
Professor, Political Science
Department
Hebrew University of Jerusalem
JEWISH DIASPORA

James F. Sheffield, Jr.
Professor, Department of Political
Science
University of Oklahoma
KEFAUVER, ESTES
KENNEDY, JOHN F.
WHITE PRIMARY

Hersh Shefrin
Mario L. Belotti Professor of Finance
Santa Clara University
PROSPECT THEORY

Kathleen Sheldon
Research Scholar, Center for the Study
of Women
University of California, Los Angeles
MACHEL, SAMORA

Mimi Sheller
Visiting Associate Professor,
Department of Sociology and
Anthropology
Swarthmore College
CARIBBEAN, THE

J. Nicole Shelton
Associate Professor
Princeton University
MULTIDIMENSIONAL
INVENTORY OF BLACK
IDENTITY
SELF-AFFIRMATION THEORY

Michael Sheppard
Professor
University of Plymouth, United
Kingdom
SOCIAL EXCLUSION

Michelle R. Sherrill vanDellen
Research Assistant
Duke University
OUGHT SELF
SELF DISCREPANCY THEORY
SELF-CONTROL
SELF-GUIDES
SELF-SCHEMATA

Michael P. Shields
Professor of Economics
Central Michigan University
HEDONIC PRICES
IMMISERIZING GROWTH
STEADY STATE
UTILITY, VON NEUMANN-
MORGENSTERN

Rob Shields
Henry Marshall Tory Chair and
Professor, Sociology/Art and Design
University of Alberta
LEFEBVRE, HENRI

Yuval Shilony
Department of Economics
Bar–Ilan University, Israel
INSURANCE

Keith Shimko
Purdue University
FOREIGN POLICY

Parker Shipton
Associate Professor of Anthropology
and Research Fellow in African Studies
Boston University
TURNER, VICTOR

Ronald Shone
Independent Researcher
Stirling, Scotland
PHASE DIAGRAMS
REVENUE, MARGINAL

Eran Shor
Graduate School, Department of
Sociology
Stony Brook University, New York
PERFORMANCE
QUANTIFICATION

Martin Shubik
Seymour Knox Professor of
Mathematical Institutional Economics
Yale University
COMPETITION, PERFECT
GENERAL EQUILIBRIUM
MONETARY THEORY
MONEY
STRATEGIC GAMES

Doron Shultziner
Politics and International Relations
Department, Lincoln College
University of Oxford
RECOGNITION

Chris G. Sibley
Postdoctoral Fellow
University of Auckland, New Zealand
PERSONALITY, AUTHORITARIAN
SOCIAL DOMINANCE
ORIENTATION

Robin C. Sickles
Department of Economics
Rice University
AVIATION INDUSTRY

John J. Siegfried
Professor of Economics
Vanderbilt University
AMERICAN ECONOMIC
ASSOCIATION

Jennifer Silva
Department of Sociology

University of Virginia
LIFESTYLES

Aliza Silver
Department of Psychology
University of Illinois at Chicago
TRAIT INFERENCE

Daniel Silver
Doctoral Candidate, Committee on
Social Thought
University of Chicago
SOCIAL THEORY

Roxane Cohen Silver
Professor of Psychology and Social
Behavior
University of California, Irvine
COPING

Paul J. Silvia
Associate Professor, Department of
Psychology
University of North Carolina at
Greensboro
SELF-AWARENESS THEORY

Josef Sima
Department of Institutional
Economics
University of Economics, Prague
ORDINALITY

Eleni Simintzi
Economic Analyst
Eurobank EFG
GROSS NATIONAL INCOME
LOANS

Katherine Simmonds
Clinical Assistant Professor
Graduate Program in Nursing, The
MGH Institute of Health Professions
REPRODUCTIVE RIGHTS

Adam F. Simon
Department of Political Science
Yale University
POLLSTERS

Lawrence H. Simon
Associate Professor of Philosophy and
Environmental Studies
Bowdoin College
PHILOSOPHY

Dean Keith Simonton
Distinguished Professor, Department
of Psychology
University of California at Davis

CLIOMETRICS
DISTRIBUTION, NORMAL
NAPOLEON COMPLEX
SELF-ACTUALIZATION

Brooks D. Simpson
Professor, Department of History
Arizona State University
GRANT, ULYSSES S.

Tyrone R. Simpson, II
Assistant Professor, Department of
English
Vassar College
BLACK CONSERVATISM

M. Thea Sinclair
Christel DeHaan Tourism and Travel
Research Institute
University of Nottingham
TOURISM INDUSTRY

Merrill Singer
Research Scientist, Center for Health,
Intervention and Prevention
University of Connecticut
ETHNO-EPIDEMIOLOGICAL
METHODOLOGY

David S. Siroky
Department of Political Science
Duke University
POLITICS, COMPARATIVE

Lenka Bustikova Siroky
Professor, Department of Political
Science
Duke University
POLITICS, COMPARATIVE

Claes-Henric Siven
Professor, Department of Economics
Stockholm University
STOCKHOLM SCHOOL

David L. Sjoquist
Professor, Department of Economics
Andrew Young School of Policy
Studies, Georgia State University
MULTI-CITY STUDY OF URBAN
INEQUALITY

Neil T. Skaggs
Professor, Department of Economics
Illinois State University
LENDER OF LAST RESORT
LOMBARD STREET (BAGEHOT)

Bonnie L. Slade
Collaborative Women's Studies
Program and Department of Adult
Education
University of Toronto
INEQUALITY, GENDER
INTERSECTIONALITY

Joel B. Slemrod
Paul W. McCracken Collegiate
Professor of Business Economics and
Public Policy and Professor of
Economics
University of Michigan
TAXES

Fred Slocum, III
Associate Professor of Political Science
Minnesota State University, Mankato
CIVIL RIGHTS
DEALIGNMENT
LAW AND ORDER
NEW DEAL, THE
POLITICS, SOUTHERN
POLLING
PUBLIC OPINION
SOUTHERN STRATEGY

La Fleur F. Small
Assistant Professor of Sociology,
Department of Sociology and
Anthropology
Wright State University
NATIONAL HEALTH INSURANCE

Timothy M. Smeeding
Founder and Director Emeritus,
Luxembourg Income Study
The Maxwell School, Syracuse
University
LUXEMBOURG INCOME STUDY

Brandy L. Smith
Department of Counseling,
Educational Psychology, and Research
University of Memphis
TRANSGENDER

Charles Anthony Smith
Assistant Professor
University of California, Irvine
DUE PROCESS

Earl Smith
Rubin Professor of American Ethnic
Studies, Professor of Sociology
Wake Forest University
DRED SCOTT V. SANFORD

Gavin Smith
Professor, Department of
Anthropology
University of Toronto
INFORMAL ECONOMY

Joanne R. Smith
School of Psychology
University of Exeter
SELF-IDENTITY

Judith E. Smith
Professor of American Studies
University of Massachusetts Boston
ELLIS ISLAND

Lahra Smith
Assistant Professor, Edmund A. Walsh
School of Foreign Service
Georgetown University
PLURALISM

Laurence D. Smith
Associate Professor, Psychology
Department
University of Maine
HULL, CLARK

Mark C. Smith
American Studies and History
University of Texas at Austin
LYND, ROBERT AND HELEN

Murray E. G. Smith
Professor of Sociology
Brock University
CREDENTIALISM
MANAGERIAL CLASS
MANDEL, ERNEST
PUTTING-OUT SYSTEM
SELF-DETERMINATION
SELF-EMPLOYMENT
VALUE, OBJECTIVE

Richard H. Smith
Department of Psychology
University of Kentucky
PRESTIGE
SOCIAL COMPARISON

River J. Smith
University of Tulsa
MULTIPLE PERSONALITIES

Steven M. Smith
Associate Professor, Department of
Psychology
Saint Mary's University
PERSUASION
PRIMACY/RECENCY EFFECTS

Tyson Smith
Department of Sociology
SUNY–Stony Brook
ADVERTISING

Wayne S. Smith
Senior Fellow and Director, Cuba
Program
Center for International Policy
BAY OF PIGS

Vassiliki Betty Smocovitis
Professor, History of Science,
Departments of Zoology and History
University of Florida
DOBZHANSKY, THEODOSIUS

Ingrid F. Smyer
The International Society for
Embodied Imagination (ISEI)
Boston, Massachusetts
ANIMISM

Ben Snyder
University of Oklahoma
SUBURBS

C. R. Snyder
Formerly the Wright Distinguished
Professor of Clinical Psychology,
Department of Psychology
University of Kansas, Lawrence,
Kansas
LOCUS OF CONTROL

Jack Snyder
Columbia University
JERVIS, ROBERT

Ted Socha
Brown University
DECENTRALIZATION

Lise Solberg Nes
Department of Psychology
University of Kentucky
OPTIMISM/PESSIMISM
PSYCHONEUROIMMUNOLOGY
STRESS

Anja Soldan
Postdoctoral Research Scientist,
Cognitive Neuroscience Division
Taub Institute for Research on
Alzheimer's Disease and the Aging
Brain, Columbia University
ALZHEIMER'S DISEASE

Sheldon Solomon
Professor of Psychology, Skidmore
College
Saratoga Springs, New York
TERROR MANAGEMENT
THEORY

Robert M. Solow
Institute Professor Emeritus
Massachusetts Institute of Technology
KLEIN, LAWRENCE
SAMUELSON, PAUL A.

Ilya Somin
Assistant Professor of Law
George Mason University School of
Law
PRIVATE INTERESTS

Lewis Soroka
Professor, Department of Economics
Brock University, St. Catharines,
Ontario, Canada
SPORTS INDUSTRY

Roberta Spalter-Roth
Director, Department of Research and
Development
American Sociological Association
AMERICAN SOCIOLOGICAL
ASSOCIATION

Aris Spanos
Department of Economics
Virginia Tech
SPECIFICATION
SPECIFICATION TESTS

Jan F. Spears
Professor, Department of Crop
Science
North Carolina State University,
Raleigh
PEANUT INDUSTRY

Robert W. Speel
Associate Professor of Political Science
Penn State Erie, The Behrend College
VOTING PATTERNS

Alan E. H. Speight
Professor, School of Business and
Economics
Swansea University
ABSOLUTE INCOME
HYPOTHESIS
PERMANENT INCOME
HYPOTHESIS

Margaret Beale Spencer
Graduate School of Education
University of Pennsylvania
CHILD DEVELOPMENT

Mark G. Spencer
Associate Professor, Department of
History
Brock University
MADISON, JAMES
VOLTAIRE

J. C. Spender
Visiting Professor
Lund University
KNOWLEDGE
KNOWLEDGE, DIFFUSION OF

Debra Spitulnik
Professor, Department of
Anthropology
Emory University
RADIO TALK SHOWS

Brenda Spotton Visano
Associate Professor of Economics
York University, Toronto, Canada
BANKING INDUSTRY
GREAT TULIP MANIA, THE
PANICS
SPECULATION

William E. Spriggs
Professor of Economics
Howard University
BLACK LIBERALISM

Annegret Staiger
Associate Professor of Anthropology
Clarkson University, Potsdam,
New York
PIMPS
RESEGREGATION OF SCHOOLS

Harold W. Stanley
Geurin-Pettus Distinguished Chair in
American Politics and Political
Economy
Political Science Department,
Southern Methodist University
SOUTHERN BLOC

Katina Stapleton
Adjunct Professor, Communication,
Culture and Technology Program
Georgetown University
CARTOONS, POLITICAL

Martha A. Starr
Department of Economics

American University
SAVING RATE

Richard Startz
Castor Professor of Economics
University of Washington
LEAST SQUARES, TWO-STAGE
MULTICOLLINEARITY

Dan Stastny
Department of Economics
Prague School of Economics
ECONOMICS, INTERNATIONAL
SCARCITY

Richard H. Steckel
Professor, Economics Department
Ohio State University
PHYSICAL QUALITY OF LIFE
INDEX

Brent J. Steele
Assistant Professor of Political Science
and International Relations
University of Kansas
INTERNATIONAL RELATIONS
LEE, ROBERT E.
MORAL SUASION
NEUTRALITY, POLITICAL

Nico Stehr
Karl Mannheim Professor of Cultural
Studies
Zeppelin University
SOCIOLOGY, KNOWLEDGE IN

Edward Stein
Professor of Law
Cardozo School of Law
SEXUAL ORIENTATION,
DETERMINANTS OF

Edward I. Steinberg
Lecturer of Economics
Columbia University
DISCOURAGED WORKERS
LAGGING, LEADING, AND
COINCIDENT INDICATORS

Stephen Steinberg
Professor, Department of Urban
Studies and PhD Program in
Sociology
Queens College and Graduate Center,
City University of New York
RACE RELATIONS

Charles Steindel
Senior Vice President
Federal Reserve Bank of New York

PROPENSITY TO CONSUME,
MARGINAL
PROPENSITY TO SAVE,
MARGINAL

Joseph E. Steinmetz
Dean, College of Liberal Arts &
Sciences; University Distinguished
Professor of Molecular Biology and
Psychology
The University of Kansas
CLASSICAL CONDITIONING

Victor J. Stenger
Emeritus Professor of Physics and
Astronomy, University of Hawaii at
Manoa
Adjunct Professor of Philosophy,
University of Colorado at Boulder
CLOCK TIME
REALITY

Thanasis Stengos
Professor of Economics
University of Guelph, Ontario,
Canada
THRESHOLD EFFECTS

Pamela Stern
Centre for Sustainable Community
Development
Simon Fraser University, British
Columbia, Canada
INUIT
KROEBER, ALFRED LOUIS

Yaakov Stern
Professor of Clinical Neuropsychology,
Departments of Neurology, Psychiatry
and Psychology
Taub Institute for Research on
Alzheimer's Disease and the Aging
Brain, Columbia University College of
Physicians and Surgeons
ALZHEIMER'S DISEASE

Charles Stewart, III
Kenan Sahin Distinguished Professor
of Political Science
Massachusetts Institute of Technology
ROLL CALLS

James B. Stewart
Pennsylvania State University
AFRICAN AMERICANS
ECONOMICS, STRATIFICATION
RACE AND ECONOMICS

Michael Stewart
Department of Anthropology

University College London
ROMA, THE

E. L. Stocks
Department of Psychology
University of Texas at Tyler
ALTRUISM
ALTRUISM AND PROSOCIAL
BEHAVIOR
EXPERIMENTS
SCALES

Kathy S. Stolley
Assistant Professor, Department of
Sociology and Criminal Justice
Virginia Wesleyan College
CENSUS

Clarence N. Stone
Research Professor of Public Policy
and Political Science, George
Washington University
Professor Emeritus, University of
Maryland
COMMUNITY POWER STUDIES
HUNTER, FLOYD

David R. Stone
Professor of History
Kansas State University
TROTSKY, LEON

Linda S. Stone
Department of Anthropology
Washington State University
KINSHIP

Chris E. Stout
Founding Director
Center for Global Initiatives
FULLER, BUCKMINSTER
RESILIENCY

Mark Strasser
Trustees Professor of Law
Capital University Law School,
Columbus, Ohio
MARRIAGE, SAME-SEX

Eugene W. Straus
Emeritus Professor of Medicine
State University of New York
Downstate College of Medicine
MEDICINE, SOCIALIZED

Carole Straw
Professor, Department of History
Mount Holyoke College, South
Hadley, Massachusetts
MARTYRDOM

Richard A. Straw
Professor, Department of History
Radford University
APPALACHIA

Warren R. Street
Professor of Psychology
Central Washington University
AMERICAN PSYCHOLOGICAL
ASSOCIATION

Rita M. Strohmaier
Research Assistant, Department of
Economics
University of Graz, Austria
LONG RUN
SOFT SKILLS

Kathie R. Stromile Golden
Professor and Director, International
Programs
Mississippi Valley State University
COLD WAR
COLLECTIVISM
COMMUNISM
KHRUSHCHEV, NIKITA
REFUGEE CAMPS

Daniel P. Strouthes
Associate Professor of Anthropology,
Department of Geography and
Anthropology
University of Wisconsin–Eau Claire
NATIVE AMERICANS

Charles B. Strozier
Professor of History and Director,
Center on Terrorism, John Jay College
City University of New York
BIN LADEN, OSAMA

Mary E. Stuckey
Professor, Communication and
Political Science
Georgia State University
AMERICAN INDIAN MOVEMENT
TAINO

Melissa Nicole Stuckey
PhD Candidate
Yale University
BLACK TOWNS

Susan Sugarman
Professor, Psychology Department
Princeton University
FREUD, SIGMUND
PIAGET, JEAN

Ronald Grigor Suny
Charles Tilly Collegiate Professor of
Social and Political History, University
of Michigan
Professor Emeritus of Political Science
and History, University of Chicago
RUSSIAN REVOLUTION
STALIN, JOSEPH

John B. Sutcliffe
Associate Professor, Department of
Political Science
University of Windsor
COMMON MARKET, THE
GOVERNMENT, UNITARY

John Swain
Professor of Disability and Inclusion,
School of Health, Community and
Education Studies
Northumbria University
DISABILITY

Natalie Swanepoel
Department of Anthropology and
Archaeology
University of South Africa
ARCHAEOLOGY

William B. Swann, Jr.
Professor of Psychology
University of Texas at Austin
SELF-VERIFICATION

Carole A. Sweeney
Goldsmiths College, University of
London
PRIMITIVISM

Deborah L. Swenson
Associate Professor, Department of
Economics
University of California, Davis
GOODS, NONTRADED
IMPORTS

Chris Swoyer
Department of Philosophy
University of Oklahoma
THEORY

Lori Latrice Sykes
Assistant Professor, Department of
African-American Studies
John Jay College of Criminal Justice,
City University of New York
BABY BOOMERS
NONBLACKS
NONWHITES

Michael Szenberg
Chair and Distinguished Professor of
Economics, Lubin School of Business
Pace University
COMMUNISM, PRIMITIVE
CONSUMPTION FUNCTION
DEBREU, GERARD
DIAMOND INDUSTRY
DISCRIMINATION, WAGE, BY
RACE
DRAVIDIANS
ECONOMETRICS
EXPECTATIONS
HAMILTON'S RULE
HICKS, JOHN R.
HILFERDING, RUDOLF
IDENTIFICATION PROBLEM
MATHEMATICS IN THE SOCIAL
SCIENCES
MINIMUM WAGE
MODIGLIANI, FRANCO
REFLECTION PROBLEM
RULES VERSUS DISCRETION
SHORT PERIOD
TÂTONNEMENT
TAYLOR RULE

Isaac T. Tabner
Lecturer in Finance, Department of
Accounting and Finance
University of Stirling, Scotland
RISK TAKERS

Isao Takei
PhD Student, Department of
Sociology
University of Texas at Austin
MIGRATION, RURAL TO URBAN

Wayne K. Talley
Frederick W. Beazley Professor of
Economics
Old Dominion University
RAILWAY INDUSTRY

SinhaRaja Tammita-Delgoda
Sri Lanka
VISUAL ARTS

Paige Johnson Tan
Assistant Professor
University of North Carolina,
Wilmington
KHMER ROUGE
KILLING FIELDS

Sandra J. Tanenbaum
Associate Professor, College of Public
Health
Ohio State University

MEDICAID
MEDICARE

Joyce Tang
Professor, Department of Sociology
Queens College of the City University
of New York
ENGINEERING
GLASS CEILING
PROFESSIONALIZATION

Raymond Tanter
Visiting Professor of Government
Georgetown University
PARTITION

Judith M. Tanur
Distinguished Teaching Professor
Emerita
Stony Brook University
NATIONAL LONGITUDINAL
SURVEY OF YOUTH
RESEARCH, LONGITUDINAL
STATISTICS

Betty T. Tao
Economist
CNA Corporation
INTEREST, NATURAL RATE OF

Nicholas C. T. Tapp
Professor, Department of
Anthropology, Research School of
Pacific and Asian Studies
The Australian National University
HMONG

Steven Tauber
Associate Professor, Department of
Government and International Affairs
University of South Florida
STAR TREK
WOODSTOCK

Craig Taylor
Lecturer, Department of Philosophy
Flinders University, Adelaide, Australia
SYMPATHY

Monique M. Taylor
Sociologist
Al Quds University, Jerusalem
HARLEM

Philip M. Taylor
Professor
University of Leeds
GULF WAR OF 1991

Timothy D. Taylor
Professor, Departments of
Ethnomusicology and Musicology
University of California, Los Angeles
POPULAR MUSIC

Erdal Tekin
Associate Professor of Economics,
Andrew Young School of Policy
Studies
Georgia State University
DISCRIMINATION
EDUCATION, RETURNS TO

Peter Temin
Professor of Economics
Massachusetts Institute of Technology
SOUTH SEA BUBBLE

Thijs ten Raa
Tilburg University
FIXED COEFFICIENTS
PRODUCTION FUNCTION
INPUT-OUTPUT MATRIX

Howard Tennen
Board of Trustees Distinguished
Professor, Department of Community
Medicine
University of Connecticut Health
Center
PERSONALITY

Thomas Teo
Associate Professor, Department of
Psychology
York University
MARX, KARL
PSYCHOLOGY
RACE AND PSYCHOLOGY
TWIN STUDIES

David G. Terkla
Professor of Economics and
Environmental, Earth and Ocean
Sciences
University of Massachusetts Boston
FISHING INDUSTRY

Heather Terrell Kincannon
PhD Candidate in Sociology
Texas A&M University
FERTILITY, HUMAN

Deborah J. Terry
Faculty of Social and Behavioural
Sciences
University of Queensland, Brisbane,
Australia
SELF-IDENTITY

Gunes Murat Tezcur
Assistant Professor of Political Science
Loyola University Chicago
IRAN-IRAQ WAR
LEBANESE CIVIL WAR
PALESTINIAN AUTHORITY

Carlyle A. Thayer
Professor of Politics
University of New South Wales;
Australian Defence Force Academy,
Canberra
HO CHI MINH

Douglas L. Theobald
Assistant Professor, Department of
Biochemistry
Brandeis University
PUNCTUATED EQUILIBRIUM

John K. Thomas
Professor, Department of Recreation,
Park and Tourism Sciences, Program
in Rural Sociology and Community
Studies
Texas A&M University
DETERMINISM,
ENVIRONMENTAL
LOVE CANAL
SOCIOLOGY, RURAL

Julie L. Thomas
Department of Gender Studies
Indiana University–Bloomington
FAMILY PLANNING

Paul Thomas
Professor of Political Science
University of California, Berkeley
HEGEL, GEORG WILHELM
FRIEDRICH
MATERIALISM, DIALECTICAL
STATISM

Raju G. C. Thomas
Allis Chalmers Distinguished Professor
of International Affairs
Marquette University, Wisconsin
JANATA PARTY
SINGH, V. P.

Vaso V. Thomas
Assistant Professor, Department of
Social Sciences
Bronx Community College, City
University of New York
WOMEN AND POLITICS

Marilyn M. Thomas-Houston
Assistant Professor of Anthropology
and African American Studies
University of Florida
AFRICAN AMERICAN STUDIES

Katrina D. Thompson
Visiting Professor
Roanoke College
BLACKFACE

Wayne Luther Thompson
Associate Professor, Department of
Sociology
Carthage College
MANKILLER, WILMA

Ruth Thompson-Miller
Doctoral Student
Texas A & M University
BROWN V. BOARD OF
EDUCATION, 1954
BROWN V. BOARD OF
EDUCATION, 1955
MINORITIES
MULATTOS
RACIALIZATION
SEGREGATION
WHITES

Sukhadeo Thorat
Professor of Economics
Jawaharlal Nehru University, New
Delhi, India
AMBEDKAR, B. R.
BRAHMINS
DALITS

Mark Thornton
Senior Fellow
Ludwig von Mises Institute
CANTILLON, RICHARD

Hillel Ticktin
Emeritus Professor, Centre for the
Study of Socialist Theory and
Movements
University of Glasgow
SOCIALISM, MARKET

Ronald Tiersky
Professor of Political Science
Amherst College
JUST WAR

William Timberlake
Professor of Psychological and Brain
Sciences, Neuroscience, and Cognitive
Science, Department of Psychological
and Brain Sciences

Indiana University, Bloomington
REINFORCEMENT THEORIES

Andrew R. Timming
Lecturer in International and
Comparative Human Resource
Management
Manchester Business School,
University of Manchester
RESEARCH, SURVEY

Gizachew Tiruneh
Assistant Professor, Department of
Political Science
University of Central Arkansas
DEMOCRACY
POWER, POLITICAL

Edward A. Tiryakian
Professor Emeritus of Sociology
Duke University
SOCIOLOGY, SCHOOLS IN

Zdravka Todorova
Assistant Professor, Raj Soin College
of Business, Department of Economics
Wright State University
FORCES OF PRODUCTION
LIQUIDITY PREMIUM
PRODUCTION

Stefan Toepler
Associate Professor, Department of
Public and International Affairs
George Mason University
FOUNDATIONS, CHARITABLE

Richard S. J. Tol
Economic and Social Research
Institute, Dublin, Ireland
GREENHOUSE EFFECTS

Donald Tomaskovic-Devey
Professor of Sociology
University of Massachusetts, Amherst
DISCRIMINATION, WAGE, BY
OCCUPATION

Kasaundra M. Tomlin
Assistant Professor
Oakland University, Michigan
EVENT STUDIES

Akinori Tomohara
Assistant Professor, International
Development Division, Graduate
School of Public and International
Affairs
University of Pittsburgh
TRANSFER PRICING

Lars Tønder
Department of Political Science
Northwestern University
EXISTENTIALISM

T. Hunt Tooley
Professor of History
Austin College
BOER WAR

Jan Toporowski
Research Associate in Economics,
School of Oriental and African
Studies, University of London
Research Centre for the History and
Methodology of Economics,
University of Amsterdam
GOODWILL
LEVERAGE

Simon Tormey
Professor of Politics and Critical
Theory
University of Nottingham, United
Kingdom
RADICALISM

José Toro-Alfonso
Associate Professor
University of Puerto Rico
HIV

Chris Toumey
Centenary Research Associate
Professor of Anthropology, USC
NanoCenter
University of South Carolina
GENDER, ALTERNATIVES TO
BINARY
NANOTECHNOLOGY

David A. Traill
University of California, Davis
SCHLIEMANN, HEINRICH

Binh Tran-Nam
Associate Professor, Australian School
of Taxation (Atax)
University of New South Wales,
Australia
TAX EVASION AND TAX
AVOIDANCE

Hans-Michael Trautwein
Professor
University of Oldenburg
INTEREST, NEUTRAL RATE OF

Andrew B. Trigg
Department of Economics

The Open University
CONSPICUOUS CONSUMPTION
SURPLUS VALUE

Rita B. Trivedi
Independent Researcher
Stamford, Connecticut
NAST, THOMAS

Klaus G. Troitzsch
Professor, Department of Information
Systems Research
Universität Koblenz–Landau,
Germany
CLASSICAL STATISTICAL
ANALYSIS
DIFFERENCE EQUATIONS
DIFFERENTIAL EQUATIONS
DISTRIBUTION, POISSON
LINEAR SYSTEMS
STYLIZED FACT

Jan Trost
Professor of Sociology
Uppsala University, Uppsala, Sweden
FAMILY

C. James Trotman
Professor of English; Director,
Frederick Douglass Institute
West Chester University
DOUGLASS, FREDERICK

J. D. Trout
Professor of Philosophy and Adjunct
Professor of the Parmly Hearing
Institute
Loyola University Chicago
DECISION-MAKING
PHILOSOPHY OF SCIENCE

Persefoni V. Tsaliki
Department of Economics
Aristotle University of Thessaloniki,
Greece
CAUSALITY
GOLDEN RULE IN GROWTH
MODELS
HETEROSKEDASTICITY
HUMAN CAPITAL
LIQUIDITY TRAP
MACHINERY
NATIONAL DEBT
RATE OF EXPLOITATION

Charles Tshimanga
Department of History
University of Nevada–Reno
MOBUTU, JOSEPH

Lefteris Tsoulfidis
Associate Professor of Economics
University of Macedonia,
Thessaloniki, Greece
CAMBRIDGE CAPITAL
CONTROVERSY
ECONOMICS, MARXIAN
FULL CAPACITY
MARX, KARL: IMPACT ON
ECONOMICS
PROFITABILITY
QUANTITY THEORY OF MONEY
RICARDIAN EQUIVALENCE

John Tucker
Professor of History
East Carolina University
MEIJI RESTORATION
MIDDLE WAY

Bryan S. Turner
Asia Research Institute
National University of Singapore
ALI, MUHAMMAD (MEMET)
COMPETITION, MANAGED
CONDORCET, MARQUIS DE
GERONTOLOGY
GLAZER, NATHAN
INFIDELS
MENDEL'S LAW
MOYNIHAN, DANIEL PATRICK
MOYNIHAN REPORT
ORGANIZATION MAN
REPATRIATION
SADAT, ANWAR
SANSKRITIZATION
SIKHISM
SKOCPOL, THEDA
TRANSNATIONALISM
VULNERABILITY

Fred Turner
Assistant Professor, Department of
Communication
Stanford University
FUTURE SHOCK

Jack Turner
Assistant Professor, Department of
Political Science
University of Washington
THOREAU, HENRY DAVID

Jonathan H. Turner
Department of Sociology
University of California at Riverside
EMOTION
SPENCER, HERBERT

Robert W. Turner, III
Sociology PhD Candidate

The Graduate Center, City University
of New York
   ATTITUDES, BEHAVIORAL

Stephen J. Turnovsky
Castor Professor of Economics
University of Washington
   THEORY OF SECOND BEST
   TRADE-OFFS

Russell H. Tuttle
University of Chicago
   JOHANSON, DONALD

Luther Tweeten
Emeritus Chaired Professor,
Department of Agricultural,
Environmental, and Development
Economics
Ohio State University
   PROTECTED MARKETS
   QUOTA SYSTEM, FARM

France Winddance Twine
Professor of Sociology,
University of California at Santa
Barbara; Goldsmiths College,
University of London
   PARDO
   RACIAL CLASSIFICATION

Jean-Robert Tyran
Professor of Economics, Department
of Economics
University of Copenhagen, Denmark
   COORDINATION FAILURE

Ian Tyrrell
Scientia Professor of History, School
of History and Philosophy
University of New South Wales
   BEARD, CHARLES AND MARY

Aman Ullah
Professor, Department of Economics
University of California, Riverside
   PROPERTIES OF ESTIMATORS
   (ASYMPTOTIC AND EXACT)
   SEMIPARAMETRIC ESTIMATION

Heidi K. Ullrich
International Centre for Trade and
Sustainable Development
   URUGUAY ROUND

LeRae S. Umfleet
Chief of Collections Management
North Carolina Department of
Cultural Resources
   WILMINGTON RIOT OF 1898

Isaac Unah
Associate Professor of Political Science
University of North Carolina, Chapel
Hill
   FEDERALISM
   JUDICIAL REVIEW

Marion K. Underwood
Professor, School of Behavioral and
Brain Sciences
University of Texas at Dallas
   AGGRESSION

Luis Urrieta, Jr.
Assistant Professor of Cultural Studies
in Education
University of Texas at Austin
   SELLOUTS

Ellen L. Usher
Assistant Professor, Department of
Educational and Counseling
Psychology
University of Kentucky
   STEREOTYPE THREAT

Tracy Vaillancourt
Associate Professor, Department of
Psychology, Neuroscience and
Behaviour
McMaster University
   PEER EFFECTS

Vamsi Vakulabharanam
Department of Economics
Queens College, City University of
New York
   PREBISCH, RAÚL

Nelson P. Valdes
Department of Sociology
University of New Mexico
   CASTRO, FIDEL

Maria G. Valdovinos
Assistant Professor, Department of
Psychology
Drake University
   PSYCHOTROPIC DRUGS

Paul Valent
Independent Researcher, Psychiatrist
Australia
   NECESSITIES

Thomas W. Valente
Department of Preventive Medicine,
Keck School of Medicine
University of Southern California
   NETWORKS, COMMUNICATION

Jeffrey C. Valentine
Assistant Professor, College of
Education and Human Development
University of Louisville
   META-ANALYSIS
   METHODS, QUANTITATIVE
   RELIABILITY, STATISTICAL

Arafaat A. Valiani
Assistant Professor of Sociology,
Department of Anthropology and
Sociology
Williams College
   VIOLENCE

Athanasios Vamvakidis
International Monetary Fund
   ECONOMICS, NOBEL PRIZE IN
   FINANCE

Pierre L. van den Berghe
Professor Emeritus of Sociology and
Anthropology
University of Washington
   POLITICAL CORRECTNESS
   RESEARCH, ETHNOGRAPHIC

Sjaak van der Geest
University of Amsterdam
   SANITATION

Frederick van der Ploeg
Professor of Economics
European University Institute,
Florence, Italy
   ECONOMICS, NEW KEYNESIAN

Adriaan H. van Zon
Senior Research Fellow, UNU-MERIT
Associate Professor of Economics,
Maastricht University, Netherlands
   VINTAGE MODELS

Drew E. VandeCreek
Director of Digital Projects
Northern Illinois University Libraries
   GILDED AGE

Ian Varcoe
Lecturer in Sociology, School of
Sociology and Social Policy
University of Leeds
   GEMEINSCHAFT AND
     GESELLSCHAFT
   GIDDENS, ANTHONY
   SOCIAL SCIENCE, VALUE FREE
   WORLD-SYSTEM

Rossen V. Vassilev
Department of Political Science
The Ohio State University

CENTRISM
CHINESE REVOLUTION
CIVIL SOCIETY
FRANKLIN, BENJAMIN
INDIVIDUALISM
MONARCHY
NEW CLASS, THE
OLIGARCHY, IRON LAW OF
OPIUM WARS
PALESTINE LIBERATION
   ORGANIZATION (PLO)
PERSONALITY, CULT OF
POLITICAL PSYCHOLOGY
POLITICAL SCIENCE,
   BEHAVIORAL
WAR

Robert P. Vecchio
Franklin D. Schurz Professor of
Management, Department of
Management
University of Notre Dame
   LEADERSHIP, CONTINGENCY
    MODELS OF

Benjamin W. Veghte
Assistant Professor, Graduate School of
Social Sciences
University of Bremen, Germany
   WELFARE STATE

Chris Veld
Professor of Finance
University of Stirling
   EQUITY MARKETS
   RISK-RETURN TRADEOFF

Yulia Veld-Merkoulova
Lecturer, Department of Accounting
and Finance
University of Stirling, United
Kingdom
   RISK NEUTRALITY

Francis Vella
Georgetown University
   SELECTION BIAS

William Veloce
Associate Professor, Department of
Economics
Brock University
   BAYES' THEOREM
   LOGISTIC REGRESSION
   MODEL SELECTION TESTS

Padma Venkatachalam
Director of Research and Evaluation,
Howard University Center for Urban
Progress

Department of Economics, Howard
University
   BRIMMER, ANDREW

Esperanza Vera-Toscano
Research Scientist, Instituto de
Estudios Sociales Avanzados
Consejo Superior de Investigaciones
Científicas, Spain
   UNDEREMPLOYMENT

Sidney Verba
Pforzheimer University Professor
Harvard University
   ALMOND, GABRIEL A.

Lucia Vergano
Department of Economic Science
"Marco Fanno"
University of Padua, Italy
   ADVERSE SELECTION

Oskar Verkaaik
Department of Anthropology and
Sociology
University of Amsterdam
   TERRORISM

Matías Vernengo
Assistant Professor
University of Utah
   EXPORT PROMOTION
   MILL, JAMES

Stephen Vertigans
Reader in Sociology
Robert Gordon University, Aberdeen,
U.K.
   SOCIALISM, ISLAMIC

Arnost Vesely
Senior Researcher, Department of
Sociology of Education and
Stratification
Institute of Sociology of the Academy
of Sciences of the Czech Republic
   KNOWLEDGE SOCIETY
   SKILL

Matt Vidal
Postdoctoral Fellow, Institute for
Research on Labor and Employment
University of California, Los Angeles
   TIME AND MOTION STUDY

M. Bess Vincent
Department of Sociology
Tulane University
   STREET CULTURE

W. Kip Viscusi
University Distinguished Professor
Vanderbilt University Law School
   OCCUPATIONAL SAFETY

P. V. Viswanath
Professor of Finance, Lubin School of
Business
Pace University
   BULL AND BEAR MARKETS
   SPREADS, BID-ASK

Erik Voeten
Peter F. Krogh Assistant Professor of
Global Justice and Geopolitics
Edmund A. Walsh School of Foreign
Service, Georgetown University
   UNITED NATIONS

William B. Vogele
Professor of Political Science, Program
in Social and Political Systems
Pine Manor College
   PASSIVE RESISTANCE

John von Heyking
Department of Political Science
University of Lethbridge
   POLITICS

Antina von Schnitzler
Department of Anthropology
Columbia University
   LIBERALISM
   NEOLIBERALISM

Roos Vonk
Radboud University Nijmegen, The
Netherlands
   INGRATIATION

Christopher Voparil
Assistant Professor, Graduate College
Union Institute & University, Ohio
   TYRANNY OF THE MAJORITY

Jack Vowles
Professor, Department of Politics
University of Exeter
   PLURALITY

Piet de Vries
Associate Professor
University of Twente, Enschede, The
Netherlands
   COASE, RONALD
   COASE THEOREM
   SOCIAL COST

Elizabeth Arbuckle Wabindato
Assistant Professor, Department of
Political Science
University of Wisconsin–Stevens Point
 MEANS, RUSSELL

Robert H. Wade
Professor of Political Economy
London School of Economics and
Political Science
 WASHINGTON CONSENSUS

Richard E. Wagner
Holbart Harris Professor of Economics
George Mason University
 FINANCE, PUBLIC

Brigitte S. Waldorf
Department of Agricultural
Economics
Purdue University
 LOG-LINEAR MODELS

Corey D. B. Walker
Assistant Professor, Department of
Africana Studies
Brown University
 FORMAN, JAMES

Sharon Wall
Assistant Professor, History Program
University of Northern British
Columbia
 GOING NATIVE

Daniel B. Wallace
Professor of New Testament Studies
Dallas Theological Seminary
 SHARP, GRANVILLE

Sally Wallace
Professor of Economics, Andrew
Young School of Policy Studies
Georgia State University
 TAX INCIDENCE

W. D. Walls
Professor, Department of Economics
University of Calgary
 ENERGY INDUSTRY
 ENTERTAINMENT INDUSTRY

Frank Walsh
School of Economics
University College, Dublin
 MONOPSONY

Margaret Walsh
Keene State College
 FEMALE-HEADED FAMILIES

William B. Walstad
John T. and Mable M. Hay Professor
of Economics
University of Nebraska–Lincoln
 NATIONAL ASSESSMENT OF
 EDUCATIONAL PROGRESS

John L. Waltman
Professor of Management and
Director, Merlanti Ethics Program
Eastern Michigan University
 COMMUNICATION

Xiaodong Wang
Research Analyst, Texas Guaranteed
Student Loan Corporation
Austin, TX
 MIGRATION, RURAL TO URBAN

Benedicta Ward
Reader in the History of Christian
Spirituality, Theology
Oxford University
 MIRACLES

Warren Waren
PhD Candidate, Department of
Sociology
Texas A&M University
 DEMOGRAPHY, SOCIAL
 GRAUNT, JOHN

Andrew J. Waskey
Professor of Social Science
Dalton State College
 CONUNDRUM
 OCCAM'S RAZOR
 SUDRAS
 VAISYAS

Frederick Wasser
Professor, Department of Television
and Radio
Brooklyn College, New York City
 TECHNOLOGY, VIDEO

Anthony M. C. Waterman
St John's College, Winnipeg
 MALTHUS, THOMAS ROBERT

Daphne C. Watkins
Research Fellow, National Institute of
Mental Health
Institute for Social Research,
University of Michigan
 SMOKING

Harry L. Watson
Professor, Department of History, and
Director, Center for the Study of the
American South
University of North Carolina–Chapel
Hill
 SOUTH, THE (USA)

Micah J. Watson
Assistant Professor
Union University
 LAW

Wendy L. Watson
Assistant Professor, Department of
Political Science
Southern Methodist University
 CONSTITUTION, U.S.
 JUDICIARY
 JURISPRUDENCE
 JURY SELECTION
 SEXUAL HARASSMENT
 SUPREME COURT, U.S.

David Harrington Watt
Associate Professor of History
Temple University
 PROTESTANTISM

Michael Watts
Class of '63 Professor
University of California, Berkeley
 EXPLOITATION

Christopher Way
Associate Professor of Government
Cornell University
 PROLIFERATION, NUCLEAR

Gifford Weary
Professor and Psychology Department
Chair
The Ohio State University
 ATTRIBUTION

Catherine Elizabeth Weaver
Assistant Professor of Political Science
University of Kansas
 LEAGUE OF NATIONS

Jennifer L. Weber
Assistant Professor, Department of
History
University of Kansas
 CONFEDERATE STATES OF
 AMERICA
 LINCOLN, ABRAHAM
 U.S. CIVIL WAR

John Weeks
Professor Emeritus, School of Oriental and African Studies
University of London
COMPETITION, MARXIST

Simone A. Wegge
Associate Professor of Economics
City University of New York
IMMIGRANTS, EUROPEAN

Seth Weinberger
Assistant Professor, Department of Politics and Government
University of Puget Sound
ARAB-ISRAELI WAR OF 1967
DETERRENCE
PUTIN, VLADIMIR

Raymond M. Weinstein
Department of Sociology
University of South Carolina Aiken
GREAT SOCIETY, THE

Rhona S. Weinstein
Professor of Psychology
University of California, Berkeley
TEACHER EXPECTATIONS

E. Roy Weintraub
Professor, Department of Economics
Duke University
MICROFOUNDATIONS

Paul Weirich
Professor, Department of Philosophy
University of Missouri–Columbia
RATIONALITY
REPLICATOR DYNAMICS
TIME PREFERENCE
UTILITY, OBJECTIVE

Avi Weiss
Professor, Department of Economics
Bar–Ilan University
MORAL HAZARD

Jillian Todd Weiss
Associate Professor of Law and Society
Ramapo College of New Jersey
HETERONORMATIVITY

Thomas E. Weisskopf
Professor, Department of Economics
University of Michigan
AFFIRMATIVE ACTION
QUOTA SYSTEMS

Paul Weithman
Professor, Department of Philosophy

University of Notre Dame
RAWLS, JOHN

Ronald Weitzer
Professor, Department of Sociology
George Washington University
PROSTITUTION

Jeffrey B. Wenger
School of Public and International Affairs, Department of Public Administration and Policy
University of Georgia
McFADDEN, DANIEL L.

Carl Wennerlind
Assistant Professor of History
Barnard College
MONEY, EXOGENOUS

Gregory J. Werden
Senior Economic Counsel, Antitrust Division
U.S. Department of Justice
ANTITRUST

James L. Werth, Jr.
Radford University, Virginia
The University of Akron, Ohio
EUTHANASIA AND ASSISTED SUICIDE

Michael Wertheimer
Professor Emeritus of Psychology
University of Colorado at Boulder
GESTALT PSYCHOLOGY

Burns H. Weston
Bessie Dutton Murray Distinguished Professor of Law Emeritus; Senior Scholar, UI Center for Human Rights, University of Iowa
Vermont Law School Visiting Distinguished Professor of International Law and Policy
CHILD LABOR

Charles J. Whalen
Editor, *Perspectives on Work*
Labor and Employment Relations Association and the University of Illinois Press
FULL EMPLOYMENT

Arthur L. Whaley
Visiting Scholar Program
Russell Sage Foundation, New York
PARANOIA

Douglas R. White
School of Social Sciences
University of California, Irvine
STANDARD CROSS-CULTURAL SAMPLE

Halbert L. White
Chancellor's Associates Distinguished Professor
University of California, San Diego
HAUSMAN TESTS

Melissa Autumn White
PhD Candidate, Women's Studies
Researcher, Center for International and Security Studies, York University
SAID, EDWARD

Paul F. Whiteley
Professor, Department of Government
University of Essex
CONSERVATIVE PARTY
(BRITAIN)

Stephen J. Whitfield
Professor, Department of American Studies
Brandeis University
ARENDT, HANNAH

Wythe L. Whiting
Assistant Professor, Department of Psychology
Washington and Lee University
MEMORY IN PSYCHOLOGY

Aaron L. Wichman
Postdoctoral Researcher and Teacher, Psychology Department
The Ohio State University
ATTRIBUTION

Krista E. Wiegand
Assistant Professor, Department of Political Science
Georgia Southern University
BORDERS
MORGENTHAU, HANS
TERRORISTS

Christopher Wilkes
Professor of Sociology
Pacific University
CASINO CAPITALISM

Steven I. Wilkinson
Associate Professor of Political Science
University of Chicago
CONGRESS PARTY, INDIA

Jennifer Willard
Doctoral Student, Department of
Psychology
Iowa State University
SELF-FULFILLING PROPHECIES

Victoria W. Willard
Graduate Student, Psychology and
Neuroscience
Duke University
PSYCHOSOMATICS, SOCIAL

Adrienne A. Williams
Research Associate, Department of
Psychology
Duke University
HITE, SHERE

Jeff Williams
Literature Professor, Department of
Humanities
National University of La Rioja,
Argentina
COMIC BOOKS
STAR WARS
WIZARD OF OZ

Joseph W. Williams
Florida State University, Tallahassee
BUDDHA
BUDDHISM
MISSIONARIES

Kim M. Williams
Associate Professor of Public Policy
John F. Kennedy School of
Government, Harvard University
MULTIRACIAL MOVEMENT

Vernon J. Williams, Jr.
Professor, Department of African
American and African Diaspora
Studies
Indiana University
BENIGN NEGLECT

Thomas A. Wills
Professor, Department of
Epidemiology and Population Health
Albert Einstein College of Medicine
DIATHESIS-STRESS MODEL
STRESS-BUFFERING MODEL

Franke Wilmer
Montana State University
SOVEREIGNTY

Daniel J. Wilson
Economist

Federal Reserve Bank of San Francisco
USER COST

Frank Harold Wilson
University of Wisconsin–Milwaukee
INTEGRATION

Harlan Wilson
Professor of Politics
Oberlin College
TECHNOCRAT
TECHNOPHOBIA

Pamela S. Wilson
Associate Professor, Department of
Communication
Reinhardt College
CHEROKEES

Paul W. Wilson
Professor, Department of Economics
Clemson University
BOOTSTRAP METHOD
CENSORING, LEFT AND RIGHT
DATA ENVELOPMENT ANALYSIS
DURATION MODELS
LARGE SAMPLE PROPERTIES
LEAST SQUARES, ORDINARY
NONPARAMETRIC REGRESSION
STATISTICAL NOISE
VARIABLES, RANDOM

Peter H. Wilson
GF Grant Professor of History
University of Hull
HOLY ROMAN EMPIRE

Vincent L. Wimbush
Professor, School of Religion; Director,
Institute for Signifying Scriptures
Claremont Graduate University
RACE AND RELIGION

Michael Winkelman
School of Human Evolution and
Social Change
Arizona State University
SHAMANS

Carol Wise
Associate Professor
School of International Relations,
University of Southern California
DEPENDENCY THEORY
ECONOMIC COMMISSION FOR
LATIN AMERICA AND THE
CARIBBEAN (ECLAC)
WORLD BANK, THE

Richard Wiseman
Professor of Psychology

University of Hertfordshire, United
Kingdom
LUCK

Edward J. Wisniewski
Associate Professor of Psychology
University of North Carolina at
Greensboro
MOOD CONGRUENT RECALL

Scott T. Wolf
Department of Psychology
University of North Carolina at
Chapel Hill
ROLE CONFLICT
SCHEMAS

Edward N. Wolff
Professor of Economics
New York University
INEQUALITY, WEALTH
RATE OF PROFIT

Kenneth K. Wong
Brown University
DECENTRALIZATION
DOCUMENTARY STUDIES

Phillip K. Wood
Professor, Quantitative Psychology,
Department of Psychological Sciences
University of Missouri–Columbia
VARIANCE-COVARIANCE
MATRIX

Edward J. Woodhouse
Professor of Political Science,
Department of Science and
Technology Studies
Rensselaer Polytechnic Institute
LINDBLOM, CHARLES EDWARD

Drexel G. Woodson
Associate Research Anthropologist,
Bureau of Applied Research in
Anthropology
University of Arizona
TROUILLOT, MICHEL-ROLPH

Frances Woolley
Professor of Economics, Department
of Economics
Carleton University, Ottawa, Ontario,
Canada
ECONOMICS, PUBLIC

Kenton W. Worcester
Chair, Division of Social Sciences
Marymount Manhattan College
JAMES, C. L. R.

Stephen Worchel
Professor of Psychology
University of Hawaii at Hilo
REACTANCE THEORY

Tiemen Woutersen
Professor, Department of Economics
Johns Hopkins University
VARIABLES, PREDETERMINED

L. Randall Wray
Professor of Economics, University of Missouri–Kansas City
Senior Scholar, Levy Economics Institute of Bard College
JOB GUARANTEE

Earl Wright, II
Chairperson and Associate Professor, Department of Sociology
Texas Southern University
SOCIOLOGY, AMERICAN

Scott Wright
Professor, Department of History
University of St. Thomas, St. Paul, MN
ALI, MUHAMMAD (USA)
HOOVER, J. EDGAR
JAMES, WILLIAM
SHINTO

Teresa Wright
Professor, Department of Political Science
California State University, Long Beach
DISSIDENTS

Raymond F. Wylie
Department of International Relations
Lehigh University
MAO ZEDONG

Clifford Wymbs
Associate Professor, Department of Marketing and International Business
Baruch College, City University of New York
LONG WAVES

Jonathan R. Wynn
Lecturer, Department of Sociology
Smith College
TRAVEL AND TRAVEL WRITING

Anastasia Xenias
Adjunct Assistant Professor, Department of Political Science
City University of New York

PEACEFUL COEXISTENCE
SYSTEM ANALYSIS
WORLD TRADE ORGANIZATION
WORLD WAR II

Nicholas Xenos
Professor, Department of Political Science
University of Massachusetts, Amherst
NEOCONSERVATISM

Yu Xie
Otis Dudley Duncan Professor of Sociology
University of Michigan
DUNCAN, OTIS DUDLEY

Xiaojian Xu
Department of Mathematics
Brock University, St. Catharines, Ontario
PROBABILITY, LIMITS IN

Elena S. Yakunina
The University of Akron, Ohio
EUTHANASIA AND ASSISTED SUICIDE

Antronette (Toni) K. Yancey
Professor, Department of Health Services, School of Public Health
University of California, Los Angeles
ROLE MODELS

Oscar Ybarra
Associate Professor of Psychology
University of Michigan
MISANTHROPY

Rosemary Yeilding
Department of Sociology
Washington State University
MARRIAGE

Kevin A. Yelvington
Associate Professor, Department of Anthropology
University of South Florida
HERSKOVITS, MELVILLE J.

John Yinger
Professor of Economics and Public Administration, The Maxwell School
Syracuse University
AUDITS FOR DISCRIMINATION

Jeremy R. Youde
Assistant Professor, Department of Political Science

Grinnell College
AMERICANISM

Alford A. Young, Jr.
Department of Sociology and Center for Afroamerican and African Studies
Univeristy of Michigan
BLACK SOCIOLOGISTS
FRAZIER, E. FRANKLIN

Brian M. Young
School of Psychology
University of Exeter, United Kingdom
ECONOMIC PSYCHOLOGY

Serinity Young
Division of Anthropology
American Museum of Natural History
NIRVĀNA

Myeong-Su Yun
Assistant Professor, Department of Economics
Tulane University
BLINDER-OAXACA DECOMPOSITION TECHNIQUE

Maria Zadoroznyj
Department of Sociology
Flinders University, Adelaide, Australia
NATURAL CHILDBIRTH

Avihu Zakai
Professor, Department of History
The Hebrew University of Jerusalem
THEOCRACY

Ernő Zalai
Professor, Department of Mathematical Economics and Economic Analysis
Corvinus University of Budapest, Hungary
VON NEUMANN, JOHN

Paul Zarembka
Professor, Department of Economics
State University of New York at Buffalo
ACCUMULATION OF CAPITAL

Arnold Zellner
H. G. B. Alexander Distinguished Service Professor Emeritus of Economics and Statistics, Graduate School of Business, University of Chicago

Adjunct Professor, Department of
Agricultural and Resource Economics,
University of California, Berkeley
  SEEMINGLY UNRELATED
    REGRESSIONS

Tao Zha
Senior Policy Advisor
Federal Reserve Bank of Atlanta
  NORMALIZATION

Li Zhang
Assistant Professor in Sociology at the
Wilder School
Virginia Commonwealth University
  FERTILITY, HUMAN
  POPULATION GROWTH

Zhongwei Zhao
Senior Fellow, Demography and
Sociology Program, Research School
of Social Sciences
Australian National University
  POPULATION CONTROL

Buhong Zheng
Department of Economics
University of Colorado at Denver and
Health Sciences Center
  POVERTY, INDICES OF

Benjamin Ziemann
Lecturer, Department of History
University of Sheffield, United
Kingdom
  PACIFISM
  PEACE MOVEMENTS

Thomas Ziesemer
Associate Professor of Economics,
Department of Economics
University of Maastricht and
UNU–MERIT
  LOAN PUSHING

Stephen T. Ziliak
Professor of Economics
Roosevelt University
  NORMATIVE SOCIAL SCIENCE
  POSITIVE SOCIAL SCIENCE
  RHETORIC

Stacy M. Zimmerman
Tufts University
  ADOLESCENT PSYCHOLOGY

Christian Zimmermann
Associate Professor, Department of
Economics
University of Connecticut
  EMPLOYMENT

Ekkart Zimmermann
Chair in Macrosociology
Dresden University of Technology
  ETHNIC FRACTIONALIZATION
  STATELESSNESS

Daniel John Zizzo
Senior Lecturer, School of Economics
University of East Anglia
  ENDOGENOUS PREFERENCES
  EXPECTATIONS, RATIONAL
  PREFERENCES,
    INTERDEPENDENT

Michael W. Zuckerman
Professor, Department of History
University of Pennsylvania
  SPOCK, BENJAMIN

Marlene Zuk
Professor, Department of Biology
University of California, Riverside
  SEXUAL SELECTION THEORY

Lorna Lueker Zukas
Associate Professor, Department of
Social Sciences
National University, Costa Mesa, CA
  G7 COUNTRIES

Sharon Zukin
Broeklundian Professor, Department
of Sociology
Brooklyn College and Graduate
School of the City University of
New York
  GENTRIFICATION

Christopher F. Zurn
Associate Professor, Philosophy
Department
University of Kentucky
  INTERSUBJECTIVITY

Todd J. Zywicki
Professor of Law
George Mason University School of
Law
  CULTURAL GROUP SELECTION

Thematic Outline

The following classification of articles, arranged thematically, gives an overview of the variety of entries and the breadth of subjects treated in the encyclopedia. Along with the index in volume 9 and the alphabetical arrangement of all entries, the thematic outline should aid in the location of topics. Ideally, this feature will facilitate a kind of browsing that invites the reader to discover additional articles, related perhaps tangentially to those originally sought. Because the rubrics used as section headings are not mutually exclusive, certain entries in the Encyclopedia are listed in more than one section below.

1. Anthropology

2. Archaeology

3. Arts, Media, and Popular Culture

4. Demography

5. Econometrics

6. Economic Development

7. Economics

8. Education

9. Geography

10. History and Historiography

11. Interdisciplinary Studies

12. International Relations, Organization, and Law

13. Law

14. Linguistics

15. Methodology

16. Personality

17. Philosophy of Science

18. Political Science

19. Professions

20. Psychiatry

21. Psychology, Applied

22. Psychology, General

23. Religion

24. Social Issues and Policy

25. Social Psychology

26. Social Sciences

27. Societies

28. Sociology

ANTHROPOLOGY

Acting White
African American Studies
African Americans
African Crisis Response Initiative
African Diaspora
African National Congress
Africville (Canada)
AIDS/HIV in Developing Countries, Impact of
Alpha-male
American Anthropological Association

American Dream
Americanism
Anthropology
Anthropology, Biological
Anthropology, British
Anthropology, Linguistic
Anthropology, Medical
Anthropology, Public
Anthropology, U.S.
Anthropology, Urban
Aryans
Asiatic Mode of Production
Birth Control
Births, Out-of-Wedlock
Black Towns
Blood and Bloodline
Borders
Brahmins
Buraku or *Burakumin*
Burial Grounds
Burial Grounds, African
Burial Grounds, Native American
Cannibalism
Caste, Anthropology of
Cherokees
Childlessness
Children
Chinese Americans
Civil Society
Civilization
Clock Time
Collective Memory
Colonialism

Communication
Communism, Primitive
Creole
Critical Theory
Cultural Group Selection
Cultural Landscape
Cultural Relativism
Cultural Resource Management
Cultural Rights
Cultural Studies
Cultural Tourism
Culture
Culture, Low and High
Dalits
Dance
Darwinism, Social
Death and Dying
Diaspora
Discourse
Distinctions, Social and Cultural
Dowry and Bride Price
Dravidians
Eroticism
Essentialism
Ethnic Conflict
Ethnicity
Ethno-epidemiological Methodology
Ethnography
Ethnology and Folklore
Ethno-methodology
Eugenics
Exoticism
Fahrenheit 9/11
Family
Fatherhood
Feminism
Fertility, Human
Female-Headed Families
Femininity
Food
Gaze, Colonial
Gaze, The
Globalization, Anthropological
  Aspects of
Going Native
Identification, Racial
Identity
Immigrants, Black
Intersectionality
Intersubjectivity
Inuit
Islam, Shia and Sunni
Japanese Americans
Kinship, Evolutionary Theory of

Kshatriyas
Leisure
Landlords
Magic
Malnutrition
Marx, Karl: Impact on Anthropology
Marxism
Masculinity
Masculinity Studies
Matriarchy
Maturation
Mecca
Medicine
Medicis, The
Memory
Minstrelsy
Modernism
Modernity
Modernization
Mulatto Escape Hatch
Music
Mysticism
Myth and Mythology
Nation
National Geographic
Nationalism and Nationality
Nationalization
Native Americans
Natives
Nativism
Navajos
Negro
Nonblacks
Nonwhites
North and South, The (Global)
Observer, Participant
Oppositionality, Schooling
Organization Theory
Orientalism
Other, The
Palestinian Diaspora
Pan-Africanism
Pan-Arabism
Pan-Caribbeanism
Peasantry
Popular Culture
Postmodernism
Plantation
Practice Theory
Pre-Columbian Peoples
Primates
Primitivism
Queer Studies
Race and Anthropology

Rape
Realist Theory
Reciprocity
Reciprocity, Norm of
Reflexivity
Relativism
Religion
Rites of Passage
Rituals
Sambo
Sanskritization
Social Theory
Standard Cross-Cultural Sample
Stare, The
Street Culture
Subjectivity
Sudras
Tally's Corner
Tourism Industry
Travel and Travel Writing
Tribalism
Tribe
Trigueño
Vaisyas
Values
Womanism
Women's Liberation
Women's Movement
Women's Studies
Work and Women
World War I
World War II
Zionism

Biographies

Benedict, Ruth
Boas, Franz
Bourdieu, Pierre
Darwin, Charles
Diop, Cheikh Anta
Dobzhansky, Theodosius
Evans-Pritchard, E. E.
Geertz, Clifford
Herskovits, Melville J.
Hurston, Zora Neale
Johanson, Donald
Kroeber, Alfred Louis
Leakey, Richard
Lewis, Oscar
Lowie, Robert
Malinowski, Bronislaw
Mead, Margaret
Mintz, Sidney W.
Montagu, Ashley

Ogbu, John U.
Ortiz, Fernando
Radcliffe-Brown, A. R.
Sahlins, Marshall
Said, Edward
Schliemann, Heinrich
Trouillot, Michel-Rolph
Turner, Victor
Wolf, Eric

ARCHAEOLOGY

Archaeology
Architecture
Burial Grounds
Burial Grounds, African
Burial Grounds, Native American
Caribbean, The
Civilization
Colonialism
Common Land
Cultural Landscape
Cultural Resource Management
Cultural Studies
Culture
Development, Rural
Diaspora
Fertile Crescent
Fertility, Land
Food
Incas
Irrigation
Metropolis
Olmecs
Pre-Columbian Peoples
Slave Lives, Archaeology of
Vinyl Recordings

Biographies

Diop, Cheikh Anta
Schliemann, Heinrich

**ARTS, MEDIA, AND POPULAR
CULTURE**

Bamboozled
Battle of Algiers, The
Birth of a Nation
Black Arts Movement
Blackface
Bluegrass
Blues
Calypso
Cartoons, Political
Classical Music
Comedy

Comic Books
Communication
Computers: Science and Society
Conundrum
Creativity
Critical Theory
Cultural Resource Management
Cultural Tourism
Culture, Low and High
Dance
Documentary Studies
Entertainment Industry
Ethnography
Ethnomusicology
Exoticism
Fahrenheit 9/11
Fiction
Film Industry
Gone With the Wind
Harlem Renaissance
Hip Hop
Internet
Jazz
Journalism
Literature
Matrix, The
Media
Medium Is the Message
Memín Pinguín
Metropolis
Minstrelsy
Modernism
Music
Myth and Mythology
Naturalism
Nature vs. Nurture
Nursery Rhymes
Objectivism
Objectivity
Obscenity
Parody
Patriotism
Persuasion, Message-based
Popular Culture
Popular Music
Postmodernism
Poststructuralism
Primitivism
Radio Talk Show
Reggae
Rock 'n' Roll
Sambo
Satire
Science Fiction

Star Trek
Star Wars
Stepford Wives
Storytelling
Stream of Consciousness
Television
Theater
Uncle Tom
Vinyl Recordings
Visual Arts
War and Peace
Wizard of Oz
World Music

Biographies

Alger, Horatio
Disney, Walt
Fanon, Frantz
Friedan, Betty
Fuller, Buckminster
Garvey, Marcus
Gobineau, Comte de
Goffman, Erving
Hall, Staurt
Hurston, Zora Neale
Jacobs, Jane
Jencks, Christopher
Kariel, Henry S.
Le Guin, Ursula K.
Leary, Timothy
Lynd, Staughton
Machiavelli, Niccolò
McLuhan, Marshall
Nast, Thomas
Ortiz, Fernando
Robeson, Paul
Said, Edward
Sartre, Jean-Paul
Solzhenitsyn, Aleksandr
Thoreau, Henry David
Voltaire

DEMOGRAPHY

Birth Control
Childlessness
Children
Club of Rome
Contraception
Demographic Transition
Demography
Demography, Social
Diversity
Fertility, Human
Gender

Gender Studies
Generation X
Genetic Testing
Genomics
Groups
Identification, Racial
Morbidity and Mortality
Nation
Natives
Nativism
Neighborhoods
Overpopulation
Population Control
Population Growth
Population Studies
Racial Classification
Zero Population Growth

Biographies

Boserup, Ester
Galton, Francis
Graunt, John
Ibn Khaldūn
Malthus, Thomas Robert

ECONOMETRICS

Bayesian Econometrics
Blinder-Oaxaca Decomposition
    Technique
Bootstrap Method
Censoring, Left and Right
Censoring, Sample
Central Limit Theorem
Chow Test
Classical Statistical Analysis
Cliometrics
Codetermination
Cointegration
Duration Models
Econometric Decomposition
Econometrics
Eigen-Values and Eigen-Vecotors,
    Perron-Frobenius Theorem:
    Economic Applications
Fixed Effects Regression
Hausman Tests
Heckman Selection Correction
    Procedure
Heteroskedasticity
Identification Problem
Inverse Matrix
Least Squares, Ordinary
Least Squares, Three-Stage
Least Squares, Two-Stage
Logistic Regression

Matrix Algebra
Maximum Likelihood Regression
Measurement Error
Multicollinearity
Ordinary Least Squares Regression
Probabilistic Regression
Properties of Estimators (Asymptotic
    and Exact)
Regression
Regression Analysis
Simultaneous Equation Bias
Specification
Specification Error
Specification Tests
Statistics
Time Series Regression
Tobit
Unit Root and Cointegration
    Regression
Variables, Latent
Variables, Predetermined
Variables, Random

Biographies

Klein, Lawrence
McFadden, Daniel L.
Solow, Robert M.
Tinbergen, Jan

ECONOMIC DEVELOPMENT

Agricultural Economics
Agricultural Industry
Appalachia
Capitalism
Capitalism, State
Collectivism
Colonialism
Community Economic Development
Democratization
Demographic Transition
Dependency Theory
Developing Countries
Development
Development Economics
Development in Sociology
Economic Growth
Economics, Classical
Feudal Mode of Production
Green Revolution
Imperialism
Industrialization
Industry
Infant Industry
Kuznets Hypothesis

Laissez Faire
Latifundia
Land Reform
Limits to Growth
Machinery
Machinery Question, The
Market Economy
Mercantilism
Migration
Migration, Rural to Urban
Mode of Production
Modernism
Modernity
Modernization
Nanotechnology
Nationalism and Nationality
Nationalization
Natural Disasters
Neighborhoods
Neocolonialism
Neoinstitutionalism
Neoliberalism
Networks, Communication
New Deal, The
North and South, The (Global)
Nouveaux Riches
Nutrition
O-Ring Theory
Offshore Banking
Operation Bootstrap
Outsourcing
Overpopulation
Peaceful Coexistence
Peasantry
Physical Quality of Life Index
Physiocracy
Planning
Population Growth
Poverty, Indices of
Prebisch-Singer Hypothesis
Protestant Ethic, The
Quota System, Farm
Research and Development
Sanitation
Slavery Industry
Socialism
Socialism, African
Socialism, Islamic
Socialism, Market
Stages of Economic Growth
Technological Progress, Economic
    Growth
Underdevelopment
Unequal Exchange

Urbanization
Washington Consensus
Work and Women

Biographies

Amin, Samir
Boserup, Ester
De Soto, Hernando
Frank, Andre Gunder
Hilferding, Rudolph
Inikori, Joseph
Ladejinsky, Wolf
Lewis, W. Arthur
Mill, John Stuart
Minsky, Hyman
Mitchell, Wesley Clair
Myrdal, Gunnar
Nkrumah, Kwame
North, Douglass
Prebisch, Raúl
Ricardo, David
Schumpeter, Joseph
Sen, Amartya
Singer, Hans
Smith, Adam
Solow, Robert M.
Sombart, Werner
Tawney, R. H.
Taylor, Lance
Weber, Max
Williams, Eric

ECONOMICS

Absolute and Comparative Advantage
Absolute Income Hypothesis
Accumulation of Capital
Adaptive Expectations
Adverse Selection
Aggregate Demand
Aggregate Demand and Supply Price
Aggregate Supply
Agribusiness
Agricultural Economics
Agricultural Industry
American Economic Association
Antitrust
Arbitrage and Arbitrageurs
Arrow Possibility Theorem
Arrow-Debreu Model
Auctions
Audits for Discrimination
Austrian Economics
Automobile Industry
Autoregressive Models

Average and Marginal Cost
Aviation Industry
Backwash Effects
Balance of Payments
Balance of Trade
Banana Industry
Banana Parable
Banking
Banking Industry
Barriers to Trade
Barro-Grossman Model
Bauxite Industry
Beauty Contest Metaphor
Beggar-Thy-Neighbor
Bequests
Beveridge Curve
Blinder-Oaxaca Decomposition
    Technique
Bribery
Bull and Bear Markets
Business
Business Cycles, Empirical Literature
Business Cycles, Political
Business Cycles, Real
Business Cycles, Theories
Butterfly Effect
Cambridge Capital Controversy
Capital
Capital Controls
Capital Flight
Capitalism, Black
Capitalist Mode of Production
Carrying Cost
Catastrophe Theory
Cattle Industry
Causality
Census
Central Banks
Change, Technological
Chaos Theory
Chicago School
Choice in Economics
Class, Leisure
Cliometrics
Coase Theorem
Cobweb Cycles
Codetermination
Coffee Industry
Colony, Internal
Common Good, The
Common Knowledge Rationality
    Games
Common Market, The
Communism

Communism, Primitive
Comparative Dynamics
Comparative Statics
Compensation, Unemployment
Competition
Competition, Imperfect
Competition, Managed
Competition, Marxist
Competition, Monopolistic
Competition, Perfect
Conditionality
Conjunctures, Transitional
Conspicuous Consumption
Constrained Choice
Consumer
Consumer Surplus
Consumerism
Consumption
Consumption Function
Contango
Cooperatives
Copper Industry
Corn Laws
Corporate Social Responsibility
Corporate Strategies
Corporations
Corporatism
Cosmopolitanism
Cost-Benefit Analysis
Cotton Industry
Creative Destruction
Crony Capitalism
Crowding Hypothesis
Cumulative Causation
Currency
Currency Appreciation and
    Depreciation
Currency Devaluation and
    Revaluation
Data Envelopment Analysis
Decentralization
Demand
Depression, Economic
Deregulation
Determinism, Biological
Determinism, Environmental
Determinism, Technological
Developing Countries
Development
Development, Rural
Development Economics
Diamond Industry
Difference Equations
Difference Principle

Differential Equations
Dirigiste
Dirty Float
Discounted Present Value
Discouraged Workers
Distortions
Divestiture
Divisia Monetary Index
Division of Labor
Dornbusch-Fischer-Samuelson Model
Dowry and Bride Price
Dual Economy
Dumping, Product
Dutch Disease
Econometrics
Economic Commission for Latin
　America and the Caribbean
　(ECLAC)
Economic Crises
Economic Growth
Economic Methodology
Economic Model
Economic Psychology
Economic Rhetoric
Economics
Economics, Behavioral
Economics, Classical
Economics, Experimental
Economics, Institutional
Economics, International
Economics, Islamic
Economics, Keynesian
Economics, Labor
Economics, Marxian
Economics, Neoclassical
Economics, Neo-Ricardian
Economics, New Classical
Economics, New Keynesian
Economics, Nobel Prize in
Economics, Post Keynesian
Economics, Public
Economics, Stratification
Economics of Control
Economies, Transitional
Efficient Market Hypothesis
Eigen-Values and Eigen-Vectors,
　Perron-Frobenius Theorem:
　Economic Applications
Elasticity
Employment
Employment, White Collar
Endogenous Preferences
Energy
Energy Industry

Energy Sector
Engineering
Enterprise
Entertainment Industry
Environmental Impact Assessment
Environmental Kuznets Curves
Equilibrium in Economics
Equity Markets
Error-correction Mechanisms
Ethics
Ethics, Business
Ethnic Enterprises
Event Studies
Evolutionary Games
Excess Demand
Excess Supply
Exchange Rates
Exchange Value
Exchangeability
Expectations
Expectations, Implicit
Expectations, Rational
Expectations, Static
Exploitation
Export Penetration
Export Promotion
Exports
Externality
Factories
Federal Reserve System, U.S.
Federal Reserve System, U.S.: Analysis
Fertility, Land
Feudal Mode of Production
Feudalism
Fields' Index of Economic Inequality
Film Industry
Finance
Finance, Public
Financial Instability Hypothesis
Financial Markets
Firm
Fishing Industry
Fixed Coefficients Production
　Function
Flexibility
Flow
Flower Industry
Food
Forces of Production
Ford Motor Company
Foresight, Perfect
Formation, Social
Forward and Futures Markets
Franchise

Free Rider
Free Trade
Full Capacity
Full Employment
Functionings
G7 Countries
G8 Countries
Game Theory
Gender Gap
General Equilibrium
Generalized Least Squares
Gini Coefficient
Glass Ceiling
Globalization, Social and Economic
　Aspects of
Gold
Gold Industry
Gold Standard
Golden Rule in Growth Models
Goods, Nontraded
Goodwill
Grameen Bank
Great Depression
Great Tulip Mania, The
Gross Domestic Product
Gross National Income
Growth Accounting
Growth Curve Analysis
Harris-Todaro Model
Health Economics
Heckman Selection Correction
　Procedure
Heckscher-Ohlin-Samuelson Model
Hedging
Hedonic Prices
Herd Behavior
Hessian Matrix
Hidden Persuaders
Human Capital
Hume Process
Ideal Type
Identification Problem
Identity Matrix
Immiserizing Growth
Import Penetration
Import Promotion
Import Substitution
Imports
In Vivo Transfers
Inada Conditions
Income
Income Distribution
Income Maintenance Experiments
Income Tax, Corporate

Industrialization
Industry
Infant Industry
Inference, Bayesian
Inflation
Informal Economy
Information, Asymmetric
Information, Economics of
Inheritance
Inheritance Tax
Initial Public Offering (IPO)
Input-Output Matrix
Insurance
Insurance Industry
Integrated Public Use Microdata Series
Interest, Natural Rate of
Interest, Neutral Rate of
Interest, Own Rate of
Interest, Real Rate of
Interest Rates
Interest Rates, Nominal
International Economic Order
International Monetary Fund
International Nongovernmental
  Organizations (INGOs)
Internet Bubble
Inventories
Investment
Investors
Investors, Institutional
Involuntary Unemployment
IS-LM Model
Isolationism
Jacobian Matrix
J-Curve
Jajmani Matrix
Job Guarantee
Kuznets Hypothesis
Labor
Labor, Marginal Product of
Labor, Surplus: Conventional
  Economics
Labor, Surplus: Marxist and Radical
  Economics
Labor Demand
Labor Force Participation
Labor Market
Labor Market Segmentation
Labor Supply
Labor Theory of Value
Lagging, Leading, and Coincident
  Indicators
Lagrange Multipliers
Laissez Faire

Landlords, Absentee
Large Sample Properties
Latifundia
Lausanne, School of
Law and Economics
Law of Large Numbers
Legacy Effects
Leisure
Lender of Last Resort
Leninism
Leverage
Lexicographic Preferences
Liberalization, Trade
Life-Cycle Hypothesis
Limits of Growth
Linear Regression
Linear Systems
Liquidity
Liquidity Premium
Liquidity Trap
Luxembourg Income Study
Loan Pushing
Loans
Lombard Street (Bagehot)
Long Period Analysis
Long Run
Long Waves
Lotteries
Luxembourg Income Study
Machinery
Machinery Question, The
Macroeconomics
Macroeconomics, Structuralist
Macrofoundations
Malthusian Trap
Management
Management Science
Managerial Class
Manifolds
Marginal Productivity
Marginalism
Marginalization
Market Clearing
Market Clearinghouse
Market Correction
Market Economy
Market Fundamentals
Markets
Markup Pricing
Mathematical Economics
Maximin Principle
Maximization
Measurement
Measurement Error

Mechanism Design
Mercantilism
Merit
Merit Goods
Microeconomics
Microelectronics Industry
Microfoundations
Middle Way
Migration, Rural to Urban
Minimization
Minimum Wage
Mining Industry
Misery Index
Mobility
Mobility, Lateral
Mode of Production
Model Minority
Models and Modeling
Modernism
Modernity
Modernization
Modigliani-Miller Theorems
Monetarism
Monetary Base
Monetary Theory
Money
Money, Demand for
Money, Endogenous
Money, Exogenous
Money, Supply of
Money Illusion
Money Laundering
Monopoly
Monopoly Capitalism
Monopsony
Mont Pelerin Society
Moral Hazard
Moral Suasion
Motivation
Multiple Equilibria
Multiplier, The
Multisector Models
Mundell-Fleming Model
Nash Equilibrium
National Debt
National Economic Association
National Family Health Surveys
National Income Accounts
Natural Rate of Unemployment
Natural Resources, Nonrenewable
Necessities
Needs
Needs, Basic
Negative Income Tax

Negotiation
Neighborhood Effects
Neoclassical Growth Model
Neoinstitutionalism
Neoliberalism
Neuroeconomics
Neutrality of Money
New Class, The
New Deal, The
Node, Stable
Nominal Income
Nominal Wages
Noncompeting Groups
Noncooperative Games
Non-expected Utility Theory
Nonzero-Sum Game
North American Free Trade
    Agreement
North and South, The (Global)
North-South Models
Ordinary Least Squares Regression
O-Ring Theory
Objectivism
Occam's Razor
Occupational Hazards
Occupational Regulation
Occupational Safety
Occupational Score Index
    (OCCSCORE)
Occupational Status
Offshore Banking
Okun's Law
Open Market Operations
Operation Bootstrap
Opportunity Cost
Optimal Growth
Optimizing Behavior
Ordinality
Organization Theory
Organizations, Peasant
Outsourcing
Overemployment
Overlapping Generations Model
Overlending
Overproduction
Overshooting
Overtime
Pareto Optimum
Partial Equilibrium
Pasinetti Paradox
Path Analysis
Peanut Industry
Penn World Table
Permanent Income Hypothesis

Petroleum Industry
Pharmaceutical Industry
Phase Diagrams
Philanthropy
Phillips Curve
Philosophy, Moral
Physical Capital
Physiocracy
Planning
Plantation Economy Model
Ponzi Scheme
Poverty
Poverty, Indices of
Prebisch-Singer Hypothesis
Predatory Pricing
Preferences, Interdependent
Price Indices
Price Setting and Price Taking
Price vs. Quantity Adjustment
Prices
Primitive Accumulation
Principal-Agent Models
Prison Industry
Prisoner's Dilemma (Economics)
Private Interests
Private Sector
Privatization
Producer Surplus
Production
Production Frontier
Production Function
Productivity
Profitability
Profits
Propensity to Consume, Marginal
Propensity to Import, Marginal
Propensity to Save, Marginal
Properties of Estimators (Asymptotic
    and Exact)
Property
Property, Private
Property Rights
Property Rights, Intellectual
Protected Markets
Protectionism
Protestant Ethic, The
Psychological Capital
Public Choice Theory
Public Goods
Purchasing Power Parity
Putting-Out System
Quality, Product
Quality Controls
Quantity Theory of Money

Quotas, Trade
Race and Economics
Railway Industry
Random Walk
Rate of Exploitation
Rate of Profit
Rational Choice Theory
Rationality
Real Income
Recession
Reciprocity
Reciprocity, Norm of
Recording Industry
Regulation
Relative Deprivation
Relative Income Hypothesis
Relative Surplus Value
Rent
Rent Control
Reparations
Repatriation
Representative Agent
Reserves, Foreign
Resource Economics
Resources
Restitution Principle
Returns
Returns, Diminishing
Returns, Increasing
Returns to a Fixed Factor
Returns to Scale
Returns to Scale, Asymmetric
Revealed Preference
Revenue
Revenue, Marginal
Ricardian Equivalence
Ricardian Vice
Risk
Risk Neutrality
Risk-Return Tradeoff
ROSCAs
Rules Versus Discretion
Russian Economics
Rybczynski Theorem
Saving Rate
Say's Law
Scarcity
Screening and Signaling Games
Seemingly Unrelated Regressions
Self-Employment
Selling Long and Selling Short
Separability
Settlement
Settlement, Negotiated

Settlement, Tobacco
Shadow Prices
Sharecropping
Shipping Industry
Shocks
Short Period
Short Run
Signals
Silicon Valley
Silver Industry
Simultaneous Equation Bias
Skill
Slave Mode of Production
Slave Trade
Slavery Industry
Social Accounting Matrix
Social Capital
Social Cost
Social Economy
Social Statics
Social Status
Social Welfare Functions
Social Welfare System
Socialization of Investment
Socioeconomic Status
Sociology, Economic
Sloar Energy
Solow Residual, The
South Sea Bubble
Space Exploration
Specification
Specification Error
Specification Tests
Speculation
Sports Industry
Spot Market
Spreads
Spreads, Bid-Ask
Stability in Economics
Stages of Economic Growth
Stagflation
Stagnation
Stakeholders
Steady State
Steel Industry
Sterilization, Economic
Sticky Prices
Stochastic Frontier Analysis
Stock Exchange
Stock Exchanges in Developing
　　Countries
Stock Options
Stockholm School
Stocks

Stocks, Restricted and Unrestricted
Stocks and Flows
Stolper-Samuelson Theorem
Strategic Behavior
Strategic Games
Student's T-Statistic
Stylized Fact
Subgame Perfection
Subsidies
Subsidies, Farm
Subsistence Agriculture
Substitutability
Sugar Industry
Supply
Surplus
Surplus Value
Syndicalism
Tariffs
Tastes
Tâtonnement
Tax Credits
Tax Evasion and Tax Avoidance
Tax Incidence
Tax Relief
Tax Revolts
Taxation
Taxes
Taxes, Progressive
Taxes, Regressive
Taylor Rule
Tea Industry
Technological Progress, Economic
　　Growth
Technological Progress, Skill Bias
Technology
Technology, Adoption of
Technology, Cellular
Technology, Transfer of
Technology, Video
Telecommunications Industry
Terms of Trade
Textile Industry
Theil Index
Theory of Second Best
Third World
Threshold Effects
Time Allocation
Time and Motion Study
Time-and-a-Half
Time on the Cross
Time Preference
Time Trends
Tobacco Industry
Tobin's Q

Tobit
Tourism Industry
Trade
Trade, Anglo-Portuguese
Trade, Bilateral
Trade Deficit
Trade Surplus
Trade-offs
Tragedy of the Commons
Transaction Cost
Transaction Taxes
Transfer Pricing
Transformation Problem
Transparency
Transportation Industry
Two-Sector Models
Uncertainty
Underachievers
Underclass
Underconsumption
Underdevelopment
Underemployment
Underemployment Rate
Unemployable
Unemployment
Unemployment Rate
Unequal Exchange
Upward Mobility
Uruguay Round
User Cost
Utilitarianism
Utility, Objective
Utility, Subjective
Utility, Von Neumann-Morgenstern
Utility Function
Value
Value, Objective
Value, Subjective
Values
Vanilla Industry
Venture Capital
Verdoorn's Law
Voluntary Unemployment
Wage and Price Controls
Wages
Wages, Compensating
Wall Street
Walras' Law
Want Creation
Wants
Water Resources
Wealth
Weapons Industry
Welfare

Welfare Analysis
Welfare Economics
Welfare State
Wholesale Price Index
Wicksell Effects
Widow's Cruse
Winner's Curse
Winner-Take-All Society
Work
Work and Women
Work Day
Work Week
Working Class
Working Day, Length of
Workplace Relations
World Bank, The
World Trade Organization
World War I
World War II
X-Crise
Yield
Yield Curve
Z-D Model

Biographies

Akerlof, George A.
Amin, Samir
Arrow, Kenneth J.
Becker, Gary S.
Bentham, Jeremy
Bhagwati, Jagdish
Boserup, Ester
Brimmer, Andrew
Cantillon, Richard
Coase, Ronald
De Soto, Hernando
Debreu, Gerard
Drucker, Peter
Engerman, Stanley
Fisher, Irving
Fogel, Robert
Frank, Andre Gunder
Friedman, Milton
Frisch, Ragnar
Galbraith, John Kenneth
Ginzberg, Eli
Harris, Abram L., Jr.
Hayek, Friedrich August
Heilbroner, Robert
Hicks, John K.
Hilferding, Rudolf
Hume, David
Hurwicz, Leonid
Ibn Khaldūn

Inikori, Joseph
Kahn, Richard F.
Kalecki, Michal
Keynes, John Maynard
Kindleberger, Charles Poor
Klein, Lawrence
Koopmans, Tjalling
Law, John
Leontief, Wassily
Lewis, W. Arthur
Lindblom, Charles Edward
Lucas, Robert E., Jr.
Lundberg, Erik
Malthus, Thomas Robert
Mandel, Ernest
Markowitz, Harry M.
Marshall, Alfred
Marx, Karl
Meade, James
Mill, James
Mill, John Stuart
Mills, Edwin
Minsky, Hyman
Mises, Ludwig Edler von
Mitchell, Wesley Clair
Modigliani, Franco
Myrdal, Gunnar
Nash, John
North, Douglass
Oaxaca, Ronald
Pareto, Vilfredo
Parnes, Herbert
Pasinetti, Luigi
Patinkin, Don
Phillips, A. W. H.
Postlethwayt, Malachy
Potron, Maurice
Prebisch, Raúl
Quesnay, Francois
Rawls, John
Reagan, Ronald
Ricardo, David
Robinson, Joan
Samuelson, Paul
Sargent, Thomas
Schumpeter, Joseph
Sen, Amartya Kumar
Simon, Herbert
Singer, Hans
Smith, Adam
Smith, Vernon L.
Solow, Robert M.
Sombart, Werner
Sraffa, Piero

Stalin, Joseph
Stigler, George Joseph
Stiglitz, Joseph E.
Tawney, R. H.
Taylor, Lance
Tinbergen, Jan
Tobin, James
Turgot, Jacques
Uzawa, Hirofumi
Veblen, Thorstein
Von Neumann, John
Walras, Léon
Weaver, Robert C.
Wolf, Eric

EDUCATION

Acting White
African Americans
Brown v. Board of Education, 1954
Brown v. Board of Education, 1955
Cambridge University
Child Development
Children
Citations
Communication
Computers: Science and Society
Correspondence Tests
Credentialism
Curriculum
Desegregation, School
Digital Divide
Disability
Diversity
Equal Opportunity
Equality
Education, Informal
Education, Returns to
Education, Unequal
Education, USA
Educational Quality
Employment
Flynn Effect
Gifted and Talented
Head Start
Head Start Experiments
Intellectualism, Anti-
Intellectuals, Organic
Intellectuals, Public
Intellectuals, Vernacular
Intelligence
Intelligence, Social
IQ Controversy
Journals, Professional
Knowledge

Knowledge, Diffusion of
Knowledge Society
Marginal Productivity
Medicine
Memory
Mentoring
Merit
Meritocracy
Multiple Intelligences Theory
National Assessment of Educational
    Progress
National Education Longitudinal
    Study
National Longitudinal Study of
    Adolescent Health
National Longitudinal Survey of Youth
Nature vs. Nurture
Neighborhood Effects
Objectivity
Oppositionality, Schooling
Pedagogy
Productivity
Programmed Retardation
Race and Education
Readiness, School
Resegregation of Schools
School Vouchers
Schooling
Schooling in the USA
Segregation, School
Separate-but-Equal
Skill
Sociology, Schools in
Talent
Teacher Expectations
Teacher-Child Relationships
Teachers
Tracking in Schools
University, The
University of Oxford
Wages
Women's Liberation
Women's Movement
Women's Studies
Work and Women

Biographies

Becker, Gary S.
Berg, Ivar E.
Bourdieu, Pierre
Chomsky, Noam
Drucker, Peter
Freire, Paulo
Hegel, Georg Wilhelm Friedrich
Lynd, Staughton

McLuhan, Marshall
Mill, John Stuart
Oaxaca, Ronald
Ogbu, John
Pettigrew, Thomas
Piaget, Jean
Smith, Adam

GEOGRAPHY

Appalachia
Architecture
Caribbean, The
Chiapas
Cities
City-State
Clock Time
Colonialism
Common Land
Commonwealth, The
Confederate States of America
Confederations
Cultural Landscape
Darfur
Deforestation
Developing Countries
Diaspora
Drought
East Indies
Ellis Island
Environmental Kuznets Curves
Ethnic Fractionalization
European Union
Fertile Crescent
Fertility, Land
Geography
Global Warming
Green Revolution
Greenhouse Effects
Gulf States
Harlem
Human Ecology
Irrigation
League of Nations
Mars
Mecca
Metropolis
Nation
National Geographic
Nationalism and Nationality
Nation-State
Nationalization
Pan-Africanism
Pan-Arabism
Pan-Caribbeanism

Plantation
Postcolonialism
Regions
Regions, Metropolitan
Resources
Solar Energy
South, The (USA)
Space Exploration
Spatial Theory
Topography
Topology
Towns
Townships
Union of Soviet Socialist Republics
United Arab Republic
Zionism

HISTORY AND HISTORIOGRAPHY

African Americans
Afrocentrism
Al-Qaeda
American Indian Movement
American Revolution
Anticolonial Movements
Anti-Semitism
Apartheid
Architecture
Battle of Algiers, The
Battle of the Little Big Horn
Bay of Pigs
Berlin Wall
Black September
Black Towns
Blackface
Blood and Bloodline
Boer War
Brown v. Board of Education, 1954
Brown v. Board of Education, 1955
Burial Grounds
Burial Grounds, African
Burial Grounds, Native American
Cannibalism
Cherokees
Child Labor
Chinese Americans
Chinese Diaspora
Chinese Revolution
Civil Disobedience
Civil Liberties
Civil Rights
Civil Rights, Cold War
Civil Rights Movement, U.S.
Civil Wars
Civilization

Civilizations, Clash of
Cliometrics
Clock Time
Cold War
Collective Memory
Colonialism
Colony, Internal
Comic Books
Communication
Communitarianism
Computers: Science and Society
Concentration Camps
Confederate States of America
Confederations
Conjunctures, Transitional
Constitution, U.S.
Contraception
Corn Laws
Cross of Gold
Cuban Missile Crisis
Cuban Revolution
Cultural Rights
Culture
Cyberspace
Daughters of the American Revolution
Declaration of Independence, U.S.
Decolonization
Democracy, Christian
Desegregation
Desegregation, School
Domino Theory
Dred Scott v. Sanford
East Indian Diaspora
Ellis Island
Enlightenment
Ethnic Conflict
Eugenics
Factories
Factory System
Falkland Islands War
False Consciousness
Famine
Feudalism
Food Crisis
French Revolution
Gilded Age
Glasnot
Going Native
Gold, God, and Glory
Gold Standard
Grameen Bank
Great Depression
Green Book, The (Libya)
Green Revolution

Grenadian Revolution
Gulags
Gulf War of 1991
Haitian Revolution
Harlem Renaissance
Haymarket Square Riot
History, Social
Holocaust, The
Holy Roman Empire
Hungarian Revolution
Identification, Racial
Illuminati, The
Immigrants, Asian
Immigrants, Black
Immigrants, European
Immigrants, Latin American
Immigrants, New York City
Immigrants to North America
Immigration
Incarceration, Japanese American
Industrialization
Industry
Internet Bubble
Interwar Years
Intifada, The
Inuit
Iran-Contra Affair
Iranian Revolution
Iran-Iraq War
Iraq-U.S. War
Irish Republican Army
Iron Curtain
Islam, Shia and Sunni
Isolationsim
Japanese Americans
Jewish Diaspora
Jim Crow
Kerner Commission Report
Khmer Rouge
Killing Fields
Korean War
Kshatriyas
Ku Klux Klan
Labour Party (Britain)
Landlords
Landlords, Absentee
Latinos
League of Nations
Lebanese Civil War
Liberal Party (Britain)
Little Red Book
Liverpool Slave Trade
Loyalists
Luddites

Lumpenproletariat
Machinery
Magna Carta
Malinchistas
Maoism
Martyrdom
Mau Mau
McCarthyism
Mecca
Medicis, The
Meiji Restoration
Memín Pinguín
Memory
Mexican Revolution (1910–1920)
Mexican-American War
Microsoft
Migrant Labor
Migration
Migration, Rural to Urban
Minstrelsy
Modernization
Monarchism
Monarchy
Monarchy, Constitutional
Monroe Doctrine
Moreno
Motherhood
Moving to Opportunity
Mulatto Escape Hatch
Mulattos
Multiculturalism
Multilateralism
Multiparty Systems
Multiracial Movement
Multiracials in the United States
Napoleonic Wars
Nation
National Health Insurance
National Security
Nationalism and Nationality
Nationalization
Nation-State
Native Americans
Natives
Nativism
Natural Disasters
Navajos
Nazism
Negro
New Deal, The
Nobel Peace Prize
Non-alignment
Nonblacks
Nonwhites

Operation Bootstrap
Opium Wars
Organization Man
Organizations, Peasant
Orientalism
Osceola
Ottoman Empire
Pacifism
Palestinian Diaspora
Pan-Africanism
Pan-Arabism
Pan-Caribbeanism
Passing
Passive Resistance
Patricians
Patriotism
Pax Britannica
Peace Movements
Peace Process
Pearl Harbor
Peasantry
Periodization
Peronism
Phalangists
Philanthropy
Plantation
Plantation Economy Model
Plumbing
Pogroms
Protectionism
Punishment
Putting-Out System
Quebecois Movement
Race Riots, United States
Raj, The
Reconstruction Era (U.S.)
Reparations
Restitution Principle
Royal Commissions
Russian Revolution
Sambo
Sandinistas
Sanitation
Scottish Moralists
Secession
Segregation
Segregation, Residential
Segregation, School
Separate-but-Equal
September 11, 2001
Shtetl
Silk Road
Slave Resistance
Slave Trade

Slave-Gun Cycle
Slavery
Slavery Hypertension Hypothesis
Social Change
Social Contract
Social Movements
Social Science
Social Structure
Social Theory
Solidarity
Solidarność
South, The (USA)
South Sea Bubble
Space Exploration
Spanish Civil War
Sterilization, Human
Stolen Generations (Australia)
Suez Crisis
Suffrage, Women's
Syndicalism
Taliban
Third World
Time on the Cross
Toilets
Tools
Trail of Tears
Triumphalism
Truth and Reconciliation
    Commissions
Tulsa Riot
Tuskegee Syphillis Study
Two-State Solution
U.S. Civil War
Uncle Tom
Union of Soviet Socialist Republics
University of Oxford
Urban Riots
Vietnam War
War
War and Peace
War of 1898
Warren Report
Wilmington Riot of 1898
Women's Liberation
Women's Movement
Working Class
World Trade Organization
World War I
World War II
Xenophobia
Yugoslavian Civil War
Zionism
Zombies

Biographies

Alger, Horatio
Ali, Muhammad (Mehmet)
Ali, Muhammad (USA)
Allende, Salvador
Ambedkar, B.R.
Amin, Idi
Anderson, Perry
Beard, Charles and Mary
Ben-Gurion, David
Benjamin, Judah P.
Bose, Subhas Chandra and Sarat
    Chandra
Bunche, Ralph Johnson
Chief Joseph
Chisholm, Shirley
Churchill, Winston
Clinton, Bill
Columbus, Christopher
Cook, James
Cortés, Hernán
Crazy Horse
Davis, Angela
Diop, Cheikh Anta
Douglass, Frederick
Forman, James
Franco, Francisco
Franklin, Benjamin
Friedan, Betty
Fuller, Buckminster
Gandhi, Indira
Gandhi, Mohandas K.
Garvey, Marcus
Gobineau, Comte de
Gorbachev, Mikhail
Gould, Stephen Jay
Gramsci, Antonio
Grant, Ulysses S.
Greenspan, Alan
Gabriel (Prosser)
Hamilton, Alexander
Hitler, Adolf
Ho Chi Minh
Hoover, J. Edgar
Houston, Charles Hamilton
Hume, David
Hussein, King of Jordan
Hussein, Saddam
Ibn Khaldūn
Inikori, Joseph
James, C. L. R.
Jefferson, Thomas
Jervis, Robert
Jinnah, Mohammed Ali

Johnson, Lyndon B.
Juárez, Benito
Kaunda, Kenneth
Kefauver, Estes
Kennedy, John F.
Kenyatta, Jomo
Khomeini, Ayatolla Ruhollah
Khrushchev, Nikita
Kimathi, Dedan
King, Martin Luther, Jr.
Kissinger, Henry
Ladejinsky, Wolf
Lafargue, Paul
Le Duc Tho
Lee, Robert E.
Lenin, Vladimir Ilitch
Lincoln, Abraham
Louverture, Toussaint
Lumumba, Patrice
Luxemburg, Rosa
Lynd, Staughton
Machel, Samora
MacMillan, Harold
Madison, James
Mahathir, Mohamad
Malcolm X
Mandela, Nelson
Marshall, Thurgood
Mandela, Winnie
Mankiller, Wilma
Mao Zedong
Marshall, Thurgood
Marx, Karl
Means, Russell
Meir, Golda
Milosevic, Slobodan
Mobutu, Joseph
Mossadegh, Mohammad
Moynihan, Daniel Patrick
Mugabe, Robert
Museveni, Yoweri
Mussolini, Benito
Nader, Ralph
Napoléon Bonaparte
Nasser, Gamal Abdel
Nehru, Jawaharlal
Nixon, Richard M.
Nkrumah, Kwame
Nyerere, Julius
Obote, Apollo Milton
Plato
Pol Pot
Poulantzas, Nicos
Pullman Porters

Putin, Vladimir
Qadhafi, Muammar al
Rabin, Yitzhak
Reagan, Ronald
Rhodes, Cecil
Robeson, Paul
Rodney, Walter
Roma, The
Roosevelt, Franklin D.
Rothschilds, The
Rousseau, Jean-Jacques
Sadat, Anwar
Schliemann, Heinrich
Seneca
Sharon, Ariel
Shklar, Judith
Sitting Bull
Skocpol, Theda
Solzhenitsyn, Aleksandr
Soros, George
Stalin, Joseph
Steinem, Gloria
Stowe, Harriet Beecher
Sun Yat-sen
Tawney, R. H.
Thatcher, Margaret
Thompson, Edward P.
Thoreau, Henry David
Thurmond, Strom
Tito (Josip Broz)
Tocqueville, Alexis de
Trotsky, Leon
Truman, Harry S.
Truth, Sojourner
Tubman, Harriet
Turner, Nat
Vajpayee, Atal Bihari
Vesey, Denmark
Villa, Francisco (Pancho)
Washington, George
White, Walter
Williams, Eric
Wilson, Woodrow
Yeltsin, Boris
Zapata, Emiliano

INTERDISCIPLINARY STUDIES

African American Studies
African Studies
Afrocentrism
Anthropology, Biological
Anthropology, Linguistic
Anthropology, Medical
Communication

Critical Race Theory
Critical Theory
Cultural Studies
Documentary Studies
Economic Psychology
Feminism
Gender Studies
Gerontology
Latino/a Studies
Marxism
Masculinity Studies
Multiculturalism
Organization Theory
Philosophy, Political
Political Economy
Postcolonialism
Postmodernism
Poststructuralism
Queer Studies
Realist Theory
Research, Trans-disciplinary
Rhetoric
Social Psychology
Social Theory
Sociology, Economic
Sociology, Political
Urban Studies
Women's Studies

Biographies

Derrida, Jacques
Diop, Cheikh Anta
Freud, Sigmund
Friedan, Betty
Fuller, Buckminster
Garvey, Marcus
Goffman, Erving
Habermas, Jürgen
Hall, Stuart
Hegel, Georg
Hurston, Zora Neale
Jacobs, Jane
James, William
Lynd, Staughton
Malcolm X
Marx, Karl
McLuhan, Marshall
Pettigrew, Thomas
Poulantzas, Nicos
Said, Edward
Simon, Herbert
Weber, Max
White, Walter

INTERNATIONAL RELATIONS, ORGANIZATION, AND LAW

Al-Qaeda
Arab League, The
Arab-Israeli War of 1967
Arms Control and Arms Race
Berlin Wall
Bracero Program
Bribery
Bureaucracy
Civilizations, Clash of
Coalition
Coalition Theory
Colonialism
Communication
Communism
Competition
Conditionality
Confiscation
Conflict
Conservative Party (Britain)
Corn Laws
Counterterrorism
Croats
Cuban Missile Crisis
Cuban Revolution
Cultural Tourism
Currency
Customs Unions
Cyberspace
Decolonization
Defense
Defense, National
Deterrence
Deterrence, Mutual
Diamond Industry
Dictatorship
Digital Divide
Dirty Float
Disarmament
Domino Theory
East Indian Diaspora
Euro, The
European Union
Exchange Rates
Export Penetration
Export Promotion
Exports
Fabianism
Factory System
Falkland Islands War
Feudalism
Food Diplomacy
Foreign Policy

Foundations, Charitable
Franchise
Free Trade
French Revolution
Fundamentalism, Islamic
G7 Countries
G8 Countries
Genocide
Government, World
General Agreement on Tariffs and Trade
Globalization, Anthropological Aspects of
Globalization, Social and Economic Aspects of
Gold
Gold Standard
Goods, Nontraded
Grameen Bank
Green Revolution
Guantánamo Bay
Guerrilla Warfare
Gulf War of 1991
Haitian Revolution
Health in Developing Countries
Hmong
Holocaust, The
Hume Process
Hungarian Revolution
Immigrants, Asian
Immigrants, European
Immigrants, Latin American
Immigrants, New York City
Immigrants to North America
Immigration
Imperialism
Import Penetration
Import Promotion
Import Substitution
Indirect Rule
International Economic Order
International Monetary Fund
International Nongovernmental Organizations (INGOs)
International Relations
Internationalism
Interrogation
Interwar Years
Intifada, The
Iran-Contra Affair
Iranian Revolution
Iran-Iraq War
Iraq-U.S. War
Irish Republican Army

Iron Curtain
Islam, Shia and Sunni
Isolationism
Japanese Americans
Jewish Diaspora
Just War
Khmer Rouge
Killing Fields
Korean War
Labour Party (Britain)
Latinos
Law and Economics
Law and Order
League of Nations
Lebanese Civil War
Liberal Party (Britain)
Liberalization, Trade
Liverpool Slave Trade
Luxembourg Income Study
Maoism
Maquiladoras
Mau Mau
Medicine
Mexican Revolution (1910–1920)
Mexican-American War
Microsoft
Migrant Labor
Migration
Migration, Rural to Urban
Militarism
Military
Mobilization
Modernism
Modernity
Modernization
Monarchism
Monarchy
Monarchy, Constitutional
Monroe Doctrine
Multiculturalism
Multilateralism
Napoleonic Wars
Nation
National Security
Nation-State
Nationalism and Nationality
Nationalization
Naturalization
Nazism
Neocolonialism
Neoconservatism
Neoimperialism
Neoinstitutionalism
Neutral States

Neutrality, Political
Nobel Peace Prize
Non-alignment
Noncooperative Games
Nongovernmental Organizations (NGOs)
North American Free Trade Agreement
North and South, The (Global)
North Atlantic Treaty Organization
Offshore Banking
Oligarchy
Oligarchy, Iron Law of
Olympic Games
Organization of African Unity (OAU)
Organization of Petroleum Exporting Countries (OPEC)
Organizations
Overpopulation
Pacifism
Palestinian Authority
Palestinian Diaspora
Pan-African Congress
Pan-Africanism
Pan-Arabism
Pan-Caribbeanism
Parliament, United Kingdom
Parliaments and Parliamentary Systems
Patriotism
Pax Britannica
Peace
Peace Movements
Peace Process
Peaceful Coexistence
Pearl Harbor
Petroleum Industry
Quotas, Trade
Raj, The
Refugee Camps
Relativism
Restitution Principle
September 11, 2001
Silk Road
Sociology, African
Sociology, European
Sociology, Latin American
Sociology, Third World
South Sea Bubble
Space Exploration
Suez Crisis
Taliban
Third World
Tourism
Tourism Industry

Transnationalism
Travel and Travel Writing
Trilateral Commission
United Nations
Uruguay Round
Vietnam War
War
Weltanschauung
World Bank, The
World Health Organization
World Music
World Trade Organization
World War I
World War II
World-System
Xenophobia
Zionism

Biographies

Ben-Gurion, David
bin Laden, Osama
Blair, Tony
Bose, Subhas Chandra and Sarat Chandra
Brezhnev, Leonid
Bunche, Ralph Johnson
Bush, George H. W.
Bush, George W.
Carter, Jimmy
Castro, Fidel
Chamberlain, Neville
Chávez, Hugo
Chiang Kai-shek
Churchill, Winston
Cortés, Hernán
Franco, Francisco
Gandhi, Indira
Gandhi, Mohandas K.
Gorbachev, Mikhail
Hitler, Adolf
Ho Chi Minh
Huntington, Samuel
Hussein, King of Jordan
Hussein, Saddam
Jervis, Robert
Jinnah, Mohammed Ali
Johnson, Lyndon B.
Kennedy, John F.
Kenyatta, Jomo
Keohane, Robert
Khomeini, Ayatollah Ruhollah
Khrushchev, Nikita
Kimathi, Dedan
Kissinger, Henry

Ladejinsky, Wolf
Le Duc Tho
Lenin, Vladimir Ilitch
Louverture, Toussaint
Lumumba, Patrice
Machel, Samora
MacMillan, Harold
Mahathir Mohamad
Mandela, Nelson
Mandela, Winnie
Mao Zedong
Meir, Golda
Milosevic, Slobodan
Morgenthau, Hans
Mossadegh, Mohammad
Moynihan, Daniel Patrick
Mugabe, Robert
Museveni, Yoweri
Mussolini, Benito
Myrdal, Gunnar
Napoléon Bonaparte
Nasser, Gamal Abdel
Nehru, Jawaharlal
Nixon, Richard M.
Nkrumah, Kwame
Nyerere, Julius
Pol Pot
Putin, Vladimir
Qadhafi, Muammar al
Rabin, Yitzhak
Reagan, Ronald
Rhodes, Cecil
Roma, The
Rousseau, Jean-Jacques
Said, Edward
Sharon, Ariel
Soros, George
Stalin, Joseph
Sun Yat-sen
Thant, U.
Thatcher, Margaret
Tito (Josip Broz)
Tocqueville, Alexis de
Trotsky, Leon
Truman, Harry S.
Walz, Kenneth
Wilson, Woodrow
Yeltsin, Boris
Zapata, Emiliano

LAW

Abortion
Abortion Rights
Activism

Activism, Judicial
Administrative Law
Affirmative Action
Antitrust
Antitrust Regulation
Apartheid
Bequests
Bioethics
Bracero Program
Bribery
Brown v. Board of Education, 1954
Brown v. Board of Education, 1955
Business
California Civil Rights Initiative
Church and State
Citations
Civil Disobedience
Civil Liberties
Civil Rights
Civil Rights, Cold War
Civil Rights Movement, U.S.
Coase Theorem
Compensation, Unemployment
Constitution, U.S.
Constitutional Courts
Constitutionalism
Constitutions
Consumer Protection
Contempt
Corn Laws
Corporal Punishment
Crime and Criminology
Decision-making
Decisive Events
Dred Scott v. Sanford
Due Process
Equal Protection
Ethics
Ethics, Business
Franchise
Freedom of Information Act
Genocide
Grutter Decision
Harassment
Hate Crimes
Hernandez v. Texas
Hot Money
Identification, Racial
Imprisonment
Indigenismo
Indigenous Rights
Informed Consent
Inheritance
Inheritance Tax

Interrogation
Jim Crow
Journals, Professional
Judicial Review
Judiciary
Jurisprudence
Jurors, Death-Qualified
Jury Selection
Justice
Justice, Distributive
Justice, Social
Labor Law
Land Claims
Law
Law and Economics
Law and Order
Legal Systems
Litigation, Social Science Role in
Lying
Magna Carta
National Organization for Women
Obscenity
Punishment
Roe v. Wade
Royal Commissions
Rule of Law
Segregation
Separate-but-Equal

Biographies

Benjamin, Judah P.
Bentham, Jeremy
Clark, Kenneth B.
Coase, Ronald
Gandhi, Mohandas K.
Hicks, John R.
Hoover, J. Edgar
Houston, Charles Hamilton
Levi-Strauss, Claude
Lynd, Staughton
Marshall, Thurgood
Morgenthau, Hans
Rawls, John
Robeson, Paul
Warren, Earl
Wells-Barnett, Ida B.

LINGUISTICS

Anthropology
Anthropology, Linguistic
Communication
Discourse
Hermeneutics
Linguistic Turn

Narratives
Obscenity
Persuasion
Psycholinguistics
Racial Slurs
Relativism
Rhetoric
Semiotics
Signals
Speech Act Theory
Storytelling
Structuralism
Symbols

Biographies

Chomsky, Noam
Nietzsche, Friedrich
Rorty, Richard
Thorndike, Edward

METHODOLOGY

Afrocentrism
Case Method
Case Method, Extended
Chaos Theory
Cliometrics
Conundrum
Data
Data Envelopment Analysis
Determinants
Difference Equations
Differential Equations
Environmental Impact Assesment
Ethno-epidemiological Methodology
Ethnography
Ethnography and Folklore
Formulas
Functionalism
Game Theory
Hypothesis and Hypothesis Testing
Ideology
Latino National Political Survey
Logic, Symbolic
Marginalism
Mathematics in the Social Sciences
Mechanism Design
Meta-Analysis
Methodology
Methods, Qualitative
Methods, Quantitative
Microanalysis
Model Selection Tests
Models and Modeling
Moving to Opportunity

Multi-City Study of Urban Inequality
Multidimensional Inventory of Black Identity
Narratives
National Assessment of Educational Progress
National Education Longitudinal Study
National Family Health Surveys
National Longitudinal Study of Adolescent Health
National Longitudinal Survey of Youth
National Sample Survey (India)
National Survey of Black Americans
Natural Experiments
Network Analysis
Neuroscience
New Immigrant Survey
New School for Social Research
Objectivism
Objectivity
Observation, Participant
Occam's Razor
Occupational Score Index (OCCSCORE)
Occupational Status
Ordinality
Panel Studies
Panel Study of Income Dynamics
Paradigm
Path Analysis
Phase Diagrams
Planning
Polls, Opinion
Pooled Time Series and Cross-sectional Data
Praxis
Prevention Science
Principal Components
Quantification
Quantity Index
Quota Systems
Quotas
Random Effects Regression
Random Samples
Recursive Models
Reflection Problem
Research, Cross-Sectional
Research, Democracy
Research, Ethnographic
Research, Longitudinal
Research, Survey
Research, Trans-disciplinary
Research and Development
Rorschach Test

Rosenberg's Self-Esteem Scale
Rotter's Internal-External Locus of Control Scale
Sample Attrition
Scales
Schemas
Semiparametric Estimation
Skinner Box
Social Statics
Sociology, Voluntaristic v. Structuralist
Sociometry
Spearman Rank Correlation Coefficient
Standard Cross-Cultural Sample
Structuralism
Subjectivity
Survey
Survey of Income and Program Participation
Surveys, Sample
Systems Theory

Biographies

Darwin, Charles
Foucalt, Michel
Galton, Francis
Hurwicz, Leonid
Kuhn, Thomas
Lakatos, Imre
Milgram, Stanley
Park, Robert E.
Parsons, Talcott
Pettigrew, Thomas F.
Popper, Karl
Robinson, Joan
Sherif, Muzafer
Tolman, Edward

PERSONALITY

Addiction
Aggression
Anxiety
Authoritarianism
Authority
Body Image
Communication
Ethics
Leadership
Lying
Mood
Mood Congruent Recall
Obese Externality
Personality
Personality, Authoritarian
Personality, Cult of

Personality, Type A/Type B
Self-Concept
Self-Efficacy
Self-Esteem
Self-Identity
Self-Perception Theory
Talent
Temperament
Values

Biographies

Allport, Gordon
Bandura, Albert
Freud, Sigmund
Gilligan, Carol
Goffman, Erving
James, William
Jung, Carl
Sherif, Muzafer
Zimbardo, Philip

PHILOSOPHY OF SCIENCE

Aesthetics
Bayesian Statistics
Behaviorism
Bioethics
Classical Statistical Analysis
Consciousness
Constructivism
Creationism
Critical Race Theory
Determinism
Determinism, Biological
Determinism, Environmental
Determinism, Genetic
Determinism, Technological
Elitism
Empiricism
Epistemology
Essentialism
Existentialism
Freedom
Gaze, The
Hegelians
Hegemony
Idealism
Ideology
Incrementalism
Inegalitarianism
Libertarianism
Liberty
Linguistic Turn
Marginalism
Meaning

Mechanism Design
Meta-Analysis
Methodology
Methods, Qualitative
Methods, Quantitative
Mendel's Law
Modernism
Modernity
Natural Experiments
Natural Rights
Natural Selection
Naturalism
Nature vs. Nurture
Occam's Razor
Orthodoxy
Particularism
Phenomenology
Philosophy
Philosophy, Moral
Philosophy, Political
Philosophy of Science
Postcolonialism
Postmodernism
Poststructuralism
Pragmatism
Praxis
Primitivism
Punctuated Equilibrium
Rational Choice Theory
Rationalism
Realism
Realism, Experimental
Realism, Moral
Realism, Political
Realist Theory
Reality
Reductionism
Revolutions, Scientific
Science
Scientific Method
Scientism
Scopes Trial
Semiotics
Social Contract
Social Constructs
Social Experiment
Social Science, Value Free
Sociobiology
Sociology, Knowledge in
Sociology, Voluntaristic v. Structuralist
State of Nature
Statistics
Stem Cells
Storytelling

Structuralism
System Analysis
Taylorism
Technotopia
Teleology
Theory
Time
Universalism
Weight

Biographies

Althusser, Louis
Bentham, Jeremy
Burke, Edmund
Castaneda, Carlos
Condorcet, Marquis de
Darwin, Charles
Davis, Angela
Derrida, Jacques
Foucault, Michel
Franklin, Benjamin
Freire, Paulo
Fromm, Erich
Fuller, Buckminster
Habermas, Jürgen
Hegel, Georg Wilhelm Friedrich
Hobbes, Thomas
Hume, David
James, William
Kant, Immanuel
Kuhn, Thomas
Lakatos, Imre
Lefebvre, Henri
Locke, John
Lukacs, Georg
Marcuse, Herbert
McLuhan, Marshall
Mead, George Herbert
Nietzsche, Friedrich
Pavlov, Ivan
Piaget, Jean
Popper, Karl
Poulantzas, Nicos
Rawls, John
Rorty, Richard
Sartre, Jean-Paul
Sen, Amartya Kumar
Skinner, B. F.

POLITICAL SCIENCE

Accountability
Activism
Affirmative Action
African National Congress

Agenda Setting
Alliances
Al-Qaeda
American Indian Movement
American National Election Studies
  (ANES)
American Political Science Association
American Revolution
Americanism
Anarchism
Annexation
Anticolonial Movements
Antitrust
Antitrust Regulation
Apartheid
Appeasement
Apportionment
Appropriations
Arab League, The
Arab-Israeli War of 1967
Aristocracy
Arms Control and Arms Race
Associations, Voluntary
Attitudes, Political
Authoritarianism
Authority
Autocracy
Ballots
Battle of Algiers, The
Battle of the Little Big Horn
Bay of Pigs
Bicameralism
Bilateralism
Bill of Rights, U.S.
Bioethics
Bioterrorism
Black Conservatism
Black Liberalism
Black Nationalism
Black Panthers
Black Power
Black September
Black Sociologists
Bloc Vote
Bolshevism
Borders
Brown v. Board of Education, 1954
Brown v. Board of Education, 1955
Bureaucracy
Bureaucrat
Business
Business Cycles, Political
California Civil Rights Initiative
Campaigning

Cartoons, Political
Censorship
Census
Central Intelligence Agency, U.S.
Centrism
Checks and Balances
Children's Rights
Chinese Revolution
Church and State
Civil Disobedience
Civil Liberties
Civil Rights
Civil Rights Movement, U.S.
Civil Rights, Cold War
Civil Society
Civilizations, Clash of
Civil-Military Relation
Cleavages
Clientelism
Club of Rome
Coalition
Coalition Theory
Collectivism
Colonialism
Colony, Internal
Coloreds (South Africa)
Common Good, The
Communalism
Communication
Communism
Communism, Primitive
Communitarianism
Community Power Studies
Compulsory Voting
Computers: Science and Society
Concentration Camps
Confederations
Congress, U.S.
Congress of Racial Equality
Congress Party, India
Consensus
Conservatism
Conservative Party (Britain)
Constituency
Constitution, U.S.
Constitutional Courts
Constitutionalism
Constitutions
Commonwealth, The
Corruption
Cosmopolitanism
Counterterrorism
Coup d'Etat
Cross of Gold

Cuban Missile Crisis
Cuban Revolution
Dealignment
Decentralization
Decision-making
Decisive Events
Declaration of Independence, U.S.
Decolonization
Defense
Defense, National
Democracy
Democracy, Christian
Democracy, Consociational
Democracy, Indices of
Democracy, Representative and
   Participatory
Democracy, Racial
Democratic Centralism
Democratic Party, U.S.
Democratization
Desegregation
Destabilization
Deterrence
Deterrence, Mutual
Development, Institutional
Diet, The
Dictatorship
Diplomacy
Direct Action
Dissidents
Diversity
Divine Right
Dixiecrats
Domino Theory
Egalitarianism
Elections
Electoral College
Electoral Systems
Elite Theory
Elitism
Environmental Impact Assessment
Ethics
Ethnic Conflict
Eugenics
European Union
Exit Poll
Exit, Voice, and Loyalty
Exploitation
Fahrenheit 9/11
False Consciousness
Fascism
Federalism
Feminism
Feminism, Second Wave

Feudalism
Filibuster
First-past-the-post
Food Diplomacy
Foreign Policy
Free Rider
French Revolution
Gaze, Panoptic
Gerrymandering
Glasnost
Government
Government, Coalition
Government, Federal
Government, Unitary
Government, World
Governmentality
Great Society, The
Green Book, The (Libya)
Guantánamo Bay
Guerilla Warfare
Gulags
Herd Behavior
Identification, Racial
Ideology
Illuminati, The
Impeachment
Imperialism
Incrementalism
Indian National Army
Indian National Congress
Indigenismo
Indigenous Rights
Initiative
Intellectualism, Anti-
Intellectuals, Organic
Intellectuals, Public
Intellectuals, Vernacular
Interest Groups and Interests
International Relations
Internationalism
Internet, Impact on Politics
Interrogation
Interventions, Social Policy
Isolationism
Jacobinism
Janata Party
Jingoism
Journalism
Just War
Kerner Commission Report
Khmer Rouge
Knesset, The
Land Reform
Latino National Political Survey

Lay Theories
Leaders
Leadership
Leadership, Contingency Models of
Left and Right
Left Wing
Lenininsm
Levellers
Liberal Party (Britain)
Liberalism
Liberty
Little Red Book
Lobbying
Loyalists
Lucas Critique
Lying
Lynchings
Machinery Question, The
Magna Carta
Majoritarianism
Majorities
Majority Rule
Majority Voting
Malinchistas
Maoism
Mau Mau
Maximin Principle
McCarthyism
Media
Medicaid
Medicare
Medium Is the Message
Meiji Restoration
Merit
Meritocracy
Meritocracy, Multiracial
Middle Way
Militants
Militarism
Military
Military Regimes
Military-Industrial Complex
Misogyny
Mobilization
Model Minority
Moderates
Modernization
Monarchism
Monarchy
Monarchy, Constitutional
Monroe Doctrine
Moynihan Report
Mulatto Escape Hatch
Multiculturalism

Multiparty Systems
Nader's Raiders
Napoleonic Wars
Nation
National Association for the
    Advancement of Colored People
    (NAACP)
National Health Insurance
National Organization for Women
National Security
National Service Programs
Nation-State
Nationalism and Nationality
Nationalization
Natives
Nativism
Natural Rights
Naturalization
Nazism
Negotiation
Neocolonialism
Neoconservatism
Neoimperialism
Neoinstitutionalism
Neoliberalism
Neutral States
Neutrality, Political
Non-alignment
Nonblacks
Noncooperative Games
Nongovernment Organizations
    (NGOs)
Nonwhites
North and South, The (Global)
Objectivism
Oligarchy
Oligarchy, Iron Law of
Olympic Games
One-Party States
Opposition
Organization Theory
Orthodoxy
Pacifism
Palestinian Authority
Palestine Liberation Organization
    (PLO)
Pan-African Congresses
Pan-Africanism
Pan-Arabism
Pan-Caribbeanism
Paradox of Voting
Parliament, United Kingdom
Parliaments and Parliamentary Systems
Participation, Political

Particularism
Partido Revolucionario Institucional
Partition
Party Systems, Competitive
Passive Resistance
Patriotism
Patronage
Peace
Peace Movements
Peace Process
Peaceful Coexistence
Peronism
Phalangists
Philosophy, Political
Pluralism
Plurality
Policing, Biased
Policy, Fiscal
Policy, Monetary
Policy Analysis
Political Conventions
Political Correctness
Political Culture
Political Economy
Political Instability, Indices of
Political Parties
Political Psychology
Political Science
Political Science, Behavioral
Political System
Political Theory
Politics
Politics, Asian-American
Politics, Black
Politics, Comparative
Politics, Gay, Lesbian, Transgender,
    and Bisexual
Politics, Gender
Politics, Identity
Politics, Latino
Politics, Southern
Politics, Urban
Poll Tax
Polling
Polls, Opinion
Pollsters
Polyarchy
Population Growth
Populism
Power, Political
Power Elite
Pragmatism
Prediction
Preemptive Strike

Presidency, The
Pressure Groups
Primaries
Prison Psychology
Prisoner's Dilemma (Psychology)
Private Interests
Progress
Progressive Movement
Progressives
Proletariat
Proliferation, Nuclear
Propaganda
Protectionism
Protest
Protestant Ethic, The
Public Administration
Public Assistance
Public Health
Public Interest
Public Interest Advocacy
Public Opinion
Public Policy
Public Rights
Public Sector
Public Sphere
Public Utilities
Public Welfare
Quebecois Movement
Race and Political Science
Rationalism
Rationality
Reactance Theory
Recall
Reconstruction Era (U.S.)
Radio Talk Show
Referendum
Relative Deprivation
Reparations
Representation
Representation in Postcolonial
    Analysis
Repressive Tolerance
Reproduction
Reproductive Politics
Reproductive Rights
Republic
Republican Party
Republicanism
Reserves, Foreign
Resistance
Restitution Principle
Retaliation
Revolution
Revolution of Rising Expectations

Revolutions, Latin American
Right Wing
Riots
Roll Calls
Russian Federation
Russian Revolution
Sandinistas
Scottish Moralists
Selective Service
Separate-but-Equal
Separation of Powers
Separatism
September 11, 2001
Silk Road
Social Capital
Social Change
Social Contract
Social Identification
Social Movements
Social Relations
Social Science, Value Free
Socialism
Socialism, African
Socialism, Christian
Socialism, Islamic
Socialism, Market
Sociology, Political
Solidarity
Solidarność
Southern Bloc
Southern Strategy
Sovereignty
Spanish Civil War
Stability, Political
Stalinism
State, The
State Enterprise
State of Nature
Statelessness
Statism
Stem Cells
Sterilization, Human
Stratification, Political
Strategy and Voting Games
Student Nonviolent Coordinating
    Committee
Supreme Court, U.S.
Syndicalism
System Analysis
Tax Revolts
Term Limits
Terrorism
Terrorists
Third World

Tolerance, Political
Torture
Totalitarianism
Tourism
Transparency
Treaty Federalism
Tribalism
Trilateralism
Triumphalism
Truth and Reconciliation
    Commissions
Two-State Solution
Tyranny of the Majority
Underrepresentation
Unilateralism
Unions
United Nations
Utilitarianism
Utopianism
Values
Veto
Vote, Alternative
Voting
Voting Patterns
Voting Rights Act
Voting Schemes
War
War and Peace
War Crimes
War of 1898
Warfare, Nuclear
Warren Report
Warsaw Pact
Washington Consensus
Watergate
Weaponry, Nuclear
Weapons of Mass Destruction
Womanism
Women and Politics
Women's Liberation
Women's Movement
X-Crise
Xenophobia
Yugoslavian Civil War
Zero-sum Game
Zionism

Biographies

Ali, Muhammad (USA)
Allende, Salvador
Almond, Gabriel A.
Ambedkar, B. R.
Arafat, Yasir
Arendt, Hannah

Aristotle
Bahro, Rudolf
Ben-Gurion, David
Benjamin, Judah P
bin Laden, Osama
Blair, Tony
Bose, Subhas Chandra and Sarat Chandra
Brezhnev, Leonid
Brimmer, Andrew
Bunche, Ralph Johnson
Burke, Edmund
Burr, Aaron
Bush, George H. W.
Bush, George W.
Cabral, Amílcar
Campbell, Angus
Campbell, Donald
Carter, Jimmy
Castro, Fidel
Chamberlain, Neville
Chávez, César
Chávez, Hugo
Chiang Kai-shek
Chief Joseph
Chisholm, Shirley
Chomsky, Noam
Churchill, Winston
Clinton, Bill
Condorcet, Marquis de
Cortés, Hernán
Dahl, Robert Alan
Davis, Angela
Davis, Jefferson
de Gaulle, Charles
Douglass, Frederick
Duvaliers, The
Easton, David
Eisenhower, Dwight D.
Fenno, Richard F.
Forman, James
Franco, Francisco
Friedan, Betty
Gandhi, Indira
Gandhi, Mohandas K.
Gorbachev, Mikhail
Gosnell, Harold
Gramsci, Antonio
Grant, Ulysses S.
Greenspan, Alan
Hamilton, Alexander
Hartz, Louis
Hitler, Adolf
Hoover, J. Edgar

Hunter, Floyd
Huntington, Samuel P.
Hussein, King of Jordan
Hussein, Saddam
James, C. L. R.
Janowitz, Morris
Jefferson, Thomas
Jervis, Robert
Jinnah, Mohammed Ali
Johnson, Lyndon B.
Juárez, Benito
Kariel, Henry S.
Kaunda, Kenneth
Kefauver, Estes
Kennedy, John F.
Kenyatta, Jomo
Keohane, Robert
Key, V. O., Jr
Khomeini, Ayatollah Ruhollah
Khrushchev, Nikita
Kimathi, Dedan
King, Martin Luther, Jr.
Kissinger, Henry
Ladejinsky, Wolf
Lafargue, Paul
Lakatos, Imre
Lasswell, Harold
Le Duc Tho
Lee, Robert E.
Lenin, Vladimir Ilitch
Lincoln, Abraham
Lindblom, Charles Edward
Lowi, Theodore J.
Lukacs, Georg
Lumumba, Patrice
Luxemburg, Rosa
Lynd, Staughton
Machel, Samora
Machiavelli, Niccolò
MacMillan, Harold
Madison, James
Mahathir Mohamad
Malcolm X
Mandela, Nelson
Mandela, Winnie
Mankiller, Wilma
Mao Zedong
Marcuse, Herbert
Marshall, Thurgood
Means, Russell
Meir, Golda
Merriam, Charles
Michels, Robert
Mill, James

Mill, John Stuart
Miller, Warren
Mills, C. Wright
Mills, Edwin
Milosevic, Slobodan
Minh, Ho Chi
Mobutu, Joseph
Moore, Barrington
Morgenthau, Hans
Moses, Robert
Mossadegh, Mohammad
Moynihan, Daniel Patrick
Mugabe, Robert
Museveni, Yoweri
Mussolini, Benito
Myrdal, Gunnar
Nader, Ralph
Napoleon
Nasser, Gamal Abdel
Nast, Thomas
Nehru, Jawaharlal
Neumann, Franz
Nixon, Richard M.
Nkrumah, Kwame
Nyerere, Julius
Obote, Apollo Milton
Pitkin, Hanna
Plato
Pol Pot
Popper, Karl
Poulantzas, Nicos
Putin, Vladimir
Qadhafi, Muammar al
Rabin, Yitzhak
Rawls, John
Reagan, Ronald
Riker, William
Robeson, Paul
Rodney, Walter
Roosevelt, Franklin D.
Rousseau, Jean-Jacques
Sadat, Anwar
Sartre, Jean-Paul
Schattschneider, E. E.
Sharon, Ariel
Shklar, Judith
Singh, V. P.
Stalin, Joseph
Steinem, Gloria
Stowe, Harriet Beecher
Sun Yat-sen
Thatcher, Margaret
Thoreau, Henry David
Thurmond, Strom

Tocqueville, Alexis de
Toussaint Louverture
Trotsky, Leon
Truman, Harry S.
Truth, Sojourner
Tubman, Harriet
Vajpayee, Atal Bihari
Verba, Sidney
Villa, Francisco (Pancho)
Walz, Kenneth
Washington, George
Williams, Eric
Wilson, Woodrow
Yeltsin, Boris
Zapata, Emiliano

PROFESSIONS

Accidents, Industrial
Agribusiness
Banking
Computers: Science and Society
Discouraged Workers
Employment
Employment, White Collar
Engineering
Entrepreneurship
Factories
Ford Motor Company
Franchise
General Electric
General Motors
Genetic Testing
Genomics
Industry
Job Guarantee
Journals, Professional
Labor Union
Machinery
Management
Management Science
Managerial Class
Media
Medicine
Microfinance
Microsoft
Music
New Class, The
Professionalization
Professoriate
Skill
Social Work
Soft Skills
Work and Women

PSYCHIATRY

Children
Hyperactivity
Hypertension
Lobotomy
Medicine
Neuroscience
Neuroticism
Psychiatric Disorders
Psychoanalytic Theory
Psychoneuroendocrinology
Psychoneuroimmunology
Psychopathology
Psychotherapy
Psychotropic Drugs
Schizophrenia
Serotonin
Steroids
Tolerance, Drug

Biographies

Bettelheim, Bruno
Brazelton, T. Berry
Freud, Sigmund
Jung, Carl
Leary, Timothy
Spock, Benjamin

PSYCHOLOGY, APPLIED

Achievement
Adolescent Psychology
Advertising
Authority
Cannibalism
Child Development
Children
Classical Conditioning
Cognition
Communication
Coping
Creativity
Determinism
Determinism, Nonadditive
Determinism, Reciprocal
Determinism, Technological
Developmental Psychology
Drugs of Abuse
Experiments
Experiments, Controlled
Experiments, Human
Experiments, Shock
Flynn Effect
Genetic Testing
Genomics

Gestalt Psychology
Gestalt Therapy
Guttman Scale
Hallucinogens
Head Start Experiments
Heredity
Likert Scale
Lobotomy
Psychology
Psychosomatics
Psychotherapy
Psychotropic Drugs
Schizophrenia
Skinner Box
Stages of Development

Biographies

Ainsworth, Mary
Bowlby, John
Erickson, Erik H.
Fromm, Erich
Jung, Carl
Lewin, Kurt
Maslow, Abraham
Piaget, Jean
Seligmann, Martin

PSYCHOLOGY, GENERAL

Achievement
Achievement Gap, Racial
Adolescent Psychology
Aesthetics
Aggression
Alienation
Alienation-Anomie
Alpha-male
Altruism
Altruism and Prosocial Behavior
Alzheimer's Disease
American Psychological Association
Anxiety
Attachment Theory
Attention-Deficit/Hyperactivity
   Disorder
Attitudes
Attitudes, Behavioral
Attitudes, Political
Attitudes, Racial
Attribution
Behavior, Self-Constrained
Behaviorism
Birth Control
Body Image
Body Mass Index

Child Behavior Checklist
Child Development
Children
Choice in Psychology
Class Consciousness
Classical Conditioning
Cognition
Cognitive Dissonance
Collective Memory
Collective Wisdom
Common Knowledge Rationality Games
Communication
Conflict
Conformity
Consciousness
Constructivism
Contact Hypothesis
Convergence Theory
Conversational Analysis
Cooperation
Coordination Failure
Creativity
Dementia
Dependency
Depression, Psychological
Developmental Psychology
Diathesis-Stress Model
Disability
Dopamine
Dreaming
Emotion
Emotion and Affect
Emotion Regulation
Empathy
Energy
Equilibrium in Psychology
Eroticism
Ethics in Experimentation
Evolutionary Psychology
Expectations
Family
Family, Extended
Family Functioning
Family Planning
Family Structure
Family Values
Farsightedness
Fatherhood
Female-Headed Families
Flynn Effect
Generosity/Selfishness
Gerontology
Guttman Scale

Habits
Happiness
Head Start Experiments
Hope
Humiliation
Identities, Deadly
Identity
Identity, Social
Identity Crisis
Identity Matrix
Illness, Mental
Inferiority Complex
Infertility Drugs, Psychosocial Issues
Ingratiation
Initiative
Institutional Review Board
Intersubjectivity
IQ Controversy
John Henryism
Knowledge
Knowledge, Diffusion of
Knowledge Society
Leadership, Contingency Models of
Learned Helplessness
Life Events, Stress
Locus of Control
Logic
Loneliness
Looking-Glass Effect
Luck
Lying
Madness
Manias
Manic Depression
Marital Conflict
Materialism
Materialism, Dialectical
Maturation
Masculinity
Masculinity Studies
Mechanism Design
Memory in Psychology
Men
Mental Health
Mental Illness
Mental Retardation
Midlife Crisis
Misogyny
Mood
Mood Congruent Recall
Moral Domain Theory
Moral Sentiments
Morality
Morality and Inequality

Morbidity and Mortality
Motivation
Multidimensional Inventory of Black Identity
Multifinality
Multiple Personalities
Murder
Music, Psychology of
Napoleon Complex
Narcissism
Need For Cognition
Neuroticism
Obedience, Destructive
Obese Externality
Obesity
Obsession
Obsessive-Compulsive Disorder
Oedipus Complex
Operant Conditioning
Oppositionality
Optimism/Pessimism
Organization Theory
Other, The
Ought Self
Overachievers
Over-attribution Bias
Overeating
Panic
Panics
Paranoia
Parent-Child Relationships
Parenthood, Transition to
Parenting Styles
Pathology, Social
Peer Cliques
Peer Effects
Peer Influence
Peer Relations Research
Perception, Person
Person Memory
Person-Situation Debate
Personal Constructs
Perspective-taking
Persuasion
Persuasion, Message-based
Phobia
Positive Psychology
Post-Traumatic Stress
Preference, Color
Preference, Gender
Preferences
Prejudice
Primacy/Recency Effects
Priming

Prospect Theory
Psychoanalytic Theory
Psycholinguistics
Psychological Capital
Psychology
Psychology, Agency in
Psychometrics
Psychoneuroendocrinology
Psychoneuroimmunology
Psychopathology
Psychosomatics
Psychosomatics, Social
Psychotherapy
Psychotropic Drugs
Pygmalion Effects
Qualifications
Race and Psychology
Rape
Recall
Recognition
Reconciliation
Reinforcement Theories
Rejection/Acceptance
Relationship Satisfaction
Resiliency
Risk Takers
Role Conflict
Role Models
Role Theory
Rorschach Test
Rosenberg's Self-Esteem Scale
Rotter's Internal-External Locus of
    Control Scale
Salience, Mortality
Satiation
Satisficing Behavior
Schizophrenia
Secrecy
Selection Bias
Selective Attention
Self-Actualization
Self-Affirmation Theory
Self-Awareness Theory
Self-Classification
Self-Concept
Self-Consciousness, Private vs. Public
Self-Control
Self-Defeating Behavior
Self-Determination
Self-Determination Theory
Self-Disclosure
Self-Discrepancy Theory
Self-Efficacy
Self-Enhancement

Self-Esteem
Self-Fulfilling Prophecies
Self-Guides
Self-Hatred
Self-Justification
Self-Identity
Self-Monitoring
Self-Perception Theory
Self-Presentation
Self-Report Method
Self-Representation
Self-Schemata
Self-Serving Bias
Self-System
Self-Verification
Script Models
Semantic Memory
Separation Anxiety
Sexual Orientation, Determinants of
Sexual Orientation, Social and
    Economic Consequences
Sexual Selection Theory
Sexuality
Shame
Shyness
Similarity/Attraction Theory
Slavery Hypertension Hypothesis
Sleeper Effects
Social Anxiety
Social Categorization
Social Cognition
Social Cognitive Map
Social Information Processing
Social Learning Perspective
Social Status
Socialization
Stability, Psychological
Stare
State Dependent Retrieval
Sterilization, Human
Stream of Consciousness
Stress
Stress-Buffering Model
Structural Adjustment
Subject/Self
Subjectivity: An Overview
Subjectivity: Analysis
Sublimate
Subliminal Suggestion
Suicide
Superordinate Goals
Sympathy
Technophobia
Temperament

Terror
Terror Management Theory
Theory of Mind
Time Allocation
Time Orientation
Trait Inference
Trait Theory
Trauma
Traumatic Bonding
Trends
Trust
Twin Studies
Undereating
Xenophobia

Biographies

Ainsworth, Mary
Allport, Gordon
Bandura, Albert
Baumrind, Diana
Bettelheim, Bruno
Bowlby, John
Clark, Kenneth B.
Dawes, Robyn
Erikson, Erik
Fanon, Frantz
Festinger, Leon
Freud, Sigmund
Fromm, Erich
Galton, Francis
Gilligan, Carol
Goffman, Erving
Hull, Clark
James, William
Jung, Carl
Kinsey, Alfred
Kohlberg, Lawrence
Leary, Timothy
Maccoby, Eleanor
Maslow, Abraham
Milgram, Stanley
Münsterberg, Hugo
Pavlov, Ivan
Scarr, Sandra Wood
Schachter, Stanley
Seligman, Martin
Skinner, B. F.
Spock, Benjamin
Steele, Claude
Thorndike, Edward
Tolman, Edward
Zimbardo, Philip

RELIGION

Agnosticism
Animism
Atheism
Authority
Brahmins
Buddhism
Christianity
Church, The
Church and State
Coptic Christian Church
Creationism
Cults
Dalits
Divine Right
Ethics
Existentialism
Fundamentalism
Fundamentalism, Christian
Fundamentalism, Islamic
Foundations, Charitable
Gold, God, and Glory
Greek Orthodox Church
Hate Crimes
Heaven
Hell
Hermeneutics
Hinduism
Holy Roman Empire
Ideology
Infidelity
Infidels
Islam, Shia and Sunni
Jainism
Jews
Jihad
Judaism
Kshatriyas
Liberation Theology
Magic
Martyrdom
Mecca
Miracles
Missionaries
Modernity
Modernization
Monotheism
Morality
Muslims
Mysticism
Myth and Mythology
Nation of Islam
Nirvāna
Occult, The

Orthodoxy
Pacifism
Political Correctness
Polytheism
Protestant Ethic, The
Protestantism
Purgatory
Purification
Race and Religion
Rastafari
Reincarnation
Religion
Religiosity
Rituals
Roman Catholic Church
Santería
Secular, Secularism, Secularization
Shamans
Shinto
Shtetl
Sikhism
Sin
Social Welfare Function
Spirituality
Sudras
Supreme Being
Taliban
Theism
Theocracy
Totemism
Tradition
Universalism
Vaisyas
Vatican, The
Veil, in African American Culture
Veil, in Middle Eastern and North
    African Cultures
Vodou
Worship
Zionism
Zombies

Biographies

Buddha
James, William
Jesus Christ
Khomeini, Ayatollah Ruhollah
Muhammad
Muhammad, Elijah
Nietzsche, Friedrich
Potron, Maurice
Sen, Amartya Kumar
Smith, Adam
Weber, Max

SOCIAL ISSUES AND POLICY

Addiction
AIDS
Alcoholism
Al-Qaeda
Anti-Semitism
Assisted Death
Bigotry
Bioterrorism
Brain Drain
Bribery
Bubbles
Business Cycles, Theories
Cannibalism
Caste
Catastrophe Theory
Child Labor
Church and State
Civil Wars
Class
Class Conflict
Class Consciousness
Colorism
Concentration Camps
Consumerism
Conundrum
Conflict
Corruption
Credentialism
Cults
Dalits
Decolonization
Desegregation
Desegregation, School
Depression, Economic
Development Economcs
Diamond Industry
Discrimination
Discrimination, Price
Discrimination, Racial
Discrimination, Statistical
Discrimination, Taste for
Discrimination, Wage
Discrimination, Wage, by Age
Discrimination, Wage, by Gender
Discrimination, Wage, by Occupation
Discrimination, Wage, by Race
Disease
Dissidents
Divorce and Separation
Drought
Drug Traffic
Drugs of Abuse
Economic Crises

Energy Industry
Ethics, Business
Ethics in Experimentation
Ethnic Conflict
Eugenics
Family Structure
Famine
Food Crisis
Foreign Policy
Free Rider
Gender Gap
Genocide
Global Warming
Great Depression
Guantánamo Bay
Hallucinogens
Harassment
Hard-core Unemployed
Hate Crimes
Health in Developing Countries
HIV
Hobos
Holocaust, The
Homelessness
Hot Money
Immigration
Imprisonment
Inequality, Gender
Inequality, Income
Inequality, Political
Inequality, Racial
Inequality, Wealth
Infidelity
International Monetary Fund
Involuntary Unemployment
Ku Klux Klan
Lotteries
Love Canal
Mafia, The
Marital Conflict
Marriage, Interracial
Marriage, Same-Sex
Medicaid
Medicare
Misanthropy
Misogyny
Model Minority
Modernity
Modernization
Money Laundering
Motherhood
Moving to Opportunity
Moynihan Report
Multi-City Study of Urban Inequality

Mulatto Escape Hatch
Multiracial Movement
Multiracials in the United States
Murder
National Association for the
    Advancement of Colored People
    (NAACP)
National Education Longitudinal
    Study
National Family Health Surveys
National Health Insurance
National Longitudinal Study of
    Adolescent Health
National Longitudinal Survey of Youth
National Organization for Women
Nationalism and Nationality
Nationalization
Natives
Nativism
Nazism
Nutrition
Obesity
Orientalism
Overeating
Overfishing
Overpopulation
Pardo
Passing
Patriarchy
Patronage
Peace
Pimps
Plantation
Pogroms
Pollution
Pollution, Air
Pollution, Noise
Pollution, Water
Population Control
Poverty
Poverty, Urban
Prejudice
Prison Industry
Prisons
Privacy
Pro-Choice/Pro-Life
Profanity
Programmed Retardation
Prostitution
Race Riots, United States
Race-Conscious Policies
Racial Slurs
Racism
Rape

Refugee Camps
Refugees
Reparations
Repression
Resegregation of Schools
Riots
Roma, The
Sambo
Segregation, Residential
Segregation, School
Sensationalism
September 11, 2001
Sexism
Sexual Harassment
Sexual Orientation, Social and
    Economic Consequences
Slave Trade
Slavery
Slavery Industry
Slums
Smoking
Social Exclusion
Social Isolation
Social Science, Value Free
Social Welfare Functions
Social Welfare System
Sterilization, Human
Stolen Generations (Australia)
Stunted Growth
Suicide Bombers
Sweatshops
Tax Revolts
Technocracy
Technocrat
Tobacco Industry
Toxic Waste
Tribalism
Tuskegee Syphillis Study
Unemployable
Urban Riots
War
War on Poverty
Weapons Industry
Wilmington Riot of 1898
Womanism
Women's Liberation
World Trade Organization
X-Crise
Xenophobia
Zionism

Biographies

Arendt, Hannah
bin Laden, Osama

Blumer, Herbert
Cox, Oliver C.
Gabriel (Prosser)
Milgram, Stanley
Milosevic, Slobodan
Mobutu, Joseph
Mugabe, Robert
Nast, Thomas
Oaxaca, Ronald
Ogbu, John U.
Pareto, Vilfredo
Park, Robert E.
Postlethwayt, Malachy
Rhodes, Cecil
Roma, The
Said, Edward
Sharp, Granville
Soros, George
Thurmond, Strom
Truth, Sojourner
Tubman, Harriet
Vesey, Denmark
Warren, Earl
Wells-Barnett, Ida B.
White, Walter

SOCIAL PSYCHOLOGY

Altruism
Altruism and Prosocial Behavior
American Dream
Americanism
Anti-Semitism
Attitudes, Racial
Audits for Discrimination
Authoritarianism
Authority
Autokinetic Effect
Case Method
Case Method, Extended
Child Behavior Checklist
Child Development
Childlessness
Children
Cognitive Dissonance
Common Knowledge Rationality
   Games
Communication
Conformity
Conspicuous Consumption
Consumerism
Cultural Relativism
Deviance
Expectations
Experiments, Shock

False Consciousness
Groupthink
Hearsay
Herd Behavior
Identity, Social
Ideology
Ignorance, Pluralistic
Inferiority Complex
Infertility Drugs, Psychosocial Issues
Intelligence, Social
Intergroup Relations
Interventions, Social Skills
Labeling Theory
Lay Theories
Loneliness
Lonely Crowd, The
Lying
Madness
Monarchy
Moral Domain Theory
Moral Sentiments
Morality
Morality and Inequality
Multiculturalism
Multifinality
Multiple Intelligences Theory
Myth and Mythology
National Security
Naturalization
Networks
Networks, Communication
Nondecision-making
Nonverbal Communication
Nonzero-Sum Game
Oppositionality, Schooling
Organization Man
Overachievers
Parent-Child Relationships
Parenthood, Transition to
Parenting Styles
Peer Cliques
Peer Effects
Peer Influence
Peer Relations Research
Perception, Person
Person-Situation Debate
Pluralism
Plurality
Pogroms
Power
Prototypes
Psychosomatics, Social
Racism
Reciprocity

Reciprocity, Norm of
Rejection/Acceptance
Relationship Satisfaction
Relative Deprivation
Riots
Sellouts
Sex, Interracial
Sex and Mating
Sexual Orientation, Determinants of
Sexual Orientation, Social and
   Economic Consequences
Sexual Selection Theory
Sexuality
Sibling Relationships
Social Comparison
Social Dominance Orientation
Social Exchange Theory
Social Exclusion
Social Facilitation
Social Identification
Social Influence
Social Judgment Theory
Social Movements
Social Psychology
Social Science
Social Science, Value Free
Social Status
Socioeconomic Status
Soft Skills
Stereotype Threat
Stereotypes
Stigma
Strategies, Self-Handicapping
Tastes
Unemployable
Unidentified Flying Objects
Vindication
War on Poverty
Weight

Biographies

Allport, Gordon
Aronson, Elliot
Asch, Solomon
Bandura, Albert
Blumer, Herbert
Fromm, Erich
Gilligan, Carol
Goffman, Erving
Hite, Shere
Jones, Edward Ellsworth
Kelley, Harold
Kinsey, Alfred
Milgram, Stanley

Mills, C. Wright
Pettigrew, Thomas F.
Rousseau, Jean-Jacques
Sherif, Muzafer
Zimbardo, Philip

SOCIAL SCIENCES

Anthropology
Archaeology
Butterfly Effect
Census
Computers: Science and Society
Economics
Elasticity
Ethics
False Consciousness
History, Social
Intergroup Relations
Mathematics in the Social Sciences
Merit
Models and Modeling
Motherhood
Motivation
Multidimensional Inventory of Black
    Identity
Multiple Births
Multisector Models
Music
Mystification
Narratives
National Education Longitudinal
    Study
National Family Health Surveys
National Geographic
National Longitudinal Study of
    Adolescent Health
National Longitudinal Survey of Youth
Natural Childbirth
Natural Experiments
Nature v. Nurture
Neighborhoods
Network Analysis
Neuroscience, Social
New Class, The
Nobel Peace Prize
Normalization
Normative Social Science
Norms
North and South, The (Global)
North-South Models
Orthodoxy
Overeating
Overfishing
Paradigm

Paradox of Voting
Pardo
Pareto Optimum
Park School, The
Participation, Political
Performance
Period Effects
Periodization
Phenotype
Planning
Political Science
Population Growth
Population Studies
Populism
Positive Social Science
Positivism
Postcolonialism
Postmodernism
Postnationalism
Poststructuralism
Protestant Ethic, The
Psychology
Quebecois Movement
Queer Studies
Race
Race Mixing
Race Relations
Race Relations Cycle
Race Riots, United States
Race-Blind Policies
Race-Conscious Policies
Racial Classification
Racial Slurs
Racialization
Racism
Radicalism
Reflection Problem
Relativism
Romance
Rumors
Satire
Seneca
Separability
Servitude
Sex, Interracial
Sex and Mating
Slavery Hypertension Hypothesis
Social Accounting Matrix
Social Anxiety
Social Capital
Social Categorization
Social Change
Social Cognition
Social Cognitive Map

Social Comparison
Social Constructionism
Social Constructs
Social Contract
Social Cost
Social Dominance Orientation
Social Economy
Social Exchange Theory
Social Exclusion
Social Experiment
Social Facilitation
Social Identification
Social Influence
Social Information Processing
Social Isolation
Social Judgment Theory
Social Learning Perspective
Social Movements
Social Psychology
Social Relations
Social Science
Social Science, Value Free
Social Statics
Social Status
Social Structure
Social System
Social Theory
Social Welfare Functions
Social Welfare System
Social Work
Socialization
Society
Sociobiology
Socioeconomic Status
Sociology
Sports
Star Trek
Star Wars
Statistics in the Social Sciences
Strategy and Voting Games
Subaltern
Suburban Sprawl
Suburbs
Suffrage, Women's
Superordinate Goals
Surplus Population
Symbols
Taboos
Tastes
Television
Theory
Toilets
Tools
Transgender

Treasury View, The
University of Texas Inequality Project
Upward Mobility
Urban Renewal
Urban Sprawl
Urban Studies
Urbanity
Urbanization
Vacations
Vagabonds
Video games
Vintage Models
Violence
Violence, Frantz Fanon on
Violence, Role in Resource Allocation
Violence in Terrorism
Virgins
Volunteer Programs
Volunteerism
Vulnerability
Whistle-blowers
White Noise
White Primary
White Supremacy
Whiteness
Whitening
Whites
Wizard of Oz
Women
Woodstock
World War I
World War II
Youth Culture

SOCIETIES

African Americans
African Diaspora
Arabs
Aryans
Boricua
Bourgeoisie
Bourgeoisie, Petty
Brahmins
Buraku or *Burakumin*
Caste
Caste, Anthropology of
Cherokees
Chinese Diaspora
Creole
Culture
Dalits
East Indian Diaspora
Ethnic Fractionalization
Garifuna

Hierarchy
Hmong
Identity
Identity, Social
Inequality, Gender
Inequality, Income
Inequality, Political
Inequality, Racial
Inequality, Wealth
Incas
Inuit
Islam, Shia and Sunni
Iroquois
Japanese Americans
Jewish Diaspora
Jews
Kshatriyas
Labeling Theory
Latinos
Majorities
Matriarchy
Mexican Americans
Minorities
Nation
Nationalism and Nationality
Nation-State
Native Americans
Navajos
Nuyoricans
Olmecs
Ottoman Empire
Palestinian Diaspora
Palestinians
Patriarchy
Seneca
Sequoyah
Serbs
Social Categorization
Social Constructs
Social Exclusion
Social Theory
Socialization
Society
Sociology
Stratification
Sudras
Taino
Vaisyas
Zionism

SOCIOLOGY

African Americans
African American Studies
African Studies

Al Jazeera
Alienation
Altruism
American Dilemma
American Dream
American Sociological Association
Anti-Semitism
Aristocracy
Asiatic Mode of Production
Assimilation
Austro-Marxism
Autonomy
Baby Boomers
Bamboozled
Benign Neglect
Bigotry
Bioethics
Bioterrorism
Birth Control
Birth of a Nation
Births, Out-of-Wedlock
Black Arts Movement
Black Conservatism
Black Liberalism
Black Middle Class
Black Nationalism
Black Panthers
Black Power
Black September
Black Sociologists
Black Towns
Blackface
Blackness
Blue Collar and White Collar
Bluegrass
Blues
Body Image
Body Mass Index
Bolshevism
Bootstrap Method
Borders
Boricua
Bourgeoisie
Bourgeoisie, Petty
Brahmins
Buraku or *Burakumin*
Bureaucracy
Butterfly Effect
California Civil Rights Initiative
Cannibalism
Capitalism
Capitalism, Black
Capitalism, Managerial
Capitalism, State

Capitalist Mode of Production
Case Method
Case Method, Extended
Casino Capitalism
Caste
Censoring, Left and Right
Censoring, Sample
Censorship
Census
Central Intelligence Agency, U.S.
Change, Technological
Chaos Theory
Chicago *Defender*
Child Development
Children
Chinese Americans
Chinese Diaspora
Chinese Revolution
Christianity
Citizenship
Civil Society
Civilization
Civilizations, Clash of
Class
Class, Leisure
Class, Rentier
Class Conflict
Class Consciousness
Cohabitation
Collective Action
Collective Action Games
Collective Memory
Collective Wisdom
Colonialism
Colony, Internal
Coloreds (South Africa)
Comic Books
Commonwealth, The
Communalism
Communication
Communism
Communism, Primitive
Communitarianism
Community Power Studies
Computers: Science and Society
Conformity
Conspicuous Consumption
Constitution, U.S.
Constitutional Courts
Constitutionalism
Constitutions
Consumerism
Contraception
Cooperation

Creaming
Creamy Layer, The
Creolization
Critical Race Theory
Critical Theory
Croats
Cults
Cultural Capital
Cultural Landscape
Cultural Rights
Cultural Studies
Culture
Culture, Low and High
Culture of Poverty
Current Population Survey
Dalits
Darwinism, Social
Data
Day Care
Death and Dying
Decentralization
Deininger and Squire World Bank
    Inequality Database
Depopulation
Desegregation
Desegregation, School
Determinism, Environmental
Determinism, Genetic
Determinism, Technological
Development
Development and Ethnic Diversity
Development in Sociology
Diet, The
Difference Principle
Digital Divide
Disability
Disaster Management
Discouraged Workers
Distinctions, Social and Cultural
Diversity
Dowry and Bride Price
Dravidians
Egalitarianism
Elite Theory
Elites
Elitism
Empire
Empiricism
Employment
Employment, White Collar
Eroticism
Ethnic Enclave
Ethnicity
Ethnocentrism

Ethnography
Ethnomethodology
Euthanasia and Assisted Suicide
Expectations
Exploitation
Fabianism
Family
Family, Extended
Family, Nuclear
Family Functioning
Family Planning
Family Structure
Family Values
Fatherhood
Female-Headed Families
Femininity
Feminism
Feminism, Second Wave
Formation, Racial
Formation, Social
Foundations, Charitable
Frankfurt School
Freedom
Friendship
Functionings
Funerals
Future Shock
Futurology
Gambling
Gautreaux Residential Mobility
    Program
Gaze, Colonial
Gemeinschaft and Gesellschaft
Gender
Gender, Alternatives to Binary
Gender and Development
Gentility
Gentrification
Gerontology
Ghetto
Globalization, Social and Economic
    Aspects of
Gold, God, and Glory
Groups
Groupthink
Habitus
Hamilton's Rule
Heterarchy
Heteronormativity
Hidden Persuaders
Hierarchy
History, Social
Human Rights
Human Sacrifice

Humanism
Hybridity
Hypothesis and Hypothesis Testing
Ideal Type
Identification, Racial
Identities, Deadly
Identity
Identity, Social
Identity Crisis
Ideology
Immigrants, Asian
Immigrants, Black
Immigrants, European
Immigrants, Latin American
Immigrants, New York City
Immigrants to North America
Immigration
Imperialism
Imprisonment
Incarceration, Japanese American
Incas
Indigenismo
Indigenous Rights
Individualism
Inegalitarianism
Institutionalism
Integrated Public Use Microdata Series
Integration
Intellectualism, Anti-
Intellectuals, Organic
Intellectuals, Public
Intellectuals, Vernacular
Interactionism, Symbolic
Intergenerational Transmission
Intergroup Relations
Intersectionality
Intersubjectivity
Interventions, Social Policy
Interventions, Social Skills
Jewish Diaspora
Kerner Commission Report
Kinship
Kinship, Evolutionary Theory of
Knowledge Society
Labeling Theory
Landlords
Landlords, Absentee
Latino National Political Survey
Latino/a Studies
Lay Theories
Leisure
Liberation
Liberation Movements
Lifestyles

Limits of Growth
Lonely Crowd, The
Lotteries
Luck
Luddites
Madness
Mafia, The
Managerial Class
Marriage
Marriage, Interracial
Marriage, Same-Sex
Martyrdom
Marx, Karl: Impact on Sociology
Marxism, Black
Masculinity
Masculinity Studies
Material Culture
Materialism
Medicine, Socialized
Meiji Restoration
Melting Pot
Men
Merit
Methods, Research (in Sociology)
Metropolis
Middle Class
Middleman Minorities
Midwifery
Minorities
Minstrelsy
Misanthropy
Miscegenation
Mixed Strategy
Mobility
Mobility, Lateral
Model Minority
Modernism
Modernity
Modernization
Monarchism
Monarchy
Monarchy, Constitutional
Moreno
Moving to Opportunity
Moynihan Report
Mulatto Escape Hatch
Mulattos
Multiculturalism
Nanotechnology
National Education Longitudinal
  Study
National Family Health Surveys
National Longitudinal Study of
  Adolescent Health

National Longitudinal Survey of Youth
Nationalism and Nationality
Nationalization
Natural Selection
Naturalism
Negro
Neighborhood Effects
Network Analysis
Networks
Networks, Communication
Neuroscience
Neuroscience, Social
Neuroticism
New Class, The
Nonblacks
Nondecision-making
Nonwhites
Normalization
Norms
Nouveaux Riches
Oppositionality, Schooling
Organization Man
Organization Theory
Organizations
Pacifism
Palestinian Diaspora
Pardo
Park Scool, The
Particularism
Passing
Patriarchy
Philanthropy
Pimps
Power Elite
Practice Theory
Prestige
Protestant Ethic, The
Punishment
Queer Studies
Rape
Reflexivity
Sambo
Secular, Secularism, Secularization
Sellouts
Signals
Skill
Social Capital
Social Constructionism
Social Constructs
Social Exchange Theory
Social Facilitation
Social Influence
Social Relations
Social Structure

Social System
Social Theory
Socialization
Society
Sociobiology
Socioeconomic Status
Sociology
Sociology, African
Sociology, American
Sociology, Economic
Sociology, European
Sociology, Feminist
Sociology, Institutional Analysis in
Sociology, Knowledge in
Sociology, Latin American
Sociology, Macro-
Sociology, Micro-
Sociology, Parsonian
Sociology, Political
Sociology, Post-Parsonian American
Sociology, Rural
Sociology, Schools in
Sociology, Third World
Sociology, Urban
Sociology, Voluntaristic vs.
    Structuralist
Sociometry
Spatial Theory
Statelessness
Statistics in the Social Sciences
Stereotypes
Stigma
Stratification
Structural Transformation
Tastes
Trigueño
Underclass
Unemployable
Unidentified Flying Objects
Upward Mobility
Utilitarianism
Utopianism
Values
Want Creation
War on Poverty
Womanism
Women and Politics
Women's Liberation
Women's Movement
Work and Women
Working Class

Biographies

Anderson, Perry

Bahro, Rudolf
Baumrind, Diana
Berg, Ivar E.
Blau, Peter M.
Blumer, Herbert
Bonacich, Edna
Bourdieu, Pierre
Comte, Auguste
Cox, Oliver C.
Drake, St. Clair
Du Bois, W. E. B.
Duncan, Otis Dudley
Durkheim, Émile
Feagin, Joseph
Frazier, E. Franklin
Gans, Herbert J.
Giddens, Anthony
Glazer, Nathan
Goffman, Erving
Habermas, Jürgen
Hall, Stuart
Hite, Shere
Ibn Khaldūn
Janowitz, Morris
Jencks, Christopher
Kinsey, Alfred
Lazarsfeld, Paul Felix
Lefebvre, Henri
Lukacs, Georg
Lynd, Robert and Helen
Lynd, Staughton
Mannheim, Karl
Marcuse, Herbert
Marx, Karl
Merton, Robert K.
Mills, C. Wright
Moore, Barrington
Moynihan, Daniel Patrick
Pareto, Vilfredo
Park, Robert E.
Parnes, Herbert
Parsons, Talcott
Pettigrew, Thomas F.
Poulantzas, Nicos
Putnam, Robert
Sherif, Muzafer
Skocpol, Theda
Sombart, Werner
Spencer, Herbert
Tawney, R.H.
Veblen, Thorstein
Wallerstein, Immanuel
Weber, Max
Wilson, William Julius

STATISTICS

Bayes' Theorem
Bayesian Econometrics
Bayesian Statistics
Census
Central Limit Theorem
Central Tendencies, Measures of
Chi-Square
Cholesky Decomposition
Classical Statistical Analysis
Cliometrics
Cluster Analysis
Covariance
Data
Data, Longitudinal
Data, Pseudopanel
Degrees of Freedom
Descriptive Statistics
Determinants
Distribution, Normal
Distribution, Poisson
Distribution, Uniform
Econometrics
Errors, Standard
Expected Utility Theory
Factor Analysis
Fixed Effects Regression
Frequency Distributions
Functional Form
Hessian Matrix
Hypothesis, Nested
Identity Matrix
Inference, Statistical
Instrumental Variables Regression
Inverse Matrix
Lags, Distributed
Latino National Political Survey
Least Squares, Ordinary
Least Squares, Three-Stage
Least Squares, Two-Stage
Logistic Regression
Log-linear Models
Loss Functions
Luxembourg Income Study
Mathematics in the Social Sciences
Matrix Algebra
Maximum Likelihood Regression
Mean, The
Measurement
Measurement Error
Meta-Analysis
Method of Moments
Methodology
Methods, Qualitative

Methods, Quantitative
Methods, Research (in Sociology)
Methods, Survey
Mode, The
Moment Generating Function
Monte Carlo Experiments
Multicollinearity
Multisector Models
Nash Equilibrium
National Education Longitudinal
    Study
National Family Health Surveys
National Longitudinal Study of
    Adolescent Health
National Longitudinal Survey of Youth
Non-expected Utility Theory
Nonlinear Regression
Nonlinear Systems
Nonparametric Estimation
Nonparametric Regression
Objective Function
Ordinary Least Squares Regression
Probabilistic Regression
Probability
Probability, Limits in
Probability, Subjective
Probability Distributions
Probability Theory

Programming, Linear and Nonlinear
Properties of Estimators (Asymptotic
    and Exact)
Psychometrics
Random Effects Regression
Random Samples
Randomness
Recursive Models
Regression
Regression Analysis
Regression Towards the Mean
Reliability, Statistical
Replicator Dynamics
Residuals
Sample Attrition
Sampling
Serial Correlation
Sociometry
Spearman Rank Correlation
    Coefficient
Standard Deviation
Standardized Tests
Stationary Process
Stationary State
Statistical Noise
Statistics
Structural Equation Models
Survival Analysis Regression

Test Statistics
Time Series Regression
Unit Root and Cointegration
    Regression
Validation
Validity, Statistical
Variability
Variables, Latent
Variables, Predetermined
Variables, Random
Variance
Variance-Covariance Matrix
Variation
Vector Autoregression
Vectors
White Noise
Z-Test

Biographies

Dawes, Robyn
Frisch, Ragnar
Galton, Francis
Mitchell, Wesley Clair
Oaxaca, Ronald
Pearson, Karl
Tinbergen, Jan
Von Neumann, John

A

ABILITY, INNATE

SEE *Intelligence.*

ABILITY, NATURAL

SEE *Intelligence.*

ABNORMALITY

SEE *Psychiatric Disorders.*

ABOLITIONISM

SEE *Slavery; Suffrage, Women's.*

ABORIGINES

SEE *Indigenous Rights; Natives.*

ABORTION

Induced abortion, in contrast to spontaneous abortion, is the deliberate termination of an established pregnancy. Induced abortion is a universal phenomenon, present in every known culture—literate or preliterate, primitive or modern. What has differed has been the safety of the methods used; how widespread the practice has been, especially relative to contraception and infanticide; and the role of church and state.

Induced abortion was certainly practiced in ancient societies. The oldest known recipe for abortifacients comes from an ancient Egyptian papyrus dating back to 1550 BCE, which lists substances that terminate pregnancy in the first, second, and third trimesters. Ancient Greeks also used herbal abortifacients, including silphium (a giant fennel), pennyroyal, and myrrh; modern analyses suggest that many of these were effective. Abortion was common in both ancient Greece and Rome, although not nearly as widespread as infanticide. The timing of animation or ensoulment was of great interest to Greek philosophers. Aristotle (384–322 BCE) hypothesized that the fetus had a succession of souls: vegetable, animal, and rational. He also believed that animation occurred in the male fetus forty days after conception and in the female fetus after eighty days. Among Romans, the prevailing view was that the fetus became a person, an entity with a soul, only at the time it began to breathe.

Abortion practices varied widely among early Christians, who generally believed that fetuses did not have a soul until sometime after conception. Saint Augustine (354–430 CE) accepted Aristotle's theory of delayed animation of the female fetus and contributed his own description of fetal development: the first six days in milky form, nine more days for it to turn to blood, twelve days for the mass of blood to solidify, and eighteen more days for the mass to become fully formed with all of its members.

During the Middle Ages, a woman was considered to have had an abortion only if a formed fetus was extracted. Abortion among Christians remained a local issue, and penances imposed for procuring abortions varied widely among localities. In the thirteenth century, the Christian philosopher Thomas Aquinas (c. 1225–1274) expanded upon the ideas of his predecessors, accepting Aristotle's view that male semen alone had the power of creation. He reasoned that since beings tend to reproduce their own kind, the products of conception ordinarily would be male. Females must result from flaws in the semen or an act of God, such as the south wind. Aquinas's ideas influenced Pope Innocent IV (d. 1254), who declared that abortion before the infusion of the soul was not homicide.

The papal position did not change again for three centuries. In 1588 Pope Sixtus V (1521–1590) declared that whoever practiced abortion, which he believed to be premeditated murder, was to be excommunicated and put to death. In 1591 Pope Gregory XIV (1535–1591) withdrew these penalties for the sin of abortion, which he believed were too severe in light of the debate on animation or ensoulment. This remained the Catholic Church's abortion policy until 1869, when Pope Pius IX (1792–1878) restored Sixtus V's declaration, thus eliminating any distinction between an animated and an unanimated fetus.

Despite its change in doctrine, the Catholic Church did not play an important role in the passage of antiabortion legislation in either England or the United States during the nineteenth century. At the beginning of the nineteenth century, English common law, which also applied in the United States, allowed induced abortion until at least quickening, that is, when the woman first feels fetal movements, usually between the fourth and fifth months of pregnancy. The change in British law occurred in 1803 when induced abortion was made illegal throughout pregnancy. The change in American law occurred somewhat later through two waves of state antiabortion legislation.

The first wave occurred between 1821 and 1841. Ten states and one territory enacted legislation to make some abortions illegal. Connecticut passed the first statute in 1821, prohibiting the administration of poisons to produce postquickening abortions. In 1828 New York banned postquickening abortions by all methods. Other than politicians and physicians, there was little popular support for these laws, and they were almost never enforced.

Massachusetts launched the second wave of antiabortion legislation in 1846 with a law that ignored the notion of quickening and included jail sentences and fines for attempted abortions. New York followed suit in the same year and passed an abortion law that also disregarded

quickening and prescribed punishments for abortionists and abortion patients. Between 1840 and 1880, forty antiabortion state laws were passed. By 1910 induced abortion at any stage was a criminal offense in every state except Kentucky. The only exception was a therapeutic abortion, performed to save the pregnant woman's life. However stringent, these state laws were ineffective in curtailing abortions—reliable estimates show that abortion rates climbed throughout the nineteenth century.

During the first half of the twentieth century, an estimated one in three pregnancies ended in abortion. Most of these abortions were illegal and unregulated, resulting in high morbidity and mortality rates for poor and rural women. The rationale for therapeutic abortions had also expanded over time. For women who had access to physician services, induced abortions became relatively safe by the mid-twentieth century. Not surprisingly, the medical profession became a principal advocate for reforming the antiabortion laws for which it had lobbied in the previous century.

Abortion was legalized in the United Kingdom in 1967 and throughout the United States in 1973. While these policy changes occurred within about five years of each other, their paths were almost totally divergent. In Britain, the law was liberalized after a fierce political campaign. In the United States, abortion reform occurred judicially rather than through legislative deliberation. In both counties, deaths from abortions plummeted after the abortion laws were liberalized, but these reformed policies have not settled the abortion debate in either country. However, abortion politics have been far more contentious in the United States than in the United Kingdom.

In 1973 the U.S. Supreme Court's decision in *Roe v. Wade* overturned existing state laws by holding that a woman's right to choose abortion was constitutionally protected as part of her right to privacy. This decision prohibited any level of government from interfering with a woman's right to obtain an abortion during the first trimester except to require that it be performed by a licensed physician. During the second trimester, the state had only the power to regulate abortion in ways designed to preserve and protect the woman's health. In the third trimester, the protection of fetal life became a compelling reason to justify state interference with a woman's right to obtain an abortion. Beyond these broad parameters, individual states were free to regulate other aspects of abortion.

By permitting considerable state discretion, *Roe v. Wade* federalized, rather than nationalized, abortion policy. Consequently, state abortion laws differ widely in terms of parental involvement, informed consent, and funding for poor women. Since *Roe*, the U.S. Supreme

Court has decided over thirty abortion-related cases emanating from the states. The changing composition of the Court has meant that American abortion case law has changed over time.

A key question that remained in the early twenty-first century was whether the U.S. Supreme Court would overturn the *Roe* decision. Such a decision would have serious ramifications. In the 2000s, about one in three women in the United States had an abortion by the age of forty-five.

SEE ALSO *Birth Control;* Roe v. Wade

BIBLIOGRAPHY

Alan Guttmacher Institute. 2006. An Overview of Abortion in the United States. http://www.agi-usa.org/media/presskits/2005/06/28/abortionoverview.html.

Devereux, George. 1967. Typological Study of Abortion in 350 Primitive, Ancient, and Pre-Industrial Societies. In *Abortion in America: Medical, Psychiatric, Legal, Anthropological, and Religious Considerations,* ed. Harold Rosen. Boston: Beacon.

Francome, Colin. 2004. *Abortion in the USA and the UK.* Hants, U.K., and Burlington, VT: Ashgate.

Luker, Kristin. 1984. *Abortion and the Politics of Motherhood.* Berkeley: University of California Press.

McFarlane, Deborah R., and Kenneth J. Meier. 2001. *The Politics of Fertility Control: Family Planning and Abortion Policies in the American States.* New York: Chatham House.

Rosenblatt, Roger. 1992. *Life Itself: Abortion in the American Mind.* New York: Random House.

Sheeran, Patrick J. 1987. *Women, Society, the State, and Abortion: A Structuralist Analysis.* New York: Praeger.

Tribe, Laurence H. 1992. *Abortion: The Clash of Absolutes.* New ed. New York: Norton.

Deborah R. McFarlane

ABORTION RIGHTS

Abortion (also known as induced abortion, to distinguish it from miscarriage) is the intentional termination of a pregnancy prior to the time when the embryo or fetus is viable. Abortion rights refers to the claim that abortion is a liberty that is or ought to be protected by law.

INTERNATIONAL ABORTION LAWS

Internationally, abortion is legal for about two-thirds of the world's population. Abortion laws vary widely. Abortion in some countries is available on demand (for any reason) throughout part or all of pregnancy. In some countries it is illegal under all circumstances. Some countries take a middle path in which access to abortion is regulated but not prohibited. In these countries legal restrictions, along with the seriousness of the reasons necessary for permitting an abortion, tend to increase along with the gestational age of the fetus. The reasons for permitting abortion may include maternal life and health (sometimes including mental health), pregnancy resulting from rape, social and economic factors, and defects in the fetus.

ABORTION LAWS IN THE UNITED STATES

In the United States, prior to the nineteenth century, early abortion was largely unregulated. Common law considered abortion at most a misdemeanor if it occurred prior to quickening (the perception of movement in the fetus, generally in the fourth month of pregnancy). Termination of early pregnancy was commonly spoken of not as abortion but as restoration of blocked menstruation, which could be accomplished by taking abortifacient herbs or drugs or by mechanical means. Between 1820 and 1900, however, laws were passed by every state prohibiting abortion at any stage of pregnancy, except to save the life of the pregnant woman. The American Medical Association (AMA) advocated for restrictive abortion laws on the grounds that pregnancy was a continuous process, that quickening was not a true indicator of the beginning of fetal life, and that to end fetal life through abortion was unethical unless the pregnant woman's life was endangered.

During the period in which abortion was illegal, it was still practiced, whether outside the law or by physicians acting within the law (sometimes broadly interpreted). Public concern with the issue of abortion increased in response to the well-publicized case of Sherri Finkbine, an Arizona woman who sought an abortion in 1962 after taking thalidomide (a drug known to cause serious birth defects) during her pregnancy. From 1962 to 1965, the birth of thousands of babies with birth defects following a rubella outbreak further contributed to public concern. By 1973 eighteen states, with the support of the AMA, had adopted less restrictive abortion laws. However, in the late 1960s and early 1970s abortion came to be identified as primarily a women's issue rather than a medical issue as it had been in the past. Women's groups such as the National Organization for Women (NOW) and the National Association for the Repeal of Abortion Laws (NARAL) were founded. These and other groups identified abortion as a right of women and called for the repeal, rather than the reform, of abortion laws.

ROE V. WADE (1973)

In 1973 the U.S. Supreme Court handed down opinions in two cases, *Roe v. Wade* (an appeal of a case filed in Texas) and *Doe v. Bolton* (a Georgia case). The majority opinion held that the right of privacy that exists in the Constitution (often attributed to the Ninth and Fourteenth Amendments) "is broad enough to encompass a woman's decision whether or not to terminate her pregnancy" (Section VIII). The court held that the right to an abortion is not absolute, meaning that it can be justifiably infringed for the sake of other interests such as those in "safeguarding health, in maintaining medical standards, and in protecting potential life" (Section VIII). The opinion held, importantly, that the word "person" in the Fourteenth Amendment did not "include the unborn" (Section IX). On the basis of these principles, the justices set up a framework for abortion laws in which each trimester (third) of pregnancy could be treated somewhat differently. In the first trimester, no state interference with abortion would be permitted. Beginning in the second, the states could regulate abortion for the sake of protecting the health of the pregnant woman, and at the point of fetal viability, the states could enact legislation designed to protect the life of the fetus, except when abortion was necessary to protect the pregnant woman's life or health.

AFTER *ROE V. WADE*

This landmark decision was celebrated by supporters of the repeal of abortion laws (pro-choice groups) and decried by groups who were pro-life (those in favor of restrictive abortion laws, such as the National Right to Life Committee). At the state level, between 1973 and 1989 several hundred laws were passed to regulate abortion, for example by allowing a spouse or parent to overrule the pregnant woman's abortion decision, requiring twenty-four-hour waiting periods, or by enacting other restrictions. Many of these laws were challenged and rejected because they did not accord with the framework set forth in *Roe*. Other laws, such as a requirement of parental notification for dependent minors, were upheld. In *Webster v. Reproductive Health Services* (1989), the Supreme Court seemed ready to reject *Roe* when it upheld a Missouri law that declared that human life began at conception and that required second-trimester tests of the fetus for viability. The decision referred to the trimester framework of *Roe* as "rigid" and "unworkable" (Devins 1996, p. 66). However, in *Planned Parenthood of Southeastern Pennsylvania v. Casey* (1992), the court affirmed the central principles of *Roe*, including "recognition of the right of the woman to choose to have an abortion before viability and to obtain it without undue interference from the State" (Section I). The court rejected the trimester framework, adopting instead the standard of an undue burden and stating, "[a]n undue burden exists, and therefore a provision of law is invalid, if its purpose or effect is to place a substantial obstacle in the path of a woman seeking an abortion before the fetus attains viability" (Section IV).

In addition to challenges from state legislatures, other challenges to (and affirmations of) the *Roe* framework came from members of Congress and from the executive branch. The Hyde Amendment to a 1976 Department of Health, Education, and Welfare appropriations bill resulted in an end to Medicaid funding for abortion. Congress considered several proposals that would have either affirmed or overturned the basic principles of *Roe*, but did not adopt any of them. Congress also used its oversight of federal judicial appointments as an occasion to question candidates concerning their views of abortion rights. Particular issues that have galvanized debate in the years following *Roe* have included that of late-term abortion and of the contraceptive RU-486, sometimes called the abortion pill.

Ethical debates concerning abortion turn on the questions of whether the fetus should be regarded as a human being with rights (and if so, at what point in its development it acquires these rights), as well as the extent to which a pregnant woman has a moral obligation to bring a fetus to term, even if doing so requires that her own interests be compromised or sacrificed. Depending on the answers to these questions, abortion may be viewed as primarily an individual woman's right, or as an area in which some degree of state regulation is warranted.

SEE ALSO *Abortion; Pro-Choice/Pro-Life;* Roe v. Wade; *Women and Politics; Women's Liberation; Women's Movement*

BIBLIOGRAPHY

Devins, Neal. 1996. *Shaping Constitutional Values: Elected Government, the Supreme Court, and the Abortion Debate.* Baltimore, MD: Johns Hopkins University Press.

Hull, N. E. H., and Peter Charles Hoffer. 2001. Roe v. Wade: *The Abortion Rights Controversy in American History.* Lawrence: University Press of Kansas.

Luker, Kristin. 1984. *Abortion and the Politics of Motherhood.* Berkeley: University of California Press.

Reagan, Leslie. 1997. *When Abortion Was a Crime: Women, Medicine, and Law in the United States, 1867–1973.* Berkeley: University of California Press.

Roe v. Wade and *Planned Parenthood of Southeastern Pennsylvania v. Casey.* Legal Information Institute of Cornell University Law School. http://www.law.cornell.edu/.

Paulette Kidder

ABSOLUTE AND COMPARATIVE ADVANTAGE

During the seventeenth and eighteenth centuries the dominant economic philosophy was *mercantilism*, which advocated severe restrictions on import and aggressive efforts to increase export. The resulting export surplus was supposed to enrich the nation through the inflow of precious metals. Adam Smith (1776), who is regarded as the father of modern economics, countered mercantilist ideas by developing the concept of *absolute advantage*. He argued that it was impossible for all nations to become rich simultaneously by following mercantilist prescriptions because the export of one nation is another nation's import. However, all nations would gain simultaneously if they practiced free trade and specialized in accordance with their absolute advantage. Table I, illustrating Smith's concept of absolute advantage, shows quantities of wheat and cloth produced by one hour's work in two countries, the United States and the United Kingdom.

Division of labor and specialization occupy a central place in Smith's writing. Table I indicates what the international division of labor should be, as the United States has an absolute advantage in wheat and the U.K. has an absolute advantage in cloth. Smith's absolute advantage is determined by a simple comparison of labor productivities across countries. Smith's theory of absolute advantage predicts that the United States will produce only wheat (W) and the U.K. will produce only cloth (C). Both nations would gain if they have unrestricted trade in wheat and cloth. If they trade 6W for 6C, then the gain of the United States is 1/2 hour's work, which is required to produce the extra 2C that it is getting through trade with the U.K. Because the U.K. stops wheat production, the 6W it gets from the United States will save six hours of labor time with which 30C can be produced. After exchanging 6C out of 30C, the U.K. is left with 24C, which is equivalent to almost five hours' labor time. Nations can produce more quantities of goods in which they have absolute advantage with the labor time they save through international trade.

Though Smith successfully established the case for free trade, he did not develop the concept of comparative advantage. Because absolute advantage is determined by a simple comparison of labor productivities, it is possible for a nation to have absolute advantage in nothing. In Table I, if the labor productivity in cloth production in the United States happened to be 8 instead of 4, then the United States would have absolute advantage in both goods and the U.K. would have absolute advantage in neither. Adam Smith, however, was much more concerned with the role of foreign trade in economic development and his model was essentially a dynamic one with variable

Absolute advantage		
	U.S.	U.K.
Wheat (bushel/hour)	6	1
Cloth (yards/hour)	4	5

Table I

factor supplies, as pointed out by Hla Myint (1977). David Ricardo (1817) was concerned with the static resource allocation problem when he defined the concept of *comparative advantage*, which is determined not by absolute values of labor productivity but by labor productivity ratios. Ricardo would have interpreted the numbers in Table I by pointing out that, whereas U.S. labor in wheat production is 1.5 (= 6/4) times as productive as it is in cloth production, the U.K.'s labor productivity in wheat is only one fifth of its labor productivity in cloth. Therefore, the United States has comparative advantage in wheat and by inverting these ratios one can show that the U.K. has comparative advantage in cloth. This pattern of comparative advantage will not be affected if the United Sates has absolute advantage in both wheat and cloth, which will be the case if we raise U.S. labor productivity in cloth from 4 to 8. This is because 3/4 will still be greater than 1/5.

The rationale of labor productivity ratios comes from Ricardo's labor theory of value. Ricardo treated labor as the only source of value, as all other factors of production (such as capital) are also produced by labor. Thus the price of a good (P) is simply equal to the wage rate (w) times the labor (L) used in production, divided by output (Q), as profit is zero in competitive markets: $P = (wL)/Q$. Because the average productivity of labor is $a = Q/L$, $P = w/a$. If the labor market is competitive, the wage rate paid in all industries will be the same. Therefore, the ratio between the price of wheat (Pw) and the price of cloth (Pc) will be equal to the ratio between average productivity of labor in cloth (ac) and average productivity of labor in wheat (aw): $[Pw/Pc] = [ac/aw]$. This creates a direct link between comparative advantage and relative commodity prices in a competitive economy. If the United States has comparative advantage in wheat production, wheat will be relatively cheaper in the United States than in the U.K., which provides the basis for trade.

Ricardo's theory of comparative advantage creates hope for technologically backward countries by implying that they can be a part of the world trading system even though their labor productivity in every good may be lower than that in the developed countries. In the Ricardian model, trade is a win-win situation, as workers in all trading countries are able to consume more of all goods. Ricardo was blissfully unaware of the complications that would be created if his model included another factor such as capital, and if the producers had responded to changes in factor price ratio in favor of the cheaper factor. It was Wolfgang Stolper and Paul A. Samuelson (1941) who later discussed the effect of international trade on income distribution. The comparative advantage model has many unrealistic assumptions, which ignore the fact that the real world consists of many countries producing many goods using many factors of production. Each market is assumed to be perfectly competitive, when in reality there are many industries in which firms have market power. Labor productivity is assumed to be fixed and full employment is guaranteed. The model assumes that technology differences are the only differences that exist between the countries. Finally, in a dynamic context, comparative advantage changes, as trade in goods and capital alters the trading countries' factor endowments. Hajime Oniki and Hirofumi Uzawa (1965) have shown in a formal model how trade and economic growth continuously change patterns of trade and specialization.

In spite of its shortcomings, some of which have been removed by subsequent research (see Chipman 1965–1966), Ricardo's model carries a message that cannot be ignored. Ricardo's most important contribution lies in the fact that he was the first economist to link specialization with opportunity cost, which is the basis of modern trade theory. As for empirical testing of Ricardo's theories, G. D. A. MacDougall (1951–1952) demonstrated that trade between the United States and the U.K. in 1937 followed Ricardo's prediction. As a matter of fact, Ricardian theory performs better in empirical testing than most other theories.

SEE ALSO *Heckscher-Ohlin-Samuelson Model; North-South Models; Ricardo, David; Smith, Adam; Trade, Anglo-Portuguese*

BIBLIOGRAPHY

Chipman, John S. 1965–1966. A Survey of the Theory of International Trade. Parts 1–3. *Econometrica* 33 (3): 477–519 (The Classical Theory); 33 (4): 685–760 (The Neo-Classical Theory); 34 (1): 18–76 (The Modern Theory).

Heckscher, Eli F. 1935. *Mercantilism*. 2 vols. London: Allen & Unwin.

MacDougall, G. D. A. 1951–1952. British and American Exports: A Study Suggested by the Theory of Comparative Costs. Parts 1 and 2. *Economic Journal* 61 (244): 697–724; 62 (247): 487–521.

Myint, Hla. 1977. Adam Smith's Theory of International Trade in the Perspective of Economic Development. *Economica*, n.s., 44 (175): 231–248.

Oniki, Hajime, and Hirofumi Uzawa. 1965. Patterns of Trade and Investment in a Dynamic Model of International Trade. *Review of Economic Studies* 32 (1): 15–38.

Ricardo, David. 1817. *On the Principles of Political Economy and Taxation*. London: J. Murray.

Stolper, Wolfgang, and Paul A. Samuelson. 1941. Protection and Real Wages. *Review of Economic Studies* 9 (1): 58–73.

Smith, Adam. 1776. *An Inquiry into the Nature and Causes of the Wealth of Nations*. 3 vols. Dublin: Whitestone.

Monica Das

ABSOLUTE INCOME HYPOTHESIS

The *consumption function*, a key behavioral relationship in macroeconomics, was first introduced by John Maynard Keynes (1883–1946) in 1936. While Keynes offered no precise functional formulation of the *propensity to consume* (in his original terminology), his analysis has come to be associated with a simple version of the consumption function that embodies only the more quantitative aspects of his considerations, popularly known as the simple *Keynesian consumption function* or *absolute income hypothesis* (AIH).

The AIH is readily described using four propositions expressed in terms of the *marginal propensity to consume* (MPC) and the *average propensity to consume* (APC), where the MPC is the change in real consumption (c) for a unit change in real disposable (after-tax) income (y), and the APC is the ratio of consumption to real disposable income:

1. That real consumption is a stable function of real disposable income.

2. That the MPC is a positive fraction.

3. That the MPC is less than the APC, and the APC declines as income rises.

4. That the MPC declines as income rises.

The most common representation of the AIH is the linear function (inclusive of an intercept) that satisfies (1), (2), and (3), but not (4) (see Figure 1). Such a simple linear consumption function is to be found in nearly all introductory macroeconomic textbooks.

While early empirical work found support for the AIH and the proposition that the APC falls as income rises, long-run data offered contrary evidence (Kuznets 1946). This indicated that the APC out of national disposable income appeared not to vary with rising income over the relatively long run; in particular, it did not fall as

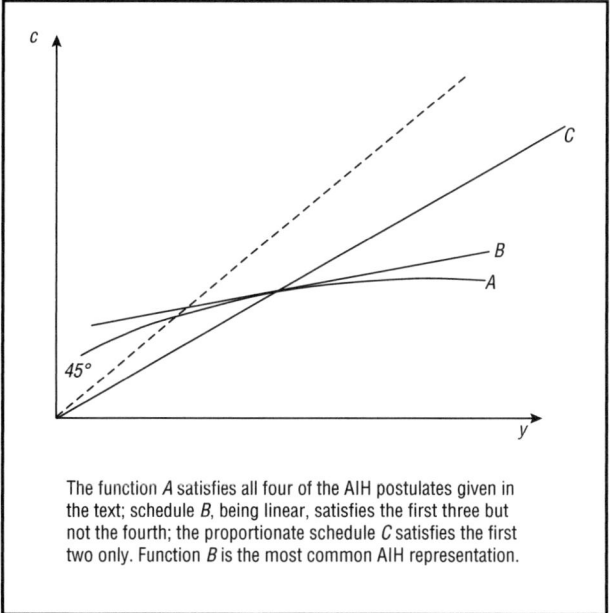

The function *A* satisfies all four of the AIH postulates given in the text; schedule *B*, being linear, satisfies the first three but not the fourth; the proportionate schedule *C* satisfies the first two only. Function *B* is the most common AIH representation.

Figure 1

disposable income rose, as predicted by the linear AIH inclusive of an intercept. Rather, the apparent constancy of the APC suggested a long-run proportional consumption function (*C*), such that the APC equals the MPC. In contrast, the examination of household budget data (Brady and Friedman 1947) revealed the cross-section consumption function to have a positive intercept, and a lower MPC than APC in any given year (*B*). The dilemma therefore arose of how to reconcile the long-run proportional consumption function with the finding from short-run and cross-section analyses that the APC exceeded the MPC.

It should also be noted that the AIH predicts a simple positive relationship between consumption and income, such that the two should not move in opposite directions, nor one change and not the other. However, data shows the two variables disobey this suggested relationship, the most prevalent of such irregularities involving an increase in consumption with a decrease in income, which the AIH is unable to account for. Moreover, the AIH consistently underpredicted consumption for the mid-twentieth century. The is partly explained by noting that during and immediately following World War II (1939–1945), increases in income could not be translated into increased expenditure due to rationing, forced holdings of liquid assets being subsequently converted into increased consumption demand following the relaxation of rationing. Such reasoning suggests that assets, and thereby wealth, may be a significant consumption determinant, and gave rise to modern theories of consumption,

such as the *life-cycle hypothesis* (Modigliani and Brumberg 1955; Ando and Modigliani 1963) and the *permanent income hypothesis* (Friedman 1957), which emphasize the role of wealth and other factors in explaining the paradoxes noted above.

SEE ALSO *Consumption; Keynes, John Maynard; Life-Cycle Hypothesis; Multiplier, The; Permanent Income Hypothesis; Relative Income Hypothesis*

BIBLIOGRAPHY

Ando, Albert, and Franco Modigliani. 1963. The Life Cycle Hypothesis of Saving. *American Economic Review* 53: 55–84; 54: 111–113.

Brady, Dorothy S., and Rose D. Friedman. 1947. Saving and the Income Distribution. In *Studies in Income and Wealth*, Vol. 10. New York: National Bureau of Economic Research.

Friedman, Milton. 1957. *A Theory of the Consumption Function.* Princeton, NJ: Princeton University Press.

Keynes, John Maynard. 1936. *The General Theory of Employment, Interest, and Money.* London: Macmillan.

Kuznets, Simon. 1946. *National Product Since 1869.* New York: National Bureau of Economic Research.

Modigliani, Franco, and Richard Brumberg. 1955. Utility Analysis and the Consumption Function: An Interpretation of Cross-Section Data. In *Post-Keynesian Economics*, ed. Kenneth K. Kurihara, 388–436. New Brunswick, NJ: Rutgers University Press.

Alan E. H. Speight

ABSTRACT THINKING
SEE *Intelligence.*

ABUSE
SEE *Torture.*

ACCIDENTS
SEE *Shocks.*

ACCIDENTS, HISTORICAL
SEE *Disaster Management.*

ACCIDENTS, INDUSTRIAL

The term *industrial accidents* refers to events involving unintended injury, harm, or damage that occur unexpectedly in the process of industrial production.

Definitions of what an accident is and theories concerning industrial accidents have evolved over time, and have differed depending on social context. Preindustrial workplaces were largely unregulated by the state. Tom Dwyer (1991) analyzed accidents in the preindustrial workplace and noted their regulation via moral practice, with Christian notions of "sin" being used to label and control the workplace. As the Industrial Revolution emerged in the United States and Europe, however, so too did new ideas about the worker and the workplace, along with an increased role for the state, rather than small groups and the individual, in defining accidents and addressing the concerns they generated.

The British coal mining industry provides a useful encapsulation of Anglo-American ideas regarding the treatment of industrial accidents in the nineteenth and twentieth centuries. Reports of British mining accidents begin to appear in the early nineteenth century (from 1812 onward), and demonstrate the social value placed on the prevention of industrial accidents. As labor unions emerged, European and American societies also came to expect the state to address concerns about deplorable working conditions in mines and large-scale industrial factories. Workers' grievances regarding accidents were addressed to some extent through the gradual introduction of state regulation. The frequency of accidents, and their pattern and types, reflected the conflict between labor and capital that existed in larger society, as well as the evolution of technology (Dwyer 1991).

Despite the introduction of regulation, life for the typical European or American industrial worker in the late nineteenth and early twentieth centuries was abysmal. Upton Sinclair's *The Jungle* (1906) is often credited with raising consciousness about problems in the industrial workplace, such as long work hours, grotesque injuries, the inability to file complaints and report accidents, and economic exploitation. The American progressive movement brought some of these issues into the political realm, though only the most severe problems were actually corrected during the early twentieth century.

The workers' movement created a new emphasis on the prevention of accidents, leading to state regulations that codified types of violation. Labor unions pressed for safety changes to reduce the incidence of accidental injuries. At the same time, the technology of the industrial workplace became highly specialized. Early workplace safety procedures made use of this increasing specialization of labor, by allowing the worker, for instance, to stop the assembly line and halt production when safety was at risk. New laws were also used to regulate lost time, lost production of goods, damaged or broken equipment, and worker claims against industrial firms. These laws generally favored the financial interests of owners and paralleled the movement toward bureaucratization of management and the workplace.

Industrialization bloomed in the United States and Western Europe in the late nineteenth and early twentieth centuries. So too did social science. The work of Frederic Taylor and the theories of Scientific Management suggested that owners of factories benefited from dividing labor into specialized jobs—that is, it was more productive to divide work into separate, repetitive jobs that could be understood and controlled on the basis of time studies. Ford's use of the assembly line created a highly specialized and linear form of production that set the model for many Western organizations. Accidents, also, came to be viewed as somewhat predictable and thus controllable, with models for prevention arising in response.

Max Weber's work analyzed the ways in which legal/rational authority was used by owners to create a new managerial class that separated owners from workers. A new salaried middle class of managers emerged, with little or no ownership of the industrial factories and firms they managed. The modern corporation shifted responsibility for the day-to-day operations of industrial organizations away from owners to managers. Management became highly specialized as well, with the separation of "thinkers" from "doers" in Scientific Management underlying this division.

Large industrial organizations instituted the complex division of labor into multiple layers of linear production (e.g., the assembly line) and other nonlinear divisions. At the same time, arguably, accidents became less visible, and workers' grievances became internalized within the structures of the organization of production, rather than being dealt with by the state (Dwyer 1991). In the United States, this created a counter-response from labor unions, which began advocating for more state regulation.

The creation of the Office of Safety and Health Administration (OSHA) in 1970, as an agency of the U.S. Department of Labor, was an attempt to codify safety regulations and to centralize the enforcement of statutes and standards in order to address the problem of accidents in industrial and other workplaces. OSHA was established through the National Institute for Occupational Safety and Health Act.

The industrial workplace had become a major locus of death and injury in the United States by the early twentieth century. The worker's means of addressing prevention of accidents were limited, and the drive for profit provided little incentive for change. It was not until the

Year/number of deaths/deaths rate (per 100,000)		
1955	14,200	8.6
1960	13,800	7.7
1965	14,100	7.3
1970	13,800	6.8
1975	13,000	6.0
1980	13,200	5.8
1985	11,500	4.8
1990	10,100	4.0
1995	5,018	1.9
2000	5,022	1.8

Table 1 Source: Bureau of Labor Statistics, Census of Fatal Occupational Injuries; reported in National Safety Council, 2006.

creation of OSHA that serious attempts were made in industrial workplaces to prevent accidents and address workers' grievances; for the first time also, inspection by outside agencies was legislated and laws were enforced with seriousness. Although accidents were reported to be beginning to drop with the incorporation of internal models of prevention, it was only after the creation of OSHA that trends were most visibly improved, especially during the post-1990 era.

Table 1 shows trends in unintentional injury death rates in the workplace—a key indicator of the rate of industrial accidents—in the United States during the postwar era.

In recent years, theories of accidents have evolved into sophisticated models, often driven by advances in models of rational choice and systems theory in economics and other social sciences. The *normal accident theory* of Charles Perrow (1984, 2000) is the most prominent of these, and is useful for the analysis of highly complex and "tightly coupled" systems of production in industry. It asserts that humans design error into systems of production, whether consciously or not, as a product of human imperfection. Failures within safeguards in system design can co-occur, beyond the imagination of those who created the systems, such that the outcomes are explosively exponential in their potential harm. Accidents thus are unavoidable in nonlinear forms of production, because of unforeseen interactions between different system failures. The accident is thus a "normal" aspect of complexly tight systems built by humans.

In developing nations, the problems associated with Western industries in the past seemingly continue: Nations such as India, China, and Thailand are experiencing many of the same social conflicts and problems surrounding industrialization that the United States and Europe did during the Industrial Revolution. Moreover, the Union Carbide accident in Bhopal, India, in 1983

brought attention to the fact that U.S. laws safeguarding workers and the environment are often ignored by U.S.-based multinationals operating abroad. Whether or not accidents are more or less probable, they are always a product of social organization, and thus in any future consideration of safety regulation, social issues must be central.

SEE ALSO *Factories; Management; Management Science; Marx, Karl; Regulation; Taylorism; Weber, Max*

BIBLIOGRAPHY

Dwyer, Tom. 1991. *Life and Death at Work: Industrial Accidents as a Case of Socially Produced Error.* New York: Plenum Press.

National Safety Council. 2006. *Injury Facts: 2005–2006 Edition.* Washington, DC: National Safety Council.

Perrow, Charles. 1984. *Normal Accidents: Living with High-Risk Technologies.* New York: Basic Books. Reprint, Princeton, NJ: Princeton University Press, 2000.

Sinclair, Upton. [1906] 2001. *The Jungle.* London: Penguin.

Steven Curtis Dreyer

ACCOUNTABILITY

In the context of education, *accountability* refers to the concept that schools are responsible for ensuring that students meet agreed-upon standards of academic achievement. While governmental entities claim accountability is essential for the allocation of resources and the evaluation of policies and budgets, the term has taken on several distinct meanings. The principal dilemma was articulated by Susan Fuhrman and Richard Elmore (2004):

> It is evident that what policy makers and the informed public *think* performance-based accountability is, differs considerably from what it *actually is*. In political discourse, it is common to hear both opponents and advocates speak as if test results were the metric of success in performance-based accountability … [but] the idea of equating student learning with test performance is suspect, both in terms of the technical characteristics of tests and the incentive effects of testing on instruction. (p. 275)

David Figlio and Cecilia Rouse (2006) suggest that accountability in the United States involves two distinct alternatives. The first is the use of test-based performance indicators, followed by sanctions for low-performing schools. The second alternative uses market forces to reward some schools and punish others as parents and students make personal resource-allocation decisions through the use of vouchers. Similar market-based accountability systems occur through the exercise of enrollment choice in charter schools, magnet schools, or open-enrollment systems (Finn et. al. 2000; Coulson et al. 2006). This article reviews accountability before recent changes in federal legislation and provides alternatives for consideration.

COMPLIANCE-BASED ACCOUNTABILITY

Until 2001 *compliance-based accountability* was the primary mechanism by which school systems and many other recipients of governmental funds were held accountable. If procedures were followed and rules were enforced, then the entity was sufficiently accountable. Despite the evidence that a lot of wasteful and counterproductive effort is spent on generating strategic plans and submitting proof of school improvement (Schmoker 2004; Reeves 2006), compliance-based accountability remains a dominant force throughout the United States and in many other national and provincial school systems.

RESULTS-BASED ACCOUNTABILITY

The prevailing example of results-based accountability is the No Child Left Behind (NCLB) Act of 2001, legislation that is scheduled for reauthorization in 2007. The essence of NCLB is a focus on results as defined by state test scores. While the law makes the National Assessment of Educational Progress (NAEP) a calibration device (Reeves 2001), it also allows each state to establish its own academic standards and its own assessment procedures. Thus, two states using the NAEP can show, respectively, 20 percent and 80 percent of students scoring at a proficient level—but show precisely the reverse when the "results" under consideration are scores generated by state-created tests. Moreover, results-based accountability emphasizes the effects of education without providing insight into the results. Wealthy schools have better results, but it does not necessarily follow that those results stem exclusively from better teaching, leadership, and policy, any more than poorer results in poor schools stem exclusively from inferior teaching, leadership, and policy (Rothstein 2004).

HOLISTIC ACCOUNTABILITY

To supplement exclusive reliance on test scores, expanded accountability systems have been employed in many school systems (see Reeves 2002, 2004a, 2004b). *Holistic accountability* is based on three tiers of indicators: system-wide indicators, including test scores; school-based indicators, including professional practices of teachers and educational leaders; and school narratives, providing qualitative context for quantitative data. One of the best examples of a governmental entity systematically examining both student achievement data and professional practices is provided by Alberta Learning, the system used in the Canadian province of Alberta (unlike the United States, Canada's educational governance is decentralized). Alberta's rigorous standards, consistent tests, holistic accountability system, public reporting, and long-term improvements in achievement suggest that accountability policies can be effective and constructive governance tools.

VALUE-ADDED ACCOUNTABILITY

A growing number of schools are using *value-added accountability*, in which progress is measured by comparing students' present performance to their performance in previous years (Sanders 1998). As of November 2006, ten states have been authorized to experiment with this system. Value-added accountability has the advantage of showing more meaningful comparisons and focusing on growth in achievement, thus encouraging low-performing schools and challenging high-performing schools. Value-added models are complex and in some cases proprietary. Moreover, any test that can show progress will, of necessity, include items below grade level and above grade level. Such tests are not consistent with the prevailing NCLB requirement that state tests reflect grade-level academic standards. This inevitably leads to tradeoffs: A test that addresses multiple grade levels in order to allow students to "show progress" will require more items in order to maintain the reliability of the test—but more test items can subject students (and teachers) to "test fatigue," which itself can impair the validity of the test. If, on the other hand, a fifth grade student takes a test with only fifth grade items on it, it would be possible for immense progress—say, from a second-grade to a fourth-grade reading level—to be substantially overlooked. Emerging models using *item response theory* are being experimentally implemented in some districts, notably by the Northwest Evaluation Association. Item response theory (IRT) is the study of test and item scores based on assumptions concerning the mathematical relationship between abilities (or other hypothesized traits) and item responses (Baker 2001). While the mathematics of IRT can be complex, the practical application in the realm of educational accountability and assessment is straightforward. Without IRT, every student would take the same test. Using IRT, each student would take a test uniquely suited to his or her abilities.

For example, if student A and B are taking a test of Grade 4 reading, student A might get the first question right, while student B gets the first question wrong. In a traditionally constructed test, both students would continue to take the same test, with student A doing well—in fact, failing to be challenged—while student B might become increasingly frustrated, perhaps to the point of enduring test fatigue and giving up on the exam. Using IRT, however, student A would proceed to a more difficult question, while the next question given to student B would be easier.

ACCOUNTABILITY GUIDELINES

As educational accountability policies are revised in future years, leaders and policymakers can learn from the successes, errors, and unintended consequences of previous policies. In a wide variety of fields, opinions hold sway over evidence, and as Jeffrey Pfeffer and Robert Sutton (2006) warn, leaders are deluded by "dangerous half-truths" and "total nonsense." Many faulty educational practices, often incorporated into detailed long-term strategic plans, continue, even though the evidence does not support them (Childress et. al 2006; Reeves 2006). While market-based accountability surely leads to definitive rewards and sanctions, the invisible hand of the market does not shed light on how accountability policies can be employed to attain their central aim—the improvement of school performance and student achievement. To advance this cause, three essential aspects of accountability need to be kept in mind:

1. The purpose of accountability is to improve performance. It is not merely a reporting vehicle used to rate, rank, and sort students, teachers, schools, and states. Therefore, of necessity, an effective accountability system must include not only results, but also inferences about how to improve results. An accountability system that includes only student test scores without a measurement of teaching and leadership practices is like a healthcare accountability system that counts death rates, but does not ask how patients died.

2. Accountability requires coherent data. To allow for hypothesis testing, data must be distributed and warehoused in a way that makes it accessible and usable. While national educational standards remain politically impossible, there should be national standards for accountability systems that would permit meaningful comparison of the data generated by them.

3. The smaller the unit of analysis, the more meaningful inferences from the data will be. The evidence on the impact of classroom teachers on student learning is overwhelming (Darling-Hammond and Sykes 1999). Goodlad (1990, 1994) also makes a persuasive case that the individual school leader can have a profound impact on student achievement. However, when considered on a larger scale, the relationship between policy and results is less clear. Attempts to track district-level "progress" are bedeviled by countless confounding variables. Even school-level accountability—the focus of present law—can lead to a label of success or failure for an entire school based on the performance of one group of students in one grade in one subject.

SEE ALSO *Bureaucracy; Corruption; Democracy; Education, Unequal; Education, USA; Government; Principal-Agent Models; Private Sector; Public Sector; School Vouchers; Schooling in the USA; Transparency; Whistle-blowers*

BIBLIOGRAPHY

Baker, Frank B. 2001. *The Basics of Item Response Theory.* 2nd ed. College Park, MD: ERIC Clearinghouse on Assessment and Evaluation.

Childress, Stacey, Richard Elmore, and Allen Grossman. 2006. How to Manage Urban School Districts. *Harvard Business Review* 84 (11): 55–68.

Coulson, Andrew J., with James Gwartney, Neal McCluskey, John Merrifield, David Salisbury, and Richard Vedder. 2006. The Cato Education Market Index: Full Technical Report. *Policy Analysis* 585, December 13. http://www.cato.org/pubs/pas/pa585tr.pdf.

Darling-Hammond, Linda, and Gary Sykes. 1999. *Teaching as the Learning Profession: Handbook of Policy and Practice.* San Francisco: Jossey-Bass.

Figlio, David N., and Cecilia Elena Rouse. 2006. Do Accountability and Voucher Threats Improve Low-Performing Schools? *Journal of Public Economics* 90 (1–2): 239–255.

Finn, Chester E., Jr., Bruno V. Manno, and Gregg Vanourek. 2000. *Charter Schools in Action: Renewing Public Education.* Princeton, NJ: Princeton University Press.

Fuhrman, Susan H., and Richard F. Elmore, eds. 2004. *Redesigning Accountability Systems for Education.* New York: Teachers College Press.

Goodlad, John I. 1990. *Teachers for Our Nation's Schools.* San Francisco: Jossey-Bass.

Goodlad, John I. 1994. *Educational Renewal: Better Teachers, Better Schools.* San Francisco: Jossey-Bass.

Pfeffer, Jeffrey, and Robert I. Sutton. 2006. *Hard Facts, Dangerous Half-Truths, and Total Nonsense: Profiting from Evidence-Based Management.* Boston: Harvard Business School Press.

Reeves, Douglas B. 2001. *Crusade in the Classroom: How George W. Bush's Education Reforms Will Affect Your Children, Our Schools.* Riverside, NJ: Kaplan/Simon & Schuster.

Reeves, Douglas B. 2002. *Holistic Accountability: Serving Students, Schools, and Community.* Thousand Oaks, CA: Corwin Press.

Reeves, Douglas B. 2004a. *Accountability for Learning: How Teachers and School Leaders Can Take Charge.* Alexandria, VA: Association for Supervision and Curriculum Development.

Reeves, Douglas B. 2004b. *Accountability in Action: A Blueprint for Learning Organizations.* 2nd ed. Englewood, CO: Advanced Learning Press.

Reeves, Douglas B. 2006. *The Learning Leader: How to Focus School Improvement for Better Results.* Alexandria, VA: Association for Supervision and Curriculum Development.

Rothstein, Richard. 2004. Class and the Classroom: Even the Best Schools Can't Close the Race Achievement Gap. *American School Board Journal* 191 (10): 16–21.

Sanders, William L. 1998. Value Added Assessment. *The School Administrator*, December. http://www.aasa.org/publications/saarticledetail.cfm?ItemNumber=4627.

Schmoker, Mike. 2004. Tipping Point: From Feckless Reform to Substantive Instructional Improvement. *Phi Delta Kappan* 85 (6): 424–432.

Douglas B. Reeves

ACCOUNTING, GROWTH

SEE *Solow Residual, The.*

ACCUMULATION OF CAPITAL

Economists have used the term *accumulation of capital* to express several conceptual ideas in economics. Avoiding those having to do with obtaining more money, more bonds, or more stocks, two principal uses remain: an increase in the amount of physical means of production within an economy or its firms, or an increase in the power of the capitalist class. The former is the usage in neoclassical or mainstream economics while the latter is often considered within Marxist economics (although the exact meaning is still subject to various considerations). It is not unusual for either consideration to lead to discussion of economic crises, specifically to what might be their origins. The issue of crises may be, in turn, connected to disproportionalities among supplies and demands across industries within the economy.

EARLY DISCUSSIONS

In 1776 the Scottish economist Adam Smith made some attempt to define capital, but not its accumulation, while in 1821 the English economist David Ricardo introduced serious discussion of the effects upon workers of the introduction of new machinery, finding that it would not necessarily be beneficial. Ricardo was probably persuaded to undertake this investigation under the influence of the Swiss economist Jean-Charles-Léonard Simonde de Sismondi (1773–1842), whom Ricardo respected enough to visit from the United Kingdom. Sismondi was quite critical of the influence of capitalism upon the population and explicitly discussed the crisis aspects of capitalist development.

The German economist and political philosopher Karl Marx discussed accumulation of capital, yet there are ambiguities in his discussion. Marx was concerned, fundamentally, with the exploitation of the working class by the capitalist class and the capitalist class's capability of earning surplus value off the workers. Surplus value is the difference between working time of workers and the time required to produce the goods workers are able to buy with their wages. His principal book *Capital* (1867) is precisely a focus on that exploitation, so his accumulation of capital ought to be understood as an increase in the numbers of workers being exploited, including the related requirement to have built the factories within which the workers would be working. Crises could result from disproportionalities in production but also from the inability to find outlets for all the products produced under capitalist relations when the standard of living for the mass of workers is continually depressed. The latter concern dates back to Sismondi and the English economist Thomas Malthus (1766–1834), yet has unique aspects of analysis in Marx. The emphasis, generally, on means of production (e.g., machinery) in referring to accumulation of capital did penetrate Marx to some extent and his writing on accumulation.

In the 1890s the Russian Communist leader Vladimir Lenin brought Marxist economic thought back toward Ricardo, and also included more emphasis on technological development and disproportionalities in production than would be consistent with Marx himself. Becoming leader of the Bolshevik Revolution in Russia in 1917, his influence on Marxist economic thought was greater than his depth of understanding of Marx's political economy. Nevertheless, Lenin was not alone as Mikhail Tugan-Baranowsky (1865–1919) and the German economist and statesman Rudolf Hilferding (1877–1941) also emphasized disproportionalities in explaining crises.

TWENTIETH-CENTURY APPROACHES

A distinct approach away from Lenin, Tugan-Baranowsky, and Hilferding was undertaken by Rosa Luxemburg, whose *The Accumulation of Capital* (1913) had a major, albeit controversial, impact. This volume was the first of only two substantial books with the words "accumulation of capital" as the title, both written by women economists. Luxemburg's focus was on the incapacity of a closed capitalist system to find sufficient markets, since workers' wages are naturally suppressed, capitalist luxury consumption has its limits (considering the massive quantities of products that can be produced), and producing more and more machines just for its own sake makes no sense. She criticized certain aspects of Marx's work for failure to recognize the problem, even as she is firmly considered to be a Marxist economist.

Following upon the development of neoclassical economics beginning in the 1870s, John Bates Clark's *The Distribution of Wealth* solidified a distinct interpretation of capital as a measure of machines, like acres of land. In other words, all those different types of machines in industrial society were to be reduced to a homogenous measure called real capital. However, unlike land, machinery is a produced element of the production process and is changing much of the time, not just in numbers, but in its very physical characteristics. This was a strange innovation on the part of Clark, but it allowed him to render a marginal productivity theory of income distribution to explain why workers, capitalists, and landowners get what they get out of the national output.

As the mathematization of mainstream economics proceeded apace, capital in the sense of Clark, including its accumulation, proceeded along with it, and the neoclassical production function became widespread, both at the microeconomic level of the firm as well as for national economies.

When Luxemburg's book was translated into English in 1951 it had an introduction by Joan Robinson, and soon thereafter Robinson published her own book, *The Accumulation of Capital* (1956). Having come out of the Keynesian tradition of the 1930s that shared concerns of Malthus, Sismondi, and Marx regarding the possible deficiencies of aggregate demand to sustain the mammoth potentials on the supply side, Robinson's work was little concerned with disproportionalities as an explanation of economic crises.

During the 1960s Clark's conception of capital came under strong criticism when the so-called reswitching controversy arose. This controversy is too involved to summarize in this entry, but it starts with a proof that a simple economy, as wages moved in one direction, could switch from one technology to a second technology, and then, as wages continued to move in the same direction, switch back to the initial technology. The significance was to question how marginal productivity à la Clark could have any meaning.

Meanwhile, the Marxist tradition continued to refer to accumulation of capital as an expression of the inherent tendency of capitalism to extend its domination, but now connected to the possibility of a falling tendency of the average profit rate and thus to economic crises. By and large, accumulation of capital as a concept was anything but well defined and often functioned similarly to the term *capitalism*, with a more serious sound to it. A resolution that refers to increasing proletarianization of the world under the thrust of capital is not well accepted as of 2006.

CONCLUSIONS

Possible empirical work on accumulation of capital follows from the conceptualization. Should capital be measured as real capital then disparate physical items are typically aggregated by some type of weighting by relative prices exhibited in product markets. The trend of capital accumulation would therefore seem to be reflected in the increasing amounts of the individual items of equipment and structures. Yet, there are deep index number problems involved, including the initial base of the weighting, changing relative prices, and, most significantly, the introduction of totally new technologies and the disappearance of old (tractors substituting for iron plows pulled by horses, mules, or oxen; electrical lighting substituting for candles; cash registers for abacuses). In spite of difficulties, a whole segment of empirical economics has developed around such accounting, sometimes additionally integrated into profit-rate calculations.

Should capital be measured by capacity to exploit the labor hours of wage workers one would first have to measure the total employed wage workers and the length of their work hours. One would need to make a distinction between those who produce for capitalists commodities to be sold in the market and those who perform functions such as selling or administrative, as well as exclude those who do not work for capitalists (such productive/unproductive distinction appears, in differing forms, in portions of Smith's and Marx's works). At the level of an enterprise, data may be available, but for national economies they are much less so. No satisfactory work has been done on a global scale.

SEE ALSO *Luxemburg, Rosa; Marx, Karl; Optimal Growth; Primitive Accumulation; Production Function; Ricardo, David; Robinson, Joan; Technological Progress, Economic Growth*

BIBLIOGRAPHY

Clark, John Bates. 1956. *The Distribution of Wealth: A Theory of Wages, Interest, and Profits.* New York: Kelley & Millman. (Orig. pub. 1899).

Hilferding, Rudolf. 1981. *Finance Capital.* Trans. Morris Watnick and Sam Gordon. London: Routledge & Kegan Paul. (Orig. pub. 1910).

Luxemburg, Rosa. 1951. *The Accumulation of Capital.* Trans. Agnes Schwarzschild. London: Routledge & Kegan Paul. (Orig. pub. 1913).

Malthus, Thomas. 1989. *Principles of Political Economy Considered with a View to Their Practical Application.* 2 Vol. Ed. John Pullen. Cambridge, U.K.: Cambridge University Press. (Orig. pub. 1820).

Marx, Karl. 1954. *Capital: A Critical Analysis of Capitalist Production.* Vol. 1. Ed. Frederick Engels. Trans. Samuel Moore and Edward Aveling. Moscow: Progress Publishers. (Orig. pub. 1867).

Ricardo, David. 1951. *On the Principles of Political Economy and Taxation.* 3rd ed. Ed. Piero Sraffa. Cambridge, U.K.: Cambridge University Press. (Orig. pub. 1821).

Robinson, Joan. 1956. *The Accumulation of Capital.* London: Macmillan.

Sismondi, Jean-Charles-Léonard Simonde de. 1991. *New Principles of Political Economy: Of Wealth in Its Relation to Population.* Trans. Richard Hyse. New Brunswick, NJ: Transaction Publishers. (Orig. pub. 1819).

Smith, Adam. 1937. *An Inquiry into the Nature and Causes of the Wealth of Nations.* New York: Modern Library. (Orig. pub. 1776).

Tugan-Baranowsky, Mikhail I. 2000. *Studies on the Theory and the History of Business Crises in England, Part I: Theory and History of Crises.* 2nd ed. Chapters 1 and 7 trans. Alejandro Ramos-Martínez. In *Value, Capitalist Dynamics and Money, Research in Political Economy.* Vol. 18, ed. Paul Zarembka, 43–110. Amsterdam: JAI/Elsevier. (Orig. pub. 1901).

Zarembka, Paul. 2000. Accumulation of Capital, Its Definition: A Century after Lenin and Luxemburg. In *Value, Capitalist Dynamics and Money, Research in Political Economy.* Vol. 18, ed. Paul Zarembka, 183–241. Amsterdam: JAI/Elsevier Science.

Zarembka, Paul. 2003. Lenin as Economist of Production: A Ricardian Step Backwards. *Science & Society* 67 (3): 276–302.

Paul Zarembka

ACHIEVEMENT

The modern scientific study of achievement began with Henry Murray's seminal study of basic human needs, *Explorations in Personality* (1938). His definition of *achievement*, influential in all subsequent work on the subject, was "To accomplish something difficult. To master, manipulate or organize physical objects, human beings, or ideas. To do this as rapidly and as independently as possible. To overcome obstacles and attain a high standard. To excel one's self. To rival and surpass others. To increase self-regard by the successful exercise of talent" (Murray 1938, p. 164). His definition of *achievement motivation* was "To make intense, prolonged and repeated efforts to accomplish something difficult. To work with singleness of purpose towards a high and distant goal. To have the determination to win. To try to do everything well. To be stimulated to excel by the presence of others, to enjoy competition. To exert will power; to overcome boredom and fatigue" (Murray 1938, p. 164).

MEASURING ACHIEVEMENT

Murray developed a list of twenty human needs. Of these, the Need for Achievement has been the most extensively studied (along with the Need for Affiliation and the Need for Power). Murray also created the most extensively used measure of achievement motivation, the Thematic Apperception Test (TAT). This test asks people to tell stories about each of several pictures of people in a variety of situations. Evaluators then code the stories for the presence of achievement themes. It is an indirect, or *implicit*, measure of interest in achievement, as opposed to an explicit measure in which people are asked to answer questions that probe for achievement motivation (as in the Achievement Motivation Inventory, an explicit adaptation of the TAT). The primary use for these measures is to discover how individuals differ in their degree of interest in achievement and, by implication, the strength of their achievement motivation.

David McClelland, using a refined version of the TAT, showed that child rearing practices have a relation to subsequent strength of achievement motivation, both at the level of the individual parent-child relationship (e.g., the extent of early independence training) and at the level of a society's dominant culture of achievement. McClelland's wide-ranging work at the level of culture-related differences between countries (in such things as the Protestant work ethic and the amount of achievement imagery in children's texts or in the works of prominent writers) to indices of economic activity. This work demonstrated a clear and consistent relation between achievement imagery and economic development among and within nations and across a span of time from ancient Greek civilization to the mid-twentieth century, with increased levels of achievement themes preceding increases in economic productivity. Murray's theory specified that the surrounding cultural context regarding achievement influenced the way that parents reared their children, which in turn created stable achievement motivation in those children as adults, eventually resulting in overall increases in the society's economic output.

John Atkinson and his colleagues developed an influential *expectancy X value* theory of achievement motivation. The tendency to strive for success is, in this formulation, a multiplicative combination of the motivation to succeed, the value placed on success, and the likelihood of success. One of the primary findings using this analysis is that when given a choice among tasks varying in difficulty (probability of success), individuals will prefer tasks of intermediate difficulty, particularly if they are high in achievement motivation. The most likely reason for this preference is that tasks of intermediate complexity are the best diagnostic tasks in that they give the most information about the meaning of success or failure for one's current level of proficiency. Another implication of this formulation is that when either the probability of success, or the value of success, is extremely low, little motivation to achieve will be generated.

UNDERSTANDING MOTIVATION

A more cognitive approach to achievement motivation emphasizes how individuals understand and explain successes and failures. Bernard Weiner proposed that explanations for performances vary in two dimensions. Explanations may be either *internal* (something about the performer) or *external* (something about the performance situation), and they also vary in whether the cause is *stable* (likely to be the same in the future) or *unstable* (likely to be different in the future). An explanation for a particular performance might be internal and stable (*ability*), internal and unstable (*effort*), external and stable (*task difficulty*), or external and unstable (*luck*). These explanations for performance affect both how individuals feel after success and failure, and how willing they are to persist in the face of an initial failure.

Initial differences in the kinds of explanations people are likely to use also have been shown to underlie the likelihood of persisting or quitting in the face of initial failure. A *mastery orientation* entails a focus on acquiring competence at the task, on the feeling of making progress and getting better. In the face of initial failure, a mastery orientation leads to attributions to effort, and supports task persistence. In contrast, with a *performance orientation* the goal is to show how good one is at the task. When a person takes this orientation, initial failure is likely to be interpreted as a sign of low ability and to lead to decreased task persistence.

STEREOTYPE THREAT

The expectations of others can strongly affect achievement. Stereotypes about how well or poorly a member of a particular group is likely to perform can strongly affect the actual achievement of members of the stereotyped group. Claude Steele and Joshua Aronson introduced the concept of *stereotype threat*. This research demonstrates that when negative performance stereotypes are present, actual performance suffers. For example, women who are quite good at math show poorer math performance in situations in which the stereotype that women are not as good at math as men is salient, showing that the stereotype itself leads to a self-fulfilling prophecy. Steele and Aronson's initial work showed that when stereotype about intelligence is made salient for African Americans in an SAT-like task, performance suffers. Underlying this

process of stereotype threat is the fear that performing consistently with the stereotype will serve to confirm it in the minds of others. Worrying about this result unfortunately creates enough anxiety to interfere with performance and paradoxically results in the very behavior about which one is worried.

Achievement and achievement motivation are essential aspects of human nature, and are influenced by learning, by expectations of the value and probability of success, by one's own explanations for task performance, and by the beliefs and expectations of others.

SEE ALSO *Locus of Control; Motivation; Narratives; Parent-Child Relationships; Parenting Styles; Psychology; Scales; Self-Fulfilling Prophecies; Steele, Claude M.; Stereotype Threat*

BIBLIOGRAPHY

Atkinson, John W., and David Birch. 1970. *The Dynamics of Action.* New York: Wiley.

Dweck, Carol. 2006. *Mindset: The New Psychology of Success.* New York: Random House.

McClelland, David C. 1985. *Human Motivation.* Glenview, IL: Scott, Foresman.

Murray, Henry A., William G. Barrett, Erick Homberger, et al. 1938. *Explorations in Personality.* New York: Oxford University Press.

Steele, Claude M., and Joshua Aronson. 1995. Stereotype Threat and the Intellectual Test Performance of African Americans. *Journal of Personality and Social Psychology* 69 (5): 797–811.

Weiner, Bernard, ed. 1974. *Achievement Motivation and Attribution Theory.* Morristown, NJ: General Learning Press.

Thane S. Pittman

ACHIEVEMENT GAP, RACIAL

The black-white achievement gap refers to disparities between African American (black) and European American (white) students on educational outcomes that include standardized test scores, grade-point averages, high school graduation rates, and college enrollment and completion rates. On each of these measures, white students typically outperform their black peers. While scholars have studied the gap in standardized test scores since the early 1900s, interest in this topic reemerged in the 1990s partly in response to a widening of the gap on the National Assessment of Education Progress in the United States after it had narrowed for nearly 20 years. This renewed interest also arose partly in response to the publication of the controversial book *The Bell Curve*, by

Richard J. Herrnstein and Charles Murray (1994), which suggested that the gap resulted from genetic differences between racial groups.

Genetic arguments have been rejected convincingly by research in which scholars identify multiple methodological flaws in such work and point out that the lack of systematic genetic variation across racial categories undermines such arguments. Other explanations for the racial achievement gap, however, have empirical support. For example, racial differences in social class as measured by parents' education, income, and wealth explain a substantial portion of the gap in test scores and educational attainment. Additionally, research shows that black and white students receive different opportunities to learn, even when attending desegregated schools, and that these differences contribute to the gap. Black students are typically placed in lower-ability groups and educational tracks, are overrepresented in special education, are underrepresented in gifted and talented programs, are taught by less experienced and less well trained teachers, and face lower teacher expectations regarding their academic potential than white students.

Additional explanations focus on psychological and cultural mechanisms associated with the gap. For instance, the stereotype threat model devised by the psychologist Claude Steele (b. 1946) demonstrates that black college students underperform on academic tasks because they fear being viewed through the lens of negative racial stereotypes about black intelligence or are apprehensive about confirming such negative stereotypes through poor test performance. Stereotype threat may lead to a process called disidentification, in which black students' personal identities become disconnected from education as a domain, leading to underachievement. More research, however, is needed to further test this hypothesis.

The oppositional culture argument provides a related explanation for the black-white achievement gap. Perhaps best articulated by the anthropologist John Ogbu (1939–2003) and his colleagues—for example, in the contribution to *Urban Review*, "Black Students' School Success" (Fordham and Ogbu 1986)—this perspective suggests that black students respond to race-based educational and employment discrimination by opposing educational achievement. As a result, high-achieving black students may confront negative feedback from their peers for investing in school and receive criticism for "acting white." While this has been an influential explanation for the gap in scholarly and popular discourse, recent research rejects its core hypotheses. Finally, while no scholarly consensus exists, some research suggests that schools, as institutions, respond favorably to and reward white students' cultural styles (such as dress, linguistic practices, and learning styles) and devalue those of black students, perhaps contributing to the gap.

WHY DID THE GAP CLOSE?

It is unclear why the test-score gap narrowed between 1970 and 1988. However, work suggests that greater access to educational resources among black students, reductions in class size, and racial desegregation efforts may have contributed to this pattern. The gap persists in desegregated schools, however, probably because of racial inequalities in opportunities to learn in such contexts. Likewise, aggressive efforts to challenge systematic racial discrimination in educational and employment opportunities following the civil rights movement of the 1950s and 1960s may have led to greater optimism about the economic returns to education among African Americans and increased their already high levels of motivation for educational achievement.

SEE ALSO *Acting White; Civil Rights Movement, U.S.; Class; Determinism, Cultural; Determinism, Genetic; Education, Unequal; Inequality, Racial; National Assessment of Educational Progress; Ogbu, John U.; Schooling in the USA; Standardized Tests; Steele, Claude M.; Stereotype Threat; Tracking in Schools*

BIBLIOGRAPHY

Ainsworth-Darnell, James W., and Douglas B. Downey. 1998. Assessing the Oppositional Culture Explanation for Racial/Ethnic Differences in School Performance. *American Sociological Review* 63 (4): 536–553.

Cook, Philip J., and Jens Ludwig. 1997. Weighing the "Burden of 'Acting White' ": Are There Race Differences in Attitudes toward Education? *Journal of Policy Analysis and Management* 16 (2): 256–278.

Fordham, Signithia, and John U. Ogbu. 1986. Black Students' School Success: Coping with the "Burden of 'Acting White.' " *Urban Review* 18 (3): 176–206.

Herrnstein, Richard J., and Charles Murray. 1994. *The Bell Curve: Intelligence and Class Structure in American Life.* New York: Free Press.

Jacoby, Russell, and Naomi Glauberman, eds. 1995. *The Bell Curve Debate: History, Documents, Opinions.* New York: Times Books.

Jencks, Christopher, and Meredith Phillips, eds. 1998. *The Black-White Test Score Gap.* Washington, DC: Brookings Institution Press.

Steele, Claude. 2003. Stereotype Threat and African American Student Achievement. In *Young, Gifted, and Black: Promoting High Achievement Among African American Students*, eds. Theresa Perry, Claude Steele, and Asa G. Hilliard III, 109–130. Boston: Beacon Press.

Tyson, Karolyn, William Darity, and Domini R. Castellino. 2005. It's Not "a Black Thing": Understanding the Burden of

Acting White and Other Dilemmas of High Achievement. *American Sociological Review* 70 (4): 582–605.

John B. Diamond

ACT TEST, THE

SEE *Standardized Tests.*

ACTING WHITE

African American adolescents sometimes ridicule their peers for behaving in ways they identify as characteristic of whites. A variety of behaviors may trigger this response: manner of speech and dress, choice of television shows or sports, and, most troubling, demonstrating a commitment to academic success by participating in class, studying hard, and enrolling in advanced classes. This phenomenon was given prominence in an article published in 1986 by ethnographers Signithia Fordham and John Ogbu, reporting a study of a predominantly black high school in Washington, D.C. Since then, the burden of "acting white" has emerged as one of the standard explanations for the black-white gap in test scores and academic achievement; gifted black students are dragged down by peer pressure. But the evidence does not provide much support for the view that peer pressure against academic achievement is especially pervasive or important in influencing the academic striving of African Americans.

Ogbu speculated that black students tend to sneer at academic striving because they are influenced by an "oppositional culture" traceable to slavery, discrimination against blacks, and persistent inequality. Academic achievement is devalued because of its association with the dominant and oppressive white culture. A contrary view notes that while both black and white adolescents may sometimes exert (or experience) peer pressure against being "nerdy" and working hard in school, this anti-intellectual norm is not usually racialized.

Fordham and Ogbu reported on their observations from a single school. Several studies based on representative national surveys of high-school students have reached contrary findings. These have demonstrated that the differences between black and white students are negligible with respect to the value placed on education. Blacks express expectations at least as high as whites for graduating from high school and attending a four-year college. On average they attend class and expend as much effort outside of class as whites, and their parents are just as involved.

Whether there is a social penalty for academic success has also been investigated from national survey data. By a number of measures relating to social rejection, top students of both races do no worse (on average) than those in the middle of the grades distribution. Being in the honor society actually appears to protect against social ostracism, especially for black students in predominantly black schools. On the other hand, research by David Austen-Smith and Roland Fryer (2005) has found that the best black students have fewer close friends than those with average grades, especially in the case of males.

Since Fordham and Ogbu's original contribution, there have been several more ethnographic studies of individual schools. These have tended to cast further doubt on the notion of the "burden of acting white." A detailed survey of students in Shaker Heights, Ohio, by Harvard economist Ronald Ferguson (2001) has been especially influential. He found no evidence of an oppositional culture among the black students. Similar proportions of black and white students reported that there was a social penalty for academic striving in this successful and long-integrated school system. Another study of eight schools in North Carolina confirmed that there was some social penalty for high achievement for both races, but in only one of the schools were there reports of a strong racial element to this stigmatization (Tyson, Darity, and Castellino 2005). It did appear that qualified black students sometimes avoided taking advanced placement classes, but that was due more to a concern with being socially isolated (as possibly the only black student in class), rather than a concern with being criticized by their black peers.

The bottom line is that the adolescent norm against academic striving and success is evident among both white and black students. In some times and places, the successful black students are accused of "acting white," but there is little evidence in support of a pervasive black cultural norm against academic striving and success. Finally, whatever the penalties, there are also social rewards for being successful, and in the rough-and-tumble of adolescent society, the top scholars are not doing any worse on average than their peers.

BIBLIOGRAPHY

Austen-Smith, David, and Roland Fryer. 2005. An Economic Analysis of "Acting White." *Quarterly Journal of Economics* 120 (2): 551–583.

Cook, Philip J., and Jens Ludwig. 1998. The Burden of Acting White: Do Black Adolescents Disparage Academic Achievement. In *The Black-White Test Score Gap*, eds. Christopher Jencks and Meredith Phillips, 375–400. Washington, DC: Brookings Institution Press.

Ferguson, Ronald. 2001. A Diagnostic Analysis of Black-White GPA Disparities in Shaker Heights, Ohio. *Brookings Papers on Education Policy*, 347–414. Washington, DC: Brookings Institution Press.

Fordham, Signithia, and John U. Ogbu. 1986. Black Students' School Success: Coping with the "Burden of Acting White." *The Urban Review* 18: 176–206.

Tyson, Karolyn, William Darity Jr., and Domini R. Castellino. 2005. It's Not "A Black Thing": Understanding the Burden of Acting White and Other Dilemmas of High Achievement. *American Sociological Review* 70: 582–605.

Philip J. Cook

ACTIVISM

Activism refers to action by an individual or group with the intent to bring about social, political, economic, or even ideological change. This change could be directed at something as simple as a community organization or institution or as complex as the federal government or the public at large. In most cases, but not all, the action is directed toward the support or opposition of a controversial issue. Such issues range from basic human rights (see Blau and Moncada 2005) to the rights of gay men and lesbians (see Hunter et al. 1992) to antiwar or prowar sentiments over the Iraq War.

The First Amendment of the U.S. Constitution guarantees the right of the people to "petition the government for a redress of grievances." While earlier drafts of the First Amendment simply addressed the needs of the people to assemble and petition, later drafts included the rights of free speech, freedom of the press, and religion. However, the right to these freedoms is a matter of debate. Laws such as the Patriot Act, passed shortly after the September 11, 2001, attacks on the World Trade Center in New York City and the Pentagon near Washington, D.C., expand the authority of U.S. law enforcement agencies under the rhetoric of terrorism and limit the constitutional rights of U.S. citizens. In addition, rights to assembly are often viewed by law enforcement agencies and government organizations as a political threat. As a result, there are countless cases in U.S. history where altercations between law enforcement and organizing groups, even peaceful assemblies, have resulted in violence. For instance, a rally in Los Angeles over immigration rights on May 6, 2007, was disrupted when police officers fired rubber bullets into the crowd and pummeled television crews and other journalists with batons (Kahn 2007).

Activism can take many forms, including such actions as civil disobedience, rioting, striking by unions, government or institutional lobbying, verbal or physical confrontation, various forms of terrorism, and the use of music and the media to draw attention to particular issues. The rise of the Internet has allowed new forms of activism to emerge and has also allowed many small, local issues to gain a wider audience and in some cases worldwide attention. Activism is a necessary vehicle for progressive and social change (see Bonilla-Silva 2006). Major movements such as the civil rights movement represent examples of what large-scale activism can accomplish given the right historical conditions and group collectivities.

In addition to individual or group-level activism, there are centers and organizations whose sole purpose is to promote social change through awareness and the bridging of theory and practice. Examples of such organizations include Loyola University–Chicago's Center for Urban Research and Learning, a public sociology center that promotes research addressing community needs and that involves community organizers at all levels of its research process. Similarly, Project South, a leadership-development organization located in the southern United States, works with communities in bottom-up activism over issues pertaining to social, racial, and economic justice.

SEE ALSO *Civil Liberties; Civil Rights; Civil Rights Movement, U.S.; Human Rights; Political Parties; Protest; Resistance; Revolution; Social Movements; Women's Movement*

BIBLIOGRAPHY

Blau, Judith, and Alberto Moncada. 2005. *Human Rights: Beyond the Liberal Vision.* Lanham, MD: Rowman and Littlefield.

Bonilla-Silva, Eduardo. 2006. *Racism without Racists: Color-Blind Racism and the Persistence of Racial Inequality in the United States.* 2nd ed. Lanham, MD: Rowman and Littlefield.

Hunter, Nan D., Sherryl E. Michaelson, and Thomas B. Stoddard. 1992. *The Rights of Lesbians and Gay Men: The Basic ACLU Guide to a Gay Person's Rights.* 3rd ed. Carbondale: Southern Illinois University Press.

Kahn, Carrie. 2007. Police Tactics at L.A. Rally Reignite Scrutiny. National Public Radio (NPR): *Weekend Edition Sunday,* May 6.

David G. Embrick

ACTIVISM, JUDICIAL

Judicial activism is a philosophy that motivates judges to depart from strict adherence to judicial precedent, statutes, and strict interpretation of the United States Constitution. The juridical reasoning behind judicial activism is that the judiciary should have latitude in creating and interpreting law to protect the rights of political minorities from majoritarian excesses. Judicial activism has frequently been contrasted with *judicial restraint.* Judicial restraint means deference to other political branches, whether by upholding precedent or strictly interpreting statutory or constitutional provisions. The issue of judicial activism versus judicial restraint is volatile because of the consequences it can have on the law and society. Therefore, charges of judicial activism have been strategically used by both conservatives and liberals as concise campaign slogans to extol either the virtue or vice of the opposing candidate or political party. Many times, individuals affiliated with particular political parties or groups who view specific judicial decisions as conflicting with their philosophies characterize the judicial decision as an example of judicial activism. However, to discuss the issue in polarizing terms and apply political labels is overly simplistic. There are numerous Supreme Court decisions in the history of the United States, arguably results of judicial activism, that many would argue were constitutional milestones and others view as setbacks. Among these decisions are some of the most important landmark rulings in ensuring equity and fairness, as well as others that were patently flawed.

The landmark case *Brown v. Board of Education* (1954) ended the segregation in public schools that previously had been directed by the "separate but equal" doctrine. The decision overruled precedents and rejected state legislative statutes that allowed racial segregation in schools. In another example, in 1971 the Supreme Court in *Reed v. Reed* determined that the Equal Protection Clause of the Fourteenth Amendment guaranteed equality for women, and that a state law that discriminated based on gender was unconstitutional despite the fact that the Fourteenth Amendment does not state on its face that women and men should be treated the same. Most people today acknowledge that these Supreme Court rulings could be considered examples of judicial activism, but few would argue that they were not fair and just and should be overturned.

Judicial activism has also produced some less desirable results. In *Dred Scott v. Sandford* (1856), commonly known as the Dred Scott decision, the Supreme Court invalidated the Missouri Compromise and interpreted the Constitution as expressly allowing slavery, and held that people of African descent, whether or not they were slaves, could not be citizens of the United States. This was in direct contrast to the will of Congress, and set the scene for the Civil War.

An example of judicial restraint that resulted in a flawed decision is the Supreme Court ruling in *Plessy v. Ferguson* (1896), which stated that "separate but equal" public facilities met the requirements of the Fourteenth Amendment guarantees. Therefore, states could segregate facilities based on the color of a person's skin. Examples of cases where judicial restraint produced positive results include the civil rights cases of 1964 in which the Supreme Court deferred to Congress and upheld the Civil Rights Act of 1964 (e.g., in *Heart of Atlanta Motel, Inc. v. United States,* 1964).

Neither judicial activism nor judicial restraint should be viewed as an absolute vice or virtue. Judicial activism and judicial restraint by the United States Supreme Court have both produced some of the wisest landmark decisions as well as some of the less desirable rulings. The U.S. experience with judicial review demonstrates that juridical philosophies defined as activism or restraint are not helpful in determining the quality of a judge or a judicial decision.

BIBLIOGRAPHY

Powers, Stephen P., and Stanley Rothman. 2002. *The Least Dangerous Branch?: Consequences of Judicial Activism.* Westport, CT: Praeger.

Smithey, Shannon Ishiyama, John Ishiyama. 2002. Judicial Activism in Post-Communist Politics. *Law and Society Review* vol 36, no. 4, 719–741.

Diana C. Noone

ADAMS, JOHN

SEE *Jefferson, Thomas.*

ADAPTIVE EXPECTATIONS

The term *adaptive expectations* refers to the way economic agents adjust their expectations about future events based on past information and on some adjustment term. This implies some sort of correction mechanism: if someone's expectations are off the mark now, they can be corrected the next time, and so on. Economists view decision rules that govern an agent's behavior as being continuously under revision. As new decision rules are tried and tested, rules that yield accurate outcomes supersede those that fail to do so. In this sense, Robert Lucas (1986) refers to the trial-and-error process through which the models of behavior are determined as "adaptive."

Suppose we want to forecast the inflation rate (Π_t), which is itself measured by variations in the price index over time, $(P_t - P_{t-1})/P_{t-1}$. An example from an economics textbook (e.g., Arnold 2005, pp. 351–352) will help illustrate the principle of adaptive expectations. Let an individual forecast the future inflation rate for Year 5 based on the previous four yearly inflation rates. Observing the declining trend in the inflation rate over time, the forecaster assigns more weight to the more immediate past as follows:

Year 1: 5% inflation rate with weight 10%

Year 2: 4% inflation rate with weight 20%

Year 3: 3% inflation rate with weight 30%

Year 4: 2% inflation rate with weight 40%

The individual's expected inflation rate, $E(\Pi_t)$, will be: $0.05\,(0.10) + 0.04\,(0.20) + 0.03\,(0.30) + 0.02\,(0.40) = 0.030$, or a 3 percent inflation rate forecast for Year 5.

More generally, inflationary expectations can be calculated by using a weighted average of past actual inflation (Π_t) and past expected inflation measured by $E(\Pi_{t-1})$:

$$E(\Pi_t) = \lambda\,\Pi_{t-1} + (1-\lambda)\,E(\Pi_{t-1}) \tag{1}$$

where: $E(.)$ is the expectations operator; and $0 < \lambda < 1$ is the weight of past inflation on current inflation expectations. Algebraic manipulation of (1) yields:

$$E(\Pi_t) = E(\Pi_{t-1}) + \lambda\,[\Pi_{t-1} - E(\Pi_{t-1})] \tag{2}$$

where the second term (in brackets) is composed by the weight and a forecast error of the previous rate of inflation. Inflationary expectations are thus the sum of the previous term inflation forecast and the forecast error. The error term is going to have a large effect on current inflationary expectations if the parameter λ is large. If λ is zero, the adjustment term vanishes and current expected inflation matches past expected inflation. If, on the other hand, λ is one, the current expected inflation rate equals the past inflation rate.

The adaptive expectations principle found plenty of applications in macroeconomics, such as in the analysis of hyperinflation by Philip Cagan (1956), in the consumption function by Milton Friedman (1957), and in Phillips curves for inflation and unemployment. The empirical success of the idea was ultimately challenged by the rational expectations hypothesis, developed by John Muth (1961) and extended by Thomas Sargent and Neil Wallace (1975) and Lucas (1976). More recent work, such as George Evans and Garey Ramey (2006), follows Muth (1960) and reconsiders the Lucas critique in the context of adaptive expectations.

SEE ALSO *Expectations; Expectations, Implicit; Expectations, Rational; Expectations, Static*

BIBLIOGRAPHY

Arnold, Roger A. 2005. *Economics.* 7th ed. Mason, OH: Thomson/South-Western.

Cagan, Philip. 1956. The Monetary Dynamics of Hyperinflation. In *Studies in the Quantity Theory of Money*, ed. Milton Friedman, 25–117. Chicago: University of Chicago Press.

Evans, George, and Garey Ramey. 2006. Adaptive Expectations, Underparametrization, and the Lucas Critique. *Journal of Monetary Economics* 53 (2): 249–264.

Friedman, Milton. 1957. *Theory of the Consumption Function.* Princeton, NJ: Princeton University Press.

Lucas, Robert, Jr. 1976. Econometric Policy Evaluation: A Critique. *Carnegie-Rochester Conferences in Public Policy* 1: 19–46. Supplemental series to the *Journal of Monetary Economics.*

Lucas, Robert, Jr. 1986. Adaptive Behavior and Economic Theory. *Journal of Business* 59 (4, pt. 2): S401–S426.

Muth, John F. 1960. Optimal Properties of Exponentially Weighted Forecasts. *Journal of the American Statistical Association* 55: 299–306.

Muth, John F. 1961. Rational Expectations and the Theory of Price Movements. *Econometrica* 29: 315–335.

Sargent, Thomas J., and Neil Wallace. 1975. "Rational Expectations": The Optimal Monetary Instrument and the Optimal Money Supply Rule. *Journal of Political Economy* 83: 241–254.

Andre V. Mollick

ADAPTIVE INTELLIGENCE

SEE *Intelligence, Social.*

ADD HEALTH

SEE *National Longitudinal Study of Adolescent Health.*

ADDAMS, JANE

SEE *Poverty, Urban.*

ADDICTION

The term *addiction*, as applied to substance use, denotes an advanced level of dependence on a substance, marked by a compulsive need to obtain and consume it despite negative consequences. Dependency may consist of physical dependency, psychological dependency, or both. Physical dependency is characterized by withdrawal symptoms that occur if the substance is discontinued. This physical dependence thus produces a cycle in which the individual continues to use the substance to prevent the withdrawal symptoms. Psychological dependency, while no less powerful than physical dependency, refers to an individual's *perceived* need for the substance. When the individual is unable to acquire the drug, negative psychological experiences may occur, prompting the individual to continue substance use. Individuals who experience addiction may find themselves unable to function effectively without the substance or substances to which they are addicted. What distinguishes addiction from less extreme forms of dependence is a loss of control and a markedly intense preoccupation with the substance.

The term *addiction* is not part of the clinical framework presented in the Diagnostic and Statistical Manual of Mental Disorders (*DSM-IV-TR*) of the American Psychiatric Association. Yet, the diagnostic classifications in the 2000 edition of the *DSM-IV-TR* acknowledge the symptoms of physical and psychological dependence, including withdrawal and tolerance. Withdrawal, the prominent feature of addiction, is characterized by physical symptoms and often by inability to function without the substance. Tolerance occurs when over time individuals experience a decreased substance effect or must increase their dosage of the substance to experience the same effect.

Individuals may develop addiction to a variety of substances, including alcohol and drugs. Drugs of addiction include both illicit drugs like heroin and prescription or over-the-counter drugs like prescription oxycodone. Whether individuals can become addicted to behaviors—such as gambling, eating, and sexual promiscuity—is, however, controversial. Scholars who favor an expanded definition of addiction argue that certain behaviors may serve an emotion-regulating function and can thus lead to addiction.

The use of potentially addictive substances is quite prevalent. According to the 2004 National Survey on Drug Use and Health (NSDUH), 7.9 percent of the population aged twelve or older used illicit drugs in 2004 (Substance Abuse and Mental Health Services Administration [SAMHSA] 2005). However, substance use and addiction are not equally prevalent in all social categories. According to the 2004 NSDUH, rates of illicit drug use among those twelve and older increase until ages eighteen to twenty, after which rates gradually decrease (SAMHSA 2005). Rates of current illicit drug use also vary by race/ethnicity, with rates highest among individuals reporting two or more racial/ethnic groups and those of American Indian or Alaskan Native descent (SAMHSA

2005). Rates are similar for whites, Hispanics, and blacks, but markedly lower among Asians (SAMHSA 2005). With regard to socioeconomic status, rates are higher for the unemployed than the employed (SAMHSA 2005).

In addition to variations by social category, distinct patterns are observed for different classes of drugs. Tobacco and alcohol use are even more prevalent than illicit drug use (SAMHSA 2005).

CAUSES OF ADDICTION

Differences in patterns of use may be due to both social and biological factors. Furthermore, factors involved in initial and in continued substance use may differ. For example, individuals may begin use as a means of social enhancement or in response to pressure from peers and may continue use to avoid negative emotions or withdrawal.

Animal models have improved understanding of addiction and, in tandem with the findings of twin studies, strongly suggest a genetic component (see Crabbe 2002 for review). Scientists have identified neurotransmitter systems that are involved in the development of addiction. In recent years, this genetic component has received increasing attention as research on addiction has shifted from the domain of sociologists and psychologists to that of geneticists and neurobiologists. This focus on the role of brain chemistry (e.g., Koob, Sanna, and Bloom 1998) and genetics (e.g., Nestler 2000) has many potential implications for the study and treatment of addiction: It may lead to revolutionary new treatments and reduce addiction's stigma. Especially useful are gene-environment interaction models in which social environments/circumstances and genetics interact to determine whether an individual develops addiction.

CONSEQUENCES AND TREATMENT OF ADDICTION

Addiction is costly to both society and the individual. At the societal level, the prevention, control, and treatment of addiction require substantial resources. The types of societal investments made depend in part on whether addiction is viewed as primarily a medical or a criminal issue. Policies based on medical models favor rehabilitation and other treatments and generally attempt to minimize the stigma of addiction. Policies based on criminal models focus on punishing addicts and deterring addiction in the same way that other crime is deterred. In practice, both policies, or elements of both policies, are observed.

Addiction usually entails a variety of social costs as well. Individuals with addictions are highly motivated to attain the substance of their addictions and may engage in self-destructive behaviors or criminal acts in this pursuit. Drugs per se do not necessarily make individuals more violent, but the need to attain the drug, often to ward off withdrawal, may disinhibit individuals and lead to unhealthy and/or criminal activity. At the familial level, parents who have an addiction may be unable to responsibly care for their children. Moreover, children of substance users are themselves at increased risk of substance use (see, e.g., White, Johnson, and Buyske 2000). At the individual level, addiction is associated with a multitude of negative health effects. This may be due to the substance itself or to the way that the substance is consumed. For example, drugs that are smoked may contribute to lung cancer, whereas drugs that are taken intravenously pose risks associated with injection (i.e., use of unsterile needles may be associated with the transmission of infectious diseases like HIV). Negative health effects also include withdrawal, which can be fatal with some drugs and with alcohol if not medically supervised.

TREATMENT OF ADDICTION

Many agencies exist to assist individuals in overcoming addiction, including outpatient facilities, residential communities, and hospital-based programs. In addition, self-help groups like Alcoholics Anonymous (AA) are quite common. The twelve-step model of AA has been embraced by the treatment community and often provides the structural framework for both inpatient and outpatient treatment. A variety of pharmacotherapies are available for treating addictions, including agonist medications, antagonists, agonist-antagonist medications, and anticraving medications (see O'Brien 1997 for discussion). Supervised medical detoxification may be required for individuals addicted to certain drugs and for alcohol-dependent individuals with medical problems. Treatment for addiction can be quite costly.

Approaches to the treatment of addiction are predominantly based on a *biopsychosocial* model, which holds that the biological, psychological, and social bases of addiction all need to be addressed. Within that approach, differences in understandings of the causes of addiction may prompt some treatment providers to favor certain approaches over others. For example, some treatment providers favor a medical model in which addiction is viewed as a disease and treated within a medical framework, whereas others may lean toward more behavioral models that conceptualize substance abuse as resulting from deficient coping skills. Some providers more than others pay special attention to social and cultural explanations for addiction and advocate culturally sensitive programs that focus on overcoming social disadvantage. Individualized treatment programs and programs that

respond to differences in gender and sexual orientation have great potential for success.

Addiction is a phenomenon with social, medical, and legal dimensions. A multifaceted public health problem, its treatment and prevention require contributions from multiple disciplines. Medical scholars, legal scholars, sociologists, psychologists, and policymakers are all needed if progress is to be made.

SEE ALSO *Drugs of Abuse; Tolerance, Drug*

BIBLIOGRAPHY

American Psychiatric Association. 2000. *Diagnostic and Statistical Manual of Mental Disorders: DSM-IV-TR.* Rev. 4th ed. Washington, DC: American Psychiatric Association.

Crabbe, John C. 2002. Genetic Contributions to Addiction. *Annual Review of Psychology* 53: 435–462.

Koob, George F., Pietro Paolo Sanna, and Floyd E. Bloom. 1998. Neuroscience of Addiction. *Neuron* 21 (3): 467–476.

Nestler, Eric J. 2000. Genes and Addiction. *Nature Genetics* 26 (3): 277–281.

O'Brien, Charles P. 1997. A Range of Research-Based Pharmacotherapies for Addiction. *Science* 278 (5335): 66–70.

Substance Abuse and Mental Health Services Administration. 2005. *Overview of Findings from the 2004 National Survey on Drug Use and Health.* NSDUH Series H-27; DHHS Publication No. SMA 05-4061. Rockville, MD: Department of Health and Human Services, Substance Abuse and Mental Health Services Administration, Office of Applied Studies.

White, Helene Raskin, Valerie Johnson, and Steven Buyske. 2000. Parental Modeling and Parenting Behavior Effects on Offspring Alcohol and Cigarette Use: A Growth Curve Analysis. *Journal of Substance Abuse* 12 (3): 287–310.

Alexis T. Franzese

ADLER, ALFRED

SEE *Inferiority Complex; Napoleon Complex.*

ADMINISTRATIVE LAW

Administrative law is a branch of public law that includes the laws and legal principles pertaining to the administration and regulation of state agencies, ministries, or departments and the relationship of the state with private individuals. It is a product of the need for a state to perform a multitude of functions for its citizens and deals with the decision making of a state agency in relation to its regulatory framework. Such regulatory frameworks perform a variety of state functions including natural resource protection, transportation regulation, and food and health safety regulations. Because all administrative law systems are not the same it is imperative for an individual to have knowledge of the political, historical, social, and economic context of the system of a particular state to fully understand its administrative law. In most systems a state's constitution or fundamental law is inextricably linked to its administrative law system and must be considered in light of the system or tradition under consideration.

All but the most oppressive administrative law systems share at least one or more of the following interests: (1) providing justice for injuries inflicted by state personnel and agencies on private citizens; (2) maintaining the legality and propriety of subordinate state agencies and actors; and (3) remedying injuries to bureaucrats by the state. Common law administrative law scholars in the United Kingdom and the United States look to the *Conseil d'Etat* in France because, at one time, French administrative law dominated continental systems. Not all administrative law systems conform, however, to this pattern. At least four other divergent themes have all been noted by H. B. Jacobini in *An Introduction to Comparative Administrative Law* (1991): "(1) the Sinitic Censorate and its derivatives, (2) the Procuracy and other administrative law procedures as found in the communist world, (3) the concept of the ombudsman, and (4) machinery for registering complaints" (p. 12).

The fundamental elements of administrative law in the United States that are similar to many European and other nations include: (1) statutory delegation of powers from an elected legislative body to the executive; (2) an administrative agency that derives its authority from the legislative body, and that implements the relevant law through rulemaking, adjudication, or other forms of administrative process; (3) judicial review by an independent judiciary of the administrative body's actions for compliance with the statutory delegation of powers by the legislative body and other applicable laws; and (4) transparency of the decisional process.

For example, in the United States, administrative agencies are said to have no inherent powers because they must act pursuant to the legal authority delegated to them by the legislative body. The legislative body empowers administrative agencies to act as agents for the executive branch of government through statutory law. The statute that delegates power to an administrative agency sets forth the scope of the agency's authority. Thus, the nature of administrative law is subconstitutional in the United States because the powers of administrative agencies are delegated through statutory law, not through constitutional law. Yet the actions of the administrative agency must ultimately comply with the U.S. Constitution, its fundamental law. In contrast the German Constitution,

the *Grundgesetz*, contains provisions specifically relevant to the development of its administrative law system.

Administrative agencies in the United States typically utilize adjudication, rulemaking, and inspection to execute their statutory authority. Adjudication can be either informal or formal and must comport to the U.S. Constitution's due process clause. Rulemaking can also be informal or formal. In addition, the power of inspection is sometimes used as a substitute for adjudication procedures or to determine whether not the existence of certain conditions warrant further administrative action. One example of an administrative agency is the Environmental Protection Agency (EPA), whose mission is to protect human health and the environment.

In many countries the courts play a large part in the development of administrative law. In the United States the power of judicial review allows courts to determine whether or not the actions of administrative agencies exceed the scope of their delegated authority or violate the Constitution. Similar processes of review are found in other countries and, although the legal standards vary, their roles are quite similar. For example, in France the Conseil d'Etat has developed general principles for administrative law. In the United Kingdom, the ordinary courts are competent in administrative law and, generally, this area is subject to common law. There, the Queens Bench of the High Court is more administrative than the ordinary court when it deals with applications of judicial review.

SEE ALSO *Bureaucracy; Government; Judicial Review; Public Administration; Separation of Powers*

BIBLIOGRAPHY

Jacobini, H. B. 1991. *An Introduction to Comparative Administrative Law*. New York: Oceana Publications.

Seerden, René, and Frits Stroink, eds. 2002. *Administrative Law of the European Union, Its Member States and the United States: A Comparative Analysis*. Antwerpen: Intersentia.

Strauss, Peter L. 2006. *Administrative Justice in the United States*. 2nd ed. Durham, NC: Carolina Academic Press.

Angelique M. Davis

ADOLESCENT HEALTH LONGITUDINAL SURVEY

SEE *National Longitudinal Study of Adolescent Health.*

ADOLESCENT PSYCHOLOGY

Adolescence spans the second decade of life, a phase social scientists describe as beginning in biology and ending in society. Adolescence may be defined as the life-span period in which most of a person's biological, cognitive, psychological, and social characteristics are changing in an interrelated manner from what is considered childlike to what is considered adultlike. When most of a person's characteristics are in this state of change the person is an adolescent.

CHANGING MODELS OF ADOLESCENCE

Since the founding of the scientific study of adolescent development at the beginning of the twentieth century the predominant conceptual frame for the study of this age period has been one of storm and stress, or of an ontogenetic time of normative developmental disturbance (Freud 1969). Typically, these deficit models of the characteristics of adolescence were predicated on biologically reductionist models of genetic or maturational determination (Erikson 1959, 1968) and resulted in descriptions of youth as broken or in danger of becoming broken (Benson, Scales, Hamilton, and Sesma 2006), as both dangerous and endangered (Anthony 1970), or as problems to be managed (Roth, Brooks-Gunn, Murray, and Foster 1998). In fact, if positive development was discussed in the adolescent development literature—at least prior to the 1990s—it was implicitly or explicitly regarded as the absence of negative or undesirable behaviors. A youth who was seen as manifesting behavior indicative of positive development was depicted as someone who was *not* taking drugs or using alcohol, *not* engaging in unsafe sex, and *not* participating in crime or violence.

Beginning in the early 1990s, and burgeoning in the first half decade of the twenty-first century, a new vision and vocabulary for discussing young people emerged. Propelled by the increasingly more collaborative contributions of scholars (Benson et al. 2006; Damon 2004; Roth & Brooks-Gunn 2003), practitioners (Floyd & McKenna 2003; Little 1993; Pittman, Irby, and Ferber 2001), and policy makers (Cummings 2003; Gore 2003), youth are viewed as resources to be developed. The new vocabulary emphasizes the strengths present within all young people and involves concepts such as developmental assets, moral development, civic engagement, well-being, and thriving. These concepts are predicated on the ideas that every young person has the potential for positive youth development (PYD).

This vision for and vocabulary about youth has evolved in the context of the growth of developmental systems, theoretical models that stress that human development derives from dynamic and systemic (and therefore bidirectional and mutually influential) relations among the multiple levels of organization that comprise the human development system. Developmental systems theory eschews the reduction of an individual to fixed genetic influences and, in fact, contends that such a hereditarian conception of behavior is counterfactual. Instead, developmental systems theory stresses the inherent plasticity of human development, that is, the potential for systematic change throughout development. This potential exists as a consequence of mutually influential relationships between the developing person and his or her biological, psychological, ecological (family, community, culture), and historical niche.

These mutually influential relations involve the influence of a young person on his or her context (e.g., his or her influences on parents, peers, teachers, and community) and the influence of the components of his or her world on him or her. Termed *developmental regulations*, these bidirectional influences constitute the key focus of empirical study in contemporary research on adolescent development. When the exchanges between individual and context are mutually beneficial, developmental regulations are termed *adaptive*, and healthy, positive individual development should occur.

Plasticity, then, is instantiated from the regulation of the bidirectional exchanges between the individual and his or her multilevel context. Thus, the concepts of relative plasticity and developmental regulation combine to suggest that there is always at least some potential for systematic change in behavior and, as such, that there may be means found to promote positive development in adolescence.

Thus, plasticity legitimizes an optimistic view of the potential for promoting positive changes in youth. The presence of plasticity in development is a key strength of human development; when combined with the concept of adaptive developmental regulation, and when there is an alignment between the assets of an individual and the assets for positive development that exist in the ecology of youth, one may hypothesize that PYD will be promoted.

The key features of adolescent development underscore the importance of focusing on developmental regulations, in person-context relations, to understand the basic developmental process during this period. This focus allows as well an understanding of how plasticity may eventuate in PYD.

FEATURES OF ADOLESCENT DEVELOPMENT

Adolescent development involves adjustments to changes in the self (e.g., pertinent to puberty, cognitive and emotional characteristics, and social expectations), and also to alterations in family and peer group relations, and often to institutional changes as well (e.g., regarding the structure of the schools within which adolescents are enrolled or opportunities or rules for community service). Not all young people undergo these transitions in the same way, with the same speed, or with comparable outcomes. Individual differences are thus a key part of adolescent development, and are caused by differences in the timing of connections among biological, psychological, and societal factors—with no one of these influences (e.g., biology) acting either alone or as the prime mover of change (Lerner 2004).

In other words, a major source of diversity in developmental trajectories is the systematic relations that adolescents have with key people and institutions in their social context; that is, their family, peer group, school, workplace, neighborhood, community, society, culture, and niche in history. These person-context relations result in multiple pathways through adolescence.

In short, intra-individual changes in development and inter-individual differences in intra-individual change typify this period of life. Both dimensions of diversity must be considered in relation to the general changes of adolescence. The following examples of such general changes illustrate the nature and importance of diversity in adolescence and that the key process within this period (as is the case as well throughout the life span) is a relational one involving mutually influential relations between the developing individual and the multiple levels of the ecology of human development.

MULTIPLE LEVELS OF CONTEXT

Adolescence is a period of extremely rapid transitions in physical characteristics. Indeed, except for infancy, no other period of the life cycle involves such rapid changes. While hormonal changes are part of the development of early adolescence, they are not primarily responsible for the psychological or social developments during this period. Instead, the quality and timing of hormonal or other biological changes influence, and are influenced by, psychological, social, cultural, and historical factors.

Good examples of the integrated, multilevel changes in adolescence arise in the area of cognitive development during this period. Global and pervasive effects of puberty on cognitive development do not seem to exist. When biological effects are found they interact with contextual and experiential factors (e.g., the transition to junior high school) to influence academic achievement. Perspectives on adolescence that claim that behavioral disruptions or disturbances are a universal part of this period of life might lead to the assumption that there are general cognitive disruptions inherent in adolescence. However, evi-

dence does not support this assumption. Rather, cognitive abilities are enhanced in early adolescence as individuals become faster and more efficient at processing information—at least in settings in which they feel comfortable in performing cognitive tasks.

Thus, relations among biology, problem behaviors associated with personality, and the social context of youth illustrate the multiple levels of human life that are integrated throughout adolescent development. For example, in 1993 researcher Avshalom Caspi and colleagues linked the biological changes of early pubertal maturation to delinquency in adolescent girls, but only among girls who attend mixed-sex schools; similarly, Hakan Stattin and David Magnusson linked pubertal maturation and delinquency with girls who socialize with older friends instead of same-age friends. Early maturation among girls in single-sex schools or in sex-age peer groups was not linked with higher delinquency.

ADOLESCENCE AS AN ONTOGENETIC LABORATORY

Given the structure and substance of the range of interrelated developments during adolescence, from the late 1970s to the mid-2000s researchers have come to regard adolescence as an ideal natural ontogenetic laboratory for studying key theoretical and methodological issues in developmental science. There are several reasons for the special salience of the study of adolescent development to understanding the broader course of life-span development.

First, although the prenatal and infant period exceeds adolescence as an ontogenetic stage of rapid physical and physiological growth, the years from approximately ten to twenty not only include the considerable physical and physiological changes associated with puberty but also mark a time when the interdependency of biology and context in human development is readily apparent. Second, as compared to infancy, the cognizing, goal setting, and relatively autonomous adolescent can, through reciprocal relations with his or her ecology, serve as an active influence on his or her own development, and the study of adolescence can inform these sorts of processes more generally. Third, the multiple individual and contextual transitions into, throughout, and out of this period, involving the major institutions of society (family, peers, schools, and the workplace), engage scholars interested in broader as well as individual levels of organization and provide a rich opportunity for understanding the nature of multilevel systemic change.

Finally, there was also a practical reason for the growing importance of adolescence in the broader field of developmental science: As noted by Laurence Steinberg and Amanda Sheffield Morris in 2001, the longitudinal samples of many developmental scientists who had been studying infancy or childhood had aged into adolescence. Applied developmental scientists were also drawn to the study of adolescents, not just because of the historically unprecedented sets of challenges to the healthy development of adolescents that arose during the latter decades of the twentieth century, but because interest in age groups other than adolescents nevertheless frequently involved this age group. For example, interest in infants often entailed the study of teenage mothers and interest in middle and old age frequently entailed the study of the middle generation squeeze, wherein the adult children of aged parents cared for their own parents while simultaneously raising their own adolescent children.

CONCLUSIONS

The theoretically interesting and socially important changes of adolescence constitute one reason why this age period has attracted increasing scientific attention. To advance basic knowledge and the quality of the applications aimed at enhancing youth development, scholarship should be directed increasingly to elucidating the developmental course of diverse adolescents.

In turn, policies and programs related to interventions must factor in adolescents' specific developmental and environmental circumstances. Because adolescents are so different from one another, one cannot expect any single policy or intervention to reach all of a given target population or to influence everyone in the same way. Therefore, the stereotype that there is a single pathway through the adolescent years—for instance, one characterized by inevitable "storm and stress"—cannot be expected to stand up in the face of contemporary knowledge about diversity in adolescence. In future research and applications pertinent to adolescence, scholars and practitioners must extend their conception of this period to focus on changing relations between the individual characteristics of a youth and his or her complex and distinct ecology.

The future of civil society in the world rests on the young. Adolescents represent at any point in history the generational cohort that must next be prepared to assume the quality of leadership of self, family, community, and society that will maintain and improve human life. Scientists have a vital role to play in enhancing, through the generation of basic and applied knowledge, the probability that adolescents will become fully engaged citizens who are capable of, and committed to, making these contributions. As evidenced by the chapters in Richard M. Lerner and Laurence Steinberg's *Handbook of Adolescent Psychology* (2004), high-quality scientific work on adolescence is being generated at levels of study ranging from the biological through the historical and sociocultural. As the work in this volume demonstrates, the study of adolescent development at its best both informs and is informed by the concerns of communities, of practitioners, and of policy makers.

BIBLIOGRAPHY

Anthony, E. James. 1970. The Behavior Disorders of Childhood. In *Carmichael's Handbook of Child Psychology*, Vol. 2, ed. Paul H. Mussen, 667–764. New York: Wiley.

Benson, Peter L., Peter C. Scales, Stephen F. Hamilton, and Arturo Semsa Jr. 2006. Positive Youth Development: Theory, Research, and Applications. In *Theoretical Models of Human Development*. Vol. 1 of *Handbook of Child Psychology*, ed. Richard M. Lerner, 894–941. 6th ed. Hoboken, NJ: Wiley.

Bornstein, Marc H., et al., eds. 2003. *Well-Being: Positive Development across the Life Course*. Mahwah, NJ: Lawrence Erlbaum.

Brandtstädter, Jochen. 1998. Action Perspectives on Human Development. In *Theoretical Models of Human Development*. Vol. 1 of *Handbook of Child Psychology*, ed. William Damon and Richard M. Lerner, 807–863. 5th ed. New York: Wiley.

Bronfenbrenner, Urie. 2005. *Making Human Beings Human: Bioecological Perspectives on Human Development*. Thousand Oaks, CA: Sage.

Caspi, Avshalom, Donald Lynam, Terrie E. Moffitt, and Phil A. Silva. 1993. Unraveling Girls' Delinquency: Biological, Dispositional, and Contextual Contributions to Adolescent Misbehavior. *Developmental Psychology* 29: 19–30.

Cummings, Elijah. 2003. Foreword. In *Promoting Positive Youth and Family Development: Community Systems, Citizenship, and Civil Society*. Vol. 3 of *Handbook of Applied Developmental Science: Promoting Positive Child, Adolescent, and Family Development through Research, Policies, and Programs*, ed. Donald Wertlieb, Francine Jacobs, and Richard M. Lerner, ix–xi. Thousand Oaks, CA: Sage.

Damon, William. 1988. *The Moral Child: Nurturing Children's Natural Moral Growth*. New York: Free Press.

Damon, William. 2004. What Is Positive Youth Development? *The Annals of the American Academy of Political and Social Science* 591: 13–24.

Dorn, Lorah D., Ronald E. Dahl, Hermi R. Woodward, and Frank Biro. 2006. Defining the Boundaries of Early Adolescence: A User's Guide to Assessing Pubertal Status and Pubertal Timing in Research with Adolescents. *Applied Developmental Science* 10 (1): 30–56.

Dowling, Elizabeth M., Steinunn Gestsdottir, and Pamela M. Anderson, et al. 2004. Structural Relations among Spirituality, Religiosity, and Thriving in Adolescence. *Applied Developmental Science* 8: 7–16.

Dryfoos, Joy. 1990. *Adolescents at Risk: Prevalence and Prevention*. New York: Oxford University Press.

Erikson, Erik H. 1959. Identity and the Life Cycle. *Psychological Issues* 1: 50–100.

Erikson, Erik H. 1968. *Identity, Youth, and Crisis*. New York: Norton.

Floyd, Donald T., and Leigh McKenna. 2003. National Youth Serving Organizations in the United States: Contributions to Civil Society. In *Promoting Positive Youth and Family Development: Community Systems, Citizenship, and Civil*

Society. Vol. 3 of *Handbook of Applied Developmental Science: Promoting Positive Child, Adolescent, and Family Development through Research, Policies, and Programs*, ed. Donald Wertlieb, Francine Jacobs, and Richard M. Lerner, 11–26. Thousand Oaks, CA: Sage.

Freud, Anna. 1969. Adolescence as a Developmental Disturbance. In *Adolescence*, ed. Gerald Caplan and Serge Lebovici, 5–10. New York: Basic Books.

Gore, Al. 2003. Foreword. In *Developmental Assets and Asset-Building Communities: Implications for Research, Policy, and Practice*, ed. Richard M. Lerner and Peter L. Benson, xi–xii. Norwell, MA: Kluwer.

Gottlieb, Gilbert. 1997. *Synthesizing Nature-Nurture: Prenatal Roots of Instinctive Behavior.* Mahwah, NJ: Lawrence Erlbaum.

Graber, Julia A., and Anne C. Petersen. 1991. Cognitive Changes at Adolescence: Biological Perspectives. In *Brain Maturation and Cognitive Development: Comparative and Cross-Cultural Perspectives*, ed. Kathleen R. Gibson and Anne C. Petersen, 253–279. New York: Aldine de Gruyter.

Hall, G. Stanley. 1904. *Adolescence: Its Psychology and Its Relations to Psychology, Anthropology, Sociology, Sex, Crime, Religion, and Education.* New York: Appleton.

Kuhn, Deanna, and Stan Franklin. 2006. The Second Decade: What Develops (and How)? In *Cognitive Perception and Language.* Vol. 2 of *Handbook of Child Psychology*, ed. Deanna Kuhn and Robert Siegler, 953–993. 6th ed. Hoboken, NJ: Wiley.

Lerner, Richard M. 1995. *America's Youth in Crisis: Challenges and Options for Programs and Policies.* Thousand Oaks, CA: Sage.

Lerner, Richard M. 2002. *Concepts and Theories of Human Development.* 3rd ed. Mahwah, NJ: Lawrence Erlbaum.

Lerner, Richard M. 2004. *Liberty: Thriving and Civic Engagement among American Youth.* Thousand Oaks, CA: Sage.

Lerner, Richard M. 2006. Editor's Introduction: Developmental Science, Developmental Systems, and Contemporary Theories. In *Theoretical Models of Human Development.* Vol. 1 of *Handbook of Child Psychology.* 6th ed. Hoboken, NJ: Wiley.

Lerner, Richard M., and Laurence Steinberg, eds. 2004. *Handbook of Adolescent Psychology.* 2nd ed. Hoboken, NJ: Wiley.

Lerner, Richard M., and Nancy L. Galambos. 1998. Adolescent Development: Challenges and Opportunities for Research Programs, and Policies. In *Annual Review of Psychology*, Vol. 49, ed. Janet T. Spence, 413–446. Palo Alto, CA: Annual Reviews.

Little, Rick R. 1993. What's Working for Today's Youth: The Issues, the Programs, and the Learnings. Paper presented at the Institute for Children, Youth, and Families Fellows' Colloquium, Michigan State University.

Offer, Daniel. 1969. *The Psychological World of the Teen-Ager.* New York: Basic Books.

Petersen, Anne C. 1988. Adolescent Development. In *Annual Review of Psychology*, Vol. 39, ed. M. R. Rosenzweig, 583–607. Palo Alto, CA: Annual Reviews.

Pittman, Karen J., Merita Irby, and Thaddeus Ferber. 2001. Unfinished Business: Further Reflections on a Decade of Promoting Youth Development. In *Trends in Youth Development: Visions, Realities, and Challenges*, ed. Peter L. Benson and Karen J. Pittman, 4–50. Norwell, MA: Kluwer.

Roth, Jodie, and Jeanne Brooks-Gunn. 2003. Youth Development Programs: Risk, Prevention, and Policy. *Journal of Adolescent Health* 32: 170–182.

Roth, Jodie, Jeanne Brooks-Gunn, Lawrence Murray, and William Foster. 1998. Promoting Healthy Adolescents: Synthesis of Youth Development Program Evaluations. *Journal of Research on Adolescence* 8: 423–459.

Sherrod, Lonnie R., Constance Flanagan, and James Youniss. 2002. Dimensions of Citizenship and Opportunities for Youth Development: The What, Why, When, Where, and Who of Citizenship Development. *Applied Developmental Science* 6 (4): 264–272.

Simmons, Roberta G., and Dale A. Blyth. 1987. *Moving into Adolescence: The Impact of Pubertal Change and School Context.* Hawthorne, NJ: Aldine.

Stattin, Hakan, and David Magnusson. 1990. *Pubertal Maturation in Female Development.* Hillsdale, NJ: Erlbaum.

Steinberg, Laurence, and Amanda Sheffield Morris. 2001. Adolescent Development. In *Annual Review of Psychology*, Vol. 52, ed. Susan T. Fiske, Daniel L. Schacter, and Carolyn Zahn-Waxler, 83–110. Palo Alto, CA: Annual Reviews.

Susman, Elizabeth J., and Alan Rogel. 2004. Puberty and Psychological Development. In *Handbook of Adolescent Psychology*, Vol. 2, ed. Richard M. Lerner and Laurence Steinberg, 15–44. Hoboken, NJ: Wiley.

Richard M. Lerner
Stacy Zimmerman
Kristen Fay
Yibing Li

ADOPTION STUDIES

SEE *Twin Studies.*

ADORNO, THEODOR

SEE *Frankfurt School; Personality, Authoritarian; Personality, Cult of.*

ADVERSE SELECTION

The concept of adverse selection is used to identify a market process in which low-quality products or customers are more likely to be selected as a result of the possession of asymmetric information by the two sides of the market transaction. In this situation the better-informed side may take trading decisions that adversely affect the other side, with unwelcome consequences for the market as a whole. Economists usually refer to this situation as a case of market failure: a case in which market dynamics do not lead to an efficient allocation of goods and services.

The notion of adverse selection is applied widely in contemporary economic literature because asymmetric information is often a common feature of market interactions. This typically occurs when the private information available to the sellers is not disclosed to the buyers or vice versa. The most classic example of adverse selection concerns the market for secondhand cars, which usually is referred to as the "market for lemons" since the pioneering work in 1970 of the Nobel laureate economist G. A. Akerlof.

In that market potential buyers cannot distinguish good cars ("peaches") from bad cars ("lemons") easily. However, the sellers are perfectly aware of the characteristics of their cars. Potential buyers are likely to offer the average market price for a particular car model. A peach owner will refuse such an offer, but a lemon owner will agree to sell his or her car for an amount that is likely to be higher than its real value. As a consequence, only sellers with bad cars will offer them for sale, and the potential buyers' willingness to pay for secondhand cars will decrease. The resulting market equilibrium will be inefficient because there will be a number of transactions that are lower than the optimal level.

The role of adverse selection in explaining market inefficiencies has been understood since the beginnings of the economic literature. In his 1776 inquiry on the wealth of nations Adam Smith implicitly applied the concept of adverse selection to the analysis of the credit market. He intuited that a legal rate for loans much above the lowest market rate probably will attract only risky borrowers who are willing to pay a high interest rate. Safe borrowers, who are willing to pay only part of what they are likely to gain through the use of money, will not venture into the competition, and most of the capital probably will be lost.

Inefficiencies in the credit market caused by adverse selection have been used more recently to explain the causes of the Third World debt crisis of the early 1980s. Much of that debt was amassed after the 1973 oil crisis, when European and North American banks lent large amounts of money from the oil revenues deposited in their accounts. The low interest rate that was demanded attracted several Third World countries whose financial capability was not observable by those banks. For some of those countries strong financial constraints resulted in the inability to repay the debt when economic conditions worsened and interest rates increased.

SEE ALSO *Banking; Insurance; Loan Pulling; Loan Pushing; Loans; Moral Hazard; Smith, Adam*

BIBLIOGRAPHY

Akerlof, G. A. 1970. The Market for "Lemons": Quality Uncertainty and the Market Mechanism. *Quarterly Journal of Economics* 84 (3): 488–500.

Mas-Colell, Andreu, Michael D. Whinston, and Jerry R. Green. 1995. *Microeconomic Theory*. New York: Oxford University Press.

Smith, Adam. [1776] 1904. *An Inquiry into the Nature and Causes of the Wealth of Nations*. 5th ed., ed. Edwin Cannan. London: Methuen.

Lucia Vergano

ADVERTISING

Advertising is a form of mass media designed to promote a specific product, service, or idea on behalf of a business or organization. Advertisers ordinarily use media such as television, radio, print (magazines, newspapers, and billboards), sponsorship of cultural and sporting events, and the Internet.

From the Industrial Revolution to the mid-twentieth century, advertising in the United States and Europe was generally straightforward and usually included an image and description of the product's function, price, and location to be purchased. According to William M. O'Barr in his 2006 article "Representations of Masculinity and Femininity in Advertising," ads were primarily directed toward women because they were responsible for the majority of consumer purchases, the exception being "big ticket" products like cars and major appliances. Since World War II, however, industries have increasingly courted the adult male consumer, and with the advent of youth culture, children, teenagers, and young adults have been targeted as well.

A common strategy for advertisers is to make the consumer feel as though the given product will remedy a specific problem or insecurity. Designers prey on a modern culture obsessed with status, self-enhancement, youth, body image, and gender identity, the latter being a favored theme now aimed at both men and women. Critics such as John Kenneth Galbraith (1969) and Christopher Lasch (1978) charged that advertising functions to create desires that previously did not exist and that advertising serves to promote consumption as a way of life.

A dialectical relationship exists between consumers and advertisers where ads face heavy skepticism and scrutiny, while at the same time receive access and appreciation in the form of high revenue, lavish award ceremonies, and TV programs devoted to airing successful commercials. In the United States, argued Michael Schudson in his 1984 book *Advertising, the Uneasy*

Persuasion: Its Dubious Impact on American Society, the culture is amenable to advertising that is "more pervasive and more intrusive than in any other industrialized country" (p. 128). Millions watch the United States's *Superbowl* programming not for the content of the football game, but rather just to see the premier of new, multimillion-dollar ads.

A crucial difference between previous eras and today is advertising's saturation. In U.S. and European cities a conservative estimate of people's daily exposure to ads is 250 messages a day, while others suggest that that number is closer to 5,000 messages a day. This ubiquity creates a more skeptical and desensitized audience. As a result marketers go to greater lengths to make their products stand out.

Advertisers now use more diverse and insidious mediums such as stickers on food, social networking websites like YouTube, motion sickness bags, and space within public schools. Guerrilla marketing practices like "product placement"—where the intended audience is unaware that they have been exposed to an advertisement, while the desired impression of the given product remains—are now everyday tactics. In 2007 blinking electronic signs promoting a television show were surreptitiously planted on highways and bridges in Boston and mistaken for terrorist bombs.

Given the use of more sophisticated technology and the expansion of the Internet, marketers can better assess the effectiveness of their pitches and the return on investment. Sophisticated techniques like data mining help identify (and subsequently create) niche consumption desires. Additionally hyperspecialized media outlets enable advertisers to target more precise demographics. For example advertisers now design ads for gay men and air them on gay-oriented cable television channels like "Here TV" and "Logo." Targeted marketing and reliable measurements of effectiveness are the holy grail of companies seeking to reduce costs.

In an era of global capitalism, advertising agencies work for clients all over the world and target niche demographics in nearly all continents. Successful advertising for multinational corporations hinges on the familiarity with local habits, symbols, and cultural differences. According to Marieke K. de Mooij in the 2005 publication *Global Marketing and Advertising: Understanding Cultural Paradoxes*, for a global brand like McDonald's—a company that sells its food via more than 30 thousand distribution points, in 119 countries, serving 47 million customers a day—particular attention must be paid to local culture for the pitch to be successful. For example, advertising for McDonald's in France tied into "Asterix and Obelisk," the most famous historical cartoon of the nation (Mooij 2005).

As more advertising proliferates in the globalized context, we are likely to see new, unforeseen forms of consumer reluctance and resistance. Companies will surely continue to manage this dialectic for their own financial advantage.

SEE ALSO *Consumerism; Galbraith, John Kenneth; Goodwill; Hidden Persuaders; Internet; Markets; Media; Television; Veblen, Thorstein; Want Creation; Wants*

BIBLIOGRAPHY

Galbraith, John Kenneth. 1969. *The Affluent Society.* 2nd ed. Boston: Houghton Mifflin.

Lasch, Christopher. 1978. *The Culture of Narcissism: American Life in an Age of Diminishing Expectations.* New York: W. W. Norton.

Mooij, Marieke K. de. 2005. *Global Marketing and Advertising: Understanding Cultural Paradoxes.* 2nd ed. Thousand Oaks, CA: Sage.

O'Barr, William M. 2006. Representations of Masculinity and Femininity in Advertising. *Advertising and Society Review* 7 (2).

Schudson, Michael. 1984. *Advertising, the Uneasy Persuasion: Its Dubious Impact on American Society.* New York: Basic Books.

Tyson Smith

AESTHETICS

The philosophy professor and writer Jerrold Levinson defines aesthetics as "the branch of philosophy devoted to conceptual and theoretical inquiry into art and aesthetic experience" (Levinson 2003, p. 3). What makes an experience an aesthetic one is a contentious matter, however, and is indeed one of the main subjects of the theoretical inquiry. Nonetheless, there is general agreement that people experience something aesthetically when, for example, they find it beautiful, elegant, or vulgar. Levinson's definition, which is a fairly orthodox one, indicates that aesthetics developed out of different, though overlapping, concerns: for art, and for an allegedly distinctive type of human experience. The two are different because not only artworks, but also natural scenes and objects encountered in "everyday life" (coffee-machines, say), may be appreciated for their aesthetic qualities, such as garishness or symmetry. In addition, not all philosophical questions about artworks are about their aesthetic properties (e.g., questions about the role of poets' intentions in determining the meaning of poems). The two concerns overlap, however, because the identification of an artwork's aesthetic qualities is often an important ingredient in its appreciation.

Levinson's definition blends two early and different ways of using the term *aesthetics*. Derived from a Greek word for "sensation," it was first introduced by the German philosopher Alexander Baumgarten in 1735 as a name for "the science of how something … is sensitively cognized" (Baumgarten 1954, §16). The scope of the term was later restricted by Immanuel Kant, in his *Critique of Judgement* (1790), to sensation-based judgements of taste or beauty. For Kant, aesthetics had nothing peculiarly to do with art. G. W. F. Hegel, however, doubted the possibility of a general "science" of beauty, and in his *Lectures on Fine Art* in the 1820s he equated the term with "the philosophy of fine art."

Of course, although *aesthetics* was an eighteenth-century coinage, the discipline it refers to has an ancient pedigree. Plato and Aristotle, for example, addressed such paradigmatically aesthetic topics as beauty and the role of emotion in art.

Reflecting the divergent approaches of Kant and Hegel, later aestheticians have often been divided between those focused primarily on the philosophy of art and those concerned with understanding the character of aesthetic experience. Attention of the latter sort has tended to concentrate on an examination of Kant's characterization of aesthetic experience as "disinterested," as disengaged from cognitive and practical interests, and therefore sensitive solely to the appearances and forms of things.

Within philosophy, the status of aesthetics is disputed. For some it is a relatively discrete subdiscipline, while for others it is necessarily parasitic on the insights of other areas of philosophy, including metaphysics. Some thinkers, such as Friedrich Nietzsche, have held that its place is central, since aesthetic concepts such as style and elegance are involved in ethical reflection on the good life and even in philosophical reflection on scientific method.

The relation of aesthetics to the social sciences is also disputed, but many philosophical questions about art and aesthetic experience are certainly closely related to social-scientific issues, and aestheticians often invoke the findings of social science. One such question is "What is art?" John Dewey and Thorstein Veblen, for example, argued against "timeless" conceptions of art. They maintained that the modern concept of art is a nineteenth-century product that reflects the predilections of a dominant and leisured social class. A related theme was developed in Pierre Bourdieu's "social critique" of such distinctions as that between aesthetic and less "pure" pleasures.

Several issues concerning aesthetic experience, especially that of beauty, also engage with cultural anthropological ones. Thus, there has been considerable debate about whether there are broadly universal standards of, say, women's beauty, explicable perhaps in terms of evolutionary factors, or whether such standards are relatively "local" ones, explained instead as functions of cultural pressures exerted by advertisers and the fashion industry. While aestheticians both contribute to and draw upon such empirical debates, most of them also maintain that these debates involve conceptual and evaluative issues that it is not for empirical enquiry to settle, but that instead call for philosophical analysis.

SEE ALSO *Bourdieu, Pierre; Cultural Studies; Culture; Distinctions, Social and Cultural; Literature; Music; Preferences; Psychology; Tastes*

BIBLIOGRAPHY

Baumgarten, Alexander. 1954. *Reflections on Poetry*. Trans. K. Aschenbrenner and W. Holther. Berkeley and Los Angeles: University of California Press.

Cooper, David E., ed. 1992. *A Companion to Aesthetics*. Oxford, U.K.: Blackwell.

Levinson, Jerrold, ed. 2003. *The Oxford Handbook of Aesthetics*. Oxford, U.K.: Oxford University Press.

David E. Cooper

AFFECT

SEE *Emotion and Affect.*

AFFECT-INFUSION MODEL

SEE *Mood Congruent Recall.*

AFFIRMATIVE ACTION

The term *affirmative action* refers to policy measures designed to reduce the marginalization of groups that have historically suffered from discrimination, exclusion, or worse, and that are underrepresented in a society's desirable positions. The measures may take the form of public laws, administrative regulations, and court orders, or of practices by private businesses and nonprofit institutions. The underrepresented groups are typically "identity groups" defined in terms of characteristics that are physical or cultural, such as race, caste, tribe, ethnicity, and gender.

Affirmative action policies are designed to benefit members of underrepresented identity groups by providing them with more favorable access to certain benefits— usually positions such as jobs, promotions, or admissions to educational institutions, but sometimes resources such as business loans and contracts, financial aid, or land rights. Membership in an identity group recognized as underrepresented is treated as a positive factor, increasing one's chances of access to such benefits. This may be accomplished by means of a quota system, in which certain benefits are reserved for members of the relevant groups, or by means of a preferential boost system, in which extra weight is accorded to group members in an explicit or implicit measure of qualifications for access to benefits.

Affirmative action in the United States owes its origin to the civil rights movement of the 1950s and 1960s, which demanded an end to the long history of injustices perpetrated against African Americans and called for their full participation as citizens in U.S. society. This movement prodded the U.S. federal government into action to curb the segregation of African Americans into inferior facilities and to provide them with access to rights and opportunities long denied. The term *affirmative action* was first mentioned by President John F. Kennedy in his Executive Order #10925 of March 1961, which established the President's Committee on Equal Employment Opportunity and described positive steps to be taken by federal agencies to root out discrimination against any identity group.

Affirmative action in this sense gained a firm legal foundation in the Civil Rights Act of 1964, championed by President Lyndon B. Johnson and enacted in the wake of the assassination of President Kennedy. Reinforcing the antidiscrimination provisions of the act, President Johnson went on to issue a series of executive orders designed to promote equal opportunity in employment, education, and government contracting. It was initially expected that the assertion of formal legal equality of all citizens, the removal of overtly discriminatory barriers, and a much wider diffusion of relevant information to members of underrepresented groups would lead to significant increases in opportunities for members of such groups—in particular, African Americans. It soon became apparent, however, that affirmative action of this kind would not have a significant impact on the numbers of African Americans in desirable jobs or schools. By the late 1960s, therefore, many government agencies and private organizations began to give some preference to African Americans in selection processes. In this context the term *affirmative action* came to denote positive action in favor of members of underrepresented groups, not simply an effort to abolish all forms of discrimination.

Following the example set by African Americans, other identity groups underrepresented in desirable positions in the United States—such as women, Hispanic Americans, and Native Americans—began to mobilize in the late 1960s and early 1970s for policies to end discrimination and to facilitate improvement of their standing in U.S. society. Soon thereafter, affirmative action programs oriented to African Americans came to include also Hispanic Americans and Native Americans as beneficiaries; and a variety of public and private affirmative action programs were established to increase the representation of women in fields that had long been dominated by men.

Affirmative action has been practiced in many countries of the world. Beyond the United States, significant affirmative action policies are in place in India, South Africa, Malaysia, and Sri Lanka; and some form of affirmative action has been implemented in another dozen countries. India was the first site of such policies—labeled "reservations" since they involved quotas of reserved seats. In the early twentieth century popular movements against Brahmins—the highest Hindu caste, whose members dominated the most elite positions open to Indians under British colonial rule—led in parts of India to the establishment of reserved seats for non-Brahmins in some public services and educational institutions. In the 1930s reservation policies were implemented throughout British India in the form of legislative assembly seats reserved for four of India's minority communities—Muslims, Christians, Sikhs, and Anglo-Indians—and later also the two most depressed communities—untouchables and tribals, officially labeled "Scheduled Castes" and "Scheduled Tribes." The constitution of independent India, completed in 1950, is unusual in making explicit provision for affirmative action in the form of reservations for Schedules Castes and Scheduled Tribes in national and provincial assemblies, as well as in public sector jobs and public institutions of higher education. The Indian constitution also permits reservations for members of "Other Backward Classes"; such reservations have been extended to a variety of groups in most Indian states and, since the 1990s, at the national level.

Wherever they have been implemented, affirmative action policies have proven to be highly controversial, generating heated debate and, at times, mass demonstrations. Where proponents see such policies as a way of rectifying historical injustices and integrating marginalized communities into the life of the society, opponents see these policies as a kind of "reverse discrimination" that contravenes the principle of equal rights for all individuals.

In recent decades academic scholarship has begun to shed light on the actual consequences of affirmative action policies, bringing empirical evidence to bear on debates most often dominated by ethical and political considerations. The evidence makes clear that the direct beneficiaries of affirmative action policies are most often relatively privileged members of underrepresented identity groups, who are in the best position to take advantage of improved access to desirable positions and resources. It has become increasingly clear that affirmative action does not compensate those individuals most disadvantaged by past injustices, nor does it redistribute effectively from rich to poor. But it does foster greater integration of the societal elite, which can serve to legitimate and energize democratic political institutions, to inspire members of marginalized groups, and to improve the performance of tasks where greater diversity among performers contributes to better quality of service for a diverse clientele. Simultaneously, however, affirmative action heightens attention to identity group status, which may exacerbate divisive identity politics.

SEE ALSO *African Americans; California Civil Rights Initiative; Caste; Civil Rights Movement, U.S.; Discrimination; Hierarchy; Inequality, Political; Inequality, Racial; Politics, Gender; Politics, Identity; Quota Systems; Racism; Underrepresentation*

BIBLIOGRAPHY

Anderson, Elizabeth S. Race, Gender, and Affirmative Action: Resource Page for Teaching. http://www-personal.umich.edu/~eandersn/biblio.htm.

Nesiah, Devanesan. 1997. *Discrimination with Reason: The Policy of Reservations in the United States, India, and Malaysia.* Delhi; New York: Oxford University Press.

Sowell, Thomas. 2004. *Affirmative Action around the World: An Empirical Study.* New Haven, CT: Yale University Press.

Weisskopf, Thomas. 2004. *Affirmative Action in the United States and India: A Comparative Perspective.* London: Routledge.

Thomas E. Weisskopf

AFFLUENT SOCIETY

SEE *Galbraith, John Kenneth.*

AFRICAN AMERICAN STUDIES

African American studies (also called black studies, African and African American studies, Africana and Pan-African studies, and African diaspora studies) combines general intellectual history, academic scholarship, and a radical movement for fundamental educational reform (Alkalimat et al. 1977). From its inception the field has embraced the focus of academic excellence and social responsibility in a unique approach that addresses traditional issues of "town and gown." Though born out of turbulence, the discipline's ability to persevere since its

formal establishment in university settings makes it a lasting testament to the legacy of the Black Power movement and the goals of a long list of black intellectuals dedicated to bringing the history and culture of African Americans into a place of prominence in the American academy.

The first concerted calls to break from disciplinary foci that ignored the culture and background of black people came during the 1930s at the annual meetings of the Association for the Study of Negro Life and History (now the Association for the Study of African American Life and History). Building on the efforts of W. E. B. Du Bois (1868–1963) and Carter G. Woodson (1875–1950), Joseph Rhoads (1890–1951) and Lawrence D. Reddick (1910–1995) called for black colleges to expand traditional departments. By the 1940s historically black institutions such as Howard University were offering courses within the traditional disciplines that addressed issues of black concern. Arturo A. Schomburg (1874–1938) joined the efforts of these early proponents of black studies with his enormous collection of materials documenting the black experience. The donation of the collection to the New York Public Library and his work as the curator of its Black Life Collection led to the establishment of the Schomburg Center for Research in Black Culture, hailed by the *New York Times* (May 11, 2007) as a "cultural anchor in a sea of ideas."

Early twenty-first century formations of African American studies at historically white institutions emerged as institutional responses to the "black studies movement." Once the numbers of black students at historically white institutions developed into a critical mass, the general unrest and civil rights movement of the 1960s fueled the dissatisfaction that often led to aggressive and violent expressions. Cornell, Howard, Michigan, Rutgers, and San Francisco State are a few of the institutions where students demanded that black studies curricula be instituted and black faculty be hired. This black studies movement led to the formation of programs, departments, institutes, and centers at numerous colleges and universities, thus marking the period as a moment of radical rupture in the evolutionary history of the discipline.

The establishment of the first department of black studies occurred under the duress of a student strike. At San Francisco State, 80 percent of the racially and ethnically diverse student body joined forces and "made or supported unequivocal demands" (Rooks 2006, p. 4). Similar strikes occurred at Howard (March 1968), Northwestern (May 1968), Cornell (April 1969), and Harvard (April 1969). San Francisco State responded to the demands with the appointment of Nathan Hare as the acting chair of the Department of Black Studies in 1969. Other universities followed this course, with James Turner at Cornell (1969), Andrew Billingsley at Berkeley (1969),

Ronald Foreman at the University of Florida (1970), Carlene Young at San Jose State University (1970), Herman Hudson at Indiana (1970), and Richard Long at Emory University (1970).

The establishment of black studies as a legitimate academic discipline required intense discussions over the direction the course of study should take. Some of the earliest texts, including *Introduction to Afro-American Studies* (Alkalimat et al. 1977), *Introduction to Black Studies* (Karenga 1982), and *All the Women Are White, All the Blacks Are Men, But Some of Us Are Brave: Black Women's Studies* (Hull et al. 1982), represented the differing perspectives and were foundational beginnings for many departments. Although the application of knowledge from a non-Eurocentric perspective is essential to the diverse intellectual frameworks that constitute the field, Africology, an Afrocentric perspective, was principally established in the work of Molefi Asante. Other (often competing) perspectives—such as St. Clair Drake's Pan-Africanist view, Maulana Karenga's cultural nationalistic Kawaida theory, Abdul Alkalimat's "paradigm of unity" and technologically focused eBlack studies, James B. Stewart's concept of the field as a disciplinary matrix, Gloria T. Hull's focus on black women's studies, Manning Marable's scholarly commitment to the assault of structural racism in the context of global capital, and Henry Louis Gates and Cornel West's focus on cultural studies—make important contributions to the intellectual trajectories of the field. Black British cultural studies in the work of Stuart Hall and Paul Gilroy generate new flows of ideas of a decentered cultural region and add to the discourse on intellectual frameworks for studying the black experience. Key to the mission of black studies throughout its evolutionary stages is the application of knowledge to promote social change, and it is at the core of the diverse intellectual and methodological approaches to the field. As with most social science disciplines, black studies scholars continue to reexamine the field.

The differences within African American studies, though important to each proponent, are far less destructive than many detractors suggest and provide evidence of the vibrancy and necessity of the discipline. Rather than leading to the demise of the field, diversity broadens and strengthens it as the research and scholarship of various practitioners contribute to a growing literature examining the complexity of the historical, social, and cultural phenomena that influence black lives in an increasingly globalized world.

A holistic view of black studies (whether under the formation of African American studies, Africana studies, Afrikan studies, etc.) reveals the focus of the discipline to be a search for understandings of what it means to be of African descent in a world where unequal power relations

developed as a result of colonial pursuits. Institutional structure (whether a department, program, center, or institute) and the extent of institutional support determine the strength of the degree programs in African American studies offered by more than three hundred American universities. While many of the programs in this field embrace similar objectives, what they are named (i.e., department, program, center, institute) sometimes signals their intellectual trajectory, programmatic foci, and institutional mission.

The value and success of African American studies can be determined by its contribution to the transformation of higher education. The commitment to blending scholarship and activism instituted by most programs of study is reflected in different ways in other disciplines. The conditions under which feminist studies, ethnic studies, postcolonial studies, gay and lesbian studies, and cultural studies could articulate their positions were established by the introduction of African American studies into the academy.

Important to the continued development of the field are the many organizations and institutions that support African American studies. In addition to repositories such as the Schomburg, the Association for the Study of African American Life and History (ASALH), the National Council of Black Studies (NCBS), the Association of Black Cultural Centers, and eBlackstudies.org are among a number of organizations dedicated to the gathering and dissemination of knowledge on the black experience. Through their meetings, journals, and public programs, these organizations (along with myriads of local community organizations and dedicated scholars) continue to address the diverse challenges facing black studies and the social sciences in the twenty-first century.

SEE ALSO *African Americans; African Studies; Afrocentrism; Black Power; Blackness; Cultural Studies; Du Bois, W. E. B.; Hall, Stuart; Pan-Africanism; Race; Race Relations*

BIBLIOGRAPHY

Alkalimat, Abdul. 2007. Africana Studies in the U.S. http://www.eblackstudies.org/su/complete.pdf.

Alkalimat, Abdul, et al. [1977] 1986. *Introduction to Afro-American Studies: A Peoples College Primer.* 6th ed. Chicago: Twenty-First Century.

Hall, Perry A. 2000. Paradigms in Black Studies. In *Out of the Revolution: The Development of Africana Studies*, eds. Delores P. Aldridge and Carlene Young, 25–38. Lanham, MD: Lexington.

Hull, Gloria T., Patricia Bell Scott, and Barbara Smith, eds. 1982. *All the Women Are White, All the Blacks Are Men, But Some of Us Are Brave: Black Women's Studies.* Old Westbury, NY: Feminist.

Karenga, Maulana. [1982] 1993. *Introduction to Black Studies.* 2nd ed. Los Angeles: University of Sankore Press.

Marable, Manning. 2000. *Dispatches from the Ebony Tower: Intellectuals Confront the African American Experience.* New York: Columbia University Press.

Rooks, Noliwe M. 2006. *White Money Black Power: The Surprising History of African American Studies and the Crisis of Race in Higher Education.* Boston: Beacon.

Woodyard, Jeffrey Lynn. 1991. Evolution of a Discipline: Intellectual Antecedents of African American Studies. *Journal of Black Studies* 22 (2): 239–251.

Marilyn M. Thomas-Houston

AFRICAN AMERICANS

The term *African American* has typically referred to descendants of enslaved and indentured black Africans transplanted by force into what is now the United States. The terms *African American, black,* and *Afro-American* are sometimes used interchangeably. *African American* has supplanted other designations, such as *Negro,* derived from the word *Negroid,* coined in the eighteenth century by European anthropologists. *African American* is sometimes applied more broadly to descendants of all ten million or more Africans forcibly transported to the Western Hemisphere from the beginning of the sixteenth century until the 1860s.

Africans shipped to the United States represented over forty ethnic groups from twenty-five different kingdoms, but constituted only 7 percent of all Africans transported to the Western Hemisphere by 1810. Over time, their descendants in the United States formed a composite identity shaped primarily by shared conditions, since historical circumstances and systematic de-Africanization efforts precluded the tracing of ancestry to precise points of origin. African American identity has been and is continuing to be constructed out of an African cultural and historical legacy, but it is shaped within the framework of intragroup cooperation and intergroup conflict within American society.

Chattel slavery contributed significantly to pre–Civil War economic growth in the United States. The invention of the cotton gin (1793) dramatically increased the demand for slaves by lowering the cost of cotton production and inducing landowners to expand production beyond coastal areas. Approximately one million African Americans were redeployed from the upper to the lower South via a well-organized urban-based internal slave trade. Slavery was a normal feature of southern American cities—in 1860 there were approximately seventy thousand urban slaves. Exploitation of African American labor resulted in a massive increase in cotton production from 300,000 bales in 1820 to nearly 4.5 million bales in 1860. Plantation owners used harsh physical punishments such as whippings, brandings, and amputations along with incentives to garner compliance. Incentives included prizes for the largest quantity of cotton picked, year-end bonuses, time off, and plots of land. Developing reliable estimates of income and wealth generated by slavery is difficult because much of the accumulated wealth of the slave regime was destroyed by the Civil War. Some income financed planters' conspicuous consumption, a portion was converted into personal wealth holdings, and another fraction provided capital for large-scale industrial ventures.

A dramatic disparity in wealth holdings between African Americans and white Americans constitutes one of the most enduring legacies of slavery. While emancipation enabled African Americans to increase the portion of income actually received from agricultural pursuits, forces reproducing wealth disparities ensured continuing subjugation. The arrangements by which most African Americans remained tied to the agricultural sector were characterized as the "tenancy system." Three different classes of tenancy emerged: cash tenancy, share tenancy, and sharecropping. Sharecroppers, the status to which African Americans were disproportionately relegated, owned nothing. Implements were supplied by the landowners on credit and the sharecropper paid half the crop as rent to the landowner. Debt peonage emerged when the croppers' share of the harvest was insufficient to repay the landlord. Landlords often charged exorbitant interest rates for supplies and failed to give croppers their full share of the harvest value. Sharecropping laws required that indebted croppers remain on landlords' land until all debts were satisfied.

Prior to World War I (1914–1918), African Americans remained overwhelmingly rural residents. In 1910 over 90 percent of the 9.8 million African Americans lived in the South and only 25 percent lived in cities of 2,500 or more. Between 1890 and 1910 the percentage of African American males employed in agriculture fell only slightly; the occupational situation of females actually worsened. The persisting effects of institutional discrimination introduced during earlier periods led to an unusual set of circumstances whereby the occupational and economic status of African Americans declined as their absolute and relative education was increasing. The opposite pattern would have been predicted by traditional economic models. Moreover, the trends in inequality that developed during this period were reproduced into the 1980s.

Spurred by floods, crop destruction by boll weevils, and the need for workers in war-related industries, the first net exodus from the South of about 454,000 African Americans occurred between 1910 and 1920. During World War I, the Division of Negro Economics was established within the U.S. Department of Labor to reduce tensions resulting from the introduction of African American workers into northern factories. The wisdom of this initiative was reinforced by race riots in Chicago, Omaha, and Washington, DC, during the summer of 1919.

Northward migration initiated a redefinition of African American identity that manifested itself most visibly in the cultural movement termed the "Harlem Renaissance" and the associated concept of the "New Negro." The negritude movement that developed in the French African and Caribbean colonies introduced similar reconceptualizations of black identity. The African American scholar Alain Locke (1886–1954) declared that this redefined identity reflected a transformation in psychology such that "the mind of the Negro seems suddenly to have slipped from under the tyranny of social intimidation and to be shaking off the psychology of imitation and implied inferiority" (1925, p. 631).

Efforts to translate this new sense of identity into economic gains proved, however, to be problematic. Throughout the interwar period, rapid technological change increasingly pushed African Americans out of the agricultural sector. By 1930 the percentages of African American males and females employed in agriculture had fallen to 45 percent and 27 percent, respectively. Opportunities for manufacturing employment for African Americans were largely restricted to nonunionized industries, prompting a resurgence of self-organizing efforts, such as those of the Brotherhood of Sleeping Car Porters, formed by the labor leader A. Philip Randolph (1889–1979).

Many African Americans capitalized on the new industrial employment opportunities generated by World War II (1939–1945), and this prospect contributed to a net southern out-migration of 1.6 million between 1940 and 1950. Between 1910 and 1950 the proportion of African American males employed as operatives increased from 6 percent to 22 percent. By 1950 the proportion of African American males and females employed in agriculture had fallen to 25 percent and 10 percent, respectively. For African American women, the decline in agricultural employment was associated with increases in employment as service workers, operatives, clerical and sales workers, and private household workers. These employment shifts contributed to a marked improvement in African Americans' economic progress after World War II. Even before the civil rights movement took center stage in 1956, one in every three urban African American families owned their own home.

The civil rights and Black Power movements signaled shifts in the political and economic consciousness of African Americans catalyzed, in part, by the emergence of a larger and more diverse middle class. The two movements offered different approaches to addressing identity and economic advancement issues. The civil rights movement promoted complete integration of African Americans through elimination of all legalized segregation and discrimination, whereas the Black Power movement emphasized group solidarity and self-determination. It is important to note that the ideologies undergirding these movements were influenced significantly by such Caribbean scholars as Frantz Fanon (1925–1961), C. L. R. James (1901–1989), and Eric Williams (1911–1981), as well as the liberation movements that developed in the African colonies. The most concrete policy outcomes of the civil rights movement were the Civil Rights Act of 1964, the Voting Rights Act of 1965, and the Equal Housing Act of 1968. Measures focusing on redistribution of economic benefits, such as affirmative action, have proved to be more controversial and less successful.

While nondiscrimination and affirmative action policies have undoubtedly contributed to increases in the relative income of African Americans, as well as significant improvements in occupational distribution, many African Americans have not experienced significant improvements in economic well-being. Moreover, data covering the mid-1990s to the first decade of the twenty-first century paint a fairly consistent picture of racial wealth disparities—namely, that the wealth of African American families is less than one-fifth that of whites. Stagnation in the quality of life of many African Americans has resulted, in part, from disproportionate vulnerability to forces associated with transformation of the U.S. economy. Between 1960 and 2000, the percentage of men working as operatives, fabricators, and laborers has declined from 46 to 29 for African Americans and from 25 to 18 for white Americans. About 50 percent of all workers displaced as a result of plant closings and relocations had been employed in manufacturing, and African Americans have been significantly overrepresented among displaced workers. In the wake of these employment shifts, African American men have a much higher unemployment rate than other groups, and between 1991 and 2000 the percentage of African American men not in the labor force has averaged 26, compared to 15 for whites.

Black Power ideology emphasizes African American self-determination, economic self-sufficiency, and black pride; these foci became a catalyst for the displacement of terms like *Negro* and *colored*. *Black* and *Afro-American* were in vogue briefly, but *African American* became the most popular term during the 1980s. Advocates of *African American* argue that this term is consistent with the nation's immigrant tradition of "hyphenated Americans," which preserves links between people and their or their ancestors' geographic origins. For many, *African American* describes cultural and historical roots and also conveys pride and a sense of kinship and solidarity with other African diasporans.

Embracing the designation *African American* is not symbolic of a commitment to the type of cultural nationalism advocated by Black Power proponents. This is especially the case in the economic arena, although some contemporary commentators claim that African Americans' disposable income constitutes a potential form of collective economic power, an argument reminiscent of those advanced in the past. However, suburbanization of a significant segment of the black middle class has stymied efforts to promote any functional type of economic development in the black community, which would require, among other conditions, the capacity to exercise sufficient control over economic resources to mobilize production processes and create markets.

Ironically, African American suburbanization has also not produced outcomes anticipated by integrationists, such as substantial reductions in residential segregation. Like their inner-city counterparts, African American suburban dwellers experience a high degree of residential segregation. In addition, middle-class suburbanization has increased the isolation experienced by inner-city African American residents, and has made it increasingly difficult to ameliorate persisting economic and social inequalities. The economic prospects of inner-city African American residents are constrained, in part, by a spatial mismatch between job location and place of residence as African Americans generally have the longest travel times to work in all regions of the country where public transportation is available.

Divergence of interests between middle-class and other African Americans creates new complications in defining African American identity. Each group accesses different configurations of "social capital," that is, the complex of resources associated with group membership that individuals can use to enhance well-being. Persisting differences in social capital can generate disparate conceptions of group identity. Conventional notions of African American identity are also challenged by phenotypical discrimination reminiscent of patterns associated with the one-drop rule operative during the slavery and Jim Crow eras that led to formal designations of the extent of African parentage—mulatto (1/2), quadroon (1/4), and octoroon (1/8).

Phenotypical discrimination results in African Americans and Latinos with the darkest and most non-European phenotype receiving lower incomes, having less stable employment, and obtaining less prestigious occupa-

tions than counterparts who are lighter or have more European physical features. In some studies, skin tone has been found to be the most important determinant of occupational status other than an individual's education. Internalization of beliefs that skin-shade differences reflect membership in different groups adds ambiguity to efforts to define African American identity. In the 1980s parents of mixed-race children lobbied for the addition of a more inclusive term in census racial designations to reflect the multiple heritages of their offspring, and the term *biracial* has become more widely used and accepted to classify people of mixed race, reintroducing divisions between black and biracial subgroups into the American social-identity fabric.

Contemporary immigration patterns also have important economic and identity consequences for those traditionally defined as *African American*. There is ongoing disagreement about the impact of international migration on African American employment, but some researchers maintain that immigration lowers the wages and reduces the labor supply of competing native workers, with the largest effects on high school dropouts. Increasingly, *African American* is applied to recent immigrants and their offspring from African and diasporan countries, irrespective of preferred self-identification. In every year between 1995 and 2003 (with the exception of 1999), over forty thousand documented immigrants from African nations entered the United States, with the largest numbers originating in Nigeria and Ghana. First-generation African and Caribbean immigrants tend to identify most strongly with their country of origin, although many of their offspring identify with domestic African Americans. Some immigrants from South American countries are also classified as *African American*, but are even less likely to identify with domestic African Americans.

To the extent that the designation *African American* and related terms are increasingly used to collect information regarding economic outcomes for diverse subgroups, researchers should practice extreme care in interpreting data to ensure that aggregate data do not mask inequalities experienced by identifiable subgroups. There are likely to be differences across subgroups in income-generating characteristics. In addition, the types of phenotypical and linguistic discrimination experienced by immigrants may parallel forms of discrimination experienced by domestic African Americans, but, a priori, it cannot be assumed that the consequences for economic outcomes are identical. As a consequence, ameliorative strategies may need to be tailored specifically to address the unique circumstances of various subgroups.

SEE ALSO *Affirmative Action; African American Studies; Black Arts Movement; Black Conservatism; Black Liberalism; Black Middle Class; Black Panthers; Black*

Power; Blackness; Capitalism, Black; Civil Rights Movement, U.S.; Discrimination; Dred Scott v. Sanford; *Ethnic Enterprises; Harlem Renaissance; Harris, Abram L.; Jim Crow; Lewis, W. Arthur; Politics, Black; Politics, Urban; Race; Race and Anthropology; Race and Economics; Race and Education; Race Relations; Racial Classification; Racism; Reconstruction Era (U.S.); Reparations; Separate-but-Equal; Slave Trade; Slavery; U.S. Civil War; Weaver, Robert C.*

BIBLIOGRAPHY

America, Richard, ed. 1990. *The Wealth of Races: The Present Value of Benefits from Past Injustices.* Westport, CT: Greenwood.

Baugh, John. 1991. The Politicization of Changing Terms of Self Reference Among American Slave Descendants. *American Speech* 66 (2): 133–146.

Borjas, George. 2003. The Labor Demand Curve Is Downward Sloping: Reexamining the Impact of Immigration on the Labor Market. *Quarterly Journal of Economics* 118 (4): 1335–1374.

Conrad, Cecilia, John Whitehead, Patrick Mason, and James Stewart, eds. 2005. *African Americans in the U.S. Economy.* Lanham, MD: Rowman & Littlefield.

Darity, William, Jr., Patrick Mason, and James Stewart. 2006. The Economics of Identity: The Origin and Persistence of Racial Norms. *Journal of Economic Behavior and Organization* 60 (3): 283–305.

Fogel, Robert. 1989. *Without Consent or Contract: The Rise and Fall of American Slavery.* New York: Norton.

Hughes, Emmet. 1956. The Negro's New Economic Life. *Fortune* (September): 127–131.

Jacobson, Louis, Robert LaLonde, and David Sullivan. 1993. *The Costs of Worker Dislocation.* Kalamazoo, MI: Upjohn Institute for Employment Research.

Keith, Verna, and Cedric Herring. 1991. Skin Tone and Stratification in the Black Community. *American Journal of Sociology* 97 (3): 760–778.

Locke, Alain. 1925. Enter the New Negro. *Survey Graphic* Harlem 6 (6) (March): 631–634.

Office of Immigration Statistics, U.S. Department of Homeland Security. 2004. *2003 Yearbook of Immigration Statistics.* Washington, DC: U.S. Government Printing Office. Editions from 1975 to 2003 available online at http://uscis.gov/graphics/shared/aboutus/statistics/ybpage.htm.

Smitherman, Geneva. 1991. What Is Africa to Me?: Language, Ideology, and African American. *American Speech* 66 (2): 115–132.

Stewart, James. 1977. Historical Patterns of Black-White Political Economic Inequality in the United States and the Republic of South Africa. *Review of Black Political Economy* 7 (3): 266–295.

Stewart, James. 2004. Globalization, Cities, and Racial Inequality at the Dawn of the 21st Century. *Review of Black Political Economy* 31 (3): 11–32.

Trotter, Joe, Jr. 2001. *The African American Experience.* Boston: Houghton Mifflin.

James B. Stewart

AFRICAN CRISIS RESPONSE INITIATIVE

The African Crisis Response Initiative (ACRI) is a program that the United States launched in 1996 to address challenges of peacekeeping and conflict management in Africa. Its formation was prompted by fears that the ethnic massacres that occurred in Rwanda in 1994 might also take place in neighboring Burundi, and by the desire of the United States to avoid getting entangled in local conflicts, as occurred in 1993 when eighteen U.S. Army rangers were killed in Somalia, where the United States had intervened to provide humanitarian assistance.

Initially, the United States wanted to establish an African force that could intervene to save lives in humanitarian crises. After consultations with numerous African and non-African officials, the United Nations, and the Organization of African Unity (OAU), the U.S. government decided to establish a program to build such a capacity among African militaries.

ACRI was established to enable selected African military forces to respond to crises through peacekeeping missions in Africa. The initiative aimed at training and equipping African peacekeepers as rapid-response contingency forces that could be quickly assembled and deployed under the auspices of the United Nations, the OAU, or subregional organizations. Participation in peacekeeping missions depends on decisions at the national level. U.S. special forces soldiers conducted the training on common peacekeeping doctrines and procedures. African militaries were trained in basic soldiering skills at individual, squad, platoon, and company levels. Military personnel received training in logistics, leadership, convoy security, roadblocks and checkpoints, human rights, humanitarian law, negotiation and mediation, protection of refugees, relations with humanitarian organizations, and civil-military relations. The units were equipped with compatible communication facilities, water purification units, night-vision binoculars, mine detectors, uniforms, boots, belts, packs, and entrenching tools.

Brigade-level training for subregional command and control structures was conducted in Senegal and Kenya in 2000 and 2001, respectively. Follow-up training was conducted twice a year after the completion of the initial training period of two and a half years.

The selection criteria for countries participating in ACRI raised questions about U.S. interests. Such an initiative carries the risk of dividing states into those that are considered pro-American and those that are not. It also risks undermining local initiatives for conflict resolution. Countries participating in the program had to have democratic governments and professional militaries with a record of previous peacekeeping. Uganda and Ethiopia did not pass the test, but were selected to participate in the initiative. Several countries that were initially considered for participation became ineligible. Follow-up training was suspended in Ethiopia, Uganda, and Côte d' Ivoire in 1998. Ethiopia was embroiled in a war with Eritrea, as was Uganda in the Democratic Republic of Congo. Côte d' Ivoire had experienced a military coup and was facing civil strife.

ACRI partners contributed to conflict resolution in Africa. Mali and Ghana sent forces to Sierra Leone as part of the ECOMOG (Economic Community of West African States Cease-Fire Monitoring Group) peacekeeping force. Benin provided a contingent to Guinea-Bissau as part of ECOMOG, and Senegal contributed troops to the UN mission in the Central African Republic. The success of ACRI was undermined by the lack of an institutionalized security framework within which it could operate. An African continental security framework for conducting peacekeeping is in its infancy, while subregional security frameworks like ECOMOG and SADC (Southern African Development Community) that have participated in peacekeeping operations are fragile. Programs like ACRI also risk contributing to the militarization of conflicts by strengthening the militaries of conflict-ridden countries and regions. It is likely that the participation of some states in ACRI was motivated by the need to strengthen their militaries to deal with internal and regional conflicts rather than a desire to engage in peacekeeping.

The African Contingency Operation Training and Assistance (ACOTA) program succeeded ACRI in 2004. ACOTA focuses on training military trainers and equipping African militaries to conduct peacekeeping support operations and to provide humanitarian relief.

BIBLIOGRAPHY

Jendayi, Frazer. 1997. The African Crisis Response Initiative: Self-Interested Humanitarianism. *Brown Journal of World Affairs* 4 (2): 103–118.

Paul, Omach. 2000. The African Crisis Response Initiative: Domestic Politics and Convergence of National Interests. *African Affairs* 99 (394): 73–95.

Paul Omach

AFRICAN DIASPORA

The *African diaspora* was the dispersal of African peoples to Asia, Europe, and the Americas. The term is used most commonly for the coerced movement in various slave trades, but the word *diaspora* has also been used to refer to voluntary migrations from Africa and for population movements within Africa.

In some ways, the most consequential movement of peoples from Africa was the first, when the early stages of human evolution took place in the highlands of East Africa. From there, over the last million and a half years, human beings spread out across Africa, gradually adapting to different environments, and then into Asia, Europe, and eventually the Americas. More recent large-scale movements of peoples have occurred within Africa. For example, over the last 2,500 years, people speaking Bantu languages have spread out from a base in the Nigeria-Cameroon borderlands over most of southern and central Africa, absorbing most preexisting populations.

THE EMERGENCE OF A MARKET FOR SLAVES

Almost six thousand years ago, complex civilizations marked by powerful imperial states began emerging in the alluvial valleys of Mesopotamia, then in Egypt and India. These were slave-using societies, though not as dependent on slave labor as some more recent societies. They were also involved in long-distance trade. They tended to obtain their slaves from warfare, from trade with less-developed neighbors, and through debt and social differentiation. Athenian Greece, the first real slave society, acquired slaves from the Balkans, the Black Sea areas, and Asia Minor. There was, however, from an early date some movement of Africans into these worlds both as slaves and free persons. Egyptians were involved in conflict with Nubia and were ruled by dynasties from the south. Nubia, and perhaps the Horn of Africa, were sources of Egyptian slaves, though slaves also came from many other groups. Statuary and paintings from ancient Egypt clearly indicate the presence, sometimes as rulers, of people with African physical features. There were certainly Africans elsewhere in the Mediterranean world. Authors of the Old Testament and from classical antiquity were clearly familiar with Africans. Trade across the Indian Ocean was also taking place at least two thousand years ago, and clearly involved some movement of people, both free and slave.

The emergence of Islam in the seventh century and the subsequent conquest of the Middle East and much of the Mediterranean world expanded the market for slaves. Although Islam forbade the enslavement of fellow Muslims, it also created a demand for slaves, particularly as concubines, servants, and soldiers, but also sometimes as laborers. There was, for example, a major revolt in ninth-century Mesopotamia among the Zanj, East African slaves who were subject to harsh labor draining the swamps of lower Mesopotamia. Exploitation of African slaves seems to have been rare, however. The Muslim empires got most of their slaves from eastern Europe and the Caucasus, as did the Christian cities of southern Europe. For the Muslim Middle East, eastern Europe remained the most important source of slaves into the eighteenth century.

A trade in slaves with Africa, however, remained significant. Christian kingdoms in the middle Nile region paid a tribute to Egypt, which was partly in slaves. Ethiopia seems to have sold slaves to Muslims. The introduction of camels in the first centuries of the Common Era increased trade across the Sahara; trade was further increased when Arab conquerors revitalized the Middle East. The trans-Sahara trade led to the emergence of Muslim states in the savanna belt known as the Sudan, which comes from the Arabic *bilad-es-sudan*, "land of the blacks." For many of these Sudanic states, slaving became a source of labor and services, as well as an export that could be exchanged for Middle Eastern products. For Ghana, Mali, and Songhai, the export of slaves supplemented a trade in gold, but for Kanem and Bornu in the central Sudan, slaves were the major export. Slaves were probably less important to the Swahili cities of the east coast, though they were a constant export.

African slaves from Ethiopia and East Africa served as soldiers and concubines in India. In 1459 there were supposedly eight thousand Africans in Bengal's army. A number of African military commanders became rulers of small states, of whom the best known was Malik Ambar (d. 1626), who was noted for his tolerance and his patronage of the arts. Communities of people of African descent known as *Habshis* or *Sidis* are still found in India and Pakistan. There were also African merchants and sailors in India.

Africans could also be found, in different roles, in many parts of the Arab world. There were, for example, a succession of poets in pre-Islamic and early Islamic Arabia known as the "black crows." One of the companions of the Prophet Muhammad (c. 570–632) was an African, Bilal, who served as the first *muezzin* for the Muslim community. In the Muslim empires, particularly that of the Ottoman Turks, black eunuchs were common. They played an important role in the Ottoman harem. African slaves were particularly important in Morocco and Tunisia and provided much of the labor in the mines and oases of the Sahara. Some scholars have estimated that African slave exports into the Middle East were as numerous as those across the Atlantic. They did not, however, leave as deep a footprint. Most were women who became concubines. As concubines, they produced few offspring and

those offspring were free members of their masters' families. Soldiers probably experienced high mortality and thus left behind few identifiable communities. As a result, few self-reproducing African communities developed in the Arab world.

THE ATLANTIC SLAVE TRADE

The Portuguese ships that cruised along the African coast were not primarily interested in slaves, but slaves could be procured. The first were taken in raids, but trade soon proved more effective. Slaves could be purchased from many African societies, and the profits from the slave trade helped pay for many early expeditions. Some slaves were exchanged within Africa—for example, for gold along the Gold Coast—but most were sold in Portugal or at Mediterranean slave markets where a shortage of slaves developed after the Ottoman conquest of Constantinople in 1453 limited Mediterranean access to eastern European slaves. African slaves became important in Lisbon, southern Portugal, and Mediterranean cities.

A more important market soon developed on the Atlantic islands, which had become underpopulated or depopulated when earlier populations were decimated by slaving and by European diseases, though many islands, like Madeira, had no native population at all. Sugar was the key to their prosperity and to the development of a particularly harsh slave system. Venetian and Genoan planters had begun the exploitation of sugar in the eastern Mediterranean during the Crusades. As improved technology reduced the cost of producing sugar, an expanding European market offered large profits, and the Atlantic islands offered European investors an opportunity to extend sugar cultivation. Madeira was briefly the world's largest sugar producer, and then São Tomé. On Madeira and in the Canaries, both slave and peasant labor was used, but the equatorial climate of São Tomé made the island unattractive to European peasants, and a plantation system developed there that depended exclusively on slave labor. In the late sixteenth century, this plantation system was extended to Brazil, where once again, the decimation of Indians by European diseases led to the use of African slave labor. The plantation model was extended to the West Indies in the seventeenth century.

The use of slaves was attractive wherever labor was in short supply and new crops offered prospects of profit. Slave labor produced rice in South Carolina and tobacco in Virginia. Slaves were also used to grow indigo, spices, and coffee. Slaves were found everywhere in the Americas and were important even in the Middle Atlantic colonies. The availability of slaves meant that they could be acquired for many purposes. They worked as servants; they worked on the docks; and after the invention of the cotton gin they provided the labor for the extension of cotton over the southeastern United States. Sugar, however, created the biggest market for slaves.

Slave exports grew from about a quarter million in the sixteenth century to over six million in the eighteenth. Only in what became the United States did natural population growth among slaves eventually make the slave trade irrelevant. As native slaves either died out or were absorbed into an African population, slavery came to be seen as the lot of the African. This is probably the first time that enslaveability was defined in terms of race.

To meet the steadily increasing demand, slave traders pushed routes deeper and deeper into the interior of Africa. Prices rose, old states were militarized, and new states appeared that were willing to provide the slaves Europe wanted. The late seventeenth and early eighteenth century saw the emergence of a series of powerful slaving states that responded to rising prices and demand in the West Indies. A smaller slave trade emerged in East Africa after islands in the Indian Ocean were colonized. The conquest of what is now the Ukraine by the Russians closed off the major source of white slaves in the late eighteenth century. Increasingly, during the last years of the international slave trade, the Middle East looked to African sources for their slaves. The East African slave trade was also stimulated by the development of a plantation economy in Zanzibar and on the East African coast, as well as economic growth in the Middle East.

THE WORLD OF THE DIASPORA

Many of the early sugar planters treated slaves as expendable. Sugar was a particularly brutal crop, and slaves worked long hours under abusive conditions. The mortality rate, particularly for men, who did the most dangerous work in pressing and boiling rooms, was high. For planters, it was often easier to buy a slave than to raise one, and many early planters literally worked slaves to death. With time, however, family life developed because planters found that slaves worked better when allowed to live in family relationships. Though mortality remained high until the end of the slavery era, the ratio of men and women gradually moved toward parity.

Family life and natural reproduction among slaves developed much more quickly elsewhere. In the tobacco areas of Virginia, the slave population had been growing since the 1720s. Slave culture was shaped by the beliefs and culture that slaves brought with them from Africa, by the conditions of slavery, and by the world of their masters. The perpetuation of slave culture was influenced by the identification of slave status with African origins. In the European world, color became an important boundary that persisted even when slaves were freed.

African roots show especially vividly in religions. Throughout the diaspora, we find religious cults of African origin: *candomblé* in Brazil, *shango* in Trinidad, *Santeria* in Cuba, vodou in Haiti, *gnawa* in Morocco, *bori* in Tunisia, and *zar* in Istanbul and southern Iran, all of them involving spirit possession and the use of music. Like the African systems from which they emerged, these cults assimilated elements of dominant religions, but also in many cases influenced those religions. This is most striking in the United States, where the African impact is found less in distinctive cults than in the way Africans shaped the practice of Christianity, particularly among Baptists. African religious practices, like the ring shout, led to a highly emotive and richly musical practice of Christianity among African Americans. Similarly, in Hindu and Muslim parts of the world, Africans were absorbed into the dominant religion but often infused it with an African approach.

African musical traditions are also prevalent throughout the diaspora: the drumming of *sides* in India, *gnawa* music in Morocco, Afro-Cuban music, and calypso in Trinidad, as well as gospel, blues, and various kinds of jazz. These different traditions have taken on a life of their own and feature a variety of musical instruments, but all have African roots. So too with language. The grammatical structure of African languages often shaped the development of pidgin languages, and African terms became a source of slang. In Maroon communities, formed by runaway slaves, African political traditions also shaped the states that were created. Some scholars see the African family structure in the kind of extended and often fictive family that evolved in the slave quarters and protected Africans from the insecurity of slavery, where a family member could be sold off at any time. African folklore and African craft skills, such as pottery or raffia work, also remained important in many diaspora communities.

FREE MIGRANTS

Not all Africans migrated in chains. Many free migrants traveled within and from Africa, including those who went to Morocco, Egypt, or the Arabian Peninsula to study at Islamic institutions. Many medieval African rulers made the pilgrimage to Mecca, and some supported hostels for their subjects who were studying at Muslim schools. Some of these travelers stayed and married. Africans also migrated to Europe. Missionaries brought Africans to Europe to study, some of whom returned to Africa. Others came as ambassadors. Free Africans also worked on oceangoing vessels in both the Indian Ocean and the Atlantic. The Kru in Liberia, for example, developed a tradition of working on European vessels. By the eighteenth century, there were small populations of free Africans in many major port cities of Europe, the Americas, and the Middle East. In the nineteenth century, the Soninke of the upper Senegal River area moved from working on riverboats to hiring on to oceangoing vessels. Most went home, but many settled in port cities of Europe.

These migrations increased with the end of slavery, particularly the migration of Africans who traveled to get an education. In the early twentieth century, there were about one hundred South Africans studying in the United States and more in Europe. The establishment of colonial rule also made it easier for Muslim Africans to travel, both for the pilgrimage and to seek an education. During the colonial period, most African migration took place within Africa, but there were also migrations from parts of the diaspora. Jamaicans, for example sought plantation work in Central America and Cuba, and some people from the West Indies immigrated to the United States and England. The number of Africans in North America and Europe increased significantly after World War II (1939–1945); this population was spearheaded by students but also included working-class economic migrants.

There was also a process that Michael Gomez calls "reconnection," as some people from the diaspora went back to Africa. Edward Blyden from the Virgin Islands, for example, became an influential intellectual in nineteenth-century Sierra Leone and Liberia. In addition, missionaries from black churches in Europe and the Americas, particularly the African Methodist Episcopal Church, took Christianity to various parts of Africa. A sense of having roots in Africa was more important to diaspora intellectuals than to those who remained in Africa. Five Pan-African congresses were held between 1900 and 1945, only the last of which included major African participation. Marcus Garvey (1887–1940) organized a "back to Africa" movement, and diaspora intellectuals in France developed the literature of *négritude*.

Migration increased dramatically after independence came to most of Africa in the 1950s and 1960s. Increasing numbers of African students sought higher education abroad during the postindependence period, and African workers started going to Europe and then to North America. Some fled oppressive political conditions, while others left because their home countries' stagnant economies offered them little future. Today, many highly skilled African professors, engineers, and scientists emigrate to better use their skills and achieve a more comfortable life. The Mourides, a Muslim religious fraternity in Senegal, have helped organize the emigration of people who work as street vendors. In the cities of Europe and North America, the different branches of the diaspora are merging, the newest migrants from Africa joining migrants from the West Indies and an indigenous population of African descent. By the beginning of the twenty-first century, these migrations, particularly of unskilled workers, were beginning to meet resistance in Europe.

SEE ALSO *African Studies; Anthropology, Linguistic; Anticolonial Movements; Caribbean, The; Colonialism; Diaspora; Ethnology and Folklore; Immigration; Imperialism; Kinship; Migration; Refugees; Slave Trade; Slavery*

BIBLIOGRAPHY

Alpers, Edward, and Amy Catlin-Jairazbhoy, eds. 2004 *Sidis and Scholars: Essays on African Indians.* Trenton, NJ: Red Sea Press.

Conniff, Michael L., and Thomas J. Davis. 1994. *Africans in the Americas: A History of the Black Diaspora.* New York: St. Martin's Press.

Gomez, Michael. 2005. *Reversing Sail: A History of the African Diaspora.* Cambridge, U.K.: Cambridge University Press.

Harris, Joseph E. 1971. *The African Presence in Asia: Consequences of the East African Slave Trade.* Evanston, IL: Northwestern University Press.

Harris, Joseph E., ed. 1993. *Global Dimensions of the African Diaspora.* 2nd ed. Washington, DC: Howard University Press.

Hunwick, John O., and Eve Troutt Powell, eds. 2002. *The African Diaspora in the Mediterranean Lands of Islam.* Princeton, NJ: Weiner.

Lewis, Bernard. 1990. *Race and Slavery in the Middle East: An Historical Enquiry.* New York: Oxford University Press.

Lovejoy, Paul. 2000. *Transformations in Slavery: A History of Slavery in Africa.* 2nd ed. Cambridge, U.K.: Cambridge University Press.

Martin Klein

AFRICAN NATIONAL CONGRESS

The origins of the African National Congress (ANC) were a conference of black South African notables assembled in 1912 to protest impending legal restrictions on African land ownership. Until the 1940s, the ANC remained decorously circumspect: lobbying, submitting memorandums, and relying heavily on white liberal intermediaries. During World War II (1939–1945), the ANC began to build a mass membership structure and attempted to mobilize popular support by contesting local "advisory board" elections in black townships. By this time, several of its leaders were also members of the Communist Party. Communists had initially concentrated on winning white worker support but switched their efforts to blacks in the late 1920s.

Within the ANC, both communists and a group of young self-professed "Africanists" who formed a Youth League helped to influence the ANC to embrace more aggressive tactics. It adopted in 1949 a "Program of Action" calling for strikes, boycotts, and civil disobedience as means toward a goal of African "self-determination." The ANC's radicalization coincided with the accession to government of the (Afrikaner) National Party (NP). In power, Afrikaner nationalists began to tighten and extend racial segregation policies. In practice, the NP's apartheid policies sought to confine black participation in the urban economy to unskilled and semiskilled labor.

The Communist Party was banned in 1950. Thereafter its members would work within the ANC. Communist influence as well as older liberal traditions instilled by the Methodist schools that trained most African political leaders ensured that although the ANC itself remained an exclusively African body, it defined its program on a broader basis. It sought allies in the Indian Congress movement, founded in Natal by Mohandas Gandhi in 1894, and in 1952 encouraged the establishment of a Congress of Democrats for white sympathizers.

The ANC's Freedom Charter, adopted in 1956, referred to a democratic future in which all races would enjoy equal rights. In 1952 a "Defiance Campaign" against new apartheid laws failed to win any concessions but succeeded in swelling membership to 100,000. Six subsequent years of mass-based militant resistance helped to convince a number of ANC principals, including its patrician but popular deputy president, Nelson Mandela, that the organization had exhausted the available options of peaceful protest. A breakaway movement, the Pan-Africanist Congress (PAC), formed in 1959 as a more radical alternative. The Pan-Africanists emphasized African racial identity and criticized the role of the Communist Party in "watering down" the ANC's nationalist predispositions. In fact, the Communist Party's influence was most evident in the mild socialism of the Freedom Charter. In 1960 the PAC committed itself to resisting the pass laws. In Sharpeville on March 21, outside Vereeniging, police were confronted by a crowd of five thousand people, and the tense standoff culminated with the police firing and killing eighty. In the national tumult that followed, the government banned both the PAC and the ANC. The ANC reconstituted itself underground and in 1961 formed an armed wing, Umkhonto we Sizwe (Spear of the Nation). In 1963 Umkhonto's high command was arrested and most of its members sentenced to life imprisonment for their leadership of a sabotage campaign.

For the next thirty years, under the leadership of Mandela's close professional associate and friend, fellow ex–Youth Leaguer and attorney Oliver Tambo, the ANC would base itself in Dar es Salaam and Lusaka. Only in the mid-1970s could it begin rebuilding its clandestine organization in South Africa. In exile, the ANC strengthened its alliance with the Communist Party, and in stages between 1969 and 1985 it opened its ranks to whites, Indians, and coloreds (in South Africa, any person of mixed racial descent). Survival in exile required discipline and authority, and communist organizational models were influential. Today, Leninist tenets of "democratic centralism" remain in the organization's constitution. After 1976, ANC guerrillas succeeded in attracting public attention with bold attacks on symbolic targets. So-called armed propaganda brought the ANC considerable public support both in South Africa and internationally, though Umkhonto's campaigning hardly represented a serious military threat to white security.

Meanwhile a charismatic cult developed around the imprisoned leaders on Robben Island, especially Nelson Mandela. Mandela's stature was a key factor in achieving for the ANC the degree of recognition or acceptance it enjoyed outside communist countries: By the late 1980s meetings between its leaders and Western statesmen served to underline its status as a government in waiting. The military command structure controlled the destinies of most of the refugees who joined the ANC after 1976. In this part of the organization communists were especially powerful.

However, around its foreign missions and its own educational establishment the ANC began to foster a group with administrative and technical skills, many of its members the recipients of U.S. and western European higher educations. Members of this group began to develop policy blueprints for a post-apartheid liberal democracy. From within this community the ANC also began to make the first cautious moves toward a negotiated settlement in the mid-1980s, a process in which Thabo Mbeki, the head of the ANC's directorate of international affairs, was a principal actor. Separately, from inside prison, Nelson Mandela began his own program of meetings and conversations with senior government officials and cabinet ministers. In February 1990 the South African government repealed its prohibitions of the ANC and other exiled organizations.

Ironically, the ANC's development over thirty years as a virtual government in exile was the key to its successful reentry into the domestic terrain of South African politics. The international recognition it received brought with it the financial resources needed to build a mass organization in South Africa of unprecedented scope and sophistication. This organization would not only absorb the exile "liberation bureaucrats" and returning soldiers but also bring together a variety of movements that had developed inside South Africa during their absence, including some of the homeland-based political parties and the vast federation of civic bodies led beginning in 1983 by the United Democratic Front.

Between 1990 and 1994 the ANC played a decisive role in negotiating a fresh constitutional dispensation. After elections in 1994, Nelson Mandela would lead a transitional Government of National Unity in which the ANC would share power with its old adversary, the National Party. The ANC won successive electoral victories in 1999 and 2004.

In power, the ANC's market-friendly economic policies, encapsulated in the GEAR (Growth, Employment and Redistribution) program, have reflected leadership concerns about retaining and attracting investment capital. The rewards of economic liberalization have included increases in GDP (currently around 3.5%) and a measure of white support especially after former National Party leaders joined the ANC and Thabo Mbeki's government in 2003. The government has also been successful in promoting a black business class. The ANC's continuing popularity is probably more a consequence of expanded access to pensions and grants. More equitable provisions are unlikely to guarantee that the ANC will hold its political base for very much longer. Free-market policies have failed to check social inequality or unemployment. After more than a decade in office, the ANC today is sharply divided by a conflict over who should succeed President Mbeki. This division reflects deep disagreements between right and left over policy.

SEE ALSO *Apartheid; Colonialism; Mandela, Nelson; Mandela, Winnie*

BIBLIOGRAPHY

Callinicos, Luli. 2004. *Oliver Tambo: Beyond the Engeli Mountains.* Cape Town, South Africa: David Philip.

Davis, Stephen, M. 1987. *Apartheid's Rebels: Inside South Africa's Hidden War.* New Haven, CT, and London: Yale University Press.

Lodge, Tom. 2004. The ANC and the Development of Party Politics in Modern South Africa. *Journal of Modern African Studies* 42 (2): 189–219.

South African Democracy Education Trust. 2004. *The Road to Democracy in South Africa*, Vol. 1 (1960–1970). Cape Town, South Africa: Zebra Press.

Walshe, Peter. 1970. *The Rise of African Nationalism in South Africa: The African National Congress, 1912–1952.* London: C. Hurst.

Tom Lodge

AFRICAN SOCIALISM

SEE *Socialism, African.*

AFRICAN STUDIES

The studies of African peoples, history, and philosophy; arts, literature, and culture; political, economic, and social organization; geography, ecology, and paleontology are and have long been contested domains of intellectual inquiry. In the modern era this is perhaps best represented by the 1969 annual meeting of the (American) African Studies Association (ASA; founded in 1957 by the anthropologist Melville Herskovits) in Montreal, at which the "highly charged emotional atmosphere" (Cowan 1970, p. 344) "came as an earthquake to Africa scholars" (Wallerstein 1983, p. 14). The outcome of an unsuccessful negotiation between the ASA and a large group of primarily African American members resulted in most of the latter leaving the ASA for the African Heritage Studies Association (AHSA) (Rowe 1970; Clarke 1976). Many of the AHSA members viewed the ASA as "an organization founded ... by European American scholars for the Eurocentric Study of Africa" that had made itself the "validating agency in the United States for all matters African, political and academic. ... Indeed, some scholars hold that ASA was and is a white, CIA/government-controlled organization" (Gray 2001, p. 70). Nevertheless, dissension in the field is not limited to the United States or the late twentieth century, and the debates continuing into the twenty-first century cannot be neatly packaged into one that is solely about "white versus black" or "African versus non-African" or "Eurocentric versus Afrocentric," although all of these are part of the story.

The reasons behind the controversies are themselves illuminating. Firstly, European scholarly interest in Africa was in part the outcome of the search for humankind's origins and the origins of "civilization." It is now known that Africa was the birthplace of *Homo sapiens sapiens* and that ancient Egypt had great influence on classical Greece (Diop 1967; Bernal 1987). Furthermore the rise of (European) African studies is inseparable from the European concept of race and races and the origins of modern racism (as well as the rise and development of both capitalism and modern science) and even the European self-concept itself. There was no concept of "European" (or "whiteness" for that matter) prior to racist capitalism (Jaffe 1985; Carew 1988; Davidson 1961). The European enslavement of Africans was not the result of racism, but rather racism was an ideological justification of that enslavement, considered necessary for capitalist development (Williams 1944; Cox 1948; Rodney 1972). The ties between anthropology and colonialism are well documented, confirming the role the Euro-American study of Africa played in wresting political and economic control of the continent, its peoples, and its resources (Asad 1973). Sir Frederick Lugard, the first governor of British Nigeria, was head of the Executive Council of the

International Institute of African Languages and Cultures (IIALC), founded in 1926 (Moore 1993). Another important figure associated with the IIALC was A. R. Radcliffe-Brown, whose functionalist approach dominated anthropological study of Africa: "Functional analyses depend on a contrast between the normal and the pathological. If what is European is defined as normal, then the non-European appears to be disordered, abnormal, and primitive" (Mudimbe 1988).

There are both Eurocentric and Afrocentric versions of Africa prior to European contact. The most extreme Eurocentric versions are of "primitive" (and "backward" and "uncivilized") "tribes" and worse—the "Niam-Niam" who had tails, according to Count de Castelnau's 1851 book *Troglodytes*, inhabiting caves and hunting unicorns (Rigby 1996). Spurious claims concerning "Hamitic" and "Caucasoid" Africans accompanied the attempts to de-Africanize ancient Egypt. The African-centered versions focus on ancient Egypt (Kmet) and Ethiopia and the empires of Ghana, Mali, and Songhai in the West and the Zimbabwe, Monomotapa, and Rozwi kingdoms in the South (Williams 1974; Du Bois 1965). Of course there are both oral and written indigenous African and Afro-Arab literatures and histories, including the writings of Ibn Khaldun and Ibn Battuta and works such as *Sundiata: An Epic of Old Mali* (Niane 1965). Since not all whites or Europeans are Eurocentric and not all black or African scholars are Afrocentric, the issues are not at all easy to disentangle. In addition African studies is not simply another branch of an "area studies" curriculum that would include Asia, Latin America, and so on. Each has its own unique history and motivations driving its research. There are also important methodological issues at stake in the various debates. These came to the fore especially during the struggles that gave rise to black studies programs, in many cases resulting in departments and programs that combine African and African American studies, such as Africana, Pan-African, and black global studies programs.

There are Euro-centered frameworks that supported African liberation or that reject race as a biological or natural category, including many Marxian approaches to African studies (of particular note are the French structuralists, e.g., Bonte 1975, 1981). There are on the other hand a variety of African-centered paradigms, some of which reject Marxism, and some that do not necessarily reject the idea of race. A number of periodizations of African studies have been put forward (e.g., Copans 1977; Temu and Swai 1981; Moore 1993), and they are in general agreement concerning colonization, decolonization, and the post–political independence periods, the latter dominated by neocolonialism and imperialism. In the face of ongoing crises on the continent (civil war, famine, epidemics, and so forth), the 1990s saw a surrender to an

"Afro-pessimism" (Hyden 1996) that ignored many important victories, large and small, from the end of apartheid in South Africa to the successes of grassroots organizations (e.g., the Green Belt movement).

Postcolonial approaches (Eze 1997) combine materialist and discursive components into an analysis that rejects determinist Marxism, while their qualms about the Afro-centered frameworks are concerned more with the "centrist" part than the African. Just as distinctions must be made between liberatory and fascist nationalisms, one may utilize Afrocentricity in a "strategic essentialist" fashion. In addition a wave of "Afro-Oriental" approaches have been increasingly appearing, going back at least as far as the Bandung Conference of 1955, promoting Afro-Asian unity and international anticolonialism based on the common historical experiences of colonialism and racism while respecting the integrity of cultural differences (e.g., Mullen 2004). "African womanism" offers a wide range of uniquely African-centered feminist perspectives (e.g., Dove 1998). These encouraging developments are examples of the vitality, originality, and creativity of African studies in the twenty-first century.

SEE ALSO *African American Studies; Afrocentrism; Anticolonial Movements; Black Nationalism; Civilization; Colonialism; Diop, Cheikh Anta; Functionalism; Ibn Khaldūn; Pan-Africanism; Radcliffe-Brown, A. R.; Slave Trade; Slavery Industry*

BIBLIOGRAPHY

Asad, Talal, ed. 1973. *Anthropology and the Colonial Encounter.* Atlantic Highlands, NJ: Humanities.

Bernal, Martin. 1987. *Black Athena: The Afroasiatic Roots of Classical Civilization.* New Brunswick, NJ: Rutgers University Press.

Bonte, Pierre. 1975. Cattle for God: An Attempt at a Marxist Analysis of the Religion of East African Herdsman. *Social Compass* 22: 381–396.

Bonte, Pierre. 1981. Marxist Theory and Anthropological Analysis: The Study of Nomadic Pastoral Societies. In *The Anthropology of Pre-Capitalist Societies*, eds. J. Kahn and J. P. Llobera, 22–56. London: Macmillan.

Carew, Jan. 1988. Columbus and the Origins of Racism in the Americas. *Race and Class* 30 (1): 33–57.

Clarke, John Henrik. 1976. The African Heritage Studies Association (AHSA): Some Notes on the Conflict with the African Studies Association (ASA) and the Fight to Reclaim African History. *Issue: A Quarterly Journal of Africanist Opinion* 6 (2–3): 5–11.

Copans, Jean. 1977. African Studies: A Periodization. In *African Social Studies: A Radical Reader*, eds. Peter C. W. Gutkind and Peter Waterman, 19–43. New York: Monthly Review.

Cowan, L. Gray. 1970. President's Report. *African Studies Review* 13 (3): 343–352.

Cox, Oliver C. 1948. *Caste, Class, and Race.* New York: Modern Reader, 1970.

Davidson, Basil. 1961. *Black Mother: A Study of the Precolonial Connection Between Africa and Europe.* London: Longman, 1970.

Diop, Cheikh Anta. 1967. *The African Origin of Civilization: Myth or Reality.* New York: Lawrence Hill.

Dove, Nah. 1998. African Womanism: An Afrocentric Theory. *Journal of Black Studies* 28 (5): 515–539.

Du Bois, W. E. B. 1965. *The World and Africa: An Inquiry into the Part Which Africa Has Played in World History.* New York: International.

Eze, Emmanuel Chukwudi, ed. 1997. *Postcolonial African Philosophy: A Critical Reader.* Cambridge, MA: Blackwell.

Gray, Cecil Conteen. 2001. *Afrocentric Thought and Praxis: An Intellectual History.* Trenton, NJ: Africa World.

Hyden, Goran. 1996. African Studies in the Mid-1990s: Between Afro-Pessimism and Amero-Skepticism. *African Studies Review* 39 (2): 1–17.

Jaffe, Hosea. 1985. *A History of Africa.* London: Zed.

Moore, Sally Falk. 1993. Changing Perspectives on a Changing Africa: The Work of Anthropology. In *Africa and the Disciplines: The Contributions of Research in Africa to the Social Sciences and Humanities,* eds. Robert H. Bates, V. Y. Mudimbe, and Jean O'Barr, 3–57. Chicago: University of Chicago Press.

Mudimbe, V. Y. 1988. *The Invention of Africa: Gnosis, Philosophy, and the Order of Knowledge.* Bloomington: Indiana University Press.

Mullen, Bill V. 2004. *Afro-Orientalism.* Minneapolis: University of Minnesota Press.

Niane, Djibril Tamsir. 1965. *Sundiata: An Epic of Old Mali.* Trans. G. D. Pickett. London: Longmans.

Rigby, Peter. 1996. *African Images: Racism and the End of Anthropology.* Oxford: Berg.

Rodney, Walter. 1972. *How Europe Underdeveloped Africa.* Washington, DC: Howard University Press, 1981.

Rowe, Cyprian Lamar. 1970. *Crisis in African Studies: The Birth of the African Heritage Studies Association.* Buffalo, NY: Black Academy Press.

Temu, Arnold, and Bonaventure Swai. 1981. *Historians and Africanist History: A Critique.* London: Zed.

Wallerstein, Immanuel. 1983. The Evolving Role of the Africa Scholar in African Studies. *Canadian Journal of African Studies/Revue Canadienne des Études Africaines* 17 (1): 9–16.

Williams, Chancellor. 1974. *The Destruction of Black Civilization: Great Issues of a Race from 4500 B.C. to 2000 A.D.* 3rd ed. Chicago: Third World, 1987.

Williams, Eric. 1944. *Capitalism and Slavery.* Chapel Hill: University of North Carolina Press, 1994.

Mathew Forstater

AFRICAN UNION

SEE *Organization of African Unity (OAU).*

AFRICVILLE (CANADA)

Africville has correctly been called Canada's most famous black community. It has been the subject of books (both scholarly and fiction), award-winning documentaries, thousands of newspaper articles (local, national, and international), hundreds of graduate student theses, poems, songs, a jazz suite, symposia, and an exhibition that traveled across Canada and is now housed permanently at the Black Cultural Centre in Halifax Regional Municipality in Nova Scotia. There remains a continuing negotiation between the city of Halifax and the Africville Genealogical Society, which speaks for the former residents of Africville and their descendants, over compensation for the people of Africville and proper recognition of the community. A United Nations committee has also weighed in on the importance of Africville, the significance of its history, the racism and neglect that eventually made its people vulnerable to the urban renewal process and relocation, and the validity of the Africville Genealogical Society's claims for compensation and recognition. Virtually all the public attention, certainly all the positive characterization, has occurred in the years since the community buildings were bulldozed out of existence and the residents scattered, mostly into neighboring areas of the former seashore site. Africville no longer exists in a physical sense, though surviving members and their descendants and friends usually gather each summer at the former site, now the Seaview Memorial Park, to renew ties, remember, and enjoy themselves.

Africville was founded by black refugees from the War of 1812 and their descendants, when blacks—some free, mostly slave—fled the United States for the promise of freedom and a better life in the British colony of Nova Scotia. Although not without some controversy, sociologists and historians have established that the first black settlers into the Campbell Road area of Halifax purchased their properties from white entrepreneurs in the 1840s. These first black families came from the areas of Preston and Hammonds Plains, where most of the refugees had settled, joining with loyalist blacks who had earlier fled the American Revolution (1775–1783). The move to Halifax was driven by economic need, since surviving on the small lots of scrubland made available to the refugees was difficult, if not impossible. Taking up a new life in the city, though at its outer peninsular edge, made possible both a bucolic lifestyle and opportunities for paid employment. The small community took hold over the next few decades with a church and a school. By the last decade of the nineteenth century, the name Africville had become widespread and the community was deemed by black leaders in Nova Scotia to be a fine community with much promise.

From the beginning of the Africville settlement, the community was constantly encroached upon by developments in the larger society. Land was expropriated for railway construction, and various facilities, such as sewage disposal pits and an infectious-diseases hospital, were established on the edges of the community in the nineteenth century, reducing the community's residential attractiveness and signaling future intrusions. By the end of World War I (1914–1918), Africville was ringed by facilities rejected by other residential areas of the city and was largely left to fend for itself with respect to housing standards, bylaw enforcement, and policing. Residents petitioned for services but mostly to no avail. City officials claimed there was a minimal tax base there and in any event the Africville area might be better utilized for non-residential development.

Africville evolved as a small community with considerable social diversity, but increasingly its reputation suffered as small numbers of squatters and transients (often white) moved into the community from the 1930s on. The establishment of an open dump on its doorstep in the 1950s, in addition to its sometimes condemned wells and lack of paved roads, sealed its public image as "the slum by the dump." It was a label that belied the community's strengths and core respectable lifestyle, but one that was widely held in the larger society among both whites and blacks and that made it impossible to resist the pressures of urban renewal, liberal welfare relocation policy, and integrationist civil rights that emerged after World War II (1939–1945) throughout Canada and the United States.

When Africville residents were relocated in 1964 to 1967, the community's population consisted of eighty households and about four hundred people. The relocation was hailed as a fine example of liberal welfare policy. The process was guided by proposals made by a leading Canadian social housing expert, with black and white representatives of an independent human rights commission involved in each relocatee's settlement, and a social worker responsible for working with the residents and developing educational and employment programs. Within a few years, however, the relocation's alleged success began to be sharply challenged as the promised benefits for many Africvilleans and their families were not realized. The educational and employment programs were minimal and ineffective; the housing conditions for many relocatees—public housing and housing in areas scheduled for redevelopment—left much to be desired; and the loss of community was much grieved.

Africville became a symbol of the need for black communities to appreciate their communal culture, build on their strengths, and resist similar pressures, and also of the hubris of a liberal welfare ideology that focused on individuals rather than communities and neglected the significance of social power in ensuring that promises become actualities. Africville became a symbol for the black community's experiences in Nova Scotia, and the lessons learned perhaps a hope for its future.

SEE ALSO *American Revolution; Black Towns; Loyalists; Modernization; Race Relations; Racism; Reparations; Slavery; Slums; United Nations; Urban Renewal; Welfare State*

BIBLIOGRAPHY

Africville Genealogical Society, ed. 1992. *The Spirit of Africville.* Halifax, Nova Scotia: Formac.

Clairmont, Donald H., and Dennis William Magill. 1999. *Africville: The Life and Death of a Canadian Black Community.* 3rd ed. Toronto: Canadian Scholars Press.

Walker, James W., and Patricia Thorvaldson. 1979. *The Black Experience in Canada.* Toronto: Gage.

Donald H. Clairmont

AFROCENTRISM

Over the last three decades or so, the production, validation, legitimation, and mediation of knowledge about peoples African and of African descent were subjects of often very heated debate. A significant number of the generations of black academics, independent scholars, and teachers who came of age during the civil rights and black power movements became especially aggressive in their efforts to subject knowledge-production and knowledge-mediation to guiding norms of *Afrocentrism.* While many of the concerns now linked with Afrocentrism have older roots—for example, in the antiracist writings of W. E. B. Du Bois (*The Negro*, 1915; *The Souls of Black Folk*, 1903), the rehabilitative historiography of J. A. Rogers (*World's Great Men of Color*, 1946–1947), and the works of George Washington Williams (*History of the Negro Race in America*, 1882)—the predominant steward of Afrocentrism in its modern form has been Molefi Kete Asante, of Temple University's department of African American studies.

Asante's call to become *Afro-centric*—that is, "African centered"—was shaped by twin forces: the politics of knowledge production, mediation, and appropriation, and resurgent black nationalism. The initial focus was on intellectual and political struggles over *black studies*: that is, on how to define, implement, and sustain systematic studies of black peoples (that is, Africans and peoples of

African descent) through the disciplines of history, sociology, political science, psychology, economics, the arts, religion, and literature. Such studies were to be corrective of the denigrating distortions of the histories, lives, achievements, contributions, and possibilities of black peoples perpetuated through centuries of racist, Eurocentric scholarship. Foundational to this corrective work, Asante and others concluded, was the necessity of ensuring that producers and consumers of knowledge of black peoples be "centered" on the values and agendas of black peoples, especially those that originated within the classical African civilizations. A corollary conviction was that the production and consumption of such knowledge must be devoted unequivocally to the liberation of black peoples from Eurocentric constrictions and denials of their humanity. A distinctive contribution made by Asante is his ongoing effort to specify epistemological norms and strategies by which to produce knowledge that is fully and properly Afrocentric.

Thus, *Afrocentrism* (and its evolving cognates *Afrocentricity* and *Afrology*) became a name with multiple references serving several related agendas. On one hand, it referred to epistemological and methodological norms and strategies by which to guide the production of knowledge by, about, and for black peoples. At the same time, the agenda was not merely scholarly: Afrocentric knowledge-production was to give guidance to history-making living in all dimensions of black life—political, sociological, and cultural.

Afrocentrism thus became a complex intellectual, social, political, and cultural movement with substantial impact on proponents and practitioners of black/African/Africana studies. While the Afrocentric orientation is by no means the only or even predominant guiding commitment, it has been an intellectual and political force to be reckoned with, especially by knowledge-workers of African descent. These scholars have felt compelled either to establish their Afrocentric credentials, or to declare their independence from or opposition to Afrocentrism. Furthermore, Afrocentric critiques of what has passed, and continues to pass, for knowledge about black peoples have compelled more than a few scholars, black and white, to undertake reviews and counter-critiques of their own. Moreover, the Afrocentric movement in the United States has spread well beyond college and university campuses and contestations among professional academics. It has challenged curricula and teaching in primary and secondary schools, with notable impact in a number of cities and states (Portland, Oregon, and New York state, for example).

In reaction to Afrocentrism's influence, critics have posed a number of important questions: Do Afrocentric commitments render what is produced more ideology and propaganda than "objective truth"? Is Afrocentric knowl-edge-work limited by the strictures of racialized epistemology and self-defeating methodological circularity? To answer these challenges, and to address Afrocentrism's potential weaknesses, a number of scholars have sought to refine the concept. Asante has contributed to this refinement through his reworking of the concept of *Afrocentricity* as *Africalogy* in *Kemet, Afrocentricity, and Knowledge* (1990). So, too, has Maulana Karenga, in his *Introduction to Black Studies* (1993). And works by strenuous critics such as Stephen Howe (1998) and Mary Lefkowitz (1997), along with the work of disciplined and deft intellectual historians such as Wilson Jeremiah Moses (1998) have helped to foster healthy reconsiderations and refinements of Afrocentrism.

Irrespective of the excesses and deficiencies of the Afrocentric quest in its various guises, one core insight remains cogent: *All* modes of knowledge-production and mediation are "centered" on particular historically and culturally conditioned values and interests. Proponents of Afrocentrism have sought to make such interests, values, and commitments explicit in terms of the agendas and communities they serve, while disclosing the racist investments in whiteness and imperialism that have distorted so much of supposedly "interest-free," "objective" knowl-edge-production and mediation.

Here, then, is Afrocentrism's historic contribution: It has compelled us to become more mindful of, and honest about, our "centerings," and, hopefully, inspired us to work much more openly and diligently for the achievement of a true "objectivity" free of the distorting limitations of invidious ethnocentrisms and racisms.

SEE ALSO *African American Studies; African Diaspora; Black Nationalism; Black Power; Blackness; Du Bois, W. E. B.; Ethnocentrism; Racism*

BIBLIOGRAPHY

Asante, Molefi K. 1980. *Afrocentricity: The Theory of Social Change.* Buffalo, NY: Amulefi.

Asante, Molefi K. 1987. *The Afrocentric Idea.* Philadelphia: Temple University Press.

Asante, Molefi K. 1990. *Kemet, Afrocentricity, and Knowledge.* Trenton, NJ: Africa World Press.

Howe, Stephen. 1998. *Afrocentrism: Mythical Pasts and Imagined Homes.* New York: Verso.

Karenga, Maulana. 1993. *Introduction to Black Studies.* 2nd ed. Los Angeles: University of Sankore Press.

Lefkowitz, Mary. 1997. *Not Out of Africa: How Afrocentrism Became an Excuse to Teach Myth as History.* New York: Basic Books.

Moses, Wilson Jeremiah. 1998. *Afrotopia: The Roots of African American Popular History.* New York: Cambridge University Press.

Lucius T. Outlaw Jr.

AGE

SEE *Period Effects.*

AGE EFFECTS

SEE *Period Effects.*

AGEISM

SEE *Discrimination, Wage, by Age; Gerontology.*

AGENCY IN ECONOMICS

SEE *Principal-Agent Models.*

AGENCY IN PSYCHOLOGY

SEE *Psychology, Agency in.*

AGENDA SETTING

Barbara Sinclair provides a concise definition of agenda setting: "the process through which issues attain the status of being seriously debated by politically relevant actors" (1986, p. 35). The study of agenda setting began as a reaction to the pluralist claim that policy outcomes are the result of competing groups (Dahl 1956, 1961; Truman 1951). E. E. Schattschneider (1960) claimed that groups would not necessarily form on both sides of an issue, given the upper-class bias in the system. Theodore Lowi (1979) highlighted this problem of imperfect competition, arguing that what gets on the congressional agenda is a process of bargaining between a few interested groups, elected officials, and administrators. Finally, Peter Bachrach and Morton Baratz (1969) argued that many issues would be relegated to nondecision-making because leaders only put safe issues on the agenda.

The next logical question is how agenda setting is achieved. Early scholars argued that an item is more likely to get on the agenda as the scope of conflict expands (Schattschneider 1960) and as the groups involved become larger (Cobb and Elder 1972). In John Kingdon's (1984) model, what gets on the agenda is a function of problem and political streams (the proposal stream presents the alternatives), where policy entrepreneurs play a key role in using their resources to push problems onto the agenda. Frank Baumgartner and Bryan Jones (1993) added to this understanding by claiming that strategic actors not only push items onto the agenda through issue definition (Riker 1986; Stone 1988) but also through the choice of policy venues.

Scholars have investigated the role of various actors in setting the agenda. Researchers have found that in the U.S. government the president is more likely to influence the congressional agenda on foreign policy issues (Peake 2001; Peterson 1994), under conditions of unified control (Taylor 1998), when he makes explicit appeals to the public (Kernell 1986) or when his political capital is high (Light 1982; Mueller 1973). Scholars of the U.S. Congress have shown that the majority party exerts negative and positive agenda control through the powers of the speaker (Cox and McCubbins 1993, 2002; also see Riker 1982). Gregory Caldeira and John Wright (1988) find that amicus curiae briefs influence whether the Supreme Court grants writs of certiorari. The media plays an agenda-setting role by influencing public perceptions about which issues are important (Iyengar and Kinder 1987; McCombs and Shaw 1972; MacKuen 1984), which in turn influences the standards used to evaluate leaders (Miller and Krosnick 2000), and by influencing preferences by framing issues (Druckman 2001; Iyengar 1987). While women and minority groups have had a harder time influencing the agenda, issues of concern to these groups are more likely to make it onto the agenda, given strong group organization, innovative policy proposals, and the presence of minorities and women in elected office (Bratton and Haynie 1999; Epstein, Niemi, and Powell 2005; McClain 1990, 1993; Miller 1990; Thomas 1994).

One of the key consequences of agenda setting is that many issues do not make it onto the agenda. This facet leads to the punctuated equilibrium model of Baumgartner and Jones (1993), where long periods of stability on an issue, are seen, followed by an abrupt shift to a new equilibrium, which can be reached as the issue becomes salient and institutional actors benefit from a new alternative.

SEE ALSO *Decision-making; Elites; Nondecision-making; Priming; Public Opinion*

BIBLIOGRAPHY

Bachrach, Peter, and Morton S. Baratz. 1969. Two Faces of Power. *American Political Science Review* 63 (4): 947–952.

Baumgartner, Frank R., and Bryan D. Jones. 1993. *Agendas and Instability in American Politics*. Chicago: University of Chicago Press.

Bratton, Kathleen A., and Kerry L. Haynie. 1999. Agenda Setting and Legislative Success in State Legislatures: The Effects of Gender and Race. *Journal of Politics* 61 (3): 658–679.

Caldeira, Gregory A., and John R. Wright. 1988. Organized Interests and Agenda Setting in the U.S. Supreme Court. *American Political Science Review* 82 (4): 1109–1127.

Cobb, Robert W., and Charles D. Elder. 1972. *Participation in American Politics: The Dynamics of Agenda-Building*. Baltimore, MD: Johns Hopkins University Press. 2nd ed., 1983.

Cox, Gary W., and Mathew D. McCubbins. 1993. *Legislative Leviathan: Party Government in the House*. Berkeley: University of California Press.

Cox, Gary W., and Mathew D. McCubbins. 2002. Agenda Power in the U.S. House of Representatives, 1877–1986. In *Party, Process, and Political Change in Congress: New Perspectives on the History of Congress*, ed. David W. Brady and Mathew D. McCubbins, 107–145. Stanford, CA: Stanford University Press.

Dahl, Robert. 1956. *A Preface to Democratic Theory*. Chicago: University of Chicago Press.

Dahl, Robert. 1961. *Who Governs? Democracy and Power in an American City*. New Haven, CT: Yale University Press. 2nd ed., 2005.

Druckman, James N. 2001. On the Limits of Framing Effects: Who Can Frame? *Journal of Politics* 63 (4): 1041–1056.

Epstein, Michael J., Richard G. Niemi, and Lynda W. Powell. 2005. Do Women and Men State Legislators Differ? In *Women and Elective Office: Past, Present, and Future*, 2nd ed., ed. Sue Thomas and Clyde Wilcox, 94–109. New York: Oxford University Press.

Iyengar, Shanto. 1987. Television News and Citizens' Explanations of National Affairs. *American Political Science Review* 81 (3): 815–832.

Iyengar, Shanto, and Donald R. Kinder. 1987. *News That Matters: Television and American Opinion*. Chicago: University of Chicago Press.

Iyengar, Shanto, Mark D. Peters, and Donald R. Kinder. 1982. Experimental Demonstrations of the "Not-so-Minimal" Consequences of Television News Programs. *American Political Science Review* 76 (4): 848–858.

Kernell, Samuel. 1986. *Going Public: New Strategies of Presidential Leadership*. Washington, DC: CQ Press. 3rd ed., 1997.

Kingdon, John W. 1984. *Agendas, Alternatives, and Public Policies*. Boston: Little Brown. 2nd ed., 2003. New York: Longman.

Light, Paul. 1982. *The President's Agenda: Domestic Policy Choice from Kennedy to Clinton*. Baltimore, MD: Johns Hopkins University Press. 3rd ed., 1999.

Lowi, Theodore J. 1979. *The End of Liberalism: The Second Republic of the United States*. 2nd ed. New York: Norton.

MacKuen, Michael. 1984. Exposure to Information, Belief Integration, and Individual Responsiveness to Agenda Change. *American Political Science Review* 78 (2): 372–391.

McClain, Paula D. 1990. Agenda Setting, Public Policy, and Minority Group Influence: An Introduction. *Policy Studies Review* 9 (2): 263–272.

McClain, Paula D., ed. 1993. *Minority Group Influence: Agenda Setting, Formulation, and Public Policy*. Westport, CT: Greenwood.

McCombs, Maxwell E., and Donald L. Shaw. 1972. The Agenda-Setting Function of Mass Media. *Public Opinion Quarterly* 36 (2): 176–187.

Miller, Cheryl M. 1990. Agenda Setting by State Legislative Black Caucuses: Policy Priorities and Factors of Success. *Policy Studies Review* 9 (2): 339–354.

Miller, Joanne M., and Jon A Krosnick. 2000. News Media Impact on the Ingredients of Presidential Evaluations: Politically Knowledgeable Citizens are Guided by a Trusted Source. *American Journal of Political Science* 44 (2): 301–315.

Mueller, John. 1973. *War, Presidents, and Public Opinion*. New York: Wiley.

Peake, Jeffrey S. 2001. Presidential Agenda Setting in Foreign Policy. *Political Research Quarterly* 54 (1): 69–86.

Peterson, Paul E. 1994. The President's Dominance in Foreign Policy Making. *Political Science Quarterly* 109 (2): 215–234.

Riker, William H. 1982. *Liberalism Against Populism: A Confrontation Between the Theory of Democracy and the Theory of Social Choice*. San Francisco, CA: Freeman.

Riker, William H. 1986. *The Art of Political Manipulation*. New Haven, CT: Yale University Press.

Schattschneider, E. E. (Elmer Eric). 1960. *The Semisovereign People: A Realist's View of Democracy in America*. New York: Holt, Rinehart, and Winston.

Sinclair, Barbara. 1986. The Role of Committees in Agenda Setting in the U.S. Congress. *Legislative Studies Quarterly* 11 (1): 35–45.

Stone, Deborah A. 1988. *Policy Paradox and Political Reason*. Glenview, IL: Scott, Foresman.

Taylor, Andrew J. 1998. Domestic Agenda Setting, 1947–1994. *Legislative Studies Quarterly* 23 (3): 373–397.

Thomas, Sue. 1994. *How Women Legislate*. New York: Oxford University Press.

Truman, David B. 1951. *The Governmental Process: Political Interests and Public Opinion*. New York: Knopf. 2nd ed., 1971.

Jennifer Merolla

AGGREGATE DEMAND

The notion of aggregate demand formally made its appearance in John Maynard Keynes's (1883–1946) *General Theory* in 1936 and, in its numerous guises, quickly rose to become a vital concept in economists' tool kit of analytical devices. Despite pleas by some economists, notably new classical economists, to reject the aggregate demand/supply framework because of lack of rigorous microeconomic foundations (see, among others, Barro 1994), the aggregate demand function has retained a central but highly debated role in macroeconomic analysis.

Though he regarded it as his major analytical innovation (King 1994, p. 5), Keynes defined his aggregate demand function in a way that would be unfamiliar to most economists nowadays. This is because the aggregate demand function was conceived as a subjective aggregate relation linking entrepreneurs' offers of employment to the anticipated overall market demand (or expected proceeds) for their firms' output. Keynes wrote: "Let D be the proceeds which entrepreneurs expect to receive from the employment of N men, the relationship between D and N being written $D = f(N)$, which can be called the *aggregate demand function*" (Keynes 1936, p. 25). Given entrepreneurial perceptions of firms' investment plans, and expected flow of household consumption arising from hypothetical employment offers, an aggregate functional relation could be delineated in a two-dimensional D-N space: "The aggregate demand function relates various hypothetical quantities of employment to the proceeds their outputs are expected to yield" (Keynes 1936, p. 55).

There is a positive relationship between aggregate income and employment because increased employment offers will bring forth higher expected proceeds from household consumption. Indeed, the greater the share of spending out of each additional dollar of income—that is, the higher the marginal propensity to consume—the higher the level of additional income associated with increased employment (Asimakopulos 1991, p. 45).

When depicted in D-N space with an aggregate supply function (the latter resting on a standard Marshallian microfoundation and representing the desired proceeds that would just make it worth the while of entrepreneurs to employ N workers), short-period equilibrium is achieved at the intersection of the aggregate demand and supply curves, dubbed the *point of effective demand*. On this basis, Keynes rejected classical-type theories founded on the Say's Law principle (that "supply creates its own demand") by arguing that the latter doctrine did not assume an independent aggregate demand function that could conceivably result in an equilibrium point at less than full employment.

While the development of his aggregate demand concept was of major theoretical and policy significance, particularly in its support of activist taxation, spending, and monetary policies of aggregate demand management, there were obvious problems with Keynes's original formulation. For instance, unless the business sector is conceived as one large firm that can envision the impact of its employment decision on its own expected proceeds, how exactly could a multitude of uncoordinated decisions by competitive firms be collectively anticipated by entrepreneurs and represented in an aggregate demand relation? As a result of such theoretical conundrums, the concept was to undergo tremendous transformations during the post–World War II (1939–1945) period as economists sought conceptually less challengeable theoretical constructs.

Even among fundamentalist Keynesians of the early postwar years, such as Sidney Weintraub (1914–1983) and Paul Davidson, the aggregate demand function, D, came to be treated no longer as an expected proceeds curve as perceived by entrepreneurs, but simply as a representation of the intended spending on the part of economic agents (consumers, firms, and governments) associated with hypothetical levels of total employment. Indeed, in the hands of numerous early postwar Keynesians such as Paul Samuelson, Keynes's original association between sales proceeds and employment was to be transformed into a relation between aggregate intended expenditures of economic agents and the level of real income or output, as depicted in the framework of the popular 45-degree diagrams found in many introductory textbooks (Dutt 2002, p. 329).

Because of its implicit assumption of fixed price, the 45-degree aggregate expenditure relation slowly succumbed to alternative formulations of the aggregate demand function as economists struggled to incorporate the effect of changes in prices within a competing analytical framework. This resulted in redefining a downward-sloping aggregate demand function within aggregate price-output space seemingly comparable to its traditional Marshallian microeconomic counterpart. However, to ensure a negative slope, this latter incarnation of the aggregate demand function had to rely on somewhat more questionable assumptions than its previous upward-sloping Keynesian aggregate expenditure relation in the context of 45-degree diagrams. This is because, as prices rise, it is assumed that the purchasing power of household wealth and cash balances declines and thereby household spending (aggregate demand) also declines. These so-called wealth effects and real balance effects assume that currency held by households plus reserves held by banks exceed the value of bank deposits. In fact, however, bank deposits greatly exceed the value of bank reserves plus currency held by households. Hence, the relevance of real balance effects has been seriously questioned. This is why modern macroeconomic textbooks have slowly been abandoning this form of aggregate demand analysis (in price-output space) and relying simply on a dynamic relation that links inflation to an economy-wide capacity utilization rate—a variant of the Phillips Curve. Unfortunately, the latter is a far cry from Keynes's unique formulation of the aggregate demand function that related aggregate expected proceeds to the level of employment.

SEE ALSO *Aggregate Supply; Economics, Keynesian; Economics, New Classical; Keynes, John Maynard; Lucas, Robert E.; Macroeconomics; Phillips Curve; Propensity to Consume, Marginal; Survey of Income and Program Participation*

BIBLIOGRAPHY

Asimakopulos, A. 1991. *Keynes's General Theory and Accumulation.* Cambridge, U.K.: Cambridge University Press.

Barro, Robert J. 1994. The Aggregate-Supply/Aggregate-Demand Model. *Eastern Economic Journal* 20 (1): 1–6.

Dutt, Amitava Krishna. 2002. Aggregate Demand-Aggregate Supply Analysis: A History. *History of Political Economy* 34 (2): 321–363.

Keynes, John Maynard. 1936. *The General Theory of Employment, Interest, and Money.* London: Macmillan.

King, John E. 1994. Aggregate Supply and Demand Analysis since Keynes: A Partial History. *Journal of Post Keynesian Economics* 17 (1): 3–31.

Mario Seccareccia

AGGREGATE DEMAND AND SUPPLY PRICE

Theories of *demand* and *supply* have their roots in the works of the English economist Alfred Marshall, who divided all economic forces into those two categories. In 1890 Marshall introduced the concepts of *supply price* and *demand price* functions to capture the demand and supply factors facing an individual firm or industry. Marshall's demand price function relates the quantity of a specific good buyers would be willing to purchase at alternative market prices. The supply price function relates the quantity of goods sellers would be willing to sell at alternative prices. In equilibrium, market price and sales (equal to purchases) would be established at the intersection of these two micro-Marshallian functions.

In his *The General Theory of Employment, Interest, and Money* (1936), John Maynard Keynes aggregated these Marshallian micro-demand and -supply concepts to achieve an aggregate supply price function and an aggregate demand price function for the macroeconomy. Keynes called the intersection of these aggregate functions the *point of effective demand*. This "point" indicates the equilibrium level of aggregate employment and output.

AGGREGATE SUPPLY PRICE

Keynes's aggregate supply price function is derived from ordinary Marshallian microeconomic supply price functions (see Keynes 1936, pp. 44–45). It relates the aggregate number of workers (N) that profit-maximizing entrepreneurs would want to hire for all possible alternative levels of expected aggregate sales proceeds (Z), given the money wage rate (w), technology, the average degree of competition (or monopoly) in the economy, and the degree of integration of firms (cf. Keynes 1936, p. 245). In other words, the aggregate supply price is the profit-maximizing total sales proceeds that entrepreneurs would expect to receive for any given level of employment hiring they reach.

Gross Domestic Product (GDP) is the measure of the gross total output produced by the domestic economy. For any given degree of integration of firms, GDP is directly related to total sales proceeds (Z). If all firms are fully integrated—that is, if each firm produces everything internally, from the raw materials to the final finished product—then aggregate sales proceeds (Z) equals GDP. If all firms in the economy are not fully integrated, then Z will be some multiple of GDP depending on the average degree of integration of all firms.

Keynes argued (1936, p. 41) that money values and quantities of employment are the only two homogeneous "fundamental units of quantity" that can be added together to provide meaningful aggregates. Accordingly, the aggregate supply price (expected sales proceeds) associated with alternative levels of employment should be specified either in (1) money terms (Z) or (2) Keynes's wage unit terms (Z_w), where the aggregate money sales proceeds is divided by the money wage rate (w). Hence the aggregate supply function is specified as either:

$$Z = f_1(N) \qquad (1)$$

or

$$z_w = Z/w = (f_1(N)/w) = f_2(N) \qquad (2)$$

The Marshallian supply curve for a single firm (s_f) relates the profit-maximizing output possibilities for alternative expected market prices. This supply price function (s_f) of any profit-maximizing firm depends on the degree of competition (or monopoly) of the firm (k_f) and its marginal costs (MC_f). In the simplest case, in which labor is the only variable factor of production, $MC_f = w/MPL_f$ where w is the wage rate and MPL_f is the marginal product of labor. Accordingly, the Marshallian microeconomic supply price function is specified as

$$s_f = f_3(k_f, MC_f) = f_3(k_f, (w/MPL_f)) \qquad (3)$$

Lerner's (1935) measure of the degree of monopoly (k_f) is equal to $(1 - 1/E_{df})$ where E_{df} is the absolute value of the price elasticity of demand facing the firm for any given level of effective demand. For a perfectly competitive firm, $k_f = 0$ and only marginal costs affect the position and shape of the firm's supply price function.

The Marshallian industry supply price function (s) is obtained by the usual lateral summation of the individual firm's supply curves

$$s = f_4(k, MC) = f_4(k, (w/MPL)) \qquad (4)$$

where the symbols without subscripts are the industry's equivalent to the aforementioned firm's variables.

Although output across firms in the same industry may be homogeneous and therefore capable of being aggregated to obtain the industry supply quantities (as in equation 4), an assumption of output homogeneity cannot be accepted as the basis for summing across industries to obtain the aggregate supply price function of total output (Keynes 1936, ch. 4). Because every point on the Marshallian industry supply function (s) is associated with a unique profit-maximizing combination of price (p) and quantity (q), the multiple of which equals total industry expected sales proceeds (z) (i.e., $pxq = z$), and because every industry output level (q) can be associated with a unique industry hiring level n (i.e., $q = f(n)$), then every point of equation 4 of the s-curve in p vs. q quadrant space can be transformed to a point on a z-curve in z vs. n quadrant space to obtain

$$z = f_5(n). \qquad (5)$$

These equation 5 industry-supply functions are aggregated across all industries to obtain Keynes's aggregate supply price function in terms of aggregate money proceeds (Z) and the aggregate quantity of employment units (N) as specified in equation 1. To achieve unique aggregation values of Z for each possible N, Keynes assumed that corresponding to any given point of aggregate supply price there is a unique distribution of income and employment between the different industries in the economy (Keynes 1936, p. 282).

Though Keynes describes the aggregate supply price function and its inverse, the employment function, in *The General Theory*, he unquestioningly accepted Marshall's microeconomic supply price concept as the basis for the aggregation he used to aggregate supply price function. Consequently, the bulk of *The General Theory* is devoted to developing the characteristics of aggregate demand price function, for it was the latter that Keynes thought was his revolutionary and novel contribution.

AGGREGATE DEMAND PRICE

Keynes's "Principle of Effective Demand" (1936, ch. 2) attacked classical theory's fundamental building block,

known as Say's Law. This law presumes that "supply (equal to total output produced and income earned) creates its own demand." Under Say's Law all income, whether spent on consumption or saved, is presumed to be spent on the products of industry. Accordingly, the total costs of aggregate production incurred by firms (by definition equal to aggregate income earned) at any level of employment is presumed to be entirely recouped by the sale of output at every possible level of employment and output. The factors determining the aggregate demand price for products are presumed to be identical to those that determine aggregate output (aggregate supply price) for every possible given level of output.

Keynes justified his position by declaring that Say's Law "is not the true law relating the aggregate demand price function and the aggregate supply price function.... [Such a law] remains to be written and without ... [it] all discussions concerning the volume of aggregate employment are futile" (1936, p. 26). Keynes's *General Theory* developed the characteristics and properties of the aggregate demand price function to explain why it was not identical with the aggregate supply function—that is, why supply does not create its own demand.

Keynes's aggregate demand price function related the expected aggregate planned expenditures of all buyers for all possible alternative levels of aggregate income and employment. An expanded taxonomy for the components of the aggregate demand price relationship was necessary to differentiate Keynes's analysis from the aggregate demand price function implicit in the classical Say's Law. Under Say's Law, all demand for producibles is collected in a single category (D_1) that is solely a function of (and is equal to) income earned (supply) at all possible alternative levels of employment. Keynes split aggregate demand price into two categories, D_1 and D_2, where D_1 represents *all* expenditures that "depend on the level of aggregate income and, therefore, on the level of employment N," and D_2 represents *all* expenditures *not* related to income and employment (1936, pp. 29–30). These two categories make up an exhaustive list of all possible classes of demand.

Unlike the Say's Law D_1 category, Keynes's D_1 spending does not necessarily equal aggregate income, because some income might be saved—and in Keynes's analysis, savings out of current income is never immediately used for the purchase of producibles. Keynes identified D_1 as the propensity to consume (i.e., consumption expenditures) using current income. Keynes argued that some portion of current income was not spent on consumption, but was instead saved in the form of money or other liquid assets to permit the saver to transfer purchasing power to the indefinite future. Moreover, an essential property of money (and all liquid assets) is that it is not producible in the private sector by the employment of labor (Keynes

1936, ch. 17). Thus, the decision to save a portion of income as money or other liquid assets involves "a non-employment inducing demand" (cf. Hahn 1977, p. 39) that is incompatible with Say's Law.

Because all income received goes either to planned consumption or planned savings, if Keynes's second expenditure category, D_2, were to be equal to the planned savings at every possible alternative level of employment, then Say's Law would be reinstalled. To demonstrate why D_2 is not equal to a planned savings function, Keynes assumed the existence of an uncertain future (i.e., a system in which the classic ergodic axiom is not applicable). By *uncertain* Keynes meant that the future can neither be known in advance nor reliably statistically predicted through an analysis of existing market price signals. Given an uncertain (nonergodic) future economy, future profits, the basis for current D_2 investment spending, can neither be reliably forecasted from existing market information, nor endogenously determined via planned savings. Instead, the expected profitability of investment spending (D_2) depends on the optimism or pessimism of entrepreneurs—what Keynes called "animal spirits." In such a world, neither in the short run nor the long run can D_2 expenditures be a function of current income and employment.

Keynes's general theory, therefore, implies that the aggregate demand price function is not identical with the aggregate supply function at every possible alternative level of employment. Thus, the possibility exists for a unique single intersection (the point of effective demand) at less than full employment.

SEE ALSO *Economics, Post Keynesian; Keynes, John Maynard; Macroeconomics; Marshall, Alfred; Z-D Model*

BIBLIOGRAPHY

Davidson, Paul. 1994. *Post Keynesian Macroeconomic Theory: A Foundation for Successful Economic Policies for the Twenty-First Century.* Cheltenham, U.K.: Elgar.

Hahn, Frank H. Keynesian Economics and General Equilibrium Theory: Reflections on Some Current Debates. In *The Microeconomic Foundations of Macroeconomics,* ed. G. C. Harcourt, 22–41. London: Macmillan.

Keynes, John Maynard. 1936. *The General Theory of Employment, Interest, and Money.* New York: Harcourt, Brace.

Lerner, Abba P. 1934. The Concept of Monopoly and the Measurement of Monopoly Power. *Review of Economic Studies* 1 (June): 157–175.

Marshall, Alfred. 1890. *Principles of Economics.* London: Macmillan.

Paul Davidson

AGGREGATE SUPPLY

Aggregate supply is an aggregate analogue of the concept of supply for individual goods and services markets that is used in microeconomic analysis. The aggregate supply of goods and services is usually taken to be related to the aggregate price level, a relationship that is called the aggregate supply function. The curve representing this relation is called the aggregate supply curve, and is a component of the popular aggregate demand–aggregate supply analysis of short-run macroeconomics, which abstracts from longer run issues such as capital accumulation and technological change.

The economist John Maynard Keynes defined the aggregate supply function as the relation between the level of employment and the aggregate supply price, which is the expectation of proceeds that makes it just worthwhile for firms to offer that level of employment, and distinguished it from the aggregate demand function that shows the relation between the proceeds that firms expect to receive and the level of employment. The modern use of aggregate supply and demand remains close to Keynes's usage but replaces the relation between the value of output (or total proceeds) and employment to that between the price level and the quantity of output. Early economics textbooks after Keynes took the aggregate supply (AS) curve to be positively sloped like its microeconomic counterpart, but as shown in Figure 1, assumed it to be relatively flat at low levels of output, having an upward slope at intermediate levels, and to become increasingly steeper as the economy approaches full employment. At low levels of output many resources, including labor, are unutilized, and increases in output can be obtained without increases in input prices and without experiencing significant diminishing returns, so that firms are willing to produce more without any increase in the price. As output expands, diminishing returns sets in and input prices begin to rise, so that firms require a higher price to produce more. Finally, when full employment of labor is reached with the corresponding output level shown by Y_f in Figure 1, no further expansion in output is possible.

In subsequent (late twentieth-century) presentations this representation has been replaced by a variety of others, the relevance of which depend on the precise assumptions made about the economy and the time horizon one has in mind. The most popular representation, common to a number of Keynesian and monetarist approaches, takes the short-run aggregate supply curve to be positively sloped, as shown by the curve AS in Figure 2, and the long-run aggregate supply curve as vertical as shown by the vertical line at Y_n (denoting the natural level of employment, which is consistent with wage-price stability) in the figure. The short-run curve can extend beyond the long-run curve as shown in the figure, implying that

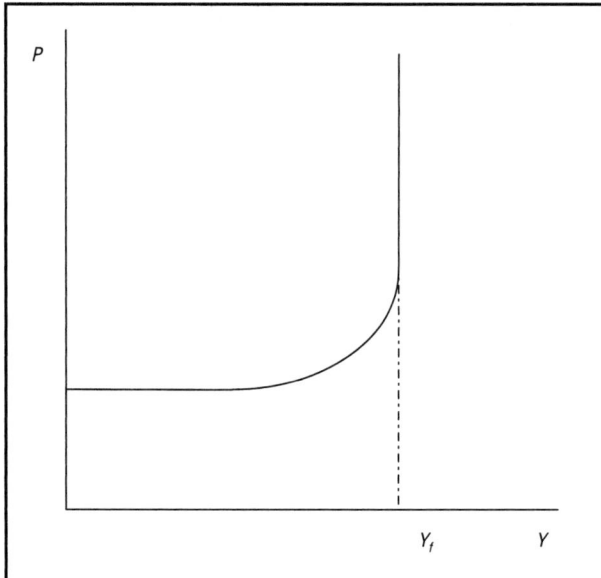

Figure 1

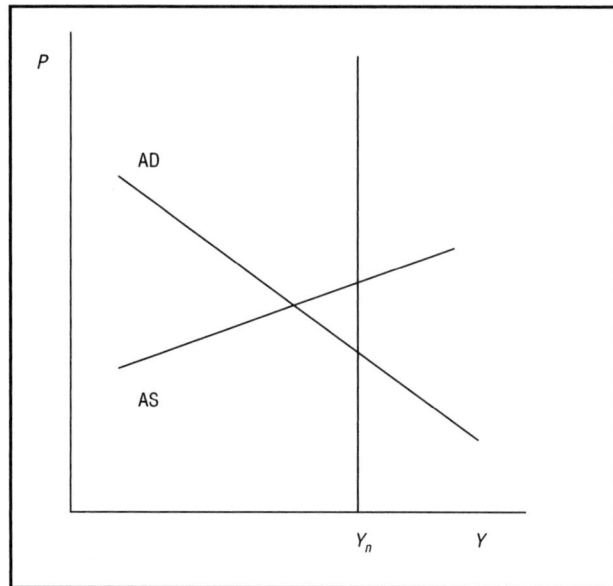

Figure 2

the economy can in fact produce beyond the level shown by the longer-run curve, for instance by hiring more workers than normal by paying overtime wages.

There are several interpretations of this configuration. One interpretation—common among the neoclassical synthesis Keynesians—assumes that firms operate in a perfectly competitive market and with diminishing returns to labor. With the money wage given in the short run, a higher price makes profit-maximizing firms increase employment and production. With the money wage flexible in the longer run, the money wage changes; if there is unemployment, the money wage falls, so that the aggregate supply curve shifts down. In the long run the economy is at full employment, where the demand for labor and the supply of labor (both of which depend on the real wage) are equal, so that the economy is at Y_n in the figure. A second interpretation—made by the early monetarists—takes the price level expected by workers to be given, but allows the money wage to adjust to clear the labor market, in the short run. A higher price increases the money wage as firms increase their demand for workers, and workers supply more labor because with the fixed expected price their expected real wage is higher. Over the longer run the expected price adapts to the actual price, which shifts the AS curve; in long run equilibrium price expectations are fulfilled and the economy is at Y_n. A similar interpretation—often made by new Keynesians—assumes that the money wage depends on the expected price and on labor market conditions reflected by the

unemployment rate, and that the price level is determined by firms as a markup on unit labor costs. In the short run, with expected price given, a higher level of output implies a lower unemployment rate, a higher money wage and a higher price. In the longer run, as expected price adapts to the actual price, the AS curve moves; for instance, if the economy produces below Y_n, the expected price falls, so that the AS curve shifts down. The long-run supply curve is given at the natural rate of unemployment at which the wage and price are stable, as determined by labor market conditions and the pricing policies of firms. Unemployment may prevail due to, for instance, firms keeping wages higher than the market, clearing one to make workers exert more effort, thereby becoming more productive.

In all of these interpretations, in the short run the economy is on the AS curve, at a position determined by the AS curve and the downward-sloping aggregate demand (AD) curve. Since the short-run position of the economy is not at Y_n, the price and wage will change; at the intersection shown in Figure 2, the price and wage falls so that AS shifts down, and the economy moves along the AD curve until long-run equilibrium is attained at Y_n, so that the vertical line can be given the interpretation of the long-run AS curve. This adjustment occurs because (as is shown by the negative slope of the AD curve) a reduction in the price reduces the demand for money (since less money is required to make transactions), which makes asset holders want to lend more thereby reducing the interest rate and inducing more spending. The nature of the short-run and long-run aggregate supply curves, given by AS and Y_n, implies that changes in the aggregate demand curve (such as fiscal and monetary policy shifts, or changes in expectations which affect investment) have an effect on output in the short run, but not in the long run.

This interpretation, however, is not accepted by all approaches. Some take the view that the economy is always on the vertical curve, so that it is the only AS curve for the economy. These views, which are associated with the new classical approach, assume that the money wage is perfectly flexible (in contrast to the neoclassical Keynesians) and that economic agents have rational expectations (in contrast to the early monetarists) and do not make systematic forecasting errors, so that it is inappropriate to take the expected price as given in the short run. In this approach, the AS curve is the vertical curve at full employment, so that aggregate demand shifts do not affect the level of output. However, this result need not hold if there are wealth effects on labor supply. With the traditional interpretation based on the supply and demand for labor and market clearing wage, a change in the price level can affect the value of real wealth, which in turn can affect the supply of labor and the level of employment.

Approaches having the rising short-run AS curve need not accept the interpretation that vertical curve is the long-run AS curve. First, the economy may not converge to Y_n, so that the vertical line cannot be given the interpretation of the long-run supply curve. For instance, if the economy is below Y_n in the short run, the downward shift in the AS curve need not take the economy to Y_n if the AD curve also shifts to the left or because it is not negatively sloped if, for instance, as the money wage falls aggregate demand falls as wage income falls (with a higher propensity to spend out of wage than out of profit income) or because firms reduce investment when the price falls. Second, even if the economy converges toward Y_n, its level may change endogenously, so that the long-run supply curve need not be vertical. For instance, according to some new Keynesian contributions, a fall in output and employment below the natural rate can make outsiders in the labor market lose their ability to reduce the wage, which increases the natural rate of unemployment and reduce Y_n. In these cases the aggregate supply side of the story implies that the aggregate demand side can have effects not only in the short run, but also in the longer run.

SEE ALSO *Aggregate Demand; Economics, Keynesian; Economics, New Classical; Keynes, John Maynard; Lucas, Robert E.; Macroeconomics*

BIBLIOGRAPHY

Dutt, Amitava Krishna. 2002. Aggregate Demand-Aggregate Supply Analysis: A History. *History of Political Economy* 34 (2): 321–363.

Keynes, John Maynard. 1936. *The General Theory of Employment, Interest and Money.* London: Macmillan.

Tarshis, Lori. 1947. *The Elements of Economics: An Introduction to the Theory of Price and Employment.* Boston: Houghton-Mifflin.

Amitava Krishna Dutt

AGGRESSION

Aggression is defined as behavior that is intended to harm others and that is perceived as harmful by the victim. Because aggression is such a broad phenomenon, subtypes of aggression have been proposed to reconcile discrepant research findings—for example, that not all aggression is angry. Subtypes of aggression abound, but two classifications are most important: reactive versus proactive aggression, and physical versus social aggression.

Reactive aggression is angry, impulsive, and typically occurs in response to provocation, whereas *proactive aggression* (sometimes called *instrumental aggression*) is more cool and deliberate and is deployed to achieve a social goal. Although reactive and proactive aggression are highly correlated, they seem to be related to different correlates and developmental outcomes (Coie and Dodge 1998). Reactive aggression is related to overattributing hostility in social interactions, whereas proactive aggression is related to expecting that physical aggression will have positive outcomes. Reactive aggression is associated with parental abuse, behavior problems in the classroom, and peer rejection and victimization. Proactive aggression is related to friendship similarity and leadership, and also predicts future antisocial behavior.

Because hurtful behavior can take nonphysical forms, perhaps especially for girls, other important subtypes to consider are physical and social aggression. *Social aggression* is behavior that hurts others by harming their social status or friendships. This form of aggression includes malicious gossip, friendship manipulation, and verbal and nonverbal forms of social exclusion (Underwood 2003). Social aggression is sometimes called *indirect* or *relational aggression*, but the construct of social aggression acknowledges that harm to relationships can be both direct and indirect, and that social exclusion can be both verbal and nonverbal. Here again, children's propensities to engage in social and physical aggression are highly correlated. Both social and physical aggression may take reactive or proactive forms.

Across almost all cultures that have been studied, boys and men are more physically aggressive than girls and women are. However, evidence for gender differences is much less clear for social aggression. Because base rates for girls' physical aggression are so low, without a doubt girls are more socially aggressive than they are physically aggressive. However, this does not necessarily mean that girls are more socially aggressive than boys are, and research findings conflict. Future research should examine whether social aggression unfolds differently in girls' groups than in boys' groups.

DEVELOPMENTAL ORIGINS AND OUTCOMES OF PHYSICAL AGGRESSION

Physical aggression emerges in the first two years of life (Tremblay et al. 2005) and may have biological correlates. Experts disagree as to whether there is a strong genetic component for physical aggression, but genes likely underlie temperamental qualities that have been shown to be related to aggression in childhood, which appears in such forms as impulsivity, negative emotionality, and reactivity. Although testosterone has long been thought to be related to physical aggression, the relation between this hormone and physical fighting is complex and at best indirect. Elevations in testosterone are more related to social ascendance than aggression specifically.

Socialization experiences may relate to a child's propensity for physical aggression. Children who experience harsh, abusive parenting may develop a bias toward interpreting ambiguous social cues as hostile, which leads them to be sensitive to slights and prone to reactive aggression. Children whose parents have an authoritarian style (punitive and low on warmth) may be more likely to have behavior and peer problems. Children who engage in coercive cycles with parents, in which the child's behavior escalates until the parent gives in, thereby reinforcing the highly noncompliant behavior, are more prone to a number of antisocial behaviors that may include physical aggression. Children may also become increasingly aggressive as a result of exposure to media violence on television or in video games, although the direction of causation is difficult to disentangle because physically aggressive children may be more drawn to violent media content.

Physical aggression is associated with a number of adjustment problems, in childhood and beyond. Children who fight are at risk for peer rejection and academic difficulties; as adolescents, they are at risk for dropping out of school, delinquency, and substance use. Although fewer girls than boys fight physically, those that do are just as much at risk for these negative outcomes (Putallaz and Bierman 2004). For girls, physical aggression in childhood is associated with adolescent childbearing, and these adolescent mothers who were aggressive as children are at heightened risk for having children with health and behavioral problems.

DEVELOPMENTAL ORIGINS AND OUTCOMES OF SOCIAL AGGRESSION

Although much less is known about the developmental origins of social aggression, interesting hypotheses are emerging. Children may learn the power of social aggression by watching their parents resolve marital conflicts in ways that involve triangulating others and threatening relationship harm, or by watching how parents refrain from open conflict with friends but instead malign others behind their backs. Children may also learn social aggression by observing peers or siblings, or perhaps even by seeing relationship manipulation and malicious gossip gleefully depicted in television and movies, not only those aimed at children and adolescents but also adult programming.

Engaging in high levels of social aggression and chronically being victimized are both associated with psychological maladjustment for children. Children, especially girls, who are frequently victimized report elevated levels of depression, loneliness, anxiety, and low self-concept. In addition, children who frequently perpetrate social aggression are disliked by peers, and they report feeling lonely and anxious. In young adult women, being nominated by peers as high on social aggression has been shown to be related to bulimia and borderline personality disorder. As suggested by Nicki Crick and Carolyn Zahn-Waxler (2003), high levels of social aggression may be associated with the psychological problems to which girls and women are most vulnerable.

FUTURE RESEARCH

Future research should examine how physical and social aggression are related and unfold together in both real and developmental time. Promising strategies to reduce physical aggression involve training parents to respond strategically to their children by rewarding positive behavior and not reinforcing aggression, and teaching children skills that will help them regulate emotions and form relationships. Some of these same strategies may be helpful for reducing social aggression, and adding components that address social aggression may enhance the effectiveness of violence prevention programs.

BIBLIOGRAPHY

Coie, John D., and Kenneth A. Dodge. 1998. Aggression and Antisocial Behavior. In *Handbook of Child Psychology*, ed. William Damon. Vol. 3, *Social, Emotional, and Personality Development*, ed. Nancy Eisenberg, pp. 779–862,. New York: Wiley.

Crick, Nicki R., and Carolyn Zahn-Waxler. 2003. The Development of Psychopathology in Females and Males: Current Progress and Future Challenges. *Development and Psychopathology* 15, 719–742.

Putallaz, Martha, and Karen L. Bierman. 2004. *Aggression, Antisocial Behavior, and Violence Among Girls: A Developmental Perspective.* New York: Guilford.

Tremblay, Richard E., Willard W. Hartup, and John Archer. 2005. *Developmental Origins of Aggression.* New York: Guilford.

Underwood, Marion K. 2003. *Social Aggression Among Girls.* New York: Guilford.

Marion K. Underwood

AGING

SEE *Gerontology.*

AGNOSTICISM

Agnosticism concerns the withholding of a person's judgment, or belief, on a matter. Such withholding entails neither believing in favor of nor believing against a phenomenon in question. With regard to the question of God's existence, for instance, an agnostic would believe neither that God exists nor that God does not exist. Agnosticism can be directed toward any alleged phenomenon. It need not be limited to the issue of God's existence. It thus is equivalent to skepticism. One might be agnostic about the external world, minds, God, non-physical entities, causal relations, and future truths, among other things. Sextus Empiricus (fl. c. 150 CE), David Hume (1711–1776), and Bertrand Russell (1872–1970) have supported influential versions of agnosticism.

Cognitive agnosticism about an alleged entity (say, God) entails that, owing to counterbalanced or at least highly mixed evidence, one should withhold belief regarding the proposition that God exists. That is, one should neither believe that God exists nor believe that God does not exist. Doxastic agnosticism about God, in contrast, entails that one actually withholds belief regarding the proposition that God exists. A doxastic agnostic can consistently say: I withhold judgment whether God exists, but I have no commitment regarding the status of the overall available evidence on the matter. So a person could be a doxastic agnostic without being a cognitive agnostic. Cognitive agnostics about God, however, are logically required to recommend doxastic agnosticism about God, at least on cognitive grounds, even if they fail at times actually to withhold judgment regarding God's existence.

A common motivation for agnosticism regarding an issue is a concern to avoid error or at least to minimize the risk of error in one's beliefs. The concern is that if relevant evidence is highly mixed, then in answering either yes or no to a question, one seriously risks falling into error, that is, false belief. The better alternative, according to agnostics, is to refrain from answering either yes or no, that is, to withhold judgment. Refraining from believing that something exists while refraining from believing that it does not exist can save one from mistaken belief. There is, however, a price to pay: One will then miss out on an opportunity to acquire truth in the area in question. For instance, it is true either that God exists or that God does not exist. Agnostics in principle forgo acquiring a truth in this area of reality.

Agnostics about the issue of God's existence do not endorse atheism about God. They do not affirm that God does not exist; nor do they propose that our overall available evidence indicates that God does not exist. Agnostics hold that (at least for their own situation) atheism goes too far in the negative direction, just as (they hold for at least their own situation) theism goes too far in the positive direction. Theism, like agnosticism and atheism, can be either cognitive or doxastic. Doxastic theists hold that God exists. Cognitive theists hold that, owing to the overall available evidence, one should believe that God exists. Agnostics hold that, at least for their own situation, theism and atheism go too far, positively or negatively, in the area of belief.

An underlying assumption of cognitive agnosticism is that God's existence would need to be more obvious to justify acknowledgment. This assumption has given rise to extensive contemporary discussion about divine hiddenness and elusiveness. The discussion shows no sign of ending any time soon.

SEE ALSO *Atheism; Monotheism; Reality; Religion; Theism*

BIBLIOGRAPHY

Copan, Paul, and Paul K. Moser, eds. 2003. *The Rationality of Theism.* London: Routledge.

Greco, John, ed. 2008. *The Oxford Handbook of Skepticism.* New York: Oxford University Press.

Howard-Snyder, Daniel, and Paul K. Moser, eds. 2002. *Divine Hiddenness: New Essays.* New York: Cambridge University Press.

Moser, Paul K. 1993. *Philosophy after Objectivity: Making Sense in Perspective.* New York: Oxford University Press.

Paul K. Moser

AGRIBUSINESS

Agribusiness is related to the production of food and fiber. Agribusiness includes agricultural input industries, commodity processing, food manufacturing and food distribution industries, and third-party firms that facilitate agribusiness operations including bankers, brokers, advertising agencies, and market information firms. Harvard Business School professor Ray A. Goldberg introduced the term *agribusiness* together with coauthor John H. Davis in 1955 in a book titled *A Concept of Agribusiness*. Food and fiber products that rely upon agricultural production, which is inherently decentralized and subject to the vagaries of weather and disease, often are perishable and require specialized economic institutions and public policies including sanitary regulations. Decentralized farmers of a particular commodity, such as milk, have organized agricultural marketing cooperatives to aggregate their product and coordinate sale to large food-manufacturing firms in a fashion that enhances product quality, economic efficiency, and fairness of the market pricing system.

Similarly, on the input side there are tightly coordinated (contract farming) arrangements for chicken and pork. In the beef and grain industries, agribusiness coordination uses complex pricing mechanisms, such as futures markets, to hedge risk and price products. Closer to the consumer, large supermarket chains have integrated back into the wholesaling of food products and developed private-label food products (such as bread with the supermarket's name on it) to countervail the power of branded food-product manufacturers who would charge a premium for their products.

Public policies toward the agribusiness sector have been critical in creating the food and fiber system that is seen throughout the world. Food safety and health regulations are critical. Agricultural commodity and pricing policies in developed countries aid in the pricing of commodities such as milk, wheat, corn, soybeans, cotton, and other products. These policies attempt to stabilize commodity price cycles and to ensure the economic health of the agricultural industries.

Public policy also aids in the organization of agricultural marketing and input supply cooperatives and the development of commodity promotion programs wherein farmers fund advertising efforts such as the "Got Milk?" program in the United States. Here the desire is to improve the incomes of farmers by enhancing their bargaining power and expanding the demand for their products.

Antitrust and competition policy also affects agribusiness. Over time the food systems in the United States and other countries have become industrialized. Relatively few large food processing firms and relatively few large retailing organizations sit between decentralized agricultural production and the general consuming public. Antitrust/competition policy examines proposed mergers and acquisitions in these concentrated industries to determine whether they would increase pricing power to the disadvantage of consumers or farmers. Those policies also prohibit price-fixing cartels and attempts to monopolize industries.

In the March-April 2000 issue of the *Harvard Business Review*, Goldberg revisited the concept of agribusiness with Juan Enriquez. He observed that ethanol, an additive to gasoline, and pharmaceutical products were made from agricultural outputs. Agribusiness in the 2000s also includes forestry and forest products and the plant nursery industry.

SEE ALSO *Agricultural Industry; Banana Industry; Cattle Industry; Coffee Industry; Cotton Industry; Flower Industry; Peanut Industry; Slave Trade; Slavery Industry; Sugar Industry; Tea Industry; Tobacco Industry; Vanilla Industry*

BIBLIOGRAPHY

Agribusiness: An International Journal. Research journal published quarterly by John Wiley & Sons, Inc., Hoboken, NJ.

Enriquez, Juan, and Ray A. Goldberg. 2000. Transforming Life, Transforming Business: The Life-Science Revolution. *Harvard Business Review* 78 (2): 94–104.

Goldberg, Ray A., and John H. Davis. 1957. *A Concept of Agribusiness.* Cambridge, MA: Harvard University Press.

Ronald W. Cotterill

AGRICULTURAL ECONOMICS

The field of agricultural economics deals with resource allocation and utilization and income distribution and growth in land-intensive activities. Traditionally such activities were confined to crops and livestock production, which, accordingly, have been the accepted domain of agricultural economics. As the relative economic importance of agriculture declines (steeply in the case of the industrialized nations) and as natural resource depletion and degradation loom large, agricultural economics has come to be seen as inseparable from the economics of renewable resources and the environment.

Established areas of study in agricultural economics include farm-level decision making, production economics and resource use efficiency, household economics and consumer behavior, agricultural markets and market outcomes, food safety and variety, international trade in agricultural commodities, and nutrition. The contemporary field includes natural resource and environmental economics, agribusiness, forestry economics, and aspects of health economics, community and rural development, food security, and economic development (see, for example, Cramer, Jensen, and Southgate, 2001).

The affinity between traditional agricultural economics and environmental and resource economics is more than a matter of their common concerns with land, water, and other natural resources; it is also rooted in shared principles and methods of research. This accounts for the reincarnation of most academic departments of agricultural economics as departments of agricultural and resource economics since the early 1980s.

Agricultural economics is a branch of neoclassicism, the reigning paradigm in economics. Its origins are coterminous with the ascendancy of neoclassicism from the 1870s on. Indeed, agricultural economics has provided its parent with the archetype of the neoclassical textbook ideal: firms without market power (farms), workers without bosses (peasant families), and products without private identities (cereal commodities). This model remains the hobbyhorse not just of agricultural economists but of economists generally; ironically, though, agricultural markets have long ceased to be guided by the invisible hand, given ubiquitous state interventionism. Nonagricultural markets ruled by competition, on the other hand, have long been exceptions, not the rule.

Apart from supplying a deceptively persuasive model bolstering neoclassical preconceptions, the theoretical significance of agricultural economics consists in its unwavering adherence to these preconceptions. Agricultural economics has always been highly micro-oriented in both theoretical and empirical analyses, relying on the standard models of rational decision making by households (as both consumers and producers) and of profit-maximizing farms (see Norton 2004).

Claiming universal validity for this paradigm, Nobel prize winner Theodore Schultz famously described developing nations' agriculture-dominated economies as "poor but efficient," a narrowly technical-economic conclusion that seemed incongruous with endemic resource underutilization, including underemployment, egregious social structures of exploitation, and momentous instances of agrarian conflict and revolution (Rao 1986).

If agricultural economics deals with the narrowly technical issues of resource allocation and utilization that arise in our relation to nature and its cultivation, agrarian economics may be taken to deal with broader issues of social structure and regulation that arise in our relation to each other as we relate to nature. Advancing socially relevant knowledge in these twin fields is vital to our future. But this will depend on conscious efforts to integrate the twin fields rather than, as agricultural economics has

done, ignoring the social dimension by hypostatizing itself.

SEE ALSO *Agribusiness; Agricultural Industry; Development Economics; Economics; Economics, Classical; Green Revolution; Harris-Todaro Model; North-South Models; Optimizing Peasant; Peasantry; Primitive Accumulation; Production; Production Frontier; Quota System, Farm; Rent; Returns, Diminishing; Returns, Increasing; Returns to a Fixed Factor; Returns to Scale; Slavery; Stages of Life; Subsidies, Farm; Subsistence Agriculture*

BIBLIOGRAPHY

Cramer, Gail L., Clarence W. Jensen, and Douglas D. Southgate Jr. 2001. *Agricultural Economics and Agribusiness.* New York: Wiley.

Norton, Roger D. 2004. *Agricultural Development Policy: Concepts and Experiences.* Hoboken, NJ: Wiley.

Rao, J. Mohan. 1986. Agriculture in Recent Development Theory. *Journal of Development Economics* 22(1): 41–86.

J. Mohan Rao

AGRICULTURAL EXTENSION PROGRAM

SEE *Development, Rural.*

AGRICULTURAL INDUSTRY

The emergence of agriculture was one of the most prominent events in human history, and transformations in agriculture have proved to be among the most significant sources of social change. Even in the postindustrial world, agriculture and agricultural change continue to have major implications for human societies. Fundamentally, humans remain absolutely dependent on agriculture for food and many other products used on a daily basis.

The emergence of and subsequent developments in agriculture have transformed human societies in at least three major ways: First, when compared to hunting and gathering, agriculture greatly increased the amount of food that could be produced and made food production much more consistent and dependable. With an ever-increasing and more dependable food supply, the human population that the earth can support has increased dramatically (Vasey 1992). Second, agriculture made permanent settlement possible because it was no longer necessary for humans to follow herds of animals or go out in search of edible plants. Third, as agriculturally based societies developed, the ownership or control of agricultural lands became perhaps the most important source of wealth and power. Extensive inequality quickly followed.

Agricultural production has always been, and continues to be, totally dependent on two broad sets of input. These include: (1) the force, energy, or labor to accomplish necessary agricultural tasks such as preparing the soil, planting seeds, removing weeds, and harvesting; and (2) environmental resources such as soil, water, and sunshine (Schlebecker 1975). From the beginning, attempts to procure these resources have had substantial societal impacts.

For most of agriculture's long history, human beings, with assistance from domesticated animals, have provided the bulk of agricultural labor. Agriculture has always faced the unique and somewhat troublesome challenge of securing an adequate labor supply: While an industrial labor force can generally be used consistently and efficiently throughout the year, the same is not true in agriculture, where the production of most commodities is seasonal. Consequently, throughout the year there are periods of extensive labor needs, primarily during planting and the harvest, followed by periods when labor requirements are minimal as biological processes unfold (Mann and Dickinson 1978). Employing an agricultural workforce large enough to meet labor requirements during peak seasons means that during most of the year this labor force will be underutilized, while the cost of feeding and housing workers remains constant. On the other hand, if a year-round workforce is not retained and attempts to secure a sufficient temporary labor force during critical labor-intensive periods fail, the results could be disastrous.

Throughout history, attempts to deal with the unique labor problems of agriculture have taken a variety of courses. Initially, approaches revolved around securing an adequate but relatively cheap human labor supply. More recently, technological solutions were sought in which machines were developed to replace human labor in the production process. Both paths have had major social consequences.

MAINTAINING AN ADEQUATE LABOR FORCE

Historically, agricultural lands have often been unequally distributed, largely controlled by wealthy and powerful landowners who sought for ways to maintain a sufficient agricultural labor force at relatively low costs. Some of the solutions have resulted in some of the darkest chapters of human history. In the past couple of centuries more equitable labor solutions have been attempted.

Feudalism During the Middle Ages in Europe, and at times in Japan, China, and other areas, feudalism emerged as a complex and varied cultural system that provided a way for the wealthy and powerful aristocracy to maintain a constant and relatively inexpensive agricultural labor force. In theory, feudalism resembled a pyramid. At the top of the pyramid was the monarch—a king, emperor, or shogun—who owned all of the land within the kingdom. Since it was impossible for the monarch to supervise or control such a large area, he or she divided the land and granted control of various segments to upper-class nobles. These nobles were the second level on the pyramid. In exchange for the land grant, the noble would swear an oath of loyalty to the monarch, collect taxes from the land to be shared with the monarch, and provide soldiers when requested. Often upper-level nobles would further subdivide the land under their control and provide land grants to lower-level nobles, who in turn, were expected to collect taxes to be shared with those above them and to provide soldiers. Further subdivisions were found in some areas. If production increased, greater levels of wealth would flow to all levels up the pyramid. The higher up the pyramid an individual resided, the greater the power, prestige, and financial benefits.

At the base of the pyramid were the peasantry and serfs, who often comprised up to 95 percent of the population. These individuals provided a constant and cheap source of agricultural labor, became soldiers when requested, and generally lived near abject poverty. They owned virtually nothing, spent their days working as day laborers on the lands of the aristocracy, and had few freedoms. The entire feudal system was based on ascribed status, where a person's position in life was almost entirely a function of his or her birth.

Slavery Slavery has a long and painful chapter in world history. While slaves have been used in a variety of economic endeavors, slavery has most prominently been a way of maintaining a consistent and cheap agricultural labor force. Although slavery has been a part of numerous cultures throughout the world, perhaps the most vivid example of slave labor in agriculture involved exporting Africans to the Americas to work as agricultural slaves. Studies by David B. Davis estimate that between 1500 and 1870, about 9.4 million Africans were transported to the Americas. About 48 percent of the slaves arrived in the Caribbean Islands, 41 percent were sent to Brazil, about 6 percent arrived in the southern United States, and the remaining 5 percent were sent to mainland Central and South America (Davis 2006).

Slavery was a part of an extremely productive agricultural system that generated great wealth to those who owned land and slaves and allowed most slaveholders to live a life of relative comfort. However, this wealth was generated by the labor of slaves who endured torture, degradation, and were treated as property. Individuals were often separated from friends and family and sold like animals. One of the lasting consequences of slavery is a legacy of racism. To justify the race-based slavery that existed in the Americas, an ideology emerged in which the slave-owning race was defined as superior while the enslaved race was defined as inferior. The ramifications of this ideology continue to have implications for human interactions in modern society.

The Family Farm When the United States became an independent nation, policies were instigated that were intended to create an agricultural system based on numerous medium-sized family farms. The traditional agricultural labor problems would be solved by having the farmer and other family members provide the vast majority of the labor. Family labor was relatively effective because family members could be used extensively when labor needs were high and idled with minimal costs when not needed (Buttel et al. 1990). A nation of family farmers would also largely eliminate the tremendous inequality inherent in a system of landed aristocracy. The Homestead Act of 1862 perhaps best exemplifies the policy of encouraging family farms in the United States. This act made it possible for a settler, after paying a small registration fee and residing on and working 160 acres of land for five years, to gain clear title to that land. The opportunity to own one's own land was the magnet that drew millions of immigrants from Europe to the United States. In time, millions of medium-sized, full-time family farming operations dominated agriculture in the United States.

Collective Agriculture Karl Marx expressed great concern over the inequality inherent in the feudally based agricultural system that prevailed in Europe. He felt the basic problem was that a few individuals owned the land while the masses provided the agricultural labor. Following the Bolshevik Revolution of 1917, the existing agricultural system was totally overturned in areas under communist control. In time a system of large state-owned, centrally controlled collective farms was developed. The manifest goal of collective agriculture was equality. All members of the collective farm worked together and shared equally in the output. Despite an egalitarian land-ownership system and production units that were conducive to machinery and other modern technology, the productivity of collective farms was never as extensive or as efficient as communist leaders hoped it would be.

THE MECHANIZATION OF AGRICULTURE

Prior to about 1800, the vast majority of the world's population lived on farms in rural areas in an economy based on subsistence agriculture. It was necessary for nearly everyone to be involved in agriculture because most farms were barely able to produce what was needed by their own workers, and thus there was little surplus. Then in the mid-eighteenth century, the Industrial Revolution emerged in Great Britain. Developments in science, technology, and machinery greatly increased the efficiency of human labor. Initially, the industry most extensively affected was agriculture. By using increasingly advanced machines, farmers were able to produce an ever-greater surplus of food and fiber. With fewer workers needed in agriculture, a labor force was available to work on the new machines coming into use in manufacturing and industry.

For many farmers, the development of machines was a welcome solution to agricultural labor problems. Machines had several advantages over human labor. Once a machine was purchased, it could be stored during periods of disuse for little additional cost and made quickly available when needed. Additionally, machines eliminated much of the back-breaking work once associated with farming.

Despite some nineteenth-century breakthroughs, a large proportion of the world's population remained directly involved in agricultural production into the early decades of the twentieth century. Between about 1940 and 1970 the mechanization of agriculture proceeded rapidly in economically advanced nations. The impact of this process was dramatic. The mechanization of agriculture changed the very nature of farm work, totally transformed the face of rural areas, and had dramatic implications for urban and nonfarm populations as well. By utilizing new technologies, the labor capacity of farmers was greatly increased, which enabled them to operate progressively larger farms. With a rapid increase in farm size, there was a corresponding decline in the number of farms (Albrecht and Murdock 1990). In the United States, Calvin Beale (1993) described the subsequent transition as the largest peacetime movement of people in history as millions of people left the farm and moved to urban areas seeking industrial employment. The industrialization of agriculture also significantly altered what was once a family-farm-based agricultural structure. Increasingly, agriculture in the United States and other advanced economies became more dualistic: Most production now comes from a number of large and highly mechanized farms, with another large segment of the farm population running small part-time retirement or hobby farms. The number of medium-sized family farms has declined substantially.

The extent to which agriculture has been transformed by industrialization varies greatly from one part of the world to another. In economically advanced nations, a highly mechanized agricultural sector is extremely productive and typically less than 5 percent of the labor force is involved in agriculture. The large nonfarm sector is then able to produce goods and services that add to the quality of life in these countries. By contrast, in less developed countries a majority of the labor force remains involved in agricultural production and the standard of living is much lower.

AGRICULTURAL ENVIRONMENT AND SOCIETY

Agricultural production has always been and continues to be closely tied to the natural environment (Albrecht and Murdock 2002). The quality and quantity of resources available play a major role in determining which commodities can be produced and in what quantity. While innumerable environmental factors influence agricultural production, a few are obviously vital. Successful agricultural production requires the appropriate combination of soil, water, and temperature. If these factors are missing or vary too widely, production will either not occur or will be somewhat limited. Although the production of agricultural commodities requires all of these essential resources, the amounts required vary substantially from one commodity to another. Wheat can be produced in areas that experience harsh winters and have relatively short growing seasons, while citrus fruits cannot, and rice production requires substantially more water than cotton production. Thus basic environmental differences severely limit farm production in some areas, and certain commodities cannot be effectively produced in other areas.

Throughout history, humans have attempted to overcome the shortcomings of their agricultural environment. Unwanted vegetation is removed, complex irrigation systems carry water to land whose natural rainfall is insufficient, and fertilizers, including animal manure, are added to the soil to improve its natural fertility. As a continuation of these efforts, scientists are seeking to overcome environmental limitations through developments in biotechnology. The implications are extensive. On the one hand, agricultural production far exceeds what it would be otherwise. On the other hand, some environmental resources have been severely depleted and other significant environmental pollution problems have emerged.

In many cases agricultural production has severely impaired the environment. Soil erosion is a classic example. Many great civilizations of the past were founded on an extensive base of fertile soil. Ample soil allowed for surplus farm production, which freed part of the population from agriculture and permitted some workers to become artisans, engineers, and artists (Dale and Carter 1955; Lowdermilk 1953). However, with few exceptions, humans have not been able to sustain a progressive civilization in one locality for more than a few hundred years. Over time the natural resource base (particularly the soil base) that permits surplus production becomes depleted. As resources are depleted, surplus production decreases and the civilization declines (Brown 1981). Lowdermilk (1953), for example, found evidence of over a hundred dead villages in Syria. These villages now stand on bare rocks with the soils completely washed or blown away. He concluded that "if the soils had remained, even though the cities were destroyed and the population dispersed, the area might have been repeopled and the cities rebuilt. But now that the soils are gone, all is gone" (p. 10). In most cases, the more technologically advanced the civilization, the shorter its period of progressive existence and expansion (Diamond 2005; Dale and Carter 1955). Similarly, in Mesopotamia, the rich soils of the Tigris and Euphrates valleys supported some of the world's greatest civilizations. Through the centuries the soils have been severely eroded and today the land supports less than one-sixth of the population that lived there during its historic peak.

Dale and Carter state:

> Let's not put the blame for the barrenness of these areas on the conquering hordes that repeatedly overran them. True, those conquerors often sacked and razed the cities, burned the villages, and slaughtered or drove off the people who populated them. But while the soil and other resources … remained, the cities were usually rebuilt. It was only after the land was depleted or exhausted that the fields became barren and the cities remained dead. (1955, p. 15)

Even today, many of the world's most severe environmental problems are a direct result of modern farming practices. These problems include soil depletion; water pollution from eroded soils, fertilizers, and pesticides; and the depletion of critical resources, including groundwater and nonrenewable energy supplies. The extent to which societies deal with these problems effectively will profoundly influence the world in years to come.

Agriculture of the future will no doubt look substantially different from the agriculture of today, and its evolution will continue to have significant societal impact. Three factors are likely to play significant roles. First, technological developments have always figured prominently in agriculture and will continue to do so. Second, the emergence of a true world economy will have massive implications for prices and production in communities throughout the world. Third, the depletion of resources and environmental change will drastically alter agriculture. Of special concern is global warming, which could significantly alter the agricultural environment in a myriad of ways. The role of social scientists in understanding these issues will be of continued significance.

SEE ALSO *Agricultural Economics; Boserup, Ester; Change, Technological; Civilization; Food; Green Revolution; Industry; Irrigation; Malthus, Thomas Robert; Overpopulation; Quota System, Farm; Slavery; Subsidies, Farm; Subsistence Agriculture*

BIBLIOGRAPHY

Albrecht, Don E., and Steve H. Murdock. 1990. *The Sociology of U.S. Agriculture: An Ecological Perspective.* Ames: Iowa State University Press.

Albrecht, Don E., and Steve H. Murdock. 2002. Rural Environments and Agriculture. In *Handbook of Environmental Sociology*, ed. Riley E. Dunlap and William Michelson. Westport, CT: Greenwood.

Beale, Calvin L. 1993. Salient Features of the Demography of American Agriculture. In *The Demography of Rural Life*, ed. D. L. Brown, D. Field, and J. J. Zuiches, 108–127. University Park, PA: Northeast Regional Center for Rural Development.

Brown, Lester R. 1981. *Building a Sustainable Society.* New York: Norton.

Buttel, Frederick H., Olaf F. Larson, and Gilbert W. Gillespie Jr. 1990. *The Sociology of Agriculture.* New York: Greenwood.

Dale, Tom, and Vernon Gill Carter. 1955. *Topsoil and Civilization.* Norman: University of Oklahoma Press.

Davis, David Brion. 2006. *Inhuman Bondage: The Rise and Fall of Slavery in the New World.* Oxford, U.K.: Oxford University Press.

Diamond, Jared M. 2005. *Collapse: How Societies Choose to Fail or Succeed.* New York: Viking.

Lowdermilk, Walter C. 1953. *Conquest of the Land Through 7,000 Years.* Agriculture Information Bulletin 99. Washington, DC: U.S. Department of Agriculture, Soil Conservation Service.

Mann, Susan A., and James M. Dickinson. 1978. Obstacles to the Development of Capitalist Agriculture. *Journal of Peasant Studies* 5(4): 466–481.

Schlebecker, John T. 1975. *Whereby We Thrive: A History of American Farming, 1607–1972.* Ames: Iowa State University Press.

Vasey, Daniel E. 1992. *An Ecological History of Agriculture, 10,000 BC–AD 10,000.* Ames: Iowa State University Press.

Don E. Albrecht

AGRICULTURE

SEE *Agricultural Industry.*

AID TO FAMILIES WITH DEPENDENT CHILDREN (AFDC)
SEE *Public Assistance.*

AIDS

As the twenty-first century moves forward, the HIV/AIDS (human immunodeficiency virus/acquired immunodeficiency syndrome) epidemic remains a major public health concern. As of 2006, a cure for HIV/AIDS remained to be found. While medical researchers focus their efforts on finding a cure and a vaccine, social scientists work hard to find ways to prevent the spread of HIV/AIDS. These efforts have emphasized reducing behaviors that increase the risk of exposure to HIV, such as having unprotected vaginal or anal sex and sharing needles when injecting drugs. Such efforts require an understanding of which groups of people are most at risk for contracting HIV.

During the late 1990s and early 2000s, the Centers for Disease Control and Prevention (CDC) estimated that approximately forty thousand new cases of HIV infection occurred each year in the United States. Among the 23,153 men diagnosed with HIV in 2003 (73 percent of all cases reported by thirty-three states), men who have sex with men (MSM) accounted for the largest proportion (63%), followed by those reporting heterosexual contact (17%) or injection-drug use (14%), MSM and injection-drug use (5%), and other-unspecified (1%). Among women diagnosed with HIV in 2003 (27% of all cases), heterosexual contact accounted for the largest proportion (79%), followed by injection-drug use (19%), with 2% reported as other-unspecified. While a much higher percentage of men are infected with HIV in the United States, women make up a rising percentage of those living with HIV/AIDS (their numbers increasing from 14% in 1992 to 22 percent in 2003), and heterosexual transmission has become an increasingly important factor for men. Race/ethnicity diagnoses in 2003 were disproportionately led by African Americans (50%), followed by whites (32%) and Hispanics (15%).

Social scientists use demographic information to design and implement prevention programs specifically tailored to minimize exposure for population groups at risk for HIV/AIDS. Because each population is primarily at risk through a single but unique means of HIV/AIDS transmission, prevention programs vary tremendously in emphasis depending on the target population. Identifying and effectively targeting those at risk for HIV/AIDS are fundamental to setting up a situation in which social prevention programs can be effective. The late 1990s and early 2000s have seen a variety of prevention programs, ranging from intense, individual therapy to group programs and public announcements addressing a large audience.

Three primary components of prevention programs appear most effective: providing attitudinal arguments, basic information, and behavioral skills training. Although attitudes do not always predict behavior, research has shown that certain attitudes can influence the likelihood that one engages in a certain behavior. For example, positive attitudes toward condoms are associated with more frequent condom use. Basic information made available in prevention programs typically includes discussions of how the virus is transmitted, how to evaluate one's personal level of risk exposure, and how to prevent transmission. Behavioral skills training allows participants to practice skills related to reducing high-risk sexual behavior. Training can include skills such as discussing condom use with partners, condom application and removal, and cleaning and disinfecting needles and syringes. Although attitudinal arguments, basic information, and behavioral skills training are common components of effective prevention programs, an individual's gender, ethnicity, age, and risk group can have an impact on that effectiveness.

Other prevention approaches have produced varied results. Programs providing only basic information have little impact on reducing risky behaviors. Fear-based approaches most often target mass audiences, but are only effective if an individual believes he or she can accomplish the desired behavior and that doing so will lead to the expected outcome. With condom use, for example, fear-based appeals only work when people believe they can use condoms and that, if they do, they won't get HIV/AIDS.

There are several barriers to HIV/AIDS prevention efforts. These barriers include, but are not limited to, religious objections to sex education, substance use, unknown HIV status, underestimating risk, denial of sexual preference, sexual inequality in relationships, and AIDS stigma. Despite the extremely low rates of HIV/AIDS in countries with rigorous sex education programs, such as the Netherlands and Sweden, religious-based objections to sex education remain an obstacle for prevention researchers. People under the influence of alcohol or drugs are more likely to engage in high-risk behaviors, such as unprotected sexual intercourse. An additional factor in the spread of HIV is people living with HIV/AIDS who are unaware of their status, an estimated 250,000 people in the United States alone. Research has shown that a high percentage of those testing positive for HIV considered themselves at low risk for the virus. This is problematic because those who underestimate their risk of infection are less likely to engage in risk-preventing behaviors. Similarly, and particularly among African

American MSM, denial of sexual preference is high. In addition to underestimating risk, these men are less likely to respond to, and thus benefit from, prevention efforts targeting MSM. Among women, perceived inequality in a relationship can reduce prevention efforts. For example, some women may fear violence or abandonment should they insist that their partners use condoms.

Perhaps the strongest barrier to prevention efforts comes from "AIDS panic" or AIDS stigma. There are three primary sources of AIDS stigma: fear of HIV infection; the labeling of risk groups (e.g., identifying AIDS as a "gay disease"); and negative attitudes toward death and dying. In addition to implementing programs aimed at reducing risky behavior, social scientists also work to eliminate stigmas associated with HIV/AIDS. By 2006, there was some evidence of positive effects from these programs; however, research in this area is limited, and the observed effects may be minor and short-lived. Nonetheless, continuing these efforts is important because of the severe negative effects stigma can have on those living with HIV/AIDS. These effects include psychological problems such as anxiety and depression, strained social relationships, abandonment by family members, loss of medical insurance, and employment discrimination.

Although most barriers to prevention are widespread, internationally the AIDS epidemic is even more troubling and the additional barriers to prevention in Africa, Asia, and third world countries have elevated the challenges facing prevention researchers. A person's religious beliefs may discourage the use of condoms for contraceptive reasons, for example. In some countries, poor economic conditions and access to medical care or antiviral medications, coupled with an even greater social stigma associated with the virus, decrease the likelihood of persons living with HIV/AIDS seeking and receiving medical treatment. The early twenty-first century is marked by a global effort to help countries where HIV/AIDS cases are alarmingly high yet medical resources are scarce.

In the absence of a vaccine, social science offers the only effective means of preventing HIV/AIDS transmission. The 1900s and early 2000s have seen great advances in the effectiveness of prevention programs, especially those targeting specific high-risk groups. Despite these efforts, HIV/AIDS remains an international epidemic requiring an international response.

SEE ALSO *AIDS-HIV in Developing Countries, Impact of; Developing Countries; Disease; Medicine*

BIBLIOGRAPHY

Albarracin, Dolores, Jeffery C. Gillette, Allison N. Earl, et al. 2005. A Test of Major Assumptions about Behavior Change: A Comprehensive Look at the Effects of Passive and Active

HIV-Prevention Interventions Since the Beginning of the Epidemic. *Psychological Bulletin* 131 (6): 856–897.

Brigham, Thomas A., Patricia Donohoe, Bo James Gilbert, et al. 2002. Psychology and AIDS Education: Reducing High-risk Sexual Behavior. *Behavior and Social Issues* 12 (1): 10–18.

Brown, Lisanne, Kate Macintyre, and Lea Trujillo. 2003. Interventions to Reduce HIV/AIDS Stigma: What Have We Learned? *AIDS Education and Prevention* 15 (1): 49–69.

Centers for Disease Control and Prevention. HIV/AIDS Prevention. http://www.cdc.gov/hiv/dhap.htm.

Dana F. Lindemann
Thomas A. Brigham

AIDS/HIV IN DEVELOPING COUNTRIES, IMPACT OF

Developing countries include low- and middle-income economies as well as those in transition from central planning. A wide diversity of political, economic, social, religious, and cultural systems is embraced within such countries, resulting in markedly different HIV/AIDS experiences between neighbors as well as within the nations themselves.

Several HIV epidemics often operate in tandem, including injecting drug-use, unprotected heterosexual or male-to-male sexual contact, mother-to-child infection (either in the womb or by breast feeding), and contaminated blood products. Even within a country, epidemics can be extremely diverse.

Ninety-five percent of the 38 million adults and 2.2 million children estimated to be living with HIV worldwide at the end of 2005 lived in developing countries. Worst affected is Sub-Saharan Africa, where an estimated 25.8 million have the disease, including the 3.2 million new infections during 2005. South and Southeast Asia follow with 8.3 million, Latin America and the Caribbean with 2.1 million, Eastern Europe and Central Asia with 1.6 million, East Asia with 870,000, and North Africa and the Middle East with 510,000. Worldwide, 26 million people have died from AIDS and related illnesses, 3 million of these in 2005 alone.

During that year some 4.8 million adults and children were newly infected with HIV in developing countries, 98 percent of the global total. The full extent of the problem is hidden because of inadequate testing and reporting facilities in some countries and regions within them. People may not want to be tested, and continue living with HIV without being aware of it, but even if test-ing positive, they may not tell their partners, seek treatment, or negotiate safer sex.

THE EMERGENCE OF EPIDEMICS

Epidemics usually pass through stages, beginning with injecting drug-users sharing needles and syringes, commercial sex workers having unprotected sex with clients, and men having unprotected sex with men. As HIV spreads more widely among these groups, it begins to percolate into the wider population, as has occurred in Indonesia, Vietnam, and Malaysia. Then, when the overall infection rate exceeds one percent, as in Thailand, Cambodia, and Myanmar, the epidemic is considered to have become generalized.

In most countries high rates of infection are associated with marginalized groups like sex workers, truck drivers, and men having sex with men. Epidemics in India, Pakistan, Libya, Uruguay, and Ukraine are being driven by injecting drug-use; in the Russian Republic HIV prevalence is four times greater in prisons than in the population at large. Some groups are especially at risk. Women and girls with little income may turn to risky commercial sex. In Sub-Saharan Africa, for example, those aged between fifteen and twenty-four are three times more likely to be HIV-positive than men in a similar age group.

The origins and early spread of HIV/AIDS remain controversial but it seems to have emerged in Central Africa toward the end of the 1970s and in the United States and Europe in the early 1980s. Elsewhere it appeared later, with the first HIV cases being reported in Thailand and the Philippines in 1984, in India and the People's Republic of China in 1985, and in Myanmar in 1988. The early data are very unreliable. In 1992, for instance, estimates of total HIV infections in Thailand ranged from 333,000 to 696,000 depending on how studies of military conscripts were analyzed and varying assumptions about the age and gender distribution of the disease. In societies where religious and political leaderships had close relationships, HIV was initially explained away as an outcome of lax morals in Western societies. Sometimes there were disputes between departments, as in Thailand, where the Tourism Ministry was concerned that health authority warnings about HIV/AIDS would deter foreign visitors.

By the mid-1990s HIV/AIDS had emerged in virtually every country. The vast differences in population make raw numbers misleading. In India the 2,095 cumulative AIDS cases in adults and children reported to the World Health Organization in December 1995 represented a rate per 100,000 population of less than one, whereas the forty-three cases in New Caledonia represented a rate of twenty-five. The wide geographical spread of the disease in Asia alone can be seen from the fact that by 1995, 570 cases had been reported in Myanmar, 292 in Vietnam, 259 in Malaysia, and 220 in the Philippines. Actual numbers were probably much higher.

Most people living with HIV/AIDS are in the prime of their working life. Industry and commerce thus suffer from absenteeism, lower productivity, and lack of investment. Police recruitment, and the maintenance of law and order, become more difficult. Dwindling government revenues and rising expenditures (on health care, for example) can put at risk decades of development progress. In twenty-five Sub-Saharan countries average life expectancy rates have fallen dramatically since about 1988, due mainly to HIV/AIDS. Worst affected is Botswana, with life expectancy expected to fall from 60 to 27 years by 2010. In Asia, the Caribbean, and the Russian Republic steep declines are also in evidence.

In Sub-Saharan Africa there are 12.1 million orphans (80 percent of the global total), children under eighteen who have lost one or both parents to AIDS. In Nigeria alone AIDS orphans number 1.8 million and in South Africa 1.1 million. Some live with relatives or in institutions, but many end up as abused street kids who will be ill-equipped as adults to become professionals such as teachers and doctors, drive industry and commerce, or run the bureaucracy.

Often the opportunity for early intervention was missed. Thus, the Chinese government maintained that homosexuality and prostitution were not only illegal but contrary to Chinese morality. Despite warnings by health officials in 1993 that 100,000 people could be living with HIV by 2000 and 20,000 with full-blown AIDS, it was not until 2001 that the government admitted to a semi-official estimate of 600,000 infections spread over almost all parts of the country. Earlier and more vigorous intervention might have slowed the spread of the disease.

Large variations exist between individual countries, between rural and urban areas, and between men and women. Thus HIV prevalence rates are below 1 percent in Mauritania and Senegal but reach almost 40 percent in Botswana and Swaziland. Prevalence among some pregnant women in Namibia exceeds 50 percent.

In Asia the main driver of HIV infection is injecting drug-use, often accompanied by unsafe sexual practices. The huge populations of some countries reduce the average adult HIV prevalence rate to only about 0.4 percent, disguising the fact that in Asia as a whole at least 8.3 million adults and children were living with the disease in 2005. During the previous year 1.1 million people were newly infected and 520,000 died of AIDS.

In most countries several epidemics are underway: in India (which had 5.1 million people living with HIV in 2003) the disease is being mainly spread by unprotected sex in the south and injecting drug-use in the northeast.

Widespread ignorance about safe sex and a growing propensity for youngsters to engage in sexual activities are further boosting the spread of HIV in countries like Indonesia, Vietnam, Pakistan, Malaysia, and Japan.

HIV/AIDS has a massive impact on societies. It places a huge financial burden on health care (even without costly antiretroviral therapy) and on medical facilities, hospitals, and nursing staff. Households and nutrition suffer when people are too ill to work, while caring for the sick reduces the time other household members can spend on activities such as farming. Children, especially girls, may be taken out of school to reduce costs or to help look after the sick, which has implications for literacy, skill development, and even dissemination of knowledge about diseases.

More than 15 million people had already died of AIDS in Sub-Saharan Africa by 2005 and, without massively expanded intervention programs and antiretroviral therapy, deaths will increase as people infected with HIV eight to ten years ago succumb to full-blown AIDS.

The AIDS epidemic continues to outstrip the global efforts to contain it. In mid-2005 only one person in ten in Africa and one in seven in Asia who needed antiretroviral treatment was receiving it. Progress is mixed. An estimated one-third of the people in need of antiretroviral treatment in Botswana and Uganda were receiving it in mid-2005, but in many African countries it is available to less than one in ten. Since 1996 Brazil has been providing free treatment, to 170,000 people in 2006, while Indian drug companies are making treatments available at more affordable prices. For most of the developing world, however, more basic initiatives are needed, with HIV/AIDS being seen as part of the wider problems of access to clean water, malnutrition, poverty, discrimination, and unemployment. Much has to be done to educate people, especially women and those living in rural areas, about this and related diseases and ways of avoiding them, but perhaps only one in ten people living with HIV has been tested and knows that he or she is infected.

SEE ALSO *AIDS; Demography; Developing Countries; Disease; Drugs of Abuse; Economic Growth; Medicine; Morbidity and Mortality; Sexual Orientation, Social and Economic Consequences; Sexuality*

BIBLIOGRAPHY

Armstrong, Sue, Chris Fontaine, and Andrew Wilson. 2004. *Report on the Global AIDS Epidemic.* XV International AIDS Conference Bangkok, July 11–16, 2004. UNAIDS. http://www.unaids.org/bangkok2004/GAR2004_html/GAR2004_00_en.htm.

Garrett, Laurie. 2005. The Lessons of HIV/AIDS. *Foreign Affairs,* July/August 2005.

Joint United Nations Program on HIV/AIDS, World Health Organization. 2004. *AIDS Epidemic Update: December 2004.* Geneva: UNAIDS.

Joint United Nations Program on HIV/AIDS, World Health Organization. 2005. *AIDS Epidemic Update: December 2005.* Geneva: UNAIDS. http://data.unaids.org/Publications/IRC-pub06/epi_update2005_en.pdf.

Linge, Godfrey, and Doug Porter, eds. 1997. *No Place for Borders: The HIV/AIDS Epidemic and Development in Asia and the Pacific.* New York: St. Martin's Press.

Godfrey Linge

AINSWORTH, MARY
1913–1999

It is difficult to overestimate the influence Mary D. Salter Ainsworth has had on the field of developmental psychology. Her work has been cited by over 7,000 social science sources, with over 2,500 of these citing her seminal work on patterns of infant attachment (Ainsworth, Blehar, Waters, and Wall 1978). Moreover, her professional life, which spanned five decades and three continents, exemplifies the gendered and circuitous career path taken by many women.

Mary Salter was born in 1913 to parents who were both college graduates. Her family moved to Toronto, Canada, when she was five, and it was there that she received her PhD in psychology from the University of Toronto in 1939, did her World War II (1939–1945) service in the Canadian Women's Army Corps, and accepted a postwar teaching appointment at her alma mater in the area of personality psychology. William Blatz, first as dissertation advisor and then as colleague, influenced Mary Salter's research interests in the contribution of a secure relationship between parent and child to healthy growth and adjustment.

Marriage to Leonard Ainsworth, a graduate student at the University of Toronto, complicated her staying at the university as a faculty member. The couple relocated to England in 1950 when Leonard was accepted to a doctoral program at University College, London. Mary Ainsworth soon began a research position at the Tavistock Clinic with John Bowlby, who was using evolutionary and ethological theory to explore the development of attachments to caregivers and the consequences of maternal separation and loss for young children.

In 1954 Leonard Ainsworth accepted a job at the East African Institute of Social Research in Kampala, Uganda. Mary Ainsworth moved to Africa with her husband and secured an appointment at the Institute. She then embarked on a longitudinal field-based study of infant-mother interactions in their natural setting using the skills she had developed in analyzing naturalistic observations at Tavistock. The commonalities she observed in the developing relationships of Ugandan infants to their mothers and the attachment development of infants in industrialized nations was striking to Ainsworth and consistent with Bowlby's theoretical explorations. When the Ainsworths returned to the United States at the completion of Leonard's two-year appointment, Mary brought back extensive field notes. A decade later these became the basis for her book *Infancy in Uganda* (1967), which provided some of the first empirical evidence supporting Bowlby's ethological theory of attachment development and in general made a significant contribution to the emerging field of infant social development.

On returning from Africa, Mary Ainsworth obtained a teaching and clinical position at the Johns Hopkins University. She also began to organize an intensive observational study of infant-mother pairs in Baltimore from birth through age one. In a series of papers, Ainsworth examined the sensitivity and responsiveness of mothers across a variety of daily contexts, such as feeding, face-to-face interaction, greetings, explorations, and the exchange of affection. She found connections between individual differences in maternal sensitivity and an infant's later responses to a series of separations and reunions from his or her mother. Compared to infants of less responsive mothers, infants of more responsive mothers evidenced more secure maternal attachment in their reaction to separation and reunion.

To quantify the infant's attachment security, Ainsworth and her colleagues developed a twenty-minute procedure (known as the Strange Situation) involving a series of separations and reunions between mother and toddler. Three main patterns of attachment were observed: (1) anxious/avoidant, in which the child tended not to be distressed at the mother's departure and to avoid her on return; (2) securely attached, in which the child was distressed by mother's departure and easily soothed by her on return; and (3) anxious/resistant, in which the child tended to become highly distressed at the mother's departure, only to seek comfort and distance simultaneously on her return by engaging in behaviors such as crying and reaching to be held, but then attempting to leave once picked up.

The Strange Situation has become one of the most commonly used procedures in child development research, and it has been extended to studies of attachment behaviors and correlates in rhesus monkeys, chimpanzees, and dogs used as pets and guide animals for the blind (Fallani, Prato-Previde, and Valsecchi 2006; Inoue, Hikami, and Matsuzawa 1992; Prato-Previde, Fallani, and

Valsecchi 2006; Stevenson-Hinde, Zunz, and Stillwell-Barnes 1980). Ainsworth's original interpretations have also prompted several lines of research to explicate the origins and meanings of behavior in the Strange Situation (e.g., Mangelsdorf, McHale, Diener, et al. 2000; Marshall and Fox 2005).

Mary Ainsworth moved from Johns Hopkins to the University of Virginia in 1975. She died in 1999, leaving behind forty published papers or books and scores of investigators whose work is securely attached to her own.

SEE ALSO *Attachment Theory; Bowlby, John; Child Development; Developmental Psychology; Parent-Child Relationships; Personality; Psychology*

BIBLIOGRAPHY

PRIMARY WORKS

Ainsworth, Mary D. (Salter). 1967. *Infancy in Uganda: Infant Care and the Growth of Love.* Baltimore, MD: Johns Hopkins University Press.

Ainsworth, Mary D. (Salter). 1969. Object Relations, Dependency, and Attachment: A Theoretical Review of the Infant-Mother Relationship. *Child Development* 40 (4): 969–1025.

Ainsworth, Mary D. (Salter). 1979. Infant-Mother Attachment. *American Psychologist* 34 (10): 932–937.

Ainsworth, Mary D. (Salter). 1983. A Sketch of a Career. In *Models of Achievement: Reflections of Eminent Women in Psychology*, eds. Agnes N. O'Connell and Nancy Felipe Russo, 200–219. New York: Columbia University Press.

Ainsworth, Mary D. (Salter). 1989. Attachments beyond Infancy. *American Psychologist* 44 (4): 709–716.

Ainsworth, Mary D. (Salter), Mary C. Blehar, Everett Waters, and Sally Wall. 1978. *Patterns of Attachment: A Psychological Study of the Strange Situation.* Hillsdale, NJ: Erlbaum.

Bell, Silvia M., and Mary D. (Salter) Ainsworth. 1972. Infant Crying and Maternal Responsiveness. *Child Development* 43 (4): 1171–1190.

Crittenden, Patricia M., and Mary D. (Salter) Ainsworth. 1989. Child Maltreatment and Attachment Theory. In *Child Maltreatment: Theory and Research on the Causes and Consequences of Child Abuse and Neglect*, eds. Dante Cicchetti and Vicki Carlson, 432–463. New York: Cambridge University Press.

Stayton, Donelda J., Robert Hogan, and Mary D. (Salter) Ainsworth. 1971. Infant Obedience and Maternal Behavior: The Origins of Socialization Reconsidered. *Child Development* 42 (4): 1057–1069.

SECONDARY WORKS

Bretherton, Inge. 1992. The Origins of Attachment Theory: John Bowlby and Mary Ainsworth. *Developmental Psychology* 28 (5): 759–775.

Fallani, Gaia, Emanuela Prato-Previde, and Paola Valsecchi. 2006. Do Disrupted Early Attachments Affect the Relationship between Guide Dogs and Blind Owners? *Applied Animal Behaviour Science* 100 (3–4): 241–257.

Inoue, Noriko, Koji Hikami, and Tetsuro Matsuzawa. 1992. Attachment Behavior and Heart-Rate Changes in an Infant Chimpanzee (Pan troglodytes) in Strange Situations. *Japanese Journal of Developmental Psychology* 3 (1): 17–24.

Mangelsdorf, Sarah C., Jean L. McHale, Marissa Diener, et al. 2000. Infant Attachment: Contributions of Infant Temperament and Maternal Characteristics. *Infant Behavior and Development* 23 (2): 175–196.

Marshall, Peter J., and Nathan A. Fox. 2005. Relations between Behavioral Reactivity at 4 Months and Attachment Classification at 14 Months in a Selected Sample. *Infant Behavior and Development* 28 (4): 492–502.

Prato-Previde, Emanuela, Gaia Fallani, and Paola Valsecchi. 2006. Gender Differences in Owners Interacting with Pet Dogs: An Observational Study. *Ethology* 112 (1): 64–73.

Stevenson-Hinde, Joan, Marion Zunz, and Robin Stillwell-Barnes. 1980. Behaviour of One-Year-Old Rhesus Monkeys in a Strange Situation. *Animal Behaviour* 28 (1): 266–277.

Doreen Arcus

AIRLINE DEREGULATION ACT

SEE *Aviation Industry.*

AIR MAIL

SEE *Aviation Industry.*

AKERLOF, GEORGE A.
1940–

American economist George Akerlof received the Bank of Sweden Prize in Economic Sciences in Memory of Alfred Nobel in 2001. He was awarded this prize jointly with economists Michael Spence and Joseph Stiglitz, for their work on *asymmetric information*—a situation in which agents in a market have differing levels of information (e.g., regarding the quality of a product). In his seminal paper "The Market for 'Lemons': Quality Uncertainty and the Market Mechanism" (1970), Akerlof demonstrates how asymmetric information is persistent in the market for used cars. In the simplest example, there are two types of cars: a high-quality car with price C^H and a "lemon," or defective car, with price C^L. Only the seller is aware of the type of car being sold, whereas the consumer faces significant uncertainty about the quality of the purchase. Given that the probability of receiving a car of high quality is q, where $0 < q < 1$, and low quality is $1 - q$, the buyer will only be willing to pay the expected value of the car, or $q \cdot C^H + (1 - q) \cdot C^L$. As a result, lemons will drive owners of high-quality cars, who have little incentive to sell at the average price, out of the market. Akerlof also suggests that institutions, such as warranties and chain brands, may help circumvent the problem of asymmetric information. Despite critical acclaim for this work, some researchers have criticized Akerlof's theoretical model for its failure to explain observed empirical patterns.

Akerlof has also made significant contributions to the understanding of *efficiency wages*—that is, wages set above the market-clearing wage as a way to induce worker efficiency and productivity. In 1967 Akerlof spent a year at the Indian Statistical Institute in New Delhi as a visiting professor. He describes what he learned in India during that time as "the keystone for [my] later contributions to the development of an efficiency wage theory" (2001). Almost twenty years after his return from India, he published "Efficiency Wage Models of the Labor Market" (1986), written with his wife, economist Janet Yellen. This paper explains the motivation behind efficiency wages, which are an oft-cited theoretical explanation for market failures resulting in involuntary unemployment. Akerlof and Yellen show that firms pay efficiency wages because they minimize the labor cost per efficiency unit.

Akerlof was born on June 17, 1940, in New Haven, Connecticut. He attended high school at the Lawrenceville School in Princeton, New Jersey, and in 1958 entered Yale University, where he earned his BA degree. He later attended the Massachusetts Institute of Technology, from which he received a PhD in economics in 1966. He has been a visiting professor at the Indian Statistical Institute (1967–1968) and the Cassel Professor of Money and Banking at the London School of Economics (1978–1980), and has also served as senior economist at the Council of Economic Advisers (1973–1974). Akerlof is currently Koshland Professor of Economics at the University of California, Berkeley.

SEE ALSO *Economics, New Keynesian; Economics, Nobel Prize in; Information, Asymmetric; Information, Economics of; Involuntary Unemployment; Productivity; Quality, Product; Stiglitz, Joseph E.; Wages*

BIBLIOGRAPHY

Akerlof, George A. 1970. The Market for "Lemons": Quality Uncertainty and the Market Mechanism. *Quarterly Journal of Economics* 84 (3): 488–500.

Akerlof, George A. 2001. Autobiography. The Nobel Foundation. http://nobelprize.org/nobel_prizes/economics/laureates/2001/akerlof-autobio.html.

Akerlof, George A. Curriculum Vitae. University of California, Berkeley Economics Department. http://elsa.berkeley.edu/~akerlof/docs/cv.pdf.

Akerlof, George A., and Janet L. Yellen, eds. 1986. *Efficiency Wage Models of the Labor Market.* Cambridge, U.K., and New York: Cambridge University Press.

Yellen, Janet L. 1984. Efficiency Wage Models of Unemployment. *American Economic Review* 74 (2): 200–205.

Mai N. Hubbard

AL JAZEERA

Al Jazeera satellite television was founded in 1996 in Doha, Qatar. Within less than two years of its founding, it dramatically transformed the media and information climate in the entire Arab world. The station capitalized on the emergence of satellite reception in the Arab world from the early 1990s, which created potentially large regional markets that began to be filled up by commercial and state-owned stations. When Al Jazeera was launched, it was clear that no Arab government was willing to tolerate uncensored news media. The founding staff of Al Jazeera was in fact recruited from the ranks of an earlier British Broadcasting Corporation Arabic television service that had been set up in Saudi Arabia, but that had its contract canceled because of the Saudi government's objection to its editorial content.

Conceived as an independent station but supported with loans or grants from the then new, reform-oriented emir of Qatar, Hamad bin Khalifa Al Thani, the station devoted itself to news and information, and became known for a daring style in which it presented issues that would have been routinely censored by any Arab government. It interviewed opposition figures and members of banned parties. It moved away from the traditional news format of staid, official news, focusing instead on items relevant to a wide pan-Arab audience. Almost all Arab governments levied complaints against the station with the government of Qatar at one point or another. The Saudi government went a step further, banning companies that advertise on Al Jazeera from operating in the country. In this way it attempted to economically undermine what seemed to be, for a few years, the freest channel of information with a pan-Arab audience. The station also drew bitter complaints from the U.S. government over its graphic coverage of the wars in Iraq and Afghanistan, as well as for allegedly inflaming Arab feeling by its equally poignant coverage of the suffering in the occupied Palestinian territories. During the Afghanistan and Iraqi wars, U.S. aircraft in fact bombed and destroyed Al Jazeera's offices in Kabul and Baghdad, killing some journalists, and in both cases the official story was that the bombings were mistakes.

Realizing that Al Jazeera was here to stay, many commercial as well as government-owned channels in the Arab world changed their formats or saw some relaxation of rigid censorship so as to compete with Al Jazeera, which by 1998 had become the most widely watched station in the entire Arab world. Even the Saudi government, once the station's severest critic, set up al-Arabiyya, a competing satellite station that mimicked Al Jazeera's style of uncensored news and reporting. In view of the station's association with the emir of Qatar and its location in that country, its coverage of Qatar appears scant, although the country itself is small and is of little importance in the context of the more pressing pan-Arab issues.

In addition to news and investigative reporting, Al Jazeera also broadcasts programs on religion and modern life, featuring modernizing and popular Muslim clergy, and provides historical education in the form of lengthy interviews with "witnesses of the age," namely important intellectuals and former government or revolutionary figures. Al Jazeera regularly interviews U.S. ambassadors, secretaries of state, and other notables from around the world and was the first Arab channel to interview Israeli officials.

SEE ALSO *Arab League, The; Arabs; Media; Pan-Arabism; Television*

BIBLIOGRAPHY

El-Nawawy, Mohammed, and Adel Iskandar. 2003. *Al-Jazeera: The Story of the Network That Is Rattling Governments and Redefining Modern Journalism.* Boulder, CO: Westview.

Rugh, William A. 2004. *Arab Mass Media: Newspapers, Radio, and Television in Arab Politics.* Westport, CT: Praeger.

Sakr, Naomi. 2002. *Satellite Realms: Transnational Television, Globalization, and the Middle East.* London: I. B. Tauris.

Mohammed A. Bamyeh

ALAMO, THE

SEE *Mexican-American War.*

ALCOHOL MYOPIA

SEE *Steele, Claude M.*

ALCOHOLISM

While those individuals who consume alcohol to the point of abuse or dependence comprise only a small per-

cent of the general public, the impact of their actions is relatively broad, as it can be felt by families, friends, and even communities as a whole. In other words, alcohol abuse and dependence on alcohol have implications not only for the health and welfare of individual drinkers, but also for the lives of persons around them. Alcoholism is therefore an important public health concern, the symptoms and effects of which are crucial to understand.

To identify alcoholism and distinguish it from alcohol abuse, researchers and clinicians in the United States typically rely on diagnostic criteria found in the American Psychiatric Association's *Diagnostic and Statistical Manual of Mental Disorders.* Alcoholism, or more appropriately *alcohol dependence*, is a chronic disease that endures throughout an affected individual's lifespan. Typically, dependence is suspected when alcohol use is coupled with the following warning signs or symptoms:

1. The strong urge or compulsion to consume alcohol. An individual experiencing such craving spends a great deal of time obtaining and using alcohol, as well as recovering from its effects.

2. Loss of control over drinking habits. When this symptom is present, individuals can no longer limit their consumption or cease drinking once beginning. Alcohol is consumed in greater quantities and over longer periods of time than intended, and there are frequent failed efforts to cut down on or control alcohol use.

3. Tolerance to the effects of alcohol. In this phase, markedly increased quantities of alcohol must be consumed in order to experience intoxicating effects (i.e., get "high"); if the amount of alcohol consumed remains constant, a noticeably diminished effect is experienced.

4. Physical dependence. This state is characterized by withdrawal symptoms, such as anxiety after drinking has stopped, nausea, and shakiness; alcohol is consumed in order to alleviate or avoid these physical manifestations.

Individuals who do not meet the diagnostic criteria for alcohol dependence, but drink despite recurrent physical, psychological, interpersonal, legal, or social problems resulting from their drinking behaviors, are categorized as *alcohol abusers.* It is important to note that someone who abuses alcohol may not necessarily be an alcoholic or ever develop alcohol dependence; however, an alcoholic is an alcohol abuser.

THE EFFECTS OF ALCOHOLISM ON THE DRINKER

Individuals who are dependent on alcohol expose themselves to numerous conditions that threaten the quality of their lives. For example, because the liver is the human body's primary organ responsible for metabolizing (i.e., eliminating) alcohol, it is particularly susceptible to alcohol-related damage. Injury to the liver due to heavy alcohol consumption is termed *alcoholic liver disease* (ALD) by researchers. ALD encompasses three stages or conditions: (1) steatosis (or "fatty liver"); (2) alcohol hepatitis; and (3) the most commonly known, cirrhosis.

While the first stage of ALD, steatosis, can occur after only a few days of heavy drinking, it can be reversed once drinking ceases. The second and more serious stage, alcohol hepatitis, occurs after longer periods of heavy drinking. The National Institute of Alcohol Abuse and Alcoholism equates the following indicators with alcoholic hepatitis: lack of appetite, nausea or vomiting, abdominal pain, fever, and jaundice. This condition can be potentially life threatening. If heavy alcohol consumption continues, inflammation due to alcoholic hepatitis will eventually lead to the final stage of ALD, cirrhosis. Cirrhosis is characterized by fibrosis, also known as scar tissue. As a result of continued abuse of the liver, scar tissue forms and takes the place of healthy liver cells. Consequently, the liver loses its ability to perform essential functions. The presence of alcoholic hepatitis is a telltale sign that cirrhosis could shortly follow.

Cognitive impairment (i.e., brain damage) is another potential consequence of alcohol dependence. Many alcoholics exhibit mild to moderate deficiencies in their intellectual performance, along with alterations to brain-cell activity in various sections of the brain. A very small percentage of long-term, heavy drinkers develop overwhelming, irreversible brain-damage conditions such as Wernicke-Korsakoff syndrome. This amnesic disorder is characterized by the inability to acquire new information or form new memories. Numerous other conditions such as gastrointestinal problems, heart disease and stroke, and carcinoma have also been associated with alcohol dependence.

THE EFFECTS OF ALCOHOLISM ON SOCIETY

In addition to documenting the damaging and potentially life-threatening consequences of alcohol dependence for the individual drinker, researchers have also identified numerous impacts of alcoholism that affect those surrounding an alcoholic. Often referred to as social consequences, these include:

1. The impact on communities: Intoxication can lead to unintentional accidents—such as automobile crashes and fires—as well as to criminal behavior or disorderly conduct, such as violence toward others and vandalism.

2. The impact on families: Alcoholics may neglect familial responsibilities, such as caring and providing for children or spouses; if they exhibit violent or aggressive behavior, this may lead to marital conflict, child or spousal abuse, or divorce. If maternal alcohol consumption occurs during pregnancy, serious birth defects such as fetal alcohol syndrome may develop.

3. The impact on the workplace: Alcoholism can result in lost workplace productivity due to time-off for alcohol-related illness or injury, in termination due to decreased job performance or absenteeism, and in increased company costs when termination makes it necessary for new employees to be recruited and trained.

OVERCOMING ALCOHOL DEPENDENCE

While some of the damage caused by alcohol dependence cannot be reversed, there are numerous treatment options available to alcohol-dependent individuals that may allow them to return to a more balanced and healthy lifestyle. It is important to note, however, that alcoholism cannot be cured. Alcoholics cannot address their affliction and the effects they experience by "cutting back" on the amount they consume. If actual progress is to take place, it is essential that an alcoholic "cut out" any and all drinking. Thus, to guard against relapse, alcoholics must avoid any contact with alcoholic beverages. Permanent sobriety is a long and arduous road; however, there are treatment options available that have shown promise in helping individuals to remain sober.

SEE ALSO *Addiction; Dependency; Disease; Drugs of Abuse; Mental Health*

BIBLIOGRAPHY

National Institute on Alcohol Abuse and Alcoholism. 2000. Research Refines Alcoholism Treatment Options. *Alcohol Research and Health* 24 (1): 53–61. http://pubs.niaaa.nih.gov/publications/arh24-1/53-61.pdf.

National Institute on Alcohol Abuse and Alcoholism. 2001. Cognitive Impairment and Recovery from Alcoholism. *Alcohol Alert* 53 (July). http://pubs.niaaa.nih.gov/publications/aa53.htm.

National Institute on Alcohol Abuse and Alcoholism. 2005. Alcoholic Liver Disease. *Alcohol Alert* 64 (January): 1–5. http://pubs.niaaa.nih.gov/publications/aa64/AA64.pdf.

National Institute on Alcohol Abuse and Alcoholism. Alcoholism: Getting the Facts. http://www.collegedrinkingprevention.gov/OtherAlcoholInformation/alcoholismFacts.aspx.

Adam E. Barry

ALGER, HORATIO
1832–1899

Horatio Alger Jr. is the author most closely associated with the American rags-to-riches story. His name has become synonymous with the experience of rising from relative poverty to substantial fortune without an inheritance; such a trajectory is often termed a "real Horatio Alger story." The son of a Unitarian minister living in Revere and Marlborough, Massachusetts, Alger graduated from Harvard University in 1852 and from the Harvard Divinity School in 1860. The Harvard Unitarians were heirs to the Calvinists, the Puritans, and the Congregationalist tradition. The Unitarians were steeped in a belief in the importance of character and the role of both the individual and the community in maintaining the character and ethical sensibility in the young. At Harvard, Alger studied Greek and Latin and read Scottish common-sense philosophers such as Francis Bacon and Thomas Reid. The Harvard Unitarian moralists of the antebellum era sought to render Plato's teachings compatible with Christianity, and as Alger saw it, Socrates believed in divine retribution for earthly sinners. Alger also studied with the poet Henry Wadsworth Longfellow (1807–1882) and later sought his favor when he published his own volume of adult poetry in 1875. One of Alger's mentors was Harvard president Edward Everett (1794–1865).

Alger served briefly as a minister in Brewster, Massachusetts, but left the ministry in 1866 and moved to New York City to earn his living by his pen. An author of modest literary talent, Alger wrote fiction aimed at pleasing large audiences, but amassed no riches in doing so. In addition to writing, Alger also tutored the sons of wealthy New Yorkers, including those of the Seligman and Cardozo families. Alger published 123 works as novels, serializations in newspapers and magazines, and books of poetry. Most of his formulaic fiction was aimed at juvenile readers. Alger created nineteenth-century characters who are "risen from the ranks," who "strive and succeed" and are "bound to rise"; they manage to transform themselves with "luck and pluck" and with the help of benevolent mentors from bootblacks, newsboys, or street peddlers to respectable adults with comfortable middle-class incomes. Some late heroes attain more remarkable fortunes, particularly in the era of the robber barons. Several novels feature heroines, such as Jenny Lindsay, the title character in *Tattered Tom*, who is saved from street life before she attains adolescence. Quite a few heroes leave New England farms and villages where their families cannot support them and go to the big city, but some heroes depart for Western adventures and one is sent, with the help of the Children's Aid Society, from the city to the countryside to be brought up in a healthier environment.

Alger kept his heroes out of the way of modern factory labor. Genteel moralists of his era believed that manliness required independence; factories were seen as both breeding dependence and bringing the young into contact with fellow workers who endangered virtue. Alger's most famous and popular work, *Ragged Dick*, was published in 1867 and featured a young, spirited, cheerful but ragged orphan bootblack who captures the attention of a benefactor who helps him attain middle-class respectability. Alger asserted that his story *Phil, the Fiddler*, featuring a very young Italian street musician, helped to end the exploitive padrone system, a system that involved the near-enslavement of young children brought from Italy to work for the benefit of those to whom they were contractually bound. The author befriended and assisted various young boys, and informally adopted at least two of them.

Alger heroes not only work hard and help themselves but also possess steadfast character, are loyal to their employers, and help others along the way who are deserving. In Alger's formula, character is capital. Its value is recognized wherever it goes. Stories arrange for accidents through which the character of the struggling young person comes to the attention of a benefactor. Foils are excessively focused on money, social status, and finery; they consume but do not produce, and have no fellow feeling. Alger's morality tales frequently arrange justice for such characters. These stories not only provided graphic detail of neighborhoods of New York but also told readers how to avoid crime and confidence games. However, by the 1890s, some moralists inveighed against juvenile fiction, including Alger's, for planting false ideas of life in the heads of impressionable young people, encouraging them to leave their homes for adventure in the city or out West. Many libraries removed Alger novels in this period.

The fiction of Horatio Alger Jr. fueled the American dream of rising through the ranks and becoming self-made. Poverty was not an insurmountable barrier to success, and character—a key ingredient of success—was under one's own control. Many Americans would subsequently conclude that failure was the individual's own fault. While it was appropriate for charitable organizations and benevolent individuals to help deserving young people along the way, for quite a few Americans the self-help creed precluded public, governmental efforts to address poverty and inequality.

SEE ALSO *American Dream; False Consciousness*

BIBLIOGRAPHY

Cawelti, John. 1965. *Apostles of the Self-Made Man*. Chicago: University of Chicago Press.

Moon, Michael. 1987. "The Gentle Boy from the Dangerous Classes": Domesticity, Pederasty, and Capitalism in Horatio Alger. *Representations* 19 (summer): 87–110.

Nackenoff, Carol. 1994. *The Fictional Republic: Horatio Alger and American Political Discourse.* New York: Oxford University Press.

Scharnhorst, Gary. 1980. *Horatio Alger, Jr.* Boston: Twayne Publishers.

Scharnhorst, Gary, with Jack Bales. 1985. *The Lost Life of Horatio Alger, Jr.* Bloomington: Indiana University Press.

Carol Nackenoff

ALGERIAN REVOLUTION

SEE *Battle of Algiers, The.*

ALI, MUHAMMAD (MEMET)
1769–1849

The history of modern Egypt opens in 1798 with Napoleon Bonaparte's (1769–1821) invasion of the Ottoman province, destroying the army of the Mamluk rulers at the Battle of the Pyramids. With the Mamluks and the Ottomans in disarray, the French troops also withdrew after the defeat of the French fleet at Abu Qir, leaving a political vacuum. Muhammad Ali (or Mehmet Ali), born in the Macedonian town of Kavalla in the Ottoman Empire, was a young officer serving with the Albanian contingent against the French. He successfully filled this vacuum by creating a power base in the villages, and by joining forces with local clerics and merchants in Cairo. He removed three successive governors sent from Istanbul. Appointed *wali* or Ottoman viceroy of Egypt in 1805, Muhammad Ali used brutal methods to establish his control over Egypt, including breaking the power of the Mamluks by massacring their leaders in 1811. Regarded as the founder of modern Egypt, he created a dynasty that ruled Egypt until 1952.

Recognizing that modern political power rests on a modern, disciplined army, Muhammad Ali conscripted peasants from Upper Egypt to train them in the Napoleonic army system. He undertook a number of military campaigns, but his military and dynastic ambitions were thwarted by British, French, or Russian intervention. These powers had their own designs on the dismemberment of the Ottoman Empire, and their interests were not compatible with the strategic objectives of Muhammad Ali. Between 1820 and 1822, he conquered the Sudan in search of gold and slaves, founding the city of Khartoum in 1823. Some thirty thousand Sudanese slaves had been

trained, and these *nizami* troops, led by Muhammad Ali's son Ibrahim (1789–1848), were sent against the Greeks in 1827 in the Greek war of independence. Although his troops were relatively effective, the Ottoman navy was destroyed at the Battle of Navarino in 1827.

To fund his military reforms, Muhammad Ali established long-staple cotton as a cash crop and modernized Egyptian agriculture for cotton production to supply the British textile industry. To secure his rule and to support cotton production, he confiscated the lands of the ruling class, made large land grants to his own family, and reclaimed uncultivated land, thereby creating a new landed class to support his political rule.

His modernization program also included the reform of educational institutions, the creation of a teaching hospital, the building of roads and canals, the construction of state factories, and the development of a shipbuilding foundry at Alexandria. These industrial developments provided the military platform that led Muhammad Ali to invade Greater Syria in 1831 and again in 1839. Alarmed by his success, the British intervened, blocked the Nile Delta and defeated him at Beirut. In the Treaty of London in 1841, he surrendered Crete and Hijaz and abandoned his military ambitions; in return, he and his descendants were given hereditary rule over Egypt. He died in 1849, being buried in the Muhammad Ali Mosque in the Citadel of Cairo, the mosque that he had commissioned.

Muhammad Ali was the last of the military adventurers who periodically seized power in the Ottoman provinces, giving their military domination a mask of legitimacy by creating a dynasty. He was fortunate to rule in a period of Ottoman decline, taking advantage of French military officers to modernize his army.

SEE ALSO *Ottoman Empire*

BIBLIOGRAPHY

Fahmy, Khaled. 1997. *All the Pasha's Men: Mehmed Ali, His Army, and the Making of Modern Egypt.* New York: Cambridge University Press.

Vatikiotis, P. J. 1991. *The History of Modern Egypt: From Muhammad Ali to Mubarak.* 4th ed. Baltimore, MD: John Hopkins University Press.

Bryan S. Turner

ALI, MUHAMMAD (USA)
1942–

Muhammad Ali was one of the greatest heavyweight boxing champions. He also stands as a powerful symbol of social and cultural change in the United States during the second half of the twentieth century.

Ali was born Cassius Marcellus Clay Jr. in Louisville, Kentucky, on January 17, 1942. He began boxing at an early age and had a distinguished amateur career that culminated in winning a gold medal at the 1960 Rome Olympics. He then turned professional, and on February 25, 1964, he defeated Sonny Liston (1932?–1970) to become heavyweight champion at the age of twenty-two.

Already at this point in his career Ali demonstrated the outspoken demeanor that reflected the changing racial climate of the times. The civil rights movement that had begun in the United States in the years following World War II (1939–1945) was coming to a climax, with widespread activism, the charismatic leadership of Martin Luther King Jr. (1929–1968), and the passage of landmark federal legislation, including the Civil Rights Act of 1964 and the Voting Rights Act of 1965. The more violently confrontational Black Power movement was about to begin. The history of the heavyweight championship and Ali's role in it serves to reflect these elements of change. Following a controversial black champion, Jack Johnson (1878–1946), in the early years of the century, no African American was allowed to fight for the heavyweight championship until the arrival of Joe Louis (1914–1981) in the 1930s. Louis, who held the title from 1937 to 1949, and other black champions who followed, most notably Floyd Patterson (1935–2006) during the late 1950s and early 1960s, were submissive and noncontroversial. The young Cassius Clay, however, was brash and outspoken. Shortly after becoming heavyweight champion, the aura of controversy surrounding him grew when he announced that he had become a member of the Nation of Islam and was officially changing his name to Muhammad Ali. In 1966, as U.S. military involvement in Vietnam became an increasingly divisive national issue, Ali announced that he was seeking exemption from military service as a conscientious objector. As a result of this, and his subsequent refusal of induction when his draft board failed to grant the exemption, he was formally stripped of his boxing title early the following year.

Ali was kept out of the sport for next three years. In 1970, however, he was again able to obtain a boxing license, and in 1971 the U.S. Supreme Court overturned his conviction for refusing induction. Returning to the ring at the age of twenty-eight, he went on to fight some of his most memorable bouts, including his stunning victory over George Foreman in Zaire in October 1974 in which he regained the heavyweight title. He continued to fight through the rest of the decade, losing and regaining the title a third time in 1978. He fought his last fight and left the ring for good in 1981.

In the latter part of his fighting career, Ali began to display the effects of his many years in boxing. In the early 1980s he was diagnosed with pugilistic Parkinson's syndrome. Despite deteriorating health following his retirement, he continued to make public appearances and to serve as a spokesperson for anti-imperialist and anticolonial movements throughout the world. During this period also, his reputation in the United States gradually underwent a transformation, from a figure of controversy to a national icon. In 1980 he was sent to Africa by President Jimmy Carter in an unsuccessful effort to gain African support for the U.S. boycott of the Moscow Olympics. A diplomatic effort in Iraq in 1990 secured the release of several of the U.S. hostages being held by Saddam Hussein (1937–2006) in the period immediately preceding the 1991 Gulf War. As the 1990s progressed, Ali's rise to iconic status continued. In 1996, with an estimated three billion people around the world watching on television, he lit the Olympic flame to open the Atlanta Summer Olympics, and nine years later, in 2005, he was awarded the Presidential Medal of Freedom at a ceremony in the White House.

It is extremely difficult to separate the real from the mythic Ali. His stature, clearly, extends far beyond his skill in the boxing ring, and is attributable to the natural charisma and sincerity of the man, to the work of the many journalists and publicists who wrote about him, and finally to the times in which he lived. Never a profound or original thinker, Ali's activities and pronouncements on various issues—his support, for example, of Republican presidential candidates Ronald Reagan (1911–2004) and George H. W. Bush in the 1980s—often appeared inconsistent and contradictory. In the end, however, it is in the transition from a figure of controversy to a national icon, and the manner in which it serves to symbolize the social and cultural change occurring in the United States during the second half of the twentieth century, that his greatest significance lies.

SEE ALSO *Black Power; Bush, George H. W.; Colonialism; Imperialism; Malcolm X; Nation of Islam; Neocolonialism; Olympic Games; Reagan, Ronald; Sports; Sports Industry; Vietnam War*

BIBLIOGRAPHY

Hauser, Thomas. 1991. *Muhammad Ali: His Life and Times.* New York: Simon & Schuster.

Marqusee, Mike. 2005. *Redemption Song: Muhammad Ali and the Spirit of the Sixties.* 2nd ed. London: Verso.

Remnick, David. 1998. *King of the World: Muhammad Ali and the Rise of an American Hero.* New York: Random House.

Scott Wright

ALIENATION

Alienation is a term that is employed commonly in a number of disciplines to describe and explain the sense of estrangement that organizes the relationship between the subject and itself on the one hand and the subject and its relationship to history, power, and authority on the other hand: estrangement from the state in Georg Hegel, from God in Ludwig Feuerbach, from labor in Karl Marx, or from essential sexuality in Sigmund Freud. Anthropology, philosophy, economic theory, sociology, and political science all refer to the tensions that result from the sense of alienation experienced by the subject. The word *alienation*, however, comes from the Latin term *alius*, meaning "other" or "another," from which the term *alienus*, meaning "of another place or person," is derived. In this way the meaning of alienation has a spatial and existential significance. In the fifteenth century it came to mean the loss of mental faculties and thus the presence of insanity, and by the mid-nineteenth century physicians who concerned themselves with mentally disturbed patients were called alienists.

Alienation is a developmental process in Hegel's *The Phenomenology of Mind* (1807) and in 1844 writings by Marx that engage two gestures: *Entfremdung* (estrangement) and *Entäuberung* (externalization). The "unhappy consciousness" of Hegel is unhappy precisely because it is conscious of its own divisions, of its alienated relationship to its world, and thus cannot attain the unity that it seeks. In the ideality of the state this unhappy consciousness materializes itself as a subject. In Marx, labor itself is an object from which the worker is alienated, a realization that becomes possible only through the development of class consciousness. This materialization of the subject in late Marx (*Grundrisse* [1867] and *Das Kapital* [1857–1858]) through the experience of alienation from the labor process acquires a materiality that is expressed in *Vergegenständlichung* (reification), enabling the transformation of Hegel's idealism into Marx's materialism, a point that later, as reification, acquires centrality in the work of Gyorgy Lukács and the Frankfurt School.

In Marx the worker experiences the object of his or her labor as alien and threatening so that, despite the fact that it has been produced through the worker's labor, it is not accessible to the worker. For Marx abstracted forms of consciousness such as religion are symptomatic of the alienating experiences of workers, and only through the recognition of those forms as symptomatic of a frustrated historical experience, along with the abolition of capitalist ownership of the means of production that will interrupt the alienation of the worker from his or her labor, can they be overcome and allow for the emancipation of the subject.

For Feuerbach (1841) religion constitutes the alienated form of human realization of the divided subject. This is a process in which the subject understands itself as having been alienated from its own human essence and has turned that essence into an abstracted object of worship. In *Future of an Illusion* ([1928] 1975), *Moses and Monotheism* (1938), and *Civilization and Its Discontents* [1930] 1962), Freud recognizes civilization as the location where the understanding of the frustrated relationship of the subject with itself takes place. The overcoming of the sense of alienation is engendered either by the recovery of the subject's relationship to the divine (in the theological tradition) or by the recovery of the libido (in Freud). However, since alienation belongs to the historical process of subject formation and recognition, a process that reveals as much as it constitutes the process of civilization itself, alienation is taken to be the ransom of civilization, a point of no return (to nature or essence) for the human subject.

In the work of the Frankfurt School, particularly in that of Theodor W. Adorno (Horkheimer and Adorno [1944] 1972), alienation is the result of the rationalization of the process of cultural production, a process that is analogous to the injustice that is produced through the rationalization of the market. In that sense Adorno sees alienation not as part of the process of subject formation that has within it the potential for emancipation, as Marx saw it becoming as part of the historical process, but as constitutive of the new, modern subject that rests on reason, a reason that in modernity has become bankrupt without any prospects of resistance.

SEE ALSO *Alienation-Anomie; Consciousness; Frankfurt School; Freud, Sigmund; Hegel, Georg Wilhelm Friedrich; Lukacs, Georg; Marx, Karl; Power; Religion; Sexuality*

BIBLIOGRAPHY

Feuerbach, Ludwig Andreas. [1841] 1957. *The Essence of Christianity*. Trans. George Eliot. New York: Harper.

Freud, Sigmund. [1928] 1975. *Future of an Illusion*. Trans. James Strachey with a biographical introduction by Peter Gay. New York: W. W. Norton.

Freud, Sigmund. [1930] 1962. *Civilization and Its Discontents*. Trans. James Strachey with a biographical introduction by Peter Gay. New York: W. W. Norton.

Freud, Sigmund. 1939. *Moses and Monotheism*. Trans. Katherine Jones. New York: Vintage.

Hegel, Georg W. F. [1807] 1967. *The Phenomenology of Mind*. Trans. with an introduction and notes by J. B. Baillie and with an introduction by George Lichtheim. New York: Harper & Row.

Horkheimer, Max, and Theodor W. Adorno. [1944] 1972. *Dialectic of Enlightenment*. Trans. John Cumming. New York: Seabury Press.

Marx, Karl. [1844] 1988. *The Economic and Philosophic Manuscripts of 1844.* Trans. Martin Milligan. Amherst, NY: Prometheus Books.

Marx, Karl. [1857–1858] 1973. *Grundrisse: Foundations of the Critique of Political Economy.* Trans. and with a foreword by Martin Nicolaus. New York: Random House.

Marx, Karl. [1867] 1967. *Capital* Vol. 1, *A Critical Analysis of Capitalist Production,* ed. Frederick Engels. New York: International Publishers.

Williams, Raymond. 1983. *Keywords: A Vocabulary of Culture and Society.* London: Fontana Paperbacks.

Neni Panourgiá

ALIENATION-ANOMIE

Since 1844, when Karl Marx (1818–1883) first used the concept, alienation has been an important instrument for social critique. Marx saw alienation as inevitable in a capitalist social order where workers were paid for the time they spent producing commodities whose value for market rests on the labor congealed within, but the worker gets very little of the market price. For the capitalist who sells the goods for profit, the accumulation of wealth is the primary value. When, however, workers sell their time as a commodity, they too become commodities—they become alienated, that is, both objectified and estranged. In producing commodities, workers are rendered powerless and their lives meaningless. They are estranged from their "species being," the innate human ability to see themselves as members of a species. Their creativity and humanity are thwarted and their social world is fragmented. Marx understood alienation as a multidimensional concept with implications for the social structure and for groups and with psychological consequences for individuals.

The discipline of sociology emerged with the tumultuous changes consequent on the French Revolution (1789–1799), industrialization, and urbanization. Avoiding a political stance, sociologists explained the upheavals in different ways. Max Weber (1864–1920) explained the process of modernization as one of relentless rationalization that trapped people in the "iron cages" of bureaucratic organization. For Georg Simmel (1858–1918), people could have little concern for one another in the superficial anonymity of urban life. For Émile Durkheim (1858–1917), the erosion of social bonds meant that people were isolated and lonely. When they could not adjust to the emergent values of a modern society, with its high division of labor and advanced technologies, they were subject to anomie, normlessness.

Sociologist Robert K. Merton (1910–2003) explored modes of response to anomie and alienation by devising a typology for different kinds of fit between cultural goals and the institutionalized means available for realizing them. When goals and means are upheld, a group demonstrates conformity, while rejection of both signals *retreatism* (a withdrawal into mental illness or addiction). Two additional types of adaptation are *innovation*, developing new means to attain agreed-upon goals, and *ritualism*, remaining fixated on means while rejecting culturally sanctioned goals. *Rebellion* is the name Merton gave to the search for new goals and means. Stemming from alienation and unrest, rebellion can feed into movements for a different kind of society.

In the late twentieth century, there was a renewed interest in alienation as a tool for critiquing globalizing late capitalism and for seeking out alternative visions of a de-alienated society. Displaced from their social moorings by global changes while facing assaults on their values, alienated people tend to resort to religious fundamentalisms and resurgent nationalisms to gain a sense of stable identity, community, and meaning. For others, consumerism and popular culture feed upon alienation, at once containing discontent and reproducing the conditions that lead to this discontent. This is not new, for the advertising industry has long exploited feelings of loneliness and frustration in order to sell goods that promise to ameliorate alienation. But there are some indications of how alienation can be overcome. Many people unite to effect liberation in movements that celebrate, for example, feminism, environmentalism, and global justice.

Formulated in the nineteenth century, the concept of alienation remains a fruitful tool for understanding the contemporary world. Rooted in Marx's critique of wage labor, the concept has been expanded to consider culture, political trends, and grassroots movements, as well as aspects of everyday life. As long as changing social conditions sustain unequal power and wealth, alienation and loneliness are likely to thwart creativity and neutralize people's power to change. And sociologists will be there to chart the expression of alienation and how we may try to overcome it.

SEE ALSO *Alienation*

BIBLIOGRAPHY

Langman, Lauren, and Devorah Kalekin-Fishman, eds. 2005. *The Evolution of Alienation: Trauma, Promise, and the Millennium.* Boulder, CO: Rowman & Littlefield.

Merton, Robert K. 1968. *Social Theory and Social Structure.* Enl. ed. New York: Free Press.

Mészáros, István. 2005. *Marx's Theory of Alienation.* 5th ed. London: Merlin.

Lauren Langman
Devorah Kalekin-Fishman

ALIGHIERI, DANTE

SEE *Purgatory.*

ALIMONY

SEE *Divorce and Separation.*

ALL DELIBERATE SPEED

SEE *Brown v. Board of Education, 1955.*

ALLAIS, MAURICE

SEE *Non-expected Utility Theory.*

ALLEGORIES

SEE *Narratives.*

ALLENDE, SALVADOR

1908–1973

Salvador Allende Gossens was the democratically elected socialist president of Chile from 1970 until his death during a military coup d'état on September 11, 1973. Allende was born in Valparaíso on June 26, 1908, to an upper middle-class family. He trained at the University of Chile as a medical doctor, but he became involved in politics as a student and spent most of his adult life in politics. He was elected to the lower house of congress in 1937, served as minister of health from 1939 to 1942, and was elected to the senate in 1945. He ran for president in 1952, 1958, and 1964, and finally won in 1970 as the leader of a coalition of leftist parties, called Popular Unity.

As president, Allende sought to lead the country through a peaceful electoral transition to socialism, an endeavor known as the *via chilena*, or Chilean path. Popular Unity's ambitious platform called for state control of much of the economy. The Chilean path was premised on nationalizing key industries such as copper. In addition, Allende accelerated the agrarian reform program initiated by the prior Christian Democratic government, promoted the creation of public-private firms, and vowed not to interfere in the affairs of small businesses, which

were numerous in Chile. Allende also promised to improve the access of poor Chileans to education and health care.

The failure of Allende's *via chilena* has inspired fierce debate among scholars. Many critics emphasize that Allende was a minority president who won only a plurality of the vote in 1970. However, minority presidents were common in Chile, with only Eduardo Frei Montalva (1911–1982) of the Christian Democratic Party winning a clear majority in the modern era (55% of the vote in 1964). In addition, the platform of the Christian Democrats in 1970 was similar to that of Popular Unity. Julio Faúndez suggests that a clear case can be made that "in 1970 more than two-thirds of the electorate voted in favor of radical reform" (1988, p. 180).

Some scholars argue that Allende's policy mistakes led to the coup. For example, Paul Sigmund (1977) questions the legality of Popular Unity's nationalization policies and emphasizes Allende's tactical error of failing to form a coalition government with the Christian Democratic Party, which would have ensured an electoral majority. Other scholars, such as James Petras and Morris Morley (1975), emphasize the role of the opposition (including the U.S. government) in thwarting Allende's policy objectives.

While scholars disagree over what ultimately caused the 1973 coup, there is a virtual consensus that the U.S. government and several large U.S.–based American businesses were determined to prevent Allende from being elected and once in office sought to destabilize his government. Allende had nearly won the presidency in 1958 as the leader of a leftist coalition. Faúndez (1988) notes that Allende's near victory led to an unprecedented degree of U.S. intervention in Chilean politics. From 1958 to 1970, the U.S. government financially supported the electoral campaigns of Christian Democratic Party candidates. The United States also helped establish conservative think tanks and helped produce and disseminate popular media criticizing a hypothetical Allende administration. In fact, Faúndez notes that from 1958 to 1970, the opposition to Allende (Christian Democrats, conservatives, and the U.S. government) worked hand-in-hand to prevent an Allende victory.

In spite of these efforts, the opposition was divided in 1970 and Popular Unity won. Once Allende was elected, Henry Kissinger, President Richard Nixon's (1913–1994) secretary of state, famously quipped, "I don't see why we need to stand by and watch a country go Communist due to the irresponsibility of its own people" (Faúndez 1988, p. 182). U.S. government documents included in the Senate report *Covert Action in Chile, 1963–1973* (1975) clearly show that Nixon and Kissinger, working with the Central Intelligence Agency, actively sought to prevent Allende's confirmation as president by the Chilean

Congress in 1970 and worked to destabilize the Allende government until its demise in 1973. That said, critics of Allende and some analysts who supported the *via chilena* (e.g., Roxborough et al. 1977) have argued that even if the U.S. government had played no role in ousting Allende, the Popular Unity government would have failed due to its own mistakes and the fierceness and unity of the opposition.

At the end of an intense battle against military forces, Allende asked those who fought alongside him to evacuate La Moneda, the presidential palace. Rather than face capture, or likely execution at the hands of the military, Allende committed suicide. In the days leading up to the coup, Allende swore to his supporters that he would die defending his presidency and, more importantly, democracy in Chile. The military government that overthrew Allende ruled Chile from 1973 until 1989, when the dictator Augusto Pinochet stepped down after a popular referendum. During and after the coup, thousands died and thousands more were tortured.

Why was the U.S. government so intent on preventing an Allende victory? On one hand, the zero-sum game of politics during the cold war dictated that success by leftists anywhere was a threat to the United States. Thus, the *via chilena* had to be undermined to maintain the status quo between the United States and the Soviet Union. However, a more plausible explanation might lie in the fact that Allende and other Latin American leftists posed a threat to the hegemonic development model for Latin America and the third world, which favored large multinational firms. Allende and other leftist leaders emphasized that the region needed development models that benefited their countries and the poor. Key to this endeavor was limiting the repatriation of exorbitant profits by U.S.–based companies. The U.S. government was determined to protect the interests of U.S.–based companies and also to undermine a new socialist government in the hemisphere.

SEE ALSO *Central Intelligence Agency, U.S.; Cold War; Developing Countries; Kennedy, John F.; Politics, Latino; Socialism; Third World*

BIBLIOGRAPHY

Faúndez, Julio. 1988. *Marxism and Democracy in Chile: From 1932 to the Fall of Allende.* New Haven, CT: Yale University Press.

Petras, James, and Morris Morley. 1975. *The United States and Chile: Imperialism and the Overthrow of the Allende Government.* New York: Monthly Review Press.

Roxborough, Ian, Phil O'Brien, and Jackie Roddick. 1977. *Chile: The State and Revolution.* New York: Macmillan.

Sigmund, Paul. 1977. *The Overthrow of Allende and the Politics of Chile, 1964–1976.* Pittsburgh, PA: University of Pittsburgh Press.

U.S. Senate, Select Intelligence Committee. 1975. *Covert Action in Chile, 1963–1973: Staff Report of the Select Committee to Study Governmental Operations with Respect to Intelligence Activities, United States Senate.* Washington, DC: U.S. Government Printing Office.

Robert Sean Mackin

ALLIANCES

Alliances are a primary form of international relations (IR) and national security policy. In conventional usage, an alliance is a formal agreement between governments to provide military support under specific political conditions. This may include military operations separately planned and executed, or highly coordinated and integrated, and other measures such as arms transfers, intelligence sharing, and the use of bases, air space, waterways, and territory. Their most important dimensions fall into three categories: (1) basic purpose and function; (2) internal politics; and (3) external affects.

BASIC PURPOSES AND FUNCTIONS

The primary function of an alliance is to combine military strength against adversaries. The combined strength may be used in various ways to advance collective and individual purposes. It is most often used for deterrence, to signal to potential aggressors that they will meet such combined resistance that aggression will not pay. But it may also be used more offensively to compel others into political submission. Both of these coercive strategies, nevertheless, hinge on the most basic alliance function, to promote cooperative war fighting, for that is what makes them credible.

Although the process is never frictionless, alliances tend to form and deform in response to shifting concentrations of power and the threats they pose. Because threats are a function of intentions as well as power, compatibility of national aims tends to drive alliance patterns. Alliances may also form along lines of ideological or religious affinity, because the shared values are likely to be endangered by common threats. In late-nineteenth-century Europe, for example, a conservative alliance based on monarchical solidarity—the Three Emperors League of Prussia, Russia, and Austria-Hungary—formed against the spread of radicalism at home and abroad. Thus the political logic of combining strength against a common threat holds, even when the calculus is not determined by external power configurations alone.

When alliances fight in general wars the common interests they stand for tend to reflect status quo or revisionist goals. The former seek to uphold the prevailing territorial divisions and political frameworks of an international system. The latter seek to overthrow them. At the start of World War II, the revisionist alliance (or "Axis") of Germany, Italy, and Japan joined in rejecting the League of Nations, and in pursuing territorial conquests and a new international economy. It was opposed by a status quo alliance composed of Britain and France, and their allies in Eastern Europe.

But allies' purposes are often more complicated than such broad generalities suggest, for partners will also seek parochial and perhaps contradictory aims, including control over each other. Once the Soviet Union and the United States joined Britain in World War II, their Grand Alliance sought not only to eliminate enemy regimes in Rome, Berlin, and Tokyo, but also to preserve fading empire, extend new spheres of influence over satellites, and create the United Nations and a multilateral liberal economic system. There were obvious tensions among these goals, and they were amply manifest in the international politics of the cold war.

INTERNAL POLITICS

Alliances require material and/or political sacrifices. They can also multiply dangers by provoking counter-alliances and new threats. Allies will thus struggle over the distribution of the costs and benefits of their enterprise, each trying to shift obligations and dangers onto the others. Two basic organizational features shape these internal politics: the number and relative strength of the allies. Increasing the number of allies makes it harder to reconcile disparate priorities. Equality of power among allies adds to the trouble by making it harder to determine whose contributions and priorities must trump. In bilateral alliances, the internal politics are least complicated between strong and weak partners, and more complicated between roughly equal ones. In multilateral alliances of unequal partners the internal politics are yet more difficult, and most difficult of all are multilateral pacts of equals. Regardless of what form an alliance takes, each partner will try to avoid two elementary risks: The first is being abandoned by one's allies at a moment of grave danger; the second is being entrapped in a fight for an ally's parochial interest that harms one's own. These twin risks pose an inherent dilemma of alliance politics, and especially during periods of international crisis, much of alliance politics reflects the strivings of each ally to navigate through it.

Although it creates the danger of entrapment, forging an alliance in peacetime is advantageous because it allows allies to send diplomatic signals and coordinate military plans and forces in ways that increase deterrence and the prospects for military victory. In principle, the more deeply allies coordinate and integrate national strategies, forces, and operations the more effective and beneficial the alliance will be. Yet even when allies agree strongly about their common political purposes, and share a high degree of trust, the business of coordinating let alone integrating military strategies, postures, and operations, can be deeply divisive—within governments as much as between them. Traditional wisdom holds that divisions will recede as common dangers increase, and grow as common dangers fade. Thus wartime alliances tend to unravel after victory, as the Anglo-American–Soviet alliance did after World War II. However, the cleverest and most menacing adversaries will incite and exploit divisions within opposing alliances; then even great danger will not mute debilitating internal politics.

Important questions in IR concern the conditions for taming corrosive alliance politics. Shared norms and transparent decision-making may help liberal democracies to make and keep stronger alliance commitments. Institutionalized alliances, possessing routine processes for political decision-making and military coordination, supported by deliberative bodies and bureaucracies, may also be more robust. Such institutionalization, especially in an alliance of democracies, may even be transforming, creating an unusually cohesive security community in which partners tend to interpret and react to world politics in increasingly convergent ways. The North Atlantic Treaty Organization (NATO)—the most institutionalized and democratic alliance in history—may for this reason have continued to function and adapt long after its main opponent, the Soviet-led Warsaw Pact, crumbled.

EXTERNAL EFFECTS

Alliances are a primary means for balancing power in international politics. Most dramatically this occurs when broad alliances form against an aggressor, like Napoleonic France, that threatens to suborn the international system. Short of such extremes, alliances may foster international order and stability by spreading deterrence and predictability among states and a sense of assurance and restraint within them. But alliances have often been seen as causing more not less international warfare. First, because competitions in alliance building can create spirals of insecurity that make war more likely. Second, because once small local wars start, alliances may widen them and make them more destructive through webs of commitments on each side. That pathology is most associated with the start of World War I in 1914 when two tight alliances, with France and Russia on one side, and Germany and Austria-Hungary on the other, became deadlocked during a crisis between Austria-Hungary and Serbia. Though both were conceived as defensive alliances to prevent war, they seem to have dragged the European powers, and much of the rest of the world, into catastrophe.

The idea that alliances promote peace and stability was boosted by NATO's cold war successes in deterring a Soviet-led Warsaw Pact attack on Western Europe, and fostering cooperation within the alliance between historical enemies West Germany and France. Expectations about reproducing the latter effect motivated NATO expansion after the cold war, when former Warsaw Pact members in Eastern Europe were left in a region of strategic uncertainty without alliance safeguards. NATO's members overcame internal disputes over the scope and pace of enlargement, and agreed to expand the alliance eastward to project stability and promote democracy within the new member states. This logic for projecting security through alliance growth thus evoked the idea that democratic alliances can instill deep bonds of common identity and security community.

In the first decade of the twenty-first century, the strongest case for such bonding remained the Anglo-American alliance: forged in world wars, it was deepened and institutionalized bilaterally and multilaterally through NATO during decades of cold war. As their security concerns shifted to nuclear proliferation and transnational terrorism, those two allies showed surprising cohesion in fighting wars in Iraq and Afghanistan. With other NATO members, however, especially concerning Iraq, there was greater political acrimony and less evident commitment to joint effort, showing that even the deeply democratic and institutionalized transatlantic security community remains vulnerable to divisive and perhaps debilitating internal politics.

As the century unfolds, two issues concerning alliances will loom largest for students and practitioners of international relations. The first is the extent to which traditional alliance frameworks can be retooled and mobilized to redress amorphous transnational terrorist threats that are less amenable to solutions based on combined military strength. The second is the extent to which traditional alliance frameworks will come into play against the largest and fastest-growing powers. Will new alliances form and tighten in reaction to preponderant American military power? Will alliances in Asia and the Pacific endure and grow—or whither and fracture—as China's military posture and prestige climbs? The broad contours of twenty-first-century international politics will be defined by answers to these questions.

SEE ALSO *Cold War; Confederations; Cooperation; Deterrence; Ideology; League of Nations; North Atlantic Treaty Organization; United Nations; War; Warsaw Pact; World War I; World War II*

BIBLIOGRAPHY

Art, Robert J. 1996. Why Western Europe Needs the United States and NATO. *Political Science Quarterly* 111 (1): 1–39.

Asmus, Ronald D. 2002. *Opening NATO's Door: How the Alliance Remade Itself for a New Era.* New York: Columbia University Press.

Dingman, Roger V. 1979. Theories of, and Approaches to, Alliance Politics. In *Diplomacy*, ed. Paul G. Lauren, 245–266. New York: Free Press.

Gaubatz, Kurt Taylor. 1996. Democratic States and Commitment in International Relations. *International Organization* 50 (1): 109–139.

Gibler, Douglas M. 2000. Alliances: Why Some Cause War and Why Others Cause Peace. In *What Do We Know About War?* Ed. John A. Vasquez, 145–164. Lanham, MD: Rowman and Littlefield.

Goldgeier, James M. 1999. *Not Whether but When: The U.S. Decision to Enlarge NATO.* Washington, DC: Brookings Institution Press.

Gordon, Phillip H., and Jeremy Shapiro. 2004. *Allies at War: America, Europe, and the Crisis over Iraq.* Washington, DC: Brookings Institution Press.

Haas, Mark L. 2005 *The Ideological Origins of Great Power Politics, 1789–1989.* Ithaca, NY: Cornell University Press.

Holsti, Ole R. P., Terrence Hopmann, and John D. Sullivan. 1973. *Unity and Disintegration in International Alliances: Comparative Studies.* New York: Wiley.

Lake, David A. 1999. *Entangling Relations: American Foreign Policy in Its Century.* Princeton, NJ: Princeton University Press.

Leeds, Brett Ashley, and Sezi Anac. 2005. Alliance Institutionalization and Alliance Performance. *International Interactions* 31: 183–201.

Liska, George. 1962. *Nations in Alliance: The Limits of Interdependence.* Baltimore, MD: Johns Hopkins University Press.

Mearsheimer, John J. 2001. *The Tragedy of Great Power Politics.* New York: Norton.

Morgenthau, Hans J. 1973. *Politics Among Nations.* 5th ed. New York: Knopf.

Morrow, James D. 2000. Alliances: Why Write Them Down? *Annual Review of Political Science* 3: 63–84.

Neustadt, Richard E. 1970. *Alliance Politics.* New York: Columbia University Press.

Niou, Emerson M. S., Peter C. Ordeshook, and Gregory F. Rose. 1989. *The Balance of Power: Stability in International Systems.* Cambridge, U.K.: Cambridge University Press.

Olson, Mancur, Jr., and Richard Zeckhauser. 1966. An Economic Theory of Alliances. *Review of Economics and Statistics* 48 (3): 266–279.

Posen, Barry R. 1984. *The Sources of Military Doctrine: France, Britain, and Germany Between the World Wars.* Ithaca, NY: Cornell University Press.

Risse-Kappen, Thomas. 1996. Collective Identity in a Democratic Community: The Case of NATO. In *The Culture of National Security: Norms and Identity in World*

Politics, ed. Peter J. Katzenstein, 357–397. New York: Columbia University Press.

Schroeder, Paul W. 2004. Alliances, 1815–1945: Weapons of Power and Tools of Management. In *Systems, Stability and Statecraft: Essays on the International History of Modern Europe*. Ed. David Wetzel, Robert Jervis, and Jack S. Levy, 195–222. New York: Palgrave Macmillan.

Schweller, Randall L. 1998. *Deadly Imbalances: Tripolarity and Hitler's Strategy of World Conquest*. New York: Columbia University Press.

Snyder, Glenn H. 1997. *Alliance Politics*. Ithaca, NY: Cornell University Press.

Walt, Stephen M. 1987. *The Origins of Alliances*. Ithaca, NY: Cornell University Press.

Waltz, Kenneth N. 1979. *Theory of International Politics*. Reading, MA: Addison Wesley.

Weitsman, Patricia A. 2004. *Dangerous Alliances: Proponents of Peace, Weapons of War*. Stanford, CA: Stanford University Press.

Timothy W. Crawford

ALLPORT, GORDON
1897–1967

Gordon Willard Allport was a leading personality and social psychologist of the mid-twentieth century. His initial fame came from his central role in establishing the scientific study of personality as a major component of academic psychology. In 1924 he taught at Harvard University what was probably the first personality course in North America. But it was his 1937 volume, *Personality: A Psychological Interpretation*, that firmly grounded the field. Immediately hailed by reviewers as a classic, this unique work offered a counter to the then-rising popularity of Freudian theory. The book legitimized personality as a scientific topic, and shaped the agenda for the study of personality for the ensuing decades.

Allport vigorously advocated an open-system theory of personality with emphases upon individual uniqueness, rationality, proaction, consciousness, and the united nature of personality. He stressed human values, dynamic traits, and the self. He focused more on the mature adult than on the early years of childhood. As such, Allport's position was less anti-Freudian than it was a correction to right the balance in the conception of personality. This is illustrated by his proposition that the bulk of human motives and the personal attributes of adult persons become *functionally autonomous* from their likely developmental roots.

In 1954 Allport published his second classic work: *The Nature of Prejudice*. It too shaped its field for half a century. This book departed from previous conceptions of prejudice and advanced an array of new insights later supported by research. Two theoretical stances proved especially important. Allport held that intergroup contact under favorable conditions could substantially reduce prejudice and offer a major means of improving intergroup relations. Research throughout the world, as well as such events as the ending of apartheid in South Africa, support the theory. Allport also countered the then-fashionable assumption that group stereotypes were simply the aberrant cognitive distortions of prejudiced personalities. Advancing the view now universally accepted, Allport insisted that the cognitive components of prejudice were natural extensions of normal processes. Stereotypes and prejudice, he concluded, were not aberrant but all too human.

Though known principally as a theorist, Allport also had an active empirical career. In his efforts to forge a broad psychology, he employed a range of methods— from the study of personal documents to nomothetic tests and ingenious experiments. His most famous test measured basic values. His influential experiments opened up research on eidetic imagery, expressive movement, radio effects, and rumor.

Critics of Allport's personality theory regard it as too static and overly oriented to the sane and mature. Social science critics regard Allport's work as too individualistic and detached from social factors. Nonetheless, he remains one of the most cited writers in the social psychological literature.

Allport's lasting influence is based on three interwoven features that characterize all his work (Pettigrew 1999). First, he offered a broadly eclectic balance of the many sides of psychology. Second, he repeatedly formulated the discipline's central problems and proposed innovative approaches to them. Typically, his suggested solutions were loosely sketched out and not readily accepted. Years later, however, his ideas often gained acceptance and were expanded with new concepts. Finally, Allport's entire body of scholarly work presents a consistent and seamless perspective both forcefully advanced and elegantly written.

SEE ALSO *Developmental Psychology; Erikson, Erik; Personality; Prejudice; Self-Esteem; Self-Identity*

BIBLIOGRAPHY

Allport, Gordon W. 1937. *Personality: A Psychological Interpretation*. New York: Henry Holt.

Allport, Gordon W. 1954. *The Nature of Prejudice*. Reading, MA: Addison-Wesley.

Pettigrew, Thomas F. 1999. Gordon Willard Allport: A Tribute. *Journal of Social Issues* 55 (3): 415–427.

Thomas F. Pettigrew

ALMON LAG

SEE *Lags, Distributed.*

ALMOND, GABRIEL A.
1911–2002

Gabriel A. Almond was one of the most creative political scientists of the latter half of the twentieth century. He carried out major work on public opinion and foreign policy; he did pioneering work on political culture, making the study of the subject much more systematic; he was the leading figure in the field of comparative politics, in which he broke down the single-country focus and made the field truly comparative; he brought sophisticated psychological analysis into the study of politics; and he ended his long career with significant work on religious fundamentalism.

The American People and Foreign Policy, published in 1950, was one of the earliest works in behavioral political science. Almond used survey data to explain the periodic swings of American public opinion toward international affairs—from idealistic to cynical attitudes, from a support for withdrawal to support for intervention, and from optimism to pessimism. In *The Appeals of Communism,* published in 1954, he used surveys and in-depth interviews to demonstrate the fundamentally different nature of the appeals of the communism in countries where it was the "normal" ideology of the working class and in countries where it was a less class-based manifestation of alienation.

Almond's most lasting contribution was to the systematic study of comparative politics. *The Civic Culture* (1963, coauthored with Sidney Verba) was one of the first large-scale cross-national survey studies. With its examination of the cultural roots of democracy in five nations, it opened the new field of comparative surveys and was one of the first attempts to study cultural factors in comparative politics systematically. In *The Politics of the Developing Areas,* Almond and James S. Coleman proposed a broad analytical framework for identifying the basic institutions and processes of social change. In *Crisis, Choice, and Change,* Almond and his collaborators considered the role of leadership and strategic choice in political change.

Almond also contributed analyses of the state of political science. In *A Discipline Divided,* he called for a political science that was open to many approaches, a political science that was empirical and whose conclusions were open to testing and falsification.

Late in life, Almond led a large-scale project on fundamentalisms sponsored by the American Academy of Arts and Sciences. The project culminated in an overview volume, *Strong Religions,* authored by Almond, R. Scott Appleby, and Emmanuel Sivan. The authors consider the role of fundamental religion most broadly, from its social roots to its political consequences. They do not simplify and reduce all forms to a single pattern, but instead allow one to see beyond the particularities of each of the forms of fundamentalism.

SEE ALSO *Political Science, Behavioral; Verba, Sidney*

BIBLIOGRAPHY

PRIMARY WORKS

Almond, Gabriel A. 1950. *The American People and Foreign Policy.* New York: Harcourt, Brace.

Almond, Gabriel A. 1990. *A Discipline Divided: Schools and Sects in Political Science.* Newbury Park, CA: Sage.

Almond, Gabriel A. 2002. *Ventures in Political Science: Narratives and Reflections.* Boulder, CO: Lynne Rienner.

Almond, Gabriel A., R. Scott Appleby, and Emmanuel Sivan. 2003. *Strong Religion: The Rise of Fundamentalisms around the World.* Chicago: University of Chicago Press.

Almond, Gabriel A, and James S. Coleman, eds. 1960. *The Politics of the Developing Areas.* Princeton, NJ: Princeton University Press.

Almond, Gabriel A., Scott C. Flanagan, and Robert J. Mundt, eds. 1973. *Crisis, Choice, and Change: Historical Studies of Political Development.* Boston: Little, Brown.

Almond, Gabriel A., Herbert E. Krugman, Elsbeth Lewin, and Howard Wriggins. 1954. *The Appeals of Communism.* Princeton, NJ: Princeton University Press.

Almond, Gabriel A., and Sidney Verba. 1963. *The Civic Culture: Political Attitudes and Democracy in Five Nations.* Princeton, NJ: Princeton University Press.

Sidney Verba
Lucian Pye

ALPHA FEMALE

SEE *Alpha-male.*

ALPHA-MALE

In 1802 P. Huber related the concept of dominance to the social behavior of bumblebees. Almost 100 years later, Thorleif Schjelderup-Ebbe (1935) wrote about "pecking orders" in chickens, describing a hierarchy in which the top-ranking chicken could peck all the others with impunity and the second-ranking could do the same thing to all except the first one, down to the last-ranking bird, which was pecked by all and could peck none in return. The idea of dominance was applied to explain the directionality of aggressive behavior in animals that live socially and was defined as a relationship learned through previous experience.

DOMINANCE IN NONHUMAN PRIMATES

Ray Carpenter applied the concept to nonhuman primates and considered it a universal principle that shapes all primate social organizations (1954). Interest quickly was focused on individual attributes that might account for the achievement of high rank and its consequences. Size and strength may contribute, but Masao Kawai and Syunzo Kawamura (1958) and Bernard Chapais (1992) demonstrated that social skills and alliances are far more important in determining the dominance positions of monkeys. Irwin Bernstein and colleagues showed that dominance ranks have meaning only in a specific social context (1980). In different groups individual ranks can be reversed, and the highest-ranking individual in one group can be the lowest-ranking in another. Dominance thus is not an attribute that can be studied in an isolated individual.

The functions of dominance were speculated to relate to instrumental aggression, a process in which aggression is used to gain something at the expense of a rival. Dominant individuals were expected to have priority of access to food, mates, and other resources. However, the existence of mixed evolutionarily stable strategies was interpreted to mean that alternative means might obscure the expected correlation between rank and resources. If dominance meant access to incentives, it was speculated that individuals would strive actively for high rank, but William Mason and Sally Mendoza found little evidence that primates fight specifically to attain rank (1993). Moreover, empirical studies of genetic fitness and high rank have not always demonstrated the expected correlation. Market theories that suggest that animals should perform "favors" for those of high rank in exchange for "services" such as agonistic aid and tolerance also have received mixed support. Although there are good correlations between grooming and dominance in some groups, the tendency for kin or other close associates to both groom and aid one another can override any tendency for lower-ranking animals to groom higher-ranking animals.

BIOLOGICAL CORRELATES AND BEHAVIOR

The search for biological correlates of dominance rank revealed that whereas some characteristics may contribute to the attainment of high rank, others may follow as a consequence of achieving that rank. Robert Rose and colleagues initially assumed that the correlation between male testosterone levels and dominance suggests that hormones contribute to dominance (1971) but later found that recent histories of winning or losing a fight account for profound changes in testosterone levels. The correlation with dominance pertained only immediately after fighting had established or changed dominance positions. Robert M. Sapolsky reported that cortisol levels were lower in dominant individuals, but only when the group was in a period of social stability (1984). Hormone levels both influence social interactions and are a result of those interactions.

Since dominance relationships are often linear, the first position is called alpha and the last is called omega. The alpha animal can be expected to be the "leader" of a primate group, but high agonistic rank does not lead routinely to leadership of group movements or other activities. The alpha individual may be assumed to be integral to the defense of the group against external and internal threats, but the "control role" often is played by individuals other than the alpha. In macaque and baboon societies sexual dimorphism in body size, canine size, and other features may contribute to a male becoming the alpha animal in the group, but sometimes a female may outrank all the males. Among the lemurs females routinely assume the alpha position. Nonetheless, with the original assumption that males would be the highest-ranking individuals, investigators asked whether females also have an "alpha" with special characteristics, as is assumed for alpha males. Of course this required separating the sexes in determining relative ranks, and some researchers went so far as to suggest that all adult males outrank all adult females. Whereas this occasionally may be true for some species, it is far from a general rule.

The focus on biological correlates of "alphaness" led to considerations of the evolutionary consequences of natural selection on behavior. If males were selected on the basis of their ability to defeat other males to obtain access to females (Charles Darwin's intrasexual selection), larger, more aggressive males would have higher genetic fitness. Aggression was expected in males, whereas females were expected to be more passive and even "coy," inciting males to demonstrate their superior prowess. Male aggression also could be directed against females to coerce mating (reducing the effect of Darwin's second principle of sexual selection: epigamic selection, or "female choice"). With a long history of natural selection favoring aggressive males that fought other males and coerced females, one would expect strong differences in the aggressiveness of the sexes, and such differences were assumed and supported by the more extreme consequences of male aggression. This, however, is a poor indicator of differential initiation, participation, and duration of aggression. Because of different anatomic capabilities, aggression by females may take forms different from those of male aggression and inflict less damage, but does this mean that verbal aggression or social ostracism (presumed to be more common in human females) is any less aggressive than physical attacks? In many species the frequency and duration of female aggression exceed those of males, although the consequences of male aggression are usually more severe.

If, however, evolution has favored males that are highly aggressive and engage in sexual coercion, it is not surprising that males, with their correlated higher levels of male hormones, are more aggressive than females. (The relationship with male testosterone is widely assumed and castration often is recommended to reduce aggression in animals and human males, but there is little proof that there is a direct correlation between testosterone levels and aggression.) If male aggression is "natural," Richard Wrangham and Dale Peterson argued in 1996, males are possessed by "demons" that drive their behavior. They fight and copulate at every opportunity because evolution has shaped them to do that. If natural selection is responsible, should they be blamed, or should researchers be more accepting of male aggression and sexual coercion? Does this excuse the inexcusable? Are people really programmed by their "hormones" and heredity so that "free will" has little influence on "typical" sex behavior? Is sexual dimorphism proof that males have greater physical fighting abilities so that they can defeat other males in contests for mating, or is it possible that other factors promote a sexual division of labor that favors larger size and fighting ability in males and/or smaller size in females? Sexual dimorphism could as easily be due to differences in the social roles of males and females with regard to group defense against predators, rival groups, or other sources of potential disturbance or even to differences in foraging patterns that reduce competition for food within a group. Plausibility seems the only argument for favoring one interpretation over another, and sexual dimorphism often is assumed to be proof of male mating patterns.

THE HUMAN ALPHA

The application of speculations about nonhuman primate behavior to the understanding of the human condition is fraught with peril. "Alphaness" is more an artifact of peo-

ple's ability to count than a matter of biology. Linear hierarchies are appealing, but the game paper, scissors, rock also can describe dominance. Researchers see an entire group, but animals may be more self-centered and see only their individual relationships with the members of the group. They may not have abstract concepts of group organization.

Dominance in human groups may be pronounced in institutions with a rank hierarchy such as the military; an alpha may be suggested when groups have a clear leader and the others are all more or less equal followers, but some human groupings do not show structures that suggest that individuals have histories of coercive relationships that lead to recognized superiors. Christopher Boehm suggested that many human social structures have specific mechanisms that preclude the development of alpha positions (1994). The existence of leadership does not require aggression or a history of aggressive contests, although that may occur in some circumstances. Superior reproductive success can correlate with high social status, but it need not. (Genetic fitness is defined by the number of replicates of an individual's genes that show up in a future generation compared to the average individual in the population—roughly equivalent to the number of grandchildren or great grandchildren that one has. For the last several decades there has been an inverse relationship between economic status and genetic fitness.) Presumed correlates of dominance or alpha status cannot be construed as evidence that alpha status exists.

If the term *alpha-male* is used to indicate a male that uses social position to obtain more mating or power over others, surely females might do the same and there would be alpha females. These concepts are a far cry from the origins of the term in animal behavior, where *alpha* was used to designate the individual that could aggress against others without fear of retaliation. Whether dominance leads to increased mating or access to resources is an empirical question, and the data do not always support such hypotheses. Thus, the relationships among dominance rank, genetic fitness, and status are empirical questions with regard to humans as well, and one cannot assume that success in any one area implies success in the others. Researchers may describe alpha individuals of either sex or of a group, but they should describe data and not assume data on the basis of theory.

SEE ALSO *Aggression; Hierarchy; Men; Military; Organization Theory; Social Dominance Orientation; Sociobiology; Violence*

BIBLIOGRAPHY

Bernstein, Irwin. 1964. Role of the Dominant Male Rhesus in Response to External Challenges to the Group. *Journal of Comparative and Physiological Psychology* 57: 404–406.

Bernstein, Irwin. 1966a. Analysis of a Key Role in a Capuchin (*Cebus albifrons*) Group. *Tulane Studies in Zoology* 13 (2): 49–54.

Bernstein, Irwin. 1966b. An Investigation of the Organization of Pigtail Monkey Groups through the Use of Challenges. *Primates* 7: 471–480.

Bernstein, Irwin. 1981. Dominance: The Baby and the Bathwater. *Behavioral and Brain Sciences* 4: 419–457.

Bernstein, Irwin, and Matthew A. Cooper. 1999. Dominance in Assamese Macaques (*Macaca assamensis*). *American Journal of Primatology* 48 (4): 283–289.

Bernstein, Irwin, and Thomas P. Gordon. 1974. The Function of Aggression in Primate Societies. *American Scientist* 62: 304–311.

Bernstein, Irwin, and Thomas P. Gordon. 1980. The Social Component of Dominance Relationships in Rhesus Monkeys (*Macaca mulatto*). *Animal Behaviour* 28: 1033–1039.

Bernstein, Irwin, Thomas P. Gordon, and Robert M. Rose. 1983. The Interaction of Hormones, Behavior, and Social Context in Nonhuman Primates. In *Hormones and Aggressive Behavior* 535–561.

Bernstein, Irwin, Peter G. Judge, and Thomas E. Ruehlmann. 1993. Kinship, Association, and Social Relationships in Rhesus Monkeys (*Macaca mulatta*). *American Journal of Primatology* 31 (1): 41–53.

Bernstein, Irwin, Robert M. Rose, and Thomas P. Gordon. 1974. Behavioral and Environmental Events Influencing Primate Testosterone Levels. *Journal of Human Evolution* 3: 517–525.

Bernstein, Irwin, Robert M. Rose, Thomas P. Gordon, and Cheryl L. Grady. 1979. Agonistic Rank, Aggression, Social Context, and Testosterone in Male Pigtail Monkeys. *Aggressive Behavior* 5: 329–339.

Bernstein, Irwin, Lawrence Williams, and Marcia Ramsay. 1983. The Expression of Aggression in Old World Monkeys. *International Journal of Primatology* 4: 113–125.

Boehm, Christopher. 1994. Pacifying Interventions at Arnhem Zoo and Gombe. In *Chimpanzee Cultures*, eds. Richard W. Wrangham, W. C. McGrew, and Frans B. M. de Waal, 211–226. Cambridge, MA: Harvard University Press.

Carpenter, C. Ray. 1954. Tentative Generalizations on the Grouping Behaviour of Non-Human Primates. *Human Biology* 3 (26): 269–276.

Chapais, Bernard. 1992. The Role of Alliances in Social Inheritance of Rank among Female Primates. In *Coalitions and Alliances in Human and Other Animals*, eds. Alexander H. Harcourt and Frans B. M. de Waal, 29–59. Oxford: Oxford University Press.

Cooper, Matthew A., and Irwin Bernstein. 2000. Social Grooming in Assamese Macaques (*Macaca assamensis*). *American Journal of Primatology* 50 (1): 77–85.

Duvall, Susan W., Irwin Bernstein, and Thomas P. Gordon. 1976. Paternity and Status in a Rhesus Monkey Group. *Journal of Reproduction Fertility* 47: 25–31.

Gordon, Thomas P., Robert M. Rose, Cheryl L. Grady, and Irwin Bernstein. 1979. Effects of Increased Testosterone Secretion on the Behavior of Adult Male Rhesus Living in a Social Group. *Folia Primatologica* 32: 149–160.

Huber, P. 1802. Observations in Several Species of the Genus Apis, Known by the Name of Bumble-Bees, and Called Bombinatrices by Linnaeus. *Transactions of the Linnean Society of London* 6: 214–298.

Kawamura, Syunzo. 1958. On the Rank System in a Natural Group of Japanese Monkeys. *Primates* 1: 111–130.

Koyama, N. 1967. On Dominance Rank and Kinship of a Wild Japanese Monkey Troop in Arashiyama. *Primates* 8: 189–216.

Kummer, Hans. 1971. *Primate Societies: Group Techniques of Ecological Adaptation*. Chicago: Aldine-Atherton.

Mason, William A., and Sally P. Mendoza. 1993. *Primate Social Conflict*. Albany: State University of New York Press.

Matheson, Megan D., and Irwin Bernstein. 2000. Grooming, Social Bonding, and Agonistic Aiding in Rhesus Monkeys. *American Journal of Primatology* 51: 177–186.

Rose, Robert M., Irwin Bernstein, and Thomas P. Gordon. 1975. Consequences of Social Conflict on Plasma Testosterone Levels in Rhesus Monkeys. *Psychosomatic Medicine* 37: 50–61.

Rose, Robert M., Irwin Bernstein, Thomas P. Gordon, and S. F. Catlin. 1974. Androgens and Aggression: A Review and Recent Findings in Primates. In *Primate Aggression, Territoriality, and Xenophobia*, ed. Ralph L. Holloway, 275–304. New York: Academic Press.

Rose, Robert M., Irwin Bernstein, and John W. Holaday. 1971. Plasma Testosterone, Dominance Rank, and Aggressive Behavior in a Group of Male Rhesus Monkeys. *Nature* 231: 366–368.

Rose, Robert M., Thomas P. Gordon, and Irwin Bernstein. 1972. Plasma Testosterone Levels in the Male Rhesus: Influences of Sexual and Social Stimuli. *Science* 178: 643–645.

Sapolsky, Robert M. 1984. Stress and the Successful Baboon. *Psychology Today* 18 (9): 60–65.

Schjelderup-Ebbe, Thorleif. 1935. Social Behavior of Birds. In *A Handbook of Social Psychology*, ed. Carl Murchison, 947–972. Worcester, MA: Clark University Press.

Wilson, Edward O. 1975. *Sociobiology: The New Synthesis*. Cambridge, MA: Belknap Press of Harvard University Press.

Wilson, Mark E., Thomas P. Gordon, and Irwin Bernstein. 1980. Serum Testosterone and Social Context Influences on Behavior of Adult Male Rhesus Monkeys. *Biology of Reproduction* 22 (1): 137A.

Wrangham, Richard, and Dale Peterson. 1996. *Demonic Males: Apes and the Origins of Human Violence*. Boston: Houghton Mifflin.

Irwin S. Bernstein

AL-QAEDA

Al-Qaeda, an Arabic word meaning "base," is an international Islamic terrorist group led by Osama bin Laden, who founded Al-Qaeda along with Abdullah Azzam (1941–1989) in Afghanistan in 1988 (*9-11 Commission Report*, p. 56). Al-Qaeda's administrative and recruitment foundation sprang from the associations of Muslim warriors (*mujahideen*) that had formed in the early 1980s to fight the Soviet invaders in Afghanistan. These fighters later became the backbone of Al-Qaeda's forces.

After the Soviet retreat from Afghanistan in February 1989, bin Laden returned to his native Saudi Arabia. When Iraq invaded Kuwait on August 2, 1990, bin Laden offered to raise a volunteer Islamic army to fight Iraq. The Saudi government refused, preferring to seek help from the United Nations. During the ensuing war, bin Laden opposed American involvement, calling the United States an "enemy invader." Following his disagreement with the Saudi regime, bin Laden and his supporters went to Sudan in 1991 (*9-11 Commission Report,* p. 57). International pressure on the Sudanese government later obliged bin Laden to return to Afghanistan in 1996, where he and his supporters remained until the Taliban government was defeated following the invasion of the American-led coalition forces in 2001.

Since 1991 Al-Qaeda has launched several attacks on various Western targets: suicide car bombings of the American embassies in Nairobi, Kenya, and Dar es Salaam, Tanzania, on August 7, 1998; the suicide attack on the USS *Cole* in the port of Aden in Yemen on October 12, 2000; the September 11 attacks on the Pentagon and the World Trade Center in the United States in 2001; and the suicide attack in Riyadh, Saudi Arabia, on May 12, 2003. When American-led coalition forces invaded Iraq on March 20, 2003, Al-Qaeda–linked groups swung into action. On October 21, 2004, they united as "Al-Qaeda in Iraq" under the leadership of Abu Musab al-Zarqawi, a Jordanian who was killed by American forces on June 7, 2006.

Al-Qaeda and its ideology were established on a background of the decline of socialism and communism in the face of Western culture and capitalism and increasing Islamic influence. Al-Qaeda was influenced mainly by the extreme ideologies of the Salafi stream of Islam, particularly those of Sayyid Qutb (1906–1966), an Egyptian religious theoretician. Qutb viewed the West and its culture as the greatest threat to Islam and advocated the establishment of an Islamic state based on Muslim religious law. This idea became associated with bin Laden's contention that Westerners violate the honor of Muslims, humiliate them, and try to possess their lands. Muslims must therefore fight against the West in a jihad holy war. The concept that best represents Al-Qaeda's ideology is that of "defensive jihad," according to which it is every Muslim's religious obligation to fight the attackers, seen as the Western countries headed by the United States.

This ideology molded Al-Qaeda's goals, which are: (1) to establish Islamic regimes like the Taliban, based on Islamic religious law, in all the Arab states; (2) to free all Islamic lands from any Western presence or influence; and (3) to establish the "pious caliphate" (a pan-Arabic Islamic kingdom) over all the Muslim lands. These goals were expressed in bin Laden's fatwa (religious legal proclamation) of February 23, 1998, although he himself has no religious authority. In the fatwa, bin Laden asserted that the United States, through its policies in Muslim lands, had declared war on God, his Messenger, and all Muslims.

Al-Qaeda is one of the few terrorist groups structured with a distinct separation between the *majlis a-shura* (the core leadership) and the action groups. This structural difference makes it easier for Al-Qaeda to function without a home country as a base that provides it with political and military sponsorship and hosts its training camps and administrative headquarters. As a result, cells of activists have become semi-independent centers of activity. Each cell is composed of a few members, some natives of their locale, all ready to die for their cause when the leadership so orders. Al-Qaeda cells are scattered throughout the world, with a conspicuous presence in Europe, and often have only Internet connections with the leadership.

SEE ALSO *Al Jazeera; Arab League, The; Arabs; Arafat, Yasir; bin Laden, Osama; Fundamentalism, Islamic; Palestine Liberation Organization (PLO); Palestinian Authority; Palestinians; Pan-Arabism; September 11, 2001; Terrorism; Terrorists; Violence in Terrorism*

BIBLIOGRAPHY

Burke, Jason. 2004. *Al-Qaeda: The True Story of Radical Islam.* Updated ed. London: Penguin.

National Commission on Terrorist Attacks upon the United States. 2004. *The 9-11 Commission Report.* http://www.9-11commission.gov/.

Sageman, Marc. 2004. *Understanding Terror Networks.* Philadelphia: University of Pennsylvania Press.

Ami Pedahzur
Alexandr Bialsky

ALTHUSSER, LOUIS
1918–1990

Born in Algeria, the troubled and reclusive French philosopher Louis Althusser revolutionized Marxist philosophy with his radical theses on Karl Marx's oeuvre and influenced several generations of students at the École Normale Supérieure, including Michel Foucault, Étienne Balibar, Jacques Ranciere, and Régis Debray. Many of Althusser's arguments, often theoretical interventions in French Communist Party (of which he was a member) and international Left debates, were published in socialist journals or articulated in public lectures and seminars (and subsequently compiled as volumes) in keeping with his determination to "intervene as much in politics as in philosophy, alone against the world" (Althusser 1993, p. 173).

Arguing that socialism was scientific and humanism ideological, Althusser challenged Hegelian and humanistic readings of Marx's work as a coherent whole, by marking an "epistemological rupture" between Marx's early (pre-1845), humanistic writings and his subsequent "mature," "scientific" works such as *Reading Capital*. The *problématique* (theoretical framework that encapsulates both presence and absence of concepts) of Marx's mature work was described as historical materialism, a "science of history" that provided a revolutionary conceptualization of social formation and change. This "History Continent" discovered by Marx, was original and unprecedented and "induced" the birth of a new, "theoretically and practically revolutionary philosophy"—dialectical materialism—distinct from historical materialism (1970a, p. 14).

Althusser's "symptomatic" reading performed the dual function of revealing the "unconscious" of Marx's texts and illuminating their underlying deep structures, while demonstrating the methodology mobilized by Marx himself in reading classical political economy. Contrary to the prevalent economically deterministic readings of *Capital*, Althusser identified a wider range of *pratique* (processes of production or transformation) that constituted a social whole or "structure in dominance" that had no essence or center. Each economic, political, ideological structure "existed in its effects," and was asymmetrically related but autonomous, the economic determining "in the last instance" which element was to be dominant. This dominance was not fixed but varied according to the "overdetermination" of the contradictions in social formation and their uneven development (1970b, p. 188).

While Althusser was influenced by his teachers such as Maurice Merleau-Ponty and Georges Canguilhem, his indebtedness to psychoanalysis was profound and particularly evident in his expositions on ideology. He distinguished between *Ideology* (eternal, omni-historical and structural, like Freud's notion of the unconscious) and *ideologies* (particular, sociohistorical). Ideology is a "representation of the imaginary relationship of individuals to their lived conditions" and has a material existence in practices and apparatuses. Of these, Ideological State Apparatuses (ISAs) such as religion, schools, and family are significant as they *interpellate* or "hail" subjects to accept their role within the system of production relations by "misrecognizing" their subjecthood as agency. Thus, an individual is simultaneously subject (of) and subject (to) ideology (1971, pp. 160–170).

Althusser consistently refuted accusations that his omni-historical, structuralist formulations disenabled revolutionary practice by insisting that he was never a structuralist but rather a Spinozist; structuralism was an accidental by-product of his antihumanist, theoreticist deviation via Spinoza's notion of structural causality. Further, his Marxism could never be structuralism because it affirmed the primacy of class struggle and thus "rests on revolutionary class theoretical positions" (1976, p. 130).

Althusser battled unbearable sadness and mental instability for much of his adult life. Althusser's murder of his wife, Helene Rytman, with whom he shared an extremely intense emotional and intellectual relationship, and his subsequent efforts to "answer charges" in his memoirs, *The Future Lasts Forever* (1993), are respectively horrific and poignant examples of the fragile balance between madness and reason upon which he constantly teetered while nevertheless always being aware of the powerful role that violent organizations had played in his life.

SEE ALSO *Lenin, Vladimir Ilitch; Leninism; Marx, Karl; Marxism; Structuralism*

BIBLIOGRAPHY

PRIMARY WORKS

Althusser, Louis. 1970a. *For Marx.* Trans. Ben Brewster. New York: Vintage Books. (Orig. pub. 1969).

Althusser, Louis. 1970b. *Reading Capital.* With Étienne Balibar. Trans. Ben Brewster. London: New Left Books.

Althusser, Louis. 1971. *Lenin and Philosophy and Other Essays.* Trans. Ben Brewster. London: New Left Books.

Althusser, Louis. 1976. *Essays in Self-Criticism.* Trans. Grahame Locke. London: New Left Books.

Althusser, Louis. 1993. *The Future Lasts Forever.* Trans. Richard Veasey. Ed. Olivier Corpet and Yann Moulier Boutang. New York: New Press.

Malathi de Alwis

ALTRUISM

One fundamental question about human nature is whether people are ever capable of genuinely altruistic acts. The term *altruism* is typically used to reflect one of two concepts. The first is *evolutionary altruism*, which refers to helping behavior that benefits another at some cost to oneself. Evolutionary altruism reflects behavior caused by many different habits and motives assumed to have evolved in a species because they promote the long-term reproduction of species members' genes. The term *altruism* is also used to reflect *psychological altruism*, which refers to a motivational state with the goal of increasing another's welfare. Psychological altruism is typically contrasted with *psychological egoism*, which refers to a motivational state with the goal of increasing one's own welfare.

There has been much debate about whether humans possess the capacity for psychological altruism. One claim that assumes psychological altruism exists is the empathy-altruism hypothesis, which states that feelings of *empathic concern* for a person in need evoke an altruistic motive. Feelings of empathic concern have been contrasted with feelings of *personal distress*. Feelings of personal distress are assumed to evoke motivation to reduce these unpleasant emotions by either escaping continued exposure to the person's suffering or by helping, whichever happens to be the least costly option in the situation. Consistent with these claims, research suggests that people feeling empathic concern tend to help even if they can easily escape exposure to the victim's suffering, whereas people feeling personal distress tend to help only when escape from continued exposure to the person's suffering is difficult or impossible.

The tendency for an observer to help a needy other as a result of evolutionary altruistic or psychological altruistic processes is also influenced by factors that affect helping behavior more generally. For example, research demonstrates that observers are more likely to help a person if they (1) notice the person and (2) recognize that the person is in need. Even then, help is likely only if observers (3) assume personal responsibility for reducing the person's need. Research also suggests that the number of observers witnessing the need situation can actually reduce the likelihood that any one observer will offer help (i.e., the *bystander effect*). However, observers who experience psychological altruism may be immune to this diffusion of responsibility because empathy may promote feelings of responsibility for the victim regardless of the number of additional bystanders present in the situation.

In development, helping behavior appears to emerge as early as two years of age in humans. However, the cause of these behaviors (e.g., evolutionary altruistic versus psychological altruistic processes, or neither) has been debated. There is also debate about the extent to which evolutionary altruistic or psychological altruistic processes influence, or are influenced by, an individual's personality characteristics. Some research shows that people scoring high on personality measures that assess altruism-relevant characteristics (e.g., perspective-taking, emotionality, and responsibility for others' welfare) are more likely to help

than people scoring low on these measures. Again, it is unclear whether such behavior reflects evolutionary altruistic processes, psychological altruistic processes, or neither. Future research will almost certainly address, and hopefully answer, these and other questions about the existence of altruism in humans.

SEE ALSO *Altruism and Prosocial Behavior; Empathy; Evolutionary Psychology; Sociobiology*

BIBLIOGRAPHY

Batson, C. Daniel, and Laura L. Shaw. 1991. Evidence for Altruism: Toward a Pluralism of Prosocial Motives. *Psychological Inquiry* 2 (2): 107–122.

Sober, Elliot, and David Sloan Wilson. 1998. *Unto Others: The Evolution and Psychology of Unselfish Behavior*. Cambridge, MA: Harvard University Press.

David A. Lishner
E. L. Stocks

ALTRUISM AND PROSOCIAL BEHAVIOR

Social scientists use the word *altruism* to describe two distinct phenomena—*motivation* and *prosocial behavior*. Although it is more common to describe altruism as a motivational state with the goal of increasing another's welfare, some researchers, especially within the field of sociobiology, use the term as a synonym for *prosocial behavior*, which refers to any behavior that benefits someone other than oneself, regardless of the motivation involved. The factors that predict when, and for whom, prosocial behavior will occur can be divided into three categories—dispositional, situational, and evolutionary.

Dispositional factors are personal characteristics that predispose an individual to engage in prosocial behavior. These include sensitivity to norms of personal and social responsibility, internalization of prosocial values, moral reasoning ability, a tendency to empathize, intelligence, nurturance, religiosity, and self-esteem. Although none of these factors alone predicts prosocial behavior well, a combination of empathic tendencies, moral reasoning ability, and sensitivity to norms of personal and social responsibility constitute what some have called an *altruistic personality*. A person may also be prone to engage in prosocial behavior as a consequence of social learning. Those who have received (or observed others receive) rewards for helping, or punishments for not helping, are more likely to help than are those who have not.

Situational factors are stimuli in an individual's environment that promote prosocial behavior. There are many situational factors that affect prosocial behavior, but only a few have received detailed scientific attention. Among these is the presence of bystanders. In an emergency situation, as the number of bystanders increases diffusion of responsibility for helping also increases, which, in turn, reduces the likelihood of prosocial behavior. Another factor is the presence of prosocial norms, which are written and unwritten rules of behavior that communicate when, how, and for the benefit of whom help is to be provided. If a situation promotes attention to prosocial norms, then prosocial behavior is more likely to occur. Information about the cause of a victim's need also affects prosocial behavior such that those viewed as not responsible for their need are more likely to be helped. Factors that increase positive mood and feelings of empathy promote prosocial behavior, as do situations that promote negative mood or personal distress, but only if prosocial behavior is perceived as rewarding or if escape from such feelings is possible only through helping.

Evolutionary factors are those that promote prosocial behavior as a consequence of natural selection. According to sociobiologists, individuals are predisposed to benefit those who are likely to share or promote their own genes. *Kin selection* suggests that people are more likely to benefit genetically related individuals because helping kin can promote the survival and reproduction of one's own genes in future generations. Similarly, *reciprocal altruism* suggests that people will help those who are likely to help them back because doing so increases the likelihood that one's own genes will be protected or promoted when in need at a later date. Research also suggests that younger individuals are more likely to receive aid (suggesting an evolved sensitivity to those displaying characteristics typical of offspring) unless essential resources are scarce, in which case only those capable of reproduction are likely to be helped.

SEE ALSO *Altruism; Empathy; Evolutionary Psychology; Mood; Norms; Reciprocity, Norm of*

BIBLIOGRAPHY

Batson, C. Daniel. 1998. Altruism and Prosocial Behavior. In *The Handbook of Social Psychology*, ed. Daniel T. Gilbert, Susan T. Fiske, and Gardner Lindzey, 4th ed., 282–316. Boston: McGraw-Hill.

Dawkins, Richard. 1976. *The Selfish Gene*. New York: Oxford University Press.

Latané, Bib, and John M. Darley. 1970. *The Unresponsive Bystander: Why Doesn't He Help?* New York: Appleton-Century Crofts.

E. L. Stocks
David A. Lishner

ALZHEIMER'S DISEASE

Alzheimer's disease (AD) constitutes about two-thirds of all dementia cases. Dementia is defined as cognitive impairment of sufficient severity to interfere with daily functioning. AD currently affects twelve million people worldwide, including over four million in the United States. These numbers could triple by 2050 due to increasing life expectancies. The prevalence of AD is approximately 1 percent among those under 70 years and increases with age to about 40 percent in those 85 years and older. It is the fourth-leading cause of death in the United States among persons older than 65 years. The term *senility* was used in the past to indicate severe age-related cognitive changes. It is now recognized that subtle cognitive changes do occur with aging, but very marked changes are unexpected unless there is an underlying disease process. The recognition of AD as a disease syndrome has transformed cognitive impairment from an expected stage of life to a medical problem, prompting public concern, new policies, and advocacy.

AD is characterized by a subtle onset and gradual decline. The most prominent early symptom is memory impairment, particularly the ability to remember recent events or names of familiar people or objects. This is accompanied by other, initially subtle, cognitive deficits, such as impaired verbal, spatial, or problem-solving skills. Other symptoms may include disorientation, increased irritability, mood lability, depression, anxiety, and sleep disturbance. Delusions are common, as are behavior problems (e.g., aggression, wandering, disregard for normative social conduct). As the disease progresses, basic activities of daily living, such as eating and dressing, become impaired. Late-stage AD is marked by the loss of recognizable speech and the inability to control bodily functions, leaving patients completely dependent on caregivers. Death occurs approximately eight to ten years after diagnosis (range three to twenty years).

The causes of AD are currently not fully understood. The most evident brain abnormalities are neuritic plaques (clumps of beta amyloid protein) and neurofibrillary tangles (Tau protein strands). Soluble forms of these abnormalities may be toxic to the brain. There is also a deficiency in the neurotransmitter acetylcholine, clogging of the NMDA-glutamate receptor, and considerable brain atrophy (shrinkage).

AD can be familial (inherited) or sporadic. Familial AD is rare and begins earlier in life (age 30 to 60 years). There are at least three genes that can cause familial AD: presenilin 1, presenilin 2, or the amyloid precursor protein gene. Sporadic AD typically occurs after age 65 and accounts for 90 percent of all AD cases. The primary risk factor for sporadic AD is age. Others include a family history of AD, carrying the E4 allele (variant) of the apolipoprotein E (ApoE) gene, being female, Down syndrome, head injury, a prolonged loss of consciousness, diabetes, and cardiovascular disease. Compared to Americans of European descent, African and Hispanic Americans are at greater risk for AD, whereas Asians and Native Americans are at lower risk. It is unclear whether these differences are due to genetic heritage, health, or social or cultural differences between ethnic groups. Protective factors include higher occupational attainment, education, literacy, physical exercise, and engagement in socially and intellectually stimulating leisure activities.

Current drug treatments of AD consist of cholinesterase inhibitors, which increase the neurotransmitter acetylcholine, and NMDA receptor antagonists, which block glutamate from activating NMDA receptors. There is some evidence that antioxidants (vitamins E), anti-inflammatory agents (ibuprofen, aspirin), and estrogen may slow the progression of AD. All current treatments are symptomatic and only marginally helpful. There is weak support for the effectiveness of cognitive interventions in improving cognitive and emotional health during early AD.

The burden of AD is enormous, both to society and to individual caregivers, who suffer from financial and emotional distress. Lack of effective treatment, high health care costs, and increasing numbers of patients make AD one of the most challenging medical conditions.

SEE ALSO *Dementia; Disease; Medicine; Mental Health; Mental Illness*

BIBLIOGRAPHY

Emilien, Gérard, Durlach, Cécile, Minaker, Kenneth L., et al., eds. 2004. *Alzheimer Disease: Neuropsychology and Neuropharmacology*. Basel, Switzerland: Birkhäuser Verlag.

Whitehouse, Peter J., Maurer, Konrad, and Ballenger, Jesse F., eds. 2000. *Concepts of Alzheimer Disease: Biological, Clinical, and Cultural Perspectives*. Baltimore, MD: Johns Hopkins University Press.

Anja Soldan
Yaakov Stern

AMBEDKAR, B. R.
1891–1956

Bhimrao Ramji Ambedkar contributed to the development of the Indian nation during the formative stages of its history in the first half of the twentieth century. Ambedkar was born into a low-caste untouchable family in Maharashtra state in western India. Because his father had been in the military service through a limited opening given by the British during the middle of the nineteenth century, young Bhimrao gained access to an education at a time when the majority of untouchables were excluded from education. He graduated in 1912 and later earned MA and PhD degrees from Columbia University in New York City and a degree in law and DSc from the University of London. His studies were facilitated by fellowships awarded in 1913 by the philanthropic king of India's Baroda state.

Untouchables in India traditionally hold a low position in Hindu social order based on the caste system, which denies basic human rights to them. They are considered polluting and suffer from social and physical segregation. Ambedkar himself faced discrimination in various stages of life as a student, as a government servant and lecturer, as a lawyer, and occasionally even when he occupied high positions of power as a minister and on other occasions in his public life.

CIVIL RIGHTS ACTIVIST AND POLITICAL LEADER

India gained independence from British colonial rule in 1947 and adopted its own constitution in 1950. Ambedkar was at the forefront of Indian politics as a scholar, a civil rights activist, and a political leader from 1920 until 1956. His nation-building contributions were multiple, and included writing books and memoranda on a number of issues of national importance and serving as a chief framer of the Indian constitution and as a policymaker. Above all, he was a leader of the excluded group of untouchables.

Ambedkar began his civil rights campaigns against caste discrimination and untouchability in the 1920s, mobilizing untouchables for access to public water tanks in the town of Mahad and entry into temples in the cities of Amravati and Nasik. With these struggles and the symbolic burning of the Manusmriti (a traditional Brahmanic law book) in 1927, the movement spread to the countryside. In the 1930s, struggles of workers and tenants against landlords were organized.

From 1930 onward, the focus shifted to seeking adequate representation for low-caste untouchables in the legislature, public employment, and in educational institutions, as well as to seeking general economic empowerment. Ambedkar published weekly papers, created associations, and established political parties. His first organization was the Bahishkarit Hitkarni Sabha (Association for the Welfare of the Ostracized), founded in 1924. In 1936 he created the Independent Labor Party, which was renamed the Scheduled Caste Federation in 1942, and converted finally into the Republican Party of India in 1956. Ambedkar also set up a Peoples' Education Society in 1946 beginning with a college in Bombay, and he organized the Indian Buddhist Council to help spread Buddhism.

SOCIAL ANALYST AND POLICYMAKER

Ambedkar was a scholar as well as a man of action. His aim was to use insights from various studies on Indian history and society to restructure Indian society on the principles of equality, liberty, and fraternity. He had differences both with contemporaries like Mahatma Gandhi (1869–1948) and with India's leftists. In Ambedkar's view, the problem of the untouchables was rooted in the caste system, which was based on the principle of inequality, isolation, and exclusion, with an ideological support from Brahmanic-Hindu religious philosophy. Gandhi, in contrast, believed that the institution of untouchability had no base in Hinduism and treated it as an aberration. The leftists, on the other hand, believed that the caste system had economic foundation and could be resolved through industrialization and a move toward socialism. Solutions differed correspondingly. Gandhi emphasized moral solutions and a change of heart among Hindus. Marxists advocated economic equality for the annihilation of caste discrimination. Ambedkar, however, favored dismantling both the religious-ideological and economic foundations of the caste system. At the social-religious level, he argued for the acceptance of the egalitarian Buddhist religious tradition in Indian society. Economically, he favored a strong state, a democratic socialism oriented to rapid economic development, and a system of compensatory affirmative action policy that included "reservations" in legislature, public services and educational institutions to ensure equal access to economic opportunities. As a minister for energy and irrigation under the last British government, Ambedkar played a major role in initiating economic planning in India.

Ambedkar turned toward Buddhism and converted with a large number of followers in 1956. Buddhism, in his view, was a harbinger of economic and social/cultural egalitarianism and political democracy. This perspective on the problems of Indian society had an immense impact on the issue of reform in Hindu society.

Ambedkar also had a profound impact on the development of policies opposing discrimination and facilitating the empowerment of discriminated groups. Because Hindu society is exclusionary and discriminatory in character, it requires policies of social inclusion. The set of measures aimed at ending discrimination and increasing equal opportunity and economic empowerment included equal rights legislation, legal safeguards against discrimination, and affirmative action to ensure fair participation to the discriminated and excluded groups of untouch-

ables. Legal safeguards against discrimination came with the Anti-Untouchability Act of 1955, and affirmative action came with the Reservation Policy for representation in legislatures, educational institutions, and public jobs, measures that were instituted in 1935 and were finally incorporated into the constitution of India in 1950. In support of economic empowerment, Ambedkar favored a particular type of socialistic economic framework, which in his view would ensure economic equality to poor and marginalized groups. Ambedkar's contribution is, thus, valuable both in social thought and in the shaping of policies against discrimination. As chairman of the drafting committee of the Indian constitution, he helped to create the basic political, economic, and social framework under which Indians live today.

Ambedkar died in 1956, and the Indian state recognized his unique contributions. He was posthumously awarded the country's highest civilian honor, the Bharat Ratna (Jewel of India) on April 14, 1990.

SEE ALSO *Buddhism; Caste; Caste System, The; Dalits; Development; Gandhi, Mohandas K.*

BIBLIOGRAPHY

Ambedkar, B. R. 1979–2003. *Dr. Babasaheb Ambedkar: Writings and Speeches.* 17 vols. Bombay: Department of Education, Government of Maharashtra.

Gore, M. S. 1993. *The Social Context of an Ideology: Ambedkar's Political and Social Thought.* New Delhi: Sage.

Jaffrelot, Christophe. 2005. *Dr. Ambedkar and Untouchability: Fighting the Indian Caste System.* New York: Columbia University Press.

Kadam, K. N., comp. and ed. 1991. *Dr. Babasaheb Ambedkar and the Significance of His Movement: A Chronology.* Bombay: Popular Prakashan.

Keer, Dhananjay. 1962. *Dr. Ambedkar: Life and Mission.* 2nd ed. Bombay: Popular Prakashan.

Kharmode, C. D. 1952–1994. *Dr. Bhimrao Ramji Ambedkar: A Biography.* 13 vols. Bombay: Maharashtra State Department of Language Art and Culture. In the Marathi language.

Omvedt, Gail. 1994. *Dalits and the Democratic Revolution: Dr. Ambedkar and the Dalit Movement in Colonial India.* New Delhi and Thousand Oaks, CA: Sage.

Omvedt, Gail. 2004. *Ambedkar: Towards an Enlightened India.* New Delhi: Penguin.

Thorat, Sukhadeo. 1997. Ambedkar and the Economic of Hindu Social Order: Understanding Its Orthodoxy and Legacy. In *The Emerging Dalit Identity: The Re-assertion of the Subalterns,* ed. Walter Fernandes, 120–129. New Delhi: Indian Social Institute.

Thorat, Sukhadeo. 1998. *Ambedkar's Role in Economic Planning and Water Policy.* Delhi: Shipra.

Thorat, Sukhadeo. 1999. Ambedkar and Nation Building: Reflection on Selected Themes. In *Nation Building in India:*

Culture, Power, and Society, ed. Anand Kumar, 257–294. New Delhi: Radiant.

Zelliot, Eleanor. 1992. *From Untouchable to Dalit: Essays on Ambedkar Movement.* New Delhi: Manohar.

Sukhadeo Thorat

AMBIGUITY AVERSION

SEE *Non-expected Utility Theory.*

AMERICAN ANTHROPOLOGICAL ASSOCIATION

The establishment of the American Anthropological Association (AAA) in 1902 was the culmination of a gradual process of professionalization in American anthropology that revealed subdisciplinary, regional, and theoretical tensions within the emerging discipline. The first anthropological society in the United States was the American Ethnological Society, founded in New York by Albert Gallatin (1761–1849) in 1842 and revived by Franz Boas (1858–1942) in the 1890s to balance the Washington-based Bureau of American Ethnology's potential stranglehold that threatened to dominate anthropology on a national scale. Section H of the American Association for the Advancement of Science, established in 1882, already provided annual meetings for anthropologists but not visibility among the social science disciplines or discrete professional identity.

Abortive efforts to establish a separate organization in 1897 floundered over Washington hegemony, with the compromise being a new series of the Bureau of American Ethnology–based journal *American Anthropologist* co-organized by W. J. McGee (1853–1912) of the bureau and Boas in New York. The diverse editorial board reinforced the revamped journal's claim to national representation and self-consciously built toward a formal professional organization in the near future. Boas wanted to wait until he had trained more professional anthropologists and solidified his organizational control over the discipline.

The American Anthropological Association that was established in 1902 compromised between Boas's insistence on professional gatekeeping and McGee's populism, a contrast reflecting their respective institutional frameworks of university and government. The Washington contingent, backed by Frederick Ward Putnam's (1839–1915) archaeological bailiwick at Harvard's Peabody Museum of American Archaeology and Ethnology, supported evolutionary theory in the mode of Lewis Henry Morgan (1818–1881), whereas Boas critiqued this paradigm in favor of historical particularism.

Boas succeeded in restricting the organizational meeting to forty carefully chosen professionals, but McGee ensured that any interested person could join. The AAA began with 175 members, including sixteen women, incorporating members of the Anthropological Society of Washington. McGee became the first president, but his successors were carefully chosen to represent alternative regional and local components of the national membership. Boas served as the third president of the AAA in 1907 to 1908, succeeding Putnam, who had long been the permanent secretary of the American Association for the Advancement of Science. When the inclusive structure rapidly proved unwieldy, the establishment of an executive council further enshrined Boas's aspirations to professionalism by limiting decision-making power to the established elite, increasingly under his patronage.

World War I (1914–1918) polarized the hyperpatriotism and racialism of the National Research Council against Boasian autonomy of science on both ethical and intellectual grounds. Boas was German and a pacifist about the war, a critic of eugenics, and ambivalent about collaboration between universities and museums. Archaeology and physical anthropology were left tacitly to Putnam at Harvard. In 1919, after the war had officially ended, Boas accused unnamed anthropological colleagues working in Mexico, representing his still powerful long-term nemeses in the Cambridge/Washington axis, of spying under cover of research. In the resulting furor, Boas was removed as anthropology's representative to the National Research Council, censured by his own professional association, and removed from its council. Despite the apparent defeat, however, this was the last time that anti-Boasian forces would challenge successfully his organizational leadership, commitment to professional credentials, and effective critique of evolution, or that the institutional core of American anthropology would be academic. Thereafter, Boas's former students and protégés edited the *American Anthropologist*, represented the AAA on the three research councils, and headed the growing number of university programs credentialing new anthropologists. The discipline and the AAA grew incrementally during the interwar years under this balanced structure.

During World War II (1939–1945), many anthropologists entered government service. At the war's end, the discipline was poised for exponential growth. The 1945 annual meeting narrowly averted schism led by archaeologists and younger anthropologists. During the annual meeting of 1946, concurrent sessions were held for the first time. The 1946 AAA meeting introduced a distinction between members and fellows that persisted until the 1970s. The new structure maintained the inclusive subdisciplinary scope of cultural, physical, archaeological, and linguistic specialization (although the three latter also participated in independent associations). This structure was intended to render anthropology competitive among the social sciences. An AAA Research Committee was established to seek philanthropic support for anthropology in the transition to government funding and beyond. Increasingly, the competition would be interdisciplinary, seeking a place for anthropology among the social science disciplines.

The political upheavals of the 1960s initiated centrifugal as well as further numerical expansion in American anthropology. By the 1970s, the academic job market had contracted and many fledgling anthropologists found themselves working outside the ivory tower. Practicing anthropology emerged as the fifth subdiscipline in the AAA structure to accommodate this growing diversity within its membership. Increasingly, the most salient internal schism was a generational conflict between activism and objective science. Many anthropologists on both sides considered these mutually exclusive.

Under the presidency of Anthony F. C. Wallace in 1972, the AAA began its restructuring to mitigate the increasing size and cumbersomeness of the organization and to incorporate its ever more diverse versions of anthropology by establishing specialized sections, while retaining the overall organization as an umbrella. As the powerful university-based old guard was challenged by younger and more radical critics, the AAA strove to legitimize both the activists and the scientists within its membership. A new constitution in 1983 formalized this structure, producing over thirty sections and numerous interest groups and committees by the mid-1990s. Sociocultural anthropology dominated, as it had throughout the history of the AAA, but the other subdisciplines retained their affiliation with the umbrella organization.

Centripetal forces perhaps have come to the forefront again with the decision that AAA membership includes subscriptions to the *American Anthropologist* as well as section publications. Many AAA members belong to multiple sections and value this acknowledgement of the diversity within their profession. The organization is active in seeking a public voice for anthropology and anthropologists and in maintaining internal dialogue among anthropologists of diverse persuasions.

SEE ALSO *Anthropology; Anthropology, Public; Anthropology, U.S.*

BIBLIOGRAPHY

Darnell, Regna. 1998. *And Along Came Boas: Continuity and Revolution in Americanist Anthropology.* Amsterdam and Philadelphia: John Benjamins.

Darnell, Regna, and Frederic W. Gleach, eds. 2002. *Celebrating a Century of the American Anthropological Association: Presidential Portraits.* Washington, DC: American Anthropological Association; Lincoln: University of Nebraska Press.

Stocking, George W., Jr. 1992. *The Ethnographer's Magic and Other Essays in the History of Anthropology.* Madison: University of Wisconsin Press.

Stocking, George W., Jr. 2001. *Delimiting Anthropology: Occasional Essays and Reflections.* Madison: University of Wisconsin Press.

Regna Darnell

AMERICAN ASSOCIATION ON MENTAL RETARDATION

SEE *Mental Retardation.*

AMERICAN CIVIL LIBERTIES UNION

SEE *Public Interest Advocacy.*

AMERICAN CREED

SEE *American Dilemma; Myrdal, Gunnar.*

AMERICAN DILEMMA

Published in 1944, amid the massive destruction and racial genocide of World War II (1939–1945), *An American Dilemma: The Negro Problem and Modern Democracy,* by the Swedish economist and sociologist Gunnar Myrdal (1898–1987), not only challenged America's democratic principles but also offered firm testament to their promise. Myrdal's epic study has framed racial discourse for more than half a century. Consistent with the times, Myrdal's research team included some of the leading black intellectuals of the era—Ralph Bunche (1904–1971), Kenneth Clark (1914–2005), E. Franklin Frazier (1894–1962), Charles S. Johnson (1893–1956), and Ira Reid (1901–1968)—who were forced by custom and discrimination to work as his racial, if not intellectual, subordinates.

Myrdal saw the American race problem as a moral dilemma, concluding that legal segregation and the racial caste system were inconsistent with the American creed and its commitment to freedom, equality, and democracy. For Myrdal, one solution was located in the American system of education. Education represented a vehicle for combating racist beliefs as well as a way to improve black people's material conditions. Increased educational opportunities for blacks, and improved education about race for whites, he argued, represented an important step toward reducing racial prejudice, ending segregation, improving black economic development, and ultimately solving the puzzle of race in America.

THE AMERICAN DILEMMA AND ECONOMICS

In *American Dilemma*, Myrdal rightly described the economic situation and prospects of black Americans at the close of the Second World War as dark. His work highlighted four barriers to black employment prevalent at the time, namely: (1) exclusion of blacks from certain industries; (2) limited mobility or segregation within industries in which they were accepted; (3) relegation to unskilled or undesirable occupations; and (4) geographical segregation, which resulted in little to no black labor in the small cities of the North and a surplus in large northern cities. Myrdal identified race prejudice as a chief explanation of these barriers, citing three ways in which prejudice operated in the economic sphere: (1) the tendency for even well meaning whites with egalitarian values to resist competition from blacks in their own industries or unions; (2) objections by white customers opposed to being served by blacks in nonmenial positions; and (3) the belief among many white employers that blacks were simply inferior for most kinds of work.

Myrdal described the conditions of economic discrimination against blacks as self-perpetuating, arguing, "the very fact that there is economic discrimination constitutes an added motive for every individual white group to maintain such discriminatory practices" (Myrdal 1944, p. 381). His argument hinged on what he referred to as two mutually reinforcing variables, "white prejudice" and blacks' "low plane of living," which he believed to interact in a "vicious cycle," a situation in which a negative factor is both cause and effect of one or more other negative factors. As he described the cycle, "on the one hand, the negroes' plane of living is kept down by discrimination from the side of the whites while, on the other hand, the white's reason for discrimination is partly dependant on the negroes' plane of living" (Myrdal 1944, p. 1066). In other words, blacks' opportunities to transcend their rela-

tively low standard of living were limited or cut off by white discrimination, while at the same time the low standard of living imposed on black Americans led to a host of negative outcomes such as poverty, low levels of education, and health problems, which whites pointed to as justification for continued discrimination.

This cycle is further explained through Myrdal's use of the theory of cumulative causation. According to Myrdal, each of the attributes described above (poverty, education, health, and white prejudice against blacks), along with a host of others, is itself in a relationship of cumulative causation with all of the other attributes. For example, if an individual is denied access to education necessary to attain employment, he or she will be unable to find work in a skilled field. With only the least skilled and lowest-paid jobs available, he or she will be forced into what may be physically demanding work for little pay. The resulting physical and mental stress and poverty is likely to lead to high levels of anxiety, a poor diet, and inadequate health care, all of which can be devastating for his or her health. Frequent illness may result in an inability to hold down even the most menial of jobs, which in turn only worsens the poverty of the individual. A person in such a state may appear to be incapable of benefiting from an education, and thus educational opportunity will continue to be denied.

In Myrdal's assessment, given the interconnected relationship among these attributes and between blacks' standard of living and white prejudice and discrimination against blacks, the welfare of individual black people and of blacks in the United States was at best in a state of unstable equilibrium. The slightest change—an increase in white prejudice, a decrease in the availability of educational opportunities, loss of employment opportunities, or the onset of an illness—could send all of these attributes spiraling downward in a vicious cycle. Despite the tendency for changes in any one of these attributes to result in a vicious cycle, Myrdal suggested that the unstable equilibrium that characterized blacks' lives, though mostly negative, offered hope for reducing white prejudice and raising black Americans' plane of living. For if any of the attributes of a black person's life were to improve, the other attributes would be expected to improve as well, and white prejudice would more than likely decrease as its justification vanished.

To this end, Myrdal proposed a campaign aimed at educating whites about their own prejudices and at attacking prejudice and discrimination everywhere they were found. In his words, "the objective of an educational campaign is to minimize prejudice—or, at least, to bring the conflict between prejudice and ideals out into the open and to force the white citizen to take his choice" (Myrdal 1944, pp. 385–386). Myrdal felt that given the choice, most whites, especially in the North, would side with their egalitarian ideals and that "the breakdown of discrimination in one part of the labor market [would facilitate] a similar change in all other parts of it," or in other words, "the vicious cycle [could] be reversed" (p. 385).

THE AMERICAN DILEMMA AND EDUCATION

Myrdal's study highlighted the extreme educational disadvantages of African Americans in 1944. Concentrating on the South, where the overwhelming majority of blacks lived, he outlined the systematic efforts of whites to limit black educational opportunities. Black schools were underfunded, black efforts at educational empowerment were thwarted, and black access to educational opportunity was denied as part of a larger strategy to prevent blacks from challenging white dominance. Myrdal's *An American Dilemma* placed much of the responsibility for solving the problems of blacks on the system of education. He argued that schools are the great levelers in American democracy, providing equal opportunity for all regardless of race, gender, ethnicity, region, or class origins. On the level playing field of fair, open competition, merit would determine who won society's choicest prizes—prestigious jobs, high salaries, fine homes, the good life. As evidenced by the persistent social and economic inequality that continues to dog blacks, Myrdal's ideal notion fails the test of reality even today.

Despite his overly optimistic vision, Myrdal's examination of black educational trends and problems seemed, for the most part, to predict accurately the years following publication of his study. However, the assimilationist political thrust of the study also limited its predictive power in important respects. Myrdal accurately foresaw the formal dissolution of the dual school system in the South. He also predicted the virulent racist reactions of lower-class whites to increased black educational access, as white racial privilege was threatened by the dissolution of segregation. On these points, Myrdal's analysis was particularly insightful and accurate. However, his assimilationist approach to solving America's race problem has not proven sufficient to address the factors that perpetuate racial inequities in education (e.g., residential segregation, unequal funding, inequity in quality of schooling).

In the chapter titled "The Negro Community as a Pathological Form of the American Community," Myrdal argued that the African American community and its culture are essentially "distorted developments" or "pathological conditions" of the general American community and culture. Under this reasoning, the assimilation of white culture is the "final solution" to overcome America's race problem. Education would serve to change African American culture fundamentally (i.e., remove its patho-

logical elements) and eventually bring blacks into the larger American community: "The trend toward a rising educational level of the Negro population is of tremendous importance for the power relations discussed in this Part of our inquiry. Education means an assimilation of white American culture. It decreases the dissimilarity of the Negroes from other Americans" (Myrdal 1944, p. 879). This analysis suggested that blacks and whites must go to school together in order for blacks to assimilate into the larger American culture. Although Myrdal's assimilationist stance saw black institutions and culture slowly disappearing or merging with those of white America, today black education in fact remains a separate and problematic issue. This is primarily due to the intractability of American racial beliefs and to structured racial disadvantage that reinforces the social, economic, and political underdevelopment of the black community.

In his final analysis of the "American Dilemma" (chap. 45), Myrdal envisioned a gradual erosion of the American caste system. While this held true with regard to formal practices and laws, the emergence of a white backlash in the late 1960s and early 1970s, coupled with the persistence of American racial beliefs, betrayed Myrdal's optimistic assimilationist view. Today, the *American Dilemma* is manifested in the continued failure of this society to deliver on its promise of equal opportunity. Despite educational gains made by African Americans since the publication of *An American Dilemma*, disproportionate black economic deprivation persists, as does de facto racial segregation and negative, stereotypic racial beliefs about black people (Brown et al. 2003; Farley and Allen 1989; Feagin 2006; Jaynes and Williams 1989; Kirschenman and Neckerman 1991; Massey and Denton 1993; Schumann et al. 1985). African Americans are disadvantaged in the quantity and quality of education made available to them over their lifespan. At the same time, their hopes for progress in a society that places a premium on educational attainment are thwarted, resulting in the continued subordination of black people in American society (Winfield and Woodard 1994).

As a primarily moral argument for addressing racism, it is on these grounds that Myrdal's work is often criticized. The sociologist Oliver Cox (1901–1974) described Myrdal's *American Dilemma* as a "mystical approach to the study of race relations," citing his repeated references to a common set of American values or the "American creed" (Cox 1959, p. 509). He argued that such an approach to the dilemma of racism in the United States fails to take into account the material interests that sustain racism and "may have the effect of a powerful piece of propaganda in favor of the status quo" (p. 538). Cox put forward that racism was in fact a system designed by the ruling political class to maintain control over the proletariat, of whatever color, by distracting them from the exploitation brought on by upper-class whites and discouraging class unity across color lines.

Describing Myrdal's stance on the solution to the American dilemma, Cox referred to the agenda of reformism, which "never goes so far as to envisage real involvement of the exploitative system with racial antagonism. Its extreme aspiration does not go beyond the attainment of freedom for certain black men to participate in the exploitation of the commonality regardless of the color of the latter" (Cox 1959, p. 535). Myrdal's *American Dilemma* then, as Cox saw it, was at best a useful source of data with no consistent theory of race relations or solution to the problem of racial discrimination. At worst, Myrdal's treatise represented a propaganda piece designed to reinforce class exploitation by framing racism as simply a moral problem.

Myrdal was correct in pointing to an American dilemma; however, he misconstrued this as a moral dilemma. Rather, the dilemma with which America wrestles—and has wrestled for centuries—is how best "to reconcile the practical morality of American capitalism with the ideal morality of the American Creed" (Ellison 1973, p. 83). That is, how can a system that is inherently exploitative be accommodated within the rhetoric of equality? This is a dilemma that goes beyond the black/white issues of Myrdal's time. Recently this dilemma includes how the American educational system has dealt with other nonwhite groups (Stanton-Salazar 2001). Although now far more diverse, the country's racial climate remains in many ways unchanged from the years of Myrdal's research, giving a new urgency to the questions that many felt had been answered by the immense undertaking of *An American Dilemma* and the subsequent period of social change. The challenge before the country now, as was the case in 1944, is "Will America commit to change and to a new, more democratic future or will the country continue to cling to its heritage of racial exploitation and oppression?" (Feagin 2006).

SEE ALSO *Cox, Oliver C.; Cumulative Causation; Myrdal, Gunnar; Mystification; Race Relations; Racism*

BIBLIOGRAPHY

Allen, Walter R., and Joseph O. Jewell. 1995. African American Education Since *An American Dilemma:* An American Dilemma Revisited. *Daedalus* 124 (1): 77–100.

Brown, Michael, et al. 2003. *Whitewashing Race: The Myth of a Color-Blind Society.* Berkeley: University of California Press.

Cox, Oliver C. [1948] 1959. *Caste, Class, & Race: A Study in Social Dynamics.* New York: Monthly Review Press.

Ellison, Ralph. 1973. *An American Dilemma: A Review.* In *The Death of White Sociology,* ed. Joyce A. Ladner, 81–95. New York: Vintage.

Farley, Reynolds, and Walter R. Allen. 1989. *The Color Line and the Quality of Life in America.* New York: Oxford University Press.

Feagin, Joe R. 2006. *Systemic Racism: A Theory of Oppression.* New York: Routledge.

Jaynes, Gerald D., and Robin M. Williams Jr. 1989. *A Common Destiny: Blacks and American Society.* Washington, DC: National Academy Press.

Kirschenman, Joleen, and Kathryn M. Neckerman. 1991. "We'd Love to Hire Them But…": The Meaning of Race for Employers. In *The Urban Underclass,* eds. Christopher Jencks and Paul E. Peterson, 203–234. Washington, DC: Brookings Institution.

Marable, Manning. 2002. *Great Wells of Democracy: The Meaning of Race in American Life.* New York: Basic Books.

Massey, Douglas, and Nancy A. Denton. 1993. *American Apartheid: Segregation and the Making of the Underclass.* Cambridge, MA: Harvard University Press.

Myrdal, Gunnar. 1944. *An American Dilemma: The Negro Problem and Modern Democracy.* 2 vols. New York: Harper.

Schumann, Howard, Charlotte Steeh, and Lawrence Bobo. 1985. *Racial Attitudes in America: Trends and Interpretations.* Cambridge, MA: Harvard University Press.

Stanton-Salazar, Ricardo. 2001. *Manufacturing Hope and Despair: The School and Kin Support Networks of U.S.-Mexican Youth.* New York: Teachers College Press.

Winfield, Linda F., and Michael D. Woodard. 1994. Assessment, Equity, and Diversity in Reforming America's Schools. *Educational Policy* 8 (1): 3–27.

Walter R. Allen
Michael W. Knox
Gerren J. Bennett

AMERICAN DREAM

The term *American Dream* traditionally has meant the ability of all Americans to attain a better standard of living, including owning a home and an automobile, and having access to higher education. The term first appeared in 1932, coined by James Truslow Adams in his book *The Epic of America.* In an indirect sense, it was a reaction to Theodore Dreiser's novel *An American Tragedy* (1925), in which the protagonist is portrayed as bent on bettering his current status in life, regardless of the consequences.

Although the term had not yet been coined, the dream became part and parcel of the national psyche during the 1920s, when consumer goods such as radios, cars, and, most importantly, homes, became readily available. To achieve widespread consumerism, manufactured items came with consumer credit offered on a revolving basis, often by the manufacturers of the goods. During that decade, about two-thirds of the gross national product became attributable to consumer spending; this share has persisted ever since.

The idea was aided immeasurably by political events from the 1930s through the 1970s. The concept of home ownership and mortgage credit was the first part of the dream to be given government assistance, beginning in the 1930s. Using a model first developed during World War I to aid farmers by providing standard mortgages, the Hoover administration, followed by the Roosevelt administration, began extending government intervention to the banks making residential mortgages. During the Great Depression many banks failed, and in order to preserve their assets and stabilize the market for home mortgages, Congress created several agencies dedicated to preserving the market for mortgages, to benefit both homeowners and banks. The Federal Housing Administration and the Federal National Mortgage Administration were created to guarantee home loans to banks, and the result was that mortgages were easier to obtain.

After World War II subsidized mortgages were offered by the Veterans Administration to returning servicemen, extending the concept into the postwar period. In 1957 higher education also benefited from intervention by the government when the Department of Education began offering student loans. As a result of the two programs and the modifications they underwent in the 1970s, homeownership and higher education were within the reach of many people who otherwise might not have been able to access them.

The concept has been extended to other sections of the economy as well, but the presence of government-sponsored enterprises dedicated to supporting residential mortgage loans and higher education loans attests to the enduring quality of the American Dream, both for politicians as well as social commentators. Its essential definition remains unchanged over the years.

SEE ALSO *Americanism*

BIBLIOGRAPHY

Caldor, Lendol. 1999. *Financing the American Dream: A Cultural History of Consumer Credit*. Princeton, NJ: Princeton University Press.

Geisst, Charles R. 1990. *Visionary Capitalism: Financial Markets and the American Dream in the Twentieth Century*. New York: Praeger Publishers.

Rivlin, Alice M. 1992. *Reviving the American Dream: The Economy, the States, and the Federal Government*. Washington, DC: Brookings Institution.

Wright, Esmond. 1996. *The American Dream: From Reconstruction to Reagan*. Cambridge, MA: Blackwell Publishers.

Charles Geisst

AMERICAN ECONOMIC ASSOCIATION

The American Economic Association is the premier organization of professional economists in the world. It was organized in 1885 at a meeting in Saratoga Springs, New York. Richard T. Ely, who was active in founding the association, was its first secretary (an administrative officer) and was later a president of the association. Francis Amasa Walker, then president of the Massachusetts Institute of Technology, was its first president.

The association has three purposes: to encourage economic research, especially historical and statistical studies; to issue publications on economic subjects; and to encourage freedom of economic discussion. Because of a controversy about whether the association would be used for political advocacy that confounded its formation, the association is prohibited by charter from taking a position on practical economic questions. The spirit of these objectives has been maintained throughout the association's history.

The association's initial membership consisted mainly of college and university economics teachers. However, with growing interest in economics in the twentieth century, the association has attracted members from business and professional groups. In 2005 membership was approximately 19,000, including over 5,000 members from beyond North America. About 60 percent of members are associated with academic institutions; 20 percent with business, industry, and consulting; and 15 percent with government and not-for-profit research organizations. More than 4,000 libraries, institutions, and firms subscribed to the publications of the association in 2005.

The association employed about thirty people full-time in 2005, most involved in producing publications and organizing an annual convention. Its headquarters is in Nashville, Tennessee, and its publications office is in Pittsburgh, Pennsylvania.

Members annually receive thirteen issues of three journals: the *American Economic Review*, the *Journal of Economic Literature*, and the *Journal of Economic Perspectives*. The *American Economic Review* publishes about 100 articles a year on various economic topics chosen from among 1,200 submissions on the basis of double-blind peer review (neither author nor reviewer know the other's identity). The *Journal of Economic Literature* annually publishes about 20 comprehensive interpretive essays on topics that synthesize the relevant literature, and about 150 reviews of recently published books on economics. The *Journal of Economic Perspectives* publishes about 50 articles a year that explain current research on topics in theoretical and empirical economics or analyze public-policy issues. Articles in the *Journal of Economic Perspectives* are written to be accessible to an audience of nonspecialists. Articles in the *Journal of Economic Literature* and the *Journal of Economic Perspectives* are commissioned by the editors. The association also produces a searchable bibliography, *EconLit*, of the economic literature.

The association organizes an annual three-day conference of economists each January. About 8,000 people attend. About 1,500 research papers are presented, many of which are subsequently published in scholarly journals. The association publishes a monthly listing of job openings for economists and awards its Clark Medal biannually to the economist under age forty who has made the most important contributions to economic research. It also annually names three distinguished fellows and runs a summer program to help prepare students from underrepresented groups for PhD study in economics.

SEE ALSO *Economic Commission for Latin America and the Caribbean; Economics; National Economic Association (NEA)*

BIBLIOGRAPHY

Coats, A. W. 1985. The American Economic Association and the Economics Profession. *Journal of Economic Literature* 23 (4): 1697–1727.

Siegfried, John J. 1998. Who Is a Member of the AEA? *Journal of Economic Perspectives* 12 (2): 211–222.

Siegfried, John J. 2002. The Economics of Regional Economics Associations. *Quarterly Review of Economics and Finance* 42 (1): 1–17.

John J. Siegfried

AMERICAN ENTERPRISE INSTITUTE

SEE *Neoconservatism.*

AMERICAN INDIAN MOVEMENT

From first contact, American Indians have striven to be treated with the respect due members of sovereign and culturally distinct nations. Governmental policy toward American Indians has shifted over the centuries from overt attempts at genocide to removal and assimilation to respect for sovereignty. By the 1950s, policy preferences were clearly in favor of acculturation and assimilation. Government boarding schools sought to help turn American Indian children into "cultural soldiers," whose mission was to help destroy indigenous cultures from within. The national government also began to combine policies of *relocation*, moving Indians off of their reservations and into urban environments, promising help with housing and employment (promises that were more often broken than kept), and *termination*, ending official recognition of tribal status.

This combination of policies—boarding schools, relocation, and the threat of termination—led to the creation of Indian ghettos in major cities, increased incidence of social problems such as alcoholism and drug addiction, and an increased awareness of the threat to Indian resident cultures and homelands. Thus, these policies also facilitated an increasing sense among peoples of diverse tribes of both a common cause and a common enemy. That realization helped forge a common identity. American Indians did not cease thinking of themselves as members of distinct tribal communities, but many of them began to also consider themselves part of a larger whole: as "Indian" as well as Kiowa or Chickasaw.

As American Indians found themselves uprooted from their land and their cultures and facing poverty, disease, overt racism, police brutality, and other forms of discrimination, their anger at these conditions began to build. They looked to the successes of the burgeoning civil rights movement, and they too began to organize.

In 1960 Vine Deloria Jr., Clyde Warrior, Mel Thom, Shirley Witt, and Herb Blatchford formed the National Indian Youth Council, an organization explicitly based on traditional American Indian values and specifically dedicated to furthering the interests of American Indian peoples. By 1964 American Indians in the Northwest began to defend their legal and historic treaty rights through "fish-ins," events that often led to confrontations with local citizens, governments, and police forces. Finally, in 1968, Vernon Bellecourt, his brother Clyde, and Dennis Banks incorporated the American Indian Movement (AIM) in Minneapolis, Minnesota. AIM was explicitly founded to protect local Indians from police brutality and other forms of discrimination. It soon became national, and its purpose expanded as well.

In November 1969 a group calling itself Indians of All Tribes claimed Alcatraz Island in San Francisco Bay "by right of discovery" and remained there in defiance of the federal government for nineteen months. The occupation of Alcatraz began a series of occupations of other government properties, as well as protests led by AIM leaders Dennis Banks and Russell Means at Mount Rushmore and, on Thanksgiving Day in 1970, at Plymouth Rock. Such protests signaled the beginning of increased media attention to what was styled "Indian militancy" or the "Red Power Movement."

These protests in turn indicated the peculiar situation of American Indian activists: changing governmental policies depended, in large part, on mobilizing public sympathy, which depended on gaining public attention. That depended on keeping the attention of the media, which often also meant staging public events and maintaining public images that relied upon the prevalent stereotypes of Indian peoples—the same stereotypes activists believed contributed to the very policies they were trying to change. And in trying to change governmental policies, they were up against a powerful array of social, bureaucratic, and economic forces.

To combat these forces, AIM organized a series of caravans in 1973 that would travel the nation by separate routes, meeting in Washington, D.C., called the Trail of Broken Treaties. The caravans arrived in Washington on November 3, 1973, with a list of Twenty Points that the activists hoped to bring to the attention of the federal government. The Twenty Points included demands that the government recognize the sovereign status of Indian nations, reestablish treaty relations, and allow an Indian voice in the formation of policies regarding Indian interests.

When housing arrangements turned out to be unsuitable, the protestors converged on the Bureau of Indian Affairs (BIA) seeking assistance. They were turned away. Some of the protestors refused to leave, and ended up taking over the building, which they held for a week. The Trail of Broken Treaties, like the Alcatraz occupation, signaled the extent of the tension between the Indians, especially AIM, and the federal government. That tension escalated as many of the AIM Indians left Washington and headed for the Lakota Sioux reservation at Pine Ridge, South Dakota. Pine Ridge had long been sharply divided between those Indians favoring assimilation and accommodation with the national government and those favoring traditional Indian ways. The tribal chair, Richard Wilson, was solidly in the assimilationist camp, and was seen by the traditionalists as unfair and often violent in his treatment of them.

On February 27, 1973, a caravan of some three hundred Indians left Pine Ridge and headed for Wounded Knee, the site of a famous massacre in 1890. They occupied the small village there, and the government responded with an unprecedented show of force. The standoff continued for seventy-three days, comprised hours of negotiations, and led to the deaths of two Indians. Both sides considered it a moral victory, but little changed.

After Wounded Knee, the government began to escalate its actions against AIM and its leaders. Through arrests, court battles, and the operations of its COINTELPRO (counterintelligence program), which was designed to infiltrate and destroy activist organizations from within, the federal government sought to bankrupt, distract, and eliminate AIM.

The final confrontation between AIM and the federal government was also the most tragic: on June 25, 1975, FBI agents claiming to be in hot pursuit of a suspect ventured into an AIM compound on the Pine Ridge reservation. A firefight broke out, and in the melee one Indian and the two agents were killed. The rest of the Indians fled. Two (Bob Robideaux and Dino Butler) were later apprehended and tried in Cedar Rapids, Iowa, for the murder of the federal agents. An all-white jury found them not guilty. Later, a third Indian, Leonard Peltier, was also tried for the murders, was convicted, and has been in prison since 1976.

The trial of Leonard Peltier marked the end of the period of Indian activism, although not the end of AIM. AIM leaders remained active, albeit in a smaller way. Many of them have been in movies, such as Michael Apted's *Thunderheart* (1992) and *Incident at Oglala* (1992) and the animated film *Pocahontas* (1995). Banks, Means, and Peltier have authored autobiographies. John Trudell, the voice of Radio Free Alcatraz, is the subject of a 2006 documentary. AIM continues to agitate, in less dramatic ways, for treaty rights, against Indian mascots, and on other issues of concern.

SEE ALSO *Activism; Civil Disobedience; Civil Rights; Native Americans; Protest; Trail of Tears; Tribalism; Tribes*

BIBLIOGRAPHY

Cornell, Stephen. 1988. *The Return of the Native: American Indian Political Resurgence.* New York: Oxford University Press.

Deloria, Vine, Jr. 1974. *Behind the Trail of Broken Treaties: An Indian Declaration of Independence.* New York: Delacorte.

Johnson, Troy, Joane Nagel, and Duane Champagne. 1997. *American Indian Activism: Alcatraz to the Longest Walk.* Urbana: University of Illinois Press.

Matthiessen, Peter. 1991. *In the Spirit of Crazy Horse.* New York: Viking.

Stern, Kenneth. 1994. *Loud Hawk: The United States versus the American Indian Movement.* Norman: Oklahoma University Press.

Mary E. Stuckey

AMERICAN INDIANS

SEE *Native Americans.*

AMERICAN NATIONAL ELECTION STUDIES (ANES)

The American National Election Studies (ANES) is a well-known, widely used, and broadly collaborative scientific study of elections. It focuses its efforts on providing high-quality data about voting, turnout, and participation to a wide range of social scientists. ANES data has served as the basis for hundreds of books and thousand of articles. Around the world, researchers, students, government agencies, and interested members of the public use ANES data to gain a deeper understanding of citizens and elections in the United States.

Angus Campbell, Philip E. Converse, Warren Miller, and Donald Stokes started the project in 1948. From 1952 to 1977 it was called the Michigan Election Studies and was run by the Center for Political Studies and the Survey Research Center of the Institute for Social Research at the University of Michigan. The founders introduced many valuable methodological and procedural innovations, and their book *The American Voter* is a focal reference in the study of American politics. In 1977, following an agreement with the National Science Foundation, the study was renamed the National Election Studies and has received its primary funding from the National Science Foundation ever since. This agreement stabilized the project's funding and instituted procedures to increase the number of political scientists who contributed to the design of ANES data collections.

Throughout its history, the focal activity of ANES has been the production of a comprehensive national survey taken before and after every major election. Collectively, these studies are known as the ANES Time Series. ANES Time Series surveys are carried out via face-to-face interviews conducted in people's homes. The combination of high response rate and carefully worded questions results in data that deeply and uniquely reflect voter perceptions and attitudes. Each survey includes many questions, including some questions that appear repeatedly over time. Such attributes allow researchers to test a wide range of hypotheses about citizen attitudes and perceptions.

In 2005 the National Science Foundation agreed to fund a substantial expansion of the project. The University of Michigan, Stanford University, and other universities are using this opportunity to give the project a new interdisciplinary emphasis. While the project's mandate continues to be providing survey-based resources for studying voting, turnout, and participation, it is now led by a team of scholars from across the social sciences. The new ANES also features a more transparent governance and consultation structure, including the ANES Online Commons, which allows scholars to make, amend, view, and review proposals for future data collections as they are being developed. New data-collection activities include a twenty-one-month panel study. This panel interviews the same people multiple times, with the interviews starting well before the onset of presidential primary elections and ending well after the election. This strategy allows original and deeper testing of hypotheses about how and when citizens make decisions about presidential candidates and how actions taken during the election year affect public views of the new president, and hence the president's ability to pursue new policies, in the initial months of the new president's term.

SEE ALSO *Elections; Electoral Systems; Political Science; Politics; Research, Survey; Survey*

BIBLIOGRAPHY

American National Election Studies Web site. http://www.electionstudies.org.

Campbell, Angus, Philip E. Converse, Warren E. Miller, and Donald Stokes. 1960. *The American Voter.* New York: John Wiley.

Arthur Lupia

AMERICAN NATIONAL ELECTION SURVEY

SEE *American National Election Studies (ANES).*

AMERICAN POLITICAL SCIENCE ASSOCIATION

The American Political Science Association (APSA) is a professional association of scholars from all over the world dedicated to the study of politics in all of its dimensions. The association was established in 1903 at Tulane University in New Orleans, Louisiana, and celebrated its one hundredth anniversary in Philadelphia in 2003. The one hundredth anniversary of the association's annual convention was held in Chicago in 2004. Originally, the association was formed to distinguish a "science of politics" from the study of history and economics. In the early years, however, close cooperation with the American Historical and American Economic Associations was encouraged. The primary purpose of a separate association for political science was to "encourage" the "scientific study of politics, public law, administration and diplomacy" (Willoughby 1904, p. 109). In 2007, the association consisted of more than 15,000 members from more than eighty countries. The objectives of the association are to promote research in the discipline of political science, to nurture quality teaching regarding the principles of good government and citizenship, to encourage diversification within the discipline, to provide challenging opportunities to members, to recognize outstanding contributions to the study of politics through awards programs, to develop and maintain high professional standards among scholars in the discipline, and to serve the public through the widespread dissemination of research findings.

The association is governed by a twenty-six-person council headed by a president. All members of the council and the president are elected by ballot by members of the association. A number of distinguished scholars have served as president of the APSA, including Woodrow Wilson, Charles E. Merriam, Charles A. Beard, Harold D. Lasswell, V. O. Key Jr., Carl J. Friedrich, Gabriel A. Almond, Robert Dahl, David Easton, Heinz Eulau, Samuel P. Huntington, Theodore J. Lowi, and Judith N. Shklar, the APSA's first woman president. Ralph J. Bunche, in addition to winning the Nobel Peace Prize in 1950, became the first African American president of the APSA in 1953. With few exceptions, the addresses of presidents, a highlight at the national convention each year, are available at the APSA Web site. These addresses examine major issues and trends in the discipline and allow students of politics at all levels to gauge the perspectives and concerns of scholars, as opposed to state officials, on changing global political dynamics.

The APSA sponsors a number of programs to further its objectives. Among these is the Congressional Fellowship Program, which since 1953 has been dedicated to expanding an understanding of Congress and its operations. Participants in this program serve on Congressional staffs and include journalists and federal executives as well as political scientists. Another program provides grants of various types, such as those to assist graduate students to attend and present papers at the annual conference, and, through the Minority Fellows Program, those to assist minority students with tuition grants. Other programs provide services both to departments of political science and to individual members, such as the ejobs Placement Service. The latter service is designed to assist recent graduates of master's and doctoral programs and current faculty on the job market to find faculty or other full-time positions.

Other major activities of the association are the publication of three journals, the *American Political Science Review, Perspectives on Politics,* and *PS: Political Science and Politics,* and the presentation of awards for outstanding scholarship in political science or outstanding public service. Among the awards are the Ralph J. Bunche Award for the best work in the previous year in the area of American ethnic studies or cultural pluralism, the James Madison Award for an American scholar who has made a particularly outstanding contribution to the study of politics, the Victoria Schuck Award for the best work in the previous year on women and politics, and the Benjamin E. Lippincott Award for a work of exceptional merit in political theory that is still considered meritorious after at least fifteen years. Awards are also given each year for the outstanding doctoral dissertations within subfields of the discipline. A highlight of the association's activities is the annual convention, which in recent years has brought together more than 7,000 scholars participating in more than 700 panels in 47 divisions of the discipline. There are also numerous affiliated societies that regularly hold their annual conferences in conjunction with the APSA annual convention.

SEE ALSO *Bureaucracy; Political Conventions; Political Science; Political Science, Behavioral; Political System; Political Theory; Politics; Professionalization*

BIBLIOGRAPHY

The American Political Science Association. Networking a World of Scholars. http://www.apsanet.org/.

Crick, Bernard R. 1959. *The American Science of Politics: Its Origins and Conditions.* Berkeley: University of California Press.

Willoughby, W. W. 1904. The American Political Science Association. *Political Science Quarterly* 19 (1): 107–111.

Timothy Hoye

AMERICAN PSYCHIATRIC ASSOCIATION

SEE *Post-Traumatic Stress.*

AMERICAN PSYCHOLOGICAL ASSOCIATION

The American Psychological Association (APA) is the world's largest scientific and professional association of psychologists, with 90,000 members and 65,000 student and teacher affiliates, international affiliates, and associate members. The APA was founded on July 8, 1892, by a small group of psychologists meeting in Professor G. Stanley Hall's study at Clark University. The thirty-one charter members, not all present at the founding meeting, were primarily scientific and academic psychologists. In the first few decades, rival associations were formed by psychologists who felt that their theoretical or professional orientations were not adequately represented in the APA. During World War II these differences were set aside and a national coordinating committee channeled the skills of the entire psychological community toward America's war effort.

In 1945 the member organizations of the coordinating committee enacted a plan to preserve the harmony of the war years by creating a reorganized APA, governed by a council of representatives of divisions and state and provincial associations and administered by a board of directors. Division status was accorded to seventeen special interest groups and formerly independent organizations, the largest being the American Association for Applied Psychology (AAAP). The basic structure of the modern APA is composed of the governance elements created in 1945. The APA constitution provides for the creation of new divisions, and by 2006 the number of divisions had grown to fifty-six.

The reorganized APA promptly hired its first professional staff and located its headquarters in Washington, D.C., where it has occupied a series of increasingly larger buildings. In 2006 the APA employed a professional staff of nearly five hundred people and administered an annual budget of about $60 million.

Since the mid-twentieth century, growing numbers of applied psychologists have joined the organization, the majority of whom are mental health service practitioners. In the 1980s a significant number of research-oriented psychologists proposed a new reorganization of the APA that would have moderated the influence of practitioner-oriented divisions. When the proposal was not approved by the membership, the reform group founded the American Psychological Society (APS). The APS draws its members primarily from the academic and scientific communities.

The contemporary APA is a vigorous leader in many domains. The APA publishes forty-nine of the most influential scientific and professional journals in the field. It publishes a comprehensive list of books for psychological scientists, practitioners, and the general public. The *APA Publication Manual*, its handbook of writing standards for published articles, first appeared in 1929 and has become the standard for professional writing in many fields. The association publishes standards for the conduct of psychologists, including standards for educational and psychological testing, for the ethical treatment of humans and nonhuman animals in research, and for ethical professional conduct by psychological service providers.

After World War II the APA developed standards for professional training programs to meet the national need for well-prepared clinical psychologists. In the early twenty-first century the APA endorsed training models that combine both scientific and professional practice skills by reviewing and accrediting doctoral educational and internship programs in clinical, counseling, and school psychology. Through its liaisons with state associations of psychology, the APA has promoted rigorous state licensure standards for psychological service providers.

Since 1894 the APA has published abstracts of the world's scientific and professional literature in psychology. This resource, called PsycINFO, is composed of more than two million abstracts and sophisticated online searching tools. The association makes full text versions of its journal articles and book chapters electronically available.

The APA has brought the science of psychology to bear on social issues. For example, it promotes awareness of ethnic minority, gender identity, and age-related concerns in educational, counseling, and clinical treatment settings, it advocates for culture-fair aptitude and achievement testing, and it promotes studies of women's social, professional, and health-related issues. When legal cases involve critical psychological matters, the APA has filed amicus curiae briefs and has supported litigants with a legal defense fund. Among the APA's advocacy goals are infusing federal public policy with the findings of behavioral science, extending drug prescription privileges to specially trained psychologists, and elevating support of psychological health services and research to equal that of physical health programs.

SEE ALSO *Mental Health; Mental Illness; Professionalization; Psychology*

BIBLIOGRAPHY

American Psychological Association. http://www.apa.org.

Benjamin, L. T., Jr., ed. 1992. The History of American Psychology. *American Psychologist* Spec. issue 47 (2).

Evans, R. E., V. S. Sexton, and T. C. Cadwallader, eds. 1992. *The American Psychological Association: A Historical Perspective*. Washington, DC: American Psychological Association.

Hilgard, E. R. 1987. *Psychology in America: A Historical Survey*. San Diego, CA: Harcourt Brace Jovanovich.

Warren R. Street

AMERICAN REVOLUTION

The American Revolution began in the early 1760s with changes in British colonial policy. Resistance opened a large problem: belonging to Britain while residing outside the British realm. The problem proved insurmountable as argument and riot led to open warfare. But virtually until independence in 1776, most rebels wanted only to stave off unwanted changes, and in this sense the Revolution was "conservative."

Abandoning British loyalty and identity forced enormous changes. Monarchy yielded to republicanism, easy to accept as an ideal but hard to work out in practice. Hierarchy beneath a king gave way to proclaimed equality. Ordinary white men who had been marginal claimed full political citizenship. White women and enslaved people of color, whom the old order had virtually excluded from public life, demanded that American liberty should apply to them, as well. Both slaves and Native Americans waged their own struggles for independence, and slavery did begin to crumble. Wartime needs gave rise to a national economy.

By the Revolution's end a separate, republican American people existed, with powerful political institutions to achieve its will. Energies had been released that would transform both the American people and the American continent. However, entirely new problems had emerged and only some of them were resolved. Others would prove as difficult as the questions on which the British Empire had foundered. In these senses, the Revolution was radical and transforming.

AN EMPIRE FALLS APART

In 1763 Britain stood triumphant over its ancient rival France. British merchant capitalism was delivering unprecedented wealth. Britons and Europeans alike celebrated British liberty, based on the premise that the British monarch could rule only with the consent of Parliament, the legislative body of Great Britain. White colonials joined in the celebrations, singing "Rule Britannia!" and huzzahing for the youthful George III (1738–1820), their "best of kings." Like their fellows in "the realm," the people of the overseas dominions were fully and proudly British.

But being British had two possible meanings. From London's viewpoint, all Britons owed obedience to the supreme authority, the king-in-parliament, which was Great Britain's absolute sovereign power. The British House of Commons represented the interests and protected the liberties of all Britons everywhere. Colonials had given little thought to such matters, but if pressed they would have said otherwise. Parliament could address large imperial questions, but their assemblies protected their local liberties and privileges. As long as Parliament did not exercise its claims, the question was effectively moot.

Defeating the French, however, had been very expensive, and British officials believed that Americans had not done their part. They also thought that the local assemblies were fractious and needed to be reined in. Some feared the northern colonies would become rivals. The answer seemed simple. Tax the colonies directly and control their economies. The money would stay in America, to pay salaries and maintain troops. But Parliament, not the local assemblies, would raise it.

The result was the Sugar Act (1764), the Stamp Act (1765), and the Townshend Acts (1767), as well as a host of administrative changes. None of the taxes matched what Britons paid at home, but they were to be paid in coin, which was scarce in America. Further, the new laws were to be enforced in vice-admiralty courts, whose judges could be fired and where no juries sat. The Stamp Act, in particular, threatened the well-being of the entire commercial economy. The act undercut the power of colonial elites to use finance as a weapon in their ongoing struggle with royal governors. It also threatened colonials with taxes on virtually all business transactions, to be payable in hard coin, which they simply did not have.

Colonials protested with words and deeds, and the British retreated twice. But at the end of 1773, when Bostonians destroyed three shiploads of valuable East India Company tea rather than pay the one import duty still in effect, Parliament decided that it had retreated enough. It would isolate Boston and Massachusetts and punish them severely. Shocked and in awe, the other colonies would retreat.

OLD ISSUES DIE, NEW PROBLEMS EMERGE

Instead, matters worsened. Troops occupied Boston, and people in rural areas refused to let Parliament's attempt to reform the province take effect. By the late summer of 1774, British authority in Massachusetts extended only where royal troops could march. Their commander, General Thomas Gage (1721–1787), was also the governor of the province, and he knew that rural armies were being formed. Acting under orders from London, he tried to seize a cache of supplies at Concord, Massachusetts, on April 19, 1775, along with rebel leaders who were there. Instead, he launched a war.

By that time the effort to isolate Massachusetts had failed. One Continental Congress (the federal legislature of the thirteen American colonies and later of the entire United States following the American Revolution) had met, and another was preparing to assemble. Provincial congresses and local committees were draining power from the old institutions. People from New Hampshire to Georgia rallied to support Massachusetts. George Washington emerged as American commander and began the long task of turning a haphazard volunteer force into an army capable of facing Britain.

But for fourteen more months Americans held on to the idea that they could turn back the clock. In January 1776 Thomas Paine's *Common Sense* argued that all monarchy needed to end and that for Americans it was "time to part." Paine's powerful language and vision of a transformed world reached people of all sorts, and they began to assert their own claims, challenging the ideas that the "better sort" deserved to rule the rest and that women should not have political voices, and that among America's precious liberties was the privilege of holding slaves. Nonetheless, for many slaves and native people, the king seemed to offer a better prospect for freedom than any congress.

The Declaration of Independence was more temperate than Paine's pamphlet. Thomas Jefferson (1743–1826), who drafted it, and Congress, which edited and adopted it, knew that attacking all monarchy would not play well with the French king, who already was giving secret aid. At the center of the document, Jefferson penned a crescendo-like indictment of "the present king of Great Britain," presenting "facts" to a "candid world." As his last count, Jefferson tried to blame the king both for forcing black slavery on unwilling white Americans and for encouraging slaves to rise. It was bad history and worse logic, written in tortured language. Congress dropped it, but it did demonstrate one point. Slavery was on the new republic's agenda, ultimately to the point that it nearly destroyed what the Revolution achieved.

THE NEW AMERICAN ORDER

Immediately, however, the revolutionaries had to confront two urgent problems. One was winning the war. Excited by early successes and convinced of their own virtue, they expected a short conflict. But what began with a firefight in Massachusetts turned into a global conflict, involving not just France, which became an American ally in 1778, but most of Europe. The main North American war ended at Yorktown, Virginia, in 1781. The very last hostilities involving Europeans were in India. French forces first intervened there in 1778, and between 1780 and 1782. The two sides fought on the Indian mainland, Ceylon, and in Indian waters. Word of the Treaty of Paris arrived just as the British were about to lay siege to the major French stronghold, at Cuddalore, south of Madras. For native people, threatened by the American victory and abandoned by the British at the Treaty of Paris in 1783, the conflict simply continued.

Secondly, the war brought major changes, requiring a national economy in order to meet the army's needs and creating a national elite, the men who went on to create the United States in its present form. It shook slavery, and it stimulated women, left to manage affairs, to think and act for themselves. It drove out thousands of loyalists, white, black, and native, who left rather than accept the Revolution's triumph.

Nobody gave any thought to calling a European prince, in the way that the English had called William and Mary to the throne when they overthrew James II in 1688. There was no question that the Americans would be republican. But creating a republican order proved very difficult. Most fundamentally, it raised the problem of how to give real meaning to the idea that "the people" now were the final authority. The earliest state constitutions were simply proclaimed into effect. Not until 1780 in Massachusetts was there a popular vote on whether to accept a state's proposed constitution. In all the states, debate raged between the idea of a remote, complex government and the idea of simple, responsive institutions. The new institutions brought men to the center of affairs who had been mere onlookers under the old order. New York split, as Vermont seceded from it, and people in the other states thought of doing the same. In 1786 Massachusetts erupted into armed conflict as farmers rose to close the courts rather than let tough fiscal policies threaten their farms. Looking around at the time, George Washington saw the danger of similar insurrections everywhere.

In 1784 Washington had seen that Americans had acquired "a mighty empire," stretching from the Atlantic to the Mississippi and from Florida to the Great Lakes. At its center was the extremely weak Confederation Congress (the immediate successor to the Second Continental Congress), where each state had one vote and every state could veto major change. Under Congress, the United States had won the war and negotiated a very successful peace. It laid down its own colonial policy, by providing for new states in the western territories, if it could force native people out.

But in peacetime, Congress withered and men like Washington worried about the states. The result was the United States Constitution, written by a special convention in Philadelphia in 1787 and brought into effect when New Hampshire became the ninth state to ratify it in June 1788. Writing the Constitution required great creativity. Ratifying it meant hard conflict among people with widely differing visions of the American future.

Farmers, city artisans, women, slaves, and natives: All of these as well as the familiar "Founding Fathers" took part in the Revolution's course. All of them had voices in what the Revolution wrought. Together, though rarely in agreement, they forged an unprecedented republic that

that was capitalistic and democratic, elitist and open, racist and egalitarian, imperial and inclusive, operating under a political settlement—the Constitution—that included all those qualities. They had abandoned the problems that went with being British. They solved many of the problems that rose from independence and republicanism. But they were only beginning to address the more profound social and ideological issues that their revolution raised.

SEE ALSO *Bill of Rights, U.S.; Burr, Aaron; Confederations; Congress, U.S.; Constitution, U.S.; Coup d'Etat; Declaration of Independence, U.S.; Empire; Franklin, Benjamin; Hamilton, Alexander; Loyalists; Monarchy; Parliament, United Kingdom; Political System; Republicanism; Revolution; Slavery; Violence; Voting; Washington, George*

BIBLIOGRAPHY

Countryman, Edward. 2003. *The American Revolution*. Rev. ed. New York: Hill and Wang.

Draper, Theodore. 1996. *A Struggle for Power: The American Revolution*. New York: Times Books.

Fischer, David Hackett. 2004. *Washington's Crossing*. New York: Oxford University Press.

Maier, Pauline. 1997. *American Scripture: Making the Declaration of Independence*. New York: Knopf.

Nash, Gary B. 2005. *The Unknown American Revolution: The Unruly Birth of Democracy and the Struggle to Create America*. New York: Viking.

Wood, Gordon S. 1992. *The Radicalism of the American Revolution*. New York: Knopf.

Edward Countryman

AMERICAN SOCIOLOGICAL ASSOCIATION

Historically, the social sciences in the United States were the province of amateurs, clergy, and practitioners who belonged to the interdisciplinary American Social Science Association. During the early twentieth century, the social sciences came to be the province of academically trained PhDs working in separate disciplines. Sociology broke away from the American Social Science Association and later became part of the American Economics Association. Finally, fifty sociologists formed the American Sociological Association (ASA) in 1905. Since its founding, the ASA has grown to an organization of nearly 14,000 members. During its first 100 years, the ASA grew in complexity as well as in size as it attempted to meet members' needs and responded to contentious as well as ordinary issues—issues that continue to affect the discipline as a whole.

PROFESSIONALISM

The professorate in sociology has become professionalized along several dimensions: its long training period terminating in a PhD, its claim to autonomy and freedom in research and in the classroom, its relative freedom from supervision, its body of specialized knowledge, and its adherence to a code of ethics. As of 2000, about 70 percent of sociology PhDs were employed in academia. Since 1933, especially during periods of economic downturn, the ASA or its members have attempted to develop positions for professional sociologists outside of the professorate. These efforts, an effort to control the labor supply, were buttressed by claims about the overproduction of PhDs. At the same time, there were strong feelings that practicing sociology outside of the academy, especially in political or business settings, compromised scientific objectivity and theoretical rigor. The distinction between scientific sociology and client-oriented sociology decreased with the growth of pressure for academics to seek outside funding and with the increase in state-mandated accountability and assessment requirements for faculty. The most recent rewriting of the ASA Code of Ethics bound both academic and nonacademic sociologists to avoid conflicts of interest, assure confidentiality, and respect people's "rights, dignity, and diversity."

ACADEMIC FREEDOM

Because norms of autonomy and control are important in research and teaching, the ASA developed institutional mechanisms for dealing with issues of academic freedom. In the early years, the ASA joined with the American Economics Association and the American Political Science Association in a Committee on Academic Freedom and Academic Tenure. This committee produced one report. During the 1950s, members of the ASA passed a resolution at the annual business meeting "deploring such discriminatory requirements" as loyalty oaths on account of the special interest of social scientists in inquiring about controversial social, political, and economic issues. In the 1980s the ASA's elected Council founded the Committee on Freedom in Research and Teaching (COFRAT) to protect individual freedom of research and teaching. During the 1980s this committee served in a fact-finding capacity on individuals' complaints against institutions and recommended institutional sanctions if warranted. These efforts became increasingly acrimonious as institutions protested COFRAT's work. A committee appointed to review COFRAT's mission recommended that COFRAT should deal with systematic abuses rather than individual cases. COFRAT reported difficulty in monitoring systematic or institutional conditions and became increasingly inactive. When the ASA restructured in the late 1990s, COFRAT was discontinued.

SPECIALIZATION

As its membership grew, there were internal pressures for the ASA to respond to members' requests for new projects, services, and processes. In so responding, the association became more a complex organization composed of an Executive Office, standing committees, and single-issue task forces. Growth also brought a proliferation of new membership subgroups, "sections" formed around substantive, theoretical, and methodological specialty areas. By 2005 there were forty-two sections, with most members joining at least one section. The larger sections include Medical Sociology; Sex and Gender; Organizations, Occupations, and Work; Sociology of Culture; Theory; and Family. Some members argue that the diversity of sections reflects the fragmentation of the discipline. Others, however, claim that the growth of sections promotes networking within the organization. While the number of specialty sections increased within the association, the ASA continued to participate in such multidisciplinary institutional efforts as the Social Science Research Council, the American Council of Learned Societies, and the Council of Social Science Associations.

SOCIAL PRACTICE

Early U.S. sociologists often engaged deeply in public issues. The writings and activism of Lester Ward, W. E. B. Du Bois, and Jane Addams affected public debate on such issues as racism, poverty, employment conditions, feminism, and social welfare. Others practiced sociology in the public arena by writing reports for courts, health departments, foundations, and government agencies. Social activism was criticized as "unscientific" by academic sociologists who enjoyed higher status, assumed leadership positions, and published in leading journals. Over time, public sociologists tried to legitimate their work. In the 1980s they petitioned for a practice section within the ASA, initiated a short-lived journal of practice, and pressed for a task force that would create bridges to the public sphere. In 2004 a new task force on "institutionalizing public sociology" was formed to provide rewards and incentives to "bring sociology to publics beyond the academy." During this time, debate resurfaced about whether the ASA should take sides on political issues. Although the membership did not endorse an antiwar resolution in 1968, they endorsed positions favoring the withdrawal of troops from Iraq in 2003 and opposing a Constitutional amendment banning gay marriage. In response to the

debate, the ASA's Council developed criteria requiring scientifically supported evidence before putting hot-button issues before the membership for final approval.

TEACHING

Since the ASA's inception, debates about the sociology curriculum concerned not only content and teaching methods but also whether the craft of teaching is rewarded and respected on par with scholarly pursuits. During the 1970s the ASA Executive Office opened a Teaching Resource Center; added teaching workshops to the annual meeting; awarded grants for enhancing teaching; formed a departmental visitation program to improve curricula, teaching, and the status of the craft; and began a new journal, *Teaching Sociology*. These activities paralleled a growing movement to develop a scholarship of teaching and learning that challenged the denigration of teaching within academia.

GENDER

Only one woman attended the founding meeting of the ASA. Since then, women's involvement within the ASA increased dramatically, though not without a struggle. By 1944 about 25 percent of PhD-level sociologists were women, although the percentage decreased until the late 1960s. As the number of sociology doctorates awarded to women increased, feminists worked to change both the substance of the field and their treatment within it. After women engaged in sit-ins, founded a separate organization (Sociologists for Women in Society), held an alternative convention, and formed a Women's Caucus, the ASA's Council responded by establishing a standing Committee on the Status of Women in Sociology in 1971. ASA members successfully petitioned to create a specialty section on the study of sex and gender, now among the largest ASA sections. Later in the decade, the first annual Jessie Barnard Award was given "in recognition of scholarly work enlarging the horizons [of sociology] to encompass fully the role of women in society." At the centennial of the ASA, women received about 60 percent of all sociology PhDs. Yet the 2004 report of the Committee on the Status of Women in Sociology to the Council presented evidence suggesting that women are a "majority minority" in the discipline—not equally represented at the discipline's highest ranks, facing chilly climates at work, experiencing uneven policies to balance work and family, and relatively ignored in ASA journals that include few articles on women's issues.

RACE AND ETHNICITY

Papers on race relations, racial attitudes, cultural differences among races, and the concept of race as a social category have been presented at every annual meeting since 1907. According to many African American and Hispanic sociologists, the growth of sociology in the United States was related to studies of the problems of racial and minority groups rather than to struggles for social justice. With the growth of the civil rights movement, an ad hoc group was formed to increase the visibility and the voice of minority sociologists within the ASA. The Black Caucus formed in 1969, and by the 1970 annual meeting it had presented a number of resolutions, including one for the establishment of a program to provide stipends for graduate training. Independently of the ASA, the Association of Black Sociologists was formed in 1970 to promote "scholarship that will serve Black people in perpetuity." The ASA responded to these efforts throughout the 1970s. A specialist in racial and minority relations was hired, the Council instituted the Du Bois-Johnson-Frazier Award, and it later created a standing Committee on the Status of Race and Ethnicity. In the wake of a Black Caucus recommendation, a training grant from the National Institute of Mental Health has provided stipends for nearly 400 doctoral students of color since 1974. The ASA has continued to address race and ethnic issues by participating in the Clinton Administration's Initiative on Race, producing the ASA Statement on the Importance of Collecting Data and Doing Research on Race, and presenting an amicus brief to the Supreme Court for *Grutter v. Bollinger*, a case concerning affirmative action at the University of Michigan's Law School. Despite these efforts, in response to a recent review of sociology in its 100th year, James Blackwell, a renowned black sociologist, noted that members of minority groups remain tokens at most traditionally white colleges and universities. That may not change in the near future. Even as late as 2003, only 32 of 106 graduate programs awarded a doctorate of sociology to an African American, and only 18 programs awarded a doctorate to a Hispanic.

In the beginning of its second hundred years, the ASA continues to face both ordinary and contentious issues raised by sociologists of diverse positions and interests as it attempts to meet their professional needs, advance the discipline, and engage the public.

SEE ALSO *Sociology*

BIBLIOGRAPHY

Bernard, Jessie. 1973. My Four Revolutions: An Autobiographical History of the ASA. *American Journal of Sociology.* 78 (6): 773–791.

Blackwell, James E. 2005. The Continuing Invisibility of Black Sociologists. Letters to the Editor. *Chronicle of Higher Education* 54 (4): B18.

Calhoun, Craig, and Troy Duster. 2005. The Visions and Divisions in Sociology. *Chronicle of Higher Education* 51 (49): B7.

Deegan, Mary Jo. 1998. *Jane Addams and the Men of the Chicago School, 1892–1918.* Somerset, NJ: Transaction Publishers.

Ferree, Myra Marx. 2005. It's Time to Mainstream Research on Gender. *Chronicle of Higher Education* 51 (49): B10.

Grant, Linda, and Lowell Hargens, cochairs. 2004. *Final Report of the Committee on the Status of Women, 2004.* Washington, DC: American Sociological Association. http://www.asanet.org/galleries/default-file/CSWS%20Final%20Report%20Oct%202004.pdf.

Kulis, Stephen. 1998. The Representation of Women in Top Ranked Sociology Departments. *American Sociologist* 19 (3): 203–217.

Kulis, Stephen, Karen A. Miller, Morris Axelrod, and Leonard Gordon. 1986. Minority Representation in U.S. Departments. *American Sociological Association Footnotes* 15 (January): 9, 11.

Levine, Felice J. 1999. The ASA's MFP—A Solid Investment. *American Sociological Association Footnotes* 27 (September/October): 2.

Research and Development Department. American Sociological Association. *Few PhDs Awarded to African Americans and Hispanics in 2003.* http://www.asanet.org/page.ww?name=Sociology+PhDs+Awarded+to+African+Americans+%26+Hispanics&section=Profession+Trend+Data.

Rhodes, Lawrence J. *A History of the American Sociological Association, 1905–1980.* Washington, DC: American Sociological Association.

Rosich, Katherine J. *A History of the American Sociological Association, 1981–2004.* Washington, DC: American Sociological Association.

Slaughter, Sheila, and Larry L. Leslie. 1997. *Academic Capitalism: Politics, Policies, and the Entrepreneurial University.* Baltimore, MD: Johns Hopkins University Press.

Roberta Spalter-Roth

AMERICANISM

Americanism is an ideology that holds that the cultural and political values of the United States are the most ideal and desirable of any in the world. It is closely linked with American exceptionalism, a phrase coined by Alexis de Tocqueville (1805–1859) in 1831. Tocqueville argued that, because of its historical evolution, national credo, historical origins, and distinctive political and religious institutions, the United States is qualitatively different from other nations. Some have characterized Americanism and its beliefs as a "civic religion."

Seymour Lipset identifies five key elements of Americanism: liberty, egalitarianism, individualism, populism, and laissez-faire. He avers, "Being an American, however, is an ideological commitment. It is not a matter of birth. Those who reject American values are un-American" (Lipset 1997, p. 31). Americanism emphasizes equality of opportunity, as opposed to equality of outcomes, and attaches greater importance to social and political individualism.

American veneration of these ideals grew out of the country's historical development and the distinctive role of Protestantism. John Winthrop (1588–1649), governor of the Massachusetts Bay Colony, described the early Puritan community in New England as a "city on a hill" with which God had made a special covenant. According to Winthrop, the early colony should serve as a moral and political example for the rest of the world. The American Revolution (1775–1783), with its emphasis on democracy, liberty, and republicanism, is often cited as proof that the United States offers unlimited potential and opportunity to those who work hard. Americanism is often associated with manifest destiny, the idea that Americans had a mission from God to spread liberty and democracy across the American frontier and around the world. Later, supporters of Americanism have pointed to the durability of the U.S. Constitution, the failure of socialist parties to take root in the United States, and the defeat of the Soviet Union in the cold war as proof of the superiority of American values.

Theodore Roosevelt (1858–1919) greatly popularized Americanism. In an 1894 magazine article, he wrote that "no other land offers such glorious possibilities to the man able to take advantage of them as does ours" (1897, pp. 38–39). He argued that any person could become an American, provided they adopted the American beliefs in democracy, hard work, capitalism, and egalitarianism; learned English; and left behind their previous sectarian identities. Roosevelt encouraged immigration to the United States, but with the proviso that immigrants fully embrace the American way of life. He also adopted these same ideals in his foreign policies, leading American military involvement in Cuba and the Philippines under the guise of bringing liberation, democracy, and the American way of life to these countries.

During both world wars, German and Japanese communities in the United States came under suspicion for not fully believing in American values and identifying too closely with their homelands. This resulted in both relatively harmless colloquial changes (renaming sauerkraut "liberty cabbage") and overtly discriminatory policies like the forced internment of twelve thousand ethnic Japanese (most of whom were U.S. citizens) in camps throughout the western United States during World War II (1939–1945). Later, during the cold war, mass media and government officials often juxtaposed Americanism with Communism as a battle between liberty and tyranny.

President George W. Bush has relied on Americanism arguments to justify American operations in Iraq, positing that the United States is freeing the Iraqi people from tyranny and delivering American-style democracy and liberty.

In recent years, Americanism has been at the heart of the debates about legal and illegal immigration. Samuel Huntington (2004) has argued that immigration, primarily from Latin America, threatens the very character of American society because recent immigrants remain too attached to their homelands, refusing to learn English or adopt American beliefs in hard work, individual responsibility, and capitalism.

Critics have long chastised Americanism for relying on a selective, uncritical reading of U.S. history. They point out that the United States itself often fails to uphold Americanist ideals for its own citizens through such means as denying voting rights, restricting citizenship, and promoting discriminatory policies. This hypocrisy not only undermines the argument that egalitarianism and liberty are at the heart of the American experience, but also calls into question whether the United States can (or should) promote these values to other countries. Others have called Americanism imperialism cloaked in a rhetoric of values and human rights. They also question the use of military force in places like the Philippines, Vietnam, and Iraq to promote democracy and liberty.

Americanism shares some commonalities with both nationalism and patriotism, as all three attach positive values to one's home country and its upholding of national beliefs and symbols. In a crucial distinction, though, Americanism specifies the nature of the United States' distinctness from the rest of the world. Further, Americanism allows that persons born outside the United States can become Americans if they adopt American beliefs; nationalism often holds that one's membership in a nation is determined by birth and remains constant throughout life.

SEE ALSO *American Dream; Nationalism and Nationality; Patriotism*

BIBLIOGRAPHY

Huntington, Samuel P. 2004. *Who Are We? The Challenges to America's National Identity.* New York: Simon and Schuster.

Lipset, Seymour Martin. [1996] 1997. *American Exceptionalism: A Double-Edged Sword.* New York: Norton.

Roosevelt, Theodore. 1897. True Americanism (1894). In *The Works of Theodore Roosevelt in Sixteen Volumes: American Ideals and Administration-Civil Service,* vol. 1, 31–50. New York: Collier.

Jeremy Youde

AMIN, IDI
c. 1925–2003

Idi Amin became the president of Uganda in January 1971 after a military coup removed the elected leader, Milton Obote, and he fled into exile to Saudi Arabia on April 11, 1979 after a war with Tanzania. In the intervening eight years his name became synonymous with mass murder, destruction, militarism, and the worst features of political misrule in Africa.

Idi Amin was born in northwest Uganda in 1925 or 1926; that his birthdate is imprecise illustrates the marginalization and isolation of the peoples of that part of Uganda under British colonial rule. Britain had claimed Uganda as a protectorate at the end of the nineteenth century, and Uganda was integrated into the East African Command of the King's African Rifles (KAR). Later the events of Amin's life became more precise—the records show that he was recruited into the KAR in 1946, one year after the end of World War II. Amin was deployed by the British to participate in the counterinsurgency war against the freedom fighters in Kenya, and there he engaged in brutality and wanton murder against Africans. Based in the Muranga region of Kenya between 1953 and 1956, Amin learned all of the techniques of low-intensity warfare when the British incarcerated more than 1.5 million Kenyans and hanged thousands.

Idi Amin was both a pugilist and militarist; from 1951 to 1960 he was the light heavyweight boxing champion of Uganda. He also rose through the colonial army, eventually attaining the rank of *effendi* (warrant officer), the highest rank that a black African could attain in the KAR at that time. The Uganda that became independent in 1962 was plagued with deep divisions based on regional, religious, and ethnic alliances. Because of uneven colonial penetration, the areas in the south of the country—including the precolonial kingdoms of Ankole, Buganda, Bunyoro, Toro, and Busoga—were more involved with colonial cash crops, and hence in these regions there was a higher proportion of Africans educated by the missionary schools. These regional differences were interpreted in ethnic terms, so much of the writings on Uganda portrayed Idi Amin as coming from the tribally backward north. This social reality was compounded by the fact that there were close to 100,000 Asians who dominated the interstices of the colonial economy and owned sugar and tea plantations. At the time of independence in 1962 there was not a single black African wholesaler on the main business street in Kampala, the capital.

Amin was promoted rapidly in the Ugandan army, becoming general and commander in 1966. By 1969 the social divisions in Uganda had deepened to the point where Obote's government increasingly depended on the military to maintain its power. The military was mobilized against trade unions, against village cooperatives, against cattle rustlers, against political opponents, and against students.

The military coup of January 25, 1971, took place while the prime minister, Milton Obote, was attending a Commonwealth summit meeting in Singapore. The military takeover immediately plunged the society into a bloodbath. The coup could not have been consolidated without the support of imperial security networks, especially those of Britain and Israel, and later, records showed that the governments of Israel and Britain were indeed involved in planning, executing, and defending the military coup in January 1971.

The relations between Britain and Uganda changed one year later, however, when Amin declared an economic war, which involved the expulsion of more than 80,000 Asian citizens who held British passports. Many Asians (primarily of Indian origin) owned businesses in Uganda, and by deporting them Amin gained domestic political support amid increased repression in the society. But their expulsion placed Amin on a collision course with the West, and brought the conditions of the people of Uganda to the attention of the international media.

At the height of the cold war, Amin became the chairperson of the Organization of African Unity (OAU). The selection of Amin was possible, in large part, because of the divisions unleashed by the cold war in Africa. The Soviet Union supported leaders who declared themselves to be anti-imperialist. When Amin had seized power in the 1971 military coup, Uganda was diplomatically allied to the United States, Israel, and the United Kingdom. After the expulsion of the Asians in 1972, Uganda became a close ally of Libya, Saudi Arabia, and the Soviet Union. Inside Africa, Amin formed a close alliance with known butchers and militarists such as Mobutu Sese Seko of Zaire and Michel Micombero of Burundi. In the same year Amin expelled the Asians, Micombrero carried out genocide in his own country, killing more than 300,000 citizens. The selection of Amin to be the chairperson of the OAU brought disgrace to the organization insofar as Amin used the clause of noninterference in the internal affairs of states to prevent pan-African intervention to stop the killings.

The killings and wanton destruction of lives in Uganda intensified between 1972 and 1978, and it has been estimated that by the end of his regime Amin had killed more than 300,000 Africans (another estimate puts the number as high as 500,000). In addition, there were more than one million Ugandans living in exile in neighboring countries.

The Ugandan army invaded Tanzania and occupied the Kagera province in October 1978, precipitating the war between Uganda and Tanzania. The Tanzanian army counterattacked and supported Ugandan exiles in launching their own counteroffensive (as the Uganda National Liberation Army, or UNLA) against the Amin regime. At the end of this war, in April 1979, when the combined forces of the Tanzanian army and the UNLA took Kampala, Amin fled the city to exile, first in Libya, then in Saudi Arabia, where he lived until his death in August 2003.

When Amin came to power in 1971 he had been hailed as an archetypal common man, and Western social scientists had declared that Uganda's military government could serve as a model for modernization in Africa; Makerere University in Kampala was a veritable laboratory for the ideas of modernization and nation-building. But Amin's regime left a tradition of destruction, low respect for human life, and cross-border warfare that is still plaguing the regions of eastern and central Africa. The continuing war between the Ugandan government and the Lord's Resistance Army, a rebel paramilitary group in northern Uganda, remains one of the outstanding legacies of this period of militarism, masculinity, and warfare.

SEE ALSO *African Studies; Colonialism; Dictatorship; Genocide; Militarism; Military Regimes; Obote, Milton*

BIBLIOGRAPHY

Anderson, David. 2005. *Histories of the Hanged: The Dirty War in Kenya and the End of Empire.* New York: W. W. Norton.

Avirgan, Tony, and Martha Honey. 1982. *War in Uganda: The Legacy of Idi Amin.* Westport, CT: L. Hill.

Campbell, Horace. 1975. *Four Essays on Neo-Colonialism in Uganda.* Toronto: Afro Carib Publications.

Elkins, Carole. 2005. *Imperial Reckoning: The Untold Story of Britain's Gulag in Kenya.* New York: Henry Holt.

Kyemba, Henry. 1977. *A State of Blood: The Inside Story of Idi Amin.* New York: Ace Books.

Mamdani, Mahmood. 1984. *Imperialism and Fascism in Uganda.* Trenton, NJ: Africa World Press.

Horace G. Campbell

AMIN, SAMIR
1931–

Samir Amin was born in Cairo, the son of two doctors, his father Egyptian and his mother French. He lived in Port Said in northern Egypt and attended the French lycée there, receiving his baccalaureate in 1947. Amin then enrolled at the Lycée Henri IV in Paris to study mathematics and at the Institut d'études Politiques to study law, which at the time was the way to study economics. He received a diploma in political science in 1952 and a license in law and economics in 1953 and then opted to pursue a doctorate in economics. He also obtained a diploma in statistics from the Institut de Statistiques de L'université de Paris in 1956. In June 1957, Amin received a doctorate in economics under the direction of Maurice Byé and with the additional guidance of François Perroux. As a student, Amin spent much of his time as a militant with various student movements and from 1949 to 1953 helped publish the journal *Étudiants Anticolonialistes*, through which he met many of the future members of Africa's governing elite.

From 1957 to 1960, Amin worked in Cairo on economic development issues for the Egyptian government, then moved to Bamako, Mali, where he was an adviser to the Malian planning ministry (1960–1963). In 1963 he moved to Dakar, Senegal, where he took a fellowship (1963–1970) at the Institut Africain de Développement Économique et de Planification (IDEP). He became a director at IDEP (1970–1980) and subsequently was named director of the Third World Forum (1980–). Amin has at various times held professorships in Poitiers, Dakar, and Paris.

The author of more than thirty books, Amin's brilliant 1957 dissertation, subsequently published in 1970 as *L'accumulation à l'échelle mondiale; critique de la théorie du sous-développement* (translated in 1974 as *Accumulation on a World Scale: A Critique of the Theory of Underdevelopment*), was the earliest significant work to argue that underdevelopment in much of the world was a direct consequence of the way the capitalist economy functions. He argued that this polarization is due to transfers of profits from the poor countries to the rich, which help alleviate potential underconsumptionist problems in the industrial economies, allowing the industrial world to pay higher salaries or offer lower prices to consumers than would be possible were the labor theory of value to work simply at the national level.

Amin's new emphasis on the global economy as a unit of analysis is intended to explain global salary and price differences within a Marxist labor theory of value. Even his later works (e.g. *Obsolescent Capitalism* and *Beyond U.S. Hegemony*) have built on this model to critique imperialist projects generally and post–September 11, 2001 U.S. hegemonic efforts more particularly. Amin argues for a polycentric world that can counteract monopolies in areas such as technology, finance, natural resources, media, and weapons production that consistently hurt poor countries.

Amin's reliance on a labor theory of value and underconsumptionist theory has limited his analytical outlook and led him to make overly simplistic predictions even as it has allowed a holistic historical materialistic perspective. Nevertheless, his criticisms of neoclassical equilibrium models and imperialistic projects have long since been joined by those of economists and social scientists from many different theoretical persuasions.

SEE ALSO *Capital; Development; Development Economics; Economics; Social Science*

BIBLIOGRAPHY

Amin, Samir. 1970. *L'accumulation à l'échelle mondiale; critique de la théorie du sous-développement.* Dakar, IFAN. Translated by Brian Pearce as *Accumulation on a World Scale: A Critique of the Theory of Underdevelopment.* New York: Monthly Review Press, 1974.

Amin, Samir. 1976. *Unequal Development: An Essay on the Social Formations of Peripheral Capitalism.* Trans. by Brian Pearce. New York: Monthly Review Press.

Amin, Samir. 1994. *Re-Reading the Postwar Period: An Intellectual Itinerary.* Trans. by Michael Wolfers. New York: Monthly Review Press.

Amin, Samir. 1997. *Capitalism in the Age of Globalization: The Management of Contemporary Society.* Atlantic Highlands, NJ: Zed Books.

Amin, Samir. 2003. *Obsolescent Capitalism: Contemporary Politics and Global Disorder.* Trans. by Patrick Camiller. New York: Zed Books.

Amin, Samir. 2006. *Beyond U.S. Hegemony? Assessing the Prospects for a Multipolar World.* Trans. by Patrick Camiller. New York: Zed Books.

Amin, Samir. 2007. *A Life Looking Forward: Memoirs of an Independent Marxist.* Trans. by Patrick Camiller. New York: Zed Books.

Thomas K. Park

AMNESTY INTERNATIONAL

SEE *Civil Liberties.*

AMOS 'N' ANDY

SEE *Minstrelsy.*

ANALYSIS OF VARIANCE (ANOVA)

SEE *Statistics in the Social Sciences.*

ANARCHISM

Anarchism is a theory and way of life rooted in the belief that the individual should be free to pursue his or her own interests without coercion, especially by the state and its laws and institutions. The term is derived from the ancient Greek word *anarkhia,* meaning "no ruler," and originally was used to denote a disruption of the normal civic order that often implied a condition of civil war. As with *democracy* and *democrat,* the words *anarchy* and *anarchist* were typically used as terms of abuse until the nineteenth century, when with the rise of commercial society and the decline of feudalism the idea of self-rule by "the people" became increasingly accepted.

The political theory of anarchism properly begins only with William Godwin (1756–1836) and Pierre-Joseph Proudhon (1809–1865), though important elements of anarchist thought can be found in the ancient Greeks, among them Aristippus of Cyrene (c. 435–c. 360 BCE) and the founder of Stoicism, Zeno of Citium (c. 334–262 BCE). Strains of anarchist thought can also be found in the medieval era, in the Anabaptists of the Reformation, and in the Diggers of the English Revolution of the mid-seventeenth century. However, Godwin is the first exponent of the philosophic doctrine of anarchism, though he does not use the term *anarchist* to describe himself; it is Proudhon who first calls himself an anarchist. In Proudhon's *What Is Property?* (1840) he lays out a vision of socialism in which the individual is liberated from the shackles of capitalist property relations, and is instead free to reap the benefits of his labor under a form of communal production. Anarchism became increasingly relevant to the political world of the late nineteenth and early twentieth centuries, first through the writings of Mikhail Bakunin (1814–1876), who opposed the overly centralized socialism of Karl Marx (1818–1883), and later through Peter Kropotkin (1842–1921) and Emma Goldman (1869–1940).

Anarchist thought is extremely diverse, but is generally characterized by opposition to the state, capitalism, and religion. Rather than seeing the legal apparatus of the state as a means of protecting individual freedom, anarchists contend that the state and its laws merely represent the self-serving interests of powerful groups in society. In this view, law is a means of oppressing the vast majority of the people, and the best way to eliminate this oppression is to do away with the institutions that create and reinforce it—especially the state and private property. Private property is a particular concern for anarchists, in that it corrupts the democratic process by controlling the inputs and outputs to the political system, and also because it directs people to think merely about their own self-interest rather than about how to cooperate with their fellow citizens. Because private property uses the state to benefit the members of the ruling class or elite, anarchists are not in favor of representative democracy as it is currently practiced.

Anarchists promote their goals by multiple means, including sometimes violent revolution, but also through democratic evolution and the creation of independent communal societies that function outside the domain of the state. In the Spanish Civil War (1936–1939) anarchists and anarcho-syndicalists (linked industrial worker-councils) formed an important element in the opposition to Francisco Franco's fascist coup, and shared governmental authority with a socialist coalition, particularly in Barcelona. This experiment, though short-lived, provided an example of anarchist "government" in practice, and was characterized by the liquidation of the landed estates and the parceling of the land into agricultural cooperatives, the establishment of a federation of worker-controlled factories, and the elimination of the social indications of class status that had marked Bourbon Spain. Although defeated in the war, Spanish anarchism continues to be a model for other nations, because it is here that one of the largest worker-run cooperatives in the world, the Mondragon Cooperative Corporation, has been functioning for more than fifty years.

Among anarchists in the early part of the twenty-first century there are several prominent trends, some of which are substantially in tension with one another. Libertarian anarchists such as Murray Rothbard (1926–1995) defend capitalism, arguing that the protection of private property under capitalism provides the surest foundation for promoting individual liberty. Unlike most libertarians, Rothbard claims that even the most minimal state is an unnecessary evil, but this is almost the only thing that unites him with anarchist-socialists such as the protesters at the World Trade Organization (WTO) and G8 meetings in Seattle in 1999 and Geneva in 2001. Though not united by a systematic program, these protesters represented groups that are dissatisfied with the current system of neoliberal trade promoted by the WTO, which to them represents an extension of the rule of private property over the globe.

Anarchism is not highly visible in most developed western nations, but it remains a powerful underground current that both the Left and the Right continue to find useful as a stimulant to political thought and political action. Anarchism will continue to be relevant as long as the meaning of the terms *democracy*, *property*, and *freedom* is not self-evident.

SEE ALSO *Austrian Economics; Capitalism; Democracy; Fascism; Franco, Francisco; Freedom; Harris, Abram L., Jr.; Liberty; Mill, John Stuart; Political Theory; Politics; Property, Private; Religion; Socialism; Spanish Civil War; State, The; Syndicalism*

BIBLIOGRAPHY

Bakunin, Mikhail. 1990. *Statism and Anarchy*, ed. Marshall Shatz. Cambridge, U.K.: Cambridge University Press.

Guerin, Daniel. 1970. *Anarchism: From Theory to Practice*. New York: Monthly Review Press.

Kropotkin, Peter. [1970] 2002. *Anarchism: A Collection of Revolutionary Writings*, ed. Roger Baldwin. Mineola, NY: Dover Publications.

Orwell, George. [1938] 1969. *Homage to Catalonia*. San Diego: Harvest Books.

Proudhon, Pierre-Joseph. [1840] 1994. *What Is Property?* eds. Donald Kelley and Bonnie Smith. Cambridge, U.K.: Cambridge University Press.

Wolff, Robert Paul. [1970] 1998. *In Defense of Anarchism*. Berkeley: University of California Press.

Stefan Dolgert

ANARCHO-SYNDICALISM

SEE *Syndicalism.*

ANDERSON, PERRY
1938–

Perry Anderson (born in 1938) is one of the most important Marxist authors of the past forty years. As the principal editor of *New Left Review* since 1962, he has introduced and shaped English-language readers' understanding of the principal Western European Marxist theorists of the twentieth century, above all the Italian Antonio Gramsci, whose concept of hegemony is now central to Marxist scholarship. Under Anderson's guidance, *New Left Review* has brought the work of European and third-world Marxists to a broader public of intellectuals and activists. *New Left Review* has also published continuous analysis of contemporary political economy and culture that seeks to find openings for leftist politics and provides criticism of contemporary social scientists, philosophers, novelists, and artists. In addition, Anderson has made a major scholarly contribution to the understanding of England's particular political development and to the analysis of European absolutism.

Anderson's political orientation was shaped by two events of 1956 (the year he arrived at Oxford University as a student): the Soviet crushing of the Hungarian Revolution and the Israeli, French, and British invasion of Egypt. He was part of the New Left, which condemned both Soviet repression and Western imperialism against

Egypt. Anderson, throughout his intellectual career, has argued that contemporary politics needs to be understood in the context of the historical development of states and classes. He has contributed to such a historical-materialist analysis through his study of the formation of the English state. His aptly titled "Origins of the Present Crisis," published in *New Left Review* in 1964, explains the failure of British socialism in terms of England's unusual historical trajectory, especially its lack of a bourgeois revolution. His analysis quickly came under attack from historian E. P. Thompson on both empirical and theoretical grounds ("The Peculiarities of the English"). Anderson responded with *Arguments within English Marxism* (1980), a book-length analysis of Thompson. Written as an appreciation and critique of Thompson's historical and political writings, Anderson sees Thompson's main contribution as a reassertion of the importance of culture and morality in socialist intellectual discussions. Anderson believes that Thompson slights the search for effective strategies of socialist politics. That is the task to which Anderson has devoted himself and *New Left Review* in recent years.

Anderson's greatest intellectual contribution is his study of absolutist states and their role in the development of the European bourgeoisie. *Passages from Antiquity to Feudalism*, the first volume of Anderson's study of transitions, provides the context for his analysis of feudalism in *Lineages of the Absolutist State*. *Passages* explores the dynamics of the slave mode of production and explains variations in feudalism across Europe in terms of divisions in the Roman Empire and the sorts of class struggle that erupted during the empire's decline. *Lineages of the Absolutist State* (1974) reconceived the social dynamics that followed the Black Death of the fourteenth century (the liberalization of peasant obligations in England and France and the reimposition of serfdom in much of Eastern Europe). Feudalism, in Anderson's analysis, was neither destroyed nor replaced by a new mode of production. Instead, feudalism was reconstituted, as the aristocracy reasserted its dominance through the larger social form of the absolutist state rather than within local manors.

Anderson views the bourgeoisie as an inadvertent outcome of absolutist state polices designed by aristocrats to safeguard their collective interests. Both state and capital grew and profited from the monetization of taxes and rents, the sale of state offices, and the establishment of protected domestic monopolies and colonial ventures. Anderson explains the different trajectories of Eastern European and Western European states, and of England and France, in terms of the strength of aristocrats' organization within estates, the extent of town autonomy, and the results of military competition. He was able to show how a new social group, the bourgeoisie, developed at particular sites within certain absolutist states, yet he never

attempted to explain why the bourgeoisie was unable to continue to pursue its interests within absolutism. As a result, *Lineages*, despite its significant insights, was not able to serve as the foundation for Anderson's planned but as yet unwritten study of the bourgeois revolutions. Since the early 1980s Anderson has moved away from historical studies and has concentrated his writings on contemporary politics and criticism.

SEE ALSO *Capitalism; Marx, Karl; Marx, Karl: Impact on Sociology; Sociology*

BIBLIOGRAPHY

PRIMARY WORKS

Anderson, Perry. 1974. *Lineages of the Absolutist State*. London: NLB.

Anderson, Perry. 1974. *Passages from Antiquity to Feudalism*. London: NLB.

Anderson, Perry. 1980. *Arguments within English Marxism*. London: NLB.

SECONDARY WORK

Elliott, Gregory. 1998. *Perry Anderson: The Merciless Laboratory of History*. Minneapolis: University of Minnesota Press.

Richard Lachmann

ANGER

SEE *Emotion.*

ANGLO-CHINESE WAR

SEE *Opium Wars.*

ANGLO-CONFORMITY

SEE *Melting Pot.*

ANIMISM

According to animism, all phenomena—everything that is seen, heard, touched, or felt; every animal, plant, rock, mountain, cloud, or star, and even tools and implements—are believed to possess a soul, which is understood to be conscious and endowed with an ability to communicate. Considered the original or first human religion, animism originates from the Latin *anima*, meaning "soul," which comes from the earlier Greek word *animus*, meaning "wind" or "breath." It is defined as belief in spiritual beings or entities that are thought to give all things, both animate and inanimate, a certain kind of potency or life force.

Animism is a primal belief system dating back to the Paleolithic era, yet it is estimated that 40 percent of the world's population still practices some form of animism, often in syncretism with Christianity, Islam, Buddhism, and Hinduism. Contemporary people find animism a belief system that infuses their real-life situation with the sacred and provides guidance in addressing everyday problems, concerns, and needs, such as healing sickness, bringing success, or receiving guidance. Animism can be practiced by anyone who acknowledges the existence of spirits, but it does not require any affiliation with an organized religion.

As the first human thought system to interface with the nonhuman or spirit realms, animism recognizes an ontological connection between material things and their spiritual source. The artifacts and remains that document the symbolic nature of animism are unimaginably old, created long before human culture gave birth to language and recorded history. For millions of years humans have deified ancestors, animals, plants, stones, rivers, and stars, each of which was thought to be enlivened by a particular "anima" or soul, having the capacity to leave the body both during life and after death.

Animism was not discovered, created, or developed by any one individual or group; instead, it was a way of living in reciprocity with the larger natural environment and not separate from it. Indigenous people followed a kind of rudimentary animism that served many functions. Not only did animism provide answers to pressing philosophical questions—how the universe came into being, the nature of the forces operating within it, the origins of the ancestors—but also it addressed more immediate issues concerning how to live, how to die, and what happens in the afterlife.

Shaman was the name given to the holy men and women who were considered sacred leaders called on to sustain the tribe's connection to the spirit realm and the land of the dead. Shamans were able to navigate through various cosmic levels so as to ensure that all things in nature were kept interdependent and integral to the whole universe. The basis of animism is an acknowledgement of a spiritual realm, within the physical world, that humans share with the cosmos. To become a shaman required that one have special proximity to the spirit world. Using preternatural powers, trance, ritual, dance, and shamanic "journeys," the shaman ensured that the relation between the human community and the natural ecosystem it cohabited was reciprocal and mutual.

Western philosophical schools have employed the term *animism* to describe an awareness of a living presence within all matter. Aristotle's idea supporting the relation of body and soul was animistic, as was Plato's belief in an immaterial force behind the universe. Gottfried Wilhelm Leibniz (1646–1716) and Arthur Schopenhauer (1788–1860) expanded the notion of animism with the assertion that all substances are essentially force, tendency, and dynamism. The modern concept of vitalism challenges the idea that all phenomena can be traced back to chemical and mechanical processes and offers a perspective that presupposes an animistic understanding of human nature and the natural world. In his work *Primitive Culture* (1871), Edward. B. Tyler coined the term *animism* to refer to the original form of human spirituality and the first primitive religion. In this book, he described primitive religion as operating at a lower level of cognitive and social development than more evolved religions with coherent, systematic theologies. Primitive religion is now understood in a less ethnocentric way and is valued for its direct link to the primal mind. Today those practicing animism see themselves as part of the natural world rather than the masters and rulers of it.

Animism is emerging as a critical voice in response to the ecological crisis and is a serious topic that science, technology, and the social sciences must consider. Many in search of a new spirituality are discovering animism to offer a world view that is naturally connected to the earth, nature, and broader ecosphere. Animism fosters an attitude that reinforces living respectfully with all things.

SEE ALSO *Buddhism; Christianity; Hinduism; Indigenous Rights; Islam, Shia and Sunni; Judaism; Philosophy; Primitivism; Religion; Rituals; Shamans; Spirituality*

BIBLIOGRAPHY

Abram, David. 1996. *The Spell of the Sensuous.* New York: Vintage.

Eliade, Mircea. 1959. *Cosmos and History: The Myth of the Eternal Return.* Trans. Willard. R. Trask. New York: Harper & Row.

Halpern, Daniel, ed. 1987. *On Nature: Nature, Landscape, and Natural History.* San Francisco: North Point Press.

Lehmann, Arthur C., and James E. Myers, eds. 1993. *Magic, Witchcraft, and Religion: An Anthropological Study of the Supernatural,* 3rd ed. Mountain View, CA: Mayfield.

Lovelock, James. 1986. Gaia: The World as Living Organism. *New Scientist* 18 (December): 25–28.

Ingrid F. Smyer

ANNEXATION

Annexation is the physical takeover of conquered territories as part of a greater state policy of expansionism. In most cases, annexation begins with the occupation of a subordinate territory through military possession and ends with formal political recognition of the acquisition by both parties involved. In some cases, the involved parties seek a cooperative agreement either to avoid war or because they recognize a common benefit through shared political, economic, and social institutions. The process of annexation, however, is usually driven by coercive measures: a compelling use or physical threat of force, intimidation or fear tactics, and other means of direct or indirect pressure. Annexation may produce either a long-lasting or a temporary political, economic, and social relationship between two states.

States that adopt annexationist policies are driven to satisfy their "land hunger" through the acquisition of lands that are outside of their original borders. These lands may be adjacent to the annexing state and represent the fulfillment of irredentist or nationalist goals. For example, Germany's annexation of Austria and the Sudetenland in 1938 was part of a larger foreign policy aiming to unite all Germanic peoples under one larger empire. This policy of national expansion also directed the United States' annexation of Texas in 1845. In this case, annexation was at the heart of the United States' greater policy of Manifest Destiny; it believed that "winning the West" was part of fulfilling its natural destiny in North America. States may also seek to expand their colonial empire through the annexation of foreign territories. The annexation of Madagascar by France in 1896 illustrates this form of expansionism. In 1868 a treaty between the Merina peoples and the French government designated Madagascar as a French protectorate. British recognition of this arrangement in 1890 legitimized the French presence on the island, but only after France's defeat of the Merina army in 1895 did Madagascar become fully annexed by France.

In either case, the expansion of national influence through the physical acquisition of land, peoples, and natural resources drives a state's annexationist policies. The absence of international laws that regulate annexation allows each state to develop its own process of annexation. Some states' annexationist policies are or have been governed by domestic national law, as was the case with Italy's 1936 annexation of Ethiopia, which occurred with a formal decree issued by the king of Italy, and the United States' acquisitions of Texas (1845) and Hawaii (1898), which were directed by joint resolutions in the U.S. Congress. Other states do not or have not constructed a legal framework for determining the process of annexation. For example, Japan completed the annexation of its Korean protectorate in 1910 through a simple proclamation by the emperor. Only the illegal use of force is condemned by the charter of the United Nations.

Annexed regions become part of the greater entity when the sovereign authority of the annexing state is recognized by both parties. Even though annexationist policy is a form of unilateral politics—a one-sided agreement imposed by the dominant party—the process of annexation is complete once a legitimization of the acquisition is accepted by the international community. In some cases, international treaties may aid in the process of annexation, as in the case of Norway's annexation of the Svalbard Islands in 1925. The terms of the country's final configuration, however, are determined solely by the annexing state. For example, the annexing state has the right to force the citizens of the annexed territory to adopt new national laws and customs. In many instances, the process of annexation leads to the destruction of the subordinate territory's cultural identity. For example, the annexation of Hawaii by the United States and the subsequent declaration of Hawaiian statehood in 1959 have resulted in the Americanization of the Hawaiian Islands. Many native populations of permanently annexed lands have dedicated themselves to the preservation of their culture through peaceful educational movements or active resistance to deculturation.

Conversely, annexationist policies may be underscored by distinct humanitarian goals. A dual desire to promote industrial growth in the South and greater racial equality in American society as a whole drove the annexationist program of Northern Radical Republicans at the end of the U.S. Civil War (1861–1865). These abolitionist politicians advocated a program of Reconstruction that included the annexation of Southern states with the express purpose of destroying plantation society and establishing a unified liberal capitalist federal nation. In this case, the politics of annexation reflected a desire for the institutionalization of Radical Republican Judge Albion Tourgée's (1838–1905) philosophy of "color-blind justice" for freed persons of the South and should be noted for its progressive commitment to social justice.

Annexation is not the inevitable outcome of military conquest, but rather one of many possible outcomes of conquest. For example, the military occupation of Germany and Japan after World War II (1939–1945) did not lead to the annexation of either country by the Allied powers. In both cases the Allies expressly rejected annexation of the subordinate territories at the time of occupation. Annexation can therefore be seen as a calculated, deliberate domestic or international policy.

SEE ALSO *Cooperation; Empire; Imperialism; Land Claims; Reconstruction Era (U.S.); Unilateralism*

BIBLIOGRAPHY

Dudden, Arthur Power, ed. 2004. *American Empire in the Pacific: From Trade to Strategic Balance, 1700–1922.* Burlington, VT: Ashgate.

Elliott, Mark Emory. 2006. *Color-Blind Justice: Albion Tourgée and the Quest for Racial Equality.* New York: Oxford University Press.

Korman, Sharon. 1996. *The Right of Conquest: The Acquisition of Territory by Force in International Law and Practice.* New York: Oxford University Press.

Wagner, Dieter, and Gerhard Tomkowitz. 1971. *Anschluss: The Week Hitler Seized Vienna.* Trans. Geoffrey Strachan. New York: St. Martin's Press.

Tracey A. Pepper

ANNULMENT

SEE *Divorce and Separation.*

ANOMIE

SEE *Alienation-Anomie; Durkheim, Émile.*

ANOREXIA NERVOSA

SEE *Body Image; Undereating.*

ANTHONY, SUSAN B.

SEE *Suffrage, Women's.*

ANTHRAX

SEE *Bioterrorism.*

ANTHROPOLOGY

Anthropology is the study, analysis, and description of humanity's past and present. Questions about the past include prehistoric origins and human evolution. Study of contemporary humanity focuses on biological and cultural diversity, including language. Compared to other disciplines that address humanity such as history, sociology, or psychology, anthropology is broader in two ways. In terms of humanity's past, anthropology considers a greater depth of time. In terms of contemporary humans, anthropology covers a wider diversity of topics than other disciplines, from molecular DNA to cognitive development and religious beliefs.

This depth and breadth correspond to the wide variety of sites and contexts in which anthropologists conduct research. Some anthropologists spend years in harsh physical conditions searching for fossils of early human ancestors. Others live among and study firsthand how people in Silicon Valley, California, for example, work, organize family life, and adapt to a situation permeated by modern technology. Anthropologists may conduct analyses in a laboratory studying how tooth enamel reveals an individual's diet, or they may work in a museum, examining designs on prehistoric pottery. Yet other anthropologists observe chimpanzees in the wild.

Research methods in anthropology range from scientific to humanistic. In the scientific mode, anthropologists proceed deductively. They formulate a hypothesis, or research question, and then make observations to see if the hypothesis is correct. This approach generates both quantitative (numeric) data and qualitative (descriptive) data. In the humanistic approach, anthropologists proceed inductively, pursuing a subjective method of understanding humanity through the study of people's art, music, poetry, language, and other forms of symbolic expression. Anthropologists working in the humanistic mode avoid forming a hypothesis, and they rely on qualitative information.

No matter whether it is conducted in a rainforest settlement or a university laboratory, or pursued from a scientific or a humanistic perspective, research in anthropology seeks to produce new knowledge about humanity. Beyond generating knowledge for its own sake, anthropology produces findings of relevance to significant contemporary issues. Knowledge in anthropology is of value to government policy makers, businesses, technology developers, health care providers, teachers, and the general public.

FOUR-FIELD ANTHROPOLOGY IN NORTH AMERICA

In North America anthropology is defined as a discipline comprising four fields that focus on separate but interrelated subjects. The subjects are archaeology, biological anthropology (or physical anthropology), linguistic anthropology, and cultural anthropology (or social anthropology). Some North American anthropologists argue that a fifth field, applied anthropology, should be added. Applied anthropology, also called practicing or practical anthropology, is the use of anthropological knowledge to prevent or solve problems, or to shape and achieve policy goals. The author of this essay takes the position that the application of knowledge is best conceived of as an integral part of all four fields, just as theory is, rather than placed in a separate field.

The depth and breadth of anthropology have both positive and negative implications. The advantages of the depth and breadth of the four-field approach are the same as those that accrue to any kind of multidisciplinary work that requires thorough dialogue across domains about theories, methods, findings, and insights. Such dialogue tends to advance thinking in original and fruitful ways. Those who do not support anthropology as a four-field discipline point to the disadvantages of combining so much depth and breadth in one discipline. The main issue here is the differences between the scientific and humanistic approaches to understanding humanity.

In North America, the four-field approach is maintained to a large extent in the departmental organization and degree requirements at larger colleges and universities, and in professional associations such as the American Anthropological Association (AAA) and the Canadian Sociology and Anthropology Association (CSAA). Some notable splits in departments occurred in the late twentieth century. In 1998, the former single Department of Anthropology at Stanford University divided into the Department of Cultural and Social Anthropology and the Department of Anthropological Sciences, with the former focusing on humanistic anthropology and the latter on scientific anthropology. Duke University has a Department of Cultural Anthropology and a Department of Biological Anthropology and Anatomy. Archaeology is housed within the Department of Classics. In some North American universities archaeology is a separate department, but archaeology is generally housed in anthropology departments.

Outside North America the four fields exist in separate academic units. The word "anthropology" in such contexts often refers only to biological anthropology. The English term "ethnology" or its equivalent in other languages corresponds to North American cultural anthropology. "Folklore" studies continue to be important in many European countries and in Japan. Linguistic anthropology is less prominent outside North America.

Archaeology Archaeology means, literally, the "study of the old," with a focus on human culture. Archaeology, which began in Europe in the nineteenth century, centers on the excavation and analysis of artifacts, or human-made remains. Depending on one's perspective about valid evidence for the first humans, the time-depth of archaeology goes back to the beginnings of early humans with the earliest evidence of human-made tools approximately two million years ago.

Archaeology encompasses two major subfields: prehistoric archaeology and historical archaeology. Prehistoric archaeology covers the human past before written records. Prehistoric archaeologists identify themselves according to major geographic regions: Old World archaeology (Africa, Europe, and Asia) or New World archaeology (North, Central, and South America). Historical archaeology deals with the human past in societies that have written documents.

Another set of specialties within archaeology is based on the context in which the research takes place. One such specialty is underwater archaeology, which is the study and preservation of submerged archaeological sites. Underwater archaeological sites may be from either prehistoric or historic times. Industrial archaeology focuses on changes in material culture and society during and since the Industrial Revolution. Industrial archaeology is especially active in Great Britain, home of the industrial revolution. In Great Britain industrial archaeologists study such topics as the design and construction of iron bridges, the growth and regional distribution of potteries and cloth mills, and workers' housing.

Worldwide, archaeologists seek to preserve the invaluable remains of humanity's cultural heritage of the past, and therefore archaeology has a strong applied component. Applied archaeologists work in a variety of domains. Many archaeologists are employed in cultural resource management, assessing possible archaeological remains before such construction projects as roads and buildings can proceed. Industrial archaeologists contribute to the conservation of endangered sites that are more likely to be neglected or destroyed than sites that have natural beauty or cultural glamour attached to them. Archaeologists are becoming increasingly involved in making findings relevant to local people and to improving their welfare. Collaborative archaeology projects that involve community members in excavation, analysis, stewardship, and financial benefits are a growing trend.

Biological Anthropology Biological anthropology, or physical anthropology, is the study of humans as biological organisms, including their evolution and contemporary variation. The history of biological anthropology was strongly influenced by the work of Charles Darwin (1809–1882), especially his theories of evolution and species survival through competition. The three subfields of biological anthropology are primatology, paleoanthropology, and contemporary human biology. The three subfields share an interest in the relationship between morphology (physical form) and behavior.

Primatology is the study of the order of mammals called primates, including human and nonhuman primates. The category of nonhuman primates includes a wide range of animals from small, nocturnal creatures to gorillas, the largest members. Primatologists record and analyze how animals spend their time; collect and share food; form social groups; rear offspring; deal with conflict; and how all of these are affected by captivity.

Paleoanthropology is the study of human evolution on the basis of the fossil record. Paleoanthropologists search for fossils to increase the amount and quality of evidence related to how human evolution occurred. Genetic evidence suggests that human ancestors diverged from the ancestors of chimpanzees between five and eight million years ago in Africa. Fossil evidence for the earliest human ancestors is scarce for this period and researchers are searching for fossils to fill the gap. An equally important activity of paleoanthropologists is labwork focused on dating, reconstructing, and classifying fossils.

Anthropologists who study contemporary human biology define, measure, and seek to explain similarities and variation in the biological makeup and behavior of modern humans. Topics include diet and nutrition, fertility and reproduction, physical growth and health over the life cycle, and urban stress and pollution. Genetic and molecular analyses are of growing interest and importance for tracing similarities and differences in human biology including susceptibility to certain health conditions such as sickle cell anemia, Down syndrome, and diabetes.

Biological anthropology has many applied aspects. Applied primatologists provide data for designing nonhuman primate conservation projects. Paleoanthropologists serve as advocates for programs to protect fossil sites from looting and to ensure that important fossils and knowledge about them are part of public education. Biological anthropologists with specialized knowledge of human anatomy work in forensics, identifying crime victims and providing expert testimony in courts. Many forensic anthropologists are involved in investigations of human rights abuses around the world. Biological anthropologists in the subfield of contemporary human biology provide knowledge relevant to development projects seeking to improve people's nutrition and health.

Linguistic Anthropology Linguistic anthropology is the study of communication, mainly among humans but also among other animals. Linguistic anthropology emerged in Europe and North America in the latter half of the nineteenth century. At that time its major topics of interest were the origins of language, the historical relationships of languages of different regions and continents, and the languages of "primitive" peoples.

Two factors shaped linguistic anthropology in its early days: the discovery that many non-European languages were unwritten and the realization that the languages of many non-European peoples were dying out as a consequence of contact with Europeans. Linguistic anthropologists responded to the discovery of unwritten languages by developing methods for recording unwritten and dying languages. They learned that non-European languages have a wide range of phonetic systems (pronunciation of various sounds) that do not correspond to those of Western languages. Linguistic anthropologists invented the International Phonetic Alphabet, which contains symbols to represent all known human sounds. In response to the discovery of dying languages, many early linguistic anthropologists devoted efforts to recording dying languages in work that is called "salvage anthropology."

Linguistic anthropology has three subfields. The first, historical linguistics, is the study of language change over time, how languages are related, and the relationship of linguistic change to cultural change. The second is descriptive or structural linguistics. This subfield is the study of how contemporary languages differ in terms of their structure, such as in grammar and sound systems. The third subfield is sociolinguistics, the study of the relationships among social variation, social context, and linguistic variation, including nonverbal communication. Sociolinguistics is closely related to cultural anthropology and some North American anthropologists rightfully claim expertise in both fields.

Beginning in the 1980s, four new directions emerged in sociolinguistic anthropology. First is a trend to study language in everyday use, or discourse, in relation to power structures at local, regional, and international levels. For example, in some contexts, powerful people speak more than less powerful people, while in other contexts more powerful people speak less. Second, globalization has prompted new areas of inquiry include the study of "world languages" such as English, Spanish, and the emerging role of Chinese. Third, study of the media is a major growth area with attention to the relationship between language and nationalism, the role of mass media in shaping culture, mass communication and violence, and the effects of the Internet and cell phones on identity and social relationships. Fourth, linguistic anthropologists are increasingly focusing on language rights as human rights.

Applied roles for linguistic anthropologists are expanding. One professional area is education policy and school curriculum. Applied linguistic anthropologists consult with educational institutions about how to meet the needs of multicultural school populations and improve standardized tests for bilingual populations. They conduct research on classroom dynamics, such as student participation and teachers' speech patterns, in order to assess possible biases related to ethnicity, gender, and class. Applied linguistic anthropologists contribute to the recovery of "dead" and declining languages as invaluable cultural heritage of descendant populations. Linguistic anthropologists work with governments, advocating for particular policies about the official status of languages in multicultural settings.

Cultural Anthropology Cultural anthropology is the study of the culture, or the learned and shared behavior and beliefs of groups of living humans. Prominent subfields within cultural anthropology are economic anthropology, medical anthropology, psychological anthropology, kinship and family studies, social organization and social stratification, political anthropology, legal anthropology, religion, communication, expressive culture, and development anthropology.

History. The earliest historical roots of cultural anthropology are in the writings of Herodotus (fifth century BCE), Marco Polo (c. 1254–c. 1324), and Ibn Khaldun (1332–1406), people who traveled extensively and wrote reports about the cultures they encountered. More recent contributions come from writers of the French Enlightenment, such as eighteenth century French philosopher Charles Montesquieu (1689–1755). His book, *Spirit of the Laws*, published in 1748, discussed the temperament, appearance, and government of non-European people around the world. It explained differences in terms of the varying climates in which people lived.

The mid- and late nineteenth century was an important time for science in general. Influenced by Darwin's writings about species' evolution, three founding figures of cultural anthropology were Lewis Henry Morgan (1818–1881) in the United States, and Edward Tylor (1832–1917) and James Frazer (1854–1941) in England. The three men supported a concept of cultural evolution, or cumulative change in culture over time leading to improvement, as the explanation for cultural differences around the world. A primary distinction in cultures was between Euro-American culture ("civilization") and non-Western peoples ("primitive"). This distinction is maintained today in how many North American museums place European art and artifacts in mainstream art museums, while the art and artifacts of non-Western peoples are placed in museums of natural history.

The cultural evolutionists generated models of progressive stages for various aspects of culture. Morgan's model of kinship evolution proposed that early forms of kinship centered on women with inheritance passing through the female line, while more evolved forms centered on men with inheritance passing through the male line. Frazer's model of the evolution of belief systems posited that magic, the most primitive stage, is replaced by religion in early civilizations which in turn is replaced by science in advanced civilizations. These models of cultural evolution were unilinear (following one path), simplistic, often based on little evidence, and ethnocentric in that they always placed European culture at the apex. Influenced by Darwinian thinking, the three men believed that later forms of culture are inevitably superior and that early forms either evolve into later forms or else disappear.

Most nineteenth century thinkers were "armchair anthropologists," a nickname for scholars who learned about other cultures by reading reports of travelers, missionaries, and explorers. On the basis of readings, the armchair anthropologist wrote books that compiled findings on particular topics, such as religion. Thus, they wrote about faraway cultures without the benefit of personal experience with the people living in those cultures. Morgan stands out, in his era, for diverging from the armchair approach. Morgan spent substantial amounts of time with the Iroquois people of central New York. One of his major contributions to anthropology is the finding that "other" cultures make sense if they are understood through interaction with and direct observation of people rather than reading reports about them. This insight of Morgan's is now a permanent part of anthropology, being firmly established by Bronislaw Malinowski (1884–1942).

Malinowski is generally considered the "father" of the cornerstone research method in cultural anthropology: participant observation during fieldwork. He established a theoretical approach called functionalism, the view that a culture is similar to a biological organism wherein various parts work to support the operation and maintenance of the whole. In this view a kinship system or religious system contributes to the functioning of the whole culture of which it is a part. Functionalism is linked to the concept of holism, the perspective that one must study all aspects of a culture in order to understand the whole culture.

The "Father" of Four-Field Anthropology. Another major figure of the early twentieth century is Franz Boas (1858–1942), the "father" of North American four-field anthropology. Born in Germany and educated in physics and geography, Boas came to the United States in 1887. He brought with him a skepticism toward Western science gained from a year's study among the Innu, indigenous people of Baffin Island, Canada. He learned from that experience the important lesson that a physical substance such as "water" is perceived in different ways by people of different cultures. Boas, in contrast to the cultural evolutionists, recognized the equal value of different cultures and said that no culture is superior to any other. He introduced the concept of cultural relativism: the view that each culture must be understood in terms of the values and ideas of that culture and must not be judged by the standards of another. Boas promoted the detailed study of individual cultures within their own historical contexts, an approach called historical particularism. In Boas's view, broad generalizations and universal statements about culture are inaccurate and invalid because they ignore the realities of individual cultures.

Boas contributed to the growth and professionalization of anthropology in North America. As a professor at Columbia University, he hired faculty and built the department. Boas trained many students who became prominent anthropologists, including Ruth Benedict and Margaret Mead. He founded several professional associations in cultural anthropology and archaeology. He supported the development of anthropology museums.

Boas was involved in public advocacy and his socially progressive philosophy embroiled him in controversy. He published articles in newspapers and popular magazines opposing the U.S. entry into World War I (1914–1918), a position for which the American Anthropological Association formally censured him as "un-American." Boas also publicly denounced the role of anthropologists who served as spies in Mexico and Central America for the U.S. government during World War I. One of his most renowned studies, commissioned by President Theodore Roosevelt (1858–1919), was to examine the effects of the environment (in the sense of one's location) on immigrants and their children. He and his research team measured height, weight, head size and other features of over 17,000 people and their children who had migrated to the United States. Results showed substantial differences in measurements between the older and younger generations. Boas concluded that body size and shape can change quickly in response to a new environmental context; in other words, some of people's physical characteristics are culturally shaped rather than biologically ("racially") determined.

Boas' legacy to anthropology includes his development of the discipline as a four-field endeavor, his theoretical concepts of cultural relativism and historical particularism, his critique of the view that biology is destiny, his anti-racist and other advocacy writings, and his ethical stand that anthropologists should not do undercover research.

Several students of Boas, including Mead and Benedict, developed what is called the "Culture and Personality School." Anthropologists who were part of this intellectual trend documented cultural variation in modal personality and the role of child-rearing in shaping adult personality. Both Mead and Benedict, along with several other U.S. anthropologists, made their knowledge available to the government during and following World War II (1939–1945). Benedict's classic 1946 book, *The Chrysanthemum and the Sword* was influential in shaping U.S. military policies in post-war Japan and in behavior toward the Japanese people during the occupation. Mead likewise, offered advice about the cultures of the South Pacific to the U.S. military occupying the region.

The Expansion of Cultural Anthropology. In the second half of the twentieth century cultural anthropology in the United States expanded substantially in the number of trained anthropologists, departments of anthropology in colleges and universities, and students taking anthropology courses and seeking anthropology degrees at the bachelor's, master's, and doctoral level. Along with these increases came more theoretical and topical diversity.

Cultural ecology emerged during the 1960s and 1970s. Anthropologists working in this area developed theories to explain cultural similarity and variation based on environmental factors. These anthropologists said that similar environments (e.g., deserts, tropical rainforests, or mountains) would predictably lead to the emergence of similar cultures. Because this approach sought to formulate cross-cultural predictions and generalizations, it stood in clear contrast to Boasian historical particularism.

At the same time, French anthropologist Claude Lévi-Strauss (b. 1908) developed a different theoretical perspective influenced by linguistics and called structuralism. Structuralism is an analytical method based on the belief that the best way to learn about a culture is by analyzing its myths and stories to discover the themes, or basic units of meaning, embedded in them. The themes typically are binary opposites such as life and death, dark and light, male and female. In the view of French structuralism these oppositions constitute an unconsciously understood, underlying structure of the culture itself. Lévi-Strauss collected hundreds of myths from native peoples of South America as sources for learning about their cultures. He also used structural analysis in the interpretation of kinship systems and art forms such as the masks of Northwest Coast Indians. In the 1960s and 1970s French structuralism began to attract attention of anthropologists in the United States and has had a lasting influence on anthropologists of a more humanistic bent.

Descended loosely from these two contrasting theoretical perspectives—cultural ecology and French structuralism—are two important approaches in contemporary cultural anthropology. One approach, descended from cultural ecology, is cultural materialism. Cultural materialism, as defined by its leading theorist Marvin Harris (1927–2001), takes a Marxist-inspired position that understanding a culture should be pursued first by examining the material conditions in which people live: the natural environment and how people make a living within particular environments. Having established understanding of the "material" base (or infrastructure), attention may then be turned to other aspects of culture, including social organization (how people live together in groups, or structure) and ideology (people's way of thinking and their symbols, or superstructure). One of Harris' most famous examples of a cultural materialist approach is his analysis of the material importance of the sacred cows of Hindu India. Harris demonstrates the many material benefits of cows, from their plowing roles to the use of their dried dung as cooking fuel and their utility as street-cleaning scavengers, underly and are ideologically supported by the religious ban on cow slaughter and protection of even old and disabled cows.

The second approach in cultural anthropology, descended from French structuralism and symbolic anthropology, is interpretive anthropology or intepretivism. This perspective, championed by Clifford Geertz (1926–2006), says that understanding culture is first and foremost about learning what people think about, their ideas, and the symbols and meanings important to them. In contrast to cultural materialism's emphasis on economic and political factors and behavior, interpretivists focus on webs of meaning. They treat culture as a text that can only be understood from the inside of the culture, in its own terms, an approach interpretivists refer to as "experience near" anthropology, in other words, learning about a culture through the perspectives of the study population as possible. Geertz contributed the concept of "thick description" as the best way for anthropologists to present their findings; in this mode, the anthropologist serves as a medium for transferring the richness of a culture through detailed notes and other recordings with minimal analysis.

Late Twentieth and Turn of Century Growth. Starting in the 1980s, several additional theoretical perspectives and research domains emerged in cultural anthropology. Feminist anthropology arose in reaction to the lack of anthropological research on female roles. In its formative stage, feminist anthropology focused on culturally embedded discrimination against women and girls. As feminist anthropology evolved, it looked at how attention to human agency and resistance within contexts of hierarchy and discrimination sheds light on complexity and change. In a similar fashion, gay and lesbian anthropology, or "queer anthropology," has exposed the marginalization of gay and lesbian sexuality and culture in previous anthropology research and seeks to correct that situation.

Members of other minority groups voice parallel concerns. African American anthropologists have critiqued mainstream cultural anthropology as suffering from embedded racism in the topics it studies, how it is taught to students, and its exclusion of minorities from positions of power and influence. This critique has produced recommendations about how to build a non-racist anthropology. Progress is occurring, with one notable positive change being the increase in trained anthropologists from minority groups and other excluded groups, and their ris-

ing visibility and impact on the research agenda, textbook contents, and future direction of the field.

Another important trend is increased communication among cultural anthropologists worldwide and growing awareness of the diversity of cultural anthropology in different settings. Non-Western anthropologists are contesting the dominance of Euro-American anthropology and offering new perspectives. In many cases, these anthropologists conduct native anthropology, or the study of one's own cultural group. Their work provides useful critiques of the historically Western, white, male discipline of anthropology.

At the turn of the twenty-first century, two theoretical approaches became prominent and link together many other diverse perspectives, such as feminist anthropology, economic anthropology, and medical anthropology. The two approaches have grown from the earlier perspectives of cultural materialism and French structuralism, respectively. Both are influenced by postmodernism, an intellectual pursuit that asks whether modernity is truly progress and questions such aspects of modernism as the scientific method, urbanization, technological change, and mass communication.

The first approach is termed structurism, which is an expanded political economy framework. Structurism examines how powerful structures such as economics, politics, and media shape culture and create and maintain entrenched systems of inequality and oppression. James Scott, Nancy Scheper-Hughes, Arthur Kleinman, Veena Das, and Paul Farmer are pursuing this direction of work. Many anthropologists use terms such as social suffering or structural violence to refer to the forms and effects of historically and structural embedded inequalities that cause excess illness, death, violence, and pain.

The second theoretical and research emphasis, derived to some extent from interpretivism, is on human agency, or free will, and the power of individuals to create and change culture by acting against structures. Many anthropologists avoid the apparent dichotomy in these two approaches and seek to combine a structurist framework with attention to human agency.

The Concept of Culture Culture is the core concept in cultural anthropology, and thus it might seem likely that cultural anthropologists would agree about what it is. Consensus may have been the case in the early days of the discipline when there were far fewer anthropologists. Edward B. Tylor (1832–1917), a British anthropologist, proposed the first anthropological definition of culture in 1871. He said that "Culture, or civilization … is that complex whole which includes knowledge, belief, art, law, morals, custom, and any other capabilities and habits acquired by man as a member of society" (Kroeber and

Kluckhohn 1952, p. 81). By the 1950s, however, an effort to collect definitions of culture produced 164 different definitions. Since that time no one has tried to count the number of definitions of culture used by anthropologists.

In contemporary cultural anthropology, the theoretical positions of the cultural materialists and the interpretive anthropologists correspond to two different definitions of culture. Cultural materialist Marvin Harris defines culture as the total socially acquired life-way or life-style of a group of people, a definition that maintains the emphasis on the holism established by Tylor. In contrast, Clifford Geertz, speaking for the interpretivists, defines culture as consisting of symbols, motivations, moods, and thoughts. The interpretivist definition excludes behavior as part of culture. Again, avoiding a somewhat extreme dichotomy, it is reasonable and comprehensive to adopt a broad definition of culture as all learned and shared behavior and ideas.

Culture exists, in a general way, as something that all humans have. Some anthropologists refer to this universal concept of culture as "Culture" with a capital "C." Culture also exists in a specific way, in referring to particular groups as distinguised by their behaviors and beliefs. Culture in the specific sense refers to "a culture" such as the Maasai, the Maya, or middle-class white Americans. In the specific sense culture is variable and changing. Sometimes the terms "microculture" or local culture are used to refer to specific cultures. Microcultures may include ethnic groups, indigenous peoples, genders, age categories, and more. At a larger scale exist regional or even global cultures such as Western-style consumer culture that now exists in many parts of the world.

Characteristics of Culture Since it is difficult to settle on a neat and tidy definition of culture, some anthropologists find it more useful to discuss the characteristics of culture and what makes it a special adaptation on which humans rely so heavily.

Culture is based on symbols. A symbol is something that stands for something else. Most symbols are arbitrary, that is, they bear no necessary relationship to that which is symbolized. Therefore, they are cross-culturally variable and unpredictable. For example, although one might guess that all cultures might have an expression for hunger that involves the stomach, no one could predict that in Hindi, the language of northern India, a colloquial expression for being hungry says that "rats are jumping in my stomach." Our lives are shaped by, immersed in, and made possible through symbols. It is through symbols, especially language, that culture is shared, changed, stored, and transmitted over time.

Culture is learned. Cultural learning begins from the moment of birth, if not before (some people think that an unborn baby takes in and stores information through sounds heard from the outside world). A large but unknown amount of people's cultural learning is unconscious, occurring as a normal part of life through observation. Schools, in contrast, are a formal way to learn culture. Not all cultures throughout history have had formal schooling. Instead, children learned culture through guidance from others and by observation and practice. Longstanding ways of enculturation, or learning one's culture, include stories, pictorial art, and performances of rituals and dramas.

Cultures are integrated. To state that cultures are internally integrated is to assert the principle of holism. Thus, studying only one or two aspects of culture provides understanding so limited that it is more likely to be misleading or wrong than more comprehensively grounded approaches. Cultural integration and holism are relevant to applied anthropologists interested in proposing ways to promote positive change. Years of experience in applied anthropology show that introducing programs for change in one aspect of culture without considering the effects in other areas may be detrimental to the welfare and survival of a culture. For example, Western missionaries and colonialists in parts of Southeast Asia banned the practice of head-hunting. This practice was embedded in many other aspects of culture, including politics, religion, and psychology (i.e., a man's sense of identity as a man sometimes depended on the taking of a head). Although stopping head-hunting might seem like a good thing, it had disastrous consequences for the cultures that had practiced it.

Cultures Interact and Change Several forms of contact bring about a variety of changes in the cultures involved. Trade networks, international development projects, telecommunications, education, migration, and tourism are just a few of the factors that affect cultural change through contact. Globalization, the process of intensified global interconnectedness and movement of goods, information and people, is a major force of contemporary cultural change. It has gained momentum through recent technological change, especially the boom in information and communications technologies, which is closely related to the global movement of capital and finance.

Globalization does not spread evenly, and its interactions with and effects on local cultures vary substantially, from positive change for all groups involved to cultural destruction and extinction for those whose land, livelihood and culture are lost. Current terms that attempt to capture varieties of cultural change related to globalization include hybridization (cultural mixing into a new form) and localization (appropriation and adaptation of a global form into a new, locally meaningful form).

ETHNOGRAPHY AND ETHNOLOGY

Cultural anthropology embraces two major pursuits in its study and understanding of culture. The first is ethnography or "culture-writing." An ethnography is an in-depth description of one culture. This approach provides detailed information based on personal observation of a living culture for an extended period of time. An ethnography is usually a full-length book.

Ethnographies have changed over time. In the first half of the twentieth century, ethnographers wrote about "exotic" cultures located far from their homes in Europe and North America. These ethnographers treated a particular local group or village as a unit unto itself with clear boundaries. Later, the era of so-called "village studies" in ethnography held sway from the 1950s through the 1960s. Anthropologists typically studied in one village and then wrote an ethnography describing that village, again as a clearly bounded unit. Since the 1980s, the subject matter of ethnographies has changed in three major ways. First, ethnographies treat local cultures as connected to larger regional and global structures and forces; second, they focus on a topic of interest and avoid a more holistic (comprehensive) approach; and third, many are situated within industrialized/post-industrialized cultures.

As topics and sites have changed, so have research methods. One innovation of the late twentieth century is the adoption of multi-sited research, or research conducted in more than one context such as two or more field sites. Another is the use of supplementary non-sited data collected in archives, from Internet cultural groups, or newspaper coverage. Cultural anthropologists are turning to multi-sited and non-sited research in order to address the complexities and linkages of today's globalized cultural world. Another methodological innovation is collaborative ethnography, carried out as a team project between academic researchers and members of the study population. Collaborative research changes ethnography from study of people for the sake of anthropological knowledge to study with people for the sake of knowledge and for the people who are the focus of the research.

The second research goal of cultural anthropology is ethnology, or cross-cultural analysis. Ethnology is the comparative analysis of a particular topic in more than one cultural context using ethnographic material. Ethnologists compare such topics as marriage forms, economic practices, religious beliefs, and childrearing practices, for example, in order to discover patterns of similarity and variation and possible causes for them. One might compare the length of time that parents sleep with their babies in different cultures in relation to personality. Researchers ask, for example, if a long co-sleeping period leads to less individualistic, more socially connected personalities and if a short period of co-sleeping produces more individualistic personalities. Other ethnological analyses have considered the type of economy in relation to frequency of warfare, and the type of kinship organization in relation to women's status.

Ethnography and ethnology are mutually supportive. Ethnography provides rich, culturally specific insights. Ethnology, by looking beyond individual cases to wider patterns, provides comparative insights and raises new questions that prompt future ethnographic research.

CULTURAL RELATIVISM

Most people grow up thinking that their culture is the only and best way of life and that other cultures are strange or inferior. Cultural anthropologists label this attitude ethnocentrism: judging other cultures by the standards of one's own culture. The opposite of ethnocentrism is cultural relativism, the idea that each culture must be understood in terms of its own values and beliefs and not by the standards of another culture.

Cultural relativism may easily be misinterpreted as absolute cultural relativism, which says that whatever goes on in a particular culture must not be questioned or changed because no one has the right to question any behavior or idea anywhere. This position can lead in dangerous directions. Consider the example of the Holocaust during World War II in which millions of Jews and other minorities in much of Eastern and Western Europe were killed as part of the German Nazis' Aryan supremacy campaign. The absolute cultural relativist position becomes boxed in, logically, to saying that since the Holocaust was undertaken according to the values of the culture, outsiders have no business questioning it.

Critical cultural relativism offers an alternative view that poses questions about cultural practices and ideas in terms of who accepts them and why, and who they might be harming or helping. In terms of the Nazi Holocaust, a critical cultural relativist would ask, "Whose culture supported the values that killed millions of people on the grounds of racial purity?" Not the cultures of the Jewish people, the Roma, and other victims. It was the culture of Aryan supremacists, who were one subgroup among many. The situation was far more complex than a simple absolute cultural relativist statement takes into account, because there was not "one" culture and its values involved. Rather, it was a case of cultural imperialism, in which one dominant group claimed supremacy over minority cultures and proceeded to change the situation in its own interests and at the expense of other cultures. Critical cultural relativism avoids the trap of adopting a homogenized view of complexity. It recognizes internal cultural differences and winners/losers, oppressors/victims. It pays attention to different interests of various power groups.

APPLIED CULTURAL ANTHROPOLOGY

In cultural anthropology, applied anthropology involves the use or application of anthropological knowledge to help prevent or solve problems of living peoples, including poverty, drug abuse, and HIV/AIDS. In the United States, applied anthropology emerged during World War II when many anthropologists offered their expertise to promote U.S. war efforts and post-war occupation. Following the end of the war, the United States assumed a larger global presence, especially through its bilateral aid organization, the U.S. Agency for International Development (USAID). USAID hired many cultural anthropologists who worked in a variety of roles, mainly evaluating development projects at the end of the project cycle and serving as in-country anthropologists overseas.

In the 1970s cultural anthropologists worked with other social scientists in USAID to develop and promote the use of "social soundness analysis" in all government-supported development projects. As defined by Glynn Cochrane, social soundness analysis required that all development projects be preceded by a thorough baseline study of the cultural context and then potential redesign of the project based on those findings. A major goal was to prevent the funding of projects with little or no cultural fit. The World Bank hired its first anthropologist, Michael Cernea, in 1974. For three decades, Cernea influenced its policy-makers to pay more attention to project-affected people and their culture in designing and implementing projects. He promoted the term "development induced displacement" to bring attention to how large infrastructure projects negatively affect millions of people worldwide and he devised recommendations for mitigating such harm.

Many cultural anthropologists are applying cultural analysis to large-scale institutions (e.g., capitalism and the media) particularly their negative social consequences, such as the increasing wealth gap between powerful and less powerful countries and between the rich and the poor within countries. These anthropologists are moving in a new and challenging direction. Their work involves the study of global–local interactions and change over time, neither of which were part of cultural anthropology's original focus. Moreover, these cultural anthropologists take on the role of advocacy and often work collaboratively with victimized peoples.

Anthropologists are committed to documenting, understanding, and maintaining cultural diversity throughout the world as part of humanity's rich heritage. Through the four-field approach, they contribute to the recovery and analysis of the emergence and evolution of humanity. They provide detailed descriptions of cultures as they have existed in the past, as they now exist, and as they are changing in contemporary times. Anthropologists regret the decline and extinction of different cultures and actively contribute to the preservation of cultural diversity and cultural survival.

SEE ALSO *AIDS; American Anthropological Association; Anthropology, Biological; Anthropology, British; Anthropology, Linguistic; Anthropology, Medical; Anthropology, Public; Anthropology, U.S.; Anthropology, Urban; Archaeology; Boas, Franz; Cold War; Colonialism; Cultural Relativism; Culture; Developing Countries; Ethnography; Ethnology and Folklore; Feminism; Geertz, Clifford; Globalization, Anthropological Aspects of; Observation, Participant; Poverty; Primates; Race and Anthropology; Social Science*

BIBLIOGRAPHY

Abélès, Mark. 1999. How the Anthropology of France Has Changed Anthropology in France: Assessing New Directions in the Field. *Cultural Anthropology* 14: 404–408.

Appadurai, Arjun. 1996. *Modernity at Large: Cultural Dimensions of Globalization.* Minneapolis: University of Minnesota Press.

Asad, Talal, ed. 1992. *Anthropology and the Colonial Encounter.* 2nd ed. Atlantic Highlands, NJ: Humanities Press.

Barnard, Alan. 2000. *History and Theory in Anthropology.* New York: Cambridge University Press.

Barrett, Stanley R. 2000. *Anthropology: A Student's Guide to Theory and Method.* Toronto: University of Toronto Press.

Barth, Fredrik, Andre Gingrich, Robert Parkin, and Sydel Silverman. 2005. *One Discipline, Four Ways: British, German, French, and American Anthropology.* Chicago: University of Chicago Press.

Beckett, Jeremy. 2002. Some Aspects of Continuity and Change among Anthropologists in Australia or 'He-Who-Eats-From-One-Dish-With-Us-With-One-Spoon.' *The Australian Journal of Anthropology* 13: 127–138.

Blaser, Mario, Harvey A. Feit, and Glenn McRae, eds. 2004. *In the Way of Development: Indigenous Peoples, Life Projects and Globalization.* New York: Zed Books.

Borofsky, Robert, ed. 1994. *Assessing Cultural Anthropology.* New York: McGraw-Hill.

Bourdieu, Pierre. 1977. *Outline of a Theory of Practice.* Trans. Richard Nice. New York: Cambridge University Press.

Cernea, Michael. 1991. *Putting People First: Social Variables in Development.* 2nd ed. New York: Oxford University Press.

Fahim, Hussein, ed. 1982. *Indigenous Anthropology in Non-Western Countries.* Durham: Carolina Academic Press.

Geertz, Clifford. 1995. *After the Fact: Two Countries, Four Decades, One Anthropologist.* Cambridge: Harvard University Press.

González, Roberto J., ed. 2004. *Anthropologists in the Public Sphere: Speaking Out on War, Peace, and American Power.* Austin: University of Texas Press.

Goody, Jack. 1995. *The Expansive Moment: Anthropology in Britain and Africa, 1918–1970.* New York: Cambridge University Press.

Gupta, Akhil, and James Ferguson, eds. 1997. *Anthropological Locations: Boundaries and Grounds of a Field Science.* Berkeley: University of California Press.

Hammond-Tooke, W. David. 1997. *Imperfect Interpreters: South Africa's Anthropologists: 1920–1990.* Johannesburg: Witwatersrand University Press.

Hannerz, Ulf. 1992. *Cultural Complexity: Studies in the Social Organization of Meaning.* New York: Columbia University Press.

Harris, Marvin. 1968. *The Rise of Anthropological Theory: A History of Theories of Culture.* New York: Thomas Y. Crowell Company.

Harrison, Ira E., and Faye V. Harrison, eds. 1999. *African-American Pioneers in Anthropology.* Urbana: University of Illinois Press.

Inda, Jonathan Xavier, and Renato Rosaldo, eds. 2002. *The Anthropology of Globalization: A Reader.* Malden, MA: Blackwell Publishing Company.

Kroeber, Alfred. L., and Clyde Kluckhohn. 1952. *Culture: A Critical Review of Concepts and Definitions.* Cambridge, MA: Harvard University Press.

Kuper, Adam. 1973. *Anthropologists and Anthropology: The British School 1922–1972.* New York: Pica Press.

Kuwayama, Takami. 2004. *Native Anthropology: The Japanese Challenge to Western Academic Hegemony.* Melbourne, Australia: Trans Pacific Press.

Lassiter, Luke Eric. 2005. *The Chicago Guide to Collaborative Ethnography.* Chicago: University of Chicago Press.

Marcus, George E., and Michael M. J. Fischer. 1986. *Anthropology as Cultural Critique: An Experimental Moment in the Human Sciences.* Chicago: University of Chicago Press.

Medicine, Beatrice, with Sue-Ellen Jacobs, ed. 2001. *Learning to Be an Anthropologist and Remaining "Native."* Champaign: University of Illinois Press.

Mingming, Wang. 2002. The Third Eye: Towards a Critique of "Nativist Anthropology." *Critique of Anthropology* 22: 149–174.

Mullings, Leith. 2005. Interrogating Racism: Toward an Antiracist Anthropology. *Annual Review of Anthropology* 34: 667–694.

Patterson, Thomas C. 2001. *A Social History of Anthropology in the United States.* New York: Berg.

Peirano, Mariza G. S. 1998. When Anthropology Is at Home: The Different Contexts of a Single Discipline. *Annual Review of Anthropology* 27: 105–128.

Restrepo, Eduardo, and Arturo Escobar. 2005. "Other Anthropologies and Anthropology Otherwise:" Steps to a World Anthropologies Framework. *Critique of Anthropology* 25: 99–129.

Robinson, Kathryn. 2004. Chandra Jayaawrdena and the Ethical "Turn" in Australian Anthropology. *Critique of Anthropology* 24: 379–402.

Roseberry, William. 1997. Marx and Anthropology. *Annual Review of Anthropology* 26: 25–46.

Ryang, Sonia. 2004. *Japan and National Anthropology: A Critique.* New York: RoutledgeCurzon.

Shanklin, Eugenia. 2000. Representations of Race and Racism in American Anthropology. *Current Anthropology* 41: 99–103.

Spencer, Jonathan. 2000. British Social Anthropology: A Retrospective. *Annual Review of Anthropology* 29: 1–24.

Stocking, George W., Jr. 1992. *The Ethnographer's Magic and Other Essays in the History of Anthropology.* Minneapolis: University of Minnesota Press.

Yamashita, Shinji, Joseph Bosco, and J. S. Eades, eds. 2004. *The Making of Anthropology in East and Southeast Asia.* New York: Bergahn Books.

Barbara D. Miller

ANTHROPOLOGY, APPLIED

SEE *Anthropology, Public.*

ANTHROPOLOGY, BIOLOGICAL

Biological anthropology is concerned with the origin, evolution and diversity of humankind. The field was called physical anthropology until the late twentieth century, reflecting the field's primary concern with cataloging anatomical differences among human and primate groups. Under the name of biological anthropology, it is an ever-broadening field that encompasses the study of: human biological variation; evolutionary theory; human origins and evolution; early human migration; human ecology; the evolution of human behavior; paleoanthropology; anatomy; locomotion; osteology (the study of skeletal material); dental anthropology; forensics; medical anthropology, including the patterns and history of disease; primatology (the study of non-human primates); growth, development and nutrition; and other related fields.

The kinds of questions that biological anthropologists ask include:

What makes humans different from other species?

Where did modern humans arise and when?

What does evidence show about the original human migrations throughout the world?

What kinds of biological differences exist between populations, including anatomical, genetic, and behavioral, or patterns of growth and development, and how did the biological differences arise?

What can we learn about human evolution and behavior from non-human primates or other species?

How did uniquely human traits such as bipedalism and language evolve?

What can molecular genetics add to the understanding of evolution and human variation?

How does normal development happen, and what can it contribute to knowledge about evolution?

METHODS

Biological anthropology has a rich collection of methods, new and old, for answering these questions. Methods used include: field methods for finding specimens; comparative anatomy and morphological measurement; fossil analysis; population genetics; demographic and epidemiologic methods; and the use of model animals such as mice or non-human primates. Modern technologies—computed tomography (CT) scanning, molecular genetic and bioinformatic analytic techniques—are used to address questions about human diversity with studies of DNA variation and its history, for example. Tiny details of bones and fossils can be visualized and compared with high-powered imaging techniques to yield clues about the evolution of various traits.

In the late twentieth century, the largest change in biological anthropology has been the rapid incorporation of modern genetics. There are genetics laboratories in anthropology departments around the world, working on a wide variety of questions concerning human origins and diversity. Anthropologists also collaborate with non-anthropologists who have expertise in a broad spectrum of technical fields in order to use a wide variety of methodologies in their research.

HISTORY

Although people have been interested for several millennia in characterizing how populations differ, the work of Swedish botanist Carolus Linnaeus (1707–1778) cataloging all known species was the first modern systematic classification of human variation. Linnaeus developed the binomial naming convention (*Homo sapiens*, for example) still used today. He classified humans into groups based on geographic origin and skin color, and subsequently on behavior. Probably not surprisingly, Europeans ranked highest in Linnaeus's schemes.

A number of people worked on cataloging human variation in the eighteenth and nineteenth centuries, including Georges Buffon (1707–1788, who published

Varieties of the Human Species in 1749), Jean-Baptiste Lamarck (1744–1829), and Georges Cuvier (1769–1832). Johann Friedrich Blumenbach (1752–1840) is often considered the founder of physical anthropology. Inspired by Linnaeus, Blumenbach was interested in documenting the anatomical differences among humans, establishing the field of comparative anatomy to do so. He published *On the Natural Variety of Mankind* in 1795, in which he proposed five distinct races.

Blumenbach's grouping became the basis of the scientific classification system for race, which was developed and expanded in the nineteenth and twentieth centuries. But, as Darwin pointed out in *The Descent of Man*, race is a slippery concept. The number of races catalogued in Darwin's day alone ranged from two to sixty-three. In modern time, race as a useful biological concept is largely considered by anthropologists to be without scientific merit. By any biological measure, even human groups long isolated geographically are more similar than they are different. Yet race is an issue that will not go away because the concept of race is as much political and social as it is biological.

Although in the twenty-first century biological anthropology is thoroughly grounded in the study of human diversity, nineteenth century biological (physical) anthropologists were preoccupied with such questions as whether humans were part of the natural world, or more than one species. Darwin's theory of evolution, first published in 1859 in *The Origin of Species*, gave biological anthropology a conceptual framework. Old questions were immediately resolvable; evolutionary theory confirms that humans are part of the natural world and share a common origin with every other species on Earth. Other questions were not resolvable. For example, the question of how many species humans comprise became a question of how many races, and this question preoccupied anthropologists, along with human geneticists, for decades.

Homo sapiens (modern human) is the only surviving species of those that comprised the 1.5 to 2.5 million year old *Homo* lineage. Paleontologists still debate what extinct species should be considered *Homo* (based on fossil evidence), or the extent to which there were contemporary *Homo* species alive during the approximately 2 million years of hominid history. If *Homo sapiens* and *Homo neanderthalensis* (a *Homo* species, commonly known as Neanderthal, that lived in Europe and parts of western Asia from about 130,000 to 24,000 years ago, now extinct) were contemporaneous 30,000 and more years ago, for example, did they interbreed? Some anthropologists believe that the tools of modern molecular genetics may help answer this question. The 2003 finding of 12,000-year-old fossils of apparently small people in a cave on the Indonesian island of Flores, *Homo floresiensis*

(Man of Flores), raises the question of whether other *Homo* species were alive until even more recently than Neanderthals. This issue will be debated for some time to come. Whatever the question of interest to contemporary biological anthropologists, from comparisons between species to the origins of human traits, biological anthropologists will continue to couch questions within the framework of evolutionary theory.

SEE ALSO *Anthropology; Anthropology, Medical; Archaeology; Burial Grounds; Darwin, Charles; Disease; Genomics; Leakey, Richard; Natural Selection; Primates; Race; Racial Classification; Racism*

BIBLIOGRAPHY

Boyd, Robert, and Joan Silk. 2006. *How Humans Evolved*, 4th ed. New York: Norton.

Brown P., T. Sutikna, M. J. Morwood, et al. 2004. A New Small-Bodied Hominin from the Late Pleistocene of Flores, Indonesia. *Nature* 431 (October):1055–1061.

Darwin, Charles. 1859. *The Origin of Species by Means of Natural Selection.* London: John Murray.

Darwin, Charles. 1871. *The Descent of Man, and Selection in Relation to Sex.* London: John Murray.

Jobling, Mark, Matthew Hurles, and Chris Tyler-Smith. 2004. *Human Evolutionary Genetics: Origins, Peoples and Disease.* New York: Garland.

Relethford, John. 2003. *The Human Species: An Introduction to Biological Anthropology.* New York: McGraw-Hill.

Weiss, Kenneth M., and Anne V. Buchanan. 2004. *Genetics and the Logic of Evolution.* Hoboken, NJ: Wiley-Liss.

Anne Buchanan

ANTHROPOLOGY, BRITISH

A. R. Radcliffe-Brown once said that anthropology has two beginnings: the first in 1748 and the second around 1870. For British anthropology, one could add a third beginning, around 1922, when both Radcliffe-Brown and Bronislaw Malinowski began teaching in earnest and published their major field monographs. Radcliffe-Brown's first date, 1748, marks the first publication, in French, of Montesquieu's *Spirit of the Laws.* Within two years an English edition appeared, and this greatly influenced the anthropological ideas of Scottish writers such as Adam Smith. His anthropological approach, modeled on Montesquieu's, became known as "conjectural history." The idea was that speculation and logical deduction, often supplemented by knowledge from early ethnographic

reports, should lead us to understand the early history of society.

Institutional anthropology in Britain began in 1843 with the founding of the Ethnological Society of London, which merged with a rival society in 1871 to become the Anthropological Institute. Major publications around that time include Sir Henry Maine's *Ancient Law* (published in 1861), J. F. McLennan's *Primitive Marriage* (1865), and Sir Edward Tylor's *Primitive Culture* (1871). Maine's book overthrew the Enlightenment notion of the "social contract" in favor of the family as the basis of society, and it also created the study of kinship as the central interest of the British tradition. One early debate centered on which came first, patrilineal or matrilineal descent? Maine favored the former, while McLennan favored the latter. Tylor's contribution included his famous definition of *culture* as "that complex whole which includes knowledge, belief, art, morals, law, custom, and any other capabilities and habits acquired by man as a member of society" ([1871] 1958, p. 1).

Polish immigrant Bronislaw Malinowski began teaching at the London School of Economics in 1922, the year of publication of his *Argonauts of the Western Pacific.* That book describes the inhabitants of the Trobriand Islands, where Malinowski spent World War I and where he created the modern style of anthropological fieldwork (working in the native language and through participating in as well as observing daily activities of the people). Meanwhile, Radcliffe-Brown had the year before obtained a professorship at the University of Cape Town. He later moved to Sydney and to Chicago before returning to Britain to take a chair at Oxford University. His major monograph, also published in 1922, was *The Andaman Islanders.* Together Malinowski and Radcliffe-Brown came to emphasize contemporary society over social evolution. Malinowski called this new approach "functionalism," and the idea was to see how each aspect of society related to other aspects. Radcliffe-Brown shied away from the word, but what others called his "structural-functionalism" emphasized further the relations between institutions in social systems, the classic four systems being kinship, politics, economics, and religion. He published his collected essays as *Structure and Function in Primitive Society* in 1952, and his theoretical approach (borrowed partly from Émile Durkheim's sociology) together with Malinowski's fieldwork methods became the twin hallmarks of the British tradition. These two men trained the first generation of professional anthropologists (most of the earlier ones having been amateur scholars), and established British anthropology as a great world tradition and the idea of the departmental seminar as the main means of teaching graduate students.

The United Kingdom became the world's most expansive imperial power in the nineteenth century, and British anthropologists through the first half of the twentieth century took advantage of this. The Malinowskian emphasis on fieldwork encouraged interaction between indigenous populations of the empire and anthropologists, and also between anthropologists and colonial officers. Some of the latter even studied anthropology in British or Commonwealth institutions, and indeed, so too did some residents of the colonies, most famously Jomo Kenyatta, later the first president of Kenya, who did his PhD under Malinowski in the 1930s.

From the 1950s other influences came in. Max Gluckman, from South Africa, and other members of the "Manchester school" that he founded, introduced an interest in conflict and dispute settlement. Fredrik Barth, a Norwegian who studied at Cambridge University, emphasized individual action and fluent group boundaries over rigid social structures. Radcliffe-Brown's successor at Oxford, Sir Edward Evans-Pritchard, pushed against functionalism from another angle. He came to see anthropology as more like the art of history-writing than like the practice of the biological sciences (Radcliffe-Brown's favorite analogy was "society is like an organism"). Especially in his study of the religion of the Nuer of Sudan, Evans-Pritchard argued that anthropologists should aim to understand things such as religious belief from the native point of view and "interpret" them so they can be understood in one's own culture.

British followers of the French structuralist Claude Lévi-Strauss became prominent in the 1960s, especially Sir Edmund Leach. In *Political Systems of Highland Burma* (1954), Leach argued that the Kachin he had lived with before and during World War II exhibited two forms of social organization, one being egalitarian and the other hierarchical. Groups oscillated between the two according to ecological influences, and the political structure too was apparent in the ways in which lineages were related through marriages. Leach, along with Rodney Needham, took to Lévi-Strauss's "alliance theory" in kinship, and the great battle of the 1960s was between this idea (stressing relations between groups through marriage) and "descent theory" (the older British approach stressing the importance of descent groups). The 1970s saw battles within the alliance theory camp, with Needham and most other British alliance theorists looking to reflect accurately ethnographic realities of what they called "prescriptive" systems of alliance (where one must marry someone of a particular category of kin), whereas French thinkers tended to prefer idealized models far removed from ethnography.

In the 1970s Marxism became a dominant force, with work such as that of Talal Asad critiquing relations that had existed between colonialism and the development of British anthropology. Other British-based anthropologists, including Maurice Bloch, Jonathan Friedman, and Joel Kahn, argued for greater awareness of historical global influences such as colonialism and capitalism on the populations anthropologists work with. Through the 1980s and 1990s the influence of American anthropology further watered down classic British interests, and today there is little difference, except in the way the history of the discipline is construed, between British anthropology and other traditions. That said, British anthropology retains particular strengths in studies of conflict, social development, and kinship (including new reproductive technologies), as well as in ethnographic writing. It also retains strong pedagogical elements from its earlier times, notably the tradition of departmental seminar as a means of teaching and of debate.

SEE ALSO *American Anthropological Association; Anthropology; Anthropology, Biological; Anthropology, Linguistic; Anthropology, Medical; Anthropology, Public; Anthropology, U.S.; Anthropology, Urban; Archaeology; Boas, Franz; Culture; Functionalism; Geertz, Clifford; Globalization, Anthropological Aspects of; Race and Anthropology*

BIBLIOGRAPHY

Barnard, Alan. 2000. *History and Theory in Anthropology.* Cambridge, U.K.: Cambridge University Press.

Kuklick, Henrika. 1992. *The Savage Within: The Social History of British Anthropology, 1885–1945.* Cambridge, U.K.: Cambridge University Press.

Kuper, Adam. 1996. *Anthropology and Anthropologists: The Modern British School.* 3rd ed. London: Routledge.

Leach, Edmund. 1954. *Political Systems of Highland Burma.* Cambridge, MA: Harvard University Press.

Maine, Henry. [1861] 2000. *Ancient Law.* Washington, DC: Beard Books.

Malinowski, Bronislaw. 1922. *Argonauts of the Western Pacific.* New York: E. P. Dutton.

McLennan, J. F. [1865] 1970. *Primitive Marriage.* Chicago: University of Chicago Press.

Radcliffe-Brown, A. R. [1922] 1964. *The Andaman Islanders.* New York: Free Press.

Radcliffe-Brown, A. R. 1952. *Structure and Function in Primitive Society.* Glencoe, IL: Free Press.

Spencer, Jonathan. 2000. British Social Anthropology: A Retrospecive. *Annual Review of Anthropology* 29: 1–24.

Tylor, Edward. [1871] 1958. *Primitive Culture*, Vol. 1. New York: Harper and Brothers.

Alan Barnard

ANTHROPOLOGY, LINGUISTIC

Linguistic anthropology examines the links between language and culture, including how language relates to thought, social action, identity, and power relations. It is one of the four traditional subfields of American anthropology, sharing with sociocultural anthropology its aims of explaining social and cultural phenomena, with biological anthropology its concern over language origins and evolution, and with archaeology the goal of understanding cultural histories. Linguistic anthropology has developed through international work across social science disciplines, as researchers attend to language as a key to understanding social phenomena. The discipline overlaps most closely with the sociolinguistic subfield of linguistics. But while sociolinguistics generally considers social factors in order to explain linguistic phenomena, linguistic anthropology aims to explain social and cultural phenomena by considering linguistic information.

Linguistic anthropology, as a part of American anthropology, has its origins in the work of Franz Boas's 1911 *Handbook of American Indian Languages*. Inspired by his work with Native American groups, Boas introduced the concept of linguistic and cultural relativism, the premise that a particular language or culture can only be understood with regard to its own internal logic. The concept of linguistic relativism was developed further by Edward Sapir and Benjamin Whorf, who argued that languages predispose the speakers to experience the world in particular ways. This axiom has come to be known as the "Sapir-Whorf hypothesis." Researchers have since explored the extent to which language shapes thought, for example, with studies of color terminologies. These trends led to "ethnoscience," a field of research founded in the 1960s that focused on the systematic ways of understanding the world that are encoded in language. This approach was strongly influenced by the work of Swiss linguist Ferdinand de Saussure, whose analysis of language as an idealized social system set the foundations for the structuralist approach in anthropology. Recognizing the unique value of every language, linguistic anthropologists continue to document the grammars, cognitive maps, and traditional knowledge of threatened cultures and their languages in an effort to preserve and revitalize them.

The interest in language as a window on thought was paralleled by an interest in language as a means of acting upon the world. This line of inquiry drew on the work of philosophers John Austin and John Searle. They examined the performative function of language in speech acts (called performativity), actions that are accomplished as words are spoken, such as promising and marrying. Linguistic anthropologists extended the concept of performativity, viewing all language in use as a constructive activity and not just a means of relaying pre-existing information. Language is social action at many levels, from the construction of personhood and beliefs, to negotiation of social status between people, to the assertion of authority and group identities at the level of nations or transnational groups.

From analysis of contextualized speech acts, anthropologists John J. Gumperz and Dell Hymes introduced the ethnography of communication in the 1960s. This approach examines the rich cultural and contextual knowledge required to communicate competently, beyond knowledge of words and grammar. The speech community was proposed as a unit of analysis based on observed interactions, in place of pre-existing idealized categories. The ethnography of communication had much in common with the ethnomethodology approach developed in sociology starting in the 1960s by Harold Garfinkel and Erving Goffman. The methods of conversation analysis were elaborated by scholars in both anthropology and sociology, relying on analysis of recordings to uncover the rules governing interactions that usually function below the level of awareness (e.g., norms for turn-taking, timing, topic control, and other factors shaping social positioning). Linguistic anthropologists examine these interactional dynamics and rules across cultures and, among other things, seek to explain the reasons for cross-cultural miscommunication.

Discourse analysis expands from a focus on conversations to include analysis of language use in any context in both verbal and written form, including speeches, storytelling, ritual, performance, television, newspapers, and the Internet. Discourse analysis methods attend to both content and linguistic forms used (e.g., active or passive grammatical construction, inclusive or exclusive pronoun choice, formality of language) to show how linguistic forms affect people's thoughts, actions, and identities. In linguistic anthropology, a major concern in the analysis of discourse is how inequalities of power are created, expressed, and manipulated through language. Also of particular interest are processes of socialization (how children or adults learn new social rules) and how agency (an individual's ability to act) is expressed and enacted in speech. At the broadest level, analysis of discourse can also refer to examination of discourse as the systems of logic pervading a society (e.g., ways of thinking and talking about things, ways of arranging things in space) that shape social differences and power inequalities. This way of thinking about discourse was proposed by philosopher Michel Foucault.

The study of language as social action has also led to a view of language as a fluid, shifting, and heterogeneous medium, replacing Saussure's notion of languages and cultures as discrete idealized units. Influential in this development was the work of Russian linguists Valentin Voloshinov (*Marxism and the Philosophy of Language*) and Mikhail Bakhtin (*Discourse in the Novel*), who theorized that language is "heteroglossic," its meanings never fixed but always emerging anew between speakers, shaped by histories of social experiences, intentions, and desires. This approach posits language as the site of struggles over social power, supporting the analysis of the role of language in political economy. This area of research examines in part how authoritative and prestigious languages are constructed, how named languages and correlating national or ethnic units and identities are defined, and how language values are negotiated in multilingual situations. Beginning in the 1990s, interest in the relationships between language, power, and identity led to a focus on language ideology, the ideological link between linguistic forms (e.g., different languages, registers, or word choices) and social forms (ethnic, gendered, socioeconomic, or other social distinctions). Researchers studying these topics examine the meaning-making processes and stances through which people construct identities, taking into account both historical trajectories and contemporary contexts of language use.

While linguistic anthropology overlaps with many other fields in its topics of inquiry, its distinctiveness as a field lays in its holistic comparative cross-cultural approach and fieldwork-based research methods.

SEE ALSO *Anthropology; Boas, Franz; Culture; Discourse; Goffman, Erving; Identity; Inequality, Political; Inequality, Racial; Linguistic Turn; Logic; Performance; Power; Racial Slurs; Socialization; Structuralism; Theory of Mind*

BIBLIOGRAPHY

Agar, Michael. 1994. *Language Shock: Understanding the Culture of Conversation*. New York: William Morrow.

Bakhtin, Mikhail M. [1934] 1981. Discourse in the Novel. In *The Dialogic Imagination: Four Essays,* ed. Michael Holquist, trans. Caryl Emerson and Michael Holquist. Austin: University of Texas Press.

Boas, Franz. [1911] 1976. *Handbook of American Indian Languages*. St. Clair Shores, MI: Scholarly Press.

Bourdieu, Pierre. 1991. *Language and Symbolic Power,* ed J. B. Thompson, trans. Gino Raymond and Matthew Adamson. Cambridge, MA: Harvard University Press.

Brenneis, Donald, and Ronald K. S. Macaulay. 1996. *The Matrix of Language: Contemporary Linguistic Anthropology*. Boulder, CO: Westview Press.

Duranti, Alessandro, ed. 2006. *A Companion to Linguistic Anthropology*. Oxford: Blackwell.

Gumperz, John J., and Dell Hymes, eds. 1972. *Directions in Sociolinguistics: The Ethnography of Communication*. New York: Holt, Rinehart and Winston.

Kroskrity, Paul V., ed. 2000. *Regimes of Language: Ideologies, Polities, and Identities*. Santa Fe, NM: School of American Research Press; Oxford: James Currey.

Sapir, Edward. 1921. *Language: An Introduction to the Study of Speech*. New York: Harcourt, Brace, and Company.

Whorf, Benjamin Lee. 1956. *Language, Thought, and Reality: Selected Writings*, ed. John B. Carroll. Cambridge, MA: Technology Press of MIT.

Voloshinov, Valentin. [1929] 1986. *Marxism and the Philosophy of Language*. Trans. Ladislav Matejka and I. R. Titunik. Cambridge, MA: Harvard University Press.

Laada Bilaniuk

ANTHROPOLOGY, MEDICAL

Medical anthropology is the subdiscipline of anthropology that focuses on the intersection of health, medicine, society, and culture. Generally thought to include the study of the impact of disease on society and the impact of society and culture on health and disease, medical anthropology encompasses several different paradigms for research, including biocultural anthropology; ethnomedicine; social and cultural factors in the incidence, prevalence, and treatment of disease, or social epidemiology; the political economy of health; and the inclusion of cultural and social concerns in the planning, implementation, and evaluation of projects, which is the core of applied medical anthropology.

ORIGINS OF MEDICAL ANTHROPOLOGY

In 1978 George Foster and Barbara Anderson, following Khwaja Hassan (1975), suggested that the field of contemporary medical anthropology has four distinct roots that came together in the mid-twentieth century to form a recognized subfield of inquiry: the interest in variation in human morphology and paleopathology that began in the mid-nineteenth century, carried out in part by anatomists and early physical anthropologists; the culture and personality movement, or psychological anthropology, that began in the early twentieth century as both an offshoot of and a critical alternative to Freudian psychology but gained strength during World War II because of increasing interest in understanding the psychological makeup of the different cultures involved in that conflict; the study of ethnomedicine, which began as part of ethnography in the nineteenth century but became a focus of study for culturally oriented medical anthropologists after the posthumous publication of W. H. R. Rivers's *Medicine, Magic, and Religion* in 1924; and the applied anthropology of public health, which arose from the post–World War II interest in improving health practices and introducing biomedicine in developing countries. The continuation of these themes can be seen in contemporary medical anthropology in the form of biocultural anthropology, ethnomedicine, critical medical anthropology (CMA), applied medical anthropology, and psychological anthropology.

REVIEWS AND ORGANIZATIONS

The first review that addressed the subfield was William Caudill's 1953 article "Applied Anthropology in Medicine." As the title suggests, it was a review of the inclusion of anthropological concepts and ethnographic methods in medical settings, or in medical sociologist Robert Straus's terms, social science *in* medicine (1957). The first review article with the title "Medical Anthropology" was published by Norman Scotch in 1963 and was more comprehensive in its approach. Subsequent reviews by Horacio Fabrega in 1971 and Anthony Colson and Karen Selby in 1974 continued to debate the nature of the field, with the latter article discussing whether medical anthropology constituted a subfield of anthropology or the intersection of anthropology and medicine.

By the mid-1970s, however, there was a well-organized association representing the field of medical anthropology that embraced the full range of work by people who called themselves medical anthropologists. The Society for Medical Anthropology (SMA) started as the Steering Committee for the Organization of Medical Anthropology, which began publication of the *Medical Anthropology Newsletter* (MAN) in 1968. MAN later became the *Medical Anthropology Quarterly* (MAQ). In 1987 MAQ achieved status as a peer-reviewed quarterly journal that publishes across the full range of research in medical anthropology.

PHILOSOPHIES AND THEORIES

Biocultural anthropology draws heavily on the work of the neoevolutionary theorists of the mid-twentieth century and the adaptation paradigm that entered medical anthropology in the 1970s after the publication in 1970 of Alexander Alland's *Adaptation in Cultural Anthropology: An Approach to Medical Anthropology*. It includes anthropologists trained in cultural anthropology and those trained in biological anthropology and generally examines the way in which adaptation to particular physical and social environmental conditions shapes the experience of disease and illness in societies and the ways in which society adapts to challenges presented by disease. It also involves researchers working in human biology, and early interest among physical anthropologists and anatomists in paleopathology is represented currently by

forensic anthropology. Biocultural anthropology has been criticized by writers with a CMA perspective for its failure to assess the assumptions in the adaptation/neoevolutionary theoretical framework critically. However, current theorists such as Goodman and Leatherman (1998) and Andrea Wiley (2004) have attempted to include a political economy approach in biocultural anthropology.

Critical medical anthropology and the political economy of health approaches draw heavily on the work of Marxist and later poststructural social theorists such as Michel Foucault (1975). The central project of CMA is a critical examination of the assumptions and practice of biomedicine, their application in medicine and health policy, and the diffusion of biomedical understandings to non-Western settings, in Straus's terms, social science *of* medicine (or ethnomedical systems). Drawing on the work of Rudolf Virchow, it also can include the application of theory from political economy to the understanding of the distribution of health and illness. Key books in this area include the works of Paul Farmer (1999, 2003), Merrill Singer (2006a, 2006b), and Nancy Scheper-Hughes (1992) and more comprehensive works such as *Medical Anthropology in the World System* (Baer, Singer, and Susser 2003).

Applied medical anthropology has its roots in the international public health movement that gained momentum after World War II. One of the first series of studies of the role of ethnomedical beliefs in the adoption of public health practices and biomedical treatment was carried out by anthropologists working for the Smithsonian Institution's Bureau of American Ethnology under contract to the Office of Special Studies, which later became the U.S. Agency for International Development. Some of this work is summarized in *Health, Culture, and Community*, edited by Benjamin Paul (1955), which argued for the inclusion of the study of ethnomedical beliefs in the design and implementation of public health programs. A number of anthropologists have worked with bilateral and multilateral health organizations such as the U.S. Agency for International Development and the World Health Organization. Interest in the study of non-Western medical systems also has been incorporated, including Mark Nichter's work on ethnomedical systems and medical change (1989, 1992). The line dividing primarily theoretically oriented and primarily applied research has become blurred. Several critical theorists, such as Merrill Singer and Paul Farmer, are deeply involved in the design and implementation of interventions and use a political economy approach to understand the epidemiology of disease and illness.

SEE ALSO *Anthropology; Anthropology, Biological; Disease; Ethno-epidemiological Methodology; Foucault, Michel; Marxism; Medicine; Poststructuralism*

BIBLIOGRAPHY

Alland, Alexander. 1970. *Adaptation in Cultural Evolution: An Approach to Medical Anthropology*. New York: Columbia University Press.

Baer, Hans A., Merrill Singer, and Ida Susser. 2003. *Medical Anthropology and the World System*. 2nd ed. Westport, CT: Praeger.

Caudill, William 1953. Applied Anthropology in Medicine. In *Anthropology Today: An Encyclopedic Inventory, Prepared under the Chairmanship of A. L. Kroeber*, ed. Alfred L. Kroeber, 771–791. Chicago: University of Chicago Press.

Colson, Anthony C., and Karen E. Selby. 1974. Medical Anthropology. *Annual Review of Anthropology* 3: 245–262.

Ember, Carol R., and Melvin Ember. 2003. *Encyclopedia of Medical Anthropology: Health and Illness in the World's Cultures*, vols. 1 and 2. New York: Kluwer Academic/Plenum Publishers.

Fabrega, Horacio, Jr. 1971. Medical Anthropology. *Annual Review of Anthropology.*167–229.

Farmer, Paul. 1999. *Infections and Inequalities: The Modern Plagues*. Berkeley: University of California Press.

Farmer, Paul. 2003. *Pathologies of Power: Health, Human Rights, and the New War on the Poor*. Berkeley: University of California Press.

Foster, George M., and Barbara Gallatin Anderson. 1978. *Medical Anthropology*. New York: Wiley.

Foucault, Michel. 1975. *Birth of the Clinic: An Archaeology of Medical Perception*. New York: Vintage.

Goodman, Alan, and Thomas Leatherman, eds. 1998. *Building a New Biocultural Synthesis: Political-Economic Perspectives on Human Biology (Linking Levels of Analysis)*. Ann Arbor: University of Michigan Press.

Hassan, Khwaja Arif. 1975. What Is Medical Anthropology? *Medical Anthropology Newsletter* 6 (3): 7–10.

Nichter, Mark. 1989. *Anthropology and International Health: South Asian Case Studies*. Dordrecht, Netherlands, and Boston: Kluwer Academic Publishers.

Nichter, Mark, ed. 1992. *Anthropological Approaches to the Study of Ethnomedicine*. Yverdon, Switzerland, and Langhorne, PA: Gordon and Breach Science Publishers.

Paul, Benjamin D., ed. 1955. *Health, Culture, and Community: Case Studies of Public Reactions to Health Programs*. New York: Russell Sage Foundation.

Rivers, W. H. R. 1924. *Medicine, Magic, and Religion: The Fitz Patrick Lectures Delivered before the Royal College of Physicians of London*. New York: Harcourt Brace.

Scheper-Hughes, Nancy. 1992. *Death without Weeping: The Violence of Everyday Life in Brazil*. Berkeley: University of California Press.

Scheper-Hughes, Nancy, and Margaret Lock. 1987. The Mindful Body: A Prolegomenon to Future Work in Medical Anthropology. *Medical Anthropology Quarterly, New Series* 1: 6–41.

Scotch, Norman A. 1963. Medical Anthropology. *Biennial Review of Anthropology* 3: 30–68.

Singer, Merrill. 2006a. *The Face of Social Suffering: Life History of a Street Drug Addict*. Long Grove, IL.: Waveland Press.

Singer, Merrill. 2006b. *Something Dangerous: Emergent and Changing Illicit Drug Use and Community Health*. Long Grove, IL: Waveland Press.

Straus, Robert. 1957. The Nature and Status of Medical Sociology. *American Sociological Review* 22: 200–204.

Trostle, James A. 2004. *Epidemiology and Culture*. Cambridge, U.K., and New York: Cambridge University Press.

Wiley, Andrea S. 2004. *An Ecology of High-Altitude Infancy: A Biocultural Perspective*. Cambridge, U.K., and New York: Cambridge University Press.

Kathleen Musante DeWalt

ANTHROPOLOGY, PHYSICAL
SEE *Anthropology, Biological.*

ANTHROPOLOGY, PRACTICING
SEE *Anthropology, Public.*

ANTHROPOLOGY, PUBLIC

Public anthropology focuses the distinctive perspectives and methods of anthropology on public issues. Since the founding of anthropology as an academic discipline in the late nineteenth century, it has changed a great deal and divided into numerous specialties and schools of thought, but certain key features abide. Anthropology is comprehensive of space and time: it covers the entire world, and it treats humankind throughout its history and prehistory, including the present. It is also comprehensive in aspect, treating biological as well as cultural features of humans, and it tends to be holistic, considering how various aspects of life fit together rather than attending mainly to one aspect, such as economics or politics. Finally, anthropology relies strongly on fieldwork, whether archaeological excavation or participant observation of all manner of contemporary situations. Public anthropology deploys these characteristic approaches of anthropology to address public issues.

Some consider public anthropology to be an extension of an older field, *applied anthropology*, which is also termed *practicing anthropology*. That is a valid perspective, but public anthropology tends to focus less on specific problems than on the issues and policies that create the problems. Applied anthropology, for example, might aid a community in correcting a problem with pollution, while public anthropology might address the policies or culture that create the pollution. Among those practicing and defining public anthropology, emphases and terminologies vary. *Public interest anthropology*, for example, emphasizes that the issues the field is concerned with are defined by public bodies' interests (Sanday), while Rob Borofsky would include the publicizing of anthropology—connecting public figures and public arenas to anthropology.

Whereas anthropologists generally attempt to understand and appreciate all human behaviors, a public anthropologist may conclude that some behaviors or situations should change. She or he may judge that some actions violate human rights and move beyond cultural relativism to take a position against torture, child slavery, or the oppression of women, for example, and then work to prevent those actions or even to change the situations and culture that support them.

Moving from scholarly understanding to advocacy and action, public anthropology may modify classic methods. Ethnographic fieldwork is excellent for in-depth analysis but may take too long to be a good way of investigating urgent problems. Holism offers breadth but can distract attention from a problem at hand. Anthropology as a discipline offers much, but the work of addressing public issues cannot be confined to a single discipline. Instead, it requires a combination of academic disciplines and necessarily reaches beyond academics to involve the entire community. Researchers may need to engage with or even become leaders, administrators, and advocates. Public anthropology welcomes such disciplinary intersections and forms of engagement (Peacock 1997).

Historically and in the early twenty-first century, a variety of anthropological efforts illustrate possibilities for public anthropology, though they are not always labeled as such. Lee Baker's account suggests that the founder Franz Boas's efforts to combat racism were an early example of public anthropology. Boas utilized careful research to demonstrate, for example, that the shape of one's head is influenced by the environment. From this, he argued against racism on the ground that the environment, including culture, is a major factor in shaping physical characteristics that many of his contemporaries identified as being specific to race. Boas's student Margaret Mead (1928) followed his lead by demonstrating through her fieldwork in Samoa that adolescence is culturally shaped and not merely biologically determined. After completing fieldwork in New Guinea and Bali, Mead went on to apply anthropology to a range of public issues, one of which was gender. She utilized her fieldwork to show how definitions of male and female depend on cultural context, and hence she argued for a more flexible understand-

ing and acceptance of wider variation in the roles of both women and men (Mead 1949).

Early twenty-first century examples of public anthropology are diverse. Paul Farmer, a physician and anthropologist, practiced in Haiti initially and addresses public-health issues globally (Kidder 2003). Johnnetta Cole is an anthropologist who has served as a college president, first of Spelman College and then of Bennett College—both historically black colleges for women that Cole has shaped into institutions that nurture positive values. Other examples range from James Peacock's (2007) efforts to build international concerns at a state university and in a regional context to the creation of a union of academics and activists (CIRA) and investigation of public issues in communities (Holland et al. 2007).

Among formal anthropological organizations, public anthropologists can be found in the National Association of Practicing Anthropologists and the Society for Applied Anthropology and among the thirty-plus sections of the American Anthropological Association (identified by specialty or cultural/ethnic focus) as well as in the Royal Anthropological Institute and many international organizations. Several universities offer programs in public anthropology, and there are publications focused on the discipline. The work also occurs in interdisciplinary and nonacademic organizations ranging from local legislatures to international bodies, such as the United Nations.

Public anthropology, then, is not easily defined by pinpointing a single organizational affiliation or any certification; one is not certified to practice public anthropology. It is best recognized as an approach or practice that utilizes anthropological training, knowledge, and perspectives in addressing societal issues.

In a global and diverse world, issues require comprehensive perspectives. More so than most disciplines, anthropology is comprehensive, encompassing a century of field experience in diverse global contexts. The challenge for public anthropology is to deploy that experience in active engagement to address pressing issues effectively. On the one hand, public anthropology must broaden its vision beyond its British and North American academic origins as diverse cultures and communities assume leadership roles; on the other, it must hone its methods to make an impact.

SEE ALSO *Activism; American Anthropological Association; Anthropology; Boas, Franz; Human Rights; Mead, Margaret; Public Policy*

BIBLIOGRAPHY

Baker, Lee. 2004. Franz Boas Out of the Ivory Tower. *Anthropological Theory* 4 (1): 29–51.

Basch, Linda G., Lucie Wood Saunders, Jagna Wojcicka Sharf, and James Peacock, eds. 1999. *Transforming Academia: Challenges and Opportunities for an Engaged Anthropology.* Arlington, VA: American Anthropological Association.

Borofsky, Rob. 2006. Public Anthropology. http://www.publicanthropology.org.

Cole, Johnnetta B. 2003. *Gender Talk: The Struggle for Women's Equality in African American Communities.* New York: Ballantine Books.

Hill, Carole E., and Marietta L. Baba, eds. 2000. *The Unity of Theory and Practice in Anthropology: Rebuilding a Fractured Synthesis.* Arlington, VA: American Anthropological Association.

Holland, Dorothy, Donald Nonini, Catherine Lutz, Leslie Bartlett, Marla Frederick-McGlathery, Thaddeus Guldbrandsen, and Enrique Murillo. 2007. *Local Democracy under Siege: Activism, Public Interests, and Private Politics.* New York: New York University Press.

Kidder, Tracy. 2003. *Mountains beyond Mountains: The Quest of Dr. Paul Farmer, a Man Who Would Cure the World.* New York: Random House.

Mead, Margaret. 1928. *Coming of Age in Samoa: A Psychological Study of Primitive Youth for Western Civilisation.* New York: William Morrow.

Mead, Margaret. 1949. *Male and Female: A Study of the Sexes in a Changing World.* New York: William Morrow.

Peacock, James L. 1997. The Future of Anthropology. *American Anthropologist* 99 (1): 9–17.

Peacock, James L. 2007. *Grounded Globalism: How the U.S. South Embraces the World.* Athens: University of Georgia Press.

Sanday, Peggy. 2003. Public Interest Anthropology: A Model for Engaged Social Science. http://www.sas.upenn.edu/~psanday/SARdiscussion%20paper.65.html.

Sanday, Peggy. 2004. Public Interest Anthropology: A Model for Engaged Research. http://www.sas.upenn.edu/~psanday/PIE.05.htm.

James Peacock

ANTHROPOLOGY, URBAN

Throughout history, cities have been important places of associated life, human diversity, and interaction. However, while twentieth-century sociologists have been at the forefront of urban studies, social and cultural anthropologists have long neglected the city as a relevant field of research. In the late 1930s a few anthropologists, such as Robert Redfield (1897–1958), shifted their attention from tribal and rural communities to peasant city-dwellers. Influenced by the Chicago school, some American anthropologists engaged in problem-centered studies that focused on poverty, ecology, and minorities; they developed such concepts as the "culture of poverty," cited by Oscar Lewis in *Five Families: Mexican Case Studies in the Culture of Poverty* (1959). Many of these studies examined rural-urban migration in slums and shanty towns in Mexico and other Latin American countries. Meanwhile, a group of anthropologists led by the South African Max Gluckman at the Rhodes Livingston Institute of Northern Rhodesia studied the effects of urbanization on tribal economy and social relations, particularly in the Copperbelt area of central Africa. Research in African cities, however, was not really considered urban research, according to Ralph D. Grillo in *Ideologies and Institutions in Urban France: The Representation of Immigrants* (1985). Although such pioneering work was later criticized for its functionalist approach, it did contribute to the development of new anthropological methods, such as case and network analysis.

More generally, anthropologists seemed to consider the city a new laboratory in which to carry out traditional studies on kinship, small-group dynamics, and belief and value systems. This trend continued throughout the 1960s, prompting Ulf Hannerz in *Exploring the City; Inquiries toward an Urban Anthropology* (1980) to question whether urban anthropology had a specific subject of study.

A more eclectic and regionally diversified urban anthropology emerged during the 1970s as field research was conducted in Japan, India, and Indonesia, and across Africa and South America. Such socioeconomic and geopolitical variety raised some confusion in precisely defining the term *urban.* For some, *urban* referred to population aggregates of a certain size. Others defined *urban* in terms of occupations other than agricultural or subsistence production. Still others defined *urban* as the density of social interaction rather than just demographic or physical density. From a Marxist perspective, it was argued that class struggle constituted the essence of urban life. Two main positions eventually emerged. One regarded the city as a totality that should be studied in itself. The other argued that the city could not be studied as an isolated unit separated from the wider national and international context. Richard G. Fox in *Urban Anthropology: Cities in Their Cultural Setting* (1977) expanded on this position by including historical analysis in the locally significant global context.

By the early 1980s anthropologists appeared to be divided between those who focused on so-called third-world societies—continuing to address town-country relations, rural migration, and urban adaptation—and those with an interest in industrial societies. The latter were mainly native anthropologists.

In Euro-American societies, urban anthropology grew in parallel to the study of the anthropologist's own society. However, many European anthropologists, especially in Britain, regarded the study of one's own society as not "distant" enough to be fit for anthropological research. In contrast, American anthropologists had a long tradition of domestic interest. Their so-called exotic subjects were American Indians, urban migrants, and immigrant ethnic communities. Hannerz, who had carried out a pioneering study of "ghetto" culture and community in *Soulside* (1969), later criticized this approach for viewing the city as a mosaic in which each piece presented different problems. In his later work, *Exploring the City* (1980), he saw the failure to bring together the various pieces as a major limitation of earlier urban research. Criticism aside, American anthropologists such as Ida Susser (1982) and Leith Mullings (1997) have produced in-depth analyses on such issues as urban poverty, ethnicity, and gender.

RELUCTANCE TURNED TO NEW METHODS

Anthropologists' reluctance to engage in urban research originated in the fear of losing their disciplinary identity and in the view that the disciplinary paradigm, which had been developed for the study of village and tribal communities, could not be applied to larger, more complex communities. This debate developed into an advocacy for new methods.

While urban geographers such as Doreen Massey (1999) and sociologists such as Herbert J. Gans (1967) have become increasingly interested in the ethnographic methodology, anthropologists such as Sandra Wallman have doubted the applicability of participant observation in metropolitan areas. In her research in East London, published in *Eight London Households* (1984), Wallman applied research methods borrowed from other disciplines, calling it "anthropology by proxy." In contrast, Italo Pardo's research in Naples in the mid-1980s, presented in *Managing Existence in Naples* (1996), eminently proved that not only was participant observation possible, but that a holistic study in the anthropological tradition could productively be done in urban Europe. Key points of Pardo's work are a focus on the agency-system relationship, on the link between micro- and macro-level analysis, and on the sociological relevance of "strong continuous interaction" (Pardo 1996, pp. 11–12) between the material and the nonmaterial in people's rational choices. New urban research followed, including that of Giuliana B. Prato (2000), on the interactions among economic, political, and cultural aspects of urban life, which contextualized local dynamics and change in national historical processes. Later works, such as that of Manos Spyridakis (2006), have used such an approach to examine the rela-

tionships between local and national processes and global restructuring.

The diversity of the societies studied by anthropologists inevitably led to different forms of urban anthropology worldwide. In the 1980s a new trend emerged in the United States. Apart from studying the poor, the marginal, and ethnic minorities, anthropologists began to examine such topics as inherited wealth, congressional patronage, and transnational migrants. Ethnographies on African societies moved to new grounds, examining the dramaturgy of power and status symbolism, the economic role of women, informal activities, ethnic conflict, the reemergence of witchcraft, and new urban segregation. Work, class, gender, religion, and bureaucracy, along with urban planning, became major topics of urban research in Asia. Many urban ethnographies on Latin America focused on economic policies, local politics, women's work, urban development and planning, and indigenous rights.

Urban research in Europe appeared more geographically diversified in the early years of the twenty-first century. Sweden was at the forefront of urban research, addressing welfare institutions, class, and culture in relation to ethnicity. In Britain, apart from a few exceptions, urban research mainly focused on ethnic groups from Commonwealth countries. Urban France attracted the attention of both British and native anthropologists. In spite of a slow start, more urban research was carried out in southern and eastern Europe.

The fields of study mentioned thus far are by no means exhaustive of urban anthropological research. They represent major trends that have developed over the years. Throughout the 1990s, new developments in urban anthropology—notably those of Pardo (2000, 2004)—have investigated the relationships among elite groups, those between ordinary people and the ruling elite, and the legitimacy of governance. In the early twenty-first century—marked by transnationalism, globalization, the reemergence of localism, and the project of multiculturalism—this trend addressed the urgent need to understand the city as a crucial arena in which citizenship, democracy, and, by extension, belonging are critically renegotiated and the morality of law and politics are increasingly questioned and scrutinized.

SEE ALSO *Anthropology; Chicago School; Cities; Class; Colonialism; Culture; Elite Theory; Elites; Ethnography; Functionalism; Geography; Ghetto; Marxism; Metropolis; Migration, Rural to Urban; Multiculturalism; Observation, Participant; Slums; Sociology, Urban; Suburbs; Urban Renewal; Urban Studies; Urbanization; Welfare State*

BIBLIOGRAPHY

Ansari, Ghaus, and Peter J. M. Nas, eds. 1983. *Town Talk: The Dynamics of Urban Anthropology.* Leiden, Netherlands: Brill.

Antoun, Richard T. 2005. *Documenting Transnational Migration.* New York: Berghahn Books.

Appadurai, Arjun. 1981. *Worship and Conflict under Colonial Rule: A South Indian Case.* Cambridge, U.K.: Cambridge University Press.

Appadurai, Arjun, and James Holston. 1999. Introduction: Cities and Citizenship. In *Cities and Citizenship*, ed. James Holston. Durham, NC: Duke University Press.

Cohen, Abner. 1981. *The Politics of Elite Culture: Explorations in the Dramaturgy of Power in a Modern African Society.* Berkeley: University of California Press.

Cornelius, Wayne, and Robert Kemper, eds. 1978. *Metropolitan Latin America: The Challenge and the Response.* Beverly Hills, CA: Sage Publications.

El-Kholy, Heba Aziz. 2002. *Defiance and Compliance: Negotiating Gender in Low-Income Cairo.* New York: Berghahn Books.

Fox, Richard G. 1977. *Urban Anthropology: Cities in Their Cultural Setting.* Englewood Cliffs, NJ: Prentice-Hall.

Gans, Herbert J. 1967. *The Levittowners; Ways of Life and Politics in a New Suburban Community.* New York: Pantheon Books.

Grillo, Ralph D. 1985. *Ideologies and Institutions in Urban France: The Representation of Immigrants.* Cambridge, U.K.: Cambridge University Press.

Hannerz, Ulf. 1969. *Soulside; Inquiries into Ghetto Culture and Community.* New York: Columbia University Press.

Hannerz, Ulf. 1980. *Exploring the City; Inquiries toward an Urban Anthropology.* New York: Columbia University Press.

Lewis, Oscar. 1959. *Five Families: Mexican Case Studies in the Culture of Poverty.* New York: Basic Books.

Makhulu, Anne-Maria. 2002. New Housing, New Dreams? Southern Delft Housing Scheme, Cape Town, South Africa. *Public Culture* 14 (3): 643.

Massey, Doreen, John Allen, and Steve Pile, eds. 1999. *City Worlds.* London: Routledge.

Mullings, Leith. 1997. *On Our Own Terms: Race, Class, and Gender in the Lives of African American Women.* New York: Routledge.

Ortega-Perrier, Marietta. 2006. The 1993 Indian Law and the Revival of Aymara Identity in Northernmost Chile. In *Political Ideology, Identity, Citizenship: Anthropological Approaches*, ed. Giuliana B. Prato, 31–43. Special issue of *Global Bioethics*, Vol. 19.

Pardo, Italo. 1996. *Managing Existence in Naples: Morality, Action, and Structure.* Cambridge, U.K.: Cambridge University Press.

Pardo, Italo, ed. 2000. *Morals of Legitimacy: Between Agency and System.* New York: Berghahn Books.

Pardo, Italo, ed. 2004. *Between Morality and the Law: Corruption, Anthropology, and Comparative Society.* Aldershot, U.K.: Ashgate.

Parry, Jonathan. 2000. The Crisis of Corruption and the Idea of India: A Worm's Eye View. In *Morals of Legitimacy: Between Agency and System*, ed. Italo Pardo, 27–55. New York: Berghahn Books.

Prato, Giuliana B. 2000. The Cherries of the Mayor: Degrees of Morality and Responsibility in Local Italian Administration. In *Morals of Legitimacy: Between Agency and System*, ed. Italo Pardo, 57–82. New York: Berghahn Books.

Redfield, Robert. 1941. *The Folk Culture of Yucatan.* Chicago: University of Chicago Press.

Spyridakis, Manos. 2006. The Political Economy of Labor Relations in the Context of Greek Shipbuilding: An Ethnographic Account. *History and Anthropology* 17 (2): 153–170.

Susser, Ida. 1982. *Norman Street: Poverty and Politics in an Urban Neighborhood.* New York: Oxford University Press.

Wallman, Sandra. 1984. *Eight London Households.* London: Tavistock Publications.

Giuliana B. Prato

ANTHROPOLOGY, U.S.

Some trace the concept of anthropology, an academic discipline devoted to understanding every aspect of humans and their societies, to the Greek culture from which its name, *anthropos* (human being) and *logos* (knowledge), derives. According to Merwyn S. Garbarino in *Sociocultural Theory in Anthropology: A Short History* (1983), it is the breadth of anthropology's coverage, and its ability to combine the categories and interests of other fields like economics, political science, social psychology, sociology and even biology that brands it as unique—a holistic approach to "the study of …[humankind] the animal and …[humankind] the social being through time and space" (Garbarino 1983, p. 2).

ORIGINS

Anthropology is very much rooted in European intellectual traditions (Herodotus's descriptions of other societies in the fifth century BCE), Europe's expansion as a colonial power (Marco Polo's *ethnographic* details of the court of Kubla Khan in Peking around 1275), and the rise of imperialism. The Enlightenment was a time of profound and systematic inquiry into the nature of humans (cast during that time as the nature of *man*), and the ideas of Enlightenment scholars shaped many of the core questions that still direct anthropology in the early-twenty-first century. Building upon the approaches of natural history, the precursor to what is now called science, scholars like Jean Jacques Rousseau, Thomas Hobbes, and John Locke attempted to explain human social and cultural variation by seeking to uncover the *natural laws* that governed the rational order of the universe. The logic behind Newton's *Principia Mathematics* and Locke's *Essay Concerning Human Understanding*, two of the most influential works of the time, could best be summarized as follows: "*The universe was rationally ordered, and laws could be discovered that explained the motions of the planets and the behavior of people*" (Garbarino 1983, p. 12, emphasis original). These principles were thought to be the key to answering two questions about humans as social creatures and human cultural and biological variation: "Why do people behave the way they do?" and "What causes human diversity?" The theories developed in anthropology were attempts to answer these two questions about human behavior and observable differences in societies and in human phenotypes using natural science methodology.

Colonial contact with non-complex, non-industrial other societies gave Europeans the understanding that such societies were *primitive* because they did not mimic European society. By the nineteenth century, social theorists, like anthropologists, adhered to a "doctrine of progress," according to editors W. L. Partridge and E. M. Eddy in *Applied Anthropology in America* (1978). As they described it, "Throughout centuries of progress, the modern, 'superior,' 'moral,' social life of nineteenth century industrialism was believed to have developed from 'primitive,' 'immoral,' 'childlike' societies" (p. 7). Anthropologists believed that by studying such societies, one could trace the progress from so-called primitive societies to their own contemporary status, always holding European social development as the ideal. The two theoretical camps that emerged in the mid-nineteenth century were those who interpreted non-western societies through a lens of *unilinealism*, and argued that "all societies passed through a single evolutionary process," and those who professed a belief in diffusionism, an attempt to explain "the spread of a cultural item from its place of origin to other places" (King and Wright 2003).

Underpinning these theories, and many of the other ideas that would shape anthropology, was the belief in cultural evolution, led by Herbert Spencer. He believed "evolution to be one of the fundamental processes in the universe" (McGee and Warms 2000, p. 7). Charles Darwin also cited Spencer's work in his theory on biological evolution. At the close of the nineteenth century, Europeans dominated the development of anthropological theories and practices: from Lewis Henry Morgan (1818–1881) and Edward Burnett Tylor (1832–1917) to Sir James Fraser (1854–1941); Karl Marx, whom Garbarino argues did not do "competent anthropology" (Garbarino 1983, p. 39); his collaborator and benefactor, Friedrich Engels; and Émile Durkheim.

Some of these great theorists, such as Fraser and Tylor, had never conducted field research, drawing their generalizations from the ethnographies of anthropologists who conducted ethnographic fieldwork as well as from the nonscholarly observations and descriptions of missionaries and travelers. In England and France, sociocultural anthropologists remained separate from those studying archaeology and physical anthropology, and colonialism, fueled by theories of unilineal evolutionism, further reinforced ethnocentric views that so-called primitive societies were at a lower scale of development than those in Europe. Durkheim's use of the cross-cultural approach to understand "social development, suicide, religion, and above all, social cohesion," moved French sociology into the realm of anthropology, and Durkheim is claimed by the discipline today as a key figure (Garbarino 1983, p. 38).

THE EMERGENCE OF AMERICAN CULTURAL ANTHROPOLOGY

Cross-cultural comparison, the culture concept, cultural relativism (introduced by Charles Louis de Secondat, Baron de la Brede and de Montesquieu [1689–1755], generally referred to as Montesquieu), the professionalization of data collection (including William H. R. Rivers's genealogical method used to trace descent and describe kinship patterns as a window onto understanding general social relations), and critiques of unilineal evolutionist approaches to explaining sociocultural variation were all part of the emerging field of anthropology. Also part of it was a belief among "British and American anthropologists … that good ethnographic information would help government personnel avoid mistakes that might be not only costly but also painful and destructive to native peoples" (Garbarino 1983, p. 44). This cozy relationship between colonial administrators and anthropology, such as the Royal Anthropological Institute's training center for colonial administrators, would come back at the end of the century to haunt anthropology, produce a distrust between former colonial people and the discipline in the so-called Third World or the Global South, and give anthropology the unfortunate, but accurate for the period in question, moniker—"child of imperialism and colonialism" (Garbarino 1983, p. 44).

In the United States, at the American Museum of Natural History, a transplanted German, Franz Boas, embarked on the Jesup North Pacific Expedition (1897–1902). The data he collected affirmed the value of anthropologists doing their own research rather than relying on the reports of others. "He encouraged his students to collect as many ethnographic data as possible—total recovery was his goal" (Garbarino 1983, p. 48). Boas turned his back on the tendencies prevalent in the discipline: sweeping and broad generalizations and comparisons. Rather, he stressed to his students that they accumulate large bodies of data using a holistic approach before venturing toward any conclusions. What set Boas apart from his peers was that "while evolutionists had searched for similarities, …[he] looked for diversity." He also paid close attention to history, "believing that each society could be understood only in light of its particular past" (Garbarino 1983, p. 48). In his 1920 essay, "The Methods of Ethnology," Boas summed up his critique of the flawed logic of both evolutionism and diffusionism in the following way: "These methods are essentially forms of classification of the static phenomena of culture according to two distinct principles, and interpretations of these classifications as of historical significance, without, however any attempt to prove that this interpretation is justified" (Boas 2000, p. 135).

According to McGee and Warms's discussion of Boas in their history of anthropological theory, Boas "pioneered the concept of cultural relativism in anthropology." Further, his approach of historical particularism emphasized the discipline's holism, and drew upon the study of "prehistory, linguistics, and physical anthropology" (McGee and Warms 2000, p.131). Boas's desire to introduce scientific rigor to this emerging academic field and his quest for holism were directly responsible for academic American anthropology acquiring the four-field signature of cultural (social) anthropology, archaeology (or prehistory), biological (or physical) anthropology, and linguistics anthropology (Miller 2004, p. 2). This holistic approach would distinguish American anthropology, going forward, from its European progenitors. Boas also brought to this emerging discipline a new "agenda for social reform" as well as theories of race that challenged the prevailing status quo beliefs. He believed that environment and nurturing were significant factors in human development. In his 1940 essay, "Anthropological Study of Children," Boas noted, "Some observations have been made that illustrate the influence of environment, not only upon growth of the bulk of the body but also upon some of the forms that develop very early in life" (Boas 1982, p. 101). Boas's students were the first generation of formally trained academic American anthropologists, and many would become leading figures in the discipline—Alfred Kroeber, Robert Lowie, Edward Sapir, and Ruth Benedict. Subsequent students included Margaret Mead and Zora Neale Hurston.

American anthropology continues to embrace holism, and although the four-field approach, the culture concept, and cultural relativism have drawn sharp criticism and debate, they remain cornerstones of the discipline's distinctiveness. American anthropology's history of contributing to social reform has also attracted new thinkers that include women, nonwhite, and gay, lesbian, bisexual, and transgendered anthropologists. Their contributions include ongoing interrogations of evolutionist theories, positivism, modernization, critiques of ethnocentrism, homophobia, sexism, and racism, both in the society and within the academy, and challenges to the scientific validity of the concept of race, while acknowledging the power of social race. Their interpretive approaches and use of identity politics support methodologies quite different from the empiricism that H. Russell Bernard (1998) claims is ubiquitous to the discipline. These characteristics, along with the persistence of the four-field approach, and a long-standing tension between humanism and science, continue to distinguish American anthropology from its British and French cousins

SEE ALSO *American Anthropological Association; Boas, Franz*

BIBLIOGRAPHY

Bernard, H. Russell. 1998. *Handbook of Methods in Cultural Anthropology*. Walnut Creek, CA: AltaMira Press.

Boas, Franz. (1920) 2000. The Methods of Enthology. In *Anthropological Theory: An Introductory History*, eds. R. Jon McGee and Richard L. Warms, 2nd ed. Mountain View, CA: Mayfield Publishing.

Boas, Franz. (1940) 1982. Anthropological Study of Children. In *Race, Language, and Culture*, ed. Franz Boas, 94–102. Chicago: University of Chicago Press.

Eddy, Elizabeth M., and William L. Partridge, eds. 1978. *Applied Anthropology in America*. New York: Columbia University Press.

Garbarino, Merwyn S. (1977) 1983. *Sociocultural Theory in Anthropology: A Short History*. Prospect Heights, IL: Waveland Press.

King, Gail, and Meghan Wright. 2003. Diffusionism and Acculturation. http://www.as.ua.edu/ant/Faculty/murphy/diffusion.htm.

McGee, R. Jon, and Richard L.Warms. 2000. *Anthropological Theory: An Introductory History*, 2nd ed. Mountain View, CA: Mayfield Publishing.

Miller, Barbara D. 2004. *Cultural Anthropology*. 3rd ed. Boston: Pearson Education.

Partridge, William L., and Elizabeth M. Eddy. 1978. The Development of Applied Anthropology in America. In *Applied Anthropology in America*, eds. Elizabeth M. Eddy and William L. Partridge, 3–45. New York: Columbia University Press.

Titiev, Mischa. 1959 *Introduction to Cultural Anthropology*. New York: Henry Holt.

Irma McClaurin

ANTICOLONIAL MOVEMENTS

During the eighteenth and nineteenth centuries the states of western Europe projected their power and their rivalries into much of Asia and Africa, establishing an "era of western domination over the rest of mankind" (Emerson 1960, p. 5). This creation of a global imperial order eventually generated a counterrevolution as colonized peoples organized anticolonial movements that asserted their rights to self-government. The age of imperialism spawned an era of nonwestern nationalism that gained great momentum during the twentieth-century world wars, thus changing the face of contemporary international politics.

The competition to acquire overseas territories was fueled by political, economic, and technological factors. European states developed military technologies, including naval maneuverability and enhanced firepower, that allowed them to prevail over the societies they sought to conquer. The search for exotic goods, raw materials, and new markets in which to trade provided a material motive for expansion. Political prestige was at stake as well, as states sometimes sought to compensate for defeats in Europe by victories abroad; doctrines such as the "civilizing mission" were invented to justify colonial empires. This gigantic historical enterprise transformed Asia and Africa, not the least by unleashing the will of the colonized to strike back.

Anticolonial movements such as the Indian National Congress, the Association of Vietnamese Revolutionary Youth, and the United Gold Coast Convention took form in individual colonies to confront different local situations. These diverse local movements were well aware of one another, prompting a transnational sentiment of solidarity against colonial rule. Although each movement adopted its own tactics and strategy according to its local circumstances, they shared a sense of common cause with one another. Some struggles for independence were violent, others primarily diplomatic, and yet other anticolonial forces shrewdly combined political and military means to achieve their goals.

A representative regional example of these historical processes can be seen in the case of North Africa. In 1830 France invaded the territory of Algeria, waging an extremely bloody war of conquest. Finally overcoming prolonged Algerian resistance, the French colonial administration encouraged European settlers to occupy the country. Once established in Algeria, France extended its power by imposing protectorates over Tunisia (in 1881) and much of Morocco (in 1912). Then as World War I (1914–1918) engulfed Europe, the French conscripted North African manpower into its army. When these soldiers returned from the trenches of Europe, they contributed to laying the early groundwork for what became national movements for independence. World War II (1939–1945) further eroded the foundations of empire as another generation of Africans was enlisted in the French war effort. In Algeria the National Liberation Front (FLN) took up arms in 1954, spurring France to negotiate the independence of neighboring Tunisia and Morocco in 1956. Through effective diplomacy as well as armed resistance, the FLN achieved the independence of their nation in 1962.

Movements such as Algeria's FLN emerged, often under the leadership of western-trained elites, throughout the colonized world. Mahatma Mohandas Gandhi and Jawaharlal Nehru mobilized the Indian people against the inherent inequalities of colonial rule in the name of certain liberal principles such as self-determination, as articulated by the U.S. president Woodrow Wilson. The Vietnamese nationalist Ho Chi Minh was inspired by both the U.S. Declaration of Independence and the anti-imperialist ideology of V. I. Lenin. Ho traveled to France and the Soviet Union on his path to organizing the anticolonial movement in Indochina. Kwame Nkrumah of Ghana studied in the United States, where he was influenced by pan-Africanism, another anticolonial doctrine. The Sorbonne trained the Tunisian lawyer Habib Bourguiba (1903–2000), who assumed the leadership of the nationalist Neo-Destour Party. East African leaders such as Jomo Kenyatta and Julius Nyerere studied in British universities. These intellectuals from developing countries found the means to turn the west's rhetorical ideals of justice and democracy into tools of liberation. Thus did the imperial powers plant the seeds of the eventual formation of anticolonial movements.

Not only European wars, but also Asian ones destabilized the imperial order, allowing room for anticolonial movements to consolidate. Japan's ambitions to become an imperial power in China in the 1930s, and later in Southeast Asia, shook the hold of the French in Indochina, the Dutch in Indonesia, and the British in South Asia. In India, where the Indian National Congress had been created as early as 1885 as a primarily elite organization, the anticolonial forces had built a mass movement incorporating a wide range of social groups by the 1920s. Thus the Congress Party was well situated to play a vanguard role in the march to independence in 1947. Nehru declared a neutralist foreign policy that offered support to other anticolonial movements. In rapid succession, Burma (now Myanmar) and Indonesia achieved independence under their prewar nationalist leaders—U Nu (1907–1995), who founded the leftist University Students' Union in the 1930s, and Ahmed Sukarno (1901–1970), who formed the Indonesian National Unity Party in 1927. In Indochina, however, the French chose to resist the anticolonial League for

Vietnamese Independence (or "Vietminh," as Ho's organization was known after 1941). France waged a costly war that lasted until the Vietnamese victory at Dien Bien Phu in May 1954.

The struggle in Vietnam was closely watched by the Algerian nationalists. The anticolonial movement in Algeria had long been divided into competing political parties and religious associations. The model provided by Vietnam's successful guerrilla war inspired the more radical wing of the Algerian movement to organize the FLN, which carried out its first military operation on November 1, 1954, just months after the fall of Dien Bien Phu. Thus did a common anticolonialism lead to common strategy across colonized continents. The Algerian war in turn became a major episode in the history of decolonization. The FLN mounted an exceptionally dynamic diplomacy in the Arab world, Africa, and Asia, enlisting both recently independent governments and sub-Saharan anticolonial political parties in support of Algerian independence in such forums as the United Nations and the Bandung Conference. The latter, held in Indonesia in April 1955, was a meeting of the independent states of Asia and Africa, most of which were former colonies. The conference both celebrated this newly won independence and issued a call for ongoing efforts to end colonialism. The "spirit of Bandung" became a major mobilizational theme for the continuing anticolonial movement. The FLN was an unofficial participant in the conference (its representatives lodged within the Egyptian delegation) and it subsequently insisted upon representation of national liberation movements in similar conferences.

The pressure exerted upon the government of France by the war in Algeria became an asset for anticolonial movements in sub-Saharan Africa, speeding the process of decolonization on the continent. Likewise, the radicalization of the anticolonial movement in Ghana under Nkrumah—who proceeded from organizing the Fifth Pan-African Conference in England in 1945 to editing a paper called *The New African* in 1946 to serving as general secretary of the United Gold Coast Convention (UGCC) in his homeland in 1947—accelerated the pace of events. Disillusioned by the moderation of the UGCC, Nkrumah formed the Convention People's Party in 1949 and promptly initiated a Gandhi-style campaign called "Positive Action," for which he was imprisoned by the colonial authorities. His popularity obliged the British to deal with his movement; by 1954 he won a promise of self-government, by 1957 Ghana was independent, and in 1958 he convened in Accra an All-African People's Conference, which was attended by anticolonial forces from around the continent. Meanwhile, Ahmed Sékou Touré (1922–1984), a trade unionist who had assumed leadership of the Democratic Party of Guinea in 1952, persuaded his compatriots to vote for independence from

France in a 1958 referendum organized by French president Charles de Gaulle in his attempt to diffuse the mounting international opposition to the French war in Algeria. Political momentum arising out of this Algiers–Accra–Conakry axis enabled anticolonial forces to sweep away the fractured colonial framework in seventeen more African countries in 1960, the "year of Africa."

The influx of former colonies into the United Nations General Assembly allowed the anticolonial movement to harness that institution to the goal of eradicating the final vestiges of colonialism. The assembly sponsored the passage of, for example, Resolution 1514, the Declaration on the Granting of Independence to Colonial Countries and Peoples (December 1960). They formed new instruments such as the Nonaligned Movement and the Organization of African Unity to pursue the remaining agenda of decolonization in the Portuguese colonies and the settler states of southern Africa. Activist states such as Algeria supported the training of guerrilla movements in Angola, Mozambique, and Portuguese Guinea; upon independence in 1975 the Frelimo government in Mozambique in turn aided the Patriotic Front in Southern Rhodesia (now Zimbabwe) and the African National Congress in South Africa, whereas Angola assisted the Southwest African People's Organization (SWAPO) in Namibia. In South Africa, whose African National Congress (ANC, organized in 1912) was one of the oldest members of the collective anticolonial movement, the release of the activist leader Nelson Mandela in 1990 led to the election of an ANC government in 1994. These were among the final battles in the long march of decolonization.

The historian Hugh Tinker has called anticolonial militants "fighters, dreamers, and schemers." Their common scheme was to build a local organization that could join a larger movement that restored self-rule to their peoples.

SEE ALSO *African National Congress; Battle of Algiers, The; Castro, Fidel; Colonialism; Cuban Revolution; Decolonization; Democracy; Haitian Revolution; Imperialism; Indian National Army; Indian National Congress; Justice; Kenyatta, Jomo; Lenin, Vladimir Ilitch; Mandela, Nelson; Mandela, Winnie; Mao Zedong; Mau Mau; Minh, Ho Chi; Neocolonialism; Nkrumah, Kwame; Nyerere, Julius; Organization of African Unity (OAU); Pan-Africanism; Revolutions, Latin American; Socialism; Union of Soviet Socialist Republics; United Nations; Vietnam War; Violence; Violence, Frantz Fanon on; War; World War I; World War II*

BIBLIOGRAPHY

Emerson, Rupert. 1960. *From Empire to Nation.* Cambridge, MA: Harvard University Press.

Mortimer, Robert. 1984. *The Third World Coalition in International Politics.* 2nd ed. Boulder, CO: Westview Press.

Tinker, Hugh. 1987. *Men Who Overturned Empires: Fighters, Dreamers, and Schemers.* Madison: University of Wisconsin Press.

Robert Mortimer

ANTIPSYCHOTICS

SEE *Psychotropic Drugs.*

ANTI-SEMITISM

Is anti-Semitism a new name for an ancient, uninterrupted phenomenon? It is a recent name, no doubt—its 1878 coinage being attributed to Swiss radical Wilhelm Marr. Yet, new names have become one of the curious features of problems that either refer to a long and obstinate history (e.g., the hatred of the Jews through the centuries) or indicate sites of resistance, the refusal to confront diverse and changing phenomena. Understandably, different interests seeking to isolate and refute or, alternatively, contextualize "anti-Semitism" necessarily run the risk of sacralizing or banalizing it. Thus, inseparable from the study and elusive comprehension of such an object (or objects), the politics of anti-Semitism have involved most manifestly the definition of the word *Semite* (along with its companion, *Aryan,* a term that was invented in German Protestant theological circles circa 1771 and quickly spread to England, France, and their respective empires) and most covertly the very representation of the West vis-à-vis its others.

HISTORY

Scholars and ideologues differ in invoking, for different periods and regions of the world, terms such as *Jew-hatred, anti-Judaism, Judeophobia,* more recently including even *anti-Zionism.* Is there, then, one history of anti-Semitism through the ages (Almog 1988)? Should one not attend instead to the distinct histories of relations between Jews and the populations among whom they have lived? A further claim has been made that some forms of anti-Semitism have thrived, in fact, in the complete absence of Jews. French philosopher Jean-Paul Sartre, for example, famously asserted that anti-Semitism is essentially independent of the Jews, that it rather "makes the Jew" ("c'est

l'antisémite qui fait le Juif") (1948, p. 84). Indeed, it now seems as if anti-Semitism has become a unified and universal, indeed global, phenomenon, one that has spread and radiated from its historical center in early Christian theology (borrowing from earlier Greek and Latin writers) and in western Europe to all corners of the planet. When considering the genocidal paroxysm that hostility to Jews reached in Europe (and, incidentally, only there), the temptation has increased to read all prior hostility toward Jews as prefiguring the horrors of the Holocaust (Bernstein 1994).

EXPLANATIONS

Clearly, anti-Semitism demands explanation—and refutation—and many compelling cases have been made in this direction. Some have sought to testify to anti-Semitism's quasi-eternal nature (Netanyahu 2001; Bein 1990) or account for its specific persistence (the recurrence of Christian theological prejudice). Others have explored vectors of change (the well-known, modern shift from religion to race described by Léon Poliakov; the teleological understanding of Daniel Goldhagen) and tried to account for historical distinctiveness (Amos Funkenstein on the changing and proximate nature of the Jewish-Christian dispute; Gavin Langmuir's criterion of "socially significant chimerical hostility" [1990, p. 341]; Jeremy Cohen's description of the medieval transformation of the Jews from "theological witness" to "demonic" figures) and geographical or cultural difference (Poliakov, again, as well as Mark Cohen). At times, Jewish thinkers themselves have gone so far as to consider Jewish "antisocial behavior" as a major source of anti-Jewish hostility (Bernard Lazare; Israel Yuval on Jewish collective suicide in the eleventh century).

Other reasons, equally contentious, have been proposed: materialist reasons, for example, and chief among them, socioeconomic ones ("Jews and money," as the old topos goes, but see also Abram Léon's notion of the Jews as a "people-class"), and political reasons (Karl Marx, but also Hannah Arendt's theory of the modern state and the role of "political anti-Semitism" in it) and psychological reasons as well (Sigmund Freud on sibling rivalry and castration, and Max Horkheimer and Theodor Adorno on mimesis). Historians of science have shown the importance of new categories of thought and classification, including those operative in Jewish self-perception (Gilman 1986; Hart 2000). There are those who have sought to locate anti-Jewish hostility within the larger frame of attitudes toward "outsiders" (Mayer 1982) or as one among numerous features of a "persecuting society" (Moore 1987). A recurring dispute continues to separate those who wish to distinguish exclusionary practices on the basis of their (real or fantasmatic) targets and those who uphold the strategic usefulness of conducting a unified analysis of (and struggle against) all agents of exclusionary practices. Should all racisms be studied and fought as the different guises of one essence or should differences be acknowledged and exposed?

RECENT DEVELOPMENTS

Hannah Arendt (1958) insisted on the numerous elements and structures that relate attitudes toward the Jews with issues of state formation, modern racism, imperialism, and colonialism. After Arendt, however, the most significant breakthrough in the study of anti-Semitism was made by Edward W. Said (1978). Arguing that the history of Orientalism (and prominent among them "western views of Islam") is the history of anti-Semitism, Said has enabled a novel understanding of the emergence of the category of "Semites" as the most obvious manifestation of an enduring theologico-political problem. This problem, which antedates modernity, is at the heart of the West's own constitution as a historical subject. Relating theological premises to political endeavors, and religion to race, Said demonstrates the necessity of understanding the distributive and dynamic distinctions between Jews and Arabs, between Judaism and Islam, strategically associating and dissociating the two from within the standpoint of Western Christendom and, later, of European colonialism (Anidjar 2003). This dynamic approach also means taking the measure of the late eighteenth-century invention of "Semites" as the unity of race and religion, of Jew and Arab (Olender 1992; Hess 2002). From this novel perspective, it becomes possible to better understand the spread of European anti-Semitism to the Arab world (described, for example, by Bernard Lewis and Geneviève Dermenjian), as well as phenomena like Zionism in its different figures, at once emancipatory and potential manifestations of covert self-hatred (Gilman 1986).

The intricate connections that tie modern anti-Semitism to Zionism may further explain the continued contaminations we witness today between the two (Wistrich 1990; Finkelstein 2005). The Zionist "negation of exile" also participated in the project to reinscribe and undo the unity of the Semites and recast it from within as either a separation of Jews from Arabs (anti-Semitism from Orientalism) or as a binational perspective—advocated by Martin Buber, Gershom Scholem, Arendt, and other members of Brit Shalom, a Jewish group founded in 1925 dedicated to promoting coexistence—seeking to invent and promote collective rights for both Jews and Arabs (Raz-Krakotzkin 2001). The debate over the persistence of anti-Semitism as anti-Zionism can therefore be better understood as the enduring effort to maintain Jews and Arabs as separate and opposed, indeed as objects of different, unrelated, exclusionary practices. Reframed as the unity of a theologico-political complex that manages both hostility to Jews and hostility to Arabs, anti-Judaism and the war on Islam, anti-Semitism and Orientalism, are revealed as indissociable: one and the same in their very difference.

SEE ALSO *Jewish Diaspora; Jews*

BIBLIOGRAPHY

Almog, Shmuel, ed. 1988. *Antisemitism Through the Ages.* Trans. Nathan H. Reisner. Oxford and New York: Pergamon.

Anidjar, Gil. 2003. *The Jew, the Arab: A History of the Enemy.* Stanford, CA: Stanford University Press.

Arendt, Hannah. 1958. *The Origins of Totalitarianism.* 2nd ed. New York: Meridian.

Bein, Alex. 1990. *The Jewish Question: Biography of a World Problem.* Translated by Harry Zohn. Rutherford, NJ: Fairleigh Dickinson University Press.

Bernstein, Michael-André. 1994. *Foregone Conclusions: Against Apocalyptic History.* Berkeley: University of California Press.

Cohen, Jeremy. 1982. *The Friars and the Jews: The Evolution of Medieval Anti-Judaism.* Ithaca, NY: Cornell University Press.

Cohen, Jeremy. 1999. *Living Letters of the Law: Ideas of the Jew in Medieval Christianity.* Berkeley: University of California Press.

Cohen, Mark R. 1994. *Under Crescent and Cross: The Jews in the Middle Ages.* Princeton, NJ: Princeton University Press.

Dermenjian, Geneviève. 1983. *Juifs et Européens d'Algérie: L'antisémitisme oranais, 1892–1905.* Jerusalem: Institut Ben-Zvi.

Finkelstein, Norman G. 2005. *Beyond Chutzpah: On the Misuse of Anti-Semitism and the Abuse of History.* Berkeley: University of California Press.

Freud, Sigmund. 1967. *Moses and Monotheism.* Trans. Katherine Jones. New York: Vintage.

Funkenstein, Amos. 1993. *Perceptions of Jewish History.* Berkeley: University of California Press.

Gilman, Sander L. 1986. *Jewish Self-Hatred: Anti-Semitism and the Hidden Language of the Jews.* Baltimore, MD: Johns Hopkins University Press.

Goldhagen, Daniel. 1996. *Hitler's Willing Executioners: Ordinary Germans and the Holocaust.* New York: Knopf.

Hart, Mitchell B. 2000. *Social Science and the Politics of Modern Jewish Identity.* Stanford, CA: Stanford University Press.

Hess, Jonathan M. 2002. *Germans, Jews, and the Claims of Modernity.* New Haven, CT: Yale University Press.

Horkheimer, Max, and Theodor W. Adorno. 2002. *Dialectic of Enlightenment: Philosophical Fragments.* Trans. Edmund Jephcott. Stanford, CA: Stanford University Press.

Katz, Jacob. 1980. *From Prejudice to Destruction: Anti-Semitism, 1700–1933.* Cambridge, MA: Harvard University Press.

Langmuir, Gavin I. 1990. *Toward a Definition of Antisemitism.* Berkeley: University of California Press.

Lazare, Bernard. 1995. *Antisemitism: Its History and Causes.* Lincoln: University of Nebraska Press.

Léon, Abram. 1970. *The Jewish Question: A Marxist Interpretation.* New York: Pathfinder.

Lewis, Bernard. 1986. *Semites and Anti-Semites: An Inquiry into Conflict and Prejudice.* New York: Norton.

Mayer, Hans. 1982. *Outsiders: A Study in Life and Letters.* Trans. Dennis M. Sweet. Cambridge, MA: MIT Press.

Moore, R. I. 1987. *The Formation of a Persecuting Society: Power and Deviance in Western Europe, 950–1250.* Oxford: Blackwell.

Netanyahu, Benzion. 2001. *The Origins of the Inquisition in Fifteenth-Century Spain.* 2nd ed. New York: New York Review of Books.

Olender, Maurice. 1992. *Languages of Paradise: Race, Religion, and Philology in the Nineteenth Century.* Trans. Arthur Goldhammer. Cambridge, MA: Harvard University Press.

Poliakov, Léon. 1965. *The History of Anti-Semitism.* Trans. Richard Howard. New York: Vanguard.

Raz-Krakotzkin, Amnon. 2001. Binationalism and Jewish Identity: Hannah Arendt and the Question of Palestine. In *Hannah Arendt in Jerusalem,* ed. Steven E. Aschheim, 165–180. Berkeley: University of California Press.

Said, Edward W. 1978. *Orientalism.* New York: Vintage.

Sartre, Jean-Paul. 1948. *Anti-Semite and Jew.* Trans. George J. Becker. New York: Schocken.

Wistrich, Robert S., ed. 1990. *Anti-Zionism and Antisemitism in the Contemporary World.* New York: New York University Press.

Gil Anidjar

ANTITRUST

Antitrust law—also called *competition law*—limits how competitors may act in the marketplace, unilaterally and especially collectively. The aim of antitrust law is to promote social welfare by protecting the competitive process. Two federal agencies are responsible for U.S. antitrust enforcement—the U.S. Department of Justice and the Federal Trade Commission. In addition, state attorneys general and private parties may bring antitrust suits to enjoin specific conduct or recover damages suffered as a result of antitrust violations.

One major antitrust law is the Sherman Act of 1890. It was the congressional response to the invention of the *trust,* a contractual coordination among competitors used to drive up prices. The U.S. Supreme Court developed two frameworks for applying Section 1 of the Sherman Act, which addresses anticompetitive agreements, including those forming trusts. The *per se rule* prohibits categories of agreements without consideration of their actual effects because they are inherently likely to eliminate competition without any offsetting social benefits. The most important of these categories are cartel agreements through which competitors fix prices, rig bids, or allocate customers. Cartels are prosecuted as felonies, and prosecu-

tion of international cartels since the mid-1990s resulted in many fines in excess of $100 million and imprisonment for many corporate executives. The *rule of reason* prohibits agreements in other categories if determined actually to harm competition.

Section 2 of the Sherman Act addresses unilateral conduct that would "monopolize" an industry. It has been applied sparingly, especially in recent decades. Landmark early cases resulted in the breakup of the American Tobacco Company and the Standard Oil Company. The most notable modern case involved Microsoft Corporation and resulted in a variety of prohibitions and requirements on its conduct.

The other major antitrust law is the Clayton Act of 1914, which contains several specific prohibitions, the most important of which applies to mergers that would substantially "lessen competition." Since the 1970s, large mergers have been reviewed by federal agencies prior to consummation. The agencies file suit against roughly a dozen mergers per year, although all but a few are later consummated after the merging parties agree to divest significant assets. Controversial cases include the Justice Department's unsuccessful challenge to Oracle Corporation's takeover of PeopleSoft, and oil industry mergers the Federal Trade Commission allowed to proceed.

Antitrust law and policy have evolved considerably, especially as insights from economics were incorporated through case law development. At the vanguard was the Chicago School, which drew attention to efficiency reasons for business practices and was instrumental in limiting the application of the per se rule. Since the early 1980s, increasingly sophisticated economic analysis has been applied. The federal agencies and the courts rely on economic analysis in predicting the competitive effects of proposed mergers and assessing the effects of ongoing business practices.

Antitrust law was unique to the United States for a considerable time, but more than one hundred countries now have antitrust laws. These laws generally prohibit cartel activity, anticompetitive mergers, various specific business practices, and what is termed *abuse of dominance.* The prohibition of abuse of dominance is similar to Section 2 of the Sherman Act. International views on antitrust have converged a great deal, although complete convergence likely never will be achieved.

Outside cartel enforcement, debates on antitrust policy continue. Nearly all agree on basic goals of antitrust policy, but the best means to achieve those goals remain controversial. Recent debates have focused mainly on the proper standards for evaluating the potentially exclusionary conduct of a single competitor. Controversial practices include 3M's use of rebates across multiple product lines in sales to retailers (found unlawful in the United States) and Microsoft's inclusion of its media player in its Windows PC operating system (found unlawful in Europe).

SEE ALSO *Antitrust Regulation; Chicago School; Deregulation*

BIBLIOGRAPHY

Bork, Robert H. 1993. *The Antitrust Paradox: A Policy at War with Itself.* 2nd ed. New York: Free Press.

Carlton, Dennis W., and Jeffrey M. Perloff. 2005. *Modern Industrial Organization.* 4th ed. Boston: Addison Wesley.

Connor, John M. 2001. *Global Price Fixing: Our Customers Are the Enemy.* Boston: Kluwer.

Hovenkamp, Herbert. 2005. *The Antitrust Enterprise: Principle and Execution.* Cambridge, MA: Harvard University Press.

Hylton, Keith N. 2003. *Antitrust Law: Economic Theory and Common Law Evolution.* Cambridge, U.K.: Cambridge University Press.

Kwoka, John E., Jr., and Lawrence J. White, eds. 2004. *The Antitrust Revolution: Economics, Competition, and Policy.* 4th ed. New York: Oxford University Press.

Posner, Richard A. 2001. *Antitrust Law.* 2nd ed. Chicago: University of Chicago Press.

Shenefield, John H., and Irwin M. Stelzer. 2001. *The Antitrust Laws: A Primer.* 4th ed. Washington, DC: AEI Press.

Gregory J. Werden
The views expressed herein are not purported to represent those of the U.S. Department of Justice.

Luke M. Froeb

ANTITRUST REGULATION

Antitrust regulation is accomplished through legal statutes that proscribe anticompetitive conduct and unfair business practices. Its major role is to protect consumers against anticompetitive behavior that raises prices, reduces output, and hinders innovation and economic growth (Baker 2003). Antitrust laws originally were formulated for the purpose of combating business trusts. A trust was a legal form of business entity that was created during the nineteenth century in the United States in which the shareholders of the companies in an industry transferred their shares to a board of trustees in exchange for dividends. That process led to the formation of giant monopoly firms such as John D. Rockefeller's Standard Oil Trust.

Eventually the term *antitrust* was used to refer to government regulation of monopolies in general.

IMPACT OF ANTITRUST REGULATION ON ECONOMIC ACTIVITY

The impact of antitrust regulation on the economy has been the subject of long-standing debate. Critics of the concept argue that excessive competition endangers the functioning of industries with high fixed costs and low marginal costs such as railroads and public utilities. In this case engaging in monopoly practices such as price discrimination may enable firms to recover fixed costs and realize economies of scale and scope (Kovacic and Shapiro 2000). There are also concerns about the way competition policy is designed and executed. Some corporate leaders feel that the laws are vague and ambiguous, whereas others think that antitrust statutes give too much power to politicians. Public choice theorists emphasize the idea that antitrust enforcement may not always serve consumers' interest but instead favor private corporate or political interests.

Despite those criticisms competition generally is thought to be desirable for a variety of reasons: It stimulates individualism and innovation, guarantees wider product choices for consumers, and promotes economic efficiency as market participants strive for business success. Competition, however, cannot sustain itself. Without regulation competitors inevitably will agree to raise prices, and the victims of that conduct will be unable to protect themselves.

ANTITRUST REGULATION IN THE UNITED STATES

The first federal antitrust law in the United States, the Sherman Act, was passed by Congress in 1890. It outlawed "every contract, combination or conspiracy in restraint of trade" as well as "monopolization." The legislation made illegal collusive arrangements such as price-fixing, bid rigging, resale price maintenance, and territorial and structural division agreements that would tend to establish a monopolistic practice. The Sherman Act gave federal judges substantial discretion in court, and that led Congress pass in 1914 two other laws to substantiate the original statute: the Clayton Act and the Federal Trade Commission Act. The Clayton Act outlined particular practices that were deemed illegal, such as price discrimination (Section 2), exclusive dealing and tying contracts (Section 3), and corporate mergers when they were intended to create a monopoly (Section 7). The Federal Trade Commission Act formed an administrative body, the Federal Trade Commission, to design antitrust policy. Today the Federal Trade Commission and the

Antitrust Division of the Justice Department are jointly responsible for the enforcement of antitrust laws in the United States. In a 1993 article B. Dan Wood and James Anderson provided a discussion of the competencies and activities of the government agencies that regulate antitrust.

ANTITRUST REGULATION IN EUROPE AND INTERNATIONALLY

The foundation of antitrust regulation in the European Union is outlined in Articles 81 and 82 of the European Community Treaty. Article 81 outlawed agreements such as price-fixing and market sharing, and Article 82 made illegal the practice of predatory pricing aimed at eliminating competitors from the market. Although similar in spirit to antitrust policy in the United States, competition policy in the European Union is intended to advance economic integration among its members.

There has been increasing cooperation among countries in acting against international cartels. The efforts of law enforcement authorities are coordinated through the International Competition Network, an international body whose goal is convergence in the enforcement of antitrust regulation laws. In the first decade of the twenty-first century more than a hundred countries adopted antitrust laws.

LENIENCY PROGRAMS

Leniency programs are legal incentive schemes that offer the members of a cartel amnesty from prosecution if they report a conspiracy and cooperate with the investigation. The purposes of these programs include detection and successful prosecution of cartel members as well as destabilization of cartels and deterrence of their formation. The United States established a leniency program in 1993; the European Union adopted a revised leniency program in 2002. Countries such as Brazil, Canada, the Czech Republic, Germany, Ireland, Korea, Sweden, and the United Kingdom have used leniency programs as part of their antitrust enforcement efforts. Economists and game theorists increasingly are involved in the design of leniency schemes.

SEE ALSO *Antitrust; Competition; Competition, Marxist; Competition, Perfect; Deregulation; Discrimination, Price; Monopoly; Regulation; Returns, Increasing; Returns to Scale*

BIBLIOGRAPHY

Baker, Jonathan B. 2003. The Case for Antitrust Enforcement. *Journal of Economic Perspectives* 17 (4): 27–50.

Kovacic, William E., and Carl Shapiro. 2000. Antitrust Policy: A Century of Economic and Legal Thinking. *Journal of Economic Perspectives* 14: 43–60.

Wood, B. Dan, and James E. Anderson. 1993. The Politics of U.S. Antitrust Regulation. *American Journal of Political Science* 37 (1): 1–39.

Damian S. Damianov

ANXIETY

Anxiety is a universally experienced emotion felt as an unpleasant, tense anticipation of an impending but vague threat. Some 18 percent of the adult U.S. population experiences anxiety symptoms to the extent that they can be diagnosed as suffering from an *anxiety disorder*. Anxious people often feel as if something bad were about to happen to them, although they might be unable to identify an immediate threat. The emotion of anxiety is in many ways similar to fear, although fear is typically defined as an emotional reaction to a clearly identifiable threat, such as a charging elephant or the possibility of falling when leaning over the edge of a tall building.

Fear and anxiety have in common several reaction patterns. One typical anxiety response is a sense of choking or constriction, felt as a lump in the throat. Indeed, the Latin root of the term *anxiety* is *angh*, meaning "constriction." Also related is the Germanic word *angst*. However, an anxiety reaction is more than a lump in the throat, as described by psychologist Stanley J. Rachman, one of the leading authorities on anxiety and anxiety disorders. Most experts agree that there are three partially integrated response systems that account for the various symptoms and therefore make up the full experience of anxiety. These are the cognitive, physiological, and behavioral response systems. Examples of each are described in Table 1.

Sigmund Freud (1856–1939), the founder of psychoanalysis in the late nineteenth century, is credited with explication of the role of anxiety in affecting people's daily lives. Freud postulated three types of anxiety. He called a reaction to a real or potential threat *reality anxiety*, whereas anxiety generated within the psychic apparatus as a threat to the ego was called *neurotic anxiety*. According to Freud, the ego keeps its instinctual sources of threat out of conscious awareness so that the true source of neurotic anxiety remains obscure and is experienced as "free-floating" or unattached anxiety. Freud also described *moral anxiety*, arising from an impending or actual violation of internalized standards. Moral anxiety is experienced as shame or guilt.

Response components that make up the experience of anxiety	
Cognitive:	Thoughts that something is wrong, a sense of dread, worry about many things, and difficulty concentrating.
Physiological:	Increased activation of the sympathetic nervous system leading to increases in heart rate, blood pressure, perspiration, respiration rate, pupil dilation, and muscle tension.
Behavioral:	Fidgeting, pacing, jittery movements, irritableness, stuttering, flight from or active avoidance of a harmless but feared situation.

Table 1

Physical conditions that can cause anxiety symptoms	
Disordered system	**Example conditions or substances**
Endocrine disorders	hypoglycemia, hyperthyroidism
Cardiovascular disorders	mitral valve prolapse, angina pectoris, arrhythmia
Respiratory disorders	hyperventilation, chronic obstructive pulmonary syndrome
Metabolic disorders	vitamin B12 deficiency
Neurologic disorders	postconcussive syndrome, vestibular dysfunction
Toxins	paint, gasoline, insecticides
Drug intake	alcohol, amphetamines, sedatives, antihistamines
Drug withdrawal	sedatives, alcohol, cocaine

Table 2

Another, more recent characterization of anxiety types is psychologist Charles Spielberger's *state-trait* distinction. *State anxiety* refers to an individual's anxious feeling at a given time: "Are you anxious right now?" *Trait anxiety* refers to one's state of anxiety in general: "Are you an anxious person?" State anxiety is more akin to fear as a response to a specific situation, whereas trait anxiety is part of one's overall personality.

The most common source of anxiety or fear is the perception that one is in imminent psychological or physical danger, or might be at some future time, such as feeling anxious about an impending dental appointment. Another common source of anxiety is concern over what other people might think of you. This social anxiety is particularly prevalent among adolescents, who worry that they might be scrutinized by others and be found lacking in appearance, skills, or behavior.

Although most anxiety is precipitated by perceived environmental threats, there are clear individual differences in how people perceive and react to potential threats. There is good evidence that some people are genetically predisposed to be more anxiety-reactive than others. Furthermore, a number of physical and medical conditions can cause anxiety symptoms that resolve when the condition is successfully treated. A sample of these anxiety inducing medical conditions is shown in Table 2.

The experience of anxiety is virtually universal among humans and most vertebrate animals. Most anxiety is experienced within the normal range, where it escalates under perceived stressful situations (e.g., taking a test) and then diminishes as the threat wanes. However, for those whose anxiety is severe enough to be diagnosed as an anxiety disorder, the experience of anxiety is chronic, debilitating, and interferes with personal, social, and occupational functioning. The various disorders have in common an exaggerated sense of fear, anxiety, and dread; yet each has a distinctive pattern to its expression.

Specific phobias are morbid and irrational (relative to the potential for actual danger) fear reactions to specific objects and situations. The phobic person attempts to avoid or escape from these objects or situations at all cost. Common examples include phobias of small animals (e.g., rats, snakes, spiders), heights, and injections of medicine. *Social phobia* involves fear and anxiety reactions to situations in which a person believes that he or she might be observed by others and be negatively evaluated or might embarrass himself or herself. Public speaking, using public restrooms, and eating in public are among the more common social phobia situations.

Generalized anxiety disorder involves a chronic state of worry, apprehension, and anticipation of possible disaster, no matter how unlikely it is that the disaster will occur. Individuals with *panic disorder* might have a sudden attack of intense anxiety or panic that hits them unexpectedly, out of the blue. In certain cases, when these unexpected panic attacks occur outside the home, people become fearful that another attack might strike if they go out again. When they become so fearful of having another attack that they cannot leave their home or safe haven, they are diagnosed as having *panic disorder with agoraphobia*. *Posttraumatic stress disorder* can occur following a terrifying event. The person might experience persistent, frightening thoughts and images as *flashbacks* to the original trauma. Individuals with *obsessive-compulsive disorder* experience anxiety-related thoughts and feel compelled to enact compulsive rituals, such as washing their hands repeatedly, lest they experience even more intense anxiety.

One of the most serious consequences of untreated chronic anxiety disorders, which are often accompanied by depression, is the increased risk of substance abuse as a form of self-medication. Other consequences of the con-

Drugs for treating anxiety disorders

Drug class	Examples of trade names
Antianxiety:	
Benzodiazepines:	Valium, Librium, Klonopin, Xanax, Ativan
Buspirone:	BuSpar
Antidepressants:	
Selective serotonin reuptake inhibitors:	Paxil, Zoloft, Prozac, Clozapine, Luvox
Tricyclic antidepressants:	Elavil, Endep, Anafranil

Table 3

stant worry and accompanying physical tension are gastrointestinal distress, insomnia, headache, high blood pressure, hyperventilation, nausea, and fatigue.

Anxiety disorders are among the most successfully treated of all mental disorders. Two basic approaches contribute to this effectiveness: psychotherapy (specifically, *cognitive-behavioral therapy*) and pharmacotherapy. The effective therapeutic processes in cognitive-behavioral therapy include helping patients alter negative anticipatory thoughts that often trigger anxiety symptoms and helping them confront their feared situations directly, which allows the anxiety symptoms to dissipate. To facilitate these processes, training in cognitive coping skills and deep relaxation are typically included in a cognitive-behavioral therapy treatment protocol.

Two classes of drugs are known to be effective in treating some anxiety disorders. Antianxiety drugs, primarily benzodiazepines, can reduce anxiety and panic symptoms but they have the serious drawback of physical dependency if taken for extended periods. Many antidepressants, particularly selective serotonin reuptake inhibitors and tricyclics, also have antianxiety properties. Examples of these antianxiety drugs are listed in Table 3.

SEE ALSO *Coping; Mental Health; Phobia; Psychotherapy; Social Anxiety; Stress*

BIBLIOGRAPHY

American Psychiatric Association. 2000. *Diagnostic and Statistical Manual of Mental Disorders* (*DSM*-IV-TR). 4th ed., text rev. Washington, DC: Author.

Barlow, David H. 2002. *Anxiety and Its Disorders: The Nature and Treatment of Anxiety and Panic.* 2nd ed. New York: Guilford.

Rachman, Stanley J. 2004. *Anxiety.* 2nd ed. East Sussex, U.K.: Psychology Press.

Ronald A. Kleinknecht

ANXIETY, SEPARATION

SEE *Separation Anxiety.*

ANXIETY, SOCIAL

SEE *Social Anxiety.*

ANXIOLYTICS

SEE *Psychotropic Drugs.*

APARTHEID

Apartheid is a word in Afrikaans that originally meant "apartness" or "separateness." Now it is the internationally recognized term for the policies of strict racial segregation and political and economic domination of blacks (Africans, "Coloreds," and Asians) pursued by the National Party government of South Africa from 1948 until its exit from power in the early 1990s.

Apartheid catapulted to prominence as a catchword used by the National Party in its successful 1948 electoral campaign to oust Prime Minister Jan Smuts and his United Party, who were accused of undermining racial segregation. The National Party, headed successively by Prime Ministers D. F. Malan, J. G. Strydom, H. F. Verwoerd, B. J. Vorster, P. W. Botha, and F. W. deKlerk, implemented an interlocking set of policies that together comprised apartheid: intensified segregation, "separate development," and harsh political repression.

Intensified segregation was manifested in a plethora of new laws. Starting with the prohibition of marriage and sexual liaisons between races (Prohibition of Mixed Marriages Act, 1949, and Immorality Act, 1950), the National Party government defined criteria for racial categorization of individuals (Population Registration Act, 1950), mandated racially based residential segregation (Group Areas Act, 1950), required segregation of public facilities (Separate Amenities Act, 1953), established separate education for Africans (Bantu Education Act, 1953), banned trade unions from representing Africans in labor negotiations (Native Labour Act, 1953), and empowered government to reserve specific jobs for particular racial groups (Industrial Conciliation Amendment Act, 1956). State power confronted blacks at almost every turn.

"Separate development" distinguished post-1948 National Party policies from previous segregation in South Africa. All blacks were segregated residentially and commercially under the Group Areas Act. Millions of blacks were forcibly removed from urban "white" areas into crowded "black" areas. Additionally Africans were assigned to ten ethnic "homelands" (based upon existing "tribal reserves") that were to be the sole legitimate space for black political expression and representation under the Bantu Authorities Act (1951) and the Promotion of Bantu Self Government Act (1959). From 1976 onward four "homelands" (Transkei, Bophututswana, Venda, and Ciskei) were granted fictive independence, recognized only by South Africa. "Coloreds" and Asians were granted nominal representation in separate political bodies.

Opposition to apartheid in the 1950s centered around the African National Congress (ANC), led by Nelson Mandela, Walter Sisulu, and Oliver Tambo. The ANC organized nonviolent campaigns of defiance and boycott in alliance with the South African Indian Congress, the South African Coloured People's Organization, and radical whites in the Congress of Democrats. In 1955 representatives of the congresses, led by the ANC, adopted the Freedom Charter, a document demanding full civil rights for all South Africans, an end to racial discrimination, and major economic reform, including selected nationalization. In 1959 the Pan Africanist Congress (PAC) broke from the ANC, accusing it of subservience to non-Africans and insufficient militancy. It echoed the ANC in calling for demonstrations against passes, the hated government control document carried by all Africans.

Following widespread demonstrations protesting the Sharpeville massacre of 1960—in which sixty-nine unarmed Africans were shot after responding to a PAC call to turn in passes and submit to arrest—the government embarked on sustained repression of opposition. Prior to 1960 it had generally respected legal norms, relying upon the Riotous Assemblies Act (1914) and its amendments (1927, 1929), under which the government could declare a state of emergency and ban individuals from political activity, and the Suppression of Communism Act (1950), which granted additional powers to block political activity deemed communist under a broad definition. In 1960 the government enacted the Unlawful Organizations Act, under which it banned the ANC and the PAC. It followed with General Laws Amendment Acts in 1962 and 1963 and the Terrorism Act of 1966, which legalized house arrest and detention without habeus corpus and provided greater penalties up to death for sabotage and terrorism. Concomitantly police adopted the practices of solitary confinement, physical and mental torture, and assassination.

In the view of the government, harsh police state measures were a necessary response to the decision of the ANC in 1961 to abandon nonviolence for armed struggle—to be led by Umkhonto we Sizwe (MK), a military

organization jointly directed by leaders of the banned ANC and the clandestine South African Communist Party (SACP)—and to attacks on whites by POQO, an offshoot of the PAC, in 1962–1963. Relentlessly deploying its strengthened arsenal of repression, the government successfully decimated its internal opposition, as symbolized by the imprisonment in 1964 of ANC leaders, including Mandela and Sisulu, on Robben Island. Tambo, who had left the country in 1960, peripatetically undertook the difficult creation of ANC and MK structures in exile.

The Soweto uprising of June 1976 and the nationwide unrest that followed exploded the government's hopes that blacks might acquiesce to apartheid. The government responded with both reform and repression. African trade union rights were recognized in 1980 and 1981, a new constitution was enacted in 1984 granting subordinate voting privileges to "Coloreds" and Asians, and there was selective relaxation of rigid segregation, including the abolition of the pass system in 1985. Repression of opposition was intensified, however, as symbolized by the 1977 death in police custody of Steve Biko, the charismatic leader who founded the Black Consciousness movement in the late 1960s. Nevertheless, opposition inside the country grew. Post-1976 boycotts, strikes, and township demonstrations metamorphosed in the 1980s into open nationally organized opposition, led by the ANC-oriented United Democratic Front (UDF), a burgeoning trade union movement, and prominent church leaders, most notably the 1983 Nobel Peace Prize winner Archbishop Desmond Tutu. Numerous acts of sabotage and armed attacks—organized by the resurgent ANC/MK underground and the ANC mission in exile—were carried out, complementing the external opposition of the worldwide antiapartheid movement and increasingly extensive economic sanctions.

On February 11, 1990, the newly elected president deKlerk freed Mandela and other ANC leaders from prison and legalized the PAC, ANC, and SACP. Negotiations between the National Party, headed by deKlerk, and its erstwhile antiapartheid opponents led by the ANC, headed by Mandela, commenced in mid-1990, leading in late 1993 to agreement upon a new nonracial democratic constitution. In 1993 the last apartheid laws were repealed.

In South Africa's first election under the new constitution in April 1994, the ANC won a majority of votes, and Mandela became president. Mandela vigorously pursued a policy of reconciliation with those who had supported apartheid. The Truth and Reconciliation Commission, headed by Archbishop Tutu, exposed the workings of the apartheid police state. The ANC-led government adopted policies to reverse the consequences of decades-long apartheid, but apartheid's entrenched legacies of inequality and black poverty proved hard to overcome.

SEE ALSO *African National Congress; Boer War; Coloreds (South Africa); Discrimination; Discrimination, Wage, by Race; Inequality, Racial; Mandela, Nelson; Mandela, Winnie; Nobel Peace Prize; Racism; Separatism; Truth and Reconciliation Commissions*

BIBLIOGRAPHY

Adam, Heribert. 1971. *Modernizing Racial Domination: South Africa's Political Dynamics.* Berkeley: University of California Press.

Beinart, William, and Saul Dubow, eds. 1995. *Segregation and Apartheid in Twentieth-Century South Africa.* London and New York: Routledge.

MacDonald, Michael. 2006. *Why Race Matters in South Africa.* Cambridge, MA: Harvard University Press.

Price, Robert M. 1991. *The Apartheid State in Crisis: Political Transformation in South Africa, 1975–1990.* New York: Oxford University Press.

Sheridan Johns

APPALACHIA

The Appalachian Mountains range southwestward from Quebec and Newfoundland in Canada to Alabama in the southeastern United States. The central and southern highlands of this ancient mountain range, consisting of the Blue Ridge and Smoky Mountain ranges, the Allegheny and Cumberland plateaus, and the Great Valley in between, are frequently thought of as comprising a distinct sociocultural region known as "Appalachia."

The Appalachian Regional Commission (ARC) defines Appalachia as 406 counties found in 13 states, including all of West Virginia plus portions of Alabama, Georgia, Kentucky, Maryland, Mississippi, New York, North Carolina, Ohio, Pennsylvania, South Carolina, Tennessee, and Virginia. A more common geographical definition of Appalachia includes the ARC-designated counties in West Virginia, Kentucky, Ohio, Maryland, Tennessee, North Carolina, Virginia, and Georgia.

EARLY POPULATION

A diverse population of Native Americans has lived in the mountain South for around three thousand years. The Iroquois, who were the dominant group in the region, came from the west around 1300 BCE and split into the northern Iroquois and the southern Cherokees. The Cherokees were farmers and hunters who lived in small independent villages.

Although Indians in the Appalachians had sporadic contacts with Europeans as early as 1540, it was not until the period 1700 to 1761 that contact between the two cultures accelerated. The Europeans looked to the backcountry for room to expand their settlements and for sources of skins for trading. The Indians opposed them in an ultimately futile attempt to save their homes and hunting grounds. The final defeat of the Cherokees by the British occurred in 1761, and after this date the number of whites in the Appalachian frontier grew rapidly. The conquest of the Indian lands encouraged settlement, and land speculation in the Appalachian frontier ran rampant.

The areas from which the earliest European settlers in Appalachia came and the routes they took into the backcountry helped form Appalachian culture. There were three major reservoirs of population from which people flowed into the Appalachian region in the eighteenth century: the central valley of Pennsylvania, the Piedmont of North Carolina, and western Pennsylvania. The earliest European immigrants into the Appalachian frontier came from eastern Pennsylvania. Around 1720 the German and Scotch-Irish populations around Philadelphia began to move first into central Pennsylvania, then southward into the Shenandoah Valley. Over time they and their descendants pushed south toward the New River, but instead of crossing the mountains into Indian country, they turned southeastward toward the Carolina Piedmont.

By the middle of the eighteenth century this area became a second population reservoir that fed migrants into the mountains. It was the source of early settlers into far southwestern Virginia, western North Carolina, and upper eastern Tennessee. By 1760 a significant number of Germans and Ulster Scots were also coming into Appalachia from western Pennsylvania. These people drifted down the Ohio River, then followed tributaries into the mountains.

By 1763, in clear violation of the English Proclamation of 1763, settlers began to migrate into the western reaches of North Carolina, the river valleys of the Tennessee-Virginia border country, and, just a few years later, even into central Kentucky. The most important of the communities they formed were the Watauga settlements in eastern Tennessee, the Holston settlements of far southwestern Virginia and western North Carolina, and the Boonesborough and Harrodsburg settlements laid out by Daniel Boone after he traversed the Cumberland Gap in 1775. Although many of these people did not own the land they lived on, and acted as agents for absentee owners, it is nonetheless significant that on the eve of the American Revolution there were scattered settlements deep in the American frontier. The population of the southern mountains grew steadily from the 1760s until the 1820s.

CIVIL WAR ERA AND INDUSTRIALIZATION

The society that emerged in the mountains was not unlike other rural American farm regions that were not far removed from their frontier origins, and that were dominated by connections between land, family, and work. Until the era of industrialization Appalachia was a region of small, open-country communities, concentrated in valleys and up into mountain coves and hollows. The separate settlements were integrated by transportation and communication systems, but only loosely. Each community of farmsteads was relatively self-sufficient socially and economically, and people tended to avoid routinely crossing mountains to reach another community, if possible.

What held these scattered farms together and molded them into some semblance of community was a shared sense of identity, common values, and shared work. People exchanged food and shelter, worshiped in small, independent congregations, engaged in cooperative community service, had a sense of belonging to a larger group of friends and neighbors, and were united in their love of the land and the place they lived.

The mountain economy was also similar in many ways to other preindustrial economies in rural America. There was a preponderance of noncommercial, semi–self-sufficient farms, although in some areas of Appalachia farming for an external market was common. Some industries also emerged in the mountains before the Civil War, but were not significant regionally and had only a marginal effect on the total economy.

Although the issue of slavery did not emerge in Appalachia as the dominant controversy of the Civil War era, the war did have an impact in the mountain areas of the South. The relative absence of slavery in the mountains was the result of the geographic and economic conditions found there. Because of the mountain terrain, it was simply not profitable to develop commercial agriculture based upon a slave workforce, and what slavery did exist in Appalachia was concentrated in the larger valleys of Virginia and Tennessee. There was considerable industrial slavery in Appalachia in the tanning works, salt mines, and iron foundries of Virginia, and in the brick mills of Tennessee and Kentucky.

As the result of their Civil War experiences, a great many northerners came into contact with the southern mountains, and many were surprised by what they found. Great mineral and timber wealth was coupled with a romantic beauty, just at a time when untamed urban growth, foreign immigration, and technological developments were beginning to unalterably change northern urban society. Capitalists responded to the call of profits, but writers, missionary workers, and teachers accompanied the industrialists into the mountains, and their work there was in some ways as substantial and the effects as long lasting as those of their entrepreneurial counterparts.

The dominant stereotype of Appalachia that was formed during this era of industrial development was ironically an image of a society that still held within it much of its late-eighteenth-century frontier heritage. Mountain people were described as noble and savage, independent, proud, rugged, and violent, but also as dirty and uneducated, yet crafty and practical. They drank too much and were lazy, but managed to produce excessively large families.

The people who were mostly responsible for this image of Appalachia were a group of writers in the Local Color Movement. They described in influential journals, short stories, novels, and travel literature a land of contemporary ancestors who were more Elizabethan than American. Violence, feuding, moonshining, and a traditional culture existed in an Appalachia that had been untouched by the forces of modernization. Appalachia began to be thought of as a region in stark contrast to the progressive, urban culture of the rest of the United States.

One of the results of this new image of Appalachia was the urge felt mostly by middle-class women who came into Appalachia from the Northeast to improve conditions in the mountains and uplift Appalachian culture. They typically perceived the regional culture as deficient in many ways, and they worked diligently to bring schools and modern middle-class values to mountain people.

A second feature of the response to this new image of Appalachia was cultural preservation. What certain cultural workers thought represented the best of mountain culture was preserved and protected from contamination by the evils of modernization. This work to preserve mountain ballads, folk crafts, and dances was carried out by traveling folklorists such as Cecil Sharp and at folk schools such as the one founded by John C. Campbell. What they chose to preserve and value did not always reflect the reality and variety of Appalachian culture, but rather the image that was created and perpetuated by the cultural workers themselves.

A third response to the backward image of Appalachia was to use economic development and industrialization to promote progress, because the local population was believed to be incapable of developing Appalachian resources on its own. Promoters of this idea asserted that economic development would provide needed discipline and order in the mountains, and that through industrialization the Appalachian people could become effective contributors to the progress of the nation. Both technological innovations and rapid urban

150

growth created demands for labor, minerals, and timber, all of which were in abundant supply in Appalachia. Industrialization depended first upon the building of an adequate transportation system into, out of, and within the mountain regions of the South.

The great era of railroad building in Appalachia lasted from 1870 to 1910. By the end of this period the rail network reached into nearly every county by either a main or branch line. The impact of the railroads on every facet of life in Appalachia is hard to overestimate, but the most immediate effect was to open the doors to full exploitation of the region's natural resources.

Coal was the primary resource that drove the Industrial Revolution in Appalachia. The ambitious men who opened and operated the mines were outsiders from middle- or upper-middle-class backgrounds who established the company town system in Appalachia and wielded enormous political and economic power in the coal fields and beyond. They manipulated the local and state political system to their industry's benefit, sometimes to the long-term detriment of the local economy. The laborers who worked in the mines and moved their families into company towns to live were a varied lot. They were primarily native Appalachians, southern blacks, and immigrants from southern and eastern Europe.

Although coal mining was certainly the most important industrial development in Appalachia, it was not the only one. From 1880 to 1930 industrialization also showed up in forestry and timber exploitation, textile mills, railroading, non-coal mineral mining, and chemicals production.

The impact of industrialization in Appalachia was tinged with good and bad features. At the end of this era, fully two-thirds of Appalachian people made their living from nonfarm work. The economy had moved, by World War I, from a local or regional orientation to a national and international one. Although most mountain people no longer gained their primary incomes from the land, an attachment to the land remained an important regional value. People still farmed on a part-time basis, growing large gardens and raising some livestock. Older values such as strong family ties and conservative religious beliefs remained central to regional culture despite the wrenching economic and social changes of the late nineteenth and early twentieth centuries.

One of the most important results of industrialization in Appalachia has been the negative impact it has had on the long-term economic health of the region. None of the industries in Appalachia, and especially not the coal industry, encouraged rival or spin-off economic development during their boom years. The effect has been sporadic economic growth without real economic development.

POSTWAR TO THE PRESENT

World War II and the years immediately following it were turning points in the history of Appalachia, just as they were for the rest of the United States. Once they returned home from their wartime experiences, many young men and women focused on the lack of economic opportunities in Appalachia, and began to move out of the region again in search of better jobs. This resulted in a great out-migration from Appalachia to the North and Midwest. Between 1945 and 1965 nearly 3.5 million people left Appalachia in search of a brighter economic future in major cities in the Midwest. Sizable subcultures of Appalachian migrants built up in these cities.

Despite the general prosperity in the United States, the 1950s was a time of extreme poverty in Appalachia. A renewed national attention to Appalachia was accelerated by the campaign for the Democratic presidential nomination in 1960 when the major candidates visited West Virginia. After he became president in 1963, Lyndon Johnson pushed the Appalachian Regional Development Act through Congress. The bill called for federal funding for secondary and vocational education programs, highway construction, timber management programs, and widespread promotion of tourism.

Most historians think that though the War on Poverty had some successes, it generally failed in Appalachia. The heritage of the billions of dollars spent on highways and industries in the mountains has been continued poverty amidst pockets of prosperity. Economic development in the 1970s consisted of the coal boom of 1974 to 1978, the tourism-generated land boom in eastern Tennessee and western North Carolina, a growth in textile production, some small-scale component-part manufacturing, and the growth of large-scale chain stores and fast-food establishments located within the more prosperous areas. Outside the few growing towns and cities, there are rural areas where poverty is still the norm.

One important result of the War on Poverty in Appalachia was the emergence by the late 1970s of a strong sense of regional identity and the need to express a positive image of Appalachia when writing or talking about its people, history, and culture. Even the word *Appalachia* became more accepted than it had ever been. To many within the region, the culmination of the organizing and turbulence of the 1960s was an Appalachian Renaissance filled with a strong dose of regional pride that was associated for this first time in American history with being from the mountains.

SEE ALSO *Great Depression; Industrialization; Migration; Mining Industry; New Deal, The; Poverty; Railway Industry; Regions; South, The (USA); War on Poverty*

BIBLIOGRAPHY

Abramson, Rudy, and Jean Haskell. 2006. *Encyclopedia of Appalachia.* Knoxville: University of Tennessee Press.

Eller, Ronald D. 1982. *Miners, Millhands, and Mountaineers: Industrialization of the Appalachian South, 1880–1930.* Knoxville: University of Tennessee Press.

Still, James. [1940] 1978. *River of Earth.* New York: Viking Press.

Straw, Richard A., and H. Tyler Blethen. 2004. *High Mountains Rising: Appalachia in Time and Place.* Urbana: University of Illinois Press.

Whisnant, David E. 1983. *All That Is Native and Fine: The Politics of Culture in an American Region.* Chapel Hill: University of North Carolina Press.

Williams, John A. 2002. *Appalachia: A History.* Chapel Hill: University of North Carolina Press.

Woolley, Bryan. 1975. *We Be Here When the Morning Comes.* Lexington: University Press of Kentucky.

Richard Straw

APPEASEMENT

Appeasement is a foreign policy strategy of making concessions to an adversary in order to avoid direct military conflict. As a foreign policy strategy it is rarely advocated today, largely as a result of the failure of British diplomacy vis-à-vis Nazi Germany in the later 1930s. It remains a central concept beyond this historical moment, however, in that it is often invoked in foreign policy debates in the United States and elsewhere as a term of opprobrium to describe concessions to adversaries. Appeasement is not necessarily a policy resulting from fear and weakness, however; it has the potential to be effective if political leaders can understand the distribution of power in the international system.

THE IDEA OF APPEASEMENT

According to the Oxford English Dictionary (1993), the term *appease* means, "to bring peace" and was first used in English around the thirteenth century. *Appeasement*, thus, means "pacification" or "satisfaction." Because it implies the satisfaction of the *demands* rather than the requests of an aggrieved party, *appeasement* has had an underlying negative connotation even when used to describe interpersonal relations. But its strongly negative connotations did not solidify in the English-speaking world until after World War II (1939–1945). Various dictionaries and encyclopedias of the social and political sciences demonstrate this negative valence quite clearly. One author, for example, describes the policy as the "surrender of a vital interest for a minor *quid pro quo*, or for no reciprocal concession at all" (Plano and Olten 1982, p. 229).

Despite this generally negative valence, however, some have described the policy in more positive ways: for example, as a form of conflict resolution (Walker 2005). Indeed, satisfying the demands of an opponent in order to avoid war need not be a negative policy, especially if the opponent is viewed as having been unfairly treated in the past. Conflict resolution often requires the granting of concessions, something that, while very few would call it appeasement, is not that far from the policies that were identified as such in the late nineteenth and early twentieth centuries.

BRITISH INTERWAR DIPLOMACY

Appeasement as a foreign policy strategy is most closely associated with British policies in the interwar years (1919–1939). Martin Gilbert in his *The Roots of Appeasement* (1966) gives the clearest analysis of British appeasement policies. He argues that they should be seen as resulting from a combination of guilt over the harshness of the Versailles treaty, liberal policies favoring economic interdependence, and an abhorrence of war. The end of the "Great War" led to the Paris Peace Conference, during which the allied powers sought to both impose a settlement on Germany and create new institutions that would, it was hoped, eliminate war in the future. Although a desire for revenge animated many at the conference, others sought to counter those impulses. During the conference David Lloyd George, the British prime minister, authored the famous Fontainebleau Memorandum, which sought to limit the harshness of the reparations scheme, a proposal that Gilbert sees as being in the spirit of appeasement.

Appeasement during the interwar period revolved around two issues: reparations and rearmament. After the Versailles settlement, British policymakers soon recognized the precarious position in which Germany had been placed by the imposition of harsh reparations. John Maynard Keynes's influential book *The Economic Consequences of the Peace* (1919) supplied the foreign policy community with strong economic reasons for decreasing reparations. In 1924 the Dawes Plan—the result of an American-led commission, but largely inspired by British attempts to improve the German economic situation—resulted in a reduction of German war reparations. The Young Plan of 1929 further reduced the burden of reparations, which were eventually abolished at the Lausanne Conference in 1932 (Carr 1947).

While the decrease in German reparations payments was generally perceived as positive, concessions on security agreements were more controversial. The Versailles settlement included the provision that the Rhineland was to be occupied for fifteen years by Allied forces and permanently demilitarized. Stringent limits were also placed on German armed forces. These limits were violated soon after Adolf Hitler came to power in 1933. Quickly dismantling any semblance of constitutional government in Germany, Hitler began the process of rearming the German nation. On March 7, 1936, Germany remilitarized the Rhineland, a move some British leaders considered acceptable, as in their view it rectified the unjust division of Europe created by Versailles (Rock 1977, p. 38). Others in the British political system, however—most prominently, Winston Churchill and Anthony Eden—were beginning to see the folly of appeasing the Nazis.

At this point, the policy of appeasement began to appear as one of weakness rather than strength. In March 1938, the Germans annexed Austria, an action that resulted in the British undertaking a high-level policy review of relations with Germany. Rather than seeing this as an opportunity to halt an aggressive dictator, however, British leaders proposed to further appease Hitler in order to avoid another shock to the fragile European system. When German troops began massing near the Sudetenland, a region of Czechoslovakia with a large percentage of German speakers, the British sought to convince Prague of the wisdom of appeasement. Failing to convince the Czechs to accept German demands, the British sought to negotiate directly with Germany. After two separate trips to Germany to convince Hitler to moderate his demands, in late September 1938 Prime Minister Neville Chamberlain flew to Munich, where an agreement was signed (without a Czechoslovakian signature) giving the Germans the Sudetenland. Germany occupied the rest of Czechoslovakia in March 1939, leading the British to finally stand up to Hitler by guaranteeing the borders of Poland. When Hitler attacked in September 1939, war erupted and appeasement lay in ruins.

APPEASEMENT SINCE WORLD WAR II

In the postwar period, *appeasement* quickly became a term used to identify a failed or misguided policy. British and American policymakers, embroiled in the cold war, refused to "appease" the Soviet Union when faced with its aggressive policies. In 1956 Prime Minister Anthony Eden, who had resigned from the British government in the 1930s over appeasement policies, intervened in Egypt with the French and Israelis because he believed that concessions to Nasser would be a new form of appeasement. American president Lyndon Johnson's unwillingness to back out of the Vietnam War resulted, in part, from his refusal to appease Ho Chi Minh. In the United States' long war with Iraq, both Democratic and Republican leaders (for example, the Democratic secretary of state

Madeline Albright and the Republican vice president Richard Cheney) claimed that to give into Saddam Hussein would be Chamberlain-esque appeasement all over again.

This reflexive view of appeasement as weakness, however, misunderstands its potential. Paul Kennedy points out that appeasement arose from a British tradition of ethical foreign policy reaching back to nineteenth century, when William Gladstone sought to create a foreign policy grounded in peace and economic prosperity. Great powers can indulge in policies of appeasement in order to manage the international system, as Kennedy argues the British did in their relations with the United States during the latter half of the nineteenth century when they allowed an emerging power to take control of the Western Hemisphere (Kennedy 1976).

If an adversary seeks a change in the international system that does not weaken but might actually improve the position of the stronger power, a policy of appeasement might well be a wise move. It is only when it is undertaken in response to the demands of a powerful state bent on aggrandizement that appeasement can be deemed a policy failure. This suggests that appeasement can only succeed if leaders can correctly appraise the distribution of power in the international system. When an adversary who is weak makes demands that will not necessarily increase its strength too much, appeasing those demands might decrease conflict in the future. At the same time, by constantly conceding to demands from different powers, a great power might eventually undermine its ability to deter others in the system.

The realist policy of maintaining a balance of power might include appeasement at key moments, in order to ensure stability. E. H. Carr, one of the leading realists of the twentieth century, suggested in his classic *Twenty Years Crisis* (1940) that British appeasement was a realist policy, in that it combined the interests of Britain with an honest appraisal of power—although in later editions, Carr excised those passages in which he justified appeasement (Hall 2006).

The normative foundations of appeasement that underlay British policies toward Germany in the interwar years correspond with the goals of modern liberal internationalism: defusing conflict, rectifying unjust settlements, and avoiding war. British policymakers' inability to appreciate the emerging power of Germany prevented them from seeing how their good intentions could lead to war. The disastrous consequences of their policy choices continue to influence how appeasement is understood today. Although it is difficult to change the word's connotations, appeasement, from a position of strength, should also be seen as a means to avoid conflict.

SEE ALSO *Annexation; Chamberlain, Neville; Churchill, Winston; Conflict; Foreign Policy; Hitler, Adolf; Keynes, John Maynard; Negotiation; Strategy; War; War and Peace; World War II*

BIBLIOGRAPHY

Carr, E. H. 1940. *The Twenty Years Crisis, 1919–1939: An Introduction to the Study of International Relations.* London: Macmillan.

Carr, E. H. 1947. *International Relations between the Two World Wars, 1919–1939.* Houndsmill, U.K.: Macmillan.

Gilbert, Martin. 1966. *The Roots of Appeasement.* London: Weidenfeld & Nicolson.

Hall, Ian. 2006. "Power Politics and Appeasement: Political Realism in British International Thought, c. 1935–1955." *British Journal of Politics and International Relations* 8 (2): 174–192.

Kennedy, Paul. 1976. "The Tradition of Appeasement in British Foreign Policy, 1865–1939." *British Journal of International Studies* 2 (3): 195–215.

Keynes, John Maynard. 1919. *The Economic Consequences of the Peace.* London: Macmillan.

Plano, Jack C., and Roy Olton. 1982. *The International Relations Dictionary.* 3rd ed. Santa Barbara, CA: ABC-Clio.

Rock, William R. 1977. *British Appeasement in the 1930s.* London: Edward Arnold.

Walker, Stephen. 2005. "Appeasement." In *Encyclopaedia of International Relations and Global Politics,* ed. Martin Griffiths: 22-24 London: Routledge.

Anthony F. Lang Jr.

APPLE

SEE *Microelectronics Industry.*

APPORTIONMENT

The term *apportionment* refers to the decennial process that divides membership in the U.S. House of Representatives among the fifty states according to the size of the states' populations. After apportionment, state governments initiate redistricting, the highly contentious process of revising the intrastate boundaries of the House districts. Article I, Section 2 of the U.S. Constitution mandates that apportionment take place every ten years, and Congress is given the responsibility of managing the procedure. Two amendments to the Constitution influence apportionment: Amendment 14, Section 2 repealed the original provision that considered nonfree persons (slaves) as three-fifths of a person for counting purposes,

and Amendment 16 released the federal government from the original bind of having to use a state's population as a basis for determining tax levies.

The Constitution entitles each state to have at least one representative in the House, with the "respective numbers" of each of the states forming the basis for the further distribution of seats. Congress has the power to define the precise manner of dividing up House seats, and this process has been a continuous source of controversy. In issuing his first presidential veto, George Washington "rejected a formula designed by New York's Alexander Hamilton for allocating seats after the 1790 census" (Prewitt 2000, p. 2). More recently, a 1998 U.S. General Accounting Office paper noted that after the number of available House seats was fixed at 435 in 1911, "a gain of representation for any one state came only with a loss of representation for another state" (p. 10). Orville J. Sweeting notes that the cap was instituted because "the House threatened to become so large, if size continued to follow population growth, that it could not properly transact its business" (1956, p. 440).

Southern and rural members of Congress were so fearful of the consequences of losing their seats due to the urban and northward shift of the population that they prevented the constitutional mandate of apportionment from taking place during the 1920s. Although apportionment has occurred in every decade since the 1930 census, the political battles associated with the process have not subsided. As currently written, Title 2 of the U.S. Code requires the use of the "method of equal proportions" to determine the allotment of seats among the states, as described in an online document produced by the Census Bureau. This method has been in place since the apportionment associated with the 1940 census, and it was upheld as constitutional by the Supreme Court in 1992 in the case of *United States Department of Commerce v. Montana.*

In the prelude to the 2000 census, there was a strong debate over whether statistical sampling to adjust for census undercounting could be used in the apportionment process. In 1999, the Supreme Court's five-to-four ruling in *Department of Commerce v. United States House of Representatives* affirmed that Section 195 of Title 13 of the U.S. Code prohibits the use of statistical sampling, but the Court explicitly declined to rule on the constitutionality of using sampling should this section of the code be repealed.

SEE ALSO *Census; Congress, U.S.; Gerrymandering*

BIBLIOGRAPHY

Prewitt, Kenneth. 2000. The US Decennial Census: Political Questions, Scientific Answers. *Population and Development Review* 26 (1): 1–16.

Rush, Mark E., and Richard Lee Engstrom. 2001. *Fair and Effective Representation?: Debating Electoral Reform and Minority Rights.* Lanham, MD: Rowman and Littlefield.

Sweeting, Orville J. 1956. John Q. Tilson and the Reapportionment Act of 1929. *Western Political Quarterly* 9 (2): 434–453.

U.S. Census Bureau. 2001. Computing Apportionment Homepage. http://www.census.gov/population/www/censusdata/apportionment/computing.html.

U.S. General Accounting Office. 1998. *Decennial Census: Overview of Historical Census Issues.* Washington, DC: U.S. Government Printing Office. http://www.gao.gov/archive/1998/gg98103.pdf.

Thomas J. Scotto

APPROPRIATIONS

Appropriations are legislative acts that authorize the withdrawal of public money from the treasury to fund government programs. Thus, appropriations measures provide the legal authority to spend government money, but are distinct from the act of spending. For example, the legislature could appropriate $100,000 for a public-works program, but the agency responsible for the work could spend only $50,000 to complete the program.

Generally, the two main types of appropriations measures in the United States are for mandatory spending and for discretionary spending. Appropriations for mandatory spending are budget authority for entitlement programs, such as Social Security, set by legal parameters (confusingly, this budget authority is generally considered outside the appropriations process). Appropriations for discretionary spending are budget authority for annual measures. The main work of the Appropriations Committees of the House of Representatives and the Senate is to hold hearings concerning appropriations measures for different areas of discretionary spending. In 2007, there were thirteen areas of discretionary spending: agriculture; commerce, justice, and state; defense; District of Columbia; energy and water development; foreign operations; homeland security; interior; labor, health and human services, and education; the legislative branch; military construction; transportation; veterans administration; and housing and urban development.

The appropriations process is distinguished from many other forms of legislation considered by Congress because of the legally proscribed budgetary cycle. The annual appropriations cycle begins near the start of each calendar year when the president submits his annual budget for the upcoming fiscal year with recommended spending levels. Congress is required by law to respond to the president by passing an annual budget resolution. This resolution provides a guide for subsequent congressional action by setting spending ceilings for the different areas of discretionary spending and by projecting appropriation levels for the next five fiscal years. Once the budget resolution is passed, the legislation is referred to the Appropriations Committees of the House and Senate, and the legislative process continues in much the typical manner.

From the mid-1990s Congress has had increasing difficulty passing separate appropriations bills for the different areas of discretionary spending. This can create problems for government operation because if Congress fails to pass appropriations legislation in time for the next fiscal year, the effected programs lose the authority to spend and must shut down. To prevent the shutdown of government operations, Congress may pass a continuing resolution to provide temporary funding. To speed the legislative process, appropriations measures have been passed with increasing frequency as omnibus legislation that packages multiple areas of spending into one bill.

Article 1, section 9, of the Constitution states, "No Money shall be drawn from the Treasury, but in Consequence of Appropriations made by Law; and a regular Statement and Account of the Receipts and Expenditures of all public Money shall be published from time to time." Because the passage of legislation requires the approval of the legislature, this provision provides a strong constitutional check on the president's ability to act without the approval of Congress. Article 1, section 8, of the Constitution gives this check additional weight in military matters by prohibiting congressional appropriations to raise and support armies for more than two years, thereby restricting the legislature's ability to cede full control over the army to the president, who already serves as commander in chief of the military.

SEE ALSO *Congress, U.S.; Gerrymandering*

BIBLIOGRAPHY

Streeter, Sandy. 2004. The Congressional Appropriations Process: An Introduction. *Congressional Research Service Report for Congress.* http://www.senate.gov/reference/resources/pdf/97-684.pdf.

Jeffrey Grynaviski

ARAB LEAGUE, THE

Officially known as the League of Arab States and consisting in 2006 of twenty-two countries, the Arab League was formed in 1945 by the governments of the then-independent or semi-independent Arab counties of Egypt,

Syria, Lebanon, Transjordan (now Jordan), Iraq, Saudi Arabia, and Yemen. Other Arab countries joined the League as they became independent, including Algeria, Bahrain, Comoros, Djibouti, Kuwait, Libya, Mauritania, Morocco, Oman, Qatar, Somalia, Sudan, Tunisia, and the United Arab Emirates. In addition, the Palestine Liberation Organization (PLO), while not ruling a sovereign territory, was granted full membership in 1976 as the representative of the Palestinians. In 2003 Eritrea became an observer, but has not pursued full membership.

The main purpose of the Arab League is to provide a forum for coordinating policies concerning education, finance, law, trade, and foreign policy among signatory members, and to help resolve their disputes. The secondary institutions that have resulted from that mandate coordinate developments in such areas as communication, transport, construction, medicine, and some minor industries. The Arab Common Market, established in 1965, has generally failed to live up to its expectations and original goals of abolishing custom duties, free movement of capital and labor among member countries, and coordination of economic development.

The most visible feature of the Arab League, however, is its political role as a governmental forum for common Arab national concerns, showcased in its highly publicized, though usually ineffectual, summit meetings. Historically the League sustained a consensus on supporting the independence of still colonized Arab countries. In the same spirit it opposed the creation of the state of Israel in 1948, and for decades supervised a joint Arab boycott of Israel and of companies doing business with it. For ten years after 1979 the League suspended Egypt's membership because of its treaty with Israel—a treaty that violated a prior principle of coordinating Arab policies regarding the Jewish state—and moved its headquarters from Cairo to Tunis, where it remained until 1991 before returning to Cairo.

The political history of the Arab League has often been characterized by factional infighting among member states, which during the cold war took the form of a split between pro-Soviet and pro–United States regimes. A unified stance vis-à-vis Israel was broken when Egypt, Jordan, and the PLO signed separate agreements with Israel, although a semblance of a common position reemerged once the peace process stalled. With the notable exception of Syria, the League also held a unified position supporting Iraq during the devastating Iran-Iraq War (1980–1988). However, it was thrown into turmoil after the Iraqi invasion of Kuwait in 1990, which highlighted a low point in inter-Arab rivalries and also violated the League's charter prohibiting the use of force by member states against each other.

Generally the Arab League is regarded not to have been successful in effectively promoting Arab unity and even coordinating policies, and many Arab governments are reluctant to agree to reforming and strengthening the League so that it could better pursue its aims. However, as a highly publicized forum for Arab governmental discussions, the League maintains an important symbolic status as a voice of a common aspiration for more Arab unity and coordination.

SEE ALSO *Arabs; Peace Process; Zionism*

BIBLIOGRAPHY

Barnett, Michael N. 1998. *Dialogues in Arab Politics: Negotiations in Regional Order.* New York: Columbia University Press.

Hudson, Michael C., ed. 1999. *Middle East Dilemma: The Politics and Economics of Arab Integration.* New York: Columbia University Press.

Mohammed A. Bamyeh

ARAB-ISRAELI WAR OF 1967

The Arab-Israeli War of 1967, also known as the Six-Day War, erupted between Israel and several of its neighbors on June 5, 1967, lasting until June 10. When the war was over, Israel had soundly defeated the militaries of Egypt, Syria, and Jordan and seized large amounts of territory, including the Old City of Jerusalem and its attendant holy sites, the Sinai Peninsula, the Gaza Strip, the West Bank, and the Golan Heights. The war transformed the political landscape of the Middle East from a military contest between Israel and its neighbors into (the 1973 Arab-Israeli War notwithstanding) what was primarily a political struggle between Israel and the more than a million Palestinians under Israeli occupation.

THE POLITICAL BACKGROUND

The Six-Day War had its roots in the creation of the Palestine Liberation Organization (PLO) by the Arab League in 1964. While Arab national armies had already been defeated twice by Israel (in 1948 and 1956), the creation of the PLO allowed Palestinian nationals to attack Israel directly and without support from the weakened Arab states in their quest to destroy the Jewish state and create a Palestinian homeland. In 1965 the PLO began attacking Israel from bases in Egypt and Jordan. Despite the fears of Egypt and Jordan that the aggression might lead to a general war, the PLO attacks increased in number and scale, from 35 in 1965 to 41 in 1966 and 37 in the first four months of 1967.

Furthermore, tensions had been steadily rising between Israel and Syria over Israel's National Water Carrier irrigation project, which channeled water through the Jordan River for use in Israel. A Syrian project begun in 1964 attempted to divert the flow of water; Israel responded in 1965 by bombing the Syrian diversionary project. In retaliation, Syria bombarded Israeli villages and farms in the northern part of the country. A particularly deadly attack on April 7, 1967, provoked Israeli retaliation and six Syrian MiG fighters were shot down.

The Soviet Union, a major patron and ally of both Egypt and Syria, issued warnings on May 13 (now known to be false) that Israel was preparing for an invasion of Syria, prompting Syria to invoke its mutual defense pact with Egypt. The reasons for the Soviet deception are still unclear. Some believe that the Soviets hoped the increasing U.S. involvement in Vietnam would prevent their assisting Israel, creating an opportunity to seriously damage Israel and bolster Egyptian president Gamal Abdel Nasser's power and prestige. It is also possible that the Soviets hoped Israel would prevail and remove Nasser from the scene, to be replaced by a more stable and predictable leader. Either way, despite assurances from UN observers that there were no signs of Israeli troop buildups or preparations for invasion on the Israeli-Syrian border, both Syria and Egypt accepted the Soviet warnings and initiated plans for an invasion of Israel.

PRELUDE TO WAR

On May 15, 1967, Egypt began moving troops into the Sinai Peninsula and massing them near the Israeli border. This was followed on May 18 by a Syrian mobilization that moved forces into position along the Golan Heights. On the same day President Nasser demanded that the United Nations Emergency Force, which had been stationed in the Sinai as a buffer between Israel and Egypt since the 1956 war, be withdrawn. United Nations Secretary-General U Thant complied with the demand, in spite of a prior promise to take any such request before the UN General Assembly.

The withdrawal of the UN troops was quickly followed by an Egyptian blockade of the Strait of Tiran, Israel's only supply route to Asia and the main shipping lane for oil from Israel's largest supplier. Israel had made it clear that any attempt to close the strait would be considered cause for war and, following the 1956 Suez Crisis, had been given assurances by the United States and the United Nations that Israel had right of access to the Strait of Tiran. However, when Israel asked the major world powers to enforce those assurances, Great Britain and France reneged. The United States offered to form an international armada to break the Egyptian blockade, a proposal Israel accepted, although it was expected to take several weeks to assemble the armada and despite the worsening situation in the Sinai and Golan Heights.

On May 30, responding to pressure for Arab unity, Jordan joined the military alliance between Egypt and Syria. This, along with the entrance of Iraq into the alliance on June 4, brought the combined size of the Arab armies to approximately 465,000 troops, 2,880 tanks, and 810 aircraft. Against that force the Israel Defense Forces (IDF) mustered 275,000 troops (including reservists), 1,100 tanks, and 200 planes. Israel's demographics (a relatively small population of around 2.3 million in 1967) and military structure (a small standing army backed by large numbers of reservists who could be called into duty when needed) made it difficult for the army to stay mobilized for long periods of time without doing massive damage to the domestic economy. Faced with hostile armies seemingly gearing up for war on all sides, the closure of a major shipping route, and the prospect of a troop mobilization with no immediate end in sight, Israel chose to launch a preemptive strike.

THE WAR

The Six-Day War officially began on June 5 when Israel launched a surprise attack on the Egyptian air force. The Israeli air force caught the vast majority of Egyptian planes on the ground and destroyed more than three hundred fighters, bombers, and helicopters in less than two hours. After decimating the Egyptian air force, Israel turned its air power against Jordan, Syria, and Iraq, destroying another 107 planes. Israeli losses totaled twenty aircraft, twelve pilots killed, five wounded, and four captured. The preemptive Israeli raids essentially decided the course of the war, leaving Israel with total air superiority. Israeli ground forces could operate without fear of air attack and enjoyed unchallenged air support.

Following the air assaults, Israeli ground forces began moving against Egyptian forces in the Sinai. Relying on its tank divisions to push the assault forward, Israeli forces moved deeply and quickly into the Sinai, without slowing to secure supply lines or transportation routes. By the end of June 6, Israel had seized the Gaza Strip and was moving quickly toward the Suez Canal. As Israeli forces drove to the canal, any Egyptian forces not retreating at top speed were encircled and destroyed. Meanwhile, in a self-proclaimed effort to spare the army total annihilation, the Egyptian commander in chief ordered the entire Egyptian army to retreat across the Suez Canal. Such an order issued so early in the conflict broke the morale of the soldiers and effectively finished the Israeli task of destroying the Egyptian army. Forty-eight hours after the beginning of the war, Israeli forces reached the Suez Canal, and by the end of June 8, the entire Sinai Peninsula was under Israeli control.

On June 9, the UN Security Council enacted a cease-fire that left Israel in control of the Sinai; Israel accepted the cease-fire immediately, and Egypt followed suit on June 10.

While Israeli tanks were driving through the Sinai, Israel was trying to keep the other major fronts in Jordan and Syria quiet, in accordance with the preferred Israeli strategy of fighting on only one front while holding the others. Israel had warned Jordan's King Hussein to stay out of the conflict, claiming that Israel had no intention of attacking Jordan, Jerusalem, or the West Bank. Israel also indicated its willingness to absorb a so-called barrage of honor, whereby Jordan could shell certain Israeli positions to fulfill its alliance commitments without provoking an Israeli response. However, when the Jordanian artillery barrage expanded and the Jordanian army moved to occupy a UN observation post in Jerusalem, Israel seized the opportunity to reunify Jerusalem and eliminate the Jordanian presence on the west bank of the Jordan River.

Israeli soldiers and paratroopers began moving toward the Old City of Jerusalem on June 5 and by June 6 had encircled the walled city. Israeli tanks also began sweeping through the West Bank, seizing the towns of Ramallah, Latrun, Jenin, and Nābulus, in the process opening the Tel Aviv–Jerusalem road for the first time since 1947. Early on the morning of June 7, Israeli paratroopers broke through Jordanian resistance, entered the Old City of Jerusalem, and seized the Temple Mount, home of holy sites for both Jews (the Western Wall, the last remaining structure from the Second Temple of King Solomon) and Muslims (the Dome of the Rock and al-Aqsa mosques), reuniting the divided city of Jerusalem. Later the same day, Israeli forces occupied Bethlehem and Hebron, placing the entire West Bank under Israeli control. Fighting between Israel and Jordan ended on June 7 as both sides accepted a UN Security Council call for a cease-fire.

On the northern front, Israel and Syria limited their exchange to artillery barrages for the first four days of the war. Israel was content to postpone an invasion of Syria until after Egypt and Jordan had been dealt with, while Syria, despite all the prewar bluster and alliances, seemed satisfied to hang back and leave Egypt to the Israelis. However, Israel began to fear that a cease-fire might take effect before Israel had the opportunity to seize the Golan Heights. On June 9 Israel began an offensive to push the Syrians away from the Syrian-Israeli border and Israel's northern villages and farms. Israeli armored units quickly punched holes in the Syrian defenses and pushed deep into the Golan. By the end of June 10, Israel had occupied

the entire Golan Heights. The acquisition of the Golan Heights, along with the Gaza Strip, West Bank, and Sinai Peninsula, more than tripled Israel's previous size. The new territory gained the country important strategic positions, but also created a perennial political problem: Israel now occupied territories inhabited by more than a million Palestinians.

Over the course of the Six-Day War, Israel defeated the combined armies of three Arab nations at a relatively low cost to its own troops. All told, Israel lost approximately 800 soldiers, with about 2,500 wounded and 18 taken prisoner or missing. Egyptian losses were the heaviest: between 10,000 and 15,000 dead, 15,000 wounded, and 5,500 taken prisoner. Jordan had about 2,000 soldiers killed and 5,000 wounded, while Syria had 700 dead, 3,500 wounded, and 500 taken prisoner.

THE POLITICAL AFTERMATH

The Six-Day War is, unquestionably, one of the seminal events in the modern Middle East. The Israeli victory redrew the political map of the region and created an intractable problem that would remain unresolved for decades.

Israel initially hoped that the destruction and humiliation of the Arab armies would pave the way for diplomatic initiatives, and on June 19 the Israeli cabinet voted to restore the prewar boundaries with Egypt and Syria and to offer the newly occupied Sinai and Golan territories back to their former owners in exchange for peace. The offers were, however, rejected by both Egypt and Syria within days. The Gaza Strip and West Bank proved even more difficult to deal with, as neither Egypt nor Jordan wanted the territories, and their Palestinian populations, back. Furthermore Israel, for security reasons, did not want to return the entire West Bank, as doing so would again put Jordan within miles of Tel Aviv and the Mediterranean. Israel held out hopes that the occupied land could be used to exchange for peace; nonetheless, Israel began settling religious Jews in the newly acquired lands. These settlements would prove to be a major obstacle to peace during negotiations between Israel and the PLO in the late 1980s and 1990s.

The major problem resulting from the Six-Day War was that Israel now occupied the land of more than a million Palestinians: 600,000 living in the West Bank, 70,000 in East Jerusalem, and 350,000 in Gaza (210,000 of whom were refugees, of which 170,000 were living in refugee camps). The occupation awakened Palestinian nationalism and led to protests, graffiti, strikes, and clashes between Palestinians and Israeli soldiers. Such displays remained relatively rare, however, until the outbreak of the first intifada, or uprising, in 1987. The PLO, founded before the war, became the de facto representative of the Palestinian people and formed the vanguard for a new guerrilla war against Israel, hoping to succeed where the conventional armies of the Arab nations had failed.

At a meeting of the Arab League in September 1967, the Arab states reacted to the war and subsequent occupation by issuing the Khartoum Resolution, whose third paragraph became known as the Three No's: no peace with Israel, no recognition of Israel, and no negotiations with Israel. In response to the Arab declaration, Israel publicly backed away from the offer to restore prewar boundaries and instead adopted policies of annexation and settlement. The international community stepped into the dispute by passing United Nations Security Council Resolution 242, which became the starting point for all future negotiations surrounding the occupied territories. Resolution 242 required that Israel withdraw from land occupied in 1967 and that the Arab nations end the war against Israel and acknowledge Israel's right to exist. However, with the exception of Egypt, little progress was made by any side in moving toward peace or resolving the problems of the occupied territories and the Palestinians until the early 1990s.

SEE ALSO *Peace Process*

BIBLIOGRAPHY

Dupuy, R. Ernest, and Trevor Dupuy. 1993. The Arab-Israeli Wars 1945–1975: The Six-Day War. In *The Harper Encyclopedia of Military History.* 4th ed. New York: HarperCollins.

Israel Defense Forces: The Official Website. The Six-Day War. http://www1.idf.il/DOVER/site/mainpage.asp?sl=EN&id=5&docid=18924&year=2&Pos=3.

Morris, Benny. 2001. *Righteous Victims: A History of the Zionist-Arab Conflict, 1881–2001.* New York: Vintage.

Oren, Michael. 2003. *Six Days of War: June 1967 and the Making of the Modern Middle East.* New York: Ballantine.

Seth Weinberger

ARABS

As an ethno-national term, *Arabs* currently designates the Arabic-speaking population that dominates North Africa and West Asia. The Arabs are considered part of the Semitic peoples, and their migrations out of the Arabian peninsula to the rest of the Middle East in large numbers began in the seventh century. Politically, the term is also applied to the twenty-two member states of the Arab League, whose population in 2005 totaled about 300 million inhabitants, and there were several million more in Europe and North America. The Arab League was originally founded in 1945 to coordinate Arab politics and resolve common issues. The common defining features of an Arab identity include the Arabic language, a sense of shared culture, and similar historical patterns.

In pre-Islamic times, and often in the Qur'an as well, the term *Arab*, or *A'rab*, was often reserved for nomadic populations. However, over time the term came to designate all Arabic-speaking peoples. The career of the Arabs in history began with Islam in the seventh century, a coincidence that continues to give rise to much confusion about the relationship between the two. Arab Muslims in fact comprise only about 20 percent of world Muslims. And while the vast majority of Arabs are Muslims, many Arabs belong to various Christian denominations, such as Coptic, Maronite, Orthodox, and Assyrian. Also, until at least 1948 many Arab countries, such as Iraq, Egypt, Morocco, and Syria, housed large Jewish communities that were fully assimilated and largely saw themselves as part of Arab culture. The Arab world also contains many Muslim but non-Arab communities, such as the Kurds in Iraq and Syria and the Imazighen (otherwise known as Berbers) in North Africa.

The rise of Islam in Arabia early in the seventh century provided the first catalyst for unifying the various tribes and communities of the Arabian peninsula into a common, religiously defined state. The Islamic conquests following the death of Muhammad (in 632) were carried out of Arabia in the name of Islam, not Arab nationalism, but they quickly changed the political and demographic makeup of the Middle East by moving Arab populations, and imprinting Arab language and culture, over much of the region. Within less than a century after Muhammad, the domain of Islam stretched as far east as the Indian subcontinent and as far west as the Iberian peninsula. The Arabic language, being the language of the Qur'an (which for Muslims consists of the literal revelations of God) and also the language of the new ruling elites and migrating population groups, spread across immense distances over the next few centuries and came to house greatly refined poetic and cultural traditions. Because the classics of the Hellenic and Roman heritage were translated into Arabic during the Abbasid caliphate, and because the new Arab-centered Muslim civilization patronized all branches of science and philosophy, the Arabic language also became the scholarly lingua franca across vast territories stretching from Central Asia to Iberia. It retained that status throughout the European Middle Ages. In fact, the first authoritative set of rules for Arabic grammar were set down during that period by a Persian scholar, Sibawayh (d. 793).

While presiding over the vast expansion of Islam throughout the region, the Umayyad caliphate, which lasted from 661 to 750 and was seated at Damascus, had a largely Arab ruling elite and sought to exclude non-

Arabs from positions of authority. As Islam became genuinely universal, the Arabs lost monopoly over it. With the rise of the Abbasid caliphate in 750, the Muslim ruling elites became ethnically mixed, reflecting the demographic mix of Muslims themselves. Reflecting the growth in importance of non-Arabs among Muslims, the Abbasids moved the center of political power farther east, establishing Baghdad and making it their capital, thereby replacing Damascus as a Muslim political center.

After more than two centuries of glory, Abbasid rule entered a long period of decline toward the end of the tenth century, even though Islam as a faith continued to spread worldwide. The remnants of the Umayyads, who had established themselves over Iberia, proclaimed a rival caliphate there, and the Fatimids, who subscribed to a version of Shi'ism, soon announced a competing claim to the caliphate after capturing Egypt. The Abbasids also lost much temporal power to successive militaristic Turkish dynasties, notably the Buyids and then the Saljuks. Nonetheless, the Abbasid caliphate was retained in Baghdad as a sort of spiritual symbol for Muslims until the Mongols captured and destroyed the city in 1258.

By that point most Arabs had already become familiar with the pattern of non-Arabs exercising effective rule over them. This pattern was exercised first by other Muslims and then by Western colonialism, and thus lasted well into the twentieth century. Insofar as most governed populations were concerned, there is little evidence that the ethnic origins of the rulers mattered much before Western colonialism. The main cities of what is now called the Arab world were ethnically mixed, although Arabs were usually the majority, and many of them were also religiously mixed, being vital nodes of global and regional trade routes.

The modern idea of Arab nationalism began to emerge in the nineteenth century, when much of the Arab World was still ruled by the Ottoman Empire, centered in Istanbul. The original tracts of Arab nationalist intellectuals show that Arabism was often viewed as compatible with an Islamic identity. The early Arab nationalists, many of whom were Christians, focused on reviving Arab high culture and called for more autonomy and local rule within the Ottoman system. Western models of nationalism clearly influenced these ideas, and within the Ottoman system concurrently informed Turkish nationalism, as it later would be advocated by the Committee of Union and Progress, or the Young Turks. The rise of Young Turks into positions of dominance in the empire shortly before World War I helped deepen Arab hostility to an empire they had lived with for four centuries, since the Young Turks tended to treat the Arab provinces more as colonies of a Turkish center. Moreover, such policies as imposing the Turkish language was at odds with the rising Arab cultural sentiment and the accompanying romanticization of an Arab golden age.

Still, at the beginning of World War I, most Arabs did not appear willing to abandon the empire, even though they had become open to suggestions. Such suggestions came during the war, when the British government persuaded Husayn Bin Ali, the Sherif of Mecca, to declare an Arab rebellion with the promise that the Arabs would gain independence after the defeat of the Ottoman Empire. Arab elites and their peoples did not take a unified stance on the rebellion, but they supported it after it became successful.

The aftermath of the war was a bitter disappointment for most Arabs. Rather than gaining independence, the Arab East was divided up between Britain and France. In addition, Egypt had been under British domination since 1882; most of the rest of north Africa had come under French control at various points during the nineteenth century; Libya was already under Italian control; the gulf region was already designated as a British protectorate. Thus virtually the entire Arab world emerged from World War I as a constellation of colonies of European powers.

Arab countries gained independence at various points over the following few decades, but the usual model of power transfer was from a colonial administration to a narrowly based national elite in each country, often clustered around a monarchy. These elites were preoccupied with survival in power, which usually meant maintaining alliances with their former colonial patrons. The failure of the Arab armies to secure Palestine for Arabs in 1948 undermined that system by vastly exposing the weakness of the new regimes, as well as their ineptitude, corruption, subservience to foreign interests, and lack of concern about national interests and common Arab issues. Further, the Palestine debacle highlighted the impotence of a divided Arab World and provided Arabs at large a single great cause around which they could make a unified stand.

During the two decades following the Palestine war of 1948, the era of older postindependence regimes came to an end in most of the Arab World, with the old systems being overthrown in Egypt, Iraq, Syria, Yemen, and Libya, and placed on the defensive in Jordan and Saudi Arabia. The new era was characterized by populism. The most successful figure here was the Egyptian leader Gamal Abdel Nasser. His adoption of pan-Arabism galvanized Arab public opinion everywhere, and his successful challenge to colonial powers by nationalizing the Suez Canal in 1956 and surviving the following tripartite invasion by Britain, France, and Israel, gave Arabs a rare vision of modern success against enemies set on controlling their national wealth and keeping them weak and divided.

The era unleashed by these new regimes also fostered the growth of ideals of social justice, socialism, agrarian reforms, and better distribution of social wealth. However, most of the new ruling elites in places such as Egypt, Syria, Iraq, or Algeria, whose members had to a great extent come from humble social backgrounds, maintained a dictatorial, albeit populist, style of rule. The catastrophic defeat of three Arab armies against Israel in 1967 revealed the continuing vulnerability of the Arabs. It also helped undermine pan-Arab ideals, whose anticolonial, anti-imperialist, and social-justice-oriented content began to be taken up by growing Islamic movements since the mid-1970s. Further undermining pan-Arab ideals were the great disparities among Arab countries caused by oil wealth, with the lion's share going to less populated countries, while the vast majority of Arabs lived in less resourceful, underdeveloped countries.

In spite of the continuing division and lack of coordination among Arab governments, a sense of common Arab identity has been maintained in the public sphere by a media revolution, which started out in the 1990s with the launching of the satellite television station Al Jazeera, based in Qatar. Its success was followed by several imitators and also forced many official governmental media outlets to exhibit more openness so that they could retain their audiences. In recent years satellite dishes have become the most striking feature of the streetscapes of many Arab cities, testifying to an intense interest in uncontrolled information, free dialogue, and a more open public sphere. Common issues include the unresolved question of Palestine and, more recently, of Iraq, which, after undergoing three catastrophic wars in about two decades, again fell under direct foreign control. The new media also foster discussions about other common issues, such as democratization and political reform, the role of Islam in politics and social life, and the status of women. Cultural life in music, the arts, and literature has also remained vibrant, with major figures in each field usually becoming celebrated across the Arab World. Novelists such as Naguib Mahfouz, Abdelrahman Munif, or Ghassan Kanafani are considered important literary figures across the Arab World, as are the poets Mahmoud Darwish or Adnois, for example. Similarly in music it is usual for some singers to attain a pan-Arab appeal in spite of differences in dialects. These include some established singers like Fairuz or Warda, along with more recent talents that are showcased on pan-Arab satellite stations—although none has surpassed the enduring appeal of Umm Kulthum. The notion that there is a common Arab culture and identity remains strong, as does the desire felt among ordinary Arabs for better governance and coordination among Arab countries. There is less conviction, however, that pan-Arab feeling can easily translate into a political union.

BIBLIOGRAPHY

Cleveland, William L. 2004. *A History of the Modern Middle East.* Boulder, CO: Westview Press.

Hitti, Philip. 2002. *History of the Arabs.* 10th ed. New York: Palgrave Macmillan.

Hourani, Albert. 2003. *A History of the Arab Peoples.* Cambridge, MA: Harvard University Press.

Mohammed A. Bamyeh

ARAFAT, YASIR
1929–2004

Yasir Arafat is best known as chairman of the Palestine Liberation Organization (PLO) and first president of the Palestinian Authority (PA). He was also one of the founding members of *Fateh* (1959), which would later become the most powerful group within the PLO. More than anything else, Arafat is viewed as one of the patriarchs of the Palestinian national movement. In the 1970s, Arafat also attained the standing of a head of state within the Arab world as a result of two events: First, in 1974, the PLO was recognized as the "official" representative of the Palestinian people by the Arab Summit Conference. Second, in 1976 Palestine was granted full membership into the League of Arab States. In 1994 Arafat was the co-recipient of the Nobel Peace Prize with Israelis Yitzhak Rabin and Shimon Peres in recognition of the successful completion of peace negotiations and the 1993 signing of the Declaration of Principles (Oslo Accords) between Israel and the PLO.

Arafat was trained as an engineer in Egypt and graduated from Cairo University. He then moved to Kuwait, where he worked as a civil engineer. It was in Kuwait that Fateh was founded. For the next forty years, Arafat moved around the region, from Kuwait to Syria to Jordan to Lebanon to Tunisia to Gaza and the West Bank, all in pursuit of his ultimate goal: the formation of a sovereign national homeland for the Palestinian people. Arafat's complete dedication to the "Palestinian cause," and the tactics used to further it, often led to tense relations not only with Israeli leaders, but also with his fellow Arab leaders. In fact, it was as a result of some of these tactics that Arafat and his operatives were either jailed (i.e., in Syria) or expelled.

Historians and political commentators have described the tactics used by Arafat and his supporters (either under the banner of Fateh, the PLO, or other organizational names such as Black September) as both guerrilla warfare and terrorism. Actions such as sabotage, infiltration into Israel, and airline hijackings were among the measures used by Arafat and these groups. While Israel was the primary target of these attacks, other Western states and assets were also targeted on occasion, particularly with respect to airline hijackings. At the same time, Jordan was also a target of some of these actions as well.

Tensions between Arafat and the leaders of the various Arab states arose from a number of factors, including destabilizing consequences of having the PLO based in one's territory—a factor that led to Arafat and the PLO being expelled from two different states (Jordan and Lebanon), and differing of opinions about how the "struggle" should be run, from where it should be directed, or if a change in strategy (i.e., negotiations with Israel) should be undertaken. By September 1970, Arafat and his followers had created a virtual Palestinian "mini-state" within Jordan and was using it as its base of operations—which was viewed by the Jordanian regime as a substantial threat—and direct clashes broke out between the Palestinian forces and Jordanian troops. As a result of this, Arafat was forced out of Jordan and eventually made his way to Lebanon via Syria.

Once in Lebanon, Arafat and the PLO used Lebanese territory as a springboard for attacks against Israel. This would eventually lead to the 1982 Israeli invasion of Lebanon and Arafat and the PLO's expulsion from that country. From Lebanon, Arafat moved to Tunisia, where he remained until the signing of the Oslo Accords, at which time he returned to take control of the newly created Palestinian Authority in Gaza and the West Bank. After a series of agreements negotiated with the Israelis that formalized elements of the Oslo Accords and established the Palestinian Council and Palestinian Authority (PA), Arafat was elected president of the PA in 1996.

As tense as his relationship was with leaders in the Arab world, he had a different type of relationship with the leadership of Israel. For many years Israeli leaders sought to marginalize him. Regardless of the international recognition granted to Arafat, Israeli leaders refused to talk to Arafat or acknowledge him as the leader of the Palestinian people. Until the 1990s Israeli leaders consistently branded him a terrorist and refused to recognize or legitimize the PLO—referring to the organization as a terrorist group rather than a government in exile. In this respect, the 1993 Oslo Accords were also a personal victory for Arafat in that, for the first time, an Israeli leader granted explicit recognition to Arafat. Rabin publicly shook Arafat's hand on the White House lawn and announced to the world that Israel "had a partner" in Arafat.

Many in Israel, however, quickly reapplied the "terrorist" label to Arafat with the collapse of the Oslo Accords and the resumption of violence in 2000. By the end of Arafat's life, the Israeli leadership had again marginalized the leader; the Israeli government arguing that Arafat was an impediment toward the implementation of a lasting peace between Israel and the Palestinians rather than a real "partner." Arafat and forces under his control were viewed as playing a direct role in the coordination of the violence, and as a result the Israelis reoccupied many areas that had been ceded to PA control. Additionally, the Israel Defense Forces (IDF) forced Arafat to remain at his Ramallah compound for two years. After he became ill in 2004, the Israeli government allowed him to be transferred to France for treatment, where he died of unknown causes that year.

While many viewed his death as an opportunity for resurrecting the peace process between Israel and the Palestinians, as of the mid-2000s this has not yet been the case. Although it is difficult to pinpoint any one culprit, the PA created by Arafat was extremely weak and fractious. In fact, some scholars have argued that the structural weaknesses inherent in the PA were deliberate creations of Arafat to keep the body subservient to his own influence and manipulation.

SEE ALSO *Meir, Golda; Nobel Peace Prize; Palestine Liberation Organization (PLO); Palestinian Authority; Rabin, Yitzhak*

BIBLIOGRAPHY

Government of Israel, Ministry of Foreign Affairs. 2002. Cabinet Communiqué: March 29. Jerusalem, Israel. http://www.mfa.gov.il/MFA/Government/Communiques/2002/Cabinet%20Communique%20-%2029-Mar-2002.

Nofal, Mamdouh. 2004–2005. Arafat: The Man, The Symbol. *Palestine-Israel Journal* 11 (3–4): 24–29.

Rubenstein, Danny. 2004–2005. The Arafat Enigma. *Palestine-Israel Journal* 11 (3–4): 19–23.

Samuels, David. 2005. In a Ruined Country. *Atlantic* 296 (2): 60–91.

Sela, Avraham, ed. 1999. *Political Encyclopedia of the Middle East*. Jerusalem: The Jerusalem Publishing House.

Rachel Bzostek

ARBITRAGE AND ARBITRAGEURS

Arbitrage is a trading strategy that is used to generate a guaranteed profit from a transaction that requires no commitment of capital or risk bearing on the part of the trader. An arbitrageur is a person who engages in this kind of trading. Arbitrage can be done when equivalent assets or combinations of assets sell for two different prices.

When the opportunity for arbitrage arises, arbitrageurs exploit that opportunity as long as it generates a profit. A simple example of an arbitrage trade would be the simultaneous purchase and sale of the same security in different markets at different prices. Another example would be cross-rate arbitrage transactions in a foreign currency market, in which three currencies are purchased and sold in different markets to exploit mispricing in the cross-exchange rate.

A third example involves the put-call parity relationship in options markets. A put is an option granting the right to sell the underlying asset at a predetermined price (the exercise price) at or before a predetermined date (the maturity date). A call is similar to a put except that it grants the right to buy. With the same underlying asset, exercise price, and maturing date, prices of European-style put options and call options should have a parity relationship in which owning a call option is equivalent to owning a put option, owning the underlying asset, and selling a risk-free bond that matures on the option's expiration day with a face value equal to the exercise price of the option. If the prices do not conform to put-call parity, an arbitrage strategy can be applied to sell the overpriced instruments and buy the underpriced instruments simultaneously, generating a guaranteed profit that is equal to the amount by which the put or call option is mispriced.

In practice, besides the requisite information, arbitrageurs deal with market imperfections such as transaction costs and limitations on short selling to generate arbitrage profit. If an opportunity is profitable after the full transaction costs have been paid, it is considered pure arbitrage. The arbitrage trade forces the prices of the overpriced assets and the underpriced assets to reach an equilibrium that eventually eliminates the opportunity to generate an arbitrage profit. When there are market imperfections, that equilibrium usually provides boundary conditions that prevent arbitrage opportunities. The principle that no arbitrage opportunities should be available for any significant length of time is one of the elementary principles of derivative pricing. Theoretical boundary conditions of derivative pricing conform to models that assume no arbitrage. That is, the price of a derivative instrument can be modeled on the return of a synthetic portfolio, which is an appropriate combination of the underlying asset and the risk-free asset constructed to replicate the derivative instrument.

Arbitrage profits are examples of abnormal returns and are violations of the principle of market efficiency. In efficient markets arbitrage opportunities are nonexistent or are eliminated quickly. Arbitrage trade facilitates flows of market information. It also forces efficiency in intertemporal resource allocation because arbitrage transactions usually take place over a period of time. The rule of no arbitrage is upheld only if arbitrageurs are vigilant in finding arbitrage opportunities.

BIBLIOGRAPHY

Chance, Don M. 2003. *Analysis of Derivatives for the CFA Program.* Charlottesville, VA: Association for Investment Management and Research.

Kolb, Robert W. 2000. *Futures, Options, and Swaps.* 3rd ed. Malden, MA: Blackwell.

Reilly, Frank K., and Kenneth C. Brown. 2000. *Investment Analysis and Portfolio Management.* 6th ed. Cincinnati, OH: South-Western/Thomson Learning.

Donald Lien
Mei Zhang

ARBITRAGEUR

SEE *Arbitrage and Arbitrageurs.*

ARCHAEOLOGY

Broadly defined, archaeology is the study of the human past through the discovery, analysis, and interpretation of the material remains of that past over space and time. The bulk of such material evidence is artifactual, which is anything made or modified by human action. Artifacts encompass everything from the stone tools discarded at Gona in Ethiopia 2.5 million years ago to the trash discarded yesterday. Immovable artifacts, such as hearths or postholes, are called features. Non-artifactual evidence that have cultural significance, such as human, faunal, or botanical remains, are called ecofacts. These material remains tend to co-occur at archaeological sites. Collectively, these traces of the past are referred to as the archaeological record. It is the province of the archaeologist to find, record, and preserve, where possible, the archaeological record in order to identify, analyze, explain, and understand past events and processes. They are also interested in contemporary material culture—ethnoarchaeologists study how modern-day people use material culture in their everyday lives. While there are a variety of scientific and other investigative techniques used to reconstruct the past based on this wealth of evidence, archaeological interpretations are constrained by issues of preservation. Not everything discarded in the past will survive in the archaeological record, and thus there will always be gaps in our knowledge.

Archaeologists attempt to bridge these gaps by making use of theoretical models, often based on data provided by ethnographic or ethno-archaeological studies. These theoretical models may vary depending on the training and context of the researcher as archaeology has developed differently in different parts of the world. As will be demonstrated below, archaeology in Europe developed from historical roots and is in some cases regarded as "long-term history." By contrast, archaeology in the United States falls under the aegis of anthropology and is seen as the study of past cultures.

Archaeology can be characterized as an omni-competent human science as it is concerned with the entire scope of human life from our hominid ancestors to the modern-day industrial age. Archaeological projects are conducted at many different scales. They range from studies of how past peoples used and perceived the landscapes that they inhabited to the re-creation of an individual's life and death, as exemplified by the work done on mummified or skeletal remains. Archaeologists study long-term change at sites that have been occupied for hundreds if not thousands of years as well as the immediate at "time capsule" sites such as shipwrecks or Pompeii. It is both a science and a humanity. Many archaeologists also have sub-specializations in the natural sciences such as zoology, botany, and chemistry while others make use of anthropological and historical methodologies and sources.

DOING ARCHAEOLOGY

Archaeologists make use of a diverse methodology. While the most important task is to place finds within a chronological and spatial framework, techniques differ depending on the scale at which the archaeologist is working. The upper end of such a scale is that of the identification of sites within a region. Many finds of archaeological sites and artifacts are still the result of accidental discovery by non-archaeologists, but there are a wide range of survey techniques in existence that allow for the location of archaeological sites within the landscape. These range from systematic pedestrian surveys of a region in search of surface traces to the use of aerial photography and other remote sensing techniques (including ground-penetrating radar, bowsing, and magnetometers) to locate buried remains. Archaeologists often cannot afford either the time or money to achieve total coverage of a region and may thus use sampling techniques designed to either maximize site location or to statistically reflect the occurrence of sites within a region.

Once a site has been located and recorded, the material remains at that site can be further explored and their relationship to one another determined by excavation. Excavation can be conducted either horizontally (clearing excavations) or vertically (penetrating excavations) depending on the nature of the site and the kinds of questions that the researcher is attempting to answer. Most excavation projects will include a mixture of both. Excavation involves the physical destruction of the site and the removal of artifacts and other remains and is thus guided by rigorous standards of recording and fieldwork practice. Most importantly, the context of finds is recorded so that their position in the site and their relationship to one another can be reconstructed once their original provenance has been destroyed.

Context is also crucial for establishing either the relative or absolute age of archaeological remains. Relative dates do not allow a specific age to be assigned to an archaeological find or excavation layer; rather they indicate the age of finds relative to one another. Relative dating was paramount until post–World War I advances resulted in a wide range of chemical and other dating techniques that allow absolute or calendar dates to be assigned to artifacts and sites. Foremost among these are radiocarbon, uranium series, potassium-argon, and thermo-luminescence dating. The most widely used of these is radiocarbon dating, which is used to date organic remains and can provide fairly reliable dates back to forty thousand years ago. The other chemical dating methods mentioned above can be used to date inorganic remains and offer a much greater chronological depth. Archaeologists working in more recent time periods can also use documents or other written evidence to date sites.

Once excavated, artifacts are sorted, classified, and analyzed in an archaeological laboratory. This analysis allows the archaeologist to create order out of a mass of data; to summarize many individual artifacts by identifying their shared characteristics; and to define the variability present within an archaeological assemblage. There are many debates about the best way to classify artifacts. They are mostly analyzed in terms of formal, stylistic, and technological attributes. Philosophically, there is a question as to whether or not the categories of artifacts that archaeologists devise reflect the emic order (items analyzed in terms of their role as structural units in a system) created by the people who produced the artifacts or if they are etic (items analyzed without consideration of their role in a system), artificial categories imposed by the archaeologist. Most archaeologists, however, recognize that the best classification systems are a combination of the two.

The suite of techniques that we associate with modern day, professional archaeology did not, of course, emerge fully fledged but developed over the course of more than a century. While many societies over the centuries displayed an interest in the material remains of the past and there are even instances of past societies excavating to uncover those remains, it was not until the nineteenth century that archaeology truly became a scientific discipline. Archaeology's roots lie in two disparate contexts: the development of classical studies from the 1500s onward and subsequent discoveries in various parts of the world; and the gradual recognition of the true age of the earth in the eighteenth and nineteenth centuries.

CLASSICAL BEGINNINGS

The fifteenth-century Renaissance in western Europe prompted interest in the Greek and Roman civilizations, particularly as their art and architecture were still highly visible. The buried Roman cities of Pompeii and Herculaneum were rediscovered in the 1700s and were excavated for art and antiquities. The foundation for art history and subsequently much of classical archaeology was laid in 1764 by the publication of Johann J. Winckelmann's *History of Ancient Art* (1764), in which he contextualized the art's production and set out the first systematic chronology for classical remains. Early excavation of these classical sites was by no means methodical. Smaller artifacts and "unimportant" structures were destroyed during the search for highly desirable works of art. It was these classical studies that provided a model for the development of Egyptology and Assyriology, which themselves evolved within a larger context of European imperial expansion.

Egyptology developed as a direct result of Napoleon Bonaparte's (1769–1821) invasion of Egypt in 1798. Accompanying the French army on this expedition was a Commission of Arts and Sciences that published multiple volumes of *Description de l'Egypte* from 1809 onward. The invasion also led to the accidental discovery of the Rosetta Stone, which featured the same passage written in hieroglyphs, Demotic (a cursive form of hieroglyphs), and Greek, thus enabling Jean François Champollion to finally decipher the hieroglyphic script in 1822. At this time there was widespread looting by both locals and foreigners in search of treasure for sale or collection, including not only easily transportable artifacts but also the wholesale removal of large monuments, such as Giovanni Belzoni's 1816 removal of the seven and a quarter ton granite head and torso of Ramesses II from Thebes to Alexandria. Belzoni, and others like him, worked as agents for the European elite and were involved in the discovery and excavation of many sites in Egypt. At this time there was little interest on the part of Egypt's rulers in preserving or investigating their past through the preservation of the remains of that past. They thus sanctioned the activities of many of the European agents at work in the country. It was not until Frenchman Auguste Mariette was appointed as the director-general of the Antiquities Service in 1858 that the sanctioned plunder and export of Egyptian antiquities ended.

There was widespread interest in the Egyptian past and many expeditions were funded, but the systematic excavation and recording of Egypt's archaeological past only began with William Matthew Flinders Petrie (1853–1942) in the 1880s. Petrie emphasized the careful recording of all artifactual material recovered in the excavations as well as the full publication thereof. Further, he developed the first typological sequence dating (based on ceramic jars recovered from graves) to be used in Egypt. His work laid the foundation for other archaeologists such as Howard Carter (1874–1939) who, funded by his patron Lord Carnarvon, discovered and carefully excavated the sealed tomb of Tutankhamun in 1922. As all other tombs discovered in the Valley of Kings had been looted, this find remains one of the most spectacular Egyptian discoveries.

As European governments began to take a political interest in places like Egypt and the Near and Middle East, historical and archaeological scholars followed suit. These areas were of especial interest to the European public because of their link to places mentioned in the Bible. Unlike in Egypt, however, there were few impressive structures that had survived the ravages of time in Asia Minor, Syria, Palestine, Mesopotamia, or Persia. Rather, explorers in the region reported the existence of large mounds that local tradition held to be biblical locations such as Babylon and Nineveh.

The first systematic work on mounds in Mesopotamia was carried out by the French consul in Mosul, Paul Emile Botta, who had previous experience in Egypt. The French government funded his excavations and paid for the transport of finds to Paris. Further research was also carried out by Henry Layard, an Englishman who is best known for his work at Nimrud. Wholesale excavation and exportation of finds was only halted after World War I (1914–1918) when much of the Near East was placed under French or British control. Museums were established, as were departments of antiquity and stratigraphic (layered) excavation, and the recording of all finds became the new standard. This standard was exemplified in Leonard Woolley's excavations at the site of Ur in the 1920s.

While these major discoveries were being made in Egypt and the Near East, the traces of civilizations of equal complexity were being discovered in the Americas. Monumental ruins were not common in North America, but large earthen mounds were often remarked upon. The question of who built these mounds—the ancestors of Native Americans or a lost race of moundbuilders—swiftly became one of the most contentious issues in American archaeology and remained so until the end of the nineteenth century. In 1781 Thomas Jefferson became the first person known to have used the principle of stratigraphy to interpret archaeological remains during his excavation of a mound on his Monticello estate. Meanwhile in South America, Antonio del Rio "discovered" the Mayan ruins of Palenque in 1786. It was not until 1896, however, that a stratigraphic excavation was conducted on that continent when Max Uhle started working at Pachacamac in Peru. Peru also yielded the well-preserved Inca site of Macchu Picchu, which was located by Hiram Bingham in 1911.

ROOTS OF PREHISTORIC ARCHAEOLOGY

While discoveries were continuing apace in the eighteenth and nineteenth centuries, intellectual trends in Europe were laying the groundwork for an archaeology of Europe's prehistory. These trends eventually led to the emergence of archaeology as an academic discipline rather than merely the occupation of adventurers and collectors, and they include the development of typological sequences, the use of stratigraphy, and the acceptance of the principles of uniformitarianism, all of which center around the key issue of chronology.

Up until the seventeenth and eighteenth centuries, it was widely accepted, based on biblical chronology, that the earth was no older than six thousand years. Several discoveries of stone tools in association with the bones of extinct animals by individuals such as John Frere in 1797 and Jacques Boucher de Crèvecoeur de Perthes in 1837 demonstrated, however, that the earth and human existence on it was much older than had previously been believed. Two theories had been advanced to explain these and other geological and paleontological finds. Catastrophism, advocated by scientists such as Georges Cuvier, was the notion that the earth had been periodically destroyed numerous times in the past, after which a new creation would occur. Uniformitarianism, put forward by geologist Charles Lyell in his *Principles of Geology, Being an Attempt to Explain the Former Changes of the Earth Surface by Reference to Causes Now in Operation* ([1830–1833] 1969), was the theory that the earth had been formed over a long period of time by a series of geological processes that are still observable in the contemporary world. It was this latter theory, in addition to the increasing fossil evidence, that contributed to the theory of biological evolution and the publication of Charles Darwin's *Origin of Species by Means of Natural Selection, or The Preservation of Favored Races in the Struggle for Life* ([1859] 1998). Lyell's work also gifted archaeology with the concept of stratigraphy, and thus the law of superposition, which states that stratigraphic layers are arranged chronologically, with the oldest layers at the bottom and the younger layers at the top, unless disturbed by later processes. This is the foundation for all interpretations of stratified archaeological deposits.

Even before the age of the earth had become widely accepted, chronological sequences for archaeological material, independent of written records, were being developed. One of the first was that of Danish scholar, Christian Thomsen (1788–1865), who was given the task of cataloguing and preparing for exhibition a collection of antiquities in 1816. He used the Three Age System, subdividing the prehistoric period into stone, bronze, and iron. While the idea was not new, Thomsen was the first to apply it to a large artifactual assemblage. He solved the problem of knowing which finds should be placed in which age by using "closed finds," artifacts that had been buried together in hoards and graves. By delineating which types and styles of artifacts were found or not found together he was able to work out a stylistic typology with chronological significance. This kind of stylistic ordering is known as seriation and is an important relative dating technique. Stratigraphic excavations of Danish burial mounds conducted by Jens Worsaae, a student of Thomsen, supported this sequence. The notion of technological progress, coupled with the ideas of biological evolution, gave rise to the unilineal cultural evolution of E. B. Tylor and L. H. Morgan and was expounded in John Lubbock's archaeological text *Pre-historic Times, as Illustrated by Ancient Remains, and the Manners and Customs of Modern Savages* ([1865] 1971).

There were further major developments in archaeological methodology at the end of the nineteenth and beginning of the twentieth centuries. Oscar Montelius refined Thomsen's seriational method of dating using a typological approach, while between 1880 and 1900, Augustus Henry Lane-Fox Pitt Rivers, a retired British general, conducted several excavations of barrows on his estate and developed the standards for excavation, recording, and publication associated with modern-day archaeology. These included the recording of all finds including those not directly related to the research questions being asked, as well as the recognition of the chronological value of even unimportant finds (potsherds, for example) if their context was correctly recorded. Later, it was a student of Pitt Rivers, R. E. M. Wheeler, who developed the grid method of excavation and, in the 1940s, went on to revolutionize the archaeology of the Indian subcontinent with his work at Mohenjodaro and other sites.

THE CULTURE-HISTORICAL APPROACH

The unilineal evolution of the nineteenth century was replaced in the early twentieth century by an interest in historical questions. This shift from an evolutionary perspective to culture-history resulted in an increased emphasis on descriptions of past cultures. In Europe there was a desire to discover how particular peoples developed in the past in order to promote national unity. In the United States, where archaeology was regarded as part of anthropology, there was an increased emphasis on data collection as the foundation for the development and testing of theory and explanations, in addition to chronologies.

Culture history, as a theoretical approach, has a normative view of culture. Basically it holds that cultures are composed of shared norms and values and that their members share a particular worldview. Artifacts are therefore seen as expressions of the shared norms and values of any given culture. This approach emphasized data collection, which allowed for the construction of site and regional chronologies. The results of these endeavors were often represented in a time-space grid. In the cultural historical view, change is most often attributed to the action of outside forces, most commonly migration and diffusion, or environmental change.

In the United States this approach was pioneered and applied par excellence by Alfred V. Kidder, who was also the first archaeologist to use the stratigraphic method on a large scale in the Southwest. The first scholar to systematically apply it to archaeological data in Europe was Gustav Kossina in his book *Origin of the Germans* (1911). Kossina argued that cultural boundaries (as reflected in material culture) were also indicative of ethnic boundaries. His work was extremely nationalistic and was later used by the Nazis in the Socialist education system. By tracing the migrations of the Indo-European people and demonstrating the supposed racial purity of the German people, he argued that the Germans were the true heirs of the Indo-Europeans and, by extension, were the true heirs of Europe. Archaeology was thus also used to establish historical rights to territory. Kossina's work had little impact outside of Germany and while British archaeologists recognized the importance of repeated invasions and migrations, they did not rigorously apply the culture concept until the appearance of V. Gordon Childe's *The Dawn of European Civilization* ([1925] 1958), after which the "archaeological culture" became central to European archaeology.

COLONIAL ARCHAEOLOGY

By the end of the nineteenth and beginning of the twentieth century, archaeological fieldwork was also increasingly conducted in colonial contexts. While much of this archaeology was essentially cultural-historical in approach and method, the situation in the colonial arena was complicated by the sociopolitical relations that existed between colonized and colonizer. Bruce Trigger in his 1984 work offers a definition of colonialist archaeology as comprising that archaeology which developed either in

countries "whose native population was wholly replaced or overwhelmed by European settlement or in ones where Europeans remained politically and economically dominant for a considerable period of time" (p. 360), specifically, an archaeology as practiced by "a colonising population that had no historical ties with the peoples whose past they were studying." Tied up as it is in land and heritage issues as well as its commentary on the supposed political or social sophistication of the cultures being studied, archaeology in these places had an increasingly political dimension.

This was especially the case in the southern African context. At sites such as Great Zimbabwe, it was denied that the ancestors of local people could have been the builders and inhabitants of what was clearly an advanced civilization. As with the myth of the moundbuilders in the United States, this made it easier to claim a civilizing mission and to take ownership of the land. Great Zimbabwe represents possibly one of the most famous examples of the misuse of the past to suit political purposes in the present. The racist theories of Zimbabwe's past have not been easily laid to rest. Claims that it was the place of King Solomon's mines or was built (variously) by the Queen of Sheba, the Sabaea Arabs, or the Phoenicians were still being disseminated well into the 1970s.

PROCESSUAL ARCHAEOLOGY

By the 1940s some North American scholars were becoming dissatisfied with the shortcomings of culture history, which was severely hampered by a lack of absolute dating techniques that would allow the refinement of chronologies. Walter Taylor called for a conjunctive approach to the past in *A Study of Archaeology* ([1948] 1983), advocating that artifacts should be looked at in their broader social contexts. His book did not spark a revolution, but in the 1960s a series of articles written by a young Lewis Binford (1962, 1967) did. Influenced by the 1950s neo-evolutionary anthropology of Julian Steward and Leslie White, Binford and his fellow "New Archaeologists" criticized the normative view of culture as inadequate in that it did not address how people interacted with their environments or how material culture was used as an adaptive tool in that environment. They emphasized the relationship of archaeology to anthropology and stressed the need to go beyond description to explanation. Culture history was seen as too particularistic and its practitioners as not being explicit enough about their research objectives, methods, and expectations.

The school of thought and methodologies for research espoused by the New Archaeology have come to be more generally known as processualism. Processualism, as an approach to archaeology, is heavily influenced by scientific positivism. It is based on a belief in "objective science" and aimed to test archaeological propositions against data in order to answer anthropological questions and to deliver broad generalizations—law-like statements—about human behavior. While the most famous processualists are undoubtedly American scholars such as Lewis Binford and Kent Flannery, many of the ideas espoused by them were also taken up by British archaeologists including Colin Renfrew. While Renfrew did not wholeheartedly embrace all aspects of processualism such as the search for law-like generalizations, its systemic approach to the study of culture and the new methodologies proved attractive.

The New Archaeology was characterized by a battery of new methods, techniques, and aids fostered by advances in scientific dating methods. The most important of these was the development of radiocarbon dating, which made internal development more likely than migration and diffusion as an explanation of change. It also meant that archaeologists were finally free to focus on broader questions of cultural and social significance rather than on the development of regional chronologies. Other scientific advances included the use of computers and, in the study of the environment, pollen diagrams and soil geomorphology. The application of these to archaeology necessitated increasing specialization on the part of archaeologists; and increased funding from bodies such as the National Science Foundation led to the scientification of archaeology, especially in the United States.

Fieldwork also became more rigorous and standardized. This was partly a response to the expansion of cultural resource management, which meant an increased need for systematic control and monitoring. Most processual archaeology has strong environmental overtones and thus new field and research methods were developed to accommodate those questions. Regional approaches—the analysis of sites in their settlement systems and environments—were developed, as well as new survey, sampling, and screening techniques to recover the most environmental evidence possible.

The New Archaeology changed the way in which archaeological research projects were administered and carried out. Advocates of this school adopted a formalized methodology that had hypothesis testing as its central emphasis. Archaeologists were expected to clearly and explicitly state the conditions and expectations of their hypotheses. Models employed by processual archaeologists include systems models, cultural ecological models, and multilinear cultural evolution models. One of the best-known case studies is Kent Flannery's use of systems theory to explain the increasing reliance on maize agriculture in Mesoamerica, which he detailed in 1968.

One of the most important aspects of processualism was the desire for an objective evaluation of ideas and research designs. To achieve this Binford developed Middle Range, or bridging, theory. This solved one of the primary problems facing archaeologists, that of inference, the linking of the (observable) present with the (unobservable) past. In order to understand what happened in the past, a way had to be found to link the dynamics of human action in the past with the static material traces of those activities in the present. Binford felt that archaeologists should observe the processes that give rise to the patterns and their variations, discernible in the archaeological record. This interest of Binford's in actualistic studies led to an increased focus on experimental- and ethno-archaeology.

The greatest contribution of processualism was methodological, in the sense that issues of sampling, inference, and research design were paramount. These were of course closely linked to the increased use of scientific techniques in archaeological fieldwork and analysis. The second contribution is seen as the shift away from description to explanation, particularly the notion of culture as adaptive and the interconnectedness of social and ecological variables. It also moved archaeology forward in the consideration of long-term processes. While processualism was seen as advancing research in some areas, it was also seen as retarding research into others. While significant advances were made in the study of prehistoric economies, topics such as the role of the individual decision-making, conflict and negotiation between different social groups, and prehistoric ideology were neglected while certain actors/interest groups were excluded from analysis. Many of these arise directly from the processual focus on entire systems and the overriding view that the environment plays the most important role in bringing about change.

POST-PROCESSUALISM

In the light of these limitations, by the late 1970s and early 1980s some archaeologists were arguing that while processual archaeology aimed to explain the past, it could not understand it. In *Reading the Past* (1986) Ian Hodder argued that material culture and past events had to be understood with reference to people's attitudes and beliefs, not just their adaptation to an external environment and, further, that archaeological remains could be "read" as a "text." Similarly, Michael Shanks and Christopher Tilley critiqued the scientific focus of processual archaeology in *Re-constructing Archaeology* (1987), arguing that archaeologists have to be critical of the context in which archaeological interpretations of the past are produced and that multiple interpretations of the past are valid. This critical approach has also been adopted by feminist archaeologists, such as Margaret Conkey and Janet Spector (1984), who have highlighted in "Archaeology and the Study of Gender" the androcentric bias in representations of the past and the practice of archaeology.

While *post-processual and cognitive archaeology* is an umbrella term incorporating many different theoretical approaches, it is characterized by its cognitive—as opposed to normative or adaptive—view of culture. Thus culture is seen as being actively constructed and reworked by individuals in order to fit the context of their own lives. The various approaches included within post-processualism can be divided into three different categories. The first deals with approaches that have at their base a concern with structure, such as structuralism, cognitive approaches, and Marxism. Second is contextual archaeology, which views material culture as a text that can be read. The third incorporates a variety of approaches that seek to offer alternative perspectives on the world and the way in which archaeological results are communicated, such as phenomenology, feminism, and postmodernism. Post-processual approaches have been especially embraced by historical archaeologists, who also have written documents to draw on. James Deetz, for example, used structuralism in his seminal study *In Small Things Forgotten* (1977) to explore the changing worldview of North American immigrants while Mark Leone has adopted a critical approach in his study of ideology in Annapolis.

Undoubtedly the post-processual critique has made contributions to the discipline. It has moved archaeology away from modeling the environment as the prime mover in past human societies and has added greatly to our ability to understand the past. The political nature of the study of the past and the sociopolitical context of the researcher have also been problematized. More attention is now paid to the way in which archaeologists interact with contemporary groups that have a stakehold in the past and how that past is represented. It remains, however, a largely Anglo-American phenomenon and has hardly affected archaeology on the European continent.

AN EVOLVING SCIENCE

Since the 1980s archaeology has been characterized by a wide diversity of approaches that draw on a range of theory from other social sciences including anthropology, sociology, geography, history, and political science. Like their counterparts, archaeologists make use of practice theory, agency theory, political economy, cultural ecology, world systems theory, and so on. Many times these viewpoints are combined or applied in interesting new ways to the archaeological record.

Archaeology is a constantly evolving discipline. New fields of study are always being created. Since the 1950s sub-disciplines such as landscape, historical (post-medieval), and industrial archaeology have grown rapidly. Further archaeological discoveries and fine-grained analy-

sis continue to make important contributions to ongoing research that include, *inter alia*: the study of human origins; the origins of agriculture; human migrations; human use (and abuse) of the environment; the rise and fall of civilizations; the processes and impact of colonialism; as well as the lives of people who are generally overlooked in major historical narratives, such as slaves. Yet there are still many parts of the world which, due to environmental, political, or economic factors, have very sparse archaeological coverage, for example sub-Saharan Africa, especially when compared with Egypt. Many times archaeologists in these countries do not have adequate resources with which to pursue research.

Archaeologists are also actively involved in cultural resource management and the conservation of archaeological sites. Sites are threatened by the ever-increasing development that results from expanding urbanization and industrialization. Many sites are destroyed without ever being recorded. Even well known monuments are under threat from wars, pollution, and vandalism. The worldwide antiquities market, which fueled wholesale looting during the early development of archaeology, remains in existence. Archaeology is also a highly politicized discipline, and the balancing of archaeological research objectives with those of other stakeholders, including conservation authorities and local communities, remains an ongoing challenge.

SEE ALSO *Agricultural Industry; Anthropology; Anthropology, Biological; Burial Grounds; Cultural Landscape; Cultural Resource Management; Culture; Feminism; Geography; Leakey, Richard; Material Culture; Migration; Postmodernism; Schliemann, Heinrich; Structuralism; World-System*

BIBLIOGRAPHY

Binford, Lewis. 1962. Archaeology as Anthropology. *American Antiquity* 28 (2): 217–225.

Binford, Lewis. 1967. Smudge Pits and Hide Smoking: The Use of Analogy in Archaeological Reasoning. *American Antiquity* 32 (1): 1–12.

Childe, V. Gordon. [1925] 1958. *The Dawn of European Civilization*. 6th ed. New York: Knopf.

Conkey, Margaret, and Janet Spector. 1984. Archaeology and the Study of Gender. *Advances in Archaeological Method and Theory* 7: 1–38. New York: Academic Press.

Darwin, Charles. [1859] 1998. *The Origin of Species by Means of Natural Selection, or, The Preservation of Favored Races in the Struggle for Life*. New York: Modern Library.

Deetz, James. 1977. *In Small Things Forgotten: The Archaeology of Early American Life*. Garden City, NY: Anchor Press/Doubleday.

Flannery, Kent. 1968. Archaeological Systems Theory and Early Mesoamerica. In *Anthropological Archaeology in the Americas*, ed. B. J. Meggers, 67–87. Washington: Anthropological Society of Washington.

Hodder, Ian. 1986. *Reading the Past: Current Approaches to Interpretation in Archaeology.* Cambridge, U.K.: Cambridge University Press.

Johnson, Matthew. 1999. *Archaeological Theory: An Introduction.* Oxford, U.K.: Blackwell.

Kossina, Gustav. 1911. *Die Herkunft der Germanen* [Origins of the Germans]. Leipzig, Germany: Kabitzsch.

Leone, Mark, P. Potter, and P. Shackel. 1987. Toward a Critical Archaeology. *Current Anthropology* 28 (3): 289–302.

Lubbock, John. [1865] 1971. *Pre-historic Times as Illustrated by Ancient Remains, and the Manners and Customs of Modern Savages.* Freeport, NY: Books for Libraries Press.

Lyell, Charles. [1830–1833] 1969. *Principles of Geology, Being an Attempt to Explain the Former Changes of the Earth's Surface by Reference to Causes Now in Operation.* New York: Johnson Reprint Corporation.

Renfrew, Colin, and Paul Bahn. 2004. *Archaeology: Theories, Methods and Practice.* 4th ed. London: Thames and Hudson.

Shanks, Michael, and Christopher Tilley. 1987. *Re-constructing Archaeology: Theory and Practice.* Cambridge, U.K.: Cambridge University Press.

Stiebing, William H. 1994. *Uncovering the Past: A History of Archaeology.* New York: Oxford University Press.

Taylor, Walter. [1948] 1983. *A Study of Archaeology.* Carbondale: Southern Illinois University Press.

Trigger, Bruce. 1984. Alternative Archaeologies: Nationalist, Colonialist, Imperialist. *Man* 19: 355–370.

Trigger, Bruce G. 1989. *A History of Archaeological Thought.* New York: Cambridge University Press.

Willey, Gordon R., and Jeremy A. Sabloff. 1993. *A History of American Archaeology.* New York: W. H. Freeman.

Winckelman, Johann J. [1764] 1969. *History of Ancient Art.* New York: F. Ungar.

Natalie Swanepoel

ARCHITECTURE

Architecture is the art and science of building the human environment. Because that environment is meant to enclose, enhance, and shape human activity, architecture thus extends beyond abstract issues of formal geometrical design and structural science into a far broader social dimension. As Winston Churchill is famous for saying to Parliament in 1943: "First we shape our buildings, and then our buildings shape us."

Exactly when the conscious, deliberate shaping of the human environment began defies dating, since the earliest structures most likely were made of organic materials that quickly returned to earth. Archaeological evidence discovered near Marseille, France, however, revealed repeated construction of wood-framed dwellings dating back as far as 300,000 to 400,000 years ago, and several skin coverings and wooden house frames from 13,500 years ago were surprisingly preserved at a Chilean site called Monte Verde. The well-known stone structures of megalithic Europe date to 6,000 years ago, but it is significant that these were almost universally built for ceremonial or religious purposes, while the construction of dwellings apparently still relied on vegetable and animal materials long since vanished. Hence, the first intentionally permanent architecture was shaped for the most fundamental of social communal purposes—to bring a sense of visible order to the cosmos and to provide a link to the dead.

Architecture is a decidedly social activity, for it involves the interactions of many individuals, beginning with the patron—individual, committee, or organization—who calls a building into being. The architect and assistants, or architectural firm, then translate the client's wishes into abstracted drawings and other construction documents that are used in turn by an army of construction specialists to fabricate the final product. At every step of this process, social exchanges, discussions, and negotiations are required to adjust the design to changing needs and costs. This multidisciplinary social process involves large numbers of people specializing in many occupations, such as drawing and computer design, materials acquisition, preparing written specifications, scheduling construction, arranging construction materials, assembling the prepared materials, and applying the interior finishes, among many others. For the most complex buildings, additional management specialists are required to ensure that materials and subassemblies arrive at the building site with optimal timing to prevent costly delays.

As a social art, architecture is subject to a range of controlling forces to ensure public safety. In ancient Rome, huge privately financed urban apartment blocks, called *insulae*, sometimes were so shoddily built that they collapsed. With the establishment of a firmer centralized authority during the Roman Empire, regulations were enforced to curb the worst of these building shortcuts. Later, during the seventeenth and eighteenth centuries, governing authorities in France and Britain similarly instituted building regulations to reduce the spread of urban fires. In the United States, following disastrous fires in Boston and Chicago in the late nineteenth century, building codes and regulations were instituted in larger cities. To ensure general public safety, nearly every community now has zoning regulations and building codes controlling where types of buildings can be located and governing density as well as engineering requirements of design and durability of building materials. These regulations apply equally to commercial and governmental buildings, as well as to private residences.

Making architecture involves the shaping of space in a way reached by no other art. Whether fully enclosed or an open external area, architectural space has several different properties. Initially designed to accommodate some function of human activity, this space is definable as square feet or meters. If the space is enclosed by glass, then the user's view extends beyond the physically enclosed space, and this larger reach constitutes perceptual space less easily quantified. If some substantial object is permanently fixed in that space—a large table, for example—the physical presence of that object emphatically conditions human use of the space, giving definition to the social parameters of behavioral space.

Beyond these three-dimensional aspects, another important spatial quality is the distance members of a particular species place between themselves. This strong determinant of social behavior, called personal space, can be seen in the way birds space themselves along a telephone wire. Seemingly genetically programmed, impinging upon personal space may produce socially aberrant behavior. Among humans, however, Edward T. Hall notes in *The Hidden Dimension* (1966) that personal space seems to be significantly determined by culture in addition to any fixed internal programming.

Making places for human use extends from the design of a single room and its interior furnishings in ever-increasing scales: from a small building to a large multi-story office or institutional structure, to a group of interconnected buildings such as a college campus, to an urban neighborhood, even to the planned organization and pattern of use of a region. Architectural design involves not only physical structures but also the landscape in which the buildings are placed.

MEANING IN ARCHITECTURE

Buildings embody wishes and aspirations on several levels, beginning with the desires of the client. Typically, images a client might envision for a building are part of a general collection of accepted communal formal qualities, evolved over time and called by a style name. These stylistic qualities are understood by most of the community and symbolize its values at any given time.

This concept is the iconography of a particular architectural style. To later historians, additional layers of meaning might be discernible, but these interpretations may not have been part of the consciousness of the original builders. This more embracing concept is the iconology of a time period.

THE SOCIAL FUNCTION OF ARCHITECTURE

In sketching the general iconological content of past architecture, one might make several observations:

- that ancient Greek architecture, particularly temples, represented humans striving to achieve the highest level of excellence in construction;

- that ancient Roman architecture borrowed details from Grecian architecture for use in buildings of vast scale devoted to public purposes;

- that the most important medieval architecture served to reinforce human religious life in anticipation of an eternity in heaven;

- that Renaissance architecture sought to fuse this inherited religious meaning with a renewed appreciation of the geometric logic of classical architecture; and

- that Baroque architecture endeavored to appeal to emotions to enhance religious mysticism (in the ecclesiastical realm) or to make a political impression through magnificence or vastness of scale (in the aristocratic realm).

Architects of the nineteenth century struggled to master new industrial technologies while attempting to understand the enormously rich and complex history of architecture around globe.

What changed in the early twentieth century was an added layer of social utopianism, an outgrowth of the Arts and Crafts movement in England. Through the exploitation of industrial production processes, and using industrial materials such as concrete, steel, and glass, architects were challenged to devise a radically new architectural style that would eliminate slum housing. Moreover, this new millennial architecture was to be shaped by an idealistic view of the way things *should be* (at least in the eyes of the architects and theorists), rather than shaped by the way things actually were. The resulting new communities were to provide fresh air, clean water, and open space in the belief that these transformations would permanently improve society. Architect and polemicist Charles-Édouard Jenneret (who called himself Le Corbusier) declared in his 1923 *Vers une Architecture* that it was either this new architecture or social revolution. He even suggested the creation of a normative type—one building type for all people everywhere. Begun in Europe at the dawn of the twentieth century, the new architecture became public policy in the 1920s and 1930s, with more limited application in the United States. Although this social utopianism was well intended, it often fell short of the objective. It may have been supremely utilitarian, but as Hannah Arendt would observe in her 1958 *The Human Condition*, utility established as meaning generates meaninglessness.

The perceived lack of referential meaning in the International Modern style (as it came to be known by mid-twentieth century) led to a reaction by a new generation of architects, particularly Robert Venturi and Denise Scott-Brown in the United States. Beginning with the use of broadly and whimsically altered historic details, post-modern architecture appeared in the mid-1960s, entering the professional mainstream by the end of the 1980s and extending worldwide by the 1990s. In referencing the past, postmodernism also validated reexamination of traditional regional architectural styles around the globe. Architects in Hungary, Egypt, Saudi Arabia, Sri Lanka, and scores of other nations began to draw inspiration from their own ancient regional traditions in new buildings of wholly original design and construction; such architecture proved rich in meaning to its users. Architecture in the late twentieth century was viewed once again as capable of being a powerful element in how people envision themselves in time and place.

NEW ARCHITECTURAL CONSIDERATIONS FOR THE TWENTY-FIRST CENTURY

The end of the twentieth century was marked by the emergence of certain mega-architects identified by their unique building forms. Most notable was Frank Gehry, known for his multiply curved, metal-clad, irregularly shaped "swoosh" buildings. Exploitation of computer-aided design has rendered such complex building forms more cost effective, marking a dramatic change in the imagining and construction of buildings and doing away with traditional drafting instruments largely unaltered for centuries. The unfolding effect of this fundamental change in design methodology will shape twenty-first century architecture.

An equally significant shift in the nature of the discipline is the emergence of women in a field dominated for centuries by men. Women began to make important contributions beginning at the dawn of the twentieth century, but their names were seldom widely known and their numbers were few. This advent of women as major players in the discipline was vividly demonstrated by the award of the prestigious international Pritzker Architecture Prize to Zaha Hahid in 2003.

Perhaps more significant for Earth's future is the movement toward sustainable "green" architecture. The traditional energy-consuming methods of making construction materials—toxic in themselves and leaving toxic residue from their manufacture—resulted in buildings that, once completed, further consumed prodigious amounts of energy for lighting, heating, cooling, and ventilating. Nowhere was this old-style architecture more evident than in the thin-walled modernist glass-sheathed boxes of the mid-twentieth century. In contrast, the emerging philosophy of sustainable green architecture promotes using less toxic materials and forming buildings in ways that allow them to work with, rather than against, nature. For example, windows can be shaded by calculating orientation and latitude to prevent internal solar heat gain, and buildings may be cooled in part by facilitating natural ventilation, practices of architect Ken Yeang. The future social implications of such a design approach, especially in the reduction of long-term operating costs, are enormous.

SEE ALSO *Archaeology; Cities; Human Ecology; Material Culture; Postmodernism; Religion; Rituals; Telecommunications Industry; Urbanization*

BIBLIOGRAPHY

Arendt, Hannah. 1958. *The Human Condition.* Chicago: University of Chicago Press.

Le Corbusier. 1977. *Vers une Architecture*, rev. ed. Paris: Arthaud. (Orig. pub. 1923).

Gauldie, Sinclair, 1969. *Architecture.* New York: Oxford University Press.

Hall, Edward T. 1966. *The Hidden Dimension.* Garden City, NY: Doubleday.

Kostof, Spiro, ed. 1977. *The Architect: Chapters in the History of the Profession.* New York: Oxford University Press.

Kostof, Spiro. 1991. *The City Shaped: Urban Patterns and Meanings Through History.* New York: Little, Brown.

Kostof, Spiro. 1995. *A History of Architecture: Setting and Rituals,* 2nd ed. New York: Oxford University Press.

Moffett, Marian, Michael Fazio, and Lawrence Wodehouse. 2004. *Buildings Across Time: An Introduction to World Architecture.* Boston: McGraw-Hill.

Norberg-Schulz, Christian. 1975. *Meaning in Western Architecture.* New York: Praeger.

Prak, Niels Luning, 1968. *The Language of Architecture: A Contribution to Architectural Theory.* The Hague: Mouton.

Rasmussen, Steen Eiler. 1962. *Experiencing Architecture*, 2nd ed. Eve Wendt, trans. Cambridge, MA: MIT Press.

Roth, Leland M. 2006. *Understanding Architecture: Its Elements, History, and Meaning*, 2nd ed. Boulder, CO: Westview.

Trachtenberg, Marvin, and Isabelle Hyman. 2002. *Architecture: From Prehistory to Postmodernity*, 2nd ed. New York: Abrams.

Watkin, David. 2005. *A History of Western Architecture*, 4th ed. New York: Watson-Guptill.

Leland M. Roth

ARENDT, HANNAH
1906–1975

A political theorist endowed with a flair for grand historical generalization, Hannah Arendt focused contemporary thought, particularly in scholarly circles, on the novelty of the tyranny that afflicted Europe in the twentieth century. Her most influential book, *The Origins of Totalitarianism*, emphasized the parallels between the Third Reich under Adolf Hitler and the Soviet Union under Joseph Stalin.

Arendt was born on October 14, 1906, to middle-class Jewish parents in Hanover, Germany. After studying theology and philosophy at the University of Marburg, she specialized in philosophy at the University of Heidelberg. As the National Socialists drew closer to power, she became a political activist and, beginning in 1933, helped German Zionists publicize the plight of the victims of Nazism. For the remainder of the decade, Arendt lived in Paris, aiding in the efforts to relocate German Jewish children to Palestine. In 1940 she married a former communist, Heinrich Blücher; later that year they were interned in southern France along with other stateless Germans and Jews after the Nazi invasion. Arendt and her husband landed in the United States in May 1941. While living in New York City during and after World War II, Arendt wrote *The Origins of Totalitarianism*, published in 1951, the year she secured U.S. citizenship.

No book traced more insightfully the steps that Hitler and Stalin took toward creating their distinctively modern despotisms, nor calculated more evocatively how grievously wounded civilization had become as a result of the concentration camps, the slave labor camps, the extermination camps. In exposing the operations of "radical evil," she demonstrated that with the superfluity of life toward which it aimed, totalitarianism marked a crucial discontinuity in the very notion of what it has meant to be human. *The Origins of Totalitarianism* asserted that the hell that medieval visionaries could only imagine had been put into practice in Auschwitz and Treblinka and in the Gulag Archipelago.

Her book exerted its greatest impact during the bleakest phase of the cold war, because of Arendt's insistence upon the resemblances between Nazi Germany and Stalinist Russia. Such claims also engendered doubt among scholars, who noted her limited access to Soviet sources. Nevertheless, her emphasis on the precariousness of European Jewry while Enlightenment ideals of human rights were collapsing, plus her argument that Nazism was conducting two wars—one against the Allies, the other against the Jewish people—became truisms in the history of the Holocaust.

In 1963 came a sequel of sorts, and her most controversial work. *Eichmann in Jerusalem: A Report on the Banality of Evil* did not portray the S.S. lieutenant colonel who had directed the transportation of Jews to their deaths as an anti-Semitic fanatic. He was instead an energetic organization man whose primary attribute was a sense of duty. Nonetheless, her book endorsed the Israeli verdict that he be hanged for his crimes. Arendt's view that Eichmann's iniquity did not stem from sadistic impulses to orchestrate genocide, but was the result rather of sheer thoughtlessness (a failure to think through what he was doing), led her back in the final phase of her career to the formal philosophical approaches that had marked her German education. Arendt died in New York City on December 4, 1975.

SEE ALSO *Totalitarianism*

BIBLIOGRAPHY

Whitfield, Stephen J. 1980. *Into the Dark: Hannah Arendt and Totalitarianism.* Philadelphia: Temple University Press.

Young-Bruehl, Elisabeth. 1982. *Hannah Arendt: For Love of the World.* New Haven, CT: Yale University Press.

Stephen J. Whitfield

ARISTOCRACY

The term *aristocracy* derives from the Greek words *aristos* and *kratos,* meaning "rule by the best." In denoting hierarchy and social differentiation, *aristocracy* has often been used synonymously with *elites* or *oligarchy.* More broadly, the term has been used in modern formulations such as "America's aristocracy" to denote a *plutocracy* of wealth and privilege in the United States, or as "labour aristocracy" in the United Kingdom to refer to a privileged stratum of skilled workers within the nineteenth-century working class. Indeed, its modern usage is so broad that many commentators have concluded that *aristocracy* is now impossible to define.

The aristocracy in preindustrial European states combined specific economic, social, and political characteristics that differentiated it from other social strata at the time, and from subsequent notions of aristocracy in industrial and postindustrial societies. For a period of over five hundred years, before the rapid spread of industrialization in the nineteenth century, predominantly agrarian societies in Europe were structured in feudal hierarchies and governed by monarchs in varying alliances with landed aristocrats. In these hierarchies, aristocrats were differentiated from monarchs in one, upward direction, and from gentry, merchants, and peasants in the opposite direction.

In economic terms, aristocracy in preindustrial societies was defined in relationship to the land. Initially in feudal systems, monarchs granted feudal lords the rights to income from large estates or manors in return for military support and local administration of justice. Thus, aristocrats derived their income primarily from land, either directly through the extraction of services and dues from peasants, or, latterly, indirectly through sharecropping contracts or lease-renting arrangements with small farmers.

The economic differentiation of the aristocracy was reinforced by social distinctiveness. Monarchs conferred not only economic rewards but also status rewards in the form of titles. Although titles were not an exact indicator of membership in the aristocracy, they were, when combined with land ownership, the most effective defining characteristic of the aristocracy. Noble rank reinforced notions of social exclusivity, and even among the aristocracy there was an internal hierarchy of titles that distinguished landed magnates from lesser nobility.

The aristocracy's combined economic and social dominance was sustained over centuries through inheritance laws based on primogeniture (where succession passes to the firstborn son). In this manner, the indivisibility and continuity of landed estates was secured and the social status of titular rank was passed from one male generation to the next.

A deliberate cult of ostentation characterized the lifestyle of most European aristocrats. "Living nobly" entailed architectural recognition in the construction of grand country residences and palatial dwellings in capital cities; cultural recognition in the patronage of the arts and music; fashionable recognition in elaborate dress and tailoring; and educational recognition in, for example, the value placed upon multilingualism by European aristocrats.

Political power was closely associated with the economic and social power of the aristocracy. Nonetheless, there were wide variations in the political relationships between monarch and aristocracy from one country to the next. By the seventeenth and eighteenth centuries, there were marked contrasts between France, where the aristocracy was politically enfeebled, and England, where the landed aristocracy effectively restricted monarchical power through representation in Parliament. Eventually, with the transition to industrial capitalist economies, the political, social, and economic ascendancy of the aristocracy was eroded in all European states. Even in the twenty-first century, however, residues of aristocratic status and wealth can still be traced in many European countries.

SEE ALSO *Authority; Conspicuous Consumption; Distinctions, Social and Cultural; Elitism; Feudalism; Gentility; Hierarchy; Landlords; Meritocracy; Monarchy; Monarchy, Constitutional; Power; Wealth*

BIBLIOGRAPHY

Clark, Samuel. 1995. *State and Status: The Rise of the State and Aristocratic Power in Western Europe.* Cardiff, U.K.: University of Wales Press.

Wasson, Ellis. 2006. *Aristocracy and the Modern World.* London: Palgrave Macmillan.

David Judge

ARISTOTLE
384–322 BCE

Aristotle was born near the Greek village of Stagira. While he was still a young man, this area came under the control of the kingdom of Macedonia. Aristotle's father was a physician in the royal Macedonian court, which led to the son's early interest in biology and, later, to his becoming the tutor of Alexander the Great (356–323 BCE). At the age of eighteen, Aristotle departed for Athens, where he attended Plato's Academy for twenty years. After Plato's death, Aristotle spent a couple of years in Asia Minor, where he married and engaged in biological research. When Alexander became king of Macedonia in 336 BCE, Aristotle returned to Athens, where he established the Lyceum, a rival school to Plato's Academy. Plato's Academy continued until it was closed by Emperor Justinian in the sixth century CE. After Alexander's death in 323 BCE, Aristotle came under suspicion as an agent of Macedonia and was forced to flee Athens.

Aristotle's works may be broadly classified into those dealing with the theoretical sciences (e.g., physics, mathematics, and metaphysics) and those dealing with the practical sciences (e.g., ethics, political science, rhetoric, and poetics). Informing all of Aristotle's works is his approach to logic. The six logical works are the *Categories, On Interpretation,* the *Prior Analytics,* the *Posterior Analytics,* the *Topics,* and *On Sophistical Refutations.* These works are traditionally collected together under the title of the *Organon.* Important works in the theoretical sciences are the *Physics, On the Soul,* and the *Metaphysics.* In the practical sciences, the *Nichomachean Ethics, Politics,* and *Poetics* are particularly noteworthy. All of these works have been influential, in varying degrees, in the development of the modern social sciences. But Aristotle's influence has been particularly important in the development of political science, and the seminal works here are the *Nichomachean Ethics* and the *Politics*.

In most of the contemporary social sciences a fact-value dichotomy is observed. That is, the researcher must carefully distinguish between facts based on empirical observation and values based on personal preferences. This distinction is denied in Aristotle's works, however, and one must read the *Nichomachean Ethics* and the *Politics* as one extended work. Thus, Aristotle distinguishes six types of states, according to qualitative as well as quantitative considerations. Monarchy is the rule of one in the interest of all, while tyranny is a corrupted form of monarchy. Similarly, aristocracy is the rule of the few in the interest of all, while oligarchy is the selfish rule of the few. Polity, finally, is the rule of the many in the interest of all, while democracy is the decayed rule of the many in their own interest. To Aristotle, human beings are political by nature, for they develop in association with others—beginning with the household, progressing through a village organization, and coming to full maturity in the *polis*, or city-state. This teleological approach to the human or social sciences pervades all of Aristotle's writings on the practical sciences.

Aristotle's influence in Western civilization is such that he was considered "the philosopher" throughout the Middle Ages. His influence has also been considerable in Christian theology, especially through the works of Thomas Aquinas (1225–1274); in philosophy, especially in his teachings regarding intellectual and moral virtues; in the physical sciences, notably as the target of extensive criticism by modern giants such as Galileo Galilei (1564–1642); and in the modern social sciences, with particular reference to political science.

SEE ALSO *Philosophy; Plato; Political Science*

BIBLIOGRAPHY

Jaeger, Werner. 1960. *Aristotle: Fundamentals of the History of His Development*, 2nd ed. Oxford, U.K.: Oxford University Press.

Voegelin, Eric. 2000. Order and History: Plato and Aristotle. In *The Collected Works of Eric Voegelin*. Ed. Dante L. Germino. Vol. 16. Columbia: University of Missouri Press.

Timothy Hoye

ARMED FORCES

SEE *Military.*

ARMS CONTROL AND ARMS RACE

Arms control is a form of international security cooperation, or "security regime," aimed at limiting, through tacit or explicit agreement, the qualities, quantity, or use of weapons. The term *arms control* has been used loosely to denote many things in international politics involving the reduction or elimination of weapons or the tensions that lead to their use, and even as a euphemism for militarily enforced disarmament, like that imposed on Iraq by the United Nations in the 1990s. But such phenomena often do not reflect the conventional meaning of the term as it is used by arms control scholars and practitioners: a meaning that implies a cooperative relationship involving reciprocity and mutually agreed restraints.

The three most important goals of arms control are (1) to lower the likelihood of war; (2) to reduce its destructive effects; and (3) to curtail the price of preparing for it. The first aim can be met by encouraging military postures that enhance deterrence and defense and thus make aggression less attractive; by reducing the instabilities of arms racing that may lead to war (see below); and by taking steps that make military "accidents" or unauthorized uses of force less liable to happen or to lead to war if they do. As for the goal of limiting damage when wars do break out, arms control measures may forbid the production, deployment, or use of certain military technologies. Finally, cost-savings can be garnered through quantitative or qualitative arms limitation agreements. Such economies are an important policy consideration, for resources not sunk into certain types of weapons can be used to promote security in other ways, or put toward other welfare-enhancing activities.

Regardless of how it mixes or prioritizes these objectives, arms control has a few essential interrelated characteristics. First, it is a political relationship between actors: Unilateral arms control is an oxymoron. This does not preclude unilateral steps toward disarmament or demobilization that one state may take in order to elicit reciprocity from others and thus launch an arms control process: The determining factor is the conception of an end-state involving mutual reductions, limitations, or other restraints. Second, arms control involves strategic interdependence—the parties engaged in it are sensitive to each other's postures and actions, and their decisions to agree and comply with arms control depend on their beliefs about each other's willingness to do likewise. Third, it involves at least tacit if not explicit bargaining because the incentives to cooperate that infuse the relationship are always mixed with some degree of conflict and incentives to compete.

TYPES OF ARMS CONTROL

It is useful to distinguish between rivalry-specific and general arms control measures. In the rivalry-specific form, adversaries seek to manage their security competition through agreements that are tailored to the shape of their strategic relationship, in order to make a more stable or at least less costly military balance. By contrast, general arms control measures aspire to universality: With a broad ambit and generic guidelines, they are meant to exert desired effects over the multitude of strategic relationships in international politics.

The 1922 Washington Naval Treaty, for example, was rivalry specific. In it, the United States, Britain, and Japan agreed to reductions in battleship fleets according to specific ratios of strength between them, and to a ten-year hiatus on new construction, as well as limitations on battleship tonnage and armaments. The goal was to stabilize the existing balance of naval forces at lower levels, and to forestall an arms race among the three parties. Similarly, in 1972, at the peak of cold war détente, the United States and the Soviet Union pledged in the first Strategic Arms Limitation Talks agreement (SALT I) to limit the number of ballistic nuclear missile launchers to then-current levels, and to abide by major limitations on the deployment of strategic missile defense systems. Behind these arrangements were mutually held cooperative and competitive goals: to slow down the arms race and reduce worrisome instabilities and to maximize restraints on the other side while minimizing those on one's own side.

As for general arms control measures, the most extensive early efforts were the conventions produced at the Hague Conferences of 1899 and 1907. Those widely endorsed conventions promulgated, among other things, prohibitions on the use of certain types of arms, such as "dum-dum" bullets, poisonous chemical weapons, or bombs dropped from balloons. In 1925, during the heyday of the League of Nations, the Geneva Protocol was added to the conventions, reinforcing the prohibition on the use of deadly gases. Later in the interwar period, participants in the World Disarmament Conference in Geneva (1932–1936) tried to enact a blanket prohibition on the use and development of "offensive" weapons, which were (and still are) thought to be conducive to war. The effort was ill fated for many reasons, but chief among them was the bane of many such qualitative exercises—the thorny and politicized issue of distinguishing between offensive and defensive weaponry. At the Geneva conference, for example, Britain, France, and the United States argued that aircraft carriers were essentially defensive; conversely, Germany, Italy, the Soviet Union, and Japan asserted that they were inherently offensive because they were useful for launching surprise attacks. In the era of the United Nations, similar attempts to foster far-reaching

agreements have been carried forward by groups of states in the General Assembly; the current locus of these efforts is the sixty-six-member Geneva Conference on Disarmament (CD). Begun in 1979, the CD has been the forum for adoption of the 1992 Chemical Weapons Convention and the 1996 Comprehensive Test-Ban Treaty, and for negotiating various additions to the 1975 Biological Weapons Convention.

The most recent general effort was the tightly focused 1997 Ottawa "Landmines" Convention, which prohibits the use, stockpiling, production, and transfer of antipersonnel mines and mandates the destruction of existing stocks. As a general measure with aspirations to universality, the treaty has had mixed success. As of 2007, 155 member states had joined, while 37 had not, including 3 permanent members of the United Nations Security Council: the United States, Russia, and China. However, although the United States has not signed the treaty, it has funded and supported demining efforts worldwide. Thus, even though many important countries have not signed the convention, it has had a tangible humanitarian impact. Demining efforts catalyzed by the convention have resulted in the removal of hundreds of thousands of mines, saving a large number of lives worldwide.

General and rivalry-specific characteristics of arms control can overlap—for example, when a rivalry-specific formula is nested within a more general arms control agreement. The most important and contentious arms control agreement of the early twenty-first century—the Nuclear Nonproliferation Treaty (NPT)—is a good illustration of this. The NPT, which first came into force in 1970, has a nearly universal membership (by 2007, 188 of the 192 members of the United Nations were signatories). Its general aims are to reduce and eventually eliminate the role of nuclear weapons in international politics. Behind these sweeping generalities are a variety of undertakings that apply specifically to two different "classes" of signatories—the Nuclear Weapons States (NWS) and the Non-Nuclear Weapons States (NNWS). The NWS parties "legitimately" possess nuclear weapons, but must work to reduce them (eventually to zero), and must not share them with states that do not possess nuclear weapons. The NNWS cannot "legitimately" possess nuclear weapons, but in return for foreswearing them, they are entitled to develop nuclear energy for peaceful purposes, and to international support for those efforts channeled through the International Atomic Energy Agency (IAEA). Thus, although the NPT is a nearly universal and general agreement, it is politically oriented toward managing a dangerous and difficult imbalance between the nuclear haves and have-nots. Similarly, the parties to the 1990 Conventional Forces in Europe (CFE) treaty were all members of either the NATO or Warsaw Pact alliances. Although a general aim of the treaty was to reduce conventional forces in

Europe, its organizing principle was military balance between the two blocs. There was thus a strong rivalry-specific core within the broader general agreement.

Yet another form of arms control is the supplier-cartel regime, in which participants who share a leading position on a given weapons technology agree to restrict its transfer to other parties outside the cartel. A formula of this sort is wired into the NPT in that the NWS agree not to transfer nuclear weapons to NNWS. But the purest example is the Missile Technology Control Regime (MCTR), which enjoins parties possessing advanced ballistic missile capabilities not to export the technology to other states. Begun in 1987 by the United States and six of its closest allies (Britain, Canada, France, West Germany, Italy, and Japan), the MCTR cartel grew to thirty-three members, including Russia, and also attracted the "unilateral" adherence of a number of other key players, most notably China and India.

PROBLEMS AND CRITIQUES OF ARMS CONTROL

The most important general critique of arms control is that if states become or threaten to become aggressive, arms control is rendered irrelevant and even pernicious: It encourages false hopes, wastes political energies on panaceas, and, worst of all, lowers defenses that need rather to be raised. By the same token, critics contend, arms control is most readily achieved and likely to work when it is least needed—that is, when international politics are placid or when foes concur that the weapons in question lack utility. In the 1991 Strategic Arms Reduction Treaty (START I), struck *after* the cold war evaporated with the end of the Warsaw Pact and the withdrawal of Soviet forces in Eastern Europe, Washington and Moscow achieved stunning success in agreeing to 30 to 40 percent cuts in the number of deployed strategic nuclear weapons: Such cuts had been impossible in the hostile and distrustful atmosphere of earlier decades. Once the political bases for enmity are removed, arms control can seem easy.

In circumstances of rivalry, in which trust and confidence-building is most needed, solutions to the verification problem (of measuring compliance with arms control agreements) can prove elusive. Insistence on highly intrusive forms of verification, moreover, can mask a basic unwillingness to reach agreement and negotiations can become a charade: Here the goal is not to find common ground but merely to avoid taking the blame for the failure to do so. Assuming a workable verification mechanism can be agreed on, there remains, as Fred Iklé famously observed, the enforcement problem—how to punish the cheaters that are caught. There is nothing about an arms control treaty that can make sanctions automatic:

Although effective verification may make it harder for cheaters to covertly "break out" of agreements, the basic political problem of when, where, and how to counter their threatening military power remains, and will be decided by the parties that are both willing and able to do something about it. Thus, although it is a form of international cooperation, arms control does not transcend power politics.

There is one more note of caution: Effective arms control agreements that do produce mutual verifiable cuts will expose new gaps and asymmetries in the balance of forces among potential rivals, and, as a result, may encourage them to channel new investments into other—and potentially more destabilizing—weapons systems. This is most likely to occur when, despite major agreements, the embers of political competition continue to smolder. One of the important effects of the Washington Naval agreements was to facilitate the parties' shift of focus and resources to competitive aircraft carrier development—with portentous consequences for the outbreak and conduct of World War II in the Pacific.

Proponents of arms control do not deny that these problems exist, but they point out that arms control is not always hostage to the vagaries of the political environment—it can shape that environment too. Arms control is more than just a means by which states press fixed national interests; it involves a political process that may permit them to learn more about each other, to deflate exaggerated images of "the enemy," and to conceive of interests in more compatible ways. If it is folly to pursue arms control with irredeemably aggressive states, it is just as foolish *not* to pursue it when the situation is less clearcut, for arms control itself may help not only to bring clarity but also to prevent potentially aggressive states from becoming aggressors.

ARMS RACE: CONCEPT AND CONTROVERSIES

An arms race occurs only when parties for whom war is a possibility engage in strategically interdependent increases in the quantity and/or quality of weapons: Their respective acquisitions and buildups are meant to match or overcome the strengths of the other side. The element of strategic interdependence is central to the identification of the arms race as a phenomenon *of* international politics, which requires states to rely ultimately on their own military forces for security, because the military forces of other states may threaten them and there is no world government to protect them. In such a milieu, where falling behind one's competitors can potentially lead to the gravest consequences, arms racing can be seen as a normal, survival-enhancing behavior.

Nevertheless, arms races are often considered harmful because they lead states that are trying to outpace each other to devote more resources to military preparations than would otherwise be necessary for their security. Increased military buildup, in turn, means that fewer resources can be devoted to other, welfare-enhancing activities. When the competitive dynamic of arms racing comes to dominate other principles for controlling acquisitions, the buildup (and concomitant waste) can mount precipitously. For example, during the most dramatic upswing of the cold war nuclear arms race, as the Soviet arsenal grew and American planners became ever more ambitious in their target selection, the U.S. nuclear warhead stockpile climbed from approximately 1,000 in 1955, to 18,000 in 1960, to 32,000 by 1967. It was very hard to understand why a much smaller (and cheaper) arsenal of warheads would not have been sufficient to achieve the main strategic purposes: deterring a Soviet nuclear strike on the United States, or a conventional assault on Western Europe.

The worst fears about arms races, however, are not that they are wasteful but that they can cause wars by feeding *conflict-spirals* that do not just reflect enmities, but create and reinforce them. In this view, arming itself may become the stuff over which states fight. The conflict-spiral premise is what makes many figurative uses of the term *arms race* inapt. It has, for example, been used to describe the spike in steroid use among the "slugger-elite" of professional baseball, and also the steady pace of miniaturization and computing-capacity innovation among microchip developers. But few would argue that the greatest danger of steroid use in baseball is that the supersized sluggers will eventually fall on each other in sudden bat-wielding melees, or that the technology race among microchip producers will lead to a cataclysmic collapse of the high-tech economy.

Two objections to the conflict-spiral conception of arms racing are often raised. The first and most intuitive is that arms races do not cause hostility but are its consequence. They reflect the maneuvering of rivals consciously seeking a margin of advantage that will permit aggression or deter it, not some unfortunate misunderstanding—and that being the case, buildups may prevent war, because they reinforce mutual caution. Second, even if an arms race between status-quo-oriented states does sometimes culminate in war, their decisions to fight are based on concrete stakes and complex political judgments that simply cannot be reduced to reciprocal fears caused by the arms race itself.

Nevertheless, there is an impressive amount of research on the connection between arms races and war, most of which has tended to focus on a few key questions: Given that some arms races culminate in wars, whereas others do not, are certain types more conducive to war than others? Do the dynamics of qualitative races (in which competitors seek innovative capabilities that will render their rival's obsolete) differ from quantitative races (in which competitors seek a numerical advantage in relatively comparable weapons)? Samuel Huntington's answer to these questions blended the two concerns by arguing that quantitative arms races are more dangerous than qualitative ones because, among other reasons, quantitative races require increasingly costly sacrifices that put pressure on states to seek a quick and violent escape from the competition. Others have suggested that arms races that generate large swings back and forth in relative strength (thus creating tempting opportunities for aggression by the temporary leader) are the most dangerous. Still others have made the intuitive point that arms races which give big advantages to states that favor the status quo are more likely to result in peace than those which give big advantages to states with aggressive intentions (although this ignores the possibility that a status-quo state may want to use its temporary margin of strength to defeat an aggressive adversary before it, in turn, becomes stronger).

During the cold war, these concerns were amplified by the fact that the arms race in question was nuclear: If it had led to war, it would truly have been a "race to oblivion." The survival of human life—let alone civilization—following a major nuclear exchange between the cold war rivals would be questionable. Furthermore, it was clear that unless effective arms control measures were taken to interrupt the competitive dynamic, the superpowers' nuclear race would metastasize, creeping into other rivalries throughout the international system. Even if arms racing increased the likelihood of war only by small margins, as the number of nuclear "racers" multiplied so too would the prospects for nuclear holocaust. Concerns such as these provided the impetus behind the rivalry-specific and general nuclear arms-control efforts discussed above, and while the politics of the NPT remain contentious, and a number of crucial nuclear-weapons states are not members (Israel, India, Pakistan, and North Korea), the NPT does appear to have helped stem the contagion of nuclear arms and arms races among states.

As the cold war recedes, and with it the chilling imagery of a nuclear-arms-race-spiral, the concept of an arms race remains useful. It has striking relevance to an important issue of international security today: the militarization of outer space. From the 1960s to the 1980s, the Soviet Union and the United States experimented with weapons designed to destroy earth-orbiting satellites, which have tremendous civilian and military utility. The feared arms race in such weapons did not then materialize, and the end of the cold war put the issue on ice. In 2007, however, China surprised the world by testing an antisatellite weapon, challenging the presumption of the

United States' military preeminence in space. Thus, the prospect of a space arms race was resurrected, and the question of whether such a race could become so intense as to raise the probability of war was reopened—along with the question of whether arms control could serve to prevent war.

Still, in the early twenty-first century concerns over the arms-race-spiral as a potential cause of nuclear war seemed to decline relative to fears of another nuclear nightmare scenario—that of "loose nukes" getting into the hands of terrorists. This perceived and perhaps real shift in nuclear risk raises important questions about the future agenda of arms control concerning nuclear weapons and other weapons of mass destruction: Can the existing nonproliferation regimes—with some clever rewiring—furnish satisfactory solutions? Or must a new matrix of rivalry-specific, general, and supplier-cartel agreements be contrived to manage risky relationships between states and nonstate actors? And if the latter is necessary, will the supportive international political context on which arms control depends take shape and be maintained? For common danger does not make security cooperation inevitable. Without a countervailing common will, a construct entirely contingent on politics, the states that oppose this danger will make a rabble, not a regime.

SEE ALSO *Cold War; Deterrence, Mutual; Gorbachev, Mikhail; Huntington, Samuel P.; League of Nations; Militarism; National Security; Politics; Reagan, Ronald; Terrorism; Union of Soviet Socialist Republics; United Nations; Weaponry, Nuclear; Weapons Industry; Weapons of Mass Destruction*

BIBLIOGRAPHY

Adler, Emanuel. 1992. The Emergence of Cooperation: National Epistemic Communities and the International Evolution of the Idea of Nuclear Arms Control. *International Organization* 46 (1): 101–145.

Betts, Richard K. 1992. Systems for Peace or Causes of War? Collective Security, Arms Control, and the New Europe. *International Security* 17 (1): 5–43.

Brennan, Donald G., ed. 1961. *Arms Control, Disarmament, and National Security.* New York: Braziller.

Brodie, Bernard. 1976. On the Objectives of Arms Control. *International Security* 1 (1): 17–36.

Bull, Hedley. 1961. *The Control of the Arms Race: Disarmament and Arms Control in the Missile Age.* New York: Praeger.

Buzan, Barry, and Eric Herring. 1998. *The Arms Dynamic in World Politics.* Boulder, CO: Lynne Rienner.

Diehl, Paul F., and Mark J. C. Crescenzi. 1998. Reconfiguring the Arms Race-War Debate. *Journal of Peace Research* 35: 111–118.

Downs, George W. 1991. Arms Races and War. In *Behavior, Society, and Nuclear War*, vol. 2, ed. Philip E. Tetlock, Jo L. Husbands, Robert Jervis, Paul C. Stern, and Charles Tilly, 73–109. New York: Oxford University Press.

Fairbanks, Charles H., Jr., and Abram N. Shulsky. 1987. From 'Arms Control' to 'Arms Reductions': The Historical Experience. *Washington Quarterly* 10 (3): 59–72.

Falkenrath, Richard A. 1995. *Shaping Europe's Military Order: The Origins and Consequences of the CFE Treaty.* Cambridge, MA: MIT Press.

Garthoff, Raymond L. 1994. *Detente and Confrontation: American-Soviet Relations from Nixon to Reagan.* Rev. ed. Washington, DC: Brookings Institution Press.

Garthoff, Raymond L. 1994. *The Great Transition: American-Soviet Relations and the End of the Cold War.* Washington, DC: Brookings Institution Press.

Glaser, Charles L. 2000. The Causes and Consequences of Arms Races. *Annual Review of Political Science* 3: 251–276.

Glaser, Charles L. 2004. When Are Arms Races Dangerous? Rational versus Suboptimal Arming. *International Security* 28 (4): 44–84.

Goldman, Emily O. 1994. *Sunken Treaties: Naval Arms Control between the Wars.* University Park: Pennsylvania State University Press.

Gray, Colin S. 1971. The Arms Race Phenomenon. *World Politics* 24 (1): 39–79.

Gray, Colin S. 1992. *House of Cards: Why Arms Control Must Fail.* Ithaca, NY: Cornell University Press.

Hafner, Donald L. 1980–1981. Averting a Brobdingnagian Skeet Shoot: Arms Control Measures for Anti-Satellite Weapons. *International Security* 5 (3): 41–60.

Huntington, Samuel P. 1958. Arms Races: Prerequisites and Results. *Public Policy* 8 (1): 41–86.

Iklé, Fred Charles. 1961. After Detection—What? *Foreign Affairs* 39 (2): 208–220.

Intriligator, Michael D., and Dagobert L. Brito. 1989. Richardsonian Arms Race Models. In *Handbook of War Studies*, ed. Manus I. Midlarsky, 219–236. Boston: Unwin Hyman.

Jervis, Robert. 1982. Security Regimes. *International Organization* 36 (2): 357–378.

Jervis, Robert. 1993. Arms Control, Stability, and Causes of War. *Political Science Quarterly* 108 (2): 239–253.

Kennedy, Paul M. 1983. Arms Races and the Causes of War, 1850–1945. In *Strategy and Diplomacy, 1870–1945: Eight Studies,* 165–177. London: Allen and Unwin.

Larsen, Jeffrey A., ed. 2004. *Arms Control: Cooperative Security in a Changing Environment.* Boulder, CO: Lynne Rienner.

Lavoy, Peter R. 1991. Learning and the Evolution of Cooperation in U.S. and Soviet Nuclear Nonproliferation Activities. In *Learning in U.S. and Soviet Foreign Policy*, ed. George W. Breslauer and Phillip E. Tetlock, 735–783. Boulder, CO: Westview.

Levi, Michael A., and Michael E. O'Hanlon. 2005. *The Future of Arms Control.* Washington DC: Brookings Institution Press.

Lieber, Keir A. 2005. Grasping the Technological Peace: The Offense-Defense Balance and International Security. *International Security* 25 (1): 71–104.

Mistry, Dinshaw. 2003. *Containing Missile Proliferation: Strategic Technology, Security Regimes, and International Cooperation in Arms Control.* Seattle: University of Washington Press.

Morrow, James D. 1989. A Twist of Truth: A Reexamination of the Effects of Arms Races on the Occurrence of War. *Journal of Conflict Resolution* 33 (3): 500–529.

Nye, Joseph S., Jr. 1989–1990. Arms Control after the Cold War. *Foreign Affairs* 68 (5): 42–64.

O'Hanlon, Michael E. 2004. *Neither Star Wars nor Sanctuary: Constraining the Military Uses of Space.* Washington DC: Brookings Institution Press.

Pringle, Peter, and William Arkin. 1983. *S.I.O.P.: The Secret U.S. Plan for Nuclear War.* New York: Norton.

Rathjens, George W. 1969. The Dynamics of the Arms Race. *Scientific American* 220 (4): 15–25.

Richardson, Lewis. 1960. *Arms and Insecurity: A Mathematical Study of the Causes and Origins of War.* Pacific Grove, CA: Boxwood Press and Quadrangle Books.

Rosenberg, David Alan. 1983. The Origins of Overkill: Nuclear Weapons and American Strategy, 1945–1960. *International Security* 7 (4): 3–71.

Sample, Susan G. 2000. Military Buildups: Arming and War. In *What Do We Know about War?* ed. John A. Vasquez, 165–195. Lanham, MD: Rowman and Littlefield.

Schear, James A. 1989 Verification, Compliance, and Arms Control: The Dynamics of the Domestic Debate. In *Nuclear Arguments: Understanding the Strategic Nuclear Arms and Arms Control Debates,* ed. Lynn Eden and Steven E. Miller, 264–321. Ithaca, NY: Cornell University Press.

Schelling, Thomas C., and Morton H. Halperin. 1961. *Strategy and Arms Control.* New York: Twentieth Century Fund.

Siverson, Randolph M., and Paul F. Diehl. 1989. Arms Races, the Conflict Spiral, and the Onset of War. In *Handbook of War Studies,* ed. Manus I. Midlarsky, 195–218. Boston: Unwin Hyman.

Talbott, Strobe. 1979. *Endgame: The Inside Story of SALT II.* New York: Harper and Row.

Talbott, Strobe. 1985. *Deadly Gambits: The Reagan Administration and the Stalemate in Nuclear Arms Control.* New York: Vintage.

Weber, Steven. 1991. *Cooperation and Discord in U.S.-Soviet Arms Control.* Princeton, NJ: Princeton University Press.

York, Herbert. 1970. *Race to Oblivion: A Participant's View of the Arms Race.* New York: Simon and Schuster.

Timothy W. Crawford

ARMSTRONG, LOUIS

SEE *Jazz.*

ARONSON, ELLIOT
1932–

Elliot Aronson is a prominent American social psychologist. Born in Revere, Massachusetts, on January 9, 1932, his career has spanned nearly fifty years. He is renowned as a creative methodologist who conducts carefully crafted, highly impactful experiments to explore the causes and consequences of human social behavior. His style of experimentation builds on the legacy of Kurt Lewin (1890–1947) and Leon Festinger (1919–1989). Aronson's textbook, *The Social Animal* (9th ed., 2003), is widely used and highly regarded for its pedagogical innovations. He is also known for his work as coeditor of two editions (1969, 1985) of the important *Handbook of Social Psychology.* He has been a highly successful mentor of doctoral students, including many who have made significant contributions to the field of social psychology during distinguished careers.

Aronson earned a bachelor's degree in 1954 at Brandeis University, where he was mentored by Abraham Maslow (1908–1970). He then earned a master of arts degree at Wesleyan University in 1956, and completed the PhD program at Stanford University in 1959, where his mentor was Festinger, known for developing the theory of cognitive dissonance. Aronson subsequently held faculty positions at Harvard University, the University of Minnesota, the University of Texas at Austin, and the University of California at Santa Cruz, where he has been professor emeritus since 1994. Since 2001 he has also been distinguished visiting professor at Stanford University.

Beginning in 1959 and continuing through the mid-1960s, Aronson published a number of widely cited experiments that tested derivations from the theory of cognitive dissonance, providing support for dissonance-theory explanations of such phenomena as effort justification (evaluating an outcome more positively after a high degree of effort was required to attain it) and insufficient deterrence (devaluing a forgone pleasure when the threatened aversive consequence was minimal). Aronson proposed a useful modification to the theory of cognitive dissonance by asserting that the dissonant cognitions must be self-relevant, and that dissonance reduction will be directed at preserving one's self image. In the 1990s he returned to this topic in experiments that show that making salient a discrepancy between the behavior that one advocates for others and one's own behavior (hypocrisy) induces dissonance that is reduced by adopting behavior more in accord with what one has advocated for others.

Aronson's contributions include his work on the effects of disconfirmed expectancies, and a substantial body of work on the antecedents of interpersonal attraction, notably the *gain-loss hypothesis*, predicting that changes in the level of esteem received from another would be a more important determinant of attraction to that person than the overall amount of esteem received. Aronson is also well known in the field of education for his work on the *jigsaw classroom*. He and his colleagues conducted field experiments demonstrating that creating interdependence within student teams working on a school assignment leads to reduced prejudice against minority students or other out-groups, while maintaining or enhancing academic achievement. This technique is widely used in classrooms at all levels of elementary, secondary, and post-secondary education.

Aronson has received many academic and scientific honors, including the American Psychological Association's Distinguished Teaching Award (1980), its Donald Campbell Award for Distinguished Research in Social Psychology (1980), and its Distinguished Scientific Contribution Award (1999). He was also elected to the American Academy of Arts and Sciences in 1992, and received the Distinguished Scientific Career Award from the Society of Experimental Social Psychology in 1994. He received a William James Fellow Award for 2006–2007 from the Association for Psychological Science.

SEE ALSO *Cognitive Dissonance; Festinger, Leon; Social Psychology*

BIBLIOGRAPHY

Aronson, Elliot. 2003. *The Social Animal.* 9th ed. New York: Worth.

Aronson, Elliot, and Shelley Patnoe. 1997. *The Jigsaw Classroom: Building Cooperation in the Classroom.* 2nd ed. New York: Longman.

Darwyn E. Linder

ARONSON, JONATHAN

SEE *Steele, Claude M.; Stereotype Threat.*

ARRANGED MARRIAGES

SEE *Marriage.*

ARROW, KENNETH J.
1921–

One of the most active, influential, and respected economists of the twentieth century, Kenneth J. Arrow was born in New York City in 1921 and remained in that city through his early adulthood. After receiving a bachelor of sciences degree in mathematics from the City College of New York in 1940, he obtained a master's degree in the same field from Columbia University in 1941. During his graduate training in mathematical statistics his teachers Harold Hotelling (born 1895) and Abraham Wald nudged him toward economics. After working at the Cowles Commission in Chicago and the RAND Corporation in Santa Monica, Arrow received a doctorate in economics from Columbia University in 1951. He started his career at Stanford University and returned to that institution after spending the years from 1968 through 1979 at Harvard University. It was during that period, in 1972, that Arrow shared the Nobel Memorial Prize with John R. Hicks "for pioneering contributions to general equilibrium theory and welfare theory." In welfare theory Arrow's impossibility theorem is a towering achievement, and in general equilibrium theory Arrow is one of the founding fathers, along with Gerard Debreu.

THEORIES

Three distinct schools can be identified in post–World War II (1939–1945) American neoclassical demand theory (Mirowski and Hands 1998): the Chicago School, the Cowles Commission (at the University of Chicago), and Paul A. Samuelson's Massachusetts Institute of Technology (MIT). All three offered different solutions to the problem of the relationship of the law of demand to utility maximization and the interdependence of income constraints and income effects.

Arrow's contributions concern the so-called Cowles approach. Arrow's impossibility theorem was developed in his doctoral dissertation and established that under certain assumptions about people's preferences between options it is always impossible to find a collective choice rule in which one option emerges as the most preferred. In other words, it is logically impossible to add up or otherwise combine the choices of individuals into an unambiguous social choice. This has major implications for welfare economics and theories of justice. Along with Debreu, Arrow gave the first rigorous proof of the existence of a market-clearing equilibrium given certain restrictive assumptions. He extended the analysis to incorporate uncertainty, evaluate stability, and assess efficiency. The restrictive conditions under which the existence of equilibriums could be established, the difficulties encountered in efforts to prove the stability and uniqueness of competitive equilibriums, and the general perception of limited usefulness have caused a shift away from Arrow-Debreu general equilibrium theory toward game theory in microeconomics.

Areas in which Arrow's legacy is most persistent are growth theory and information economics. In growth theory his research on innovation and learning by doing has served as a major inspiration for endogenous growth theory. For instance, Arrow was the first to construct a theoretical model of learning by doing, which was followed by many empirical studies by others. Yet whereas Arrow had imposed the restriction that increasing only capital (or only labor) does not lead to increasing returns, endogenous growth theorists such as Paul Romer (b. 1955) have gone to great lengths to disqualify that restriction. In information economics Arrow's evaluations of problems caused by asymmetric information in markets endure in analyses of moral hazard, adverse selection, and so on. Arrow's asymmetric information insights are of further importance for analyzing specific topics such as discrimination and education. For instance, Arrow offered the best and most complete model of racial wage differentials that are not based on productivity by making the phenomenon compatible with competitive equilibrium theory, more specifically by developing a model that includes signaling and screening mechanisms under conditions of asymmetric information.

CRITICISMS

Arrow's insights have not gone without criticism. His impossibility theorem in particular has sparked a literature that has found other impossibilities as well as some possibility results. For example, if one weakens the requirement that the social choice rule must create a social preference ordering that satisfies transitivity and instead only requires acyclicity, there exist social choice rules that satisfy Arrow's requirements. In addition, Amartya Sen (1982) has suggested at least two other alternatives based on relaxation of transitivity and removal of the Pareto principle. This has enabled Sen to show the existence of voting mechanisms that comply with all of Arrow's criteria but supply only semitransitive results. In response to Arrow's model of racial discrimination, others have developed a long list of criticisms and countered that the phenomenon must be understood in terms of the dual labor market hypothesis or radical models that build on the work of multiple labor analysts yet have added twists of their own. In spite of or perhaps as a result of these critical responses, Arrow's legacy within the economics profession is as rich as his work.

SEE ALSO *Adverse Selection; Arrow Possibility Theorem; Arrow-Debreu Model; Debreu, Gerard; Discrimination, Statistical; Economics, Nobel Prize in; Equilibrium in Economics; General Equilibrium;*

Information, Asymmetric; Information, Economics of; Moral Hazard; Samuelson, Paul A.

BIBLIOGRAPHY

PRIMARY WORKS

Arrow, Kenneth J. 1951. *Social Choice and Individual Values.* New York: Wiley.

Arrow, Kenneth J. 1962. The Economic Implications of Learning by Doing. *Review of Economic Studies* 29: 155–173.

Arrow, Kenneth J. 1963. Uncertainty and the Welfare Economics of Medical Care. *American Economic Review* 53: 941–973.

Arrow, Kenneth J. [1953] 1964. The Role of Securities in the Optimal Allocation of Risk-Bearing. *Review of Economics Studies* 31: 91–96.

Arrow, Kenneth J. 1971. *Essays in the Theory of Risk Bearing.* Chicago: Markham Publishing.

Arrow, Kenneth J. 1974. *The Limits of Organization.* New York: Norton.

Arrow, Kenneth J., and Gerard Debreu. 1954. The Existence of an Equilibrium for a Competitive Economy. *Econometrica* 22 (3): 265–290.

Arrow, Kenneth J., and Frank H. Hahn. 1971. *General Competitive Analysis.* San Francisco: Holden-Day.

SECONDARY WORKS

Feiwel, George R., ed. 1987. *Arrow and the Ascent of Modern Economic Theory.* New York: New York University Press.

Marshall, Ray. 1974. The Economics of Racial Discrimination: A Survey. *Journal of Economic Literature* 12: 849–871.

Mirowski, Philip, and D. Wade Hands. 1998. A Paradox of Budgets: The Postwar Stabilization of American Neoclassical Demand Theory. In *From Interwar Pluralism to Postwar Neoclassicism*, eds. Mary Morgan and Malcolm Rutherford, 260–292. London and Durham, NC: Duke University Press.

Sen, Amartya. 1982. *Choice, Welfare, and Measurement.* Oxford: Blackwell.

Esther-Mirjam Sent

ARROW-DEBREU MODEL

The Arrow-Debreu Model is named after the Nobel laureates Kenneth Arrow (b. 1921) and Gerard Debreu (1921–2004). It is a formalized Walrasian economic equilibrium system, and the existence of its competitive equilibrium was proven by Arrow and Debreu in their joint work in 1954. Solving the long-standing problem of proving the existence of equilibrium in a Walrasian system, the Arrow-Debreu Model has been the central piece of the general equilibrium theory of economics since the 1950s.

At around the same time, the economist Lionel McKenzie (b. 1919) proved the existence of a competitive equilibrium of a general equilibrium model using a similar set of techniques, so the Arrow-Debreu model is sometimes also referred to as the Arrow-Debreu-McKenzie model.

The Arrow-Debreu model specifies a competitive economy in which there are finite numbers of consumers, commodities (some being used as production inputs), and production units. Consumers have a set of well-defined preferences (continuous, nonsatiated, and convex), and each consumer holds an initial endowment of the commodities, with a positive quantity of at least one commodity. The technology that converts inputs into outputs is either nonincreasing returns to scale or constant returns to scale. In this economy, every producer maximizes profit and every consumer maximizes utility over their budget sets. The equilibrium of the economy is characterized by a set of prices at which the excess demand is zero for every commodity, and producers make zero profit. These market-clearing prices are reached through a *tâtonnement* process, in which "a fictitious price-setter" facilitates the price adjustment following a set of rules that resembles the way in which prices are reached in the real competitive economy.

Formulated in a purely mathematical form, the Arrow-Debreu model can be easily modified into spatial or intertemporal models with proper definition of the commodities based on the commodity's location or time of delivery. When commodities are specified to be conditional on various states of the world, the Arrow-Debreu model can easily incorporate expectation and uncertainty into the analysis. Theoretical extensions and applications have been made to analyze financial and monetary markets and international trade, as well as other subjects. With a general equilibrium structure, the model is applicable in assessing the overall impact on resource allocation of policy changes in areas such as taxation, tariff, and price control.

The model has been subject to the criticism that many of the assumptions it makes do not fit the workings of the real economy. However, this criticism is not unique to the Arrow-Debreu model; it also applies to all general equilibrium models that are heavily dependent upon rigorous mathematical proofs. In the case of the Arrow-Debreu model, the assumption that each consumer has to have in the initial endowment at least a positive quantity of all commodities (strong survival assumption) or of at least one commodity (weak survival assumption) has drawn substantial criticism. The *tâtonnement* process, which requires that all purchases be made when the competitive equilibrium is reached, is also claimed to be incompatible with the workings of a real economy, where purchasing at non-market-clearing price is often observed.

SEE ALSO *Arrow, Kenneth J.; Debreu, Gerard; General Equilibrium; Market Clearing; Prices;* Tâtonnement

BIBLIOGRAPHY

Arrow, Kenneth J., and Gerard Debreu. 1954. Existence of an Equilibrium for a Competitive Economy. *Econometrica* 22 (3): 265–290.

Arrow, Kenneth J., and F. H. Hahn. 1971. *General Competitive Analysis.* San Francisco: Holden Day.

Debreu, Gerard. 1959. *Theory of Value.* New York: Wiley.

Chung-Ping A. Loh

ARROW IMPOSSIBILITY THEOREM
SEE *Arrow Possibility Theorem.*

ARROW POSSIBILITY THEOREM

The Arrow (im)possibility theorem can be viewed as a generalization of the Condorcet paradox. Assume that three girls, Ann, Beryl, and Cathy, wish to have dinner together in a restaurant. They have a choice of three restaurants: a Chinese (*c*), a French (*f*), and an Italian (*i*). Ann, Beryl, and Cathy have different preferences and unanimously decide that they will choose the restaurant on the basis of majority rule: a restaurant *x* will be ranked before a restaurant *y* if at least two of them prefer *x* to *y*. But Ann prefers the Chinese to the French and the French to the Italian (and, of course, the Chinese to the Italian); Ann's ranking is *cfi* (*c* is ranked first, *f* ranked second, and *i* ranked third). Beryl prefers the French to the Italian and the Italian to the Chinese (and the French to the Chinese); Beryl's ranking is *fic*. Cathy prefers the Italian to the Chinese and the Chinese to the French (and the Italian to the French); Cathy's ranking is *icf*. Using majority rule, the Chinese is ranked before the French, the French is ranked before the Italian, and the Italian is ranked before the Chinese (*cfic* ...). A choice is impossible.

For Arrow's theorem, one considers a set *X* of alternatives (social states, candidates to an election, etc.) and a set of individuals (in the case of an election, voters), the number of individuals being a positive integer. Individuals have preferences over alternatives. If the number of alternatives is a positive integer (i.e., if *X* is finite), they rank these alternatives from the most preferred to the least preferred with possible ties. For instance, with three alternatives, one can have a first ranked, a second ranked, and a third ranked (six possibilities), or two alternatives ranked first and the third alternative ranked last (three possibilities), or an alternative ranked first and the other two ranked second (three possibilities), or the three alternatives tied. This makes thirteen possibilities (thirteen complete preorders or *weak orderings* as they are indifferently known in mathematics). The main question of social choice is to associate a social preference or a choice—an alternative in X or a subset of X—to the individual rankings (one ranking by individual). An Arrovian social welfare function is a rule that associates a social preference that is a weak ordering (i.e., a social ranking if X is finite) to the individual weak orderings (i.e., individual rankings if X is finite). Among these rules, one can consider the rule saying that the social weak ordering is the weak ordering of some specified individual, or the rule saying that the social weak ordering is fixed whatever are the individual weak orderings. To avoid these kinds of rules, Arrow imposes four conditions.

Condition U (Universality). This condition states that the individuals can have any weak ordering (there is no extra rationality condition where some weak orderings could be excluded due, for instance, to some homogeneity in the preferences of the individuals). Consequently, for three alternatives and three individuals, there are 13^3 data of individual weak orderings and 13^{2197} social welfare functions (10^{2000} is 1 followed by 2,000 zeros!).

Condition I (Independence). The social preference between two alternatives, say a and b, depends only on the individual preferences between a and b. For instance, the social preference between a and b, given five alternatives a, b, c, d, and e, other things being equal, will be the same whether some individual ranks the alternatives *abcde* or *acdeb*. Majority rule satisfies this property, but scoring rules where points are attributed to alternatives according to their ranks in the individual rankings and the social preference is based on the sums obtained do not. This excludes, in particular, the standard American and British voting rules and the famous Borda's rule. (For Borda's rule, if individuals rank k alternatives without ties, the alternative ranked first in an individual ranking gets $k-1$ points, the alternative ranked second gets $k-2$ points, and so forth, and the alternative ranked last gets no point. The social ranking is determined by the sum of points obtained by the alternatives, with the alternative socially ranked first being the alternative whose sum of points is the greatest. Ties are possible in the social ranking; to avoid ties, one can use some tie-breaking device. For instance, if alternatives are election candidates, their age may be used to break a tie.)

Condition P (Pareto Principle). If the individuals unanimously prefer any alternative, say a, to any other alternative, say b, then in the social preference a is preferred to b. This condition, given Condition U, excludes constant rules. In particular, rules that would be imposed by a moral or religious code are excluded.

A dictator is an individual who imposes the "strict" part of his preference, that is, of his weak ordering (he does not impose indifferences—ties); a is socially preferred to b whenever he prefers a to b.

Condition D (Nondictatorship). There is no dictator.

The Theorem can now be stated: If there are at least two individuals and at least three alternatives, there is no social welfare function satisfying Conditions U, I, P, and D. The enormous number of social welfare functions has been "reduced" to none.

A common but somewhat dishonest interpretation is that democracy is impossible or possible only in a two-party system. It is clear that, from a formal point of view, one can challenge Condition U. This is done by restricting individual weak orderings—for instance, the concept of single-peaked preferences introduced by Duncan Black (1958) just does this. One can also challenge Condition I. This has been done by Donald Saari (1995) in his studies on scoring rules.

Kenneth Arrow's book and papers on this topic are among the most brilliant scientific works of the last century. They were crucial in the introduction of the use of modern logical and mathematical concepts in economics and other social sciences, and were at the origin of a new scientific domain, social choice theory, that is now flourishing at the frontier of economics, political science, mathematics, philosophy, psychology, and sociology.

SEE ALSO *Arrow, Kenneth J.; Choice in Economics; Preferences; Social Welfare Functions*

BIBLIOGRAPHY

Arrow, Kenneth J. 1963. *Social Choice and Individual Values.* 2nd ed. New York: Wiley.

Arrow, Kenneth J., Amartya K. Sen, and Kotaro Suzumura, eds. 2002. *Handbook of Social Choice and Welfare.* Vol. 1. Amsterdam: Elsevier.

Arrow, Kenneth J., Amartya K. Sen, and Kotaro Suzumura, eds. 2006. *Handbook of Social Choice and Welfare.* Vol. 2. Amsterdam: Elsevier.

Austen-Smith, David, and Jeffrey S. Banks. 1999. *Positive Political Theory I: Collective Preference.* Ann Arbor: University of Michigan Press.

Black, Duncan. 1958. *The Theory of Committees and Elections.* Cambridge, U.K.: Cambridge University Press.

Saari, Donald G. 1995. *Basic Geometry of Voting.* Berlin: Springer.

Sen, Amartya K. 1970. *Collective Choice and Social Welfare.* San Francisco: Holden-Day.

Maurice Salles

ARTIFICIAL INTELLIGENCE

SEE *Computers: Science and Society.*

ARYANS

The term *Aryan* is derived from the Indic word *ārya* (noble). The ancient Hindu *Rig Veda* (variously dated 4000–1200 BCE) uses ārya as a self-designation of its authors. According to another Hindu text, the *Manu Smriti* (c. sixth century BCE), the inhabitants of the *āryā-varta* (the Hindu heartland) were setting the standards for *dharma.* In the *Bhagavad Gita* (c. second century BCE), the Hindu god Krishna tells the warrior Arjuna that it would be *an-ārya* not to fight a just war. In Buddhism, *ariya* has an ethical connotation: not birth but high moral standards make one an ariya. Gautama Buddha (c. sixth century BCE) taught the *ariya saccāni,* or the "(four) noble truths." Jains also use the word as an expression of moral excellence. The word ārya also occurs in the *Zend-Avesta,* the oldest scripture of the Zoroastrians, which states that Iran is the "ariya country." In 1875 Swami Dayananda Saraswati (1824–1883) founded the Ārya Samāj, a Hindu reform movement aimed at restoring Vedic religion by eliminating all later accretions to sacred Hindu writings known as Purana and excluding all foreign influences.

"Aryan" entered European scholarly discourse in the mid-nineteenth century through philology as a generic name for Indo-European languages. A major international interdisciplinary enterprise appeared under the title "Indo-Aryan research." The Sanskrit scholar F. Max Müller (1823–1900) cautioned other scholars not to load the linguistic term with racial overtones, as had already been done by some anthropologists of his time. Joseph Arthur Conte de Gobineau (1816–1882) maintained that within the "white race," the "master race," the blue-eyed, blond-haired, dolichocephalic Aryans constituted the highest variant. Variously Scandinavia, Lithuania, the (dried-out) North Sea, northern Germany, southeastern Russia, the North Pole, and the (mythical) Atlantis were claimed as the cradle of the Aryans. For at least two thousand years, Europeans, relying on ancient Greco-Roman traditions and on the *Genesis* story of the peopling of the earth after the great flood, assumed that their ancestors

had migrated westward from the East. By the nineteenth century, when it had become accepted that the earth and humankind were much older than six thousand years and the claim of European cultural superiority seemed to have been established, the direction of migration was reversed. The Aryan Invasion Theory (AIT) that arose in England in the second half of the nineteenth century specifically suggested that "Aryan" conquerors brought horses, iron, Sanskrit, and the Vedas to India around 1500 BCE.

By the early twentieth century, it had become impossible to find any scholarly agreement on either the identity or the origin of an Aryan race: now ideology took over. Widespread racism in Europe and North America led to the creation of "scientific" race theories that not only justified white-black segregation, but also supported an increasingly militant anti-Semitism. Houston Stewart Chamberlain's (1855–1927) *The Foundations of the Nineteenth Century* (1899) inspired the Nazi ideologue Alfred Rosenberg (1893–1946) to claim in his 1930 book *Der Mythos des 20. Jahrhunderts* (The Myth of the Twentieth Century) that the preservation of the purity and dominance of the Aryan race was the main agenda of the twentieth century. Rosenberg also used the publications of the racist-nationalist Gustaf Kossinna (1858–1931) and Hans Reinert (1900–1990), who held the chair for "Prehistory and Early Germanic history" at the University of Berlin, to prove his thesis. The so-called Aryan race, or *Herren Rasse,* included besides the North Germans also the Scandinavians, the English, and the (Nordic) North Americans. Rosenberg's *Mythos* offered "scientific" grounding to the *Arier Paragraphen* (legislation requiring pure Aryan ancestry) through which the Nazi government in early 1933 forced all German Jewish civil servants into retirement; it also provided theoretical support for the genocide later carried out on Jews, Gypsies (Roma), and other so-called inferior races.

For many years following the Holocaust, the term "Aryan" rarely appeared in scholarly literature. It resurfaced in the 1990s in a controversy about the Aryan Invasion Theory in connection with the early history of India. While archaeological, anthropological, and DNA research has proven the (AIT) all but untenable, some philologists, such as Michael Witzel, and some historians, such as Romila Thapar, defend it. Karl Marx (1818–1883) had also believed in it.

In a different context, but related to the older race ideologies, the "Aryan Nations" movement in the United States, founded in 1974 by Richard G. Butler (1918–2004), has revived the issue through its use of Nazi symbols and vocabulary to promote its white supremacist anti-Semitic agenda. The Aryan Nations movement openly advocates the aims and strategies of Adolf Hitler

(1889–1945), and supporters strive to establish a worldwide "Fourth Reich" dominated by "Aryans."

SEE ALSO *Anti-Semitism; Gobineau, Comte de; Hinduism; Jews; Myth and Mythology; Nazism; Race; Racism; Roma, The; White Supremacy; Whiteness*

BIBLIOGRAPHY

Aryan Nations. http://www.aryan-nations.org/about.htm.

Elst, Koenraad. 1999. *Update on the Aryan Invasion Debate.* New Delhi: Aditya Prakashan.

Sieferle, Rolf Peter. 1987. Indien und die Arier in der Rassenkunde. *Zeitschrift fur Kulturaustausch* (3): 444–467.

Klaus K. Klostermaier

ASANTE, MOLEFI KETE

SEE *Afrocentrism.*

ASCH, SOLOMON
1907–1996

Solomon Elliott Asch was a Polish-born American psychologist noted for his dedication to psychology as a natural science, his talent for designing arresting experiments, and a humanism that embraced cultural knowledge and sensitivity. For Asch, behaviorists and Freudians were alike in their reductionism. Asch aimed instead to represent the breadth and depth of *Homo sapiens* in a Gestalt psychology that focused on context and relationships.

Asch was born in Warsaw in 1907 and moved to the United States as a teenager. At City College of New York he majored in both literature and science. While completing his graduate studies in psychology at Columbia University, he took an interest in anthropology and attended seminars with Ruth Benedict (1887–1948) and Franz Boas (1858–1942). In 1930 Asch married Florence Miller and took her with him on a summer fellowship to study Hopi children and their culture in Arizona. Although these experiences laid the foundation for Asch's humanist interests, his graduate work was more conventional. Henry E. Garrett (1894–1973) supervised his Ph.D. research and, in the custom of the day, gave Asch his thesis problem: to find out whether all learning curves had the same form.

After completing his doctorate in 1932, Asch became a faculty member at Brooklyn College. Soon after taking up this position, he met Max Wertheimer (1880–1943), a Gestalt psychologist who became the major intellectual influence in Asch's life. When Wertheimer died in 1943, Asch succeeded him as chairman of psychology at the New School for Social Research.

Asch moved to Swarthmore College in Pennsylvania in 1947 and spent twenty productive years there. At Swarthmore, Asch was in daily contact with two of the brightest stars of Gestalt psychology: Wolfgang Kohler (1887–1967) and Hans Wallach (1904–1998). It was in this environment that Asch developed his classic studies of social psychology: "Forming Impressions of Personality" (1946); "The Doctrine of Suggestion, Prestige, and Imitation in Social Psychology" (1948); and "Studies of Independence and Conformity: I. A Minority of One against a Unanimous Majority" (1956). Each of the three investigations joins an elegantly simple method with a question of surprising depth, and each poses a striking conflict.

For personality impressions, the conflict is between positive and negative traits in descriptions of a single person. Perhaps the most important result is that students given inconsistent information (that a person is both cold and friendly) have no difficulty producing a unified impression (friendly manner, cold eyes). One can imagine a world in which students complain that they can do no more than repeat back the trait list—how can they say more? Creativity in integrating information about others is so natural that it takes an experiment to make us wonder at our capacity.

For prestige suggestion, the conflict is between evaluation of a quotation ("a little rebellion, now and then, is a good thing, and as necessary in the political world as storms are in the physical") and evaluation of the source to which the quotation is attributed (Thomas Jefferson or Vladimir Lenin). Others had found that agreement with an argument was higher when the source held a higher status. These studies had concluded that humans are irrational in attending to the source associated with an argument. Asch showed that the perceived meaning of the quotation is different, depending on the source: Jefferson's rebellion is reform; Lenin's is blood in the street. The difference in agreement comes not from blind associations but from creative interpretation of the combination of statement and source information. (Asch's irony was that the quotation came, in fact, from Jefferson, and, in context, Jefferson meant blood in the streets.)

For conformity research, the conflict is between social and sensory information, as a phony majority contradicts visual reality about the length of a line. In the standard situation, the real subject has to render a judgment after six "fellow students" give the same obviously wrong answer. These conformity test trials are interspersed among numerous trials in which all give the correct judgment. Overall, subjects remain independent on two-thirds of the test trials, but three-quarters of subjects conform to the majority on at least one test trial. Many have understood this result as indicating human weakness in the face of social pressure. Asch emphasized instead that independence was twice as likely as conformity and noted that social life requires sensitivity to the opinions of others.

These experiments are revealing because, in all of them, conflicting inputs elicit the human capacity for creative integration of these inputs. During the decades in which psychology was dominated by stimulus-response psychology and behaviorism, Asch was an inspiration for those who could still see the complexity of human perception and the richness of human culture. Asch's 1952 textbook, *Social Psychology*, conveyed his experimental humanism to generations of undergraduate students and remains worth reading today.

SEE ALSO *Autokinetic Effect; Norms; Social Psychology*

BIBLIOGRAPHY

PRIMARY WORKS

Asch, Solomon E. 1946. Forming Impressions of Personality. *Journal of Abnormal and Social Psychology* 41: 258–290.

Asch, Solomon E. 1948. The Doctrine of Suggestion, Prestige, and Imitation in Social Psychology. *Psychological Review* 55: 250–276.

Asch, Solomon E. 1952. *Social Psychology*. New York: Prentice-Hall. Reprint. 1987. New York: Oxford University Press.

Asch, Solomon E. 1956. Studies of Independence and Conformity: I. A Minority of One against a Unanimous Majority. *Psychological Monographs* 70: 1–70.

Clark McCauley

ASHKENAZIM

SEE *Jews.*

ASIATIC MODE OF PRODUCTION

In twentieth-century Marxist politics and social sciences, the concept of the Asiatic mode of production was at the center of debates and controversies over how to apply the idea of *mode of production* to non-Western societies. Marxist theorists also turned to the Asiatic mode of production to argue for different revolutionary strategies in societies subject to colonial and imperialist domination.

The concept's status within Marx's own work is uncertain. The young Marx's references to Asian societies are influenced by a political tradition that, from Aristotle (384–322 BCE) to Charles Montesquieu (1689–1755) and Georg W. F. Hegel (1770–1831), saw the Asian continent as characterized by political despotism and socioeconomic stagnation. The initial theorization of modes of production in Marx's *German Ideology* (1845) makes no mention of an "Asian" mode. His *Misery of Philosophy* (1847), however, discusses India as a society where village-based production coexists with common land property. After 1850 Marx's view of Asia became more systematic, and he outlined a specific mode of production for the region. A series of articles he wrote in 1853 for the *New York Daily Tribune* dealt in detail with the Indian case, and to a lesser degree with China. The chapter on "precapitalist economic formations" in the *Grundrisse* (1857–1858) inserted the Asiatic mode of production into a theory of stages of social development, where it followed "primitive communism." Marx tended to chronologically overlap the Asiatic mode of production with slavery and feudalism as two other, successive precapitalist societies where laborers are not separated from the means of production.

Marx's definition of the Asiatic mode of production included the absence of private ownership of land, autonomous village communities, and a despotic centralized state in charge of public works, especially irrigation. To finance public infrastructure, the state extracts, mainly through coercion and the control of the armed forces, an economic surplus produced by local communities in the form of tributes and collective work. Once surplus is extracted, village communities remain relatively independent within their "self-sustaining" economies.

After the first volume of *Capital* (1867), the Asiatic mode of production almost disappears from Marx's writings. Friedrich Engels's (1820–1895) analysis of precapitalist societies in *The Origins of Family, Private Property, and the State* (1884) did not mention it. In the early twentieth century, socialist reformists of the Second International took the concept as a metaphor for Asia's backwardness; they saw in colonialism a force of development and modernization. Fervent disputes on the Asiatic mode of production reemerged in the aftermath of the Russian Revolution (1917). Vladimir I. Lenin (1870–1924) had, in fact, stigmatized the "Asiatism" of czarist Russia. The Stalinist Third International (Comintern), however, rejected the Asiatic mode of production in 1921 when in colonial societies it chose to support alliances between the proletariat and nationalist bourgeoisies against imperialism and indigenous ruling classes. The Comintern defined the latter as "feudal," avoiding in this way the concept of the Asiatic mode of production, which was seen as too closely associated with political despotism and therefore liable to be used against the Stalinist regime itself.

The critical positions of Leon Trotsky (1879–1940) and Evgenij Varga (1879–1964) nonetheless alluded to the Asiatic mode of production in proposing anticolonial alliances of workers and peasants against both foreign imperialism and local bourgeoisies. The concept was finally expunged from orthodox Marxism after 1930, as Stalin codified a rigid, mechanical succession of modes of production. Conversely, in *Oriental Despotism* (1957) the former Marxist sinologist Karl Wittfogel (1896–1988) employed Marx's original formulation as a polemical indictment of the Soviet state, which he characterized as a manifestation of totalitarianism akin to Asia's "hydraulic civilizations."

The Asiatic mode of production resurfaced in Marxist historiography and anthropology during the 1960s in a context of intensified anticolonial and anti-imperialist resistance. Maurice Godelier and other contributors to the French journal *La pensée* (Thought) asserted that this mode of production remained central throughout the work of Marx and Engels. Jean Chesneaux did not limit the concept's validity to Asia, but extended it to a variety of traditional societies. At the same time, these authors argued for a dynamic perspective to depart from the Eurocentric bias of orthodox Marxism, which saw precapitalist non-Western societies as stagnant and undeveloped. The Asiatic mode of production has also been severely criticized in Marxist debates. Barry Hindess and Paul Hirst refused to define it as a mode of production because it presupposes the state rather than explaining it through the analysis of social relations. Maxime Rodinson considered the concept a blunt and simplified way to encase highly complex societies. Claude Meillassoux noted the concept's excessive generalization as it conflates diverse social formations that share a tributary extraction of surplus. The distinctiveness of African realities led Catherine Coquery-Vidrovitch to propose an "African," kinship-based, mode of production-reproduction. Finally, postcolonial studies have rejected the Asiatic mode of production concept, following Edward Said's *Orientalism* (1978), seeing it as a reflex of the cultural stereotypes that underpinned European imperial expansion.

BIBLIOGRAPHY

Dunn, Stephen P. 1982. *The Fall and Rise of the Asiatic Mode of Production*. London: Routledge and Kegan Paul.

Godelier, Maurice. 1978. The Concept of the "Asiatic Mode of Production" and Marxist Models of Social Evolution. In *Relations of Production: Marxist Approaches to Economic Anthropology*, ed. David Seddon, 209–257. London: Frank Cass.

Hindess, Barry, and Paul Hirst. 1975. *Pre-capitalist Modes of Production*. London: Routledge and Kegan Paul.

Sofri, Gianni. 1969. *Il modo di produzione asiatico: Storia di una controversia marxista*. Turin, Italy: Einaudi.

Franco Barchiesi

ASSEMBLY LINE

SEE *Factories.*

ASSETS

SEE *Wealth.*

ASSIMILATION

Assimilation is the process by which individuals or groups adopt (either voluntarily or forcedly) the language and cultural norms and values of another group. In most cases, it is the minority group that is expected to conform to the normative practices and ideals associated with the majority group. Additionally the issue of assimilation is often an issue of racial supremacy. That is, who is allowed to assimilate into the dominant culture largely depends on the whether that group will fit into the political, social, and economic desires of the dominant group, a group that historically has been (and continues to be) comprised of European white ethnic groups. In the United States, for example, Native Americans, African Americans, and Mexican Americans have lived in the United States much longer than most European American groups, but instead of being viewed as the normative culture (or part of the normative culture), these groups are viewed as "others" outside the "American" culture.

WHY SOME GROUPS ASSIMILATE MORE QUICKLY THAN OTHERS

There are three main factors that explain why some racial and ethnic groups tend to assimilate more quickly than others. The first explanation, which is especially relevant for understanding assimilation in the United States but also instrumental for understanding assimilation in countries that have faced European colonialism, can be summed up as having to do with racial discrimination and in particular white supremacy. For instance, although many European ethnic groups that immigrated to the United States in the 1800s faced racial and ethnic discrimination and prejudice, eventually they were able to integrate into American society as "whites." Groups that were unable to pass as whites because of skin color, phenotype, or even accent remained largely excluded from full assimilation into American society.

Much research has been conducted on the relationship between minority group size and racial prejudice and discrimination. Some scholars have suggested that a perceived "racialized" threat to the dominant group from a minority group, even if the threat is unfounded, leads to increased prejudice against the minority group (Quillian 1995; Burr, Galle, and Fossett 1991; Fossett and Kiecolt 1989; Blumer 1958; Blalock 1967).

The second factor involves socioeconomic status or class. Groups that have economic resources tend to assimilate into society more quickly than groups that have few or limited resources. Groups with large financial resources are able to have greater access to education, jobs, and even politics. In the United States, for example, Cubans have achieved a greater level of assimilation compared to Mexicans (Saenz 2004). Although skin color is a factor explaining the relatively higher success of assimilation for Cubans (they tend to have lighter skin tones compared to Mexicans), the fact that Cuban Americans tend to be better off economically allows them greater mobility and access to good jobs and better education.

Finally, a third factor has to do with the historical context of a society. A number of scholars have argued that prejudice against immigrant groups is higher during economic downturns than in times when the economy is prosperous (Becker 1971). During economic difficulties, there is a tendency for the majority group to blame minority groups for a perceived loss of jobs, economic insecurities, and threat of job competition, and the level of hostility toward racial and ethnic minorities tends to rise. In other words, there is an inverse relationship between a society's economic prosperity and discrimination against minority groups.

Although all three factors provide plausible explanations for understanding why some groups are more likely than others to assimilate, more contemporary analysis of assimilation reveals that a complex intersectionality exists between race, class, and the economy. However, many scholars have argued pointedly that race and colorism continue to be the most salient reasons why many minority groups are still referred to as "hyphenated Americans" (e.g., African Americans or Mexican Americans) rather than simply "Americans" (Bonilla-Silva 2001).

EARLY ASSIMILATION THEORIES

Robert Erza Park (1864–1944), one of the first American sociologists and scholars to focus on ethnic relations, is considered a founding father of early assimilation theories, although his take on assimilation can be traced to the works of earlier social scientists, such as Herbert Spencer, Hermann Schneider, William Sumner, Franz Boas, and

Ruth Benedict, among others. Indeed it was Herbert Spencer's analysis and explanation of how larger societies capture and integrate other peripheral cultures and societies into their own, often forcing them to adapt to the larger and more powerful society's normative climate and values, that enticed Park into thinking more about the role race and ethnicity played in the larger equation. Other influential scholars who helped to shape Park's sociological imagination were John Dewey, George Simmel, and Booker T. Washington.

Before Park, racial implications of assimilation were minimally discussed at best, but there were models centered on cultural or national levels of assimilation. For example, Hermann Schneider in his two-volume book *World Civilizations* (1931) developed (albeit on a very macro-level) one of the earliest models of assimilation, though he never used that term. According to Schneider, as civilizations advance technologically, they grow larger and begin to incorporate other cultures in a three-stage process. At stage one it is through migration, invasion, or conquest that civilizations progress. At stage two, a period of miscegenation and amalgamation takes place in which the two cultures physically mix with one another. Finally, stage three begets a period of internal conflict in which class dynamics are restratified and there is a re-creation of new cultural symbols in the form of art, music, literature. Schneider never envisioned this process as a linear one but rather as a cycle that repeated itself every time a civilization progressed.

Park's assimilation theory, widely referred to as the "race relations cycle," was one of the first to incorporate the term *assimilation* into a model. Park suggested that immigrants are incorporated into a given society in four stages: contact, conflict, acculturation, and assimilation. His theory was that all immigrants face hostility and struggles initially, but gradually they are able to shed their ethnic identities and conform to the normative climate of the dominant group in society. Eventually, then, the group melts right in with the dominant group (i.e., A + B = A). At the time that Park was conceptualizing his cycle of race relations theory, a massive number of immigrants from European countries (e.g., Irish, Italians, Jews) were slowly being incorporated into the social, economic, and political spheres of the United States. However, it remained unclear whether African Americans and other non-European groups would be able to do the same. Park assumed that, given time, non-European groups would be able to assimilate into the dominant culture in the same manner that European groups were already doing.

Park's theory was widely accepted (Duncan and Duncan 1955; Burgess 1928), but not everyone agreed with the simplicity of his model. For instance, Emory Bogardus developed his own model in which he proposed seven steps toward assimilation, including the native population's curiosity about immigrants, followed by an economic welcoming, then competition, legislative antagonism, fair play, quiescence, and finally partial second- and third-generation assimilation (Bogardus 1930). The last stage of Bogardus's model is worthy of attention because he never claimed that immigrants would be able to assimilate fully into the receiving society but rather that second and succeeding generations would be accepted partially yet still sometimes scrutinized depending on their country of origin (i.e., A + B = A + b). Here the little *b* represents the partial acceptance of certain second- and third-generation immigrants and their cultures. This is different from the concept of cultural pluralism, or the "salad bowl theory," which suggests that both cultures remain intact and get along with each other. Bogardus's model has some of the same problems as Park's in that he made too many assumptions, particularly in regard to the initial acceptance of immigrants as mostly favorable. Bogardus is better known for his social distance scale (the "Bogardus scale") used to measure the preferred distance between two groups of people. Although Bogardus's model of assimilation has remained relatively unknown, especially in comparison to the works of other assimilation scholars of his time, his social distance scale has been widely adopted as a measurement tool for racial and ethnic attitudes and levels of intimacy between groups, and both of these factors have been used as indicators of assimilation.

Milton Gordon dramatically overhauled and expanded Park's theory in the 1960s with a more complex model of two main stages along a mostly linear path to assimilation: acculturation and social assimilation. Stage one, acculturation, deals with the initial contact and the conflicts experienced by immigrants coming into another society. Stage two, social assimilation, is the interaction and slow process of developing friends, social networks, and intermarriage within the dominant culture, eventually leading to total assimilation, which is broken down into seven substages: cultural (acculturation), structural (participating in education, church, etc.), marital (amalgamation), identificational (self-identifying and shedding of ethnic background), attitudinal changes (prejudice), behavioral changes (discrimination), and finally civic assimilation.

As minority groups went through these stages, Gordon theorized three possible assimilation outcomes: Anglo conformity, cultural pluralism, and the melting pot. Anglo conformity, which Gordon dealt with in *Assimilation in American Life: The Role of Race, Religion, and National Origins* (1964), refers to the idea that the assimilation of the minority group into the majority group (i.e., Anglos) results in a loss of the norms, values, language, and culture of the minority group (i.e., A + B = A). Outcome two, cultural pluralism (also referred to as the "salad bowl theory" or "multiculturalism"), refers to the idea that minority groups are able to assimilate into the dominant groups' social structures (e.g., schools) while continuing to maintain their own cultures, traditions, and languages (i.e., A + B = A + B). Finally, Gordon's notion of the melting pot theory refers to idea that the culture of a society changes as elements of minority groups are taken and incorporated into the values, norms, and institutions of the dominant group (i.e., A + B = C).

ASSIMILATION'S ROLE IN SCHOLARSHIP

Assimilation theorists took a beating in the 1960s and 1970s from scholars who argued that many racial and ethnic groups remained unassimilated in the United States, even though in some cases they had been in the country for three generations (Glazer and Moynihan 1963; Novak 1972). However, starting in the middle to late 1980s and continuing in the early twenty-first century, research on assimilation has been picked up and expanded upon by a whole new group of scholars. Changing the notion of what it means to be assimilated into the dominant culture, scholars such as Lisa Neidert and Reynolds Farley (1985) argued that although they have not achieved assimilation as defined by Park in his race relations cycle model, newer immigrant groups in the United States have achieved some level of socioeconomic success. Edward Murguia (1975) has suggested that anti-Anglo-conformity practices, such as those initiated by the Chicano movement in the 1960s, could also have drastic consequences for Mexicans and other immigrants who were seen as troublemakers and discriminated against because of their culture and heritage. A groundbreaking article by Richard Alba and Victor Nee (1997) offered a staunch counterargument to scholars critical of the assimilation concept. Their basic argument was that it is unnecessary to abandon the concept of assimilation in favor of new terminology, especially considering that the assimilation model is still useful in studying contemporary immigration in the United States.

One the best known assimilation theories, introduced in the early 1990s by Alejandro Portes and Min Zhou (1993), was segmented assimilation. Segmented assimilation refers to the idea that there are multiple routes to assimilation and that these routes are not necessarily positive in their outcomes. Depending on their national origins, wealth, skin colors, phenotypes, accents, social networks, and opportunities, some groups may be able to assimilate more quickly or easily than other groups. Historically western European and other lighter-skinned immigrants have been more successful in assimilating into mainstream American society compared to their darker-skinned counterparts. Mary Waters's *Black Identities* (1999) rocked assimilation theorists still using methods derived from Park and Gordon by suggesting that there are some immigrants (e.g., English-speaking Caribbeans) who are doing better than native-born Americans. Other authors, such as Portes and Ruben Rumbaut (1996), suggested that some second- and third-generation immigrants, because they are losing their cultural identities, fare less well compared to their parents and grandparents, who are viewed, for example, as hard workers.

Although Park's assimilation model has proven unsuccessful at predicting assimilation of groups such as African Americans or Mexican Americans, it remains debatable whether assimilation theories have outlived their usefulness in the social sciences. Nonetheless, for many immigration experts, such as Richard Alba and Reynolds Farley, assimilation models are still a good predictor of future outcomes, because many social scientists predict that the United States will one day have a "majority minority," which will change the pattern of who gets assimilated into the system and who does not.

SEE ALSO *African Americans; Benedict, Ruth; Boas, Franz; Business Cycles, Theories; Class; Colorism; Discrimination, Racial; Immigrants to North America; Immigrants, European; Immigrants, Latin American; Immigration; Mexican Americans; Minorities; Native Americans; Park School, The; Park, Robert E.; Race Relations; Race Relations Cycle; Spencer, Herbert; White Supremacy*

BIBLIOGRAPHY

Alba, Richard, and Victor Nee. 1997. Rethinking Assimilation Theory for a New Era of Immigration. *International Migration Review* 31 (4): 826–874.

Becker, Gary S. 1971. *The Economics of Discrimination.* Chicago: University of Chicago Press.

Blalock, Hubert. 1967. *Toward a Theory of Minority-Group Relations.* New York: Capricorn.

Blumer, Herbert. 1958. Race Prejudice as a Sense of Group Position. *Pacific Sociological Review* 1: 3–7.

Bogardus, Emory S. 1930. A Race-Relations Cycle. *American Journal of Sociology* 35 (4): 612–617.

Bonilla-Silva, Eduardo. 2001. *White Supremacy and Racism in the Post-Civil Rights Era.* Boulder, CO: Lynne Rienner Publishers.

Burgess, Ernest W. 1928. Residential Segregation in American Cities. *Annals of the American Academy of Political and Social Science* 140: 105–115.

Burr, Jeffrey A., Omer R. Galle, and Mark A. Fossett. 1991. Racial Occupational Inequality in Southern Metropolitan Areas, 1940–1980: Revisiting the Visibility-Discrimination Hypothesis. *Social Forces* 69 (3): 831–850.

Duncan, Otis D., and Beverly Duncan. 1955. Residential Distribution and Occupational Stratification. *American Journal of Sociology* 60: 493–503.

Fossett, Mark A., and K. J. Kiecolt. 1989. The Relative Size of Minority Populations and White Racial Attitudes. *Social Science Quarterly* 70: 820–835.

Glazer, Nathan, and Daniel P. Moynihan. 1963. *Beyond the Melting Pot.* Cambridge, MA: MIT Press.

Gordon, Milton M. 1964. *Assimilation in American Life: The Role of Race, Religion, and National Origins.* New York: Oxford University Press.

Murguia, Edward. 1975. *Assimilation, Colonialism, and the Mexican American People.* Austin: University of Texas Press.

Neidert, Lisa J., and Reynolds Farley. 1985. Assimilation in the United States: An Analysis of Ethnic and Generation Differences in Status and Achievement. *American Sociological Review* 50 (6): 840–850.

Novak, Michael. 1972. *The Rise of the Unmeltable Ethnics.* New York: Macmillan.

Park, Robert E. 1923. A Race Relations Survey. *Journal of Applied Sociology* 8: 195–205.

Park, Robert E. 1924. Experience and Race Relations. *Journal of Applied Sociology* 9: 18–24.

Park, Robert E. 1950. *Race and Culture.* Glencoe, IL: Free Press.

Portes, Alejandro, and Ruben Rumbaut. 1996. *Immigrant America: A Portrait.* Berkeley: University of California Press.

Portes, Alejandro, and Min Zhou. 1993. The New Second Generation: Segmented Assimilation and Its Variants. *Annuals of the American Academy of Political and Social Science* 530: 74–96.

Quillian, Lincoln. 1995. Prejudice as a Response to Perceived Group Threat: Population Composition and Anti-Immigrant and Racial Prejudice in Europe. *American Sociological Review* 60: 586–611.

Saenz, Rogelio. 2004. *Latinos and the Changing Face of America.* New York: Russell Sage Foundation and Population Reference Bureau.

Schneider, Hermann. 1931. *The History of World Civilization from Prehistoric Times to the Middle Ages.* London: Routledge.

Waters, Mary. 1999. *Black Identities: West Indian Immigrant Dreams and American Reality.* Cambridge, MA: Harvard University Press.

David G. Embrick

ASSISTED DEATH

Assisted death is an umbrella term for a death that requires an intentional act or omission on the part of a second person. There are five categories of assisted death.

Withholding of potentially life-sustaining treatment is the failure to start treatment that has the potential to sustain the life of a person (for example, not providing cardiopulmonary resuscitation to a person having a heart attack).

Withdrawal of potentially life-sustaining treatment is the stopping of treatment that has the potential to sustain the life of a person (for example, removing a feeding tube from a person in a persistent vegetative state).

Potentially life-shortening symptom relief is pain- or suffering-control medication given in amounts that may but are not certain to shorten a person's life (for example, ever-increasing levels of morphine necessary to control an individual's pain from terminal cancer where the morphine is known to potentially depress respiration even to the point of causing death, but it is not known precisely how much is too much as the levels are slowly increased).

Assisted suicide is the act of intentionally killing oneself with the assistance (i.e., the provision of knowledge or means) of another (for example, a person is bedridden with ALS, also known as Lou Gehrig's disease, and her sister brings her a lethal dose of a barbiturate ground up in a glass of orange juice, and the bedridden person drinks it through a straw).

Euthanasia is an act undertaken by one person with the motive of relieving another person's suffering and the knowledge that the act will end the life of that person (for example, a person is bedridden with ALS and her physician gives her a lethal injection of potassium chloride).

CONTENTIOUS ISSUES

It has been widely accepted for some time that the withholding and withdrawal of potentially life-sustaining treatment are both legally and ethically acceptable. Indeed, courts, legislatures, and professional health-care bodies have recognized that patients have a right to refuse treatment and that free and informed refusals made by competent individuals (or substitute decision makers on behalf of individuals) should be respected. However, two areas of significant tension remain. First, there is debate about whether artificial hydration and nutrition are different from other forms of treatment (e.g., cardiopulmonary resuscitation) and therefore should be treated differently. Second, there is debate about whether health-care professionals have the authority to unilaterally withhold or withdraw potentially life-sustaining treatment—for example, where the family of a patient in a persistent vegetative state believes that ongoing treatment is what the patient would have wanted or is in the patient's best interests, while the health-care team claims that the treatment would be "futile." Can the health-care team proceed against the family's wishes and stop treatment? This is a question that has not yet been settled in either law or in ethics.

It has also been widely accepted that the provision of potentially life-shortening symptom relief can be appro-

priate end-of-life care. However, there is still a great deal of uncertainty at the margins. That is, how much medication is too much? When does symptom relief shade into euthanasia? Are there limits on when such symptom relief is appropriate? For example, does a patient need to be terminally ill or could potentially life-shortening symptom relief be provided to someone with a chronic illness? There is also growing controversy over the practice of total or terminal sedation (sedation to the point of unconsciousness). The practice is controversial largely because it creates a physical dependence on artificial hydration and nutrition, which can then be withheld, leading to certain death.

Both assisted suicide and euthanasia are clearly illegal in the United States (with the notable exception of Oregon, which has legalized physician-assisted suicide). Many books and articles have been written about the legal and ethical arguments for and against decriminalization of euthanasia and assisted suicide. Opponents frequently emphasize beliefs about the sanctity of life, dignity, and slippery slopes. Proponents frequently emphasize beliefs about autonomy and dignity and reject slippery-slope arguments. A sharp divide can be found on the issue of whether there is a valid moral distinction between the withholding and withdrawal of potentially life-sustaining treatment, and the provision of potentially life-shortening symptom relief on the one hand and euthanasia and assisted suicide on the other. Public opinion is certainly split but, with consistency over a significant period of time, a strong majority of Americans support both euthanasia and assisted suicide.

SEE ALSO *Death and Dying; Euthanasia and Assisted Suicide; Murder*

BIBLIOGRAPHY

Dworkin, Gerald, R. G. Frey, and Sissela Bok. 2004. *Euthanasia and Physician-Assisted Suicide (For and Against)*. Cambridge, MA: Cambridge University Press.

Oregon Department of Human Services. 2006. *Eighth Annual Report on Oregon's Death with Dignity Act*. Portland, OR: Office of Disease Prevention and Epidemiology. www.oregon.gov/dhs/ph/pas/docs/year8.pdf.

Rubin, Susan. 1998. *When Doctors Say No: The Battleground of Medical Futility*. Bloomington: Indiana University Press.

Jocelyn Downie

ASSOCIATION OF BLACK SOCIOLOGISTS

SEE *Black Sociologists.*

ASSOCIATIONS, VOLUNTARY

Voluntary associations are associations that people voluntarily join. Voluntary associations may be religious, fraternal or sororal, economic, social, cultural, or political. There are three types of membership incentives: social solidary (a term used by James Q. Wilson), purposive, and material (Wilson 1995). Social solidary incentives include the satisfaction of getting to know other people and networking with others. Purposive incentives involve working with an association to fulfill a social, political, or economic interest in society. Material incentives provide members with some tangible benefit (e.g., a discount card).

Associations facilitate people's participation in civil society. Such civic engagement makes for a more connected society. As people get to know one another by way of their civic associations, they can in turn use their relationships to help accomplish other goals or objectives. People thus gain capital socially, what is also referred to as *social capital*. Social capital is composed of those "features of social organization, such as trust, norms, and networks that can improve the efficiency of society by facilitating coordinated actions" (Putnam 1993, p. 167). As one's social networks increase, one's ability to organize and effect change in one's interests is also increased (Putnam 1993, 2000). Increased interconnectedness is believed to increase social productivity. Yet social capital may be used for positive or negative circumstances. Positive uses of social capital contribute to a better society.

Those who participate in organizations face problems of collective action (Olson 1971). They have to overcome problems related to coordinating tasks among group members and problems related to limited resources. Limited resources can exist in the form of smaller memberships, limited financial resources, limited communication between members, and limited networks with other associations or institutions. Trust is a resource that can reduce some of the problems related to collective action. Those who are more trusting in others, who exhibit more social trust, can associate with others more freely and can later use these relationships to their benefit by asking for reciprocation.

While trust is an important resource in social relations, it is also important in the relationships between people and government, where it is referred to as *political trust* (Hetherington 1998, 2001, and 2005). When citizens trust in government, the relationship between citizens and government is more positive (Hardin 1998). Political efficacy affects perceptions of trust in government: Those who feel that they have a say in government or who feel that they have some effect on changes in government tend to trust in government more (Brehm and

Rahn 1997). Those who exhibit more social trust also trust in government more (Brehm 1998). Over time, social trust (Putnam 2000; Rahn and Transue 1998) and political trust (Putnam 2000; Hetherington 2005; Rahn and Transue 1998) have been declining in the United States. Since their heyday in the late nineteenth and early twentieth centuries, memberships in associations have also been declining (Gamm and Putnam 1999).

Distrust of people or government may have a deleterious effect on society. As social networks decrease, memberships in associations also decrease. Distrust leads citizens to feel less connected to government, but it also protects people against the possibility that their relationships with others or with government might be abused (Hardin 2004).

Collective action can also be important for countering government actions that disfavor people's interests. People, however, also may face collective action problems when they try to coordinate large numbers of people to participate in activities to represent their interests. Despite the organization of associations, some people may be more likely to participate in associational activities than others. This leads to those who do not participate in associational activities free-riding on the work of those who do participate and still reaping the benefits of collective action (Olson 1965). The power of collective action, however, is also evident by way of social movements, when large numbers of people and sometimes several associations and their members can protest en masse for change. Moreover, social movements can connect the networks of many people and many associations to represent their interests more broadly (Tarrow 1994).

SEE ALSO *Social Capital*

BIBLIOGRAPHY

Brehm, John. 1998. Who Do You Trust? People, Government, Both, or Neither. Paper presented at the Duke University International Conference on Social Capital and Social Networks, Durham, NC, October 30–November 1.

Brehm, John, and Wendy Rahn. 1997. Individual-Level Evidence for the Causes and Consequences of Social Capital. *American Journal of Political Science* 41 (July): 999–1023.

Gamm, Gerald, and Robert D. Putnam. 1999. The Growth of Voluntary Associations in America, 1840–1940. In Patterns of Social Capital: Stability and Change in Comparative Perspective: Part II, special issue, *Journal of Interdisciplinary History* 29 (4): 511–577.

Hardin, Russell. 1998. Trust in Government. In *Trust and Governance*, ed. Valerie Braithwaite and Margaret Levi. New York: Russell Sage Foundation.

Hardin, Russell. 2004. Introduction. In *Distrust*, ed. Russell Hardin. New York: Russell Sage Foundation.

Hetherington, Marc. 1998. The Political Relevance of Political Trust. *American Political Science Review* (December).

Hetherington, Marc. 2005. *Why Trust Matters: Declining Political Trust and the Demise of American Liberalism.* Princeton, NJ: Princeton University Press.

Hetherington, Marc, and John D. Nugent. 2001. Explaining Public Support for Devolution: The Role of Political Trust. In *What Is It about Government that Americans Dislike?*, ed. John R. Hibbing and Elizabeth Theiss-Morse. Cambridge, U.K.: Cambridge University Press.

Olson, Mancur. 1971. *The Logic of Collective Action: Public Goods and the Theory of Groups.* Cambridge, MA: Harvard University Press.

Putnam, Robert D. 1993. *Making Democracy Work: Civic Traditions in Modern Italy.* Princeton, NJ: Princeton University Press.

Putnam, Robert D. 2000. *Bowling Alone: The Collapse and Revival of American Community.* New York: Simon and Schuster.

Rahn, Wendy M., and John Transue. 1998. Social Trust and Value: The Decline of Social Capital in American Youth, 1976–1995. *Political Psychology* 19 (3): 545–565.

Tarrow, Sidney. 1994. *Power in Movement: Social Movements, Collective Action, and Politics.* Cambridge, U.K.: Cambridge University Press.

Wilson, James Q. 1995. *Political Organizations.* 2nd ed. Princeton, NJ: Princeton University Press.

Shayla C. Nunnally

ASYMPTOTES

SEE *Probability Theory.*

ASYMPTOTIC NORMALITY

SEE *Properties of Estimators (Asymptotic and Exact).*

ASYMPTOTIC THEORY

SEE *Probability, Limits in.*

ATHEISM

Atheism, put simply, is the view that God does not exist. Cognitive atheism entails that, owing to the direction of the overall available evidence, people should believe that God does not exist. Doxastic atheism, in contrast, entails that one actually believes that God does not exist. A doxastic atheist can say: I believe that God does not exist, but

I have no view regarding the status of the overall available evidence regarding God's existence. A person could thus be a doxastic atheist without being a cognitive atheist. Cognitive atheists about God, however, are logically required to recommend doxastic atheism about God, at least on cognitive grounds, even if they fail at times actually to believe that God does not exist. In the history of philosophy, Democritus (c. 460–c. 370 BCE), Epicurus (341–270 BCE), Ludwig Feuerbach (1804–1872), and Friedrich Nietzsche are widely regarded as supporters of atheism.

Theism is the denial of atheism. Cognitive theists hold that, owing to the overall available evidence, people should believe that God exists. Doxastic theists, in contrast, hold that God exists, even if they have no position on the overall available evidence regarding God. Cognitive theists must recommend doxastic theism about God, at least on cognitive grounds, even if they fail at times actually to believe that God exists. Another alternative to atheism is agnosticism, whose cognitive version entails that, owing to highly mixed overall evidence, people should withhold judgment (neither believe nor disbelieve) that God exists. Cognitive atheism entails that cognitive theism and agnosticism get the available evidence wrong. It implies that the evidence counts decisively against the existence of God.

If reality is just material bodies in motion, then atheism is true, since God would not be just a material body in motion. That would be a quick case for atheism, but a problem arises: decisive evidence for holding that reality is just material bodies in motion is lacking. At least this is a topic of ongoing controversy among philosophers.

Another case for atheism would be: If God exists, the evil found in this world would not exist; this world's evil does exist; so God does not exist. Here, again, the case would not be decisive. No decisive reason exists to think that God would not allow the evil found in this world. Certainly God could allow for various kinds of beings with free wills, and they could be causally responsible for much, if not all, of the evil in this world. A problem arises from the limited cognitive resources of human beings. People are simply not in a position to know that God would not allow the evil found in this world. God would be a moral tyrant in causing the evil in this world, but theism does not imply otherwise.

A big issue concerns whether cognitive atheism allows for due cognitive modesty for humans. Can one reasonably suppose that all available evidence has been canvassed in a way that calls for belief that God does not exist? This is a tall order, and it seems doubtful that one can plausibly answer yes. At any rate, God might seek to be elusive for various reasons, as recent work on divine hiddenness indicates. So atheism invites reasonable doubt about itself, owing at least to the limited cognitive resources available to humans.

SEE ALSO *Agnosticism; Monotheism; Polytheism; Reality; Religion; Theism*

BIBLIOGRAPHY

Copan, Paul, and Paul K. Moser, eds. 2003. *The Rationality of Theism.* London: Routledge.

Howard-Snyder, Daniel, and Paul K. Moser, eds. 2002. *Divine Hiddenness: New Essays.* New York: Cambridge University Press.

Martin, Michael. 1990. *Atheism: A Philosophical Justification.* Philadelphia: Temple University Press.

Paul K. Moser

ATROCITIES

SEE *Battle of Algiers, The; Conformity; Darfur; Genocide; Guantánamo Bay; Interrogation; Killing Fields.*

ATTACHMENT THEORY

Attachment theory, formulated by British psychiatrist John Bowlby (1907–1990), focuses on the child-parent relationship and the influence of that relationship on subsequent child development (Bowlby 1969/1982, 1973, 1980). Since Bowlby's original writings were published, attachment theory and research have burgeoned, largely bearing out Bowlby's tenets about the importance of attachments to human development across the life span.

BOWLBY'S ATTACHMENT THEORY

According to attachment theory, the infant-parent attachment is an evolutionarily adaptive relationship whose principal function is the protection of the child. Bowlby argued that all people are genetically predisposed to form enduring and preferential relationships with principal caregivers because in the earliest environments of human beings such relationships were evolutionarily advantageous.

In addition to his concern with all people's attachments, Bowlby focused on differences between individuals. At the heart of Bowlby's thinking about individual differences is the notion of *internal working models.* Specifically, Bowlby argued that individuals draw on their earliest experiences to create mental maps, or internal working models, to guide their behavior. Internal working

models guide people's expectations, attention, interpretations, and memories. These processes then guide behavior.

According to attachment theory, it is the responses of parents to their infants' earliest behaviors (crying, looking, reaching) that most heavily influence the development of the infants' internal working models. Specifically, Bowlby asserted that repeated daily interactions between infant and parent lead the infant to develop expectations about the parent's caregiving. These expectations are gradually organized into internal working models of the caregiver and of the self in relation to this caregiver. Sensitive, supportive caregiving leads to the development of an internal working model of the caregiver as trustworthy and helpful, and of the self as deserving of supportive care. Insensitive, unsupportive caregiving leads to working models of the caregiver as unavailable and untrustworthy, and of the self as unworthy of supportive care.

With continual use, internal working models come to operate automatically and unconsciously. Over time, individuals are more likely to define their experiences using existing working models than to modify their internal working models to accommodate new, possibly inconsistent information. In particular, people's working models guide the development of subsequent relationships. This occurs initially by their guiding the individual's expectations about others' emotional availability: "the kinds of experiences a person has, especially during childhood, greatly affect . . . whether he expects later to find a secure personal base, or not" (Bowlby 1979, p. 104). Barring major changes in the environment or the individual, the principal qualities of the infant-parent attachment(s) will be replicated in subsequent close relationships: infants who received sensitive, supportive care will subsequently form supportive, nurturing, close relationships; infants who received insensitive, unsupportive care will form close relationships in which the giving and receiving of care is distorted.

It is important to note that internal working models are not considered to be immutable. As environments and individuals change and develop, working models are likely to require updating; major changes in the environment or in the person require the reformulation of internal working models. Factors such as traumas, losses, and new attachments are those most likely to alter internal working models.

PATTERNS OF ATTACHMENT

American psychologist Mary Ainsworth (1913–1999) was a lifelong collaborator with Bowlby. Ainsworth's development of the laboratory Strange Situation procedure galvanized the systematic study of individual differences in infant-parent attachment (Ainsworth et al. 1978). The Strange Situation is a twenty-minute videotaped assessment with a twelve- to twenty-month-old infant, the infant's parent, and an unfamiliar female "stranger." There are two brief infant-parent separations during which the infant remains in a laboratory playroom with a selection of toys. Based largely upon the infant's response to the parent during the two reunion episodes, the Strange Situation classification system distinguishes three main patterns of infant-parent attachment: secure, insecure-avoidant, and insecure-ambivalent.

Approximately 65 percent of infants in most nonpathological samples are classified as secure. During reunion, these infants actively seek to reestablish contact with their parent. Comforted by their parent's return, secure infants then return to play. In their inclination to seek and receive comfort from their parent and then resume exploration, secure infants are thought to use their parent as a "secure base from which to explore."

Approximately 20 percent of infants in most nonpathological samples are classified as insecure-avoidant. Infants classified as avoidant are unlikely to cry during the separations. During reunion, these infants actively avoid interaction with the parent and may appear to ignore their parent completely. In their lack of comfort-seeking, avoidant infants appear less able than secure infants to rely on their parent as a secure base.

Approximately 15 percent of infants in most nonpathological samples are classified as insecure-ambivalent. Infants classified as insecure-ambivalent are highly likely to express distress during the separations. During reunion, however, these infants appear to derive little comfort from their parent's return. These infants demonstrate ambivalence about interacting with the parent that is frequently accompanied by angry, resistant behavior. In their inability to be soothed by their parent, ambivalent infants appear less able than secure infants to rely on their parent as a secure base.

Following Ainsworth's identification of these three patterns, Mary Main and Judith Solomon (1986) identified a fourth group: insecure-disorganized. Disorganized, disoriented, and frightened reunion behaviors characterize the infants in this group. When an infant is classified as disorganized, the infant is also assigned to the principal attachment pattern (secure, avoidant, or ambivalent) that most strongly coexists with or underlies the infant's disorganization.

The four patterns of attachment are especially valuable for understanding human development because, as demonstrated by a large body of research, early patterns of attachment consistently forecast later development (Thompson 1999). In brief, children who are classified as secure during infancy later appear more socially competent than children who were classified as insecure. They have more positive interactions with friends and peers;

they are also more empathic and less hostile, aggressive, or withdrawn. Infants classified as disorganized are considered most at risk for future emotional and social problems. In addition, consistent with Bowlby's earliest predictions, these four patterns are also consistently predicted by specific patterns of parenting behavior (Berlin and Cassidy 2000). The disorganized pattern is consistently associated with parental maltreatment (abuse or neglect).

Since the advent of the Strange Situation, numerous other assessments of individual differences in attachment have been developed: the Attachment Q-Sort is an adult-report measure of attachment in infants and young children (Waters et al. 1995). Using modified Strange Situation procedures, researchers have also developed systems for classifying attachment patterns in preschool children (Cassidy and Marvin 1992; Crittenden 1994) and in five- to seven-year-old children (Main and Cassidy 1988). (See Solomon and George [1999] for a discussion of these and other measures.)

After the Strange Situation, the second most widely used assessment of attachment is the Adult Attachment Interview (AAI) (George et al. 1985; Hesse 1999), a one-hour semistructured interview that assesses the adult's current "state of mind with respect to attachment" (i.e., the current internal working models). During the AAI, adults are asked to discuss early childhood experiences and their influences on adult personality. Although the AAI draws heavily on recollections of early attachment experiences, it is the ways in which the interviewee discusses these experiences that figure most importantly in the individual's classification into one of four patterns: secure, insecure/dismissing, insecure/preoccupied, or insecure/unresolved. Consistent with the theory, adults' patterns of attachment reliably predict: (1) the adults' parenting behaviors, and (2) the quality of their child's attachment to them. A second arm of adult attachment theory and research uses adults' self-reports about the way they usually feel and act in romantic relationships to assess "adult attachment style," both in terms of romantic attachments and more generally (Bartholomew and Horowitz 1991; Hazan and Shaver 1987; Rholes and Simpson 2004).

CLINICAL APPLICATIONS

Since the late 1980s, interventions based on attachment theory and research have proliferated in various settings across the United States and abroad. The field of attachment-based interventions has only just begun to gain order and systemization, especially with respect to the use of theory- and research-based protocol (Berlin et al. 2005). Attachment theory and research are also beginning to be integrated into the diagnosis and treatment of children with *reactive attachment disorder*, a set of seriously aberrant and problematic attachment behaviors typically associated with parental maltreatment or disruptions in early caregiving relationships Theory- and research-based interventions to enhance early attachments among high- and low-risk parents and children are a promising avenue toward supporting human development on the whole.

SEE ALSO *Ainsworth, Mary; Bowlby, John; Parenting Styles; Relationship Satisfaction; Separation Anxiety*

BIBLIOGRAPHY

Ainsworth, Mary D. Salter, Mary C. Blehar, Everett Waters, and Sally Wall. 1978. *Patterns of Attachment: A Psychological Study of the Strange Situation.* Hillsdale, NJ: Erlbaum.

Bartholomew, Kim, and Leonard Horowitz. 1991. Attachment Styles Among Young Adults: A Test of a Four-Category Model. *Journal of Personality and Social Psychology* 61: 226–244.

Berlin, Lisa J., and Jude Cassidy. 2000. Parenting and Attachment. In *The Handbook of Infant Mental Health.* Vol. 3: *Parenting and Childcare,* eds. Joy D. Osofsky and Hiram E. Fitzgerald, 137–170. New York: Wiley.

Berlin, Lisa J., Yair Ziv, Lisa Amaya-Jackson, and Mark T. Greenberg, eds. 2005. *Enhancing Early Attachments: Theory, Research, Intervention, and Policy.* New York: Guilford.

Bowlby, John. 1973. *Attachment and Loss.* Vol. 2: *Separation: Anxiety and Anger.* New York: Basic Books.

Bowlby, John. 1979. *The Making and Breaking of Affectional Bonds.* New York: Methuen.

Bowlby, John. 1980. *Attachment and Loss.* Vol. 3: *Loss: Sadness and Depression.* New York: Basic Books.

Bowlby, John. [1969] 1982. *Attachment and Loss.* Vol. 1: *Attachment.* 2nd ed. New York: Basic Books.

Cassidy, Jude, and R. S. Marvin. 1992. *Attachment Organization in Preschool Children: Procedures and Coding Manual.* Unpublished manual.

Crittenden, Pat M. 1994. *Preschool Assessment of Attachment.* 2nd ed. Unpublished manuscript.

George, Carol, Nancy Kaplan, and Mary Main. 1985. *Adult Attachment Interview.* 2nd ed. Unpublished manuscript.

Hazan, Cindy, and Phillip Shaver. 1987. Romantic Love Conceptualized as an Attachment Process. *Journal of Personality and Social Psychology* 52: 511–524.

Hesse, E. 1999. The Adult Attachment Interview: Historical and Current Perspectives. In *Handbook of Attachment: Theory, Research, and Clinical Applications,* eds. Jude Cassidy and Phillip R. Shaver, 395–433. New York: Guilford.

Main, Mary, and Jude Cassidy. 1988. Categories of Response with the Parent at Age 6: Predicted from Infant Attachment Classifications and Stable Over a 1-Month Period. *Developmental Psychology* 24: 415–426.

Main, Mary, and Judith Solomon. 1986. Discovery of a New, Insecure-Disorganized/Disoriented Attachment Pattern. In *Affective Development in Infancy,* ed. T. Berry Brazelton and Michael Yogman, 95–124. Norwood, NJ: Ablex.

Rholes, W. Steven, and Jeffrey A. Simpson, eds. 2004. *Adult Attachment: Theory, Research, and Clinical Implications.* New York: Guilford.

Solomon, Judith, and Carol George, 1999. The Measurement of Attachment Security in Infancy and Early Childhood. In *Handbook of Attachment: Theory, Research, and Clinical Applications,* ed. Jude Cassidy and Phillip R. Shaver, 287–309. New York: Guilford.

Thompson, Ross A. 1999. Early Attachment and Later Behavior. In *Handbook of Attachment: Theory, Research, and Clinical Applications,* ed. Jude Cassidy and Phillip R. Shaver, 265–286. New York: Guilford.

Waters, Everett, Brian E. Vaughn, German Posada, and Kiyomi Kondo-Ikemura, eds. 1995. *Caregiving, Cultural, and Cognitive Perspectives on Secure-base Behavior and Working Models: New Growing Points of Attachment Theory and Research.* Chicago: Society for Research in Child Development.

Lisa J. Berlin

ATTENTION-DEFICIT/ HYPERACTIVITY DISORDER

Attention-deficit/hyperactivity disorder (ADHD) is a diagnostic label describing children and adults who demonstrate developmentally inappropriate levels of inattention, hyperactivity, and impulsivity. This disorder has been identified by many different names in the past, including attention-deficit disorder (ADD) with and without hyperactivity. It is one of the most commonly diagnosed disorders of childhood and accounts for a significant percentage of referrals to mental health and primary care clinics. Once considered a childhood disorder that one would "grow out of," it is now recognized that symptoms and impairment persist across the lifespan for many individuals, with an increasing number of adults seeking treatment. Although prevalence rates vary as a function of diagnostic method, it is estimated that 5 to 8 percent of children and 1 to 3 percent of adults meet criteria for ADHD as outlined by the American Psychiatric Association (1994). ADHD is more often diagnosed in boys, but prevalence rates are fairly consistent across diverse geographic and racial populations.

DIAGNOSIS

The *Diagnostic and Statistical Manual of Mental Disorders* (*DSM-*IV), the primary reference for mental health professionals in the United States (APA 1994), identifies three subtypes of ADHD: predominantly inattentive, predominantly hyperactive-impulsive, and combined. At least six of nine inattentive or hyperactive-impulsive symptoms must be present for at least six months for diagnosis, with the subtype determined by which symptoms are predominant. Inattentive symptoms include inattention to details or making careless mistakes, difficulty sustaining attention, not listening, not following through and completing tasks, avoiding or disliking tasks requiring sustained mental effort, disorganization, forgetfulness, losing things, and distractibility. Hyperactive symptoms include fidgeting, difficulty remaining seated, being "on the go," running or climbing excessively (feelings of restlessness in adults), difficulty playing quietly, and talking excessively. Impulsive symptoms include blurting out, difficulty waiting, and interrupting or intruding on others. These symptoms must be sufficiently maladaptive and developmentally inappropriate to warrant diagnosis.

DSM-IV criteria also require that at least some of the symptoms must have caused impairment for the individual before the age of seven. Although symptoms may be overlooked in some children when they are younger, particularly those who are higher functioning, the developmental nature of the disorder requires a chronic and pervasive pattern of difficulties across time. Thus, one cannot develop "adult onset" ADHD. When symptoms present in adulthood for the first time, there is often an alternative explanation for them, such as anxiety, depression, or another medical condition. Because inattention and hyperactivity-impulsivity can have numerous causes, diagnosis actually requires that symptoms are not better accounted for by another psychiatric disorder and that they do not occur solely in the context of a pervasive developmental disorder, schizophrenia, or other psychotic disorder. Finally, ADHD-related impairments must occur across settings (i.e., in the home, during social activities, and at school or work) and there must be evidence of clinically significant impairment in social, academic, or occupational functioning. That is, the symptom severity is more than mild and interferes in individuals' daily lives and activities. Although these criteria have limitations, notably their appropriateness for different ages and subtypes, they are the most rigorous and empirically derived in the history of ADHD.

When the *DSM*-IV criteria are carefully followed using well-defined practice parameters for children (AACAP 1997; AAP 2000), ADHD can be reliably diagnosed. The parent interview lies at the core of the assessment process and covers questions regarding symptoms, impairment, history (medical, developmental, psychiatric, and family), and alternative explanations for the child's behavior. Developmental history forms, symptom screening checklists, and diagnostic interviews are useful tools in collecting this information. Standardized parent and teacher rating scales that include ADHD-specific items aid in documenting developmental deviance and perva-

siveness of symptoms. Additional feedback from the child's school, including testing reports and observations, may also be obtained. Although medical and cognitive tests are not routinely indicated, they may help identify coexisting conditions. Assessment of ADHD in adults includes the same basic components, with age-appropriate interviewing tools and the use of rating scales completed by the adult and another informant, such as a spouse or coworker (Weiss and Murray 2003). The reliability and validity of these measures are less well established, however.

Despite concerns about large-scale overdiagnosis, epidemiological studies have found little evidence of this. According to the 2003 National Survey of Children's Health that assessed over 100,000 U.S. children through parent phone interviews, approximately 7.8 percent of 4–17 year olds were reported to have been identified by a professional as having ADHD (Centers for Disease Control 2005). Similarly, William J. Barbaresi, Slavica K. Katusic, Robert C. Colligan, et al. (2002) found that 7.5 percent of children in a birth cohort of over 5,000 in Minnesota had received clinical diagnoses of ADHD according to medical record documentation. These numbers closely resemble prevalence rates found in carefully conducted diagnostic studies (Barkley 2006), suggesting that there is not substantial over-identification in practice. The American Medical Association came to a similar conclusion after reviewing over 20 years of literature using a National Library of Medicine database (Goldman et al. 1998). Rather, more children, particularly girls and adolescents, are being identified than in the past, particularly with recently changed and expanded diagnostic criteria. Nonetheless, some practitioners who do not conduct thorough evaluations using validated diagnostic criteria may be inappropriately diagnosing and treating children. Dramatically increasing prescription rates for medications to treat ADHD are also believed to represent more effective treatment patterns, although concerns of misuse and diversion are recognized.

COURSE, IMPACT, AND COMORBIDITY

Children with ADHD experience frequent learning difficulties and are more likely than others to be placed in special education, retained, and suspended; they are also more likely to fail to graduate. Furthermore, they are at higher risk for peer rejection, physical injury, delinquency, and substance use (Barkley 2006). Adults with ADHD are also at higher risk for smoking, drug abuse, driving citations and accidents, and poorer physical and mental health. They often experience higher levels of anxiety and depression, more job-related turmoil, and relationship difficulties (Wender 1995).

Outcomes for children with ADHD vary based on risk factors and the presence of coexisting psychiatric conditions, which commonly include oppositional behavior and conduct problems, anxiety, depression, tic disorders, and learning disorders. Overall, 15 to 20 percent of children with ADHD appear normalized as adults; 20 to 30 percent experience marked impairments in occupational, relational, and mental health functioning, and the remainder exhibit persistent symptoms with mild to moderate difficulties (Biederman et al. 1998). Factors predicting a worse outcome include psychosocial adversity, a family history of ADHD, and the presence of oppositional behavior (Biederman et al. 1996).

HISTORY OF THE DISORDER AND ITS TREATMENT

First described in the early 1900s, thousands of studies on ADHD were conducted in the latter half of the twentieth century, making this the most well-researched childhood disorder. Significant advances have been made in our understanding of the nature of ADHD, resulting in changes to diagnostic criteria and ongoing exploration of risk factors and prognosis. Once attributed to brain injuries or environmental maladjustment, the neurobiological nature of the disorder is now well established (Barkley 2006). Research suggests that the causes of ADHD are complex, although most cases can be accounted for by heredity. Neuroimaging research has identified frontal lobe functioning deficits and structural brain abnormalities associated with ADHD, and molecular genetics studies are investigating specific genes that may be implicated, with a goal of developing more sophisticated treatment strategies (Biederman 2005).

A wide range of treatments for ADHD has been developed, with many having little or no empirical basis (e.g., dietary interventions, biofeedback, and optometric training). Proven treatments for ADHD include parent-management training, direct behavior modification in schools and specialty camps, and stimulant medications, primarily methylphenidate products (AACAP 1997; Pelham et al. 1998). More recently, efficacy has been demonstrated for specific norepinepherine reuptake inhibitors such as atomoxetine. A multimodal treatment approach is generally considered the best practice, although knowledge of long-term benefits and methods for individualizing treatments is limited. There is also a lack of information on the availability and effectiveness of typical community and school services for ADHD. Use of stimulant medications remains controversial, although there is considerable evidence of short-term benefit for core symptoms in children (MTA Cooperative Group 1999) and growing support for the use of these medications in adults. Psychosocial treatments for adults that incorporate behavioral compensation skills and cognitive-behavioral modification are being developed but have not yet been well evaluated.

SEE ALSO *Anxiety; Disability*

BIBLIOGRAPHY

American Academy of Child and Adolescent Psychiatry (AACAP). 1997. Practice Parameters for the Assessment and Treatment of Children, Adolescents, and Adults with Attention-Deficit/Hyperactivity Disorder. *Journal of the American Academy of Child and Adolescent Psychiatry* 36 (10) Suppl.: 85S–121S.

American Academy of Pediatrics (AAP). 2000. Clinical Practice Guideline: Diagnosis and Evaluation of the Child with Attention-Deficit/Hyperactivity Disorder. *Pediatrics* 105 (5): 1158–1170.

American Psychiatric Association (APA). 1994. *Diagnostic and Statistical Manual of Mental Disorders.* 4th ed. Washington, DC: Author.

Barbaresi, William J., Slavica K. Katusic, Robert C. Colligan, et al. 2002. How Common Is Attention-Deficit/Hyperactivity Disorder? Incidence in a Population-Based Birth Cohort in Rochester, MN. *Archives of Pediatrics and Adolescent Medicine* 156: 217–224.

Barkley, Russell. 2006. *Attention-Deficit Hyperactivity Disorder: A Handbook for Diagnosis and Treatment.* 3rd ed. New York: Guilford.

Biederman, Joseph. 2005. Attention-Deficit/Hyperactivity Disorder: A Selective Overview. *Biological Psychiatry* 57 (11): 1215–1220.

Biederman, Joseph, et al. 1996. Predictors of Persistence and Remission of ADHD into Adolescence: Results from a Four-Year Prospective Follow-up Study. *Journal of the American Academy of Child and Adolescent Psychiatry* 35 (3): 343–351.

Biederman, Joseph, Eric Mick, and Stephen Faraone. 1998. Normalized Functioning in Youths with Persistent Attention-Deficit/Hyperactivity Disorder. *Journal of Pediatrics* 133 (4): 544–551.

Centers for Disease Control and Prevention. 2005. Mental Health in the United States: Prevalence of Diagnosis and Medication Treatment for Attention-Deficit/Hyperactivity Disorder–United States, 2003. *Morbidity and Mortality Weekly Report* 54 (34): 842–847.

Goldman, Larry S., Myron Genel, Rebecca J. Bezman, and Priscilla J. Slanetz. 1998. Diagnosis and Treatment of Attention-Deficit/Hyperactivity Disorder in Children and Adolescents. *Journal of the American Medical Association* 279 (14): 1100–1107.

MTA Cooperative Group. 1999. A 14-month Randomized Clinical Trial of Treatment Strategies for Attention-Deficit/Hyperactivity Disorder. *Archives of General Psychiatry* 56: 1073–1086.

Pelham, William, Trilby Wheeler, and Andrea Chronis. 1998. Empirically Supported Psychosocial Treatments for Attention Deficit Hyperactivity Disorder. *Journal of Clinical Child Psychology* 27 (2): 190–205.

Weiss, Margaret, and Candice Murray. 2003. Assessment and Management of Attention-Deficit Hyperactivity Disorder in Adults. *Canadian Medical Association Journal* 168 (6): 715–722.

Wender, Paul. 1995. *Attention-Deficit Hyperactivity Disorder in Adults.* New York: Oxford University Press.

Desiree W. Murray
Rachel E. Baden

ATTITUDES

Attitude, one of the key concepts of social psychology, refers to people's evaluations of entities in their world. Formally defined, attitude is a psychological tendency that is expressed by evaluating a particular entity with some degree of favor or disfavor. An individual's evaluation is directed to some entity or thing that is its object—such as a person (Oprah Winfrey), a city (Chicago), or a theory (Darwinian evolution). The entity that is evaluated, known as an *attitude object,* can be anything that is discriminable or held in mind, sometimes below the level of conscious awareness.

Attitudes are initially formed when an individual's first reaction to an exemplar of an attitude object leaves a mental residue that predisposes the individual to respond with the same degree of evaluation on subsequent encounters with the attitude object. This mental residue is a *tendency* to respond with some degree of positivity or negativity to an attitude object. Once an attitude is formed, it is expressed through the cognitive, affective, and behavioral responses that the attitude object elicits. The cognitive aspect of attitudes consists of associations that people establish between an attitude object and various attributes that they ascribe to it. The affective aspect of attitudes consists of feelings and emotions and physiological responses that accompany affective experience. The behavioral aspect of attitudinal responding refers to overt actions toward the attitude object as well as to intentions to act. These cognitions, affects, and behaviors all express positive or negative evaluations of attitude objects.

As people form attitudes based on cognitive, affective, or behavioral responding to an attitude object, they form associations between the attitude object and these responses. As evaluative meaning is abstracted from these associations, an overall abstract attitude may be derived from these more elementary associations. Yet attitudes do not necessarily take the form of simple, unitary evaluations. To represent attitudes' complexity, psychologists have assumed that the mental associations underlying attitudes can have structural properties. For example, mental associations may be more or less *ambivalent,* or evaluatively inconsistent with one another. In addition many important structural properties derive from attitudes' links to other attitudes—for example, attitudes may form *ideologies* when they are linked by a common theme, such as liberalism or conservatism.

Attitudes may be implicit or explicit. Explicit attitudes are evaluations that are consciously experienced and may be reported by the person who holds the attitude. In contrast, implicit attitudes are those that people do not consciously recognize. These implicit attitudes may be automatically activated by the attitude object or cues associated with it. Regardless of whether attitudes are explicit or implicit, they are a source of motivational and cognitive bias and therefore generally foster attitude-consistent beliefs, affects, and behaviors.

Attitudes are usually assessed through questionnaire techniques that elicit respondents' endorsement of statements or other stimuli (called *items*) that imply positive or negative evaluation of an attitude object. Researchers typically combine each respondent's reactions to these items according to a mathematical model that scales the reactions along an evaluative continuum that extends from very negative to very positive. Implicit measures of attitudes seek to assess attitudes without asking respondents for direct verbal reports of these attitudes. Such techniques may disguise attitude measures as tests of knowledge, assess physiological responses, or monitor the speed with which respondents associate an attitude object with positive or negative stimuli.

ATTITUDE CHANGE

Attitudes can be changed on the basis of cognitive, affective, and behavioral processes. Most research on change has concerned persuasion by informational messages. Classically the independent variables studied by persuasion researchers are categorized as source, message, channel (or medium), recipient, and context variables. Variables within a single category do not necessarily affect persuasion similarly, nor do they necessarily act on attitudes through similar processes or through similar processes in varying circumstances. The reasons for this empirical complexity lie in the multiple psychological processes that can mediate attitude change.

Persuasion theory, which has a long history in social psychology, examines psychological processes that serve as mediators of the effects of information on attitudes. Some of these theories have emphasized what can be termed *systematic processing,* that is, the detailed processing of a communication's content that produces acceptance of its conclusions. Yet dual-process models of persuasion emphasize that, in addition to careful, systematic scrutiny of the content of messages, people may use simple decision rules or cognitive heuristics to assess the validity of messages. For example, the decision rule that "experts' statements can be trusted" might underlie persuasion by an individual expert communicator. A key assumption of dual-process theories is that people process information superficially and minimally unless they are motivated to turn to more effortful, systematic forms of processing. Furthermore systematic processing can only take place if they have the capacity or ability to evaluate the argumentation contained in messages. Therefore persuasion theory's predictions about the effects of variables such as the characteristics of message sources are contingent on the ability and motivation of members of the target audience.

Another technique for changing attitudes is to induce people to engage in behavior that has implications for their attitudes. This research has featured competing theoretical positions that make differing assumptions about the psychological processes that produce such change. The best-known theory, cognitive dissonance theory, took the view that the behavior of advocating a position inconsistent with one's attitude creates *cognitive dissonance*, an unpleasant state of arousal that motivates attitude change. Behavior inconsistent with an attitude changes this attitude toward the behavior, but only when the incentive for the behavior is not seen as the main reason for the behavior. Dissonance is particularly motivating when an individual accepts personal responsibility for his or her behavior bringing about an unwanted consequence. An example of such an unwanted consequence is provided by the case of a speaker who persuades audience members to adopt a viewpoint that he or she does not privately endorse. If the inducement for this behavior is small and personal responsibility is present, the speaker would be likely to show attitude change toward the position advocated. This attitude change occurs because such behavioral acts threaten the speaker's self-identity or integrity unless attitude change makes the advocacy seem more consistent with his or her attitudes.

THE EFFECTS OF ATTITUDES ON BEHAVIORS

One of the greatest successes of attitude research is the substantial progress made in predicting behavior from attitudes. Relatively good prediction can be readily achieved if researchers design their measures of attitudes and behaviors appropriately. However, debates have ensued concerning the psychological processes by which attitudes influence behaviors. Many theories have assumed that people take the utility of behaviors into account in a rational cost-benefit calculation that determines behavior. However, other theorists have emphasized automatic links between attitudes and behaviors as well as the more deliberative route involving analysis of the utility of behaviors. According to the automaticity approach,

attitudes can be formed automatically and then cause behavior to follow without any conscious reasoning process. Increasing the plausibility of relatively automatic attitude-behavior links is research suggesting that implicit measures of attitudes—but not explicit measures—can predict a variety of relatively spontaneous and subtle behaviors, such as nonverbal behaviors, that are for the most part not consciously controlled.

SCOPE OF ATTITUDE THEORY AND RESEARCH

In summary, many specific research topics are encompassed within the broad area of attitudes, which in general pertains to the evaluative aspects of human experience. Researchers are concerned with the causes of attitudes and their effects. A wide range of causes can form and change attitudes. The attitude itself can have various structural properties and may be implicit or explicit. Attitudes in turn influence cognition, affect, and behavior.

SEE ALSO *Attitudes, Behavioral; Attitudes, Political; Behaviorism; Cognition; Cognitive Dissonance; Communication; Ideology; Lay Theories; Personality; Persuasion; Research, Survey; Scales; Self-Perception Theory; Social Influence; Social Psychology; Values*

BIBLIOGRAPHY

Albarracin, Dolores, Blair T. Johnson, and Mark P. Zanna, eds. 2005. *Handbook of Attitudes and Attitude Change.* Mahwah, NJ: Erlbaum.

Eagly, Alice H., and Shelly Chaiken. 1998. Attitude Structure and Function. In *The Handbook of Social Psychology*, 4th ed., eds. Daniel T. Gilbert, Susan T. Fiske, and Gardner Lindzey, vol. 1, 269–322. New York: McGraw-Hill.

Petty, Richard E., and Duane T. Wegener. 1998. Attitude Change: Multiple Roles for Persuasion Variables. In *The Handbook of Social Psychology*, 4th ed., eds. Daniel T. Gilbert, Susan T. Fiske, and Gardner Lindzey, vol. 1, 323–390. New York: McGraw-Hill.

Alice H. Eagly

ATTITUDES, BEHAVIORAL

Attitudes are judgments people have about ideas, experiences, and other people. They can be conscious (explicit) or unconscious (implicit) beliefs that may influence behavior and decisions. Behavioral attitudes are attitudes that develop as a direct result of certain behaviors. However, because one may hold a negative attitude toward a specific behavior yet still engage in that behavior, a person's behavior does not always reflect his or her attitudes.

Social research on nonconformity at the group and societal level has yielded insights into attitude formation and behavior. An early and influential work was Oscar Lewis's *La Vida: A Puerto Rican Family in the Culture of Poverty, San Juan, and New York* (1966). Lewis intended to show that the behavior of poor people—his book's subjects—revealed key insights into how poverty itself generated a way of life that Lewis described as a distinct "culture of poverty." Lewis's work set off a highly politicized controversy in social scientific and policy circles over the causes of poverty and the complex issue of which social groups set and define the "norms" used to judge behavior as favorable or unfavorable. According to Lewis, poverty's enduring nature cannot be attributed to structural constraints only, but also to poor peoples' own attitudes and beliefs that prevent them from succeeding according to mainstream standards.

Research on unfavorable behavior has revealed the key role that norms play in all attitude formation, whether these norms are sanctioned at the group level, the societal level, or both (see for example Erikson 1966; Becker 1991). Many social scientists emphasize the way in which shared or socially held beliefs and attitudes—"norms"—link the individual to society (Tesser and Shaffer 1990). In contrast to a singular or independently developed attitude, belief systems are larger structures that link individual attitudes together. Human behavior is thus continuously mediated between socially situated attitudes (norms) and an individual's attitudes. Jary and Jary (1991), integrating various definitions, argue that attitudes contain three elements: the cognitive, the affective, and the behavioral. Using the framework of behavioral action and attitudes, social scientists have focused their empirical research on the societal and group context in which attitudes and beliefs, and their attendant actions, occur. Some social scientists differ over the weight to ascribe to the individual, group, or society in attitude formation, but generally their numerous studies of behaviors—both conforming and deviant—have revealed the complex nature of the interactions between the various levels at which attitudes are formed, beliefs are generated, and behaviors are enacted. The behavioral attitudes exhibited by Lewis's subjects, for example, may not have been a reflection of their individual-level "positive regard" for the behaviors so much as the group-level "coping strategy" for dealing with the results of generations of poverty.

SEE ALSO *Culture; Culture, Low and High; Culture of Poverty; Moral Sentiments; Norms, Social; Values; Youth Culture*

BIBLIOGRAPHY

Becker, Howard. [1966] 1991. *Outsiders: Studies in the Sociology of Deviance.* New York: Free Press.

Erikson, Kai T. 1966. *Wayward Puritans: A Study in the Sociology of Deviance.* New York: Macmillan.

Jary, D., and J. Jary. 1991. *The Harper Collins Dictionary of Sociology.* New York, Harper Collins Publishers.

Lewis, Oscar. 1966. *La Vida: A Puerto Rican Family in the Culture of Poverty, San Juan, and New York.* New York: Random House.

Tesser, Abraham, and David R. Shaffer. 1990. Attitudes and Attitude Change. *Annual Review of Psychology* 41: 479–523.

Robert Turner
Juan Battle

ATTITUDES, POLITICAL

Political attitudes can be broadly defined as the opinions and values individuals hold about political issues, events, and personalities. Social scientists first began the systematic study of these attitudes in the 1930s and 1940s. Surveys had been used sporadically prior to this time, but it was not until the publication of *The Peoples Choice* in 1944 that scholars began to examine the impact of media exposure and campaign-related events on evaluations of the major party presidential candidates. This study by Paul Lazarsfeld, Bernard Berelson, and Helen Gaudet of the 1940 U.S. presidential election focused on a single community in Ohio and found that political messages conveyed through the mass media were not especially persuasive. That is, instead of media messages influencing voters to support a candidate they might otherwise have opposed, it simply reinforced existing predispositions.

Other studies followed with essentially the same conclusion. Messages conveyed through the mass media could be effective in passing along information, but not in changing opinions. Subsequent research modified this finding somewhat by uncovering a variety of indirect effects from media exposure. It turns out that, although the media cannot effectively tell individuals what to think, it can often influence them as to what to think about. This effect, known as *agenda setting*, stipulates that when the mass media focus on a particular topic—for example, defense spending—those exposed to the message are more likely to think this issue is an important one for the country. Similarly, when the media highlight a particular issue or set of issues, these matters become more important in the evaluation of political candidates. For example, a variety of experimental and survey-based studies have found that emphasizing racial considerations in the media results in attitudes about race being more heavily correlated with attitudes about crime, welfare, or candidate preferences. In short, the mass media tend to have greater indirect effects rather than direct effects on public opinion.

GROUP DIFFERENCES IN PUBLIC OPINION

One common theme in the study of public opinion is the examination of various social group differences in political attitudes. Scholars have typically focused on age, gender, class, and racial group differences. Often, attitudinal differences across these demographic groups are relatively small and inconsistent. For example, the elderly and the nonelderly rarely differ on matters of public policy. The elderly are more attentive to perceived threats to programs such as Social Security or Medicare, but the overall levels of support are virtually indistinguishable. Gender differences in public opinion are also less pronounced than some might think. On a wide variety of issues, the views of men and women are remarkably similar. There are some exceptions, however. In terms of partisanship and ideology, women are somewhat more likely than men to identify as Democrats and liberals. Similarly, since at least 1980, women have been somewhat more likely than men to support Democratic presidential candidates. The differences usually range from ten to fifteen percentage points. In the area of policy preferences, the most prominent gender differences are with issues concerning violence and the use of force. Women tend to be less supportive of these issues (e.g., war, capital punishment, permissive gun control, etc.) than men. Women are also more supportive of gay rights and slightly more liberal on social welfare spending, some measures of racial attitudes, and environmental issues. Interestingly, men and women do not differ dramatically in their levels of support or opposition to abortion, although women do tend to regard the issue as more important than men.

The effects of social class on political attitudes are also uneven. On balance, voters in the bottom half of the income distribution tend to vote for Democratic presidential candidates but this association is not strong and it has been declining over time. In terms of pubic opinion, studies show that citizens with lower incomes are more likely to support social welfare programs. These differences are usually on the order of ten to fifteen percentage points. Less affluent citizens are not, however, more likely to favor a progressive income tax or other taxes that disproportionately affect the wealthy. On most noneconomic issues there are virtually no class differences.

Racial differences in public opinion represent, by far, the largest demographic divide in political attitudes. This is especially true in the case of the views of whites and African Americans. On a range of racially tinged issues, such as efforts to end employment discrimination, sup-

port for school desegregation, and affirmative action in the workplace and in higher education, blacks and whites have differed by as much as fifty percentage points. Racial differences also emerge, of only slightly smaller magnitudes, on ostensibly nonracial issues, such as funding for welfare, food stamps, education, and Medicare. Donald R. Kinder and Nicholas Winter explored these differences in a 2001 article and tried to isolate the causes. Their results differ depending on whether the issue domain involves race-based policies or social welfare issues. In the case of the former, the racial divide is primarily explained by differences between African Americans and whites in political principles (e.g., egalitarianism and limited government), as well as in-group identification and out-group resentment. Class differences do not play a significant role. In the case of social welfare attitudes, the racial divide is mostly driven by all of the previous factors listed along with, to a lesser extent, social class differences between blacks and whites.

One final feature of public opinion with respect to groups is worth mentioning. Since the early part of the twentieth century, there has been a dramatic change over time in attitudes about disadvantaged groups in society. This is perhaps best illustrated in the case of attitudes about women's rights and tolerance toward African Americans. In both cases, these changes are due, at least in part, to the conscious efforts of social movements to change public opinion. For example, Howard Schuman and his colleagues (1997) report that in 1942, 68 percent of whites in a nationally representative sample endorsed the idea that black students should go to separate schools from whites. By 1995, however, this figure had declined to a mere 4 percent. Similarly, in the case of attitudes about gender roles, Virginia Sapiro notes that in the early 1970s roughly one-third of Americans agreed that women should "take care of running the homes and leave running the country up to men" (2002, p. 35). By 1998, only about 15 percent of respondents adopted this position.

SEE ALSO *Ideology*

BIBLIOGRAPHY

Kinder, Donald R., and Nicholas Winter. 2001. Exploring the Racial Divide: Blacks, Whites, and Opinion on National Policy. *American Journal of Political Science* 45 (2): 439–456.

Lazarsfeld, Paul, Bernard Berelson, and Helen Gaudet. 1944. *The People's Choice: How the Voter Makes Up His Mind in a Presidential Campaign.* New York: Duell, Sloane, and Pearce.

Sapiro, Virginia. 2002. It's the Context, Situation, and Question, Stupid: The Gender Basis of Public Opinion. In *Understanding Public Opinion*, eds. Barbara Norrander and Clyde Wilcox, 21–41. 2nd ed. Washington, DC: CQ Press.

Schuman, Howard, Charlotte Steeh, Lawrence Bobo, and Maria Krysan. 1997. *Racial Attitudes in America: Trends and*

Interpretations. Rev. ed. Cambridge, MA: Harvard University Press.

Vincent L. Hutchings

ATTITUDES, RACIAL

Attitude is one of the oldest concepts in the field of social psychology, but its proper meaning has often remained obscure. The basic understanding has been that, when presented with an "object of thought" regarding a person, group, policy, or idea, an individual will possess an attitudinal judgment on a scale of favorableness. However, this definition is contested; others argue that attitudes are much more complex cognitive structures than simple judgments regarding an object of thought (e.g., van Dijk 1987). Nevertheless, social psychologists most often use the former definition and measure racial attitudes, and how they change over time, using survey methods. In many ways, this dominant form of measurement downplays the complexity within people's belief systems.

PROBLEMS WITH MEASUREMENT

The study of racial attitudes arose in the 1930s from concerns over anti-Semitism and the European Holocaust. The first major study of racial attitudes linked individual possession of anti-Semitic views with authoritarian personality traits (Adorno et al. 1950). These early researchers conceptualized racist views as stemming from the larger society but as choice items a person could choose to either adopt or decline, based on one's psychological needs. The continued focus by social psychologists on individual characteristics of the attitude-holder has been criticized, because the historical, social, and rhetorical aspects of the attitudes are often ignored. In other words, thinking itself is a cultural product rather than an individual process, which emerges from a certain social context (Billig 1991).

The most well-known, comprehensive study of racial attitudes in the United States analyzes changes in survey data from the early 1940s until the mid-1990s (Schuman et al. 1997). The findings show a consistent liberalization of racial attitudes of white Americans toward African Americans. One major problem with this and other studies of racial attitudes is that much of the alteration in survey responses over time could be attributed to changes in social norms, not necessarily attitude changes.

A related problem occurs when old survey questions are reused for the sake of longitudinal analysis, but, eventually, their relevance diminishes. All questions are created within a certain context, and the social environment inevitably changes over time. For example, a question asked throughout six decades in the United States is: "Do you think white students and Negro/black students should go to the same schools or to separate schools?" This question found nearly 70 percent in favor of separate schools in 1942, and by 1996, decades after the matter had been settled by federal law and public schools were integrated, only 4 percent retained a preference for separate schools—to which they would admit when surveyed.

Some changes in attitude trends can be attributed to changing social norms, but it is likely that another significant factor in the apparent liberalizing trend is people learning how to express themselves in a way that will prevent them from sounding racist. In a society like the United States, where being a "racist" is now equated with being a bad person, many people try to avoid sounding racist, even if they do hold some strong, prejudiced views (Bonilla-Silva 2006).

Traditionally, attitude theorists see the views that people express in surveys as representing the inner thoughts and feelings of respondents. Rather, in people's talk there is evidence that responses to abstract objects ("blacks") rely on specifics (e.g., marriages between whites and blacks)—the context of the question in the discussion or the particular social issues of the day. Additionally, people express their views in much more complex ways than can be predicted by traditional attitude theory (e.g., Billig 1991; Potter and Wetherell 1987; van Dijk 1987). For example, an initial positive reflection on the object of thought may in actuality be a *disclaimer*, after which the individual, if allowed, will explain why they do not actually feel completely favorable on the issue (Potter and Wetherell 1987; Bonilla-Silva 2006). Because of this, survey responses may be better viewed as discursive acts instead of attitudinal expressions, and they should be used in conjunction with in-depth interviews whenever possible.

However, there are additional factors to consider within the more in-depth interview format. For example, how the question is framed will affect the respondent's interpretation; the object of thought may not be consistent between researcher and respondent (Potter and Wetherell 1987). Additionally, whether it is within the format of a survey, interview, or focus group, the researcher (a stranger) may not put respondents sufficiently at ease to answer openly in an artificial environment.

ATTITUDES AND BEHAVIOR

A final critique of racial attitude research is that the correlation between attitudes and behavior is indirect and unclear (Fishbein and Azjen 1975). Research frequently finds inconsistencies between people's behavior and their stated attitudes. One major factor in this dynamic is that behavior arises not simply from attitudes but is also shaped significantly by social norms (van Dijk 1987). "Social behavior is controlled to a considerable extent by exactly the same norms that control the expression of attitudes in surveys, and one should not look to either for final evidence of what goes on in the hearts of men and women" (Schuman et al. 1997, p. 7). Thus, even when there is consistency between behavior and expressed attitude, there is no assurance that the attitudes themselves are dictating the behavior. Furthermore, there is evidence in social psychological research that one's behaviors can affect attitudes and feelings; people observe their own behavior and make inferences about their internal motivation for such acts.

How important are racial attitudes if their correlation to behavior is not direct? From the perspective of those experiencing racial oppression, gauging the internal feelings of oppressors may not seem nearly as important as understanding, in a practical way, the behaviors of racially dominant group members. From this understanding, strategies may be devised to challenge the way dominant groups treat subordinate groups. These are the tangible battles that can be fought in courtrooms—places where people are held accountable for their actions, not their attitudes, or emotions, or fears, which they may or may not reveal to others, no matter the circumstances.

SEE ALSO *Affirmative Action; Anti-Semitism; Authoritarianism; Holocaust, The; Ideology; Norms; Personality, Authoritarian; Prejudice; Race-Blind Policies; Race-Conscious Policies; Racism; Self-Presentation; Self-Representation*

BIBLIOGRAPHY

Adorno, Theodor W., Else Frenkel-Brunswik, Daniel J. Levinson, and R. Nevitt Sanford. 1950. *The Authoritarian Personality.* New York: Harper.

Allport, Gordon W. 1935. Attitudes. In *Handbook of Social Psychology*, Vol. 2, ed. Carl A. Murchison, 798–884. London: Oxford University Press.

Billig, Michael. 1991. *Ideology and Opinions: Studies in Rhetorical Psychology.* London: Sage.

Bonilla-Silva, Eduardo. 2006. *Racism without Racists: Color-blind Racism and the Persistence of Racial Inequality.* 2nd ed. Lanham, MD: Rowman & Littlefield.

Fishbein, Martin, and Icek Azjen. 1975. *Belief, Attitude, Intention, and Behavior: An Introduction to Theory and Research.* Reading, MA: Addison-Wesley.

Potter, Jonathan, and Margaret Wetherell. 1987. *Discourse and Social Psychology: Beyond Attitudes and Behaviour.* London: Sage.

Schuman, Howard, Charlotte Steeh, Lawrence Bobo, and Maria Krysan. 1997. *Racial Attitudes in America: Trends and Interpretations.* Rev. ed. Cambridge, MA: Harvard University Press.

van Dijk, Teun A. 1987. *Communicating Racism: Ethnic Prejudice in Thought and Talk.* Newbury Park, CA: Sage.

Kristen Lavelle

ATTRACTION
SEE *Similarity/Attraction Theory.*

ATTRIBUTION

It is important to understand why things happen in order to control outcomes or prevent future undesirable occurrences. *Attributions* answer the question of "why" something happens. People tend to seek attributions for unexpected events, and generally infer that things happen either because of factors internal to the actor (personality or dispositional factors) or because of situational influences.

This distinction between situational and personality attributions can be traced to Fritz Heider's seminal book, *The Psychology of Interpersonal Relations* (1958). Heider further identified a stability dimension of attributions. That is, stable situational forces, such as test difficulty, can cause outcomes—but so too can unstable forces, such as a chance opportunity for cheating. Personality can be conceptualized similarly. Stable personality factors include such forces as ability or intelligence. Examples of unstable personality factors are motivation and effort, both of which can change over time and across situations.

Inspired in part by Heider's ideas, Edward Jones and Keith Davis (1965) developed *correspondent inference theory* (CIT) to predict whether observers of an event will make personality or situational attributions for the actor's behavior. According to CIT, the more clearly a person has freely chosen to do something unexpected, and the more clear the intended effects of the activity are, the more likely perceivers are to make personality attributions. When free choice of behavior is limited, when the behavior is not perceived to depart from the norm, and when the intention of the behavior is unclear, perceivers are less likely to make personality attributions.

Another early attribution theory based on Heider's work is Harold Kelley's *covariation theory* (1967). This theory explains that effects are attributed to causes with which they "covary." That is, perceived causes will differ, depending on whether or not an effect is associated uniquely with a particular object, a class of objects, or other people. If a person were happy after seeing a movie, one would attribute the happiness to the person's liking of that particular movie. However, if one knew this person was happy after most movies, one would attribute the happiness to the person being a movie buff.

Given the complexity of the reasoning involved in making attributions in accord with Jones and Davis's and Kelley's notions, it is not surprising that attributions do not always follow theoretical predictions. Such departures often are referred to as *attributional biases*. Well-known biases include the *fundamental attribution error* (FAE)—the tendency to overestimate personal, and underestimate situational, causes for behavior—and the *actor-observer effect*, or the tendency to commit the FAE more strongly when explaining others', rather than one's own, behavior. Additionally, the *self-serving bias*, identified by Gifford Weary Bradley in 1978 as reflecting self-esteem concerns, is the tendency of people to attribute good outcomes to causes that are internal, do not change over time, and have global implications for success in other areas. When bad things happen, however, people tend to invert this pattern. They attribute failures to external, temporary causes that have few implications outside of the specific context they take place in. All together, much research has focused on attributional biases. Together with an understanding of past theories, new findings permit ever more accurate models of how people ask "why?"

SEE ALSO *Causality; Kelley, Harold*

BIBLIOGRAPHY

Gilbert, Daniel T. 1998. "Ordinary Personology." In *The Handbook of Social Psychology*, 4th ed., vol. 2, eds. Daniel T. Gilbert, Susan T. Fiske, and Gardner Lindzey, 89–150. New York: McGraw Hill.

Aaron L. Wichman
Gifford Weary

ATTRITION, SAMPLE

SEE *Sample Attrition.*

AUBURN SYSTEM

SEE *Prisons.*

AUCTIONS

The word *auction* is derived from the Latin *augere*, which means, "to ascend" or "increase." The concept of auctioning, however, is not confined solely to bidding processes in which the price is raised successively until only one bid-

der remains. Rather, the term encompasses a variety of trading methods and is broadly understood as "a market institution with explicitly set rules, which determine resource allocation and prices on the basis of bids from market participants" (see McAfee and McMillan 1987, p. 701).

HISTORY OF AUCTIONS

Auctions have been used since antiquity and have a colorful history. One of the earliest written records of an auction is a description by Herodotus and dates back to 500 BCE (see Cassady 1967, p. 26). At that time in Babylon, women were sold annually as brides in auctions. Auctions were also used in ancient Rome for commercial trade and for the sale of almost anything from slaves to plundered booty and debtor's property. Martin Shubik (1983) provides an entertaining sketch of the history of auctions in the Roman and Babylonian empires, while Ralph Cassady Jr. (1967) discusses the types of auctions used in England and America in the seventeenth and eighteenth centuries and the establishment of the world-renowned auction houses Sotheby's and Christie's.

STANDARD AUCTION TYPES

Despite the variety of auction methods, only four basic types of auctions are commonly used: the *ascending bid auction*, the *descending bid auction*, the *first-price auction*, and the *second-price auction*. In the ascending-bid auction (also called *English* or *open outcry auction*), the price is successively raised until only one bidder remains, and that bidder wins the auction at the final price. This auction form is most familiar to the general public and is usually used to sell art and other collectibles. In the descending-bid auction (also called *Dutch auction*, as it has been used for the sale of flowers in the Netherlands), the auctioneer starts at a very high price. The price is gradually lowered until one bidder accepts paying the current price for the auctioned item. This auction is commonly used to sell perishables like fish or flowers. In the other two standard auction formats—first-price sealed bid and second-price sealed bid auctions—bids are submitted in sealed envelopes. In both sealed bid auction formats, the winner is the person with the highest bid. The auctions differ in their payment requirements, however: In the first-price auction, the winner pays the amount they have bid; in the second-price auction, the winner pays the second-highest bid. These auctions are most commonly used for procurement of government contracts.

AUCTION THEORY

Although auctions have existed for many centuries, the theory of auctions is a relatively new field in economics.

Auctions are market institutions with well-defined rules that determine how the winner is selected and what the payments are, depending on the bids. For that reason auctions are typically modeled and analyzed as bidding games of incomplete information. The first treatment of auctions, which identified the strategic aspect of bidding, is found in the work of William S. Vickrey (1961). Vickrey assumed that each bidder knows precisely how highly he values the item, but does not know anyone else's valuation of the item. The other bidders' valuations are perceived to be uncertain; they are drawn from the same probability distribution and are stochastically independent. All bidders are considered risk neutral. Vickrey's major contribution is the celebrated *revenue equivalence theorem*. It states that under the above premises all four auctions generate the same average revenue for the seller. His model is known as the *independent private value model* and is well suited to situations in which consumers buy an item for their own use. If the item is bought for the purpose of resale, however, it has a single, objective value (the resale value), though bidders may have different guesses about what this value would be. To analyze such a situation, one would need to employ a *common value model*. The most general treatment of the auction problem, which allows for interdependence among bidder's valuations and includes the common value and the private value models as special cases, was developed by Paul R. Milgrom and Robert J. Weber (1982). This entry will establish a revenue ranking for the four standard auction formats, and show that on average, revealing information about the quality of the item put up for sale increases equilibrium bids and, consequently, seller's proceeds.

The purpose of auction theory is twofold. On the one hand, auction theory attempts to explain the existence of certain trading institutions and the functioning of the price formation and exchange processes. On the other hand, it provides a guide on how to tailor the trading mechanism to certain information environments and suggests improvements in already existing institutions. A line of inquiry of both practical and theoretical interest is the design of *optimal* auctions—auctions generating the highest expected revenue for the seller. In an influential paper, Roger B. Myerson (1981) introduced a method that allows one to design the best-performing trade mechanism for a wide class of environments. Jeremy I. Bulow and D. John Roberts (1989) made Myerson's approach accessible to a much broader audience of economists by recasting it in terms of marginal revenues and marginal cost and linking it to the theory of monopoly pricing. The theoretical work on auctions continues to grow rapidly—by December 2006 the Econ Lit Database contained more than two thousand entries with the words *auction* or *auctions*, about half of them theoretical.

AUCTION EXPERIMENTS AND COMPUTER SIMULATIONS

Experimental studies of competitive bidding in auctions first appeared in the early 1980s, with a primary focus on testing the theoretical properties of the standard auction formats. The experimental results established several facts about behavior relative to the theoretical predictions. For instance, the revenue equivalence theorem concerning private value auctions fails in the laboratory. Bids in first-price auctions are higher than in Dutch auctions and bids in second-price auctions are higher than in English auctions. These results remain consistent when the number of bidders is changed. The comparative static predictions of the equilibrium model, however, remain valid. Bidders with higher valuations bid higher and bids generally increase with an increased number of bidders. This picture changes in common value auction environments. In a common-value auction, bidders face a more complicated strategic problem because such auctions involve a combination of competitive bidding and value estimation. Inexperienced bidders often fall prey to the *winner's curse*: The bidder who ends up winning the auction has the most optimistic estimate of the value of the auctioned item. This leads to excessively high bids and to winners who pay prices higher than the value of the item on sale. John H. Kagel (1995) provides a comprehensive overview of the experimental literature on auctions. The use of computer simulations to study the performance of market institutions has been proposed by researchers on the crossroad between economics and engineering (for a discussion, see Roth 2002.)

ONLINE AUCTIONS: PHENOMENA AND PSYCHOLOGY OF BIDDING

Since the 1990s online auction sites have been a popular place to trade a variety of goods. By far the most popular online auction site is eBay, which was founded in 1995 and has evolved from a simple online mechanism for buying and selling collectibles to a major marketplace, where in 2001 about $9 billion worth of goods were traded. This is three times more than, for instance, the total sales of Amazon for that year. A phenomenon widely observed on eBay is the tendency of bidders to submit bids in the last seconds of bidding. (This phenomenon, called *last-minute bidding* or *sniping*, is pertinent only to eBay-style auctions, which have a predetermined deadline. Amazon-style auctions do not have a hard close. Rather, they have an automatic extension rule that allows bidding to continue if bidding activity is registered in the last ten minutes of an auction.) Explanations for the practice of last-minute bidding have fallen into two categories. One idea, advanced by Patrick Bajari and Ali Hortacsu (2003), attributes this effect to the existence of experts, who wait until the very end of the auction because they do not want to reveal their interest in the item on sale. This argument is valid for common value auctions where expert opinion matters. The late bidding phenomenon also exists in private value auctions and Roth and Axel Ockenfels (2006) provide another rationale for bidding close to an auction's end in these circumstances. Waiting until the end allows bidders to acquire an item at a lower price by preventing "bidding wars" (the successive escalation of bids). Other issues of interest to both psychologists and economists are the effect of minimum bid and secret reserve prices on bidding behavior. Bajari and Hortacsu (2004) provide an extensive review of the economic research on Internet auctions.

SEE ALSO *Economics, Experimental; Game Theory*

BIBLIOGRAPHY

Bajari, Patrick, and Ali Hortacsu. 2003. The Winner's Curse, Reserve Prices, and Endogenous Entry: Empirical Insights from eBay Auctions. *Rand Journal of Economics* 4 (2): 329–355.

Bajari, Patrick, and Ali Hortacsu. 2004. Economic Insights from Internet Auctions. *Journal of Economic Literature* 42 (2): 457–486.

Bulow, Jeremy I., and D. John Roberts. 1989. The Simple Economics of Optimal Auctions. *Journal of Political Economy* 97 (5): 1060–1090.

Cassady, Ralph, Jr. 1967. *Auctions and Auctioneering*. Berkeley: University of California Press.

Kagel, John H. 1995. Auctions: A Survey of Experimental Research. In *Handbook of Experimental Economics*, ed. John H. Kagel and Alvin E. Roth, 501–585. Princeton, NJ: Princeton University Press.

McAfee, R. Preston, and John McMillan. 1987. Auctions and Bidding. *Journal of Economic Literature* 25 (2): 699–738.

Milgrom, Paul R., and Robert J. Weber. 1982. A Theory of Auctions and Competitive Bidding. *Econometrica* 50 (5): 1089–1122.

Myerson, Roger B. 1981. Optimal Auction Design. *Mathematics of Operations Research* 6 (1): 58–73.

Roth, Alvin E. 2002. The Economist as Engineer: Game Theory, Experimentation, and Computation as Tools for Design Economics. *Econometrica* 70 (4): 1341–1378.

Roth, Alvin E., and Axel Ockenfels. 2006. Late and Multiple Bidding on Second Price Internet Auctions: Theory and Evidence Concerning Different Rules for Ending an Auction. *Games and Economic Behavior* 55 (2): 297–320.

Shubik, Martin. 1983. Auctions, Bidding, and Markets: An Historical Sketch. In *Auctions, Bidding, and Contracting: Uses and Theory*, ed. Richard Engelbrecht-Wiggans, Martin Shubik, and Robert M. Stark, 33–52. New York: New York University Press.

Vickrey, William S. 1961. Counterspeculation, Auctions, and Competitive Sealed Tenders. *Journal of Finance* 16 (1): 8–37.

Damian S. Damianov

AUDITS FOR DISCRIMINATION

An audit is a survey technique that isolates the impact of a person's group membership on the way he or she is treated in the marketplace. Audits, also called tests, first appeared in the 1950s. Since then they have been used to study racial, ethnic, or gender discrimination in car sales, hiring for entry-level jobs, home insurance quotes, preapplication treatment in the mortgage market, house sales, and apartment rentals. National audit studies of housing discrimination were conducted in the United States, for example, in 1977, 1989, and 2000, and audits have been used to help enforce civil-rights laws, particularly in the housing market.

AUDIT METHODOLOGY

In an audit study, people from two groups are selected, trained, and paired so that they are equally qualified in the market being studied. Audit teammates may be equally qualified to buy a house or a car, for example. One member of the team belongs to a legally protected minority group and the other belongs to the comparable majority group. A sampling frame, such as newspaper advertisements, is then selected; a sample is drawn; and an audit is conducted for each observation in the sample. Audit teammates paired for an observation successively visit the associated economic agent, usually in random order, to engage in the relevant market activity, such as applying for a job or inquiring about an available apartment. Each teammate then independently records how he or she was treated. Discrimination exists if minority auditors are systematically treated worse than their teammates. Most audit studies observe several types of agent behavior; discrimination may exist for some types and not for others.

Audits are an alternative to regression studies, which use statistical procedures to determine whether some economic outcome is less favorable for people in a minority group, after controlling for relevant individual characteristics. This approach leads to biased results if key characteristics are omitted from the regression. An audit study minimizes the possibility of omitted-variable bias by matching similar individuals; giving them the same training; assigning them similar or identical characteristics, such as income or education, for the purposes of the audit; and sending them to visit economic agents in response to the same advertisement within a short time of each other. These procedures ensure that audit teammates do not differ significantly in terms of any characteristic, other than group membership, that might influence their treatment in the marketplace.

Audit studies face many challenges of design and management. Researchers must decide, for example, whether audits should be "blind" in the sense that teammates are unaware of the purpose of the study or that they have a teammate. Some scholars believe that this step is needed to protect the integrity of audit results. Discriminatory treatment is sometimes so egregious, however, that it can upset auditors to the point of compromising their ability to fill out the audit survey forms. To preserve the accuracy of the audit information, therefore, it sometimes makes sense to tell auditors the purpose of the study and train them to fill in the forms as objectively as possible, no matter what happens during the audit.

Audit results must be interpreted with care. An audit study indicates the discrimination that occurs when members of a certain minority group with certain assigned traits visit a random sample of economic agents identified through a particular sampling frame. Because discrimination may not be the same under all circumstances, however, the discrimination experienced by the average member of a group may not be the same as the differential treatment of that group in an audit study. Moreover, audit studies do not provide comprehensive measures of discrimination, but instead measure discrimination only in certain types of behavior, and they may not be not feasible for complex market transactions.

Audit studies also face challenging statistical issues. Different statistical procedures are required to measure discrimination for different types of agent behavior, for example, and statistical tests need to recognize that some factors relevant to the treatment of auditors, such as the skill or mood of the agent being audited may be shared by teammates but not observed by the researcher. In addition, audit studies must recognize that people in a legally protected minority are sometimes favored, for either systematic or random reasons. This fact leads to two different measures of the incidence of discrimination, which serve as upper and lower bounds. The gross incidence of discrimination is the share of audits in which the nonminority auditor was favored. The net incidence is the gross incidence minus the share of audits in which the minority auditor was favored. The net incidence measure is accurate if all favorable treatment of minority auditors is due to random factors, so that subtracting this favorable treatment is a correction for randomness. Minority auditors might be favored for systematic reasons, however. Systematic favoring of minority auditors is troubling in its own right, of course, but it should not be subtracted from

gross incidence to determine systematic unfavorable treatment of minorities; a real estate broker who refuses to show any houses to black customers is discriminating regardless of whether or not another broker fails to show white customers any houses in black neighborhoods.

Finally, audit studies raise ethical questions because they make demands on economic agents, including many agents who do not practice discrimination. In 1982 the U.S. Supreme Court decided in *Havens Realty Corporation vs. Coleman* that housing audits are a legitimate investigative technique. Nevertheless, scholars conducting audits have a responsibility to make certain that their studies are well managed and do not make unnecessary demands on the economics agents being audited.

RESULTS FROM AUDIT STUDIES

Audit studies have uncovered racial, ethnic, and gender discrimination in several countries. Recent audits studies in the United States have found discrimination against blacks and women in car sales, against blacks and Hispanics in hiring for entry-level jobs, against women in hiring for servers at expensive restaurants, and against blacks and Hispanics in preapplication mortgage procedures. The 2000 national housing audit study found, among other things, that both blacks and Hispanics receive less information about available housing units than do non-Hispanic whites in both the sales and rental markets. In the sales market, for example, white auditors but not their black teammates were shown additional units similar to the advertised unit in 22.9 percent of the audits (gross incidence), whereas black auditors were favored over their white teammates on this measure of treatment in 16.0 percent of the audits. The difference between these measures, 6.9 percent, is the net incidence of discrimination.

Not all audit studies find discrimination, however, and some audit studies find that certain types of discrimination are declining. An audit study of the home insurance industry, for example, found no clear evidence of discrimination. Moreover, a comparison of the results of the 1989 and 2000 national housing studies reveals significant declines in many types of discrimination, including several associated with housing availability. This comparison also reveals increased discrimination against blacks and Hispanics in some other types of agent behavior, including the number of housing units shown and steering, which is defined as directing different customers to different types of neighborhoods based on their race or ethnicity. Real estate agents were more likely, for example, to steer black customers away from white neighborhoods in 2000 than in 1989.

Finally, audit studies provide some insight into the causes of discrimination. One study found, for example, that the more expensive a house, the more likely it is to be withheld from black customers. Because black and white teammates in this study had the same qualifications and made the same requests, this result suggests that some real estate brokers act on the basis of a stereotype that black households cannot afford expensive houses, rather than on the basis of a customer's stated income and wealth.

SEE ALSO *Correspondence Tests; Discrimination; Inequality, Gender; Inequality, Racial*

BIBLIOGRAPHY

Ayres, Ian, and Peter Siegelman. 1995. Race and Gender Discrimination in Bargaining for a New Car. *American Economic Review* 85 (June): 304–321.

Fix, Michael, and Raymond Struyk. 1993. *Clear and Convincing Evidence: Testing for Discrimination in America.* Washington, DC: Urban Institute.

Ondrich, Jan, Stephen Ross, and John Yinger. 2003. Now You See It, Now You Don't: Why Do Real Estate Agents Withhold Houses from Black Customers? *Review of Economics and Statistics* 85 (4): 854–873.

Riach, Peter A., and Judith Rich. 2002. Field Experiments of Discrimination in the Market Place. *Economic Journal* 112 (November): F480–F518.

Ross, Stephen L., and Margery Austin Turner. 2005. Housing Discrimination in Metropolitan America: Explaining Changes between 1989 and 2000. *Social Forces* 52 (2): 150–180.

Wissoker, Douglas A., Wendy Zimmerman, and George Galster. 1997. Testing for Discrimination in Home Insurance. Washington, DC: Urban Institute. http://www.urban.org/publications/307555.html.

Yinger, John. 1996. *Closed Doors, Opportunities Lost: The Continuing Costs of Housing Discrimination.* New York: Russell Sage Foundation.

John Yinger

AUSTRIAN ECONOMICS

Austrian economics, so named for its country of origin, is distinguished by its methodological precepts and by its theories of capital, money, and the business cycle. Carl Menger (1840–1926), who taught at the University of Vienna, is the acknowledged founder of this school of thought. Menger's writings, particularly his *Principles of Economics* (1871) and his *Investigations into the Method of the Social Sciences* (1883), set out the principles and methods that guided the development of a worldwide Austrian tradition.

Menger rejected the German historicism of Wilhelm Roscher (1817–1894), which offered an inductive approach to economic understanding; and he deviated markedly from the eighteenth-century British classicism of David Ricardo (1772–1823) and John Stuart Mill (1806–1873), which featured long-run relationships among the different economic classes of people (workers, capitalists, and landlords). Menger's theory of economic institutions does bear a striking resemblance to the invisible-hand theorizing of Adam Smith (1723–1790). However, given Smith's cost-based theory of value, the appropriateness of linking Menger and his followers to the reputed father of economic science is a contentious issue among contemporary Austrian economists.

Menger focused on the individual market participant and on his or her choices as governed by perceived needs and wants. This general approach to economics was termed *methodological individualism* by the sociologist Max Weber (1864–1920). Menger's notion of economic value derives from the purposes of the individuals doing the valuing rather than from the qualities of the objectively defined goods being valued. Menger's value theory, termed *methodological subjectivism* and now embedded (though not consistently) in modern economics, stood in contrast to Marxism's labor theory of value and classicism's cost-of-production theory of value.

Methodological individualism and the closely related methodological subjectivism allow for a straightforward accounting of the gains from trade. Individuals value various goods differently, such that trading goods allows both traders to gain. Direct exchange (goods for goods) leads quite naturally to indirect exchange (goods for more-easily-tradable goods for actually-sought-after goods). The more-easily-tradable goods are called *media of exchange.* Over time, the practice of indirect exchange gives rise to *a most commonly accepted medium of exchange.* This is Menger's theory of money—with early monies taking the forms of salt or cattle and later monies, silver or gold. (The fact that modern paper money is a result of governmental institutions overriding the would-be choices of market participants is seen as supporting Menger's theory.)

Whether exchange is direct or indirect, market values never pertain to the whole of the supply, such as the diamond supply or the water supply. Rather, they pertain to the smallest quantities of the goods subject to potential trades, that is, the marginal unit. Because of relative scarcities, the value of the marginal unit of diamonds exceeds the value of the marginal unit of water—despite water's being the more useful of the two goods. This is Menger's resolution of the so-called diamond-water paradox, which was identified by Adam Smith (who distinguished value in use from value in exchange) but not satisfactorily resolved until the "Marginalist Revolution" of the 1870s. Menger was one of three revolutionists, the others being British economist William Stanley Jevons

(1835–1882) and French economist Leon Walras (1834–1910). The latter two formulated the issues mathematically by writing the equations for total and marginal utility (Jevons) and for the equilibrium relationships among all the prices in a frictionless market economy (Walras).

Historians of economic thought sometimes see the Austrian theory as applying only to the demand side of the market—with supply and demand finally being juxtaposed by Alfred Marshall (1842–1924), who drew supply from the classicists and demand from the marginal revolutionists. But Menger applied his value theory to the means of production as well as to the ends. Consumption goods were designated as *goods of the first order*. Markets for goods of the second, third, and higher orders guide the time-consuming production activities that proceed from the highest to the lowest order. This reckoning, together with the concept of *opportunity costs* introduced by Friedrich von Wieser (1851–1926), established the Austrian supply-side relationships.

Eugen von Böhm-Bawerk (1851–1914) developed Menger's conception of the production process into a theory that he explicated in *Capital and Interest* (vol. 2, 1889). The rate of interest governs the extent to which resources can profitably be tied up in the production process: The lower the interest rate, the more roundabout, or time-consuming, the production process. Unfortunately, Böhm-Bawerk's use of a crude arithmetic reckoning of roundaboutness (the average period of production) diverted attention from the otherwise Mengerian construction and played into the hands of critics who questioned the relevance of such a metric.

In his *Theory of Money and Credit* (1912) Ludwig von Mises (1881–1973) used marginalist thinking to account for the value of money and, drawing on Böhm-Bawerk's capital theory, set out a theory of the business cycle. Interest rates held artificially low by central banks stimulate investment and cause production processes to be unduly roundabout. In the absence of sufficient resources to complete all of the production processes, the boom eventually gives way to a bust. In essence, the boom-bust cycle is an instance of economic discoordination attributable to an interest rate that does not accurately reflect the valuations and choices of market participants.

Mises systematized Austrian economics in his *Human Action* (1949), calling its method *praxeology*, which literally means "action logic." He distinguished between economics and history, denying that there is a unilateral testing of economic theory with historical data but recognizing that the two disciplines are essential complements in our understanding of real-world economies. Mises's praxeology, an exclusively deductive system of logic based on self-evident axioms (e.g., human action is purposeful),

stands in contrast to Milton Friedman's "methodology of positive economics" (1953), according to which contrary-to-fact assumptions can be used in the formulation of theory, which can then be accepted or rejected on the basis of empirical evaluation. In Mises's hard-drawn Austrianism, empirical studies serve to identify cases or episodes in which a particular theory is applicable.

In his *Prices and Production* (1935), Friedrich A. Hayek (1899–1992) developed the business-cycle theory, offering this means-ends theorizing about booms and busts as an alternative to the circular-flow theorizing of John Maynard Keynes (1883–1946). By many accounts, Hayek's theory lost out to Keynes's primarily because of its lack of politically attractive policy prescriptions. Israel M. Kirzner (b. 1930) developed the essential entrepreneurial aspects of the Austrian theory and, along with Hayek, offered a market-as-a-process view that stands in contrast with the more conventional mathematics of market equilibria. In both microeconomic and macroeconomic contexts, the Austrians have argued that governments are ill-advised to override market forces with central planning or to supplement those forces with economic stimulants. The policy prescription of laissez-faire is emphasized by Murray Rothbard (1826–1995) in his *Man, Economy, and State* (1962).

Through his introduction and selection of articles, Israel Kirzner offers, as an Austrian sampler, a three-volume *Classics in Austrian Economics* (1994). Dating from the mid-1970s, numerous books and articles have made Austrian economics a living tradition. Some developments and extensions are intended to compete with modern mainstream thinking; others to reconcile with it. In the contemporary world of economics, the Austrian principles of microeconomics (the subjectivity of value and opportunity costs) are widely accepted, although they are often observed in the breach because of considerations of mathematical tractability and data availability. By contrast, Austrian macroeconomics, which is rooted in capital theory and focuses on the allocation of resources over time, has been neither widely accepted nor well understood. Dating from the Keynesian revolution, capital theory is seen as foundational for theories of economic growth but as largely irrelevant for macroeconomics, which deals instead with overall levels of output and inflation.

SEE ALSO *Austro-Marxism; Hayek, Friedrich August; Libertarianism; Mises, Ludwig Edler von*

BIBLIOGRAPHY

Böhm-Bawerk, Eugen von. [1889] 1959. *Capital and Interest* Vol. 2: *Positive Theory of Capital*. Trans. George D. Huncke and Hans F. Sennholz. South Holland, IL: Libertarian Press.

Friedman, Milton. 1953. The Methodology of Positive Economics. In *Essays in Positive Economics*, ed. Milton Friedman, 3–43. Chicago: University of Chicago Press.

Hayek, Friedrich A. [1935] 1967. *Prices and Production*. 2nd ed. Clifton, NJ: Augustus M. Kelley.

Kirzner, Israel M. 1973. *Competition and Entrepreneurship*. Chicago: University of Chicago Press.

Kirzner, Israel M. 1994. *Classics in Austrian Economics: A Sampling in the History of a Tradition*. 3 vols. London: William Pickering.

Menger, Carl. [1871] 1981. *Principles of Economics* [*Grundsätze*]. Trans. James Dingwall and Bert F. Hoselitz. New York: New York University Press.

Menger, Carl. [1883] 1985. *Investigations into the Method of the Social Sciences with Special Reference to Economics*. Trans. Francis J. Nock. New York: New York University Press.

Mises, Ludwig von. 1949. *Human Action: A Treatise on Economics*. New Haven, CT: Yale University Press.

Rothbard, Murry N. 1962. *Man, Economy, and State*. 2 vols. Princeton, NJ: Van Nostrand.

Roger W. Garrison

AUSTRO-LIBERTARIANISM

SEE *Libertarianism.*

AUSTRO-MARXISM

The term *Austro-Marxism* was probably introduced by the American socialist Louis Boudin to characterize a specific Austrian version of Marxism. Established at the turn of the twentieth century, Austro-Marxism became a powerful political and cultural movement during the Austrian First Republic (1918–1934). For analytical purposes, Gerald Mozetič (1987) distinguishes three versions of Austro-Marxism. First, there was the political Austro-Marxism put forth by political intellectuals such as Otto Bauer, Karl Renner, Rudolf Hilferding, Max Adler, and Friedrich Adler. This version represents what might be called a third way of thinking, located between (or beyond) socialist revisionism and Leninism. It was more radical than the First Socialist International as well as more democratic (or moderate) than the Bolshevist approach to Marxism. In contrast to other Marxist conceptions, Austro-Marxism was not based on Hegelian dialectics but on two rather distinctive philosophies: the materialism of natural scientist and philosopher Ernst Mach (1838–1916), and the idealism and ethics of Immanuel Kant (1724–1804).

Second, there was Austro-Marxism as scholarship. Outside the universities that were dominated by conservatives, and even suffused with anti-Semitism, there were institutions offering extramural teaching and adult education at which a large number of socialist intellectuals were active in various academic disciplines, such as economics, law, sociology, history and, last but not least, the natural sciences. Their institutional and personal cooperation established interdisciplinary work and combined scholarship with political commitment and activism. A number of scholars and social scientists, such as Otto Neurath, Paul Lazarsfeld, and Marie Jahoda, worked in this particular context, which has been referred to as an "alternative institutionalization" of social sciences and cultural studies (cf. Sandner 2006).

Third, mention must also be made of Austro-Marxism as a way of life. Austrian socialism was organized into a number of political and cultural associations that claimed to establish within bourgeois society a counterculture based on socialist values and attitudes, such as solidarity, class consciousness, and the socialist reform of everyday life.

In a way, Austro-Marxism was the political theory of the socialist camp (in contrast to the Catholic-conservative and the pan-German camps), although not all Austrian socialists were Austro-Marxists. However, Austro-Marxism existed not only on a theoretical level; it was closely connected with the socialist counterculture in "Red Vienna" (the socialist-governed capital of Austria) between 1918 and 1934 (cf. Gruber 1991; Rabinbach 1983, 1985). In certain political fields, such as housing and adult education, its practitioners were able to bring about remarkable improvements in the social and cultural conditions of the working class.

Theoretical Austro-Marxism's rather nondeterministic and undogmatic approach enabled it to broadly partake of and to absorb modern intellectual currents—including psychoanalysis and empirical sociology—and led to a wide-ranging intellectual exchange, even among nonsocialist politicians and scholars. In actual practice, both its strict parliamentary strategy and the socialist-governed Red Vienna project worked successfully for a long period. It eventually collapsed, in contrast to other socialist-oriented experiments, through no fault of its own (i.e., undemocratic practices), under the weight of the violent policies of Austro-Fascism (1934–1938) and National Socialism (1938–1945). By the end of World War II, most of Austro-Marxism's representatives were dead, while the majority of those that emigrated did not return to Austria.

SEE ALSO *Marxism; Socialism*

BIBLIOGRAPHY

Blum, Mark E. 1985. *The Austro-Marxists, 1890–1918: A Psychobiographical Study.* Lexington: University Press of Kentucky.

Bottomore, Thomas B., and Patrick Goode, eds. 1978. *Austro-Marxism.* Oxford, U.K.: Clarendon Press.

Gruber, Helmut. 1991. *Red Vienna: Experiment in Working-Class Culture 1919–1934.* New York: Oxford University Press.

Mozetič, Gerald. 1987. *Die Gesellschaftstheorie des Austromarxismus. Geistesgeschichtliche Voraussetzungen, Methodologie und soziologisches Programm.* Darmstadt, Germany: Wissenschaftliche Buchgesellschaft.

Rabinbach, Anson. 1983. *The Crisis of Austrian Socialism: From Red Vienna to Civil War, 1927–1934.* Chicago: University of Chicago Press.

Rabinbach, Anson, ed. 1985. *The Austrian Socialist Experiment: Social Democracy and Austromarxism, 1918–1934.* Boulder, CO: Westview Press.

Sandner, Günther. 2006. *Engagierte Wissenschaft: Austromarxistische Kulturstudien und die Anfänge der britischen Cultural Studies.* Münster, Germany: Lit Verlag.

Günther Sandner

AUTHORITARIANISM

Authoritarianism is one of the three main types of political systems (or *regimes*), democracy and totalitarianism being the other two. Social science scholars have identified a number of features of authoritarianism in its *ideal type* form. The ideal criteria may not be present in practice in actually existing authoritarian systems. Rather, descriptions of the ideal type provide a measuring stick for analysts to assess how authoritarian a particular system is. Scholars also increasingly recognize a hybrid between authoritarianism and democracy as forming its own ideal type regime, generally called either *semi-authoritarian* or *semi-democratic* systems (Ottaway 2003).

DEFINING FEATURES OF AUTHORITARIANISM

Defining features of authoritarianism include the existence of a single leader or small group of leaders with ultimate political authority. Believing in the supremacy of the authority of the state over all organizations in society, authoritarian leaders make all important government policy decisions. The state's needs are paramount; individualism is encouraged only to the extent that it benefits the state. Ideal type authoritarianism lacks both official and unofficial limitations on its power, although Mark Hagopian (1984, p. 118) has argued that, in practice,

powerful social groups can maintain unofficial, "extralegal" constraints over authoritarian leaders.

Whereas totalitarianism strongly emphasizes an official and overarching ideology serving as a blueprint for the remaking of society, authoritarianism is less concerned with ideology. When authoritarian leaders come to power, they often have a set of policy goals—such as eliminating corruption or resurrecting the economy—as well as what Juan Linz (1975) calls a "mentality" about the purpose of their rule. But this is quite different from the kind of ideology present in an ideal type totalitarian system.

Authoritarian systems commonly emerge in times of political, economic, and social instability, and thus, especially during the initial period of authoritarian rule, authoritarian systems may have broad public support. The stereotype of an authoritarian leader as uniformly despised by the general population is rarely accurate. In the majority of authoritarian systems, however, these public (and publicly supported) goals take a back seat to the maintenance of the regime's power if the latter is threatened. Over time, if the government fails to achieve its policy goals, the public may withdraw its support.

Because of the government's control of the state's repressive mechanisms, declining support need not translate into popular unrest and antigovernment mobilization. Indeed, another of authoritarianism's defining features is the limiting of mass political participation. Democratic and totalitarian systems encourage the general public's political participation, although in the totalitarian case the state or ruling party controls all aspects of mass political mobilization. Authoritarian leaders typically prefer a population that is apathetic about politics, with no desire to participate in the political process. Authoritarian governments work to develop such attitudes, both by fostering a sense of a deep divide between society and government and by repressing expressions of dissent, violently if necessary. Consequently, authoritarian leaders view the rights of the individual, including those considered to be "human rights" by the international community, as subject to the needs of the government. Concern about the possible emergence of potential political opposition can become an obsession of authoritarian leaders, weakening their effectiveness as leaders and the policy performance of the government.

TYPES OF AUTHORITARIANISM

Just as social scientists identify various types of democratic systems, scholars highlight three types of authoritarianism. A *military authoritarian* system is one in which the military is not only privileged—as it typically is in all authoritarian systems—but actually in control of all major aspects of government decision-making. The rule of

Augusto Pinochet in Chile from 1973 to 1988 is the classic example of a military authoritarian regime.

In *party authoritarian* systems, on the other hand, a single political party dominates the system. Though this is also true of totalitarian systems (e.g., Stalin's USSR or Hitler's Germany), party authoritarian systems penetrate into society less than totalitarian systems. Party authoritarian systems may even tolerate small opposition parties and use mechanisms of democracy like elections in an effort to increase their legitimacy with the public. Mexico's authoritarian system prior to the reforms of the 1990s and 2000s is an example of a party authoritarian system.

Bureaucratic authoritarian systems are run by the military but rely heavily on experts in the fields of economics and other policy areas, often allowing them significant autonomy to set and oversee government policy. Social scientists often label these officials *technocrats*. Military leaders point to the technical expertise of these bureaucrats as a key component of their economic modernization policies, which are introduced under harsh authoritarian conditions to prevent opposition to economic reforms. Guillermo O'Donnell identifies Argentina from the mid-1960s to the mid-1970s as the classic example of bureaucratic authoritarianism.

SEE ALSO *Bureaucracy; Democracy; Democratization; Dictatorship; Human Rights; Leadership; Military Regimes; Oligarchy; State, The; Technocrat; Totalitarianism*

BIBLIOGRAPHY

Hagopian, Mark N. 1984. *Regimes, Movements, and Ideologies: A Comparative Introduction to Political Science.* 2nd ed. New York: Longman.

Linz, Juan J. 1975. Totalitarian and Authoritarian Regimes. In *Macropolitical Theory*, Vol. 3 of *Handbook of Political Science*, eds. Fred I. Greenstein and Nelson W. Polsby, 175–411. Reading, MA: Addison-Wesley.

O'Donnell, Guillermo A. 1973. *Modernization and Bureaucratic-Authoritarianism: Studies in South American Politics.* Berkeley: University of California, Institute of International Studies.

Ottaway, Marina. 2003. *Democracy Challenged: The Rise of Semi-Authoritarianism.* Washington, DC: Carnegie Endowment for International Peace.

Lowell W. Barrington
Anne Mozena

AUTHORITARIAN PERSONALITY

SEE *Personality, Authoritarian.*

AUTHORITATIVENESS
SEE *Parent-Child Relationships.*

AUTHORITY

In the first volume of *Economy and Society* (1978), Max Weber defines authority as the belief in the legitimacy of individuals to exercise power, such that they are able to influence others to do their will even with resistance, and a specific group will likely follow those orders.

Weber develops a schema of legitimate authority, identifying three pure forms. Legal authority, sometimes referred to as rational authority, is based on rules and laws. Under these laws, people have the right to exercise authority through the office they occupy. It is the position itself that holds authority, with obedience being owed to the office, such as chief executive officer or the presidency. The office continues to hold authority after the office-holder vacates it. Traditional authority is based on tradition or custom. Obedience is owed to individuals such as tribal leaders or kings through tradition. When the individual vacates the position, tradition determines who will fill the position. Finally, charismatic authority is based on dedication to the extraordinary personality of an individual and the standard or norm he or she establishes. Obedience is owed to the individual charismatic leader. Weber considered charismatic authority to be a revolutionary force in that it renounces tradition and submission is guaranteed through proof or the display of a miracle.

Jürgen Habermas notes the importance of discourse, or speech, as it relates to authority. Mark Warren (1995) recounts Habermas's argument that authority is created through discourse, particularly in those settings that prevent other forms of authority from intruding. Through discourse, citizens in a democracy make known the issues that concern them and are able to understand others. The result is a form of consensus by which laws are created and normative changes are instituted.

Theodor Adorno and colleagues, in *The Authoritarian Personality* (1950), notes that an individual's submission to the authority of a parent may be linked to submission to authority in general. In particular, he finds that opposition toward parents' authority is often evidenced as resistance to authority in general. As a result of this study, Adorno identified an authoritarian personality type. As James M. Henslin (2005) summarizes, this individual is highly prejudiced against minority groups, while also being highly conformist and respectful of authority.

Ralf Dahrendorf, in *Class and Class Conflict in Industrial Society* (1959), identifies authority in relation to class. One class exercises authority in industry yet may also be subject to authority from others. Others are subject to authority from supervisors but do not exercise their own authority. The classless do not exercise authority and are not subject to authority, such as independent workers. Thus, class is determined by the degree of authority one holds. Since industry plays a large role in one's life, a person's authority may be influential in other spheres, including the family.

Stanley Milgram (1974) experimentally tested individual obedience to authority. Authority is contextual in nature, meaning that a person with authority in one situation will not necessarily have the same authority in another. Authority comes from a person's power in a social situation, not from personality. In certain situations, there is an expectation that an authority will exist. The authority becomes apparent through (1) self-identification of the individual with authority; (2) external objects, such as uniforms, identifying the individual as an authority; (3) the lack of a competing authority; and (4) the lack of obvious inconsistencies. In his infamous shock experiments, Milgram found that individuals, who may have protested against the shocking of individuals, were willing to continue with the experiment when an authoritative individual encouraged them on.

Organizational theory has further developed the notion of authority. Philippe Aghion and Jean Tirole (1997) note the distinctions between formal and real authority. They define formal authority as "the right to decide" while real authority is defined as "the effective control over decisions" (p. 1) with the former not necessarily granting the latter.

SEE ALSO *Aggression; Alpha-male; Conformity; Experiments, Shock; Leadership; Legal Systems; Milgram, Stanley; Personality; Power; Social Dominance Orientation; Social Psychology; Weber, Max*

BIBLIOGRAPHY

Adorno, Theodor, Else Frenkel-Brunswik, Daniel J. Levinson, and R. Nevitt Sanford. 1950. *The Authoritarian Personality.* New York: Harper and Row.

Aghion, Philippe, and Jean Tirole. 1997. Formal and Real Authority in Organizations. *Journal of Political Economy* 105 (1): 1–29.

Dahrendorf, Ralf. 1959. *Class and Class Conflict in Industrial Society.* Stanford, CA: Stanford University Press.

Hagan, John, John Simpson, and A. R. Gillis. 1987. Class in the Household: A Power-Control Theory of Gender and Delinquency. *American Journal of Sociology* 92 (4): 788–816.

Henslin, James M. 2005. Politics. In *Sociology: A Down-to-Earth Approach,* 7th ed., 421–424. New York: Allyn and Bacon.

Henslin, James M. 2005. The Authoritarian Personality. *Sociology: A Down-to-Earth Approach,* 7th ed., 335. New York: Allyn and Bacon.

Meyer, Marshall W. 1968. The Two Authority Structures of Bureaucratic Organization. *Administrative Science Quarterly* 13 (2): 211–228.

Milgram, Stanley. 1974. *Obedience to Authority: An Experimental View.* New York: Harper and Row.

Presthus, Robert V. 1960. Authority in Organizations. *Public Administration Review* 20 (2): 86–91.

Robinson, Robert V., and Jonathan Kelley. 1979. Class as Conceived by Marx and Dahrendorf: Effects on Income Inequality and Politics in the United States and Great Britain. *American Sociological Review* 44 (1): 38–58.

Warren, Mark E. 1995. The Self in Discursive Democracy. In *The Cambridge Companion to Habermas,* ed. Stephen K. White, 167–200. New York: Cambridge University Press.

Weber, Max. 1947. *The Theory of Social and Economic Organization.* Trans. A. M. Henderson and Talcott Parsons. New York: Oxford University Press.

Weber, Max. 1978. *Economy and Society: An Outline of Interpretive Sociology,* eds. Guenther Roth and Claus Wittich. 2 vols. Los Angeles: University of California Press.

Gabriela Guazzo

AUTISM
SEE *Theory of Mind.*

AUTOCORRELATION
SEE *Serial Correlation.*

AUTOCORRELATION FUNCTION
SEE *Time Series Regression.*

AUTOCRACY

From the Greek word *autokratôr* meaning self-ruler, or ruler of oneself, the term *autocracy* refers to one-person rule, or a government led by a single person with unlimited power. The autocrat has uncontrolled and undisputed authority over the people and others in the government, controlling all aspects of social, economic, and political life. Autocracies come in two forms: an inherited autocracy is also referred to as a monarchy while a nonheredity autocracy is a dictatorship. Autocracy is often used interchangeably with the terms despotism, tyranny, and dictatorship.

Autocracies did not develop in a formal way until the emergence of the state. Human culture has experienced four basic political organizations: bands, tribes, chiefdoms, and states. Band societies are characterized by being nonstratified, essentially egalitarian, kin-based groups whose leadership is based on ability. They are highly local and, because they are kin-based, have very small membership groups. Decision-making in band society is typically done by consensus, meaning that members of the group discuss an issue until everyone agrees on a particular course of action. Tribes are larger, more regionalized groups that share many of the characteristics of bands with the exception of size. As regionalized groups, tribes are linked together and often act together in times of conflict or need. Chiefdoms and states, unlike bands and tribes, are hierarchical or stratified. The head of state or chief rules by the power of their office and can command armies and exact tribute (taxes are a form of tribute). The difference between chiefdoms and states is that chiefdoms are kin-based while states are bureaucracies. Bureaucracies are formalized public bodies that perform particular tasks such as law-making. Chiefdoms and states have large memberships and leaders may not have direct contact with most of their followers or members. Members may also have no authority in choosing those who are in positions of leadership. This is generally the case with an autocratic form of government.

In Roman times the terms *imperator, Caesar,* and *Augustus* were used to signify an autocratic form of government. *Autokratôr* was often used in place of *imperator.* Perhaps the best example historically of an autocracy would be the Russian Czarist (Tsarist) system of government. The czars were referred to as *Imperator i Samodyerzhets Vserossiysky,* which translates as "all-Russian emperor and autocrat." Late-twentieth-century forms of autocratic rule (though often challenged by subjects) include the government of Saddam Hussein in Iraq. Hussein, a member of the Ba'ath party, often ruled Iraq through intimidation and acts considered to be crimes against humanity. Because of this, many people in Iraq lived in fear, many were executed and murdered, and many others rose to positions of power within his government. This contrasts with other forms of government such as democracies in which leadership is decided by the people and where there are clear limits on the power of the chief executive and members of the government. The United States is technically a democracy, but is administered as a republic, wherein representatives are elected to serve the people in the House of Representatives and the Senate. There are three branches of government: the executive branch (president and the cabinet), the judicial (Supreme Court and federal court system), and the legislative (House and Senate). This configuration is designed to prevent any single branch of government from wielding too much power, including that of the executive branch and the president. Despite this, the president holds the power of veto, wherein decisions of the other branches may be overruled, and the president may also make decisions in times of emergency without consultation with or support from the other branches of government. Ultimately, this power could lead to autocratic-like authority. In the twenty-first-century United States, President George W. Bush has been compared to an autocrat in some of his decisions regarding the Iraq War, the imposition of a democratic-style government in Iraq, and in his relationship with the other branches of government in the United States.

BIBLIOGRAPHY

Lincoln, W. Bruce. 1990. *The Great Reforms: Autocracy, Bureaucracy, and the Politics of Change in Imperial Russia.* DeKalb, IL: Northern Illinois University Press.

MacKay, Sandra. 2003. *The Reckoning: Iraq and the Legacy of Saddam Hussein.* New York: W.W. Norton.

McDaniel, Tim. 1988. *Autocracy, Capitalism and Revolution in Russia.* Berkeley: University of California Press.

McDaniel, Tim. 1991. *Autocracy, Modernization and Revolution in Russia and Iran.* Berkeley: University of California Press.

Rotberg, Robert I. 2001. *Ending Autocracy, Enabling Democracy: The Tribulations of Africa.* NY: World Peace Foundation.

Kelli Ann Costa

AUTOKINETIC EFFECT

The autokinetic effect is an optical illusion. It occurs when a perceiver staring at a stationary pinpoint of light in an otherwise completely dark visual field believes that the light moves from its fixed position. This "self-motion" (auto-kinetic) is caused, in part, by the nearly imperceptible movements of the eye known as saccades. Ordinarily the visual system compensates for these naturally occurring motions of the eye, but when only a single light is visible with no frame of reference, the light appears to wander in unpredictable directions and at variable speeds. This illusion was first noted by astronomers when viewing a single star on a very dark night.

Muzafer Sherif made use of the autokinetic effect in his 1936 studies of the development of social norms. Norms provide individuals with frames of reference that guide their thoughts, emotions, and actions in social situations. Individuals sometimes conform to others' responses deliberately, but norms also emerge spontaneously in ambiguous settings as people gradually align their behaviors until consensus in actions emerges. Sherif examined this process by asking men seated in an otherwise completely dark room to state aloud their estimates of the distance a tiny dot of light moved. Individuals who made judgments alone came to fix their estimates within a specific range, which varied from one to ten inches. When people made their judgments with other people, however, their personal estimates converged with those of other group members until a consensus was reached. The men eventually accepted a socially shared estimate in place of their own idiosyncratic standard. Moreover, in subsequent individual sessions subjects still relied on the group's standard, suggesting that they had internalized the norm. Sherif, by capitalizing on the natural ambiguity of the autokinetic situation, succeeded in creating a social norm in an experimental setting.

Sherif's procedures provided a paradigm for subsequent studies of social influence, such as Solomon Asch's (1907–1996) 1955 discovery that individuals sometimes conform to a group's decision even when they know that others' judgments are biased or in error. Subsequent studies also confirmed that once norms develop they become stable frames of reference that resist change. When an individual with extreme judgments joined the group, other group members' judgments shifted so that a more extreme norm formed. Once this arbitrary standard was created a new member took the place of the source of the norm. The group continued to base its judgments on the group norm, however, and the newest member gradually adapted to the higher standard. As members were replaced with naive subjects, the new initiates continued to shift their estimates to match the group norm. The arbitrary norm eventually disappeared, but not before the group's composition changed many times. This finding shows how norms, once they are established, can become part of the group's social structure. Even when individuals who fostered the norm are no longer present, their normative innovations remain a part of the organization's traditions, and newcomers change to adopt that tradition.

SEE ALSO *Asch, Solomon; Norms; Sherif, Muzafer; Social Psychology*

BIBLIOGRAPHY

Asch, Solomon E. 1955. Opinions and Social Pressures. *Scientific American* 193 (5): 31–35.

Sherif, Muzafer. 1936. *The Psychology of Social Norms*. New York: Harper and Row.

Donelson R. Forsyth

AUTOMOBILE INDUSTRY

The turn of the twentieth century witnessed the dawning of the automobile industry. Tinkering by bicycle, motorcycle, buggy, and machinery entrepreneurs in Europe and the United States led to the first prototypes of automobiles in the late nineteenth century. French woodworking machinery makers Rene Panhard and Emile Levassor built their first car in 1890 with an engine designed in Germany by Gottlieb Daimler and Wilhelm Maybach. Armand Peugeot, a French bicycle maker, licensed the same engine and sold his first four lightweight cars in 1891. German machinist Carl Benz followed the next year with his four-wheeled car and in 1893 Charles and Frank Duryea built the first gasoline-powered car in the United States. Ransom Olds is credited as the first mass producer of gasoline-powered automobiles in the United States, making 425 "Curved Dash Olds" in 1901. The first gasoline-powered Japanese car was made in 1907 by Komanosuke Uchiyama, but it was not until 1914 that Mitsubishi mass-produced cars in Japan.

Each region in the triad—North America, Europe, and Asia—has made significant contributions to process, product, and organization throughout the twentieth century. These innovations together have shaped the competitive structure of the automotive industry that exists today. The organization of production inputs—such as labor and suppliers of components and materials—as well as the configuration of distribution channels are also important dimensions of the growth and evolution of the industry. Furthermore, various forces outside the industry shape industry structure and strategies: trade flows; regional and international movement of capital; regional and global policies on trade, environmental regulation, and intellectual property, particularly in emerging economies; and the infusion of information technology throughout the procurement, production, and distribution systems.

The automotive industry is dynamic and vast, accounting for approximately one in ten jobs in industrialized countries. Developing countries often look to their local automotive sector for economic growth opportunities, particularly because of the vast linkages that the auto industry has to other sectors of their economy.

MODERN ECONOMIC ORIGINS OF THE AUTOMOBILE INDUSTRY

The auto industry has passed through several stages: (1) craft production (1890–1908), in which dozens of small enterprises vied to establish a standard product and process; (2) mass production (1908–1973), precipitated by Henry Ford's moving assembly lines, which became the standard operating mechanism of the industry; and (3) lean production (1973–present), which was initially developed at Toyota under the leadership of Taichi Ohno during the 1950s, and which introduced a revolutionary management process of product-development and production.

Mechanization of auto production has also been transformed over the past century, led by the need for faster and lower-cost production on the supply side of the industry. Ford's mass-production system relied on standardized designs to enable the construction of assembly plants that were fully automated and utilized interchangeable auto parts. In its heyday, between 1908 and 1920, Ford streamlined the assembly process to the point where it took just over an hour and a half to produce one car. Setting the industry standard for production enabled Ford to take the lead in market share, but it also led to a complacent mindset that hindered innovation. In the 1920s General Motors improved on Ford's assembly line process by introducing flexibility into the production system, enabling faster changeovers from one model to the next. However, it took half a century after Ford stopped mass producing Model T's in 1927 for another production paradigm to emerge as the standard in the global automotive industry. Toyota's lean production system—which had its beginnings in 1953—drove productivity to new heights by replacing the "push" system with a "pull" system. Instead of producing mass quantities of vehicles and pushing them through to dealerships to sell to customers or hold as inventories, the lean system pulled vehicles through the production process based on immediate demand, minimizing inventories at suppliers, assemblers, and dealerships. Just-in-time production also gave a larger responsibility for product design, quality, and delivery to assembly workers and suppliers than did the mass-production system. Suppliers were not vertically integrated into auto assembler operations, but rather networked to the assemblers via long-term contracts. This total system of cost-minimization and responsiveness to customer demands revolutionized auto manufacturing on a global scale, although the model has been adapted to regional conditions.

Product innovation in the automotive industry has mainly been a response to customer demands, although product positioning is a critical strategic variable for automakers. Ever since General Motors began producing different types of vehicles for different product segments, thereby ending the reign of Ford's low-price, monochromatic Model T, the ability to vary products on several dimensions has been the main strategic variable of auto producers. U.S. automakers have mainly been responsive to customers' desires for comfort, speed, and safety, and have developed rugged drive trains, plush suspensions and interiors, and stylish chassis and bodies. In contrast, European auto producers have focused their attentions on performance and agility features of vehicles, such as steel-belted radial tires, disc brakes, fuel injection, and turbo diesel engines. For Japanese producers, the miniaturization culture and the scarcity of fuel, materials, and space largely determine the specifications of cars.

Organizational innovations have also occurred over the past century. In concert with the introduction of mass production techniques came the vertical organization of production processes. Auto assemblers internalized the production of critical components in an effort to minimize transaction costs associated with late deliveries and products that were not produced to exact specifications. For example, the share of components purchased from outside suppliers relative to the wholesale price of an American car dropped from 55 percent in 1922 to 26 percent in 1926. During the Great Depression, this propensity to internalize production eased, with suppliers gaining independence and importance in the replacement parts market. Automakers found that a highly vertical organizational structure did not permit the flexibility in operations necessary for product innovation. In the 1930s, Ford's vertically integrated and centrally controlled organizational structure gave way to the multidivisional organizational structure that was implemented by Alfred Sloan at General Motors Corporation (GM). Sloan's decentralized configuration of GM fostered an independent environment for the development, production, and sales of a wide variety of vehicles. With the lean production revolution came the introduction of organizational reform referred to as the *extended enterprise system*. Although Japanese auto manufacturers established and diffused efficient mechanisms of supply chain management throughout the industry, Chrysler Corporation is credited with successfully implementing these innovations in the American venue.

COMPETITIVE STRUCTURE

Rivalry among assemblers in the automotive industry, once contained within national boundaries, has evolved into global competition. First movers established market dominance in the early 1900s, and their brands are still the most recognized by consumers today. The fact that auto producers choose market strategies based on what their rivals are doing indicates that this is an oligopolistic industry. What is interesting here is that market leadership remains dynamic: It is not a given that General Motors or Toyota or DaimlerChrysler will be the market leader of tomorrow.

Before industry standards for products and production were established, hundreds of automakers existed, each vying to establish a beachhead in the industry. In the United States, for example, the year 1909 saw the largest number of automakers in operation in a given year—272 companies. It is estimated that in the first twenty years of the industry's existence, over five hundred firms entered the industry in the United States alone. The 1920s brought a wave of precipitous exits by auto manufacturers, with many firms merging into more profitable companies. In the 1930s General Motors became the market leader, with Ford slipping to second place because of a yearlong changeover in production from the Model T to the Model A. By 1937 General Motors, Ford, and Chrysler—long referred to as the Big Three—had 90 percent of total sales in the U.S. market, forming a dominant-firm oligopoly (General Motors accounted for 44.8%, Chrysler 25%, and Ford 20.5%). By the 1960s, only seven domestic auto producers remained.

In the late 1990s Japanese auto manufacturers took over more than a quarter of the U.S. market, and Big Three market share slipped below 70 percent. Today, there are only two-and-a-half U.S. automakers—General Motors, Ford, and DaimlerChrysler—collectively capturing 58.7 percent of the U.S. market. GM still has the largest share of the U.S. market (27.3%), but Toyota's market share in the United States is just one percentage point below Chrysler's (13%). Worldwide, market concentration has also been declining since the mid-1980s, with entrants such as Hyundai/Kia diluting the collective market share held by dominant automakers.

Market rivalry in the auto industry centers on two strategic variables: (1) product variety and quality, and (2) transactions price, which is manipulated to boost sales. The tension between shareholder concerns about short-term profitability and a company's desire for long-term viability is palpable. Automakers must attract and maintain a solid customer base, building allegiance to brand name in an effort to maximize earnings in the long term. Maintaining high customer repurchase rates is critical to long-term profitability in the industry. Therefore, automakers attempt to attract and keep customers from the purchase of their first car in their late teens until retirement and thereafter. Product variety at all of the major automakers spans the full spectrum from small to full-sized cars, although some automakers are better known in particular market niches. For example, Mercedes, BMW, Lexus, Infiniti, and Acura capture a third of the upscale market in the United States, whereas Buick, Ford, Mercury, and Toyota are known for their family-styled traditional cars. Turnkey reliability is the hallmark of Japanese makes, whereas Ford, Chevrolet, and Toyota appeal to buyers of small or sporty vehicles. The fastest growing market segment in the United States in recent years has been sport utility vehicles (SUVs). By the early 2000s, SUVs captured 55 percent of vehicle sales.

Auto producers have used various means to develop a full line of product offerings for a broad spectrum of customers. For example, GM has historically used acquisition or shareholdings to offer a variety of brands—including Chevrolet, Oldsmobile, Pontiac, Buick, GMC, and Cadillac. In the late 1970s, GM purchased shares in Suzuki and Isuzu subcompacts and imported those vehicles, in part to satisfy Corporate Average Fuel Efficiency requirements. In recent years, Ford-Mercury-Lincoln has also diversified its portfolio by acquiring Volvo and Jaguar. Toyota, Honda, and Nissan initiated a clever marketing ploy in the 1980s aimed at selling luxury vehicles in the United States: They named their luxury brands Lexus, Acura, and Infiniti, respectively, even though these cars are built on the same platforms as their other vehicles.

Product quality has been converging over time. As recently as 1998, European and Japanese makes had fewer vehicle defects than average for cars in their first few months on the road, whereas U.S. and Korean cars had more defects than average. By 2004 vehicles from all four regions were within ten defects per hundred vehicles of the average, which had fallen from 176 to 119 defects per hundred vehicles. Interestingly, both the Japanese and the South Korean newcomers outperformed U.S. and European vehicles on this quality scale.

To attract customers to a brand, small cars are at times used as a loss leader; that is, a firm will sell their low-end vehicle at a price below invoice, while recuperating large returns on SUVs, luxury brands, and specialty cars. Another pricing strategy that is often used by automakers to clear inventories and to get the customer in the door is discounting. At particular times of the model year (which typically begins in October and ends in September of the following year) direct assembler-to-customer discounts as well as dealer-to-customer discounts are used to adjust transaction prices to ebbs and flows in demand. If the revolutionary pull system becomes pervasive in the auto industry, the need to manage inventories through end-of-model-year discounting could become obsolete. However, product positioning will continue to be an important competitive variable for automakers because demographic attributes drive the needs and desires of customers.

Automotive suppliers have been gaining global importance in the automotive industry, taking on the primary responsibility for product development, engineering, and manufacturing for some critical systems in the automobile. In its initial stage of development, the auto industry was comprised of auto assemblers that integrated parts production into the enterprise. Independent auto parts producers mainly supplied aftermarket parts. Throughout the twentieth century, this vertically integrated structure within assemblers has been replaced by a more network-oriented tiering structure. Here, assemblers coordinate design and production efforts with premier first-tier suppliers, while these suppliers are responsible for global coordination of the supply of their subassemblies and for the coordination of production by sub-tier parts manufacturers. Thus, first-tier suppliers have been rivaling automakers in market power and in share of value added to any given vehicle. While it seems unlikely at this time that such suppliers will evolve into complete vehicle manufacturers, the profit generated by the sale of a vehicle is shifting toward the supplier and away from the traditional assembler. Automakers, therefore, face stiff rivalry both from other automakers and from dominant suppliers. Only a select few suppliers have achieved "true global competency" in the production of automotive systems, but the industry trend is pointing in this direction. The "Intel Inside" phenomenon seen with computers—in which the supplier's brand identity is critical for the sale of the final product—has not yet taken over the automotive industry, although "Hemi Inside" could be an emerging example.

As manufacturing momentum shifted toward auto parts suppliers, so too did the share of labor. Since the early 1960s, total employment in the U.S. auto industry has ranged between 700,000 and just over 1 million workers. Up until the mid-1980s, auto assemblers employed the majority of those workers, but from then on the employment share for automotive parts suppliers in the United States has consistently been greater than the share of workers at assembly plants. Between 1987 and 2002, the share of automotive sector employment at assembly plants declined from 44 percent to 36 percent, whereas the share of workers at automotive suppliers increased from 46 percent to 54 percent. Add to this change the influx of mostly non-unionized automotive transplants (foreign suppliers and assemblers), the outsourcing of parts and assembly to foreign nations, and the general sectoral shift away from manufacturing toward the service sector, and it is clear that the 1980s marked a turning point for labor in the U.S. auto industry.

Labor unions that represent autoworkers in the United States have had to weather a myriad of undulations in domestic business cycles since 1935, when the United Auto Workers (UAW) was founded. (Other unions that represent auto workers in the United States include the International Association of Machinists and Aerospace Workers of America, the United Steelworkers of America, and the International Brotherhood of Electrical Workers.) Recent changes in the organization of the auto industry and in the ownership of domestic firms, however, present uniquely formidable challenges to union strength. First, the implementation of lean manufacturing techniques and the drive to achieve globally competitive prices, quality, and delivery standards is likely to precipitate job cuts as suppliers strive to increase productivity. Second, only a few automotive transplants in the United States allow union status—namely, NUMMI (GM-Toyota), Diamond Star (Chrysler-Mitsubishi), and Auto Alliance (Ford-Mazda), all of which are joint ventures with U.S. companies. Yet, total transplant employment is rising: Between 1993 and 2003 employment at transplants in the United States rose from 58,840 to 93,408. The UAW continues to strive to organize labor at transplants and is targeting supplier parks near unionized assemblers in an attempt to maintain locational control. Third, outsourcing of production in a continuously globalizing industry diminishes the bargaining power of unions not just in the United States, but in Europe as well. Fourth, auto assemblers and suppliers are increasing their utilization of temporary workers. In Germany, BMW has a pool of temporary workers that can be utilized at different factories as needed, and in the United States auto assemblers are increasingly employing contract workers to reduce costs.

The globalization of the auto industry appears to challenge the status quo for labor in traditional regions of vehicle production. As employment in the industry shifts toward the supplier sector and toward emerging economies, the attempt to maintain good wages at traditional plants is paramount for autoworkers. Total hourly labor cost at GM and Ford for 2005 was estimated at $65.90, with $35.36 in wages and $30.54 in benefits, healthcare, and retirement costs. Other estimates for 2004 show earnings of production workers at assembly plants at $1,217 per week, whereas workers at parts plants earn $872 weekly, and workers in all manufacturing industries make an average of $529 per week. Autoworkers—particularly those who work in assembly plants in developed countries—certainly have a great deal at stake as the industry continues to globalize.

By contrast to labor, the power that dealerships exert on assemblers has historically been minimal. The push system of production meant that dealerships were the repositories for the inventory overruns of auto assemblers. Also, up until the 1960s, dealerships could legally be controlled by automakers. Therefore, auto dealers earn the majority of their profits from aftermarket sales of parts, accessories, supplies, and service, all of which are a small portion of their business. With the movement toward a pull system of production, dealerships could play a more important role in the automotive industry. However, the countervailing threat to dealerships is Internet-based sales, an innovation that stands to mitigate the market power of dealerships vis-à-vis auto assemblers.

MAJOR COUNTRIES OF PRODUCTION AND CONSUMPTION

The Worldwide Big Three automakers are General Motors, Toyota Motor Corporation, and Ford Motor Company. In 2004 these companies had worldwide market shares of 13 percent, 11 percent, and 10 percent, respectively, and production shares that closely mirrored these numbers. Interestingly, the geocenter of automotive production is the Asia-Pacific region, with over 23 million units produced in 2004. Japan was the dominant producer, with China a distant second at half of Japan's output that year. Western Europe and North America ranked a distant second and third in worldwide production, respectively, producing between 16 and 17 million vehicles in 2004. Germany is the dominant producer in western Europe, while the United States produces the lion's share of vehicles in North America.

The biggest consumers of vehicles are North Americans, with Asian Pacific and western European customers a close second and third. Although per-capita ownership of vehicles in China is very small (1.5 vehicles per 100 households compared to 50 vehicles per 100 households in Japan in 2001), the number of vehicles sold in China in 2004 fell only a few hundred thousand short of vehicle sales in Japan. In addition, the growth rate of sales in Japan between 2003 and 2004 was a sparse 0.1 percent, whereas China experienced a 17.2 percent growth in vehicle sales during that period. The other countries with over a million in vehicle sales per year that also had double-digit growth in vehicle sales in 2004 were Russia (24 percent), India (18.2%), Brazil (17%), Mexico (11.8%), and Spain (10.2%). Market opportunities in these countries are highly dependent on macroeconomic performance and policies. Hence, automakers pursue a portfolio approach to production and marketing, given the fragility of economic growth in these regions.

Since the 1960s, auto analysts have looked to a few regions for sources of new productive capacity: Eastern Europe, Latin America, India, and China. By 1980, however, the eastern European motor industry had stagnated and during the 1980s severe economic and political turmoil caused halting growth in the Latin American automotive sectors. In the 1990s liberalization of trade and investment policies gradually emerged in India and China. Today, China has captured attention as the location for new automotive productive capacity. Beginning with Volkswagen's investment in 1985, all of the major automakers have established productive capacity in China through joint-venture relationships with local automakers.

In the mid 1970s passenger car production was practically nonexistent in China. Thirty years later, sales and profit rates had soared, although capacity utilization is low (between 50% and 60%) and inventories are high relative to their Japanese, European, and U.S. competitors. If China continues on its pathway from centrally planned economy to modest marketization, and continues to become more fully integrated into the global economy,

then its domestic automotive industry will most likely steadily expand.

IMPORTANCE OF THE INDUSTRY FOR MACROECONOMIC ACTIVITY AND INTERNATIONAL TRADE

The automotive industry is an important sector of the overall economy, particularly in industrialized countries. For example, the automobile is second only to a house in purchase value for the average American household. The average manufacturing job in the automotive sector pays 60 percent more than the average U.S. job. It is estimated that the industry generates 10.4 jobs for every worker directly employed in automotive manufacturing and support services (excluding auto dealers) in the United States. Employment spillovers are seen in manufacturing and nonmanufacturing industries, including retail trade and services. In 2000 motor vehicles and equipment (assemblers and suppliers) expenditures on research and development (R&D) outpaced R&D spending in many of the thirty-nine largest industry groups, including pharmaceuticals and medicines, semiconductors and other electronic components, communications equipment, and computers and peripheral equipment.

Motor vehicles are also a major component of international trade and foreign direct investment between countries. In 2000 the share of automotive products in world trade was 9.4 percent, unchanged from its share a decade earlier. Western Europe, North America, and Asia in declining order are the global leaders in exports and imports. While western Europe and Asia are net exporters of vehicles, North American imports far outpace exports. In North America, exports have remained relatively flat since the 1980s, whereas imports have ratcheted up. North America, eastern Europe, the Middle East, and Africa are all net importers of automotive products. Intraregional trade figures show that intra–western European trade was the largest in value at almost US$200 billion that year, intra–North American trade was second at US$87.7 billion, and intra-Asian trade was the lowest at US$19.6 billion. Interestingly, intra–North American trade declined by 10 percent compared to 1990. The fastest growing region-to-region trade was North America's trade with its European and Latin American partners.

From time to time barriers have been erected around the globe to protect local automotive sectors. For example, over the past twenty years, countries in North America and Europe have erected tariff and non-tariff barriers specifically applied to trade in automobiles. Between 1981 and 1988, the United States and Japan "voluntarily" agreed on a fixed number of vehicle units that Japan would export to the United States. The European Union and Japan also entered a voluntary export agreement (VER) between 1990 and 1999, as Japanese imports to Europe began to surge. In both cases, the VERs were partly responsible for an increase in transplant production, as Japanese auto producers jumped over the trade barriers to erect manufacturing plants in the United States and Europe. Although the transplants have become a critical component of the local manufacturing landscape, the jobs and exports that they generate are weighted against their dampening effect on wages and the costs that some local governments incur to attract foreign firms to their region.

In developing countries, trade and investment restrictions in the automotive sector take the form of local content rules, tariffs, and quotas. The impetus behind these protectionist measures is to give local producers a chance to develop before they face competition from world-class auto producers that are more productive and therefore have lower unit costs. In recent decades, regional trade pacts have been implemented that liberalize many of these local content, investment, and trade restrictions. The North American Free Trade Agreement (NAFTA), which was implemented in 1994, is one significant example. When the United States and Canada included Mexico in their free trade pact on trade in automobiles and parts, Mexico reduced tariffs for its northern partners and lifted restrictions on local investment for all foreign companies, allowing domestic status for transplant operations.

One of the critical determinants of the location of assembly plants and their related suppliers is production cost. Production costs and market opportunities are the primary reasons why jobs are shifting away from the traditional geographic centers of vehicle production. At the same time, implementation of the lean production paradigm is shifting the operational center of vehicle production toward first-tier suppliers with global capabilities. Variable costs of production—costs that depend on the number of vehicles produced—include expenditures on materials and labor. In the automotive industry, material costs range between 22 and 50 percent, whereas labor costs range from 10 to 20 percent. Because these costs vary by region and product produced, auto assemblers and suppliers are actively engaged in assessments and adjustment processes that lead to changes in the configuration and operations of their plants. Yet, the evolution of North American, European, Asian, and South American trading blocs has significant implications for the geographic configuration of production and trade flows. While it remains an important factor, comparative advantage is not the sole determinant of trade patterns in the automotive industry.

CHANGES AND CHALLENGES IN THE AUTOMOBILE INDUSTRY

Auto industry analysts anticipate major organizational and geographical changes in the global auto industry in response to innovations in auto-manufacturing techniques, reconfigurations in the loci of demand for vehicles, and growing environmental concerns. A new model of labor utilization will develop as suppliers and automakers adjust to flexible manufacturing practices and the globalization of their operations.

As of 2007, overcapacity in the global automotive industry is estimated at 20 million units, which is approximately one-third of global annual production or the productive capacity of the western European automakers. With minimum efficient scale of production at an assembly plant estimated at 200,000 vehicles, dozens of assembly plants are likely to close as automakers strive to improve their profitability. Capacity unitization of about 75 percent is the tipping point below which automakers are in jeopardy of experiencing financial losses.

Overcapacity, therefore, has triggered mergers, acquisitions, and network alliances. Auto companies are consolidating and simplifying control and development functions, and attempting to minimize new investment initiatives, the number of unique parts in their vehicles, the number of design and production tools used, the number of components made in-house, and the number of direct supplier relationships. Assemblers are also utilizing modularization to simplify final assembly processes, and they are experimenting with various organizational designs as part of the restructuring process. Automakers and parts suppliers are utilizing vertical and horizontal strategic alliances with the expectation that they will facilitate the development of new products and the spread of automotive productive capacity to new geographic regions. These ventures, however, will also create new competitors, particularly in emerging economies.

However, consolidation has not proven to be a panacea for optimizing productive capacity in the industry. Mergers have typically occurred between companies that have complementary product lines and therefore the opportunities for retiring some plants are diminished. Effective rationalization brings job losses. Yet mergers between companies from different countries (such as Germany's Daimler-Benz and Chrysler in the United States) have not typically brought capacity reduction, because political forces strive to maintain domestic jobs.

Analysts anticipate that production will shift away from traditional regions in North America, Europe, and East Asia to Brazil, China, India, and countries in Southeast Asia. Trade liberalization will facilitate this geographical shift in production, as well as increased *commonilization*—the sharing of principal components and platforms—although consumer tastes will militate against the full introduction of a homogeneous "world car" from each automaker. Commonilization—coupled with the differentiation of products based on regional tastes—is already practiced by Ford and Honda, and other automakers are also adopting this practice. There is no clear evidence, however, that automakers are converging on one comprehensive paradigm of production.

Economic growth in East and South Asia is also expected to influence the locational decisions of auto producers. For example, economic and political developments in China during the past decade have had considerable influences on global sourcing and production decisions of German, American, and Japanese automakers. Growing disposable income among middle- and upper-income citizens, burgeoning industrial development in coastal regions, and the periodic liberalization of personal finance markets are driving demand for passenger cars and commercial vehicles in China. Given these trends and the size of the market, automakers anticipate good returns from their productive capacity in the Far East. Yet, exuberance over the potentially hot auto market in China is tamed from time to time by the prospect that the underpinnings of that market rests importantly on government fiat.

The automobile industry will also need to continue to address a range of environmental concerns related to carbon dioxide levels and other health risks. While estimates vary widely as to the impact that vehicle emissions have on the global environment, automakers have made emissions and safety adjustments to their automobiles over time. In the United States, rules and guidelines that originated in the 1970s—such as the Corporate Average Fuel Efficiency Standards (CAFE) and federal safety regulations—have brought about significant emission reductions. Thirty years since CAFE standards were put in place, new cars in the United States emit approximately 1 percent of the smog-producing compounds emitted by new cars in the 1970s. This progress is not solely the result of government regulations, however. The Alliance of Automobile Manufacturers—a trade association of nine automakers from the United States, Germany, and Japan—has identified clean energy technologies as a means to further economic growth in the industry. It is important to note, however, that increased use of vehicles and persistent use of vehicles with old technology mitigate some of these important strides.

Automakers around the globe are also engaged in developing new technologies and products, such as electronic fuel cells, navigational systems that manage congestion problems, and "telematics" (telecommunications capabilities). Information technology networks will be fully integrated into the R&D, procurement, manufacturing, and distribution functions of the enterprise structure. The Internet and Web-based communications are expected to drive the next transformation in the automobile industry. The next frontier in distribution channels is fully to implement a build-to-order system. While dealerships might not become obsolete, the efficiency of the pull system will reduce their inventories and associated costs. Implementing a system similar to the Dell Direct model could mean significant cost reductions in the distribution and purchasing functions of firms in the industry.

SEE ALSO *Ford Motor Company; General Motors*

BIBLIOGRAPHY

Automotive News. 2005. *Automotive News Market Data Book 2005.* http://www.autonews.com.

Boyer, Robert, Elsie Charron, Ulrich Jürgens, and Steven Tolliday, eds. 1998. *Between Imitation and Innovation: The Transfer and Hybridization of Productive Models in the International Automobile Industry.* Oxford: Oxford University Press.

Dassbach, Carl H. A. 1994. Where Is North American Automobile Production Headed? Low-Wage Lean Production. *Electronic Journal of Sociology* 1 (1). http://www.sociology.org/content/vol001.001/dassbach.html.

Easterbrook, Gregg. 2006. Case Closed: The Debate about Global Warming Is Over. *Governance Studies* 3 (June). Brookings Institution Working Paper. Washington, DC: Brookings Institution.

Federal Trade Commission. 1939. Part 1. General Investigations: Motor-Vehicle Industry. *Annual Report of the Federal Trade Commission.* Washington, DC: Federal Trade Commission/Government Printing Office.

Fine, Charles H., and Daniel M. G. Raff. 2000. Internet-Driven Innovation and Economic Performance in the American Automobile Industry. MIT Sloan School of Management and International Motor Vehicle Program Working Paper. Cambridge, MA: IMVP/MIT Press.

Fine, Charles H., and Daniel M. G. Raff. 2001. Innovation and Economic Performance in the Automobile Industry over the Long Twentieth Century. In *Technological Innovation and Economic Performance*, eds. Benn Steil, David G. Victor, and Richard R. Nelson, 416–432. Princeton, NJ: Princeton University Press.

Freyssenet, Michel, and Yannick Lung. 2000. Between Globalization and Regionalization: What Is the Future of the Automobile Industry? In *Global Strategies and Local Realities: The Auto Industry in Emerging Markets*, eds. John Humphrey, Yveline Lecler, and Mario Sergio Salerno, 72–94. New York: St. Martin's Press.

Freyssenet, Michel, Andrew Mair, Koichi Shimizu, and Giuseppe Volpato, eds. 1998. *One Best Way? Trajectories and Industrial Models of the World's Automobile Producers.* Oxford: Oxford University Press.

Freyssenet, Michel, Koichi Shimizu, and Giuseppe Volpato, eds. 2003. *Globalization or Regionalization of the American and Asian Car Industry?* New York: Palgrave-Macmillan.

Fulton, George A., Donald R. Grimes, Lucie G. Schmidt, et al. 2001. *Contribution of the Automotive Industry to the U.S. Economy in 1998: The Nation and Its Fifty States*. Prepared by the Institute of Labor and Industrial Relations, University of Michigan; Office for the Study of Automotive Transportation, University of Michigan Transportation Research Institute; and Center for Automotive Research, Environmental Research Institute of Michigan. Ann Arbor: University of Michigan Press.

Holweg, Matthias, Jianxi Luo, and Nick Oliver. 2005. The Past, Present, and Future of China's Automotive Industry: A Value Chain Perspective. International Motor Vehicle Program Working Paper, for UNIDO's Global Value Chain Project. Cambridge, MA: IMVP/Center for Competitiveness and Innovation/MIT Press.

Katz, Harry C., John Paul MacDuffie, and Frits K. Pil. 2002. Autos: Continuity and Change in Collective Bargaining. In *Collective Bargaining in the Private Sector*, eds. Paul F. Clark, John T. Delaney, and Ann C. Frost, 55–90. Ithaca, NY: Cornell ILR Press.

Klepper, Steven. 2002. The Capabilities of New Firms and the Evolution of the U.S. Automobile Industry. *Industrial and Corporate Change* 11 (4): 645–666.

Klepper, Steven, and Kenneth L. Simons. 1997. Technological Extinctions of Industrial Firms: An Inquiry into Their Nature and Causes. *Industrial and Corporate Change* 6 (2): 379–460.

Langlois, Richard N., and Paul L. Robertson. 1989. Explaining Vertical Integration: Lessons from the American Automobile Industry. *Journal of Economic History* 49 (2): 361–375.

Laux, James M. 1992. *The European Automobile Industry*. New York: Twayne Publishers.

Luo, Jianxi. 2005. The Growth of Independent Chinese Automotive Companies. International Motor Vehicle Program Working Paper. Cambridge, MA: IMVP/MIT Press.

McAlinden, Sean P., Kim Hill, and Bernard Swiecki. 2003. Economic Contribution of the Automotive Industry to the U.S. Economy—An Update. Ann Arbor, MI: Center for Automotive Research.

McAlinden, Sean P., and Bernard Swiecki. 2005. The Contribution of the International Auto Sector to the U.S. Economy: An Update. Ann Arbor, MI: Center for Automotive Research.

Ohno, Taiichi. 1988. *Toyota Production System: Beyond Large-Scale Production*. Cambridge, MA: Productivity Press.

Saripalle, Madhuri. 2005. Competing through Costs versus Capabilities: Organizational Transformation of the Indian Automobile Industry. Department of Agricultural and Resource Economics, University of Connecticut Working Paper/International Motor Vehicle Program Working Paper. Cambridge, MA: IMVP/MIT Press.

Sturgeon, Timothy, and Richard Florida. 2000. Globalization and Jobs in the Automotive Industry. Final Report to the Alfred P. Sloan Foundation. Cambridge, MA: IMVP/MIT Press.

U.S. Department of Labor, Bureau of Labor Statistics. 2005. The 2006–2007 Career Guide to Industries: Motor Vehicle and Parts Manufacturing. Bulletin 2601. Washington, DC: Bureau of Labor Statistics/Government Printing Office.

Verband der Automobilindustrie. VDA Auto Annual Report 2006. http://www.vda.de/en/service/jahresbericht/files/VDA_2006_en.pdf.

White, Lawrence J. 1971. *The Automobile Industry since 1945*. Cambridge, MA: Harvard University Press.

Wibbelink, R. P., and M. S. H. Heng. 2000. Evolution of Organizational Structure and Strategy of the Automobile Industry. Faculty of Economics, Vrije Universiteit Amsterdam, Research Memorandum 2000-12. ftp://zappa.ubvu.vu.nl/20000012.pdf.

Womack, James P., Daniel T. Jones, and Daniel Roos. 1990. *The Machine That Changed the World*. New York: Rawson Associates.

Kaye Husbands Fealing

AUTONOMY

Since the Enlightenment, the concept of autonomy has implied the capacity for self-regulation, and as a corollary of this capacity, the right to self-determination. Although many early thinkers from both the East and the West espoused the idea of self-regulation in some form, including Tertullian (second and third centuries), Thomas Aquinas (thirteenth century) and the Chinese philosopher Lao-tzu (sixth century BCE), it is generally associated with the development of Kantian philosophy and with the liberalism of the English philosophers John Stuart Mill (1806–1873) and John Locke (1632–1704), as well as the Scottish economist Adam Smith (1723–1790).

The most significant figure in the development of autonomy as a grounding concept of moral philosophy is undoubtedly Immanuel Kant (1724–1804), whose critical philosophy rests on the presumption that all human beings are rational beings and that reason is defined by the capacity for self-regulation. Reason, in Kant's analysis, is a faculty that permits individuals to subject themselves to law, not merely because it is their desire to do so, but because moral law, as the product of reason rather than empirical deduction, has a quality of necessity that is independent of any question of ends and, hence, of the desires felt by individual subjects. A crucial aspect of Kant's moral philosophy, one that was later developed by Karl Marx (1818–1883), was the notion that reason and desire could be opposed to one another, and indeed, that the autonomy of moral law implies the independence of reason from desire.

Like Jean-Jacques Rousseau (1712–1778), who influenced him greatly, Kant felt that the implications of moral autonomy extended to the political realm: The development of individual capacities for self-regulation required freedom from restraint by those forces that might otherwise cultivate desire against reason. Accordingly, he is often interpreted as an advocate of limited government—though his conception of what constituted limited government should not be confused with that of the political liberals following Mill and Locke, or the Smithian economists.

Mill in particular shared with Kant a sense that the opposite of moral autonomy is "servile dependence." Significantly, then, it was not society per se so much as the hierarchy of obligation and indebtedness that threatened the autonomy of the individual and his or her capacity to make free judgments. In the political realm, Mill's theory implied that individuals exercise their freedoms in relation to other individuals, and it is this cooperation that provides the means by which consensual governments are constituted.

It fell to Adam Smith to explicate the processes by which individual freedom and the complex organization of society could be accommodated and sustained independently of any legislative authority. He theorized a natural tendency to "truck, barter, and exchange" as the ground of those processes by which the division of labor develops naturally. In the forms of economic liberalism that owe their debt to Smith, the idea of autonomy was thus closely linked to one of spontaneous self-order. And it was used to legitimate arguments against governmental intervention in markets and other forms of economic life.

Kant was never fully able to extend the formalism of his own argument to all persons (he withheld the faculty of reason from Africans and aboriginals, and he doubted the capacities of women or servants to exercise free judgment). Moreover, the formalism that was intrinsic to his argument also encouraged a conflation between the presumption of a universal faculty (reason) and the universal equality of all to exercise this faculty of judgment in the actual social sphere. Smith's argument, like that of the liberal political economists who followed him, presumed that government exercises a more coercive and inhibiting influence on individuals than do other social forces, such as capital or organized labor. This presumption—that only states (through their legislative bodies) interfere with individual autonomy—has been one of the major objects of critique within radical political philosophy, from Marx forward. The crux of such critique has been a recognition of the complex social determinants of the very consciousness within which reason appears as a faculty, and a value as such. Even within liberal traditions, there is disagreement as to whether individual autonomy is better served by a government that regulates capital and other social institutions, or by one that allows corporations (including not only economic but also religious institutions) to be considered as individuals, and hence as entities whose regulation would constitute a violation of their rights.

Politically, the concept of autonomy no longer applies exclusively to the relationship between individuals and social institutions; it also describes the status of recognized minority communities within larger social contexts, and particularly state formations. In this case, autonomy is closely linked to the idea of a collective right to self-determination, and as such is provided for by the United Nations under the terms of the International Covenant on Economic, Social and Cultural Rights (adopted in 1966 and entered into force in 1976). This covenant not only provides for a right to self-determination, but also recognizes the right of "all peoples to freely dispose of their natural wealth and resources." However, just as liberal theory is conflicted in its assertion of the rights of individuals while it insists that these rights cease to exist when they intrude upon the rights of another individual, the rights of "peoples" may conflict with the perceived prerogatives of states. This is especially likely when such states comprise several distinct ethnolinguistic communities, and when one or another community dominates numerically, economically, or historically through the exercise of force. The structure by which states "grant" autonomy to regions within their territorial jurisdiction expresses the ambivalence of this concept of autonomy.

BIBLIOGRAPHY

Kant, Emmanuel. 1998. *Critique of Pure Reason.* Trans. and ed. Paul Guyer and Allen W. Wood. Cambridge, U.K.: Cambridge University Press.

Mill, John Stuart. 2002. *The Basic Writings of John Stuart Mill.* Ed. J. B. Schneewing, with notes by Dale E. Miller. New York: Modern Library.

Rousseau, Jean-Jacques. 1994. *Discourse on Political Economy; and The Social Contract.* Trans. Christopher Betts. Oxford, U.K., and New York: Oxford University Press.

Schneewind, J. B. 1992. Autonomy, Obligation, and Virtue: An Overview of Kant's Moral Philosophy. In *The Cambridge Companion to Kant,* ed. Paul Guyer, 309–341. Cambridge, U.K.: Cambridge University Press.

Smith, Adam. 1976. *An Inquiry into the Nature and Causes of the Wealth of Nations.* Ed. W. B. Todd. Oxford: Clarendon Press.

United Nations. 1966. International Covenant on Economic, Social, and Cultural Rights. http://www.unhchr.ch/html/menu3/b/a_cescr.htm.

Rosalind C. Morris

AUTOREGRESSIVE CONDITIONAL HETEROSKEDASTICITY (ARCH) MODEL

SEE *Autoregressive Models.*

AUTOREGRESSIVE INTEGRATED MOVING AVERAGE (ARIMA) MODEL

SEE *Autoregressive Models.*

AUTOREGRESSIVE MODELS

The statistical analysis of "time series" data, which are common in the social sciences, relies fundamentally on the concept of a *stochastic process*— a process that, in theory, generates a sequence of random variables over time. An autoregressive model (or autoregression) is a statistical model that characterizes or represents such a process. This article provides a brief overview of the nature of autoregressive models.

BACKGROUND

In the discussion to follow, I will use the symbol y_t to represent a variable of interest that varies over time, and that can therefore be imagined as having been generated by a stochastic process. For example, y_t might stand for the value of the gross domestic product (GDP) in the United States during a particular year t. The sequence of the observed values of GDP over a range for t (say, 1946 to 2006) is the *realization*, or *sample*, generated from the process y_t. One can imagine that, before they are known or observed, these values are drawn from a probability distribution that determines the likelihood that y takes on particular numerical values at any point in time. Time-series analysis is the set of techniques used to make inferences about this probability distribution, given a realization from the process. A key aspect of time series, especially when compared to cross-sectional data, is that for most time series of interest, probable values at a particular point in time depend on past values. For example, observing a larger than average of GDP in one year typically means observing a larger than average value for GDP in the following year. This time, or serial, dependence implies that the sequential order of a stochastic process matters. Such an ordering, however, is usually not important for observations on, say, individual households at a point in time because this ordering is arbitrary and uninformative.

A general way to characterize a stochastic process is to compute its *moments*—its means, variances, covariances, and so on. For the scalar process above, these moments might be described as:

$$E(y_t) = \mu \qquad (1)$$

$$E(y_t - \mu)(y_{t-k} - \mu) = v_k. \qquad (2)$$

Equation 1 defines the (unconditional) mean of the process, while equation 2 defines the (unconditional) covariance structure—the *variance* for $k = 0$, and the *autocovariances* for $k > 0$. (Some distributions, such as the well-known normal distribution that takes on the shape of a "bell-curve," are fully characterized by means and covariances; others require specification of higher-order moments.) Autocovariances measure the serial dependence of the process. If $v_k = 0$ for all $k \neq 0$, then the process is serially uncorrelated, which implies that past values of the process provide no information that will help predict future values. Such a process is called *white noise.*

The moments in equations 1 and 2 are quite general, but they are often difficult to estimate and use in practice. Time-series models, on the other hand, impose restrictions on this general structure in order to facilitate estimation, inference, and forecasting. Typically, these models focus on conditional probability distributions and their moments, as opposed to the unconditional moments in equations 1 and 2 above.

AUTOREGRESSIVE MODELS

An autoregression (AR) is a model that breaks down the stochastic process y_t into two parts: the conditional mean as a linear function of past values (to account for serial dependence), and a mean-zero random error that allows for unpredictable deviations from what is expected (given the past). Such a model can be expressed as:

$$y_t = a_0 + a_1 y_{t-1} + \cdots + a_p y_{t-p} + \varepsilon_t. \qquad (3)$$

Here, a_0 is a constant, a_1 through a_p are parameters that measure the specific dependence of y on its past (or lagged) values, p is the number of past values of y needed to account for the serial dependence in the conditional mean (the lag order of the model), and ε_t is a white-noise process with variance $E\varepsilon_t^2 = \sigma^2$. The value ε is interpreted as the error in forecasting the current value of y based solely on a linear combination of its past realization. The lag order p can take on any positive integer value, and in principle it can approach infinity. Because y_{t-1} depends only on random errors dated $t-1$ and earlier, and because ε_t is serially uncorrelated, ε_t and y_{t-k} must be uncorrelated for all t and whenever k exceeds zero.

Equation 3 is a pth order autoregressive model, or AR(p), of the stochastic process y_t. It is a complete representation of the joint probability distribution assumed to generate the random variable y at each time t. These models originated in the 1920s in the work of Udny Yule,

Eugen Slutsky, and others. The first known application of autoregressions was that of Yule in his 1927 analysis of the time-series behavior of sunspots (Klein 1997, p. 261). An autoregression explicitly models the conditional mean of the process. Because the mean of the error term ε is zero, the expected value of y_t, conditional on its past, is determined from equation 3 as:

$$E(y_t \mid y_{t-1}, y_{t-2}, \cdots) = a_0 + a_1 y_{t-1} + \cdots + a_p y_{t-p} \quad (4)$$

There is, however, a unique correspondence from the unconditional moments in equations 1 and 2 to the parameters in the AR model. This correspondence is most easily seen for the AR(1) process (i.e. $p = 1$, so that only the value of the process last period is needed to capture its serial dependence). For the AR(1) model, the unconditional mean and covariance structure are, respectively,

$$\mu = \frac{a_0}{1 - a_1} \quad (5)$$

$$\nu_k = a_1^k \left(\frac{\sigma^2}{1 - a_1^2} \right) \text{ for all } k. \quad (6)$$

This correspondence clarifies how the AR model restricts the general probability distribution of the process. (Note that a large number of unconditional moments can be concisely represented by the three parameters in the model, a_0, a_1, and σ^2.)

STATIONARITY AND MOVING AVERAGES

A stationary stochastic process is one for which the probability distribution that generates the observations does not depend on time. More precisely, the unconditional means and covariances in equations 1 and 2 are finite and independent of time. (Technically, these conditions describe covariance stationarity; a more general form of stationarity requires all moments, not just the first two, to be independent of t.) For example, if GDP is a stationary process, its unconditional mean in year 2006 is the same as its mean in, say, 1996, or any other year. Likewise, the autocovariance between GDP in 2006 and 2005 (one year apart) is the same as the autocovariance between GDP in 1996 and 1995 (one year apart), or any other pair of years one year apart. Stationarity is an important condition that allows many of the standard tools of statistical analysis to be applied to time series, and that motivates the existence and estimation of a broad class of linear time series models, as will be seen below.

Stationarity imposes restrictions on the parameters of autoregressions. For convenience, consider once again the AR(1) model. A necessary condition for the AR(1) process

y_t to be stationary is that the root (z) of the following equation be greater than one in absolute value:

$$1 + a_1 z = 0. \quad (7)$$

Since the root of equation 7 is $1/a_1$, this condition is identical to the condition $|a_1| < 1$. The proof of such an assertion lies beyond the scope of this article, but equation 6 shows, heuristically, why the condition makes sense. From this equation, we can see that if $a_1 = 1$, then the variance of the process approaches infinity; if a_1 exceeds 1 in absolute value, then the variance is negative. Neither of these conditions is compatible with a stationary process. The general condition for the stationarity of the AR(p) model is that the p roots of the following equation be greater than one in absolute value (Hamilton 1994, p. 58):

$$1 - a_1 z - a_2 z^2 - \cdots - a_p z^p = 0. \quad (8)$$

For an autoregressive process of any order that satisfies this condition, the qth order moving average (MA) representation of the process can be written as:

$$y_t = \mu + \varepsilon_t + c_1 \varepsilon_{t-1} + c_2 \varepsilon_{t-2} + \cdots + c_q \varepsilon_{t-p}. \quad (9)$$

Here, ε is the white-noise forecast error, and the parameters $c_1, c_2, \ldots, c_k$ approach 0 as k gets large. For example, using the tools of difference equation analysis, we can show that, for the AR(1) model, $c_1 = a_1$, $c_2 = a_1^2$, $\ldots, c_k = a_1^k$, and so on. Clearly, the limit of a_1^k as k gets large is zero given the stationarity condition above. The correspondence between the MA coefficients and the autoregressive coefficients in the more general AR(p) case is more complex than for the first-order case, but it can be obtained from the following iteration, for values of k that exceed 1 (Hamilton 1994, p. 260):

$$c_k = a_1 c_{k-1} + a_2 c_{k-2} + \cdots + a_p c_{k-p}. \quad (10)$$

(When applying this iteration, recall that $c_0 = 1$.) As with the autoregressive form, the order of the MA process may approach infinity.

The MA model is an alternative way to characterize a stochastic process. It shows that a stationary process can be built up linearly from white-noise random errors, where the influence of these errors declines the farther removed they are in the past. Indeed, Herman Wold (1938) proved that any stationary process has such a moving average representation.

Wold's theorem has an interesting implication. Suppose we start with the assumption that the stochastic process y_t is stationary. We know from Wold that a moving average exists that can fully characterize this process. While such a moving average is not unique (there are many MA models and forecast errors that are consistent with any given stationary stochastic process), only one such MA model is invertible. *Invertibility* means that the MA process can be inverted to form an autoregressive model with lag coefficients a_1, a_2, ..., a_k that approach zero as k gets large. Thus, the use of moving average and autoregressive models can be justified for all stationary processes, not just those limited to a specific class.

RANDOM WALKS AND UNIT ROOTS

Although economists and other social scientists mostly rely on stationary models, an interesting class of nonstationary autoregressive models often arises in time-series data relevant to these disciplines. Suppose that for the AR(1) model $y_t = a_0 + a_1 y_{t-1} + \varepsilon_t$, the parameter a_1 is equal to the value one. As seen in equation 7, such a process is nonstationary. However, the first difference of this process, $y_t - y_{t-1}$, is serially uncorrelated (the *first difference* of a stochastic process is simply the difference between its value in one period and its value in the previous period). If the constant term a_0 is zero, this process is called a "random walk." If a_0 is not zero, it is called a "random walk with drift." (Actually, for a process to be a random walk, its first difference must be independent white noise, which is a stronger condition than the absence of serial correlation. A process for which the first difference is serially uncorrelated, but not necessarily serially independent, is called a martingale difference.)

The change in a random walk is unpredictable. A time-series plot of such a process will appear to "wander" over time, without a tendency to return to its mean, reflecting the fact that its variance approaches infinity. If the process has, say, a positive drift term, it will tend to grow over time, but it will deviate unpredictably around this growth trend.

Although the idea of a random walk dates back at least to games of chance during the sixteenth century, the British mathematician Karl Pearson first coined the term in 1905 in thinking about evolution and species diffusion (Klein 1997, p. 271). The French mathematician Louis Bachelier (1900) led the way in using the notion of the random walk (although he did not use the term) to model the behavior of speculative asset prices. This idea was picked up by Holbrook Working in the 1930s, and it was formally developed in the 1960s by Paul Samuelson, who showed that when markets are efficient—when prices quickly incorporate all relevant information about underlying values—stock prices should follow a random walk.

The random walk is actually a special case of a more general nonstationary stochastic process called a *unit root* (or *integrated*) process. As seen above, for the AR(p) to be stationary, the roots of equation 8 must exceed one in absolute value. If at least one of these roots equals one (a

unit root) while the others satisfy the stationarity condition, the process has infinite variance and is thus nonstationary. The first difference of a unit-root process is stationary, but it is not necessarily white noise. In general, if there are $n < p$ unit roots, differencing the process n times will transform the nonstationary process into a stationary one. David Dickey and Wayne Fuller (1981) developed appropriate statistical tests for unit roots (see also Hamilton 1994, chapter 17), while Charles Nelson and Charles Plosser (1982) first applied these tools to economic issues.

ESTIMATION AND FORECASTING

The AR(p) model in equation 3 can be seen as representing all possible probability distributions that might generate the random sequence y_t. *Estimation* refers to the use of an observed sample to infer which of these models is the most likely to have actually generated the data. That is, it refers to the assignment of numerical values to the unknown parameters of the model that are, in some precise sense, most consistent with the data.

Ordinary least squares (OLS) is an estimation procedure that selects parameter estimates to minimize the squared deviations of the observed values of the process from the values of the process predicted by the model. Under certain conditions, OLS has statistical properties that are deemed appropriate and useful for inference and forecasting, such as *unbiasedness* and *consistency*.

If an estimator of unknown parameters is unbiased, its expected value is identical to the true value no matter how large the sample is. Clearly, this is a desirable property. Unfortunately, the OLS estimator of the autoregressive parameters in equation 3 is not unbiased, because the random error process ε is not independent of the lagged values of the dependent variable. When the error and lagged dependent variables are not independent, the OLS estimator of the AR parameters will systematically underestimate or overestimate their true values.

Nonetheless, OLS remains the common method for estimating AR models, because the OLS estimator, though biased, is a consistent estimator of the actual values. With a consistent estimator of a parameter, the probability that it will deviate from the true value approaches zero as the sample size becomes large. For a stationary process, all that is needed for consistency of the OLS estimator of the autoregression is that ε_t be uncorrelated with $y_{t-1}, y_{t-2}, ..., y_{t-p}$ for all t in the sample. As noted above, in theory this condition will hold because of the assumption that ε is serially uncorrelated. In practice, the condition is likely to hold if a sufficient number of lags are included in the estimated model. The upshot is that OLS will provide good estimates of the AR parameters, provided the sample is sufficiently large and the model is properly specified.

In the social sciences, the primary use of estimating AR models is to help forecast future values of a random variable by extrapolating from past behavior (using the conditional mean in equation 4). The foundations for exploiting the structure of AR and MA models for forecasting are based on the work of George Box and Gwilym Jenkins (1976). Although newer techniques have supplanted the exact methods of Box and Jenkins, their work has been extremely influential.

Because the true model of a particular stochastic process is unknown, forecasters must first determine the model they will estimate. The overriding rule of model determination suggested by Box and Jenkins is *parsimony*, which involves finding a model with the fewest parameters possible to fully describe the probability distribution generating the data. For example, while the data may, in concept, be generated by a complicated autoregressive process, a slimmed-down mixture of autoregressive and moving average components—an ARMA model—may provide the most efficiently parameterized model, and thus yield the most successful forecasts:

$$y_t = a_1 y_{t-1} + \cdots + a_p y_{t-p}$$
$$+ \, \varepsilon_t + c_1 \varepsilon_{t-1} + \cdots + c_q \varepsilon_{t-q}. \quad (11)$$

Here, the autoregressive component contains p past values of the process, while the moving average component contains q past values of the white noise error; hence this model is expressed as an ARMA(p,q).

With the methods of Box and Jenkins, it is important that the data be stationarity since unit-root nonstationarity can overwhelm and mask more transitory dynamics. The autoregressive-integrated-moving average process, or an ARIMA(p,d,q) model, is an ARMA(p,q) model applied to a process that is integrated of order d; that is, the process contains d unit roots. For example, the simple random walk model above can be described as an ARIMA(0,1,0) process, because it is white noise after being transformed by taking its first difference.

EXTENSIONS TO THE BASIC AUTOREGRESSIVE MODEL

Thus far, the focus here has been on univariate autoregressive models (those having only one random variable). It is often advantageous to consider dynamic interactions across different variables in a multivariate autoregressive framework. The AR model is easily generalized to a vector stochastic process:

$$y_t = A_1 y_{t-1} + \cdots + A_p y_{t-p} + \varepsilon_t. \quad (12)$$

In this case, y_t is now taken to be an $n \times 1$ vector of random variables, each of which varies over time, and each of the A matrices is an $n \times n$ matrix of coefficients. The random behavior of the process is captured by the vector white noise process ε_t, which is characterized by the $n \times n$ covariance matrix $E \varepsilon_t \varepsilon'_t = \Sigma$. This model is commonly denoted as a vector autoregressive (VAR) model.

To get a clear idea of the nature of this multivariate generalization of the scalar AR model, suppose that each of the coefficient matrices (A_k, for $k = 1, \ldots, p$) is diagonal, with zero values in the off-diagonal cells. The VAR is then simply n separate univariate AR models, with no cross-variable interactions. The important gain in using VAR models for forecasting and statistical inference comes from the type of interaction accounted for by nonzero off-diagonal elements in all the A_k matrices. VAR models can also capture *cointegrating* relationships among random variables, which are linear combinations of unit-root processes that are stationary (Engle and Granger 1987).

In economics, VAR models have been effective in providing a framework for analyzing dynamic systems of variables. For example, a typical model of the macro economy, potentially useful for implementing monetary policy or forecasting business cycles, might be set up as a VAR with the four variables ($n = 4$) being gross domestic product, the price level, an interest rate, and the stock of money. The VAR would capture not only the serial dependence of GDP on its own past, but also on the past behavior of prices, interest rates, and money. Christopher Sims (1980) produced the seminal work on the use of VAR models for economic inference, while James Stock and Mark Watson (2001) have reviewed VAR models and their effectiveness as a modern tool of macroeconometrics.

Finally, many random variables exhibit serial dependence that cannot be captured by simple, linear autoregressive models. For example, returns on speculative asset prices observed at high-frequency intervals (e.g., daily) often have volatilities that cluster over time (i.e., there is serial dependence in the magnitude of the process, regardless of the direction of change). The autoregressive conditional heteroskedasticity (ARCH) model of Robert Engle (1982) can account for such properties and has been profoundly influential. If the scalar ε_t follows an ARCH(p) process, then the conditional variance of ε varies with past realizations of the process:

$$\varepsilon_t = z_t h_t^{\frac{1}{2}} \quad (13)$$

$$h_t = E(\varepsilon_t^2 \mid \varepsilon_{t-1}, \ldots) = \alpha_0 + \alpha_1 \varepsilon_{t-1}^2 + \cdots + \alpha_p \varepsilon_{t-p}^2. \quad (14)$$

Indeed, it is straightforward to show that an ARCH process is tantamount to an autoregressive model applied to the square of the process, in this case ε^2. Tim

Bollerslev's (1986) generalized ARCH (GARCH) model extends Engle's ARCH formulation to an ARMA concept, allowing for parsimonious representations of rich dynamics in conditional variance:

$$h_t = \alpha_0 + \alpha_1 \varepsilon_{t-1}^2 + \cdots + \alpha_p \varepsilon_{t-p}^2$$
$$+ \beta_1 h_{t-1} + \cdots + \beta_q h_{t-q}. \qquad (15)$$

Even this model has been extended and generalized in many ways. Numerous applications of the GARCH family of models in economics, finance, and other social sciences have substantially broadened the reach of autoregressive-type models in the statistical analysis of time series.

BIBLIOGRAPHY

Bachelier, Louis. (1900) 1964. Theory of Speculation. In *The Random Character of Stock Market Prices*, ed. Paul Cootner. Cambridge, MA: MIT Press.

Bollerslev, Tim. 1986. Generalized Autoregressive Conditional Heteroskedasticity. *Journal of Econometrics* 31: 307–327.

Box, George E. P., and Gwilym M. Jenkins. 1976. *Time Series Analysis: Forecasting and Control*, rev. ed. San Francisco: Holden-Day.

Dickey, David A., and Wayne A. Fuller. 1981. Likelihood Ratio Statistics for Autoregressive Time Series with a Unit Root. *Econometrica* 49: 1057–1072.

Engle, Robert. 1982. Autoregressive Conditional Heteroskedasticity with Estimates of the Variance of United Kingdom Inflation. *Econometrica* 50: 987–1007.

Engle, Robert, and Clive Granger. 1987. Co-Integration and Error Correction: Representation, Estimation, and Testing. *Econometrica* 55: 251–276.

Hamilton, James D. 1994. *Time Series Analysis*. Princeton, NJ: Princeton University Press.

Klein, Judy L. 1997. *Statistical Visions in Time: A History of Time Series Analysis, 1662–1938.* Cambridge, U.K.: Cambridge University Press.

Nelson, Charles, and Charles Plosser. 1982. Trends and Random Walks in Macroeconomic Time Series: Some Evidence and Implications. *Journal of Monetary Economics* 10: 139–162.

Pearson, Karl. 1905. The Problem of the Random Walk. *Nature* 72: 294–342.

Samuelson, Paul. 1965. Proof that Properly Anticipated Prices Fluctuate Randomly. *Industrial Management Review* 6: 41–49.

Sims, Christopher. 1980. Macroeconomics and Reality. *Econometrica* 48: 1–48.

Slutsky, Eugen. 1937. The Summation of Random Causes as the Sources of Cyclic Processes. *Econometrica* 5: 105–146.

Stock, James, and Mark Watson. 2001. Vector Autoregressions. *Journal of Economic Perspectives* 15 (4): 101–115.

Wold, Herman. 1938. *A Study in the Analysis of Stationary Time Series*. Stockholm: Almqvist and Wiksell.

Working, Holbrook. 1934. A Random-Difference Series for Use in the Analysis of Time Series. *Journal of the American Statistical Association* 29: 11–24.

Yule, Udny. 1927. On a Method of Investigating Periodicities in Disturbed Series with Special Reference to Wolfer's Sunspot Numbers. *Philosophical Transactions* 226: 267–298.

William D. Lastrapes

AUTOREGRESSIVE MOVING AVERAGE (ARMA) MODEL

SEE *Autoregressive Models.*

AVERAGE AND MARGINAL COST

Total (or global) cost, represented mathematically as C_T, represents the total expenses needed to produce a given output. It is the sum of two kinds of costs: Fixed costs, represented as C_F, are independent of the volume of output; they include expenses such as rents, insurance, maintenance of equipment, interest payments, and that portion of overhead and labor costs that is independent of the level of activity.

Variable costs, represented as C_V, increase with activity. In the short run, modifications in the level of output are realized by modifying employment and raw material spending, with fixed equipment and plant costs. Some costs may be strictly proportional to production (for instance, raw material consumption); in other cases, cost variation may be more complicated, either for technical reasons (e.g. fuel consumption is not strictly proportional to speed), or for financial reasons (e.g. paying overtime hours). Let $C_V = \psi(Q)$. A frequent assumption is that the rate of increase is always positive ($\psi' > 0$) but variable: In a first phase of activity it decreases ($\psi' < 0$), and increases in a second phase ($\psi' > 0$); consequently, and obviously, it goes through a minimum ($\psi' = 0$) between the two. In some cases, variable cost is considered as a constant, independent of the activity level for some production ranges.

Average total cost, or C_A, is unit cost, that is, total cost divided by number of units produced: $C_A = \dfrac{C_T}{Q} = \dfrac{C_F + C_V}{Q}$. In a similar way, one can define average fixed cost as $C_{AF} = C_F / Q$ and average variable cost as $C_{AV} = C_V / Q$.

Marginal cost (C_m) is the additional cost of producing one more output unit. It depends on cost in the fol-

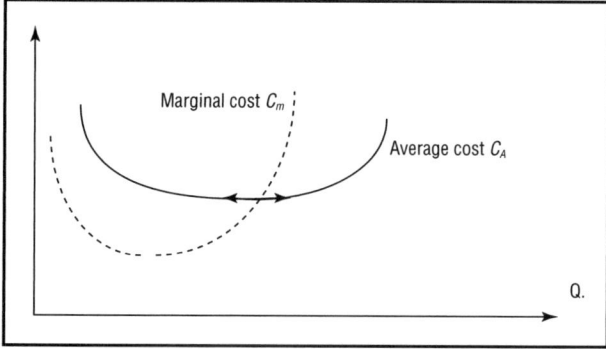

Figure 1

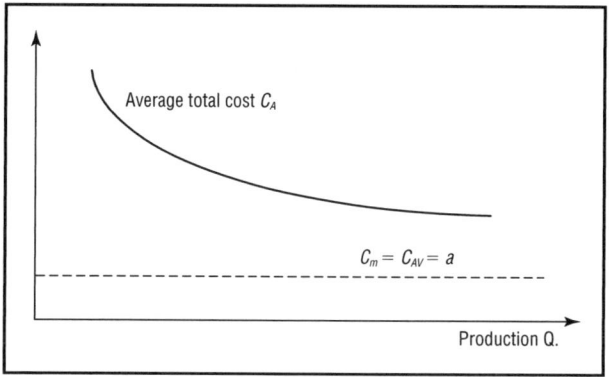

Figure 2

lowing way: An additional production of δQ units means an additional cost of δC_T euros (or dollars), thereby marginal cost is represented as $C_m = \delta C_T / \delta Q$. Given infinitely small increases of output, marginal cost is defined as derivative of total cost function: $C_m = \delta C_T / \delta Q = \varphi(Q)$. Marginal cost is independent of fixed cost and depends only on variable cost.

The following two cases will illustrate these principles: one using variable average costs, another using (total) variable costs strictly proportional to production, and, consequently, linear variable cost function.

VARIABLE AVERAGE COSTS

When production starts, the average cost curve decreases because fixed costs are recouped through increasing sales of production units. With further production increases, however, variable costs increase more than proportionally to the output level because of increasing production difficulties; eventually this factor prevails and the cost curve increases. Consequently, at a given production level average cost reaches a minimum.

The marginal cost curve in such cases follows the course indicated in Figure 1 decreasing at first when production starts and then increasing with output level. When production starts, any increase in production level implies a decrease of average cost; consequently marginal cost is inferior to average cost, and the marginal cost curve is under the average cost curve. With high production levels, marginal cost is superior to average cost (since it is very costly to produce additional output). Consequently, marginal cost curve intersects average cost curve on the minimum of this one.

This can be demonstrated mathematically as follows:

$$C_A = \frac{C_T}{Q} = \frac{C_F + C_V}{Q} = \frac{C_F + \varphi(Q)}{Q}$$

By derivation of C_A to Q (using standard rules of functions derivation), we arrive at the following:

$$\frac{d(C_A)}{dQ} = \frac{Q\varphi'(Q) - [C_F + \varphi(Q)]}{Q^2} = 0 \text{ for } \varphi'(Q) = \frac{C_F + \varphi(Q)}{Q} = C_A$$

VARIABLE COSTS STRICTLY PROPORTIONAL TO PRODUCTION

When costs are considered in strict proportion to production, the variable cost function is linear, and with a as a proportionality factor, $C_V = aQ$ and $C_T = C_F + C_V = C_F + aQ$.

Marginal cost is here constant, independent of production level

$$C_m = \frac{d(C_T)}{dQ} = \frac{d(aQ)}{Q} = a$$

and equal to average variable cost defined as $C_{AV} = \dfrac{C_V}{Q} = \dfrac{aQ}{Q} = a$.

Both functions are identical and represented by one parallel to the quantity axis.

Average total cost C_A is a constantly decreasing curve with two asymptotes, the vertical axis on one hand and the marginal cost line, or variable cost line, on the other (Figure 2).

This representation may be considered characteristic of cost functions for new products and especially for new technologies in information and communication. Development of new exploitation systems, new software, new aircraft, new medicines, cars, or drugs can cost millions of dollars. Reproduction may be quite cheap: a few dollars to manufacture a software program, more to produce a car; but the representation is also relevant since variable cost may in some cases amount to only 10 or 15 percent of total cost; the difference represents the costs of research and development, marketing, patent registration, and of course corporate profit. All these examples are characterized by very high fixed costs and constant marginal cost at very low level for large production ranges.

In the long run (which is not necessarily the same as a long time) changes in equipment and physical plant must be taken into account. The distinction between fixed and variable costs is no longer relevant because all production factors can be considered variable. With an increase in output, the average cost of production may decrease because of economies of scale due either to technical factors (improvement in task specialization, better division of labor, utilization of bigger and/or more specialized equipment) or for financial reasons (larger firms have more bargaining power with banks and suppliers).

Inversely, an excessively large production scale may create expenses: "diseconomies of scale" caused by administrative complexity, bureaucratic red tape, or organizational difficulties that may lead to increases in production costs. Such increases or decreases in costs are typical of internal economies (or diseconomies) of scale because they are the result of a firm's own decisions. But costs may increase or decrease because of factors external to the firm that may modify its cost functions. Better organization of national production factors (raw material, labor), improvements to infrastructure such as the construction of roads and highways, or reductions in input prices or taxes qualify as external economies because they can improve a firm's production costs regardless of the firm's decisions. Conversely, external diseconomies may have a negative effect on production cost, such as deterioration in infrastructures, traffic jams, pollution, and tsunamis.

BIBLIOGRAPHY

Ferguson, Charles E. 1969. *The Neoclassical Theory of Production and Distribution.* London: Cambridge University Press.

Henderson, James M., and Richard E. Quandt. 1980. *Microeconomic Theory: A Mathematical Approach.* 3rd ed. New York: McGraw-Hill.

Samuelson, Paul A., and William D. Nordhaus. 2005. *Economics.* 18th ed. Boston: Irwin/McGraw-Hill.

Varian, Hal R. 2006. *Intermediate Microeconomics: A Modern Approach.* 7th ed. New York: Norton.

Gilbert Abraham-Frois

AVERAGE REVENUE

SEE *Revenue.*

AVERSION THERAPY

SEE *Psychotherapy.*

AVIATION INDUSTRY

The aviation industry is defined as the design, manufacture, use, or operation of aircraft; the term *aircraft* refers to any vehicle capable of flight. Aircraft can either be heavier than air or lighter than air. Lighter than air craft include balloons and airships, and heavier than air craft include airplanes, autogiros, gliders, helicopters, and ornithopters.

As early as 400 BCE the Greek scholar Archytas built a wooden pigeon that moved through the air, which is the earliest aviation experiment. The Americans Orville Wright and Wilbur Wright are generally credited with making the first controlled, powered, heavier than air human flight on December 17, 1903. In 1905 Charles and Gabriel Voisin, two French fliers, started the world's first aircraft company. The military value of aircraft was quickly recognized during World War I (1914–1918), and production increased significantly to meet the rising demand. More powerful motors, enabling aircraft to reach speeds of up to 130 miles per hour, were developed. After World War I, thousands of military planes were converted to civilian use. By 1917 the U.S. government adopted something totally new: airmail. The Contract Air Mail Act of 1925 was the first major legislative step toward the creation of the private U.S. airline industry. Henry Ford, the automobile manufacturer, jumped into aircraft manufacturing and produced one of the first all-metal planes. On May 21, 1927, the pilot Charles Lindbergh flew across the Atlantic Ocean. This event made aviation an established industry by attracting millions of private investment dollars. For the airlines to attract more passengers away from the railroads, larger, faster, and safer airplanes were needed, and aircraft manufacturers responded to the challenge. There were so many improvements to aircraft in the 1930s that many believe it was the most innovative period in aviation history. Newton's Third Law theorizes that a rearward-channeled explosion can propel a machine forward at a great rate of speed. The British pilot Frank Whittle applied this law to the first jet engine in 1930. During World War II, aircraft production became the world's leading manufacturing industry.

Aviation is broadly grouped into three categories: general aviation, air transport aviation, and military aviation. By 1947 all the basic technology needed for aviation had been developed, including jet propulsion, aerodynamics, and radar. Civilian aircraft orders drastically increased from 6,844 in 1941 to 40,000 by the end of 1945. Among the minor military contractors was the

Boeing Company, which later became the largest aircraft manufacturer in the world. With all the new technologies developed by this time, airliners were larger and faster and featured pressurized cabins. New aerodynamic designs, metals, and power plants resulted in high-speed turbojet airplanes. By 1950 the airliner was well on the way to replacing the railroad and the ocean liner as the primary means of long-distance travel. The economic, social, and political consequences included the creation of global markets, opportunities for global travel undreamed of a generation before, and increasing cultural homogeneity.

In 1938 the Civil Aeronautics Authority, an independent regulatory bureau, was developed. The airline industry resembled a public utility, with a government agency determining the routes each airline flew and overseeing the prices charged. On October 24, 1978, the Airline Deregulation Act was approved, and the industry became market driven, with customer demand determining the levels of service and price. A major development that followed deregulation was the widespread development of hub-and-spoke networks, which enable the airlines to serve far more markets than they could with the same size fleet if they offered only direct, point-to-point service. Another important development following deregulation was the advent of computer reservation systems. These systems help airlines and travel agents keep track of fare and service changes, which occur rapidly. The systems also enable airlines and travel agents to efficiently process the millions of passengers who fly each day. In manufacturing, several mergers in the 1990s led to the disappearance of several historic U.S. airplane builders, such as McDonnell Douglas, which merged into Boeing. International partnerships became increasingly significant, with Airbus capturing one-third of the world market in jet airliner sales in the 1990s.

A number of researchers examined the impact of the 1978 Deregulation Act on the productivity of U.S. carriers and the demand for their services as well as how the international deregulation of the industry that accelerated in the ensuing years impacted the supply and demand for airline service worldwide. The studies pointed to an increase in efficiency of airline carriers due to increased competition, a provision of more service at lower prices, and an eroding of service quality as carriers competed on the basis of price instead of on the basis of in-flight amenities and flight frequency with relative low load factors.

On September 11, 2001, terrorists hijacked four commercial airplanes and deliberately crashed two into the towers of the World Trade Center in New York City and one into the Pentagon building in Washington, D.C. The fourth hijacked plane crashed in Somerset County, Pennsylvania. After the hijackings, U.S. airports and airlines sought new ways to protect against terrorist attacks.

Congress passed legislation requiring federal employees to handle all passenger and baggage inspection in U.S. airports by the end of 2002.

Fears of terrorism and a sluggish world economy contributed to a decline in air travel in the early 2000s. In 2003 British Airways and Air France discontinued all Concorde flights because the flights were no longer profitable.

Although many countries continue to operate state-owned airlines, most large airlines in the early twenty-first century are privately owned and therefore governed by microeconomic principles to maximize shareholder profits. The airline industry as a whole has a cumulative loss during its history, once subsidies for aircraft development and airport construction are included in the cost. The lack of profitability and continuing government subsidies are justified with the argument that positive externalities, such as higher growth due to global mobility, outweigh microeconomic losses. A historically high level of government intervention in the airline industry can be seen as part of a wider political consensus on strategic forms of transport, such as highways and railways, both of which are also publicly funded in most parts of the world.

U.S. airlines face substantial upheavals in the forms of mergers, failures, bankruptcy filings, reorganizations, and operating loss reports. This situation has raised concern that the future is bleak in terms of the number of carriers that will survive and prosper. Profitability is likely to improve as carriers find ways to be more cost-efficient and more competitive low-cost carriers proliferate.

SEE ALSO *Automobile Industry; Externality; Military; Railway Industry; September 11, 2001; Shipping Industry; Space Exploration; Terrorism; Transportation Industry; World War I; World War II*

BIBLIOGRAPHY

Ahn, Seun, David H. Good, and Robin C. Sickles. 1998. Assessing the Relative Efficiency of Asian and North American Airline Firms. In *Economic Efficiency and Productivity Growth in the Asia-Pacific Region*, ed. Tsu-Tan Fu, Cliff J. Huang, and C. A. Knox Lovell, 65–89. Northamptom, MA: Elgar.

Captain, Purvez, and Robin C. Sickles. 1997. Competition and Market Power in the European Airline Industry: 1976–1990. *Managerial and Decision Economics* 18: 209–225.

Färe, Rolf, Shawna Grosskopf, and Robin C. Sickles. 2007. Productivity? of U.S. Airlines after Deregulation. *Journal of Transport Economics and Policy* 41: 93–112.

Good, David H., M. Ishaq Nadiri, and Robin C. Sickles. 1993. Efficiency and Productivity Growth Comparisons of European and U.S. Air Carriers: A First Look at the Data. *Journal of Productivity Analysis* 4: 115–125.

Good, David H., Lars-Hendrik Röller, and Robin C. Sickles. 1993. U.S. Airline Deregulation: Implications for European

Transport. *Economic Journal, Royal Economic Society* 103: 1028–1041. Reprinted in *Recent Developments in Transport Economics*, ed. Kenneth Button. Northhampton, MA: Elgar, 2003.

Good, David H., Lars-Hendrik Röller, and Robin C. Sickles. 1994. Integration and the Structure of the Franco-American Airline Industries: Implications for Efficiency and Welfare. In *Models and Measurement of Welfare and Inequity*, ed. Wolfgang Eichhorn, 643–665. Heidelberg, Germany: Springer-Verlag.

Good, David H., Lars-Hendrik Röller, and Robin C. Sickles. 1995. Airline Efficiency Differences between Europe and the U.S.: Implications for the Pace of EC Integration and Domestic Regulation. *European Journal of Operations Research* 80: 508–518.

Longyard, William H. 1994. *Who's Who in Aviation History: 500 Biographies.* Shrewsbury, MA: Airlife.

McAllister, Bruce, and Jesse Davidson. 2004. *Wings across America: A Photographic History of the U.S. Air Mail.* Boulder, CO: Roundup.

Morrison, Stephen, and Clifford Winston. 1986. *The Economic Effects of Airline Deregulation.* Washington, DC: Brookings Institution.

Morrison, Stephen, and Clifford Winston. 1995. *The Evolution of the Airline Industry.* Washington, DC: Brookings Institution.

Perloff, Jeffrey, Robin C. Sickles, and Jesse Weiher. 2002. An Analysis of Market Power in the U.S. Airline Industry. In *Measuring Market Power*, ed. Daniel J. Slottje, 309–323. Amsterdam: Elsevier.

Postert, Anthony, and Robin C. Sickles. 1999. Air Liberalization: The Record in Europe. In *Taking Stock of Air Liberalization*, ed. Marc Gaudry and Robert Mayes, 39–59. Boston: Kluwer Academic.

Sickles, Robin C. 1987. Allocative Inefficiency in the U.S. Airlines: A Case for Deregulation. In *Studies in Productivity Analysis*, vol. 7, ed. by Ali Dogramaci, 149–162. Boston: Kluwer-Nijhoff.

Sickles, Robin C., David H. Good, and Richard L. Johnson. 1986. Allocative Distortions and the Regulatory Transition of the U.S. Airline Industry. *Journal of Econometrics* 33: 143–163.

Williams, James W. 2005. A History of Army Aviation: From Its Beginnings to the War on Terror. IUNIVERSE.

Robin Sickles
Ying Fang

AXIOMATIC THEORY OF PREFERENCES

SEE *Tastes.*

B

BA'ATH PARTY

SEE *Hussein, Saddam.*

BABY BOOMERS

The baby boom in the United States, which occurred between 1946 and 1964, took many social scientists by surprise, especially demographers. Few social scientists expected that the general fertility rate in the United States would rise from a record low in the mid-1930s to a record high in 1957 and then fall to a new record low in 1976. About 75 million more babies were born during the baby boom than expected, based upon previous fertility rates. Social scientists have pointed to two events that may have contributed to the baby boom: the Great Depression and World War II. The economic hardship that accompanied the Great Depression had a profound impact on American families, inducing the conscious decision by many to limit family size or to remain childless altogether. Births were postponed not only during the Great Depression but also during World War II, when many men were fighting overseas and many women working outside of the home (Macunovich 2002).

The conclusion of World War II brought a feeling of optimism and a period of prosperity, manifested in part by a rise in births. After World War II, soldiers returned home with entitlements that enabled them to participate in a housing boom that was one of the single greatest opportunities for wealth accumulation ever. Women who had been working in the labor force, some for the first time, returned home, and many remained there for decades to come. Individuals and families enjoyed a growth of pensions and Social Security for retirement. This feeling of great affluence and hope removed, at least temporarily, an interest in postponing childbearing. The resulting baby boom created a population bulge, the impact of which would be felt for years to come.

At the beginning of the twenty-first century, baby boomers represented about 33 percent of the total U.S. population. They have left their mark on various social institutions as they reached key points in the life cycle. School-aged baby boomers resulted in overcrowded educational facilities. As baby boomers became teenagers and young adults, crime rates increased, especially crimes committed by individuals 15 to 24 years of age. Thanks to the relative prosperity of their parents, baby boomers became the first ever generation of children and teenagers with significant buying power.

Many baby boomers came of age during a time of immense social change marked by such historic events as the civil rights movement. Baby boomers were observed to have different lifestyles and attitudes relative to previous generations. Unlike their parents, baby boomers delayed marriage and childbearing while simultaneously increasing their educational levels.

There is evidence that even with increases in education and accompanying increases in incomes, baby boomers are a diverse group (Sykes 2003). About 18 million baby boomers (24%) are racial minorities. Racial minorities in general have lower levels of income, education, and wealth than their white counterparts. Even families with similar income levels often have very different levels of wealth. Baby boomers are more likely than their parents to be sole heads of households. Single-headed households are disproportionately found among the poor. About 10 percent of baby boomers never graduated from high school.

By 2030 the youngest baby boomers will have reached retirement age, yet some will not be financially ready (U.S. Congressional Budget Office 2003). About 25 percent of baby boomers will not have adequate savings to finance their own retirement and will place a strain on existing social programs such as Social Security and Medicare. By 2019 Social Security will provide as much as 70 percent of the retirement funds for baby boomers at the lowest levels of income, and there will be 3 retired baby boomers for every 10 workers—facts that compromise the ability of this safety-net program to meet the needs of current and future workers. Policy makers have debated about the impact that aged baby boomers will have on Social Security and other programs. Plans to address the issue include privatizing Social Security, which some argue would place the retirement futures of at-risk groups like African Americans, Native Americans, Hispanics, women, the poor, and the elderly in economic peril.

The baby boom was a tremendous population shift occurring not only in the United States but also in other parts of the industrialized world. Individuals born between 1946 and 1964 have altered the age ratios of various populations and have profoundly affected social institutions and social programs as they reach various milestones. Proposed changes to long-standing social programs like Social Security and Medicare are thought to have a disproportionate negative impact on those at greatest risk, namely racial minorities and the elderly.

SEE ALSO *Demography; Population Growth*

BIBLIOGRAPHY

Macunovich, Diane. 2002. *Birth Quake: The Baby Boom and Its Aftershocks.* Chicago: University of Chicago Press.

Sykes, L. L. 2003. Income Rich and Asset Poor: A Multilevel Analysis of Racial and Ethnic Differences in Housing Values among Baby Boomers. *Population Research and Policy Review* 22:1–20.

U.S. Congressional Budget Office. 2003. *Social Security and Medicare.* Washington, DC: U.S. Government Printing Office.

Lori Sykes

BACHELIER, LOUIS
SEE *Efficient Market Hypothesis.*

BACK TO AFRICA
SEE *Repatriation.*

BACKWASH EFFECTS

Economic growth provides benefits and costs in the region in which it occurs. It has a positive impact on nearby localities if jobs, population, and wealth spill over into these communities. Alternatively, it has adverse effects on the nearby localities if growth in the core region attracts people and economic activity away from these peripheral areas. *Spread* refers to the situation where the positive impacts on nearby localities and labor markets exceed the adverse impacts. *Backwash* occurs if the adverse effects dominate and the level of economic activity in the peripheral communities declines.

The idea of backwash originated in international-trade theory in a book by Gunner Myrdal (1957). Myrdal noted that an increase in exports from a region may stimulate capital and labor flows into the region to the detriment of the localities from which the resources came. Thomas Vietorisz and Bennett Harrison (1973) later proposed that spread and backwash feedbacks between labor markets contributed to a divergence of technology levels, labor productivity, and wages in these markets. Gary Gaile (1980) used backwash concepts to describe the potential negative effects of urban growth on peripheral areas.

A renewed interest in backwash effects was stimulated by the "new economic-growth theory." An enhanced role for innovative activity and increasing returns to scale in economic development increase the competitive advantage of larger urban areas as the location for economic activity. This growth in urban (core) areas may lead to a decline in rural (peripheral) population and employment (a back-wash effect) if rural-to-urban flows weaken rural economies. Five types of flows contribute to backwash: Rural funds are invested in urban areas to take advantage of entrepreneurial activities and relatively rapidly growing markets for goods and services. Spending in rural trade and service markets declines owing to increased competition from urban businesses. Rural residents move to the expanding urban areas for improved access to jobs and urban amenities. Rural firms in the innovative stage of their life cycle move to urban areas to benefit from proximity to specialized services, skilled labor, and expanding markets. And finally, political influence and government spending may shift to the more rapidly growing core areas.

The adverse rural-to-urban flows occur in conjunction with the spillover of people, jobs, and funds from the growing core to peripheral areas (spread effects). The size and geographical extent of the beneficial and adverse forces on rural areas depend on the characteristics of the rural and urban areas and the nature of rural-urban linkages. In general, the beneficial forces are stronger for rural areas near urban cores, while the adverse flows dominate in regions more peripheral to the growing urban areas. Thus, backwash is more likely in rural areas outside of the rural-to-urban commuting zones.

The policy implications of backwash are that localities distant from urban growth centers will likely be adversely affected by regional economic-development policies that focus on innovation and entrepreneurial development in urban areas. These remote regions will need to devise economic-development programs that emphasize competitive advantages specific to their economies.

SEE ALSO *Cumulative Causation; Myrdal, Gunnar; Stockholm School*

BIBLIOGRAPHY

Gaile, Gary L. 1980. The Spread-Backwash Concept. *Regional Studies* 14: 15–25.

Myrdal, Gunner. 1957. *Economic Theory and Undeveloped Regions*. London: Methuen & Co.

Vietorisz, Thomas, and Bennett Harrison. 1973. Labor Market Segmentation: Positive Feedback and Divergent Development. *American Economic Review* 63: 366–376.

David L. Barkley

BAHRO, RUDOLF
1935–1997

Rudolf Bahro was born November 18, 1935, in Bad Flinsberg in Lower Silesia (now Poland). As a child refugee at the end of World War II (1939–1945), fleeing the advance of the Soviet armies, Bahro lost his mother and both his sisters. Bahro studied philosophy at Humboldt University in Berlin from 1954 to 1959, during which time he joined the East German Communist Party. He worked as an editor for municipal and party papers, and later became a consultant to the presiding board of directors at the only trade union academy in East Germany. In 1965 Bahro took over the post of acting head editor for the newspaper *Forum*. The unauthorized publication of a critical piece, Volker Braun's "Kipper Paul Bauch," led to his resignation in 1967. Afterward, he worked at the paper as a production supervisor.

By the 1970s Bahro had emerged as a prominent critic of the East German Communist Party (Sozialistische Einheitspartei Deutschlands, abbreviated SED). It was entirely clear, however, that the leadership of the SED had absolutely no intention of entering into a

dialogue with Bahro on the issue of basic reform in late-Stalinist East Germany. Robert Havemann, the other prominent critic of the East German regime, was under house arrest in Grünheide near Berlin, guarded by operatives of the East German security police (the Stasi). On August 23, 1977—shortly after publishing "Against Oneself and against One's People" in the West German news magazine *Der Spiegel* and discussing his forthcoming book, *The Alternative*, in several television interviews—Bahro was arrested by the Stasi.

Bahro, who developed his critique within a Marxist framework, accused the Communist Party leadership of betraying socialist ideals. Characterizing the states of Eastern Europe as systems of organized irresponsibility, he analyzed their political economy and aspects of their industrial production. He recommended far-reaching reforms of the administrative apparatus—indeed, an overhaul of the entire political structure. In Bahro's view, the Eastern Bloc was not merely an example of deformed socialism, but rather a social reality based on entirely different principles. He accused the Soviet leadership of having, through its invasion of Czechoslovakia in 1968, robbed itself and the peoples of Eastern Europe of the experience of socialism with a human face. He demanded true economic democracy, without wage privileges for tiny elites, and also the elimination of the existing division of labor. Genuine institutional self-rule, Bahro declared, must gradually develop from below, with freedom of personal development a necessary condition. He believed that a coalition drawing from all political tendencies could lead the way out of self-imposed imprisonment. All this was conceived as a new vision of communism. Altogether some 300,000 copies of *The Alternative* were sold, and the book was translated into numerous other languages.

Bahro was sentenced to eight years in prison. The international league for human rights awarded him the Carl von Ossietzky medal, and numerous authors and political figures demanded his release. Bahro was granted amnesty in 1979 and left for West Germany, where he became one of the cofounders of the Green Party. Believing that a political solution to the ecological crisis could only be achieved through a broad coalition spanning existing political divisions, he embraced everyone from the left-wing student activist Rudi Dutschke to the right-wing ecologist Herbert Gruhl. In his early years in West Germany, Bahro also devoted much of his time to the peace movement. He favored unilateral disarmament for both sides.

Because the Greens operated on the basis of an "eco-cosmetic" and reformist mode of power-sharing, Bahro left that party in 1985. Bahro's second major work, *Logik der Rettung* (The logic of salvation, 1987; revised and translated as *Avoiding Social and Ecological Disaster*,

1994), traced the connections between the ecological crisis facing civilization and Western political-economic systems. The industrial capitalist "megamachine" was globally overstepping the boundaries of nature, causing irreparable climate change. It would be necessary to decrease industrial production tenfold, through changes in economic structures and lifestyles. There would have to be a sociopsychological alteration of the attitudes characteristic of business, so that a new spirit could be born. Bahro also asserted the need for a democratically run ecological superauthority, to monitor and enforce ecological change.

In 1990 Bahro returned to East Germany. Between 1990 and 1997, he gave well-attended lectures at Humboldt University, in which he addressed questions of spirituality and communal action in a socioecological context, drawing on influential thinkers from Lao-Tse to Martin Heidegger to Erich Fromm. His lectures and interviews were published in several books: *Rückkehr* (The return, 1991), *Apokalypse oder Geist einer neuen Zeit* (Apocalypse or the spirit of a new age, 1995), and *Wege zur ökologischen Zeitenwende* (Means of the end of an ecological era, 2002). In another book that remains unpublished, he set out his views and asked which elements of Marxism and of the collapsed East German state ought to be maintained.

Bahro died of leukemia in 1997. In 2002, in Germany, Guntolf Herzberg and Kurt Seifert brought out a comprehensive biography of this prophetic thinker.

SEE ALSO *Marxism*

BIBLIOGRAPHY

Alt, Franz, Rudolf Bahro, and Marko Ferst. 2002. *Wege zur ökologischen Zeitenwende: Reformalternativen und Visionen und für ein zukunftsfähiges Kultursystem* [Means of the end of an ecological era: Alternative reforms and visions for an outstanding future culture]. Books on Demand.

Bahro, Rudolf. 1978. *The Alternative in Eastern Europe*. Trans. David Fernbach. London: NLB.

Bahro, Rudolf. 1982. *Socialism and Survival: (Articles, Essays, and Talks, 1979–1982)*. London: Heretic Books.

Bahro, Rudolf. 1984. *From Red to Green: Interviews with* New Left Review. Trans. Gus Fagan and Richard Hurst. London: Verso.

Bahro, Rudolf. 1986. *Building the Green Movement*. Trans. Mary Tyler. London: GMP.

Bahro, Rudolf. 1991. *Rückkehr: Die In-Weltkrise als Ursprung der Weltzerstörung* [The return: The global crisis as the beginning of the end of the world]. Berlin: Altis.

Bahro, Rudolf. 1994. *Avoiding Social and Ecological Disaster: The Politics of World Transformation: An Inquiry into the Foundations of Spiritual and Ecological Politics*. Trans. David Clarke. Bath, U.K.: Gateway Books. Revised version of book originally published as *Logik der Rettung: Wer kann die Apokalypse aufhalten? Ein Versuch über die Grundlagen ökologischer Politik* (Stuttgart: K. Thienemanns, 1987).

Bahro, Rudolf. 1995. *Apokalypse oder Geist einer neuen Zeit* [Apocalypse or the spirit of a new age]. Berlin: Das Neue Berlin.

Bahro, Rudolf. 1995. *Das Buch von der Befreiung aus dem Untergang der DDR* [The book of deliverance after the fall of East Germany]. (Unpublished.)

Herzberg, Guntolf, and Kurt Seifert. 2002. *Rudolf Bahro: Glaube an das Veränderbare: Eine Biographie*. Berlin: Christoph Links.

Marko Ferst
Translated by Ray Lukens

BAKER, ELLA
SEE *Student Nonviolent Coordinating Committee.*

BAKKE DECISION
SEE Grutter *Decision.*

BALANCE OF PAYMENTS
The balance of payments is an accounting statement that records transactions (trade in goods, services, and financial assets) between a country's residents and the rest of the world. Those transactions consist of receipts and payments—credits (entries that bring foreign exchange into the country) and debits (entries that record a loss of foreign exchange), respectively—that are recorded through the use of double-entry bookkeeping. Balance-of-payments data usually are reported quarterly in national publications and also are published by the International Monetary Fund.

THE CURRENT, CAPITAL, AND FINANCIAL ACCOUNTS
The balance of payments consists of the current account, the capital account, and the financial account (see the illustration). The current account includes trade in merchandise (raw materials and final goods), services (transportation, tourism, business services, and royalties), income (from salaries and direct, portfolio, and other types of investment), and current transfers (workers' remittances, donations, grants, and aid). The current account is related to the national income accounts because the trade balance corresponds broadly to the net export value recorded in the national income accounts as one of the four components of the gross national product

(GNP), along with consumption, investment, and government expenditures.

The capital account records all international capital transfers. Those transfers include the monetary flows associated with inheritances, migrants' transfers, debt forgiveness, the transfer of funds received for the sale or acquisition of fixed assets, and the acquisition or disposal of intangible assets. The financial account records government-owned international reserve assets (foreign exchange reserves, gold, and special drawing rights with the International Monetary Fund), foreign direct investment, private sector assets held abroad, assets owned by foreigners, and international monetary flows associated with investment in business, real estate, bonds, and stocks.

The balance of payments should always be in equilibrium. The current account should balance with the sum of the capital and financial accounts. However, because in practice the transactions do not offset each other exactly as a result of statistical discrepancies, a separate line with those discrepancies is included in the statistical presentation.

If the current account is in equilibrium, the country will find its net creditor or debtor position unchanging because there will be no need for net financing. Equilibrium in the capital and financial accounts means no change in the capital held by foreign monetary agencies and reserve assets. In the case of disequilibrium arising when a country buys more goods than it sells (i.e., a current account deficit), the country must finance the difference through borrowing or sale of assets (i.e., there is an inflow of capital and thus a capital and financial account surplus). In other words, the country uses foreign savings to meet its consumption or investment needs. Similarly, if a country has a current account surplus, the capital and financial accounts record a net outflow, indicating that the country is a net creditor. The exchange rate regime is an important determinant of the adjustment toward the new equilibrium. With fixed exchange rates, central banks must finance the excess demand for or supply of foreign currency at the fixed exchange rate by running down or adding to their reserve assets. Under floating exchange rates, balance of payments equilibrium is restored by movements in the exchange rate.

THEORIES AND ASSESSMENT OF THE BALANCE OF PAYMENTS

A number of theories have been developed to explain the adjustment process of the balance of payments. In a world without capital flows the elasticities approach provides an analysis of how changes in the exchange rate affect the trade balance, depending on the elasticities of demand and supply for foreign exchange and/or goods. An exchange rate depreciation increases the domestic price of imports and lowers the foreign price of exports. However, depreciation reduces imports only if import demand is

---

United States balance of payments, 1970–2005

(In millions of U.S. dollars)

	1970	1980	1990	2000	2005
Current account					
Exports of goods and services and income receipts	**68,387**	**344,440**	**706,975**	**1,421,515**	**1,749,892**
Exports of goods and services	56,640	271,834	535,233	1,070,597	1,275,245
Income receipts	11,748	72,606	171,742	350,918	474,647
Imports of goods and services and income payments	**259,901**	**−333,774**	**−759,290**	**−1,778,020**	**−2,455,328**
Imports of goods and services	−54,386	−291,241	−616,097	−1,448,156	−1,991,975
Income payments	−5,515	−42,532	−143,192	−329,864	−463,353
Unilateral current transfers, net	**−6,156**	**−8,349**	**−26,654**	**−58,645**	**−86,072**
U.S. Government grants	−4,449	−5,486	−10,359	−16,714	−31,362
U.S. Government pensions and other transfers	−611	−1,818	−3,224	−4,705	−6,303
Private remittances and other transfers	−1,096	−1,044	−13,070	−37,226	−48,407
Capital account					
Capital account transactions, net	**—**	**—**	**−6,579**	**−1,010**	**−4,351**
Financial account					
U.S.-owned assets abroad, net (increase/financial outflow (−))	**−8,470**	**−85,815**	**−81,234**	**−560,523**	**−426,801**
U.S. official reserve assets, net	3,348	−7,003	−2,158	−290	14,096
U.S. Government assets, other than official reserve assets, net	−1,589	−5,162	2,317	−941	5,539
U.S. private assets, net	−10,229	−73,651	−81,393	−559,292	−446,436
Foreign-owned assets in the U.S., net (increase/financial inflow (+))	**−6,359**	**62,612**	**141,571**	**1,046,896**	**1,212,250**
Foreign official assets in the United States, net	6,908	15,497	33,910	42,758	199,495
Other foreign assets in the United States, net	−550	47,115	107,661	1,004,138	1,012,755
Statistical discrepancy (Sum of above items reversed)	**−219**	**20,886**	**25,211**	**−70,213**	**10,410**

SOURCE: Bureau of Economic Analysis, International Economics Accounts, U.S. Department of Commerce, http://www.bea.gov/international, Washington, D.C., 2006.

---

elastic; the same is the case for the behavior of exports after a decline in export prices. Thus, the final impact on the current account balance depends on the elasticity of demand in each country for the other country's goods and services.

The absorption approach emphasizes the way in which domestic spending on domestic goods changes relative to domestic output: The trade balance is viewed as the difference between what the economy produces and what it spends. In an economy that is operating below its full potential an exchange rate depreciation tends to increase net exports (given the elasticity conditions noted above) and bring about an increase in output and employment. In an economy operating at full potential, in contrast, a depreciation tends to increase net exports, but because it is not possible to increase output, the result is higher prices of domestically produced goods.

In the modern global economy with well-developed financial markets and large-scale capital flows, financial assets play an important role in the analysis of the balance of payments. The lifting of controls on the movement of capital and financial flows has been fundamental to promoting world trade and eventually greater incomes. The unrestricted movement of capital allows governments, businesses, and individuals to invest capital in other countries, thus promoting not only foreign direct investment but also portfolio investment in the capital market.

With perfect capital mobility, monetary and fiscal policies affect the balance of payments through the interest rate channel. Under fixed exchange rates an increase in the money supply will reduce interest rates and lead to capital outflows, tending to cause a depreciation that will have to be offset by sales of foreign exchange by the central bank. This will then reduce money supply until it reaches its original level. Thus, monetary policy is ineffective in increasing output. Fiscal policy, however, is highly effective because a fiscal expansion tends to raise interest rates, leading the central bank to increase the money supply to support the exchange rate, reinforcing the impact of the expansionary fiscal policy. Under floating exchange rates, monetary policy is highly effective and fiscal policy is ineffective in changing output. A monetary expansion leads to depreciation and higher exports and output. Fiscal expansion, in contrast, causes an appreciation of the exchange rate and crowds out net exports.

The introduction of interactions between prices and changes in the exchange rate leads to a model that postulates that price flexibility ultimately moves an economy to full employment. The mechanism involves changes in the domestic money supply that take place as the central bank keeps selling foreign exchange to domestic residents in exchange for domestic currency. A monetary contraction thus reduces prices, improves competitiveness, and increases net exports and employment. Under floating exchange rates, in the short run a monetary expansion increases output and reduces interest rates, causing a depreciation of the exchange rate. In the long run, however, a monetary expansion increases the price level and the exchange rate, keeping real balances and the terms of trade unchanged.

The monetary approach to the balance of payments postulates that disequilibrium in the balance of payments is essentially a monetary phenomenon. It emphasizes the central banks' balance sheet identity—a change in net foreign assets equals the difference between changes in high-powered money and in domestic credit—which shows that sufficient contraction of domestic credit will improve the balance of payments. This improvement comes about through higher interest rates and lower domestic income and employment. Finally, the asset market (or portfolio) approach incorporates assets besides money. In recognition of the fact that asset markets across countries are well integrated, changes in the demand for and supply of assets will affect interest rates, exchange rates, and the balance of payments.

MACROECONOMIC STABILITY

Maintaining a favorable balance-of-payments position is important for macroeconomic stability, and countries gear their policies toward achieving that goal. Although current account deficits that are financed through non-debt-creating capital flows may not pose an immediate threat, large and unsustainable deficits can transform into chronically unfavorable balance-of-payments positions that may affect the stability of the currency. Correcting such unfavorable positions is done through the adoption of stabilization programs that sometimes are supported by the International Monetary Fund through the provision of short-term financing to ease the burden of temporary problems.

SEE ALSO *Balance of Trade; Capital Controls; Capital Flight; Equilibrium in Economics; Exchange Rates; Exports; Imports; Interest Rates; International Monetary Fund; Mundell-Fleming Model; Policy, Fiscal; Policy, Monetary; Reserves, Foreign; Trade Deficit; Trade Surplus*

BIBLIOGRAPHY

Dornbusch, Rudiger, Stanley Fischer, and Richard Startz. 2004. *Macroeconomics*, 8th ed. Boston: McGraw-Hill.

Frenkel, Jakob, and Harry G. Johnson, eds. 1976. *The Monetary Approach to the Balance of Payments*. Toronto: University of Toronto Press.

Husted, Steven, and Michael Melvin. 2007. *International Economics*, 7th ed. Boston: Pearson/Addison-Wesley.

International Monetary Fund. Various years. *Balance of Payments Statistics Yearbook*. Washington, DC: Author.

Costas Christou

BALANCE OF TRADE

A nation's balance of trade, also called "net exports," is a measure of the net flow of goods and services between that country and the rest of the world. Given domestic output (or income) (Y), domestic spending on domestic output (D), exports (X), and imports (M), the balance of trade is $B = Y - D = X - M$. The balance of trade is in surplus if $B > 0$, and it is in deficit if $B < 0$. This formulation suggests that fluctuations in domestic output can be absorbed by fluctuations in the trade balance, keeping domestic spending relatively stable. In 2005, the balances of trade relative to GDP (gross domestic product) for the United States, South Korea and Brazil was –5.7 percent, 2.6 percent, and 4.6 percent, respectively.

A nation's income, the income of its trading partners, and the relative price of domestic goods (compared to foreign goods) determine its balance of trade. As domestic income (Y) rises, expenditure on all goods—including foreign-produced goods—increases. Thus, imports increase and the balance of trade decreases. Similarly, when the income of a nation's trading partners increases, so do its exports, thus increasing the balance of trade. The relative price (R) of domestic to foreign goods is $R = SP/P^*$, where S is the spot exchange rate (the foreign currency price of the domestic currency) and P and P^* denote the native currency prices of domestic and foreign goods, respectively. With short-run price inflexibility, a change in the exchange rate (S) is fully reflected in a change in the relative price.

Since domestic and foreign outputs have a degree of substitutability, the nominal exchange rate affects both exports and imports. Generally, an exchange-rate depreciation (a decrease in S) switches spending away from foreign goods toward domestic goods and increases the balance of trade.

Reflecting an excess of domestic spending over domestic income, a balance-of-trade deficit may be offset by a net inflow of labor and asset incomes from abroad. Otherwise, overspending must be funded through a depletion of national wealth, possibly in the form of increased indebtedness to foreign entities through the sale of domestic bonds or of outright sales of equity or other assets. This net inflow of foreign capital requires that foreign savers be willing to lend against, or buy, domestic assets. If they are unwilling to do so or if they are not allowed to do so because of domestic capital controls, the domestic currency will depreciate and eliminate the deficit. If this does not occur and if the exchange rate is fixed, the central monetary authority must sell its gold or foreign currency reserves, causing the domestic money supply and, over time, the domestic price level to decrease and reverse the deficit.

A nation may sustain a balance-of-trade deficit for short periods but not persistently. Rising indebtedness would cause foreign lenders to fear that their claims would not be honored, leading to a reduction of further investment in domestic assets. Moreover, the government's corpus of gold and foreign currency reserves is finite. The existence of a long-term trade imbalance that is not offset by factor-income inflows is of concern because it reflects a fundamental divergence between domestic income and domestic spending. Many countries have learned, sometimes from bitter experience, that persistent failure to harmonize income and spending can lead to corrective forces, sometimes resulting in economic crises in the form of large increases in interest rates, unemployment, or a sharp depreciation of domestic currency.

Policymakers must balance short-run conflicts in maintaining the trade balance at a targeted level B^* (possibly zero), while also maintaining domestic output at a level Y^* consistent with full employment and constant inflation. In a fixed-exchange-rate regime, these goals can be met by judiciously mixing domestic demand and exchange-rate levels. Assuming stability, the relationships $Y^* = D + B (Y^*, S)$ and $B^* = B (Y^*, S)$ together yield unique values of domestic demand and exchange rate, D_0 and S_0, consistent with the goals. The level D_0 is achieved by adjusting fiscal policy; monetary policy cannot be used independently under a fixed exchange rate regime.

It may be inferred that if fiscal policy is set at D_0 but the exchange rate is overvalued ($S > S_0$), a trade deficit will result, accompanied by unemployment. It may also be inferred that if the exchange rate is undervalued ($S < S_0$), a trade surplus will accrue, along with inflationary pressure. Similarly, if the exchange rate is set at S_0 but fiscal policy is too restrictive ($D < D_0$), a trade surplus will coexist with unemployment, while an expansive fiscal policy ($D > D_0$) results in a trade deficit and inflationary pressure.

If the exchange rate is flexible, both fiscal and monetary policies will quite likely affect the balance of trade. Both affect the interest rate (r) and, thereby, the exchange rate, which moves to equilibrate international asset markets by equating the expected returns on domestic and foreign assets. If the foreign interest rate exceeds the domestic interest rate, the difference is offset by an expected appreciation of the domestic currency; otherwise, the foreign asset yields excess returns. Given an unchanged expected future exchange rate, a decrease in r

causes the domestic currency to depreciate (it decreases *S*) immediately, thus generating expectations of a forthcoming appreciation. The depreciation increases the balance of trade.

Fiscal and monetary expansions, by increasing *Y*, cause an incipient worsening of the trade balance, which works to depreciate the domestic currency. Additionally, a monetary expansion decreases *r* and causes capital outflows, compounding this depreciation and causing the balance of trade to improve. However, a fiscal expansion increases *r*, stimulates capital inflows, and appreciates domestic currency. The appreciation caused by sufficiently high capital mobility can overwhelm the depreciation effect of output expansion and worsen the balance of trade. Thus, a budget deficit can give rise to a trade deficit, invoking the label "twin deficits."

SEE ALSO *Mundell-Fleming Model; Trade Deficit; Trade Surplus*

BIBLIOGRAPHY

Appleyard, Dennis R., Alfred J. Field Jr., and Steven Cobb. 2006. *International Economics.* 5th ed. Boston: McGraw-Hill.

Krugman, Paul R., and Maurice Obstfeld. 2006. *International Economics: Theory and Policy.* 7th ed. Boston: Addison-Wesley.

Mundell, Robert. 1963. Capital Mobility and Stabilization Policy under Fixed and Flexible Exchange Rates. *Canadian Journal of Economics and Political Science* 29 (4): 475–485.

Swan, Trevor W. 1963. Longer-Run Problems of the Balance of Payments. In *The Australian Economy: A Volume of Readings,* eds. H. W. Arndt and W. M. Corden, 384–395. Melbourne, Australia: F. W. Cheshire Press.

Vikram Kumar

BALLET

SEE *Dance.*

BALLOTS

A ballot is a device for casting a vote. Traditionally, the word referred exclusively to a piece of paper, but modern usage also applies the term to electronic voting methods. Generally, ballot format covers both how the choices for various electoral contests are arranged and how choices (votes) are recorded.

The information conveyed on a ballot varies by voting system. Some electoral rules require rankings of multiple candidates, others require the selection of one or more alternatives from a set, and others involve multiple choices, such as picking one party from a list and also ranking various individuals from that party. There is also much variation in how access to the ballot is gained, precisely what information about candidates is listed, how choices are ordered, and whether voters check boxes, punch out perforated tabs of paper, press buttons, write out numbers or names, and so on.

Probably the most fundamental aspect of ballots is whether they are cast in secret. Voting in early democracies was done openly, and ballots were even produced by parties in distinct colors and shapes, to allow observers to determine how individuals voted.

Secret ballots were first introduced in Australia, and the term *Australian ballot* is still often used to refer to any ballot cast privately, even in places that share no other electoral rules with modern Australia. Many polities have made early and absentee voting (usually done by mail) easier in recent decades, in an effort to boost turnout. However, since absentee ballots are not cast in secret, they make old-style fraud, such as vote buying, much easier.

American elections usually feature many contests. In parliamentary democracies, it is more common for ballots to feature few races, sometimes only one. When ballots do cover multiple races, an important distinction is whether all candidates seeking a given office (as representatives of different parties) are grouped together or, instead, all candidates from a given party (seeking different offices) are grouped together. Sometimes ballots include an option to vote for all candidates from a party in a single stroke, though this so-called straight-ticket option has gradually become less common in American states.

In the 2000 American presidential election, Palm Beach County, Florida, used the now-famous butterfly ballot, wherein the names of competing candidates alternated from appearing to the left or the right of their associated punch-holes as one moved down the list. Analysis later suggested that many voters were confused by the format.

On a spoiled ballot, the choice(s) of the voter cannot be discerned. More complicated electoral systems and ballots featuring more contests tend to see higher rates of spoilage (including overvoting, the selection of more candidates than are legally permitted) and of undervoting (selective abstention, which is usually allowed).

As jurisdictions increasingly employ varieties of electronic voting, new issues with ballot formats have emerged. One important issue is whether computer voting systems generate a hard paper copy of the choices of voters along with the electronic copy, as a means of limiting fraud or accidental vote loss.

SEE ALSO *Compulsory Voting; Elections; Electoral Systems; Party Systems, Competitive; Voting; Voting Patterns; Voting Rights Act; Voting Schemes*

BIBLIOGRAPHY

Albright, Spencer D. 1942. *The American Ballot*. Washington, DC: American Council on Public Affairs.

Evans, Eldon Cobb. 1927. *A History of the Australian Ballot System in the United States*. Chicago: University of Chicago Press.

Fredman, Lionel E. 1968. *The Australian Ballot: The Story of an American Reform*. East Lansing: Michigan State University Press.

Wand, Jonathan N., et al. 2001. The Butterfly Did It: The Aberrant Vote for Buchanan in Palm Beach County, Florida. *American Political Science Review* 95 (4): 793–810.

Brian J. Gaines

BAMBOOZLED

Shelton Jackson ("Spike") Lee (1957–) and his 40 Acres and a Mule production company have made thirty-five films since 1983. Two of his films—*Do the Right Thing* (1989) and *Four Little Girls* (1997*)*—have been nominated for Academy Awards (Best Original Screenplay and Best Feature Documentary, respectively). Lee's films are known for their social commentary, sometimes presented in excessively didactic fashion, and their edgy exploration of recent developments in popular culture and politics. Extremely outspoken about social issues and public policy, Lee has made especially strong statements about the Tuskegee Syphilis Study and the U.S. government's labored response to the impact of Hurricane Katrina on Gulf Coast communities. Indeed, his much acclaimed recent documentary, *When the Levees Broke* (2006), specifically addresses the failure of state, local, and federal authorities to address the needs of the citizens of New Orleans when Hurricane Katrina flooded the city.

In 2000, Lee released the film *Bamboozled*, which tells the story of Pierre Delacroix, played by Damon Wayans. Delacroix is a black television writer who has grown frustrated with the business. Tired of repeatedly having his "best-foot-forward" black pilots rejected for less positive fare, Delacroix recreates "The New Millenium Minstrel Show" show in hopes of getting fired. He heads to the office of his white boss, Dunwitty (played by Michael Rappaport), accompanied by his assistant Sloan (played by Jada Pinkett) and Womack and Man Ray (played by Tommy Davidson and tap dancer Savion Glover, respectively), two homeless squatters he finds performing on the street. Dunwitty, whose office is a verita-

ble museum of black sports history and whose wife is black, is the iconic, self-described white man who knows more about black people than black people know themselves.

After pitching his show as a satire and casting the pilot from dozens of actors who attend the audition, Delacroix shoots the pilot. To his surprise, despite featuring actors in blackface and scenes of chicken and watermelon stealing, the show is an immediate hit, much to the dismay of black activists Jesse Jackson and Al Sharpton, who make cameo appearances as themselves. The show also angers the Mau Maus, a misguided group of militants led by Sloan's brother, who make plans to sabotage the show after being rejected at their audition to serve as the program's house band. As the show and Man Ray—now known as Mantan—grow in popularity at the hands of a stable of white writers, the Mau Maus plot to end his career by whatever means they have at their disposal.

Their goal comes to fruition as they succeed in kidnapping and killing Mantan on a live broadcast shortly before being gunned down by the police themselves. Only one-sixteenth black, the member of the Mau Maus who is phenotypically white is spared by the police despite his pleas for them to kill him also. Here Lee is evoking an actual event: In the early 1990s a California street gang was shot by the police and only two gang members survived, one emerging unscathed and the other suffering a leg wound. Both were white. The sight of her brother's and his comrades' deaths drives Sloan to enter a despondent Delacroix's home and shoot him fatally. Delacroix's final acts are to wipe her fingerprints off of the gun and lament his decision to develop the minstrel show that resulted in tragedy.

While Lee's films *Do the Right Thing* (1989) and *Malcolm X* (1992) are more heralded, *Bamboozled* stands as his most shrewd social critique and, excluding the magnificent documentaries *Four Little Girls* and *When the Levees Broke*, his lone masterpiece. Disturbing, terrifying, and polarizing, *Bamboozled* opened to little fanfare in 2000. Early trailers for the film elicited uncomfortable squirms from audiences and prayers that the sight of black characters on screen in blackface meant that a hearty satire was in store. Lee even begins the film with a Damon Wayans voiceover reciting the definition of satire. What Lee has in fact constructed is a horror story.

In Pierre Delacroix, Lee creates a modern Dr. Frankenstein. Mary Shelley's allegory plays out as Delacroix's creation—the minstrel show—spirals out of control and wreaks havoc. Delacroix even refers to himself as Frankenstein before the show's premier. Lee has been criticized for the movie's somber ending, but, in keeping with Shelley's template, the monster and the monster's creator must suffer. Both must be perpetrators and victims of the destruction that has been released.

The character Man Ray exemplifies this theme. Literally lifted off the streets, he and Womack are savvy enough to recognize that what they are doing is ethically wrong but hungry enough to ignore their reservations. Man Ray's simultaneous status as victim and perpetrator becomes the metaphor for the general condition of the black artist in the entertainment world. Ironically, Man Ray accuses Delacroix of sounding like a packaged voice from the popular media without realizing that that is precisely who Delacroix is and who Man Ray himself is becoming. Indeed, it is Delacroix's parents who expose Delacroix to the audience as a fake whose given name at birth was Peerless Dotham.

By naming Savion Glover's character Man Ray and then renaming him as Mantan, Lee pays homage to black artists who were denied proper credit for their comic talents during their lives, like Mantan Moreland. Womack is called "Sleep 'n' Eat" on Delacroix's minstrel show. The character name refers to the billing assigned to Willie Best, who for a large part of his film career was called only "Sleep 'n' Eat," if he was listed at all. Moreland, Best, and Lincoln Perry (known widely as Stepin Fetchit) were gifted actors, but their comedic talents were devoted exclusively to roles in which they portrayed the most demeaning stereotypes associated with black men—lazy, foot-shuffling, slow thinking, cowardly, and wholly subservient to whites. They were consistently the "Uncle Toms" or "Coons" (Bogle 2001), posing no danger to whites no matter the magnitude of the latter's acts of racist indignity.

The Mau Maus exemplify well-intentioned but misguided revolutionaries everywhere, and their behavior culminates in the killing of the target they can reach most easily. But, Man Ray/Mantan was really no more than a well-paid pawn in a programming venture executed by studio executives. As Delacroix's auditions demonstrate, there is always a long list of actors eager to play any part.

Bamboozled actually resembles a documentary because its tiny budget resulted in the film being shot with fifteen MiniDV digital cameras. While the budget permitted only a relatively low-quality print, Lee and consultant Michael Ray Charles used this limitation to their advantage in creating the film's motif. Visual artist Charles used his experience both as a historian and as an actual subject in a documentary to lend accuracy and a gritty, eerie look to the film. His artwork adorns Sloan's living room, but that room, like the offices in Delacroix's building, including Dunwitty's office with its prints of black athletes, still seems lifeless and barren.

The film's music also contributes to the chilling tone. The minstrel show's theme song, "I Wish I Was in Dixie"—performed by the Roots—is obvious, but the smooth Terrence Blanchard horn riffs that play during Mantan's death and Delacroix's subsequent moment of shame and remorse are a sonic counterpoint to the horrific images on the screen. Delacroix chooses to black his own face in this moment of mourning. In contrast to the actors on his minstrel show or their audience, there is nothing celebratory about his act of blackface; it is, instead, an act of penance manifesting his spiritual and moral nadir.

If the film can be faulted, it is for being overly ambitious. Arguably, the film tries to skewer too many subjects at once. The commercials for "Bomb" malt liquor and "Timmy Hilnigger" jeans are overkill. However, Lee is not interested in subtlety. He has stated publicly that he believes the movie does not overstate conditions in the film or television industry and that the characters are the types of people he encounters daily in Hollywood. Furthermore, he says that the idea of a live prime-time snuff broadcast is not that far in the future, comparing it with graphic war or riot footage that is aired frequently.

Bamboozled grazes over the subject of gender inequality. Lee's movies have often been criticized for their gender politics, but in this film Sloan is dynamic and complex, not just a victim or opportunist. Her initial objections to Delacroix's plan are mollified by his caress on her shoulder. He refers to her as his "little lamb," and it is only in the third act that the actual history of her relationship with Delacroix is made known.

Like all the characters in the film, Sloan raises the ethical question of how far a person will go and at what price. Is ignorance of the full consequences an excuse? Do black artists have a responsibility to be conscious of racial representation in everything they do? Are black artists during the first half of the twentieth century granted clemency because of the constraints of their times, and, if so, what is the point when forgiveness ends and pointed criticism begins? Womack/Sleep 'n' Eat does leave the minstrel show, but only after he has made a substantial sum of money. Sloan also withholds her own moral concerns and personally teaches Man Ray and Womack how to black their faces correctly, voicing objections based only on the potential adverse community reaction.

When the film was made, Lee may have intended it to convey a dystopic vision of a not-so-distant future, but many viewers in the years following its release recognized familiar images in real-life entertainment. Created in a post–Rodney King, pre-9/11 era, the film shows how easily the public can become desensitized. The audience at the opening of the minstrel show moves quickly from appalled silence to reluctant nervous laughter to full participation in the racist skits. The transition is eased by the fact that the performers are talented (as were Moreland,

Best, and Perry), and the skits are, despite their political and social ramifications, inspired and funny.

Ultimately, the film is an extended cautionary tale for the American media's continuing to put forth images that are similar to the minstrel tradition. It serves as a warning to individuals who bear direct or proximate responsibility for perpetuating stereotypes. In *Bamboozled* Lee is confronting the actions of producers, directors, and established actors, not just the desperate dirt-poor squatters, represented by Mantan and Sleep 'n' Eat, eager for a break.

SEE ALSO *Blackface; Blackness; Disaster Management; Film Industry; Humiliation; Jim Crow; Mau Mau; Memín Pinguín; Militants; Minstrelsy; Parody; Race; Racial Slurs; Racism; Sambo; Satire; Shame; Stereotypes; Tuskegee Syphilis Study; Uncle Tom; Whiteness; Whitening*

BIBLIOGRAPHY

Bogle, Donald. 2001. *Toms, Coons, Mulattoes, Mammies, and Bucks: An Interpretive History of Blacks in American Films*, 4th ed. New York: Continuum International.

Bogle, Donald. 2005. *Bright Boulevards, Bold Dreams: The Story of Black Hollywood*. New York: Random House.

Morris, Susan Booker. 2003. *Bamboozled*: Political Parodic Postmodernism. *West Virginia University Philological Papers* 50: 67–76.

Aden L. M. Darity

BANANA INDUSTRY

The production, consumption, and sale of bananas are important activities for many developing and low-income countries, generating employment, sustaining rural livelihoods, enhancing nutrition, and contributing to food security. The banana in 2002 was the fourth most important food crop in terms of value and ranked highest among fresh fruit exports in volume and in terms of export revenue to developing countries. Most bananas produced are consumed locally, with only 11 percent exported. At the start of the twenty-first century 85 percent of production was carried out by small producers using limited technological inputs.

COMPETITIVE STRUCTURE

Banana production for export employs a variety of systems, including small-scale, labor-intensive production on farms between 0.1 and 10 hectares and large-scale plantations ranging from 100 to 4,000 hectares. The latter produce 80 percent of fruit traded, employing high levels of technological innovation, including cable cars and exten-

sive irrigation. These systems result in varying levels of efficiency, evident in a wide range of yields from as high as 60 tonnes per hectare on modern plantation systems to a low of 4 tonnes on smaller farms. The banana trade is highly concentrated. In 2002 four transnational corporations (TNCs), Del Monte, Chiquita, Dole, Fyffes, and Noboa, an Ecuadorian company, controlling more than 80 percent of the trade, which includes shipping, ripening, and distribution. Dole, Chiquita, and Del Monte, whose predecessors United Fruit Company and Standard Fruit and Steamship Company pioneered the vertically integrated production and distribution system that characterized the origins of the industry in Latin America and the United States, continue their involvement in fruit production, accounting for over 50 percent of the fruit traded. Independent banana producers often engage in contract arrangements with banana companies to export their bananas. The structure of the market is grossly unequal, with international trading companies, distributors, and retailers earning 88 percent of the retail price, producing countries under 12 percent, and laborers less than 2 percent.

The conditions of workers involved in banana production vary widely. Low labor costs and cheap prices for bananas are key features of the industry's competitiveness. The first is oftentimes achieved by poor working conditions, restrictions on workers' rights to join trade unions of their choice, discrimination against women, and the use of child labor. Low prices, which result from the intense competition for markets, characterize the industry and translate to poor wages for workers, and increase the survival challenge for small-scale, independent producers.

INTERNATIONAL TRADE IN BANANAS

Developing countries are the main suppliers of banana exports and developed countries the main markets for imports, accounting for over 80 percent in 2002. There are three main markets for banana exports: Europe, North America, and Asia, in order of importance. The European Union (EU) became the largest market for banana imports in 2004 with the accession of ten new member states, absorbing one-third of the world trade in 2005. Together the EU and the United States accounted for over 60 percent of imports, while Japan and the Russian Federation combined imported roughly 12 percent.

Latin America (Ecuador, Costa Rica, Colombia, and Panama) is the largest exporting region, with Ecuador being the largest exporter in the world, exporting 4,653,900 tonnes in 2005. The Philippines was a distant second, exporting 1,904,700 tonnes, followed by Costa Rica. Latin American producers supply most of the United States and the Russian Federation. Ecuador and the Philippines are the major suppliers of the Japanese market. Latin America supplied 67 percent of the EU market in 2004; African Caribbean Pacific (ACP) countries (Cameroon, Ivory Coast, and several Caribbean countries, including the Windward Islands) supplied 17 percent; and producers within the EU (Martinique and Guadeloupe, Canary Islands, Madeira) supplied 16 percent.

REGIMES GOVERNING THE IMPORTATION OF BANANAS

A variety of arrangements govern the importation of bananas, ranging from wholly unregulated to highly regulated markets. The U.S. market is the most open, with no tariffs, quotas, or sanitary and phytosanitary (SPS) requirements (to ensure food safety and animal and plant health and product standards). Japan operates a seasonal preferential tariff rate. The European Community (EC), up to January 2006, was the most regulated market for bananas, with a complex system of quotas, tariffs, and licenses designed to provide preferential access to suppliers from the ACP countries.

EC Council regulation 404/93, which brought into being the Common Market Organisation for bananas and unified the EU banana market in 1993, changed significantly after the United States, on behalf of banana companies, and Ecuador, Honduras, Guatemala, and Mexico successfully challenged the legitimacy of some of its provisions under World Trade Organization (WTO) rules. It is now a simple tariff quota system, with a tariff of euro 176 per metric ton, and a duty-free quota of 775,000 tonnes for ACP producers on a first come, first served basis. This represents a significant reduction in the protection ACP countries had enjoyed. Latin American producers, particularly Ecuador, and some ACP producers are the main beneficiaries of this change at the expense of higher-cost, small farm driven production systems that exist in some Caribbean ACP exporting countries. In the Windward Islands, which has some of the smallest farming systems, production declined by 46 percent between 1994 and 2004, and the industry is not expected to survive further tariff reductions.

ANTICIPATED CHANGES IN THE INDUSTRY

The international trade in bananas is dynamic, with a steady increase in production but fluctuating prices. The output in the period between 1984 and 2000 saw a dramatic growth in the industry, which resulted in an increase in banana exports of 5.3 percent, more than twice that of the previous twenty-four years. This growth has been attributed to increased areas of production and, to a lesser extent, an increase in yields, rising demand in newly

liberalized markets in eastern Europe and China, and increased income in major banana importing countries in the 1990s. Projections to 2010 show the banana trade growing from 12.6 million tonnes in 2004 to 15 million tonnes, although at a slower rate than the previous decade, with Ecuador and the Philippines continuing to lead production.

Increasing Chinese domestic production suggests that China may become an important player in the export trade. The EU is expected to continue the trend of attracting a greater share of imports, especially in light of the reorganization of its market. Developing countries and transition countries, however, are expected to play a larger role as import markets for bananas, with some developing countries becoming major players after 2010. The production of bananas under organic and fair-trade labels is expected to increase. This market remains small, however, with organic bananas accounting for only 1 percent of the trade in 2002 and fair-trade bananas largely confined to the EU market. The evolution of supermarkets as major players in the production process, especially in standard setting, intensifying price competition, and the increasing use of contractual arrangements with suppliers is likely to strengthen, resulting in a further concentration of the trade at all stages: production, supply, and retail.

ENVIRONMENTAL AND LABOR PRACTICES

The extensive use of inputs to enhance quality and to control diseases and pests has contributed to concerns about the industry's impact on the environment. These surround the monocultural cultivation of the crop, which increasingly is focused on a single variety, the Cavendish, and its implications for biodiversity and vulnerability to disease and adverse weather; the intensity of production and the implications for soil fertility; the heavy usage of agrochemicals, including pesticides, fungicides, and fertilizers, and the dangers they hold for contaminating water supplies and for workers' health; and the proper disposal of plastic bags and other waste products.

Cultivation of organic and fair-trade bananas has developed in response to these concerns. Both systems are geared at mitigating the negative effects of production on the environment, with fair trade also focused on improving labor conditions, especially low wages, which can potentially increase the sustainability of small scale production. Environmental and food safety concerns have also led to a proliferation of standards to address some of the more egregious aspects of cultivation. The main standard setting institutions are the International Organization for Standardization (ISO 14001), the Food and Agriculture Organization/World Health Organization (FAO/WHO)

Codex Alimentaris Commission for organic bananas, and the Fair Trade Labelling Organisation (FLO).

CHALLENGES FACING THE INDUSTRY

The main challenge facing the industry, to quote the Costa Rican union leader Gilberth Bermudez Umana from a paper delivered at the International Banana Conference II, lies in "achiev[ing] a system of banana production based on social justice and on a development model in harmony with nature" (Umana 2005). Such a system should also result in a more equitable sharing of profits along the banana production and distribution chain in favor of laborers and small-scale producers. The difficulty, however, is that this is to be accomplished in an industry where cheaper fruit is attained at the expense of the living conditions of banana producers and the environment.

SEE ALSO *Agricultural Industry; Caribbean, The; Colonialism; Dependency; European Union; Industry; Irrigation; World Trade Organization*

BIBLIOGRAPHY

Arias, Pedro, Cora Dankers, Pascal Liu, and Paul Pilkauskas. 2003. The World Banana Economy 1985–2002. http://www.fao.org/docrep/007/y5102e/y5102e01.htm#TopOfPage.

Clegg, Peter. 2002. *The Caribbean Banana Trade: From Colonialism to Globalization.* Houndsmill, Basingstoke, Hampshire, U.K., and New York: Palgrave Macmillan.

Food and Agriculture Organization. 2006. Banana Market Situation in 2005 and Early 2006. http://www.fao.org/es/ESC/en/20953/20987/highlight_107821en_p.html.

Grossman, Lawrence S. 1998. *The Political Ecology of Bananas: Contract Farming, Peasants, and Agrarian Change in the Eastern Caribbean.* Chapel Hill: University of North Carolina Press.

Lewis, Patsy. 2000. A Future for Windward Island Bananas? Challenge and Prospect. *Journal of Commonwealth and Comparative Politics* 38 (2): 51–72.

Roche, Julian. 1998. *The International Banana Trade.* Abington, Cambridge, U.K.: Woodhead.

Slocum, Karla. 2006. *Free Trade and Freedom: Neoliberalism, Place, and Nation in the Caribbean.* Ann Arbor: University of Michigan Press.

Striffler, Steve, and Mark Moberg, eds. 2003. *Banana Wars: Power, Production, and History in the Americas.* Durham, NC: Duke University Press.

Umaña, Gilberth Bermudez. 2005. Foreword from the Secretariat. http://www.ibc2.org//images/stories/textibc/finadoc.pdf.

Patsy Lewis

BANANA PARABLE

The banana parable is found both in *A Treatise on Money* (Keynes 1930) and in John Maynard Keynes's exposition to the McMillan Committee, which was established in 1930 by Prime Minister Ramsay MacDonald to evaluate the performance of the economy in Great Britain. The committee consisted of senior ministers and outside experts, of which Keynes was one. In the *Treatise* it is presented as an illustration that saving by itself does not guarantee that investment will increase proportionally. In the explanation to the MacMillan Committee it is presented in relation to a closed or an open economy with a gold standard and in the context of an evaluation of the role of the banking system in effecting saving and investment.

In the 1920s Great Britain experienced high levels of unemployment with large fluctuations in its economy. Keynes turned his attention to those issues in *A Treatise on Money*, in which he attempted to reexamine the relationships among money, prices, and unemployment. He believed that the main cause of unemployment and economic fluctuations was the relationship of saving to investment. When individuals save more than the amounts businesses want to invest, that leads to excess capacity and too few buyers of the goods produced.

The saving-investment relationship was an important concern that was brought out in Keynes's "banana parable." In the story Keyes envisions a simple economy that produces and consumes only bananas and in which "ripe" bananas keep only for a week or two. There is a thrift campaign in that closed economy to increase saving with no corresponding increase in investment in bananas. With the same amount of bananas being produced as before the thrift campaign, savings will lower demand, causing the price to fall. This might seem desirable, Keynes points out, for it may increase saving and reduce the cost of living. However, if wages have not changed along with the falling price, the cost of production becomes greater than the revenue represented by the price and businesses will lose an amount of money equal to the saving rate. The consequence is that businesses need to cut costs by lowering wages or by firing workers, and this only makes matters worse. As the overall income level falls, this pushes the economy into a deeper recession. Keynes argued that the best way out of the economic downturn is for the central bank to pump more money into the economy to increase investment.

This parable presented a significant critique of classical economics by showing that flexible wage rates do not lead automatically to full employment. It also raised questions about the classical view of Say's law and the relationship between saving and investment. The parable also can be looked at as a demonstration of the neutrality of money wages as brought out in Keynes's *General Theory*, in which money wages follow falling prices so that the real wage remains relatively unchanged. The importance of this parable and the way in which it led Keynes to his views in the *General Theory* on the consumption function and the principle of effective demand is explained by Ingo Barens (1989).

The parable also provides insights into the debate between Friedrich Hayek and Keynes about the market economy. Hayek believed that market forces always align saving and investment in a smooth way unless there are distortions in the markets caused primarily by monetary policy. Keynes saw the economic landscape quite differently, positing that monetary policy and credit creation are absolutely necessary to stabilize the relationship between saving and investment, as is brought out in the parable.

SEE ALSO *Involuntary Unemployment; Keynes, John Maynard; Unemployment; Wages*

BIBLIOGRAPHY

Barens, Ingo. 1989. From the "Banana Parable" to the Principle of Effective Demand: Some Reflections on the Origin, Development and Structure of Keynes' *General Theory*. In *Perspectives on the History of Economic Thought; 20th- Century Economic Thought: Selected Papers from the History of Economics Society Conference,* ed. Donald Walker, 111–132. Cheltenham, U.K.: Edward Elgar.

Keynes, John Maynard. 1930. *A Treatise on Money.* New York: Harcourt Brace.

Keynes, John Maynard. [1936] 1973. *The General Theory of Employment, Interest and Money.* Vol. 7. London: Macmillan.

Keynes, John Maynard. 1983. *The Collected Writings of John Maynard Keynes,* Vol. 20. London: Macmillan.

Ric Holt

BANDITOS

SEE *Villa, Francisco (Pancho).*

BANDURA, ALBERT
1925–

Considered by some to be the father of behavioral psychology, Albert Bandura was born on December 4, 1925, in Mundare, a small town in Alberta, Canada. As a teenager, Bandura decided to take a psychology course to fill a space in his high school schedule. The result was a love for the subject that extended through his college years. He received his PhD in 1952 from the University of Iowa.

Promoted to full professor at Stanford University in 1964, Bandura often attributed his motivation for research to his collaborations with researchers such as Jack Barchas and Craig Barr Taylor. The joint research allowed them to combine different expertise and laboratory resources. One outcome of these research efforts was the finding that people regulate their level of physiological arousal (i.e., hormonal release) through their belief in self-efficacy. Bandura's contributions to personality theory and therapy incorporated a three-way interaction between the environment, behavior, and psychological processes at a time when dynamic systems theory had yet to be defined. Bandura focused on observational learning, or modeling, and he showed that children learn behavior through watching others. His most famous study, known as the *Bobo dolls* study, established that children do not need punishment or reward to learn. With his then doctoral student Richard Walters, Bandura found that hyperaggressive adolescents often had parents who modeled hostile attitudes; the results led to Bandura's first book, *Adolescent Development* (1959).

Bandura's decision to relabel his theoretical approach from *social learning* to *social cognition* was due to his growing belief that the breadth of his theorizing and research had expanded beyond the scope of the social learning label. Bandura presented a social cognitive vision of the origins of human thought and action and the influential role of self-referential processes to motivation, affect, and action. He depicted people as self-organizing, proactive, self-reflective, and self-regulative in thought and action, rather than as merely reactive to social environmental or inner cognitive-affective forces. A major focus of Bandura's theorizing addressed the extraordinary ability of humans to use imagery and symbolism. Drawing on their symbolic capabilities, people can comprehend their environment, construct guides for action, solve problems cognitively, support forethoughtful courses of action, gain new knowledge by reflective thought, and communicate with others at any distance in time and space. By symbolizing their experiences, people give structure, meaning, and continuity to their lives.

A further distinctive feature of social cognitive theory that Bandura singles out for special attention is the capacity for self-directedness as well as forethought. People plan courses of action, anticipate their likely consequences, and set goals and challenges for themselves to motivate, guide, and regulate their activities. The focus that Bandura gave to self-efficacy brought the term into mainstream conversation. Social learning theory is a general theory of human behavior, but Bandura and people concerned with mass communication have used it specifically to explain media effects. Bandura warned that children and adults acquire attitudes, emotional responses, and new styles of conduct through filmed and televised modeling. Bandura's warning struck a responsive chord in parents and educators who feared that escalating violence on television and other forms of media would transform children into bullies. Although Bandura does not think this will happen without the tacit approval of those who supervise the children, he regards anxiety over televised violence as legitimate. That stance caused him to be blackballed by network officials from taking part in the 1972 *Surgeon General's Report on Violence.* The psychologist Kevin Durkin, who reviewed the research on violent video games in 1995, reported that studies had found "either no or minimal effects." Indeed, he added, "some very tentative evidence indicates that aggressive game play may be cathartic (promote the release of aggressive tensions) for some individuals" (Durkin 1995, p. 2). Durkin and Kate Aisbett reported in a 1999 follow-up survey that "early fears of pervasively negative effects" from video games "are not supported"; "several well designed studies conducted by proponents of the theory that computer games would promote aggression in the young have found no such effects" (Durkin and Aisbett 1999, p. 3). These findings were echoed by other scholars.

To combat public policy problems, Bandura presided over the founding of the Association for the Advancement of Psychology as an advocacy group for promoting the influence of psychology in public policy initiatives and congressional legislation. He was elected to the presidencies of the American Psychological Association in 1974 and the Western Psychological Association in 1981. He was also appointed honorary president of the Canadian Psychological Association. In August 1999 Bandura received the Thorndike Award for Distinguished Contributions of Psychology to Education from the American Psychological Association (APA). In 2001 he received the Lifetime Achievement Award from the Association for the Advancement of Behavior Therapy. In August 2004 he received the APA's Outstanding Lifetime Contribution to Psychology Award. He has written seven books and edited two others, which have been translated into numerous languages.

SEE ALSO *Social Learning Perspective*

BIBLIOGRAPHY

Durkin, Kevin. 1995. *Computer Games: Their Effects on Young People.* Sidney: Australian Office of Film and Literature Classification.

Durkin, Kevin, and Kate Aisbett. 1999. *Computer Games and Australians Today.* Sidney: Australian Office of Film and Literature Classification.

Loftus, Elizabeth. A Life in Memory. In *History of Psychology in Autobiography*, ed. Garnder Lindzey and William Runyan. Vol. 9. Washington, DC: American Psychological Association.

Pajares, Frank. 2004. Albert Bandura: Biographical Sketch. http://des.emory.edu/mfp/bandurabio.html.

Zimmerman, Barry, and Dale Schunk. 2002. Albert Bandura: The Man and His Ideas. In *Educational Psychology: A Century of Contributions.* Mahwah, NJ: Erlbaum.

Sarah Holland Brown-Omar

BANKING

Banking is the name given to the activities of banks. The word *bank* is derived from the Italian *banca*, which means bench. Moneylenders in Northern Italy originally did business in open rooms or areas, with each lender working from his own bench or table. In the modern era banks are financial firms that simultaneously issue deposits, make loans, and create money.

A deposit is issued when a household or a business brings cash or currency to a bank in exchange for an equivalent amount of stored value, which can either be used to meet payment obligations or saved for future expenditure needs. Loan making is a form of credit. Credit comes into being when one economic unit (the creditor) authorizes another (the debtor) to acquire goods prior to paying for the goods received. A bank makes a loan when it authorizes a borrower to make expenditures on the bank's account up to a contractually agreed maximum level, in exchange for repayment of these advances later in time. Loans are usually made for expenditure purposes that are agreed on in advance (for example, the purchase of housing or of education services). Borrowers are normally authorized to use loan funds for a certain period of time and are required to repay the amount of the loan plus some amount of interest, which reflects the cost of the loaned funds. Common types of loans are working-capital loans, used by businesses primarily for buying supplies and making wage payments, and mortgage loans, which provide long-term funds (often for a duration of thirty years) for purchasing residences.

There are two principal types of bank deposits. Demand deposits are used primarily to handle transaction needs. They are completely liquid, as they can be withdrawn at will and without notice by the deposit holder. Time deposits are used primarily to store savings. They are less liquid than demand deposits, as they are normally contracted for fixed time periods (often six months or one year). In compensation for this loss of liquidity, those holding time deposits receive compensation in the form of (higher) interest payments.

The process of making loans may create money. A financial institution creates money in making loans when it creates demand deposits that can be spent by its borrowers. These borrowers did not possess these deposits before receiving loans, nor were these deposits taken from any of the bank's deposit customers. The ability to create money by making loans makes banks' behavior procyclical: Their loan making tends to expand when the economy is growing, further accelerating growth, and to slow when the economy does.

Banking is heavily regulated for two reasons. First, maintaining an orderly economy requires maintaining reliable transaction processes and financial markets, and banks are at the heart of these processes and markets. Second, banks are a source of instability within the economy. The default risks inherent in loan making interact with banks' ability to expand the money supply through loan making. In a worst-case scenario, unsound bank loan making (or choices of other assets) can weaken an economy and subject it to bank or currency runs, and/or expose an economy to stagnation, deflation, and even recession.

Banking has always been a heavily regulated field of activity. For one, banks typically require a bank charter issued by regulators. Moreover, every economy normally has a central bank, which attempts to control money and credit growth and which is responsible for rescuing the banking system in times of acute crisis. Regulation is especially important at the beginning of the twenty-first century, because banks' behavior in loan making has changed so much over time. From the 1930s to the 1960s, banks were relatively cautious. They made loans up the amount of their excess reserves, that is, the amount of currency on hand beyond that needed to meet its deposit customers' normal withdrawal demands. Over time, banks became more aggressive in finding funds to lend. Banks evolved the practice of liability management, in which they set targets for asset and loan growth and reach those targets by borrowing reserves, primarily from other banks in the interbank market.

Banks have also become more aggressive in loan making, as a result in part of their deepening links to financial centers such as Fleet Street and Wall Street. Since the late 1970s, banks have competed to make loans in hot markets, including overseas borrowers. This has led to severe crises of loan repayment and refinancing, the most spectacular cases being the Latin American debt crisis of the 1980s and the East Asian financial crisis of 1997–1998 (Stiglitz 2003). Despite these recurring crises, banks continually push into new areas of loan making, searching for new ways to earn revenue. In the 1990s and 2000s, banks have increasingly extended personal credit (often via credit cards), and have gotten involved in such nonbanking activities as derivatives and options, mutual funds and insurance.

The recurring problems in loan markets have made banking behavior a central topic in economic research. One key question is why lending booms and busts occur; another is why borrowers default (that is, are unable to repay loans according to their contractual obligations). Economists focusing on the first question have emphasized that banks are driven by competition to overlend in boom periods, leading to rising financial fragility (more debt obligations relative to available income), which eventually triggers a downturn (Minsky 1982). Economists addressing the second question focus on the distribution of information in credit markets; they emphasize that borrowers may seek to cheat lenders, and that banks may not accurately determine which potential borrowers are competent and which are not (Freixas and Rochet 1997). Banks can avoid default by extracting timely information about borrowers, their competence, and their intentions. Yet the social neutrality of the criteria that banks use to decide which borrowers are creditworthy has been called into question. Economic studies have generated substantial evidence that banks sometimes treat racial minorities, residents of minority and lower-income communities, and even disadvantaged regions unfairly in their credit-market decisions (Austin Turner and Skidmore 1999).

SEE ALSO *Financial Markets; Loans; Overlending*

BIBLIOGRAPHY

Austin Turner, Margery, and Felicity Skidmore, eds. 1999. *Mortgage Lending Discrimination: A Review of Existing Evidence.* Washington, DC: Urban Institute.

Freixas, Xavier, and Jean-Charles Rochet. 1997. *The Microeconomics of Banking.* Cambridge, MA: MIT Press.

Minsky, Hyman. 1982. *Can "It" Happen Again?* Armonk, NY: M. E. Sharpe.

Stiglitz, Joseph E. 2003. *Globalization and Its Discontents.* New York: Norton.

Gary A. Dymski

BANKING INDUSTRY

The modern banking industry is a network of financial institutions licensed by the state to supply banking services. The principal services offered relate to storing, transferring, extending credit against, or managing the risks associated with holding various forms of wealth. The precise bundle of financial services offered at any given time has varied considerably across institutions, across time, and across jurisdictions, evolving in step with changes in the regulation of the industry, the development of the economy, and advances in information and communications technologies.

FUNCTIONS

Banks as financial intermediaries are party to a transfer of funds from the ultimate saver to the ultimate user of funds. Often, banks usefully alter the terms of the contractual arrangement as the funds move through the transfer process in a manner that supports and promotes economic activity. By issuing tradable claims (bank deposits) against itself, the bank can add a flexibility to the circulating media of exchange in a manner that enhances the performance of the payments system. These deposits may support the extension of personal credit to consumers (retail banking) or short-term credit to nonfinancial businesses (commercial banking). If so, the bank aids the management of liquidity, thus promoting household consumption and commerce. By facilitating the collection of funds from a large number of small savers, each for a short period, the bank promotes the pooling of funds to lend out in larger denominations for longer periods to those seeking to finance investment in larger capital projects. Financing investment may take the form of underwriting issues of securities (investment banking) or lending against real estate (mortgage banking). By specializing in the assessment of risk, the bank can monitor borrower performance; by diversifying across investment projects, the bank minimizes some types of risk and promotes the allocation of funds to those endeavours with the greatest economic potential. By extending trade credit internationally (merchant banking), the bank can facilitate international trade and commerce. As one last example, by lending to other banks in times of external pressures on liquidity, the bank can manage core liquidity in the financial system, thus potentially stabilizing prices and output (central banking).

To discharge its various functions, banks of all types manage highly leveraged portfolios of financial assets and liabilities. Some of the most crucial questions for the banking industry and state regulators center on questions of how best to manage the portfolio of deposit banks, given the vital role of these banks in extending commercial credit and enabling payments. With bank capital (roughly equal to the net value of its assets after deduction of its liabilities) but a small fraction of total assets, bank solvency is particularly vulnerable to credit risk, market risk, and liquidity risk. An increase in non-performing loans, a drop in the market price of assets, or a shortage of cash reserves that forces a distress sale of assets to meet depositors' demand can each, if transpiring over a period of time too short for the bank to manage the losses, threaten bank solvency.

ORIGINS OF MODERN BANKING

The modern banking industry, offering a wide range of financial services, has a relatively recent history; elements of banking have been in existence for centuries, however. The idea of offering safe storage of wealth and extending credit to facilitate trade has its roots in the early practices of receiving deposits of objects of wealth (gold, cattle, and grain, for example), making loans, changing money from one currency to another, and testing coins for purity and weight.

The innovation of fractional reserve banking early in this history permitted greater profitability (with funds used to acquire income earning assets rather than held as idle cash reserves) but exposed the deposit bank to a unique risk when later paired with the requirement of converting deposits into currency on demand at par, since the demand at any particular moment may exceed actual reserves. Douglas Diamond and Philip Dybvig have, for example, shown in their 1983 article "Bank Runs, Liquidity, and Deposit Insurance" that in such an environment, a sufficiently large withdrawal of bank deposits can threaten bank liquidity, spark a fear of insolvency, and thus trigger a bank run.

Means of extending short-term credit to support trade and early risk-sharing arrangements afforded by such devices as marine insurance appear in medieval times. Italian moneychangers formed early currency markets in the twelfth century CE at cloth fairs that toured the Champagne and Brie regions of France. The bill of exchange, as a means of payment, was in use at this time as well.

Over the course of the seventeenth and eighteenth centuries, the industry transformed from a system composed of individual moneylenders financially supporting merchant trade and commerce, as well as royalty acquiring personal debt to finance colonial expansion, into a network of joint-stock banks with a national debt under the control and management of the state. The Bank of England, for example, as one of the oldest central banks, was a joint-stock bank initially owned by London's commercial interests and had as its primary purpose the financing of the state's imperial activities by taxation and the implementing of the permanent loan. This period was also marked by several experiments with bank notes (with John Law's experiment in France in 1719–1720 among the most infamous) and the emergence of the check as simplified version of the bill of exchange.

Eighteenth-century British banking practices and structures were transported to North America and formed an integral part of the colonial economies from the outset. The first chartered bank was established in Philadelphia in 1781 and in Lower Canada in 1817. Experiments with free banking—as a largely unregulated business activity in which commercial banks could issue their own bank notes and deposits, subject to a requirement that these be convertible into gold—have periodically received political support and have appeared briefly in modern Western financial history. Public interest in minimizing the risk of financial panics and either limiting or channelling financial power to some advantage has more often, however, dominated and justified enhanced industry regulation.

BANK REGULATION

Various forms of bank regulation include antitrust enforcement, asset restrictions, capital standards, conflict rules, disclosure rules, geographic and product line entry restrictions, interest rate ceilings, and investing and reporting requirements. The dominant view holds that enhanced regulation of this industry is necessary because there is clear public sector advantage, or for protecting the consumer by controlling abuses of financial power, or because there is a market failure in need of correction.

Where public sector advantage justifies the need for regulation, government intervention may appear in the form of reserve requirements imposed on deposit-taking institutions for facilitating the conduct of monetary policy or in the various ways in which governments steer credit to those sectors deemed important for some greater social purpose. Limiting concentration and controlling abuses of power and thus protecting the consumer have motivated such legislation as the American unit banking rules (whereby banks were limited physically to a single center of operation) and interest rate ceilings (ostensibly designed to prohibit excessive prices), as well as various reporting and disclosure requirements.

The latent threat of a financial crisis is an example of a market failure that regulation may correct. Here, the failure is in the market's inability to properly assess and price risk. The systemic risk inherent in a bank collapse introduces social costs not accounted for in private sector decisions. The implication is that managers, when constructing their portfolios, will assume more risk than is socially desirable; hence, there exists a need for government-imposed constraint and control. State-sanctioned measures designed to minimize the threat of bank runs include the need for a lender of last resort function of the central bank to preserve system liquidity and the creation of a government-administered system of retail banking deposit insurance.

Regulation explicitly limiting the risk assumed by managers of banks includes restrictions that limit the types and amounts of assets an institution can acquire. A stock market crash will threaten solvency of all banks whose portfolios are linked to the declining equity values. Investment bank portfolios will be, in such a circumstance, adversely affected. The decline in the asset values

of investment banks can spill over to deposit banks causing a banking crisis when the assets of deposit banks include marketable securities, as happened in the United States in the early 1930s.

The Bank Act of 1933 (the Glass-Steagall Act) in the United States as well as early versions of the Bank Act in Canada, for example, both prohibited commercial banks from acquiring ownership in nonfinancial companies, thus effectively excluding commercial banks from the investment banking activities of underwriting and trading in securities. This highly regulated and differentiated industry structure in twentieth-century North America contrasts sharply with the contemporaneous banking structures of Switzerland and Germany, for example, where the institutions known as universal banks offer a greater array of both commercial and investment banking services. The question for policymakers then is which industry structure best minimizes the risk of banking crises and better promotes macroeconomic stability and growth.

BANKING AND MACROECONOMIC ACTIVITY

The relationship between credit, bank notes, bank deposits, and macroeconomic stability has been the focus of much debate in the history of Western monetary thought. This debate grows more vigorous in the wake of financial panics and crises, when its focus turns to causality between banking crises and economic downturns.

Between 1929 and 1933 more than 40 percent of the American banks existing in 1929 failed. With no deposit insurance, bank failures wiped out savings and forced a severe contraction of the money supply. Milton Friedman and Anna Schwartz (1963) maintain that inaction by the American central bank permitted the sudden contraction of liquidity and magnification of real economic distress. Ben Bernanke (1983), too, believes that monetary conditions lead real economic activity, arguing that bank failures raise the cost of credit intermediation and therefore have an effect on the real economy. Charles Kindleberger (1986) alternatively suggests that non-monetary forces lie at the root of the problem, but that it was the failure of the Credit-Anstalt bank in Austria that proximately forced a sudden withdrawal of credit from the New York money markets and, in domino fashion, a contraction of credit throughout the United States. For Hyman Minsky (1982), the evolving margins of safety between the streams of asset income in relation to the contemporaneous changes in the cost of credit both characterize and explain financial instability.

Whichever the direction of primary causation, there is substantial agreement on the fact that there exists an important relationship between a sudden contraction of credit and liquidity and a considerable decline in economic activity. Consensus arises also around the likelihood that central bank last resort lending, in the manner suggested by Henry Thornton (1802) or by Walter Bagehot (1873), had it been exercised, might have substantially mitigated these effects.

Despite being subjected to similar nonmonetary shocks, and despite existing in an economy that roughly mirrored the American economy at the time, the Canadian banking system of the 1930s proved itself less vulnerable to collapse. Two factors may explain the relative stability of the Canadian banking sector: a lower level of integration of commercial and investment banking activities and a much more highly concentrated industry, with only a few large banks dominating the Canadian banking landscape. While Richard Sylla (1969) suggests that monopolistic elements in the post-bellum U.S. banking industry were present and may explain the apparent inefficiencies he observes in the data, Michael Bordo, Hugh Rockoff, and Angela Redish (1994), for example, argue for an absence of evidence in support of any similar claim that Canadian bank cartels created gross differences in pricing. Contrary to common suspicion, stability, it appears, was not at the cost of any significant loss in efficiency, at least in the Canadian industry. Nevertheless, American apprehension about concentrations of financial power continued to prevail. Legislation designed to minimize the future possibility of such crises focused instead on enforced portfolio adjustments.

The relationship between crises and economic downturns has its counterpart in a later debate about the financial structure and economic growth. In broad strokes, as an economy develops in scale and scope, formal financial arrangements gradually (however incompletely) replace informal ones. As the economy's need for larger amounts of funds to finance larger capital projects rises, the increasing inefficiency of many informal financial systems yields to the efficiency of formal codified transactions. As Rondo Cameron and Hugh Patrick (1967, p. 1) explain in *Banking in the Early Stages of Industrialization, A Study in Comparative Economic History*, the proliferation of the number and variety of financial institutions and a substantial rise in the ratio of money and other financial assets relative to total output and tangible wealth are "apparently universal characteristics of the process of economic development in market-oriented economies."

In "Finance and Growth: Theory and Evidence" Ross Levine (2005, p. 867) examines the theory and evidence and concludes, "better functioning financial systems ease the external financing constraints that impede firm and industrial expansion, suggesting that this is one mechanism through which financial development matters for growth." Whether the industry is segmented (with an enhanced role for capital markets) or not (as with universal banking systems, and their greater role for banks), does not seem to matter much, however. Several mutually reinforcing changes have stimulated a renewed public interest in this question about the preferred industrial structure.

POST-1980 INDUSTRY DEVELOPMENTS

The period from 1980 onward has been marked by increasing consolidation of banks, substantial loss in the share of financial activity to financial markets (disintermediation), greater market concentration, and considerable blurring of the traditional distinctions between banks and other financial institutions. Banks are increasingly offering a broader array of financial services in an increasing number of jurisdictions. The result is that banks in many countries where their scope was once limited are becoming more like universal banks.

Forces of change affecting the financial system since 1980 include market forces, legislative changes, and technological advances affecting communication and information. The dynamic tension and interplay between these forces have contributed significantly to the growth of new markets, new institutions, and new instruments, many of which fall outside the purview of existing regulation by virtue of their location or definition or both. The result is that an increasing amount of financial activity escapes regulation of any kind.

National responses have been largely to advocate and initiate deregulation of the domestic financial systems, justified by the same arguments that once supported the regulation. The elimination of interest rate ceilings, for example, should increase choice and competition, result in better and cheaper services for the customer, and increase the efficiency with which the economy allocates scarce funds. Permitting the integration of commercial and investment banking activities should produce greater efficiencies by permitting firms to capture greater economies of scale and scope. Notably, the legal separation of these activities was repealed in the United States with the 1999 Financial Services Modernization Act.

To date, international financial regulation is limited to the right-of-access rules negotiated by the European Union member states and by Canada, Mexico, and the United States, as part of the North American Free Trade Agreement, for example. Other international efforts have been largely and significantly restricted to international agreements to incorporate proposed rules into national legislation. The 1988 Basel Accord on the international convergence of capital measurements and standards, for example, recommended minimum common levels of capital for banks conducting international business. The twelve original signatories gradually adopted these capital requirements, as did several other countries. The second Accord, reached in 2004, broadened the scope of the earlier agreement and increased its flexibility to meet the objective of setting standards for minimizing both credit and operational risks. There remain, however, several markets and instruments in the international arena that have yet to be regulated or at least have the relevant national regulation coordinated.

FUTURE DIRECTIONS

The future may well see an increased extent and variety of the bundling of financial services as techniques and technologies of securitization, networking, and outsourcing offer new organizational possibilities. The result thus far has been a blurring of the traditional distinctions between banking and non-banking financial activity. Bank mergers and mergers of banks with other financial firms are occurring with increasing frequency and magnitude, suggesting that the future may well witness both a greater dominance of universal banking structures and a greater international concentration of financial assets.

Perhaps more profound is the potential for the blurring of any clear distinction between financial and nonfinancial activities. Nonfinancial retailers are joining forces with banks or opening their own lending facilities outright. Developments in electronic communications and software have the potential to erode the banking industry's relative monopoly over bank deposits as the nation's dominant medium of exchange. It may only be a matter of time before the provision of commercial and retail credit already offered by some nonfinancial communications companies effectively challenges even these most traditional of banking activities. Whatever the precise institutional details—and they will continue to vary from jurisdiction to jurisdiction—the difference between financial and nonfinancial enterprises may be expected to become increasingly difficult to define and regulate as the banking industry continues to evolve.

SEE ALSO *Financial Instability Hypothesis; Regulation*

BIBLIOGRAPHY

Bagehot, Walter. 1873. *Lombard Street, a Description of the Money Market.* Homewood, IL: Richard D. Irwin, 1962.

Bernanke, Ben S. 1983. Nonmonetary Effects of the Financial Crisis in Propagation of the Great Depression. *American Economic Review* 73 (3): 257–76.

Bordo, Michael D., Hugh Rockoff, and Angela Redish. 1994. The U.S. Banking System from a Northern Exposure: Stability versus Efficiency. *The Journal of Economic History* 54 (2): 325–341.

Cameron, Rondo E., and Hugh T. Patrick. 1967. Introduction. In *Banking in the Early Stages of Industrialization, A Study in Comparative Economic History*, eds. Rondo E. Cameron, Olga Crisp, Hugh T. Patrick, and Richard Tilly. New York: Oxford University Press.

Diamond, Douglas, and Philip Dybvig. 1983. Bank Runs, Liquidity, and Deposit Insurance. *Journal of Political Economy* 91 (3): 401–419.

Friedman, Milton, and Anna Jacobson Schwartz. 1963. *A Monetary History of the United States, 1867–1960.* Princeton, NJ: Princeton University Press.

Kindleberger, Charles P. 1986. *The World in Depression, 1929–1939.* Rev. and enl. ed. Berkeley: University of California Press.

Levine, Ross. 2005. Finance and Growth: Theory and Evidence. In *Handbook of Economic Growth*, eds. Philippe Aghion and Steven N. Durlauf, 865–934. Amsterdam: Elsevier.

Minsky, Hyman. 1982. The Financial Instability Hypothesis: Capitalistic Processes and the Behavior of the Economy. In *Financial Crises: Theory, History, and Policy*, eds. Charles P. Kindleberger and Jean-Paul Laffargue, 13–39. Cambridge, U.K.: Cambridge University Press.

Sylla, Richard. 1969. Federal Policy, Banking Market Structure, and Capital Mobilization in the United States, 1863–1913. *Journal of Economic History* 39 (4): 657–86.

Thornton, Henry. 1802. *An Enquiry into the Nature and Effects of the Paper Credit of Great Britain*, ed. Friedrich A. von Hayek. New York: Kelley, 1962.

Brenda Spotton Visano

BARDS

SEE *Storytelling.*

BARGAINING

SEE *Negotiation; Screening and Signaling Games.*

BARRIERS TO TRADE

Barriers to trade include those made by policy and those posed by nature. Both policy barriers and natural barriers include several important types. Overall, despite much talk of globalization, barriers to trade of both types remain high (see Anderson and van Wincoop 2004 for a review of evidence).

POLICY BARRIERS

Policy barriers include tariffs and quotas. In past years and still in many countries, these have been substantial barriers to international trade. Tariffs and quotas discriminate in the treatment of goods between those produced at home and those produced abroad. Other policy barriers can also be discriminatory.

Product standards, such as health and safety requirements, are on the surface nondiscriminatory. All autos sold in the United States must meet emissions standards. Under the surface, however, product standards are often used to discriminate. It is very difficult to make systematic evaluations of the effect of discrimination in product standards. Anecdotes abound, as in the notorious exclusion of Mexican trucking firms via discriminatory use of safety standards from the North American trade they are entitled to under the North American Free Trade Agreement.

The legal system's treatment of aliens is often different than that of nationals, even though the laws themselves are mostly formally nondiscriminatory. Fair treatment of aliens is to some degree a policy choice. Again, anecdotes abound, but systematic evaluation of the effective policy discrimination is very difficult. Statistical inference that relates the pattern of bilateral trade to economic variables and to the quality of institutions (as measured by surveys of businessmen) suggests that bad-quality institutions harm international trade. For example, Anderson and van Wincoop (2004) report that Latin America's institutional deficit relative to European norms reduces its imports by as much as Latin America's tariffs.

NATURAL BARRIERS

Nature too imposes barriers to international trade. Most obviously, trade requires shipping, which increases in cost with distance. Distance reduces international trade relative to domestic trade because markets within nations are closer together on average than markets between nations. Transportation costs between most international markets are larger, usually much larger, than tariffs or tariff equivalents of quotas. Distance may also be associated with higher nontransportation trade costs, as it appears to reduce trade by more than can be accounted for by transportation.

Asymmetric information is another natural barrier to trade. Businessmen tend to know more about local markets than foreign markets. Information can be discovered at a cost, and this constitutes another trade cost. Statistical inference suggests that information costs can be large. Language differences, cultural differences, and institutional differences all reduce trade while ethnic ties increase it.

Attempts to infer the size of border barriers of all types give some idea of the size of barriers to trade. Inference can be done by comparing trade between regions of a single country with trade between regions in different countries, controlling for other influences, such as distance, on the size of trade. The average trade reduction associated with crossing a border implies very substantial border barriers that are a large multiple of tariffs

and the tariff equivalents of quotas (see Anderson and van Wincoop 2004 for detailed discussion).

SEE ALSO *Liberalization, Trade; North American Free Trade Agreement; Quotas; Quotas, Trade; Tariffs; Trade; Trade, Bilateral*

BIBLIOGRAPHY

Anderson, James E., and Eric van Wincoop. 2004. Trade Costs. *Journal of Economic Literature* 42: 691–751.

Bordo, Michael, Alan M. Taylor, and Jeffrey G. Williamson. 2003. *Globalization in Historical Perspective*. Chicago: University of Chicago Press.

James E. Anderson

BARRO-GROSSMAN MODEL

The Barro-Grossman model, proposed by Robert J. Barro and Herschel I. Grossman, was first published in 1971 in what was to become, seventeen years later, the most frequently cited article in the *American Economic Review*. It was further developed in Barro and Grossman's *Money, Employment, and Inflation* (1976), though this latter work never became a dominant graduate textbook, as it was overtaken by what has been called the rational expectations revolution. Barro himself largely abandoned the Barro-Grossman model in the late 1970s. Though work based on the model continued to appear, and in that sense the model never disappeared, it was taught in very few graduate programs and fell out of fashion in the early 1980s.

The central idea of the model is that of an *equilibrium with rationing*, sometimes called the *economics of disequilibrium*. Suppose that for some reason—such as an external shock—an economy develops a significant level of unemployment. Workers will find that they cannot sell as much labor as they would normally expect to sell, and they will have to cut back on their purchases of consumption goods. Firms will find that they cannot sell the goods they wish to sell at the prevailing prices, and so will not be willing to employ more labor. The economy gets stuck in a "Catch 22" situation, in which spending cannot rise because workers cannot find jobs, even if they offer to work for a lower wage, and firms will not employ more workers, because even if they lower prices, they cannot increase their sales revenue. Both groups are *rationed*— that is, they face constraints on the quantities they can sell at the prevailing prices.

The key to the model is a distinction introduced by Robert Clower (1965) between *effective* and *notional* demands, the former being calculated with quantity constraints taken into account, the latter with constraints ignored (notional demands are sometimes called *Walrasian*). In an equilibrium with rationing, effective demand equals supply. For example, workers may wish to sell more labor and purchase more consumption goods, but they cannot do so. Thus, if price changes depend on effective demands, there is no pressure to change prices. It is therefore possible to have an equilibrium with rationing in which there is high unemployment, even if wages and prices are at the level consistent with full employment. Market forces will not bring the economy back toward full-employment equilibrium.

The Barro-Grossman model was a fixed-price model in the sense that prices were taken as a parameter when determining quantities of employment and output. They were not necessarily constant—the 1976 version of the model allowed for inflation by having prices change in response to effective excess demands—but they adjusted much more slowly than quantities. In the late 1970s, Barro interpreted this as meaning that prices were fixed by long-term contracts, and when it was shown that it would not be optimal for such contracts to specify "sticky" prices (that is, prices that do not change immediately to eliminate potential differences between supply and demand), he abandoned the approach. However, other users of such models interpreted equilibrium with rationing differently. Clower had been interested in dynamic price-adjustment mechanisms in markets that were typically not perfectly competitive. Axel Leijonhufvud (1968), who had done more than anyone to popularize the idea of disequilibrium macroeconomics, was more interested in the idea of intertemporal disequilibrium. Jacques Drèze (1975), who pioneered the incorporation of quantity constraints in general equilibrium models, came to them through problems of information.

The folklore in macroeconomics is that the Barro-Grossman model went out of fashion in the 1970s because it did not make sense to assume rigid prices when inflation was running at levels that exceeded 25 percent in some OECD countries. However, paradoxically, it was precisely because of inflation that some economists turned to such models. Edmond Malinvaud (1977) used a model of equilibrium with rationing (not the Barro-Grossman model, but a member of the same family of models) because it was the only framework he could find in which to make sense of *stagflation*—that is, of simultaneously rising inflation and unemployment. Taking the wage rate and the price level as parameters was the first step in discussing what might cause an economy to move between different regimes: Keynesian unemployment (unemployment accompanied by a surplus of goods), classical unemployment (unemployment and a shortage of goods), and repressed inflation (shortages of labor and goods).

Possibly the main significance of the Barro-Grossman model in the history of macroeconomics is that it was an important part of the search for microfoundations of macroeconomics. Barro and Grossman wanted to construct a macroeconomic model with rigorous microeconomic foundations (rigorous in the sense of being based on maximizing behavior by individual firms and households). It should be seen as parallel to the search for microfoundations of Edmund Phelps and his collaborators (1970). Because macroeconomics was at that time synonymous with Keynesian economics, Barro and Grossman created a Keynesian model. Their model comprised a representative household and a representative firm. When Barro abandoned the fixed-price approach, he retained those elements, and when household and firm were combined, there emerged the representative agent model that is characteristic of modern macroeconomics.

SEE ALSO *Economics, New Keynesian; Excess Demand; Excess Supply; Inflation; Macroeconomics; Microfoundations; Prices; Shocks; Stagflation; Stocks; Unemployment*

BIBLIOGRAPHY

Barro, Robert J., and Herschel I. Grossman. 1971. A General Disequilibrium Model of Income and Employment. *American Economic Review* 61 (1): 82–93.

Barro, Robert J., and Herschel I. Grossman. 1976. *Money, Employment, and Inflation.* Cambridge, U.K.: Cambridge University Press.

Clower, Robert W. 1965. The Keynesian Counterrevolution: A Theoretical Appraisal. In *The Theory of Interest Rates*, eds. Frank H. Hahn and Frank P. R. Brechling, 103–125. London: Macmillan.

Drèze, Jacques H. 1975. Existence of an Exchange Equilibrium under Price Rigidities. *International Economic Review* 16 (2): 301–320. Reprinted in Drèze's *Underemployment Equilibria: Essays in Theory, Econometrics, and Policy.* Cambridge, U.K., and New York: Cambridge University Press, 1991.

Leijonhufvud, Axel. 1968. *On Keynesian Economics and the Economics of Keynes: A Study in Monetary Theory.* Oxford and New York: Oxford University Press.

Malinvaud, Edmond. 1977. *The Theory of Unemployment Reconsidered.* Oxford: Basil Blackwell.

Phelps, Edmund S., et al. 1970. *Microeconomic Foundations of Employment and Inflation Theory.* London: Macmillan.

Roger E. Backhouse

BASEL BAN AMENDMENT

SEE *Toxic Waste.*

BASEL CONVENTION

SEE *Toxic Waste.*

BASIC NEEDS

SEE *Needs, Basic.*

BA'TH ARAB SOCIALIST PARTY

SEE *Hussein, Saddam.*

BATISTA, FULGENCIO

SEE *Cuban Revolution.*

BATTLE OF ALGIERS, THE

Often presented as an account of the Algerian struggle for freedom, Italian director Gillo Pontecorvo's 1966 film *The Battle of Algiers* (*La battaglia di Algeri*) is in fact more precisely defined as an analysis of the strengths and limitations of counterinsurgency measures during the Algerian War (1954–1962) for independence from France and, as such, remains very relevant to the early twenty-first-century "global war on terror." Though one of the major films of the 1960s, rightly rewarded with the top prize, the Lion of Saint Mark, at the Venice Film Festival in 1966, *The Battle of Algiers* is, in terms of its production, a marginalized film. Coproduced by Igor Films in Rome and shot in Algeria with an Italian crew, it is a key work of the Italian post-neorealist generation. Yet it is ignored (along with its director) in such standard English-language studies of Italian cinema as Millicent Marcus's *Italian Film in the Light of Neorealism* (1986) and Pierre Sorlin's *Italian National Cinema, 1896–1996* (1996). At the same time, it is self-evidently, with its Italian director, not part of Algerian national cinema, despite the major contribution of Yacef Saadi.

Saadi was the National Liberation Front (FLN) leader for the autonomous zone of Algiers, and it was his arrest by French General Jacques Massu on September 24, 1957, that brought to an end the Battle of Algiers, which had begun in January of that year with an eight-day general strike called by the FLN. Saadi's book of memoirs, *Souvenirs de la bataille d'Alger* (Memories of the Battle of Algiers, 1962), is often cited as the source of the film (though it is not mentioned in the credits). Saadi also coproduced the film through his own company, Casbah Films, the only independent production company allowed to operate in postliberation Algeria, and he plays the role of the (fictional) insurgent leader, Djafar. But Saadi's direct experience has been shaped into a knowingly constructed film narrative, which, far from offering the Algerian experience from within, presents instead a reflection on this experience from the outside perspective of two committed Italian Marxists, Gillo Pontecorvo and his regular scriptwriter, Franco Solinas.

The film begins at the end of a torture sequence, when the Algerian victim has been broken and has given the required information, and, for the opening credits, shifts smoothly into a French military raid over the roofs and through the alleyways of the casbah to the hiding place of Ali la Plante, the last FLN leader to remain at large. This opening sequence sets the tone and style of the entire film: grainy black-and-white photography and location shooting, but at the same time fast-paced, action-film editing and the emotive use of music. The film's ambiguous attitude to the French torturers is apparent early in the film: they are men doing their job without personal animosity, and the colonel, their leader, is a man who tolerates no joking at the expense of the victim. Italian composer Ennio Morricone's music for the French assault is jaunty and positive, echoing the music used for scenes of Italian partisan raids in neorealist films a decade and a half earlier. From a close-up of the trapped Ali's faced framed in darkness, there is a dissolve into a flashback to Algiers in 1954 and the start of Ali's career.

Ali's story is the conventional tale of a petty criminal who discovers his political awareness when he witnesses a prison execution. The film follows his rise within the FLN from impetuous newcomer to resourceful leader. His story is intercut with scenes of a trio of women who take on the key role of placing bombs in the French quarter of the city, which is ringed with barbed wire and accessible only through heavily guarded checkpoints, but is otherwise unsuspecting and unprepared. There is no attempt to minimize the horror of bomb attacks on defenseless men, women, and children or in any way to condone the French settlers' revenge attacks, which occur with police connivance. The choice of Ali as protagonist—rather than the true leader and planner, Djafar—means that we never see the terror attacks as part of any coherent strategy, with thought-out objectives and tactics, on the part of the FLN. Within the film, the suffering of the Algerian people is depicted as leading "naturally" to the violence, so that the notoriously murderous internecine struggles within the FLN leadership are simply airbrushed out of the picture. Djafar is seen and heard only when he is a man on the run, aware that his very presence within the city brings danger to his followers. Thus the uprising in *The Battle of Algiers* is shown in narrative terms as an enigma: How is all this violence organized and how can it be stopped?

The man to resolve the enigma and deal with the stalemate of violence and counterviolence, Colonel Mathieu, makes his stirring entry into the film marching proudly at the head of his paratroopers past crowds of cheering settlers. Though we are notionally still within Ali's flashback, it is Mathieu who is the driving force in the film from this point onward. His briefings to his troops are lessons in counterterrorism and his press conferences present the justification for the use of torture by the French. If politicians will the outcome, they have to accept the necessary methods, however distasteful these may be. There is nothing personal about torture: it is just part of a job that has to be done. It is also Mathieu who lucidly points out—as the film takes on an increasingly didactic tone—that winning a battle is not the same as winning a war, and he goes to his next assignment "in the mountains" aware that none of his efforts can ultimately defeat a united Algerian people. His insights form a context in which Ali's choice of death rather than surrender can seem a fitting resolution to his personal story, while the audience can derive a wider emotional satisfaction from the spontaneous popular uprising in Algiers in 1960, which presaged the ending of French rule and with which the film concludes.

BIBLIOGRAPHY

Celli, Carlo. 2005. *Gillo Pontecorvo: From Resistance to Terrorism.* Lanham, MD: Scarecrow.

Hennebelle, Guy, ed. 1997. *La guerre d'Algérie à l'écran.* Paris: Corlet-Télérama-CinémAction 85.

Mellen, Joan. 1973. *Filmguide to* The Battle of Algiers. Bloomington: Indiana University Press.

Mimoun, Mouloud, ed. 1992. *France-Algérie: Images d'une guerre.* Paris: Institut du Monde Arabe.

Saadi, Yacef. *Souvenirs de la bataille d'Alger, décembre 1956–septembre 1957.* Paris: R. Julliard, 1962.

Solinas, Franco. 1973. *Gillo Pontecorvo's* The Battle of Algiers: *A Film Written by Franco Solinas.* New York: Scribners.

Roy Armes

BATTLE OF THE LITTLE BIG HORN

The Battle of the Little Big Horn took place from June 25 to June 27, 1876, along the river of the same name in what is now south-central Montana. The result is well known. Lakota Sioux, Northern Cheyenne, and a handful from other Northern Great Plains tribes defeated the 7th U.S. Cavalry regiment. The battle included several fights. In a separate engagement, the companies led by Major Marcus Reno (1834–1889; the regiment's second-in-command) weathered a thirty-six-hour siege after warriors thwarted their attack on the Indian camp.

The Custer fight is historically the most visible event of the Little Big Horn affair. Shortly after Reno retreated, on a river bluff about four miles from Reno's defense site, warriors wiped out to the man five companies (approximately 210 men) and their acting regimental commander, Lieutenant Colonel (Brevet Major General) George Armstrong Custer (1839–1876).

The event is indelibly fixed in the American social consciousness. It has been a symbol of bravery and spirit, of folly, and of oppression. This symbolism is largely a function of Custer's presence. Its perception as folly, most visible during socially liberal times, is amply illustrated in the motion picture *Little Big Man* (1970; Dustin Hoffman, Faye Dunaway), and in various biographies, such as Frederic Van de Water's *Glory Hunter* (1934), that portray Custer as an egotist willing to sacrifice others in his pursuit of glory.

Negative conceptions of the Battle of the Little Big Horn have their roots in the attitudes of Custer's contemporaries. Custer had achieved national prominence for his often daring (and usually highly successful) Civil War exploits (see Urwin's *Custer Victorious* [1983]). With success came jealousy, criticism, and accusations. Little Big Horn reinforced such views, ensuring their survival to this day. Conversely, the battle guaranteed Custer and his men symbolic immortality. At a time when the nation was celebrating its centennial, many Americans saw their deaths as noble sacrifices in the service of Manifest Destiny.

Promoters of Custer capitalized on these emotions, especially Custer's widow, Elizabeth (née Bacon; 1842–1933). Libbie (as Custer affectionately called her) never remarried and spent the rest of her long life, as Shirley Leckie chronicles in *Elizabeth Bacon Custer and the Making of a Myth* (1993), carefully constructing the image of an heroic last stand—a steadfast fight to the final man against hopeless odds.

This image of the Battle of the Little Big Horn as a "last stand" has also been promoted by historians and Custer biographers. Charles Kuhlman's *Legend into History* (1951) and Frederick Whittaker's *Complete Life of General George A. Custer* (1876) are but two examples from a voluminous literature. Generally "last stand" symbolism assumes prominence during socially conservative periods; the wartime film epic *They Died with Their Boots On* (1941; Errol Flynn, Olivia de Havilland) exemplifies this. Here the doomed men fight bravely to the last man, in this case Custer himself.

Whatever the collective social mood of a given period, Custer's "last stand"—as Brian Dippie argues in *Custer's Last Stand: The Anatomy of an American Myth* (1976)—has for the majority of Americans come to symbolize an indomitable American spirit. This is not the case in Native American circles. Rather, the Custer battle symbolizes triumph over oppression, perpetrated against not only Native Americans but also minorities in general (see Deloria's *Custer Died for Your Sins*, 1969). Such symbolism is not confined to the Lakota and Cheyenne; it exists among Native Americans in general, and circulates widely among non-natives as well.

The symbolic value of the Battle of the Little Big Horn dwarfs its military importance. The battle, one of many during the Northern Plains Indian War Period (1862–1877), was a minor event. It had no influence on Indian policy, the foundations of which were formulated over two decades earlier. Nonetheless, followed as it was by the Army's relentless winter campaign (1876/1877), it did indirectly hasten the surrender of Lakota and Northern Cheyenne bands (spring and summer of 1877). The defeated tribes were confined to reservation tracts, including the Great Sioux Reservation (originally the western half of present South Dakota, then reduced to small tracts in the Dakotas and Montana), established in 1868, and the Northern Cheyenne reserve (in south-central Montana), formed by Congress in 1884.

Custer the man permeates studies of the Little Big Horn battle, typically at great peril to objective analysis. Apologists are driven to absolve Custer of blame, most frequently by constructing events in ways that finger Major Reno. Like apologists, anti-Custer factions sometimes go to absurd lengths—but in order to blame Custer for the debacle, not one of his subalterns. Ultimately, the two sides find common ground in "last stand" imagery—whatever the chain of events, and whoever is blamed, Custer's battalion fights to the end against impossible odds.

Only comparatively recently has the venerable notion of a "last stand" been challenged, by Douglas Scott, Richard Fox, and others in two books, *Archaeological Insights into the Custer Battle* (1987) and *Archaeological Perspectives on the Battle of the Little Bighorn* (1989). Using forensic analysis of firing pin marks on spent cartridges systematically recovered from the Custer battlefield, Fox shows in *Archaeology, History, and Custer's Last Battle* (1993) that instead of mounting a resolute stand, Custer's battalion fell apart. Cartridge case patterns show the command maintained tactical order (skirmish lines) initially, but subsequently lost cohesion. Denouement came amid panic and fear. Numerous eyewitness reports by Indian

warriors support this interpretation. They speak of soldiers who "acted as if drunk," "threw down their guns," and so on. Native testimonies also indicate the end came in half an hour or so.

In the new synthesis, two independent lines of evidence—the material and documentary records—converge, providing interpretive confidence. Before the gathering of archaeological evidence, studies of the Battle of the Little Big Horn relied solely on highly contradictory historical documentation, which was easily manipulated in support of one or another preconceived notion of Custer and his men.

The historical-archaeological synthesis has not ended debate in Custer battle studies—but the case for a "last stand" is now far more difficult to argue. Authors who wish to keep this image of the battle alive—for example, Gregory Michno in *Lakota Noon* (1997)—are typically compelled to resort to special pleading, circular reasoning, revision, and selective use of evidence.

SEE ALSO *Archaeology*

BIBLIOGRAPHY

Deloria, Vine, Jr. 1969. *Custer Died for Your Sins: An Indian Manifesto.* New York: Macmillan.

Dippie, Brian W. 1976. *Custer's Last Stand: The Anatomy of an American Myth.* Lincoln: University of Nebraska Press.

Fox, Richard A., Jr. 1993. *Archaeology, History, and Custer's Last Battle.* Norman: University of Oklahoma Press.

Kuhlman, Charles. 1951. *Legend into History: The Custer Mystery: An Analytical Study of the Battle of the Little Big Horn.* Harrisburg, PA: Old Army Press.

Leckie, Shirley A. 1993. *Elizabeth Bacon Custer and the Making of a Myth.* Lincoln: University of Nebraska Press.

Michno, Gregory F. 1997. *Lakota Noon: The Indian Narrative of Custer's Defeat.* Missoula, MT: Mountain Press.

Scott, Douglas D., and Richard A. Fox Jr. 1987. *Archaeological Insights into the Custer Battle: An Assessment of the 1984 Field Season.* Norman: University of Oklahoma Press.

Scott, Douglas D., Richard A. Fox Jr., Melissa A. Connor, and Dick Harmon. 1989. *Archaeological Perspectives on the Battle of the Little Bighorn.* Norman: University of Oklahoma Press.

Urwin, Gregory J. W. 1983. *Custer Victorious: The Civil War Battles of General George Armstrong Custer.* Lincoln: University of Nebraska Press.

Van de Water, Frederic. 1934. *Glory-Hunter: A Life of General Custer.* Indianapolis, IN, and New York: Bobbs-Merrill. Reprint, Lincoln: University of Nebraska Press, 1988.

Whittaker, Frederick. 1876. *A Complete Life of General George A. Custer.* New York: Sheldon. Reprint, 2 vols., Lincoln: University of Nebraska Press, 1993.

Richard A. Fox

BAUER, BRUNO

SEE *Imperialism.*

BAUMRIND, DIANA
1927–

Diana Baumrind's seminal work on research ethics and parenting styles has shaped research and practice since the 1960s. Baumrind earned her undergraduate degree from Hunter College in 1948 and her PhD from the University of California, Berkeley, in 1955. Following a postdoctoral residency at Cowell Hospital, Baumrind joined the Institute of Human Development at the University of California, Berkeley, where she heads the Family Socialization and Developmental Competence Project as of 2007.

RESEARCH ETHICS

In response to Stanley Milgram's 1963 study of obedience to authority, Baumrind published an influential commentary on research ethics (1964). Baumrind has continued to address ethical issues in research on humans through consultation with the American Psychological Association and published work. On the use of deception in research, Baumrind has emphasized multiple levels of potential harm: to the participant, to the credibility of psychology as a profession, and to society.

PARENTING STYLES

In 1966 Baumrind published a ground-breaking article on parenting styles, followed by a 1967 article with Allen Black examining the effects of parenting styles on girls' and boys' development. Baumrind's three parenting styles involve different combinations of parental demand and control (confrontation, monitoring, consistent discipline, punishment) and responsiveness and affection (warmth, attachment, reciprocity, friendly discourse). Authoritative parents are moderately to highly demanding and highly responsive. Their children tend to be assertive, able to regulate themselves, socially responsible, and respectful to adults. Authoritarian parents are highly demanding and unresponsive to their children. Children of authoritarian parents tend to be moody, fearful of new situations, and low in self-esteem. Permissive parents are undemanding and nondirective. They are responsive to their children and avoid confrontation. Their children tend to be creative, sociable, and friendly, but may also be impulsive, aggressive, and resistant to limit setting. In 1983 Eleanor Maccoby and John Martin proposed a fourth style, uninvolved parenting. Uninvolved parents are undemanding and unresponsive, and their children may participate in deviant or high-risk behaviors.

Baumrind's typology has formed the foundation for much research on parental socialization of children and children's developmental outcomes. In her own work, Baumrind has examined parenting styles in parents of children of preschool age through adolescence. Outcomes that Baumrind has examined encompass academic achievement, emotion regulation, moral development, peer relations, social skills, substance abuse, and teenage sexuality. Baumrind has found authoritative parenting to be associated with better outcomes for children. This parenting style provides a model for children of care and concern for others' needs and of confident and controlled behavior. Beginning in the late 1980s, researchers expanded Baumrind's paradigm to families with low incomes and from diverse cultural backgrounds. Despite cultural differences in the degree of endorsement of different parenting styles and in the strength of the association of authoritative parenting with better outcomes in children, Baumrind's typology has been largely supported.

More controversial has been Baumrind's stance on physical punishment. While Baumrind argues that occasional, mild physical punishment may not lead to negative long-term outcomes in children when used as part of an overall authoritative parenting style, other researchers contend that parents' greater use of physical punishment is associated with negative outcomes in children and that such use may escalate to physical abuse (Gershoff 2002b, p. 609). A point of agreement is that cultural norms regarding physical punishment influence the extent to which such punishment is perceived as harsh and is likely to have negative outcomes.

SEE ALSO *Milgram, Stanley; Parenting Styles*

BIBLIOGRAPHY

Baumrind, Diana. 1964. Some Thoughts on Ethics of Research: After Reading Milgram's "Behavioral Study of Obedience." *American Psychologist* 19 (6): 421–423.

Baumrind, Diana. 1966. Effects of Authoritative Control on Child Behavior. *Child Development* 37 (4): 887–907.

Baumrind, Diana. 1996. Parenting: The Discipline Controversy Revisited. *Family Relations* 45 (4): 405–414.

Baumrind, Diana, and Allen E. Black. 1967. Socialization Practices Associated with Dimensions of Competence in Preschool Boys and Girls. *Child Development* 38 (2): 291–327.

Gershoff, Elizabeth Thompson. 2002a. Corporal Punishment by Parents and Associated Child Behaviors and Experiences: A Meta-analytic and Theoretical Review. *Psychological Bulletin* 128 (4): 539–579.

Gershoff, Elizabeth Thompson. 2002b. Corporal Punishment, Physical Abuse, and the Burden of Proof: Reply to

Baumrind, Larzelere, and Cowan (2002), Holden (2002), and Parke (2002). *Psychological Bulletin* 128 (4): 602–611.

Maccoby, Eleanor, and John Martin. 1983. Socialization in the Context of the Family: Parent-Child Interaction. In *Socialization, Personality and Social Development*, ed. E. Mavis Hetherington. Vol. 4 of *Handbook of Child Psychology*. New York: Wiley.

Milgram, Stanley. 1963. Behavioral Study of Obedience. *Journal of Abnormal and Social Psychology* 67: 371–378.

Julie C. Dunsmore
Sarah Holland Omar

BAUXITE INDUSTRY

Bauxite is the only commercially viable ore used as a source material for primary aluminum production. After iron, aluminum is the world's second most used metal, having a wide variety of applications in transportation and packaging. Most of the world's bauxite reserves and production are found in a wide belt around the equator, with Australia, Brazil, Guinea, China, Jamaica, and India being the world's leading producers. While short-term demand for bauxite depends upon the demand for aluminum and is therefore cyclical, supplying countries have sufficient reserves to meet long-term projected demand for the foreseeable future.

The separation of primary aluminum from the other elements found in bauxite involves a distinct two-stage production process. First, 4 to 5 tons of bauxite is chemically refined into 2 tons of the white powder alumina (aluminum oxide), then these 2 tons of alumina are smelted into 1 ton of aluminum ingot. Both processes are highly capital intensive, and smelting is also highly electricity intensive. Of the bauxite mined worldwide, about 95 percent is converted to alumina; the remaining 5 percent is used in other applications such as abrasives and cement additives.

The world aluminum industry, from mining to fabrication, is both highly concentrated and vertically integrated. Multinational aluminum companies typically mine bauxite, which then feeds their alumina refinery operations, which then often feeds their own smelters. As a result, open markets do not generally exist for bauxite. Nearly all bauxite consumed in the United States is imported, mostly from Guinea and Jamaica.

Most of the world's bauxite reserves are found in developing countries, but these countries account for a much smaller percentage of world alumina production and very little of the world's aluminum production. Although bauxite and alumina production can typically play significant roles in terms of foreign exchange and gross domestic product in these economies, these capital-intensive production processes do not typically have significant macroemployment effects.

Nearly all of the world's bauxite is produced through opencast mining. This can have significant environmental effects, including detrimental effects on flora and fauna, water runoff resulting in groundwater contamination and soil erosion, and generation of dust affecting surrounding areas. The *Third Bauxite Mine Rehabilitation Survey*, published by the International Aluminum Institute in 2004, details these impacts and the progress that the industry has made at protection and reclamation.

Jamaica provides an example of the importance to the industry of a relatively small country and the key role that the industry plays in a supplying country's economy. Bauxite and alumina account for more than half of Jamaica's exports, and they are the country's second leading source of foreign exchange after tourism. The country's relationship with the industry has been historically confrontational. In the 1970s Jamaica was instrumental in forming an attempted bauxite cartel, the now defunct International Bauxite Association, while simultaneously but unilaterally implementing a domestic bauxite production levy. At the time, Jamaica was the world's leading producer of bauxite. After periods of industry stagnation and even contraction, the government changed approaches, and now directly participates in consortia with several of the world's leading aluminum companies in the country's bauxite and alumina operations. It has also replaced the bauxite levy with taxation on profits.

Two major issues face the industry: environmental impacts, and the desire by supplying countries to accrue a larger share of the benefits (income and employment) resulting from the downstream processing of their bauxite. The experiences of Jamaica and other countries have taught supplying countries and multinationals that direct equity participation in bauxite and alumina consortia by private or public supplying country partners is the most effective way to protect various stakeholders' interests.

SEE ALSO *Caribbean, The; Mining Industry*

BIBLIOGRAPHY

International Aluminum Institute. 2004. Third Bauxite Mine Rehabilitation Survey. http://www.world-aluminum.org.

Plunkert, Patricia. 2004. Bauxite and Alumina. *U.S. Geological Survey.* http://minerals.usgs.gov/minerals/pubs/commodity/bauxite/bauximyb04.pdf.

James P. McCoy

BAY OF PIGS

The Bay of Pigs invasion flowed from a directive signed by Republican President Dwight D. Eisenhower on March 17, 1960, authorizing the U.S. Central Intelligence Agency (CIA) to begin operations to remove the Castro government from power in Cuba (Kornbluh 1998, p. 269). This quickly evolved into a plan to land an invasion force of some 1,200 Cuban exiles near the city of Trinidad, Cuba, at the foot of the Escambray Mountains. The invasion force, called the Brigade 2506, trained in Central America and by the end of 1960 was making final preparations for the landing.

Meanwhile, however, presidential elections had been held in the United States. Vice President Richard Nixon, the Republican candidate, lost, and the Democratic candidate, Senator John F. Kennedy, won. The latter might have been expected to cancel the invasion plan, once informed of it, but this would have been difficult for him to do. During the election campaign, he had sharply criticized the Eisenhower-Nixon administration for allowing this Communist foothold to emerge only 90 miles to the south of the United States. Had he canceled the invasion, the Republicans would doubtless have gone public and pointed out that they had had a plan to remove the "foothold," but Kennedy had abandoned it.

Further, Kennedy quickly developed confidence in Richard Bissell (1910–1994), the CIA's deputy director for plans, who was masterminding the operation (Wyden 1979, p. 96). Thus, Kennedy let the invasion plan go forward. He did insist, however, that a landing so near the city of Trinidad would be "too spectacular," and requested that it be moved to a more remote location (Wyden 1979, p. 100). Bissell obligingly moved the site some 70 miles to the west, to the Bay of Pigs (Bahía de Cochinos). This meant, however, that if the invasion failed, the invaders could not melt away into the mountains and become guerrillas, as Bissell had suggested to Kennedy, for the mountains were now far away across impenetrable swamps (Wyden 1979, p. 102).

The invasion force of approximately 1,200 exiles seemed totally inadequate to the task at hand, given that they would face a regular army of 60,000 armed with Soviet tanks and artillery, and backed by a militia force of 100,000. Bissell assured Kennedy, however, that the invasion would spark a massive popular uprising against Fidel Castro. Unfortunately, this assurance was not based on any hard intelligence. Indeed, it turned out to be utterly baseless (Kornbluh 1998, p. 12).

Preparatory air strikes against Cuban airfields, flown by exile and CIA pilots operating from Central America, were quickly revealed to be exactly that and not strikes by defecting Cuban pilots, as the United States claimed.

Adlai Stevenson (1900–1965), the U.S. ambassador to the United Nations (UN), was deliberately misinformed by the White House, however, and gave a speech in the UN saying the raids had been carried out by defecting Cuban pilots. Outraged when he found out the truth, he complained to Kennedy, who ordered the next day's air cover to be canceled. Nevertheless, as the CIA's own report on the operation later stated, this was not "the chief cause of failure" (Kornbluh 1998, p. 12). The chief cause, rather, was the glaring disparity between the numbers of the invading force and the number of defenders. The former never really had a chance. They went ashore in the early morning hours of April 17, 1961, and by 2 p.m. of April 19, facing overwhelming odds, were forced to surrender. In retrospect, that surrender seemed so inevitable that the Bay of Pigs invasion came to be described as that rarest of all things—a perfect failure (Smith 1987, p. 70).

The failure of the United States at the Bay of Pigs had three crucial consequences. First, it solidified Castro in power. Second, seeing that if the United States used its own forces, he would need Soviet support to survive, to persuade Moscow to provide that support, Castro announced on April 16 that Cuba was a "socialist" state and he began to transform it into one, with a system patterned after the Soviet Union. And third, flowing in part from this transformation, Nikita Khrushchev the next year decided to place missiles in Cuba, thus leading to the October missile crisis of 1962.

SEE ALSO *Castro, Fidel; Central Intelligence Agency, U.S.; Cold War; Communism; Cuban Missile Crisis; Cuban Revolution; Democratic Party, U.S.; Eisenhower, Dwight D.; Kennedy, John F.; Republican Party; Socialism*

BIBLIOGRAPHY

Kornbluh, Peter, ed. 1998. *Bay of Pigs Declassified: The Secret CIA Report on the Invasion of Cuba.* New York: New Press.

Smith, Wayne S. 1987. *The Closest of Enemies: A Personal and Diplomatic Account of U.S.-Cuban Relations since 1957.* New York: Norton.

Wyden, Peter. 1979. *Bay of Pigs: The Untold Story.* New York: Simon and Schuster.

Wayne S. Smith

BAYES' THEOREM

With one posthumous publication on probability, Reverend Thomas Bayes inspired the development of a new approach to statistical inference known as Bayesian

Inference. "An Essay Toward Solving a Problem in the Doctrine of Chances" was published in 1764, but its impact was not felt until nearly two hundred years after his death, when in the 1950s Bayesian statistics began to flourish. His work remains at the center of one of the main intellectual controversies of our time.

Bayes was the first to solve the problem of inverse probability. In its simplest form, given two events *A* and *B* with nonzero probability, the probability of *A* and *B* can be written as:

(1) Pr(*A* and *B*) = Pr(*A*|*B*)*Pr(*B*) or

(2) Pr(*A* and *B*) = Pr(*B*|*A*)*Pr(*A*)

Equating both right hand sides of (1) and (2) yields:

(3) Pr(*A*|*B*) = Pr(*B*|*A*)*Pr(*A*)/Pr(*B*)

In words, given the conditional probability of *B* given *A*, Pr(*B*|*A*), one can obtain the reverse conditional probability of *A* given *B*, Pr(*A*|*B*). For example, given that *r* heads out of *n* coin flips are observed, what is the probability of a head in a single coin flip? This allows one to work backwards, given the outcome or effect, to discover what is the probability of the cause. Viewed in this manner there is no controversy concerning Bayes' theorem. It is a direct consequence of the laws of probability. However, viewing *A* as the parameters θ and *B* as the sample *D* one obtains the following result from Bayes' theorem:

(4) P(θ|*D*) = P(*D*|θ)*P(θ)/P(*D*)

where P(θ|*D*) = posterior distribution of the parameters given the information in the sample

P(*D*|θ) = likelihood function summarizing the information in the sample

P(θ) = prior distribution of the parameters before the data is observed

and P(*D*) = normalizing constant so that one obtains a proper posterior distribution.

In words, (4) states that:

(5) posterior distribution α likelihood *x* prior distribution,

where $\propto$ represents the relation "is proportional to."

This relation is the foundation of Bayesian statistical inference, with the posterior distribution being the main component of statistical analysis. This provides a formal process of subjective learning from experience by showing how one can revise or update prior beliefs about parameters in the light of relevant sample evidence. The role of judgment or outside information in statistical modeling is made explicit in the Bayesian approach. The Bayesian approach views the parameters of the model as being random, and thus one can make meaningful probability statements about the parameters.

There are two major issues of contention in the Bayesian approach. The first is the subjective, or reason-able degree of belief, view of probability, which differs from the classical view of probability as the limit of the relative frequency of an event occurring in infinite trials. The second issue is the necessity and choice of an accurate prior distribution incorporating known information. The controversy over views of probability is a philosophical one that has yet to be resolved. Bayesians have suggested a wide variety of possible approaches for obtaining the prior distribution. The Bayesian approach requires more thought and effort, and thus the classical approach has a significant advantage in that it is much easier to apply in practice. The debate and interaction between these two contrasting approaches to statistical inference promises to lead to fruitful developments in statistical inference. Donald Gillies asks the interesting question, "Was Bayes a Bayesian?" and concludes, "Yes, he was a Bayesian, but a cautious and doubtful Bayesian" (1987, p. 328).

SEE ALSO *Bayesian Econometrics; Bayesian Statistics; Classical Statistical Analysis; Probability Theory; Statistics*

BIBLIOGRAPHY

Bayes, Thomas. 1764. An Essay Towards Solving a Problem in the Doctrine of Chances. By the late Rev. Mr. Bayes, communicated by Mr. Price, in a letter to John Canton, M.A. and F.R.S. *Philosophical Transactions of the Royal Society of London* 53: 370–418. Reprinted in *Biometrika* 45 (1958): 293–315, with a biographical note by G. A. Barnard.

Gillies, Donald A. 1987. Was Bayes a Bayesian? *Historia Mathematica* 14: 325–346.

Kennedy, Peter 2003. The Bayesian Approach. In *A Guide to Econometrics*, 230–247. Cambridge, MA: MIT Press.

William Veloce

BAYESIAN ECONOMETRICS

Bayesian econometrics employs Bayesian methods for inference about economic questions using economic data. In the following, we briefly review these methods and their applications.

Suppose a data vector $X = (X_1, \ldots, X_n)$ follows a distribution with a density function $p_n(x|\theta)$ which is fully characterized by some parameter vector $\theta = (\theta_1, \ldots, \theta_d)'$. Suppose that the prior belief about θ is characterized by a density $p(\theta)$ defined over a parameter space Θ, a subset of a Euclidian space $\mathbb{R}^d$. Using Bayes's rule to incorporate the information provided by the data, we can form posterior beliefs about the parameter θ, characterized by the posterior density

$$p_n(\theta \mid X) = p_n(X \mid \theta)p(\theta)c,$$
$$c = 1 / \int_\Theta p_n(X \mid \tilde{\theta})p(\tilde{\theta})d\tilde{\theta}. \qquad (1)$$

The posterior density $p_n(\theta|X)$, or simply $p_n(\theta)$, describes how likely it is that a parameter value θ has generated the observed data X. We can use the posterior density to form optimal point estimates and optimal hypotheses tests. The notion of optimality is minimizing mean posterior loss, using various loss functions. For example, the posterior mean

$$\hat{\theta} = \int_\Theta \theta\, p_n(\theta)\, d\theta, \qquad (2)$$

is the point estimate that minimizes posterior mean squared loss. The posterior mode θ^* is defined as the maximizer of the posterior density, and it is the decision that minimizes the posterior mean Dirac loss. When the prior density is flat, the posterior mode turns out to be the maximum likelihood estimator. The posterior quantiles characterize the posterior uncertainty about the parameter, and they can be used to form confidence regions for the parameters of interest (Bayesian credible regions). The posterior α-quantile $\hat{\theta}_j(\alpha)$ for θ_j (the j-th component of the parameter vector) is the number c such that $\int_\Theta 1\{\theta_j \le c\} p_n(\theta)d\theta = \alpha$.

Properties of Bayesian procedures in both large and small samples are as good as the properties of the procedures based on maximum likelihood. These properties have been developed by Pierre-Simon Laplace (1818), Peter Bickel and J. A. Yahav (1969), and Il'dar Ibragimov and R. Z. Has'minskii (1981), among others. With mild regularity conditions (which hold in many econometric applications), the properties include:

(1) consistency and asymptotic normality of the point estimates, including asymptotic equivalence and efficiency of the posterior mean, mode, and median;

(2) asymptotic normality of the posterior density;

(3) asymptotically correct coverage of Bayesian confidence intervals; and

(4) average risk optimality of Bayesian estimates in small and hence large samples.

The regularity conditions for properties (1) and (2) require that the true parameter θ_0 is well identified and that the data's density $p_n(x|\theta)$ is sufficiently smooth in the parameters. Mathematically, property (1) means that

$$\sqrt{n}(\hat{\theta} - \theta_0) \approx \sqrt{n}(\theta^* - \theta_0) \approx$$
$$\sqrt{n}(\hat{\theta}(1/2) - \theta_0) \approx_d N(0, J^{-1}), \qquad (3)$$

where J equals the information matrix $\lim_n -\dfrac{1}{n}\dfrac{\partial_2 E \ln p_n(X \mid \theta_0)}{\partial\theta\partial\theta'}$, $\approx$ indicates agreement up to a stochastic term that approaches zero in large samples, and $\approx_d N(0, J^{-1})$ means "approximately distributed as a normal random vector with mean 0 and variance matrix J^{-1}." These estimators are asymptotically efficient in the sense of having smallest variance J^{-1} in the class of asymptotically unbiased estimators. Property (2) is that $p_n(\theta)$ is approximately equal to a normal density with mean $\hat{\theta}$ and variance J^{-1}/n. Property (3) means that in large samples

$$Prob[\hat{\theta}_j(\alpha/2) \le \theta_{0j} \le \hat{\theta}_j(1 - \alpha/2)] \approx 1 - \alpha. \qquad (4)$$

In nonregular cases, such as in structural auction and search models, consistency and correct coverage properties also continue to hold (Chernozhukov and Hong 2004). Property (4) is implied by the defining property of the Bayes estimators that they minimize the posterior mean risk (Lehmann and Casella 1998). The property continues to hold in nonregular cases, which proved especially useful in nonregular econometric models (Hirano and Porter 2003; Chernozhukov and Hong 2004).

The explicit dependency of Bayesian estimates on the prior is both a virtue and a drawback. Priors allow us to incorporate information available from previous studies and various economic restrictions. When no prior information is available, diffuse priors can be used. Priors can have a large impact on inferential results in small samples, and in any other cases where the identifiability of parameters crucially relies on restrictions brought by the prior. In such cases, selection of priors requires a substantial care: See Gary Chamberlain and Guido Imbens (2003, 2004) for an example concerning simultaneous equations, and Harald Uhlig (2005) for an example dealing with sign restrictions in structural vector autoregressions. Conversely, priors should have little impact on the inferential results when the identifiability of parameters does not crucially rely on the prior and when sample sizes are large.

The appealing theoretical properties of Bayesian methods have been known for many years, but computational difficulties prevented their wide use. Closed-form solutions for estimators such as (2) have been derived only for very special cases. The recent emergence of Markov Chain Monte Carlo (MCMC) algorithms has diminished the computational challenge and made these methods attractive in a variety of practical applications; see for example, Christian Robert and George Casella (2004) and Jun Liu (2001). The idea of MCMC is to simulate a possibly dependent random sequence, $(\theta^{(1)}, \ldots, \theta^{(B)})$, called a chain, such that stationary density of the chain is the posterior density $p_n(\theta)$. Then we approximate integrals such as (2) by the averages of the chain, that is, $\hat{\theta} \approx \Sigma_{k=1}^B \theta^{(k)}/B$. For computation of posterior quantiles, we simply take empirical quantiles of the chain. The leading MCMC method is the Metropolis-Hastings (MH) algorithm, which includes, for example, the random walk algorithm with Gaussian increments generating the candidate points for the chain. Such random walk is characterized by an initial point u_0 and a one-step move that consists of drawing a point η according to a Gaussian distribution centered on the current point u with covariance matrix $\sigma^2 I$, then moving to η with probability $\rho = \min\{p_n(\eta)/p_n(u), 1\}$ and staying at u with probability $1 - \rho$. The MH algorithm is often combined with the Gibbs sampler, where the latter updates components of θ individually or in blocks. The Gibbs sampler can also speed up computation when the posterior for some components of θ is available in a closed form. MCMC algorithms have been shown to be computationally efficient in a variety of cases.

The classical econometric applications of Bayesian methods mainly dealt with the classical linear regression model and the classical simultaneous equation model, which admitted closed-form solutions (Zellner 1996; Poirier 1995). The emergence of MCMC has enabled researchers to attack a variety of complex nonlinear problems. The recent examples of important problems that have been solved using Bayesian methods include:

1. discrete choice models (Albert and Chib 1993; Lancaster 2004);

2. models with limited-dependent variables (Geweke 2005);

3. nonlinear panel data models with individual heterogeneity (McCulloch and Rossi 1994; Lancaster 2004);

4. structural vector autoregressions in macroeconomics, including models with sign restrictions (Uhlig 2005);

5. dynamic discrete decision processes (Geweke, Keane, and Runkle 1997; Geweke 2005);

6. dynamic stochastic equilibrium models (Smets and Wouters 2003; Del Negro and Schorfheide 2004);

7. time series models in finance (Fiorentini, Sentana, and Shephard 2004; Johannes and Polson 2003); and

8. unit root models (Sims and Uhlig 1991).

Econometric applications of the methods are rapidly expanding.

There are also recent developments that break away from the traditional parametric Bayesian paradigm. Jayanta Ghosh and R. V. Ramamoorthi (2003) developed and reviewed several nonparametric Bayesian methods. Chamberlain and Imbens (2003) developed Bayesian methods based on the multinomial framework of Thomas Ferguson (1973, 1974). In models with moment restrictions and no parametric likelihood available, Victor Chernozhukov and Han Hong (2003) proposed using an empirical likelihood function or a generalized method-of-moment criterion function in place of the unknown likelihood $p_n(X|\theta)$ in equation (1). This permits the application of MCMC methods to a variety of moment condition models. As a result, there are a growing number of applications of the latter approach to nonlinear simultaneous equations, empirical game-theoretic models, risk forecasting, and asset-pricing models. The literature on both theoretical and practical aspects of various nonparametric Bayesian methods is rapidly expanding.

SEE ALSO *Econometrics; Least Squares, Ordinary; Regression; Regression Analysis; Simultaneous Equation Bias*

BIBLIOGRAPHY

Albert, James H., and Siddhartha Chib. 1993. Bayesian Analysis of Binary and Polychotomous Response Data. *Journal of the American Statistical Association* 88 (422): 669–679.

Bickel, Peter J., and J. A. Yahav. 1969. Some Contributions to the Asymptotic Theory of Bayes Solutions. *Zeitschrift fur Wahrscheinlichkeitstheorie und Verwandte Gebiete* 11: 257–276.

Chamberlain, Gary, and Guido Imbens. 2003. Nonparametric Applications of Bayesian Inference. *Journal of Business and Economic Statistics* 21 (1): 12–18.

Chamberlain, Gary, and Guido Imbens. 2004. Random Effects Estimators with Many Instrumental Variables. *Econometrica* 72 (1): 295–306.

Chernozhukov, Victor, and Han Hong. 2003. An MCMC Approach to Classical Estimation. *Journal of Econometrics* 115 (2): 293–346.

Chernozhukov, Victor, and Han Hong. 2004. Likelihood Estimation and Inference in a Class of Nonregular Econometric Models. *Econometrica* 72 (5): 1445–1480.

Del Negro, Marco, and Frank Schorfheide. 2004. Priors from General Equilibrium Models for VARs. *International Economic Review* 45: 643–673.

Ferguson, Thomas S. 1973. A Bayesian Analysis of Some Nonparametric Problems. *Annals of Statistics* 1: 209–230.

Ferguson, Thomas S. 1974. Prior Distributions on Spaces of Probability Measures. *Annals of Statistics* 2: 615–629.

Fiorentini, Gabriele, Enrique Sentana, and Neil Shephard. 2004. Likelihood-Based Estimation of Latent Generalized ARCH Structures. *Econometrica* 72 (5): 1481–1517.

Geweke, John. 2005. *Contemporary Bayesian Econometrics and Statistics*. Hoboken, NJ: Wiley Interscience.

Geweke, John F., Michael P. Keane, and David E. Runkle. 1997. Statistical Inference in the Multinomial Multiperiod Probit Model. *Journal of Econometrics* 80 (1): 125–165.

Ghosh, Jayanta K., and R. V. Ramamoorthi. 2003. *Bayesian Nonparametrics*. New York: Springer-Verlag.

Hirano, Keisuke, and Jack R. Porter. 2003. Asymptotic Efficiency in Parametric Structural Models with Parameter-Dependent Support. *Econometrica* 71 (5): 1307–1338.

Ibragimov, Il'dar A., and R. Z. Has'minskii. 1981. *Statistical Estimation: Asymptotic Theory*. Trans. Samuel Kotz. New York: Springer-Verlag.

Johannes, Michael, and Nicholas Polson. 2006. MCMC Methods for Continuous-Time Financial Econometrics. In *Handbook of Financial Econometrics*, ed. Yacine Ait-Sahalia and Lars Peter Hansen. Amsterdam: North-Holland.

Lancaster, Tony. 2004. *An Introduction to Modern Bayesian Econometrics*. Malden, MA: Blackwell.

Laplace, Pierre-Simon. [1818] 1995. *Théorie analytique des probabilités*. Paris: Editions Jacques Gabay.

Lehmann, E. L., and George Casella. 1998. *Theory of Point Estimation*. New York: Springer.

Liu, Jun S. 2001. *Monte Carlo Strategies in Scientific Computing*. New York: Springer-Verlag.

McCulloch, Robert, and Peter E. Rossi. 1994. An Exact Likelihood Analysis of the Multinomial Probit Model. *Journal of Econometrics* 64 (1–2): 207–240.

Poirier, Dale J. 1995. *Intermediate Statistics and Econometrics: A Comparative Approach*. Cambridge: Massachusetts Institute of Technology Press.

Robert, Christian P., and George Casella. 2004. *Monte Carlo Statistical Methods*. 2nd ed. New York: Springer-Verlag.

Sims, Christopher A., and Harald Uhlig. 1991. Understanding Unit Rooters: A Helicopter Tour. *Econometrica* 59 (6): 1591–1599.

Smets, Frank, and Raf Wouters. 2003. An Estimated Dynamic Stochastic General Equilibrium Model of the Euro Area. *Journal of the European Economic Association* 1: 527–549.

Uhlig, Harald. 2005. What Are the Effects of Monetary Policy on Output? Results from an Agnostic Identification Procedure. *Journal of Monetary Economics* 52: 381–419.

Zellner, Arnold. [1971] 1996. *An Introduction to Bayesian Inference in Econometrics*. New York: Wiley Interscience.

Victor Chernozhukov

BAYESIAN INFERENCE

SEE *Inference, Bayesian.*

BAYESIAN STATISTICS

Bayesian statistics is concerned with the relationships among conditional and unconditional probabilities. Suppose the sampling space is a bag filled with twenty black and eighty white balls. The probability of a white ball being drawn at random is .8, as defined by the relative frequency of such balls. If three more bags with seventy black and thirty white balls each are in play and a ball is drawn at random from one bag, the probability of it being white is $.8 \cdot .25 + .3 \cdot .75 = .425$. Once a white ball is in evidence, the probability that it was drawn from the bag containing mostly white balls is larger than .25, and the probability that it was drawn from a bag containing mostly black balls is less than .75. The estimation of these *inverse probabilities* is the object of Bayes's theorem.

Let the idea that the obtained white ball came from the bag containing mostly white balls be H, for "hypothesis," and the idea that the ball came from a bag containing mostly black balls be ~H; let the drawing of a white ball be E, for "evidence." Bayes's theorem states

that $p(H|E) = \dfrac{p(E|H) \cdot p(H)}{p(E|H) \cdot p(H) + p(E|\sim H) \cdot p(\sim H)}$

$= \dfrac{p(E|H)}{p(E)} \cdot p(H)$, here .471. The ratio of $\dfrac{p(H|E)}{p(H)}$

expresses the degree to which the probability of H changes in light of the evidence. This degree of probability change can be seen before the posterior probability of H is calculated because $\dfrac{p(H|E)}{p(H)}$ is equal to the ratio $\dfrac{p(E|H)}{p(E)}$, here 1.882.

The prior probability of a hypothesis constrains the degree to which it can be changed by evidence. If the evidence supports the hypothesis, the magnitude of the Bayesian revision decreases as the prior probability becomes larger. Consider the odds version of Bayes's

theorem, which is $\dfrac{p(H|E)}{p(\sim H|E)} = \dfrac{p(E|H)}{p(E|\sim H)} \cdot \dfrac{p(H)}{p(\sim H)}$.

Now, $\dfrac{p(H|E)}{p(H)} = \dfrac{p(E|H)}{p(E|\sim H)} \cdot \dfrac{p(\sim H|E)}{p(\sim H)}$, which is equal

to $\dfrac{p(E|H)}{p(E|\sim H)} \cdot \dfrac{p(E|\sim H)}{(pE|\sim H) \cdot p(\sim H) + (pE|H) \cdot p(H)}$. Note

that a larger p(H) reduces the second ratio, and thus reduces the product of the two ratios (where the first ratio > 1 if the evidence supports H). Analogously, a large p(H) leads to a stronger updating if the evidence is contrary to H.

The Reverend Thomas Bayes (1702–1761) worked out his eponymous theorem, but his solution was only published two years posthumously (see Stigler 1999). The validity of the theorem is given by its mathematical coherence. Any of its constituent probabilities can be recovered if the others are known. As a model of scientific and of everyday inference, the theorem formalizes inductive reasoning. Scientists seek to corroborate or discredit certain hypotheses, and laypeople (and animals) need to mold their beliefs at least in part with reference to the observations they make. For inductive reasoning, not only the probable truth of certain beliefs is of interest, but also the probability that certain events will recur. In the previous example, the sampling of one white ball not only alters the probability that any particular bag was sampled, it also increases the probability that a white ball will be sampled again (assuming the next draw will be made from the same bag).

In the short run, the revision of the probability of the evidence may not reduce uncertainty. In the present example, where p(E) rises from .425 to .535, one would be slightly less confident to bet on any particular color for the next draw. Over repeated sampling, however, p(E) converges on either p(E|H) or on p(E|~H), and p(H) converges on 0 or 1. Prior uncertainty is greatest when there are many equiprobable hypotheses. If there were 101 bags, each with the different proportion of white balls, p(E) = .5. Pierre-Simon Laplace's (1749–1827) *rule of succession* states that once a sample is drawn, the probability that the next draw (after replacement) will replicate the result is $\frac{k+1}{n+2}$, where k is the number of successes and n is the sample size. For an infinite number of hypotheses, this rule is obtained with integral calculus.

Bayesian alternatives to conventional hypothesis testing, confidence-interval estimation, meta-analysis, and regression are available, though computationally cumbersome. In practice, most researchers remain committed to orthodox methods that exclude prior knowledge. Fisherian null hypothesis significance testing, for example, yields the probability of the evidence under the null hypothesis, p(E|H). What the researcher really wants, namely p(H|E), cannot be estimated because, in the absence of p(E|~H), the likelihood ratio remains undefined. If, however, the researcher specifies ~H (as in the Neyman-Pearson approach) and assigns a probability to it, p(H|E) can be quantified. Indeed, prior probabilities can be represented as a distribution over possible outcomes. The mean of the posterior distribution is given by the weighted average of the prior mean and the empirical mean of the data, where the weights depend on the relative precision (i.e., the reciprocals of the variance of the means) of the prior mean and the mean of the data. Likewise, the standard deviation of the posterior distribution becomes smaller as the precision of the prior distribution or the distribution of the data increases (see Howard et al. [2000] for formulas and a numerical example).

Despite their reluctance to use Bayesian statistics for data analysis, many social and cognitive psychologists model the reasoning processes of their research participants along Bayesian lines (Krueger and Funder 2004). Any reasoning activities involving decisions, categorizations, or choices are natural candidates. Given some probative evidence, people need to decide, for example, if a person is male or female, guilty or innocent, healthy or sick. Likewise, they need to decide whether they should attribute a person's behavior to dispositional or situational causes, and how much they should yield to a persuasive message. Even strategic choices between cooperation and defection in social dilemmas depend on what people assume others will do, given their own presumed choices.

The question of whether everyday reasoning satisfies Bayesian coherence remains controversial. In some contexts, such as jury deliberations, people appear to form their beliefs on the basis of narrative, not probabilistic, coherence. In other contexts, such as the Monty Hall problem, they fail to see how Bayes's theorem can be readily applied. These difficulties can partly be overcome by altering the presentation of the problem. For example, diagnostic decisions in medicine are improved when the data are presented as frequencies instead of probabilities.

Many orthodox significance testers, who disavow the estimation of inverse probabilities, reveal implicit Bayesianism in their research practice. After a series of successful experiments, the probability of the null hypothesis being true becomes very small, and reasonable researchers desist from wasting further resources. The evidence of the past becomes the theory of the present, thus blurring the distinction between the two. Other hypotheses, such as the idea that a concerted mental concentration of a collective of people can alter the earth's magnetic field, are so improbable a priori that even devout Fisherians would not consider testing them.

SEE ALSO *Prediction; Probability; Psychometrics; Regression*

BIBLIOGRAPHY

Howard, George S., Scott E. Maxwell, and Kevin J. Fleming. 2000. The Proof of the Pudding: An Illustration of the Relative Strengths of Null Hypothesis, Meta-analysis, and Bayesian Analysis. *Psychological Methods* 5: 315–332.

Krueger, Joachim I., and David C. Funder. 2004. Towards a Balanced Social Psychology: Causes, Consequences, and Cures for the Problem-seeking Approach to Social Behavior and Cognition. *Behavioral and Brain Sciences* 27: 313–376.

Stigler, Stephen M. 1999. *Statistics on the Table: The History of Statistical Concepts and Methods.* Cambridge, MA: Harvard University Press.

Joachim I. Krueger

BEAR MARKET

SEE *Bull and Bear Markets.*

BEARD, CHARLES AND MARY

The American historian Charles Austin Beard (1874–1948) in 1900 married Mary Ritter (1876–1958), a fellow Indiana-born DePauw student who became his lifelong intellectual companion and in her own right a pioneering historian of women. Mary followed Charles to Oxford University in 1900 and later enrolled for graduate work at Columbia University (1902), but pressures of child rearing and her growing involvement in Progressive community causes ended her work there. Charles Beard studied British legal institutions for his PhD in political science at Columbia, where he taught history (1904–1917); there he also wrote textbooks on European history with James Harvey Robinson and joined the New History movement to revitalize historical practice. Members of the New History movement, or Progressive historians, as they were also known, reoriented history toward solving current problems and integrated social, economic, and intellectual subjects into their political narratives. Beard was not only a Progressive but also a political activist seeking reform of government through the application of academic knowledge when he joined the New York Bureau of Municipal Research in 1914. Resigning from Columbia in protest over the dismissal of an antiwar colleague in 1917, Beard became increasingly dissatisfied with conventional academia as too intellectually conservative, and he helped to found the interdisciplinary and Progressive-oriented New School for Social Research (1919).

Though trained as an historian, Beard's contribution straddled the porous borderland between the politics and history disciplines of the era. He wrote, among other works, *American Government and Politics* (1910), *American City Government* (1912), and *The Economic Basis of Politics* (1922). In 1927 he became president of the American Political Science Association, though historians continued to claim his allegiance, and he served as American Historical Association (AHA) president in 1933. Beard assumed a key role in the AHA's attempted reform of high school history curricula as part of the Carnegie-funded Commission on the Social Studies in Schools (1929–1934). While working on the commission, he advocated in *A Charter for the Social Sciences in the Schools* (1932) the integration of the social sciences around Progressive history.

Beard was an avowed exponent of the economic interpretation of history as the study of interest groups, though he was not committed to class analysis in a Marxist sense. His controversial *An Economic Interpretation of the Constitution* (1913) examined the relationship of economics and politics at the Federal Convention of 1787, showing a clash of landed and mercantile property interests. His study of Treasury records revealed that those favoring the Federalist position held securities likely to be repaid if a federal government with a stronger financial basis were established; in a similar interpretive vein, he also wrote *Economic Origins of Jeffersonian Democracy* (1915). Empirical studies and a counter-Progressive trend in historiography eventually challenged his account of the Constitution, revealing a much more complex array of economic interests within the Federal Convention. His larger intellectual dominance faded by the 1950s, but in the meantime, he had influenced a generation of scholars from the 1920s. Increasingly he had become a public intellectual, reaching a wide audience through popular history books written with his wife.

Mary Beard not only served as a coworker, but also influenced his intellectual vision. She was herself an activist who worked in the suffrage and trade union movements before World War I. Seeing supposedly "objective" scientific history as biased because historians did not recognize women's past contributions to human society, she stimulated Charles Beard's relativist views. These later became a foundation for his presidential address to the AHA, "Written History as an Act of Faith," which enunciated his "frame of reference" approach to historical knowledge. Mary and Charles collaborated on *The Rise of American Civilization* (1927), a work that sold more than 130,000 copies in early editions and won wide acclaim along with its successor volumes *America in Midpassage* (1939) and *The American Spirit* (1942). *The Rise of American Civilization* innovatively interpreted the Civil War (1861–1865) and Reconstruction (1865–1877) as a second American Revolution in which the forces of a (Northern) industrial civilization overcame the agrarian South. The volumes together sought to capture a synthetic view of a holistic and unique civilization shaped by American material abundance, thus linking the economic interpretation to cultural and social history. Mary added much social and cultural history thematic material and textual evidence to these works that examined media, urban life, and social reform.

Mary Beard also wrote on her own, most notably *Woman as Force in History* (1946), in which she argued that women as much as men had shaped society over the course of human social evolution, and she criticized male historians for neglecting to recognize those contributions. The book did not achieve the success that she had hoped for, but later feminist scholars rediscovered its pioneering ideas. Her efforts to stimulate collection of women's history archives, begun in 1935, added to this legacy concerning her pioneering role.

In their later years the Beards became increasingly alienated from the American mainstream as Charles espoused political isolationism and attacked the foreign policy of Franklin Roosevelt in *President Roosevelt and the*

Coming of the War: A Study in Appearances and Realities, 1941 (1948), but their legacy continued to influence the "consensus" historians of the 1950s, who tried to transcend the Beards' work.

SEE ALSO *Gilded Age*

BIBLIOGRAPHY

PRIMARY WORKS

Beard, Charles A. 1910. *American Government and Politics.* New York: Macmillan.

Beard, Charles A. 1912. *American City Government.* New York: Century.

Beard, Charles A. 1913. *An Economic Interpretation of the Constitution.* New York: Macmillan.

Beard, Charles A. 1915. *Economic Origins of Jeffersonian Democracy.* New York: Macmillan.

Beard, Charles A. 1922. *The Economic Basis of Politics.* New York: Knopf.

Beard, Charles A. 1932. *A Charter for the Social Sciences in the Schools.* New York: Scribner.

Beard, Charles A. 1948. *President Roosevelt and the Coming of the War: A Study in Appearances and Realities, 1941.* New Haven, CT: Yale University Press.

Beard, Charles A., and Mary Ritter Beard. 1927. *The Rise of American Civilization.* New York: Macmillan.

Beard, Charles A., and Mary Ritter Beard. 1939. *America in Midpassage.* New York: Macmillan.

Beard, Charles A., and Mary Ritter Beard. 1942. *The American Spirit.* New York: Macmillan.

Beard, Mary Ritter. 1946. *Woman as Force in History: A Study in Traditions and Realities.* New York: Macmillan.

SECONDARY WORKS

Cott, Nancy F. 1991. *A Woman Making History: Mary Ritter Beard through Her Letters.* New Haven, CT: Yale University Press.

Des Jardins, Julie. 2003. *Women and the Historical Enterprise in America: Gender, Race, and the Politics of Memory, 1880–1945.* Chapel Hill: University of North Carolina Press.

Hofstadter, Richard. 1968. *The Progressive Historians: Turner, Beard, Parrington.* New York: Knopf.

Nore, Ellen. 1983. *Charles A. Beard: An Intellectual Biography.* Carbondale: Southern Illinois University Press.

Ian Tyrrell

BEAUTY CONTEST METAPHOR

John Maynard Keynes, in his famous chapter 12 of the *General Theory of Employment, Interest, and Money* (1936), wrote of the ways in which "enterprise" (the attentive study of fundamentals) would become less important to the workings of the stock market, and of the ways that "speculation" (predicting the psychology of the crowd under conditions of radical uncertainty) would increasingly determine market outcomes. In doing so, he likened speculation to a beauty contest run by a newspaper, where the winner is not the candidate that is the most beautiful (by some set standard), but the candidate that most people think is the most beautiful. If one wants to win, therefore, one does not choose the candidate one actually thinks is the most beautiful, but the candidate one thinks most other people will think is the most beautiful.

But there is a problem. As soon as one thinks this way, one imagines others may be thinking this way as well. One must then choose not the candidate one thinks most people think is the most beautiful, but the candidate one thinks most people think most people think is most beautiful. But as soon as one thinks this way, one again imagines others will think this way as well, and so on and so forth. This phenomenon, when agents consider not only their own forecasts but the forecasts of others and their forecasts of others, has been referred to as higher-order beliefs (Monnin 2004) or endogenous uncertainty (Kurz 1974).

It is easy to see how this approach can be used as a metaphor for the stock market. A trader is not interested, strictly speaking, in the "fundamentals" of a company, such as market outlook and technological capabilities, because if no one else buys that stock it really doesn't matter. Its price will not rise. On the other hand, even if the fundamentals of a company do not look promising, if others believe that it is a good buy, for whatever reason, they will buy the stock and its price will rise. The lesson is not to buy the stock of a company one thinks is the best by some particular standard, but to buy the stock of a company one thinks others think is the best. But this soon leads to the same conundrum as occurs in the beauty contest, with the investor perpetually trying to stay one step ahead of everyone else. Keynes wrote that on a normal day this could expand to up to "four or five" iterations. In other words, a trader will be trying to anticipate what stocks on average "people think that people think that people think that people think that people think" are the best. At this point, values are completely separated from underlying fundamentals, and some of the best minds are engaged not in productive enterprise but guessing at mass psychology, subject to waves of optimism and pessimism, sometimes in response to phenomena difficult to get a handle on, or even to seemingly irrelevant factors. It has been shown, both theoretically and empirically, that such markets are highly volatile (see Monnin 2004).

SEE ALSO *Casino Capitalism; Economic Psychology; Economics, Keynesian; Financial Instability*

Hypothesis; Financial Markets; Keynes, John Maynard; Speculation; Stock Exchanges; Stocks

BIBLIOGRAPHY

Keynes, John Maynard. 1936. *General Theory of Employment, Interest, and Money.* New York: Harcourt Brace.

Kurz, Mordecai. 1974. "The Kersten-Stigum Model and the Treatment of Uncertainty in Equilibrium Theory." In *Essays on Economic Behavior Under Uncertainty*, ed. M. S. Balch, et al. Amsterdam: North-Holland.

Monnin, Pierre. 2004. "Are Stock Markets Really Like Beauty Contests?" IEW Working Paper No. 202. Zurich: Institut für Empirische Wirtschaftsforschung (IEW—Institute for Empirical Research in Economics).

Mathew Forstater

BECKER, GARY S.
1930–

Born in Pottsville, Pennsylvania, Gary Becker obtained his undergraduate education at Princeton University. He did his graduate work in the economics department at the University of Chicago, where his interest in social issues was reinforced by the intellectual prowess and encouragement of his mentors, foremost Milton Friedman, but Gregg Lewis and T. W. Shultz as well. There he wrote his dissertation on the economics of discrimination in 1957.

After serving a few years as assistant professor, he moved to Columbia University in New York City, where he spent twelve years combining teaching with research at the National Bureau of Economic Research. During this period Becker produced perhaps his most influential work, *Human Capital* (1964), and published his seminal papers on fertility in 1960, the allocation of time in 1965, and crime and punishment in 1968. He returned to Chicago in 1969, where he produced his *Treatise on the Family* (1981, expanded in 1991), and has continued to develop his economic way of looking at behavior.

Becker received the John Bates Clark Medal in 1967. His contributions won him the Nobel Prize in economic sciences in 1992. His professional and public contributions include serving as President of the American Economic Association in 1987, writing the Economics Viewpoint column in *BusinessWeek* from 1985 to 2004, and co-authoring the popular Becker-Posner Internet Blog with Richard Posner.

METHODOLOGY

Becker remains one of the most creative and influential economists in the early-twenty-first century. To character-ize his vast theoretical contributions is a daunting task, which is helped by Becker's own characterization of his work, as well as by attempts by others, including Sherwin Rosen, Agnar Sandmo, Ramon Febrero and Pedro Shwartz, and the Nobel Committee, to assess it. All recognize at least four areas of impact: discrimination, crime and punishment, human capital, and the family, to which should be added Becker's work on economic growth. Another way to characterize Becker's impact is by the methodological features that unite his work. For example, he applies the basic principle of rational behavior—preference maximization subject to objective opportunities or constraints—to all human behavior rather than merely behavior in the marketplace. Becker facilitates such applications by enriching the specification and interpretation of relevant opportunities and preferences, including explicit and implicit markets in which economic agents interact. He expanded both the *opportunity set* to incorporate time as a major scarce resource, and the structure of preferences to allow for material self-interest, as well as altruism, hate, discrimination, and moral values, emphasizing also the role of past experiences and social interactions in shaping these preferences.

Armed with these methodological innovations Becker expanded the boundaries of economics into areas that were traditionally the domain of sociology and political science. He pursues human behavior *from cradle to old age*, more or less in that order: discrimination, fertility, investment in human capital, time allocation, illegal behavior, self-protection, family behavior, politics, addiction, demographic change and economic growth, and social economics. More recently, Becker shifted his interest to health and aging issues.

MODELS: HUMAN CAPITAL, HUMAN BEHAVIOR, FAMILY BEHAVIOR

Another feature of Becker's work is the formulation of models that produce empirically testable implications, in the tradition of Friedman's positive economics. He explains variations in human behavior by focusing on the role of varying opportunities and market conditions rather than shifting tastes or deviations from rationality.

Becker's work on discrimination was his first undertaking of an important social problem. By its economic definition, discrimination in the marketplace exists when employers, employees, or consumers are willing to incur costs in order to refrain from entering into transactions with other agents because of their race, gender, or religion. Such behavior yields private utility to those with a taste for discrimination but creates misallocation of resources and lowers economic efficiency. The theory explains not only why discrimination exists but also the variations in its prevalence and impact on segregation and wage disparity over time and space based on varying production technologies, competition, population shares of the discriminating and discriminated groups, distribution of tastes for discrimination, government intervention, and economic growth.

The literature on human capital did not begin with Becker. However, he formulated and formalized the basic micro foundations and equilibrium analysis that transformed it into a theory of investment in various forms of human capital, wage differentials, and earning distribution. Becker's model, bolstered by the parallel development of Jacob Mincer's human-capital-earnings functions, has had a profound impact on the measurement of private and social rates of return to schooling and training and offered important insights concerning *general* and *specific* training, bonding between employers and employees, optimal wage contracts, and the sources of inequality in the distribution of labor income. The overarching importance of human capital has made the work relevant in virtually all areas of economic inquiry.

Crime and punishment was an area of inquiry of classical economists such as Cesare Beccaria, William Paley, and Jeremy Bentham, but Becker offered a systematic treatment of crime and public law enforcement, using optimization analysis and welfare theory. Taking offenders to be responsive to incentives, he applied the basic principles of rational behavior to specify their reaction to probability and severity of punishment. The main thrust of the work has been to derive propositions about optimal enforcement strategies concerning the balance between probability and severity of punishment, imprisonment and fines, compensations in civil litigations, and private enforcement, based on maximization of social income. Becker's work led to the development of a vast literature on the *economics of crime*, and influenced the *law and economics* movement.

Becker's fascination with the economics of the household and the family started with the economics of fertility and the allocation of time, and evolved into a wide range of family issues involving marriage, divorce, allocation of tasks within the family, parental altruism, inheritance, and investment in children, culminating in his expanded edition of *A Treatise on the Family* (1991). Becker also considered the long-term effects of human capital investments within the family. Following Robert Lucas's 1988 work on endogenous growth, in which human capital is identified as the engine of long-term sustainable growth of an infinitely lived agent, Becker and his colleagues offered a dynastic framework where altruistic parents make investments in children by partly trading off fertility and human capital investments. The work explains the process of development as a transition between stages of economic development, from a Malthusian Trap to a steady state of perpetual growth, over which period fertility declines.

IMPACT BEYOND ECONOMICS

Becker's influence transcends economics. At the outset, his work was met with skepticism and distrust, to some extent inside economics, as in Sandmo (1993), but mainly outside the profession where the controversy centered largely on the applicability of the rigorous economic methodology to complex social issues. Some even found the now universally established term *human capital* to be offensive, on the grounds that it likened humans to machines. Despite this, Becker persevered in his research and gradually gained wide acceptance among economists, as judged by the frequency with which his work is cited in, and augmented by, the research of others. Specific aspects of demography and health economics constitute one example, the economics of crime and law constitute another, and the literature on labor issues has been dominated by Becker's work on discrimination, time allocation within households, and human capital. But Becker also made inroads into other social sciences where sociologists and political scientists more frequently work with models based on rational choice. His belief in the widest applicability of economics as a social science links Becker, perhaps more than any other modern economist, with major classical economists who also adopted an all-embracing approach to social issues. His quest for a truly general science of society is continuing.

SEE ALSO *Bentham, Jeremy; Crime and Criminology; Discrimination, Racial; Economic Growth; Economics, Nobel Prize in; Family; Fertility, Human; Friedman, Milton; Human Capital; Law and Economics; Optimizing Behavior; Punishment; Rational Choice Theory; Rationality; Time Allocation*

BIBLIOGRAPHY

PRIMARY WORKS

Becker, Gary S. 1960. An Economic Analysis of Fertility. In *Demographic and Economic Change in Developed Countries, Conference of the Universities-National Bureau Committee for Economic Research, a Report of the National Bureau of Economic Research*, 209–240. Princeton, N.J.: Princeton University Press.

Becker, Gary S. [1957] 1971. *The Economics of Discrimination*, 2nd ed. Chicago: University of Chicago Press.

Becker, Gary S. [1964] 1993. *Human Capital*. 3rd ed. New York: Columbia University Press.

Becker, Gary S. 1965. A Theory of the Allocation of Time. *Economic Journal* 73 (299): 493–517.

Becker, Gary S. 1968. Crime and Punishment: An Economic Approach. *Journal of Political Economy* 76 (2): 169–217.

Becker, Gary S. [1981] 1991. *A Treatise on the Family.* Expanded ed. Cambridge, MA: Harvard University Press.

Becker, Gary S. 1983. A Theory of Competition Among Pressure Groups for Political Influence. *Quarterly Journal of Economics* 98 (3): 371–400.

Becker, Gary S. 1993. Nobel Lecture: The Economic Way of Looking at Behavior. *Journal of Political Economy* 101 (3): 385–409.

Becker, Gary S. 1996. *Accounting for Tastes.* Cambridge, MA: Harvard University Press.

Becker, Gary S., and Robert J. Barro. 1988. A Reformulation of the Economic Theory of Fertility. *Quarterly Journal of Economics* 103 (1): 1–25.

Becker, Gary S., and Kevin M. Murphy. 1988. A Theory of Rational Addiction. *Journal of Political Economy* 96 (4): 675–700.

Becker, Gary S., and Kevin M. Murphy. 2000. *Social Economics: Market Behavior in a Social Environment.* Cambridge, MA: Harvard University Press.

Becker, Gary S., and Guity Nashet-Becker. 1996. *The Economics of Life.* New York: McGraw-Hill.

Becker, Gary S., and George J. Stigler. 1974. Law Enforcement, Malfeasance, and Compensation of Enforcers. *Journal of Legal Studies* 3 (1): 1–18.

Becker, Gary S., and Nigel Tomes. 1986. Human Capital and the Rise and Fall of Families. *Journal of Labor Economics* 4 (3, pt. 2): S1–S39.

Becker, Gary S., Michael Grossman, and Kevin M. Murphy. 1994. An Empirical Analysis of Cigarette Addiction. *American Economic Review* 84 (3): 396–418.

Becker, Gary S., Kevin M. Murphy, and Robert Tamura. 1990. Human Capital, Fertility, and Economic Growth. *Journal of Political Economy* 98 (5, pt. 2): S12–S70.

Becker, Gary S., Tomas J. Philipson, and Rodrigo R. Soares. 2005. The Quantity and Quality of Life and the Evolution of World Inequality. *American Economic Review* 95 (1): 277–291.

Ehrlich, Isaac, and Gary S. Becker. 1972. Market Insurance, Self-Insurance and Self-Protection. *Journal of Political Economy* 80 (4): 623–648.

SECONDARY WORKS

Ehrlich, Isaac, and Zhiqiang Liu, eds. 2006. *The Economics of Crime.* Northampton, MA: Edward Elgar Publishing.

Fabrero, Ramon, and Pedro S. Shwartz, eds. 1995. *The Essence of Becker.* Stanford, CA: Hoover Institution Press.

Lucas, Robert E., Jr. 1988. On the Mechanics of Economic Development. *Journal of Monetary Economics* 22 (1): 3–42.

Mincer, Jacob. 1974. *Schooling, Experience, and Earnings.* New York: National Bureau of Economic Research.

Posner, Richard A. 1993. Gary Becker's Contributions to Law and Economics. *The Journal of Legal Studies* 22 (2): 211–215.

Rosen, Sherwin. 1993. Risk and Reward: Gary Becker's Contributions to Economics. *The Scandinavian Journal of Economics* 95 (1): 25–36.

Sandmo, Agnar. 1993. Gary Becker's Contributions to Economics. *The Scandinavian Journal of Economics* 95 (1): 7–23.

Isaac Ehrlich

BEGGAR-THY-NEIGHBOR

In economics, the term *beggar-thy-neighbor* describes economic policies that aim to enrich one country at the expense of other countries. Most commonly, the term *beggar-thy-neighbor* is used in relation to such international trade policies as the application of tariffs and other restrictions on imports, as well as currency devaluations that are intended to improve the international competitiveness of the goods the country is exporting. The policy is considered to be beggar-thy-neighbor when the welfare gain in the country imposing the policy is offset by the welfare loss in the countries affected by the policy.

Beggar-thy-neighbor trade policies could be aimed at protecting domestic industries that compete against imported goods. These policies may take the form of import quotas or import tariffs, both of which are aimed at restricting imports and also making them more expensive. For example, an import tariff will benefit the country because the tariff improves the nation's terms of trade. That is to say, by raising the price of imports the tariff causes the ratio of export prices to import prices to fall and thus makes the country's sales to others (exports) cheaper, while simultaneously making the price of purchases from its trading partners (imports) more expensive. Thus, an import tariff is a beggar-thy-neighbor policy (Feenstra 2004, chap. 7).

One of the roles of the World Trade Organization is to prevent such beggar-thy-neighbor trade policies. However, it should be noted that if import tariffs or currency devaluations are accompanied by other policy measures designed to increase economic growth in the country, they might not be beggar-thy-neighbor. The tariff, for example, will reduce imports but economic growth encourages an increase of imports.

Currency devaluations are considered beggar-thy-neighbor if they are conducted solely for the purpose of boosting the country's exports by making them cheaper for foreigners to buy and therefore increasing the country's global market share. The trading partners of the country that undertakes a beggar-thy-neighbor devaluation may retaliate by devaluing their currency as well. Such a phenomenon, known as *competitive devaluation*, is an example of a beggar-thy-neighbor policy. Similarly, wage repression policies could be beggar-thy-neighbor if their sole purpose is to increase a country's competitiveness in the international markets, which forces their competitors to repress wages as well.

During the Great Depression, the countries that were adhering to the gold standard, fixing the value of their currency to the value of gold, engaged in a series of competitive devaluations. In addition, many countries, including the United States, imposed protective import tariffs (the Smoot-Hawley Tariff Act of 1930 raised U.S. tariffs to historically high levels). Many economists have argued that such beggar-thy-neighbor policies worsened the economic decline during the Great Depression. Nevertheless, Barry Eichengreen showed that "competitive devaluations of the 1930s redistributed the Depression's effects across countries but did not worsen it overall" (1988, p. 90).

In July 1944 the delegates of forty-four countries met at the United Nations Monetary and Financial Conference at Bretton Woods, New Hampshire, and established the system of fixed exchange rates known as the *Bretton Woods system*. In addition, the conference instituted the International Monetary Fund and the World Bank. One of the purposes of the creation of these institutions was to avoid the return of the beggar-thy-neighbor policies of the 1930s.

In the early 2000s exports from China increased substantially. Some economists argue that such a fast increase can be partly attributed to the Chinese policy of keeping Chinese currency, the renminbi, at an artificially depreciated level in order to make exports from China very competitive. If this is the only reason the Chinese government keeps the value of the renminbi low, the policy could be classified as beggar-thy-neighbor.

BIBLIOGRAPHY

Eichengreen, Barry. 1988. Did International Economic Forces Cause the Great Depression? *Contemporary Economic Policy* 6 (2): 90–114.

Feenstra, Robert. 2004. *Advanced International Trade: Theory and Evidence.* Princeton, NJ: Princeton University Press.

Galina Hale

BEHAVIOR, SELF-CONSTRAINED

Self-imposed constraint or restraint has typically been defined in terms of willpower or other personal attributes assumed to be completely within the control of the individual, such as abstinence from pleasurable (sex) or unpleasurable (pain/illness) behaviors and conditions and the ability to cope with stress and dysfunction in one's life. For the vast majority of students of self-restraint, there are significant moral and social features of the behavior, and much research has attempted to address and even control these conditions. Featured below are some examples of what is known or believed about personal self-restraint from this research.

Research on self-restraint runs the gamut from the most basic (e.g., monitoring of food intake) to a middle range of investigations of control over sexual promiscuity or aggressive impulses, to the most serious forms of behavior, such as drug addiction or child abuse. Most research in food intake has addressed dieting behaviors and disorders, such as obesity or anorexia nervosa/bulimia, and these have largely been studied through genetics or other biological conditions. Much less work has been done on the most severe forms of problem restraint, with the exception of addictive disorders, where often an imprisoned or similarly institutionalized population is more readily available to be studied. The heaviest concentration of studies have been in the area in the middle, which tries to understand the triggers—personal, psychosocial, and environmental—that lead to initiation, maintenance of, or abstinence from risky or healthy behaviors. Most research links the problems to interventions to help solve them.

Additional work has addressed the efforts of individuals and their professional "helpers" to regulate their potentially excessive behavior. In the medical field, it is increasingly common for patients to ask their doctors to impose constraints by limiting or removing the opportunity for pain relief. For example, women who fear harmful side effects of anesthesia will preemptively insist that their doctors not administer drugs. Identified as "anticipatory self-command" and associated with rational choice theory, this behavior highlights the tension between individual preference and professional responsibility. The doctor is charged with minimizing discomfort and maximizing healthy outcomes. But it is, after all, not the doctor's body that is in question. In this case, both parties must or choose to administer self-constraints in order to ensure a desirable outcome. Lest this example seem isolated, think of how often people ask family or close friends to help them not do something, such as smoking ("you hold my cigarettes"), overspending ("hide my credit card from me"), or eating badly ("if you bring those into the house, don't tell me where they are"). Similar work has emphasized the need to acknowledge past behaviors and choices and build a present around this knowledge—that is, to constrain choices mostly by better understanding the self.

There is a vast literature about youth aggression and violence, much of it around sport, leisure, and play, which tries to understand adolescent impulses toward healthy or risky behaviors. Generally researchers agree that a combination of personal factors, including gender and age, and social factors, including home/family environment, school setting, and peer relationships, affect youth participation in aggression/violence, delinquency, drug or alcohol use, sexual behavior, and the like. Studies show strong connections between personal qualities, such as a resilient personality, adaptive learning, and coping/resistance skills, and higher achievement in school, less problem behavior, and lifelong success. Many of these same studies show strong associations between social-environmental influences, such as strong bonds to healthy community institutions (e.g., school, family, neighborhood) and positive life outcomes. This research has led to a number of strong programs for youth that help build skills and strengthen the social environment, including Life Skills Training, All Stars, and Family Strengthening. Critical to the success of these programs is the skills building and environmental strengthening they combine with information sharing—information alone does not help and may actually hurt the people it is aimed at.

Another significant body of literature shows connections between personal (including DNA) and social-environmental forces and the most severe problem behaviors, such as eating disorders, HIV/AIDS, and drug addiction. Much of the genetic research that has been done on animals focuses on individual stimulus-response (Skinnerian) behaviors. For instance, scientists have been able to decrease desires for a substance (something as simple as sugar) by combining it with an unpleasant one (such as morphine). Many studies have shown that releasing addicts or criminals from prisons back to their unhealthy environments arouses the same "cravings" in them and is likely to lead to re-offending or re-abusing substances; some of these cravings can be controlled with "safe" stimulation and personal control practices that help internalize the value of abstinence. Research on dopamine, naturally produced by the body, suggests it can be regulated to affect drug and eating disorders and may hold a key to reducing problems of obesity and addiction. Similar studies point to the importance of serotonin, or seroconversion, in HIV/AIDS intravenous drug users. Even heavily individual and biological studies, however, point to the glut of social and environmental forces that are beyond the control of the individual and suggest the need to improve this environment. For instance, two cardinal features of human eating disorders are binge eating and body weight/body image, so understanding the social norms around a healthy body, controlling the availability of unhealthy eating patterns (e.g., "Supersize me"), and providing mechanisms to control behavioral and neurochemical abnormalities are critical.

SEE ALSO *Choice in Psychology; Obesity; Optimizing Behavior; Overeating; Rationality; Self-Monitoring; Undereating*

BIBLIOGRAPHY

Diana, Augusto. 2001. *Youth at Play: Preventing Youth Problem Behavior through Sport and Recreation.* Eugene, OR: International Institute for Sport and Human Performance.

Hawkins, J. David, Richard F. Catalano, and J. Y. Miller. 1992. Risk and Protective Factors for Alcohol and Other Drug Problems in Adolescence and Early Adulthood: Implications for Substance Abuse Prevention. *Psychological Bulletin* 112 (1): 64–105.

Hayes, Stephen. 2007. Acceptance and Commitment Therapy, Relational Frame Theory, and the Third Wave of Behavior Therapy. *Behavior Therapy* 35: 639–665.

Poundstone, Katharine E., S. A. Strathdee, and D. D. Celentano. 2004. The Social Epidemiology of Human Immunodeficiency Virus/Acquired ImmunoDeficiency Syndrome. *Epidemiological Review* 26: 22–35.

Schelling, Thomas C. 1984. Self Command in Practice, in Policy, and in a Theory of Rational Choice. *American Economic Review* 74 (2): 1–11.

Schinke, Steven, Paul Brounstein, and Stephen E. Gardner. 2003. *Science-Based Prevention Programs and Principles, 2002.* U.S. Department of Health and Human Services, Substance Abuse and Mental Health Services Administration, Center for Substance Abuse Prevention, Publication (SMA)03-3764. Washington, DC: U.S. Department of Health and Human Services.

Steinglass, Joanna E., and B. Timothy Walsh. 2006. Habit Learning and Anorexia Nervosa: A Cognitive Neuroscience Hypothesis. *International Journal of Eating Disorders* 39 (4): 267–275.

Tobler, Nancy S., Michael R. Roona, Peter Ochshorn, et al. 2000. School-Based Adolescent Drug Prevention Programs: 1998 Meta-analysis. *Journal of Primary Prevention* 20 (4): 275–336.

Volkow, Nora D. 2004. Beyond the Brain: The Medical Consequences of Abuse and Addiction. *NIDA Notes* 18 (6): 3.

Augusto Diana

BEHAVIORISM

Behaviorism is a twentieth-century term, made popular by the psychologist John Watson (1878–1958) in 1913. Although Watson introduced *psychological behaviorism*, there is also a version called *philosophical behaviorism*.

Psychological behaviorism is the view that psychology should study the behavior of individual organisms. Psychology should be defined not as the study of the mind and internal mental processes via introspection, but as the science of behavior. The most famous proponents of psychological behaviorism were John Watson and B. F. Skinner (1904–1990). Other notable behaviorists were Edwin Guthrie (1886–1959), Edward Tolman (1886–1959), Clark Hull (1884–1952), and Kenneth Spence (1907–1967).

Philosophical behaviorism, by contrast, is a research program advanced primarily by philosophers of the twentieth century. This school is much more difficult to characterize, but in general, it is concerned with the philosophy of mind, the meaning of mentalistic terms, how we learn this meaning, and how we know when to use these terms. Important philosophical behaviorists include Bertrand Russell (1872–1970), Gilbert Ryle (1900–1976), Ludwig Wittgenstein (1889–1951), Rudolf Carnap (1891–1970), Otto Neurath (1882–1945), Carl Hempel (1905–1997), and W. V. O. Quine (1908–2000). Other philosophers such as Daniel Dennett (b. 1942), Wilfrid Sellars (1912–1989), Donald Davidson (1917–2003), and Richard Rorty (b. 1931) have behavioristic sympathies to varying degrees.

Besides these two generic versions of behaviorism, there are several subvarieties (see Kitchener 1999; Zuriff 1985). *Eliminative behaviorism* is the denial that there are any mental states at all; there is just behavior. *Methodological behaviorism* is the view that it does not matter whether there is a mind or not; psychologists should just study behavior. *Logical behaviorism* (also called *analytic behaviorism* or *semantic behaviorism*) is the view that all mentalistic terms or concepts can be defined or translated into behavioral terms or concepts. *Epistemological behaviorism* and *evidential behaviorism* hold roughly the view that the only way to know about a mental state is by observing behavior.

A BRIEF HISTORICAL OVERVIEW

It should be noted that in the intellectual history of western culture there have been individuals who held views very similar to theories supported by one or both of these movements, even though they did not use the term *behaviorism*; others have championed views that may not be characterized as "behavioristic," but which have had a strong impact on behavioristic ways of thinking (see Peters 1973–1974; Harrell and Harrison 1938). The writings of Aristotle (384 BCE–322 BCE), in particular his *De Anima*, his account of practical rationality in the *Nicomachean Ethics*, and his scientific work on animals (*De Motu Animal*), contain ideas that were assimilated by later behaviorists. Likewise, the writings of the Stoics and the Skeptics contain several theoretical accounts that are sympathetic to a general behavioristic approach, especially their views about animal cognition.

Several seventeenth- and eighteenth-century works inspired behavioristic followers, including Thomas Hobbes's generally mechanistic account of the mind, *The Leviathan* (1651), René Descartes's 1637 account of animal behavior, *Discourse on Method*, and the writings of several individuals who belonged to the French Encyclopedists tradition of the Enlightenment, such as Julien de La Mettrie's *Man a Machine* (1748), Pierre Cabanis's *On the Relations between the Physical and the Moral Aspects of Man* (1802), and Baron d'Holbach's *The System of Nature* (1770), among others.

The Cartesian Tradition A major philosophical issue emerging in the seventeenth and eighteenth centuries concerned the question of the nature of the human mind and the animal mind: Is it possible to provide a mechanistic, materialistic, and deterministic account of the human mind, or must one appeal to principles that are quite different from those used in modern physics? Descartes argued that the human mind is made of a substance different from any found in the natural world, one that operates by principles at odds with the ordinary causal processes of inorganic matter. Although humans possess this special kind of spiritual being, animals do not; they are, quite simply, machines that operate by ordinary "matter in motion" (Descartes 1637). Humans are radically different from such animals because the human mind is made of a quite different substance that is not observable by ordinary naturalistic methods; however, humans have a kind of special access to their own minds, found by means of internal reflection or introspection. None of this was true of animals, all of whose behavior can be explained mechanistically in terms of simple mechanical principles (see Rosenfeld 1941).

The question that arose, therefore, was this: If Descartes was correct about his animal psychology, was he also correct about human psychology? Do we need to appeal to a special nonmaterial substance to explain the behavior of humans, or can all of their behavior be explained in the same ways we explain animal behavior? Although Descartes's answer was widely accepted, there were a few individuals who argued that humans are no different from animals, and hence if animal behavior can be explained along naturalistic lines—by observing their behavior and trying to explain it by deterministic laws of matter in motion—the same is true of humans. This was the view of some eighteenth-century thinkers who championed a purely naturalistic, materialistic, deterministic, and mechanistic account of humans. They were the forefathers of mainstream psychological behaviorism.

The nineteenth century produced philosophers and scientists who, in one form or another, contributed ideas that were fuel for the behaviorists' fire. An example are the post-Kantian German idealistic philosophers, many of whom stressed the importance of *praxis*, or human action. These ideas in turn strongly influenced members of the philosophical/psychological school of pragmatism, including Charles Sanders Peirce (1839–1914), William James (1842–1910), and John Dewey (1859–1952). These pragmatists were concerned with understanding and providing an account of humans and animals that focused on their action—something that organisms did, something they tried to accomplish as they interacted in their physical and social environment. Strongly influenced by the Darwinian revolution, the pragmatists employed a Darwinian model of organisms adapting to their environments to understand action. Such an approach at once stressed the problem-solving nature of human and animal mentality and the assumption that everything that exists must be understood in a "functional" way—that is, how entities such as ideas are useful in an organism's struggle to survive in its environment. All intelligence was to be explained in this way, as an "instrument of action."

Although Sigmund Freud was no behaviorist, he did aid the behaviorist cause by challenging the reigning Cartesian model of the mind that maintained that humans had an immediate and privileged access to the inner workings of their minds that employed a first-person rather than a third-person perspective on the mind, and that tended to draw a sharp distinction between the human mind and the animal mind. Freud argued that the mind is not transparent to our internal gaze because most of our mental activity is going on below the surface at the level of the unconscious (Freud 1900). If this is correct, then the method of psychology cannot be assumed to be introspective. This opened the way to alternative methods of psychological investigation.

The work of Ivan Pavlov on the conditioned reflexes of dogs ([1927] 1960), as well as the work of other Russian physiological scientists, provided behaviorists with scientific accounts of behavior. Behavior occurs, persists, and changes as a result of *classical conditioning*. An original stimulus elicits some response; another stimulus is subsequently paired with the original stimulus, thereby acquiring the power to elicit the response. This version of S-R psychology is the paradigm for at least early behaviorism, providing an explanation of behavior. The other kind of learning employed by behaviorists was instrumental conditioning (operant conditioning, trial and error learning), first introduced in 1898 by Edward Thorndike (1874–1949). In instrumental conditioning, a response is learned because it is reinforced by a stimulus—the reward—where the response is instrumental in obtaining the reward. Classical and instrumental learning promised to explain all of behavior. None of this seemed to require private internal workings of a special kind of substance.

Psychology could take its place among the objective natural sciences.

PSYCHOLOGICAL BEHAVIORISM

In psychology, behaviorism began with John Watson, who coined the term *behaviorism* and set forth its initial premises in his seminal article "Psychology as the Behaviorist Views It" (1913). Behaviorism, Watson suggested, should be considered an objective, natural science, one that studies the public, observable behavior of organisms. Rejecting the method of introspection practiced by his predecessors, Watson suggested a different method to be used by psychologists: Study the observable behavior of others, and to explain it, given the stimulus, predict the response; given the response, predict the stimulus. The aim of psychology, therefore, was the prediction and control of behavior. What then of the mind, that special substance that Descartes claimed was the special province of humans? Watson gave several different answers over the course of his career, including eliminative behaviorism, methodological behaviorism, and, later, the view that the mind exists but is the same as behavior. In short, Watson's argument was this: Humans and animals are not radically different from each other, and since the behavior of animals can be explained without appealing to consciousness, the behavior of humans can be explained without appealing to consciousness, too. With the rise of the cognitive sciences in the 1960s, this conclusion was denied, and so was the claim that the behavior of animals can be explained without appealing to consciousness.

The key question is, what did Watson mean by "behavior"? Was it a mechanical physical movement of the body or something more complex—the intentional, purposive action of a rational agent? If the latter, then how can a purely mechanistic science account for it? This perplexing question remained at the center of discussion for decades. Doubts about a mechanistic approach gave impetus to versions of *purposive behaviorism* found in the writings of William McDougall (1912), Edwin Holt (1915), and E. C. Tolman (1932). Indeed, McDougall and Holt had been proposing a kind of teleological behaviorism before Watson had appeared on the scene.

We can divide the history of psychological behaviorism into several periods: (1) classical behaviorism, (2) neobehaviorism, (3) operant behaviorism, and (4) contemporary behaviorism. The first period (1912–1930) introduced the theory of behaviorism championed by John Watson and several other early advocates of behaviorism, including Max Meyer, Albert Weiss, Walter Hunter, and Karl Lashley. These behavioristic accounts were, by and large, naive, sketchy, and inadequate, but they set forth the general program of psychological behaviorism.

The second period (1930–1950) was the era of *neobehaviorism*, so called because its philosophical underpinnings were somewhat different from its predecessors. Neobehaviorism was wedded to classical learning theory (see Koch 1959), and neobehaviorists were concerned with what form an adequate theory of learning should take. The main figures were Edwin Guthrie, Edward Tolman, Clark Hull, B. F. Skinner, and Kenneth Spence. All of these individuals spent a great deal of time laying out the philosophical bases of their respective kinds of behaviorism, and in doing so, they borrowed heavily from the school of logical positivism, which was influential at the time (but see Smith 1986). This resulted in an emphasis on the importance of operational definitions, a preference for a hypothetico-deductive model of theory construction, and a focus on issues about intervening variables versus hypothetical constructs, and the admissibility of neurological speculation. This move toward postulating internal mediating responses continued with later Hullian neobehaviorists such as Charles Osgood, Neal Miller, O. H. Mowrer, Frank Logan, and others.

The last two phases of behaviorism are more difficult to characterize. Skinner's version of behaviorism—operant behaviorism—is markedly different from most of the other neobehaviorists, and yet he is perhaps the best-known behaviorist. Indeed, after the demise of Hullian learning theory in the 1960s, the main thrust of the movement switched to Skinner's distinctive version of behaviorism.

Denying he was an S-R psychologist, Skinner championed an operant account of learning, in which a response that occurs is reinforced and its frequency is increased (1938). The response—for example, a bar press or a key peck—is not elicited by any known stimulus, but once it has occurred, its rate of response can be changed by various kinds of reinforcement schedules. The response can also be brought under experimental control when it occurs in the presence of a discriminative stimulus (e.g., light). Such a relationship—discriminative stimulus, response, reinforcement—is sometimes called a contingency of reinforcement, and it holds a central place in Skinner's brand of behaviorism. Skinner himself characterized his behaviorism as a "radical behaviorism" because rather than ignoring what is going on inside the organism, it insists that such events are still behavior (1974). However, such behavior still is caused by environmental variables.

Skinnerian behaviorism was the dominant version of behaviorism in the 1970s, and Skinner extended his approach to consider more and more complex behavior, including thought processes and language. His 1957 book *Verbal Behavior*, an example of this extrapolation, was reviewed by the linguist Noam Chomsky, who subjected it to devastating criticism (Chomsky 1959). Skinner declined to respond to Chomsky, and many individuals took this as a sign of the demise of behaviorism. This was not completely true, as can be seen in the current era of behaviorism, which features teleological behaviorism, interbehaviorism, empirical behaviorism, and so on (see O'Donohue and Kitchener 1999). Although behaviorism does not have the hegemony it once did, it continues to exist, but is restricted to pockets of research. Indeed, there are several scientific journals devoted to behaviorism, including the *Experimental Analysis of Behavior* and *Behavior and Philosophy*.

Philosophical Behaviorism Although psychological behaviorism can be described relatively clearly, philosophical behaviorism cannot. Fundamentally, a philosophical behaviorist is one who has a particular theory of the philosophical nature of the mind. All philosophical behaviorists are opposed to the Cartesian theory of mind: that the mind is a special kind of nonphysical substance that is essentially private, and introspection is the only or primary way of knowing about the contents of the mind, such that the individual has a privileged access to his mind. One or more of these tenets is denied by the philosophical behaviorist, who believes that there is nothing necessarily hidden about the mind: It is not essentially private, not made of a special substance, not known by any special method, and there is no privileged access to the mind.

In effect, the philosophical behaviorist claims that the mind is essentially something public, exemplified in one's actions in the world, and that mentalistic properties are those displayed in certain kinds of public behavior. Such a view was championed by Bertrand Russell (1921, 1927; see Kitchener 2004). But what particularly distinguishes twentieth-century philosophical behaviorism is its commitment to *semantic behaviorism*, the view that philosophy is concerned with the analysis of the meaning of mentalistic terms, concepts, and representations. This "linguistic turn" in philosophy (Rorty 1967) means that instead of talking about the nature of the mind as an object in the world, philosophers should be concerned with our linguistic representations of the mind. This type of philosophical behaviorism is called logical (analytic, conceptual) behaviorism. Philosophical behaviorism, therefore, is different from psychological behaviorism.

Ludwig Wittgenstein is sometimes called a behaviorist, largely because he was critical of the Cartesian model of the mind, especially its assumption that the meaning of a mentalistic term must be given in terms of one's private sensations or states of consciousness. Such an account would amount to a private language because only the individual can know the meaning of a mentalistic term, an item of his necessarily private experience. Private languages are not possible according to Wittgenstein, because any language must (initially) be a public language; the meaning of mentalistic terms must be intersubjective and public (1953). In order to use a word correctly, Wittgenstein claimed, there must be public criteria for its correct employment. Most individuals insist that Wittgenstein's kind of behaviorism is radically different from the psychological behaviorism of Watson and Hull. Whether it is fundamentally different from Skinner's behaviorism is still an open question.

Gilbert Ryle is also sometimes characterized as an analytic or logical behaviorist. Also rejecting the Cartesian conception of the mind, Ryle showed that mentalistic terms have to have public criteria for their correct use, and hence that mentalistic terms and states are not essentially private to the individual, but must be understood (largely) as complex behavioral dispositions, or actions (and tendencies to act) in certain kinds of physical and social situations (1949). According to Ryle, therefore, mentalistic terms are to be understood in the same way we understand the meaning of, for example, the term *punctual*. An individual is punctual if she shows up to class on time, regularly meets her appointments, and so on. Ryle had strong reservations about calling his views "behavioristic," largely because he thought behaviorism was committed to a mechanistic account of bodily movements and this was certainly not what behavior (or better, action) was.

As Ryle was influenced by Wittgenstein, so were other philosophical behaviorists. Rudolf Carnap and Carl Hempel were members of the group of philosophers known as logical positivists. According to a fundamental principle of logical positivism, the meaning of a statement consists of its method of verification. The meaning of a mentalistic term must be verifiable to be meaningful, and in principle, its meaning consists in how one verifies it by means of empirical observation. For example, the statement "Paul has a toothache" is (approximately) equivalent in meaning to the procedures one uses to verify that Paul has a toothache. Although this might consist in observing Paul's physical behavior, it might also consist in observing the state of Paul's tooth. Hence, for logical positivists, analytic behaviorism merged into the identity theory of mind and central state materialism—the view that mental states are central states of the brain. It remains unclear, therefore, to what extent they should be called "logical behaviorists"; certainly their version of logical behaviorism was quite different from Wittgenstein's and Ryle's.

The last notable philosophical behaviorist was Willard Quine, who was strongly influenced by Carnap (and Wittgenstein); nevertheless, his views are not easily assimilated with theirs. His views about meaning (and hence the meaning of mentalistic terms) were verification-

ist in spirit (because he was an epistemological behaviorist), but he did not share certain of Carnap's views about how to give a behavioral translation of mental terms. It cannot be done atomistically, but only holistically: One cannot give the meaning of single mentalistic term by giving observational conditions for its use. Indeed, Quine was suspicious of the very notion of "meaning" because such things, if they do exist, would be difficult to reconcile with naturalism and physicalism, and therefore the meaning of a mentalistic term cannot be equivalent to some item of behavior. Quine was also skeptical of the very possibility of verifying a statement by means of a set of observations; scientific observation is a much more theoretical affair than this. Nevertheless, Quine insisted that any science is committed to the observation of behavior (epistemological behaviorism, evidential behaviorism), and hence that mentalistic terms are, in some sense, equivalent to behavior. This is, in part, due to the public nature of language (Quine 1960). We obviously do learn what words mean in the process of learning a language, but all of this occurs in the public arena. We are taught how to use words by our linguistic community: In the presence of a public object such as snow, we learn (by principles such as those indicated by Skinner) to utter the word *snow*. Hence, Quine's behaviorism is sometimes called a *linguistic behaviorism* because he insisted that all we have to go on when we teach and learn a language is the public behavior of individuals. This is closely tied to the importance of empirical observation and verification. Furthermore, Quine was committed to *semantic behaviorism*, the view that the meaning of words is necessarily tied to (or consists of) public behavior. Meanings are, therefore, not "in the mind." This is a close cousin to the logical behaviorism of earlier philosophers.

With the rise of computer science and artificial intelligence in the 1960s, an interesting question arose concerning how one could decide if a machine such as a computer was intelligent or not (i.e., whether it "had a mind"). Alan Turing proposed a test—the "Turing test"—for deciding this question (Turing 1950). Basically, the Turing test holds that if you cannot distinguish a computer from a human in terms of its behavior, for example by asking them both questions and reading their answers, then because the human is intelligent, it would be difficult to deny that the machine is intelligent too.

The Turing test raises the issue of behaviorism once more, this time in the context of computers: Is it the actual behavior of the computer that is decisive in ascribing intelligence to it, or are the internal workings of the computer (e.g., using a lookup table) important? Those who answer yes to the latter question might be considered mentalists rather than behaviorists (Block 1981). There is reason to believe that Turing himself thought the internal processing of the computer were important, something most behaviorists have never really denied.

OBJECTIONS TO BEHAVIORISM
Psychological behaviorism and philosophical behaviorism have been criticized since the beginning of the twentieth century.

Objection: Behaviorism Ignores or Denies Consciousness Critics charge that because the behaviorist focuses on behavior—and this means external behavior—he or she ignores or dismisses the private internal realm of consciousness.

Let us assume that consciousness does exist, that individuals are aware of their internal mental thoughts and sensations. The methodological behaviorist argues that this realm can be ignored (from a scientific point of view) by simply refusing to consider it. Radical behaviorists argue behaviorism does not have to ignore this realm; instead, one can simply treat consciousness as internal behavior not unlike the behavior of one's stomach when it digests food. Or, a behaviorist might reply that consciousness is not actual occurrent internal behavior, but rather a behavioral disposition. This is what we ordinarily mean when we say things such as, for example, "the cat is awake and thinking about the mouse."

One property of consciousness that it is particularly difficult for the behaviorist to accommodate are *qualia*—the internal "feel" of certain mental states or events, like the taste of chocolate or the feeling of a sharp pain. A related problem is how a behaviorist can handle images, for example, the image I have of my morning breakfast.

Objection: Behaviorist Explanations Are Inadequate Most behaviorists take behavior as that which needs to be explained—why it occurs, what its form consists of, why it ceases, and so on. But what provides the explanation of such behavior? The standard answer is that stimuli—external stimuli—provide explanations, together with psychological principles concerning the relation of such stimuli to responses. But according to the critic, it remains doubtful that external stimuli can provide such all-encompassing explanations. Instead, one must refer to certain kinds of internal states—typically cognitive states—to explain the behavior.

A very sketchy behaviorist reply would be that all explanatory internal states—including all "cognitive" states—can be explained in terms of the ordinary concepts of stimulus and response, as long as these terms are suitably modified. This typically has taken the form of saying that there are internal states occurring between the external stimulus and the external response but that these internal states are understood to be internal stimuli and

internal responses; for example, according to Hull, internal states might be fractional anticipatory goal responses together with sensory feedback from them. These internal mediating mechanisms are not popular by contemporary cognitive standards, but if behaviorism is to be a viable research program, it must clearly postulate such an internal mechanism or something analogous. Whether these behavioristic models are sufficiently cognitive or representational remains an open question.

Objection: The Behaviorist Concept of *Behavior* Is Inadequate According to one popular argument (Hamlyn 1953), the behaviorist sees ordinary behavior as a mechanistic, physical response, like the movement of an arm. But this is an inadequate conception of human behavior, which is better thought of as an action, such as waving, signaling, flirting, or gesturing. The behaviorist cannot handle this kind of conception because actions are not mechanistic but rather intentional, teleological, rule-governed, governed by social norms, and so on, and these are incompatible with the behavioristic program.

The standard behaviorist reply is to deny the distinction between movements and actions and/or to argue that the behaviorist has always been interested in actions (Kitchener 1977), and that such a concept is consistent with a causal account.

Objection: The Behaviorist Cannot Adequately "Analyze" or Define a Single Mentalistic Term by Means of a Set of Behaviors Logical behaviorists attempted to translate a mentalistic term such as *belief* into a corresponding set of behaviors, for example, a verbal response. But such a translation is only plausible if we assume other mental states in our account, for example, other beliefs, desires, and so on. Hence we have not gotten rid of mentalistic terms (Chisholm 1957; Geach 1957) because there is no term-by-term reduction or elimination.

This objection carries little weight because logical behaviorists such as Carnap and Hempel very early in their careers gave up such a term-by-term approach in favor of a more holistic, theoretical approach, and this commands a central place in Quine's holistic behaviorism.

Objection: The Spartan Objection and the Dramaturgical Objection A mental state, such as pain, is not equivalent to a set of public behaviors because it is possible for one to be stoic about pain: I might be in intense pain but never show it because, say, it is not "macho" to show pain. Likewise, I might manifest pain behavior but not really be in pain, as when I simulate pain as an actor in a play. Hence pain behavior is neither sufficient nor necessary for being in pain (Putnam 1975).

Both of these objections assume a very naive, "peripheral" behaviorism in which the behavior in question is publicly observable. It is necessarily restrictive because behaviorists can hold more sophisticated forms involving "internal" (covert) behavior along with the inclusion of behavioral "dispositions." Secondly, the behaviorist has insisted that one learns the meaning of the term *pain* and to use the word correctly only in the context of public behavior, a view shared by Wittgenstein, Carnap, Quine, Sellars, and Skinner. There must be public criteria for the correct use of *pain*. So originally a certain kind of behaviorism must be correct; later, we may learn how to suppress such behavior and to internalize it. The basis of this claim concerns the learning of language and is based on Wittgenstein's arguments against a private language, or on arguments similar to his.

CONCLUSION

Few individuals would claim that behaviorism today enjoys the popularity it once had. Indeed, many (or most) argue that behaviorism is dead—both in psychology and in philosophy. The claim is easier to make with respect to psychology, particularly in the aftermath of the cognitive revolution. Nevertheless, the reports of the death of behaviorism are somewhat exaggerated. Not only are there viable and interesting research programs that are behavioristic in name, there are signs that even in cognitive science and cognitive psychology there is a reemergence of behaviorism, for example, in connectionism (neural nets), robotics, and dynamic systems theory. In fact, according to some, it remains unclear how cognitive psychology differs from behaviorism, since most behaviorists have also been concerned with central cognitive states. Still, psychological behaviorism is currently a minor opinion.

In philosophy the matter is somewhat different. This is because of the centrality of language learning in analytic philosophy, which seems to demand something like a rule-following conception that presupposes a public or social conception of behavior. This view is shared by those sympathetic to Ryle, Wittgenstein, or Quine. The logical behaviorism of Carnap and Hempel is passé because it was abandoned early in favor of a central state theory of mind. But although psychological behaviorism may have seen its day, philosophical behavior, in one form or another, still claims the strong allegiance of many philosophers (depending on how one characterizes *behaviorism*).

BIBLIOGRAPHY

Baum, William M. 1994. *Understanding Behaviorism: Science, Behavior, and Culture*. New York: Harper.

Block, Ned. 1981. Psychologism and Behaviorism. *The Philosophical Review* 90: 5–43.

Boakes, Robert A. 1984. *From Darwin to Behaviorism*. Cambridge, U.K.: Cambridge University Press.

Cabanis, Pierre J. G. [1802] 1980. *On the Relations between the Physical and the Moral Aspects of Man*. Trans. Margaret Duggan Saidi. Baltimore, MD: Johns Hopkins University Press.

Carnap, Rudolf. [1932] 1959. Psychology in Physical Language. Trans. G. Schick. In *Logical Positivism*, ed. Alfred Jules Ayer, 165–198. New York: Free Press.

Chomsky, Noam. 1959. Review of *Verbal Behavior* by B. F. Skinner. *Language* 35: 26–58.

Chisholm, Roderick. 1957. *Perceiving*. Ithaca, NY: Cornell University Press.

Davidson, Donald. 1963. Actions, Reasons, and Causes. *Journal of Philosophy* 60 (23): 685–700.

Descartes, René. [1637] 1984. Discourse on Method. Trans. John Cottingham, et al. In *The Philosophical Writings of Descartes*, vol. 1, 109–176. New York: Cambridge University Press.

Descartes, René. [1642] 1984. Meditations on First Philosophy. Trans. John Cottingham, et al. In *The Philosophical Writings of Descartes*, vol. 2, 1–62. New York: Cambridge University Press.

D'Holbach, Paul-Henri Thiry. [1770] 1970. *The System of Nature*. Trans. H. D. Robinson. New York: B. Franklin.

Freud, Sigmund. [1900] 1965. *The Interpretation of Dreams*. Trans. James Strachey. New York: Basic Books.

Geach, Peter. 1957. *Mental Acts: Their Content and Their Objects*. London: Routledge and Kegan Paul.

Hamlyn, D. W. 1953. Behaviour. *Philosophy* 28: 132–145.

Harrell, W., and R. Harrison. 1938. The Rise and Fall of Behaviorism. *The Journal of General Psychology* 18: 367–421.

Hayes, Linda J., and Patrick Ghezzi, eds. 1997. *Investigations in Behavioral Epistemology*. Reno, NV: Context Press.

Hempel, Carl. 1949. The Logical Analysis of Psychology. In *Readings in Philosophical Analysis*, eds. Herbert Feigl and Wilfrid Sellars, 373–384. New York: Appleton-Century-Crofts.

Hobbes, Thomas. [1651] 1994. *The Leviathan*. Indianapolis, IN: Hackett.

Holt, Edwin. 1915. *The Freudian Wish and Its Place in Ethics*. New York: Holt.

Hull, Clark. 1943. *Principles of Behavior*. New York: Appleton-Century-Crofts.

Hunter, Walter. 1919. *Human Behavior*. Chicago: University of Chicago Press.

Kitchener, Richard F. 1977. Behavior and Behaviorism. *Behaviorism* 5: 11–72.

Kitchener, Richard F. 1999. Logical Behaviorism. In *Handbook of Behaviorism*, eds. W. O'Donohue and Richard Kitchener, 399–418. New York: Academic Press.

Kitchener, Richard F. 2004. Russell's Flirtation with Behaviorism. *Behavior and Philosophy* 32: 273–291.

Koch, Sigmund. 1964. Psychology and Emerging Conceptions of Knowledge as Unitary. In *Behaviorism and Phenomenology*, ed. T. W. Wann, 1–41. Chicago: University of Chicago Press.

La Mettrie, Julien Offray de. [1748] 1996. *Man a Machine.* Trans. Richard Watson. Indianapolis, IN: Hackett.

Lashley, Karl. 1923. A Behavioristic Interpretation of Consciousness. *Psychological Review* 23: 446–464.

MacKenzie, Brian D. 1977. *Behaviorism and the Limits of Scientific Method.* London: Routledge and Kegan Paul.

McDougall, William. 1912. *Psychology: The Study of Behavior.* New York: Holt.

Meyer, Max. 1921. *The Psychology of the Other One.* Columbus: Missouri Book Company.

O'Donnell, John M. 1985. *The Origins of Behaviorism: American Psychology, 1870–1920.* New York: New York University Press.

O'Donohue, William, and Richard Kitchener, eds. 1999. *Handbook of Behaviorism.* San Diego, CA: Academic Press.

Pavlov, Ivan. [1927] 1960. *Conditioned Reflexes.* Trans. Gleb V. Anrep. New York: Dover.

Peters, R. S. 1973–1974. Behaviorism. In *Dictionary of the History of Ideas,* ed. Philip Wiener, 214–229. New York: Scribner.

Putnam, Hilary. 1975. Brains and Behavior. In *Philosophical Papers,* vol. 2: *Mind, Language, and Reality,* 325–341. Cambridge, U.K.: Cambridge University Press.

Quine, W. V. O. 1960. *Word and Object.* Cambridge, MA: MIT Press.

Rachlin, Howard. 1991. *Introduction to Modern Behaviorism.* 3rd ed. New York: Freeman.

Rorty, Richard, ed. 1967. *The Linguistic Turn.* Chicago: University of Chicago Press.

Rosenfeld, Leonora C. 1941. *From Beast-Machine to Man-Machine: Animal Soul in French Letters from Descartes to La Mettrie.* New York: Oxford University Press.

Russell, Bertrand. 1921. *An Analysis of Mind.* London: Allen and Unwin.

Russell, Bertrand. 1927. *An Outline of Psychology.* New York: W. W. Norton.

Ryle, Gilbert. 1949. *The Concept of Mind.* New York: Barnes and Noble.

Schwartz, Barry, and Hugh Lacey. 1982. *Behaviorism, Science, and Human Nature.* New York: Norton.

Skinner, B. F. 1938. *The Behavior of Organisms.* New York: Appleton-Century-Crofts.

Skinner, B. F. 1957. *Verbal Behavior.* New York: Appleton-Century-Crofts.

Skinner, B. F. 1974. *About Behaviorism.* New York: Knopf.

Smith, L. 1986. *Behaviorism and Logical Positivism: A Reassessment of Their Alliance.* Stanford, CA: Stanford University Press.

Staddon, John. 2001. *The New Behaviorism: Mind, Mechanism, and Society.* Philadelphia: Psychology Press.

Tolman, Edwin C. 1932. *Purposive Behavior in Animals and Men.* New York: Appleton-Century-Crofts.

Turing, Alan. 1950. Computing Machinery and Intelligence. *Mind* 59: 433–490.

Watson, John. 1913. Psychology as the Behaviorist Views. *Psychological Review* 20: 158–177.

Watson, John. 1914. *Behavior: An Introduction to Comparative Psychology.* New York: Holt, Rinehart, and Winston.

Watson, John. 1919. *Psychology from the Standpoint of a Behaviorist.* Philadelphia: J. B. Lippincott.

Watson, John. 1925. *Behaviorism.* New York: W. W. Norton.

Weiss, Albert. 1925. *A Theoretical Basis of Human Behavior.* Columbus, OH: Adams.

Wittgenstein, Ludwig. 1953. *Philosophical Investigations.* Trans. G. E. M. Anscombe. Oxford, U.K.: Blackwell.

Zuriff, Gerald. 1985. *Behaviorism: A Conceptual Reconstruction.* New York: Columbia University Press.

Richard F. Kitchener

BELIEF SYSTEMS
SEE *Lay Theories.*

BELL, DERRICK
SEE *Critical Race Theory.*

BELL CURVE
SEE *Distribution, Normal.*

BEM, DARYL
SEE *Self-Perception Theory.*

BENEDICT, RUTH
1887–1948

One of the major figures in the development of American cultural anthropology, Ruth Benedict was educated at Vassar College (AB, 1909) and Columbia University (PhD, 1923), where she studied under the American anthropologist Franz Boas. Starting in the late nineteenth century, Boas and his students mounted an attack on social-evolutionary theories of human history. Boasian anthropologists showed that the evolutionists' hypothesis of universal stages of development ("primitive," "barbarian," "civilized") were belied by historical facts, especially by the diffusion of cultural materials and the movements of people. That people borrowed language and culture from one another meant that no group of people, and no cultural whole or stage, had an identity that remained fixed over time. But this concept left open the question of what Benedict came to call "cultural integration." Given that cultures were ceaselessly changing, how were anthropologists to talk about the coherence that people experienced in their life-worlds? Benedict's two masterworks, *Patterns of Culture* (1934) and *The Chrysanthemum and the Sword* (1946), provide elegant answers to that question.

Benedict begins *Patterns* by pointing out that because the possibilities for a viable way of life are almost limitless, "selection" becomes a "prime necessity" of human history (p. 23). A group of people creates, borrows, and selects materials that it "integrates" into a consistent pattern, a cultural totality. In Benedict's approach, the meaning of any item that has been incorporated into the whole depends upon its place within that whole; over time, disparate culture traits are woven together in a fundamental pattern such that any one of them can be understood only in terms of its relationship to all the others. Moreover, because cultural wholes are patterns of values in terms of which humans understand the world, people tend to understand (and misunderstand) other cultures by interpreting them in terms of their own. There is, therefore, a tension in Benedict's anthropology between scientifically authoritative descriptions of integrated cultural patterns and ironic reflections on the way Western cultural values structure her readers' (and her own) understandings of other cultures.

This tension is exemplified in *Chrysanthemum*, a book that came out of Benedict's work analyzing cultures for the United States government during World War II. *Chrysanthemum* begins with a discussion of Japanese conceptions of hierarchy and indebtedness, for these contradict the crucial American values of equality and freedom. For example, because Japanese understand family relationships as grounded in indebtedness, they accept both filial and parental duties that to Americans seem overly severe and lacking in love. Similarly, civic duty in Japan is understood as repayment of debt to the supreme authority at the apex of the social hierarchy (the emperor). A person's self-respect is bound to his fulfillment of such duties. By contrast, American self-respect depends on freedom, hence Americans tend to view governmental regulation as a violation of their dearest values—leading Japanese to find Americans to be lawless. Each culture misunderstands the other because apparently similar traits take on different significances in each.

As her study of Japan illustrates, Benedict believed that anthropology, by helping people to see their culture in a new light, could lead them to change customs that were no longer useful or humane. But such reforms were not to be imposed by force; rather, they should emerge, Benedict thought, from democratic discussion, both

nationally and internationally. Benedict herself was willing to assert strong value judgments in her work, as, for example, in her critique of the obstacles women of her time and milieu experienced trying to balance family and career (a balance that was difficult for her to achieve, as her biographers make clear). Moreover, the work of Benedict and other anthropologists on the Japanese (carried out while Japanese Americans were being placed in internment camps) has come to seem problematic to historians and anthropologists who, since Vietnam, have become increasingly dubious that social science in the service of political power can promote democratic ends. Yet, as American difficulties in places like Iraq at the turn of the twenty-first century make clear, there is a place for the kind of anthropologically informed understanding of other cultures that Benedict did so much to advance. It is no surprise, therefore, that a *New York Times* essay on the rebuilding of Iraq concludes with the question, "Where are the new Ruth Benedicts?"

SEE ALSO *Anthropology, U.S.; Boas, Franz; Mead, Margaret*

BIBLIOGRAPHY

Caffrey, Margaret. 1989. *Ruth Benedict: Stranger in This Land*. Austin: University of Texas Press.

Mead, Margaret. 1959. *An Anthropologist at Work: Writings of Ruth Benedict*. Boston: Houghton Mifflin.

Stille, Alexander. 2003. Experts Can Help Rebuild a Country. *New York Times*, July 19.

Richard Handler

BEN-GURION, DAVID
1886–1973

David Ben-Gurion, along with Theodor Herzl (1860–1904) and Chaim Weizmann (1874–1952), is considered one of the three architects of Zionism and the most effective figure in founding the state of Israel. An early convert to Zionism, Ben-Gurion migrated to then Ottoman Palestine in 1906 at a point when the territory housed about 55,000 Jewish inhabitants—only about 1 percent of whom were Zionist pioneers—as opposed to nearly 700,000 Muslim and Christian Arabs. He devoted himself fully to organizing the *Yishuv*, or Jewish community, in Palestine prior to 1948 and to encouraging Jewish immigration to create a sufficient demographic basis for a Jewish state. In 1921 he became the secretary general of the *Histadrut*, the General Federation of (Jewish) Labor in Palestine, a position he retained until becoming the chairman of the Jewish Agency in 1935 before finally becoming the first prime minister and minister of defense of Israel in 1948, positions he held, except for a brief period (1953–1955), until his retirement in 1963. After the creation of the State of Israel in 1948, Ben-Gurion adopted a more confrontational policy with Arab states than many of his compatriots in the leadership of labor, and his return to the cabinet in 1955 corresponded with preparations for the Sinai Campaign in 1956 in which Israel sought to invade Egypt in collaboration with Britain and France during the Suez crisis.

Ben-Gurion also played a key role in formulating a synthesis of labor ideology and Zionist nationalism, as evident in his early affiliation with *Poalei Zion* (Workers of Zion), which he represented during a three-year stay in the United States from 1915 to 1918, then the *Mapai* party and the Labor Party and as the first leader of the *Histadrut*. The *Histadrut* functioned as both a trade union and large employer in its own right, representing Jewish workers and creating Jewish economic enterprises. Its membership was exclusively Jewish, and it actively discouraged Jewish businesses from hiring non-Jewish inhabitants of Palestine. During the British Mandate period following World War I until 1948 when Palestine was administered by Britain, Ben-Gurion developed a working relation with the British administration, which allowed him to emerge as the face of the more "moderate" section of the Zionist movement at the same time that it facilitated his building of the paramilitary Haganah, which by 1948 had become the strongest and best organized military group in the land.

While far more pragmatic than other Zionist leaders, notably Ze'ev Jabotinsky (1880–1940) and, later, Menachem Begin (1913–1992), Ben-Gurion's vision of Zionism made, in fact, little accommodation to the Palestinians. Throughout his life Ben-Gurion regarded the Arab Palestinians as economically, socially, and culturally inferior to the Jewish immigrants. Early in his career he believed that Arab Palestinians had no collective sense of nationalism and that a Jewish state could be built without infringing on them. He never accepted that they had political rights. Significantly, while he was versed in nine languages, he never made an effort to learn Arabic. Thus, in addition to being one of the greatest figures in the history of Zionism, he was also one of the main architects of an enduring conflict.

SEE ALSO *Zionism*

BIBLIOGRAPHY

Ben-Gurion, David. 1971. *Israel: A Personal History* [*Medinat Yiśra'el ha-mehudeshet*]. Trans. Nechemia Meyers and Uzy Nystar. New York: Funk & Wagnalls, 1971.

Cohen, Mitchell. 1987. *Zion and State: Nation, Class, and the Shaping of Modern Israel*. New York: B. Blackwell.

Sternhell, Zeev. 1998. *The Founding Myths of Israel: Nationalism, Socialism, and the Making of the Jewish State*. Trans. David Maisel. Princeton, NJ: Princeton University Press.

Mohammed A. Bamyeh

BENIGN NEGLECT

The concept of benign neglect was coined by the late Senator Daniel Patrick Moynihan (D-NY) in a January 1970 memo to President Richard M. Nixon while he served as the latter's Urban Affairs counselor. The widely circulated memo, which was leaked to the press in March of that same year, read: "The time may have come when the issue of race could benefit from a period of 'benign neglect'." At that historical juncture, Moynihan declared, Americans needed "a period in which Negro progress" continued and "racial rhetoric" faded. Moynihan believed that the antipoverty programs of the "Great Society" of the 1960s had failed miserably, not only because they had attempted to use money alone to solve the nation's inability to properly educate the African American poor but also because they did not raise issues in reference to the viability of integration as a solution to U.S. racial problems. To most liberals—especially many civil rights leaders of the period—Moynihan had provided the rationalization for what Swedish political economist Gunnar Myrdal, in his classic *An American Dilemma* (1944), labeled a "laissez-faire" or "do-nothing" approach to racial problems. Most liberals at the time thought—and they thought correctly—that Moynihan's concept was fatalistic—that is, that the intervention of the federal government on behalf of the African American could not alter the inexorable social forces that could only be assuaged by local initiatives. In short, the concept of benign neglect for all intents and purposes suggested that social programs that were endorsed and funded by the federal government created attitudes of dependency among the African American poor.

In contradistinction to Moynihan's dire assessments, the recent research on antipoverty programs, conducted by such persons as Lisbeth B. Schorr, Daniel Schorr, Phoebe Cottingham, David T. Ellwood, James Comer, and many others, which were based on substantive, empirically verifiable data, demonstrated that social programs, when properly planned and executed, succeeded in reducing infant mortality and the incidence of low birth weight. Furthermore, programs such as Head Start and Job Corps succeeded in helping to remedy such problems as chronic unemployment and poor school achievement; and aided in the prevention of teenage pregnancy. The aforementioned programs, which had their origins in Lyndon B. Johnson's Great Society initiatives, helped many African Americans break the cycle of disadvantage. In essence, the concept of benign neglect, which was not based on empirical reality, ultimately blamed the victim and thus ignored the effects of the flawed structure of society in this nation.

Nevertheless, there has been a recent revival of the benign neglect arguments, which resulted in the 1996 welfare reforms and the introduction of the rhetoric of a "compassionate conservatism" into the presidential campaign of 2000. Furthermore, conservative black politicians and spokespersons have promulgated variants of the concept, which rationalized a terribly flawed social system.

SEE ALSO *Culture of Poverty; Great Society, The; Lewis, Oscar; Moynihan, Daniel Patrick; Neoconservatism; Nixon, Richard M.; Race; Racism; Welfare; Welfare State*

BIBLIOGRAPHY

Lemann, Nicholas. 1992. *The Promised Land: The Great Black Migration and How It Changed America.* New York: Vintage.

Schorr, Lisbeth B., and Daniel Schorr. 1989. *Within Our Reach: Breaking the Cycle of Disadvantage.* New York: Anchor.

Vernon J. Williams Jr.

BENJAMIN, JUDAH P.
1811–1884

Judah P. Benjamin, lawyer, U.S. senator, and Confederate official, was called "the dark prince of the Confederacy" and "the brains of the Confederacy." Born in St. Thomas, Virgin Islands, a British subject, Benjamin achieved greater political power than any other Jew in the United States in the nineteenth century. His struggling Sephardic Jewish family settled in Charleston, South Carolina, in 1813. When Judah was fourteen, a wealthy Jewish merchant sponsored him at Yale University to study law. He mysteriously left after two years and in 1831 moved to New Orleans to begin his life as an apprenticed young lawyer. A strategic marriage to Natalie Martin, whose family belonged to the Catholic Creole aristocracy in New Orleans, and the 1834 publication of his book of reported Orleans and Louisiana Supreme Court decisions propelled him into financial success as an appellate lawyer, largely in commercial cases, and subsequently into a political career. But his wife humiliated Benjamin with her affairs and left him in 1845, in the midst of scandal, to move to Paris with their daughter.

In 1852 Benjamin was elected to the U.S. Senate. Before he was sworn in, he declined an offer from President Millard Fillmore for a seat on the U.S. Supreme Court. He was more interested in a political career. Soon Benjamin met Jefferson Davis (1808–1889), beginning a long friendship. With his reasoned and eloquent oratory, Benjamin became the most celebrated spokesman for the southern moderates. He was reluctant to leave the Union and favored compromise to head off war. He was quick to answer critics who attacked his religious background. "When my ancestors were receiving their Ten Commandments from the immediate Deity," he said during a Senate debate on slavery, "the ancestors of my opponent were herding swine in the forests of Great Britain" (Kohler 1905, pp. 83–84). It was a rare reply. Usually when newspapers, political enemies, or military leaders ridiculed his Jewishness, he never answered but simply retained "a perpetual smile."

After secession, Benjamin became attorney general of the Confederacy and Davis's lieutenant and chief "implementer," writing thousands of memoranda and orders and many speeches for the president. At times he seemed almost to be Davis and even was able to convene the cabinet and ask for a vote to give him constitutional authority to act in the president's name, seeking presidential approval later. He was the only member of the cabinet without slaves, having sold his plantation with 140 slaves after his election to the Senate.

Soon promoted to secretary of war, Benjamin became the scapegoat when the war went badly and was bitterly attacked with anti-Semitic slurs—one newspaper referred to him as "Mr. Davis's pet Jew" (Woodward 1981, p. 233)—and Confederate military officers groused publicly that he knew "as much about war as an Arab knows about the Sermon on the Mount" (Hunter 1905, p. 566). But Davis stood by him and made him secretary of state in 1862.

When the quick collapse of the Confederacy left Richmond in flames, Benjamin traveled south by train and then on horseback with the Confederate leadership. Soon he complained of saddle weariness and left Davis and his guard to escape in a broken-down horse and wagon, posing as a French doctor named "Monsieur Bonfals" (Cajun French for "a good disguise"). Sympathizers smuggled him to the Caribbean and then to London, as he fled the false accusation of involvement in the assassination of Abraham Lincoln.

Especially after the publication of his 1868 treatise on mercantile law, quickly known as "Benjamin on Sales," Benjamin developed a flourishing law practice in international trade. He served in the House of Lords as a queen's counsel, becoming familiar with the leading figures in English cultural and political life. Benjamin never spoke publicly about the war again and ignored charges that the fortune he built in England resulted from his escape with the Confederate gold.

After more than thirty years apart from his wife, Benjamin finally joined her in Paris in 1883. Benjamin died there on May 6, 1884, and was buried in Père Lachaise Cemetery with the great figures in French history.

Benjamin was the main beneficiary of the nineteenth-century emancipation of the Jews and its most visible symbol in the United States. Though he was a nonpracticing Jew, he never attempted to deny his faith, and his contemporary society treated him as Jewish. His election to the Senate was a watershed for American Jews, and because of the Civil War, he became the first Jewish figure to be projected into the national consciousness.

Benjamin has fascinated historians because of the extraordinary role he played in southern history and the ways Jews and non-Jews reacted to him. He remains as he always was—the prototype of the contradiction of the Jewish southerner, a stranger in the Confederate story.

SEE ALSO *Caribbean, The; Confederate States of America; Davis, Jefferson; Jews; Secession; Slavery; U.S. Civil War*

BIBLIOGRAPHY

Chestnut, Mary Boykin. 1905. *A Diary from Dixie.* New York: Appleton.

Evans, Eli N. 1973. *The Provincials: A Personal History of Jews in the South.* New York: Atheneum. Reissue with photographs, Chapel Hill: University of North Carolina Press, 2005.

Evans, Eli N. 1988. *Judah P. Benjamin: The Jewish Confederate.* New York: Free Press.

Foote, Shelby. 1958–1974. *The Civil War: A Narrative.* 3 vols. New York: Random House.

Hunter, Alexander. 1905. *Johnny Reb and Billy Yank.* New York: Neale Publishing.

Kohler, Max J. 1905. *Judah P. Benjamin: Statesman and Jurist.* Publications of the American Jewish Historical Society, no. 12. Baltimore, MD: Lord Baltimore Press.

Korn, Bertram. [1951] 2001. *American Jewry and the Civil War.* Philadelphia: Jewish Publication Society.

Meade, Robert D. 1943. *Judah P. Benjamin: Confederate Statesman.* Oxford: Oxford University Press.

Reznikoff, Charles, and Uriah Engleman. 1950. *The Jews of Charleston.* Philadelphia: Jewish Publication Society.

Woodward, C. Vann, ed. 1981. *Mary Chestnut's Civil War.* New Haven, CT: Yale University Press.

Eli N. Evans

BENTHAM, JEREMY
1748–1832

Jeremy Bentham, a philosopher and reformer, was born in London, entered Oxford University in 1760, and was admitted to the bar in 1769. Rather than practicing law,

he devoted himself to its reform. His first major publication, *A Fragment on Government* (1776), attacked the jurist William Blackstone's (1723–1780) *Commentaries on the Laws of England* (1765–1769) for failing to distinguish between description and criticism of the law and for adopting a nonexistent moral standard, the natural law.

Bentham argued that the only proper moral standard was the principle of utility, of which he gave his best-known exposition in *An Introduction to the Principles of Morals and Legislation* (printed 1780, published 1789). An action was morally right to the extent that it promoted the greatest happiness of the greatest number. Happiness consisted in a balance of pleasure over pain. The utilitarian legislator, by means of punishments and rewards, would encourage those actions that promoted happiness and discourage those that led to suffering.

The task of the legislator was to promote the "subends" of utility, namely subsistence, abundance, security, and equality. Security for person, property, reputation, and condition in life was essential for civilized existence, and, therefore, took priority. To promote equality at the expense of security of property would, for instance, prove counterproductive, since the disappointment of fixed expectations would produce pain in the individuals concerned, and ultimately threaten social stability. Nevertheless, Bentham recognized that inequality was in itself an evil, and he understood and applied the principle of diminishing marginal utility, advocating an equal distribution of resources insofar as this could be achieved without infringing security. Furthermore, in determining the utility of an action, the interests of each individual (irrespective of gender, religious beliefs, or social status) had to be given equal weight. From here, it was a short step to democracy, which Bentham first advocated in writings composed in 1788 and 1789 on the subject of the French Revolution (1789–1799). As the revolution became more extreme, Bentham, like most of his countrymen, became worried by the threat to social order and for many years put aside any consideration of political reform.

In the 1790s Bentham's life was dominated by his attempt to build a panopticon prison in London. The panopticon consisted of a circular building, with the cells arranged around the circumference. The cells were thereby made visible at all times from a central inspection tower. The rejection of the scheme by the government in 1803 propelled Bentham into political radicalism. In writings on judicial evidence and procedure, he concluded that lawyers pursued their own selfish goals rather than the happiness of the community. In 1809 he began to extend this analysis to the political establishment, eventually calling for democratic reform in *Plan of Parliamentary Reform* (1817). He thereafter committed himself to republicanism, and concentrated on writing the *Constitutional Code* (1830), a blueprint for representative democracy.

Bentham's most sustained period of writing on economic questions took place from 1787 to 1804. The promotion of abundance, or the creation of wealth, which was both a security for subsistence and a source of pleasure in itself, was the subject of economic policy. In general, Bentham adhered to the free market principles associated with Adam Smith (1723–1790), on the grounds that individuals were the best judges of how to deploy their own resources. He also accepted Smith's principle that trade was limited by capital, arguing that there should be no prohibitions, bounties, or monopolies on foreign trade. There were, moreover, no economic advantages to the mother country in colony-holding, and those colonies able to govern themselves should be emancipated. Bentham advocated state interference in certain well-defined areas, including the provision of grain stores, encouragement of research, and dissemination of information. He was totally opposed to slavery and the slave trade, though he recognized that the abolition of the former would, in practice, require careful planning and execution.

Bentham's political thought, with its emphasis on the individual and democratic sovereignty, has contributed significantly to the development of liberalism. In economics, his notion of a calculation of utilities inspired the economist W. S. Jevons (1835–1882), and through him Alfred Marshall (1842–1924), in their development of the modern technique of cost-benefit analysis. Bentham's influence on the doctrines of classical economics is, however, less clear. His conception of economics was opposed both to the strand of political economy associated with Thomas Malthus (1766–1834), in that he rejected theology as an appropriate basis for legislation of any kind, and to the scientific strand associated with David Ricardo (1772–1823), in that he rejected the attempt to divorce economics from ethics. A proper assessment of Bentham's place in the history of economics will need to await the production of an authoritative collection of his writings on the subject.

When Bentham died, his body, following his instructions, was dissected for the benefit of anatomical research. His remains were then used to create the "auto-icon," the combination of skeleton, clothes, and wax head that is today displayed at University College London. The story that Bentham generally attends meetings of the College Council, and that the minutes record "Mr. Bentham present but not voting," is unfounded.

SEE ALSO *Ethics; Gaze, Panoptic; Malthus, Thomas Robert; Marginalism; Marshall, Alfred; Ricardo, David; Utilitarianism*

BIBLIOGRAPHY

Dinwiddy, John R. 2004. *Bentham: Selected Writings of John Dinwiddy*. Ed. William Twining. Stanford, CA: Stanford University Press.

Schofield, Philip. 2006. *Utility and Democracy: The Political Thought of Jeremy Bentham*. Oxford: Oxford University Press.

Philip Schofield

BEQUESTS

A bequest is the act of leaving personal wealth to a person or heir by a will. The distribution of bequests not only has potentially important consequences for the distribution of wealth but also the distribution of income. Bequests often take the form of income yielding assets, such as farms, businesses, rental property, financial assets, and more. The income from such assets is an important component of total household income, and the proportion of total household income from nonlabor sources increases as total income increases. In other words, high income households receive a higher proportion of their total income from nonlabor sources than low income households. Thus, inequality in the distribution of bequests not only contributes to wealth inequality but income inequality as well.

The impact of bequests on the observed wealth inequality depends on the importance of bequests in total household wealth. If bequests are a large share of household wealth, then bequests may be an important factor in explaining the observed inequality in the distribution of wealth. And vice versa, if bequests are only a small share of household wealth, then the unequal distribution of bequests may play only a minor role in explaining the observed wealth inequality. Accordingly, considerable effort has been devoted to gauging the importance of bequests in household wealth. Economists Keiko Shimono and Hideaki Otsuki provide a review of the empirical evidence for Japan, the United Kingdom, and the United States in the early-twenty-first century. They report that the empirical evidence is mixed, with a wide range of estimates for each country. Generally speaking, some researchers find that bequests make up a large proportion of household wealth, with estimates as high as 80 percent; whereas others estimate that bequests are only a minor share, with estimates as low as 20 percent. The disparity in estimates for a given country derives mainly from the varying treatment of the interest income from bequests.

EXPLAINING BEQUESTS

In addition to gauging the potential effects of bequests on the distribution of household wealth, there are a variety of theories in the economics literature attempting to explain what motivates individuals to leave bequests. In other words, why don't people simply consume all of their wealth during their lifetime? A prominent explanation for bequest behavior is that parents may be altruistically motivated to save and thereby accumulate wealth in order to leave a bequest to their children and thus increase their children's future happiness. This is often referred to as the bequest motive for saving. Formally, the parents' utility or happiness may be a function of their children's utility, and, in turn, each child's utility is assumed to be a function of the bequest received from their parents.

Such theories can have interesting twists. The Samaritan's dilemma, as explained by Ritsuko Futagami and his colleagues, describes a situation in which a child may save an inadequate amount of money in order to maximize the bequest from their parents, and the *rotten kid* theorem suggests that parents may give larger bequests to their delinquent or rotten children in order to elicit *good* behavior from them in the future. In any event, such theories suggest that the so-called bequest motive of saving may be an important explanation of household saving. As such, there is an extensive literature attempting to model the bequest motive as well as measure its importance in explaining household savings and the accumulation of wealth.

Mohamed Jellal and Francois-Charles Wolff find that parents who themselves are given bequests are more likely to give bequests to their children. As such any policy that affects current bequests to children may affect the bequest behavior of future generations. In this view, any program that currently affects the level of public taxes and subsidies will have a long-term impact on the provision of bequests due to habits passed on to them by the example set by their parents. In other words, parents who are net-beneficiaries of government programs will redistribute more resources to their children because they have higher incomes and the social safety-net provided by government programs reduces the need for precautionary bequests. In addition, by making a bequest, parents shape the preferences of their children, who in turn leave larger bequests to their own children.

BEQUESTS AND PUBLIC POLICY

Modeling the bequest motive is not merely of academic interest; the nature of the bequest motive also may have important implications for public policy. For example, according to the bequest motive of savings, a change in government tax or transfer programs may influence the future welfare of future generations. If parents care about the future happiness of their progeny, then households may adjust their savings behavior to leave a bequest which partially or fully offsets the anticipated change in govern-

ment policy on the future welfare of their children, and, perhaps, their children's children. For example, if parents and grandparents perceive that a government financed retirement program has made them better off at the expense of higher current or future taxes on their children and grandchildren, they may leave larger bequests in order to offset the deleterious effects of the program on their children and grandchildren's welfare.

The bequest motive of savings also has important implications for the economic effects of inheritances taxes and government deficits. If parents save in order to leave a bequest, then changes in inheritances taxes may change their savings behavior because it changes the cost or net-of-tax price to the individual of a bequest of a given amount. More specifically, if the inheritance tax rate is 50 percent, then a $1.00 transfer net-of-taxes requires a $2.00 transfer. David Joulfaian traces the effects of income and estate and gift taxes on the net-of-tax price of wealth transfers. His estimates suggest that taxes may have a significant effect on the timing of transfers, which suggests that the wealthy are influenced by taxes in setting their lifetime transfers, adding another dimension to the literature on bequests.

Regarding the implications of bequests for government deficits, many economists maintain that deficit financing of government expenditures may result in higher interest rates and thereby crowd out private investment. If the return to private investment is higher than the return to public investment, then the crowding-out effect of deficits could be harmful to economic growth. According to Robert Barro a deficit-financed cut in current taxes leads to higher future taxes. Parents, however, may adjust their savings in order to leave larger bequests to their children in order to offset the effect of future tax liabilities on their children's future income (wealth). In this case, there is no crowding-out effect from deficit financing because the future tax liabilities are offset by an increase in current savings; there is no change in the interest rate, and private investment is unaffected.

SEE ALSO *Altruism; In Vivo Transfers; Income Distribution; Inequality, Income; Inequality, Wealth; Inheritance; Wealth*

BIBLIOGRAPHY

Barro, Robert J. 1989. The Ricardian Approach to Budget Deficits. *Journal of Economics Perspectives* 3 (2): 37–54.

Futagami, Ritsuko, Kimiyoshi Kamada, and Takashi Sato. 2004. Government Transfers and the Samaritan's Dilemma in the Family. *Public Choice* 118 (1–2): 77–86.

Jellal, Mohamed, and Francois-Charles Wolff. 2002. Altruistic Bequests with Inherited Tastes. *International Journal of Business and Economics* 1 (2): 95–113.

Joulfaian, David. 2005. Choosing Between Gifts and Bequests: How Taxes Affect the Timing of Wealth Transfers. *Journal of Public Economics* 89 (11–12): 2069–2091.

Shimono, Keiko, and Hideaki Otsuki. 2006. The Distribution of Bequests in Japan. *Journal of the Japanese and International Economies* 20 (1): 77–86.

Mark Rider

BERG, IVAR E.
1929–

Ivar Berg is a sociologist who has made important contributions to the study of education (especially higher education), labor markets and social stratification, human resources, managers and corporations, and industrial sociology generally. In more than a dozen well-known books and more than seventy articles and chapters, Berg has addressed a variety of scholarly issues related to these topics. He is best known for his pathbreaking study *Education and Jobs: The Great Training Robbery* (1970), which posed a significant challenge to conventional economic theory's treatment of human capital and income distribution.

Berg was born on January 3, 1929, in Brooklyn, New York, where he attended kindergarten through high school. His undergraduate education was interrupted twice by service in the U.S. Marine Corps: He was on active duty from 1946 to 1948 and 1950 to 1952, serving in infantry communications in the First and Second Marine Divisions (he resigned in 1965 at the rank of major). He obtained his AB with high honors in political science from Colgate University in 1954. Returning to his Norwegian roots, he was a National Woodrow Wilson fellow and a Fulbright scholar at the University of Oslo from 1954 to 1955. He did his doctoral work at Harvard University from 1955 to 1959, receiving his PhD in 1959 under the tutelage of Alex Inkeles.

He has been a member of the faculties of Columbia University and Vanderbilt University, where he was a professor of economics and sociology, and in the sociology department at the University of Pennsylvania. Toward the end of his sixteen-year-long stay at Columbia University he served as the associate dean of Columbia's fourteen faculties in an interim administration following the upheavals in 1968 related to the Vietnam War. Berg later chaired the University of Pennsylvania's Department of Sociology (1979–1983), and served as dean of Penn's College of Arts and Sciences from 1984 to 1989 and as dean of Social Sciences from 1989 to 1991. In 2001 he was awarded the University of Pennsylvania's Ira Abrams Award for Excellence in Undergraduate and Graduate Teaching. Berg is also a member of Phi Beta Kappa, and has been elected a Fellow of the American Association for the Advancement of Science, the New York Academy of Sciences, and the International Academy of Management.

Berg's research focuses primarily on the relationship of education to work, as well as on the work structures (e.g., organizations, industries, unions, occupations) that characterize industrial societies. He has argued forcefully for the importance of studying the social bases of market phenomena, maintaining that analyses of social institutions and employers' motivations are needed to supplement economists' emphases on supply-side dynamics to understand labor market outcomes (Berg 1981). Moreover, Berg has consistently urged that it is essential to study work and its correlates at multiple levels of analysis (see Berg 1979; Kalleberg and Berg 1987). Explanations should include work structures and institutions operating at macroscopic (such as government policies and relations among nations in a world economy), mezzoscopic (such as industry sectors and labor force developments), and microscopic (such as the job definitions and human resource practices that take place within organizations) levels of analysis.

Berg's classic book *Education and Jobs: The Great Training Robbery* still exerts a profound impact upon the ways employers, academic leaders, and public policy makers have come to think about the linkages between education, personal development, income distribution, and employment. He argued that despite the claims of human capital theory in economics, peoples' educational attainment does not always correspond to their skill levels. On the contrary, Berg's analyses found evidence that employers frequently hire people with certain required levels of education to work in jobs that do not make use of their education (hence, the "great training robbery"), and that employees with more education are not necessarily more productive, and in some cases are actually less productive than workers with less education. Moreover, Berg's results showed that the rise in educational requirements for jobs in the United States reflected primarily the increase in educational attainments of workers (and an emphasis on "credentials"), not the actual technical requirements of jobs.

Berg's study cast doubt on economists' assertions that people with more education earn more because they are more skilled and productive. It also cautioned against using educational credentials as indicators of skills, an insight that played a major role in a landmark civil rights decision by the U. S. Supreme Court, *Griggs v. Duke Power Company* (1971). Moreover, Berg's notion of credentialism was credited with providing the bases of the formal theory of market signaling, for which George A. Akerlof, A. Michael Spence, and Joseph E. Stiglitz shared the 2001 Nobel Prize in Economics.

SEE ALSO *Education, Returns to; Human Capital; Marginal Productivity; Productivity; Schooling*

BIBLIOGRAPHY

Berg, Ivar. 1970. *Education and Jobs: The Great Training Robbery.* New York: Praeger. Reissue with new introduction by the author 2003. New York: Percheron Press.

Berg, Ivar. 1979. *Industrial Sociology.* Englewood Cliffs, NJ: Prentice-Hall.

Berg, Ivar, ed. 1981. *Sociological Perspectives on Labor Markets.* New York: Academic Press.

Kalleberg, Arne L., and Ivar Berg. 1987. *Work and Industry: Structures, Markets, and Processes.* New York: Plenum.

Arne L. Kalleberg

BERGMANN, BARBARA
SEE *Crowding Hypothesis.*

BERLE AND MEANS
SEE *Capitalism, Managerial.*

BERLIN WALL

On the night of August 13, 1961, police officers strung barbed wire along the border of East Berlin to keep East German citizens from fleeing to West Germany. During the previous half year about 160,000 refugees had escaped from the German Democratic Republic (GDR), bringing the total to over three million who had sought a better life and more freedom in West Germany. Because the Soviet leader Nikita Khrushchev had failed to neutralize the western sectors of the former capital of Germany in the Berlin crisis of 1958, he allowed the East German leader, Walter Ulbricht, to seal the border under the guise of protection against capitalist subversion to stop the outflow.

The barrier gradually was turned into an insurmountable concrete wall that averaged 12 feet high and 96 miles long, dividing neighborhoods, streets, and even houses. An elaborate system of fortifications with a back wall, a minefield, a jeep road, guard dogs, watchtowers, and searchlights made the wall impenetrable, and those who wanted to get out had to build tunnels, break through with trucks, fly across in balloons, or forge passports. More than 125 people died in the attempt because the border guards had orders to shoot all escapees. Because the GDR had built the wall on its side, angry Western

governments could only insist on their right to cross at Checkpoint Charlie and reassure the residents of their sectors that they would not abandon them. In 1963 President John F. Kennedy expressed his solidarity with the words "I am a Berliner."

The political effect of the wall was ambivalent. In the short run it increased cold war tensions, culminating in the Cuban missile crisis. In the medium term it stabilized the Communist regime by closing off the "exit" option and forcing East Germans to come to terms with the dictatorship of the SED (Socialist Unity Party). The wall also compelled West German leaders to accept the existence of a second German state and sign agreements with it to permit some travel through a handful of crossing points such as Friedrichstrasse. In the long run, however, the ugly edifice demonstrated symbolically that the GDR was forced to imprison its people because it remained rather unpopular. Anti-Communist leaders never tired of demanding, like President Reagan in 1987, "Mister Gorbachev, tear down this wall."

The inhumanity of the wall eventually prompted its fall. Many East Germans continued to try to leave, supported by a West German policy that recognized them as citizens and paid ransom for their release. When the Hungarian government opened its Austrian border in the summer of 1989, tens of thousands fled, sparking mass demonstrations among those left behind in the GDR. Because that democratic awakening overthrew Erich Honecker, his successor, Egon Krenz, attempted to initiate a more liberal travel policy. Its premature announcement on November 9 inspired citizens to mass at the crossing points and force them to open, thus toppling the wall. Not only East and West Berliners but many people around the world celebrated its fall, which signified the collapse of communism and allowed Germans to reunify and Europeans to reunite.

SEE ALSO *Communism*

BIBLIOGRAPHY

Hertle, Hans-Hermann, Konrad H. Jarausch, and Christoph Klessmann, eds. 2002. *Mauerbau und Mauerfall: Ursachen, Verlauf, Auswirkungen.* Berlin: Ch. Links.

Hilton, Christopher. 2001. *The Wall: The People's Story.* Stroud, U.K.: Sutton Publishing.

Konrad H. Jarausch

BERNOULLI, DANIEL
SEE *Expectations; Expected Utility Theory; Utility, Von Neumann-Morgenstern.*

BEST, LLOYD
SEE *Lewis, W. Arthur.*

BETTELHEIM, BRUNO
1903–1990

The lifework of Austrian-born American psychologist Bruno Bettelheim was devoted to what he called "helping others in their becoming"—improving the treatment of severely disturbed children (1950, 1955, 1967, 1974) and the parenting of all children (1962, 1976, 1987, 1993) through careful attention to their inner experience and developmental needs. His greatest achievement was his pioneering work in *milieu therapy*, developed when he served as director (1944–1973) of the University of Chicago's residential Orthogenic School, whose philosophy and functioning he first described in *Love Is Not Enough* (1950).

Bettelheim's thinking was strongly influenced by his experience as a concentration camp prisoner in Germany during the late 1930s (see *The Informed Heart* 1960). He coined the term *extreme situation* to describe the self-disintegrating trauma of the camp experience, where prisoners knew they might be killed any moment at the whim of the guards, but they were unable to take meaningful action because there was no predictable relationship between the prisoners' behavior and how the guards treated them. Experiencing his own personality disintegrating under these dehumanizing conditions, Bettelheim understood that the Nazis were trying to destroy individuality—in the camps and in Germany generally—and he began to realize the centrality of autonomy in mental health. If an environment designed to promote terror, unpredictability, helplessness, and hopelessness could destroy personality, he reasoned that a therapeutic environment designed to promote safety, predictability, autonomy, and hope ("love is not enough") could heal personality. This became the model for the Orthogenic School.

Recognizing that the "symptoms" prisoners developed—often resembling those of schizophrenia and autism—were actually survival mechanisms, Bettelheim developed an overall adaptational viewpoint that stresses active mastery and that views symptoms as adaptations to complex internal and external conditions rather than pathological dysfunctions. In *The Empty Fortress* (1967), his groundbreaking study of autism, Bettelheim outlined a formal developmental theory that regards autonomy as one of the two core needs of the self (along with intimacy), adumbrating an original "self-psychology" signifi-

cantly different from that of Heinz Kohut (1913–1981) (Frattaroli 1994).

Bettelheim's important contribution to the phenomenology and treatment of autism has unfortunately been overshadowed by the controversy over his theory of etiology. He viewed autism as the child's adaptive response to the mortal terror and powerlessness of growing up in an extreme situation created by inadequate or pathological mothering. He emphasized, however, that "it is not the maternal attitude that produces autism, but the child's spontaneous reaction to it" (Bettelheim 1967, p. 69). He thought that autistic children might have a neurologically based hypersensitivity to sensory and emotional stimuli, such that they experience ordinary negative emotions (including their own anger) as overwhelming and life-threatening. They then "try, in defense, to blot out what is too destructive an experience for them" (Bettelheim 1967, p. 398) by withdrawing into the self-protective "empty fortress" of autism.

Contrary to modern theories that autistics are neurologically impaired in their ability to recognize emotional cues, their hypersensitivity to emotions is now well documented. As Karen Zelan (2003, 2006) describes, this is much more hopeful for treatment. A collaborator with Bettelheim in his study of autism, Zelan has built on his positive contribution in her subsequent work with autistic children, but she rejects his ideas about bad parenting. Autistic children feel overwhelmed by—and need to withdraw from—any sensory and emotional stimulation, whether from the outside world or from within. Their development is stalled when they cannot tolerate the overstimulating presence of the very people they love—their parents. Parents may develop negative attitudes *in reaction to* the autistic withdrawal, but once they understand the underlying problem of hypersensitivity, Zelan finds that most parents are quite sensitive to their children's needs and become crucially important partners in the treatment.

Shortly after Bettelheim's death, several former students alleged that he was a sadistic tyrant who had beaten them abusively (Sutton 1996, prologue). They were students during Bettelheim's last years at the Orthogenic School, when he was preoccupied with medical problems that forced his retirement and was worried about the school's survival. As Sutton suggests, they may have felt cheated by his withdrawal and emotional disengagement during those years. Perhaps they felt betrayed when he killed himself after a life of preaching hope. And perhaps in the heat of these understandable emotions, they reacted, in a one-sidedly negative way, to real experiences with Bettelheim, who could be autocratic, impatient, and intimidating, and who did hit the children.

Ironically, Bettelheim's therapeutic rationale for hitting children was to make himself a frightening but manageable object for just this sort of extreme negative emotion, so that staff members could maintain their vital positive role in the children's lives. Psychological healing requires an atmosphere of safety, in which staff treat children with respect, acceptance, and understanding. But in any residential setting, the atmosphere will be charged with the children's intense negative emotions—rage, hate, paranoia, shame, guilt, self-loathing, and so on—and with tension generated by their impulsive, potentially destructive or self-destructive acting-out of these emotions. In such an atmosphere, staff can easily lose their therapeutic attitude, reacting to patients' negativity and acting-out with their own negativity, provoking further acting-out and creating an unsafe atmosphere. To protect staff members from being overwhelmed in this way, Bettelheim intentionally made himself the focus of all the negativity by assuming the role of feared and hated "big bad wolf" disciplinarian (Sutton 1996, chap. 14).

The perspective expressed in this article reflects the professional and personal experience of the writer, who was inspired to become a psychiatrist and psychoanalyst through working with Bettelheim during Bettelheim's last years at the Orthogenic School (1970–1973). He experienced the school under Bettelheim's direction as a loving, magical, transformative place, very much the "home for the heart" described in Bettelheim's 1974 book (Frattaroli, 1994). He has also written about Bettelheim's contributions to psychoanalytic theory, as well as his clinical teaching and therapeutic philosophy (Frattaroli 1992; 2001, chaps. 5, 6).

The writer saw Bettelheim hit children many times, but never maliciously or abusively. He hit them when their behavior was unsafe or threatened the staff's ability to manage groups. Bettelheim's practice of hitting was deliberate, controlled, predictable, and safe.

As former student Stephen Eliot (2003, chap. 7) describes, the children knew exactly what to expect from Bettelheim, an open-handed slap on the face that was humiliating enough to be a deterrent, but not physically harmful.

Bettelheim often said that because his hitting of children was not done in anger, it was much kinder than what the children would otherwise have done to themselves—out of guilt and self-hatred—or what they may have provoked staff to do to them in anger. Bettelheim's regular practice, immediately after hitting a child, was to talk with staff members about the situation that had required his intervention, pointing out where they had missed or misunderstood important signals that could have told them what the child needed. His keen sense of the children's needs and vulnerabilities in these discussions confirms that he was not angry with them. One cannot be in an

abusive rage at a child one minute and show a thoughtful, empathic respect for that child the next minute.

Standard methods of behavioral control used in hospitals nowadays—any of which can become abusive in the angry impulse of the moment—include leather restraints, locked and padded seclusion rooms, and powerful psychotropic drugs, often used indiscriminately, always without regard for their long-term impact on growth and development (about which nothing is known). Having experienced all these methods in action as a psychiatrist, this writer considers Bettelheim's approach to have been more humane and less destructive to patients' trust and self-esteem. The writer does not advocate such a treatment approach for anyone else, but it was appropriate for Bettelheim and the unique conditions of the Orthogenic School, which functioned more like an extended family than a hospital.

The above account is entirely this writer's, but it is consistent with Sutton's (1996, chap. 14) more detailed and well-documented discussion of Bettelheim's practice of hitting. At stake in this controversy is arguably the most important twentieth-century contribution to the wise, humane, ethical, and effective treatment of severely disturbed patients.

BIBLIOGRAPHY

PRIMARY WORKS

Bettelheim, Bruno. 1950. *Love Is Not Enough: The Treatment of Emotionally Disturbed Children.* Glencoe, IL: Free Press.

Bettelheim, Bruno. 1955. *Truants From Life: The Rehabilitation of Emotionally Disturbed Children.* Glencoe, IL: Free Press.

Bettelheim, Bruno. 1960. *The Informed Heart: Autonomy in a Mass Age.* Glencoe, IL: Free Press.

Bettelheim, Bruno. [1962] 1971. *Dialogues with Mothers.* New York: Avon.

Bettelheim, Bruno. 1967. *The Empty Fortress: Infantile Autism and the Birth of the Self.* New York: Free Press.

Bettelheim, Bruno. [1974] 1985. *A Home for the Heart.* Chicago: University of Chicago Press.

Bettelheim, Bruno. 1976. *The Uses of Enchantment: The Meaning and Importance of Fairy Tales.* New York: Knopf.

Bettelheim, Bruno. 1987. *A Good Enough Parent: A Book on Child-Rearing.* New York: Knopf.

Bettelheim, Bruno, and Alvin Rosenfeld. 1993. *The Art of the Obvious: Developing Insight for Psychotherapy and Everyday Life.* New York: Knopf.

SECONDARY WORKS

Eliot, Stephen. 2003. *Not the Thing I Was: Thirteen Years at Bruno Bettelheim's Orthogenic School.* New York: St. Martin's Press.

Frattaroli, Elio. 1992. Orthodoxy and Heresy in the History of Psychoanalysis. In *Educating the Emotions: Bruno Bettelheim* and *Psychoanalytic Development*, ed. N. Szajnberg, 121–150. New York: Plenum.

Frattaroli, Elio. 1994. Bruno Bettelheim's Unrecognized Contribution to Psychoanalytic Thought. *Psychoanalytic Review* 81: 379–409.

Frattaroli, Elio. 2001. *Healing the Soul in the Age of the Brain: Becoming Conscious in an Unconscious World.* New York: Viking.

Sutton, Nina. 1996. *Bettelheim: A Life and a Legacy.* Trans. David Sharp. New York: Basic Books.

Zelan, Karen. 2003. *Between Their World and Ours: Breakthroughs with Autistic Children.* New York: St. Martin's Press.

Zelan, Karen. 2006. *Amazing Stories of Families with Autistic Children.* Unpublished manuscript.

Elio Frattaroli

BEVERIDGE CURVE

The term *Beveridge curve* describes the negative relationship between the unemployment rate and the vacancy rate in an economy's equilibrium. It is named after William Henry Beveridge (1879–1963), a British economist and reformer and one of the preeminent inspirers of postwar British welfare state. His seminal reports to Parliament in 1942 and 1944 (*Social Insurance and Allied Services* and *Full Employment in a Free Society*) promoted a comprehensive social program aimed at reaching full employment, and they laid the foundation for the later development of an improved social security system to support people "from the cradle to the grave," as well as the National Health Service in Britain.

Labor markets in equilibrium are characterized by the coexistence of people seeking jobs and vacant jobs employers want to fill. This is the result of frictions that make the process of matching job seekers to job vacancies costly and time consuming. This process can be approximated through a matching function that relates the number of hires (or job matches) M to the number of unemployed workers U and job vacancies V: $M=M(U,V)$. The function is increasing in both arguments; that is, it assumes that the number of hires rises when more workers and employers search in the labor market. In equilibrium, when the number of job separations equals the number of matches, it is possible to identify a negative relationship between unemployment and job vacancies. This negative relationship is known in the literature as the *Beveridge curve*.

Cyclical labor market dynamics are commonly reflected by movements along the Beveridge curve. Expansions are characterized by higher vacancy rates and lower unemployment rates, whereas the opposite is true for contractions. Positive comovements of the job vacancy rate and the unemployment rate can be interpreted instead as the result of changes in the structural properties of the underlying job matching process—that is, in the capacity of the unemployed to be matched to job vacancies. These structural changes can be imputed to a number of factors, such as institutional change, mismatch between the skills of the unemployed and the skills required by new jobs, search effort, or effectiveness. According to this interpretation, a shift to the right of the Beveridge curve may be associated with an increase in equilibrium unemployment. Economic policy then should be aimed at increasing the effectiveness of job matching, shifting the Beveridge curve to the left and thus alleviating the underutilization of the available labor resources in the economy.

On the empirical side, there are a number of difficulties that complicate the estimation of a Beveridge curve. First, the researcher often lacks proper vacancy data and therefore resorts to vague approximations, using available series whose relationship with the vacancy rate may not be constant over time. Second, the pool of workers available for a match may include other categories of workers in addition to the unemployed, such as employed workers searching for new jobs, or even individuals only temporarily out of the labor force. Third, shifts in the Beveridge curve are usually hard to detect in a nonarbitrary way.

SEE ALSO *Business Cycles, Empirical Literature; Macroeconomics; Unemployment; Unemployment Rate*

BIBLIOGRAPHY

Blanchard, Olivier, and Peter Diamond. 1989. The Beveridge Curve. *Brookings Papers on Economic Activity* 1989–1: 1–76.

Pissarides, Christopher. 2000. *Equilibrium Unemployment Theory.* 2nd ed. Cambridge, MA: MIT Press.

Luca Nunziata

BEVERIDGE MODEL
SEE *Welfare State.*

BHAGWATI, JAGDISH
1934–

Jagdish Bhagwati was born and raised in India. He went to Cambridge University in 1954 and graduated from there in 1956 with a first in Economics Tripos (*Tripos* refs to the system of honors degrees and examinations at Cambridge). He then studied at the Massachusetts Institute of Technology (MIT) and Oxford, returning to India in 1961 as professor of economics at the Indian Statistical Institute in New Delhi. In 1963, he moved to the Delhi School of Economics as professor of international trade. He visited Columbia University during 1966–1967 and joined the permanent faculty of MIT in 1968, where he later became the Ford International Professor of Economics. In 1980, Bhagwati joined Columbia as Arthur Lehman Professor of Economics and Professor of Political Science. In 2001, he became a University Professor at Columbia University.

Bhagwati has served as economic policy adviser to the director-general of the General Agreement on Tariffs and Trade (GATT) (1991–1993), as special adviser to the United Nations (UN) on Globalization (2001), and as an external adviser to the World Trade Organization (WTO). He also recently served as a member of UN secretary-general Kofi Annan's advisory group on New Partnership in Africa's Development (NEPAD) and was a member of the Eminent Persons Group on the future of the UN Conference on Trade and Development (UNCTAD).

Bhagwati has published more than 300 articles and fifty volumes. He is regarded as one of the foremost international trade theorists of his generation. His very first article, "Immiserizing Growth: A Geometrical Note," published in the *Review of Economic Studies* in 1958, is regarded a classic and spawned a large body of literature. In it, he showed that growth that expanded a country's export sector could so drastically worsen its terms of trade as to actually lower its real income and welfare.

Bhagwati's most influential scientific contribution is "Domestic Distortions, Tariffs, and the Theory of Optimum Subsidy" (1963), written jointly with V. K. Ramaswami. This paper was written at a time when the relevant analytic literature was characterized by ambivalence with respect to the superiority of trade over autarky. It had been pointed out that when domestic distortions such as unionized wage or externalities existed, there was no guarantee that free trade would be superior to autarky. Bhagwati and Ramaswami demonstrated that once an appropriate policy was adopted to eliminate the existing distortion, the case for free trade was restored. They also introduced the idea of policy ranking. In the context of the wage-distortion model, they showed that from a welfare perspective, wage subsidy was the first best instrument, followed by output subsidy and tariff in that order.

Subsequently, Bhagwati led the way in numerous areas of research, including brain drain, illegal international trade, noneconomic objectives and optimal policy interventions, directly unproductive profit-seeking (DUP) activities, nonequivalence of tariffs and quotas, and preferential versus multilateral trade liberalization. He coauthored many of the contributions in these and other areas with T. N. Srinivasan of Yale University. The two together also wrote the influential book *Foreign Trade Regimes and Economic Development: India.*

Currently, Bhagwati is the foremost advocate of free trade. His critics have sometimes argued that he only cares about free trade and does not pay social issues such as labor and environmental standards, income equality, and the gender gap the importance they deserve. Yet such criticisms are the result of a superficial reading of his writings. In his recent celebrated book *In Defense of Globalization* (2004), he carefully dissects all of the important and controversial social issues and advocates their promotion rather than playing them down in favor of free trade. Where he differs from his critics is in the use of trade protection or trade sanctions as instruments for achieving these objectives. Instead, he advocates the use of multiple instruments to achieve multiple objectives. Thus, for example, he recommends using the instrumentality of the International Labour Organization and nongovernmental organizations to promote labor standards and the World Trade Organization to promote trade liberalization.

SEE ALSO *Brain Drain; Free Trade; Immiserizing Growth; International Nongovernmental Organizations (INGOs); Nongovernmental Organizations (NGOs); Protectionism; World Trade Organization*

BIBLIOGRAPHY

Bhagwati, Jagdish. 1971. The Generalized Theory of Distortions and Welfare. In *Trade, Balance of Payments and Growth: Papers in International Economics in Honor of Charles P. Kindleberger*, eds. Jagdish Bhagwati, R. W. Jones, R. A. Mundell, and J. Vanek, 69–90. Amsterdam: North-Holland.

Bhagwati, Jagdish. 1988. *Protectionism.* Cambridge, MA: MIT Press.

Bhagwati, Jagdish. 2004. *In Defense of Globalization.* New York: Oxford University Press.

Bhagwati, Jagdish, and V. K. Ramaswami. 1963. Domestic Distortions, Tariffs, and the Theory of Optimum Subsidy. *Journal of Political Economy* 71 (1): 44–50.

Bhagwati, Jagdish, and T. N. Srinivasan. 1982. The Welfare Consequences of Directly Unproductive Profit-Seeking (DUP) Lobbying Activities: Price versus Quantity Distortions. *Journal of International Economics* 13 (1–2): 33–44.

Arvind Panagariya

BHOPAL

SEE *Disaster Management.*

BICAMERALISM

Parliaments are unicameral or bicameral. In a unicameral parliament all members of parliament sit in the same chamber and vote on major policy decisions. In a bicameral parliament members meet and vote in two separate chambers, usually called the lower house and upper house. The lower house is usually based proportionally on population with each member representing the same number of citizens in each district or region. The upper house varies more broadly in the ways in which members are selected, including inheritance, appointment by various bodies, and direct and indirect elections.

In most bicameral legislatures, the lower chamber predominates. Especially in parliamentary systems, in which the cabinet is responsible for the parliament, ensuring that the cabinet is responsible only to one chamber is critical. Usually, the upper house is able only to delay legislation passed by the lower house. Sometimes the upper house can veto certain types of legislation. In Germany, for instance, the Bundesrat has veto power over legislation that affects the power of the states (the Länder). In Britain the House of Commons is the dominant partner: Ministers and governments emerge from the lower chamber and remain accountable to it.

A majority of the world's parliaments are unicameral. However, in 2000, 37 percent of the world's 178 parliaments had two chambers. This proportion has decreased since World War II as several established democracies have abolished their second chamber, and as new, unitary, and postcommunist states have adopted unicameral assembly. On all continents unicameral assemblies are more common than bicameral ones. For the most part bicameral systems may be found in South and North America and Europe. On the contrary, in Africa and Asia bicameral systems are rather unusual.

According to the political scientist Andrew Heywood (1997), the major benefits of bicameralism are:

- Second chambers check the power of first chambers and prevent abuses of majoritarian rule.
- Bicameral assemblies more effectively check the power of the executive, because there are two chambers to expose the failings of government.
- Two-chamber assemblies widen the basis of representation, allowing each house to articulate a different range of interests and respond to different groups of voters.

- Second chambers act as a constitutional safeguard, delaying the passage of controversial legislation and allowing time for discussion and public debate.

The major drawbacks are:

- Unicameral assemblies are more efficient, because the existence of a second chamber can make the legislative process unnecessarily complex and difficult.
- Second chambers often act as a check on democratic rule, particularly when their members are nonelected or indirectly elected.
- Bicameral assemblies are a recipe for institutional conflict in the legislature, as well as government gridlock.
- Second chambers introduce a conservative political bias by upholding existing constitutional arrangements and, sometimes, the interests of social elites.

In terms of authority and political power bicameral legislatures show large variation. The weakest upper chambers are hardly more than retirement posts for politicians of great merit. On the other hand, with respect to political influence the strongest upper chambers are comparable with the lower chamber or the executive power.

SEE ALSO *Congress, U.S.; Parliament, United Kingdom; Parliaments and Parliamentary Systems*

BIBLIOGRAPHY

Heywood, Andrew. 1997. *Politics*. Houndmills, U.K.: Macmillan Press Ltd.

Tsebelis, George, and Jeanette Money. 1997. *Bicameralism*. Cambridge, U.K: Cambridge University Press.

Guy-Erik Isaksson

BIG BROTHER

SEE *Personality, Cult of.*

BIG PUSH

SEE *Threshold Effects.*

BIGOTRY

Throughout human history, civilizations have been plagued by the problems that result from people's prejudice and bigotry toward one another. In this context, *prejudice* is a negative attitude that occurs when people prejudge disliked others, and *bigotry* is an extreme form of it. Social scientists have written extensively about the correlates of prejudice because of its relationship to group conflict and violence (e.g., Janowitz 1969). Much of this attention has focused on the connections between group conflict and a host of social phenomena that are associated with prejudice, including though not limited to stereotyping, rioting, terrorism, and, not the least among them, bigotry (e.g., Hovland and Sears 1940; Green et al. 1998). Common terms related to bigotry include *ethnocentrism* and *intergroup hatred.*

Bigotry refers to extreme intolerance of members of a socially recognized and vilified out-group. An *out-group* is a group other than the one in which individuals perceive themselves to belong. Prejudice refers to negative attitudes toward members of a group that may or may not be expressed. Though similar (e.g., they both refer to a bias in perception of others), the two terms—bigotry and prejudice—may be distinguished, with bigotry representing a more extreme and brazen form of prejudice.

Bigotry, though not an intractable problem, is one that has shaped the nature of interaction between groups of people throughout history and around the world. For example, intergroup relations between blacks and whites in the United States, Germans and Jews in twentieth-century Europe, Israelis and Palestinians in the Middle East, Africans and Afrikaners in South Africa, heterosexual and gay people, and men and women have all been affected by bigotry and bigoted attitudes. Bigotry and the corresponding problems that ensue from it remain high on the list of "social evils," and most people perceive the bigot to be a person who is obstinately narrow minded, antisocial, and lacking the moral acuity that many believe themselves to possess.

In general, researchers who study bigotry recognize the difficulties involved in identifying its causes. This is because there are often important related variables to consider, including differences (or similarities) in cultural orientation, national identity, and religious background, as well as contact and familiarity—all of which can be associated with bigotry. Not surprisingly, more is known about the consequences of bigotry (e.g., harassment, assault, riots, terrorism) than about the factors that give rise to it.

Researchers have employed a host of methods to assess the presence of bigotry. In earlier years, attempts to measure bigotry often involved direct questionnaires in which respondents indicated the degree to which they liked or disliked an out-group. More recently, changing social norms prohibit direct expression of prejudice and bigotry in most settings. Consequently, researchers have employed more covert measures, such as reaction-time tests in which the time needed to respond to a stimulus is taken as an indirect indicator of a person's attitude. In other cases, behavioral measures, such as seating choice and proximity to a member of an out-group, have been used as indicators of bigotry.

STUDIES OF BIGOTRY

Importantly, some of the earliest social science research addressing the problem of bigotry focused on patterns of interaction and violence perpetrated by whites against African Americans in the United States. Until the late 1950s, blatant racism and physical violence directed at African Americans was normative and well entrenched within the social fabric of American society. Whereas some blamed white fears about miscegenation (i.e., interracial sexual relations) for the collective violence directed at the newly freed class of citizens, others generally attributed the problem to the expanding rights of African Americans.

Contemporary research and theory on bigotry can be conceptualized along a continuum. At one end are those theories that locate the causes of bigotry outside of the individual at the societal level (i.e., the macro level of analysis). These types of theories are largely context dependent. At the other end of this conceptual continuum are explanations for bigotry that attribute causality to internal factors such as deficiencies in the individual's personality, limitations in information-processing capacities, or physiological and biological mechanisms.

Many of the efforts toward understanding the problem of bigotry have involved individualistic accounts of prejudice focusing on such cognitive processes as stereotyping, categorization, and learning. In the U.S. tradition of social psychology, researchers have tended to focus on the individual's thought processes and experiences while overlooking or minimizing ways that the wider social context can instigate bigotry (Bar-Tal and Teichman 2005). In contrast, researchers outside of the United States, as well as many of those within the discipline of sociology (e.g., Feagin and Feagin 1986), have focused upon the institutional and structural factors that can be both causes and effects of bigotry. According to this approach, current institutional policies and organizational structures continue to discriminate because they were established in the past by those most privileged by discriminatory policies. Because of these policies, people who were targets of prejudice in the past continue to experience discrimination long after explicit expressions of bigotry and acknowledgement of prejudice have ceased to occur.

Although interest in studying bigotry has varied over the years, a renewed interest in the topic is evident among researchers addressing issues related to cyberhate, terrorism, and religious and nationalistic fanaticism. In the case of cyberhate, the speed of the Internet and its widespread accessibility make the spread of bigotry almost instantaneous and increasingly available to vulnerable populations (Craig-Henderson 2006). As for the relationship between bigotry and nationalism, there are a host of researchers studying the Arab-Israeli conflict in the Middle East (e.g., Bar-Tal and Teichman 2005). That particular conflict has roots in the Zionist occupation of the country of Israel, formerly known as Palestine. Because of the historical realities that have created the state of Israel, today's Arabs and Jews in that region have very distinct group identities that have given rise to their intergroup conflict. Social science researchers who study this kind of group conflict have demonstrated that the strength of identification with one's in-group is associated with one's expressed bigotry toward the out-group. In many situations, the more strongly one identifies with an in-group, the more bigoted one is against members of the out-group.

Bigotry can be minimal and manifested in avoidance or social exclusion of the out-group, or it can be severe and deadly. In 1998 James Byrd Jr., an African American man in Jasper, Texas, was murdered by white supremacists who dragged him to death behind their pickup truck after offering him a ride home. As members of a white supremacist group, Byrd's murderers were extreme in their bigotry. As a black man, Byrd was perceived by his murderers to be a member of a despised out-group.

Similarly brutal attacks have targeted sexual minorities. In 1998 the murder of the college student Matthew Shepard near Laramie, Wyoming, was attributed to anti-gay bigotry. Most public opinion polls reveal continuing evidence of this form of bigotry (Herek 2000). Shepard's bigoted murderers were highly prejudiced toward gay people. Other examples of well-known bigots include David Duke, the former leader of the Knights of the Ku Klux Klan; Nazi chancellor of Germany Adolph Hitler (1889–1945); and French politician Jean-Marie Le Pen.

RESOLVING BIGOTRY

One popular and long-standing idea within the social psychological literature has been that bigotry can be reduced with intergroup contact. That is, through contact with one another under ideal conditions, formerly bigoted out-groups could come to look favorably upon one another and thereby attenuate conflict and bigotry. However, this optimistic outlook has fallen out of favor in recent years as its theoretical underpinnings have been challenged by a number of researchers studying bigotry. For example, when one considers the pervasiveness of gender bias

against women and the paradoxical intimacy that characterizes relations between heterosexual males and females, it becomes clear that contact, while necessary, is not sufficient to eliminate bigotry. Furthermore, there is relatively little research investigating the extent to which contact between different real-world racial and ethnic groups can actually breed harmony. How then to solve the problem of bigotry? The best strategy is one that includes education, interaction, and legislation. Indeed, any efforts aimed at eliminating bigotry must involve attention to each aspect of this tripartite approach.

SEE ALSO *Ethnocentrism; Prejudice; Racism*

BIBLIOGRAPHY

Bar-Tal, Daniel, and Rona Teichman. 2005. *Stereotypes and Prejudice in Conflict: Representations of Arabs in Israeli Jewish Society.* Cambridge, U.K.: Cambridge University Press.

Bramel, Dana. 2004. The Strange Career of the Contact Hypothesis. In *The Psychology of Ethnic and Cultural Conflict*, eds. Yueh-Ting Lee, Clark McCauley, Fathali Moghaddam, and Stephen Worchel, 49–67. Westport, CT: Praeger.

Craig-Henderson, Kellina M. 2006. Hate on the Net: Bigotry + Computer Technology = Cyber Hate. *International Journal of Knowledge, Culture, and Change Management* 6 (4): 29–36.

Feagin, Joe R., and Clairece Booher Feagin. 1986. *Discrimination American Style: Institutional Racism and Sexism.* 2nd ed. Malabar, FL: Krieger.

Green, Donald P., Jack Glaser, and Andrew Rich. 1998. From Lynching to Gay Bashing: The Elusive Connection Between Economic Conditions and Hate Crime. *Journal of Personality and Social Psychology* 75: 85–92.

Herek, Gregory M. 2000. The Psychology of Sexual Prejudice. *Current Directions in Psychological Science* 9 (1): 19–22.

Hovland, Carl J., and Robert R. Sears. 1940. Minor Studies in Aggression: VI. Correlations of Lynchings with Economic Indices. *Journal of Psychology* 9: 301–310.

Janowitz, Morris. 1969. Patterns of Collective Racial Violence. In *The History of Violence in America: Historical and Comparative Perspectives*, eds. Hugh Davis Graham and Ted Robert Gurr, 412–443. New York: Bantam.

Kellina M. Craig-Henderson
Any opinion, findings, or conclusions expressed in this material are those of the author and do not necessarily reflect the views of the National Science Foundation.

BILATERALISM

Bilateralism concerns relations or policies of joint action between two parties. It can be contrasted with unilateralism (where one party acts on its own) and multilateralism (where three or more parties are involved). Typically, the term has applications concerning political, economic, and security matters between two states. Bilateralism has both costs and benefits, and there is a debate on its merits relative to unilateral or multilateral approaches.

States have traditionally related to each other on a bilateral basis. They recognize each other as states and agree to send ambassadors to each other's capital. Diplomatic relations can be unilateral, of course, but unless relations are bilateral, some tensions are likely. China and the United States concluded a Joint Communiqué on the Establishment of Diplomatic Relations on January 1, 1979, and formally established embassies in Beijing and Washington, DC, on March 1, 1979. The result was a normalization of relations, which had often been turbulent between 1949 and 1972.

Economic bilateralism is common. In trade, for example, countries have struck bilateral agreements in which they mutually agree to lower their tariffs. The effect is to encourage trade between the two sides to their mutual benefit. Such arrangements can also lead, however, to conflict with third parties excluded from such benefits. Bilateral agreements tend to be more common during or just after periods when economic nationalism (unilateralism) dominates or when multilateral options are stalled.

In security affairs, bilateralism is also found in agreements between states to come to each other's defense if attacked or threatened by a third party. Otto von Bismarck negotiated such a treaty with the Austrian Habsburg Empire in 1879. That treaty also antagonized Russia and helped fuel insecurities that gave rise to World War I. During the cold war, the United States and the Soviet Union concluded a number of agreements to mutually limit nuclear weapons, such as the Strategic Arms Limitation Treaty (SALT) and the Strategic Arms Reduction Treaty (START).

Bilateralism has advantages and disadvantages in comparison with the alternatives. With respect to unilateralism, it offers less freedom of action. Yet it also offers the ability to realize mutual gains that may be available only from acting jointly, for example, greater economic activity from freer trade, reduced armament burdens from agreed limitations, and greater security from cooperation against external threats.

With respect to multilateralism the calculus reverses itself. Bilateralism affords greater freedom and efficiency of action because fewer actors are involved. The League of Nations and its successor, the United Nations, have often been criticized for ineffectiveness because too many parties are involved.

Yet bilateralism is too costly and is insufficient to deal with some world problems. For example, the multilateral World Trade Organization is a much easier way to organize free trade than to have every country negotiate bilateral free-trade agreements with each other. And bilateral agreements would be unwieldy and not comprehensive enough for a systemic problem like global warming. The efficacy of bilateralism depends on the issue and the situation.

SEE ALSO *International Relations*

BIBLIOGRAPHY

Caporaso, James A. 1992. International Relations Theory and Multilateralism: The Search for Foundations. *International Organization* 46 (3): 599–632.

Hardin, Garret. 1968. The Tragedy of the Commons. *Science* 162: 1243–1248.

Krugman, Paul. 1991. Is Bilateralism Bad? In *International Trade and Trade Policy*, ed. Elhanan Helpman and Assaf Razin. Cambridge, MA: MIT Press.

Jeffrey W. Legro

BILL OF RIGHTS, U.S.

The first ten amendments to the U.S. Constitution are known as the Bill of Rights. The guarantees of the Bill of Rights include freedom of religion, the rights of expression and association, the right to privacy, the right to due process, and freedom from unjust restraint or trial and from cruel and unusual punishment. The U.S. Bill of Rights has served as a model for other nations in the development of their own constitutions.

The U.S. Constitution was shaped in large part by compromises between Federalists who advocated a strong, centralized government, and Anti-Federalists who believed that the balance of power should favor the states. One of these compromises involved the adoption of a bill of rights—an enumeration of the fundamental and inalienable rights of citizens.

A proposal to include a bill of rights was rejected by the Constitutional Convention of 1787. The Federalists believed that a bill of rights was unnecessary since the government possessed only those powers enumerated in the Constitution. They asserted that state constitutions protected individual rights and that the federal Constitution did not repeal those protections. The Federalists also feared that a listing of specific rights would endanger rights that were not listed. Not persuaded by these arguments, some Anti-Federalists withheld their signatures from the final document because of the absence of a bill of rights. Others proposed that a second constitutional convention be held to draft a bill of rights.

At state conventions to consider ratification of the Constitution, opposition focused on the failure to include a bill of rights. Anti-Federalists asserted that the

Constitution lacked sufficient safeguards for individuals against abuses of power by the federal government, and they pushed to postpone ratification until the Constitution was amended appropriately. The Federalists stood their ground initially, but when it became apparent that ratification was in jeopardy, they agreed to a compromise—they would accept proposed amendments for inclusion in a bill of rights with the ratification instruments of the states.

James Madison (1751–1836), who was elected to represent Virginia in the First Congress, had made a campaign pledge to his Anti-Federalist constituents that he would sponsor a bill of rights and work toward its passage. In June 1789 Madison introduced a proposed bill of rights in the U.S. House of Representatives. Madison's bill of rights reflected the recommendations of the state ratifying conventions, but it also drew upon the Magna Carta of 1215, the English Bill of Rights of 1689, and the Virginia Declaration of Rights of 1776. Congress approved twelve of Madison's proposed amendments, and ten were ratified by the states. The Bill of Rights was added to the Constitution in 1791.

The Bill of Rights limits the powers of the federal government, but in the late nineteenth century the U.S. Supreme Court began using the Fourteenth Amendment to make the Bill of Rights applicable to state governments as well. According to the Court's incorporation doctrine, the Fourteenth Amendment prohibits states from violating those provisions of the Bill of Rights that represent the "fundamental principles of liberty and justice which lie at the base of all our civil and political institutions" (*Hebert v. Louisiana* 1926). Between 1897 and 1969, the Supreme Court made nearly all of the protections of the Bill of Rights binding upon the states.

SEE ALSO *Civil Liberties; Civil Rights*

BIBLIOGRAPHY

Labunski, Richard E. 2006. *James Madison and the Struggle for the Bill of Rights.* New York: Oxford University Press.

Schwartz, Bernard. 1977. *The Great Rights of Mankind: A History of the American Bill of Rights.* New York: Oxford University Press.

Malia Reddick

BIN LADEN, OSAMA
1957–

Osama bin Laden was born the seventeenth of Muhammed bin Laden's fifty-two children and the seventeenth of his twenty-four sons, in Riyadh, the capital of Saudi Arabia, on March 10, 1957. Osama bin Laden was, however, the only child of Alia Ghanem of Syria, perhaps the most beautiful of Muhammed bin Laden's many wives, but different and separate from the Saudi clan and soon to be divorced by her husband. Muhammed bin Laden began life as a poor Yemeni bricklayer, uneducated and one-eyed. He became an enormously wealthy building contractor in Saudi Arabia after crafting intimate ties with the royal family.

Osama bin Laden's youth was spent in Hejaz, a southern Arabian province. In 1976 he graduated from private school, the Al Thagher Model School, near the port town of Jedda where he grew up. Described by former teachers and classmates as an outstanding student, bin Laden spent his extra time involved in a for-credit after school Islamic study group for exceptional students. Many believe it could be there that he first acquired a formal education in jihad. Classes were on the principles of the Muslim Brotherhood, an Islamist organization founded in Egypt in the 1920s and based on Islamic activism, political consciousness, and jihad. Bin Laden graduated from Jedda's prestigious King Abel Aziz University with a degree in civil engineering. The stories of bin Laden as a hard-drinking partygoer in Beirut in his youth are almost certainly wrong (and probably confuse him with one of his many brothers or other family members). On the contrary, at the university bin Laden was earnest and studious. He took the Qu'ran, at least his fundamentalist reading of it, to heart.

In 1979 the Soviet Union invaded Afghanistan in what would turn out to be a disastrous war that would lead to Soviet defeat and the collapse of the empire. There immediately arose throughout the Muslim world a mythic call for jihad—embraced by the Saudi royal family itself—in defense of the Islamic peoples of Afghanistan against the godless "infidel" Russians. Osama bin Laden responded warmly to that call. At first he raised money for the cause, then in the early 1980s, with his spiritual mentor, Abdullah Azzam (1941–1989), established the Maktab al-Khidamat (services offices) in Pakistan's University of Peshawar to direct support and resources to the fighters out in the field. In 1986 the twenty-nine-year-old Osama bin Laden added a heroic battlefield experience to his expanding mythic vita at the battle of Jaji. In his account, which is probably as much inspirational fairy-tale as actual history, he and the Afghan fighters were thirty meters from the Russians. He came close to being captured, but was so peaceful in his heart that he went to sleep for a while. Mortars fell around him and miraculously failed to explode. "We beat the Soviet Union," he said (bin Laden, 2005). "The Russians fled."

Bin Laden's Islamist triumphalism and his insistence on the continuation of jihad made him a nuisance in

Saudi Arabia, which forced him to leave the country in 1991 and finally revoked his citizenship in 1994, despite his impeccable family ties. He spent the next half-decade in Sudan, a remote and lawless land in which he could operate mostly outside of international control as he plotted his next move. One important event in these years that led to his further radicalization was the Gulf War of 1991. He was appalled that Saudi Arabia would allow American troops to be based on what he saw as sacred Saudi soil as they massed troops for an attack against a fellow Muslim country. He personally despised Iraqi president Saddam Hussein (1937–2006) but regarded Iraqis as brethren in faith. Bin Laden became so extreme in his extravagant rhetoric against the royal family that the Saudi government in 1994 finally revoked his citizenship and tried to strip him of all of his assets, though by then his considerable fortune was invested in many global enterprises and out of their reach.

But Sudan in turn eventually succumbed to pressure from the United States, and in 1996 bin Laden was expelled. A man without a country, he chose to relocate in what was by then an Afghanistan controlled by the fundamentalist Taliban. It was there that bin Laden breathed new life into Al-Qaeda, or base, for global terrorist operations, an organization founded in 1988 as the Soviets were pulling out of Afghanistan. For the next five years he operated with virtual impunity in a remote land under Islamist control. In the Afghan camps, thousands of jihadis received training in terrorism. They were committed to the ideals of global jihad and to Osama bin Laden, to whom they took a personal vow of loyalty. Most of those in the camps were foot soldiers, but some, such as Khalid Sheikh Mohammed (who devised what was called the "planes projects" or what became the terrorist attacks of September 11, 2001) and Mohammed Atta (the head of operations for the 9/11 attacks) were central figures in the Afghan camps.

Bin Laden's chief lieutenant was Ayman al-Zawahiri, an Egyptian medical doctor who had been tortured in Cairo prisons. Al-Zawahiri had been inspired in the 1950s and 1960s by the writings of Sayyid Qutb (1906–1966), an Islamist intellectual who was hanged in prison by Egyptian president Gamal Abdel Nasser (1918–1970). It was Qutb who resurrected an idea at least seven centuries old that violent jihad was at the center of the faith, that purification of Islam went along with eradication of infidels, and that the only goal worth pursuing was the re-creation of a world modeled on that which the Prophet specifically created. Bin Laden, of course, knew the writings of Qutb, though probably mostly through others inspired by Qutb, such as al-Zawahiri and Azzam. Al-Zawahiri, however, was important in other ways to bin Laden. Al-Zawahiri was not an effective leader himself, and in 1996 he merged his Al-Jihad into bin Laden's Al-

Qaeda, formally joining the long Egyptian tradition of the Muslim Brotherhood with Wahhabi fundamentalism. Al-Zawahiri proved a formidable ally, able to conceptualize a global jihad and help implement it organizationally.

Al-Qaeda was structured along the lines of a multinational corporation. Bin Laden was the CEO, and each unit, which could thrive apart from the other divisions, was headed by the equivalent of a vice president. It was a structure intended to survive attack and disruption. Funding came in part from bin Laden himself, though his personal fortune was far less than most imagined and probably not more than a million or so dollars a year. Most funding came from donations and a global network of "charities." Until 9/11 bin Laden did not seem short of funds.

It was his ideology of jihad that made bin Laden remarkable in these years. He was a religious fanatic and a well-organized businessman, a mystic and master of bureaucratic detail, a man plotting mass destruction and death, and a soft-spoken dreamer who reinvigorated an Islamist movement in ways that have not been seen in the Muslim world since Saladin in the twelfth century. On August 23, 1996, in his "Declaration of Jihad" bin Laden called on all his "Muslim brothers" to help him share in the jihad against the "enemies of God, your enemies the Israelis and Americans" (bin Laden 2005, pp. 23–30). And on February 23, 1998, in his declaration of the World Islamic Front, bin Laden declared a kind of universal declaration of war against "Jews and Crusaders" and declared it was an "individual duty incumbent on every Muslim in all countries" to kill Americans and their allies (bin Laden 2005, pp. 58–62). This declaration of war took the fight outside of the sectarian battles in the Middle East and into the very heart of the enemy lands. Bin Laden wanted concrete political things: American troops out of Saudi Arabia, the defeat of Israel and the liberation of the Palestinians, and the overthrow of corrupt secular Muslim rule in the Middle East. But he also harbored millennial dreams involving the annihilation of American, Western, and Jewish culture in a forge of violence that was redemptive and purifying.

On September 11, 2001, Al-Qaeda struck New York City and the Pentagon near Washington, D.C., in an extraordinarily successful terrorist attack. That the attacks worked as well as they did was also in large part due to pure luck on bin Laden's part. The World Trade Center collapsed in an inferno of fire mainly due to failures in the architectural conception of the buildings themselves. The whole operation cost well under half a million dollars, and it has caused several hundred billion dollars in direct and indirect damage.

But the spiritual and political costs of 9/11 are incalculable. The 2,749 people who died that day in New York lingered in the air, literally, and many were inhaled by New Yorkers with dust from the collapsed towers. It all made for incomplete mourning that certainly lasted through the months of clearing away the debris but also into the two wars that soon followed, the second of which is the extended war in Iraq. Many live with a special dread from that day, and it serves to symbolize the malevolence of contemporary history. Most Americans believe, if asked in the right way, that if Osama bin Laden had possessed nuclear weapons before 9/11 he would have placed one on a plane crashing into those towers.

Thankfully, Osama bin Laden did not possess such a weapon. As of 2007, he was hiding somewhere, probably in the mountainous border region of Pakistan and Afghanistan, basically out of commission, though by remaining alive he inspires others to act in his name and may even continue to direct some actual operations. Bin Laden's legacy is mixed. There is no question he has changed the world and the violence he directed may occasion a realignment of power in the relationship between the West and the Muslim Middle East. It also energized the new terrorism for many years and disrupted advanced economies in ways few could have imagined possible before 9/11. On the other hand, the violence of bin Laden and Al-Qaeda may backfire for the Muslim world, leading to disruption and civil war and further isolation, rather than renewal along the lines of Islamist fantasies. It may be many years before we will know with any degree of certainty whether the twenty-first century will be relatively free of terrorism and violence.

SEE ALSO *Central Intelligence Agency, U.S.; Fundamentalism, Islamic; September 11, 2001; Terrorism; Terrorists*

BIBLIOGRAPHY

Anti-Defamation League. Osama bin Laden: ADL Backgrounder. http://www.adl.org/terrorism_america/bin_l.asp.

Bergen, Peter L. 2001. *Holy War, Inc.: Inside the Secret World of Osama bin Laden.* New York: Free Press.

bin Laden, Osama. 2005. *Messages to the World: The Statements of Osama bin Laden,* ed. Bruce Lawrence. London: Verso.

Coll, Steve. 2004. *Ghost Wars: The Secret History of the CIA, Afghanistan, and Bin Laden, from the Soviet Invasion to September 10, 2001.* New York: Penguin.

Hoffman, Bruce. 2003. The Leadership Secrets of Osama Bin Laden: The Terrorist as CEO. *Atlantic Monthly* 291 (3): 26–27.

Hoffman, Bruce. 2006. *Inside Terrorism.* Rev. ed. New York: Columbia University Press.

Jacquard, Roland. 2002. *In the Name of Osama bin Laden: Global Terrorism and the Bin Laden Brotherhood.* Trans. George Holoch. Durham, NC: Duke University Press.

Juergensmeyer, Mark. 2003. *Terror in the Mind of God: The Global Rise of Religious Violence.* 3rd ed. Berkeley: University of California Press.

Kepel, Gilles. 2002. *JIHAD: The Trial of Political Islam.* Trans. Anthony F. Roberts. Cambridge, MA: Belknap.

Randal, Jonathan C. 2004. *Osama: The Making of a Terrorist.* New York: Knopf.

Scheuer, Michael. 2006. *Through Our Enemies Eyes: Osama bin Laden, Radical Islam, and the Future of America.* 2nd rev. ed. Washington, DC: Potomac Books.

Stern, Jessica. 2003. *Terror in the Name of God: Why Religious Militants Kill.* New York: HarperCollins.

Weaver, Mary Anne. 2005. The War on Terror: Four Years On: Lost at Tora Bora. *New York Times Magazine.* September 11: Sec 6: 54.

WGBH Boston, with *New York Times* Television. 2003. *Frontline: Chasing the Sleeper Cell.*

Williams, Paul L. 2004. *Osama's Revenge: The Next 9/11, What the Media and the Government Haven't Told You.* New York: Prometheus.

Charles B. Strozier
Renee Cummings

BINARY OPPOSITIONS
SEE *Symbols.*

BIOETHICS

The field of bioethics, as distinct from medical ethics, has existed since the 1960s. Unlike medical ethics, which for centuries has examined the duties and responsibilities of physicians to their patients and to other doctors, the development of bioethics can be traced to the rapid progress in technology and science experienced in the United States in the 1960s. Organ transplantation, chemotherapy, kidney dialysis, respirators, the contraceptive pill, genetic screening, and intensive care units were extraordinary medical breakthroughs that were seen as highly beneficial but also costly and sometimes harmful. This explosion of technological success brought in its wake a set of daunting ethical dilemmas that medicine, academics, legislators, and the public had never previously been forced to face.

In the wake of these developments, issues of healthcare access and rationing, withdrawal and withholding of lifesaving care, dignity in dying, and how to define death and manage the high cost of medical care now loomed large as urgent ethical quandaries. At the same time, societal changes placed greater emphasis on individual autonomy and rights, which prompted the public to press the field of medicine for more patient involvement and control over medical treatment. The ethical dilemmas generated by these advances in science and medicine required interdisciplinary study and reflection that traditional academic disciplines were ill-equipped to handle. In response to these pressing ethical problems, scholars began to venture outside of their traditional subject matter to discuss, debate, and write about these new dilemmas, and bioethics became a new area of academic attention.

Some of the original dilemmas are still at the core of bioethics today. The field now focuses ethical problems in clinical, preventive, and research medicine that involve truth telling, informed consent, confidentiality, end-of-life care, conflicts of interest, nonabandonment, euthanasia, and substituted judgment for incompetent persons. Bioethics has established both the right to informed consent and the right to control one's medical treatment as key tenets of American law and ethics. With each new technological breakthrough, the field of bioethics expands its scope to address new ethical dilemmas, most recently those involving the human genome project, stem cell research, artificial reproductive technologies, the genetic engineering of plants and animals, the prospect of human reproductive cloning, preimplantation genetic diagnosis of embryos, nanotechnology, and xeno-transplantation. Bioethics has also more recently begun to reflect on the health-care challenges faced in developing nations, such as whether national or local standards should govern the conduct of medical research or the problems of rationing access to innovative treatments in nations besieged by devastating epidemics such as malaria or AIDS.

Since the 1960s, the field of bioethics has gained legitimacy as an independent academic discipline, and that new status has brought significant changes in the structure and institutions of the field. Originally, the institutions of bioethics were independent think tanks. Today, the trend is the creation of academic bioethics departments, either within a medical school or school of arts and sciences. The professionalization of bioethics has taken it from the academic margins to an accepted place within universities, hospitals, regulatory bodies, the media, and industry.

SEE ALSO *Medicine*

BIBLIOGRAPHY

Callahan, Daniel. 1973. Bioethics as a Discipline. *Hastings Center Studies* 1 (1): 66–73.

Fox, Daniel. 1985. Who Are We: The Political Origins of the Medical Humanities. *Theoretical Medicine* 6: 327–341.

Jonsen, Albert. 1998. *The Birth of Bioethics*. New York: Oxford University Press.

Potter, Van Rensselaer. 1971. *Bioethics: Bridge to the Future*. Englewood Cliffs, NJ: Prentice Hall.

Reich, Warren, ed. 1978. *Encyclopedia of Bioethics*. New York: Free Press. 3rd ed., 2004. Ed. Stephen G. Post. New York: Macmillan.

Reich, Warren. 1994. The Word "Bioethics": Its Birth and the Legacies of Those Who Shaped Its Meaning. *Kennedy Institute of Ethics Journal* 4: 319–336.

Arthur Caplan
Autumn Fiester

BIOLOGICAL ANTHROPOLOGY
SEE *Anthropology, Biological.*

BIOLOGICAL WEIGHT
SEE *Obesity; Body Image; Body Mass Index; Obese Externality; Overeating; Undereating; Weight.*

BIOTERRORISM

Terrorism is the intentional use or threat to use violence against civilians or civilian targets in order to attain political ends. Bioterrorism uses microorganisms or toxins that are derived from living organisms to produce death or disease in humans, animals, or plants. Animals and plants are of concern because of the economic consequences of terrorism on food production and exports.

Historically, terrorists have relied primarily on conventional weapons such as guns and explosives to further their objectives. While conventional weapons will continue to be the most accessible, biological weapons are becoming increasingly available, and terrorists have turned from low-casualty, high-visibility targets to targets that can result in mass casualties, where biological weapons are an ideal choice. One of the most important advantages of biological weapons is cost. One dollar's worth of anthrax can kill as many people as $2,000 worth of conventional explosives.

Biological agents had been used as weapons only twice in the United States. On September 9, 1984, a religious cult, the Rajneeshees, sprayed *Salmonella typhimurium* on salad bars in The Dales, Oregon, causing 751 cases of food poisoning. No deaths occurred. The second U.S. attack occurred in September 2001, when *Bacillus anthracis* spores were distributed through the U.S. Postal Service. This attack resulted in twenty-two cases of anthrax infection and five deaths. The production of this weapons-grade anthrax required a high degree of scientific knowledge and sophisticated equipment. Approximately two grams of the anthrax spores, if aerosolized effectively, could kill tens of thousands of people. Although the 1995 subway attack in Tokyo by the religious extremist group Aum Shinrikyo used a chemical agent, Aum had previously attempted to use anthrax and botulinum toxin.

Terrorists have access to hundreds of potential biological agents to use as weapons. These weapons can be in liquid or powder form, and they can be dispersed successfully as an aerosol if particle sizes are small enough to enter the lungs. The particles can be aerosolized from a stationary location or from a moving source either outdoors or indoors. Furthermore, many biological agents can be delivered in food or water.

The North Atlantic Treaty Organization (NATO) has identified thirty-one potential agents that bioterrorists can use. The United States Army Medical Research Institute of Infectious Diseases (USAMRIID), has reduced this list to six primary agents: anthrax, smallpox, plague, tularemia, botulinum toxin, and agents of viral hemorrhagic fever. Many of these agents cause diseases that present-day physicians have never seen, decreasing the likelihood that they can be rapidly diagnosed.

The United States, United Kingdom, and other countries have developed national response plans to deal with natural disasters and acts of terrorism, including bioterrorism. These plans will be important for mounting a coordinated response to a bioterrorist attack. Equally important are plans to respond to a global outbreak of an infectious disease because similar response mechanisms will be used for bioterrorism. Both the World Health Organization and the United States released plans in 2005 for responding to a pandemic of influenza. Other countries are developing similar plans, and these plans will be important not only for a naturally occurring infectious disease but also for a bioterrorist attack.

An effective response to an attack will also require modifying existing laws so that governments can maximize their response efforts. Governors must be able to suspend provisions that regulate how state agencies do business in order for them to rapidly respond to public health emergencies. Public health authorities must be able to close and order the decontamination of buildings and destroy or safely dispose of any material or human remains that have been contaminated. They must also be able to take every available measure to prevent the transmission of infectious disease, including the use of isolation and quarantine, and to ensure that all cases of contagious disease are properly controlled and treated. Laws will also need to be modified to allow for the rapid purchase of pharmaceutical agents and the rationing of scare supplies. Public health authorities must be able to provide tempo-

rary licenses to out-of-state health care providers and modify liability laws to protect state officials and health care providers during a declared emergency.

Although extreme measures are called for during an emergency such as a bioterrorist attack, civil liberties must be protected. Gross negligence or willful misconduct should not be exempt from liability. Provisions of the law must be in place for rescinding the emergency orders when health conditions that caused the emergency no longer pose a high probability of a large number of deaths. Lawyers have developed a model emergency health powers act that can be used to strengthen government's ability to respond to bioterrorism and at the same time protect civil liberties.

SEE ALSO *Terrorism*

BIBLIOGRAPHY

Alibek, K., and S. Handelman. 1999. *Biohazard.* New York: Random House.

Diamond, Jared M. 1997. *Guns, Germs, and Steel: The Fates of Human Societies.* New York: Norton.

Gostin, Lawrence O., J. W. Sapsin, S. P. Teret, et al. 2002. The Model State Emergency Health Powers Act: Planning for and Response to Bioterrorism and Naturally Occurring Infectious Diseases. *Journal of the American Medical Association* 288 (5): 622–628.

Miller, J., S. Engelberg, and W. Broad. 2001. *Germs: Biological Weapons and America's Secret War.* New York: Simon and Schuster.

Tucker, J. B., ed. 2000. *Toxic Terror: Assessing the Terrorist Use of Chemical and Biological Weapons.* Cambridge, MA: MIT Press.

R. Gregory Evans

BIPOLAR DISORDER

SEE *Manias; Manic Depression; Schizophrenia.*

BIRTH CONTROL

Birth control refers to the means used to limit or space human fertility. The technological development of these means, the organization of their use, and the fairness of their application are the province of scientists, policymakers, religious leaders, and the users of birth control. The definition includes recent methods such as condoms, sterilization, intrauterine devices, and the birth control pill. It also includes older methods, such as abortion, prolonged nursing of infants, periodic abstinence from sex, herbal tonics, and coitus interruptus.

The question of the comparative effectiveness of various techniques often comes up in discussions of birth control. Abortion, some forms of surgical sterilization, and complete abstinence from intercourse are the most effective at preventing births. Yet, effective birth prevention is only one of the goals considered by users of birth control and by the persons and institutions promoting its use. Safety and ease of use are, for example, other important dimensions of birth control technologies. In fact, limiting births is sometimes not even the main goal of a birth control practice, but its side effect. For example, inducing an abortion could be a means to save a woman's life. Likewise, the contraceptive effect of prolonged nursing may be subordinate to a woman's inclination to breastfeed. Moreover, practitioners of periodic abstinence and coitus interruptus can see these actions as enhancing their own self-worth because of the sacrifices they entail.

In 1798 the English economist Thomas Robert Malthus (1766–1834) argued for the eventual scarcity of natural resources given the rate of population growth worldwide. This argument became the basis of the first organized efforts to limit population sizes in the West. The fact that most of these efforts were directed at the poor, the ill, and the criminal made for an enduring link between birth control and eugenics, the belief that only the "fittest" humans should reproduce. Among the methods touted for their effectiveness were condoms, which became increasingly popular after 1860 with the use of rubber in their manufacture, replacing animal intestines and silk sheaths. Douching solutions and vaginal pessaries also became more effective in the nineteenth century. Sterilization required developments in medical antisepsis and anesthesia, which were only coming of age in the 1870s.

Opponents to organized birth control emerged in the 1870s; they included Anthony Comstock (1844–1915), founder of the New York Society for the Suppression of Vice, and the Catholic Church. To them, birth control was bound to a deep moral crisis in society. Yet the number of users of birth control grew, and ideas about family size and women's roles in society changed. Activists like Margaret Sanger (1883–1966) aided in the popularization of birth control, linking it to greater freedom for women. Sanger coined the term *birth control* in 1913 to replace the label of *neo-Malthusianism*. As the birth control movement became more popular, it attracted allies that began to reframe birth control as more than just fertility limitation. This is how the notion of birth control became associated with that of family planning by the 1930s.

Birth control acquired an additional political meaning in the 1950s with the Cold War. While population growth stabilized in Europe and North America, it accelerated in the so-called third world. The contraceptive pill emerged in this context and was promoted not only as a convenient contraceptive but also as a tool to lower population growth rates. Devised by the biologist Gregory Pincus (1903–1967) with funds from philanthropist Katharine McCormick (1875–1967) and Sanger's support, and marketed by G. D. Searle, the pill became the most popular form of birth control by 1965 in the United States.

During the late 1960s, the prospect of misery, anarchy, and socialist advances in the third world led to international development policies like the U.S. Alliance for Progress and the involvement of philanthropies like the Rockefeller Foundation in population control programs. The latter were tied to the intervention of governments in the developing world, some of which applied policies throughout the 1960s, 1970s, and 1980s to quickly lower population growth rates to match objectives set by medical and social science experts in industrialized nations. As was evident following the United Nations World Population Conference of 1974 in Bucharest, however, third world nations often suspected that population control programs were implemented only for the benefit of developed nations, while hurting the interests of the third world and failing to address the root causes of poverty and inequality. Third world nations also claimed often that population control programs sometimes conflicted with local and personal beliefs about the worth of individual births. Today, with the exception of China's "one-child policy," instituted in 1978, birth control programs in most countries have retreated from the aggressive promotion of some methods in favor of voluntarism, informed choice of contraceptives, sex education, and the insertion of birth control provisions within broader systems for health care delivery, particularly maternal and infant health. This trend began as early as the mid-1960s. Yet, even now, as in the eighteenth century, the free choices and additional services implied in family planning are part of a complex process involving individual decisions, social values, and material constraints.

SEE ALSO *Contraception; Demography; Population Control; Population Studies*

BIBLIOGRAPHY

Ginsburg, Faye, and Rayna Rapp, eds. 1995. *Conceiving the New World Order: The Global Politics of Reproduction.* Berkeley: University of California Press.

Tone, Andrea. 2001. *Devices and Desires: A History of Contraceptives in America.* New York: Hill and Wang.

Raúl Antonio Necochea López

BIRTH OF A NATION

D. W. Griffith's film *Birth of a Nation* appeared in 1915 to the outrage and dismay of the National Association for the Advancement of Colored People and other supporters of black Americans' citizenship rights. The film was an adaptation of Thomas Dixon's novels *The Clansman* (1905)—the film's original title—and, to a lesser extent, *The Leopard's Spots* (1902), which, along with *The Traitor* (1907), formed Dixon's self-consciously white supremacist trilogy. Following Dixon's novels, the film advanced a relentlessly proslavery narrative of the slaveholding South, the Civil War, and especially Reconstruction. It depicted blacks either as simple and ignorant ciphers or as brutish fiends driven by compulsions to put on airs and accost white women. Abolitionists and whites aligned with the freedpeople after the Civil War appeared as irresponsibly naive, venal, or malevolent, motivated by greed or base desires to humiliate and destroy the South through the agency of black dupes. In this depiction, black enfranchisement was a travesty that enabled degenerate whites and incompetent blacks to dominate the formerly secessionist South's governance and to impose a corrupt tyranny on the region's whites.

The interpretation put forward in Dixon's novels and Griffith's film was propagated aggressively by southern elites during the years between their successful campaign to disfranchise blacks and many poor whites and the onset of the First World War. This interpretation became scholarly historical orthodoxy, in no small measure through the work of Columbia University historian William A. Dunning. Dunning's book, *Reconstruction, Political and Economic: 1865–1877* (1907), systematized the southern white supremacist view and gave it the appearance of academic objectivity. Instructively, epigraphs from the book are interspersed throughout the film, which stands as an epic cultural expression of the Dunning school's line. In this regard, the film, along with Dixon's novels, is also the direct lineal ancestor of Margaret Mitchell's *Gone with the Wind* and the film adapted from it. In addition to striking structural parallels between the two films' narratives, Mitchell had been an avid reader of Dixon's novels, and he wrote her a gushing fan letter on her novel's publication.

Birth of a Nation has been widely celebrated for its technical cinematic innovations. Griffith's film is typically credited with pioneering use of such techniques as deep focus, the jump cut, and facial close-ups. Its large-scale battle scenes were also unprecedented. Its use of seemingly authentic daguerreotypes that shifted into live action also fed an illusion of historical accuracy. For these and other such accomplishments—as well, presumably, as its popularity at the box office (it was by far the highest grossing film of its era)—the American Film Institute lists Griffith's melodrama as one of the most important films of the twentieth century. However, although the film's technical achievements no doubt contributed to its visibility when it was released, its inflammatory politics are what generated the strongest reaction. *Birth of a Nation*'s opening provoked riots in many cities, as groups of whites were moved by the film, or took the occasion of its screening, to rampage against blacks. The film was banned in several other cities, including Chicago, and in the state of Ohio.

The film's story line is a conventional, heavy-handed romance that is a thinly allegorical template for projecting southern elites' vision of sectional reconciliation on explicitly white supremacist grounds. The plot follows two upper-status families—the northern Stonemans and the southern Camerons—from the late antebellum period through Reconstruction. The northern family's patriarch is modeled to evoke Pennsylvania Radical Republican Thaddeus Stevens; the southern family embodies the sympathetic stereotype of a planter class defined by grand manners and genteel paternalism. The families are linked socially before the Civil War, and one of the Stoneman sons falls in love with a Cameron daughter on a visit to the latter family's antebellum plantation. However, the war divides the two families and disrupts the potential romance. Both families lose sons in the war, which also further entwines their fates. A Cameron son is wounded and captured in battle and, in a Union hospital, encounters and falls in love with Stoneman's daughter, who is volunteering as a nurse. In this narrative love thus transcends and is disrupted by the sectional conflict, which brings the film's first part to a close.

Establishment of the romantic story line drives *Birth of a Nation*'s first part. In the film's second part, shown after an intermission, the romance becomes a platform for an equally sentimentalized narrative of the respectable white South's suffering under Reconstruction. This account is a purely partisan fantasy of the years after the Civil War. Conniving and malcontented mulattoes aspire to reach above their station, ultimately through intermarriage. Ignorant and brutish blacks make a travesty of the exercise of government. They and their base white allies reduce patient, suffering upper-class white southerners to poverty and heap one indignity after another upon them. Tellingly, in Griffith's narrative, having to extend the routine civilities of social etiquette to blacks, acknowledge their equal citizenship, and confront their unwanted sexual advances are interchangeable affronts, and the first two inevitably lead to the third.

The melodramatic story line feeds this linkage. In one of the film's more incendiary sequences, Flora, the Cameron's spirited but virginal daughter—whose very name identifies her as a flower of southern womanhood—is mortified by a proposal of marriage from Gus, a Union soldier and former slave. She flees hysterically with Gus in pursuit and leaps to her death to preserve her honor. Gus, whom Griffith describes as "a renegade, a product of the vicious doctrines spread by the carpetbaggers," is captured and summarily lynched by the Ku Klux Klan. The Klan subsequently rides to the rescue of the beleaguered whites, rises to overthrow the Reconstruction tyranny, and forcibly disfranchises blacks. This resolves to a happy ending that unites the Cameron and Stoneman lovers and restores the natural social order to the South. Gus's character was portrayed by a white actor in blackface, as were all the black characters who had physical contact with whites. Thus the film featured both black and white actors playing black characters.

Griffith's melodrama, by grounding its Reconstruction narrative in the personal story of the Cameron and Stoneman families, conveniently sidesteps the potentially troublesome issue that disfranchisement violated black southerners' constitutional rights under the Fifteenth Amendment. Just as the first part of the film's depiction of the South Carolina plantation world gives no hint that slavery was fundamentally a system of coerced labor, the second part obscures the fact that the foundation of post–Civil War southern politics was a struggle between the freedpeople and their allies to craft a social order based on free labor and equal citizenship and the dominant planter class's desire to restore a social and economic system as near as possible to the slave society that Union victory had destroyed.

Instead, *Birth of a Nation* propounds a view in which race is the single fulcrum of politics, the authentic basis of identity and allegiance. Such views were prevalent among Americans of all sorts during the early twentieth century, perhaps more so than at any other time before or since. Putatively scientific race theories purported to link human capacities, including the capacity for democratic government, hierarchically to racial classification. Several features of the social landscape at the time helped to give such views of the bases and significance of human difference presumptive credibility, particularly among opinion-shaping elites. Upper-status reactions against labor and populist insurgencies fueled a political conservatism readily open to arguments that manifest social inequalities were rooted in immutable natural differences. Advocates of imperialist expansion also asserted unabashedly racial arguments, typically adducing an irrepressible Anglo-Saxon or Teutonic racial spirit for conquest, along with a racialized notion of American providential entitlement, to justify international adventurism in Latin America and the Pacific. Especially in the North and Pacific West, intensifying anxiety about increasing immigration from the margins of Europe and Asia further propelled racialist discourse, as race scientists and courts sought to determine whether immigrants originated from groups capable of assimilating to "American" civilization. Fears concern-

ing immigrants' dilution of nativist American cultural authority also contributed to a growing conviction among elites that voting and political participation should be seen not as a right but as a privilege, that fitness to vote should be proven, not assumed, and that the respectable classes are the natural stewards of the polity.

The political and ideological environment that took shape during that period also supported those tendencies within the national Republican Party and northern opinion that argued for retreat from aggressive support for the southern freedpeople's rights and for sectional reconciliation on lines that favored the southern planter and merchant class. That sentiment underwrote the withdrawal of federal military occupation in 1877 and a shift in the courts' willingness over the ensuing decades to protect blacks' rights. In its ruling in the 1883 *Civil Rights Cases*, the U.S. Supreme Court invalidated the 1875 Civil Rights Act, and in its 1896 *Plessy v. Ferguson* ruling the Court legitimized legally imposed racial segregation, enunciating the infamous "separate but equal" doctrine. Residual northern liberal inclinations to defend southern blacks were further assuaged by Booker T. Washington's emergence as a prominent voice of black acquiescence to white supremacy in the South and his endorsement of blacks' expulsion from the region's civic life.

Griffith's film reflected and exploited this environment. In a clear effort to appeal to northern sensibilities, the film's first part ends with a mournful depiction of the assassinated Abraham Lincoln as a kindly figure who would not have permitted the white South to be abused. The fabrication of Austin Stoneman as a stand-in for Thaddeus Stevens similarly rationalizes sectional reconciliation. The real Stevens never wavered in his Radical Republican convictions, to the point that he insisted on being buried in a black cemetery. Griffith's fictional character, on the other hand, abjures his support of blacks' rights once he is confronted by his mulatto protégé's attempt to marry his daughter. The film's message is clear: Decent northerners who had been abolitionists were misguided, and even the staunchest of them would come to see the need for white supremacy. This message drives the film's climax. In building to the crescendo of the Klan's rescue, the fleeing white victims are given refuge in a rude shack occupied by former Union soldiers who had remained in South Carolina after the war, living as modest yeomen. The northern men respond to the situation from the race loyalty that unites Americans from both sections, and they take up arms to fend off the pursuing black militia. This, then, is the definitively racial basis on which *Birth of a Nation* proposes sectional reconciliation. As Griffith narrates, "The former enemies of North and South are united again in common defence [sic] of their Aryan birthright."

Instructively, the film quotes Woodrow Wilson, then president of the United States, explaining that "The white men were roused by mere instinct of self-preservation … until at last there had sprung into existence a great Ku Klux Klan, a veritable empire of the South to protect the Southern country" (Wilson 1902, pp. 59–60). Wilson had been Thomas Dixon's classmate at Johns Hopkins University and enjoyed a private screening of *Birth of a Nation* at the White House. Wilson embodied the victory of the white supremacist politics *Birth of a Nation* advocates. A native southerner, he was at different times president of Princeton University and governor of New Jersey, as well as president of both the American Political Science Association and the American Historical Association, as Dunning had been some years before him. Wilson's scholarly writing and his public actions were shaped fundamentally by the race theories of the day and the presumptions of white supremacist ideology in particular. As president of Princeton, he sought to impose white-only admissions; as president of the United States, he more consequentially imposed full racial segregation on the District of Columbia and drove blacks from federal employment.

SEE ALSO *Blackface; Ku Klux Klan; Race Relations; Racism*

BIBLIOGRAPHY

Anderson, James. 1988. *The Education of Blacks in the South, 1860–1935.* Chapel Hill: University of North Carolina Press.

Dixon, Thomas. 1994. *The Reconstruction Trilogy: The Leopard's Spots; The Clansman; The Traitor.* Newport Beach, CA: Noontide Press.

Du Bois, W. E. B. 1935. *Black Reconstruction in America: An Essay Toward a History of the Part Which Black Folk Played in the Attempt to Reconstruct Democracy in America, 1860–1880.* New York: Russell & Russell.

Dunning, William A. 1907. *Reconstruction, Political and Economic, 1865–1877.* New York and London: Harper and Brothers.

Foner, Eric. 1988. *Reconstruction: America's Unfinished Revolution, 1863–1877.* New York: Harper & Row.

Kousser, J. Morgan. 1974. *The Shaping of Southern Politics: Suffrage Restriction and the Establishment of the One-Party South, 1880–1910.* New Haven, CT, and London: Yale University Press.

Lofgren, Charles. 1988. *The Plessy Case: A Legal-Historical Interpretation.* New York: Oxford University Press.

Stein, Judith. 1973–1974. "Of Mr. Booker T. Washington and Others": The Political Economy of Racism in the United States. *Science & Society* 38 (4): 422–463.

Storace, Patricia. 1991. Look Away, Dixie Land. *New York Review of Books* 38 (December 19): 24–37.

Warren, Kenneth. 1993. *Black and White Strangers: Race and American Literary Realism.* Chicago and London: University of Chicago Press.

West, Michael Rudolph. 2006. *The Education of Booker T. Washington: American Democracy and the Idea of Race Relations.* New York: Columbia University Press.

Wilson, Woodrow. 1902. *Reunion and Nationalization.* Vol. 5 of *A History of the American People.* New York: Harper and Brothers.

Adolph Reed Jr.

BIRTHS, MULTIPLE
SEE *Multiple Births.*

BIRTHS, OUT-OF-WEDLOCK

Every society has mechanisms and institutions for birthing and rearing children. These may or may not be similar to what we call *wedlock*. In describing domestic groups, sociologists traditionally treated as normative those households made up of a man and a woman who are formally joined in a long-term relationship and jointly raising their shared biological children. However, from a broader historical and cultural perspective, we know that this is just one of scores of possible domestic arrangements. In numerous cultures, the husband-wife relationship is less important than the extended multigenerational family in terms of child-rearing responsibilities. Households in many societies are polygynous, with children of multiple wives, concubines, or slaves fathered by the same man. In some societies a young woman is not considered an attractive marriage candidate until she has proven her fertility by bearing one or more children. In some societies the biological contribution of fatherhood is not acknowledged; rather, the spiritual or social father is salient. And in some societies the mother's brother normatively functions as the significant man in the lives of children.

While all societies have ideas and rules concerning who is encouraged, allowed, discouraged, or forbidden to bear or raise children, these vary from place to place and over time. Distinctions between legitimate and out-of-wedlock childbearing are not universal, nor are they always consistently applied within a particular society. It tends to be the case that the domestic arrangements of higher-status or wealthier households are considered nobler, more moral, or in some other way better. However, the wealth and day-to-day functioning of those households may depend upon the services and labor provided by people whose domestic arrangements are not in line with whatever constitutes the so-called "ideal" in a particular time or place.

ATTITUDES TOWARD OUT-OF-WEDLOCK BIRTH IN THE UNITED STATES: HISTORICAL TRAJECTORY

The history of out-of-wedlock childbearing in the United States must be understood in the context of the racialized social, economic, and political structures that both preceded and followed independence. Nonmarital birth was an integral part of the slave system: White men married white women but entered into non-legal unions with women who were black or "colored." While policies varied over time, until the early-to-mid-nineteenth century slave marriages were rarely allowed.

For the free and white population in colonial America, "bastardy" was considered a sin. While the notion that out-of-wedlock childbearing constitutes a moral failure never totally disappeared, during the eighteenth and early nineteenth centuries, nonmarital births increasingly came to be framed in terms of the economic burdens borne by communities forced to support fatherless children. By the end of the nineteenth and beginning of the twentieth century, public discourse, at least regarding white women, shifted from concern with "fallen women" (a pejorative moral category) to concern with "ruined girls" (an innocent population deserving of help). Progressive reformers understood that out-of-wedlock childbearing was a product as well as a cause of social disorder, and thus advocated sex education and better wages for women so that women would be less susceptible to the sexual advances of wealthy men.

The belief that unmarried mothers are at fault for their situation took on new life in the 1920s as experts began treating out-of-wedlock childbearing as "sex delinquency." Using a new language of psychology and the unconscious, authorities diagnosed sexually active girls as unable to govern their impulses, and growing numbers of young women were sent into the newly created juvenile justice system. Throughout the twentieth century and into the twenty-first, the policy of incarcerating women because of sexual crimes (e.g., prostitution) has continued.

Intertwined moral and economic discourses reached new levels of codification when Congress passed the 1996 welfare reform known as the Personal Responsibility Act. The Act opens by proclaiming that, "Marriage is the foundation of a successful society," and goes on to link various issues—teenage pregnancy, out-of-wedlock births, children raised in single-parent homes, and fathers who fail to pay child support—to high rates of violent crime, children with low cognitive skills, and other highly negative putative outcomes. According to Sharon Hays,

> a reading of this statement of the law's intent would lead one to believe that the problem of poverty itself is the direct result of failures to live up to the family ideal.... Single mothers on welfare are effectively punished for having children out of wedlock or for getting divorced. The punishment they face is being forced to manage on their own with low-wage work. [The Act sets a five-year lifetime limit for public aid regardless of need and a two-year limit for finding full-time employment]. (2004, pp. 17–18)

Race has continued to play a key role in attitudes and policies toward out of wedlock birth in the United States. Criticism of high rates of single-mother families often seems to be thinly disguised criticism of black single mothers, who are variously portrayed as sexually promiscuous, addicted to drugs, or out to "cheat the system" by having more babies for the state to support. Kenneth J. Neubeck and Noel A. Cazenave coined the term "welfare racism" to describe the stereotyped discourse and discriminatory programming associated with the welfare system: "Today, the words *welfare mother* evoke one of the most powerful racialized cultural icons in contemporary U.S. society" (2001, p. 3).

In the last decades of the twentieth century, "Fathers' Rights" organizations and evangelical Christian groups have been vocal in asserting that female-headed families are psychologically and socially pathological and that children raised without their fathers are more likely to fail in school, use drugs, and end up in jail. Sociological studies tend not to support this view. The absence of the father does not have a significant impact on the psychological well-being of either daughters or sons. More important than physical presence or absence is how children perceive their relationships with their parents (Wenk et al. 1994). Moreover, given the high divorce rates in the United States, children born to a married mother and father have no guarantee of growing up with their two biological parents. In fact, studies show that unwed U.S. fathers actually see their children more often than do divorced fathers who have remarried.

RATES OF OUT-OF-WEDLOCK BIRTHS IN THE UNITED STATES AND EUROPE

In the United States in 1970, 10.7 percent of all live births were to non-married women. The percent rose throughout the 1980s, leveling out at about 32 to 33 percent in the mid-1990s, and going up to 34.6 percent in 2003. The biggest increase was among white women for whom rates rose from 5.5 percent in 1970 to 29.4 percent in 2003. For black women, the percent of out-of-wedlock births doubled from 37.5 percent in 1970 to 68.2 percent in 2003. Among Hispanic women, the rate increased from 23.6 percent in 1980 to 45 percent in 2003.

Over these years, the age distribution of out-of-wedlock childbearing indicates a shift toward purposeful out-of-wedlock childbearing among more mature women. In 1970, 50.1 percent of live births to unmarried women were to women under the age of twenty, 31.8 percent to women twenty-one to twenty-four, and 18.1 percent to women twenty-five and older. By 2003 only 24.3 percent of out-of-wedlock births were to women under the age of twenty, while 38.8 percent were to women twenty-one to twenty-four, and 36.9 percent to women twenty-five and older.

In 2004 nearly a third of the 4.8 million babies born in the European Union were born out-of-wedlock. The phenomenon is particularly noticeable in Scandinavia and the three Baltic member-states with a ratio of 57.8 percent in Estonia, 55.4 percent in Sweden, 45.4 percent in Denmark, and 45.3 percent in Latvia. The lowest levels of children born out of wedlock are in southern Europe with 3.3 percent in Cyprus, 4.9 percent in Greece, and 14.9 percent in Italy.

It should be noted that in statistics from Europe and the United States, the term *out-of-wedlock* means only that the newborn's parents are not registered with the government as "married"; it does not mean that the child is being raised only by its mother. In the Scandinavian countries, in particular, nonmarital births generally take place in long-term committed relationships to parents uninterested in church weddings and not in need of government-issued marriage certificates in order to have pensions or other benefits. Americans too are much more likely than ever before to bear children in reasonably stable partnerships—including same-sex partnerships—that are not legally recognized marriages.

EXPLAINING NONMARITAL BIRTHS

Efforts to explain rates of out-of-wedlock births in the United States have been characterized more by sentiment than scientific evidence. Conservatives typically attribute the increase to overly generous federal welfare benefits that encourage poor women to have children. However, a comparison of out-of-wedlock birth rates with changes in welfare benefits over time does not show a correlation between the two. Liberals have tended to attribute the increase to declines in the marriageability of black men due to shortages of jobs for less-educated men, the disproportionate deaths of black men in the military, and high rates of incarceration of young black men. Demographic studies indicate, however, that only a small percentage of the decline in black marriage rates can be explained by the shrinking of the pool of eligible men.

A popular set of explanations maintains that single parenthood has increased because of changes in attitudes toward sexuality. While some analysts blame sex education

in schools for encouraging early sexual activity, others advocate the benefits of sex education in helping teens make informed decisions regarding sexuality and contraception. Still others argue that the legalization of abortion and increased availability of contraception (birth control pills) give women tools to control the number and timing of their children. These tools empower women to make choices regarding childbearing and curb customs such as "shotgun marriages" that traditionally reduced rates of out-of-wedlock births (though not of out-of-wedlock conception).

SEE ALSO *Birth Control; Marriage; Slavery; Welfare*

BIBLIOGRAPHY

Akerlof, George A., Janet L. Yellen, and Michael L. Katz. 1996. An Analysis of Out-of-Wedlock Childbearing in the United States. *Quarterly Journal of Economics* 111 (2): 277–317.

Anderson, Elijah. 2000. *Code of the Street: Decency, Violence, and the Moral Life of the Inner City.* New York: Norton.

Christian Party. Father's Manifesto Home Page. http://christianparty.net/home.htm.

Edin, Kathryn, and Maria Kefalas. 2005. *Promises I Can Keep: Why Poor Women Put Motherhood before Marriage.* Berkeley: University of California Press.

Gough, Kathleen. 1968. The Nayars and the Definition of Marriage. In *Marriage, Family, and Residence,* ed. Paul Bohannan and John Middleton, 49–71. Garden City, NY: Natural History Press.

Hays, Sharon. 2004. *Flat Broke with Children: Women in the Age of Welfare Reform.* New York: Oxford University Press.

Hertz, Rosanna. 2006. *Single by Chance, Mothers by Choice: How Women Are Choosing Parenthood without Marriage and Creating the New American Family.* New York: Oxford University Press.

Luker, Kristin. 1996. *Dubious Conceptions: The Politics of Teenage Pregnancy.* Cambridge, MA: Harvard University Press.

National Center for Health Statistics. 2005. *Health, United States, 2005; with Chartbook on Trends in the Health of Americans.* Hyattsville, MD: U.S. Department of Health and Human Services.

Neubeck, Kenneth J., and Noel A. Cazenave. 2001. *Welfare Racism: Playing the Race Card against America's Poor.* New York: Routledge.

Wenk, DeeAnn, Constance L. Hardesty, Carolyn S. Morgan, and Sampson Lee Blair. 1994. The Influence of Parental Involvement on the Well-being of Sons and Daughters. *Journal of Marriage and the Family* 56 (1): 229–234.

Susan Sered

BIRTH STRIKE

SEE *Demographic Transition.*

BISHOP, MAURICE

SEE *Grenadian Revolution.*

BISMARCKIAN MODEL

SEE *Welfare State.*

BITKER, BORIS

SEE *Restitution Principle.*

BLACK AMERICANS

SEE *African Americans.*

BLACK ARTS MOVEMENT

Characterized by African American poet, activist, and theorist Larry Neal as "the aesthetic sister of the Black Power concept" (Neal 1989, p. 62), the Black Arts Movement (BAM) is one of the most controversial cultural movements of the modern era due to its racialist intellectual bases; its commitment to economic, political, and cultural autonomy for African America; and its overtly revolutionary intentions. It carried through the African American educator and writer W. E. B. Du Bois's 1926 call for art "about us," "by us," "for us," and "near us" (Du Bois 1926, pp. 134–136). It was, in poet Kalamu ya Salaam's words, "the only American literary movement to advance 'social engagement' as a sine qua non of its aesthetic" (Salaam 1997, p. 70). Initiated in the early 1960s, though rooted in a radical tradition dating back at least to the Haitian Revolution of 1791, it flourished, suffered setbacks in the mid-1970s from federal government harassment via the FBI's counterintelligence program and from economic downturn, and continues in the early twenty-first century. Such continuity challenges the African American scholar Henry Louis Gates Jr.'s contention that the BAM was the "shortest and least successful" cultural movement in African American history (Gates Jr. 1994, pp. 74–75).

Although other media such as painting, poetry, dance, and music were significant, theater and drama played a preeminent role due to their communal nature, focus on transformation, and institutional, organizational, and economic demands. Neal writes, "Theater is potentially the most social of all the arts. It is an integral part of the socializing process" (Neal 1989, p. 68). Especially influential were Amiri Baraka's *Dutchman* (1964) and the institution he co-founded in 1965, Harlem's Black Arts Repertory Theatre/School. This focus on aesthetic innovation within institutional development reflects the thinking of social scientists such as John Henrik Clarke, C. Eric Lincoln, and Harold Cruse. A generation of artists was fostered in organizations such as BLKARTSWEST, the African Commune of Bad Relevant Artists, Spirit House, and the New Lafayette Theatre, and in the many black studies programs created in universities and colleges across the United States in part due to the actions of BAM artists and intellectuals.

Other significant influences can be identified. First, within the movement there was a focus on popular and folk culture via Du Bois (1868–1963), the African American educator and critic Alain Locke (1886–1954), the Italian Marxist theorist Antonio Gramsci (1891–1937), the black Trinidadian historian and activist C. L. R. James (1901–1989), the African American writer and ethnographer Zora Neale Hurston (1903–1960), and the Chinese theorist of cultural warfare Mao Zedong (1893–1976). The Black Muslim leader Malcolm X (1925–1965) was perhaps the most influential in the formation of the movement: "Our cultural revolution must be the means of bringing us closer to our African brothers and sisters" (Malcolm X 1970, p. 427). This is a matter of content, but also production conditions—where, by whom, and for whom the art is created. It is also a matter of technique: In *Performing Blackness: Enactments of African-American Modernism* (2000, p. 28), Kimberly Benston argued for the primacy of methexis ("communal helping-out of the action by all assembled") over mimesis ("the representation of an action"). In practice, this meant: (1) participatory works such as the National Black Theatre's *A Revival! Change! Love! Organize!* (1969) or Sonia Sanchez's "a/coltrane/poem" (1970), which supplies directions such as "sing loud & long with feeling" (Sanchez 1991, p. 184); (2) a call to action, as in the agitation-propaganda poetry of Don L. Lee or Nikki Giovanni or the "revolutionary commercials" of Ben Caldwell; and (3) invitation to the audience to discuss and criticize, most notably the public discussion panel convened at the New Lafayette Theatre in the fall of 1968 to discuss its controversial production of Ed Bullins's *We Righteous Bombers*, a play that scathingly critiques those who advocate revolutionary violence.

A second influence was radical theology, the assumption being that the most invidious effect of slavery and colonialism was spiritual. As James T. Stewart asserted, "[E]xisting white paradigms or models do not correspond to the realities of Black existence. It is imperative that we construct models with different basic assumptions" (Stewart 1968, p. 3). Ritual dominated the stages and periodicals of black theater in the late 1960s. Religious content was a constant in the visual arts, as in Margo Humphrey's Afrocentric take on *The Last Supper, The Last Bar-B-Que* (1988–1989). That said, religion was not universally appreciated; Caldwell showed no sympathy for the theologically minded in *Prayer Meeting, or, The First Militant Minister* (1969). It depicts a hilarious bit of subterfuge by a quick-on-his-feet burglar and a hopelessly gullible liberal preacher who mistakes the intruder for God. Likewise, Joyce Green criticized her compatriots—especially men—for their tendency to cloak misogyny in metaphysical vestments.

Finally, music—popular and avant-garde—enabled the dynamic of tradition and innovation called for by cultural revolutionaries such as Amilcar Cabral, Kwame Nkrumah, Mao, and Malcolm X. Blues, rhythm-and-blues, gospel music, and jazz were considered the "key," as Neal put it, to expanding the movement's connections to local, national, and international currents (Neal 1968, p. 653). Studied with an eye to their aesthetic, conceptual, and communal dimensions, traditions such as the blues were understood to be modes of critical discourse whose contours could be mapped onto other aesthetic and critical-theoretical forms.

Too often, as Cedric Robinson demonstrated in his *Black Marxism: The Making of the Black Radical Tradition* (1983), the continuity of the black radical tradition has been obscured. As in music, such continuity exists not only between BAM artists and critics and their forebears, but also to the post-BAM generation. To adequately account for the success or failure of the BAM, one must understand it as merely the epiphenomenon of a history that preceded it and continues in the twenty-first century.

SEE ALSO *Black Power; Blackness; Culture; Social Movements*

BIBLIOGRAPHY

Benston, Kimberly. 2000. *Performing Blackness: Enactments of African-American Modernism*. New York: Routledge.

Cruse, Harold. 1967. *The Crisis of the Negro Intellectual*. New York: Quill.

Du Bois, W. E. B. 1926. Krigwa Players Little Negro Theatre. *The Crisis* 32 (July): 134–136.

Gates, Henry Louis, Jr. 1994. Black Creativity: On the Cutting Edge. *Time*, October 10.

Gayle, Addison, Jr., ed. 1972. *The Black Aesthetic*. Garden City, NY: Anchor.

Kelley, Robin D. G. 2002. *Freedom Dreams: The Black Radical Imagination*. Boston: Beacon.

Malcolm X. 1970. The Organization of Afro-American Unity: For Human Rights and Dignity. In *Black Nationalism in America*, ed. John H. Bracey Jr. et al. Indianapolis, IN: Bobbs-Merrill.

Neal, Larry. 1968. And Shine Swam On. In *Black Fire: An Anthology of Afro-American Writing*, ed. LeRoi Jones and Larry Neal. New York: William Morrow.

Neal, Larry. 1969. Any Day Now: Black Art and Black Liberation. *Ebony*, August.

Neal, Larry. 1989. The Black Arts Movement. In *Visions of a Liberated Future*, ed. Michael Schwartz. New York: Thunder's Mouth. (Orig. pub. 1968).

Robinson, Cedric J. 1983. *Black Marxism: The Making of the Black Radical Tradition*. London: Zed.

Salaam, Kalamu ya. 1997. Black Arts Movement. In *Oxford Companion to African American Literature*, ed. William L. Andrews et al. New York: Oxford University Press.

Sanchez, Sonia. [1970] 1991. a/coltrane/poem. In *The Jazz Poetry Anthology*, ed. Sascha Feinstein and Yusef Komunyakaa. Bloomington: Indiana University Press.

Sell, Mike. 2005. The Black Arts Movement: Text, Performance, Blackness. In *Avant-Garde Performance and the Limits of Criticism: Approaching the Living Theatre, Happenings/Fluxus, and the Black Arts Movement*. Ann Arbor: University of Michigan Press.

Stewart, James T. 1968. The Development of the Black Revolutionary Artist. In *Black Fire: An Anthology of Afro-American Writing*, ed. LeRoi Jones and Larry Neal. New York: William Morrow.

Mike Sell

BLACK CONSERVATISM

Despite its seeming novelty and the monolithic nature of its contemporary precepts, black conservatism has a history that reaches back to at least the late eighteenth century and is capacious enough to include figures as diverse as Frederick Douglass, Zora Neale Hurston, Malcolm X, and Bill Cosby. The tradition, often but not exclusively peopled by the middle class, constellates around three key features. The first is a deep desire for racial autonomy that, in being effected, would ultimately result in personal independence. In short, black conservatives take a citizen's constitutional prerogative to pursue happiness very seriously. The second is the commitment to obliterate race as a limiting factor or indexical feature of human achievement. Toward this end, black conservatives are quick to repudiate theses that pathologize African American life, producing a defensive posture that once impelled Ralph Ellison to famously question, "Can a people live and develop for over 300 years simply by reacting to white racism?" (Ellison 1995, p. 339). The third is a compulsion toward social respectability, one that includes obeisance to society's laws, a hearty work ethic, religious piety, family values, sexual morality, and a kind of "role model" politics that if unable to exemplify admirable black behavior to other blacks, would at least prevent the race from being embarrassed in the eyes of the (white) American public. This ethos not only resulted in Rosa Parks rather than the impoverished, less refined, single mother Claudette Colvin becoming the cause célèbre of the 1955 Montgomery bus boycott; it also at times has inspired impassioned jeremiads that scold the black masses for behavior conservatives deem dissolute and licentious. This policing practice has also at times kept an unnecessary harness on more demonstrative resistances to U.S. racism.

For conceptual purposes, the tradition, like most other American phenomena, can be divided into its modern and postmodern versions, with the assassination of Martin Luther King Jr. marking the decisive break. Black conservatism of the past pragmatically accepted racial segregation as a fact of American life and sought to thrive despite its imposed social constraints. Consequently, there is a manifest enthusiasm toward exclusively black institutions. Starting with the accomplished shipbuilder James Forten and through the agrarian wizardry of Booker T. Washington, the marketing genius of Madame C. J. Walker, and the urban entrepreneurialism of Elijah Muhammad, black conservatism saw racially homogeneous business relations, education, and religious life as an existential and economic antidote to their social marginalization, thus creating the irony that the lion's share of this epoch's black conservative politics proffered radical opposition to the will of the American mainstream.

In distinction from this strain, postmodern conservatism is a child conceived in the political atmosphere following the putative fall of legalized segregation and thus does not find its grounding in institutions that organically emerged from a discrete black body politic. Instead its birth site may be located in the strategic conference rooms of the Republican National Congress in 1968 when party leaders founded Heritage Groups (later to become the Heritage Foundation) to increase minority membership among its ranks. More beholden to American individualism and noninterventionist government than their predecessors, theorists such as Thomas Sowell, Shelby Steele, Alan Keyes, and Angela McGlowan find in the passing of civil rights legislation in the 1960s the indisputable end of American racism. With race no longer impeding black accomplishment, these commentators encourage African Americans to defrock themselves of long-standing resentments about discrimination and embrace what they see as a future of unlimited opportunity. Leader of the antipreference movement the Civil Rights Initiative, Ward Connerly, asks blacks to assume the following empowered, optimistic posture that he has perpetually donned: "I have made my commitment not to tote that bag of racial grievances and I've made it more frequently than I'd like to admit because the status of victim is so seductive and so available to anyone with certain facial features or a certain cast to his skin" (Connerly 2000, p. 18).

Bent on preventing past black victimization from entering contemporary discussions about social justice, today's black conservatives saturate the public discussion with diatribes about black victimization in the present, which they believe come in the form of government welfare programs that allegedly enfeeble black ambition and limit black achievement. They claim that whatever black failure persists does so because of the dependent, lower class culture that such programs perpetuate.

This generation of black conservatives has been criticized for silencing their outrage toward blatant gestures of racism, accommodating the avarice of neoliberal economics, and supporting the neonationalism that underwrites the aggressions of contemporary U.S. imperialism. Though officeholding conservatives have only been tepidly responsive to the appeals of their black supporters (Republican administrations have continued to tolerate affirmative action programs), the latter are viewed by Americans with both skepticism and seriousness because of the largesse they command from powerful mainstream organizations such as the Heritage Foundation, the Hoover Institute, and the Fox News Corporation.

SEE ALSO *Black Liberalism; Black Power; Capitalism, Black; Conservatism; Imperialism; Libertarianism; Liberty; Race-Blind Policies; Racism*

BIBLIOGRAPHY

Boston, Thomas D. 1988. *Race, Class, and Conservatism.* Boston: Unwin Hyman.

Connerly, Ward. 2000. *Creating Equal: My Fight Against Race Preferences.* San Francisco: Encounter Books.

Eisenstadt, Peter, ed. 1999. *Black Conservatism: Essays in Intellectual and Political History.* New York: Garland.

Ellison, Ralph. 1995. *The Collected Essays of Ralph Ellison*, ed. John F. Callahan. New York: Modern Library.

Hurston, Zora Neale. 1995. Court Order Can't Make Races Mix. In *Zora Neale Hurston: Folklore, Memoirs, and Other Writings*, ed. Cheryl A. Wall. New York: Library of America.

McGlowan, Angela. 2007. *Bamboozled: How Americans Are Being Exploited by the Lies of the Liberal Agenda.* Nashville, TN: Thomas Nelson.

Thindwa, James. How Black Conservatives Hurt Their Cause. *Black Commentator* 154 (October 13, 2005). http://www.blackcommentator.com/154/154_thindwa_black_conservatives_pf.html.

West, Cornel. 2001. *Race Matters*, 2nd ed. New York: Vintage.

Tyrone Simpson II

BLACK IMMIGRANTS

SEE *Immigrants, Black.*

BLACK LIBERALISM

While the term *black liberalism* is often seen as a pejorative favored by black conservatives and black nationalists, it is better understood as part of the epistemology of black political thought. In his 2001 work on contemporary black political ideologies, Michael Dawson distinguishes black liberals from black nationalists and black Marxists by the liberals' belief in race-neutral constitutional order, liberal democracy, and capitalism. Dawson sees the tension black liberals face in trying to avoid the pessimism of black nationalists and black Marxists, who believe that liberal democracies or capitalism cannot be free of the implicit racist constructs of the white hierarchy. He defines black liberals as unique from white liberals in the black liberal belief that the liberal construct of equal rights includes economic, social, and political egalitarianism; and that America will be better if it can fulfill that egalitarian ideal for blacks. Put succinctly, Dawson quotes Malcolm X to say that black liberals have "a version of freedom larger than America's prepared to accept" (p. 239).

In Dawson's view, black liberals see racism as a potent force that is contradictory to and independent of liberal democracy and capitalism. Black nationalists believe that liberal democracies, born at a time of European colonialism and American slavery, not only fail to handle the contradiction between liberalism and colonial subjugation and slavery, but also implicitly incorporate the contradiction by enshrining racial hierarchies. Black Marxists see capitalism as inherently racist, based on models of capitalist exploitation.

W. Avon Drake (1991) offers another perspective, contrasting black liberals with social democrats. In Avon's view, black liberals see racism as the primary impediment to black social progress, while social democrats stress class differences, with neither seeing either liberal democracy or capitalism as inherently racist. Social democrats see impediments to blacks as based on differences in class: Racial disparities are viewed primarily as economic class disparities. Thus programs designed to address poverty and issues of inequality are seen as more useful than programs aimed directly at racial disparities. Proponents of black social democracy include Abram Harris and, later, William J. Wilson.

The major triumphs of black liberalism include the 1954 Supreme Court decision in *Brown v. Board of Education*, the Civil Rights Act of 1964, and the Voting Rights Act of 1965. Research shows that these policies dramatically reduced racial income inequality in the southern United States (McCrone and Hardy 1978; Donohue and Heckman 1991). In 1965 the poverty rate for black children stood at 65.6 percent and fell to 39.6 percent by 1969. Principle architects of black liberalism include W. E. B. Du Bois in his earlier writings, Charles Houston, Thurgood Marshall, Martin Luther King Jr., and A. Philip Randolph.

Black liberalism has faced several challenges. The rise of the American conservative movement and the dominance of conservative ideology on the national level put black liberals at odds with the American political establishment. Cornel West (1994) has pointed out that the crisis for black liberalism has been its inability to handle the increase in economic inequality resulting from the deindustrialization of the U.S. economy. The poverty rate for black children remained above 40 percent from 1975 to 1992, rising as high as 47.3 percent in 1982. *Crisis* magazine, the official organ of the NAACP, pointed to an earlier conflict addressed by black liberalism, when between 1933 and 1953—from the time of the New Deal to the *Brown* decision—the fruits of the white liberal agenda in the New Deal excluded the black community (Anderson 1980).

The conservative challenge to black liberalism rests on one of three arguments: (1) blacks have developed a pathological culture in opposition to mainstream culture that fails to reward the elements needed to succeed in a capitalist system; (2) blacks are inherently inferior, an argument based on a genetic definition of race; (3) blacks for various reasons of history and culture lack the requisite skills to succeed in a capitalist system because market forces make discrimination in the marketplace of minimal importance. On the basis of these arguments, government intervention to combat racism is seen as an unwarranted intrusion of the government into the marketplace. (William Darity and Patrick Mason refute these points in their 1998 work, arguing that the evidence fails to support the belief that blacks have a pathologic culture and that discrimination within the marketplace is substantial.)

Black liberals view blacks as "liberal man"—rational in the liberal sense of acting consistently to advance black well-being and economic success (as opposed to irrational, or pathological, failing to act in their economic interests). Black liberals explain racial disparities in economic and political life as the result of racism and, in a nod to black nationalists and Marxists, posit that there are institutional barriers born of the implicit racist pact that allows for legal segregation and slavery in a liberal democracy. The conservative argument views blacks as not rational, as making choices not in their best interest. The resulting caricature by conservatives is that black liberals portray blacks as victims, and the term *black liberal* has often come to be defined by this pejorative view. Conservatives also allege that the black liberal agenda creates a dependency on government, which is what makes black culture pathological and is the real source of racial disparities in economic and political life.

SEE ALSO *Black Conservatism; Black Power; Capitalism, Black; Du Bois, W. E. B.; Harris, Abram L.; King, Martin Luther, Jr.; Liberalism; Pathology, Social; Radicalism; Wilson, William Julius*

BIBLIOGRAPHY

Anderson, James D. 1980. Black Liberalism at the Crossroads: The Role of the Crisis, 1934–1953. *The Crisis: A Record of the Darker Races* 87 (November): 339–346.

Darity, William A., Jr., and Patrick L. Mason. 1998. Evidence on Discrimination in Employment: Codes of Color, Codes of Gender. *Journal of Economic Perspectives* 12(2):63–90.

Dawson, Michael C. 2001. *Black Visions: The Roots of Contemporary African-American Political Ideologies.* Chicago: University of Chicago Press.

Donohue, John J., III, and James Heckman. 1991. Continuous Versus Episodic Change: The Impact of Civil Rights Policy on the Economic Status of Blacks. *Journal of Economic Literature* 29 (December):1603–1643.

Drake, W. Avon. 1991. Black Liberalism, Conservatism, and Social Democracy: The Social Policy Debate. *Western Journal of Black Studies* 14 (2): 115–122.

McCrone, Donald J., and Richard J. Hardy. 1978. Civil Rights Policies and the Achievement of Racial Economic Equality, 1948–1975. *American Journal of Political Science* 22 (1):1–17.

West, Cornel. 1994. Demystifying the New Black Conservatism. In *Race Matters*, 47–61. New York: Vintage.

William E. Spriggs

BLACK MIDDLE CLASS

In the United States, where blacks have comprised a sizable minority in relation to a white majority, and in South Africa, where blacks have comprised a considerable majority in relation to a white minority, the growth of a black middle class has been regarded as an important benchmark for blacks' social and economic standing. A growing black middle class would seem, at least, to indicate improving social mobility, greater affluence, and expanded life chances for blacks.

In fact, the social science literature suggests that middle-class status, with all that it promises, is precarious for those blacks who have achieved it, and still out of reach for many others. As members of a minority group, middle-class blacks face historical and persistent marginalization, discrimination, and racism; consequently, their experience differs from that of the white middle class. Scholars have struggled to decide who among minority black populations should actually be considered middle class. Nevertheless, studies dedicated to defining and describing the black middle class confirm that inequities

persist between blacks and whites in the United States and South Africa, as well as between middle-class blacks and poor blacks, despite the dismantling of legal structures that discriminate against blacks.

UNITED STATES

Prior to the civil rights movement in the United States, a small black elite emerged that often was defined by skin color—that is, lighter-skinned blacks had greater opportunities for social advancement than darker-skinned blacks. This elite has been called the "black bourgeoisie" (the title of a controversial book by E. F. Frazier) and the "old black middle class" (a term used by the academic Bart Landry). It was associated with the educated strata of the black population, which W. E. B. Du Bois hoped would produce a "talented tenth" to serve as intellectual leaders for American blacks. Members of this group typically engaged in professional services to the black community, holding occupations such as teacher, social worker, pastor, mortician, and, occasionally, doctor or lawyer, as well as business owner. The success of these business owners was contingent in part on the existence of a market protected by segregation. Because they were excluded from working with or for whites, this "old" black middle class relied on the limited resources of black patrons and enjoyed only limited social mobility.

The civil rights era gave rise to a "new" black middle class. Some scholars have traced the origins of the black middle class to an earlier period, when restrictions on immigration (especially the Immigration Act of 1924) were introduced after World War I (1914–1918). These restrictions created opportunities for black workers to move in great numbers from the agricultural economy of the South to the industrial economy of the North. However, the scholarly literature generally attributes the growth of the black middle class chiefly to increased economic prosperity following World War II (1939–1945); to improved job opportunities for blacks after civil rights, especially in the public sector; and to the expanding economy of the 1960s.

Defining the Black Middle Class Scholars have struggled to define the black middle class. The most commonly employed criteria for membership have been income, education, occupation, and wealth. These measures are used either in combination or independently. The difficulty with using these measures to define the black middle class is that pronounced disparities between blacks and whites exist for all these variables. A black middle class defined by the middle range of black incomes, for instance, is not comparable to a white middle class defined by the middle range of white incomes. The 2000 U.S. census reported that whereas half of all black households have incomes of

$29,423 or more (based on 1999 dollars), the corresponding figure for white households is $44,687, a difference of more than $15,000. In addition, scholars have disagreed about which occupations should be defined as "middle class"; opinions range from a strictly white-collar criterion to a less restrictive one that includes protective services, skilled craftsmen, and clerical and sales workers. Furthermore, discrimination in the workplace prevents occupational prestige from being a reliable marker of blacks' social positions, especially the social position of middle-class blacks. Several scholars have proposed that lifestyle, values, and behaviors are much more meaningful measures of black middle-class experience than income, education, occupation, and wealth. Other social scientists have questioned whether it is appropriate to classify blacks as members of the middle class at all, given the pronounced disparities between the black and white middle classes, as well as broader problems with defining *class*.

Describing Black Middle-Class Experience An extensive literature characterizes the black middle class in terms of the inequities that middle-class blacks experience in relation to middle-class whites. These inequities include unequal residential patterns, occupational profiles, wages and wealth, and family structures. Middle-class blacks live in less socioeconomically attractive neighborhoods, close to the black poor; this phenomenon, dubbed *racial residential segregation*, may prevent social mobility. Middle-class blacks work disproportionately in the public sector, especially in city, state, and federal government. Of blacks who work in the private sector, the majority are pigeonholed into positions where they interact chiefly with black patrons.

Although middle-class blacks have moved increasingly into white-collar occupations, they have not received wages comparable to their white counterparts: In the closing decades of the twentieth century, blacks made 70 percent of what their white counterparts made. One consequence of this disparity in wages is that blacks receive less of a financial return on their personal investments in education than do whites. One study found that the black/white disparity is even more pronounced for men with more education (Tomaskovic-Devey, Thomas, and Johnson 2005). The black/white disparity is evident when comparing not only wages (income) but also wealth (assets). Home ownership is a primary means for individuals to establish and maintain their wealth status, but black home ownership lags behind white home ownership. In 2000, 46 percent of blacks and 71 percent of whites were homeowners. A few years earlier, a study reported that blacks had only 15 percent of the wealth that their white counterparts had. Thus, although the cohort whom scholars call the black middle class has

grown historically, members of that cohort remain at a disadvantage compared to their white counterparts.

Related to labor and wealth are three characteristics of the black middle-class family structure that make that middle-class status precarious. First, black wives have to participate in the labor force to secure and maintain middle-class status for their families. Second, wealth disparities relative to whites leave middle-class blacks with fewer assets to bequeath to the next generation. Third, middle-class blacks have an extended family structure that emphasizes their moral obligation and social responsibility to invest assets in the larger black underprivileged community. These factors contribute to continuing economic disadvantages for the black middle class in the United States as compared to the white middle class.

SOUTH AFRICA

Apartheid had produced a South African black elite that was employed in—but confined to—serving a black clientele. Opportunities for social mobility expanded momentously after the end of apartheid in the 1990s. On winning control of government in 1994, the African National Congress (ANC), guided by the National Democratic Revolution theory, set out to foster a black middle class. The ANC pursued this goal by promoting growth and redistribution of wealth and by transforming social institutions and economies through "equality employment" and "Black Economic Empowerment." These developments (which were similar to affirmative action programs in the United States) enabled South African blacks to move into the public sector. While some blacks gravitated to government employment, others obtained degrees and found work in the private sector.

Despite the new opportunities for blacks that opened in the post-apartheid period, scholars have remained concerned about the relatively small size of the black middle class and about growing gaps between the black middle class and the black poor. Although opinions vary as to size of the black middle class, the consensus is that this group is quite small relative to the larger population. Out of a total population of 44 million, the black middle class comprises somewhere between 2.5 to 3.6 million. Black employees in South Africa are highly unionized, a fact that both increases wages and improves work conditions; however, these benefits do not extend to poor unskilled blacks, who are prevented from unionizing and thus have greater difficulty in securing fair wages. As a result, though unionization has decreased inequality between whites and blacks, it has increased inequality between middle-class and poor blacks. South Africa presents the same problem seen in the United States: The black middle class is making modest strides toward parity with the white middle class, whereas a class of impoverished blacks falls further and further behind.

SEE ALSO *Acting White; Apartheid; Class; Jim Crow; Middle Class; Racism; Sellouts*

BIBLIOGRAPHY

Frazier, E. Franklin. 1957. *Black Bourgeoisie.* New York: Free Press.

Kochhar, Rakesh. 2004. *The Wealth of Hispanic Households: 1996 to 2002.* Washington, DC: Pew Hispanic Center.

Landry, Bart. 1987. *The New Black Middle Class.* Berkeley: University of California Press.

Oliver, Melvin L., and Thomas M. Shapiro. 1997. *Black Wealth/White Wealth: A New Perspective on Racial Inequality.* New York: Routledge.

Pattillo-McCoy, Mary. 1999. *Black Picket Fences: Privilege and Peril Among the Black Middle Class.* Chicago: University of Chicago Press.

Seekings, Jeremy, and Nicoli Nattrass. 2005. *Class, Race, and Inequality in South Africa.* New Haven, CT: Yale University Press.

Southall, Roger. 2004. The ANC and Black Capitalism in South Africa. *Review of African Political Economy* 31 (June): 313–328.

Tomaskovic-Devey, Donald, Melvin Thomas, and Kecia Johnson. 2005. Race and the Accumulation of Human Capital Across the Career: A Theoretical Model and Fixed-Effects Application. *American Journal of Sociology* 111 (July): 58–89.

Kris Marsh

BLACK NATIONALISM

In the strictest meaning of the term, *black nationalism* refers to those ideas and movements that are associated with the quest to achieve separate statehood for African Americans. The goal of statehood was especially important during the "classical" period of black nationalism—the time of Marcus Garvey (the 1920s) and of the early activists who preceded him. During the "modern" period, especially after World War II, black nationalism encompasses more broadly both those who favored true political sovereignty through separate statehood, and those who favored more modest goals like black administration of vital private and public institutions—the latter being the common cause of those who invoked the slogan of "Black Power" after 1966. Black nationalism must always be understood in its historical context, therefore, as particular ideas and movements invariably bear the marks of their respective eras.

CLASSICAL BLACK NATIONALISM

Classical black nationalists advocated political sovereignty and they insisted that such a goal required the creation of a nation-state with clear geographical boundaries. There was not much support for this idea before the passage of the Fugitive Slave Act of 1850. Part of the Compromise of 1850, this act denied captured slaves (or those simply accused of being fugitive slaves) the right to a trial and granted marshals the power to force citizens to assist in the recapture of runaway slaves. It also prohibited testimony by those accused, and thus raised the possibility that free blacks could be captured into slavery. This was an era in which the U.S. political elite defined the meaning of citizenship in "white nationalist" terms. Justice Taney stated this perspective forcefully in the infamous 1857 *Dred Scott* case. Concerning the phrase "all men are created equal," Justice Taney commented that "it [was] too clear for dispute that the enslaved African race [was] not intended to be included and formed no part of the people who framed this declaration." The African race, Taney argued, had "no rights which the white man was bound to respect." Until the eve of the Civil War, politicians worked to expand and secure rights for the majority of whites (males), while at the same time they increasingly restricted the rights of free blacks with prohibitions against intermarriage, rules that barred the migration of blacks to different states, and laws that denied suffrage and that even established formal segregation. Thus, by the mid-nineteenth century Martin Delaney, James T. Holly, and others began to argue that black people should leave the United States for Canada, Haiti, or other destinations.

What set apart these "nationalists" from other black historical actors of the period were their positions on emigration and nation-building, not their views of culture. As Wilson Moses explains in his *Golden Age of Black Nationalism* (1978) and other writings, classical black nationalists were Christians, and they believed that Western civilization was the measure of progress when it came to letters, arts, commerce, and governance. All free black Americans of this period shared these views. It was not until after World War II that black (cultural) nationalists began to try to break entirely from Western convention.

Marcus Garvey founded the Universal Negro Improvement Association (UNIA) in 1918, and built the largest black nationalist movement in the history of the United States. The movement originated in Harlem, New York, and grew out of the social, economic, and political experience of native and foreign-born blacks of the period. Garvey's nationalism was "classical" in the sense that his final goal was political autonomy, and he was Western in orientation. In terms of ideas and practice, however, the UNIA also reflected developments unique to its era. The 1920s was a period of heightened anticolonial, nationalistic consciousness among many oppressed peoples of the world, and thus in tone, if not in substance, the arguments advanced by supporters of Garvey's vision was akin to arguments against colonial domination seen in, say, Ireland or India—especially in the Caribbean region, where the UNIA established a number of chapters. The 1920s might also have represented the height of white American nationalism in the United States. The Ku Klux Klan peaked in membership (at several million), by defending "pure womanhood" and opposing immigration and all forms of labor activism. This was also the period when, in 1924, the U.S. government instituted immigration quotas that favored Northern Europeans over all others. In terms of membership numbers and visibility, the UNIA's apex was congruent with the rise of white American nationalism of its time.

In terms of its program, the UNIA was conservative socially, economically, and politically. Although Garvey initially explained the ambitions of the organization in language that clearly reflected the influence of revolutionary (Bolshevik) thought, as well as anticolonialism, very quickly after the founding of the UNIA his message (in the United States) reflected conventional, even reactionary, thinking about race and political empowerment in the United States. Echoing conventional wisdom about the enduring significance of "racial" identity, Garvey argued for racial purity. While Garvey and his followers articulated a kind of racial chauvinism, a pride in black identity, that few had previously articulated, he nevertheless was reproducing the racist ideology of that period. After all, it was the Klan who argued most forcefully for racial purity. Starting with an organic view of racial identity—which ignored diversity *among* black people— Garvey eschewed talk of class struggle and union organization and argued for a strategy of building black businesses, believing the race would find redemption in the economic marketplace. The most prominent of the UNIA business ventures was the unsuccessful Black Star Line. Unlike the National Association for the Advancement of Colored People (NAACP), Garvey and the UNIA did not devote much effort toward expanding civil rights for blacks in the United States. In this respect, the organization foreshadowed the Nation of Islam, arguably the most successful black nationalist organization in the postwar period.

Garvey is known for his "back to Africa" philosophy, but his organization was working for selective emigration, not mass return. Garvey argued that full equality in the United States was illusory at best, and so he supported a "Negro Zionism." Black people in the Western hemisphere, he argued, should support the creation of an African nation in the eastern hemisphere (his choice was Liberia); by ensuring the development of the Negro Zion, black people in the United States, the Caribbean, and Africa would elevate their status. This reasoning was similar to that of James T. Holly and others of the antebellum period.

Black nationalism must also be understood with a number of spectra in mind. Since the second decade of the twentieth century, there have been disagreements among nationalists on "social" issues like "racial purity," and religious belief. There have also been differences in terms of economic philosophy—specifically whether black equality could be achieved under capitalism. Nationalists have differed over political tactics—for example, they have argued over whether black people could win emancipation through lobbying and electoral strategies or only through armed insurrection. During the 1920s, the UNIA vastly dwarfed another organization, the African Blood Brotherhood (ABB), which combined racial nationalism with a socialist critique of capitalism. The ABB's founder, Cyril Briggs—a native of St. Kitts in the West Indies—argued that black people constituted a separate nation, but unlike Garvey he sought to establish political sovereignty by revolutionary means. The Fenian Irish Republican Brotherhood was the likely model for the ABB. At its peak, the organization claimed several thousand members. It was eventually absorbed by the Communist Party.

MODERN BLACK NATIONALISM

Of the "modern" black nationalist organizations operating in the postwar period, the National of Islam (NOI) has been the largest and most enduring. The Nation of Islam expanded in size and significance largely due to the efforts of one convert, Malcolm X. Born Malcolm Little, Malcolm X converted to Islam while in prison, abandoned his slave name, and adopted the *X* to represent the African name lost as a result of slavery. Malcolm X's organizing skills and street savvy helped to expand the organization and vastly increase its visibility in the United States, while his oratorical gifts helped spread Elijah Muhammad's message. In some respects this message was a form of neo-Garveyism: It endorsed black pride, self-help through economic enterprise, and the creation of a separate territory in the American South. However, the NOI's unique, heretical interpretation of Islam—Elijah Muhammad was believed to be a prophet—set the organization apart from other black nationalist groups of the period. The NOI established mosques in cities across the country. Among their business activities were laundromats, restaurants, and a newspaper, *Muhammad Speaks.* The NOI also established separate schools for the children of its members.

The fact that the organization eschewed political engagement might have been its most striking feature. The late 1950s and 1960s was the period of civil rights struggle, and the NOI did not participate in any of the major campaigns of the era. Indeed, in his *Autobiography* (1965) Malcolm X makes it clear that he was bothered by the common criticism of NOI—that it was all talk, and little action. After leaving the organization, he spent the final years of his life seeking to fashion a secular, and *engaged* version of black nationalism that was represented in his short-lived Organization for Afro-American Unity (OAAU). The OAAU called for black control of the various institutions that touched black life. Malcolm X, who was assassinated in 1965, might have had his greatest impact in death. Most nationalists of the Black Power era (post-1965) drew inspiration from the life and martyrdom of Malcolm X—especially his explicit rejection of integration as a goal of the black freedom struggle, and his questioning of nonviolence as a political strategy.

Among the groups operating during the 1960s and early 1970s that adopted and propounded an explicitly nationalist agenda were the post-1965 Student Nonviolent Coordinating Committee (SNCC) and Congress of Racial Equality (CORE), Mualana Ron Karenga's US organization, the Revolutionary Action Movement (RAM), and the Black Panther Party for Self-Defense (BPP).

These organizations and activists were influenced by the anticolonial struggles of the 1950s, and especially the independence of a number of sub-Saharan African nations, starting with Ghana in 1957. Part of the inspiration came out of the fact that black activists in the United States and around the African Diaspora had long embraced Pan-Africanism—the idea that black people of the African Diaspora shared a common destiny. For nationalists of the period, the significance of these anticolonial struggles was also theoretical. First, activists understood anticolonial efforts as analogous to the struggle for civil and economic rights in the United States: Throughout the Diaspora, "African" liberation meant transforming, if not rejecting, Western social, political, and economic beliefs. Second, the nature of anticolonial struggle informed discussions of tactics within the United Sates. In some cases independence came peacefully. In other cases Africans gained political sovereignty through armed and bloody confrontation.

While proponents of black nationalism all pondered the same general questions during the 1960s, they arrived at different conclusions. Karenga, US, and "cultural" nationalists of the period believed that liberation was tied to the recovery of an "African" identity. Karenga therefore urged his followers to learn and speak Swahili, to dress in traditional African garb, and to live according to seven principles (the Kawaida) that distilled elements of an African cosmology. The Black Panther Party hoped to topple capitalism, and rejected the view that black equal-

ity could be achieved by changes in lifestyle that did not directly change political and economic realities. To help change those realities, they published a newspaper and established schools, health clinics, and free breakfast programs. US and the BPP were fierce rivals, and this rivalry (which in part was fueled by the FBI) proved deadly in 1969 when members of US shot and killed a member of the Los Angeles chapter of the BPP.

Both organizations, along with other black nationalist groups of the era, were active in what is known as the "Black Power" phase of the civil rights struggle. "Black Power," first proclaimed as a slogan in 1966, had as many definitions as it did adherents. At base, its meaning was captured by another popular slogan of the time—"black faces in previously white places." The basic idea—that blacks as a group should organize and pursue power collectively as other "ethnic" populations had done previously—was elaborated in Stokely Carmichael and Charles Hamilton's *Black Power* (1967). Black Power demands for control of school curricula and city administrations coincided with the rioting (or urban rebellions) that marked the era—outbreaks that affected hundreds of cities across the United States. By the early 1970s, however, it was clear that Black Power represented conventional tendencies far more than radical ones. For a number of reasons, starting with the success of U.S. intelligence in undermining the strength of radical black nationalist organizations, Black Power soon looked more like "ethnic pluralism" than like a programmatic orientation that could transcend the terms of and limitations of urban politics in the United States (Allen 1970).

THE POST–CIVIL RIGHTS ERA

In the post–civil rights context, the NOI has been the principal representative of black nationalism as a political movement. After the death of Elijah Muhammad in 1975, one of his sons, Warith Deen Muhammad, took control of the organization and adopted Sunni Islamic beliefs and practices. This meant, among other things, that the organization was no longer racially separatist, nor working toward political sovereignty. Louis Farrakhan subsequently led a group of defectors out of that organization and reestablished the NOI along traditional lines.

Farrakhan enjoyed considerable popularity among black Americans, especially during the early to mid-1990s. He drew large audiences to hear his lectures/sermons. Farrakhan organized the Million Man March in 1996, which drew upward of 750,000 black men to Washington, D.C. The Million Man March was intended to serve as a catalyst for the creation of a broad-based political movement that would tackle the problems that continued to plague black America—disproportionately high levels of unemployment, high rates of incarceration, unequal access to capital, and so on. However, the fundamental theme of the march was "atonement," and so—unlike the famous march on Washington of 1963, which demanded "Jobs and Freedom"—it demanded nothing but greater black male responsibility. It did not trigger a new wave of grassroots mobilization, and indeed might have had the opposite effect. By maintaining a view of political action that depends on "group consciousness" and eschews collaboration with movements that cross racial and class lines, such as organized labor, the NOI has not been able to transcend limitations that have hampered the organization from its inception.

Less overtly political, but also quite visible during the late 1980s and 1990s was the academic push for an "Afrocentric" paradigm. *Afrocentric* had once been synonymous with Pan-Africanist, but by the 1990s the term had developed a narrower connotation. Molefi Kete Asante of Temple University was the chief architect of this new usage. He insisted that to study "African" people—be they black Americans in Detroit, black West Indians in Barbados or Dominica, or the Wolof of Senegal—scholars must look to "classical" Africa, by which he meant ancient Egypt, or "Kemet." Just as Ancient Greek thought provides the basis of Western philosophy, so too, he argued, did ancient Egypt serve as the basis of "African" philosophy. For Asante, this was more than an intellectual point. Rather, this counter-epistemology was a first step toward black empowerment. In this regard, Asante and proponents who shared his views extended the arguments of cultural nationalists of the 1960s—and of the NOI—who had insisted that black empowerment depended on an embrace of a lost cultural identity. Asante was not the first to emphasize an understanding of black or "African" history, nor to suggest that proper knowledge of identity could be emancipatory; however, Afrocentricity as Asante and other proponents spelled it out added ingredients of its time—especially the theoretical bent toward "post-structural" modes of understanding. In the end, though, his was only an *attempt* at a counter-epistemology. Despite Asante's claim that Afrocentricity was a first step toward black empowerment, the conservative aspects of this ideology should be clear: This was fundamentally an intellectual, as opposed to a political, movement.

CONCLUSION

In a very broad sense, black nationalism and Black Power are not uniquely American phenomena. South Africa and more recently Brazil are other countries where activists have pushed for a consciousness about (black) identity as a way to catalyze and organize for social change. However, a proper understanding of black nationalism in *any* context requires special attention to the specificity of a given political and historical context. Simple analogies between

movements that emphasize black or African identity invariably miss crucial differences. When scholars who revisit the Black Power era in the United States, or Black Consciousness in South Africa, focus on what activists did as well as what they said, the significance of *local* context becomes clear. Analogies to anticolonial struggle, or Pan-African solidarity, or black pride do not change the fact that black nationalists ultimately face the challenge of building social movements within national boundaries.

SEE ALSO *African Americans; Afrocentrism; Black Conservatism; Black Panthers; Black Power; Blackness; Capitalism, Black;* Dred Scott v. Sanford; *Garvey, Marcus; Ku Klux Klan; Malcolm X; Marxism, Black; Nation of Islam; Nationalism and Nationality; Pan-African Congresses; Pan-Africanism; Reconstruction Era (U.S.); Separatism; U.S. Civil War*

BIBLIOGRAPHY

Allen, Robert L. 1970. *Black Awakening in Capitalist America: An Analytic History.* Garden City, NY: Anchor Books.

Carmichael, Stokely, and Charles V. Hamilton. 1967. *Black Power: The Politics of Liberation in America.* New York: Random House.

Hill, Robert A., ed. 1983. *The Marcus Garvey and Universal Negro Improvement Association Papers.* Berkeley: University of California Press.

Malcolm X, with Alex Haley. [1965] 1992. *The Autobiography of Malcolm X.* 1st Ballantine Books ed. New York: Ballantine Books.

Moses, Wilson Jeremiah. 1978. *The Golden Age of Black Nationalism, 1850–1925.* Hamden, CT: Archon Books.

Moses, Wilson Jeremiah. 1990. *The Wings of Ethiopia: Studies in African-American Life and Letters.* 1st ed. Ames: Iowa State University Press.

Pinkney, Alphonso. 1976. *Red, Black, and Green: Black Nationalism in the United States.* Cambridge, U.K., and New York: Cambridge University Press.

Robinson, Dean E. 2001. *Black Nationalism in American Politics and Thought.* Cambridge, U.K., and New York: Cambridge University Press.

Dean E. Robinson

BLACK PANTHERS

The Black Panther Party (BPP) was conceived as the next stage in the evolution of the African American struggle, building off of a trajectory that is mistakenly divided into two discrete movements: civil rights and Black Power (Hill 2004; Tyson 1999). Fusing the political thought of Robert F. Williams on armed self-defense with the philosophy of Malcolm X on black self-determination, Max

Stanford developed a unique approach to activism that would become the Black Panther Party (BPP) (Marable 2007). The basic goal was to advance Black Power and national liberation throughout the United States in general but especially in the North by improving the political, economic, social, and psychological well-being of African Americans (Hilliard and Cole 1993; Holder 1990; Jones 1998). This was to be achieved through a diverse repertoire of activities, but it was the ideas of armed self-defense and guerrilla warfare (if deemed necessary) that garnered the most attention.

From the beginning the organization was divided by a fundamental split based on important tactical differences. On the East Coast the first BPP chapter was created in New York City by Stanford in 1965 (see Marable 2007). This organization advocated a clandestine approach and opted to remain underground until it could more effectively pursue its claims openly. On the West Coast the second BPP chapter was created by Huey P. Newton and Bobby Seale in Oakland, California, in 1966 (see Seale 1970). This chapter advocated a more public presence and attempted to garner as much attention as possible. Both wings of the party developed chapters throughout the United States (especially during a period of particularly rapid growth between 1967 and 1968). In late 1969 and 1970, in an effort to avoid negative publicity and the attention of authorities, the Panther name was changed to the National Committee to Combat Fascism in many locales.

Because it drew the primary focus of the media as well as of political leaders, activists, and academics, the West Coast faction has largely shaped our understanding of the BPP. This bias is perhaps inevitable, because the West Coast faction was involved in many of the most dramatic incidents and activities associated with the Panthers. These include the storming of the California State Assembly in Sacramento in 1967, numerous shoot-outs with the police throughout Oakland (especially those involving Newton, Eldridge Cleaver, and "Li'l" Bobby Hutton), the Free Huey movement, the Chicago 8 trial, the shooting of George Jackson in San Quentin Prison, and the failed kidnapping of a judge in a Marin County courtroom by Jackson's brother Jonathan (see Holder 1990; Seale 1970; United States Congress 1971). In addition the West Coast Panthers developed numerous high-profile programs that were later imitated, such as the free breakfast program, the liberation school, sickle cell anemia tests, and the Black Panther Intercommunal News Service (see Abron 1993; Cleaver and Katsiaficas 2001). Also highly influential was the imagery associated with West Coast Panthers: Their military berets, leather gloves and hats, bright powder-blue shirts, and Afro hairstyles were as symbolically important to the Black Power movement as the phrase "Power to the People." The impact of this imagery was immediate and resonated across the United States as well as throughout the world.

Although in some respects the BPP was part of a continuum of black struggle, in other respects it represented a major divergence from the traditional black nationalist program. For example, the BPP was hesitant about calling for a black "nation"—a major goal for black nationalists. Newton, the main theoretician for the Panthers, suggested that until "the oppressive state of America" was wiped out, there would be no freedom for blacks even with a separate state. The disagreement, then, was over timing, not over nationhood per se. The BPP members were also somewhat disdainful of those who believed that the path to African American salvation was the adoption of African culture or a return to the African continent—both major planks of the black nationalist program. Indeed the Panthers were quite American and Western in their objectives and in many of the means used to attain them. Finally, the BPP decided relatively early on that coalitions should be formed with white liberals, radicals, and any other groups that wished to bring about political-economic change—a stance that further distanced them from other black nationalists.

Divided tactically and organizationally from the rest of the Black Power movement, the BPP soon became the target of a highly repressive campaign. This effort extended from J. Edgar Hoover's Federal Bureau of Investigation, which in 1968 identified the party as "the greatest threat to the internal security of the United States" (Cunningham 2004), to "red squad" and antisubversive units in local police departments throughout the country (Donner 1990). These organizations engaged in a wide variety of actions: setting up physical and electronic surveillance; sending false letters; planting informants and agents provocateur; conducting raids; making arrests for a multitude of offenses, from murder to running an intercom without a license; and even carrying out targeted assassination. The actions of both the state and the Panthers escalated to such a level of violence over several years that diverse citizens' alliances began to form calling for an end to the conflict.

By 1973, due to the efforts of the U.S. government to eliminate it and the difficulties of managing a high-profile and contentious organization, the original BPP was effectively dismantled (Calloway 1977; Goldstein 1978; Hopkins 1978; Johnson 1998; Jones 1998). In its place there developed an organization with new leadership (most of the original governing committee was no longer involved), new tactics (confrontation was replaced by electoral and civil service efforts), and new members (largely female).

The Panthers were by no means finished at this time, however. Several of their earlier programs persisted up until 1980 (Abron 1993). Ideologically and tactically, to both good and bad effect, the Panthers influenced the white Left (who considered them to be the "vanguard" of the revolution), other African American organizations (the New Black Panther Party), Latinos (the Young Lords), Native Americans (especially the American Indian Movement), diverse activists around the world (e.g., the Black Panther Parties in Australia and Israel as well as the Dalit Panthers in India), and even the social service programs of diverse state and local governments. Additionally, through popularization in film, television, music, poetry, and fiction, the BPP and its legacy continue to exert an influence on America and the rest of the world (Cleaver and Katsiaficas 2001; Kelley 2002). Indeed as one of the most visible and aggressive responses to the diverse problems confronting blacks in the United States, the Black Panthers are likely to remain inspirational to those resisting racism, the U.S. government, or capitalism for some time to come.

SEE ALSO *African Americans; Black Power; Civil Rights Movement, U.S.; Human Rights; King, Martin Luther, Jr.; Malcolm X; Marxism, Black; Militants; Repression; Resistance*

BIBLIOGRAPHY

Abron, Jonina. 1993. Raising the Consciousness of the People: The Black Panther Intercommunal News Service, 1967–1980. In *Insider Histories of the Vietnam-Era Underground Press*, vol. 1 of *Voices from the Underground*, ed. Ken Wachsberger, Sanford Berman, William Moses Kunstler, and Abe Peck, 356–357. Tempe, AZ: Mica.

Calloway, Carolyn R. 1977. Group Cohesiveness in the Black Panther Party. *Journal of Black Studies* 8 (1): 55–74.

Cleaver, Kathleen, and George N. Katsiaficas, eds. 2001. *Liberation, Imagination, and the Black Panther Party: A New Look at the Panthers and Their Legacy*. New York: Routledge.

Cunningham, David. 2004. *There's Something Happening Here: The New Left, the Klan, and FBI Counterintelligence*. Berkeley: University of California Press.

Donner, Frank J. 1990. *Protectors of Privilege: Red Squads and Police Repression in Urban America*. Berkeley: University of California Press.

Goldstein, Robert Justin. 1978. *Political Repression in Modern America: From 1870 to the Present*. Cambridge, MA: Schenkman.

Hill, Lance E. 2004. *The Deacons for Defense: Armed Resistance and the Civil Rights Movement*. Chapel Hill: University of North Carolina Press.

Hilliard, David, and Lewis Cole. 1993. *This Side of Glory: The Autobiography of David Hilliard and the Story of the Black Panther Party*. Boston: Little, Brown.

Holder, Kit Kim. 1990. The History of the Black Panther Party, 1966–1972. PhD diss., University of Massachusetts, Amherst.

Hopkins, Charles William. 1978. The Deradicalization of the Black Panther Party, 1967–1973. PhD diss., University of North Carolina at Chapel Hill.

Johnson, Ollie. 1998. Explaining the Demise of the Black Panther Party: The Role of Internal Factors. In *The Black Panthers (Reconsidered)*, ed. Charles E. Jones, 391–409. Baltimore, MD: Black Classic.

Jones, Charles E., ed. 1998. *The Black Panther Party (Reconsidered)*. Baltimore, MD: Black Classic.

Kelley, Robin D. G. 2002. *Freedom Dreams: The Black Radical Imagination*. Boston: Beacon.

Marable, Manning. 2007. The Malcolm X. Project at Columbia University. http://www.columbia.edu/cu/ccbh/mxp/index.html.

Seale, Bobby. 1970. *Seize the Time: The Story of the Black Panther Party and Huey P. Newton*. New York: Random House.

Tyson, Timothy B. 1999. *Radio Free Dixie: Robert F. Williams and the Roots of Black Power*. Chapel Hill: University of North Carolina Press.

United States Congress, House Committee on Internal Security. 1971. *Gun Barrel Politics: The Black Panther Party, 1966–1971*. Washington, DC: U.S. Government Printing Office.

Christian Davenport

BLACK POLITICS

SEE *Politics, Black.*

BLACK POWER

The Black Power movement is one of the most misunderstood and understudied protest movements in American history (Jeffries 2006). Many whites believed that Black Power was synonymous with violence and black racism. Some black leaders viewed the movement as separatist, following a similar path to that of such earlier movements as Marcus Garvey's (1887–1940) Universal Negro Improvement Association (UNIA), the National Movement for the Establishment of the Forty-ninth State, the Peace Movement of Ethiopia, and the National Union for People of African Descent.

The Black Power movement emerged at a time when the modern civil rights movement was in its final stage as a viable movement for social, political, and economic change. While some contend that the civil rights and Black Power movements were vastly different endeavors, the latter was indeed a logical extension of the former. In fact, many have maintained that Willie Ricks, a civil rights activist, introduced the Black Power slogan during a march in 1966. In 1968 Kwame Ture (then Stokely

Carmichael, 1941–1998) defined Black Power as "the ability of black people to politically get together and organize themselves so that they can speak from a position of strength rather than a position of weakness" (quoted in Ladner 1967, p. 8). It is apparent though, that while the Black Power movement was a continuation of the struggle waged by the civil rights movement, it was distinct in many ways.

Black Power organizations such as the Black Panther Party, US, the Republic of New Africa, the League of Revolutionary Black Workers, the Revolutionary Action Movement, and others saw themselves as the heirs to Malcolm X (1925–1965). Malcolm had argued that the nonviolent tactics of Dr. Martin Luther King Jr. (1929–1968) were not a viable option for black people. Malcolm viewed integration as a surrender to white supremacy, for its aims of total assimilation into white society implied that African Americans had little that was worth preserving.

Malcolm's candid and fiery rhetoric appealed to many urban blacks, and his autobiography was devoured by Black Power advocates. Nat Turner (1800–1831), Che Guevara (1928–1967), Frantz Fanon (1925–1961), Amílcar Cabral (1924–1973), Kwame Nkrumah (1909–1972), Patrice Lumumba (1925–1961), Sékou Touré (1922–1984), and Toussaint Louverture (1743–1803) were also held in high regard. Black Power advocates were inspired by the struggle for African independence.

For many in the Black Power movement, Fanon's *The Wretched of the Earth* (1961) was considered a blueprint for revolution in America. *The Wretched of the Earth* distilled the lessons of the Algerian war for anticolonial movements everywhere. In terms of organization building, Garvey's UNIA served as a model for many Black Power advocates.

The 1965 assassination of Malcolm X coupled with the urban uprisings of 1964 and 1965 ignited the Black Power movement. Some young black activists committed themselves to continuing the unfinished work of Malcolm X's Organization of Afro-American Unity by forming their own organizations. During the summer of 1965, the predominantly black Watts district in Los Angeles reached its boiling point and erupted in violence in response to the mistreatment of a black motorist by members of the California Highway Patrol. This uprising was arguably the most catastrophic of its era; it signaled to America that some blacks were willing to lash out against the establishment in a violent way when consistently denied the most basic of human rights. Ironically, this rebellion occurred just a few days after the passing of the Voting Rights Act of 1965. Consequently, for many blacks it was clear that oppression was too deeply entrenched in America's institutions to be overcome by civil rights legislation that addressed the symptoms and symbols of black inequality rather than the root causes.

By 1968 the Black Power movement was in full gear. Thousands of blacks all over the country took to the streets in response to the killing of Dr. King. Months later, black athletes staged protests at the Olympic Games in Mexico City as a way of bringing attention to the plight of African Americans in the United States.

The Black Power movement was dispersed throughout the United States. The civil rights movement, on the other hand, was to a large extent a southern-based movement. Unlike the civil rights movement, whites were prohibited from joining any of the Black Power organizations. With the exception of the Black Panther Party, Black Power organizations did not form alliances with white groups. Black Powerites sought to be free of any white influence or interference.

While all of the Black Power organizations believed in black control of their communities, they were not monolithic in their approach to that end. The civil rights movement sought to dismantle desegregation in public accommodations and to exercise the right of black Americans to vote. For many Black Powerites, integration was a nonissue and nonviolence was out of the question. The political philosophy of the organizations that comprised the Black Power movement ran the gamut. Some were black nationalist, others were cultural nationalist, while still others considered themselves Marxist-Leninist.

The Black Power movement was preoccupied with increasing black people's level of consciousness. Black people began calling themselves *black* instead of *negro*. Congressman Adam Clayton Powell (1908–1972) of New York spoke of Black Power at a rally in 1965 in Chicago and elaborated on it in his Howard University commencement speech the following year. He exclaimed that Black Power was "a working philosophy for a new breed of cats … who categorically refuse to compromise or negotiate any longer for their rights … who reject the old-line established white financed, white controlled, white washed Negro leadership" (quoted in Muse 1970, p. 242).

The Black Power movement not only represented a change in tactical strategy, but also a change in mind-set. For instance, the black music industry, with its roots in gospel and rhythm and blues became nationalist in an extraordinary way. Songs like James Brown's "Say It Loud, I'm Black and I'm Proud" (1968), the Temptations' "Message to a Black Man," (1969) and the Impressions' "We're a Winner" (1967) established a distinctive sound that became the preferred expression for a generation of politically conscious young black Americans. Some blacks chose to don African garb and adopt African names. Some chose to wear their hair in ways that were more distinctively nonwhite. In the fall of 1966, Howard University students elected as homecoming queen a woman who ran on a Black Power platform and wore the emerging Afro hairstyle. "Black Is Beautiful" became the mantra among Black Powerites.

Young black activists from Cornell University in Ithaca, New York, to the University of California at Berkeley established black student unions and demanded black studies programs, more black faculty, and proactive recruitment and admissions policies. Black Power advocates claimed that most African Americans knew little about their history. Carter G. Woodson (1875–1950) had made the same point years earlier: "The Negro knows practically nothing of his history and his 'friends' are not permitting him to learn it.... And if a race has no history, if it has no worth-while tradition, it becomes a negligible factor in the thought of the world, and it stands in danger of extermination" (Wiggins 1987, p. 45; Young 1982, p. 100).

Black Power advocates felt little need to prove to whites that they were deserving of the same rights. From their standpoint, to whom were whites to be equal? They believed that their time would be better spent educating the community, building institutions, and meeting the daily needs of the people by providing protection, food, shelter, and clothing.

The Black Power movement did not grow out of a vacuum; it was firmly rooted in the rich tradition of black protest. Like the slave rebellions and the Garvey movement, it was extensively organized. Its use of the written word, art, and culture to heighten the consciousness of the black community also linked the movement to the Harlem Renaissance (or the New Negro Renaissance), which relied heavily on these black expressive endeavors.

The Black Power movement also heightened the consciousness of other oppressed peoples throughout the world and greatly influenced the direction of their movements. The Black Power movement had a profound impact, for example, on the struggle for equality in the Caribbean, where freedom fighters started the Afro-Caribbean movement, activists in Barbados formed the People's Progressive Movement, and grassroots organizers in Bermuda launched the Black Beret group (Jeffries 2006).

By the mid-1970s, the Black Power movement was for all intents and purposes over. Government repression, which included assassinations of Black Panthers Mark Clark and Fred Hampton in Chicago, and Carl Hampton of Houston, raids, arrests, and harassment of many of the movement's members, gets much of the credit for the decline of the Black Power movement. In addition to repression, by 1973 African American activists had begun to concentrate their efforts on getting blacks and progressive whites elected to public office. Some saw the electoral process as a significantly less dangerous undertaking. Intragroup squabbles and government programs such as welfare (which underwent a loosening of eligibility requirements) also worked to dampen militant activism. While a few Black Power organizations remained active well into the mid-1970s, by the time of the election of President Jimmy Carter in November 1976, the Black Power movement was dead.

SEE ALSO *Black Panthers; Civil Rights Movement, U.S.; Congress of Racial Equality; Student Nonviolent Coordinating Committee*

BIBLIOGRAPHY

Jeffries, Judson L., ed. 2006. *Black Power in the Belly of the Beast.* Urbana: University of Illinois Press.

Ladner, Joyce. 1967. What "Black Power" Means to Negroes in Mississippi. *Transaction* (November): 7–15.

Muse, Benjamin. 1970. *The American Negro Revolution: From Nonviolence to Black Power, 1963–1967.* New York: Citadel.

Ogbar, Jeffrey O. G. 2004. *Black Power: Radical Politics and African American Identity.* Baltimore, MD: Johns Hopkins University Press.

Van DeBurg, William L. 1992. *New Day in Babylon: The Black Power Movement and American Culture, 1965–1975.* Chicago: University of Chicago Press.

Wiggins, William H. 1987. *O Freedom! Afro-American Emancipation Celebrations.* Knoxville: University of Tennessee Press.

Young, Alfred. 1982. The Historical Origin and Significance of the Afro-American History Month Observance. *Negro History Bulletin* 45: 100–101.

Judson L. Jeffries

BLACK SEMINOLES

SEE *Osceola.*

BLACK SEPTEMBER

The Black September Organization (BSO) was a Palestinian terrorist group most active in the early 1970s. The BSO named itself after the particularly bloody month in 1970 when King Hussein of Jordan declared military rule, expelling and killing thousands of Palestinian *fedayeen* (self-sacrificers). These *fedayeen* threatened to undermine Hussein's power in working with a "state within a state," the Palestine Liberation Organization (PLO), established to mobilize the Palestinian population against Israel. Black September most likely began as the

Revenging Palestinians, a group dedicated to avenging the death of Abu Ali Iyad, the last charismatic leader of the *fedayeen*, whose torture and murder was intended as a symbol of defeat for the Palestinian guerrillas. After regrouping in Lebanon, where they were given control of fifteen refugee camps by the government, the Revolutionary Council of al-Fatah (the PLO's military force) met in Damascus, Syria, and debated whether it should continue using the tactics of Iyad's followers. The council, it is suspected, agreed to remain affiliated with the group, which later renamed itself Black September, and agreed to operate as a clandestine arm of al-Fatah.

Black September carried out its first act of violence on November 28, 1971, with the assassination of Jordanian Prime Minister Wasif al-Tali. Al-Tali, believed to have personally killed Abu Ali Iyad, was attending the Arab League summit in Cairo, Egypt, when four gunmen shot him outside the Sheraton Hotel. The BSO also attempted to assassinate King Hussein and Zaid al-Rifai, Jordan's ambassador to London and former chief of the Jordanian royal court, in December 1971. These acts of revenge foreshadowed several bold attempts that the BSO would make to alter the political landscape of the Middle East and advance the cause of the Palestinian people.

The BSO is probably best known for taking members of the Israeli team as hostages on September 5 of the 1972 Munich Olympics. In return for the hostages, the BSO demanded the release of roughly 220 prisoners (mostly Palestinian) from West German and Israeli jails. After attempts to negotiate failed, the BSO members demanded to be transported by helicopters, with the Israelis in tow, to the nearby military base of Furstenfeldbruck, where they hoped to board a jetliner that would allow them to escape to an Arab country. Shooting broke out between German officials and the BSO at Furstenfeldbruck as West Germany made its last attempt to prevent the hostages from being taken out of the country. By the end of the bloody ordeal early September 6, all eleven Israeli hostages were dead (two at the Olympic village, the other nine at Furstenfeldbruck). Also killed were five members of the BSO and one German police officer, shot at the airbase.

In response to the massacre at Munich, Israel declared war on terrorist activity and targeted Black September and al-Fatah equally. Some of Israel's immediate retaliatory acts included killing hundreds of people, most of whom are believed to have been unaffiliated with the terrorist group, during raids of Palestinian refugee camps in Lebanon and Syria. These attacks added to already existing tensions between Israel and its neighboring Arab nations, and they would ultimately lead to further military conflict. In the fall of 1973 the PLO dissolved Black September. A year later Yassir Arafat, the PLO's leader, ordered his followers to withdraw from acts of violence outside Israel, the West Bank, and the Gaza Strip.

SEE ALSO *Palestine Liberation Organization (PLO)*

BIBLIOGRAPHY

Dobson, Christopher. 1974. *Black September: Its Short, Violent History*. New York: Macmillan Publishing.

Morris, Benny. 2001. *Righteous Victims: A History of the Zionist-Arab Conflict, 1881–2001*. New York: Vintage Books.

Tehama Lopez

BLACK SOCIOLOGISTS

Because race and social inequality have been central points of concern in sociology, it is not surprising that the discipline has a rich and deep history of contributions from African American sociologists. Indeed, prior to the emergence of sociology as a formal field of inquiry, African Americans were constructing and applying what would later become bedrock tools for sociological research. One such individual was Ida B. Wells (1862–1931), a journalist and social activist who documented and advocated against the lynching of African Americans in the postbellum South. In order to make her case she conducted what may have been the first formal field studies of lynchings. She accumulated statistics on the frequencies of lynchings and assessed that data in terms of the rationals given (at least in public records) for these events and the socioeconomic conditions of the communities where such events occurred. Ultimately, she discovered that occurrences of lynchings were not so much due to perceived or actual incidents of sexual interaction between African American men and white American women, but to vast increases in the business activity and economic success of African Americans residing in or near communities where lynchings occurred. Having conducted her investigations in the late 1800s, Wells stands as a pioneer figure in the statistical analysis of causal relationships.

A few years after Wells's foray into social analysis, W. E. B. Du Bois (1868–1963) initiated a more formal sociological agenda for research on black Americans. In publishing *The Philadelphia Negro* (1899), Du Bois introduced a multimethod approach (including ethnography, demographic and document analysis, and historical inquiry) for the purpose of producing a comprehensive study of an urban-based, African American residential community. Du Bois also published *The Souls of Black Folk* (1903), which helped establish, among other objectives, a tradition of social theoretical considerations or the social significance of race, racial identity, and race relations.

Anna Julia Cooper (1858?–1964) was a much-less recognized, but still highly significant, contributor to a black sociological tradition. She was the first African American woman to obtain a PhD in sociology (receiving one in 1925 from the Sorbonne in France, decades after she completed the majority of her writings). In her work, mostly published in the late nineteenth century, she argued for a feminist perspective on the African American condition by exploring what she believed to be the rightful place of women in both civic affairs and on the home front.

In the decades following the contribution of these figures, and after the founding of the first department of sociology in the United States (at the University of Chicago in 1895), other African Americans emerged in the discipline to advance research on, and interpretation of, the African American social condition. In the first half of the twentieth century, the University of Chicago's Department of Sociology produced: E. Franklin Frazier (1894–1962), who pursued a social-organizational approach to studying the African American family and African American adjustment to the urban sphere as a result of the southern to northern migration; Charles S. Johnson (1893–1956), who studied the social-psychological impact of racism and discrimination on African Americans; St. Clair Drake (1911–1990), perhaps more formally known as an anthropologist, but who, with sociology student Horace Cayton (1903–1970), explored the cultural and social-interactive dimensions of African American adjustment to the urban sphere; and Oliver C. Cox (1901–1974), who introduced a Marxist-informed paradigm for exploring what he regarded to be the caste-like arrangement of racial groups in the United States, which he also situated in a larger world-systems framework for understanding how capitalism encouraged racial subordination and conflict. Other African American sociologists who published between 1910 and 1950 also contributed to a canon of African American sociology that largely focused on the social problems and prospects associated with African American migration to metropolitan regions (e.g., Ira de Augustine Reid [1901–1968] and George Edmund Haynes [1880–1960]).

By the post–World War II era, many African American sociologists began expressing frustration with the dominant sociological paradigm that emphasized assimilation and adaptation to a rapidly maturing Western capitalist society. Their frustrations were not only based on the historical exclusion of African American sociologists from the canon of the discipline, but also the perceived inadequacy of assimilation perspectives for interpreting the social condition and possibilities of the African American community. This frustration, coupled with the motivation to pursue new frames of thinking, were captured in *The Death of White Sociology* (1973)

edited by Joyce Ladner. In this and other works produced between 1960 and the early 1970s, many African American sociologists began calling for studies of the positive aspects of African American identity and the virtues of varied patterns of family formation, peer associations, and other social processes and organizational dynamics that reflected strong differences between black Americans and others in the American landscape.

While some of the claims and arguments made during this period were challenged in later years for being more polemical than scholarly, the efforts of many African American sociologists during that time did result in the creation of the Association of Black Sociologists in 1972 (which, itself, had origins in the Black Sociology Caucus, which was created following the 1969 American Sociological Association meetings in San Francisco). The creation of the association resulted in there being a more pervasive sense that African American sociologists had achieved a visible and durable status in the mainstream areas of the discipline. Since the 1960s, some African American sociologists assumed central positions in the discipline as they helped introduce or define areas of inquiry that constitute much of the contemporary agenda of the discipline. For instance, urban poverty research became a major subfield in sociology as a result of the publications of William Julius Wilson, who emphasized the importance of taking a structural perspective on the social location and concentration of the urban poor as a foundation for better understanding certain behavioral and cultural dynamics that became manifest for this constituency. Furthermore, Patricia Hill Collins has advanced African American feminist theory in sociology through her publications. Moreover, Lawrence Bobo has advanced survey research on racial attitudes in the post–civil rights era in the United States.

Professors Wilson, Collins, and Bobo represent some of the most visible African American sociologists in American sociology. One reason for their visibility is that rather than trying to advance a distinct and autonomous field of African American sociology, they have striven to incorporate the ideas, arguments, and methods of sociology more generally into specific considerations of African Americans. The changing American racial landscape, largely a by-product of the civil rights era, created the space for these sociologists to function more effectively as mainstream scholars. Despite their rich and varied contributions, the African American sociologists of previous periods were often relegated to African American higher educational institutions in a segregated southern region of the country, where their work was not incorporated into the mainstream canon of the discipline. Accordingly, the methodological, theoretical, and empirical contributions of these early figures often do not get registered (or do not get registered as fully as they should) as significant moments in the progression of American sociological thought.

The success of figures such as William Julius Wilson and Elijah Anderson in achieving mainstream status has not come without certain criticism. Contemporarily, those and other higher-profile black sociologists have been read as traditionally liberal rather than critical analysts of American social inequality. Consequently, it has been argued that their achieving of mainstream status came about through their promoting or implying more passive and sanitized assessments of mainstream American society rather than the progressive, critically centered, and Marxist-infused perspectives of early figures such as Du Bois and Cox, who indicted American and global capitalism and its cultural manifestations more directly and fully as causal factors for the enduring social predicament of African Americans.

SEE ALSO *American Sociological Association; Sociology*

BIBLIOGRAPHY

Blackwell, James, and Morris Janowitz, eds. 1974. *Black Sociologists: Historical and Contemporary Perspectives.* Chicago: University of Chicago Press.

Bracey, John, August Meier, and Elliott Rudwick. 1971. *The Black Sociologists: The First Half Century.* Belmont, CA: Wadsworth.

McKee, James B. 1993. *Sociology and the Race Problem: The Failure of a Perspective.* Urbana: University of Illinois Press.

Young, Alford A., Jr., and Donald R. Deskins Jr. 2001. Early Traditions of African-American Sociological Thought. *Annual Review of Sociology* 27: 445–477.

Alford A. Young Jr.

BLACK STUDIES

SEE *African American Studies.*

BLACK TOWNS

African Americans have a long history of forming separate settlements and towns in what is today the United States. More than eighty black towns and settlements were established in the United States in the nineteenth and twentieth centuries. Prior to the Civil War, most black settlements were informally organized. Brooklyn, Illinois, founded in 1830 by runaway slaves and Quakers, was an exception to this general rule. Most black towns were formed after the Civil War and could be found all over the United States from Eatonville, Florida, to Allensworth,

California. However, most of these towns were established in the Midwest and Southwest between the end of Reconstruction and World War I. During this period, often referred to as the "nadir" of African American history, many black southerners lost hope that their rights and freedoms would ever be protected in white-dominated communities. Some African Americans contemplated emigrating from the United States to escape the violence, racism, and discrimination they were forced to endure, but others attempted to form separate enclaves within the United States. Although these towns were usually very small, their citizens owned property, governed themselves, educated their children, and ran their own farms and businesses. Like other small towns, over the years black towns often struggled to remain economically viable. Most black towns lasted only a few decades, but a few continue to survive today.

Two of the oldest and longest surviving black towns in the South were Eatonville, Florida, and Mound Bayou, Mississippi. Founded in 1886 and incorporated in 1887, Eatonville was the beloved childhood home of Zora Neale Hurston. Mound Bayou was founded in 1887 by Isaiah T. Montgomery but has its roots in an antebellum slave community known as Davis Bend. Booker T. Washington was a strong supporter of Mound Bayou. Although their development and growth were curtailed by racism and limited economic opportunities, both Eatonville and Mound Bayou continue to function today.

The history of Rosewood, another Florida black town, demonstrates the extreme effects of racism that black towns could be subject to. In January 1923, a white woman from a neighboring community accused a black man of attacking her. Over a period of several days, white vigilantes sought out residents of Rosewood whom they believed aided the alleged attacker. Their attacks escalated from lynching individuals to an all-out assault on the town and its residents. As the town was torched, residents escaped to nearby swamps where they hid for days. Those who did not escape to the swamps, including the elderly and infirm, were murdered. Seventy years later the state of Florida granted reparations to the surviving victims of the riot.

One of the best known black towns in the west, Nicodemus was founded in Kansas in 1877. It was a popular destination for Exodusters, southern blacks led into Kansas by Benjamin "Pap" Singleton. Singleton, a former slave from Tennessee, helped lead a movement of 10,000 to 20,000 blacks from Louisiana and other southern states into Kansas. Although most of the migrants settled in cities, others continued on to live in Nicodemus or one of the other black colonies founded by Singleton and other African Americans in western Kansas. In 1879, at the height of the Kansas migration movement, Nicodemus had a population of about 700 people. Early settlers endured difficult conditions, including bad crops, but they held on to the belief that the railroad would come through their town and make it an economically viable place. Unfortunately, Nicodemus could not survive the decision of the Union Pacific Railroad to build away from the town, and it began to decline by 1887.

Oklahoma was home to more black towns than any other state in the nation. Some of these towns predate 1889, the year the Oklahoma Territory officially opened to non-Indian settlement. Others were founded in Indian Territory before or after Oklahoma statehood in 1907. In the early days of black settlement in Oklahoma, some blacks, led by Edward P. McCabe, lobbied to make the future state all black. McCabe was a native New Yorker, but he had moved to Kansas in 1878, been part of Nicodemus, and then was elected Kansas state auditor. Although his efforts to be appointed territorial governor of Oklahoma failed, McCabe moved to Oklahoma Territory in 1890 and founded the town of Langston, which became home to Langston University in 1897. The choice by founders to give these settlements such names as Langston, Vernon, and Bookertee, in honor of important black statesmen such as John Mercer Langston, William T. Vernon, and Booker T. Washington, reflected the inspirations and aspirations of their inhabitants.

The largest and most famous of Oklahoma's black towns was Boley, founded in 1903 by an interracial group. Unlike many black towns, Boley had a railroad, which brought in new settlers by the carload and shipped their cotton to market. Boley and several other black towns had newspapers that were sold all over the South and used to encourage black Southerners to emigrate to them. By 1910, Boley had a population of over 1,000 with as many as 5,000 black farmers living around the town.

When Oklahoma became a state in 1907, the hopes of black townspeople came to a halt. The first law passed by the new state congress segregated public schools and public conveyances such as trains and streetcars. Then in 1910, the state passed a law that disenfranchised blacks. These laws were accompanied by an increase in violence against blacks. There were lynchings, and some towns and counties tried to run all African Americans out of their borders. In spite of these setbacks, Boley's population remained strong until the late 1920s and 1930s, when the Great Depression forced many of its residents to head to cities in the North and West.

BIBLIOGRAPHY

Crockett, Norman. 1979. *The Black Towns*. Lawrence: Regents Press of Kansas.

Hamilton, Kenneth. 1991. *Black Towns and Profit: Promotion and Development in the Trans-Appalachian West, 1877–1915.* Urbana: University of Illinois Press.

Rose, Harold M. 1965. The All-Negro Town: Its Evolution and Function. *Geographical Review* 55 (3): 362–381.

Melissa Nicole Stuckey

BLACKFACE

Blackface, which dates back to as early as the Middle Ages, is the theater performance practice of wearing soot, cosmetics, paint, or burnt cork to blacken the face. In medieval and Renaissance English theater, blacking up was prevalent in religious cycles and morality plays, where it was used to represent evil, badness, or damnation. Evil characters were portrayed with the color black in order to suggest that they were the antithesis of white, which stood for goodness, purity, or salvation. Blackface was also commonly used as a signifier of negative attributes in other realms of English life. As European global exploration progressed, blackface on the stage began to be used to represent newly encountered peoples of the world.

The sixteenth century witnessed a rise in the variety of blackface characters as a result of the popularity of William Shakespeare's plays. In one of the most famous of Shakespeare's plays, *Othello*, the main character is a Moor, who was often portrayed by a white man in blackface. Shakespeare's plays brought a change in the role of blackface characters from merely symbolizing evil, to signifying the social expectations and ideals of black people. At the same time, the negative attributes of blackface were reflected in the development of the African as the "exotic other" in Western society.

BLACKFACE IN NORTH AMERICA

In the New World, the institution of slavery contributed to the continuance and evolution of blackface characters on the theater stage. In the eighteenth-century United States, white traveling actors known as Ethiopian Delineators, who used burnt cork to blacken their faces, sang slave songs between the acts of plays. These performances, which were given in England as well, slowly began to grow in popularity and developed into lengthy spectacles known as *minstrels* (or *minstrel shows*).

The first mainstream minstrel character, Jim Crow, was introduced in the 1830s by Thomas Dartmouth Rice on a Northern stage. The minstrel show consisted of satirical portrayals of black Southern plantation slaves, presented by white male performers with blackened faces, lips colored to suggest exaggerated size, wooly wigs, and ragged clothing. Minstrel shows were one of the most popular forms of entertainment in the United States from the 1840s to the 1880s, and did much to disseminate and perpetuate negative stereotypes of blacks in America. After the Civil War, African Americans themselves began to blacken up their faces and perform on the minstrel stage. Blackface was also adapted by European immigrants: Irishmen, Italians, and Jews began to blacken their face in minstrel shows during the early twentieth century and developed some of the most popular blackface characters. Blackface offered to these European immigrants a way to become accepted as American whites through their embrace of the racist ideology dominant in the United States. Immigrants erased the negative stereotypes associated with their ethnic group by using blackface to highlight their "normalcy" in comparison to blacks. For blacks in America, however, minstrel shows functioned as venues for their public humiliation and degradation.

The emergence of film as the new dominant entertainment medium led to the transitioning of blackface characters from theater stage to screen. In the 1920s and 1930s, films continued the tradition of the blackface minstrel show. One of the most famous blackface performers was the Jewish actor Al Jolson. The negative stereotypes of blacks that blackface actors created and perpetuated were manifested beyond stage and film in literature, advertisements, comic strips and comic books, postcards, cookie jars, lawn accessories, and other consumer products. The popularity of blackface in American culture influenced its extension to the international community.

INTERNATIONAL BLACKFACE

Traveling theater troupes introduced the blackface satirical performances of the American minstrel to several countries. Ironically, blackface shows that were initiated in England returned within the American minstrel in the mid-nineteenth century. British audiences consumed the blackface performances from the United States and created their own national variant through blackface characters such as the Golliwog.

U.S. influence on the internationalization of blackface is demonstrated by the development of the Cape Town Coon Festival in Cape Town, South Africa. In the late nineteenth century, Orpheus M. McAdoo and the Virginia Jubilee Singers traveled to South Africa, where they remained for almost five years. These traveling troupes introduced the American blackface minstrel performance style and greatly influenced the emergence of the blackened Coon disguise used in a grand festival held in the city center of Cape Town, the origins of which can be traced back to the late 1880s. This festival, the name of which was changed to the Cape Town Minstrel Carnival in 2003, continues to present blackface displays and is one of the area's most famous tourist attractions.

Traveling American minstrel troupes also influenced the development of Cuba's *teatro bufo*, a form of comedic blackface performance featured in musical and theatrical entertainment. Blackface performances first appeared in Cuba in the mid-nineteenth century, as part of a range of satirical representations of the African found throughout Cuban literature, theater, and music.

The broad influence exerted by the American blackface minstrel also contributed to the development of blackface characters in Mexico. Memín Pingüín, a fictional and stereotypical Mexican blackface character, first appeared in a comic book in the 1940s. He was a popular, if controversial, figure, and the comics he was featured in continued to be published until the 1970s. In June 2005, the Mexican Postal Service issued character stamps with images of Memín, sparking international controversy.

The above-mentioned countries are only a few of the many that incorporated blackface: It was also performed in Jamaica, Nigeria, Ghana, India, China, Ukraine, Indonesia, Australia, the Netherlands, and Spain, among numerous other countries. Blackface, which still continues to be performed throughout the world, has done much to continue and disseminate negative stereotypes of African Americans throughout the globe.

SEE ALSO Bamboozled; Birth of a Nation; *Exoticism; Film Industry; Immigrants to North America; Jim Crow; Memín Pinguín; Minstrelsy; Other, The; Racism; Representation; Satire; Stereotypes; Uncle Tom; Whiteness*

BIBLIOGRAPHY

Baxter, Lisa. 2001. Continuity and Change in Cape Town's Coon Carnival: The 1960s and 1970s. *African Studies* 60 (1): 87–105.

Brown, T. Allston, and Charles Day. 1975. Black Musicians and Early Ethiopian Minstrelsy. *The Black Perspective in Music* 3 (1): 77–99.

Cole, Catherine M. 1966. Reading Blackface in West Africa: Wonders Taken for Signs. *Critical Inquiry* 23 (1): 183–215.

Lane, Jill. 2005. *Blackface Cuba, 1840–1895*. Philadelphia: University of Pennsylvania Press.

Rehin, George F. 1975. Harlequin Jim Crow: Continuity and Convergence in Blackface Clowning. *Journal of Popular Culture* 9 (3): 682–701.

Toll, Robert C. 1974. *Blacking Up: The Minstrel Show in Nineteenth-Century America*. New York: Oxford University Press.

Vaughan, Virginia Mason. 2005. *Performing Blackness on English Stages, 1500–1800*. Cambridge, U.K., and New York: Cambridge University Press.

Katrina D. Thompson

BLACKNESS

Blackness is first a descriptive category that refers to people of African descent and the degree to which they look like the African stereotype before and after their biological mixture with other groups in the Atlantic world. The mixtures referred to here began with Africa's contact with Europe and continued with the slave trade, the creation of African communities in the New World, and the rise of colonialism. The varying shades of blackness created competing and contradictory definitions of whiteness and blackness. The phenotypical attributes of individuals—hair texture, dark skin, blunt features, and body type—became the physical markers of blackness, but as these markers were compromised by racial mixture, it became necessary to certify whiteness.

Racial mixture required new terms to ensure the "purity" of whiteness. For example, in Europe, Latin America, and Africa, terms such as *preto* (black), *mulatto* (half-white, or brown), *mestizo* (Indian and white), and many more were commonplace by the eighteenth century. Another means to certify whiteness was to define blackness legally. In the United States, for example, the "one drop rule" rendered anyone with even one known drop of black blood as legally, fractionally black. Racial mixture was codified in law. Mulatto (one-half black), quadroon (one-quarter black), and octoroon (one-eighth black) were social and legal categories to determine who was not fully white. As more and more individuals had features that suggested white ancestry—straight or wavy hair, thin features, or brown to very light skin—blackness based on physical type alone was unstable. In the United States blackness had to include mixtures. In Latin America and elsewhere, mixture was often a means of distancing oneself from blackness but rarely allowing one to be white. In the United States, the only option was to pretend to be white or present oneself as white, provided the physical markers and cultural bearing allowed the deception. This practice was known as "passing" and hundreds, perhaps thousands, managed to pull off the deception.

In South Africa, in contrast, "black" referred to all those of African appearance, and "colored" signaled those of mixed background, with whites as the pure, uncontaminated group. East Indians in South Africa were also a separate group, but in England, East Indians embraced their own version of blackness. Their physical darkness had meaning in this context. Blackness and whiteness are therefore linked in these societies to the extent that who is black can only be ascertained by determining who is white. But blackness also exists in societies with no significant white population. In Guyana and Trinidad, for instance, blackness exists in a population that is dominated by other dark-skinned people: East Indians. Physical features other than color become salient in these societies, and culture takes on profound meaning.

BLACK CONSCIOUSNESS

Blackness, secondly, is a conscious mental attitude expressed in political practice, social organizations, and commitment to the group. It is embraced by those who by law or custom experience racial discrimination and identify themselves as a group in the struggle toward the realization of their aspirations. Black consciousness is also concerned with the consequences of defining oneself as black. It forms the basis for a transnational politics and subjectivity that creates relationships between Africans in Africa and the African diaspora.

In the eighteenth and nineteenth centuries black consciousness was expressed in slave revolts and runaway slave communities known as "maroons." Free blacks organized against slavery as well as struggled for their rightful place in society. After slavery ended, black consciousness took many forms that were grounded in an affirmative black identity. In the postbellum U.S. South, black towns emerged to form self-sustaining communities that remained relatively free from the harsher elements of Jim Crow society. But in this segregated world, the act of choosing separation and becoming economically independent invited the very violence that blacks sought to avoid. By the 1920s not only was lynching commonplace, but inhabitants in all-black towns and the "black backside" of white towns were targets of white terror. The all-black section of Tulsa, Oklahoma, was leveled in 1921 by angry whites who destroyed black businesses, churches, banks, and all signs of black independence. In the same decade, the black inhabitants in Rosewood and Ocoee, Florida, were massacred, their homes and businesses destroyed. Black consciousness that resulted in economic and political parity was not to be tolerated. This racial violence and the discrimination that it supported were key elements in forging a black consciousness and a sense of group affiliation and pride that led to an activism characterized by black self-help and political formations that spoke to needs of the black underclass. Organizations such as the National Association for the Advancement of Colored People (NAACP), the Nation of Islam, the United Negro Improvement Association, the African Blood Brotherhood, the black women's club movement, black unions, and many more fought for black rights and achievement in the early part of the century.

This assertive black mentality found expression in the modern black freedom struggle and the black power movements of the 1960s and 1970s. In the United States, with boycotts of segregated institutions, freedom marches, and political activism, blacks achieved the removal of the most egregious forms of segregation, if not complete economic and social parity. These movements were possible in large measure because of the deep sense of historical and cultural separateness blacks feel as a people. Pride and a commitment to the freedom struggle underpinned a race-based black nationalism that had been evident in the nineteenth century and flowered dramatically in the twentieth century.

Similarly, in Brazil after slavery ended in 1888, former slaves and free blacks struggled to challenge the racial discrimination that relegated them to second-class citizens. Black Brazilians (*pretos*) found themselves locked at the bottom of a hierarchy defined by gradations of color with whites at the top. Morenos, mulattos, and mestizos (mixed race), in contrast, fared better socially and economically. As in all of Latin America, whites in Brazil held political and economic power while colored folk jockeyed for positions relative to whites, often using their distance from blackness as a measure of social and political success. Yet, by the twentieth century, blacks in Brazil had formed organizations that specifically addressed racial discrimination and their position as blacks. In the 1930s they formed the Frente Negra Brasileira (Black Brazilian Front), an organization concerned with racial uplift, integration, and Afro-Brazilian mobility. In the 1970s and 1980s a flurry of organizations appeared in Brazil focusing on blackness and black issues, the most important being the Movimento Negro Unificado (United Black Movement).

In Spanish-speaking America, too, black groups pushed for inclusion through activism and protest. In Cuba, for example, during slavery the *cabildos da nacions* (council of nations) retained ethnic identities and created new ones based on memories from an African past. The survival of African belief systems and cultural forms facilitated an African ethnic consciousness well into the twentieth century. But alongside these African cultural forms, a more generalized black consciousness also emerged that unified free and slave populations. From these formations, leaders with a distinct black consciousness emerged in the late nineteenth century to challenge slavery and efforts to subject black people to white racist domination. One organization that grew from these slave nations and the revolutions in 1868 and 1898 against slavery and Spain was the Partido Independiente de Color, the first black political party in the Americas (1908). Its purpose was to work for inclusion within the Cuban state and a national identity that embraced black people as Cuban. Both Africans (i.e., dark-skinned persons) and mulattos were members of this organization, and they affirmed a black political identity as Afro-Cuban. The efforts to create a Cuban identity that was both black and Cuban resulted in a violent backlash in the race war of 1912, when members of the Partido were massacred by white Cubans. In the aftermath of this massacre, blacks did not abandon their black consciousness, but were forced to articulate that consciousness culturally and intellectually rather than in political organization.

Black voices were more audible in the years after the Cuban Revolution in 1959. Although the economic and social situations improved, racism has not been eliminated and, in some respects, has increased particularly in moments of extreme economic distress. The strength of Afro-Cuban culture and the long tradition of black consciousness in Cuba has created a black Cuban identity that is both black and Cuban.

In other parts of Spanish America, attempts to forge a black identity have met considerable resistance, historically. In Puerto Rico and the Dominican Republic, for example, blackness was not only denied, but also challenged with the powerful ideology of *mestizaje* (the racial and cultural mixing of Amerindians and Europeans), which excludes both blacks and indigenous people. Yet, black groups in each society have maintained their autonomy and challenge the official interpretation of their heritage as Spanish and not African.

The migration of so many Puerto Ricans to the United States has aided the continuation of a black consciousness among both dark-skinned and mixed-race members that often brings them into conflict with white Puerto Ricans. Class differences as well as the overt racism in the United States and Puerto Rico are also important factors in the development of black consciousness among Puerto Ricans. *Mestizaje* has had an even more powerful impact upon Dominicans, and their location in the United States has exposed the contradictions inherent in their physical blackness and their determination to claim a mestizo consciousness despite the racism that they experience in the United States.

In the English-speaking Caribbean, a consciousness based on color emerged during and after slavery. A white colonial class and a colored elite dominated a peasant and working-class black majority. In Jamaica, efforts to challenge this domination took shape in many movements such as Rastafarianism, the Garvey movement, and the black power movements of the 1970s. In Trinidad as well, black consciousness found expression in organizations and challenges to colonial authority. A black power movement emerged there in the 1970s, as it did in several other islands. These movements testify not only to black consciousness in the islands, but also to the links between African societies in the diaspora.

BLACK CULTURAL TRADITION

Blackness, thirdly, is a cultural signature that transcends physical markers, and often transcends, under certain historical conditions, national identifications. It is expressed in language, mannerisms, dress, hairstyles, cultural forms, social organization, and religious practices. Languages formed from the amalgamation of African, European, and Indian languages pepper the west coast of the Atlantic. Dialects and tonal cadences of blackness in English, French, Spanish, Portuguese, and other European languages are spoken in African communities, and often are rejected as part of the larger culture in which the group resides—that is white or European culture.

Black intellectual traditions in all of these societies emphasize the heroic efforts of slave rebels and military leaders such as Haiti's Toussaint Louverture (c. 1739–1803) and Jean-Jacques Dessalines (1758–1806); freedom fighters such as Jamaica's Sam Sharpe (1801–1832) and Marcus Garvey (1887–1940); civil rights giants such as the United States' Martin Luther King Jr. (1929–1968); and revolutionary leaders such as Guyana's Walter Rodney (1942–1980), Puerto Rico's Jesús Colón (1901–1974), Mozambique's Amílcar Cabral (1924–1973), and Ghana's Kwame Nkrumah (1909–1972). Radical thinkers such as the Americans W. E. B. Du Bois (1868–1963) and Richard Wright (1908–1960), the Barbadian Richard B. Moore (1893–1978), the Trinidadian C. L. R. James (1901–1989), the Puerto Rican Arturo Schomburg (1874–1938), the Martinican Frantz Fanon (1925–1961), and the American Malcolm X (1925–1965), among others, established the norms of black thought.

This approach to black consciousness often denies the importance of gender and sexual difference. Feminists and homosexual members of the group also embrace blackness, but in so doing, critique the masculine bias often inherent in notions of race pride, authenticity, and stigmatization. Black intellectual traditions have tended to construct the black subject as masculine and North American, thereby erasing the feminist and diasporic perspectives on black consciousness. These traditions have been equally resistant to homosexual perspectives. The perspectives of women and homosexuals in black communities render black consciousness as a contested terrain of gender and sexual politics, where the very definition of consciousness is at stake.

SEE ALSO *African Americans; African Diaspora; Black Nationalism; Black Power; Coloreds (South Africa); Colorism; Identification, Racial; Jim Crow; Miscegenation; Moreno/a; Mulattos; Pardo; Passing; Phenotype; Racial Classification; Racism; Rastafari; Slavery; Stigma; Whiteness; Whites*

BIBLIOGRAPHY

Hall, Gwendolyn Midlo. 2005. *Slavery and African Ethnicities in the Americas: Restoring the Links.* Chapel Hill: University of North Carolina Press.

Levine, Lawrence W. 1977. *Black Culture, Black Consciousness: Afro-American Folk Thought from Slavery to Freedom.* New York: Oxford University Press.

Naro, Nancy Priscilla, ed. 2003. *Blacks, Coloureds, and National Identity in Nineteenth-Century Latin America.* London: Institute of Latin American Studies.

Nwankwo, Ifeoma Kiddoe. 2005. *Black Cosmopolitanism: Racial Consciousness and Transnational Identity in the Nineteenth-Century Americas.* Philadelphia: University of Pennsylvania Press.

Stinchcomb, Dawn F. 2004. *The Development of Literary Blackness in the Dominican Republic.* Gainesville: University of Press of Florida.

Wright, Michelle M. 2004. *Becoming Black: Creating Identity in the African Diaspora.* Durham, NC: Duke University Press.

Tiffany Ruby Patterson

BLACKS

SEE *African Americans; Blackness.*

BLAIR, TONY
1953–

Born on May 6, 1953, in Edinburgh, Scotland, Tony Blair was elected Member of Parliament (MP) for Sedgefield in 1983. He became leader of the Labour Party in 1994, and prime minister of the United Kingdom (UK) in 1997. He played a key role in resetting Labour Party policy in the early 1990s, a resetting designed to address three things: Labour's inability to win general elections; the impact of Prime Minister Margaret Thatcher's neoliberal policies on UK politics and society; and the need to reposition the United Kingdom in the new global age. Blair responded to four election defeats in a row by reaching out to median floating voters, and by making real and symbolic breaks with Labour's previous policy stance. He responded to Margaret Thatcher's powerful legacy by linking her passion for markets to Labour's traditional commitment to social justice. He actively welcomed globalization as a trigger to UK economic competitiveness and as an arena in which a Labour government could play a more active and ethical role.

Blair led the Labour Party to three election victories in a row, the first two (1997, 2001) with huge majorities (179 and 167 seats in the House of Commons, respectively). The 1997 victory came after a relabeling of the Labour Party as New Labour, and the rejection of what had hitherto been many of Labour's defining policies. Out went public ownership, "tax and spend" welfare policies, unilateral nuclear disarmament, and withdrawal from the European Union. In came private funds for public investment, a freeze on direct taxation, a welfare-to-work program, and a new pro-European ethical foreign policy.

Over time, New Labor under Blair traded increased spending on health and education for public service agreements linking resources to the achievement of rising performance targets. His government made extensive use of private funds for capital projects in the public sector, and increased the degree of market competition allowed between public service providers. Blair governments also developed social policies that traded rights for responsibilities, tackling social exclusion and child poverty while simultaneously toughening the criminal code, restricting immigration, and even punishing parents for the truancy of their children.

New Labour under Blair's leadership played a crucial leadership role in the European response to the crisis in the Balkans, in the wake of which Blair spoke regularly of the need for the international community to be proactive to avoid crimes against humanity. Accordingly, he was the key architect of the broad coalition of support for the U.S.-led invasion of Afghanistan after the September 11, 2001, terrorist attacks; and, more controversially, he remained President George W. Bush's main ally in the subsequent invasion of Iraq.

Blair's final years in office were blighted by growing unease—in party circles and the wider electorate—with the consequences of privatization in the welfare sector and of his close alliance with the United States in Iraq. That unease was compounded by tensions with his chancellor of the exchequer over a deal, struck in 1994, that Blair would eventually cede the premiership to him. Relationships soured over time between the factions formed around each man, eventually forcing Blair reluctantly to announce that he would resign office in 2007.

SEE ALSO *Iraq-U.S. War; Labour Party (Britain); Parliament, United Kingdom; Social Exclusion; Thatcher, Margaret*

BIBLIOGRAPHY

Coates, David. 2005. *Prolonged Labour: The Slow Birth of New Labour Britain*. Houndmills, U.K.: Palgrave.

Coates, David, and Joel Krieger. 2004. *Blair's War*, Cambridge, U.K.: Polity.

David Coates

BLAMING THE VICTIM

SEE *Culture of Poverty.*

BLANQUEMIENTO

SEE *Whitening.*

BLAU, PETER M.
1918–2002

Peter M. Blau, the son of nonpracticing Jews, was born on February 7, 1918, the year that the Austro-Hungarian Empire fell. While in high school, Blau wrote articles for the underground socialist worker's newspaper. Arrested at age 17, he was convicted of high treason and incarcerated by the Austrian fascist government. Meanwhile, Hitler was attempting to build the Nazi Party in Austria. That same year, 1936, the Austrian chancellor Kurt Schuschnigg conceded to Hitler that he would lift the ban on political activity, and so freed all political dissidents. Blau was allowed to finish high school.

Hitler and his troops officially took over power of Austria on March 13, 1938. Blau, having applied for a visa to emigrate, attempted to cross the Czech border. There the Nazi border patrol captured him and tortured and detained him for two months.

He lived in Prague until the Nazis invaded Czechoslovakia. Peter returned to visit his family for one night. He managed to go by the last train to France, where he was arrested and detained in a labor camp as an "enemy alien." When his visa number came up, he waited in Le Havre for passage and had the good fortune to meet theologians who, to his great surprise and exceeding pleasure, gave him a refugee scholarship to attend Elmhurst College.

Blau attended Elmhurst College in Illinois, majoring in sociology. After completing his BA, Blau volunteered for the U.S. Army and served in the Normandy Invasion. He later learned that his family had been murdered in Auschwitz in May 1942, the same year he graduated from college.

His sociological writings amplify his conviction that democracy and human reason will prevail and his belief that one can judge a society by the extent that it fosters fairness and equality. He was profoundly skeptical of claims to personal authority, as distinct from ethical imperatives that emanated from widely shared norms. For his achievements, Blau received notable distinctions: election to the National Academy of Sciences, the American Philosophical Society, the American Academy of Arts and Sciences, and the presidency of the American Sociological Society. He taught at the University of Chicago, Columbia University, the State University of New York at Albany, Tianjin University, and the University of North

Carolina at Chapel Hill. Blau continued to enjoy teaching into his eighties.

Blau did pioneering work in four areas of sociology: organizations, social exchange, stratification, and intergroup relations. While his empirical work on organizations of many kinds was central to the development of organizational sociology, and *Exchange and Power in Social Life* (1964) continues to influence research on interpersonal interaction, here only the latter two areas are highlighted.

With his coauthor Otis Dudley Duncan, Blau, in *The American Occupational Structure* (1967), developed a radical new way of studying intergenerational social mobility. This work examined how social stratification occurs across generations and how factors such as education, occupation, and income determine an individual's status to a lesser or greater degree than the parents' status. This work stimulated an entire field of substantive research on occupation and mobility while developing new methods of structural equation modeling and processes of analyzing multidimensional data that remain in use.

Inequality and Heterogeneity (1977) and *Crosscutting Social Circles*, coauthored with Joseph Schwartz (1984), deal thematically with the sorts of social conditions in metropolitan communities that best bridge group differences. In *Inequality and Heterogeneity*, Blau lays out three parameters of communities: the extent to which communities are diverse along multiple dimensions; the extent to which there are prevailing inequalities; and the extent to which inequalities cut across group differences or are confounded with group differences. In *Crosscutting Social Circles*, Blau and Schwartz examine variation within 125 metropolitan communities, focusing on the extent to which inequalities are random or vary systematically across and within groups. Next they ask how such variation affects intergroup relations, as measured by intermarriage, and how heterogeneity promotes social equality.

In a career of more than fifty years, Blau played an important role in shaping the field of modern sociology. Many of the inquiries upon which he embarked became the basis for new fields and methodologies of mainstream sociology. His theories of social exchange, social structure, wealth distribution, diversity, and social reproduction are still widely used.

Blau conveyed in his writings a confidence that American institutions are inherently reasonable and that American educational institutions are open. He was optimistic that American society would be increasingly inclusive. As a private citizen, he was a socialist, supported dissenters and activists, and was impatient with the United States for being less than what he dreamed it to be in his early years. His political and social convictions are veiled in his work, as perhaps was the case with other social scientists of his generation.

Except in *Exchange and Power in Social Life*, which advances a number of sensitizing concepts, Blau used statistical techniques to answer the questions he posed. Heavily influenced by Karl Popper's approach to scientific reasoning and falsification of hypotheses, much of Blau's work illustrates how rigorous social science can be, while it masks his understanding of the important role that an author's passion for truth and justice plays in scholarly pursuits.

SEE ALSO *Networks*

BIBLIOGRAPHY

PRIMARY WORKS

Blau, Peter. 1955. *The Dynamics of Bureaucracy.* Chicago: University of Chicago Press, Rev. ed., 1963.

Blau, Peter. 1956. *Bureaucracy in Modern Society.* New York: Random House.

Blau, Peter. 1962. *Formal Organizations* (with W. Richard Scott). San Francisco: Chandler.

Blau, Peter. 1964. *Exchange and Power in Social Life.* New York: Wiley.

Blau, Peter. 1967. *The American Occupational Structure* (with Otis Dudley Duncan). New York: Wiley.

Blau, Peter. 1971. *The Structure of Organizations* (with Richard A. Schoenherr). New York: Wiley.

Blau, Peter. 1973. *The Organization of Academic Work.* New York: Wiley.

Blau, Peter. 1974. *On the Nature of Organizations.* New York: Wiley.

Blau, Peter. 1977. *Inequality and Heterogeneity.* New York: Free Press.

Blau, Peter. 1984. *Crosscutting Social Circles* (with Joseph E. Schwartz). Orlando, FL: Academic Press.

Blau, Peter. 1994. *Structural Contexts of Opportunities.* Chicago: University of Chicago Press.

SECONDARY WORK

Calhoun, Craig, Marshall W. Meyer, and W. Richard Scott, eds. 1990. *Structures of Power and Constraint: Papers in Honor of Peter M. Blau.* New York: Cambridge University Press.

Reva Blau
Judith Blau

BLINDER-OAXACA DECOMPOSITION TECHNIQUE

The Blinder-Oaxaca decomposition technique, or simply the Oaxaca decomposition, decomposes wage differentials into two components: a portion that arises because two comparison groups, on average, have different qualifications or credentials (e.g., years of schooling and experience in the labor market) when both groups receive the same treatment (explained component), and a portion that arises because one group is more favorably treated than the other given the same individual characteristics (unexplained component). The two portions are also called *characteristics* and *coefficients effect* using the terminology of regression analysis, which provides the basis of this decomposition technique. The coefficients effect is frequently interpreted as a measure of labor market discrimination. For a comprehensive review of issues related to labor market discrimination, see Joseph Altonji and Rebecca Blank (1999).

The Blinder-Oaxaca decomposition technique is named after two economists, Alan Blinder and Ronald Oaxaca, who introduced it to economic literature in the early 1970s. A similar version of this technique was explored in sociology during the late 1960s and early 1970s in order to examine sources of racial wage differentials (e.g., Duncan 1969; Althauser and Wigler 1972). The Blinder-Oaxaca decomposition technique has provided a practical way to apply economist Gary Becker's (1971) definition of discrimination as unequal treatment among equivalent people due to race or gender. This decomposition technique has become a basic tool for studying racial and gender wage differentials and discrimination, and it has been allowed in court litigation on discrimination (Ashenfelter and Oaxaca 1987).

ILLUSTRATION

Suppose that only years of schooling affect the determination of wages for men and women. The illustration can be easily extended to a more complicated model in which several variables help determine wages. A linear equation is estimated using a regression technique in statistics. The two equations, the first for men and the second for women, are: $W_M = \alpha_M + \beta_M S_M + e_M$, and $W_F = \alpha_F + \beta_F S_F + e_F$, where W is wages; α and β are the intercept and the coefficient of years of schooling (S); e is an error term; and subscript M and F are men and women, respectively. Economists usually use the natural logarithm of wages for W, while sociologists usually use level wages.

In order to examine sources of wage differentials between men and women, a counterfactual equation is constructed where women are treated as men. In other words, the intercept and coefficient in the women's equation are replaced by those of the men's equation. The counterfactual equation becomes $W_F^* = \alpha_M + \beta_M S_F + e_F$. Wage differentials between men and women, on average, can be decomposed into a characteristics effect $\overline{W}_M - \overline{W}_F^* = \beta_M(\overline{S}_M - \overline{S}_F)$, that is, differences between men's wages and counterfactual wages, and a coefficients effect $\overline{W}_F^* - \overline{W}_F = (\alpha_M - \alpha_F) + (\beta_M - \beta_F)\overline{S}_F$, that is,

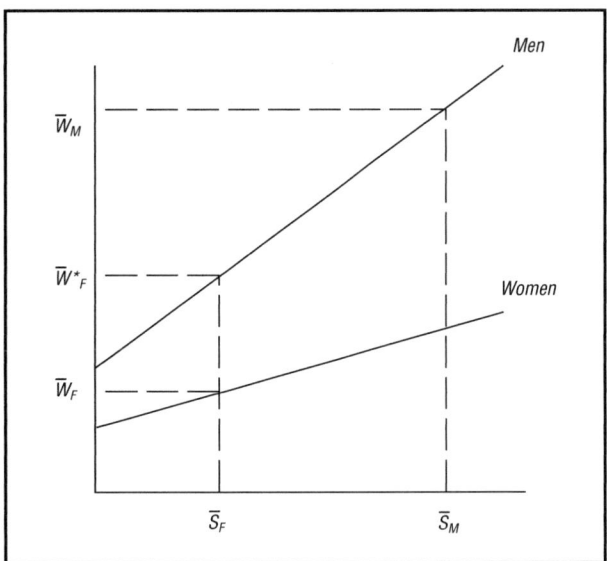

Figure 1

differences between counterfactual wages and women's wages. The Blinder-Oaxaca decomposition equation is:
$$\overline{W}_M - \overline{W}_F = [\beta_M(\overline{S}_M - \overline{S}_F)] + [(\alpha_M - \alpha_F) + (\beta_M - \beta_F)\overline{S}_F].$$

Figure 1 shows the intuition behind the Blinder-Oaxaca decomposition technique. The diagram depicts a situation where men start off at higher wages without schooling (higher intercept) and receive a bigger payoff for each year of schooling (steeper slope). The wage differentials due to differences in intercepts and coefficients $\overline{W}_F^* - \overline{W}_F$, that is, the increases in wages when women are treated as men, are attributed to coefficients effect or discrimination. The remaining wage differentials $\overline{W}_M - \overline{W}_F^*$, the characteristics effect, arises because women have fewer years of schooling than men, although women are treated as men.

INTERPRETATION

The existence of discrimination and its measurement using the Blinder-Oaxaca decomposition technique has been a center of controversy. Those who believe that discrimination does not exist in the labor market or that the Blinder-Oaxaca decomposition technique overestimates the degree of discrimination point out that the wage equation cannot include all relevant variables measuring skills and individual productivity; hence, observationally equivalent people based on the characteristics in the wage equation may not be equivalent. In Figure 1, for example, the same years of schooling do not guarantee that both men and women are equally productive because men may be more motivated for work; therefore, the coefficients effect is not due to discrimination but to unobserved differences in productivity between men and women. As long as people believe that the two comparison groups possess systematically different but difficult to observe characteristics, such as motivation, ability, and effort, they will argue that the measure of discrimination from the Blinder-Oaxaca decomposition technique is biased, and gross wage differentials can be explained by differences in skills and productivity between the two groups.

On the other hand, those who believe that there is prevalent discrimination or that the magnitude of discrimination is bigger than the coefficients effect itself argue that even differences in qualifications and credentials may be the result of premarket discrimination. In Figure 1, for example, it is possible that women were discouraged against pursuing higher education due to existing discriminatory barriers in the labor market (e.g., the glass ceiling) and elsewhere in the economy. Though current employers are not responsible for the different levels of schooling between men and women, society is. Therefore, those who believe in widespread discrimination in society may argue that the coefficients effect underestimates the magnitude of discrimination; hence, gross wage differentials may be an outcome of discrimination.

EXTENSIONS

In spite of the difficulties in interpreting the Blinder-Oaxaca decomposition equation, this decomposition technique has provided a starting point for studying racial and gender wage differentials and discrimination since its introduction in the early 1970s. Although the Blinder-Oaxaca decomposition technique was introduced to decompose racial and gender wage differentials, this technique is also suitable for studying changes in wages over time. In this case, the characteristics effect represents wage growth arising from changes in qualifications and credentials over time, and the coefficients effect shows changes in wages due to structural changes in wage determination over time. In principle, the Blinder-Oaxaca decomposition technique can be applied to decomposing differentials or changes of any continuous variable, such as hours of work. The flexibility of this technique is further demonstrated by extending it to decomposing differences or changes in binary choice variables, such as the labor-market participation rate (e.g., Yun 2004), and differences or changes in wage inequality measured with variances of log wages (e.g., Yun 2006). The Blinder-Oaxaca decomposition technique has been and will continue to be widely used in studying differences and changes in various socioeconomic variables due to its simplicity and flexibility in implementation, and the insights it offers.

SEE ALSO *Discrimination; Economics, Labor*

BIBLIOGRAPHY

Althauser, Robert P., and Michael Wigler. 1972. Standardization and Component Analysis. *Sociological Methods and Research* 1 (1): 97–135.

Altonji, Joseph G., and Rebecca M. Blank. 1999. Race and Gender in the Labor Market. In *Handbook of Labor Economics*, Vol. 3C, eds. Orley Ashenfelter and David Card, 3143–3259. Amsterdam: Elsevier.

Ashenfelter, Orley, and Ronald Oaxaca. 1987. The Economics of Discrimination: Economists Enter the Courtroom. *American Economic Review* 77 (2): 321–325.

Becker, Gary S. 1971. *The Economics of Discrimination*. 2nd ed. Chicago: University of Chicago Press.

Blinder, Alan S. 1973. Wage Discrimination: Reduced Form and Structural Estimates. *Journal of Human Resources* 8 (4): 436–455.

Duncan, Otis D. 1969. Inheritance of Poverty or Inheritance of Race. In *On Understanding Poverty: Perspectives from the Social Sciences*, ed. Daniel P. Moynihan, 85–110. New York: Basic Books.

Oaxaca, Ronald L. 1973. Male-Female Wage Differentials in Urban Labor Markets. *International Economic Review* 14 (3): 693–709.

Yun, Myeong-Su. 2004. Decomposing Differences in the First Moment. *Economics Letters* 82 (2): 273–278.

Yun, Myeong-Su. 2006. Earnings Inequality in USA, 1969–1999: Comparing Inequality Using Earnings Equations. *Review of Income and Wealth* 52 (1): 127–144.

Myeong-Su Yun

BLOC VOTE

The term *bloc voting* (or *block voting*) refers to a set of voting systems used to elect several representatives from one constituency. Although there are significant variations in types of bloc voting, they all allow voters to cast multiple votes for one or more candidates and have the potential to result in several officials being elected based on one specific distribution of voter choices. Among the variables associated with different types of bloc voting are the number of votes available to each voter, the possibility of candidate ranking, and the decision rule for determining winners (Farrell 2001). These variables have consequences with regards to the advantages and disadvantages experienced by different aggregations of voters (see the excellent essays in Grofman and Lijphart 1986).

In *plurality bloc voting*, all candidates compete with one another. Each voter is allowed to cast one vote per candidate. The total number of votes available to a voter is the same as the number of seats to be filled. The candidates who are victorious are those who receive the highest number of votes. In some systems with plurality bloc voting, voters are required to cast all five of their votes for any one of their votes to count. This is sometimes referred to as a full ballot requirement. Plurality bloc voting allows one majority of voters, if it has a consistent set of preferences, to select all candidates to office. Such voting can be especially detrimental to the interests of a minority of voters who have preferences different from those of the majority.

Preferential bloc voting is a system in which voters are required to rank candidates by first-choice preference to the *n*th preference, with *n* referring to the number of positions to be filled. No two candidates can receive the same preference ranking from any one voter. Candidates who receive the smallest number of first-choice rankings are eliminated in the first round of counting. The second-choice preferences of these voters are then counted as their first-choice preferences and distributed to the relevant candidates. The process of elimination of the candidates with the lowest first-choice preferences continues until the top *n* redistributed first-choice candidates are identified.

Another type of bloc voting is referred to as *cumulative voting*. In this system, each voter is given a number of votes equal to the total number of positions to be filled. Voters, however, are able to express the intensity of their preferences for candidates by casting all of their votes for one candidate or otherwise distributing one, two, three, or four votes for one or more candidates. In such a system, tactical voting through strategic aggregation to enhance the probability that a voter's first choice candidate(s) will be chosen is possible.

A related type of bloc voting is *limited voting*. In this system, voters are given a number of votes smaller than the total number of elected positions to be filled. Voters can either be required to cast one vote per candidate or group their votes as in cumulative voting. Among the identified advantages of limited voting is the way that it prevents one majority of voters from electing all of their highest-choice candidates to office. As a result, aggregations of voters with preferences distinct from this majority are guaranteed some success. Limited voting can result in a selection of officials that is more consistent with the proportional distribution of voter preferences.

Specific aggregations of voter choices, especially when two such groupings are in opposition to one another, are sometimes referred to as manifestations of a bloc vote. As discussed above, different types of bloc-voting systems can directly affect the chances that a specific type of block vote will appear.

SEE ALSO *First-past-the-post; Plurality; Voting; Voting Schemes; Winner-Take-All Society*

BIBLIOGRAPHY

Farrell, David M. 2001. *Electoral Systems: A Comparative Introduction*. New York: St. Martin's Press.

Grofman, Bernard, and Arend Lijphart, eds. 1986. *Electoral Laws and Their Political Consequences*. New York: Agathon Press.

Luis Ricardo Fraga

BLOCK RECURSIVE MODELS
SEE *Recursive Models.*

BLOOD AND BLOODLINE

"Blood" is a historical explanation for inherited traits that were believed to pass through "bloodlines," meaning lines of kinship descent. This understanding of heredity derives from the ancient Greek concept that eventually became known as pangenesis. Hippocrates believed that "pangenes" formed throughout the human body. The Greeks conceived of pangenes as tiny pieces of body parts, which moved through bodily fluids into the genitals, from which they were passed on to offspring.

The theory of pangenesis was revitalized by European scientists in the seventeenth century. In the mid-nineteenth century, American racial scientists began to posit a scientific link between bloodlines, culture, and racial groups. According to this view, bloodlines determined one's behavioral traits as well as physiological traits. This theory of heredity profoundly influenced European conceptions of kinship and group identity and formed a scientific justification for racism. Modern science did not fully supplant pangenesis until the twentieth century.

As biologists began in the late nineteenth century to move away from pangenetic theories, the parallel science of biometrical eugenics emerged. Eugenics preserved the notion of blood heredity, thus permitting scientific racism to hold sway well into the mid-twentieth century. Francis Galton (1822–1911), a pioneering eugenicist, argued that human intervention was needed "to give to the more suitable races or strains of blood a better chance of prevailing speedily over the less suitable than they otherwise would have had" (Field 1911). Such intervention—or eugenics—would involve ensuring that people of different races did not intermarry or interbreed, thus preserving the blood purity of the superior races, thereby ensuring the continuing transmission of their superiority through their bloodlines.

At the peak period of the eugenics movement's influence in the United States between 1910 and 1930, numerous federal and state laws were passed that reflected the obsession with purity of blood and the desire to regulate bloodlines. Existing antimiscegenation laws were strengthened and more rigorously enforced. Madison Grant (1865–1937), a leading eugenicist, wrote in *The Passing of the Great Race* (1916): "When it becomes thoroughly understood that the children of mixed marriages between contrasted races belong to the lower type, the importance of transmitting in unimpaired purity the blood inheritance of ages will be appreciated at its full value."

Consequently, a recent cultural innovation—the "one drop" definition of nonwhiteness—was institutionalized into law in a number of American states. The one-drop doctrine held that a person with any nonwhite ancestry whatsoever in his or her ancestral bloodlines could not legally be classified as white. Virginia's Racial Integrity Act of 1924 was the classic expression of one-drop doctrine, holding that "the term 'white person' shall apply only to such person as has no trace whatever of any blood other than Caucasian." Virginia's act prohibited interracial marriage, mandated that the race of every newborn be recorded and registered with the state government, and provided for a penalty of up to a year in prison for making a false report of racial identity.

Eugenic initiatives eventually moved beyond segregation and antimiscegenation laws. From the 1920s through the 1940s, a number of states in the United States set up programs to medically sterilize people defined as inferior—primarily on the basis of perceived mental disability—to ensure that they would not reproduce their traits in offspring. The Eugenics Record Office constructed pedigrees on thousands of families and determined that people who were mentally disabled came mostly from poor and minority families. Such findings only reinforced stereotypes of inferior bloodlines.

Eugenics principles were also invoked to justify anti-immigrant initiatives and exclusionary laws in the United States. Most notable was the Immigration Restriction Act of 1924, which was specifically intended to drastically reduce the flow of immigration of Italians and eastern European Jews, whom eugenicists considered to be of inferior stock. Australia, Canada, and New Zealand also passed exclusionary laws based on race, motivated by scientific racist notions of inferior bloodlines. Eugenics also took hold in some Latin American countries, where elites advocated increased immigration from Europe and the eradication of indigenous groups. The goal was to "whiten" society by reducing the number of nonwhite bloodlines. In Brazilian Portuguese this process was known as *branqueamento*. In Argentinean Spanish it was called *blanqueamiento*.

The most extreme form of eugenics took place in Nazi Germany, where Adolph Hitler's obsession with blood purity led not only to antimiscegenation and sterilization programs but also an expansion into full-blown genocide against minority groups. The notion of a "Final Solution"—the extermination of inferior bloodlines—was not original to Hitler. It had already been entertained by Madison Grant, the prominent American eugenicist.

While scientific racism was significantly discredited in the late twentieth century, the use of blood as a metaphor for kinship remains firmly ensconced in popular discourse. The use of "blood quantum" persists in federal law, which mandates a requisite minimum of one-quarter Indian blood to qualify for some services reserved to American Indians. Most American Indian tribes have written their own laws mandating a minimum blood quantum as a requirement for tribal citizenship.

Some people have found ways to take advantage of American culture's unresolved relationship with the notion of bloodlines. There are numerous cases in which an apparently white person claims an invisible "one drop" of black or Indian blood in order to gain access to minority entitlements. For example, in 1985 Boston firefighters Philip and Paul Malone were found guilty of "racial fraud" for falsely claiming a black grandmother in order to receive affirmative action employment advantages. More recently, Ward Churchill enjoyed a long career as a Cherokee academic and activist before being exposed by the Indian tribe in which he falsely claimed enrollment.

The archaic and scientifically discredited notion of blood as racial-ethnic identity persists in contemporary culture, bolstered by the historical echoes of pangenesis to be found in popular misunderstanding of DNA research. Many new business enterprises sprang up in the early twenty-first century that were designed to capitalize on this misconception, playing on the old theme of racial-ethnic bloodlines. For a fee, one can submit a DNA sample that firms purport to use to determine the percentages of various racial and ethnic identities in a person's ancestral pedigree.

SEE ALSO *Ethnicity; Eugenics; Heredity; Hitler, Adolf; Kinship; Miscegenation; Multiracials in the USA; Nationalism and Nationality; Nazism; Race Mixing; Racial Classification; Racism; Social Exclusion; Whitening*

BIBLIOGRAPHY

Field, James A. 1911. The Progress of Eugenics. *The Quarterly Journal of Economics* 26 (1): 1–67.

Gould, Stephen Jay. 1996. *The Mismeasure of Man*. Rev. ed. New York: Norton.

Grant, Madison. 1970. *Passing of the Great Race, Or, the Racial Basis of European History* (American Immigration Collection, Ser 2). Ayer Co Pub; Reprint edition (October 1970).

Smith, J. David. 1993. *The Eugenic Assault on America: Scenes in Red, White, and Black*. Fairfax, VA: George Mason University Press.

Thomas F. Brown

BLOODY LEGISLATION

SEE *Primitive Accumulation*.

BLUE COLLAR AND WHITE COLLAR

Studies of the nature of blue-collar and white-collar work are conducted in a variety of social sciences, most notably economics and sociology. Although methodologies often differ in those disciplines—for example, sociologists are more likely to perform case studies, whereas economists generally use statistical analyses—the underlying phenomena are the same. Both fields study the decision-making behavior of workers, including how they choose an occupation and what constrains their choices. Those occupational choices affect their work lives, their social class, and the society as a whole. For instance, in 1945 the humorist and poet Odgen Nash observed, "People who work sitting down get paid more than people who work standing up." Many people who work standing up are employed in blue-collar jobs, and most people who work sitting down are in white-collar occupations.

DEFINING BLUE-COLLAR AND WHITE-COLLAR WORK

The distinction between blue collar and white collar arose from the blue uniforms traditionally worn by men performing manual labor, in contrast to the white button-down shirts worn by men in professional occupations. These uniforms have become less prevalent with time, but it is possible to observe important differences between those occupational classifications. Blue-collar work can be unskilled, low-skilled, or highly skilled, ranging from relatively simple assembly-line manufacturing to the use of computerized equipment by automobile mechanics. Unskilled work does not require a great deal of training or human capital formation. Human capital is a worker's productive capacity: his or her knowledge and skill in per-forming tasks. Common methods of acquiring human capital include formal schooling, apprenticeship programs, and on-the-job training. In addition, blue-collar jobs generally involve manual labor and physical tasks. Some of the occupations in this category are construction, maintenance, carpentry, assembly, plumbing and heating, typesetting, and truck driving.

Blue-collar workers often are paid an hourly rate and are eligible for overtime pay. Traditionally, many union jobs have been blue collar, and union bargaining power has contributed to higher wages for those workers.

Some aspects of blue-collar jobs are unpleasant, such as the risk associated with construction, fire fighting, and law enforcement. In general blue-collar work is often standardized and less autonomous than other types of work. Particularly in manufacturing, workers have seen periods of low job security for many reasons, including the substitutability of physical capital, which is the machinery and equipment used in production. Throughout the twentieth century production processes became much more capital-intensive as machines were introduced to perform tasks that previously had been done by workers. Another important characteristic is that blue-collar work has been done mostly by men. For instance, in 1999, 38 percent of male workers were employed in blue-collar occupations whereas only 9 percent of women were.

White-collar jobs generally require a fair amount of formal schooling, including college degrees ranging from associate's degrees through professional degrees such as medicine and jurisprudence and academic degrees such as doctorates. Much of this white-collar work is performed sitting at a desk in an office environment, such as engineering, architecture, and bookkeeping. Many of these jobs are well paid, largely because of the amount of education and skill building required to enter these occupations. The acquisition of human capital also spurs greater income growth over time.

Highly educated workers who develop expertise receive promotions within the corporate hierarchy. White-collar jobs often require strong communication skills, either written or oral, for working in teams, communicating with clients or customers, and conveying information within the company. Many white-collar jobs, particularly professional and technical jobs such as accountancy, law, and computer technology, are paid on a salaried basis. Hours worked per week tend to be very high in highly skilled white-collar jobs, with some employees spending more than sixty or seventy hours per week working. Corporate culture and promotion goals account for the long hours, and companies have an incentive to encourage salaried employees to work more hours because those workers are not eligible for overtime pay.

Throughout the twentieth century the majority of job growth was in the service sector. According to definitions from the U.S. Department of Labor, service occupations include health-care support jobs such as nursing and physical therapy; protective service jobs such as police and security work; food preparation; building and grounds maintenance; and personal services provided by hairstylists, child-care workers, flight attendants, and animal care workers. The service sector is not uniformly blue collar or white collar. For instance, washing dishes in a restaurant clearly involves manual labor and little training, but nurses are highly skilled professionals. Many of these workers are paid an hourly wage, but few are unionized. Some jobs, such as chefs, require not only strong communication skills but also the ability to manage a large staff.

TRENDS IN BLUE-COLLAR AND WHITE-COLLAR JOBS

In the mid-1950s well over 30 percent of American jobs were in manufacturing, and in the next fifty years that declined to 17 percent, whereas nongovernment services rose from 48 percent to 67 percent of all jobs. In the late twentieth century American employment in agriculture and manufacturing declined substantially, whereas construction and transportation jobs became more prevalent, revealing a new composition of blue-collar work in the United States. At the same time there have been vast increases in professional and technical work as well as work in the service sector and retail trade. There are also substantial differences in hourly pay rates across types of jobs. As is shown in the illustration, white-collar jobs are very well paid, with professional and technical workers earning approximately $30 per hour on average in 2005. In contrast, blue-collar workers received $15 on average, with those working in skilled craft and repair fields earning more and laborers earning less. The lowest-paid work was in the fastest-growing sector; service workers earned an average hourly wage of $11.

There are many sources of the changing mix of jobs from traditional blue-collar to white-collar work. One of the most important factors has been the steady increase in educational attainment in the U.S. population. In the early 1900s, 38,000 Americans earned bachelor's degrees. By 2000, well over one million Americans completed that level of education. Both men and women have pursued higher education in greater numbers. In 1940 just over 5 percent of men age twenty-five and over and nearly 4 percent of similarly aged women earned college degrees. By 2000 those proportions grew to 29 percent and 24 percent, respectively. In the early twenty-first century many students entered college because it appeared that a college degree was necessary for a good job: one with a high salary, good benefits, and pleasant working conditions. Therefore, the characteristics of the labor force (the labor

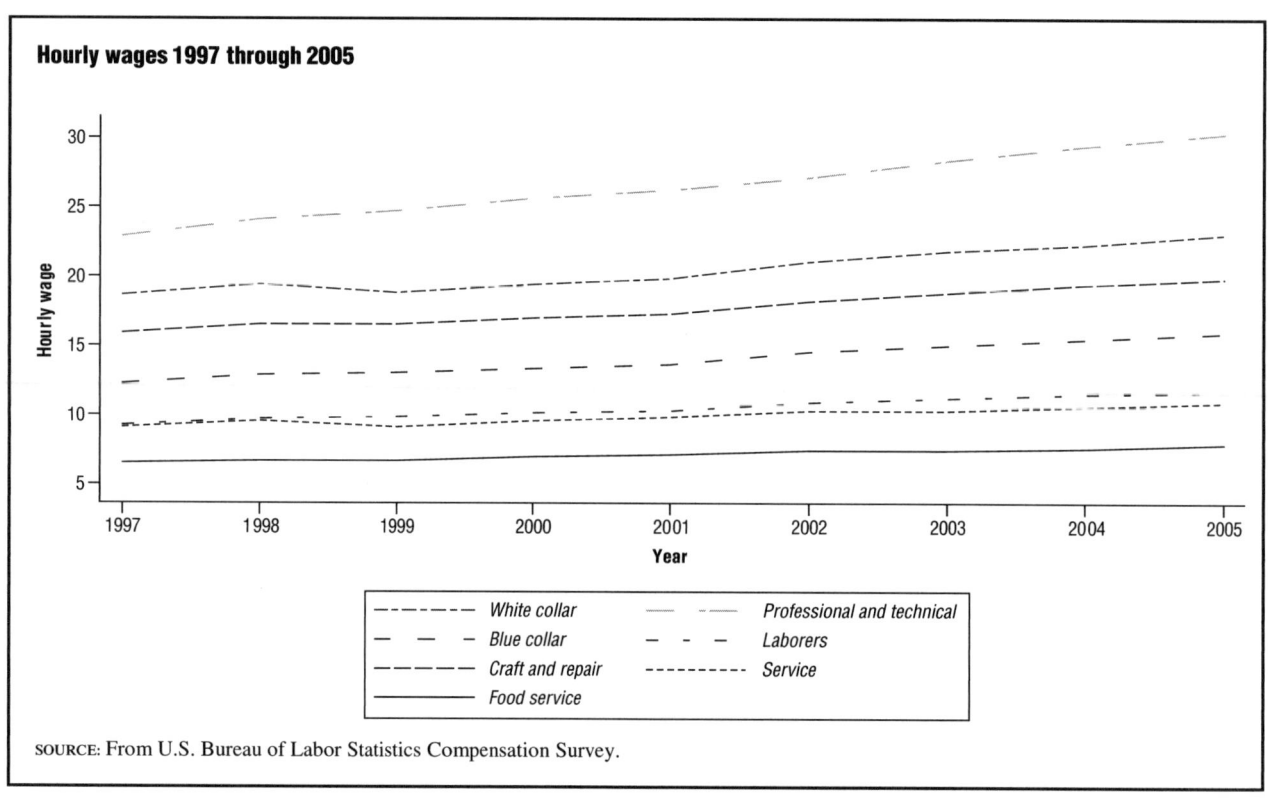

Hourly wages 1997 through 2005

Legend:
- White collar
- Blue collar
- Craft and repair
- Food service
- Professional and technical
- Laborers
- Service

SOURCE: From U.S. Bureau of Labor Statistics Compensation Survey.

supply) have changed substantially. Though some blue-collar jobs are highly skilled, few require a college degree. The majority of highly educated workers seek and usually find white-collar jobs.

In basic labor economic theory it is expected that vast increases in the supply of a certain type of labor will coincide with downward pressure on wages. If companies have a seemingly endless stream of potential hires, there is an incentive to lower costs by offering lower wages. However, the data reveal that the earnings of college graduates have grown substantially so that the premium for degree recipients compared with those with only a high school diploma has remained high. Many researchers have focused on estimating the returns to formal schooling to better understand this dynamic. For example, in 1974 Jacob Mincer found that each year of schooling provides 10 percent higher earnings on average for white men. Furthermore, those returns to college education are greater in the United States than in most other Organization of Economic Cooperation and Development (OECD) countries, helping explain why increasing numbers of young people pursue those degrees and fewer work in manufacturing and trades.

In addition, the technology used in production has changed significantly. During the nineteenth and twentieth centuries electricity and internal combustion engines fueled the transition from a mostly agrarian society to a highly industrialized nation. Into the twenty-first century advances in telecommunications and computers have led workers away from manufacturing and into more service jobs. The use of technology has coincided with more productive workers, but there is also more capital that substitutes for workers, particularly in traditionally blue-collar jobs. Increased use of computers has led to consistently increasing demand for white-collar workers who use that physical capital in production, particularly employees who use personal computers at work.

It is assumed that companies consistently maximize profit and lower production costs. Common methods of cutting costs have had a disproportionately negative impact on blue-collar workers. In the 1970s and 1980s the United States saw many mass layoffs in manufacturing, most prevalently during times of recession, when many companies coped with deficient demand by closing plants. In some cases plants were moved out of the Northeast and Midwest and into the South for cheaper labor. In the 1990s layoffs were used more commonly to restructure firms and increase competitiveness. Some already profitable firms used layoffs to generate even more profit. Overall, in the last decades of the twentieth century over 10 percent of American jobs were lost through business contractions and plant closings.

Workers who have been laid off generally face a permanently lower standard of living. The workers who find a new job earn 15 to 40 percent lower wages than they had previously. One reason for this has been the prevalence of seniority-based raises in the manufacturing sector. Workers who displayed loyalty to the firm were rewarded with higher earnings and more vacation time during their long tenure. A worker who begins at a new plant therefore starts over with a lower wage. In addition, layoffs can cause persistent unemployment if workers have obsolete skills. This happened with many blue-collar jobs as the mix of production in the United States moved from manufacturing to service.

In the twenty-first century, firms continued to move production processes in order to become more profitable. Rather than move within the country, it is increasingly common to move offshore. This practice of offshoring is related to outsourcing. Outsourcing entails moving a business function (often administrative) out of the firm, and many companies do this with human resources or marketing. Offshoring occurs when a company moves some of the business (managerial, administrative, or production) to another country. Many jobs have been moved to Asia. In fact, after China entered the World Trade Organization in 2001, many manufacturing jobs were relocated there from the United States. The majority of American jobs lost to offshoring have been in blue-collar manufacturing, but white-collar workers have not been immune to this trend. For instance, advances in technology and computer support in India have led many American firms to employ white-collar workers there.

PRIMARY AND SECONDARY LABOR MARKETS

In the early twentieth century John Stuart Mill (1909) observed a lack of competition across segments of the labor market. He described one sector that required a fair amount of training and another that did not. Basically, the direct and indirect costs associated with the training kept some workers from competing in the market for well-paid jobs. Direct costs include out-of-pocket costs for training and the related supplies and materials. The indirect cost of forgone earnings arise because the time devoted to skill building is not devoted to work that earns a wage. Many in Mill's class of "labourers" therefore were unable to take the time necessary to pursue higher-status occupations because they could not afford the associated costs. Thus, the labor market is seen as being segmented into two parts: a primary market and a secondary market.

Primary labor market jobs are characterized by good earnings, job security, a reasonable probability of promotion, good benefits, and agreeable working conditions such as autonomy and a pleasant working environment.

Many white-collar jobs match this description, and those jobs are plentiful and growing. Blue-collar jobs that are within the primary market appear in construction, mining, durable goods manufacturing, and transportation. In contrast, secondary labor market jobs have low earnings, few or no fringe benefits, high turnover, little job security, and few or no promotions. Many blue-collar and service jobs fit this description, and continuing increases in the service sector could create a larger secondary labor market. In this market, there are no clear returns to education and in some cases there are negative returns to experience.

OCCUPATION, INCOME INEQUALITY, AND SOCIAL MOBILITY

A person's social class is defined by many factors, including income, wealth, education, location of residence, and family background. Occupation is also a main determinant of social class in terms of prestige (for example, surgeon versus construction worker), education required, and earnings received. White-collar jobs traditionally have paid well and carried more prestige than blue-collar jobs, contributing to common attributions of working-class or middle-class Americans. In the mid-twentieth century many working-class Americans had relatively good blue-collar primary market jobs in manufacturing. In contrast, working-class jobs around the year 2000 were more common in the service sector. Those secondary market jobs are not prestigious or well paid, in stark contrast to the growth of quality white-collar jobs for middle-class and upper-class Americans.

Concurrent with changes in class in the United States was the rise of income inequality throughout the twentieth century. To understand the nature of this inequality, it is valuable to make comparisons within the OECD countries, which include nations in North America, Europe, and some parts of Asia. Approaching the year 2000, the United States had the most unequal distribution of post-tax income. Many developing countries have even more inequality, but the best comparison group appears to consist of countries that are similar in industry mix and economic health: those in the OECD.

There are many sources of the unequal distribution of income in the United States. From the 1940s to the 1970s real mean wages rose, but in the next thirty-five years real wages were stagnant. The overall income distribution became more unequal, and more Americans lived in poverty. One of the commonly cited reasons for this is the lack of increases in the minimum wage over that period. Because minimum wages are raised only by government mandate, the legislature must vote on increases. No adjustments are made for purchasing power. If there are no legislated increases for a lengthy period, any wage gains are eroded by inflation (higher prices). At the same time more highly paid white-collar workers saw increased earnings, and in the United States the rich did become richer in the twentieth century.

Another factor explaining low wages for blue-collar workers is the decline in unionization. Compared with most West European countries, the United States has low union rates. In 2004 the percentage of workers covered by collective bargaining agreements was 68 percent in Germany, 33 percent in the United Kingdom, 93 percent in France, and only 14 percent in the United States. However, some strong U.S. unions remain in transportation, utilities, and construction jobs. In contrast, the growing service sector has few unions, and attempts to unionize those workers are generally unsuccessful. Labor economists debate the value of unions. Some cite unions as a potential source of gains for low-paid workers, whereas others believe that unions cause unfair restraints for businesses. When both blue-collar jobs and unions were more prevalent in the United States, the ratio of white-collar to blue-collar wages was lower than it became in the early twenty-first century; the premium to white-collar work grew as unions became weaker. In light of trends in wages and employment for white-collar, blue-collar, and service sector jobs, it appears that the U.S. income distribution is likely to continue expanding, with more inequality over time.

SEE ALSO *Class; Class Conflict; Class Consciousness; Employment; Employment, White Collar; Income Distribution; Labor; Labor Market; Labor Market Segmentation; Labor Union; Middle Class; Mills, C. Wright; Occupational Status; Organization Man; Sociology; Stratification; Unions; Working Class*

BIBLIOGRAPHY

Blau, Francine, Marianne Ferber, and Anne Winkler. 2006. *Economics of Women, Men, and Work.* 5th ed. Upper Saddle River, NJ: Pearson/Prentice Hall.

Card, David. 1999. Causal Effects of Education on Earnings. In *Handbook of Labor Economics*, Vol. 3, eds. Orley Ashenfelter and Richard Layard. Amsterdam and New York: North-Holland.

Farber, Henry S. 2004. Job Loss in the United States, 1981–2001. In *Accounting for Worker Well-Being*, Vol. 23 of Research in Labor Economics, ed. Solomon W. Polachek, 69–117. Amsterdam: Elsevier.

Mill, John Stuart. [1848] 1909. *Principles of Political Economy.* 7th ed.

Mincer, Jacob. 1974. *Schooling, Experience and Earnings.* New York: National Bureau of Economic Research.

Nash, Ogden. 1945. "Will Consider Situation." In *Many Long Years Ago.* Boston: Little, Brown.

U.S. Bureau of Labor Statistics. http://www.bls.gov/.

U.S. Department of Labor. 2001. *Report on the American Workforce*. 5th ed. Washington, DC: U.S. Government Printing Office.

Sherrilyn M. Billger

BLUEGRASS

Bluegrass is a highly stylized genre of American popular country music, ostensibly created in the late 1930s and early 1940s by the mandolinist Bill Monroe (1911–1996). Indeed, Monroe is the widely accepted Father of Bluegrass. However, the genre has diverse antecedents in the Scots-Irish fiddle tradition, "old-time" country music, country blues, small-group jazz performance, stereotyped "barn-dance" radio entertainment, and vaudeville. Monroe channeled and refined these influences into a tightly arranged, high-energy, radio-performance genre later termed *bluegrass*, which mediated between the rural and the newly urban on WSM radio's widely broadcast *Grand Ole Opry*, a program that also functioned as a savvy popular representation of supposed "country ways" during a time of great urban relocation.

Today, due to its acoustic instrumentation, its highly foregrounded adherence to its own aesthetic tenets, and its widespread performance by passionate amateur musicians, bluegrass functions as a marker of musical authenticity in the world of country music more generally. This perceived authenticity is as much a part of bluegrass's identity as any of its sonic features.

Following a dip in popularity due to the emergence of rock and roll in the 1950s, bluegrass has experienced periodic revivals, functioning as a badge of country legitimacy at points of overcommercialization or political uncertainty. It has thus become associated, on one hand, with radical populist movements (such as the so-called folk scare of the McCarthy era), as well as with proud nationalism, traditionalism, and social conservatism, on the other.

HISTORY

Bluegrass is inextricably linked to three groups of musicians living and performing in the Appalachian piedmont during the late 1930s. These groups played a common style that became an extremely popular genre in the 1940s and early 1950s. Mandolinist and singer Bill Monroe and his older brother had played so-called hillbilly music on the guitar and mandolin, touring professionally as the Monroe Brothers during the 1930s. After they parted ways, Bill Monroe founded a new band, the Blue Grass

Boys, named after his home state of Kentucky (the Blue Grass State), and the band soon held a regular position on Nashville's *Grand Old Opry*, one of country music's most acclaimed radio shows. The classic sound of what came to be known as *bluegrass* crystallized in 1946 as the band's repertoire and core group of musicians stabilized. This group included Earl Scruggs, who immediately popularized an impressive new technique for the five-string banjo, in which chords are arpeggiated and ornamented extremely rapidly with three picking fingers (rather than strummed or played more melodically). The appearance of this new banjo style on the radio helped generate a wave of popular enthusiasm for the Blue Grass Boys across the Southeast.

Citing fatigue, Scruggs and vocalist/guitarist Lester Flatt (1914–1979) left the band at the height of its popularity, and soon formed their own group, the Foggy Mountain Boys, the second of the classic bluegrass triumvirate. Trading on Scruggs's vaunted virtuosity and Flatt's smooth vocal style and engaging stage presence, Flatt and Scruggs quickly achieved widespread success. The third of these widely acknowledged innovators was the Stanley Brothers, Ralph (b. 1927) and Carter (1925–1966), who initially imitated the sound of Monroe's Blue Grass Boys, whom they had heard on the radio and on records. However, the Stanley Brothers soon began to emphasize older musical traditions, such as balladry, thus cementing history and nostalgia as integral to the bluegrass aesthetic.

Despite its origins as a new sort of sophisticated country music (the Blue Grass Boys all wore unconventionally formal attire), and its dependence on modern mass media for its dissemination and popularity, the core of bluegrass's identity has come to rely on concepts of nostalgic authenticity, linked to ostensibly bygone ideals of purity, straightforwardness, and honesty. These tropes of purity are expressed lyrically, through themes that emphasize labor, family, nostalgia, pathos, regret, and grim prospects, and musically through the use of string instruments that do not require "modern" electricity (though the sounds of these instruments are commonly electrically amplified). This instrumentation typically includes the five-string banjo, mandolin, fiddle (violin), steel-string acoustic guitar, upright (double) bass, and often the resophonic guitar (Dobro), with the occasional pragmatic addition of light percussion or electric bass.

PERFORMANCE

Professional bluegrass performance is mostly executed on summer tours, supported by an informal network of locally organized festivals. These festivals specialize in bluegrass, though other closely related genres may be represented. Local groups are typically given earlier slots on festival schedules, and participating professional and amateur musicians commonly congregate and play before and after performances. Casual "parking-lot picking" on festival grounds is an important aspect of these events, as amateur performance is a highly valued aspect of bluegrass music. Amateur performance is also widely sustained through informally organized (but highly regular) jam sessions and "pickin' parties."

GENRE FEATURES

Bluegrass has proven to be a remarkably robust genre, maintaining a generic coherence over many decades. It is notable for its foregrounded adherence to its own genre rules, commonly stated among practitioners thus: "If it don't have *X*, it ain't bluegrass." However, it exists both as a generic template that can be applied to other kinds of music (a successful series known as Pickin' On markets bluegrass-style versions of the music of nonbluegrass artists, such as *Pickin' on Dylan, Pickin' on R.E.M.*), as well as a flexible paradigm that can absorb other musical parameters without losing its identity (for example, Pete Wernick's 2002 recording *Live Five* interpolates clarinet and vibraphone).

Emerging from vernacular musical traditions, the bulk of the bluegrass repertoire has typically been written in keys that allow for playing in open or first positions, utilizing open strings for accompanying drones and full, ringing chords or double (or triple) stops. However, fast tempi and tight arrangements have bred a sense of virtuosic pride into bluegrass performers, and many pieces written in formerly "awkward" keys are now commonplace.

Instrumentals are commonly written as tunes to be repeated with different musicians playing the melody in sequence. Typical repeatable forms are AABB or AABA. Vocal pieces are commonly in verse/chorus A(A)BABA form, though strophic ballads, true to bluegrass's nostalgic bent, are also common (AA … A). As noted above, however, the pride of bluegrass musicians in their technical abilities has allowed for many idiosyncratic song forms.

SEE ALSO *Music; Music, Psychology of*

BIBLIOGRAPHY

Goldsmith, Thomas, ed. 2004. *The Bluegrass Reader*. Urbana: University of Illinois Press.

Rosenberg, Neil. 2005. *Bluegrass: A History*. Rev. ed. Urbana: University of Illinois Press.

Jonathan T. King

BLUES

The blues, a term coined by the writer Washington Irving in 1807, is defined by *Webster's Dictionary* as a type of music "marked by recurrent minor intervals"—so-called *blue notes*—and by "melancholy lyrics." These lyrics reflect the oppression experienced by people of African descent in the United States: slavery, prison, chain gangs, and the indignities of the Jim Crow era.

Blues is a typically American music with its earliest roots in African forms. It originated with the slaves that were brought over from West Africa. The contemporary Malian musician Ali Farka Touré considers blues to be the type of music most similar to his own; specifically, Touré hears echoes of Tamascheq music in the music of blues artists such as John Lee Hooker. Because slaves were forbidden to use drums, they turned to traditional African "ring shouts" and created rhythms with their hands and feet. Through ring shouts slaves worshipping in "praise houses" connected the newly imposed Christianity to their African roots. "Field hollers," produced by slaves as a means of communication, were another early vocal style that influenced the blues. Work songs sung by prison road gangs also highly influenced the blues in its early days. The art of storytelling is another important element of the blues. Lyrically, the blues ranges from forms based on short rhyming verses to songs using only one or two repeated phrases.

Over time, the blues evolved from a parochial folk form to a worldwide language. The influence of the blues can be found in most forms of popular music, including jazz, country, and rock and roll. The lines between blues and jazz are often blurred. Kansas City jazz, for example, is known for its bluesy sound. Certain artists, such as Charles Brown, Jimmy Smith, Jimmy McGriff, and Mose Allison—all masters of the keyboard—make music that is hard to categorize as either purely jazz or purely blues. Likewise, gospel is closely related to the blues. The music of the "father of gospel," Thomas A. Dorsey, was a blend of blues and spirituals.

Ashenafi Kebede (1982) assigns the blues to four categories: country blues, city blues, urban blues, and racial blues. Country blues was traditionally performed by street musicians without any formal training. City blues is a standardized version of country blues. During the 1940s, as a result of the impact of communication media, city blues evolved into the more commercialized and formalized urban blues, a style characterized by big band accompaniment, modern amplification devices, and new instruments like the saxophone and electric guitar. Racial blues are songs based on racial distinctions between blacks and whites.

The great composer and musician W. C. Handy (1873–1958) was one of the first to bring blues into the popular culture, around 1911. Instrumental blues was first recorded in 1913. Aaron Thibeaux (T-Bone) Walker—whose recording debut, "Wichita Falls Blues," was cut in 1929 for Columbia Records—is believed to be the first bluesman to use an amplified acoustic guitar.

The first vocal blues was recorded by an African American woman, Mamie Smith, in 1920. Angela Davis (1998) argues that in the early 1920s African American females were given priority over African American males as recording artists due to their initial success (p. xii). Bessie Smith is said to be the greatest and the most influential blues singer of the 1920s. Bessie Smith's catalogue of blues recordings still stands as the yardstick by which all other female blues singers are evaluated. Gertrude "Ma" Rainey is also regarded as one of the best of the classic 1920s blues singers. She was "most likely the first woman to incorporate blues into ministerial and vaudeville stage shows, perhaps as early as 1902" (Santelli 2001, pp. 386–387). Alberta Hunter is identified as helping to bridge the gap between classic blues and cabaret-flavored pop music in the 1920s (Santelli 2001, p. 226).

Artists such as Buddy Guy, Otis Rush, and Magic Sam moved the blues guitar into the modern era. Other prominent figures of the second half of the twentieth century include Son Seals, one of the leading guitar stylists of Chicago's post-1960s blues generation; Muddy Waters, who has been dubbed the "patriarch of post–World War II (1939–1945) Chicago blues"; and Howlin' Wolf, who was a singer, a songwriter, a guitarist, and a harmonica player. Sonny Boy Williamson was responsible for the transformation of the harmonica (or blues "harp") from a simple down-home instrument into one of the essential parts of the Chicago blues sound. Little Walter is noted for his revolutionary harmonica technique, and was also a guitarist. Blues guitarist Luther Allison, from the late 1960s, was influenced by Freddie King, who was considered to be one of the linchpins of modern blues guitar. Albert King, who played left-handed and holding his guitar upside down, was one of the premier modern electric guitar artists. Jimmy Reed sold more records in the 1950s and early 1960s than any other blues artist except B. B. King, who is the most successful blues concert artist ever. Bobby "Blue" Bland is considered one of the creators of the modern *soul blues* sound. Blues giant John Lee Hooker is known as the father of the *boogie*—an incessant one-chord exercise in blues intensity and powerful rhythm.

While the blues was historically an African American form, in the early 1960s the urban bluesmen were "discovered" by young white American and European musicians. Prior to this discovery, black blues artists had been unable to reach a white audience. Among the best-known English blues artists are Eric Clapton and John Mayall; celebrated white American bluesmen include Paul Butterfield,

Charlie Musselwhite, Johnny Winter, and Stevie Ray Vaughan. All were heavily influenced by the great African American blues artists.

At the start of the twenty-first century, the blues is still going strong, as evidenced by the numerous national and international blues societies, publications, and festivals.

SEE ALSO *Bluegrass; Jazz; Music; Music, Psychology of; Popular Music; Rock 'n' Roll; World Music*

BIBLIOGRAPHY

Belafonte, Harry. 2001. *The Long Road to Freedom: An Anthology of Black Music.* Rochester, NY: Riverside Group. Book accompanying 5-CD set released by BGM/Buddha Records.

Davis, Angela Y. 1998. *Blues Legacies and Black Feminism: Gertrude "Ma" Rainey, Bessie Smith, and Billie Holiday.* New York: Random House.

Garon, Paul. 1975. *Blues and the Poetic Spirit.* San Francisco: City Lights.

Kebede, Ashenafi. 1982. *Roots of Black Music: The Vocal, Instrumental, and Dance Heritage of Africa and Black America.* Englewood Cliffs, NJ: Prentice-Hall.

Pareles, Jon, and Patricia Romanowski, eds. 1983. *The Rolling Stone Encyclopedia of Rock and Roll.* New York: Rolling Stone Press.

Santelli, Robert. 2001. *The Big Book of Blues: A Biographical Encyclopedia.* Rev. ed. New York: Penguin Books.

Dorothy Hawkins
Shakuntala Das

BLUMER, HERBERT
1900–1987

Herbert George Blumer earned his doctorate in 1928 at the University of Chicago and went on to teach there until 1951. He later became the founding chair of the Department of Sociology at the University of California, Berkeley. In 1983 the American Sociological Association honored him with its Career of Distinguished Scholarship Award, acknowledging the importance of his codification of the fundamental theoretical and methodological tenets of the sociological perspective that he called *symbolic interactionism*.

While it is not possible to capture the great range and significance of his contributions to the study of human group life in a single quotation, this oft-cited passage from his most influential and widely read work, *Symbolic Interaction: Perspective and Method*, sets out the cardinal premises of symbolic interactionism and the central message of his scholarship:

The first premise is that human beings act toward things on the basis of the meanings that the things have for them.... The second premise is that the meaning of such things is derived from, or arises out of, the social interaction that one has with one's fellows. The third premise is that these meanings are handled in, and modified through, an interpretative process used by the person in dealing with the things he encounters (Blumer 1969, p. 2).

Accordingly, individual and collective actions of any scale or complexity reflect the meanings that people assign to things, as these meanings emerge in and are transformed within the context of human group life. Blumer incorporated these assumptions into his vision of social life as an ongoing stream of situations handled by people through self-indication and definition.

Blumer synthesized the pragmatist philosophy of George Herbert Mead (1863–1931) with Charles Horton Cooley's (1864–1929) notion of sympathetic introspection, particularly as it informs contemporary ethnography, to develop a sociologically focused approach to the study of human lived experience. In opposition to behaviorist, structuralist, and positivist views that have dominated the social sciences, Blumer championed using an interpretivist perspective when examining social life. He contended that theoretical and methodological approaches to the study of human behavior must recognize human beings as thinking, acting, and interacting entities and must, therefore, employ concepts that authentically represent the humanly known, socially created, and experienced world.

Blumer's pioneering sociological perspective informed his analysis of a broad array of subjects including collective behavior, social movements, fashion, social change, social problems, industrial and labor relations, public opinion, morale, industrialization, public sector social science research, social psychology, and race relations. And, because his rendition of symbolic interactionism invariably portrays people as possessing agency, as reflective interactive participants in community life, he routinely called into question analyses of social life that rely on more stereotypical factors-oriented approaches.

Although Blumer's 1958 article "Race Prejudice as a Sense of Group Position" challenges psychological and psychoanalytic explanations of race relations by emphasizing social processes entailed in conflict, institutionalized power relations, and collective definitions of the situation, his most consequential contribution to the study of intergroup relations was his 1971 article "Social Problems as Collective Behavior."

SEE ALSO *Behaviorism; Groups; Industrialization; Intergroup Relations; Mead, George Herbert; Meaning; Positivism; Pragmatism; Prejudice; Public Opinion; Race; Race Relations; Racism; Social Psychology; Sociology; Stereotypes; Structuralism; Sympathy*

BIBLIOGRAPHY

PRIMARY WORKS

Blumer, Herbert. 1958. Race Prejudice as a Sense of Group Position. *Pacific Sociological Review* I (Spring): 3–7.

Blumer, Herbert. 1969. *Symbolic Interactionism: Perspective and Method.* Englewood Cliffs, NJ: Prentice-Hall.

Blumer, Herbert. 1971. Social Problems as Collective Behavior. *Social Problems* 18 (Winter): 298–306.

Blumer, Herbert. 2004. *George Herbert Mead and Human Conduct.* Ed. Thomas J. Morrione. Walnut Creek, CA: AltaMira Press.

SECONDARY WORKS

Lyman, Stanford M., and Arthur J. Vidich, eds. 2000. *Selected Works of Herbert Blumer.* Urbana: University of Illinois Press.

Morrione, Thomas J. 1999. Blumer, Herbert George. In *American National Biography*, eds. John A. Garraty and Mark C. Carnes, 73–76. New York: Oxford University Press.

Thomas J. Morrione

BLYDEN, EDWARD

SEE *Pan-Africanism; Socialism, African.*

BOAS, FRANZ
1858–1942

Franz Boas is recognized widely as the "father of American anthropology" because at Columbia University he trained a generation of graduate students who transformed an assortment of classificatory schemes based on evolutionary hierarchies into a comprehensive four-field discipline that integrated linguistics and archaeology with biological anthropology and cultural anthropology. In addition, Boas was a pioneering public intellectual who used science to challenge ideas of racial inferiority and the barbarism of certain cultures by employing empirical research to demonstrate how racism, the environment, and the history of specific cultures can explain difference and diversity.

EDUCATION AND WORKS

Born in Minden, Germany, Boas attended universities in Heidelberg, Bonn, and Kiel. His first academic appointment was in 1888 at Clark University, where he initiated a comprehensive research program that began to challenge some of the basic assumptions of racial categories; those efforts culminated in a major project for the U.S. Immigration Commission and were published as *Changes in Bodily Form of Descendants of Immigrants* (1912). In that work Boas demonstrated that the environment plays a significant role in determining physical attributes, such as head size, that often were used at that time to demarcate racial difference.

During the late nineteenth century racial categories were classified by head size, body type, and skin color and were linked to behavior, language, customs, and morality. Boas asserted that body type and race are discrete modalities and are not linked to customs and belief systems. Furthermore, he argued, one could not demarcate distinct racial categories accurately and cultures could not be rank-ordered within the then-current terminology as savage, barbarian, and civilized. His most definitive treatment of these issues was in *The Mind of Primitive Man* (1911).

The foundation of that theoretical paradigm shift in the natural and social sciences was Boas's understanding that cultures and languages should be evaluated in the context of their own complex histories and on their own terms as opposed to analyzing societies in terms of stages of evolution along a singular road to a civilization or an apex of culture. Much of Boas's research and theory was grounded in empiricism, participant observation, and detailed transcription of grammars, myths, kinship terminology, and folklore, using the interpretive framework of the people he studied.

Opposed to imposing an analytical framework on a set of traits and tendencies to deduce laws of culture, Boas instead relied on the use of inductive methods to identify patterns in process and the diffusion of material culture or folkloric themes through time and between cultural groups. Most of his ethnographic fieldwork was focused on the complex indigenous communities of the Pacific Northwest. To achieve such exhaustive empirical studies Boas relied on key informants who served as important collaborators. One of the most influential of those collaborators was George Hunt (Lingít), who was raised among the Kwakwaka'wakw near Fort Rupert on Vancouver Island in British Columbia. Hunt was instrumental in helping Boas develop his definitive work on the Kwakiutl language and kinship.

In 1896 Boas began to lecture at Columbia University, and in 1899 he became its first professor of anthropology. At that university he developed the distinctly North American four-field approach to anthropology. He also helped curate anthropological exhibits at the American Museum of Natural History, where he worked from 1895 to 1905.

In addition to his ethnographic work Boas conducted detailed studies on the growth of children and the head sizes of immigrants. Between 1908 and 1910 he measured 18,000 adults and children, using the data to produce the study *Changes in Bodily Forms of Descendants of Immigrants* (1912). Although there has been debate about the validity of his data, that study, among others Boas conducted, demonstrated that the physical metrics used to demonstrate the putative superiority and inferiority of racial groups and thus justify Jim Crow segregation and selective immigration restrictions were erroneous. African American intellectuals and early civil rights organizations welcomed the new science, and Boas actively supported the National Association for the Advancement of Colored People and formed lasting working relationships with scholars such as Carter G. Woodson (1875–1950) and W. E. B. Du Bois. Boas was also a champion of peace, academic freedom, and equal opportunity.

INFLUENCE

Perhaps Boas's greatest contribution to the field of anthropology was inspiring and training a generation of students who shaped the field in enduring ways. Many were women, and several were people of color. The list of students and colleagues whom Boas influenced at Columbia is impressive. Alfred Kroeber and Robert Lowie established the anthropology program at the University of California at Berkeley, Edward Sapir (1884–1935) and Faye-Cooper Cole (1881–1961) developed anthropology at University of Chicago, Leslie Spier (1893–1961) brought anthropology to the University of Washington, and Melville J. Herskovits organized an anthropology program at Northwestern. Other notable students include Margaret Mead, Ruth Benedict, and Zora Neale Hurston whose collective influence on American science and letters is much greater than his male students. Others included William Jones (1871–1909), a member of the Fox Nation and one of the first American Indian anthropologists; the Mexican anthropologist Manuel Gamio (1883–1960); the African American ethnographer Eugene King (1898–1981); Elsie Clews Parsons (1875–1945); Gene Weltfish (1902–1980); Gladys Reichard (1893–1955); and Alexander Goldenweiser (1880–1940). Together they went well beyond Boas's careful empirical studies to develop an understanding that cultures are dynamic and fluid, language is an integral aspect of culture that has internal structures and logics, history and ethnographic methods are central facets of anthropological research, and racial categories are scientifically untenable bases of analysis.

SEE ALSO *Anthropology, Biological; Anthropology, U.S.; Benedict, Ruth; Culture; Du Bois, W. E. B.; Ethnography; Ethnology and Folklore; Herskovits, Melville J.; Hurston, Zora Neale; Jim Crow; Kroeber, Alfred; Lowie, Robert; Mead, Margaret; National*

Association for the Advancement of Colored People (NAACP); Race

BIBLIOGRAPHY

PRIMARY WORKS

Boas, Franz. 1911. *The Mind of Primitive Man; A Course of Lectures Delivered before the Lowell Institute, Boston, Mass., and the National University of Mexico, 1910–1911.* New York: Macmillan.

Boas, Franz 1912. *Changes in Bodily Form of Descendants of Immigrants.* New York: Columbia University Press.

SECONDARY WORKS

Baker, Lee D. 1994. The Location of Franz Boas within the African American Struggle. *Critique of Anthropology* 14 (2): 199–217.

Baker, Lee D. 2004. Franz Boas Out of the Ivory Tower. *Anthropological Theory* 4 (1): 29–51.

Bashkow, Ira. 2004. A Neo-Boasian Conception of Cultural Boundaries. *American Anthropologist* 106 (3): 443–458

Bunzl, Matti. 2004. Boas, Foucault, and the "Native Anthropologist." *American Anthropologist* 106 (3): 435–442

Cole, Douglas. 1999. *Franz Boas: The Early Years, 1858–1906.* Seattle: University of Washington Press.

Darnell, Regna. 1998. *And Along Came Boas: Continuity and Revolution in Americanist Anthropology.* Amsterdam and Philadelphia: J. Benjamins.

Kuper, Adam. 1988. *The Invention of Primitive Society: Transformations of an Illusion.* London and New York: Routledge.

Lewis, Herbert. 2001. The Passion of Franz Boas. *American Anthropologist* 103 (2): 447–467

Stocking, George W., Jr. 1968 *Race, Culture, and Evolution: Essays in the History of Anthropology.* Chicago: University of Chicago Press.

Stocking, George W., Jr., ed. 1996. *Volksgeist as Method and Ethic: Essays on Boasian Ethnography and the German Anthropological Tradition.* Madison: University of Wisconsin Press.

Lee D. Baker

BODY IMAGE

Body image is a familiar phrase in contemporary American culture. The fourth edition of the *American Heritage Dictionary* (2000) defines it as "the subjective concept of one's physical appearance based on self-observation and the reactions of others." In the scientific literature, body image is considered a multidimensional construct encompassing self-perceptions and attitudes regarding one's physical appearance across cognitive, affective, perceptual, and behavioral domains.

The systematic study of body image began in the 1960s when psychiatrist Hilde Bruch (1904–1984) posited that negative body image was a causal mechanism in the development of anorexia nervosa. Since that time, numerous studies have linked body-image disturbance to the development of eating disorders and the onset of dieting. Although studies of non-treatment-seeking obese individuals indicate that there is no difference in the prevalence of psychopathology among obese and normal weight individuals, obese people consistently report higher dissatisfaction with body image and physical appearance than normal weight individuals (Rosen 2002). Furthermore, negative body image in treatment-seeking obese individuals is associated with psychological distress (Friedman et al. 2002).

A renewed interest in body image arose in the 1980s. Judith Rodin and colleagues (1984) described the widespread concerns about body image among women as a "normative discontent." This early research found a greater risk for body dissatisfaction among Caucasian women than men and women of color. Among females body-image dissatisfaction tends to be associated with the desire to lose weight, whereas among males body-image dissatisfaction is often associated with the desire to increase muscularity (McCreary and Sasse 2000). Recent evidence suggests that ethnic differences in body-image dissatisfaction may be decreasing, although more research is needed (Shaw et al. 2004). Sexual orientation is another factor that is associated with body-image concerns: homosexual males are more likely to report body dissatisfaction than heterosexual males and homosexual women (Siever 1994).

Body-image concerns typically surface with the onset of puberty. Adolescence may be an especially challenging time for girls because the thin-body ideal is inconsistent with normal pubertal changes such as increased body fat (Bearman et al., 2006) In contrast, muscle development associated with puberty in boys is more consistent with the athletic male body ideal. Normal growth and gender-specific social ideals may help explain the discrepancy in the prevalence of body dissatisfaction between females and males.

Interpersonal relationships during adolescence also appear to be related to negative body image. In particular, being teased about one's body by peers and family is associated with body-image disturbance (Keery et al. 2005; Eisenberg et al. 2003). Perceived pressure about weight from friends and parents also may play a strong role in promoting body dissatisfaction (McCabe and Ricciardelli 2005). Sociocultural theories suggest that the cultural emphasis on female appearance, especially weight, contributes to the development of body-image dissatisfaction. The impact of the mass media on body image seems to depend on the extent to which individuals internalize messages about beauty (Stice and Whitenton 2002).

SEE ALSO *Body Mass Index; Obesity*

BIBLIOGRAPHY

Bearman, Sarah Kate, Katherine Presnell, Erin Martinez, and Eric Stice. 2006. The Skinny on Body Dissatisfaction: A Longitudinal Study of Adolescent Girls and Boys. *Journal of Youth and Adolescence* 35 (2): 217–229.

Bruch, Hilde. 1962. Perceptual and Conceptual Disturbances in Anorexia Nervosa. *Psychosomatic Medicine* 24: 187–194.

Eisenberg, Marla E., Dianne Neumark-Sztainer, and Mary Story. 2003. Associations of Weight-Based Teasing and Emotional Well-being Among Adolescents. *Archives of Pediatric and Adolescent Medicine* 157: 733–738.

Friedman, Kelli E., Simona K. Reichmann, Philip R. Costanzo, and Gerard J. Musante. 2002. Body Image Partially Mediates the Relationship Between Obesity and Psychological Distress. *Obesity Research* 10: 33–41.

Keery, Helene, Kerri Boutelle, Patricia van den Berg, and J. Kevin Thompson. 2005. The Impact of Appearance-related Teasing by Family Members. *Journal of Adolescent Health* 37: 120–127.

McCabe, Marita P., and Lina A. Ricciardelli. 2005. A Prospective Study of Pressures from Parents, Peers, and the Media on Extreme Weight Change Behaviors Among Adolescent Boys and Girls. *Behavior Research and Therapy* 43: 653–668.

McCreary, Donald R., and Doris K. Sasse. 2000. An Exploration of the Drive for Muscularity in Adolescent Boys and Girls. *Journal of American College Health* 48: 297–304.

Rodin, Judith, L. Silberstein, and R. Striegel-Moore. 1985. Women and Weight: A Normative Discontent. In *Psychology and Gender: Nebraska Symposium on Motivation*, ed. T.B. Sonderegger, 267–307. Lincoln: University of Nebraska Press.

Rosen, James C. 2002. Obesity and Body Image. In *Eating Disorders and Obesity: A Comprehensive Handbook*, ed. Christopher Fairburn and Kelly Brownell, 2nd ed. New York: Guilford.

Shaw, Heather, Lisa Ramirez, Ariel Trost, et al. 2004. Body Image and Eating Disturbances Across Ethnic Groups: More Similarities than Differences. *Psychology of Addictive Behaviors* 18: 12–18.

Siever, Michael D. 1994. Sexual Orientation and Gender as Factors in Socioculturally Acquired Vulnerability to Body Dissatisfaction and Eating Disorders. *Journal of Consulting and Clinical Psychology* 62: 252–260.

Stice, Eric, and Kathryn Whitenton. 2002. Risk Factors for Body Dissatisfaction in Adolescent Girls: A Longitudinal Investigation. *Developmental Psychology* 38: 669–678.

Thompson, J. Kevin, Leslie J. Heinberg, Madeline Altabe, and Stacey Tantleff-Dunn. 1999. *Exacting Beauty: Theory, Assessment, and Treatment of Body Image Disturbance.* Washington, DC: American Psychological Association.

Kelli Friedman
Erin E. Martinez

BODY MASS INDEX

Body Mass Index, or BMI, is a common measure of weight status in adults. BMI can be calculated by multiplying weight in pounds by 703, divided by height in inches squared, and it serves as an index of weight-for-height measured in kg/m^2. BMI indicates overweight between 30 kg/m^2 and 34.9 kg/m^2; obesity between 35 kg/m^2 and 39.9 kg/m^2; and clinically severe obesity above 40 kg/m^2. BMI is an indirect estimate of body fat and is highly correlated with body fat at about .7 (Gray and Fujioka 1991). Although there are more accurate measures of body fat (e.g., underwater weighing and DXA), they are more expensive, inaccessible, and cumbersome compared to BMI (Blew et al. 2002). The widespread use of BMI is likely due to its cost-effectiveness and ease of calculation.

The measurement and definition of overweight and obesity has varied over time. For much of the twentieth century, physicians and researchers referenced Metropolitan Life Insurance Company (MLIC) tables, which recommended ideal weight-for-height. The MLIC tables suffered from limitations (e.g., unstandardized and inaccurate measurement protocols) that prompted the government to adjust the weight guidelines in the 1980s (Kuczmarski and Flegal 2000). In the mid-1980s BMI became the preferred measurement of weight status, and recommendations were based upon data from national epidemiological surveys such as the National Health and Nutrition Examination Survey. BMI emerged in the first annual federal report on the prevalence of obesity in the United States, and a National Institutes of Health (NIH) panel defined overweight in terms of sex-specific BMI cutoffs (Kuczmarski and Flegal 2000; National Center for Health Statistics 1984; National Institutes of Health Consensus Development Panel 1985).

The current classification system adopted by the National Heart, Lung, and Blood Institute uses BMI to determine weight category. Classification of weight status is important because numerous medical comorbidities are associated with increased BMI. The BMI cutoff for overweight has decreased over time from 30 to 27, and most recently 25. Further, BMI provides a relative index of growth stunting, a condition that may result in significant developmental delays and adverse physiological effects (Dickerson 2003).

Weight category	BMI (kg/m2)
Underweight	<18.5
Normal	18.5–24.9
Overweight	25.0–29.9
Obesity Class I	30.0–34.9
Obesity Class II	35.0–39.9
Obesity Class III	40+

There is empirical evidence that BMI may be more predictive of body fatness in certain subgroups (e.g., younger adults, Caucasians) than others (Baumgartner, Heymsfield, and Roche 1995; Gallagher et al. 1996). Thus, two individuals with an identical BMI may have a different percentage of body fat depending on factors such as age, gender, body shape, and ethnicity (Prentice and Jebb 2001). BMI also overestimates body fat in persons who are very muscular (e.g., athletes), does not distinguish lean mass (muscle and bone) from fat mass, and does not determine the distribution of body fat. In children, BMI must be adjusted for growth. Despite these shortcomings, BMI classifications are still valuable for research and health care.

BMI is used to diagnose and make treatment recommendations. Epidemiological studies measure BMI to identify population trends in growth retardation and obesity along with associated adverse health consequences. Mounting evidence indicates an increased risk of mortality among obese individuals. Increased BMI has been associated with medical comorbidities including cardiovascular disease, reduced fertility, sleep apnea, metabolic syndrome, hypertension, type 2 diabetes, and certain cancers. In addition to medical risks, evidence suggests that there is a powerful social stigma associated with obesity. Discrimination affects overweight individuals in numerous facets of life, including employment, education, and psychological well-being (Friedman et al. 2005; Puhl and Brownell 2003).

SEE ALSO *Body Image; Obesity*

BIBLIOGRAPHY

Baumgartner, Richard N., Steven B. Heymsfield, and Alex F. Roche. 1995. Human Body Composition and the Epidemiology of Chronic Disease. *Obesity Research* 3: 73–95.

Blew, Robert M., Luis B. Sardinha, Laura A. Milliken, et al. 2002. Assessing the Validity of Body Mass Index Standards in Early Postmenopausal Women. *Obesity Research* 10: 799–808.

De Onis, Mercedes. 2004. The Use of Anthropometry in the Prevention of Childhood Overweight and Obesity. *International Journal of Obesity* 28: 581–585.

Deurenberg, Paul, Jan A. Weststrate, and Jaap C. Seidell. 1991. Body Mass Index as a Measure of Body Fatness: Age- and Sex-specific Prediction Formulas. *British Journal of Nutrition* 65: 105–114.

Dickerson, John W. T. 2003. Some Aspects of the Public Health Importance of Measurement of Growth. *The Journal of the Royal Society for the Promotion of Health* 123: 165–168.

Forbes, Gilbert B. 1999. Body Composition: Overview. *Journal of Nutrition* 129 (1): 270S–272S.

Friedman, Kelli E., Simona K. Reichmann, Philip R. Costanzo, et al. 2005. Weight Stigmatization and Ideological Beliefs: Relation to Psychological Functioning in Obese Adults. *Obesity Research* 13: 907–916.

Gallagher, Dympna, Marjolein Visser, Dennis Sepulveda, et al. 1996. How Useful is Body Mass Index for Comparison of Body Fatness Across Age, Sex, and Ethnic Groups? *American Journal of Epidemiology* 143: 228–239.

Gray, David S., and Ken Fujioka. 1991. Use of Relative Weight and Body Mass Index for the Determination of Adiposity. *Journal of Clinical Epidemiology* 44: 545–550.

Greenberg, Isaac, Frank Perna, Marjory Kaplan, and Mary Anna Sullivan. 2005. Behavioral and Psychological Factors in the Assessment and Treatment of Obesity Surgery Patients. *Obesity Research* 13: 244–249.

Headley, Allison A., Cynthia L. Ogden, Clifford L. Johnson, et al. 2004. Prevalence of Overweight and Obesity Among U.S. Children, Adolescents, and Adults, 1999–2002. *Journal of the American Medical Association* 291: 2847–2850.

Kuczmarski, Robert J., Katherine M. Flegal. 2000. Criteria for Definition of Overweight in Transition: Background and Recommendations for the United States. *American Journal of Clinical Nutrition* 72: 1074–1081.

National Center for Health Statistics. 1984. *Health, United States, 1984*. Washington, DC: U.S. Government Printing Office.

National Center for Health Statistics Consensus Development Panel on the Health Implications of Obesity. 1985. Health Implications of Obesity. *Annals of Internal Medicine* 103: 1073–1077.

National Heart, Lung, and Blood Institute. 1998. Clinical Guidelines on the Identification, Evaluation, and Treatment of Overweight and Obesity in Adults: The Evidence Report. Rockville, MD: National Institutes of Health.

Pietrobelli, Angelo, Steven B. Heymsfield, ZiMian M. Wang, and Dympna Gallagher. 2001. Multi-component Body Composition Models: Recent Advances and Future Directions. *European Journal of Clinical Nutrition* 55: 69–75.

Prentice, Andrew M., and Susan A. Jebb. 2001. Beyond Body Mass Index. *Obesity Reviews* 2: 141–147.

Puhl, Rebecca, and Kelly D. Brownell. 2003. Psychosocial Origins of Obesity Stigma: Toward Changing a Powerful and Pervasive Bias. *Obesity Reviews* 4: 213–227.

Seidell, Jaap C., Henry S. Kahn, David F. Williamson, et al. 2001. Report from a Centers for Disease Control and Prevention Workshop on Use of Adult Anthropometry for Public Health and Primary Health Care. *American Journal of Clinical Nutrition* 73: 123–126.

U.S. Department of Agriculture and U.S. Department of Health and Human Services. 1980. *Nutrition and Your Health: Dietary Guidelines for Americans*. Washington, DC: U.S. Government Printing Office.

Kelli Friedman
Erin E. Martinez

BOER WAR

The Boer War (or Anglo-Boer War) was a conflict in which the British Empire fought the forces of two "Boer Republics" from 1899 to 1902 in southern Africa. The

Boers lost the war, but resistance gained them concessions even in defeat. One of many conflicts that heightened international tensions before 1914, the war accelerated patterns of violence that came to mark twentieth-century warfare, especially violence toward civilians.

The "Boer" population—mostly of Dutch Calvinist background—originated with a Dutch East India Company colony planted at the Cape of Good Hope in the seventeenth century. Britain acquired the Cape Colony during the Napoleonic Wars. After clashes with the British administration, many settlers migrated northward in the "Great Trek" between 1835 and 1841, establishing two "Boer republics": the South African Republic (or the Transvaal) and the Orange Free State. The term *Boer* means "farmer" in Dutch and in the related language that developed among these settlers, which today is called *Afrikaans*.

The earlier war associated with the terms *Boer War* and *Anglo-Boer War* (1880–1881) was the result of British attempts to establish control over the republics. The British lost militarily but gained Boer agreement to nominal British rule over the autonomous republics. The conflict more commonly called the *Boer War* began in 1899 and was connected to the discovery of gold in the territory of the Transvaal in 1886. Europeans poured in to run the mines and recruit African labor. In the nineties, colonial authorities pushed to gain the vote for resident "foreigners" (*uitlanders*), a measure that would have enabled the *uitlanders* to vote the republics into dissolution. Transvaal President Paul Kruger (1825–1902) opposed the plan vehemently. The Jameson Raid of 1895, sponsored by Cecil Rhodes (1853–1902; Cape Colony premier), was an effort to establish British control by force. After the defeat of the filibuster, German Emperor Wilhelm II (1859–1941) sent a telegram congratulating Kruger, to the irritation of the British. More concretely, the Germans also sent arms to the Boers in an attempt to counter their imperial rival, Britain.

Assisted by mining interests, in the late 1890s British Colonial Secretary Joseph Chamberlain (1836–1914) and British High Commissioner Sir Alfred Milner (1854–1925) pressured the republics to give full citizenship to all resident British subjects. An attempt at reconciliation at the Bloemfontein Conference in mid-1899 failed, and the sides exchanged ultimata. The Boers struck first, invading the Cape Colony and Natal with a force based on the militia-like pattern of Boer defense, the commando system. The keys to their powerful blows against professional British units were expert marksmanship, good weapons, and mobility (mostly on horseback). From October 1899 to February 1900, Boer forces enjoyed success, defeating larger British units in a series of conventional battles, climaxed by the Battle of Spioenkop (earlier,

Spion Kop), where British troops failed to carry the Boer lines after assaulting them for two days and losing 1,683 men, compared to 198 on the part of the Boers.

The tide of the war turned in February 1900, when British Field Marshall Lord Frederick Sleigh Roberts (1832–1914) arrived with reinforcements. Though the British continued to sustain high losses, they were now able to overpower Boer forces, which retreated back to the Transvaal and the Orange Free State. Roberts followed and captured the Boer capitals by early June. The largest remaining Boer force was defeated in August 1900. Yet the Boers had already decided to move away from conventional warfare and adopt a guerrilla war of raids and ambush; by June this campaign was in full swing. Several capable commanders emerged, especially Christiaan de Wet (1854–1922) and Jan Smuts (1870–1950). The British columns were deadly, but the Boer commandos were frequently elsewhere by the time the British were ready to strike.

Hence, although they nominally occupied the republics, British forces seemed stymied. Soon 250,000 British troops were engaged, but this number still represented a relatively low ratio of troops to area: The territory of the Transvaal alone (111,196 square miles) almost equaled that of the British Isles. The British military compensated for this low density of troops with a network of hundreds of "blockhouses," outpost structures giving protection to small garrisons and linked by barbed-wire fences, designed to disrupt Boer movements.

Lord Roberts resigned in November 1900 because of sickness, and Herbert Lord Kitchener (1850–1916) took command. Kitchener intensified the "scorched-earth" policy that Roberts had already begun, which paralleled similar strategies in other contemporary colonial conflicts. His plan was to destroy Boer homes and crops and appropriate their livestock to deny the commandos food, supplies, and hiding places; in two years the army burned some 30,000 Boer dwellings.

A byproduct of the "scorched-earth" policy was the creation of "concentration camps" to house those made homeless. Among the refugees were Boer women, children, and elderly, but also black Africans associated with Boer farming economies, or simply those displaced by military operations. British commanders also hoped that holding the refugees in tent camps surrounded by barbed wire, with limited food and rough hygiene, would bring about Boer surrender. Kitchener built forty concentration camps containing 116,000 prisoners, most of them women and children. Malnutrition and disease killed a high percentage. In a year and a half, well over 26,000 Afrikaners died, over 20,000 of them children under sixteen. The British also rounded up black Africans into camps, where as many as 17,000 died of disease and poor conditions. Some 12,000 of those seem to have been children. The total of black African deaths caused by the war is unknown. Nearly all the relevant mortality figures have been disputed, but it is not in dispute that the primary killer, even in the case of military deaths, was disease.

Whatever the effect of British tactics on the outcome of the war, it is clear that the Boers did not have the resources to fight on indefinitely. Several larger-scale battles in 1902 led to losses that thinned the already sparse commando ranks. The Boers surrendered in the spring of 1902, and the war ended with the Treaty of Vereeniging, signed on May 31, 1902. The two republics became undisputed British possessions, but they emerged with considerable autonomy, allowing for self-government and continued use of the Dutch (later redefined as Afrikaans) language in schools, courts, and other institutions. The British agreed to pay a large sum for reconstruction in compensation for war damage. On the question of the enfranchisement of black Africans in the region, the treaty stipulated that no discussions of the issue would be held until after the region had been granted self-government.

Historians generally understand the war to have promoted and accelerated social trends marginalizing black African and racially mixed populations in South Africa. Hence, the institutionalization of *apartheid* (separateness) after World War II is seen as a later stage in developments resulting from the settlement of the Boer War. New legal restrictions based on race appeared in South Africa in the following decades. The Boer War also seems to have set in motion or intensified dislocation and the breakup of traditional cohesions among black South African ethnic groups, trends that shaped later racial relations in South Africa.

The war was an international affair, particularly on the British side. Some 22,000 soldiers of the British Empire died, and hundreds of thousands served. Yet, thousands were not from the British Isles. Africans served in various capacities. Many Indians living in South Africa likewise served in the war (Mohandas Gandhi [1869-1948] was a stretcher-bearer in the volunteer Indian Ambulance Corps). Australia's involvement in the Boer War became a significant part of Australian history and identity. Over 10,000 Australians served in Australian units alone, and many others in British units. Some 500 Australians died in the war, about half from disease. Nearly 7,500 Canadians served, with deaths totaling 219, and New Zealand sent some 6,500 troops, with 229 resulting deaths. The war was, after all, an imperial effort.

The unity implied by these contributions did not reflect universal support back home. In Britain pacifists, liberals, socialists, and others were outspoken opponents of the war. Among the best known was political activist Emily Hobhouse (1860–1926). Opposing the war forcefully, she organized the Relief Fund for South African Women and Children in 1900 and traveled to South Africa to visit the concentration camps. Her efforts led to official inquiries and eventually a lowering of the mortality rates in the camps. Another prominent opponent was economist John A. Hobson (1858–1940), who produced a critique that far outlasted the events he observed. Covering the war for the *Manchester Guardian*, he wrote in *The South African War: Causes and Effects* (1900) that the war had been foisted on Britain by a "small confederacy of international mine-owners and speculators" lobbying for the war to support their own investments in South Africa. Hobson later generalized these and other arguments to apply to the whole of European imperialism in *Imperialism* (1902). Vladimir I. Lenin (1870–1924) adapted some of Hobson's ideas in writing *Imperialism: The Highest Stage of Capitalism* (1916).

SEE ALSO *Apartheid; Concentration Camps; Imperialism*

BIBLIOGRAPHY

Judd, Denis, and Keith Surridge. 2002. *The Boer War*. New York: Palgrave Macmillan.

Nasson, Bill. 1999. *The South African War, 1899–1902*. New York: Oxford University Press.

Pakenham, Thomas. 1979. *The Boer War*. New York: Random House.

Reitz, Deneys. 1930. *Commando: A Boer Journal of the Boer War*. New York: C. Boni.

Warwick, Peter, and S. B. Spies, eds. 1980. *The South African War: The Anglo-Boer War, 1899–1902*. Burnt Hill, U.K.: Longman.

Wilcox, Craig. 2002. *Australia's Boer War: The War in South Africa, 1899–1902*. South Melbourne: Oxford University Press.

T. Hunt Tooley

BOGARDUS, EMORY

SEE *Assimilation.*

BOLL WEEVILS

SEE *Southern Bloc.*

BOLSHEVISM

The Bolsheviks were the party that V. I. Lenin created in exile in 1903 and then used to conduct the successful Bolshevik Revolution in November 1917. *Bolshevism* is a western intellectual construct that helped to focus a debate on whether the Stalinist system was the logical consequence of Lenin's principles, or whether Bolshevism was a more subtle and complex phenomenon with which Stalinism had only a tangential relationship.

Lenin firmly rejected the growing movement that promoted a peaceful evolution of socialism. In 1902 he split with his closest revolutionary allies over control of their newspaper, *Iskra*, and over who could join their party: Lenin insisted that the party membership be limited to those who accepted strict party discipline and the duty to work actively for the revolution. The opposition had a more western view of a decentralized party that accepted anyone who would support the party program and pay dues. When it was put to a vote, Lenin had a (narrow) majority, so he called his supporters the *Bolsheviks* (from *bolshinstvo*, "majority") and his opponents the *Mensheviks* (from *menshinstvo*, "minority").

The tsar responded to the Revolution of 1905 by creating a limited parliament, the Duma, and expanding political rights. Lenin was willing to use these institutions only tactically, to promote revolution, but the Mensheviks gradually became a western, social-democratic party that saw capitalism as the next long-term stage in Russian history. Other issues became politically crucial. Lenin's centralized party implied a strong Russian empire, whereas the Mensheviks' position implied a looser one. Lenin's rigid orthodoxy implied that modern western culture was the tool of bourgeois rule, and his rejection of cooperation with liberals appealed to those who rejected westernization.

When Russia's failure in World War I led to the overthrow of the tsar in March 1917, plunging Russia into chaos, Lenin rallied a large coalition—his traditional worker-peasant support, intellectual radicals, and antiwar forces, including some in the military. In these conditions, the party was opened to all applicants, and this continued during the civil war. There is still debate about whether the broader membership of the party, together with Lenin's toleration of private agriculture and trade in the New Economic Policy, would have produced a more tolerant one-party system in the Soviet Union had Lenin or an appropriate successor been chosen. Some historians contend that Lenin's massive purge of party members from 1921 to 1923 and his decision to rule through the party apparatus under Stalin's control suggest that the openness in 1917 and during the civil war was an aberration. The answer is unknowable.

During the late Soviet period, reformers painted a softer picture of Lenin in order to claim they were true Leninists: The modern generation is less concerned about "what if" questions about Lenin and more likely to focus on Bolshevism's appeals. The successes of both Lenin and Stalin rested on the peasants and first-generation workers who flowed into the cities in massive numbers. Around the world, Communism was most successful at that stage of history, and it collapsed in Russia when the nation reached a new stage of development. In other countries, however, frightened peasants moving to the cities continued to be attracted to leaders who appealed to their grievances with a rigid doctrine, a centralized control of disorder, and antiwesternism. Other doctrines that appealed to the same social forces took hold, and religious fundamentalism was the first of them.

SEE ALSO *Lenin, Vladimir Ilitch; Leninism; Peasantry; Revolution; Russian Revolution; Stalin, Joseph; Stalinism*

BIBLIOGRAPHY

Cohen, Stephen F. 1973. *Bukharin and the Bolshevik Revolution.* New York: A.A. Knopf.

Fitzpatrick, Sheila. 2001. *The Russian Revolution.* New York: Oxford University Press.

Haimson, Leopold H. 2005. *Russian Revolutionary Experience, 1905-1917.* New York: Columbia University Press.

Jerry Hough

BONACICH, EDNA
1940–

Edna Bonacich is one of the leading scholars on race and class in the United States. Her work focuses on social inequality, labor, immigration, sweatshops, and global production. She gained prominence in the 1970s based on the publication of three seminal articles in the *American Sociological Review*. Bonacich later coauthored books on middlemen minorities and immigrant entrepreneurs (with John Modell and Ivan Light, respectively) and she coedited two volumes on Asian immigration. She also coedited a book on the apparel industry in the Pacific Rim region and coauthored (with Richard Appelbaum) *Behind the Label* (2000), an award-winning book that examines the Los Angeles garment industry and the resurgence of sweatshop labor.

Bonacich was born in Connecticut in 1940. She lived in New York City for several years before moving with her father (a Jewish reform rabbi), mother, and two siblings to South Africa in 1950. Witnessing the "world's most racist regime" first-hand profoundly influenced her career as a sociologist. While living in South Africa, she joined a Zionist youth organization that focused on establishing collective farms (*kibbutzim*) in Israel. After graduating from high school, she lived in Israel for a year, living on two separate *kibbutzim*, before she became disillusioned with Zionism (Bonacich 2005). She eventually moved back to South Africa and became a student at the University of Natal, where she graduated with a Bachelor's of Social Science degree in sociology, psychology, and English in 1961. She obtained her master's and doctoral degrees in sociology from Harvard University in 1966 and 1969, respectively. In 1970 she started working in the Sociology Department at the University of California, Riverside (UCR), and she stayed there until her retirement in 2006.

Bonacich's experiences in South Africa and Israel strongly shaped her views about race and class. Those views included the well-known but controversial claim that racism and capitalism emerged nearly simultaneously, and that both systems of inequality should therefore be concurrently challenged and abolished. Split labor markets (in which one group of workers is paid more than another) and middlemen minorities prevented these changes from taking place, however. Rather than create coalitions with mostly lower-paid workers of color, higher-paid white workers have typically favored exclusionary legislation in the United States. Meanwhile, both white workers and workers of color have often singled out middlemen minorities, who occupy an intermediate strata (or "buffer") between capital and labor. These middlemen minorities are treated as scapegoats as both white workers and workers of color blame them for their problems in the workforce. Before World War II (1939–1945), for example, Japanese American farmers faced racist legislation that prevented them from owning land. During the war, they were put into concentration camps and lost nearly all their possessions.

More recently, many Korean-owned businesses in Los Angeles established a vibrant middlemen minority community in the 1970s and 1980s (Bonacich and Light 1988), only to have them targeted and burned down during the 1992 riots. Capitalism's longevity is thus largely based on these racial and ethnic antagonisms.

This perspective, while theoretically and empirically rich, has generated concerns among some Marxist-oriented sociologists and historians. Bonacich, these scholars claim, mistakenly assumes that the working-class was primarily responsible for creating and sustaining racism. Michael Omi and Howard Winant (1994), in contrast, find Bonacich's "economic determinism" and "class reductionism" troubling. Miles and Brown (2003), moreover, suggest that racism exists autonomously from capitalism, meaning that it predates capitalism and persists in socialist societies. It has also been claimed that class is no more important than gender, race, or sexuality, and that social movements and nation-states socially construct "race" around certain practices, projects, and discourses (Anderson and Collins 2006; Omi and Winant 1994). The fact that Omi and Winant's "racial formation paradigm" became so influential in the 1980s and 1990s is extremely ironic because discussions about class—that supposedly "anachronistic" and "old-fashioned" concept—made a "comeback" as economic inequality rose in the United States and around the world during that same time period.

Globalization, or what some Marxists call imperialism, is largely responsible for this latter trend. Capitalism reproduces itself through imperialism, which generates poverty and misery within the "Third World," leading to migration into developed countries like the United States. This fact, coupled with U.S. support for neoliberal economic policies and right-wing dictatorships, facilitated significant migration from Mexico and Central America in the 1980s and 1990s. These Latino migrants made up the backbone of the Los Angeles garment industry, which became the nation's largest site for apparel production in the 1990s.

Los Angeles garment workers have endured "sweatshop" conditions, involving very long hours and extremely low pay. The "return of the sweatshop" resulted from the restructuring of the U.S. economy following the worldwide economic crisis of the 1970s. "Restructuring" involved cutting back social programs, attacking labor unions, and rolling back legal protections for workers. The resistance efforts of workers have not been very effective, however, because garment workers sometimes see their immediate employer, typically an Asian immigrant contractor, as their "enemy" (Bonacich and Appelbaum 2000). But the real power brokers in the garment industry are giant retailers and manufacturers like Wal-Mart and Nike, which are usually controlled by wealthy white men. Class conflict, therefore, is played out along racial lines. The middlemen minority group (Asian contractors) is blamed for labor's woes, while capital goes largely unchallenged.

Bonacich and Appelbaum note that even when capital is challenged—such as when the U.S. garment workers union, UNITE, targeted Guess Inc. in the mid-1990s—it can simply shut down and move someplace else. The Guess campaign and many others inside and outside the United States were undermined by capital mobility in the 1990s. Because the garment industry is so mobile, better opportunities for labor organizing may lie within nonmobile sectors like the logistics industry. Bonacich, along with Jake B. Wilson, has been studying the possibility of organizing longshore, trucking, transportation, rail, and warehouse workers (mostly people of color), who could potentially bring global capitalism to a standstill if they refused to handle goods that came through the ports of Los Angeles and Long Beach.

These have been the hallmarks of Professor Bonacich's distinguished career. She has not only interpreted the world, but, as Marx famously said, she has worked to change it for the better through her research, teaching, mentoring, and involvement with the labor and anti-sweatshop movements. Her provocative work on split labor markets, middlemen minorities, immigration, sweatshops, and global production has influenced numerous scholars and activists. Split labor market theory, for instance, is mentioned in most introductory sociology textbooks, while her studies on the Los Angeles garment and logistics industries have been invaluable for labor unions and community organizations. She is a true role model for progressive academics who wish to combine scholarship with activism.

SEE ALSO *Middleman Minorities; Migrant Labor; Textile Industry*

BIBLIOGRAPHY

PRIMARY WORKS

Bonacich, Edna. 1972. A Theory of Ethnic Antagonism: The Split Labor Market. *American Sociological Review* 37: 547–559.

Bonacich, Edna. 1973. A Theory of Middlemen Minorities. *American Sociological Review* 38: 583–594.

Bonacich, Edna. 1976. Advanced Capitalism and Black/White Relations in the United States: A Split Labor Market Perspective. *American Sociological Review* 41: 34–51.

Bonacich, Edna. 1989. Inequality in America: The Failure of the American System for People of Color. *Sociological Spectrum* 9 (1): 77–101.

Bonacich, Edna. 2005. Working with the Labor Movement: A Personal Journey in Organic Public Sociology. *American Sociologist* 36 (3–4): 105–120.

Bonacich, Edna, and Richard Appelbaum. 2000. *Behind the Label: Inequality in the Los Angeles Apparel Industry.* Berkeley: University of California Press.

Bonacich, Edna, and Lucie Cheng. 1984. *Labor Immigration Under Capitalism: Asian Workers in the U.S. Before World War II.* Berkeley: University of California Press.

Bonacich, Edna, and Ivan Light. 1988. *Immigrant Entrepreneurs: Koreans in Los Angeles, 1965–1982.* Berkeley: University of California Press.

Bonacich, Edna, and John Modell. 1980. *The Economic Basis of Ethnic Solidarity: Small Business in the Japanese American Community.* Berkeley: University of California Press.

SECONDARY WORKS

Anderson, Margaret, and Patricia Hill Collins. 2006. *Race, Class, and Gender: An Anthology*, 6th ed. Belmont, CA: Thomson Higher Education.

Armbruster-Sandoval, Ralph. 2005. *Globalization and Cross-Border Labor Solidarity in the Americas.* New York: Routledge.

Burawoy, Michael. 1981. The Capitalist State in South Africa: Marxist and Sociological Perspectives on Race and Class. *Political Power and Social Theory* 2: 279–335.

Cox, Oliver C. 1948. *Caste, Class, and Race: A Study in Social Dynamics.* New York: Monthly Review Press.

Hamilton, Nora, and Norma Chinchilla. 2001. *Seeking Community in a Global City: Salvadorans and Guatemalans in Los Angeles.* Philadelphia: Temple University Press.

Miles, Robert, and Malcolm Brown. 2003. *Racism*, 2nd ed. New York: Routledge.

Omi, Michael, and Howard Winant. 1994. *Racial Formation in the United States: From the 1960s to 1990s*, 2nd ed. New York: Routledge.

Rodney, Walter. 1972. *How Europe Underdeveloped Africa.* London: Bogle-L'Ouverture.

Roediger, David. 1991. *The Wages of Whiteness: Race and the Making of the American Working Class.* London: Verso.

Williams, Eric. [1944] 1994. *Capitalism and Slavery.* Chapel Hill: University of North Carolina Press.

Ralph Armbruster-Sandoval

BOOTSTRAP METHOD

The *bootstrap method,* introduced by Bradley Efron (1979, 1982), is a technique for making statistical inference. In the typical estimation scenario, one draws a sample $Y = [y_1, \ldots, y_n]$ from an unknown distribution F and then computes an estimate $\hat{\theta} = g(Y)$ of some parameter or quantity θ that is of interest. If the distribution of $(\hat{\theta} - \theta)$ were known, it would be straightforward to find values c_1, c_2 such that

$$P(c_1 \leq \hat{\theta} - \theta \leq c_2) = 1 - \alpha \qquad (1)$$

for some small value of α, say 0.1 or 0.05. Rearranging terms inside the parentheses results in a confidence interval, $\hat{\theta} - c_2 \leq \theta \leq \hat{\theta} - c_1$, for the quantity θ. The distribution of $(\hat{\theta} - \theta)$ is unknown in most situations, however. In some cases, the finite-sample distribution of $(\hat{\theta} - \theta)$ can be approximated by the limiting distribution, but this may not work well in some cases.

The bootstrap method is based on the idea of replicating the estimation scenario described above by drawing B samples $Y^* = [y_1^*, \ldots, y_n^*]$ from an estimate $\hat{F}$ of F and computing estimates $\hat{\theta}_b^* = g(Y^*)$, $b = 1, \ldots, B$. Given the B values $\hat{\theta}_b^*$, it is straightforward to find values c_1^*, c_2^* such that

$$P(c_1^* \leq \hat{\theta}^* - \hat{\theta} \leq c_2^*) \approx 1 - \alpha \qquad (2)$$

by finding appropriate percentiles of the differences $(\hat{\theta}_b^* - \hat{\theta})$. Substituting the values c_1^*, c_2^* into (1) yields

$$P(c_1^* \leq \hat{\theta} - \theta \leq c_2^*) \approx 1 - \alpha. \qquad (3)$$

Rearranging terms inside the parentheses in (3) yields an estimated confidence interval

$$\hat{\theta} - c_2^* \leq \theta \leq \hat{\theta} - c_1^*.$$

Here, confidence intervals have been estimated based on the differences $(\hat{\theta}_b^* - \hat{\theta})$, but other approaches may also be used (see Efron and Tibshirani [1993] for examples). The approximation in (2) is due to the fact that B must be finite, while the approximation in (3) is due to the fact that the original estimate $\hat{\theta}$ is based on a finite sample of size n; the first approximation improves as $B \rightarrow \infty$, and the second approximation improves as $n \rightarrow \infty$.

Variants of the bootstrap method also differ according to how the bootstrap samples Y^* are constructed. In the *naive* bootstrap, Y^* is constructed by drawing from the empirical distribution of the original data Y. This approach "works" in the sense of yielding estimated confidence intervals with correct coverages whenever the limiting distribution of $\hat{\theta}$ is normal, as proved by Enno Mammen (1992). However, the naive bootstrap often fails in other situations (see Bickel and Freedman [1981] for examples). In cases where data are bounded, constructing bootstrap samples by drawing from a smooth estimate of F, rather than the empirical distribution function, often yields confidence intervals with correct coverages; this approach is called a *smooth* bootstrap. The smooth bootstrap has been used with data envelopment analysis (DEA) estimators to estimate confidence intervals for measures of technical efficiency (see Simar and Wilson [1998, 2000] for details).

The bootstrap method has been increasingly used as computers have become faster and cheaper. It is particularly useful in situations where limiting distributions involve unknown parameters that may be difficult to estimate, which is often the case with nonparametric estimators such as DEA. The method is also useful in situations where limiting normal distributions provide poor approximations to finite-sample distributions of estimators. By constructing bootstrap samples by drawing from either the empirical distribution or a smooth estimate of the distribution of the original data, the bootstrap method incorporates information about higher moments (e.g., skewness, kurtosis, etc.) that is ignored when limiting normal distributions are used to approximate finite sample distributions. This sometimes leads to bootstrap confidence interval estimates with better coverage properties than more conventional confidence interval estimates.

SEE ALSO *Data Envelopment Analysis; Econometric Decomposition; Frequency Distributions*

BIBLIOGRAPHY

Bickel, Peter J., and David A. Freedman. 1981. Some Asymptotic Theory for the Bootstrap. *Annals of Statistics* 9: 1196–1217.

Efron, Bradley. 1979. Bootstrap Methods: Another Look at the Jackknife. *Annals of Statistics* 7: 1–16.

Efron, Bradley. 1982. *The Jackknife, the Bootstrap, and Other Resampling Plans.* Philadelphia: Society for Industrial and Applied Mathematics.

Efron, Bradley, and Robert J. Tibshirani. 1993. *An Introduction to the Bootstrap.* London: Chapman and Hall.

Mammen, Enno. 1992. *When Does Bootstrap Work? Asymptotic Results and Simulations.* Berlin and New York: Springer-Verlag.

Simar, Léopold, and Paul W. Wilson. 1998. Sensitivity Analysis of Efficiency Scores: How to Bootstrap in Nonparametric Frontier Models. *Management Science* 44: 49–61.

Simar, Léopold, and Paul W. Wilson. 2000. A General Methodology for Bootstrapping in Non-parametric Frontier Models. *Journal of Applied Statistics* 27: 779–802.

Paul W. Wilson

BOOTSTRAPS

SEE *Alger, Horatio.*

BORDERLANDS

SEE *Borders.*

BORDERS

All territorial entities have borders, defined as the area where one territory ends and another begins. Borders can be delineated along natural divisions such as mountain ranges or rivers or they can be artificially created. Once delineated, governments demarcate significant portions or all parts of a border with actual markings such as fences, posts, or border checkpoints. The majority of the world's borders are agreed upon, but border disputes exist in all regions of the world. Because border disputes can escalate to armed conflict or war, governments pay significant attention to borders. For this reason, the study of borders is primarily a political issue, but also involves economic and cultural issues.

Politically, borders are most significant for states to signal where their sovereign power exists. Borders are important to states both in actual and symbolic terms. In actual terms, borders protect the state and its population from foreign intrusions and potential threats. Most states maintain strict border controls, mandating that foreigners apply for entry or check in with government officials at the borders. Borders are also often secured to prevent potential attacks from hostile neighboring states or individuals. In a few cases, states such as those in the European Union have demilitarized their borders and opened them to allow for the free flow of people, goods and services, and money, making state borders less relevant. In symbolic terms, borders act as clear indicators to neighboring states that they should not interfere in the governing of territory beyond the border. A key component of sovereignty is territorial control as delineated by a state's borders.

A territorial dispute exists when one state challenges the recognized location of a border. Some of the best-known border disputes have been between India and Pakistan, Ethiopia and Eritrea, Israel and Lebanon, and China and Vietnam. States can resolve border disputes in a variety of ways. The challenging state can attempt to use armed force to move the location of the border, creating an armed conflict. The competing states can also work through bilateral or multilateral negotiations, mediation, arbitration, or adjudication through the World Court. Once a border dispute is settled, the competing states sign a treaty agreeing to the delineation and demarcation of the revised location of the border.

In economic terms, borders signify where a state's economic control exists regarding its gross national product, standard of living, economic policies, currency use, and imports and exports. Borders act as checkpoints for the movement of workers, goods, and services, preventing the ease of sharing labor between states. Culturally, borders often separate distinct cultural groups, both in real terms and metaphorically. In most cases, crossing a border indicates a shift in language, religious practices, social practices, customs, traditions, and food. Borders can also divide one cultural group so that members of a group live in two or more states. In some cases, divided cultural groups seek to reunite through secession or irredentism, causing tension or armed conflict. Borders have both positive and negative connotations, depending on which side of the fence one is located.

BIBLIOGRAPHY

Allcock, John, ed. 1992. *Border and Territorial Disputes.* 3rd ed. Essex, U.K.: Longman Press.

Anderson, Malcolm. 1996. *Frontiers: Territory and State Formation in the Modern World.* Oxford: Polity Press.

Day, Alan J., ed. 1987. *Border and Territorial Disputes.* 2nd ed. Essex, U.K.: Longman Press.

Gottman, Jean. 1973. *The Significance of Territory.* Charlottesville: University Press of Virginia.

Murphy, Alexander. 1990. Historical Justifications for Territorial Claims. *Annals of the Association of American Geographers* 80 (4): 531–548.

Krista E. Wiegand

BORICUA

The ethnic expression Boricua describes someone or something native to Boriken, Borique, Boriquén, Borinquén, Boriquí, or Boriquer—all variations of the Arawak name for the island that Christopher Columbus claimed for Spain in 1493 during his "discovery" of the Americas. While the Iberians later christened it Puerto Rico (Rich Port) in the mistaken belief that it was a veritable gold mine, in 1552 the chronicler Francisco López de Gómara referred to it as "San Juan del Boriqua." Maintaining that the aboriginal population had died out, Spanish colonial authorities made only sporadic use of either Borinquen or Boricua during the next two centuries. Their tallies rarely took into account the undercounting of Tainos by colonists seeking to dodge taxes and import "sturdier" African captives, nor of Tainos who fled into the interior or were reclassified as mestizos. Although some 2,000 "indios" still existed in Puerto Rico at the start of the nineteenth century, Boricuas had undergone a significant ethnogenetic transformation since 1493 as a result of miscegenation with poor, persecuted whites and enslaved Africans who also fled to the mountainous interior.

Over time, a pluricultural population of rural mulatto-mestizo peasants known as *jíbaros* emerged in Spanish colonial Puerto Rico. Characterized by a conscious rejection of Roman Catholic orthodoxy, forced labor, and Iberian cultural hegemony, they dwelled on the periphery of their colonial overseers where they evoked, celebrated, and perpetuated the original pre-Columbian names for the island and its aboriginal people. The *jíbaros* embraced a libertarian ethos that appealed to anticolonial and antislavery causes. For instance, an independence conspiracy led by the German general Ducoudray Holstein in the early 1820s called for the establishment of a República Boricua. An 1853 novel by ardent abolitionist and pro-independence militant Ramón Emeterio Betances was titled, *Les Deux Indiens. Episode de la Conquête de Borinquen.* Even the national anthem of Puerto Rico, "La Borinqueña," a *danza* penned in the 1860s, retained the Antillean appellation. A vast number of modern-day rural barrios, neighborhoods, roads, urban communities, streets, and avenues across the island are called Borinquen. Countless literary, artistic, and musical productions make use of Borinquen and/or Boricua instead of their Spanish counterparts.

Puerto Rican separatists operating in the United States starting in the late 1860s, among them Betances, laid the groundwork for the first Hispanic Caribbean enclaves in New York. By the early 1890s, Francisco Gonzalez Marín y Shaw, Inocencia Martínez Santaella, Sotero Figueroa Fernández, Bernardo Vega, Arturo Alfonso Schomburg, and Eugenio María de Hostos became prominent members of the embryonic Boricua *colonia*. Fittingly, the asylees congregated at the New York clubs Borinquen and Dos Antillas. Other Boricuas joined them following the 1898 Cuban-Spanish-American War, their numbers swelling slowly but perceptively after the passage of the 1917 Jones Act that conferred U.S. citizenship on Puerto Ricans. The pre–World War II (1939–1945) writings of Schomburg (1874–1938) and William Carlos Williams (1888–1963), whose mother was born in Mayagüez and father in England but raised in the Dominican Republic, spoke to a number of Antillean diasporan concerns such as race, identity, and colonialism. Significantly, Schomburg self-identified as *"afroborinqueño"* and named one of his U.S.-born children after the Taino *cacique* (chief or political leader) Guarionex, who led the 1511 uprising against the Spanish colonizers. The expansion of the New York's Boricua community in the post-1950s eventually led to the founding of the Museo del Barrio (1969), Taller Boricua (1970), and Boricua College (1974). There, local Boricua artists, musicians, poets, educators, and community activists further fashioned a Nuyorican (stateside Puerto Rican) expressive culture built largely but not exclusively on Puerto Rico's suppressed Taino and African heritage. Today, the Boricua identity has become a vehicle of cultural affirmation and cultural nationalism as diasporic Puerto Ricans continue to forge a place for themselves in the United States.

SEE ALSO *Blackness; Colonialism; Harlem; Identity; Immigrants, New York City; Nuyoricans; Race; Taino; War of 1898*

BIBLIOGRAPHY

Alvarez Nazario, Manuel. 1977. *El influjo indígena en el español de Puerto Rico.* Río Piedras, Puerto Rico: Editorial de la Universidad de Puerto Rico.

Aparicio, Frances R. 2004. U.S. Latino Expressive Cultures. In *The Columbia History of Latinos in the United States since 1960*, ed. David G. Gutierrez, 355–390. New York: Columbia University Press.

Sánchez González, Lisa. 2001. *Boricua Literature: A Literary History of the Puerto Rican Diaspora.* New York: New York University Press.

Toledo, Josefina. 2000. Ramón Emeterio Betances en la génesis de los clubes Borinquen y Mercedes Varona. In *Pasión por la libertad. Río Piedras,* eds. Félix Ojeda Reyes and Paul Estrade. San Juan, Puerto Rico: Editorial de la Universidad de Puerto Rico/Instituto de Estudios del Caribe.

Jorge L. Chinea

BOSE, SUBHAS CHANDRA AND SARAT CHANDRA

Political leaders from Bengal involved in the Indian nationalist movement in the first half of the twentieth century, Sarat Chandra Bose (1889–1950) and Subhas Chandra Bose (1897–1945) were brothers from a successful high-caste family headed by their father, Janaki Nath Bose. The two brothers attended Presidency College, Calcutta, one of the leading colleges of British India.

Sarat Bose went to Great Britain and was called to the bar from Lincoln's Inn and had a lucrative legal career before the Calcutta High Court for more than three decades. Meanwhile, his more impetuous and devoted younger brother was dismissed from college for involvement in an attack on a British professor who had insulted India. However, Subhas Bose continued his education at Scottish Churches College, graduated, and went on to secure a high position in the examination for the Indian Civil Service in 1920.

Preferring to work in the nationalist movement led by Mahatma Gandhi (1869–1948), Subhas Bose resigned from the civil service and joined the struggle against British rule in his home province of Bengal. In 1924 he became chief executive officer of the Calcutta Corporation (city government), but was arrested soon thereafter for suspicion of smuggling arms. He was imprisoned in Burma and released in 1927. Meanwhile, his activity drew his older brother into nationalist politics and Calcutta affairs.

After his release, Subhas Bose became an important leader of the younger, socialist-inclined nationalists in the Indian National Congress (INC), the main nationalist organization. Although he worked with the nonviolent Gandhian movement, he also had links to underground nationalists who committed acts of violence against their British rulers. In 1930 Subhas Bose was elected mayor of Calcutta and participated in Gandhi's civil disobedience movement. Again arrested in 1932, Subhas Bose was released to go to Europe for medical treatment. Sarat Bose was also arrested and spent 1932 to 1935 in prison.

In the late 1930s Subhas Bose became president of the INC at Gandhi's behest and his brother Sarat was leader of the opposition in the Bengal Legislative Assembly. A conflict with Gandhi led to Subhas Bose's resignation from his INC leadership post in 1939 and then his suspension for disobeying INC strictures about demonstrations. Sarat Bose continued playing an important role in Bengal politics until December 1941. The opening of World War II (1939–1945) changed everything in India.

Believing that the British would never leave India peacefully, Subhas Bose departed India secretly in January 1941 and made his way to Germany, where he set up a propaganda center and organized a small force of Indians into the Indian Legion. He decided to cooperate with the enemies of the British Empire to help destroy it. Because his younger brother was working with the enemy, Sarat Bose was imprisoned from 1941 to 1945.

In 1943 Subhas Bose traveled to Southeast Asia and with Japanese help organized the provisional government of free India and reorganized the Indian National Army (INA) to oppose the British. The Japanese and the INA invaded India in 1944 but were defeated by the Allies. Subhas Bose died in a plane crash in Taiwan in August 1945 as the war ended. Members of the INA were tried for treason, convicted, but then released by the British. In death, Subhas Bose (called "Netaji" or revered leader) became more beloved than in life. Some even disputed that he had ever died in the plane crash.

Sarat Bose was briefly a cabinet minister in the interim government in 1946 and worked to prevent the partition of India as the British prepared to leave the country. After independence and partition in August 1947, Sarat Bose became an opponent and critic of the ruling Congress Party in India, but he died shortly thereafter in 1950.

SEE ALSO *Indian National Army; Indian National Congress*

BIBLIOGRAPHY

Bose, Sisir K., and Sugata Bose, eds. 1997. *The Essential Writings of Netaji Subhas Chandra Bose.* Delhi: Oxford University Press.

Gordon, Leonard A. 1990. *Brothers against the Raj: A Biography of Indian Nationalists Sarat and Subhas Chandra Bose.* New York: Columbia University Press.

Leonard A. Gordon

BOSERUP, ESTER
1910–1999

Ester Boserup was born in Copenhagen in 1910 and graduated from the University of Copenhagen in 1935 in theoretical economics within a broad social science background. Her research work began with a decade at the United Nations and its agencies in the late 1940s; she spent the remainder of her career as a consultant and independent researcher. She died in 1999.

Boserup's primary focus is the relationship between population growth and food supply. The English economist Thomas Robert Malthus (1766–1834) and his followers believed that food supply can only grow slowly and is the main factor governing the rate of population growth. Population growth is therefore seen as the result of previous changes in agricultural productivity. Boserup approaches the problem from the opposite direction. She sets out to demonstrate that the primary stimulus to agricultural productivity is population growth itself.

Boserup groups land use into five different types in order of increasing intensity. The first is *forest-fallow*, in which plots of land are cleared in the forest and planted for a year or two. The land is then left fallow for twenty to twenty-five years in order for the forest to regenerate. With *bush-fallow*, this period is only six to ten years, in which time the land is covered in bush and small trees. *Short-fallow* is a system in which the fallow period is one or two years, during which the land is invaded by wild grasses. With *annual cropping*, the land is left uncultivated for only several months between harvest and planting. Finally, *multicropping* occurs when the same plot of land bears two or more crops every year. But Boserup does not mean the land-use typology to be a classification scheme only; rather, it is meant to characterize the main stages of the evolution of agriculture from prehistoric times to the present.

Once "frequency of cropping" is used as a measure of intensification, theories of the development of agriculture can be directly linked with changes in local landscape, flora, and fauna. For example, as people shorten the fallow period, forests deteriorate and bushes take over the land. Further intensification will bring wild grasses. In this way, many forest and bush areas gradually became savannah as a result of the intensification of agriculture. These new grasslands provide food for cattle, horses, and other animals suitable for domestication.

Both the methods of cultivation and fertilization must become more labor intensive with the shortening of fallow. While such methods produce more crops per acre, they also require far more human labor to produce these yields—and the increase in yield is not commensurate with effort. The short-term effect of intensification, Boserup maintains, necessarily lowers output per manhour. The investments in labor are so large that they are not likely to be made unless population increase makes them necessary. But there are "secondary effects" of the growth of population that lead to real economic growth in the long term. These secondary effects include a compulsion to work harder and more regularly, changing work habits that raise overall productivity, and the facilitation of urbanization, communication, education, the division of labor, and the further intensification of agriculture.

Yet another major contribution Boserup made to the literature on development was her book *Woman's Role in Economic Development* (1970). In this book, Boserup made clear that gender is one of the main criteria for the division of labor in all societies; but, she argued, there is a great diversity in this division of labor between the sexes across societies. The primary factors that are related to the work and subsequent status of women are population density and the availability of land. This division of labor in farming systems carries over into nonfarm activities as well.

Boserup does not so much refute Malthus as round him out by providing a more complete picture of the multitude of relationships between population, agricultural production, and the environment. While Malthus focused upon the necessity to keep human numbers in line with the food that could be produced, Boserup focuses upon how the amount of food that can be produced is dependent upon human numbers. She demonstrates that agricultural production is quite responsive to increased labor. Malthus, on the other hand, also recognized that the production of food could be increased, but he asserted that such intensification could never equal natural population growth for long. Boserup did not dispute this; she did document the fact, however, that a growing population often stimulates an intensification of agricultural production. Malthus made similar assertions in his *Essay on the Principle of Population* (1798). For Malthus, the principle of population "keeps the inhabitants of the earth always fully up to the level of the means of subsistence; and is constantly acting upon man as a powerful stimulus, urging him to the further cultivation of the earth, and to enable it, consequently, to support a more extended population" (Malthus [1798] 2001, p. 281). Boserup's main contribution is in clearly positing these relationships and empirically verifying them throughout the social evolutionary process. Her basic model had great influence on the social evolutionary theory of Mark Cohen, Marvin Harris, and Gerhard Lenski.

BIBLIOGRAPHY

Boserup, Ester. 1965. *The Conditions of Agricultural Growth: The Economics of Agrarian Change under Population Pressure.* New York: Aldine.

Boserup, Ester. 1970. *Woman's Role in Economic Development.* London: Allen and Unwin.

Boserup, Ester. 1999. *My Professional Life and Publications, 1929–1998.* Copenhagen: Museum Tusculanum Press, University of Copenhagen.

Malthus, T. Robert. [1798] 2001. An Essay on the Principle of Population as It Affects the Future Improvement of Society, with Remarks on the speculations of Mr. Godwin, M. Condorcet, and Other Writers. In *A Commentary on Malthus'*

1798 Essay on Population as Social Theory, by Frank W. Elwell, 127–294. Lewiston, NY: Mellen.

Frank W. Elwell

BOURDIEU, PIERRE
1930–2002

Pierre Bourdieu was one of the most prolific and influential social theorists of the second half of the twentieth century. Not only was his output astonishing, but his work has been cited continuously and approvingly by an array of scholars from many disciplines. His initial work intervened in sociology, but as his scholarship broadened, he sought to influence philosophy, anthropology, cultural criticism, psychology, gender studies, linguistics, economics, and finally, for the last two decades of his life, the political arena itself. He is well known for introducing a number of important sociological concepts that have since gained wide currency.

The son of a postal employee, Bourdieu spent his earliest years in a small town in southwestern France, speaking the provincial language, Gascon. At eleven he moved to a boarding school, and by sixteen he was attending the Lycée Louis-le-Grand in Paris. From there he gained entrance to the prestigious École Normale Supérieure. After this background at the top schools of the nation, Bourdieu became a teacher himself; but military service took him to Algeria (then still a colony of France), where he secured a teaching post.

His earliest study, *Sociologie de l'Algérie* (1958, translated as *The Algerians* in 1962), published in the midst of the war of independence in Algeria, established Bourdieu as an important and daring sociologist. In this first book, he divided the peoples of Algeria into four major ethnic categories and showed how colonization had impacted their lives, in effect causing what he called "the total disruption of society." In this book's core distinction between traditional and modern life, the former being swept aside by the latter, one can already see the seeds of Bourdieu's major theoretical concerns with social domination and practice theory. His lifelong ethical commitment to the notions of autonomy, fairness, and equality also gained its first footing in this study.

After returning from his five-year stay in Algeria in 1960, Bourdieu taught at the Sorbonne and was later appointed director of studies at the École des Hautes Études en Sciences Sociales in 1964. In 1975 he launched his influential journal, *Actes de la recherche en sciences sociales* (Records of Research in the Social Sciences), and by 1981 he had attained the prestigious chair of sociology at the Collège de France.

While still publishing influential articles and books on Algeria, he also became interested in social reproduction and began to look deeply into the French educational system and the culture of the Bearn, the part of France where he grew up. As he admitted in several interviews, his own dramatic social trajectory along these same paths contributed much to the sparks of insight that led to his most illuminating theories.

In his much-cited *Outline of a Theory of Practice* (1977), Bourdieu sets forth many of his central ideas, including *symbolic capital, doxa, habitus,* and *misrecognition.* His signal contribution in advancing these ideas was to overcome the limits of subjectivism and objectivism then current in much social thought, divided as it was between the phenomenological tradition and the structuralist one. As a major contributor to the emergent school of poststructuralism, Bourdieu continued to rely heavily on the central dichotomies and contradictions that he found prevailing throughout social life, but he attempted to return agency to the individual within these "objective" structures; this was masterfully displayed, for example, in his analysis of the gift in the *Outline.*

Bourdieu's *Distinction: A Social Critique of the Judgement of Taste* (1984) remains as influential as the *Outline* (it was named one of the "books of the century" by the International Sociological Association); in it, he uses extensive empirical data to show that cultural preference is constituted by endless competition over scarce symbolic, cultural, and economic capital. *Distinction* also stands as strong testimony to Bourdieu's commitment to inductive research methods.

In many ways, Bourdieu was a stalwart defender of the scientific heritage of the social sciences. He issued methodological statements concerning the best way to maintain an objectivist stance while undertaking necessarily subjectivist research, and his central belief in the process of misrecognition revealed that, for Bourdieu, the social world was clouded and distorted by the interests of specific powerful players. The task of sociology was then to unveil the actual reality lying underneath these strategies.

Late in life, Bourdieu joined with another French scholar, Loïc Wacquant, in applying these theories to the social world of scholarship itself. In a salvo titled "On the Cunning of Imperialist Reason" (1999), Bourdieu and Wacquant accused American social science of employing its financial and social clout in order to export American folk theories of race to the rest of the globe, much as he had documented the French state's exportation of social categories to Algeria long ago. In this manner, the misrecognized American system of race was insidiously imposing

itself abroad and was seen to be creating racial categories where perhaps none existed previously. John French, a scholar of Brazil, strongly rebuked Bourdieu and Wacquant, not least by pointing out that their argument rested upon an idealized French folk theory that imagines the creation of a social world devoid of all forms of prejudice. Further, the debate revealed a central weakness of the concept of misrecognition by showing that it is built upon the problematic idea that good scientists can gain access to a non-socially produced, and therefore "objective," reality.

In this regard, Bourdieu can be seen as an heir to Auguste Comte (1798–1857) and Johann Fichte (1762–1814), for he strongly believed that a rationalist social science could liberate humankind from its current "objective conditions." Bourdieu put this belief into practice consistently in the latter part of his life, as he became one of the more outspoken and articulate opponents of neoliberalism and globalization.

SEE ALSO *Lévi-Strauss, Claude*

BIBLIOGRAPHY

PRIMARY WORKS

Bourdieu, Pierre. 1962. *The Algerians.* Trans. Alan C. M. Ross. Boston: Beacon.

Bourdieu, Pierre. 1977. *Outline of a Theory of Practice.* Trans. Richard Nice. Cambridge, U.K.: Cambridge University Press.

Bourdieu, Pierre. 1984. *Distinction: A Social Critique of the Judgement of Taste.* Trans. Richard Nice. Cambridge, MA: Harvard University Press.

Bourdieu, Pierre. 1990. *In Other Words: Essays towards a Reflexive Sociology.* Trans. Matthew Adamson. Stanford, CA: Stanford University Press.

Bourdieu, Pierre. 2000. *Pascalian Meditations.* Trans. Richard Nice. Cambridge, U.K.: Polity.

Bourdieu, Pierre, and Loïc Wacquant. 1999. On the Cunning of Imperialist Reason. *Theory, Culture, and Society* 16 (1): 41–58.

SECONDARY WORKS

Calhoun, Craig, Edward LiPuma, and Moishe Postone, eds. 1993. *Bourdieu: Critical Perspectives.* Chicago: University of Chicago Press.

Grenfell, Michael. 2004. *Pierre Bourdieu: Agent Provocateur.* New York: Continuum.

Gustav Peebles

BOURGEOIS MODE OF PRODUCTION

SEE *Capitalist Mode of Production.*

BOURGEOISIE

In classical Marxian theory, *bourgeoisie* refers to the ruling class of capitalist society. Superseding the feudal aristocracy, its origins have been traced to a relatively early stage in capitalist development, when it was defined by ownership of the means of production. Since the 1800s the functions of management and ownership have become separated, however. As this has occurred, the explanatory value of the term *bourgeoisie* has become attenuated, particularly in discussions of advanced or late capitalism in the era of finance.

In French, *bourgeoisie* originally referred to the society of free men in towns, implying a citizen subject to civil law. The German political philosopher Karl Marx (1818–1882) and his collaborator, the German socialist Friedrich (also spelled Frederick) Engels (1820–1895), understood the bourgeoisie to have emerged from the class of "chartered burghers" in medieval towns, and in their works they trace the development of this class through several stages, from relative oppression under the feudal nobility, to militarized self-governing associations, to independent republics and taxable estates. They also linked the rise of this class to the simplification of class antagonism into a fundamentally binary opposition between the bourgeoisie and the proletariat. Marx never described the actual composition of the bourgeoisie as completely as he described the proletariat, and often the term appears to be interchangeable with *capitalist*.

The factors facilitating the rise of the bourgeoisie were both economic and geopolitical, and these two were related. In Marx's analysis, the drive to accumulation inherent in capitalism must be understood in terms of two kinds of capital, including constant capital (the value of the means of production) and variable capital (the value of labor power). Any expansion in total capital requires a growth in variable capital, which is generally achieved through the enhancement of technological means enabling the increased productivity of labor. A contradiction lies at the heart of this relation, however, for the variable portion of the capital grows more slowly than does the constant portion. This is overcome, says Marx, by increasing the scale of production; the larger the enterprise, the more capacity for accumulation it will have.

The process is, nonetheless, not linear. To begin with, the drive to accumulation generates competition among different capitalists. The result is a complex dialectic between accumulation and concentration, as well as centralization. In this environment, large-scale capital is not only advantaged in relation to smaller capital, because it can control more labor, but it grows at the expense of smaller capital. Such centralization is made possible by the credit system. Moreover, as the economist Rudolf Hilferding has argued, it is the merging of banking and industrial capital that permits and actualizes this centralizing dynamic—though not without countervailing pressures.

Through the credit system, the idle money that accumulates in the course of production is gathered together and made available for investment in production. Time is of the essence here, for the period during which money is not invested in production is, from the perspective of capital, lost. What the banks do, then, is permit enterprises to keep their own money in production, while still being able to draw on it for enhancement or expansion when opportunity arises. When assisted by banking institutions, the corporations no longer have to keep their money in reserve for such opportunities. There is, then, a phantomatic extension of the corporation through credit.

At the same time, other institutions, such as the stock market, permit the creation of joint-stock companies in which collectivities rather than individuals come to function as owners. This "special institution," as Hilferding termed it, provides a market for "titles to interest, or *fictitious capital*" (1981, pp. 107–180). Money is transformed into productive capital through the stock market because the shareholders only expect a return on the yield of the company, and their sale of title does not lead to a withdrawal of money from the corporation's productive machinery.

In this sense, the shareholder is not an owner of the means of production. He is, rather, representative of a new kind of capitalist, a money capitalist, defined by Hilferding as one liberated from the status of industrial entrepreneur. Like the manager, his actions serve the interests of the company and hence of corporate capital, but only in an extremely mediated fashion. Accordingly, many thinkers, most notably Nicos Poulantzas, argue for a reconceptualization of the bourgeoisie as a class defined not by ownership of the means of production but by the function of economic control. Others have disputed this and have preferred to see managers as special kinds of wage laborers.

With the rise of the stock market, and speculation more generally, the creation of value appears to become increasingly separated from the question of production. Initially, this market sought to attract large-scale capital, accumulated by members of a relatively conventional bourgeoisie. Other institutions, such as mutual funds, have extended this process however and, consequently, helped to disseminate the capitalist ideal even among those who are merely wage laborers. They represent a profound cultural transformation and may perhaps help explain the subversion of class consciousness in social milieus defined by financialization. Nonetheless, it is important to understand that industrial capital continues to play a crucial rule even in financialized contexts, and the vast majority of the world's labor remains engaged within it, even though a disproportionate amount of value is produced in and by financial capital.

The forces that would ultimately lead to the political and social transformation of capitalism were, Hilferding thought, internal to capitalism itself. Other, liberal theorists agreed, though for different reasons. Adolf Berle, for example, saw the concentration and centralization of capital in the huge corporations of the United States in the mid-twentieth century as a direct product of joint stock organization. But while relying upon state regulation, which, for example, provides tax incentives for philanthropic giving, Berle argued that the new corporations themselves assumed a "quasi-political" role. He argued further that the greatest incentive to corporate growth and rationalization is the threat of competition from state enterprises. Corporate investment in local infrastructural development and education as well as international diplomacy carried out by corporate representatives constitutes, for Berle, the hallmark of a specifically American form of corporatist capitalism whose defining attribute is its antipathy to statism.

Berle's conception of what might be termed, in an idiom coined by the French philosopher Michel Foucault, corporate "governmentality" may be contrasted to Marx's original conception of the relationship between bourgeois political and economic form. Marx had argued that the bourgeoisie assumed economic predominance partly through its development of a political form capable of representing its interests, namely bourgeois democracy. Although a national entity, the bourgeois democratic state was nonetheless made possible only by the reordering of local economies in colonial territories—to produce markets for European goods and to permit the extraction of natural resources for processing in metropolitan centers or, later, to serve as export processing zones. Hilferding went so far as to argue that the inhibiting influences of cartelization and protectionism within European states could only be overcome by outward expansion, and hence that the development of European capital led inevitably to imperialism, a thesis shared in different ways by both the Russian Communist thinkers Nikolay Bukharin (1888–1938) and Vladimir Lenin (1870–1924).

Toward the end of the twentieth century, economic theorists began to observe a rupture in the relationship between nation-states and corporate capital, and a supersession of the bourgeois nation-state by regional trade bodies and economic consortia (such as the North American Free Trade Agreement, the European Union, and the G8) that, while backed by the governmental authority of nation-states, attempt to ensure that domestic protectionism, which might have been deployed by national capital, does not inhibit the expansion of capital,

per se. As Hilferding anticipated, financial institutions have assumed an increasingly dominant role in such contexts, and access to credit has become a significant index of economic power for both corporations and individual persons. The development of a sphere of value-creation relatively unmoored from production, through currency trading, real estate speculation, and derivatives trading, suggests that the old bourgeoisie has not only been liberated from the function of industrial entrepreneur but that the money capitalist has become the new bearer of capital's own self-interest.

SEE ALSO *Capitalism; European Union; G8 Countries; Globalization, Social and Economic Aspects of; Marx, Karl; Marxism; North American Free Trade Agreement; Poulantzas, Nicos*

BIBLIOGRAPHY

Berle, Adolf. 1932. *The Modern Corporation and Private Property.* New York: Commerce Clearing House.

Berle, Adolf. 1954. *The Twentieth-Century Capitalist Revolution.* New York: Harcourt Brace.

Hilferding, Rudolf. 1981. *Finance Capital: A Study of the Latest Phase of Capitalist Development.* Trans. Morris Watnick and Sam Gordon. Boston: Routledge and Kegan Paul.

Mandel, Ernest. 1978. *Late Capitalism.* Trans. Joris de Bres. New York: Verso.

Marx, Karl. 1978. The Class Struggles in France, 1848–1850. In *Karl Marx, Frederick Engels: Collected Works*, Vol. 10, 45–145. New York: International Publishers. (Orig. pub. 1850).

Marx, Karl. 1992. *Capital.* Vols. 1 and 3. Ed. and intro. C. J. Arthur. London: Lawrence and Wishart. (Orig. pub. 1867, 1885, 1894).

Marx, Karl, and Frederick Engels. 1998. *The Communist Manifesto.* New York: Verso. (Orig. pub. 1848).

Poulantzas, Nicos. 1978. *Classes in Contemporary Capitalism.* Trans. David Fernbach. New York: Verso.

Rosalind C. Morris

BOURGEOISIE, PETTY

The term *petty bourgeoisie* originally referred to the class of people involved in small-scale commercial enterprises who owned their means of production. It included merchants and traders, and, in some cases, wealthier land-owning farmers. Thus conceived, this class partakes of the structures of private property on which capitalist society is grounded, but it does not own sufficient capital to reap the benefits of large-scale industrialization and workplace rationalization. Moreover, its members are not dependent upon the sale of their own labor-power. They occasionally employ others, although, unlike capitalists, they themselves must also work, and often do so alongside their employees, including family members.

The petty bourgeoisie has been assigned a particularly significant role in Marxian historiography by virtue of Karl Marx's (1818–1883) claim that, during the failed revolution of 1848 in France, they transferred their allegiance from the proletariat to the bourgeoisie. In the mid-1840s, a period of famine and widespread discontent throughout Europe but especially in France, the petty bourgeoisie had fought alongside members of the urban proletariat and students to demand workers' rights and liberal political reform. However, when this conflict began to assume anarchic dimensions, they joined with the bourgeoisie, the conservative peasantry, and residual feudal powers to support a counterrevolution whose outcome was the establishment of the Second Republic and a new era of European despotism.

By the late twentieth century, the term had receded from usage, and has been replaced in large measure by *middle class*. This has occurred at the same time that the term *middle class* has come to be dissociated from its original referent of the bourgeoisie. The reasons for this development, particularly in the United States, reveal much about both the nature of economic life in contemporary capitalist society and the ideology by which it is sustained. This ideology can be described as one that valorizes the middle class, that sees its expansion as the necessary condition of economic growth and democratization, and that links middle classness to upward mobility.

Significantly, this understanding rests on a slippage in the definition of the middle class from Marx's time. Friedrich Engels (1820–1895) had warned against this possibility in a letter to Marx in 1852. There, he distinguished the middle class as that group between the nobility, which it had superseded, and the proletariat, which would ultimately displace it. In this sense, *middle class* meant *transitional class* for Engels, rather than simply the class of small business people and professional managers now typically associated with the term.

However, the question of transition has itself become problematic in economic history. The joint stock company, which Marx believed to be a mere stage in the development and transformation of capital, now dominates capitalist enterprise, and its professional managers (as well as their support service workers) now form the core of what is sometimes referred to as the "new petty bourgeoisie."

Like the more classically conceived proletariat, these individuals are also employees of capitalist enterprises. However, they do not own the means of production in the sense that enables them to alienate it, and they are somewhat contradictorily positioned as the representatives of capitalist interests. Various theorists have tried to exclude

this new form of the petty bourgeoise from the categories of both the bourgeoisie and the working class, on the basis that they perform "unproductive" mental labor which is antithetical to the interests of the proletariat (Poulantzis 1975); that they do not own the means of production despite exercising the "function" of capital (Carchedi 1977); or, more generally, because older notions of property ownership no longer describe the ambiguous distribution of rights over property that define modern joint stock companies today (Olin Wright 1978). In each of these cases, the managerial classes are thought of as a problem for both theory and radical political organization. Allin Cottrell (1984) nonetheless suggests that the variability in forms of ownership, social roles, and ideological commitments that characterize the managerial classes in contemporary capitalist societies requires a new conception of class, and prohibits any predictive model identifying the new petty bourgeoisie with any particular political orientation.

The older model of the petty bourgeoisie nonetheless retains great ideological force in many neoliberal societies, where the idea of the self-employed businessperson who is free from the demand to sell his or her own labor continues to occupy a dominant position in popular representations of the middle classes. It is often associated with radical individualism, as well as the values of personal autonomy and rational decision making. Moreover, it is frequently imagined as the ideal form of immigrant assimilation—and serves as a counter-image to balance other immigrant economies, including those of short term contract labor in the agricultural or energy sectors, and the feminized economies of domestic and sexual labor.

SEE ALSO *Bourgeoisie; Capitalism; Class; Liberalism; Marx, Karl; Marxism; Middle Class; Neoliberalism; Welfare State*

BIBLIOGRAPHY

Carchedi, G. 1977. *On the Economic Identification of Social Classes.* London: Routledge and Kegan Paul.

Cottrell, Allin. 1984. *Social Classes in Marxist Theory.* London: Routledge and Kegan Paul.

Marx, Karl. [1850] 1978. *The Class Struggles in France, 1848–1850.* In *Karl Marx, Frederick Engels: Collected Works*, Vol. 10, 45–145. New York: International Publishers.

Marx, Karl. [1852] 1951. *Eighteenth Brumaire of Louis Bonaparte*, with explanatory notes. New York: International Publishers.

Olin Wright, E. 1978. *Class, Crisis and the State.* London: New Left Books.

Poulantzis, N. 1975. *Social Classes in Contemporary Capitalism.* London: New Left Books.

Rosalind C. Morris

BOWLBY, JOHN
1907–1990

John Mostyn Bowlby was a British child psychiatrist who developed *attachment theory*, which posited that poor relationships (attachments) to caregivers in early childhood are the primary cause of most childhood disorders. When first introduced in the 1940s, attachment theory was shunned by the psychoanalytic movement because it conflicted with some principles of psychoanalysis that were popular at the time. Attachment theory is now highly regarded as a well-established and well-researched explanation of childhood behavioral and emotional problems.

Born in 1907 to an upper-middle-class family in London, Bowlby was raised in traditional British fashion by nannies, until he was sent to boarding school at age seven. After his 1928 graduation from the medical college at the University of Cambridge, he volunteered at two homes serving "maladjusted and delinquent" children. While there, he began to investigate the early influences of the family on later childhood difficulties. To further develop his ideas on the impact of family relationships on the mental health of children, Bowlby returned to school to study child psychiatry, psychoanalysis, and psychotherapy.

At the British Psychoanalytic Institute, Bowlby trained with instructors who were among the most influential analysts of the time, including Melanie Klein (1882–1960). Although trained primarily in adult psychiatry, Bowlby returned to his work with the London Child Guidance Clinic in 1937.

In 1940 Bowlby wrote the first of several controversial papers demonstrating his divergence from contemporary psychoanalytic trends. Bowlby stated that psychoanalysts should study the "nature of the organism, the properties of the soil, and their interaction" (1940, p. 23) rather than the unconscious drives or urges that characterized the Freudian approach to understanding childhood behaviors and emotions. While at the London Clinic, Bowlby began systematic research using patient case histories to link symptoms to parental "deprivation and separation" (Bretherton 1992, p. 761).

After World War II (1939–1945), Bowlby headed the Children's Department at the Tavistock Clinic and began studying homeless children and children separated from their parents by hospitalization. In 1952 Bowlby and colleague James Robertson (1911–1988) filmed the documentary *A Two-Year-Old Goes to Hospital*, which alarmed clinicians regarding the impact of maternal separation, and influenced hospitals to change strict visitation policies.

In 1957 Bowlby presented the first formal statement of his theory that the mother-child attachment has an ethological-evolutionary foundation—that is, children, like the young of most animals, have innate behaviors promoting contact with the parent to enhance survival. Bowlby concluded that a child's survival is more likely when the child is emotionally connected and in proximity to the mother. Bowlby eventually split completely from the Kleinian psychoanalytic school and established a research unit focused on mother-child separation, continuing his work with influential researchers, including Mary Ainsworth (1913–1999). Ainsworth's research on the normative child-mother relationship across various cultures complemented Bowlby's research. Ainsworth's findings supported Bowlby's theory of the importance of early parental relationships on the behavioral and emotional well-being of children.

Bowlby continued to develop attachment theory, and spent the last decades of his life, until his death in 1990, refining the clinical application of the theory.

SEE ALSO *Ainsworth, Mary; Attachment Theory; Separation Anxiety*

BIBLIOGRAPHY

Bowlby, John. 1940. The Influence of Early Environment in the Development of Neurosis and Neurotic Character. *International Journal of Psycho-Analysis* 21: 154–178.

Bretherton, Inge. 1992. The Origins of Attachment Theory: John Bowlby and Mary Ainsworth. *Developmental Psychology* 28: 759–775.

van Dijken, Suzan. 1998. *John Bowlby: His Early Life, a Biographical Journey into the Roots of Attachment Theory.* London: Free Association.

van Dijken, Suzan, René van der Veer, Marinus van Ijzendoorn, and Hans-Jan Kuipers. 1998. Bowlby Before Bowlby: The Sources of an Intellectual Departure in Psychoanalysis and Psychology. *Journal of the History of Behavioral Sciences* 34 (3): 247–269.

Melissa D. Grady

BOX-COX TRANSFORMATION
SEE *Regression Analysis.*

BOYD, RICHARD
SEE *Realist Theory.*

BRACERO PROGRAM

In August 1942, more than ten thousand men converged on Mexico City. They were answering the government's call to combat fascism by signing up to do agricultural work in the United States. Although initiated as a temporary measure to alleviate a tightening U.S. labor market brought on by World War II, the Mexican–U.S. Program of the Loan of Laborers lasted for 22 years and awarded more than 4.5 million work contracts to nearly two million Mexican men. Competition for contracts also stimulated undocumented migration of at least that many. Many Mexican men (women could not participate) benefited economically from this regulated migration, but the biggest beneficiary of the Bracero Program, the unofficial name for the series of binational agreements, were large growers. The availability of thousands of desperate braceros, as the migrants were called, generated massive corruption in both countries, acted as a downward push on farm wages, undercut unionization efforts, and enabled growers to delay mechanization until it was cost-effective.

Soon after entering World War II, the U.S. government approached Mexico about the possibility of bringing laborers north. Most important to Mexico was that the U.S. government, not individual growers, be responsible for men migrating under the program, and that both governments monitor the proper functioning of the program and investigate abuses. For all but a brief interlude (1948–1951) did this condition stand. Complaints multiplied during this interlude, and the condition was reinstituted with the start of the Korean War, when Mexico's bargaining hand was strengthened because of a contraction in the U.S. labor market due to the war. Bracero agreements also contained wage guarantees (braceros were to be paid the area's prevailing wage for the crop picked) and requirements for sanitary housing, access to medical care, and a minimum of weeks for which they would be paid, regardless of weather conditions, making braceros' protections far stronger than those extended to U.S. domestic farm workers. Although the agreement stipulated that growers prove they had attempted to recruit U.S. workers before their request for Mexican laborers be granted, in practice this requirement was waived or ignored. Generally growers, relying on long relationships with local government officials, had only to say they could find no U.S. laborers to work for the advertised wage and their request for braceros would be granted. Over time these practices depressed wages and undermined unionization.

The United States always controlled the maximum number of bracero spots offered, and Mexico could allocate these spots (or fewer ones) according to domestic needs. Thus, Mexico theoretically retained the right to decide where braceros worked. It acted on this right initially when it refused to send men to Texas, citing a history of discrimination against Mexican citizens and Mexican Americans. In response, in 1943 Coke R. Stevenson, the governor of Texas from 1941 to 1947, instituted the Good Neighbor Commission to investigate the problem. Convinced that Texas was taking steps to address the problem or merely recognizing that undocumented migrants were crossing into the United States anyway, Mexico consented and by 1947 state-sanctioned braceros were heading to that state. Also negotiated by the two countries was the location of reception centers where the final bracero selection would occur. Mexico repeatedly pushed to place centers a great distance from the United States' preferred locations at the border. Mexico also sought to reduce costs—Mexico paid men's transportation and board to reception centers, after which the United States took over—and to control the outflow of migrants to prevent its own farm-labor shortage in northern Mexico, where workers were poorly paid and scarce. As reception centers moved closer to the border, undocumented migration increased. This move also drew men away from less well-paid farm labor in northern Mexico and aroused the ire of these large landholders. Initially the binational agreement also contained a provision that 10 percent of workers' wages be put in escrow until the men returned. Mexico fought hard for this provision, in force between 1942 and 1948, as it wanted to guarantee that, in contrast to earlier migrations, the men would return home with funds that could be used to purchase tractors and other equipment. While Mexico was heavily invested in this provision, few workers knew of it, and most have yet to recoup these funds.

With alarmist discussion of a labor shortage, growers pressured the U.S. government to replicate the informal contract system that had prevailed during World War I, when labor agents recruiting in Mexico promised workers wages and living conditions that were too often unmet. The United States recognized, however, that Mexico would not agree to any program of regulated migration without certain conditions. Furthermore, the United States was not in a position to ignore conditions sought by Mexico, for much had changed since the earlier informal program. Not only did the United States government initiate the formal exchange of workers, but President Franklin Roosevelt (in office 1933–1945) had entered office determined to establish better relations with Latin America. In contrast to earlier doctrines, his Good Neighbor Policy emphasized cooperation and guaranteed the sanctity of each sovereign American nation. As well, the Mexican president, Lázaro Cárdenas (in office 1934–1940), had, in a show of national sovereignty, nationalized oil fields in 1938, many of which had been owned by U.S. companies. Although Cárdenas had offered compensation according to the value companies listed on earlier tax rolls, the companies balked, saying that nationalized fields were worth more. Thus, in exchange for the Bracero Program and a recognition of Mexico's sovereignty, the United States had not much earlier settled the compensation issue and conceded to some of Mexico's demands. Over the course of the program, Mexico lost its leverage because its economy could not offer enough jobs, leading many men to migrate.

AFTER THE BRACERO PROGRAM

In the forty-plus years since the end of the Bracero Program, there have been numerous calls to bring it back in various forms. The most recent was President George W. Bush's push to institute a guest-worker program similar to the Bracero program. An idea proposed during his 2000 campaign for president, it was put on hold immediately after September 11, 2001, then resurfaced in 2003. By then, his expanded proposal added a post-9/11 heavy dose of border security (including a physical and virtual fence), increased enforcement of laws already on the books, and the removal of all persons in the country without the proper documentation in exchange for his guest worker program; it was also part of a larger package of changes to immigration laws.

President Bush's revised proposal garnered attacks from all sides. Citing downward pressure on workers' wages and fearing the cultural impact of largely poor immigrants of color, the anti-immigration faction countered the Bush proposal by demanding that only the removal and enhanced-security conditions be instituted. This anti-immigration position is best exemplified by the Minutemen Civil Defense Corps and Congressman Jim Sensenbrenner of Wisconsin. The Minutemen, an armed volunteer force and a visible symbol of a growing nativist sentiment operating largely in border states, have taken it upon themselves to secure U.S. borders that they see the federal government leaving unprotected. Sensenbrenner spotlighted a focus on security with a bill called the Border Protection, Anti-terrorism, and Illegal Immigration Control Act of 2005. This legislation, which passed the House by a vote of 239 to 182, would have made it a felony for anyone to "assist" an undocumented person to "remain in the United States." Although the bill stalled in the Senate, it generated a strong reaction, not only from pro-immigration groups, but from the immigrants themselves. On May 1, 2006, hundreds of thousands of immigrant protesters took to the streets in Chicago, Los Angeles, and other parts of the country in reaction to Sensenbrenner's restrictive legislation; they demanded a comprehensive reform package that included a path to legal residency and citizenship. This immigration debate also heightened simmering tensions between Latinos and African Americans. Often pitted against Latinos and recent immigrants for low-wage jobs and shrinking economic resources more generally, many African Americans see themselves ever more on the losing end of a direct competition with Latinos and immigrants.

Immigrants again turned out across the United States for peaceful May Day 2007 marches as federal officials increased their investigations of job sites known or thought to cater to immigrants. These raids have brought quick arrests of undocumented workers. In the aftermath, children—often United States citizens—have been separated from undocumented parents and wives from husbands, sending reverberations through immigrant communities. In 2007 another immigration bill, the Security through Regularized Immigration and a Vibrant Economy Act of 2007 (or STRIVE Act), was introduced in Congress. Although it was not guaranteed passage in the Democrat-controlled Congress, this compromise between pro- and anti-immigration factions has sought to combine heightened border security and a Bracero Program–like guest-worker program with a real path to citizenship for the estimated 12 million undocumented persons living in the United States.

SEE ALSO *Fascism; Immigrants, Latin American; Korean War; Labor; Migrant Labor; Nationalization; World War II*

BIBLIOGRAPHY

Anderson, Henry P. 1963. *Fields of Bondage; Mexican Contract Labor System in Industrialized Agriculture.* Martinez, CA: self-published.

Anderson, Henry P. 1976. *The Bracero Program in California.* New York: Arno Press.

Calavita, Kitty. 1992. *Inside the State: The Bracero Program, Immigration, and the I.N.S.* New York: Routledge.

Cohen, Deborah. 2001. Masculine Sweat, Stoop-Labor Modernity: Gender, Race, and Nation in Mid–Twentieth Century Mexico and the U.S. PhD dissertation, University of Chicago.

Craig, Richard B. 1971. *The Bracero Program: Interest Groups and Foreign Policy.* Austin: University of Texas Press.

García y Griego, Manuel. 1983. The Importation of Mexican Contract Laborers to the United States, 1942–1964. In *The Border That Joins: Mexican Migrants and U.S. Responsibility,* eds. Peter G. Brown and Henry Shue, 45–85. Totowa, NJ: Rowman and Littlefield.

Grove, Wayne A. 1996. The Mexican Farm Labor Program, 1942–1964: Government-Administered Labor Market Insurance for Farmers. *Agricultural History* 70 (2): 302–320.

Mize, Ronald Lee. 2000. The Invisible Workers: Articulations of Race and Class in the Life Histories of Braceros. PhD dissertation, University of Wisconsin, Madison.

Ngai, Mae M. 2004. *Impossible Subjects: Illegal Aliens and the Making of Modern America.* Princeton, NJ: Princeton University Press.

Ngai, Mae M. 2005. Braceros, "Wetbacks," and the National Boundaries of Class. In *Repositioning North American Migration History: New Directions in Modern Continental Migration, Citizenship, and Community,* ed. Marc S. Rodriguez, 206–264. Rochester, NY: University of Rochester Press.

Rasmussen, Wayne D. 1951. *A History of the Emergency Farm Labor Supply Program, 1943–47.* Washington, DC: U.S. Department of Agriculture, Bureau of Agricultural Economics.

Deborah Cohen

BRAHMINS

The word *Brahmin* appeared for the first time in Purush-Sukta, a section of the Rig Veda. The Purush-Sukta described the divine origin of human beings into the four social groups, or castes, that comprise Hindu society: Brahmin, Kshatriya, Vaishya, and Sudra. According to the Purush-Sukta, God Brahma gave birth to the divinities associated with each caste: Brahmin was born from the mouth, Kshatriya from the arms, Vaishya from the thighs, and Sudra from the calves of Brahma. Later on this concept of the divine origin of Brahmins and other castes was repeated in numerous religious texts, including the Manusmriti, the famous Hindu religious compendium of customary laws.

The Manusmriti codifies the Hindu social order—that is, the caste system. The caste system assigns rights to each of the four castes. These civil, cultural, and economic rights are divided in an unequal manner; however, Brahmin are placed at the top of the hierarchy of castes and given special privileges over the other castes, while basic rights are denied to other castes.

The Manusmriti makes it clear that Brahmin is the best of all creations on earth. Manu prescribed six main deeds for Brahmins: learning, teaching, performing *yajña*, getting *yajña* performed, giving donations, and taking donations. Kshatriyas were assigned the duty of war and defense, Vaishyas were directed to conduct business, and Sudras were enjoined to serve the three other castes.

The Brahmin was treated as the supreme creation based on the concept of purity, whereas other castes, especially the Sudras, were declared impure and hence inferior. This social construct was spread through a variety of subsequent religious texts, such as the Purānas. The mythical concepts underlying caste divisions became so powerfully resonant that even in the early twenty-first century some people carry the notion of the supremacy of Brahmins due to their blind faith in the Purānas.

The concept of Brahmin emerged in ancient India. References to the cultural and religious practices of early Brahmins reveal that they were basically a ritualistic group following a variety of primitive faiths. They invented numerous religious rituals around their philosophy of *yajña* (a religious ritual to satisfy the god). In the initial stage of their development, *yajñas* were associated with the sacrificing of animals and a few other rituals. They also became the source of earnings for the Brahmins through the religious concept of *daan-dakshina* (donation). Over time rituals became associated with more and more aspects of social and cultural life, as Brahmins began to prescribe rituals for every social and individual event, from birth to death. This development made the Brahmin community into a priesthood that also became divine. On the basis of this priesthood, the Brahmins claimed to be mediators between God and humans. Such ideas created the belief that God could be pleased only through Brahmins. Even kings became subservient to Brahmins. In this context it is interesting to note that Brahmins did not assign the office of king to themselves. They believed that kings would never go to heaven, because they have to engage in sinful activity to run the state. For this reason Brahmins chose Kshatriya, the next in the caste hierarchy after them, to become kings. At the same time Brahmins exerted indirect control over kings by acting as their advisers or prime ministers. Through this system, Brahminism became the rule of law not only in terms of religious practice but also in the day-to-day affairs of the state and society.

The divinity attributed to Brahmins and the caste system created huge inequities in society, such as the denial of certain basic rights to other castes and extreme forms of deprivation, particularly for the low-caste Sudras (the former untouchables). In reaction to these circumstances, Gautama Buddha challenged the Brahmin claim to a divinely based supremacy over other people and castes. According to Buddha, no one was born a Brahmin or a Sudra and anyone could become Brahmin or Sudra through his or her actions. He also challenged the infallibility of Vedas that had been declared divine by Brahmins. Buddha propounded the principle of social equality and argued that Brahmin, Kshatriya, Vaishya, and Sudra were all born similarly from the same part of the body as a result of biological union between man and woman. He also denied the existence of God and the soul.

Buddha's teachings spread among all levels of the Indian population, which ultimately resulted in the rapid deterioration of the Brahminical order and the supremacy of Brahmins. There was, however, a revival of Vedic rituals in the last quarter of the ninth century associated with

Adi Shankarcharaya. This led to a corresponding decline in the influence of Buddhism. As Brahminism reemerged, the caste system became more rigidly based on an extreme form of untouchability. B. R. Ambedkar has described this victory of Brahminism over Buddhism as a cultural counterrevolution.

In the early twenty-first century the Indian constitution provides for equal individual rights and does not recognize distinctions based on the caste system and the traditional superiority of Brahmins. However, the residual consequences and effects of caste traditions are still felt in some cultural, social, and religious spheres if not all.

SEE ALSO *Buddha; Buddhism; Caste; Caste, Anthropology of; Dalits; Hierarchy; Kshatriyas; Purification; Religion; Rituals; Stratification; Sudras; Vaisyas*

BIBLIOGRAPHY

Ambedkar, B. R. 1996. *Buddhist Revolution and Counter-Revolution in Ancient India.* Delhi: B. R. Pub. Corp; New Delhi: Sales Office, D. K. Publishers, Distributors.

Sukhadeo Thorat

BRAIN DRAIN

Approximately 3 percent of the world's population were immigrants in 2000 (International Organization for Migration [IOM] 2005). Within this group was a significant proportion of highly skilled and educated individuals who left their country of birth and settled elsewhere. This process is referred to as the *brain drain* because the sending countries in many instances lose a significant number of their most highly skilled people.

The economists' approaches to discussing the brain drain were laid out in the early 1970s in a series of articles coauthored by Jagdish Bhagwati (1973, 1974, 1975, 1976). Although he was not the first economist to address the brain drain (see for example Grubel and Scott 1966, Johnson 1967, and Berry and Soligo 1969), Bhagwati and his coauthors were the first to address it systematically at a theoretical, empirical, and policy level. And many of the issues raised in these articles have become staples of the debate surrounding the phenomenon of the brain drain.

Although worldwide estimates of the proportion of immigrants who contribute to brain drain are not available, reliable estimates of immigrants and education status in Organization for Economic Cooperation and Development (OECD) countries are available. While highly skilled immigrants do immigrate to other countries, these OECD countries represent a significant destination. These estimates report that approximately 35 percent of immigrants over twenty-five years of age to OECD countries had a tertiary education, while only 11 percent of the worldwide labor force had the equivalent education (Docquier and Marfouk 2006). This means that on average those who emigrated were more highly educated than the population they left. In most instances the sending countries tend to be developing countries, which have lower rates of highly skilled workers in the population, while the receiving countries are developed countries. This occurs because most of this type of emigration is driven by the wage and opportunity differentials between countries and the preference given to the immigration of skilled labor by developed countries.

The magnitude of this phenomenon increased during the 1990s, and all evidence suggests a continuation of this trend (Docquier and Marfouk 2006). This is cause for worry for policymakers in developing countries, as they lose significant parts of their most educated individuals. For example, while individuals with tertiary degrees make up only 3 percent of the sub-Saharan African population, 43 percent of the emigrants have this level of education. Other regions face a similar problem. According to the World Bank in 2005, the numbers for tertiary educated individuals and emigrants with tertiary degrees are 6 and 47 percent respectively for Asia and 9 and 39 percent for the island nations of the Caribbean. These are not only significant proportions of the emigrants but can also be very large proportions of the stock of educated individuals within the country. For example, most Caribbean nations lose between 61 and 89 percent of their tertiary educated individuals to emigration, while numerous African countries lose over 30 percent (Docquier and Marfouk 2006).

While there are numerous concerns for sending countries, and often these may differ by country, three main concerns have been identified. The first is that these countries lose individuals who are important in the delivery of crucial public services such as health and education. Compounding this loss is that in these areas the sending countries do not have sufficient personnel. The second concern is that the individuals lost are among those most capable of contributing to the dialogue for both progressive political and socioeconomic change in the country. The third concern is that in most instances the significant cost of training these individuals has been primarily borne by the public sector and is now not recoverable in taxes these individuals would have paid and services they would have provided to the community (IOM 2005; Ozden and Schiff 2006). In contrast, receiving nations gain by filling in gaps in skilled personnel at a lower cost than they would have otherwise, and gaining in the different knowledge and insights that the immigrants bring. For example it has been estimated that a reduction in visas for graduate students and skilled immigrants to the United States would result in a reduction in both patent and grant applications (Chellaraj, Maskus, and Mattoo 2006).

The concern with brain drain has also resulted in the discussion of two related phenomena, brain gain and brain waste. Brain gain is the idea that because emigration raises the rate of return of education in the sending country, more investment might take place in education and could possibly lead to a net gain in educated personnel. This idea was formalized in the literature by Bhagwati and Hamada (1974). The most recent and comprehensive study, however, finds that the gains are small and do not replace the loss due to brain drain (Ozden 2006). Brain waste is a concern, raising the question of whether the receiving countries are efficiently using the skilled emigrants they receive. From the data available it appears that a large number of skilled immigrants to OECD countries often end up in jobs for which they are significantly overqualified. This can be the result of language or cultural barriers or lack of understanding of how to interpret qualifications from different educational institutions.

The brain drain has evaded easy policy prescription because successful policy that maintains an individual's right to emigrate and recognizes the society's loss from this emigration would require the collaboration of both receiving and sending nations. One of the more interesting and thought-provoking proposals addressing a number of the concerns raised by brain drain is a "brain tax" initially proposed by Bhagwati and Hamada (1974). The proposed tax was to be imposed on the émigrés and the funds collected administered by an international organization such as the United Nations Development Programme (UNDP) for development in less industrialized countries. The strength of this proposal was that it did not interfere with an individual's right to migrate, but by taxing the individual it recovered some of the cost and positive externalities that the sending country had lost. It also marginally reduced the incentive to migrate by reducing the post-tax income of émigrés.

SEE ALSO *Bhagwati, Jagdish; Globalization, Social and Economic Aspects of; Human Capital; Immigration*

BIBLIOGRAPHY

Berry, R. A., and R. Soligo. 1969. Some Welfare Aspects of International Migration. *Journal of Political Economy* 77 (5): 778–794.

Bhagwati, Jagdish N. 1976. The Brain Drain. *International Social Science Journal* 28 (4): 691–729.

Bhagwati, Jagdish, and William Dellalfar. 1973. The Brain Drain and Income Taxation. *World Development* 1: (1–2): 94–101.

Bhagwati, Jagdish, and Koichi Hamada. 1974. The Brain Drain, International Integration of Markets for Professionals and Unemployment: A theoretical Analysis. *Journal of Development Economics* 1 (1): 19–42.

Bhagwati, Jagdish, and Carlos A. Rodriguez. 1975. Welfare-Theoretical Analyses of the Brain Drain. *Journal of Development Economics* 2 (3): 195–221.

Chellaraj, Gnanaraj, Keith E. Maskus, and Aaditya Mattoo. 2006. Skilled Immigrants, Higher Education and U.S. Innovation. In *International Migration, Remittances, and Brain Drain*, ed. Caglar Ozden and Maurice Schiff, 245–326. Washington, DC: World Bank and Palgrave Macmillan.

Docquier, Fredric, and Abdeslam Marfouk. 2006. International Migration by Education Attainment. In *International Migration, Remittances, and Brain Drain*, ed. Caglar Ozden and Maurice Schiff, 151–201. Washington, DC: World Bank and Palgrave Macmillan.

Grubel, Herbert G., and Anthony D. Scott. 1966. The International Flow of Human Capital. *American Economic Review* May: 268–274.

Hamada, Koichi, and Jagdish Bhagwati. 1975. Domestic Distortions, Imperfect Information and the Brain Drain. *Journal of Development Economics* 2 (3): 265–279.

International Organization for Migration. 2005. *World Migration 2005*. Geneva, Switzerland: Author.

Johnson, H. G. 1967. Some Economic Aspects of Brain Drain. *Pakistan Development Review* 3: 379–411.

Ozden, Caglar. 2006. Educated Migrants: Is There Brain Waste? In *International Migration, Remittances and Brain Drain*, ed. Caglar Ozden and Maurice Schiff, 227–244. Washington, DC: World Bank and Palgrave Macmillan.

Ozden, Caglar, and Maurice Schiff. 2006. Overview. In *International Migration, Remittances and Brain Drain*, ed. Caglar Ozden and Maurice Schiff, 1–18. Washington, DC: World Bank and Palgrave Macmillan.

Schiff, Maurice. 2006. Brain Gain: Claims About Its Size and Impact on Welfare and Growth Are Greatly Exaggerated. In *International Migration, Remittances, and Brain Drain*, ed. Caglar Ozden and Maurice Schiff, 201–226. Washington, DC: World Bank and Palgrave Macmillan.

Mwangi wa Gĩthĩnji

BRANDING
SEE *Advertising.*

BRAZELTON, T. BERRY
1918–

In his roles as researcher, clinician, and advocate for parents, T. Berry Brazelton has been one of the formative influences on pediatrics in the United States for over fifty years. For much of the earlier part of the twentieth century, it was assumed that the newborn infant was a "blank slate," operating at a brain-stem level, and the care of the newborn seemed to reflect this assumption. It can be argued that one of the most important advances in the study and treatment of the newborn infant was the development and publication of the Neonatal Behavioral Assessment Scale (NBAS) by Brazelton and his colleagues in 1973. Unlike the classic neurological scales, which were designed to identify abnormalities in newborn functioning, the NBAS examines the competencies of the newborn infant while at the same time identifying areas of concern. It has been used in hundreds of research studies to assess the effects of a wide range of prenatal and perinatal influences on newborn behavior, including prematurity and low birthweight and prenatal substance abuse. From the time it was first published, the NBAS has been used to document cultural variation in newborn behavior across a wide range of cultures. In recent years, it has also been successfully used as a method of helping parents understand and relate to their infants.

Critics acknowledge that whereas the NBAS provides the most comprehensive description of the newborn's current level of neurobehavioral functioning, and although a number of studies have reported a relationship between patterns of change in newborn behavior and future parent-child relations and developmental outcome, the NBAS's predictive validity has not been convincingly established. Moreover, although many population studies have been conducted with the NBAS, it has never been standardized. Because of its emphasis on "examiner flexibility" and the importance of eliciting the infant's "best performance," the scale does not have a standard order of item administration and thus is judged by some researchers to lack the objectivity required by the classic psychometric assessment tradition. Brazelton and his colleagues maintain that careful training of examiners to the 90 percent inter-rater agreement level ensures the reliability of the results across settings.

Brazelton was born in Waco, Texas, on May 10, 1918, and graduated from Princeton in 1940. In 1943 he graduated from the Columbia University College of Physicians and Surgeons in New York City, where he accepted a medical internship. In 1945 he moved to Boston to serve his medical residency at Massachusetts General Hospital, before undertaking pediatric training at Children's Hospital. His interest in child development led to training in child psychiatry at Massachusetts General Hospital and the James Jackson Putnam Children's Center. With Professor Jerome Bruner, he was a Fellow at the Center for Cognitive Studies at Harvard University. The process of integrating his dual interests—primary care pediatrics and child psychiatry—culminated in 1972, when he established the Child Development Unit, a pediatric training and research center at Children's Hospital in Boston.

Like Benjamin Spock, to whom he has been compared, Brazelton has written books for parents that have influenced the beliefs and practices of parents everywhere. What characterizes Brazelton's writings for parents is his focus on the nature of individual differences in behavior. Indeed, in the preface to Brazelton's classic book *Infants and Mothers*, Jerome Bruner remarks, "What delights me most is Dr. Brazelton's unflagging sense of human individuality." Brazelton has published many other books for parents, including the *Touchpoints* and *Brazelton Way* books, and his work also includes the development of a fourth edition of the *Neonatal Behavioral Assessment Scale* with his colleague J. Kevin Nugent.

Brazelton is a professor emeritus of clinical pediatrics at Harvard Medical School and a professor of psychiatry and human development at Brown University. In 1995 Harvard University Medical School established the T. Berry Brazelton Chair in Pediatrics. Brazelton is founder of the Brazelton Touchpoints Center at Children's Hospital, Boston. Established in 1993, Touchpoints is a preventative outreach program that trains professionals to better serve families of infants and toddlers.

SEE ALSO *Child Development; Developmental Psychology; Motherhood; Parent-Child Relationships; Parenthood, Transition to; Parenting Styles; Psychoanalytic Theory; Spock, Benjamin*

BIBLIOGRAPHY

Brazelton, T. Berry, and J. Kevin Nugent. 1995. *The Neonatal Behavioral Assessment Scale*. 3rd ed. London: McKeith Press.

Brazelton, T. Berry, with Joshua Sparrow. 2006. *Touchpoints: Birth to Three: Your Child's Emotional and Behavioral Development*. 2nd rev. ed. Cambridge, MA.: Perseus Publishing.

J. Kevin Nugent

BRETTON WOODS

SEE *Exchange Rates; Gold Standard; International Monetary Fund.*

BREZHNEV, LEONID
1906–1982

Leonid Brezhnev, leader of the Soviet Union from 1964 until his death in November 1982, was at the Soviet helm longer than anyone besides Joseph Stalin (1879–1953). Brezhnev grew up in Ukraine in an industrial working-class family (his father worked in a steel plant). Not intellectually inclined, Brezhnev was a hard worker, a good organizer, and a decent student; moreover, he showed early signs of leadership and political ambition, quickly joining the Komsomol (communist youth group) and the Communist Party. Professionally, Brezhnev trained in both industrial and agricultural sectors. He worked in factories, certified as a land surveyor (1927), and received an engineering degree (1935), all while demonstrating leadership within his trade union and party organizations.

In 1936 in Ukraine, Brezhnev's political career began, oddly thanks to Stalin's "Great Terror," which left high-ranking posts empty, allowing eager beginners like Brezhnev to advance quickly. By 1941 he had achieved the post of regional party secretary for defense industries and, crucially, made a lasting, good impression on Nikita Khrushchev (1894–1971), Ukrainian first secretary. During World War II (1939–1945), Brezhnev was assigned to the political administration of the Red Army. Though political administration was physically safer than other wartime assignments, Brezhnev later tended to exaggerate his heroic war performance, heaping an absurd number of medals on himself.

In 1950 Brezhnev began his ascent to the highest echelons of Soviet power when he was named first secretary of Moldova, charged with "Sovietizing" it. Two years later Stalin promoted Brezhnev to candidate member of the Presidium (Politburo), possibly to replace another lieutenant scheduled for removal by purge. Despite Stalin's death in 1953, Brezhnev lost little political momentum, thanks to his Ukrainian connections to the new leader, Nikita Khrushchev. Khrushchev named him first secretary of Kazakhstan in 1955 in charge of the "Virgin Lands" scheme, and elevated him to full membership of the Presidium in 1957. By 1963 Brezhnev had become a secretary of the Central Committee, controlling daily party organization. From that powerful position, Brezhnev helped plan and execute Khrushchev's overthrow in 1964, condemning Khrushchev's impulsiveness and excessive power. Brezhnev then became one of three leaders, until he consolidated his paramount position by the mid-1970s. From then on, Brezhnev was clearly the most authoritative figure within a collective leadership.

Those eighteen years—the Brezhnev era—saw the Soviet Union rise to become one of the two global superpowers dominating the world. Living standards increased, while classes of modern, educated professionals expanded. There were no terrors, cataclysms, or major conflicts; life was stable for two decades. Accordingly, when Russians are asked to assess the best time to have lived in their country in the twentieth century, the Brezhnev era usually comes out on top. Yet, Brezhnev's regime was a one-party dictatorship with no regard for human rights. It ruled

through security police and censorship, and kept Eastern European nations in captivity. It brutally crushed the 1968 reform movement in Czechoslovakia, and invaded Afghanistan in 1979. The time of stability was also an era of stagnation and economic and social rot. Brezhnev's collective leadership style led to extreme bureaucratic inertia, a government of enervated gerontocracy. When Brezhnev died, Yuri Andropov (1914–1984) inherited a superpower in deep decline. Though he made initial stabs at correcting those problems, Andropov's protégé, Mikhail Gorbachev, would go further than anyone ever imagined.

SEE ALSO *Cold War; Communism; Gorbachev, Mikhail; Khrushchev, Nikita; One-Party States; Stalin, Joseph; Union of Soviet Socialist Republics; Warsaw Pact*

BIBLIOGRAPHY

Bacon, Edwin, and Mark Sandle, eds. 2002. *Brezhnev Reconsidered.* New York: Palgrave Macmillan.

Garthoff, Raymond. 1994. *Detente and Confrontation: American-Soviet Relations from Nixon to Reagan.* Rev. ed. Washington, DC: Brookings Institution.

Julie M. Newton

BRIBERY

In the strictest sense, *bribery* is defined as the giving of money or other valuables to public officials in exchange for that official not performing his or her required duties. For example, traffic police may be paid to overlook a traffic violation, or a judge to render a decision favorable to the briber. The concept of bribery often is used outside the context of government officials to include any instance of a person disregarding the obligations of his or her position in return for a payment; for example, a salesperson may pay the purchasing manager at a client firm to continue to order their goods. A useful working definition is given by Harvey James (2002): "any payment made to an agent is a bribe if the agent retains the payment" (p. 199). A payment made to a government official that stays with that official and is not deposited into government coffers is considered a bribe.

As is often the case in economics, James's definition does not distinguish between bribery and extortion. *Extortion* refers to a situation in which an agent demands payment for a good or service that the payee has a right to have without any payment; in contrast, in *bribery* the agent demands payment for an *extra* benefit. Although there may be philosophical, moral, or ethical differences between the two terms, for economists they often fall under the same category, largely because of the similar effects of these types of payments in competitive situations. If all of a firm's competitors offer to bribe a government official to speed up the delivery of a required permit, then that firm must also pay the bribe in order to avoid falling behind the competition. Here the distinction between bribery and extortion is blurred.

Andrei Shleifer and Robert Vishny (1993) suggest that bribery harms firms more than an equivalent tax because of the secrecy associated with bribery. Government officials may encourage firms to produce goods or invest in sectors that are more easily subject to bribery. The effort to create bribe opportunities can make economies more inefficient. Paolo Mauro (1995) finds that countries with higher levels of corruption have lower investment and lower economic growth. At the micro-level, Simon Johnson, John McMillan, and Christopher Woodruff (2002) find that firms that are faced with paying bribes reinvest less of their profits back into their business. Bribery can cause firms to make inefficient decisions that can interfere with the overall growth of an economy.

International agencies such as Transparency International and the World Bank have focused international attention on the problem of bribery. Both publish country rankings based on perceived levels of corruption and bribery. Developing countries usually occupy the lower rungs of these rankings. These rankings, along with the evidence on the correlation between low growth and corruption, have made bribery a key issue in economic development. Although bribery is conceptualized as primarily an interaction between two individuals, a bribe-payer and a bribe-taker, it has far-reaching effects for firms and entire economies.

SEE ALSO *Corruption; Ethics, Business*

BIBLIOGRAPHY

James, Harvey S. 2002. When Is a Bribe a Bribe? Teaching a Workable Definition of Bribery. *Teaching Business Ethics* 6 (2): 199–217.

Johnson, Simon, John McMillan, and Christopher Woodruff. 2002. Property Rights and Finance. *American Economic Review* 92 (5): 1335–1356.

Mauro, Paolo. 1995. Corruption and Growth. *Quarterly Journal of Economics* 110 (3): 681–712.

Shleifer, Andrei, and Robert W. Vishny. 1993. Corruption. *Quarterly Journal of Economics* 108 (3): pp. 599–617.

Larry W. Chavis

BRIDE PRICE

SEE *Dowry and Bride Price.*

BRIMMER, ANDREW
1926–

Andrew Felton Brimmer, born in Louisiana in 1926 to sharecropping parents, became one of America's premier public economists, serving as a member of the Board of Governors of the Federal Reserve System from 1966 to 1974 and as chairman of the Financial Control Board of the District of Columbia in 1996. He also founded and manages Brimmer and Associates, a private consulting company with many corporate clients since 1977.

In 1944 the young Brimmer moved to the state of Washington and worked as an electrician's helper in the shipyards before joining the U.S. Army for two years. He later earned his BA (1950) and MA (1951) degrees in economics from the University of Washington. After a year of scholarly work in India supported by a Fulbright grant, he completed his PhD in economics in 1957 at Harvard University. Following a second Fulbright grant in 1958 that allowed him to help establish the Central Bank of Sudan, he served for five years as an economist at the Federal Reserve Bank of New York.

In 1963 President John F. Kennedy (1917–1963) appointed Brimmer to the post of deputy assistant secretary for economic affairs in the U.S. Department of Commerce. In this position, he authored an influential study documenting the effects of racial discrimination in public accommodations on interstate commerce, thus providing the constitutional justification for federal regulation of activities that otherwise might have been considered purely local matters to be left to the states. Brimmer summarized his contribution by noting that:

> What I did was to design an [e]conomic [m]odel which enabled me to examine the differential impact of segregation and discrimination on African Americans—from the point of view of travel, entertainment, consumer expenditure patterns, and the level of money income.… I was able to do computer simulations that tracked travel along three separate routes from Washington, D.C., … to Miami, Florida, … New Orleans, and … Chicago. The net result was that we were able to demonstrate that African Americans had to travel about twice as far and roughly twice as long as white Americans. This violated the Guidelines of the National Safety Council.

> Once the Public Accommodations Section of the Civil Rights Bill became law in the summer of 1964, it was challenged by the defenders of segregation. The case quickly got to the U.S. Supreme Court, which unanimously upheld its constitutionality. The Court based its decision substantially on the testimony I prepared. (U.S. Supreme Court 1964; Brimmer 2006)

Brimmer has returned frequently to issues of black economic progress, arguing strenuously for more black entrepreneurship, increased adoption of the corporate mode of organization (Brimmer 1973), strong educational achievement (Horatio Alger Association 1974), and careful attention to personal finances. He has simultaneously noted that the economic costs of unequal treatment accorded African Americans has significantly hampered access to higher-paying jobs and slowed the rate of black entry to managerial professions. Noting the national interest in ending unequal treatment, he argued that such discrimination deprived the U.S. economy of $215 billion in 1991, roughly 3.8 percent of GDP (Brimmer 1995).

In 1966 President Lyndon B. Johnson (1908–1973) appointed Brimmer to a fourteen-year term with the Federal Reserve Board of Governors (of which he served eight). He was the first African American to serve in this elite position. Recognizing Brimmer's objectivity and analytical skills, President Johnson declared:

> I do not expect Dr. Brimmer to be an easy-money man or a tight-money man.... I expect Dr. Brimmer to be a right-money man, one who, I believe, will carefully and cautiously and intelligently evaluate the Nation's needs and the needs of all of its people, and recommend the policies which his conscience and his judgment tells him will best serve the national interest. (Johnson 1966)

Brimmer returned to public service in 1996. Willing to grapple with the daunting budgetary crisis of the nation's capital, Brimmer accepted President Bill Clinton's appointment to serve as chairman of the District of Columbia Financial Responsibility and Management Assistance Authority (the Control Board) in 1996. The Control Board was given sweeping authority over nine major city departments, including public works, health, education, and welfare. The Control Board met with resistance from some sectors of the District, including from those who resented the loss of the limited sovereignty that the District had obtained in 1973 and from public sector trade unions that objected to the fiscal austerity that was the federal mandate given to the Control Board.

As chairman of the Control Board, Brimmer was vested with a wide range of powers to deal with the fiscal deficits that the city had incurred. It was a contentious period. For instance, during his tenure, Brimmer sought as a top priority to improve the D.C. school system, which was in shambles (District of Columbia Financial Responsibility and Management Assistance Authority 1996). The Control Board took the institutional step of transferring authority from the Board of Education to an Emergency Transitional Education Board of Trustees that

it had created. The U.S. Court of Appeals for the District of Columbia Circuit found that the Control Board could not legally do this, modifying Brimmer's efforts at educational reform. Brimmer's critics were harsh on both his management style and his policies. One even argued that "Brimmer's imperiousness runs up and down the organization: never retreat, never admit you were wrong, and never, ever say you're sorry. Brimmer believes that he and his cohorts are on a mission and that he has a sovereign right to run over all objections" (Stabile et al. 1998). During this period, controversies were legion. For instance, in 1997 Brimmer was forced by outraged District residents, Control Board members, and members of Congress to withdraw approval of a $625,000 lease of a luxury suite requested by the city's elected mayor. At the end of his term, Brimmer was succeeded by Alice Rivlin. Brimmer returned to his consulting and scholarly role, proud that he had, in his view, resisted the politicization of important economic and management issues facing the District of Columbia.

A pioneering economist, Brimmer was elected to the Washington Academy of Sciences in 1991 and has held leading elected roles in the American Economics Association, the Eastern Economics Association, and the North American Economics and Finance Association. He has served as an economics professor at Michigan State University, the Wharton School of Finance, and Harvard University, and holds a faculty position as the Wilmer D. Barrett Professor of Economics at the University of Massachusetts, Amherst. Brimmer has also been a member of the Black Enterprise Board of Economists and the Board of Overseers of Harvard University, and he continues to serve as chairman of the Tuskegee University Board of Trustees.

Brimmer's scholarly interests have focused on monetary issues (see, e.g., Brimmer 1986, 1989, 1993, 1998) and the economic costs to society of racial discrimination (Brimmer 1973, 1995, 2000). Brimmer has long been known for his rigorous mentorship of promising young economists, especially African American scholars. He has brought many of them into his firm, where they have absorbed the critical role of rigorous evaluation of data in advancing their professional economics careers.

No stranger to the private sector, Brimmer's firm has provided expert economic analysis and testimony for many of the nation's leading corporations. He has held board positions in such companies as DuPont, Gannett, United Airlines, BlackRock Mutual Funds, and Bank of America. He remains a leading force in the economics profession and corporate America.

SEE ALSO *American Economic Association; Discrimination, Racial; Federal Reserve System, U.S.;*

INTERNATIONAL ENCYCLOPEDIA OF THE SOCIAL SCIENCES, 2ND EDITION

Johnson, Lyndon B.; National Economic Association; Policy, Monetary; Supreme Court, U.S.

BIBLIOGRAPHY

PRIMARY SOURCES

Brimmer, Andrew F. 1973. The Road Ahead: Prospects for Blacks in Business. *Journal of Negro History* 58 (2): 187–203.

Brimmer, Andrew F. 1986. *International Banking and Domestic Economic Policies: Perspectives in Debt and Development.* Berkeley: University of California Press.

Brimmer, Andrew F. 1989. Central Banking and Systemic Risks in Capital Markets. *Journal of Economic Perspectives* 3 (2): 3–16.

Brimmer, Andrew F. 1993. *Origins and Causes of the S&L Debacle: A Blueprint for Reform.* Washington, DC: National Commission on Financial Institution Reform, Recovery, and Enforcement.

Brimmer, Andrew F. 1995. Economic Costs of Discrimination against Black Americans. In *Economic Perspectives on Affirmative Action*, ed. Margaret C. Simms, 11–29. Washington, DC: Joint Center for Political and Economic Studies.

Brimmer, Andrew F. 1998. Financial Regulation and the Fragility of the Banking System. *North American Journal of Economics & Finance* 9 (1): 105–119.

Brimmer, Andrew F. 2000. *Economic Prospects for African Americans, 2001–2010: Politics and Promises.* Washington, DC: Joint Center for Economic and Political Studies.

Brimmer, Andrew F. 2006. Andrew F. Brimmer: Kenneth Boulding Fellow. Speech delivered at the American Academy of Political and Social Science Installation of Fellows. http://www.aapss.org/section.cfm/1141/1143.

SECONDARY SOURCES

District of Columbia Financial Responsibility and Management Assistance Authority. 1996. *Children in Crisis: A Report on the Failure of D.C.'s Public Schools.* Washington, DC: Author.

Horatio Alger Association of Distinguished Americans. 1974. Andrew F. Brimmer. http://www.horatioalger.com/members/member_info.cfm?memberid=bri74.

Johnson, Lyndon B. 1966. Remarks at the Swearing In of Andrew F. Brimmer as a Member, Federal Reserve Board, March 9. The American Presidency Project, eds. John Woolley and Gerhard Peters. University of California at Santa Barbara. http://www.presidency.ucsb.edu/ws/?pid=27477.

Stabile, Tom, Ken Cummins, Jonetta Rose Barras, et al. 1998. Step Down. *Washington City Paper* (February 20).

U.S. Supreme Court. 1964. *Heart of Atlanta Motel, Inc. v. United States et al.* 379 U.S. 241. Appeal from the United States District Court for the Northern District of Georgia. No. 515.

Padma Venkatachalam
Rodney D. Green

BRITISH BROADCASTING COMPANY
SEE *Television.*

BRITISH PARLIAMENT
SEE *Parliament, United Kingdom.*

BROWN V. BOARD OF EDUCATION, 1954

Legal segregation under "Jim Crow" was a social system that whites developed after the abolition of slavery. Jim Crow's primary function was to continue the social system of servitude, the racial caste hierarchy, and the economic control of African Americans. After 1896 all aspects of public accommodations, such as transportation, schools, hotels, and parks, were legally segregated in the United States. The legal segregation laws declared that African Americans could not vote, testify against whites, or serve on juries and could attend only segregated schools, orphanages, and hospitals. According to Joe Feagin, "The legal and informal Jim Crow practices meant racial subordination and an imposed badge of degradation on all African Americans in many areas of the United States" (Feagin 2006, p. 123).

In southern states and some northern states legal segregation operated like the system of slavery it replaced. Segregated government agencies exercised extreme control over every aspect of the lives of African Americans. Exploitation and oppression were enshrined by racial violence and discrimination in foundational legal, economic, and social institutions. Numerous challenges to segregated public schools were made before *Brown v. Board of Education* (1954) ended up in the Supreme Court. Peter Irons notes that the first challenge to segregated public schools began in "1849 with a lawsuit filed in Boston by Benjamin Roberts, after his five-year-old daughter, Sarah, was turned away from the primary school nearest her home on the ground of her being a colored person" (Irons 2002, p. ix). The court decided it was best that she continue to attend a segregated school. This Massachusetts Supreme Judicial Court decision preceded the landmark 1896 Supreme Court case of Homer Plessy, an African American man, who refused to sit in the "colored" section on a train, which reinforced local U.S. segregation laws. The decision in *Plessy v. Ferguson* (1896) paved the way for segregation by affirming that separate facilities for blacks and whites could be "separate but equal," including racially segregated public schools. The U.S. Constitution and federal court decisions created contemporary forms of the racist institutions functioning in the early twenty-first century.

According to Derrick Bell (2004), in the years leading up to the *Roberts* and *Brown* cases, there were pressures from leaders and protestors in the black civil rights movement to end legal segregation. Using a strategy that focused on exposing the actual racial inequality that existed in educational institutions, the National Association for the Advancement of Colored People (NAACP) attorneys Thurgood Marshall and Charles Houston had successfully litigated several cases that led to desegregation in graduate schools. These successes were the inspiration that led them to attempt to dismantle all official segregation in the educational system by arguing that racially segregated schools could never be equal. Marshall combined several cases from states in which racially segregated education was mandated by law, and these cases led to the Supreme Court decision in *Brown v. Board of Education of Topeka, Kansas* (1954) (Kluger 2004).

THE 1954 CASE

Brown v. Board of Education combined five cases: *Belton v. Gebhardt* (1951) in Delaware, *Brown v. Board of Education* (1951) in Kansas, *Briggs v. Elliott* (1947) in South Carolina, *Davis v. Prince Edwards County School Board* (1951) in Virginia, and *Bolling v. Sharpe* (1951) in the District of Columbia. Even though *Brown* was a class-action suit, Oliver L. Brown, the father of the third-grader Linda Brown, was named as the first plaintiff in the case. Several attorneys were instrumental in the successful litigation of the case, including Robert L. Carter, Marshall, Spottswood W. Robinson, Houston, Charles S. Scott, Louis L. Redding, Charles Bledsoe, Jack Greenberg, George E. C. Hayes, James M. Nabrit, Harold P. Boulware, Oliver W. Hill, and George M. Johnson. The NAACP Legal Defense Fund worked with scholars such as John A. Davis, Kenneth Clark, John Hope Franklin, and C. Vann Woodward to formulate a strong argument against the "separate-but-equal" doctrine.

In 1954 the landmark decision in *Brown* overturned the infamous "separate-but-equal" doctrine of *Plessy v. Ferguson*. The decision was based on the tireless work of African American men, women, and children, including members of the NAACP. Irons notes that once parents of African American children in South Carolina, Virginia, the District of Columbia, Delaware, and Kansas bravely challenged legal segregation in public schools, at great personal risk to themselves and their families, "the Supreme Court finally agreed to decide whether school segregation violated the Constitution's promise that every American—black or white—will receive *the equal protection of the laws*" (Irons 2002, p. xi).

THE IMPACT OF *BROWN V. BOARD OF EDUCATION*

At the center of the *Brown v. Board of Education* 347 U.S. 483, 495 decision are the words of Chief Justice Earl Warren: "We conclude that in the field of public education 'separate but equal' has no place. Separate educational facilities are inherently unequal. Therefore, we hold that the plaintiffs and others similarly situated for whom the actions have brought are, by reason of the segregation complained of, deprived of the equal protection of laws guaranteed by the Fourteenth Amendment" (Feagin 2004, p. 68).

Warren specifically focused and based his decision to end school segregation on the social science research of Clark, who showed that when given a choice, black children viewed white dolls as superior to black dolls. Fundamentally the finding of the Clark research project showed that there was deep psychological damage done to the psyche of black children who were forced to attend segregated schools. The *Brown* decision impacted school systems and changed American institutions forever. It focused on the public school systems, but its effects reached far beyond the educational institutions. According to Bell, for months following the *Brown* decision, African Americans participated in organized acts of resistance against other public facilities that were segregated, such as buses and restaurants. The elected white officials of local communities refused to desegregate public facilities, and the violent white responses to peaceful protestors were televised regularly for the entire world to witness. "In addition to publications and the Voice of America broadcasts, the government encouraged and often sponsored Black leaders to travel to foreign countries and convey positive reports about race relations" (Bell 2004, pp. 60–61).

The United States was painfully cognizant of the fact that foreign countries such as Russia were utilizing the heightened racial violence to encourage African Americans to join Communist forces against the country that was denying them their civil rights. Ironically, an unforeseen benefit of the *Brown* decision was that it mobilized ordinary white citizens, who were horrified by the display on television of brutal attacks against peaceful black civil rights protestors—in most instances women and children—and who joined in public resistance against segregation.

THE CIVIL RIGHTS MOVEMENT

James Patterson (2001) points out that African American men and women who were involved in the civil rights movement were inspired by the 1954 *Brown* decision. With the support of liberal whites, African Americans began to fight harder for their civil rights in hopes that legal segregation would finally come to an end. After the *Brown* decision, African Americans organized sit-ins, boycotts, and demonstrations to end legal segregation. "The civil rights movement was heroic.... it inspired even higher expectations than *Brown* had in 1954" (Patterson 2001, p. xxi). Bell affirms this point: "*Brown* was the primary force and provided a vital inspirational spark in the post–World War II civil rights movement. Defenders maintain *Brown* served as an important encouragement for the Montgomery bus boycotters, and that it served as a key symbol of cultural advancement for the nation" (Bell 2004, p. 130).

BROWN V. BOARD OF EDUCATION REVISITED

Bell notes that Warren used extremely ambiguous language in his ruling, stating that because of the "wide applicability of this decision, and because of the great variety of local conditions, the formulation of decrees in these cases present problems of considerable complexity" (Bell 2004, p. 18). With these words, the Court postponed ordering any immediate action and ordered the plaintiffs to return to court later to address the issue of implementation.

Consequently the 1954 *Brown* decision had to be revisited one year later. But even after the courts revisited the issue of implementation, the Supreme Court never provided a specific legal remedy for the desegregation of schools. White southerners objected to the ruling of the Supreme Court and violently resisted the integration of the public school system. Furthermore the consensus in the local courts and among the general white public was that school desegregation could not be achieved. The Supreme Court faced resistance from local legislative and executive levels of government. Seeming to fear the threat of mass resistance to its ruling in *Brown*, the Supreme Court in the *Brown II* decision issued an extremely vague directive holding that the implementation of desegregation plans must be conducted "with all deliberate speed."

IS SEPARATE-BUT-EQUAL BEST?

In 1935 W. E. B. Du Bois expressed grave concerns about the possible outcomes of black children going to white schools where "white children, white teachers, and white parents despised and resented the dark child ... and literally rendered its life a living hell" (Du Bois 1935, p. 330). There was no consensus in the African American community about how to proceed with ensuring that their children had schools and resources that were equal to those of white children. "A separate Negro school, where children are treated like human beings, trained by teachers of their own race, who know what it means to be black ... is infinitely better than making our boys and girls doormats to be spit and trampled upon and lied to by ignorant social climbers whose sole claim to superiority is ability to kick 'niggers' when they are down" (Du Bois 1935, p. 335).

African American community leaders, parents, and the NAACP worried about the future of their teachers, schools, and universities, and they initially fought to ensure that their institutions were equal to white schools (Patterson 2001). However, in 1950, "after much debate within the NAACP ... Marshall [dared] to demand the demolition of Jim Crow in the schools" (Patterson 2001, p. 7).

There have been numerous discussions among scholars who question the success of school integration, the possibility of Marshall and his attorneys fighting for "separate-but-equal" instead of fighting for school integration, and the possible outcomes for African American children. Many parents who attended integrated schools feel positively about the benefits they received and feel good about their children attending integrated schools. The lives of millions of Americans, white and black, have been profoundly influenced by the *Brown* decision. The failure of the federal and state courts to preserve the gains since *Brown v. Board of Education* is as deeply troubling as the false notion that segregated schools are more beneficial for children (Boger and Orfield 2005).

THE RESEGREGATION OF SCHOOLS

In the early twenty-first century public schools are more racially segregated. The Harvard Civil Rights Project (2006) reports that more than 70 percent of African American students attend public schools that are overwhelmingly nonwhite. There have been significant challenges against affirmative action in federal and state courts. According to Gary Orfield and Chungmei Lee of the Harvard Civil Rights Project:

> Since the Supreme Court authorized a return to segregated neighborhood schools in 1991 [*Board of Education of Oklahoma City v. Dowel* (1991)], the percentage of black students attending majority nonwhite schools increased in all regions from 66 percent in 1991 to 73 percent in 2003–2004.... Over the twelve-year period, the percent of Southern black students in majority non-white schools rose from 61 percent to 71 percent, and the percent of black students in such schools grew from 59 to 69 percent in the Border States. (Orfield and Lee 2006, pp. 9–10)

In 2006 the Supreme Court agreed to hear two cases, *Parents Involved in Community Schools v. Seattle School District* and *Meredith v. Jefferson County Board of*

Education. Based on the Supreme Court's decision, these cases could overturn *Brown.* The two cases focus on the right of public schools to decide, in their efforts to promote diversity, where children should go to school based on their race. The white parents in both cases want their children to go to their neighborhood schools. In response to the Supreme Court's agreement to hear these cases, over 500 social scientists signed a statement urging the Supreme Court to allow American public schools to maintain their ongoing efforts to diversify public schools. Crystal Meredith, the mother of one of the students and the person who filed the *Meredith v. Jefferson County Board of Education* lawsuit, thinks that a policy that color codes any child denigrates and damages that child's self-esteem (Benac 2006). The issue of self-esteem, self-worth, and feeling inferior was a central part of the doll research conducted by Clark that was instrumental in the 1954 Supreme Court decision.

Margaret Beale Spencer (1982, 1984), however, criticized Clark and his doll studies research. She conducted extensive research into the relationship between identity and the self-esteem of African American children. Her findings indicate that even though "preschoolers show majority group racial attitudes[,] eighty percent of the sample obtained positive self-concept scores, while demonstrating pro-white biased cultural values on a racial attitude and preference measure" (Spencer 1984, p. 440). Therefore the children in the Clark doll study who chose the white doll were not necessarily demonstrating that their self-esteem was damaged or that they felt inferior because they picked the white doll. Spencer felt that black children chose the white doll because they knew it was valued by society. "Even the Clarks found that seven-year old black children had largely shifted in preference behavior; they more frequently preferred the black dolls" (Harpalani 2004, p. 6).

In the 1940s some scholars criticized the implementation of Clark's test and the difference in the aesthetics of the dolls. Since black dolls were difficult if not impossible to find in the 1940s, the white doll was more aesthetically appealing and thus one of the reasons black children picked it (Harpalani 2004). However, in 2005 the high school student Kiri Davis created a video, *A Girl like Me,* that demonstrated that young African American children are still choosing the white doll over the black doll, even though both dolls are aesthetically similar. Indeed there was not a consensus in the African American community about what to do in the 1950s, and there is not a consensus in the early twenty-first century about the success of *Brown v. Board of Education* in assuring quality education for black children.

SEE ALSO Brown v. Board of Education, *1955; Civil Rights; Civil Rights Movement, U.S.; Civil Rights,* Cold War; Clark, Kenneth B.; Cold War; Desegregation; Desegregation, School; Integration; Marshall, Thurgood; National Association for the Advancement of Colored People (NAACP); Schooling in the USA; Segregation; Separate-but-Equal; Supreme Court, U.S.; Warren, Earl

BIBLIOGRAPHY

Bell, Derrick. 2004. *Silent Covenants:* Brown v. Board of Education *and the Unfulfilled Hopes for Racial Reform.* New York: Oxford University Press.

Benac, Nancy. 2006. High Court to Hear School Diversity Case. *Washington Post,* December 2: A4.

Board of Education of Oklahoma City v. Dowell, 498 U.S. 237. 1991. http://caselaw.lp.findlaw.com/scripts/getcase.pl?navby=case&court=us&vol=498&page=237.

Boger, John Charles, and Gary Orfield, eds. 2005. *School Resegregation: Must the South Turn Back?* Chapel Hill: University of North Carolina Press.

Brown v. Board of Education of Topeka, 347 U.S. 483, 495. 1954. http://supreme.justia.com/us/347/483/case.html.

Brown v. Board of Education, 349 U.S. 294. 1955. http://caselaw.lp.findlaw.com/scripts/getcase.pl?court=us&vol=349&invol=294.

Du Bois, W. E. B. 1935. Does the Negro Need Separate Schools? *Journal of Negro Education* 4 (3): 328–335.

Feagin, Joe. 2004. Heeding Black Voices: The Court, *Brown,* and Challenges in Building a Multiracial Democracy. *University of Pittsburgh Law Review* 66: 57–81.

Feagin, Joe. 2006. *Systemic Racism: A Theory of Oppression.* New York: Routledge.

Harpalani, Vinay. 2004. Simple Justice or Complex Injustice? American Racial Dynamics and the Ironies of *Brown* and *Grutter. Penn GSE Perspectives on Urban Education* 3 (1): 1–14. http://www.urbanedjournal.org/archive/vol3issue1/notes/notes0014.html.

Irons, Peter. 2002. *Jim Crow's Children: The Broken Promise of the* Brown *Decision.* New York: Penguin.

Kluger, Richard. 2004. *Simple Justice: The History of* Brown v. Board of Education *and Black America's Struggle for Equality.* Rev. ed. New York: Knopf.

Orfield, Gary, and Chungmei Lee. 2006. Racial Transformation and the Changing Nature of Segregation. Cambridge, MA: The Civil Rights Project at Harvard University. http://www.civilrightsproject.harvard.edu/research/deseg/deseg06.php.

Patterson, James T. 2001. Brown v. Board of Education*: A Civil Rights Milestone and Its Troubled Legacy.* New York: Oxford University Press.

Plessy v. Ferguson, 163 U.S. 537. 1896. http://caselaw.lp.findlaw.com/scripts/getcase.pl?court=US&vol=163&invol=537.

Spencer, Margaret Beale. 1982. Personal and Group Identity of Black Children: An Alternative Synthesis. *Genetic Psychology Monographs* 106: 59–84.

Spencer, Margaret Beale. 1984. Black Children's Race Awareness, Racial Attitudes, and Self-Concept: A Reinterpretation. *Journal of Child Psychology and Psychiatry and Allied Disciplines* 25 (3): 433–441.

Ruth Thompson-Miller

BROWN V. BOARD OF EDUCATION, 1955

The original intent of the 1954 Supreme Court decision in *Brown v. Board of Education of Topeka* was to dismantle the separate-but-equal policy in American public schools. Joe Feagin (2004, p. 68) argues that the language used by Chief Justice Earl Warren (1891–1974), who wrote the *Brown* opinion, intentionally focused only on public schools: "in the field of public education, the doctrine of 'separate but equal' has no place. Separate educational facilities are inherently unequal." However, the landmark *Brown* decision did not put an end to segregation in public schools due to the hostile response the decision received from white elites.

Derrick Bell (2004, p. 18) argues that Warren's use of extremely ambiguous language in his opinion hindered the implementation of desegregation. Specifically, Warren stated that "because of the wide applicability of this decision and because of the great variety of local conditions, the formulation of decrees in these cases presents problems of considerable complexity." With these words, the Supreme Court postponed any immediate action and ordered the plaintiffs to return to court at a later date to address the issue of implementation.

Consequently, the 1954 *Brown* decision had to be revisited one year later in the *Brown* II case, which specifically addressed the issue of remedying racial segregation in American educational facilities. White southerners objected to the Supreme Court's 1954 ruling, and openly expressed racist sentiment, insisting that they had no intention of integrating the public school system. Furthermore, the consensus among local courts and the white public generally was that school desegregation could not be achieved. The Supreme Court faced outright resistance from state and local branches of government and from lower courts. With this social backdrop, the Court heard legal arguments in 1955 concerning the issue of implementation, and issued the *Brown* II decision.

According to Bell:

The Court expected a prompt and reasonable start toward full compliance, with defendants carrying the burden of showing that requests for additional time were necessary in the public interest and consistent with good faith compliance at the … earliest practicable date.… The court returned the cases to the district courts with the admonition that orders and decrees be entered to admit plaintiffs to public schools on a racially nondiscriminatory basis, "with all deliberate speed." (Bell 2004, p. 18)

Bell suggests that the Court, in using such weak language as "all deliberate speed," confirmed that its earlier *Brown* decision was "more symbolic than real" (2004, p 19). The phrase "with all deliberate speed" was met with a wide range of responses. As Paul Finkelman points out, "*Brown* II might have been more forceful and direct. In hindsight we might argue that there should have been more emphasis on speed and less on deliberate" (2004, p. 36).

Bell describes how federal judge J. Harvie Wilkinson III, "two decades after *Brown*, offered practical details why *Brown* II was a mistake.… The enormous discretion of the trial judge in interpreting such language as all 'deliberate speed' and 'prompt and reasonable start' made his personal role painfully obvious" (2004, p. 19). Judges who wanted to implement desegregation were often met with violent opposition from local whites when they used the words of the Supreme Court. Mindful of the history of racial violence against African Americans in the South, these judges cautiously phrased how the implementation of school desegregation would take place to avoid a violent backlash against African American communities. Furthermore, the failure of the Court to delineate a specific remedy for school desegregation allowed judges who favored racial segregation the means to stall, thus perpetuating segregation in education (Kluger 2004).

In the face of massive resistance from white southerners and from southern courts and legislatures, it took nearly twenty years for the United States to begin large-scale implementation of the *Brown* decision (Feagin 2004). Today, although racial segregation in schools can no longer be legally imposed, many American schools from kindergarten through twelfth grade remain racially segregated, and in some regions even more segregated than they were before *Brown*. Education scholars have suggested that this segregation is largely the result of the successful stalling techniques employed in the South, combined with de facto racism in the North, all of which was facilitated by the "all deliberate speed" phrasing of the Supreme Court in 1955 (Orfield and Eaton 1997).

SEE ALSO *Brown v. Board of Education, 1954; Desegregation, School; Education, USA; Racism; Segregation; Supreme Court, U.S.*

BIBLIOGRAPHY

Bell, Derrick. 2004. *Silent Covenants:* Brown v. Board of Education *and the Unfulfilled Hopes for Racial Reform.* New York: Oxford University Press.

Brown v. Board of Education, 349 U.S. 294 (1955). http://caselaw.lp.findlaw.com/cgi-bin/getcase.pl?court=us&vol=349&invol=294.

Brown v. Board of Education of Topeka, 347 U.S. 483, 495 (1954). http://caselaw.lp.findlaw.com/scripts/getcase.pl?court=US&vol=347&invol=483.

Feagin, Joe. 2004. Heeding Black Voices: The Court, *Brown,* and Challenges in Building a Multiracial Democracy. *University of Pittsburgh Law Review* 66: 57–81.

Finkelman, Paul. 2004. The Radicalism of *Brown. University of Pittsburgh Law Review* 66: 35–56.

Kluger, Richard. 2004. *Simple Justice: The History of* Brown v. Board of Education *and Black America's Struggle for Equality.* Rev. and expanded ed. New York: Knopf.

Orfield, Gary, and Susan E. Eaton. 1997. *Dismantling Desegregation: The Quiet Reversal of* Brown v. Board of Education. New York: New Press.

Ruth Thompson-Miller

BRYAN, WILLIAM JENNINGS

SEE *Scopes Trial.*

BUBBLES

Bubbles occur when there is excessive investment in financial assets, such as stocks, or in real assets, such as housing. The bubble "bursts" when the value of the investment plummets. The value of the investment may plummet for several reasons, including (1) investors realizing that they previously had overvalued the investment, resulting in a massive selling of the investment, and/or (2) the price of what the investment produces falls.

One of the most famous speculative bubbles in history is Dutch Tulipmania (1634–1638), which involved people mortgaging their homes and industries to buy tulip bulbs, which they expected to resell at higher and higher prices. These expectations were based on past increases in prices. In early 1637 prices for some bulbs fell from a peak of several times a typical person's annual income to almost

nothing. The Mississippi Bubble (1719–1720) and the South Sea Bubble (1720) involved the taking over of part of (respectively) France's and England's national debts by powerful trading monopolies. Expected monopoly profits from expanding trade drove these bubbles. When people lost faith in those monopolies, the value of their stocks plummeted. The U.S. stock market enjoyed spectacular growth during the 1920s, and people hoping to get rich through the stock market used ever increasing amounts of credit to buy more stocks. The bursting of this stock market bubble in 1929 ushered in the Great Depression. Likewise, the bursting of the Japanese bubble in the 1980s ushered in the worst recession that Japan had suffered since World War II. The Japanese bubble was driven partially by Japanese companies using the money from selling stocks for speculative purposes rather than to produce goods and services that could be sold to the public.

Although Albert Frederick Mummery and John Atkinson Hobson only briefly mention "bubble companies" in *The Physiology of Industry* ([1889] 1989, p. 140), their book provides one of the earliest analyses of what causes excessive investment (bubbles). They argue that the ultimate goal of investment is to produce goods for consumption. If there is no one to consume what the investment produces, then there is no ultimate value gained by investing. A bubble occurs when excessive savings leads to excessive investment that causes excessive production of goods that will not be bought due to insufficient consumption. If one person increases his or her savings, then others must increase their consumption in order to make the first person's savings valuable. If everyone saves more, then the goods produced by using the increased savings will not sell, making the increased savings worthless. According to Mummery and Hobson, excessive investment is synonymous with underconsumption. To produce sustainable growth, a correct mix must be found between savings, which is needed to finance investment, and consumption, which is needed to buy what the investment produces.

A global perspective can be added to the above analysis by noting that a correct mix of savings and consumption needs to be found on an international level. In a globalized world, countries with excess savings can export their extra savings to countries with excess consumption. One way to export savings is by fixing the exchange rate below its true value to another currency (such as the U.S. dollar), thereby encouraging exports and discouraging imports and thus lowering national savings.

Because bubbles involve "excessive" investment, they logically involve people making mistakes. These mistakes can be based on overreacting, following the herd (fads), decision making by inexperienced traders, viewing investments as a gamble (and enjoying the gambling), or basing future expectations solely on performance in the recent past. However, contemporary social science is built on an assumption of "rationality," and the above explanations imply that people make "irrational" mistakes. Thus, many theorists either deny that bubbles occur, or they try to find a rational basis for bubbles.

One explanation that denies that bubbles occur is based on the premise that asset markets adjust more quickly than goods markets. Because of this, a shock in the goods markets can create what appears to be an exaggerated reaction (bubble) in the asset market; however, contrary to appearances, these reactions actually involve the entire system trying to achieve a new equilibrium as quickly as possible. Similar models have been built based on capital, money, and cash-in-advance constraints. Taking a different tack, some explanations hold that high uncertainty about the future productivity of a new technology can cause what looks like a bubble, but that it will go away once the uncertainty is eliminated.

Some explanations that attempt to find a rational basis for bubbles are based on different investors having different beliefs (or information) and on short-selling constraints. Simon Gilchrist, Charles P. Himmelberg, and Gur Huberman show that, under these conditions, firms can issue new shares at inflated prices (2005). By so doing they reduce the cost of capital and increase real investment. Furthermore, they show that even large bubbles are not eliminated in equilibrium. Another group of theories argue that the "results" of bubbles may be "rational" due to the bubbles causing dynamically inefficient states (states with excess investment) to become more efficient (i.e., to reduce their excess investment).

Despite this last group of theories, most experts agree that it is best to avoid bubbles. The chairmen of the central banks of the United States and Japan in the 1990s (Alan Greenspan and Yasushi Mieno, respectively) both emphasized reducing speculative bubbles. One way to reduce the chance of speculative bubbles is to warn investors of excessive investment; Greenspan is well known for repeatedly condemning "irrational exuberance" in the U.S. stock market in the 1990s. Other policy responses are to increase taxes on investment and, for countries with excess investment, to promote consumption. Because the rich tend to invest more than the poor and the poor tend to consume more than the rich, policies that create a more equitable income distribution help.

To the extent that some speculative bubbles are based on incomplete or misleading information, the government can play a role in improving information. Furthermore, the punishments should be severe for corporate leaders who are found guilty of misleading investors, and insider trading should be prohibited because it gives insiders an incentive to create a speculative bubble and then exit right before the bubble bursts.

BIBLIOGRAPHY

Chancellor, Edward. 1999. *Devil Take the Hindmost: A History of Financial Speculation.* New York: Penguin.

Chirinko, Robert S., and Huntley Schaller. 2001. Business Fixed Investment and "Bubbles": The Japanese Case. *American Economic Review* 91 (3): 663–680.

Gilchrist, Simon, Charles P. Himmelberg, and Gur Huberman. 2005. Do Stock Price Bubbles Influence Corporate Investment? *Journal of Monetary Economics* 52 (4): 805–827.

Mummery, Albert Frederick, and John Atkinson Hobson. [1889] 1989. *The Physiology of Industry: Being an Exposure of Certain Fallacies in Existing Theories of Economics.* Fairfield, NJ: Augusta M. Kelley.

Jonathan E. Leightner

BUCK, CARRIE

SEE *Sterilization, Human.*

BUDDHA

Though often used in a general sense to identify any individual who has achieved enlightenment without the aid of others, the term *Buddha* usually denotes the historical founder of Buddhism, Siddhārtha Gautama. Scholars generally deem Gautama a historical figure who passed along to his followers the foundations of Buddhist philosophy and practice. Frequently referred to as "the Buddha," or the "Enlightened One," most Buddhists believe Gautama to be the Buddha for this age (though there have been numerous buddhas throughout history). Accurately reconstructing the precise details of the Buddha's life and teaching, however, proves difficult. The first biographies of his life did not appear until centuries after his death and it is often impossible to ascertain exactly where the biographies reconstruct the Buddha's life according to ideal patterns as opposed to historical realities.

LIFE

Conventionally, the Buddha was believed to have lived circa 560–480 BCE, though more-recent scholarship suggests the later dates of circa 485–405 BCE. Born in northern India (present-day Nepal), Gautama's father was king of the city of Kapilavastu. Just prior to his birth, Gautama's biographers hold that Gautama's mother dreamed of a white elephant coming into her womb; this in turn led soothsayers to predict Gautama's future as a buddha. Prepared throughout his previous lives for this his final reincarnation, Gautama could walk and talk immediately following his birth. Throughout his youth, however, Gautama's father, Śuddhodana, sought to guard him against suffering and prepared Gautama to succeed him as king. Gautama also married during this period and had a son, Rāhula (according to some traditions Rāhula [literally "fetter"] was not born until the day Gautama achieved enlightenment).

At age twenty-nine, however, Gautama's life profoundly changed when he ventured outside the palace and encountered "four signs": an old man, a sick person, a corpse, and a mendicant (Buddhist sources indicate that the gods orchestrated these events). Troubled by what he saw, Gautama then took on the life of an ascetic for the next several years and searched for an answer to the suffering he had encountered. In his search for enlightenment, Gautama excelled in meditation and asceticism (at one point it was said that he lived off a daily ration of one pea). Two teachers, Udraka Rāmaputra and Alāra Kālāma, guided him during this period. Gautama eventually rejected the positions of his mentors, though, and concluded that strict self-denial did not free an individual from suffering.

According to Gautama's biographers, six years after leaving the palace he finally experienced enlightenment. One night he sat under a bodhi tree determined not to leave until he found an answer to the perennial problems of suffering and death. A period of temptation ensued as Māra, the god of desire, assailed him through various means. Gautama resisted these assaults, however, and meditated throughout the night. By dawn, Gautama's meditation culminated in a breakthrough. Though some traditions differ as to the exact nature of his enlightenment that night, the biographers agree that Gautama achieved the status of a buddha; he eliminated the ignorance that trapped individuals in the suffering (*duḥkha*) associated with the endless cycle of reincarnation.

TEACHINGS

Following this experience, the Buddha's biographers indicate that he basked in his experience for several weeks and stayed near the tree; soon thereafter he preached his first sermon at Deer Park in Sarnath, passing along to others his insight into the dharma (the truth). This first sermon is often referred to as the "first turning of the wheel of dharma." Though it is important to note that many of the Buddha's teachings reflect the influence of Hinduism, the Buddha thoroughly modified various Hindu concepts and did not embrace the Hindu caste system. The theme of his teaching revolved around the Four Noble Truths. The first

Noble Truth stipulated the reality of suffering. Put simply, suffering persists throughout all the various stages of life. The second Noble Truth indicated that desire (*tṛṣṇā*) originated from ignorance (*avidyā*) and inevitably caused suffering. According to the Buddha, humans mistakenly posit the existence of an autonomous, permanent self (*ātman*). As such, they inevitably experience suffering as they try to maintain a permanent hold on things that are constantly changing and impermanent. Instead, the Buddha's teachings advanced the doctrine of "no-self" and insisted on the impermanence of all things. The third Noble Truth, the cessation of suffering (*nirvāṇa*, literally "blowing out"), claimed it was possible to eliminate desire and ignorance and free an individual from suffering. Finally, the fourth Noble Truth pointed to the path that brings about the cessation of suffering, often referred to as the Eightfold Path. The path includes (1) right view, (2) right intention, (3) right speech, (4) right conduct, (5) right livelihood, (6) right effort, (7) right mindfulness, and (8) right concentration. This "Middle Path" avoids both the extreme of self-denial and the extreme of self-indulgence, and leads an individual to recognize the impermanence of all things.

Often, the different parts of the Eightfold Path are grouped under three main headings: moral precepts, concentration, and wisdom. The moral precepts (*śila*) usually include basic prohibitions against killing, stealing, lying, sexual promiscuity, and intoxication (these are commonly accepted by most Buddhists, though monks and nuns usually adhere to more stringent guidelines). Concentration (*samādhi*) involves various forms of meditation that differ among Buddhist traditions. Generally, however, Buddhist meditation requires careful control of the process of breathing and discipline of the mind. Finally, wisdom (*prajñā*) reflects the necessary insights required to eliminate desire and ignorance and achieve enlightenment.

The Buddha would continue to teach throughout northeastern India for the next forty-five years of his life, and he soon attracted a cadre of followers. Many of his biographies say relatively little about this period of the Buddha's life. Tradition indicates that the Buddha formed a magical double of himself, that he ascended to heaven to teach his mother who had died, and that he tamed a wild elephant. The Buddha also formed a monastic order of monks and nuns, though the Buddhist community (*saṇgha*) included laymen and laywomen as well. During this time, other accounts also suggest that the Buddha's authority was challenged by his cousin Devadatta.

At age eighty, the Buddha died. Just prior to his death, the Buddha delivered one final message and lay down between two trees. According to tradition, the Buddha's death signaled his *parinirvāṇa*, or his release from the cycle of birth and rebirth. Following this event, his followers cremated his body and distributed his relics to be enshrined in what are known as stupas.

With no named successor, a council of elders formed and orally perpetuated the Buddha's teachings. Centuries later, canonical collections of his teachings were created, such as the Tripiṭaka. These scriptures contain material directly attributed to the Buddha (*buddhavacana*) as well as authoritative commentaries. Elaborate works of art depicting various events from the Buddha's life were also developed. Devotees lavished gifts on relics associated with the Buddha and annually celebrated his birth, enlightenment, and entrance into nirvana. Sites associated with the Buddha's life served as places of pilgrimage. These included his birthplace (Lumbinī), the setting where he achieved enlightenment (Bodh Gayā), the location of his first sermon (Deer Park), and his place of death (Kuśinagara).

GROWTH OF BUDDHISM

Because Buddhism—unlike Hinduism—operated outside of the caste system, allowing its followers to interact freely with others, this helped it to spread beyond India and into other parts of Asia following the Buddha's death. Different Buddhist traditions eventually took shape, spreading and elaborating on the Buddha's teachings within various cultural contexts. The Theravāda tradition (literally "doctrine of the elders") claims to adhere strictly to the Buddha's original teachings. The Mahāyāna tradition, however, often referred to as the "Great Way," recast many of the more traditional positions. In one key example, the Mahāyāna give a higher priority to the bodhisattva—the person who puts off nirvana to help others achieve enlightenment—as opposed to the arhat ideal, in which individuals focus on achieving enlightenment for themselves. The Buddha's life, then, was reread as the quintessential model of the bodhisattva ideal. Numerous other traditions would follow as the religion initiated by the Buddha spread, ultimately attracting followers across the globe. By the nineteenth and twentieth centuries, for example, many Westerners became fascinated by the Buddha's life and teachings, as can be seen in the popularity of *Siddhartha* (1922), a novel by Hermann Hesse. As Buddhism attracted adherents in countries such as the United States, however, many criticized Westerners for promoting superficial forms of Buddhism and of the Buddha's teachings.

At the start of the twenty-first century there were approximately 400 million Buddhist adherents worldwide. Though the various Buddhist schools differ on the exact nature of the Buddha's teachings and how to interpret them, the Buddha remains a venerated figure for all Buddhists; his life and teachings continue to shape the religious sensibilities of numerous followers around the world.

SEE ALSO *Buddhism; Hinduism; Orientalism; Reincarnation; Religion; Visual Arts*

BIBLIOGRAPHY

Bechert, Heinz, ed. 1995. *When Did the Buddha Live?: The Controversy on the Dating of the Historical Buddha.* Delhi, India: Sri Satguru Publications.

Foucher, A. 1949. *La vie du Bouddha.* Paris: Payot. Trans. Simone Brangier Boas as *The Life of the Buddha, according to the Ancient Texts and Monuments of India* (Middletown, CT: Wesleyan University Press, 1963).

Lamotte, Étienne. 1988. *History of Indian Buddhism: From the Origins to the Saka Era.* Trans. Sara Webb-Boin under the supervision of Jean Dantinne. Louvain-la-Neuve, Belgium: Université Catholique de Louvain, Institut Orientaliste.

Ñāṇamoli, Bhikku, trans. 1972. *The Life of the Buddha, as It Appears in the Pali Canon, the Oldest Authentic Record.* Kandy, Sri Lanka: Buddhist Publication Society.

Strong, John S. 2001. *The Buddha: A Short Biography.* Oxford: Oneworld.

Joseph W. Williams

BUDDHISM

With roughly 400 million adherents worldwide, Buddhism represents one of the world's largest religious traditions. Originating in India, the majority of Buddhists are now found in China, Japan, North and South Korea, Mongolia, Sri Lanka, Thailand, Tibet, and North and South Vietnam. Buddhism also spread to Western nations such as the United States and Canada beginning in the nineteenth century. Since its inception, Buddhism has developed along numerous trajectories and in different cultural settings. Though certain commonalities historically unite the various Buddhist communities—such as a commitment to the "Three Jewels of Refuge" (i.e., the Buddha, his teachings, and the Buddhist monastic community)—it is difficult to isolate a definitive set of beliefs and practices shared by all Buddhists.

EARLY HISTORY AND PRACTICES

The history of Buddhism begins with the career of Siddhārtha Gautama. Scholars generally deem Gautama a historical figure who passed along to his followers the foundations of Buddhist philosophy and practice. Traditionally, Gautama was believed to have lived circa 560–480 BCE, while more-recent scholarship suggests the later dates of circa 485–405 BCE. Though Buddhists maintain that there have been numerous buddhas throughout history, most consider Gautama the Buddha for this age (though some hold that there can be more than one buddha per age). Accurately reconstructing the precise details of the Buddha's life and teaching, however, proves difficult. The first biographies of his life did not appear until centuries after his death and it is often impossible to ascertain exactly where the biographies reconstruct the Buddha's life according to ideal patterns as opposed to historical realities.

According to tradition, Gautama's previous lives prepared him for his final reincarnation before achieving the status of Buddha. At age twenty-nine, Gautama's life was profoundly altered when he ventured outside the palace and encountered "four signs": an old man, a sick person, a corpse, and a mendicant (Buddhist sources indicate that the gods orchestrated these events). Troubled by what he saw, Gautama embraced the life of an ascetic for the next several years and searched for an answer to the suffering he had encountered. According to Gautama's biographers, six years after leaving the palace he finally experienced enlightenment. One night he sat under a bodhi tree, determined not to leave until he found an answer to the perennial problems of suffering and death. Though some traditions differ as to the exact nature of his enlightenment that night, the biographers agree that Gautama achieved the status of a buddha; he eliminated the ignorance that trapped individuals in the suffering (*duḥkha*) associated with the endless cycle of reincarnation.

Following this experience, the Buddha preached his first sermon, often referred to as the "first turning of the wheel of dharma." Though it is important to note that many of the Buddha's teachings reflect the influence of Hinduism, the Buddha thoroughly modified various Hindu concepts and did not embrace the Hindu caste system. The theme of his teaching revolved around the Four Noble Truths. The first Noble Truth stipulated the reality of suffering. Put simply, suffering persists throughout all the various stages of life. The second Noble Truth indicated that desire (*tṛṣṇā*) originated from ignorance (*avidyā*) and inevitably caused suffering. According to the Buddha, humans mistakenly posit the existence of an autonomous, permanent self (*ātman*). As such, they inevitably experience suffering as they try to maintain a permanent hold on things that are constantly changing and impermanent. Instead, the Buddha's teachings advanced the doctrine of "no-self" and insisted on the impermanence of all things. The third Noble Truth, the cessation of suffering (*nirvāṇa*, literally "blowing out"), claimed it was possible to eliminate desire and ignorance and free an individual from suffering. Finally, the fourth Noble Truth pointed to the path that brings about the cessation of suffering, often referred to as the Eightfold Path. The path includes (1) right view, (2) right intention, (3)

right speech, (4) right conduct, (5) right livelihood, (6) right effort, (7) right mindfulness, and (8) right concentration. This "Middle Path" avoids both the extreme of self-denial and the extreme of self-indulgence and leads an individual to recognize the impermanence of all things.

Often, the different parts of the Eightfold Path are grouped under three main headings: moral precepts, concentration, and wisdom. The moral precepts (*śila*) usually include basic prohibitions against killing, stealing, lying, sexual promiscuity, and intoxication (these are commonly accepted by most Buddhists, though monks and nuns usually adhere to more stringent guidelines). Concentration (*samādhi*) involves various forms of meditation that differ among Buddhist traditions. Generally, however, Buddhist meditation requires careful control of the process of breathing and discipline of the mind. Finally, wisdom (*prajñā*) reflects the necessary insights required to eliminate desire and ignorance and achieve enlightenment.

Following his experience of enlightenment, the Buddha continued to teach throughout northeastern India for the next forty-five years. With no named successor upon his death, a council of elders formed and orally perpetuated the Buddha's teachings. Centuries later, the oral traditions associated with the life of the Buddha were codified in Buddhist scriptures; these scriptures contained material directly attributed to the Buddha (*buddhavacana*) as well as authoritative commentaries. The earliest extant canon, the Pāli canon (also referred to as the Tripiṭaka), consists of Vinaya (monastic law), Sūtras (the Buddha's discourses), and Abhidhamma (commentaries). The Chinese canon and the Tibetan canon took shape at later dates and incorporated new material.

As Buddhism grew following the Buddha's death, ritual practices developed along various trajectories. For example, though differences appeared among the various Buddhist traditions regarding their view of the Buddha, he remained a venerated figure for all Buddhists. Devotees lavished gifts on relics associated with the Buddha and annually celebrated his birth, enlightenment, and entrance into nirvana. Sites associated with the Buddha's life soon became places of pilgrimage. These included his birthplace (Lumbinī), the setting where he achieved enlightenment (Bodh Gayā), the location of his first sermon (Deer Park), and his place of death (Kuśinagara). Beginning in the common era, artists created images of the Buddha. Furthermore, Buddhist monastic communities (*sangha*) quickly formed after the Buddha's death. Ordination ceremonies took shape for both monks and nuns, signaling their abandonment of worldly pursuits. Laypersons also began to venerate monks for their spiritual attainments and frequently showered them with gifts and offerings. Buddhist funeral and protective rites also emerged.

In time, Buddhism spread beyond India and also began to influence the activities of states. Beginning in the third century BCE, for example, Aśoka (c. 300–232 BCE, the emperor in India, took on the title of "righteous king" (*dharmaraja*) and formally supported the monasteries. Aśoka's son, Mahinda (c. 270–c. 204 BCE), then carried the Buddhist message outside his homeland and attracted followers in Southeast Asia. At the beginning of the common era, Buddhist missionaries entered China and spread their message through the efforts of figures such as Bodhidharma (c. early fifth century CE) and Kumārajīva (350–409/413 CE). While early Hindu missionaries also accompanied traders and merchants and helped spread Hinduism to Southeast Asia during the same period, Buddhism had key advantages that facilitated its growth. In particular, unlike Hinduism, Buddhism operated outside of the caste system, allowing its followers to interact freely with others. (This advantage carried over into the twentieth century as the Indian politician B. R. Ambedkar gained a large following among fellow Dalits ["untouchables" within the Hindu caste system]; Ambedkar viewed Buddhism as a solution to the social inequality associated with the Hindu caste system and encouraged Hindus to convert.) Through these missionary efforts, different Buddhist traditions formed as Buddhist practices and beliefs often underwent significant modification as they took root in various cultural contexts.

MAJOR BUDDHIST TRADITIONS

The Theravāda (literally "doctrine of the elders") tradition claims to adhere strictly to the Buddha's original teachings. It treats the Pāli canon as the only authoritative Buddhist scriptures and perpetuates the Hīnayāna tradition from the earliest days of Buddhism (within Buddhist literature, Hīnayāna, literally the "Inferior Way," served as a pejorative term directed at more conservative Buddhists in contrast to followers of the later Mahāyāna tradition). Very strong in Burma (now Myanmar), Cambodia, Laos, Sri Lanka, and Thailand, Theravāda first spread to Southeast Asia with the missionary activities of Mahinda in Sri Lanka. Unlike other Buddhist traditions that recognize several present buddhas and bodhisattvas, Theravāda focuses solely on the life of the historical Buddha. Ideally, every individual should imitate the Buddha's example and achieve enlightenment through self-effort. For this reason, the monastic ideal of achieving personal enlightenment (arhat) serves as the focal point of Theravāda Buddhism. Monastic complexes—often consisting of a bodhi tree and images of the Buddha, as well as stupas where relics associated with the historical Buddha are enshrined—facilitate the veneration of the Buddha. According to tradition, it is impossible for laypersons to achieve enlightenment (in some locales, however, a form of temporary ordination has

arisen that serves as a rite of passage into adulthood). For nonelite practitioners, ritual and meditation often provide a means to gain merit and improve their lot in life when reincarnated, or to better their present circumstances.

The Mahāyāna tradition (literally the "Great Way") developed later than the Theravāda tradition and recast many of the more traditional Buddhist positions; it also eventually attracted a larger following than the Theravāda tradition. Particularly strong in China, Japan, Korea, and Tibet, many scholars date the beginning of Mahāyāna to around the second or first century BCE. Groups within this Buddhist tradition usually focus on particular teachings of the Buddha, referred to as the "second turning of the wheel of the dharma," believed to have been passed along by a select group of Buddhists for centuries following his death. Unlike Theravāda Buddhism, Mahāyāna allows for the possibility of multiple buddhas to exist at the same time. Not surprisingly, alongside the historical Buddha, a number of other buddhas and bodhisattvas have appeared over the centuries. Accordingly, various Mahāyāna festivals have developed to venerate these figures. In general, Mahāyāna gives a higher priority to the bodhisattva, the person who puts off nirvana to help others achieve enlightenment; it also stresses the virtues of compassion (*karuṇā*) and wisdom (*prajñā*). The Buddha's life is reread as the quintessential model of the bodhisattva ideal that values highly a strong sense of communal responsibility. Usually, the Mahāyāna sense of communal responsibility is read as a reaction to the Theravāda arhat ideal in which Buddhists focus on achieving enlightenment for themselves in an individualistic quest for nirvana. Some scholars, however, have begun to complicate the sharp historical distinctions between the Mahāyāna and Theravāda traditions.

A third major tradition in Buddhism, Vajrayāna (literally the "Diamond Way," also referred to as tantric Buddhism) emerged around the third or fourth century CE as an amalgamation of Buddhism, Hinduism, and other popular religious practices in the region. According to Vajrayāna teachings, principles in the world that appear to be fundamentally opposed are actually united and one. Enlightenment occurs when individuals grasp this reality. Whereas earlier Buddhist sources emphasized a long path to enlightenment, Vajrayāna offers instead enlightenment in this lifetime through the disciplined practice of meditation. Often, adherents visualize various deities during meditation. Among elite practitioners, these deities are often considered representations of inner states within the individual, though this is less often the case for the average adherent.

Vajrayāna proved very influential in the formation of Tibetan Buddhism, though the two terms are not synonymous. (Tibetan Buddhism is often considered a branch of

Mahāyāna Buddhism, as is Vajrayāna.) According to Tibetan sources, Buddhism arrived in the region during the reign of the first Buddhist emperor Songtsen Gampo (Tib., Srong-btsan sgam-po, d. 649/650). By the twelfth century various Tibetan Buddhist sects emerged. One particular religious order, the Gelukpa (Tib., Dge-lugs-pa, literally "Virtuous Ones"), began to rule in Tibet by the mid-seventeenth century.

Tibetan Buddhists consider the Dalai Lama (a member of the Gelukpa school) an incarnation of the lord of compassion (Avalokiteśvara) and the rightful spiritual and temporal leader of the state. Each Dalai Lama is believed to be a reincarnation of the first Dalai Lama, Gedun Drupa (Tib., Dge-'dun-grub-pa, 1391–1474). As a result of the Dalai Lama's role, Buddhism has historically been intimately tied to politics in Tibet more so than in any other state. The current Dalai Lama (b. 1935), however, lives in Dharmsala, India, following the Chinese invasion of Tibet in 1950 and his exile from there in 1959. Nevertheless, he has gained international recognition for his nonviolent protests against Chinese abuses of Tibetans and received the Nobel Peace Prize in 1989.

Various schools within the three main traditions named above (Theravāda, Mahāyāna, and Vajrayāna) have developed over time. In Japan, for example, the Shingon school represents a form of tantric Buddhism, whereas the eclectic Tendai school adheres more closely to traditional Buddhist practices. Tendai was eventually overshadowed by its more popular offshoots: Pure Land Buddhism, Zen Buddhism, and Nichiren Shōshū, a particularly mission-oriented form of Buddhism that was reinvigorated beginning in the twentieth century through the Sōka Gakkai organization. Numerous other schools have also formed as distinct Buddhist movements within different Asian countries.

MODERN BUDDHISM

Buddhism has undergone important changes during the modern era. Beginning in the sixteenth century, Buddhist nations for the first time came into contact with Western culture as well as Western imperialism. At times, adherents adapted Buddhist practices to Western—and particularly Christian—ways, as can be seen in the adoption of Sunday meetings and Sunday schools by some Buddhists (in the West, some Buddhist groups also called themselves "churches"). In another sign of changes brought about through globalization, Buddhist societies formed to unite Buddhists worldwide. These include the Maha Bodhi Society (1891), the World Fellowship of Buddhists (1950), and the World Buddhist Sangha Council (1966).

Ultimately, Buddhism spread to the West during the nineteenth and twentieth centuries. One form of Mahāyāna Buddhism, Pure Land Buddhism, would eventually find a significant following in the United States. One of the most prominent subbranches of the Mahāyāna tradition, Pure Land Buddhism focuses on the figure of Amida Buddha, who was believed to have formed the "Pure Land" once he achieved buddhahood. In turn, individuals who devote themselves to the Amida Buddha are reborn in this Pure Land and achieve enlightenment. In a significant revision of traditional Buddhist teachings, Pure Land Buddhism emphasizes trust in the Amida Buddha as the key to enlightenment and places less stress on self-effort. Scholars often point to the strong similarities between these teachings and aspects of Christianity to help explain the success of Pure Land Buddhism in the West.

Zen Buddhism, another Mahāyāna school, has also been successful in the West. Literally Japanese for "meditation," the Zen tradition grew out of the Chan school in China and traces its lineage back to the historical Buddha. The movement stresses experience through the disciplined practice of meditation and often plays down the importance of Buddhist scriptures. There are three contemporary schools in Japan—Rinzai, Sōtō, and Ōbaku—that perpetuate these highly specialized forms of meditation.

In the West, Rinzai Zen first gained attention when Shaku Sōen (1859–1919) attended the World's Parliament of Religions in Chicago, Illinois, in 1893. He wrote books extolling Zen as a rational religion that fit well with modern trends. During the first half of the twentieth century, Shaku Sōen's disciple, D. T. Suzuki (1870–1966), then continued to promulgate a form of Zen in the United States that was less rigorous than traditional Zen. As awareness of Zen grew in the United States, it eventually became incorporated into popular culture. Though sometimes criticized for promoting a superficial form of Zen, figures such as Allen Ginsberg (1926–1997), Jack Kerouac (1922–1969), Gary Snyder (b. 1930), and Alan Watts (1915–1973) developed what is commonly referred to as "Beat Zen." Focusing on Rinzai Zen, which stresses sudden enlightenment, these figures embraced a popularized form of Zen during the social upheavals of the 1950s and 1960s in the United States. Here, Zen represented the ideals of liberation and freedom and served as a tool to combat the perceived materialism, imperialism, and consumerism of American society. In addition to Rinzai Zen, Sōtō Zen (which lacks Rinzai Zen's focus on sudden enlightenment and instead emphasizes quiet meditation) has also attracted a significant number of adherents in various parts of the United States as individuals such as Suzuki Shunryū (1904–1971) established meditation centers. The growth and popularity of both Rinzai and Sōtō Zen in the United States during the twentieth century reflect the increased awareness of Buddhism in the West.

The very practical, empirical nature of Buddhism has also facilitated various forms of spirituality that intermix elements from other religious traditions with Buddhism. Thomas Merton (1915–1968) serves as a prominent example. Merton, an American Catholic monk, sought to develop a dialogue between Christian and Buddhist forms of meditation during the mid-twentieth century (see, for example, his *Mystics and Zen Masters* [1967]). Also indicative of combinative trends, many Jews have either embraced Buddhism or sought to combine Buddhist insights with their own heritage (see, for example, Rodger Kamenetz's *The Jew in the Lotus: A Poet's Rediscovery of Jewish Identity in Buddhist India* [1994]). Some individuals have also combined Buddhist concepts with various aspects of Western science. While figures such as Watts sought to explain Zen using the terminology of Western science and psychology, others such as Mark Epstein (b. 1953) have also used Buddhist concepts to inform psychotherapeutic models.

Finally, Engaged Buddhism (sometimes referred to as Socially Engaged Buddhism) also represents a recent development within Buddhism. Initiated by figures such as the Vietnamese monk Thich Nhat Hanh (b. 1926), the movement is in part a reaction to a perceived passivity in the contemporary practice of Buddhism. Followers attempt to enlist Buddhism on behalf of various causes and address social and ecological ills. Engaged Buddhism has attracted attention from Buddhist laypersons and monks in both the Eastern and Western world, and had an impact on mainstream Buddhism as a whole. Diverse in its forms and dispersed across the globe, Buddhism has shaped the religious sensibilities of countless adherents throughout history.

SEE ALSO *Ambedkar, B. R.; Buddha; Caste; Hinduism; Reality; Reincarnation; Religion*

BIBLIOGRAPHY

Gethin, Rupert. 1998. *The Foundations of Buddhism*. New York: Oxford University Press.

Harvey, Peter. 1990. *An Introduction to Buddhism: Teachings, History, and Practices*. Cambridge, U.K.: Cambridge University Press.

Powers, John. 1995. *Introduction to Tibetan Buddhism*. Ithaca, NY: Snow Lion Publications.

Queen, Christopher S., and Sallie B. King, eds. 1996. *Engaged Buddhism: Buddhist Liberation Movements in Asia*. Albany: State University of New York Press.

Spiro, Melford E. 1970. *Buddhism and Society: A Great Tradition and Its Burmese Vicissitudes*. New York: Harper & Row.

Strong, John S. 2001. *The Buddha: A Short Biography*. Oxford: Oneworld.

Tweed, Thomas A., and Stephen Prothero, eds. 1999. *Asian Religions in America: A Documentary History*. New York: Oxford University Press.

Williams, Paul. 1989. *Mahāyāna Buddhism: The Doctrinal Foundations*. New York: Routledge.

Joseph W. Williams

BULIMIA
SEE *Body Image.*

BULL AND BEAR MARKETS

The origin of the terms *bull* and *bear markets* is unclear. Don Luskin (2001) cites an English book by a Thomas Mortimer, printed in 1785 (*Every Man His Own Broker, or, A Guide to Exchange Alley*), that identifies a "bull" with a trader who invests heavily in stocks on borrowed money in the hope of selling at a profit before the loan repayment date. In contrast, a "bear" was a short-seller, that is, someone who borrows shares and sells them in the present and perhaps lends out as the proceeds at interest because he expects the price of stocks to decline after which he can buy the securities cheaply and return them to the lender. In any case, the terms *bull* and *bear markets* are popularly used and understood to mean durations of successive large stock price increases and large stock price decreases, respectively. The implication is that there is duration dependence in stock prices—that is, once prices begin increasing in a bull market, they tend to continue increasing, whereas decreasing prices in a bear market tend to continue decreasing.

However, there has been disagreement amongst researchers as to whether bull and bear markets exhibiting such duration dependence even exist. It is known that even if price changes are independent, they can after the fact seem to exhibit bull and bear phases; theories based on this idea hold that bull and bear markets are simply the result of after the fact categorization of stock market data. Other theories hold that bull and bear markets do exhibit predictability. And even if there is predictability in prices, they can be of two kinds—rational and irrational. Irrational cycles might be fueled by fads that ignite an increase in stock purchases and then die out, leading to mean reversion in prices. Rational cycles might exhibit bubble-like characteristics—although they might satisfy no-arbitrage conditions, they might still be influenced by nonfundamental factors.

One example of stock price predictability is an economy where, for some reason, a bubble develops, that is, asset prices differ from the present value of all future expected dividends. Prices each period are, nevertheless, equal to the sum of the present values of next period's expected dividend and next period's expected asset price. Each period, the economy finds itself in one of two regimes—one where the bubble persists and another where the bubble bursts; the greater the size of the bubble, the greater the probability of the bubble bursting. Simon van Norden and Huntley Schaller (2002) use U.S. stock market returns to test the (irrational) fads hypothesis set in a regime-switching model against a (rational) bubble alternative. They find in favor of the bubble alternative. However, the power of such tests depends strongly on the auxiliary assumptions used, as well as the alternative hypothesis specified. As a result, it is very difficult to reject the "irrationality" hypothesis entirely. For example, Jerry Coakley and Ana-Maria Fuertes (2006) find that market sentiment does play an important transitory role.

There is also a parallel literature that looks at mean reversion in stock prices and the existence of momentum effects in the context of investment strategies (e.g, Jegadeesh and Titman 1993). This literature finds negative autocorrelation in stock prices at short intervals and positive autocorrelation at longer intervals. In any case, there is now a solid body of work that seeks to use quantifiable rules to document and measure the bull and bear markets. There are two widely used algorithms—one by Gerhard Bry and Charlotte Boschan (1971) that mimics the qualitative rules used by the National Bureau of Economic Research to decide upon turning points of business cycles, and another that uses a Markov regime switching model (Maheu and McCurdy 2000).

Asset prices are used as signals by economic agents in several ways. First, because asset prices are considered to be aggregators of information and generally forward-looking, higher asset prices in a given sector are interpreted as greater growth potential in that sector, or concomitantly as a reduction in the cost of capital; this then allows investment to go where there is the greatest potential. Second, they are used as measures of value in various other contexts, such as in executive compensation. Third, asset prices, particularly real estate values, are also used by individuals as measures of wealth to help plan consumption. Finally, the Federal Reserve also uses asset prices to set monetary policy. When asset prices are divorced from true value, all these uses are affected. This is also true when there is a lot of asset price volatility, because the signal to noise ratio drops.

The integrity of the financial infrastructure can also be affected if there is an unexpected swing in asset prices, particularly downward, such as in October 1987, when the U.S. stock market dropped 23 percent in one day. The payments system could be affected, as well as the mechanisms for settling trades in securities markets. Also, because bank loans are often tied to property and stock market values, swings in asset prices are related to swings in lending and hence to swings in consumption and investment. These effects vary across countries. In financial systems characterized by a greater degree of arm's-length transactions, households are more sensitive to asset prices because market forces are used more than customary relationships for borrowing and investment purposes. Of course, such systems are overall more resilient and able to adjust to changes in growth opportunities. The empirical validity of asset market price swings causing swings in real activity is difficult to establish because any correlation in asset prices and real activity might be due simply to the reflection of future real activity in forward-looking asset prices.

There is also research that shows the generally negative effect of fluctuations in economic activity, that is to say business cycles on growth and human welfare. However, Matthew Rafferty (2005) shows that although unexpected volatility is related to lower growth, expected volatility is related to higher growth. Similarly, Jaume Ventura (2004) suggests that asset price bubbles could moderate the effect of financial market frictions and improve the allocation of investment across countries.

There has been more work recently on the globalization of business cycles and asset price cycles. This is related to the issue of correlation between different geographical asset markets, because lower correlation implies greater value for international portfolio diversification. François Longin and Bruno Solnik (2001) find that correlation between international equity markets has increased in bear markets, but not in bull markets. Javier Gómez Biscarri and Fernando Pérez de Gracia (2002) find that European stock markets seem to have become more concordant over time, as would be expected from the continuing integration of European financial markets. Furthermore, Christian Dunis and Gary Shannon (2005) find that, at least for the United Kingdom and the United States, there are still benefits from diversifying over emerging economy stock markets, ranging from Indonesia, Malaysia, and the Philippines to Korea, Taiwan, China, and India. However, the extent of such benefits may drop off with the continuing integration of India and China into world security and product markets.

SEE ALSO *Beauty Contest Metaphor; Bubbles; Business Cycles, Real; Economic Crises; Federal Reserve System, U.S.; Financial Instability Hypothesis; Financial Markets; Herd Behavior; Keynes, John Maynard; Market Correction; Speculation; Stock Exchanges; Stocks; Wealth*

BIBLIOGRAPHY

Biscarri, Javier Gómez, and Fernando Pérez de Gracia. 2002. Bulls and Bears: Lessons from Some European Countries. Working Paper, University of Navarra.

Bry, Gerhard, and Charlotte Boschan. 1971. *Cyclical Analysis of Time Series: Selected Procedures and Computer Programs.* New York: National Bureau of Economic Research.

Coakley, Jerry, and Ana-Maria Fuertes. 2006. Valuation Ratios and Price Deviations from Fundamentals. *Journal of Banking and Finance* 30 (8): 2325.

Dunis, Christian L., and Gary Shannon. 2005. Emerging Markets of South-East and Central Asia: Do They Still Offer a Diversification Benefit? *Journal of Asset Management* 6 (3): 168–190.

International Monetary Fund. 2006. World Economic Outlook: Financial Systems and Economic Cycles. Ch. 4. September 14.

Jegadeesh, Narasimhan, and Sheridan Titman. 1993. Returns to Buying Winners and Selling Losers: Implications for Stock Market Efficiency. *Journal of Finance* 48: 65–91.

Longin, François, and Bruno Solnik. 2001. Extreme Correlation of International Equity Markets. *Journal of Finance* 56 (2): 649–676.

Luskin, Don. 2001. The History of "Bull" and "Bear." http://www.thestreet.com/comment/openbook/1428176.html.

Maheu, John M. and Thomas H. McCurdy. 2000. Identifying Bull and Bear Markets in Stock Returns. *Journal of Business and Economic Statistics* 18 (1): 100–112.

Rafferty, Matthew. 2005. The Effects of Expected and Unexpected Volatility on Long-Run Growth: Evidence from 18 Developed Economies. *Southern Economic Journal* 71 (3): 582–591.

Van Norden, Simon, and Huntley Schaller. 2002. Fads or Bubbles? *Empirical Economics* 27 (2): 335–362.

Ventura, Jaume. 2004. Bubbles and Capital Flows. Working Paper, Centre de Recerca en Economia Internacional, Barcelona.

P. V. Viswanath

BULL MARKET

SEE *Bull and Bear Markets.*

BUNCHE, RALPH JOHNSON
c. 1904–1971

Ralph Johnson Bunche was an American social scientist and statesman. Two weeks after the State of Israel was established in May 1948, the United Nations Security Council sent a delegation to restore peace between the Arabs and Israelis. Under the leadership of Bunche, the delegation would be singularly successfully in achieving direct negotiations between the two groups over territory, an armistice, and a UN peacekeeping force. Yet, fate would have to intervene to put Bunche in the Nobel Prize–winning position when the original head of the delegation, the Swedish diplomat Folke Bernadotte (1895–1948), was assassinated, along with everyone in his car, on an Israeli road. Fortunately for Bunche, he was delayed by the police on his way to meet Bernadotte in their efforts to strengthen the UN role in the region.

Long before going to the Middle East, Bunche had built an academic foundation for his influential career in political science and international relations. That foundation is illustrated by his involvement with a diverse group of Howard University colleagues in a 1935 national conference on "race" in New York. In concert with sociologist E. Franklin Frazier (1894–1962), economist Abram Harris (1899–1963), and philosopher Alain Locke (1886–1954), among others, Bunche gave definition to the second (professorial) phase of his scholarly leadership. For much of his life he would engage in an evolving struggle to balance race-conscious and class-conscious approaches to political and economic analysis. At the same time, he could never easily abandon political engagement for scholarly detachment. He wanted to "change the world" enough to join leftist labor union protests as a young professor and to participate in civil rights demonstrations even after retirement. Yet, he often withdrew to Howard University social science conferences or immersed himself in African- or African American–oriented research. By 1953, however, when he returned to campus for the inaugural Phi Beta Kappa lecture, he had already reached the pinnacle of the third and defining phase of his career: he was a celebrated United Nations diplomat.

Somewhere between his work as a U.S. delegate in the formative weeks of the United Nations in the 1945 talks in San Francisco, and his mediation of the 1949 negotiations leading to an agreement on the Palestinian issues and a foundation for the State of Israel, Bunche left academics to become a renowned international peacemaker. However fragile the peace resolutions he helped fashion in Israel and Africa, they were as solid as any that followed. For example, he labored under hopeless circumstances with limited success in the former Belgian Congo to bring Patrice Lumumba (1925–1961) into reconciliation with military and separatist Congolese factions.

Although his indefatigable pursuit of international conflict resolution earned him the 1950 Nobel Peace Prize, he repeatedly expressed skepticism about the primacy of peace in the foreign policies of UN member states. In addition to cautions about nuclear war in his speeches, he warned in his Nobel lecture that "some in the world ... are prematurely resigned to the inevitability of war." He added: "among them are the advocates of the so-called 'preventive war,' who ... wish merely to select their own time for initiating it" (Bunche 1950).

Returning to the United States, the discomfort he had long felt with American racism had become more difficult to tolerate. The optimism of his successful schooldays in Los Angeles had long since faded. He had gone from valedictorian at UCLA (1927) to become the first black PhD (1934) in political science, graduating from Harvard University. Although it had not been easy, raised largely by his grandmother in Los Angeles after his early years in Detroit, he worked his way through the universities with some critical scholarship assistance. While supporting his wife, Ruth, with whom he would later have three children, he began working at Howard before he completed his doctorate. Yet the global demands of his career would continually place strains on his family life.

Once settled in the Political Science Department chairmanship at Howard, the black experience and the international exposure came together for him when he worked on the 1940s publication of the groundbreaking study of race relations with the Swedish sociologist Gunnar Myrdal (1898–1987). Although Bunche is not credited as an author of Myrdal's *An American Dilemma* (1944), the 3,000-plus pages of research he contributed to the Carnegie report attest to his indispensable role. Better suited to his earlier years than to the second phase of his life, when he saw class conflict as a pivotal issue, the study was optimistic about race relations. The country was increasingly coming to recognize the contradiction for the "democratic creed" that racial discrimination entailed, according to Myrdal, and a positive resolution of this "moral dilemma" could soon be expected. As for Bunche's views, they were less reflected in this conclusion than they were in his own short book, *A World View of Race* (1936), which suggests a more deeply rooted material basis for racial inequality (Henry 1995).

While Bunche continued to break racial barriers—for example, becoming the first black president of the American Political Science Association in 1954—he grew more race conscious. He shared the stage with Martin Luther King Jr. (1929–1968) in the 1963 March on Washington, and he shared King's reservations about the progress made and to be expected in American race relations. Ironically, the complexity of his thought and beliefs on this and many social issues was largely obscured by his success in world affairs. Still, given the breadth of his political views, he could not escape the intrusive attention of the Senate Judiciary Subcommittee on Internal Security in the heat of Washington's anticommunist hysteria. He

was interrogated in 1953 about his presumed association with black communists and communist sympathizers. In particular, his 1930s organizing role in the National Negro Congress was targeted. An FBI initiative to charge him with perjury for denying membership in the Communist Party fell through because it was built on a misunderstanding of his civil rights politics.

In 1904, when Bunche was born, the United States was an isolationist country internationally that further isolated African Americans internally from access to society's resources. When he died in 1971, the United States was internationally engaged and interracially progressing, and he, far more than most leaders, had helped to make the changes possible.

SEE ALSO *Myrdal, Gunnar; Nobel Peace Prize*

BIBLIOGRAPHY

Bunche, Ralph J. 1950. Nobel Lecture: Some Reflections on Peace in Our Time. http://nobelprize.org/nobel_prizes/peace/laureates/1950/bunche-lecture.html.

Henry, Charles P., ed. 1995. *Ralph J. Bunche: Selected Speeches and Writings*. Ann Arbor: University of Michigan Press.

Henry, Charles P. 1999. *Ralph Bunche: Model Negro or American Other?* New York: New York University Press.

Holloway, Jonathan Scott. 2002. *Confronting the Veil: Abram Harris Jr., E. Franklin Frazier, and Ralph Bunche, 1919–1941*. Chapel Hill: University of North Carolina Press.

Morris, Lorenzo. 2006. Ralph J. Bunche and His Intellectual Offspring. *Government & Politics* 3: 8–9.

Myrdal, Gunnar. 1944 *An American Dilemma: The Negro Problem and Modern Democracy*. New York: Harper.

Urquhart, Brian. 1993. *Ralph Bunche: An American Life*. New York: Norton.

Walton, Hanes. 2004. The Political Science Educational Philosophy of Ralph Bunche. *Journal of Negro Education* 73 (2): 147–158.

Lorenzo Morris

BURAKU OR *BURAKUMIN*

The *buraku* people, or *burakumin* (literally, "village people"), are a group of approximately three million ethnic Japanese that is discriminated against by the majority Japanese population. This discrimination manifests itself in higher illness rates and higher unemployment than for mainstream Japanese, lower wages for the same jobs, the existence of illegal blacklists that corporations buy and use to avoid hiring *buraku* people, the discouragement of marriage between *burakumin* and non-*burakumin* Japanese, and the historic complicity of Japanese religious bodies in segregating temples and bestowing prejudicial death names (*kaimyo*). From the 1990s to 2006, the Internet has been used to post defamatory statements against the *buraku*.

The discrimination ostensibly is based on historic, familial occupations that were deemed "unclean" by Japanese religions (Buddhism and Shinto), such as butchery, tanning, and leatherwork; however, in modern Japan, although descent is an operative factor, the primary determinant of *buraku* identity is location, as many *buraku* people live in designated government-supported housing and support areas (*dōwa chiku*). Today, an emergent issue is the question of what constitutes *buraku* identity: some residents of *dōwa chiku* claim ancestral *buraku* lineages, and others are socially defined as *buraku* people simply because they live in areas designated for *burakumin*.

There is scholarly debate as to the historical origin of *buraku* discrimination. During the Heian period (794–1185) the lowest in society (*senmin*, as opposed to the *ryomin*, the "good") often handled leather armor for warlords (*daimyo*), and in return they usually were provided with some tax relief and poor land. They were also given "unclean" jobs such as jailer and executioner, and were expected to be the first line of defense in case of attack. Some scholars conjecture that this social segmentation was the beginning of what came to be the *buraku* designation; however, it was distinctly in the Tokugawa period (1603–1867) when the discriminatory policies and structure were established in a stratified social order (samurai, farmer, artisan, and merchant) that excluded the *eta* and the *hinin*. (These discriminatory terms, which respectively mean "much filth" and "nonhuman," were used as social designations at the time.) The ostracized *eta* and *hinin* groups are considered the precursors of today's *burakumin*. In 1871 discrimination against this subgroup was abolished by the Emancipation Edict (*Eta Kaihō Rei*), but the edict had little effect on bettering conditions.

In March 1922 the National Levelers Association (*Zenkoku Suiheisha*) was founded to address the persistent discrimination against the *buraku* people. With the rise of the Japanese military establishment, the organization was outlawed in 1937, then reinstituted itself in 1946 as the National Committee for Buraku Liberation (then the Buraku Liberation League in 1955). In 1969, through sustained political activism by the *buraku* organizations and their supporters, the Japanese government enacted special legislation (Laws on Special Measures for Dowa Region) that dramatically bettered conditions for the *buraku* people. It remains to be seen how the expiration of this legislation in 2003 will continue to affect the *buraku*

community and the notable advances they have made in such areas as education, housing, and employment. While living conditions have improved and exogamous marriage increases, the major issue for the *buraku* liberation effort—as with many human rights efforts across the globe—is how to sustain the energy and communal effort to improve the majority Japanese attitude toward the *buraku* people into the next generation.

SEE ALSO *Caste; Discrimination; Minorities; Racism*

BIBLIOGRAPHY

Buraku Liberation and Human Rights Research Institute. http://blhrri.org/index_e.htm.

Kitaguchi, Suehiro. 1999. *An Introduction to the Buraku Issue: Questions and Answers.* Trans. and intro. Alastair McLauchlan. Richmond, Surrey, U.K.: Curzon Press.

McLauchlan, Alastair. 2003. *Prejudice and Discrimination in Japan—The Buraku Issue.* Lewiston, NY: Edwin Mellen.

Meerman, Jacob. 2003. The Mobility of Japan's Burakumin Militant Advocacy and Government Response. In *Boundaries of Clan and Color: Transnational Comparisons of Inter-group Disparity*, ed. William Darity Jr. and Ashwini Deshpande, 130–151. London: Routledge.

Neary, Ian. 2003. Burakumin at the End of History. *Social Research* 70 (1): 269ff.

Leslie D. Alldritt

BURDIAN'S ASS

SEE *Conundrum.*

BUREAUCRACY

History discloses political orders different from each other. These orders evolve as a result of each society's self-organization toward representative structures that confer validity on its rules and continuity. It was German sociologist Max Weber's insight that these structures rely on systems of authority, such that every system attempts to establish and cultivate the belief in its legitimacy, as the grounds of authority, for which he found three pure types: charisma, tradition, and instrumental reason.

Bureaucracy, a term that literally means government by offices or agencies with prescribed functions, exemplified for Weber the organizational structure associated with legitimacy grounded in instrumental reason. He devoted considerable attention to bureaucracy in part because he believed that, despite exhibiting no unilinear development or progress, history had demonstrated a trend toward increasing rationalization, or what he referred to as a "disenchantment," so that bureaucracy represents in organizational structure a deeper cultural tendency, especially in the West. In order to grapple with increasing rationalization, he had to understand what it meant for the ordering of society.

Bureaucracy has a distinct character, which Weber delineated. Individuals with documented qualifications fill positions circumscribed by rules, in order to ensure the perpetual fulfillment of the bureau's function. These rules tend to be stable and exhaustive. The resulting structure trends toward hierarchy. Incumbents are expected to keep their work separate from their private lives, so they can concentrate on their duties, which are based more on the processing of documents or files in the abstract and not on interactions with individual persons directly. Consistent with this tendency toward abstraction, the official is then rewarded abstractly by means of job security and a salary in a money economy, thereby making this career a distinct profession.

James Burnham examined the significance of bureaucratic administration as a profession in *The Managerial Revolution,* published in 1941. Burnham worried as a disillusioned leftist that the managerial revolution would derail the transition from capitalism to socialism. His work influenced the British futuristic novelist George Orwell, author of *Animal Farm* (1944) and *1984* (1949). It also inspired social scientists to conduct empirical studies of his primary thesis, and even in the 2000s Burnham's book "occupies a prominent place in postindustrial theories of society" (Demers and Merskin 2000, p. 105). Burnham foresaw the rise of a new ruling elite composed of managers with organizational skill and technical knowledge. These managers were going to displace owners and capitalists in day-to-day operations. The research conducted since tends to bear him out.

The economist John Kenneth Galbraith extended Burnham's argument in *The New Industrial State* (1967), noting that managers as a ruling elite had given way to a group even more embedded in the staff of bureaucracy, a group named by Galbraith as the technostructure. Due to increasing complexity, decision making in bureaucracy requires the specialized scientific and technical knowledge, talent, and experience of multiple persons exchanging and testing information. In this group, one might include engineers, accountants, and lawyers. Without the requisite mastery and information, managers must rely on the resulting apparatus for group decision. Although the apparatus known as the technostructure puts a check on individual initiative and ambition, taken as a whole it works toward its collective survival, autonomy, and growth, in that order. For Galbraith, the technostructure is the decision-making apparatus emblematic of bureaucracy. Seventeen years later, Galbraith saw no reason to amend these findings, except to emphasize the technostructure's "deteriorative tendencies" (1988, p. 375).

At one time, scholars such as Ludwig von Mises might have wanted to isolate bureaucracy as a phenomenon that thrives only in the public sector, in government, but the evidence suggests that it is precisely in the technostructure described by Galbraith that the public and private sectors intertwine to share an overlapping fate, as large firms in the private sector attempt to manage their environment and as the government increasingly executes the laws by means of the technostructure within private firms. According to Galbraith, bureaucracy has emerged in every sector.

Bureaucracy not only has a distinct character, it also plays a distinct role in the routinization of charisma, the ordering of society into a rational form. Bureaucracy exerts pressure to domesticate creativity and genius, removing the element of mystification that accompanies charisma, in order to bring it into service without allowing it to supplant instrumental reason as the legitimating ground for authority. Bureaucracy thereby tends to channel or frustrate freedom, with astonishing success, which is why Weber famously lamented the "iron cage" that rationalization was building throughout society.

In the second chapter of *Images of Organization* (1986), Gareth Morgan echoed Weber by associating bureaucracy with an image of organizations that would be construed as mechanistic, structures invented and developed to perform a goal-oriented activity. Not surprisingly, with the mechanization of the Industrial Revolution came the widespread mechanization of organizational structures. Writers such as Frederick Taylor then made the process conscious, offering a scientific approach to managing organizations, on the principle that mechanistic thinking had succeeded in so many other aspects of life. And it had.

Bureaucracy contributes to the goal-oriented activities of any organization. Weber listed these advantages: "[p]recision, speed, unambiguity, knowledge of the files, continuity, discretion, unity, strict subordination, reduction of friction and of material and personal costs...." (1958, p. 214). In contradistinction to previous structures, bureaucracy exists to remove less predictable elements such as individual favor from the conduct of business. This means it offers stability to a regime. Disputes are more easily resolved by appeals to reason and rules, which guide officials in their work. Bureaucracy also fits many purposes of large-scale government especially, where other bases of legitimacy have been outlawed or discredited. Since the Enlightenment, Western culture especially has preferred legitimacy based on instrumental reason.

Despite its promise of efficacy, bureaucracy meets with considerable resistance, especially from two sources. One source of resistance has been the concern previously expressed already by Max Weber that bureaucracy inhibits freedom and all that freedom promises. Ralph Hummel sharpened the critique in *The Bureaucratic Experience* (1994): Over time, given its prevalence and power, bureaucracy shapes human psychology, language, and culture, transforming what it means to be human in exchange for values including security and efficiency. Critics such as Orwell, Franz Kafka, Aldous Huxley, and in cinema Terry Gilliam (e.g., *Brazil,* 1985) have depicted an implicit terror and malaise in bureaucratic regimes that can only be described as inhuman. In his 1995 book *Kinds of Power,* for example, psychologist James Hillman cited the predatory practices of bureaucratic fascism and communism as the logical extension of the Enlightenment's emphasis on instrumental reason.

The resistance to bureaucracy from this source emphasizes the trade-off that comes with empowering an elite of professionals at the expense of democratic participation in the decisions that affect our lives, since bureaucrats are not supposed to be directly responsive to voters, to markets, or even to beneficiaries of the services provided by that bureau. Weber noted that bureaucracy accompanies the rise of mass democracy, in that it promises status only in exchange for meritorious service and not kinship, for example, or race, yet bureaucracy by no means enhances the power of the people to govern themselves directly.

Principles of diversity challenge the basis for choosing officials as somehow biased in favor of certain privileged social groups who acquire credentials disproportionate to their numbers in the population.

The second source of resistance to bureaucracy derives from the claim that there are more effective ways for organizations to work, since bureaucracy has a number of limitations. For instance, bureaucracy tends to hide its work from scrutiny, even from one bureau to another, whereas in an information age secrets impede innovation and cast doubt on a bureaucracy's legitimacy. Bureaucracy also offers persistence at times that organizational structures should adapt to changing circumstances. The bureaucrat's loyalty to the bureau might displace his or her loyalty to the bureau's originating purpose; accusations leveled at fascist administrators who were "only doing their jobs" have been especially vivid.

Since the 1970s, organizational theorists such as Gifford and Elizabeth Pinchot have called for flattened hierarchies, cross-functional coordination, greater transparency, and shorter timelines than a conscientious bureaucracy can meet. These theorists borrow principles from the marketplace, urging bureaucracies to cultivate a more entrepreneurial spirit, taking risk and competing. Theorists also notice the power of flexible networks, rather than rigid silos. Writing in 1999, Richard Brinkman uncovered as evidence of bureaucracy's weakening hold the tendency of management to pursue short-term profit in part by downsizing elements of the technostructure, yet it can be said that reports of bureaucracy's demise are greatly exaggerated.

SEE ALSO *Bureaucrat; Weber, Max*

BIBLIOGRAPHY

Brinkman, Richard. 1999. The Dynamics of Corporate Culture: Conception and Theory. *International Journal of Social Economics* 26 (5): 674–694.

Burnham, James. 1960. *The Managerial Revolution.* Bloomington: Indiana University Press. (Orig. pub. 1941).

Demers, D., and D. Merskin. 2000. Corporate News Structure and the Managerial Revolution. *The Journal of Media Economics* 13 (2): 103–121.

Galbraith, John Kenneth. 1988. Time and the New Industrial State. *The American Economic Review* 78 (2): 373–376.

Galbraith, John Kenneth. 1971. *The New Industrial State.* 2nd ed. Boston: Houghton-Mifflin. (Orig. pub. 1967).

Hillman, James. 1995. *Kinds of Power.* New York: Currency Doubleday.

Hummel, Ralph. 1994. *The Bureaucratic Experience: A Critique of Life in the Modern Organization.* 4th ed. New York: St. Martin's Press.

Morgan, Gareth. 1986. *Images of Organization.* New York: Sage.

von Mises, Ludwig. 1983. *Bureaucracy.* Grove City, PA: Libertarian Press. (Orig. pub. 1944).

Weber, Max. 1958. *From Max Weber: Essays in Sociology.* Trans. H. H. Gerth and C. W. Mills. New York: Oxford University Press. (Orig. pub. 1922).

Nathan W. Harter

BUREAUCRAT

The term *bureaucrat* refers to a professional administrator, a career official employed to serve a bureau or office. Often used pejoratively, the term describes a predominantly stabilizing function in which the career interests of the administrator align with the bureau's norms and values.

The German sociologist Max Weber (1864–1920) embedded in his classic analysis of bureaucracy in *Economy and Society* (originally published in 1925 and translated in 1958) a section on the position of the official whose activities are fixed and ordered by rules, so that authority will be seen to derive from a rational and impersonal basis. For Weber, the bureaucrat is simply intrinsic to this process of rationalization that so typifies modernity. Such an official would have been expected to possess certain qualifications in order to occupy the position in the first place, presumably as a result of rigorous training in management generally and in the rules of the bureau. At all times, official activities are supervised by a higher authority within the organization; nevertheless, the official owes loyalty not to the supervisor, but to the bureau and its purpose. A bureaucrat assumes appointment to the office by accepting "a specific obligation of faithful management in return for a secure existence" (Weber 1958, p. 199). As a result, the official is meant to enjoy a status commensurate with rank. An official's expertise and authority will tend to protect the officeholder from "arbitrary dismissal or transfer" (Weber 1958, p. 202). Weber held that for the sake of stable employment the bureaucrat will accept a lower salary compared to the private sector, although presently bureaucrats appear in every sector, including the private sector—to the consternation of critics. One critic, James Burnham, famously warned in 1941 against their domination as a class.

According to the economist Ludwig von Mises in *Bureaucracy* (1944), allegiance to the bureau and relative insulation from "arbitrary dismissal or transfer" contributes to the perception that bureaucrats tend to be unresponsive to external complaint. The primary reason is that there exists no way to calculate the bureaucrat's performance, except of the extent to which he or she adheres to the prescribed rules and stays within budget.

Bureaucrats stabilize the office in part because they learn not to take risks. Ralph Hummel explains in *The Bureaucratic Experience* that the supervisor assumes the role of conscience and ego function, deciding what needs to be done and how, and leaving it to the bureaucrat to fulfill the explicit terms of the employment contract. Any other than instrumental rationality is not required. Mises spoke for many critics when he argued that bureaucracy "kills ambition, destroys initiative and the incentive to do more than the minimum required" (Mises 1983, p. 61). Rather than undertake risk, a prudent bureaucrat will not only conform but also take steps to secure the future by protecting the bureau from threat of dissolution. For this reason, whatever the originating and legitimating purpose had been for the creation of the bureau, the bureaucrat owes a primary allegiance to the perpetuation of the bureau itself. Keeping a job becomes more important than doing the job, which is goal displacement. For example, in 1978 the communist Rudolf Bahro identified bureaucrats in socialist states as jealous and exploitative rulers, responsible for alienated consciousness and preventing further liberation.

The virtue of bureaucrats, according to Gareth Morgan (1986), lies in professionalism based on expertise, concentration, a relatively transparent mission, and the impersonal nature of workplace relationships—all of which fulfilled the ambition of rational administration consistent with a mechanistic model of organizations, in contrast to prior models based for example on kinship, personal loyalty, or profit seeking.

BIBLIOGRAPHY

Bahro, Rudolph. 1978. *The Alternative in Eastern Europe.* London: New Left Books.

Burnham, James. 1960. *The Managerial Revolution.* Bloomington: Indiana University Press. (Orig. pub. 1941).

Hummel, Ralph. 1994. *The Bureaucratic Experience: A Critique of Life in the Modern Organization.* 4th ed. New York: St. Martin's Press.

Mises, Ludwig von. 1983. *Bureaucracy.* Grove City, PA: Libertarian Press. (Orig. pub. 1944).

Morgan, Gareth. 1986. *Images of Organization.* New York: Sage.

Weber, Max. 1958. *From Max Weber: Essays in Sociology.* Trans. Hans H. Gerth and C. Wright Mills. New York: Oxford University Press. (Orig. pub. 1922).

Nathan W. Harter

BURIAL GROUNDS

A burial ground is a place of interment. It is a tract of land, a yard, or an enclosure for the subterranean deposition of human remains. Often the objects of legend, burial grounds have varied throughout time according to the cultural practices and religious beliefs of different peoples. Whereas Aubrey Cannon (1989) maintains that human expressions of death in burial grounds follow a general cross-cultural pattern that cycles between elitism and emulation, James Deetz (1996) suggests that burial grounds showcase culturally specific symbols that are evident in every aspect of a given society's lifeways.

The first hominids to bury their dead were probably Neanderthals that lived between 20,000 and 75,000 years ago. In fact, many Neanderthal interments exhibited evidence of burial customs that are still practiced, including the placement of flowers and other grave goods with the deceased and the orientation of the dead along an east-west axis. Group interments in large earthen mounds, also called *tumuli, kofun, barrows,* or *kurgans* in different cultural contexts, became common across Europe, Asia, and the Americas in the centuries before and after 1 BCE. Gigantic stone temples that housed burial chambers also occurred across the globe during this time. These mammoth structures included Egyptian and Mayan pyramids and ancient Greek necropolises.

In the centuries leading up to the 1700s, Westerners buried their dead in sacrosanct churchyards according to specific spatial norms that tied directly to their faith in resurrection. Wealthy individuals were interred within the church itself and on the east side in order to get the most direct view of the rising sun on Judgment Day, the poor were laid to rest to the south of the church, and the north churchyard was reserved for stillborns, bastards, and individuals who committed suicide. Even though these shallow churchyards often teemed with bones, scavengers, and maggots, they were still a center of social activity and frequently hosted markets, gaming events, and other gatherings. It was not until the late 1600s that the English Parliament linked these unsanitary practices with the spread of the plague and outlawed shallow graves, large funerals, and unnecessary burial-ground activities. A chronic shortage of space in churchyards in the 1700s forced a change to burial strategies. The north side of the church was no longer for social outcasts, all of the deceased were packed closer together, and numerous coffins were stacked on top of one another under the topsoil, leading many churchyards to tower a dozen feet or more above the floor of the church.

Just as the stone walls surrounding many European churchyards began to collapse under the pressure of the overcrowded burial ground, Parisian officials enacted a drastically different interment policy, transporting the bones of millions of deceased individuals into catacombs beneath the French capital. This initial act of the eighteenth-century cemetery reform movement also led to the creation of the first garden cemetery—the Père-Lachaise—which spanned hundreds of acres in an uninterrupted picturesque landscape that was far away from the church and the crowded urban city center. Père-Lachaise was the first municipal cemetery, as the government now controlled burial procedures and planning instead of the church. Others quickly followed suit; Boston's Mount Auburn Cemetery, established in 1831, was the inaugural cemetery in the Western hemisphere to embrace this change in burial-ground planning, and it set the standard for large rural garden cemeteries in the United States that persists into the present day.

SEE ALSO *Burial Grounds, African; Burial Grounds, Native American*

BIBLIOGRAPHY

Cannon, Aubrey. 1989. The Historical Dimension in Mortuary Expressions of Status and Sentiment. *Current Anthropology* 30 (4): 437–458.

Deetz, James. 1996. *In Small Things Forgotten: An Archeology of Early American Life*. Expanded ed. New York: Anchor.

Seth W. Mallios

BURIAL GROUNDS, AFRICAN

The final resting places of enslaved and free people of African descent have been examined in diverse contexts throughout the New World. Ranging from late sixteenth-century Mexico to postemancipation Arkansas, these sites reflect the range and complexity of the African diasporic experience. Although many of these sites were examined within a historical forensic paradigm, the greater involvement of African Americans as both clients and producers of burial ground studies is fostering a historically and culturally grounded biocultural approach that is more responsive to the needs and interests of the descendant communities (Blakey 2001; Epperson 1999).

In 2000 construction activity in the city of Campeche on Mexico's Yucatan peninsula resulted in discovery of the foundation of an early cathedral and an associated multiethnic burial ground that was used from the mid-sixteenth century until the construction of a new cathedral in the late seventeenth century. Some 180 individuals were interred at this site, including at least 10 of African ancestry. The presence of dental modifications, in conjunction with strontium isotopic analysis, indicates that at least four of these individuals were born in West Africa. Although there is ample documentary evidence of African slavery in the Campeche region during this period, it should not necessarily be assumed that these individuals were enslaved (Handler and Lange 2006).

At the site of the Newton Plantation in southern Barbados the remains of 104 African-descent individuals interred between 1660 and 1820 have been analyzed. Of particular interest is Burial 72, a male about fifty years old who was buried during the late 1600s or early 1700s with a distinctive assemblage of grave goods suggestive of status as a healer/diviner (Handler 1997; Handler and Lange 1978). In a very different plantation context, investigation of the Belleview Plantation near Charleston, South Carolina, included a sample of twenty-seven individuals who died between 1840 and 1870. These individuals had a high incidence of anemia and infection as well as skeletal changes associated with very demanding physical labor (Rathbun and Scurry 1991).

Excavations in the multiethnic St. Peter Street Cemetery in the French Quarter of New Orleans recovered remains of eighteen individuals, at least ten of whom were of African descent. This cemetery was in use as early as 1720 until the end of the eighteenth century. Within the African American burials, investigators noted the presence of Roman Catholic grave goods and suggested the presence of two occupational groups: house servants and laborers (Owsley et al. 1987).

The African Burial Ground in New York City was in use from the late seventeenth century until about 1795.

Excavations conducted in 1991–1992 recovered the remains of more than four hundred African-born and African American individuals. Analysis of these remains revealed evidence of the rigors of urban slavery as well as the survival and nurturance of West African cultural traditions. Pressure from the descendant community resulted in the development of a research design that placed greater emphasis on the historical and cultural context of the burial ground. The remains were reinterred on the site in 2003 (General Services Administration 2006; LaRoche and Blakey 1997).

Analysis of over 140 burials recovered from the First African Baptist Church Cemetery (in use c. 1822–1848) in downtown Philadelphia, Pennsylvania, revealed that antebellum free African Americans shared many of the rigors of their enslaved kin, suffering high infant and childhood mortality, periodic malnutrition and infectious diseases, and degenerative joint diseases (Angel et al. 1987; Rankin-Hill 1997). Similarly, the rural Cedar Grove Cemetery in southwest Arkansas provides stark evidence that the health of African Americans did not improve during the postemancipation period. Cortical bone analysis of a sample of fifteen females and fourteen males indicates a population that was under extraordinary disease and nutritional stress (Martin, Magennis, and Rose 1987).

SEE ALSO *African Diaspora; Anthropology, Biological; Archaeology; Burial Grounds; Immigrants to North America; Slave Lives, Archaeology of; Slavery Industry*

BIBLIOGRAPHY

Angel, J. Lawrence, Jennifer Olsen Kelley, Michael Parrington, and Stephanie Pinter. 1987. Life Stresses of the Free Black Community as Represented by the First African Baptist Church, Philadelphia, 1823–1841. *American Journal of Physical Anthropology* 87 (2): 213–229.

Blakey, Michael L. 2001. Bioarchaeology of the African Diaspora in the Americas: Its Origins and Scope. *Annual Review of Anthropology* 30: 387–422.

Epperson, Terrence W. 1999. The Contested Commons: Archaeologies of Race, Repression, and Resistance in New York City. In *Historical Archaeologies of Capitalism*, eds. M. P. Leone and P. B. Potter, Jr., 3–20. New York: Plenum.

General Services Administration. 2006. *African Burial Ground Final Reports (Includes Archaeology, History, and Skeletal Biology)*, October 13, 2006. http://www.africanburialground.gov/ABG_FinalReports.htm

Handler, Jerome S. 1997. An African-Type Healer/Diviner and His Grave Goods: A Burial from a Plantation Slave Cemetery in Barbados, West Indies. *International Journal of Historical Archaeology* 1 (2): 91–130.

Handler, Jerome S., and Frederick W. Lange. 1978. *Plantation Slavery in Barbados: An Archaeological and Historical Investigation*. Cambridge, MA: Harvard University Press.

Handler, Jerome S., and Frederick W. Lange. 2006. On Interpreting Slave Status from Archaeological Remains. *African Diaspora Archaeology Network Newsletter*, June 2006. http://www.diaspora.uiuc.edu/news0606/news0606.html

LaRoche, Cheryl L., and Michael L. Blakey. 1997. Seizing Intellectual Power: The Dialogue at the New York African Burial Ground. *Historical Archaeology* 31: 84–106.

Martin, Debra L., Ann L. Magennis, and Jerome C. Rose. 1987. Cortical Bone Maintenance in an Historic Afro-American Cemetery Sample from Cedar Grove, Arkansas. *American Journal of Physical Anthropology* 74 (2): 255–264.

Owsley, Douglas W., Charles E. Orser, Jr., Robert W. Mann, Peer H. Moore-Jansen, and Robert L. Montgomery. 1987. Demography and Pathology of an Urban Slave Plantation from New Orleans. *American Journal of Physical Anthropology* 87 (2): 185–197.

Rankin-Hill, Lesley M. 1997. *A Biohistory of 19th-Century Afro-Americans: The Burial Remains of a Philadelphia Cemetery*. Westport, CT: Bergin & Garvey.

Rathbun, Ted A., and J. D. Scurry. 1991. Status and Health in Colonial South Carolina: Belleview Plantation, 1738–1756. In *What Mean These Bones? Studies in Southeastern Bioarchaeology*, ed. M. L. Powell, P. S. Bridges, and A. M. Mires, 148–164. Tuscaloosa: University of Alabama Press.

Terrence W. Epperson

BURIAL GROUNDS, NATIVE AMERICAN

In nearly every culture—and certainly in every religion—there is some promise of life after death. It is often necessary, therefore, to connect one's mortal remains with after-existence, whether by freeing the soul from its worldly dwelling or preparing those remains for their later state. The meaning attributed to such preparations and the forms they take mirror much of the society they serve and often carry, through the intensity of their attendant emotions, the ideas upon which a culture depends when death threatens the very order of things.

The disposition of the dead by American Indians is as varied as the organization of the groups themselves. For many ancient peoples (c. 1000–200 BCE), as seen particularly in the eastern United States, elaborate burial mounds probably replicated the social order of settlements or the vision of the cosmos at large; for others, like the Choctaw, Plains Indians, or Northwest Coast tribes, the spirits of the dead could only be released by first exposing them to the elements, the scattered remains sometimes being subject to secondary interment; for still others, as among those groups of the Southeast, the dead were often placed in large earthenware jars before burial. As many Indians and Aleuts were converted to Christianity by Hispanics,

Europeans, or Russians, burial in cemeteries, with appropriate religious insignia, became far more common. To the extent that one can generalize, for Native Americans, locale and cosmos came together in the rituals of daily life, including, with special force, the treatment of the place with which the remains of one's predecessors were associated.

Just as white Americans will go to extravagant lengths to recover the bodies of their dead or visit their final resting place, so, too, for Native Americans, deprivation of their dead has been felt with special intensity. The forced removal of Indians from the East, the creation of reservations, and the loss of Indian lands exacerbated the sense of separation from ancestors. Throughout the Indian wars of the nineteenth century, the remains of fallen Indians were collected by the U.S. Army, the bodies stripped of their flesh, and the bones sent back to Washington, D.C. Housed for decades in government and private institutions, thousands of skulls and bones were hidden away or subjected to every passing scientific notion—from the relation of cranial size to intelligence, to the development of civilization as determined by denture, diet, or DNA. Often, too, the remains were placed on view in public or private museums, commonly with unflattering labels or surroundings. To Indians, these collections and exhibits, whether for science or for profit, were nothing short of the desecration to which, they argued, non-Indian remains were never subjected.

Many of these issues came to a head in the 1970s and 1980s, when Indian legal groups filed lawsuits seeking the discontinuance of offensive displays and the return of Indian remains. There was, however, no clear legal right to the return of such remains—whether the 18,500 sets of remains in the Smithsonian Institution or the hundreds of skeletons plundered in the late 1980s from a site in Kentucky. In 1990, therefore, the U.S. Congress passed the Native American Graves Protection and Repatriation Act (NAGPRA), which explicitly classifies human remains as "cultural items" that could be returned to related successor tribes. As museum and university inventories were constructed and tribes asserted the right of return, archaeologists and native groups sometimes came into conflict: Most native peoples object to any scientific studies of their ancestors' remains, while scholars often asserted the benefits of allowing their studies to go forward. A number of states (e.g., California) also passed statutes or entered into agreements with tribes allowing the return of burial remains even from private sites. Further federal protection criminalizing the illegal excavation or trafficking in human remains is afforded by the Archaeological Resources Protection Act of 1978. Tribes themselves have also adopted codes affecting archaeological work on their reservations, and have even sought to make their laws extend to remains housed off Indian lands. Several international human rights conventions have proved an effective basis for the return of remains to peoples of the South Pacific, but since the United States is not a signatory to some of these treaties, international standards have yet to be applied to Native Americans.

Perhaps most difficult has been the question of ancient remains. When a set of 8,000- to 9,000-year-old-bones, known as Kennewick Man, was discovered in Washington State, the Army Corps of Engineers sought to transfer the bones to the five tribes who claimed a connection to them. In 2004 the Ninth Circuit Court of Appeals (in *Bonnichsen v. United States*) held that the requirement that there be some relation of the remains to an existing tribe, people, or culture had not been met in this case, and the court permitted scientists to gain access to the materials. Other cases may also test the meaning of *indigenous* and the criteria for showing *cultural affiliation*, terms that are not clearly defined in the statutes themselves. Nevertheless, where historical connections can be asserted, the capacity of tribes to regain control over their people's burial remains has significantly increased since the 1980s.

Americans have long had a deep-seated ambivalence toward their native peoples. From the restraints that Chief Justice John Marshall (1755–1835) sought to place on the federal government's care of its "domestic dependent nations" to the willingness of white Americans who would never adopt a black child to extend their kinship boundaries to include Indians, the course of American history has never been a simple story of conquest and oppression. The question of science versus heritage, identity versus property, replicates much of white-Indian relations and the ambivalence with which each approaches the actions and intentions of the other. The idea that Indians are like the miner's canary—that they give an early indication of the quality of the environs in which everyone operates—is no less true where archaeological remains are concerned than where land, natural resources, or the constitutional limits of indigenous sovereignty are also at issue.

SEE ALSO *Burial Grounds; Indigenous Rights*

BIBLIOGRAPHY

Bushnell, David Ives, Jr. 1920. *Native Cemeteries and Forms of Burial East of the Mississippi.* Washington, DC: U.S. Government Printing Office.

Mihesuah, Devon, ed. 2000. *Repatriation Reader: Who Owns American Indian Remains?* Lincoln: University of Nebraska Press.

Mitchell, Douglas R., and Judy L. Brunson-Hadley, eds. 2001. *Ancient Burial Practices in the American Southwest: Archaeology, Physical Anthropology, and Native American Perspectives.* Albuquerque: University of New Mexico Press.

Thomas, David Hurst. 2000. *Skull Wars: Kennewick Man, Archaeology, and the Battle for Native American Identity.* New York: Basic Books.

Lawrence Rosen

BURKE, EDMUND
1729–1797

Edmund Burke was an Irish Protestant author and member of the British House of Commons. Burke's legacy rests on his profundity as a political thinker, while his relevance to the social sciences lies in his antirevolutionary tract of 1790, *Reflections on the Revolution in France,* for which he is considered the founder of conservatism.

Born in Dublin to a Protestant father and Catholic mother, Burke was raised as an Anglican and received his education at a Quaker school and Trinity College. Rejecting a career in law, Burke wrote a treatise on aesthetics, *A Philosophical Enquiry into the Origin of Our Ideas of the Sublime and Beautiful* (1757), and edited the political review *Annual Register*. Burke's talents as an intellectual attracted the attention of a politically powerful patron, the marquis of Rockingham, for whom Burke worked as private secretary and to whom Burke owed his entry into Parliament.

As a member of Parliament from 1765 to 1794, Burke employed his oratorical skills and propensity to connect legislative policy to political philosophy in the interests of the Whig party. Foremost among his causes was the mitigation of harsh penal laws in Ireland. Although a steadfast member of the Anglican Church, Burke's experience in Ireland and his Catholic connections made him deplore the discrimination against Irish Catholics. Burke also urged reconciliation with American colonists, opposing the Stamp Act of 1765 as bad policy even as he defended the theoretical right of Parliament to tax. Throughout his career Burke condemned the East India Company's mismanagement, calling after 1782 for parliamentary control of that body and for the impeachment of Bengal's governor-general, Warren Hastings. In addition, Burke's position in the opposition led to repeated cries for "economical reform," or a diminution in the power of the Crown by limiting the number of government employees who sat in Parliament. Finally, Burke contributed to British constitutional theory in important ways: He defended the formation of political parties, defined as "bod[ies] of men united for promoting by their joint endeavours the national interest" (Ayling 1988, p. 48); and he insisted that in Parliament he represented the common good rather than simply the interests of his Bristol electors.

Burke's *Reflections on the Revolution in France* offered a conservative interpretation of Britain's Glorious Revolution in 1688 and a condemnation of France's revolution in 1789. For Burke, the Whig-led Glorious Revolution merely protected civil liberties and Protestantism by overthrowing the tyrannical and popish James II; it did not usher in an era of natural rights, democratic politics, and the separation of church and state. As such, 1688 constituted a restoration of British liberties under the protection of strong institutions, notably the Church of England and a constitution balanced between a hereditary monarchy and a governing class of landed aristocrats.

Burke excoriated the French Revolution for its radical destruction of the past. Considering society a complex historical development—"a partnership not only between those who are living, but between those who are dead, and those who are to be born" (Burke 1987, p. 85)—he rejected contemporary theories of the social contract. Convinced of the limitations of human reason, he mocked the revolutionaries' reconstruction of the polity on abstract philosophical principles as a chimerical "new conquering empire of light and reason." Viewing rights and liberties as historical patrimony (for example, English liberties founded in the Magna Carta), he recoiled at the notion of universal human rights enshrined in the French *Declaration of the Rights of Man and Citizen*. Reckoning "the restraints upon men" to be among their rights, Burke found such restraints in religion and the establishment of a state church that sanctified the social and political order. Unmoved by paeans to equality, he insisted that "the natural order of things" entitled men of ability and property to govern. In sum, Burke saw the French Revolution as a rejection of the handiwork of God as expressed in the slow development of institutions in history.

Standing at the threshold of a new age of democratic politics, Burke exclaimed: "I put my foot in the tracks of our forefathers, where I can neither wander nor stumble" (Burke 1889). Although such reverence for the past might justifiably merit Burke the title "founder of conservatism," several points are in order. First, *conservative* is not synonymous with reactionary; Burke was no arch-conservative enslaved by the status quo, as evidenced by his advocacy of issues ranging from Catholic relief to the abolition of the slave trade. His guiding principle was conservation and correction, by which he meant that reform was necessary to preserve institutions. Second, Burke's conservatism was British (or "Anglo-American"); in rejecting the French Revolution, he sought to conserve what he considered the liberal and modern order in eighteenth-century Britain. Subsequent thinkers have employed Burke's suspicion of reason; his respect for the past; his insistence on religion and property as the foundations of society; and his antipathy to democracy in order to defend absolute monarchy, a hereditary nobility, and religious discrimination—but their doing so only serves as a reminder of the differences between what and why Burke wrote and how he was read.

SEE ALSO *Aesthetics; American Revolution; Church and State; Conservatism; Democracy; Freedom; French Revolution; Liberty; Natural Rights; Parliament, United Kingdom; Political Theory; Revolution*

BIBLIOGRAPHY

Ayling, Stanley. 1988. *Edmund Burke: His Life and Opinions.* New York: St. Martin's.

Burke, Edmund. [1775] 1889. Speech on Conciliation with America. *The Works of the Right Honorable Edmund Burke,* 9th ed., 12 vols. Boston: Little, Brown.

Burke, Edmund. [1790] 1987. *Reflections on the Revolution in France,* ed. J. G. A. Pocock. Indianapolis, IN: Hackett Publishing.

O'Brien, Conor Cruise. 1992. *The Great Melody: A Thematic Biography and Commented Anthology of Edmund Burke.* Chicago: University of Chicago Press.

Anthony Crubaugh

BURR, AARON
1756–1836

Grandson of Jonathan Edwards and son of the second president of the College of New Jersey (Princeton), Aaron Burr seemingly showed great promise. He sided with the revolutionary cause and served with courage and skill in various campaigns. The real leadership skills he displayed, however, were overshadowed by George Washington's (and Alexander Hamilton's) distrust, which somehow Burr earned in his first contacts with Washington. After the American Revolution he began a career in law and quickly became immersed in politics. His political views, to the extent that they are known, tended toward radical republicanism. Burr was a vigorous opponent of slavery early in his career, and he supported expanding the rights of women. But his enlightened views were tarnished by his ambition and political opportunism. He was elected to the Senate in 1791, where he served one undistinguished term. He was included on the Republican ticket in 1800 in order to secure a victory in New York, where he had created an effective political machine. The outcome of the election plunged the nation into crisis because Burr received the same number of electoral votes as Jefferson.

Rather than step aside, as might have been expected from someone who was almost universally held to be the vice-presidential candidate, Burr forced the election into the House of Representatives. Jefferson was eventually victorious in the House, but by then his suspicions of Burr had hardened into hatred and for the next four years he simply ignored his vice president. Burr did preside with competence and fairness over the Senate, including the impeachment trial of Supreme Court Justice Samuel Chase.

Hamilton had thrown his political weight behind Jefferson in the struggle of 1800. Again in 1804 Hamilton worked actively to thwart Burr's campaign to become governor of New York. Burr had had enough. He and Hamilton met on the dueling field on July 11, 1804. Hamilton's death at Burr's hands was the death knell for Burr's conventional political career. He then embarked on the unconventional political career in the American Southwest that would see him charged with treason. The goals of Burr's extensive and well-documented efforts to put together a private military force remain unclear. Did he mean to dismember the Union? Or did he mean only to subvert Spain's empire? Were his goals in some way republican? Or would he have preferred to become the Napoléon of the Southwest? Would he have liberated slaves in the territories he conquered? Was he indifferent among these alternatives?

Significant doubts remain regarding the answers to all of these questions. Burr's own most unequivocal statement as to his intentions came late in his life when, after the Battle of San Jacinto paved the way for an independent Texas, he is said to have remarked, "I was only thirty years too soon. What was treason in me thirty years ago is patriotism today." Whatever the case, rumors of Burr's plans swept the country and, after a period of inaction, Jefferson pursued Burr ruthlessly. He had Burr captured and charged with the capital offense of treason. A spectacular and controversial trial followed. Chief Justice John Marshall strictly construed the constitutional provisions on treason. Only an "overt act" of "levying war" against the United States witnessed by two persons could amount to treason. The jury found that Burr's various plans and meetings fell short of this standard and rendered a verdict of not guilty. After the trial Burr left for Europe, where he spent four years and continued to seek support for his southern scheme.

The rest of Burr's life was sad and uneventful. Burr had admirers such as Andrew Jackson, and impressive figures such as Marshall and John Jay did not view Burr with the same hostility as did Jefferson and Hamilton. Yet it is hard not to conclude that Burr was an anomaly in his generation. When many Americans thought they were walking with history, Burr seemed strangely detached from the great republican experiment that was going on around him. This is perhaps one key reason why his life is full of extraordinary episodes but his lasting contributions are negligible.

SEE ALSO *American Revolution; Hamilton, Alexander; Jefferson, Thomas; Nationalism and Nationality; Nation-State; Republicanism*

BIBLIOGRAPHY

Freeman, Joanne. 2001. *Affairs of Honor: National Politics in the New Republic.* New Haven, CT: Yale University Press.

Lomask, Milton. 1979–1982. *Aaron Burr.* 2 vols. New York: Farrar, Straus and Giroux.

Melton, Buckner F., Jr. 2002. *Aaron Burr: Conspiracy to Treason.* New York: Wiley.

Rogow, Arnold. 1999. *A Fatal Friendship: Alexander Hamilton and Aaron Burr.* New York: Hill and Wang.

Peter McNamara

BUS BOYCOTT (1955, SOUTH AFRICA)

SEE *Apartheid; Townships.*

BUSH, GEORGE H. W.
1924–

When George Herbert Walker Bush became the forty-first president of the United States on January 20, 1989, he entered the Oval Office as one of the most experienced political figures to become president in modern times. He had just completed eight years as Ronald Reagan's vice president, and before that had served as U.S. ambassador to the United Nations and to China, had headed both the Central Intelligence Agency and the Republican National Committee, and had been a member of the U.S. House of Representatives from Texas. When he left the White House four years later, Bush's presidency seemed far more successful in terms of foreign policy than in economic policy.

Bush, born into one of the United States' most influential families, graduated Phi Beta Kappa from Yale University after flying fifty-eight missions as a naval aviator during World War II (1939–1945). After graduation Bush moved to Texas to enter the oil business and, eventually, Republican politics. He first ran for president as a Republican moderate in 1980 and became Ronald Reagan's running mate despite criticizing Reagan's fiscal policies as "voodoo economics." Despite Reagan's reliance

on Bush throughout the 1980s, the vice president became the 1988 G.O.P. nominee only after defeating several more conservative rivals. Bush then defeated Democrat Michael Dukakis of Massachusetts in a tough campaign waged over prison furloughs and flag burning and marked by Bush's vow: "Read my lips: no new taxes."

As president, Bush pursued a centrist course legislatively, winning support from Democratic majorities in Congress for social programs such as the Americans with Disabilities Act and the 1990 Clean Air Act. As the federal budget deficit expanded, Bush agreed in 1990 to tax increases that he previously had vowed to oppose.

Bush's four years as president were marked by many foreign policy challenges, most notably the collapse of communist governments across Eastern Europe and the dissolution of the Soviet Union itself. Bush's diplomatic negotiating secured reductions in superpower nuclear arsenals, a peaceful end to the cold war, the reunification of Germany, and the development of democratic nation-states in areas that had been under Soviet control for decades. Bush had less success in handling China, which brutally crushed prodemocracy demonstrators in Tiananmen Square in 1989, killing or injuring thousands. When Iraqi president Saddam Hussein invaded Kuwait in August 1990, the diplomatically oriented president built an international coalition that dislodged the dictator from Kuwait.

Bush's 89 percent approval rating after the first Gulf War in early 1991 deterred many prominent Democrats from running for president in 1992. The eventual Democratic nominee, Arkansas governor Bill Clinton, focused on public anxieties over the state of jobs under Bush. Ross Perot, an independent presidential candidate, also attacked Bush's economic policies, saying the president's policies would trigger "a giant sucking sound" as U.S. jobs moved to Mexico. Voters did focus on the economy, not on Bush's foreign policy performance. In addition, some Republicans were angered by what they viewed as Bush's broken promise on taxes. In the end, Clinton received 43 percent of the vote, Bush received 38 percent, and Perot received 19 percent.

SEE ALSO *Bush, George W.; Gorbachev, Mikhail; Gulf War of 1991; Hussein, Saddam*

BIBLIOGRAPHY

Bush, George H. W. 1999. *All The Best: My Life in Letters and Other Writings.* New York: Scribner.

Bush, George H. W., and Brent Scowcroft. 1998. *A World Transformed.* New York: Vintage.

Campbell, Colin, and Bert A. Rockman, eds. 1991. *The George W. Bush Presidency: First Appraisals.* Chatham, NJ: Chatham House.

Farnsworth, Stephen J., and S. Robert Lichter. 2006. *The Mediated Presidency: Television News and Presidential Governance.* Lanham, MD: Rowman and Littlefield.

Fitzwater, Marlin. 1995. *Call The Briefing!* New York: Times Books.

Greene, John Robert. 2000. *The Presidency of George Bush.* Lawrence: University Press of Kansas.

Pomper, Gerald M., ed. 1989. *The Election of 1988: Reports and Interpretations.* Chatham, NJ: Chatham House.

Pomper, Gerald M., ed. 1993. *The Election of 1992: Reports and Interpretations.* Chatham, NJ: Chatham House.

Woodward, Bob. 1999. *Shadow: Five Presidents and the Legacy of Watergate.* New York: Simon and Schuster.

Stephen J. Farnsworth

BUSH, GEORGE W.
1946–

George Walker Bush, the forty-third president of the United States, presided over the country during the September 11, 2001, terrorist attacks and led the nation in the resulting overthrow of the Taliban regime in Afghanistan and the invasion and occupation of Iraq.

The son of George H. W. Bush, the forty-first president of the United States, George W. was born in New Haven, Connecticut, in 1946 and grew up in Texas before attending the Philips Academy prep school in Andover, Massachusetts. In 1968 Bush earned a bachelor's degree from Yale University, his father's alma mater. After serving in the Texas Air National Guard, Bush received a Masters of Business Administration degree from Harvard Business School in 1975 and moved to Texas, where he was an executive in a series of oil-exploration ventures. He also ran unsuccessfully for the U.S. House of Representatives in 1978.

In 1989 Bush bought a stake in the Texas Rangers baseball team and became the managing general partner of the team. The public visibility of this position helped him secure the Republican nomination in the 1994 Texas race for governor. He subsequently defeated the incumbent Democrat, Ann Richards, in the general election.

After being reelected as governor in 1998 by a wide margin, Bush became the leading Republican contender for the U.S. presidency. Fighting off a strong primary challenge from Senator John McCain of Arizona, Bush won the GOP nomination. During the 2000 campaign against Bill Clinton's vice president, Al Gore, Bush carefully positioned himself as a "compassionate conservative," who supported education reform, tax cuts, and private accounts in Social Security.

On election night Gore won the popular vote, but it appeared that Bush had won the Electoral College and thus the presidency. However, Gore's aides discovered that Florida was essentially tied, and the vice president retracted the concession he had offered Bush. Gore's campaign quickly requested hand recounts in several counties and the election shifted into a legal battle. The Florida Supreme Court issued a decision allowing the results of such recounts to be incorporated into statewide vote totals, but the U.S. Supreme Court halted the recounts in a controversial 5 to 4 decision. With Bush still ahead in the official state count, the election was over. Bush and his father became the second father and son to both serve as president, following John Adams and John Quincy Adams.

Some observers expected Bush to govern as a centrist and seek bipartisan cooperation in response to the circumstances of his election. Instead, Bush, a self-proclaimed conservative, pushed ahead with his campaign plan for a sizeable tax cut, which was passed into law by June 2001 with significant Democratic support.

Then on September 11 of that year, members of the Al-Qaeda terrorist organization struck the United States, flying jetliners into the World Trade Center in New York and the Pentagon in Washington, D.C., and crashing a fourth jet in a field in Pennsylvania. More than three thousand Americans were killed. After this national trauma, the public united behind Bush, pushing his approval ratings to unprecedented levels. Within months, U.S. air strikes helped the Northern Alliance overthrow the Taliban regime in Afghanistan, which had provided safe haven to Al-Qaeda's leader Osama bin Laden and his followers. However, the United States failed to capture bin Laden.

In the fall of 2002 the Bush administration began to push for an invasion of Iraq, arguing that Iraq's leader Saddam Hussein was an evil dictator who posed a grave threat to the United States due to his possession of weapons of mass destruction and links to Al-Qaeda. Bush and British Prime Minister Tony Blair secured a United Nations Security Council resolution calling on Saddam to disarm and submit to weapons inspections. Yet Saddam continued to resist the inspections, and in response the United States and the United Kingdom called for military action against Iraq. Independent observers and many foreign countries questioned the Bush administration's claims about Saddam's possession of weapons of mass destruction and ties to Al-Qaeda. The United States and the United Kingdom failed to secure a second United Nations resolution approving military action against Iraq, but decided to invade without it, beginning the attack on March 20, 2003. Saddam's regime quickly fell with minimal casualties, and Saddam himself was captured on December 13.

The occupation of Iraq proved more difficult than anticipated. A governing regime was set up, and elections were held, but an insurgency composed of disaffected Iraqis and foreign jihadists became an increasingly deadly threat to coalition forces. By spring 2006, more than two thousand U.S. troops had died in Iraq, and a majority of Americans told pollsters that the war had been a mistake. In addition, convincing evidence that Saddam possessed weapons of mass destruction at the time of the invasion was never found, nor was hard evidence of operational links between Iraq and Al-Qaeda. Over time, Bush increasingly emphasized the cause of creating a democracy in Iraq, which had received relatively little attention before the war.

In the domestic arena, Bush passed several major initiatives after September 11, including the No Child Left Behind Act (which enacted a new accountability regime of school testing), a second tax cut, and a bill adding prescription-drug coverage to Medicare.

In 2004 he defeated his Democratic opponent, Senator John Kerry, in a reelection campaign that emphasized security concerns and such social issues as gay marriage. Bush won 51 percent of the vote and 286 electoral votes in the narrowest presidential reelection victory since Woodrow Wilson in 1916.

The first major initiative of Bush's second term was an effort to create private investment accounts in Social Security, but his proposal failed to gain significant momentum in Congress. By spring 2006 Bush's approval ratings had plunged to less than 40 percent; conservative discontent with his presidency had grown; and calls for U.S. withdrawal from Iraq had begun to mount. However, Al-Qaeda had not successfully attacked the United States again and economic growth remained relatively strong.

SEE ALSO *Al-Qaeda; bin Laden, Osama; Bush, George H. W.; Electoral College; Hussein, Saddam; Iraq-U.S. War; Republican Party; September 11, 2001; Taliban; United Nations*

BIBLIOGRAPHY

Boston Globe Web site. Campaign 2004: George W. Bush. http://www.boston.com/news/politics/president/bush/.

Washington Post Web site. 2004 election: George W. Bush. http://www.washingtonpost.com/wp-dyn/politics/elections/2004/georgewbush/.

Brendan Nyhan

BUSINESS

Business is a commercial activity engaged in as a means of livelihood or profit, or an entity that engages in such activities. The concept mainly applies to activities that are designed to supply commodities (goods and services). The term *business* pertains broadly to commercial, financial, and industrial activity. Business involves managing people to organize and maintain collective productivity toward accomplishing particular creative and productive goals, usually to generate revenue and profit. The etymology of the term refers to the state of being busy, in the context of the individual as well as the community or society. In other words, to be busy is to be doing a commercially viable and profitable activity.

Business is distinguished from households and government, the remaining economic actors in any economy. Households play a pivotal role as suppliers of resources and demanders of final products. Household consumption is the total expenditure by the household sector, which is financed by the sale of resources, mainly labor, in return for income. As society is deeply concerned, on normative grounds, with the equity of income distribution as well as with efficiency of production, the role of government is indispensable to a market economy. The market system generates a range of inefficiencies as a result of market failure (failure to produce goods and services efficiently, or failure to produce goods and services demanded), so ongoing regulatory and redistributive roles are defined for government in a market-driven economy.

PRIVATELY OWNED BUSINESS

The term *business* has at least three usages, depending on the scope of analysis: the aforementioned general usage; the singular usage to refer to a particular company or corporation; and the usage to refer to a particular market sector, such as *agricultural business* or *the business community*, that is, the aggregation of suppliers of goods and services. The singular business can be a legally recognized entity within a market-based society, wherein individuals are organized based on expertise and skills to bring about social and technological progress. In this case, the term *business* is associated with a corporation in which a number of shares are issued, and the firm is owned by shareholders who have limited liability. These corporations are legal entities. The businesses or corporations owned by the shareholders are treated by law as an artificial person.

The corporation becomes a legal entity through registration as a company and through compliance with company law. The owners of the company are issued shares in the company entitling them to any after-tax company profits in proportion to their share ownership. A major advantage of the corporation is that many individuals can pool their resources to generate the finances needed to initiate a business. An additional advantage is limited liability, meaning shareholders' liability for any losses is limited to the value of their shares. A final advantage of this form of organization is that the corporation has a life as a legal entity, separate and apart from those of the owners. The company continues to exist even if ownership changes hands, and it can be taxed and sued as if it were a person. A corporation's shareholders may not know anything about the actual production of the firm's product, whereas the managers of the firm may not be concerned about the current state of the share market.

With some exceptions, such as cooperatives, nonprofit organizations, and government institutions, in predominantly capitalist economies, privately owned businesses are formed to earn profit and grow the personal wealth of their owners. In other words, the owners and operators of a business have as one of their main objectives the receipt or generation of a financial return in exchange for their work, that is, the expenditure of time, energy, and money. Private business is the foundation of the market capitalist economies.

GOVERNMENT-OWNED BUSINESS

Private business is in contrast to government ownership of business enterprises. Since ancient times, governments have owned and conducted many businesses, such as water systems, sports, theaters, mining, and public baths. In the United States, government units own and manage the public school system, public highways and bridges, dams, land, power, and many other businesses. The importance of public utilities to the community has frequently led to municipal ownership of water, sewerage, electricity, power, gas, and transportation systems. In Europe, where public ownership is more extensive and of longer duration than in the United States, it may include railroads, telephone, radio and television, coal mining, other power resources, and banking. Since World War II, many nations in Europe and North America have practiced public ownership of business through public corporations such as Amtrak. Many developing countries also have large-scale public ownership, especially of vital industries and resources. The distinct characteristic of a government-owned business is that its goal is to serve the wider community by offering services as efficiently as possible, but at the same time as inexpensively as possible. In other words, a government-owned business has a mandate to maximize social welfare, not make a profit, which is the goal of a private business.

Frequently it is argued that government ownership is necessary when private businesses fail to work effectively and fairly. Private businesses may fail to safeguard private property and enforce contracts, or collude to avoid competition. Certain industries may be most efficiently organized as private monopolies, but the market may allow such industries to charge prices higher than are socially optimal. Private businesses may not find it profitable to produce public goods. Prices set solely by the market often

fail to reflect the costs or benefits imposed by externalities. Private businesses operating in markets can lead to an extremely unequal distribution of income. Finally, private business behavior does not guarantee full employment and price stability.

When private businesses yield socially undesirable results, governments may intervene to address these market failures. Government programs are designed to (1) promote full employment, price stability, balance of trade equilibrium, and sustainable economic growth in real gross domestic product (GDP); (2) promote competition; (3) regulate natural monopolies; (4) provide public goods and externalities; (5) discourage negative externalities and encourage positive externalities; (6) provide a more equitable distribution of income; and (7) protect private property and enforce contracts.

NONPROFITS

In contrast to a private business, a nonprofit business is a business that supports private or public interests for noncommercial purposes. Nonprofit organizations may be involved in numerous areas, most commonly relating to charities, education, religion, sports, arts, and music. Another class of business is the nongovernmental organization (NGO), an organization that is not directly part of the structure of any government. Many NGOs are also nonprofit organizations and may be funded by private donations, international organizations, or the government itself, or some combination of these. Some quasi-autonomous NGOs may even perform governmental functions. Many NGOs are key sources of information for governments on issues such as human rights abuses and environmental degradation.

COOPERATIVES

A cooperative is an autonomous association of people united voluntarily to meet their common economic, social, and cultural needs and aspirations through a jointly owned and democratically controlled enterprise. Cooperative members usually believe in the ethical values of honesty, openness, social responsibility, and caring for others. Cooperatives are often seen as an ideal organizational form for proponents of a number of sociopolitical philosophies. A cooperative comprises a legal entity owned and democratically controlled by its members. Under this structure, ownership and control are exercised by all members of the cooperative in the form of group property. All members of the cooperative have equal rights to participate in the decision-making process. The fundamental characteristic of a cooperative is that it is democratically administered. The decision-making process in cooperative firms is based on the democratic principle of one vote per person, rather than one vote per share. This is the standard the International Co-operative Alliance requires its members to embrace, and it is also the rule assumed in the theoretical literature.

In private business firms, management employs labor and has the ultimate decision-making power, whereas in cooperatives, labor employs management and ultimate decision-making power remains with the cooperative. In small cooperative firms the cooperative is able to carry out all managerial functions. However, as the size of the firm increases the complexity of organization also increases. Large cooperative firms need some delegation of authority; that is, the appointment of managers. Using their specialized skills, which are distinct from labor skills, managers assist in the formulation of decision-making by the collective; however, decision-making power still resides with the cooperative. Hence, managers are hired and dismissed by the cooperative. Whereas in private business firms managers are ultimately accountable to shareholders, in cooperatives managers are ultimately accountable to the collective.

The cooperative firm requires from its members loyalty, self-monitoring, solidarity, and commitment to the firm and to the ideas of cooperative management. As a result, cooperative firms do not need to dedicate so many resources to monitoring. Bowles and Gintis (1996, p. 320) and Doucouliagos (1995) argued that the proposition that cooperatives are inherently inefficient was not accurate. Participation in decision-making and productivity are positively related. Cooperatives can be as efficient as capitalist firms. Cooperatives do not suffer undue problems associated with investment, monitoring, and incentives, or face higher transaction costs, as assumed in the traditional literature. The dominance of capitalist firms in mature market economies and the relative scarcity of the cooperatives are independent of efficiency considerations. Institutional bias, credit rationing, path-dependent behavior, and the impact of the forces of conformity contribute to cooperative firms being outnumbered in mature market economies (Doucouliagos, 1995, pp. 1097–1098). In mature market economies the prevailing institutions, and not market oscillations, reinforce the duplication of capitalist firms. Therefore, cooperative firms must be considered an alternative to private property.

INTERNATIONAL BUSINESS

International business consists of business transactions (private and governmental) between parties from more than one country. (Daniels et al. 2004, p. 3). International business can differ from domestic business for a number of reasons, including the following: the countries involved may use different currencies, forcing at least one party to convert its currency into another; the legal systems of the countries may differ, forcing one or more parties to adjust their practices to comply with local laws; the cultures of the countries may differ, forcing each party to adjust its behavior to meet the expectations of the other; the availability of resources may differ among countries; and the way products are produced and the types of products produced may vary among countries.

The significance of business, and especially of international business, in the twenty-first century is largely determined by the following: globalization and economic integration; technological improvements in communications, information processing, and transportation; new organizational structures and restructuring processes adopted by companies in order to become more competitive and effective; the changing framework of international competition; and finally the deregulation of key sectors such as telecommunications, which led to the liberalization of capital flows among countries. The increase in international business was largely related to the sharp increase in investments and especially in foreign direct investments in the high-tech and telecommunication sectors in the advanced economies, and in the increase of mergers and acquisitions and cross-border transactions. In addition, developing and transition countries were increasingly liberalizing their economies, opening their borders, and abolishing barriers and obstacles in order to receive decisive foreign direct investment (FDI) flows. Increased FDI flow and international business is also supported by the abolition of monopolies, the elimination of tariffs and quotas, and by increased free-trade transactions as a complement to FDI flows (Bitzenis 2005, pp. 550–551).

E-BUSINESS

E-business (electronic business) is a term used when transactions for business purposes take place online on the World Wide Web. E-business, a name derived from such terms as *e-mail* and *e-commerce*, describes the conduct of business on the Internet, not only for buying and selling, but also for servicing customers and collaborating with business partners. In addition, companies are using the Web to buy inputs from other companies, to team up on sales promotions, and to initiate joint research. Companies are exploiting the cost saving, convenience, availability, and world-wide reach of the Internet to reach customers. Companies such as Amazon.com, originally only a bookseller, are diversifying into other areas and using the Internet profitably. The term *e-commerce* also describes business using the Internet, but *e-business* generally implies a presence on the Web. An e-business site may be extremely comprehensive and offer more than just products and services: some feature general search facilities or the ability to track shipments or have threaded discussions. IBM was among the first to use the term *e-business* when, in 1997, it initiated a campaign around the new term.

SEE ALSO *Capitalism; Consumer; Cooperatives; Corporations; Firm; Investment; Organizations; Profits; Venture Capital*

BIBLIOGRAPHY

Bitzenis, Aristidis P. 2005. Company Oriented Investment Interest and Cross-Border Transactions under Globalisation: Geographical Proximity Still Matters. *European Business Review* 17 (6): 547–565.

Bowles, Samuel, and Herbert Gintis. 1996. Efficient Redistribution: New Rules for Markets, States, and Communities. *Politics & Society* 24 (4): 307–342.

Daniels, John D., Lee H. Radebaugh, and Daniel P. Sullivan. 2004. *International Business: Environments and Operations.* 10th ed. Upper Saddle River, NJ: Prentice Hall.

Doucouliagos, Chris. 1995. Institutional Bias, Risk, and Workers' Risk Aversion. *Journal of Economic Issues* 29 (4): 1097–1118.

Aristidis Bitzenis
John Marangos

BUSINESS CYCLES, EMPIRICAL LITERATURE

Business cycle researchers study the temporary deviation of macroeconomic variables from their underlying trend. During the nineteenth century, theories explaining business cycles were typically driven by real factors (as opposed to monetary factors), invariably of agricultural origin. Of course, given the relative size and importance of the agricultural sector at that time, these theories had some degree of success. However, as agriculture began to decline in importance, macroeconomists searched for other driving forces for the business cycle. Friedrich August von Hayek (1899–1992) suggested monetary policy, while John Maynard Keynes (1883–1946) surmised that business cycles were driven by a force he called "animal spirits," with nontrivial roles for sticky prices and wages.

The 1970s saw the birth of the rational expectations approach to macroeconomics, coming mainly out of the new classical economics school of thought. In fact, the rational expectations revolution is often credited with returning real driving factors to the forefront of business cycle research. According to this school of thought, given that people are rational and can accurately forecast future events and the actions of policymakers, monetary and fiscal policies are likely to be ineffective in stimulating the economy (one could say that money is neutral in the former case of monetary policy, and that Ricardian equivalence holds in the latter case of fiscal policy). Additionally, in the absence of market frictions (all markets clear), an assumption held by new classical economists, sticky prices and wages are rendered nonfactors in causing macroeconomic variables to deviate from trend. Therefore, the following questions naturally arise. What are the sources of business cycle movement if people can correctly (or with a great degree of accuracy) anticipate the actions of policymakers? And given that the economy is perpetually self-adjusting so that all markets quickly return to equilibrium (no market friction), how do business cycles arise? That is, given the well-functioning macroeconomy proposed by the new classical school, what causes macrovariables to temporarily deviate from trend? The answer, according to new classical macroeconomists, is that observed cycles are driven by (unanticipated) shocks to real factors, specifically by supply-side factors that alter factor productivity and the capital-labor ratio. This led to the rebirth of *real business cycle* (RBC) theory with technology shock as its driving force, instead of agricultural factors as previously suggested.

In order to assess the applicability of the RBC theory, it should readily lend itself to empirical testing, as should any good economic theory. Economic theory, therefore, should be parsimonious while containing (enough) important features that, when estimated, the theory produces results that accord with the data, in some statistical sense. The RBC theory is no exception, and its success, hitherto, has been the ease with which it lends itself to estimation. To be clear, the purpose of RBC research, the narrow focus of this entry, is to investigate how much output variation or, more broadly, the degree to which cyclical fluctuations in key macroeconomic data over business cycle frequency, can be accounted for by technology shocks.

Calibration and regression methods are the commonly used techniques for empirically testing the RBC paradigm. Each technique, if properly applied, can be a useful tool in testing the merit of a particular model or in differentiating among various classes of models. Unfortunately, however, within the RBC framework, each tool can be subject to abuse by the researcher who wants to promote his or her own agenda at the expense of science. However, such blatant misuse of the empirical tools has been the exception rather than the rule, and the Cowles Commission (a research institute established in 1932 by businessman and economist Alfred Cowles, dedicated to linking economic theory to mathematics and statistics) should be proud to see both theory and estimation, of one form or another, appearing in more and more published articles. If only macroeconomists could agree on a particular theory or method!

BUSINESS CYCLE FACTS

There are four facts that any RBC model should be able to capture (see, for example, Hansen and Wright 1992, p. 3, Tables 1 and 2), namely:

1. Investment is three times as volatile as output.

2. Consumption (nondurable goods) is less volatile than output.

3. Labor input is nearly as volatile as output.

4. Labor and productivity are essentially uncorrelated.

Another auxiliary feature of business cycles is that most variation in output, at business cycle frequency, is due to labor input. In addition, macroeconomic data exhibit a high degree of persistence over the cycle. Researchers invariably interpret the former as implying that movements in capital are unimportant at business cycle frequency and can thus be ignored when modeling business cycle fluctuations, whereas the latter points to the use of driving forces in our model economy that display some degree of persistence. The persistence of the driving forces will find its way into the model data via what is commonly called the *transmission mechanism*. (See Cogley and Nason [1995] for reasons why having the persistence in the data solely due to the driving process is a weakness rather than strength of the model.)

CALIBRATION

Made popular by Finn Kydland and Edward Prescott (1982), *calibration* is defined as the estimation of some parameters of a model, under the assumption that the model is correct, as a middle step in the study of other parameters. Thomas Cooley (1997) describes it as a strategy for finding numerical values for the parameters of artificial economic worlds. Basically, the researcher chooses values for certain parameters (the parameters that he has no interest in making economic predictions) and has the model spit out values for those parameters, left free in the exercise, for which he wants the model to make predictions.

Prescott in his 2004 Nobel Prize lecture lays out what a sound calibrating exercise of an RBC model would entail and closes by stressing the need for scientific discipline during the process by the researcher (see also Cooley 1997). Such discipline can generally be thought of as choosing the relevant parameter values based on sound microeconomic evidence and choosing functional forms for technology and preferences that display properties characteristic of the economy of interest. For example, Prescott (1986) chose his utility function based on the observation that per capita leisure displays no observable trend over time, and he used a Cobb-Douglas production

function because of the constancy of capital share over the said period.

In an attempt to match the aforementioned business cycle facts, Prescott calibrates a baseline one-sector neoclassical growth model emphasizing technology shock as the main driving force behind cyclical fluctuations. He found that such a model was able to match not only the magnitude of output fluctuations but also the relative volatilities of both consumption and investment to output. The model failed, however, in its inability to match the facts pertaining to labor (facts three and four in the previous section). The ability of such a simple model, driven solely by technology shock, to match so many elements of the data is what led Kydland and Prescott (and others) in many of their papers, together and singly, to strongly advocate for technology shock and the RBC paradigm as being the impetus behind cyclical fluctuations in macroeconomic data.

An attractive feature of the calibration approach to estimation is its flexibility. A calibrated RBC model can be judged a success or failure depending on how many, and which, of the key business cycle facts it can capture. To be fair, one will scarcely find a model that is able to mimic *all* features of an economy—that is why it is a model. Therefore, economic researchers have to be prepared to judge a model as successful even though it fails on certain grounds—this is where calibration and calibrated RBC models fall short, since no goodness-of-fit statistic is provided with which to judge a model's success. However, this too is where calibration has been unfairly criticized, since any unmatched moment can be considered essential depending on the reader. That said, calibration can prove useful in pointing out dimensions along which existing models can be improved. For example, to improve upon the baseline RBC model, Gary Hansen and Randall Wright (1992) incorporated additional shocks, specifically to fiscal policy, and other features to technology and preferences (for example, accounting for household production) that mainly affected the moments of labor market while leaving the other (successful) elements of the model economy intact. These modifications resulted in modified RBC models that came closer to mimicking the actual U.S. economy. However, Hansen and Wright did not promote one particular modification over another; they left that up to the reader.

There are advantages and disadvantages of calibration over its econometric counterpart. Promoters of calibration usually point to the selection of parameters based on microeconomic evidence as an indication of the strength of the exercise. They claim that more information can be incorporated into the calibration exercise (compared to the econometric approach), which allows the calibrated model to be held to higher standards. The second issue, alluded to earlier, is the meaning of rejection or acceptance of a model based on statistics. A model that fits the data well along every dimension except one (unimportant) may be rejected based on some statistical test, or a model may fail to be rejected because the data is consistent with a wide range of possibilities (see Chari et al. 2005).

Those opposed to using calibration as an estimation device usually point to the extreme faith that one has to have in the model. Pure calibrators literally accept their model as truth. They also point to the fact that calibrated models are bad for forecasts (making predictions of the future), since they assume constancy of the selected parameters over time. Finally, calibration is only useful in times of structural stability, a point related to the lack of forecast ability.

REGRESSION METHODS

The most popular regression approach to the study of real business cycles and measures of technological innovation was developed by economist Robert Merton Solow (1956). The Solow approach measures inputs to capital and labor, and it labels as technology (more precisely, *total factor productivity*, or TFP) the difference between output and the measured inputs. In a more recent paper, Susanto Basu, John Fernald, and Miles Kimball (2004) modify the Solow approach by incorporating capital utilization and effort on the part of labor. They then measure technology shocks as the difference between output and measures of inputs, capital and labor, at both the extensive and intensive margins.

A more direct approach to the measure of technology shocks can be found in John Shea (1998). Shea uses estimates of research and development and patents to gauge technological changes over time.

More recently, macroeconomists have used the structural vector autoregressive (SVAR) approach to study the technology-driven RBC paradigm (see Gali 1999; Francis and Ramey 2005). Researchers using this method take key identifying assumptions from the theoretical model and impose them on the data. They then perturb the technology shocks identified this way and examine the responses of key macroeconomic variables to such perturbation. The responses are then compared to the business cycle facts in order to make a judgment about the plausibility of the RBC model in driving economic fluctuations.

Overall, the studies employing one or the other regression approach have not been good for the RBC model. These studies have failed to match the business cycle facts and have thus put into question the validity of the technology-driven RBC paradigm.

CONCLUSION

Other empirical RBC studies have brought to life the study of business cycles. The debates have centered on two important themes: (1) finding the correct empirical approach to use when studying this phenomenon; and (2) coming up with an answer to the question of what happens after a technology shock. As of 2006, there was no resolution for either of these problems, leaving room for clever young macroeconomists to shed new light and ideas on a long-standing subject at the heart of the work of many policymakers and academics.

SEE ALSO *Business Cycles, Political; Business Cycles, Real; Business Cycles, Theories; Economic Crises; Financial Instability Hypothesis; Long Waves; Mitchell, Wesley Clair*

BIBLIOGRAPHY

Basu, Susanto, John Fernald, and Miles Kimball. 2004. Are Technology Improvements Contractionary? NBER Working Paper No. 10592. Cambridge, MA: National Bureau of Economic Research.

Chari, V. V., Patrick J. Kehoe, and Ellen R. McGrattan. 2005. A Critique of Structural VARs Using Real Business Cycle Theory. Working Paper 631. Minneapolis, MN: Federal Reserve Bank of Minneapolis.

Cogley, Timothy, and James M. Nason. 1995. Output Dynamics in Real-Business-Cycle Models. *American Economic Review* 85: 492–511.

Cooley, Thomas F. 1997. Calibrated Models. *Oxford Review of Economic Policy* 13 (3): 55–69.

Francis, Neville, and Valerie A. Ramey. 2005. Is the Technology-Driven Real Business Cycle Hypothesis Dead? Shocks and Aggregate Fluctuations Revisited. *Journal of Monetary Economics* 52 (8): 1379–1399.

Galí, Jordi. 1999. Technology, Employment, and the Business Cycle: Do Technology Shocks Explain Aggregate Fluctuations. *American Economic Review* 89: 249–271.

Hansen, Gary, and Randall Wright. 1992. The Labor Market in Real Business Cycle Theory. *Federal Reserve Bank of Minneapolis Quarterly Review* 16 (2): 1–12.

Kydland, Finn, and Edward Prescott. 1982. Time to Build and Aggregate Fluctuations. *Econometrica* 50: 1345–1370.

Prescott, Edward. 1986. Theory Ahead of Business-Cycle Measurement. *Federal Reserve Bank of Minneapolis Quarterly Review* 10 (4): 9–22.

Prescott, Edward. 2004. Nobel Prize Lecture: The Transformation of Macroeconomic Policy and Research. *Journal of Political Economy* 114 (2): 203–235.

Shea, John. 1999. What Do Technology Shocks Do? In *NBER Macroeconomics Annual 1998*, eds. Ben S. Bernanke and Julio J. Rotemberg, 275–310. Cambridge, MA: MIT Press.

Solow, Robert. 1956. A Contribution to the Theory of Economic Growth. *Quarterly Journal of Economics* 70: 65–94.

Neville Francis

BUSINESS CYCLES, POLITICAL

Understanding why the economy contracts and expands at regular intervals, commonly called a business cycle, has puzzled economists for centuries. One explanation, dubbed the political business cycle theory, posits that the economy shifts or cycles during presidential election years, or when power is transferred from president to president. Partisan varieties of political business cycle theories associate the political business cycle with the president's political party. The opportunistic approach argues that the desire to be reelected drives the cycle without reference to political party affiliation.

POLITICAL BUSINESS CYCLE THEORIES

Michal Kalecki in *Political Quarterly* (1943) pioneered the idea that governments stimulate the economy prior to elections to garner constituency support and capitalists reverse the stimulus after elections. Kalecki hypothesized that capitalists were opposed to interventionist government spending to create full employment. Capitalists would therefore exploit their influence on politicians after elections creating a political business cycle. His idea was extended decades later by William Nordhaus in the *Review of Economic Studies* (1975). Nordhaus posited that as an election approaches, incumbents reduce unemployment by exploiting the short-run tradeoff between inflation and unemployment described by a Phillips curve. Once elected, the party in power follows a policy of austerity to reduce the inflation that was created earlier by the expansionary policy. The early "opportunistic" models predicted that output growth increases in the year-and-a-half before each election as incumbents stimulate economic growth to improve their chance of reelection. However, if the public is rational then it would be impossible for incumbents to systematically fool the public, and so more advanced models were developed.

In the second wave of these models Ken Rogoff and Anne Sibert, in the *Review of Economic Studies* (1988), demonstrated that opportunistic cycles can occur when voters are assumed to be rational, as long as individual leaders had private information about their competence; that is, the ability to provide government services at a low cost.

The second class of political business cycle models (termed partisan models) requires differences in policy objectives of political parties to be the impulse for the cycle. Left-wing governments stimulate the economy once elected whereas right-wing governments contract the economy due to ideological differences concerning aversion to higher inflation versus higher unemployment. In the most widely accepted specification adopted by Alberto Alesina in the *Quarterly Journal of Economics* (1987), only the unanticipated effects of monetary policy differences between the two parties can be a cause of the political business cycle.

These two approaches to understanding political business cycles generate the following important predictions. First, the partisan model predicts that left-wing governments expand while right-wing governments contract early to midway through their terms. Second, according to the opportunistic model, presidents whose parties subsequently hold on to the presidency at the following election (either by reelection or another member of their party winning) will have expanding economies as the election approaches.

EVIDENCE ON POLITICAL BUSINESS CYCLES

Since World War II the real U.S. economy has grown more rapidly after every Democratic president has begun his term and has grown more slowly after every Republican president has begun his term, providing support for the partisan approach. There is less consistent empirical support for the opportunistic approach to the political business cycle.

Although establishing the empirical regularities of output is an important first step for establishing the existence of a political business cycle, the transmission mechanism through prices is less evident in the data. Inflation should be higher under Democratic administrations than under Republican administrations. For the United States, there is little evidence to support this conclusion. As Allan Drazen noted in *Political Economy in Macroeconomics* (2000), "Democratic administrations have lower average inflation than Republican administrations in the first half of their terms, exactly opposite what the rational partisan theory of inflation surprises predicts" (p. 262).

An alternative theory of the political business cycle, termed the real political business cycle, is found in the *Journal of Public Economics*, in a 2003 article by S. Brock Blomberg and Gregory Hess. Rather than explain the political business cycle as the natural consequence of shifts in regime between two parties who have different tastes for inflation, Blomberg and Hess model the political business cycle as a dynamic process that responds to both partisan and individual leader characteristics in the size and scope of the government. While the parties themselves differ on the size of government, individual leaders also differ in their abilities to deliver on their promises at the lowest cost. Methodologically, their article blends a partisan and opportunistic explanation for the political business cycle with fiscal policy being the impulse for the cycle.

There appears to be stronger empirical support for the transmission mechanism in the real political business cycle. Both tax revenue and spending reveal a strong partisan influence: there is a sharp increase in spending and taxes for Democrats in the second or third years of the election term, with a symmetric decrease in spending and taxes by Republicans. These fiscal changes coincide with the business cycle movements consistent with a real political business cycle. Still, given the mixed evidence supporting certain aspects of real business cycle models, future research is necessary to explain these same aspects in the real political business cycle.

SEE ALSO *Business Cycles, Empirical Literature; Business Cycles, Real; Business Cycles, Theories; Economic Crises*

BIBLIOGRAPHY

Alesina, Alberto. 1987. Macroeconomic Policy in a Two-Party System. *Quarterly Journal of Economics* (August): 651–677.

Blomberg, S. Brock, and Gregory Hess. 2003. Is the Political Business Cycle for Real? *Journal of Public Economics* (July): 1091–1121.

Drazen, Allan. 2000. *Political Economy in Macroeconomics.* Princeton, NJ: Princeton University Press.

Kalecki, Michal. 1943. Political Aspects of Full Employment. *Political Quarterly* XIV (October): 322–331.

Nordhaus, William. 1975. The Political Business Cycle. *Review of Economic Studies* 42: 169–190.

Rogoff, Kenneth, and Anne Sibert, 1988. Elections and Macroeconomic Policy Cycles. *Review of Economic Studies* (January): 1–16.

S. Brock Blomberg

BUSINESS CYCLES, REAL

It is accepted knowledge in empirical macroeconomics that aggregate data are typically characterized by trend and cyclical components. A natural by-product of this is a dichotomy of (empirical) macroeconomics into those who concentrate on growth and those whose main concern is with the cyclical aspects of the data. Although this entry focuses exclusively on the cyclical side of the dichotomy, the business cycle and growth processes are not mutually exclusive features of macroeconomics. That is, one cannot draw any meaningful conclusion about one feature of the data without a comprehensive understanding of the other. It is invariably the case that empirical results hinge on the methodology used to isolate the trend and cyclical components of the data.

What drives business cycles is an important issue for economists and policymakers alike. In his 1994 article

"Shocks," John Cochrane reiterated R. E. Lucas's 1977 assertion that "business cycles are all alike" (p. 296) in that each cycle exhibits co-movements among macroeconomic variables that are so remarkably similar that the cycles are more likely to be driven by a common force and less so by a composite of several shocks. To that end macroeconomic theories have been written suggesting one shock or another that could possibly explain this cyclical phenomenon.

With abundant research devoted to real business cycles (RBC), the search for that one driving force is still ongoing, and from the early-twenty-first-century state of the literature little progress has been made. (Even though the literature does not seem to be converging on one particular shock the search process has resulted in the development of solution techniques that have contributed greatly to macroeconomics and other related literature. For example, researchers have witnessed the birth of dynamic general equilibrium models and the use of dynamic programming to solve such models.) The literature has presented a gamut of candidate shocks responsible for business cycle movements; shocks to individual preferences and tastes (fads), oil price shocks (e.g., OPEC crises in the 1970s and the Gulf War in 1990), monetary policy shocks, government spending and tax shocks, and technology shocks (shocks that shift the production possibility frontier of a nation). All these shocks, with the exception of technology shocks, have been discredited on grounds of either failing to qualitatively match actual business cycle movements or failing to explain a sizeable portion of the forecast error variance in output. That is, they fail to match the data on quantitative grounds. However, since 1999, empirical studies have begun to question the role of technology shocks in the real business cycle. A host of studies finds results that contradict the technology-driven real business cycle hypothesis. However, Finn Kydland and Edward Prescott received the Nobel Prize in economics in 2004 "for their contribution to dynamic macroeconomics: the time consistency of economic policy and the driving forces to business cycles." It is obvious, therefore, that there is indeed some benefit to real business cycle research.

The remainder of this entry provides a brief history of business cycle research and the transition of the literature over the years. This account of the history and transition of the literature to the present will be deliberately brief and could be considered an injustice without any objections from the author of this entry. However, this allows the entry to devote more time to the recent developments in real business cycle research. In the end this entry provides suggestions as to where real business cycle theory should be heading.

A BRIEF HISTORY

Business cycle research examines the periodic upswings and downswings in macroeconomic activity that is a feature of industrialized nations. The notion that business cycles are driven by real factors—termed the real business cycle hypothesis—has itself experienced periods of high and low activity over the years. Prior to the Great Depression real theories was the cornerstone of macroeconomics. The onset of the Great Depression then turned the tide in favor of monetary theory. In fact, monetary policy, more accurately monetary policy errors, was believed to be the impetus behind the devastation of the 1930s and it was widely believed at the time that corrective monetary policy and/or more active fiscal policy were the most likely candidates to turn around the economy.

Since the late twentieth century, real shocks have been the focus of macroeconomists and since the 1970s and early 1980s real business cycle research can be characterized as a period in which candidate shocks began to be eliminated for one reason or another. For example, shocks to government policy fail to deliver the requisite co-movements among macro variables by predicting a fall in household consumption in time of economic expansion. Changes in capital and labor income taxes occur too infrequently to make them serious candidates for business cycle fluctuations. Oil price shocks, even with volatile energy prices are too small a fraction of value added in production to have any sizeable effect. Monetary policy shocks, even with the addition of some type of economic friction, have small effects. However, research conducted in the 2000s has shown that monetary policy used in tandem with technology shocks can produce responses very similar to those observed in the post–World War II U.S. economy.

Technology shock has been the only survivor of this elimination process and thus the literature has accepted it as the main driving force of business cycles. The argument is that when there is a positive technology shock, peoples' marginal productivity increases, causing real wages to rise; workers will work more hours and output subsequently rises. The opposite holds when the technology shock is negative. This is a pattern economists have observed for industrialized economies since the beginning of the nineteenth century.

Kydland and Prescott (1982) have convincingly argued that a dynamic stochastic general equilibrium model driven by technology shocks can mimic the main statistical features of U.S. macroeconomic time series when calibrated using means and variances of macroeconomic data (using reasonable parameter values to fit the real world) from the U.S. economy. An oft-quoted statement used in support of technology shocks attributed to Prescott (1986) can be found on page 7 of Rebelo (2005), asserting that such shocks "account for more that half the fluctuations in the postwar period with a best point estimate near 75%." This conclusion has received its fair share of criticisms but somehow the technology-driven paradigm has addressed any serious criticism hitherto levied against it: the theory survived by adding new features such as labor hoarding, indivisible labor, or capital utilization, which make technology shocks less volatile (thus reducing the probability of technological regress) and enable the theory to better match microeconomic measures of labor supply elasticities.

However, since 1999 a new wave of attacks on the real business cycle hypothesis appears to have delivered the biggest blow yet. These recent studies have found that positive technology shocks, identified using an econometric technique known as structural vector autoregressions, are contractionary on the part of labor input, contrary to business cycle experiences. Contemporary research conducted by Neville Francis and Valerie A. Ramey (2005a) has concluded that the technology-driven real business cycle hypothesis appears dead. The reaction to such a bold statement has been swift and numerous, giving the literature new life. Real business cycle research has reemerged to the forefront of macroeconomics since the mid-1990s.

CONTEMPORARY DEVELOPMENTS

In 1999 Jordi Galí published an article in the *American Economic Review* that empirically challenged the notion that all factors of production should respond positively to positive technological innovations. Using the econometric technique, structural vector autoregression, Galí identified as technology that shock which has positive effects on labor productivity in the long run. Such identifying assumption is a feature of most RBC models. Using this technique to identify technology shock leads to a fall in per capita hours and not a rise as predicted by the standard RBC theory and as evidenced from actual business cycles experiences. Therefore, the empirical prediction for the role of technology shocks in driving business cycles contradicts the underlying theory. In this regard the literature seems to have undergone a paradigm shift and the search for a new theory of business cycle, which matches with the empirics, should be under way.

However, proponents of the technology-driven RBC paradigm have not taken this blow lightly and have tried to save one of the hitherto cornerstones of macroeconomics. Their criticisms of Galí's approach are twofold. First, they state that the manner in which the trend in hours per capita is removed is erroneous. In fact they assume that per capita hours being a bounded series should not be treated as having a long run trend and thus no attempt of removing any such trend should be made. If one agrees with this suggestion one will recover, using said structural vector autoregressions, the result from standard theory that all factor inputs rise after a technological innovation—here is an example of where the method used to remove trend has implication for the cyclical results as stressed in the opening of this entry. The second point they make is that the tool used in the empirical search, structural vector autoregression, is inappropriate and introduces bias into the results.

In their work in 2004 and 2005, Francis and Ramey address the "trend versus no trend" issue in per capita hours for the United States, both for the post–World War II era and the late twentieth century. They suggest that in order to align the theory to the data there are certain demographic features of the data that are absent from the theory, for example, trends in schooling, aging of the population, and the composition of workers into private and public enterprises. Since the real business cycle theory does not address these issues and they factor so prominently in the data, one might consider removing them from the data. Their removal will make the theory and empirics more compatible. The prediction of labor hours after this exercise is not beneficial to supporters of the technology-driven real business cycle hypothesis as per capita hours again respond negatively to a positive technological innovation.

FUTURE DIRECTION

The search for the driving force of business cycles is ongoing. While researchers have been unsuccessful in finding the candidate shock responsible for this phenomenon they have made some strides in macroeconomics along the way. In particular, research efforts have developed tools like dynamic programming that should figure prominently in economics for some time to come. They have also gone beyond static models and have begun to write models in more dynamic settings. Certainly, this is a practice that is good for the profession, though some researchers have taken it to the extreme by being so mathematical in their approach they have neglected the economics.

The driving force(s) of business cycles is an interesting concept and it will definitely continue. Some have suggested that researchers should first refine the existing model to account for the demographics that are absent from the theory. They maintain that it should not be too much of a stretch to incorporate schooling, aging, and employment composition in the commonly used models of the early twenty-first century. Finally, there are perhaps other shocks out there that have not yet been eliminated. For example, in 1997 Jeremy Greenwood, Zvi Hercowitz, and Per Krusell suggested technology shocks that work through investment goods; however, as of 2006 no consensus has been reached on the plausibility of these types of shocks.

SEE ALSO *Business Cycles, Empirical Literature; Business Cycles, Political; Policy, Monetary*

BIBLIOGRAPHY

Barro, R. J., and R. G. King. 1984. Time-Separable Preferences and Intertemporal Substitution Models of Business Cycles. *Quarterly Journal of Economics* 99: 817–839.

Chriastiano, L., and M. Eichenbaum. 1992. Liquidity Effects and the Monetary Transmission Mechanism. *American Economic Review* 82: 346–353.

Cooley, T., and G. Hansen. 1989. The Inflation Tax in a Real Business Cycle Model. *American Economic Review* 79: 733–748.

Cochrane, John. 1994. Shocks. *Carnegie-Rochester Conference Series on Public Policy* 41: 295–364.

Francis, Neville, and Valerie A. Ramey. 2004. The Source of Historical Economic Fluctuations: An Analysis using Long-Run Restrictions. NBER working paper 10631.

Francis, Neville, and Valerie A. Ramey. 2005a. Is the Technology-Driven Real Business Cycle Hypothesis Dead? Shocks and Aggregate Fluctuations Revisited. *Journal of Monetary Economics* 52 (8): 1379–1399.

Francis, Neville, and Valerie A. Ramey. 2005b. Measures of Hours Per Capita and Their Implications for the Technology-Hours Debate. NBER working paper 11694.

Galí, Jordi. 1999. Technology, Employment, and the Business Cycle: Do Technology Shocks Explain Aggregate Fluctuations. *American Economic Review* 89: 249–271.

Galí, Jordi, J. David Lopez-Salido, and Javier Valles. 2003. Technology Shock and Monetary Policy: Assessing the Fed's Performance. *Journal of Monetary Policy* 50 (4): 723–743.

Greenwood, Jeremy, Zvi Hercowitz, and Per Krusell. 1997. Long-Run Implications of Investment-Specific Technological Change. *American Economic Review* 87 (3) (June): 342–362.

Kydland, F., and E. Prescott. 1982. Time to Build and Aggregate Fluctuations. *Econometrica* 50: 1345–1370.

Lucas, R. E., Jr. 1977. Understanding Business Cycles. In *Stabilization of the Domestic and International Economy*. Vol. 5 of *Carnegie-Rochester Conference Series on Public Policy*, ed. K. Brunner and A. H. Meltzer. Amsterdam: North Holland Company.

Prescott, Edward. 1986. Theory Ahead of Business-Cycle Measurement. *Federal Reserve Bank of Minneapolis Quarterly Review* 10: 9–22.

Rebelo, Sergio. 2005. Real Business Cycle Models: Past, Present and Future. NBER Working Paper 11401.

Neville Francis

BUSINESS CYCLES, THEORIES

Economic crises of various kinds (financial and commercial failures, crop failures or overabundance, etc.) have afflicted agricultural and industrial societies for centuries. Toward the mid-nineteenth century, however, it was becoming apparent that crises linked to industrial production were recurring with some regularity, with common features, and with approximate periodicity. While previous debates on such crises focused on the partiality or generality of "gluts," the emphasis slowly started shifting from the explanation of individual crises (whose cause could be attributed to one or another historical accident) to the determinants of the general pattern. The theory (or theories) of crises gradually gave place to theories of the *recurrence* of crises, and eventually to theories of cycles.

The first stages in the transition were the recognition that crises tended to come in "waves" (Tooke 1823, vol. 1, p. 6), mainly described in terms of prices rising and abruptly falling instead of gently gravitating toward their natural level. The distinction of a number of phases regularly succeeding each other followed: Lord Overstone (1837) and S. Mountiford Longfield (1840), for instance, listed ten, but quickly the list boiled down to three to five. Then, estimates of the average period were formulated. An anonymous American reported in 1829 that "an opinion is entertained by many" that the average period of these "fluctuations" that "do take place, and … always will take place in countries, where paper money has been extensively introduced" is about fourteen years (pp. 303–304). In 1833 John Wade estimated it at about seven years, while a few decades later most writers agreed on a period of about seven to eleven years (see Jevons [1878] 1884, pp. 222–224; Miller 1927, pp. 192–193). The seminal intuition that the explanation of the whole sequence requires phases to be linked to each other seems to be due to Clément Juglar (1862). This now paved the way for theorists to look for a cause, set of causes, or at least some premises common to all crises.

During the latter part of the nineteenth century, however, the emphasis remained on crises. Whether conceived as anomalies and interruptions in the normally smooth working of the system, or as the result of intrinsic malfunctioning of industrial economies, crises—with the havoc they brought—remained the focus of theorists' and practical people's concerns. This is reflected in the asymmetry of the explanations, often focusing on the interruption of the phase of advance, in the asymmetry of the division in phases, and in the asymmetry of the cycle itself, as almost all authors stressed the abrupt and destructive character of the crisis as opposed to the gentleness of the recovery. This is also witnessed by the terminology of the time; in most languages, the subject was named "theory of crises."

In truth, the terminology (especially in German, Italian, and French) was slow to adapt to the theoretical change that rapidly intervened at the turn of the century and was completed in the interwar years. In the hands of authors such as Mikhail Tugan-Baranovsky (1865–1919), Dennis Holme Robertson (1890–1963), Arthur Spiethoff

(1873–1957), Albert Aftalion (1874–1956), and others, the explanation of the sequence of events became more and more detailed; the other phases were described not only as a launching pad for, or consequences of, crises, but as phenomena of interest on their own ground; and the focus gradually shifted from the crisis to the overall movement. Crises at first became the name of the upper turning point (Lescure [1907], quickly followed by Aftalion [1913] and Mitchell [1913]), and eventually disappeared altogether. Finally, in the hands of the "econometricians" who formulated the first mathematical theories of the cycle in the early 1930s, the cycle became symmetrical, with an even number of phases, all of which were equally important in the overall sine-curve representation of the cycle. Gradual and smooth transitions from one phase to the next substituted for the violence and suddenness of the crises. The prevalent metaphor also changed: while in the prewar literature crises were frequently depicted as a disease of the system (the normal, healthy state of which corresponded to the prosperous phase), the analogy introduced by mathematical economists was that of the pendulum (or rocking horse).

The cycle was thus becoming a new phenomenon: no longer a sequence of crises, but an entity of its own. It became identified by related fluctuations (not necessarily synchronous nor simultaneous, lags were actually called to play a relevant role) in a number of variables, among which prices gradually lost importance (only to regain the center of the stage with the real and equilibrium business cycles theories). Accordingly, the cycle deserved a proper name of its own: the term *cycle* evokes the returning of the system to a same round of states. The attribute "business" seems to be due to Wesley Clair Mitchell (1874–1948), and reflects his institutionalist creed that the cycle is a phenomenon rooted in the nature of capitalist economies and his emphasis on processes rather than equilibrium. The expression was first used in a number of articles that appeared between 1909 and 1913 and was quickly established in the American literature after the publication of Mitchell's *Business Cycles* (1913). The expression *trade cycle* was already in use in 1879 (Arthur Ellis); it appeared in an article title in 1902 (George Charles Selden), but became established in British usage after the publication of Frederick Lavington's book with the same title in 1922. The term takes up the emphasis on "commercial crises," widely spread in Britain, Germany (*Handelskrisen*) and France (*crises commerciales*).

CYCLES AND EQUILIBRIUM

Almost anyone who counted anything in economics in the first three decades of the twentieth century contributed to the debate on the causes of the business cycle. Not surprisingly, there are as many theories as there are economists, each emphasizing different mechanisms capable of explaining how the system could go out of gear. New doctrines were formulated, but some of those propounded in the nineteenth century were further elaborated. Among these doctrines are to be cited those relying on the mechanisms of credit and banking, which often blamed overspeculation, and especially the tradition focusing on the lack of demand with respect to supply, whether in the form of underconsumption or of overproduction. The denomination of these and other causes, with its stress on excesses or shortages, reveals the general attitude of arguing in terms of a comparison to some norm, not always explicitly identified but providing nonetheless a reference point.

Other authors focused on the development of vertical or horizontal imbalances, overinvestment, overindebtedness, or psychological mechanisms. The result is a plethora of causal explanations of variegated (and sometimes irreconcilable) character giving rise to currents of thought based on different views as to the working of the economic system, in particular between those who blamed the supply side of the economy and those who lamented the lack of sufficient demand. (For a still-classical classification of theories based on the alleged causes of cycles see Gottfried Haberler [1937], who also attempted to synthesize what is good in these explanations.)

Parallel to the proliferation of cycle theories and models, the interwar years were also marked by reflections on the ultimate nature of crises and cycles and the possibility of theorizing the phenomenon. The divide between two mutually exclusive groups became apparent. On one side, the "orthodox" approach conceived of equilibrium as a state toward which the system ultimately tends. In this view, fluctuations can only be explained as the result of some external force temporarily maintaining the system in disequilibrium. Accordingly, the system's rhythmic movement results from the variable's tendency to return toward its "natural" state (or to move toward a new position, to become the "natural" one), perhaps with some kind of impediment (such as Aftalion's construction lag) in response to an exogenous disturbance to equilibrium. The latter is the cause of the crisis, while the system's structure determines the mode in which movement takes place. The "heretics," on the contrary, believed that the economic system does not have an intrinsic tendency to move toward a position of rest (or a path of balanced growth), but tends instead to further depart from it. In this view, movement is the "natural" state of the system, and the problem is that of explaining how movement is constrained and why the system does not explode or collapse. The cycle results from endogenous forces, although exogenous events can be called to explain the specificity of individual cycles.

The "heretics" themselves (the terminology is due to John Maynard Keynes [1883–1946], who in 1934 claimed to be one of the dissidents) were keen to stress that the "orthodox" assumed cycles and crises away from their premises, and some clearly pointed out that this exclusion regarded the relationship of cycles and equilibrium (e.g., Keynes 1934; Löwe 1987; Bouniatian 1922). Two aspects were involved. One concerned the possible divergence between the individuals' optimizing behavior and the system's capacity of reproducing its own state. While most orthodox economists argued that the individuals' maximization of utility or profit brings an overall satisfactory state of affairs by clearing all markets, a number of heretics argued that this is not necessarily so, and found in this divergence one of the possibility of crises.

The second aspect concerns the stability of equilibrium. The most explicit discussion is due to Adolf Löwe (1893–1995; name changed to Adolph Lowe), who argued that a theory of the cycle is impossible within the premises of equilibrium economics because "the structure of a *process* which is always in equilibrium over time cannot undergo any change by definition" ([1926] 1997, p. 269); Löwe concluded that the presupposition of the stability of equilibrium should be rejected (see also Kuznets 1930). Friedrich Hayek (1899–1992) agreed that the logic of equilibrium theories (he referred to the general equilibrium theory as developed in Lausanne; the argument, however, applies in a wider sense) requires that the disturbances of equilibrium must come from outside. However, he disputed Löwe's conclusion by arguing that the proper procedure is to examine how a suitable disturbance of equilibrium—in particular an expansionary banking policy—gives rise, by the operation of the fundamental forces tending to bring the system back to equilibrium, to permanent oscillations (Hayek [1929] 1933, pp. 42–43). Roy Harrod (1900–1978) dispensed with Hayek's concern with the departure from equilibrium and, as Löwe, focused on the possibility and the persistence of disequilibrium. Harrod's "instability principle," that is, a destabilizing factor introduced at the outset, is a premise to the "very kind of explanation" required for a "rational account of the trade cycle" (Harrod 2003, p. 304; 1934, pt. 3).

The stability issue, in relation to the necessity of relying on exogenous factors, was also one of the main methodological issues among macrodynamic mathematical theorists, whose contribution was also notable for the introduction of modeling in terms of functional equations, linked to a definition of dynamics as the description of "how a situation grows out of the foregoing" (Frisch 1933, 1936). Michal Kalecki's (1899–1970) mathematical model producing constant-amplitude fluctuations (1935) is perhaps the best-known case: it was criticized as being structurally unstable and dependent upon a special configuration of parameters (Frisch and Holme 1935). Ragnar Frisch (1895–1973), who had originally postulated that one should distinguish the impulse from the propagation problems (1933), suggested instead that Kalecki's interesting model should be damped but kept alive by exogenous shocks. Kalecki struggled all his life with this problem, but failed to solve it to his own satisfaction. Nicholas Kaldor (1908–1986) criticized one of Kalecki's attempts by arguing, similarly to Harrod, that equilibrium must be unstable if the system is to generate endogenous fluctuations (1940).

Richard M. Goodwin (1913–1996) showed that the problem of the persistency of fluctuations, to which Frisch's proposal was a solution, is rooted in the assumption of linear relationships and incapable of giving rise to fully endogenous sustained cycles (1951). If this assumption is relaxed, it is possible to deal at once with cycles and growth (an issue dear to a number of interwar economists, particularly Robertson [1915, 1926] and Joseph Alois Schumpeter [1883–1950, from 1910]). In addition, persistent cycles consist in oscillations (or chaotic movement) around an unstable stationary state—precisely the point advocated, in more generic and intuitive terms, by the "heretics"—kept within bounds by endogenous or semi-exogenous constraints, such as population or resources.

Equilibrium and real business cycle theories took a different route, reviving the "orthodox" approach by taking up two different threads: Hayek's (Lucas [1977]; who, however, eventually admitted [1994] he had misread Hayek) and the impulse approach (more Slutsky's [1937] than Frisch's; see Lines [1990]). The cycle is viewed as the result of the economic agent's rational reaction to signals, transmitted via the price system (in conditions of imperfect information, in the monetary business cycle theory) triggered by exogenous impulses coming either from the monetary system or the real economy (productivity shocks, in particular), respectively. The cycle is no longer the result of a tendency to equilibrium: each configuration of the system is understood as an equilibrium state—as defined by the rational expectations hypothesis.

The contrasts among contemporary business cycle theories therefore reflect the same fundamental conflict of views on the working of an economic system that has characterized the long history of attempts to explain fluctuations. Some believe depressions to be the result of frictions or to be caused by external forces or by mismanagement of the economy on the part of the government. Others, on the contrary, interpret them as the result of the intrinsic absence (or, at least, serious and systematic failures) of self-regulating properties of economic systems (to which, perhaps, only public intervention can give remedy). It would not seem that these lines of thought, relying not only on different worldviews but also on

antagonistic methodologies and having different objects of research, can be reconciled. Perhaps this is all for the good of the discipline, for actual crises have always been the stimulus of fruitful theoretical debates, which can only thrive insofar as different viewpoints are held.

SEE ALSO *Business Cycles, Empirical Literature; Business Cycles, Political; Business Cycles, Real; Depression, Economic; Financial Instability Hypothesis; Long Waves; Lucas Critique; Panics; Recession; Say's Law; Shocks*

BIBLIOGRAPHY

Aftalion, Albert. 1913 *Les crises périodiques de surproduction*. 2 vols. Paris: Marcel Rivière.

Anonymous (Condy Raguet?) 1829. Untitled report datelined Philadelphia, May 9. *The Free Trade Advocate and Journal of Political Economy* 1 (9): 303–304.

Bouniatian, Mentor. 1922. *Les crises économiques: Essai de morphologie et théorie des crises économiques périodiques et de théorie de la conjoncture économique*. Paris: Giard.

Ellis, Arthur. 1879. *The Rationale of Market Fluctuations*. 4th ed. London: Effingham Wilson.

Frisch, Ragnar. 1933. Propagation Problems and Impulse Problems in Dynamic Economics. In *Economic Essays in Honour of Gustav Cassel*, 171–205. London: Allen & Unwin.

Frisch, Ragnar. 1936. On the Notion of Equilibrium and Disequilibrium. *Review of Economic Studies* 3 (2): 100–105.

Frisch, Ragnar, and Harald Holme. 1935. The Characteristic Solutions of a Mixed Difference and Differential Equation Occurring in Economic Dynamics. *Econometrica* 3: 225–239.

Goodwin, Richard M. 1951. The Non-linear Accelerator and the Persistence of Business Cycles. *Econometrica* 19: 1–17.

Haberler, Gottfried. 1937. *Prosperity and Depression: A Theoretical Analysis of Cyclical Movements*. Geneva, Switzerland: League of Nations. 2nd ed., 1938.

Harrod, Roy F. 1934. Doctrines of Imperfect Competition. *Quarterly Journal of Economics* 48: 442–470.

Harrod, Roy F. 2003. *The Collected Interwar Papers and Correspondence of Roy Harrod*. Ed. Daniele Besomi. 3 vols. Cheltenham, U.K.: Elgar.

Hayek, Friedrich A. 1929. *Geldtheorie und Konjunkturtheorie*. Vienna: Hölder-Pichler-Tempsky. English translation: 1933. *Monetary Theory and the Trade Cycle*. Trans. Nicholar Kaldor and H. M. Croome. London: J. Cape.

Jevons, William Stanley. 1878. Commercial Crises and Sun-Spots. Pt. 1. *Nature* 19 (14): 33–37. Reprinted in: Jevons. 1884. *Investigations in Currency and Finance*. Ed. H. S. Foxwell, 221–235. London: Macmillan.

Juglar, Clément. 1862 *Des crises commerciales et de leur retour périodique en France, en Angleterre, et aux États-Unis*. Paris: Guillaumin. 2nd ed., 1889. Paris: Alcan.

Kaldor, Nicholas. 1940. A Model of the Trade Cycle. *Economic Journal* 50: 78–92.

Kalecki, Michal. 1935. A Macrodynamic Theory of the Business Cycle. *Econometrica* 3: 327–344.

Keynes, John Maynard. 1934. Poverty in Plenty: Is the Economic System Self-Adjusting? *The Listener* 21 (November). Reprinted in: Keynes. 1971–. *The Collected Writings of John Maynard Keynes*, vol. 13, 485–492. London: Macmillan.

Kuznets, Simon. 1930. Equilibrium Economics and Business Cycle Theory. *Quarterly Journal of Economics* 44 (3): 381–415.

Lavington, Frederick. 1922. *The Trade Cycle: An Account of the Causes Producing Rhythmical Changes in the Activity of Business.* London: King.

Lescure, Jean. 1907. *Des crises générales et périodiques de surproduction.* Paris: Domat-Montchrestien.

Lines, Marji. 1990. Slutzky and Lucas: Random Causes of the Business Cycle. *Structural Change and Economic Dynamics* 1 (2): 359–370.

Longfield, S. Mountiford. 1840. Banking and Currency. *Dublin University Magazine* 1: (15): 1–15; 2 (15): 218–233; 3 (16): 371–389; 4 (16): 611–620.

Löwe, Adolf. 1926. Wie ist Konjunkturtheorie überhaupt möglich? *Weltwirtschaftliches Archiv* 24. English translation: 1997. How Is Business Cycle Theory Possible at All? *Structural Change and Economic Dynamics* 8: 245–270.

Löwe, Adolf. 1987. *Essays in Political Economics: Public Control in a Democratic Society.* Brighton, U.K.: Wheatsheaf.

Lucas, Robert E., Jr. 1977. Understanding Business Cycles. In *Stabilization of the Domestic and International Economy*, eds. Karl Brunner and Allan H. Meltzer, 7–29. Amsterdam: North-Holland.

Lucas, Robert E., Jr. 1994. Interview. In *A Modern Guide to Macroeconomics: An Introduction to Competing Schools of Thought*, eds. Brian Snowdon, Howard R. Vane, and Peter Wanarczyk, 188-235. Cheltenham, U.K.: Elgar.

Mitchell, Wesley Clair. 1913. *Business Cycles.* Berkeley: University of California Press.

Miller, Harry E. 1927. *Banking Theories in the United States Before 1860.* Cambridge, MA: Harvard University Press.

Overstone, Lord (Samuel Jones Loyd). 1837. *Reflections Suggested by a Perusal of Mr. J. Horsley Palmer's Pamphlet on the Causes and Consequences of the Pressure on the Money Market.* London: P. Richardson.

Robertson, Dennis Holme. 1915. *A Study of Industrial Fluctuation: An Enquiry into the Character and Causes of the So-Called Cyclical Movement of Trade.* London: King.

Robertson, Dennis Holme. 1926. *Banking Policy and the Price Level: An Essay in the Theory of the Trade Cycle.* London: King.

Schumpeter, Joseph Alois. 1910. Über das Wesen der Wirtschaftskrisen. *Zeitschrift für Volkswirtschaft, Sozialpolitik und Verwaltung* 19: 271–325. English translation: 2005. On the Nature of Economic Crises. In *Business Cycle Theory: Selected Texts, 1860–1939*, ed. Mauro Boianovsky, vol. 5, 5–50. London: Pickering & Chatto.

Selden, George Charles. 1902. Trade Cycles and the Effort to Anticipate. *Quarterly Journal of Economics* 16 (2): 293–310.

Slutsky, Eugene. 1937. The Summation of Random Causes as the Source of Cyclic Processes. *Econometrica* 5: 105–146.

Tooke, Thomas. 1823. *Thoughts and Details on the High and Low Prices of the Last Thirty Years*, London: Murray.

Wade, John. 1833. *History of the Middle and Working Class.* London: E. Wilson.

Daniele Besomi

BUSINESS ETHICS

SEE *Ethics, Business.*

BUTTERFLY EFFECT

The technical name for the *butterfly effect* is *sensitive dependence on initial conditions.* It was first proposed in meteorology but has an impressive array of implications in a variety of fields. Simply put, the butterfly effect occurs when a very small event has exceedingly large and far-reaching impact. The metaphor of the butterfly is used because a butterfly's wings, fragile as they are, do not stir up much air as they flap, but even that minute movement may initiate a series of changes that grow such that they eventually cause a large storm thousands of miles away. In broad terms, then, the butterfly effect implies that large events may be tied to small, or even minuscule, occurrences.

The butterfly effect was used initially to explain why weather forecasts were frequently inaccurate. Initial conditions, sometimes quite subtle, tended to go unnoticed, so forecasters did not take them into account—yet those minute conditions eventually created hurricanes or similar sizeable changes in the weather. It is this insight concerning the large potential impact of minor occurrences that gives the butterfly effect broad appeal in many other fields, including psychology: It explains why predictions are often inaccurate. Recognizing the importance of initial conditions can dramatically improve the accuracy of scientific predictions.

The butterfly effect was discovered serendipitously and shows the benefits of interdisciplinary research efforts. The meteorologist Edward Lorenz, who first described the butterfly effect, saw meaningful patterns in what appeared to be random events in weather patterns. He studied them mathematically, and eventually caught the attention of other meteorologists. These ideas contributed significantly to the new science of *chaos.* To simplify, what appears to be chaotic may in fact reflect a nonlinear pattern in which seemingly negligible events have dramatic impact. This process is chaotic neither in the sense of being unpredictable, nor in the sense that the contributing factors cannot be determined. Instead, causes are related to effects in a nonlinear fashion, and although the results may appear to be chaotic, they are in fact deducible if nonlinear reasoning is applied.

Physicists, biologists, epidemiologists, ecologists, and psychologists now consider the butterfly effect, chaos, and nonlinear reasoning when making certain predictions. This has proven to be very useful in various social and behavioral sciences, as well as the physical and biological sciences. Data from a measles epidemic in New York City, for example, supported the new ideas of chaos and the butterfly effect, as did studies of the population variations of the Canadian lynx. Lightning and clouds showed the same trends and patterns, as did phenomena on much smaller scales, such as blood vessels and proteins, and on much larger scales, such as oceans, stars, and galaxies. This is one of the attractions of chaos theory: It applies regardless of scale.

The implications for the social sciences are suggested by the population patterns noted above, but implications for individuals are at least as clear. The butterfly effect in particular has been used to describe a variety of seemingly unpredictable behaviors and seemingly unpredictable thinking patterns. What may appear to be random or meaningless ideation, such as that of some psychotics, can, for example, be understood as a result of nonlinear reasoning. Along much the same lines, creative insights, which are by definition original, may be understood by taking initial perspective into account and allowing for nonlinear cognitive processes that may lead to a surprising insight or creative solution to a problem. Behavioral tendencies such as these were for many years difficult to understand, but the butterfly effect has improved our understanding of them in dramatic fashion.

SEE ALSO *Chaos Theory; Differential Equations; Hurwicz, Leonid; Nonlinear Systems; Path Dependence; Phase Diagrams; Stability in Economics*

BIBLIOGRAPHY

McCarthy, Kimberly A. 1992. Indeterminacy and Consciousness in the Creative Process: What Quantum Physics Has to Offer. *Creativity Research Journal* 6 (3): 201–219.

Richards, Ruth. 1991. A New Aesthetic for Environmental Awareness: Chaos Theory, the Beauty of Nature, and Our Broader Humanistic Identity. *Journal of Humanistic Psychology* 41 (2): 59–95.

Vandervert, Larry, ed. 1997. *Understanding Tomorrow's Mind: Advances in Chaos Theory, Quantum Theory, and Consciousness in Psychology.* Special issue. *Journal of Mind and Behavior* 18 (2–3).

Zausner, Tobi. 1998. When Walls Become Doorways: Creativity, Chaos Theory, and Physical Illness. *Creativity Research Journal* 11 (1): 21–28.

Mark A. Runco

C

CABRAL, AMÍLCAR
1924–1973

Amílcar Lopes Cabral was born on September 12, 1924, in Bafatá, Guinea-Bissau. His father, a Cape Verdean, was a poet, polemicist, and schoolteacher; his mother was a shopkeeper, guest house owner, and later, seamstress. The family moved to the Cape Verde when Cabral was four. He was home-schooled until twelve. He did his primary schooling in Praia and subsequently went to Gil Eanes Lyceum in Mindelo, São Vincente Island. Gil Eanes was then a literary and social beehive, alive with discussion groups and social activists examining Cape Verde's social and economic deprivation amid continuing droughts and famine. Cabral was deeply influenced by these discussions and the reality surrounding him. By the time he left for Portugal to pursue university studies in the autumn of 1945, he was transformed, committed to leading an active, socially transformative life.

During his seven years in Portugal Cabral studied agronomy. He developed an aptitude for detailed field-work and quantitative analysis. He deepened his qualitative analytical skills and mastered the art of public speaking and diplomacy. And he proved highly successful at organizing discussions, meetings, and study groups while foiling surveillance.

Cabral graduated in 1952. He subsequently returned to Guinea-Bissau, where he stayed intermittently until 1959. While there, he helped found Partido Africano da Independência de Guinea e Cabo Verde (PAIGC), or the African Party for the Independence of Guinea and the Cape Verde Island.

Cabral and his leadership have attracted wide-ranging views. As a doer, however, Cabral is more graspable. He helped found the PAIGC as a binationalist party, tying the Cape Verde Island's political future and logistical fate to that of Guinea-Bissau. As a political strategist he was said to have masterminded a countrywide mobilization campaign preparing Guinea-Bissauans for liberation. As the PAIGC's chief negotiator and diplomat, he traveled internationally for nearly thirteen years, paying over eighty visits to twenty-odd countries, logging some 600,000 miles. These visits brought in much-needed military aid and humanitarian assistance vital to sustain the war effort and nation building.

Cabral was shot dead at point blank range on January 20, 1973, just as he was getting out of his vehicle outside his home in Conakry. His killing was politically motivated. His murderer, Innocencio Kani, led a group of dissidents who wanted Cabral replaced with someone less "Cape Verdean" and more "Guinea-Bissauan." On the other hand, the Portuguese armed forces, then led by General António Spinola, aided and abetted this group to have Cabral replaced with someone willing to reach a negotiated settlement for Guinea-Bissau only.

Cabral wrote extensively. His poems sought to capture the travails of Cape Verdeans, the fragility of their culture in a rapidly emaciating economy, and the social and emotional consequences of such hardships on culture, identity, and social cohesion. Of his numerous professional monographs, none surpass in importance the 1956 200-page fieldwork document evaluating Guinea-Bissau's agricultural demography. The study took several years to complete and entailed traveling some 37,000 miles to visit 2,248 peasant holdings.

Cabral's work on race and colonialism is steeped in his lived-in experience. He deeply felt the need for Africans, and for that matter anyone under colonial rule, to "re-racialize"—to return to the source. He saw this as an imperative for self-determination, a preconditional rediscovery of one's identity and culture, as it were, to begin the real overt fight to set oneself free from coloniality and colonialism.

SEE ALSO *Anticolonial Movements; Colonialism; Geography; Identity; Liberation; Liberation Movements; Self-Determination*

BIBLIOGRAPHY

Cabral, Amílcar. 1976–1977. *Unidade e Luta.* 2 vols. Lisbon, Portugal: Seara Nova.

Dhada, Mustafah. 1993. *Warriors at Work: How Guinea Was Really Set Free.* Niwot: University Press of Colorado.

Mustafah Dhada

CAIRNS, ROBERT
SEE *Social Cognitive Map.*

CALIFORNIA CIVIL RIGHTS INITIATIVE

The California Civil Rights Initiative, a 1996 ballot measure also known as Proposition 209, ended affirmative action for women and minorities in California public education and contracting. It gained little attention when it was first written by two California academics, Thomas E. Wood and Glynn Custred, in the early 1990s. However, during their second attempt to put the initiative on the 1996 ballot, it won the support of Governor Pete Wilson and the financial backing of the state Republican Party. Both Wilson and the party saw it as a potent way for the Republicans to win California's fifty-four electoral votes in the 1996 presidential election. They hoped it would become the same type of political wedge issue that the anti-immigrant Proposition 187 became in 1994, the year the Republican Party took control of Congress and nearly every state office in California.

Midway through the 1996 campaign, the conservative African American businessman Ward Connerly, appointed to the University of California (UC) Board of Regents by Wilson, became the chair and chief spokesman

for the initiative. The language of the initiative and the campaign were both designed to take advantage of what polls have consistently demonstrated: that whereas in general a slight majority of Americans support affirmative action for women and minorities, the vast majority will oppose it if it is described as preferences for women and minorities. Both the initiative's language and the political campaign to support it used the word *preferences* and omitted any mention of affirmative action.

The opposition campaign, run by a collection of grassroots organizations—the Feminist Majority, NOW, the ACLU, and the NAACP Legal Defense and Education Fund—began its fight early, but never earned the political or financial support of the state or national Democratic Party. President Clinton, who visited California several days before the vote, never urged voters to reject the initiative.

In the end, the initiative won approval with 54.6 percent of the vote, including 58 percent of white women voters and 66 percent of white men. Although some voters remained confused on Election Day about the initiative's intent, it was the use of the word *preferences*, and the public's long aversion to affirmative action when described using this word, that insured the measure's victory.

Moreover, voters who benefited from affirmative action or preferences no longer connected their success to these programs. White women, for example, had been the main beneficiaries of affirmative action or preferences, but polling by both campaigns showed that white women no longer connected their success to these programs and many believed that affirmative action hurt job prospects for their male children and husbands.

A *Los Angeles Times* exit poll showed that the initiative was rejected by 74 percent of African Americans voters, 76 percent of Latinos, and 61 percent of Asians. The Asian vote surprised some analysts because Asians are well represented at the state's premiere universities, but their own experience of facing discrimination after graduating from college and the leadership of the late UC Berkeley chancellor Chang-Lin Tien encouraged Asians to support affirmative action.

The impact of the California Civil Rights Initiative has been tremendous. Latino and African American enrollment at UC Berkeley and UCLA has never recovered. State contracting for firms owned by women and minorities has dropped sharply. Copycat initiatives have failed in Florida and Houston, but succeeded in Washington and in Michigan.

SEE ALSO *Affirmative Action; Elites; Equal Opportunity; Equality; Inequality, Gender; Inequality, Racial; Meritocracy*

BIBLIOGRAPHY

Arnold Steinberg and Associates, Inc. 1996. Campaign Plan, California Civil Rights Initiative for November/1996.

Brennan, John. 1991. Key Words Influence Stands on Minorities; Polls Find Whites Favor Remedial Programs—Until Quotas or Preferences Are Mentioned. *Los Angeles Times*, August 21.

Chávez, Lydia. 1998. *The Color Bind: California's Battle to End Affirmative Action.* Berkeley: University of California Press.

The Feldman Group, Inc. 1996. Strategic Memorandum, No on CCRI Campaign, June.

Lydia Chávez

CALIFORNIA V. BAKKE

SEE Grutter *Decision.*

CALYPSO

Calypso is a style of Caribbean music associated with the island of Trinidad in the West Indies and linked very closely to the annual celebration of the pre-Lenten carnival. The music, as well as the name itself, has uncertain roots, yet scholars generally agree that calypso is an example of a hybrid musical form resulting from the interactions of colonizers, slaves, and others from the eighteenth century onward. While calypso grew out of a myriad of traditions, it has spawned a number of separate musical genres such as soca, rapso, talkalypso, chutney soca, and others.

Although there is no general agreement as to the origin of the term, there are references in Trinidadian newspapers of the nineteenth century to *cariso* and *kaiso*, both song forms characterized by the performance of extemporaneous, satirical lyrics. The term *kaiso*, which was shouted to encourage or praise successful singers, is considered a possible source for the word *calypso*, and indeed is still used instead of *calypso*. The *cariso* is only one of many song forms to emerge from the colonial era in Trinidad. Creole slaves and free Africans contributed a variety of songs and dances, including the *bel air* (derived from both African and French sources), the *juba*, the *bamboula*, the *calinda* (both a martial art and a song style), and the *lavway* (a road chant performed during carnival processions). Combined with these forms were British ballads, French folk songs, Venezuelan string music, and other types of Creole West Indian songs. Furthermore, as new musical forms were created or introduced to the island—American jazz, Venezuelan *paseos*, and ultimately such diverse forms as Hindi film music, reggae and dance-hall, soul, and rhythm and blues—they were incorporated into calypso.

HISTORICAL BACKGROUND

Claimed for Spain by Christopher Columbus in 1498, Trinidad has played host to colonizers, slaves, indentured laborers, and immigrants from diverse cultural backgrounds, many of whom contributed their own musical forms to the mix. However, the African musical forms of the slaves and the musical styles of French, English, and Spanish colonizers exercised perhaps the greatest influence.

Trinidad was opened by Spain to French colonists first in the 1770s and later in 1783. The French dominated the cultural life of the island up to and even beyond the English conquest in 1797. The French imported their pre-Lenten festival of carnival, and much of the earliest carnival music was sung in Creole or patois. During the nineteenth century, English culture, language, and religion increased in importance and influence, and many of the folk musical styles gradually changed from French Creole to English. As the English extended their hegemony over the island, they also embarked on a mission of reforming the carnival. By the 1880s unruly masqueraders and riots against police repression resulted in a massive campaign of controlling and channeling the public celebration into a manageable event. By the early 1900s calypso music, marked lyrically now by social satire, political commentary, humor, and sexual innuendo, was largely being performed in "calypso tents," temporary venues in which calypsonians competed against each other for prizes offered by private sponsors.

The first calypso recordings were made in 1914, and by the 1920s and 1930s Trinidad's finest calypso singers, such as Attila the Hun, Roaring Lion, and Lord Invader, were regularly recording and performing in the United States. "Rum and Coca-Cola" (1944) by the Andrews Sisters, a sanitized reinterpretation of a Lord Invader song, became an American hit. It also spawned a landmark lawsuit by Lord Invader against the American actor Morey Amsterdam, who illegally copyrighted the lyrics. Invader won the suit.

Although they faced routine censorship by the British colonial authorities, the calypsonians of this period, sometimes referred to as the golden age of calypso, displayed enormous creativity and invention in circumventing restrictions placed on them and creating songs rife with double entendre, inside jokes, and subtle parody. Audiences relied on clever calypsonians for insight into the ironies of colonial rule, the hypocrisy of the ruling classes, the meaning of certain scandals and outrages, and so on. Savvy politicians could often "take the temperature" of the public by the attitudes of their calypsonians.

SOCIAL COMMENTARY

From its earliest days, calypso music served as a forum for the expression of social and political views within the Caribbean. Remarkably, the criticism mounted by calypsonians was not limited to broad appeals against inequality, racism, poverty, and oppression, but tackled precise specificity laws, domestic policy, proposed legislation, foreign policy, labor relations, actions by public figures, and even speeches given by notable persons. Thus, in addition to humorous rivalries between singers, songs about the beauty of the land, and compositions with a ribald flavor, calypsos were composed with such titles as "Prison Improvement," "Shop Closing Ordinance," "The Commissioner's Report," "The European Situation," "Devaluation," "Slum Clearance," "Reply to the Ministry," and, fittingly, "The Censoring of Calypsoes Makes Us Glad."

AFRICAN-INDIAN RELATIONS

The arrival of indentured laborers from South Asia from the 1840s until 1917 dramatically changed the ethnic makeup of Trinidad. Competition for work and land created tensions between the island's Africans and South Asians that ultimately manifested in political divisions being drawn along ethnic lines. Although never reaching the violence and discord of Guyana, where a similar immigration took place, the presence of Indians in Trinidad was closely followed by calypsonians. Initially, many calypsos dealing with Indians discussed "strange" customs, delicious food, and beautiful women. Creole calypsonians often commented in song on how they fell in love with an Indian girl or how they were able to participate in an Indian feast. As political tensions heated up during the 1950s, however, calypsos became more pointedly political. By 1961 the calypsonian Striker, registering his dismay at the deep ethnic division present in local politics, remarked in song that "Negro can't get a vote from Indian." Today there are a number of noted Indian calypsonians, both men and women, as well as African artists performing in the Indian-influenced genre of *chutney soca*. Even so, tensions between the two communities persist and are often played out musically over the airwaves and in the calypso tents of Trinidad.

In addition to the rebellious and resistant side of calypso, there was a strong dose of patriotism (songs in favor of England during the Boer War [1899–1902], World War I [1914–1918], and World War II [1939–1945], for instance, were common). Furthermore, calypsonians recorded the achievements of the British Empire and the royal family with great enthusiasm. Compositions in favor of the Empire coexisted with little discomfort alongside songs detailing the often oppressive conditions under which the children of the Empire labored.

Although not technically a calypso, the well-known "Banana Boat Song," a traditional Jamaican folksong whose best-known rendition was recorded by Harry Belafonte on his 1956 album *Calypso*, helped to make that album the first to sell more than a million copies.

CALYPSO SINCE INDEPENDENCE

In 1956 a calypsonian known as the Mighty Sparrow penned "Jean and Dinah," a commentary in song about the sudden availability and desperation of prostitutes in Port of Spain after the departure of the free-spending American sailors stationed in Trinidad during World War II. While the song became an international hit, and won the calypso "crown" for Sparrow, it is perhaps even more important as a testimony to the renewed sense of cultural and political confidence then being experienced across the Caribbean as independence movements were flourishing. The 1950s marked a pivotal point in the development of calypso and perhaps inaugurated what might be called the "independence period" in calypso.

As Trinidad, Jamaica, Barbados, and other English-speaking islands continued their drive toward independence from the United Kingdom, folk idioms such as calypso, carnival, steel band, the musical form ska, and even sports such as cricket began to take on a nationalist tone. Nation-building calypsos, as they are sometimes called, emerged to praise the efforts of certain political parties and politicians and to encourage proper behavior and decorum among the populace.

The 1960s brought to the Caribbean not only independence but also the Black Power movement. Calypso reflected this new cultural consciousness lyrically; it also reflected the cultural source from which it came—the United States. One of the most important figures to emerge at this time was the Mighty Chalkdust, a teacher and calypsonian who obtained his Ph.D. from the University of Michigan and has, under his given name, Hollis Liverpool, researched and published widely on calypso, carnival, and Trinidadian culture in general.

Traditionally accompanied by acoustic music, calypso increasingly came to incorporate electronic instrumentation and the influence of North American musical styles such as rhythm and blues and soul. Alongside Black Power came the women's liberation movement and increasing (though still small) numbers of women singers. Indeed, women as calypsonians are not given nearly the attention they deserve in the literature. Although largely excluded from the ranks of early recorded calypsonians, and often derided in songs such as "Jean and Dinah," women have been instrumental in the development of Trinidadian music as *chantwells* (praise singers for stickfighters and singers of road marches) and in religious music. In the 1960s, attitudes toward women calypsonians began to change, and it was, perhaps ironically, the Mighty Sparrow who gave the then-unknown singer Calypso Rose her start. Along with Singing Francine and Denyse Plummer, Rose has become one of the most popular calypsonians of all time.

With the rise of outside influences from North America came further influences from diverse musical sources, including Jamaican reggae and (due to the presence of a large and thriving Indian population) Hindi film music. The result has been the development of new musical forms, such as soca, chutney soca, rapso, raga, and others.

Born in 1941, Garfield Blackman, known as Lord Shorty, would become the creator of soca music. Concerned that calypso was declining in relation to reggae, Lord Shorty experimented with the calypso rhythm. He combined Indian instruments such as the dholak, tabla, and dhantal with traditional calypso instrumentation. The result was a new musical hybrid that he called *solka*. With his 1974 album *Endless Vibrations* and the single "Shanti Om," Shorty sparked a revolution in Caribbean music. Initially the term *solka* referred to an attempt to recapture the "soul of calypso," which he felt was one of inclusion, common struggle, and resistance to oppression. Shorty hoped that the "Indianization" of calypso would bring together the musical traditions of Trinidad and Tobago's two major ethnic groups, the descendants of African slaves and of indentured laborers from India. The name was later changed to *soca*, and it is routinely if erroneously explained as a fusion of soul and calypso.

By the turn of the 1980s soca was rapidly becoming the music of choice for Trinidadians during carnival time. The Montserratian singer Arrow did much to popularize soca internationally with his 1983 number-one soca classic "Hot Hot Hot." Due to the globalization of the music industry, soca has evolved swiftly and has incorporated many outside influences, spawning such diverse subgenres as ragga soca and chutney soca. Although soca has become increasingly popular, many critics within the region have pointed to its reluctance to be anything more than "party music." The political and social commentary once so central to calypso has had to find a new home in other Caribbean musical genres. In Trinidad this mantle has largely been taken up by *rapso*. Rapso is a unique style of street poetry from Trinidad and Tobago that originated in the 1970s (although it was not named *rapso* until the 1980s by Brother Resistance). Often credited to Lancelot Layne, rapso was created in a spirit of political protest and social justice. Layne's 1970 hit "Blow Away" is considered

the first rapso recording. Layne is also well remembered for his 1971 recording "Get Off the Radio."

Beginning as a folk music of protest, social commentary, and political satire, calypso has emerged as one of the most important, internationally recognized, and fecund musical forms of the twentieth century.

SEE ALSO *Caribbean, The; Music; Popular Music*

BIBLIOGRAPHY

Cowley, John. 1996. *Carnival, Canboulay, and Calypso: Traditions in the Making*. Cambridge, U.K.: Cambridge University Press.

Hill, Donald R. 1993. *Calypso Calaloo: Early Carnival Music in Trinidad*. Gainesville: University Press of Florida.

Hill, Errol. 1972. *The Trinidad Carnival: Mandate for a National Theatre*. Austin: University of Texas Press.

Manuel, Peter, with Kenneth Bilby and Michael Largey. 2006. *Caribbean Currents: Caribbean Music from Rumba to Reggae*. Rev. ed. Philadelphia: Temple University Press.

Quevedo, Raymond. 1983. *Atilla's Kaiso: A Short History of Trinidad Calypso*. Saint Augustine, Trinidad and Tobago: University of the West Indies.

Rohlehr, Gordon. 1990. *Calypso and Society in Pre-Independence Trinidad*. Tunapuna, Trinidad and Tobago: Author.

Warner, Keith Q. 1999. *Kaiso! the Trinidad Calypso: A Study of Calypso as Oral Literature*. 3rd ed. Pueblo, CO: Passeggiata.

Philip W. Scher

CAMBRIDGE CAPITAL CONTROVERSY

The Cambridge capital controversy refers to a debate that started in the 1950s and continued through the 1970s. The core of the debate concerns the measurement of capital goods in a way that is consistent with the requirements of neoclassical economic theory. The debate involved economists such as Piero Sraffa, Joan Robinson, Piero Garegnani, and Luigi Pasinetti at the University of Cambridge in England and Paul Samuelson and Robert Solow at the Massachusetts Institute of Technology in Cambridge, Massachusetts. In a now-famous *Quarterly Journal of Economics* publication from 1966, Samuelson admitted the logical validity of the British critique of the neoclassical theory of capital (Samuelson 1966). Yet, Solow (1963) claimed the debate was largely a sideshow to the core of neoclassical analysis.

The essence of the debate revolved around the fundamental premises of the theories of value, distribution, and growth, each of which depends upon an aggregate production function where the inputs or factors of production for capital and labor are aggregated in some fashion prior to the determination of the rate of profit (interest) and the wage rate. According to neoclassical theory, the price of each factor of production is determined by its marginal contribution to production; furthermore, there exists substitutability between factors of production that gives rise to diminishing returns. As a consequence, the rate of profit (or interest) is the price of capital and as such reflects capital's relative scarcity; more specifically, a relative abundance of capital, in combination with the law of diminishing returns of a factor of production (whereby the greater use of an input will imply a lower marginal product, other things being equal) will give rise to a low rate of profit (interest). The opposite would be true in the case of a relative scarcity of capital. Capital income would amount to the product of the rate of profit times the amount of capital employed.

Piero Sraffa pointed out that there was an inherent measurement problem in applying the neoclassical model of value and income distribution, because the estimation of the rate of profit requires the prior measurement of capital. The problem is that capital—unlike labor or land, which can be reduced to homogenous units stated in their own terms (for example, hours of the same skill and intensity or land of the same fertility)—is an ensemble of heterogeneously produced goods, which must be added in such a way as to enable a cost-minimizing choice of techniques. From the various alternatives, neoclassical theory chooses to measure capital goods in value terms; that is, the product of physical units (buildings, machines, etc.) times their respective (equilibrium) prices. Joan Robinson (1953), inspired by Sraffa's teaching and early writings, and later Sraffa himself (1960), argued that the value measurement of capital requires the prior knowledge of equilibrium prices, which in turn requires an equilibrium rate of profit that cannot be obtained unless we have estimated the value of capital.

Clearly, there is a problem of circularity here that the Cambridge, Massachusetts, economists sought to resolve. Paul Samuelson, in particular, presented a model based on the heroic assumption that capital-intensity is uniform across sectors, which is equivalent to saying that there is a one-commodity world. In such an economy, as income distribution varies, the subsequent revaluation of capital gives rise to results that are absolutely consistent with the requirements of neoclassical theory. In fact, Samuelson derived a straight-line wage–profit rate frontier (the mirror image of the usual convex isoquant curves), each one representing a cost-minimizing technique, and this gave rise to a well-behaved demand-for-capital schedule. Parenthetically, Samuelson attacked Marxian value theory for its alleged inability to explain relative prices. However, if one applies Samuelson's heroic assumption of an equal capital intensity across all industries to Marx's labor the-

ory of value, then all of Samuelson's criticisms of Marx become irrelevant. This irony was not unnoticed by the British participants in the capital debates.

Samuelson's assumption was attacked for lack of realism by Garegnani, Pasinetti, and Amartya Sen, among others, who showed that once we hypothesize different capital intensities across industries, the neoclassical results do not necessarily hold. The idea is that as relative prices change the revaluation of capital can go either way, and it is possible for an industry that is capital-intensive in one income distribution to become labor-intensive in another. As a consequence, we no longer derive Samuelson's straight-line wage–profit rate frontiers, which are consistent with the cost-minimizing choice of technique and give rise to well-behaved demand-for-capital schedules. In the presence of many capital goods and various capital intensities across industries it follows that the wage profit rate frontiers are nonlinear and may cross over each other more than once, which means that for a low rate of profit one may choose a capital-intensive technique. As the rate of profit increases, the technique with a lower capital intensity may be chosen, and for a higher rate of profit the original technique of higher capital intensity is chosen again. We observe that a capital-intensive technique may be chosen for both low and high rates of profit, a result that runs contrary to the neoclassical theory of value and income distribution. Under these circumstances we cannot determine a well-behaved demand for capital schedule and so the whole neoclassical construction is under question.

It is important to point out that the capital theory critique does not affect the classical theory of value and income distribution, because the classical theory does not claim that relative prices of factors of production reflect relative scarcities; additionally this theory assumes one of the distributive variables, usually the real wage, as a datum that in combination with the given technology and output level determines the relative equilibrium prices together with the equilibrium rate of profit. Furthermore, the evaluation of heterogeneous capital goods can be achieved in terms of labor values; hence there might be a problem of consistency because variables estimated in terms of labor values will differ from those estimated in terms of equilibrium prices. This, however, is mainly an empirical question and the empirical research has shown that the two types of prices are close to each other, and variables estimated in labor values or equilibrium prices are approximately equal to each other (Shaikh and Tonak 1994, p. 143).

The capital controversy had an initial effect on neoclassical economics, but soon it was forgotten to the point that the new generation of neoclassical economists either dismisses it or simply does not know it. As a result, both theoretical and empirical neoclassical research makes use of aggregate production functions, where capital is still used along with labor in the determination of output and the marginal products of these inputs are estimated on the assumption of substitutability between factors of production, as if the capital controversy never happened. At the close of the twentieth century, there were new efforts by the so-called modern classical economists to revive the classical approach, and once again the capital theory began to surface in mainstream journals, which may revive theoretical questions that puzzled the best Cambridge economists in England and the United States.

The Cambridge capital controversy revived interest in Marxian economics, contributed to the founding of neo-Ricardian or Sraffian economics, and inspired the development of post-Keynesian economics. Indeed, it was Sraffa's 1920s critique of the neoclassical theory of the firm and Sraffa's proto-critique of neoclassical value theory that greatly influenced Keynes's *General Theory of Employment, Interest, and Money* (1936). British interpretation of Keynes's influential publication assumed a classical theory of value and distribution, while the U.S. interpretation sought to integrate Keynes into the neoclassical theory of value and distribution. This difference in understanding Keynes led Joan Robinson to refer to her American counterparts as "bastard Keynesians" (Harcourt 1982, p. 347). Finally, in another famous barb, Robinson once said that because she never learned math she was always forced to think. Robinson's mathematics never went beyond basic algebra and very elementary geometry—the kind of math mastered by many American students in the first two years of high school. On the other hand, Samuelson's economic analysis has led the way in the use of calculus, linear algebra, differential equations, real analysis, and mathematical programming. Robinson's biting comment is a warning to economists to not allow mathematical technique to triumph over substantive understanding of how real-world economies operate.

SEE ALSO *Capital; Pasinetti, Luigi; Robinson, Joan; Samuelson, Paul A.; Sen, Amartya Kumar; Solow, Robert M.; Sraffa, Piero; Substitutability*

BIBLIOGRAPHY

Cohen, Avi J., and G. C. Harcourt. 2003. Whatever Happened to the Cambridge Capital Theory Controversies? *Journal of Economic Perspectives* 17 (1): 199–214.

Harcourt, Geoffrey. 1982. *The Social Science Imperialists.* London: Routledge & Kegan Paul.

Keynes, John Maynard. 1936. *General Theory of Employment, Interest, and Money.* New York: Harcourt, Brace and World.

Robinson, Joan. 1953. The Production Function and the Theory of Capital. *Review of Economic Studies* 21 (2): 81–106.

Samuelson, Paul A. 1966. A Summing Up. *Quarterly Journal of Economics* 80 (4): 568–583.

Shaikh, Anwar, and Tonak Ahmet. 1994. *Measuring the Wealth of Nations.* Cambridge, U.K.: Cambridge University Press.

Solow, Robert. 1963. *Capital Theory and the Rate of Return.* Amsterdam: North-Holland.

Sraffa, Piero. 1960. *Production of Commodities by Means of Commodities: Prelude to a Critique of Economic Theory.* Cambridge, U.K.: Cambridge University Press.

Lefteris Tsoulfidis

CAMBRIDGE UNIVERSITY

The University of Cambridge, it is generally accepted, came about as a result of a migration from the University of Oxford in 1209. The existence of a *studium* at Cambridge was recognized by a papal degree of Gregory IX dated June 14, 1233, and by about 1250 a draft of its statutes had arrived in Rome (Anglica MS 401). These were preceded by recognition from the Crown in 1231. The university's first college, Peterhouse, was founded in 1284, and today there are thirty-one colleges, the latest, Robinson, founded in 1977.

The earliest studies of the university followed the usual pattern for medieval universities, with a particular emphasis on canon law, a trend encouraged by the foundation in Cambridge of large Franciscan and Dominican houses, to be followed by several other orders.

In 1381, in a manifestation of the Peasants' Revolt, the townspeople of Cambridge made assaults on both the university and the colleges, notably on Corpus Christi College which, uniquely, had been founded by the amalgamated town gilds of St. Mary and of Corpus Christi (in 1352). This resulted, ironically, in royal charters greatly increasing the university's dominance of the town, including the oversight of weights and measures and other day-to-day business.

Although royal and papal recognition came earlier to Cambridge than it did to Oxford, Cambridge was certainly the lesser of the two universities until the English Reformation in the sixteenth century. Cambridge men were dominant in both church and state under Henry VIII (e.g., Thomas Cranmer) and Elizabeth I (e.g., William Cecil and John Whitgift), but during the English Civil War (1642–1649), when the royal court removed to Oxford, the balance was reversed.

Academically, Cambridge's eminence was enhanced in the early eighteenth century by the pupils of Isaac Newton, and for more than a century thereafter mathematics was the prime field of study and the only subject in which examinations for degrees were conducted. In the nineteenth century degrees became available in law (1816) and classics (1824), and later in the century other honors courses were introduced, natural sciences first, then moral sciences (philosophy) and gradually others. Although students of the natural sciences were at first few, it was this school that from the 1870s raised Cambridge to the status of a world-class university, with researchers coming from far and wide to work with the physicists James Clerk Maxwell (Cavendish Professor of Experimental Physics, 1871–1879) and his successors J. W. Strutt, Baron Rayleigh, J. J. Thomson, and Ernest Rutherford. Since Thomson (1906), Cambridge has been home to some thirty Nobel laureates, including Francis Crick and James Watson, the discoverers of DNA, and since Rayleigh and Kelvin (1902) some forty holders of the British Order of Merit. A roll call of the many earlier luminaries connected with Cambridge must include the teachers Erasmus of Rotterdam, St. John Fisher, Roger Ascham, Sir John Cheke, Richard Bentley, William Whewell, Lord Acton, Sir James Frazer, G. H. Hardy, Bertrand Russell, John Maynard Keynes, E. M. Forster, F. R. Leavis, and Ludwig Wittgenstein; and the alumni Oliver Cromwell, Charles Darwin, and the poets, to name but a few, Edmund Spenser, Christopher Marlowe, John Milton, Alfred Lord Tennyson, Samuel Coleridge, and William Wordsworth.

Barring several false starts in the medieval period and one (Durham) in the seventeenth century, Cambridge and Oxford were the only English (as opposed to British) universities until the 1840s. Given that, they have naturally been the universities of choice for long-established families and schools, and although there was always a variable amount of scope for the admission of the less affluent, in recent years the catchment of both universities has expanded vastly. Except in the sixteenth century, Oxford historically maintained closer relations with church and state (thus sending out more future prime ministers and archbishops), but Cambridge was never very far behind, sending out mathematicians and poets, as well as competing with Oxford for places in the civil service, seats in Parliament, and other influential positions. Some of this perception of prestige continues today, but it has been amply supported by recent national and international rankings that attract students, especially graduate students, from all over the world.

The colleges of the university, in order of foundation, are:

1284: Peterhouse

1326: Clare

1347: Pembroke

1348: Gonville Hall; refounded 1557 as Gonville and Caius College

1350: Trinity Hall

1352: Corpus Christi College

1441: King's College

1448: Queen's College; previously St. Bernard's College (1446); refounded 1465; and known as Queens' College from c. 1831

1473: St. Catharine's College

1496: Jesus College

1505: Christ's College, incorporating Godshouse (1439)

1511: St. John's College

1542: Magdalene College, incorporating Buckingham College (1428)

1546: Trinity College, incorporating King's Hall (1317) and Michaelhouse (1324) and expropriating Physwick Hostel (1393) from Gonville Hall

1584: Emmanuel College

1596: Sidney Sussex College

1800: Downing College

1869: Girton College

1871: Newnham College

1882: Selwyn College

1885: Cambridge Training College for Women, now known as Hughes Hall, Recognised Institution of the University 1949

1892: Fitzwilliam Hall, housing noncollegiate students, known as Fitzwilliam House from 1924; full college status as Fitzwilliam College (1966)

1894: Homerton College, moved to Cambridge (formerly in London from 1822) as a teacher training college; recognized by the university as an Approved Society (1977)

1896: St. Edmund's House, a Roman Catholic training college recognized as a House of Residence; recognized as an Approved Society (1965); known as St. Edmund's College from 1985

1954: New Hall

1960: Churchill College

1964: Darwin College

1965: Lucy Cavendish College

1965: University College, known as Wolfson College from 1973

1966: Clare Hall

1977: Robinson College

Of these, Newnham, New Hall, and Lucy Cavendish are for women only, and Darwin, Wolfson, and Clare Hall are for graduate students.

BIBLIOGRAPHY

Brooke, Christopher. 1992. *A History of the University of Cambridge*, Vol. 4: *1870–1990*. Cambridge, U.K.: Cambridge University Press.

Leader, Damien Riehl. 1988. *A History of the University of Cambridge*, Vol. 1: *The University to 1546*. Cambridge, U.K.: Cambridge University Press.

Leedham-Green, Elisabeth S. 1996. *A Concise History of the University of Cambridge*. Cambridge, U.K.: Cambridge University Press.

Morgan, Victor, with contribution by Christopher Brooke. 2004. *A History of the University of Cambridge*, Vol. 2: *1546–1750*. Cambridge, U.K.: Cambridge University Press.

Searby, Peter. 1997. *A History of the University of Cambridge*, Vol. 3: *1750–1870*. Cambridge, U.K.: Cambridge University Press.

Elisabeth Leedham-Green

CAMPAIGN REFORM

SEE *Congress, U.S.; Elections.*

CAMPAIGNING

Campaigning is the art and science of "selling" political candidates to voters. Candidates engage in a variety of campaign activities aimed at winning elections, including raising money, building name recognition, making public appearances, purchasing political advertisements, and debating with other candidates. Social scientists who study politics are interested in campaigns and elections because they are important components of American democracy. Elections allow citizens to select leaders and hold them accountable.

Campaigns for public office generally have two stages: the primary election and the general election. The goal of the primary campaign is to gain endorsement from a political party in order to advance to the general election. Primary campaigns appeal to the *party faithful*, that is, voters who identify with a certain political party.

Candidates will often present more extreme policy positions during the primary campaign because they have to appeal to party members who are more ideologically extreme in their views than the general public. During the general election phase, candidates adopt more moderate voter appeals to market themselves to the broader public.

THE EVOLUTION OF CAMPAIGNING

Campaigning techniques changed significantly in the late twentieth century as a result of the popularity of mass communication, namely, television and the Internet. The 1960 presidential race between Richard Nixon and John F. Kennedy marked a turning point in American politics where television gained prominence as a medium for reaching and persuading voters. During this election, listeners who heard the Kennedy-Nixon debate on the radio believed that Nixon had won the debate, whereas viewers who saw the television broadcast thought that Kennedy was the victor.

In addition to requiring candidates to be camera-friendly, television enabled candidates to reach voters directly instead of relying on their political party. The rise of candidate-centered campaigns deflated the power of the major parties in American politics. In response, party officials have come up with new and creative ways to maintain relevance in the electoral process, namely, by providing candidates with media assistance and funding. The political parties' ability to raise funds is crucial for candidates given that a contemporary national election costs about twenty times more than elections did in the 1950s.

The Internet has played an increasingly important role in campaigns for political office. Voters turn to political blogs and other online resources to get information about elections and candidates. For example, the Web site YouTube makes it possible for people to look at campaign ads from across the country with the click of a button. Not surprisingly, a growing number of candidates for public office are using Internet appeals to reach voters. Experts anticipate that the Internet will become an influential campaigning tool as this medium becomes a popular means of distributing tailored information to voters.

CAMPAIGN FINANCE AND REGULATION

The rise of media-centered campaigns has brought about an increase in the cost of campaigning. According to the Center for Responsive Politics, the 2004 presidential contest cost over $1.2 billion. Some scholars argue that the high price tag attached to winning public office is antidemocratic in that only wealthy candidates have the necessary resources. Others counter that the electoral process remains democratic because a majority of campaign contributions come from private individuals. Lawmakers passed several campaign finance reform laws in the late twentieth century and early twenty-first century in an effort to limit the amount of special interest money in campaigns.

The 1971 Federal Election Campaign Act (FECA) limited campaign contributions and required candidates for federal office to disclose all of their financial contributions. FECA also outlawed financial contributions from corporations to candidates. In response, corporate-related organizations—Political Action Committees (PACs)—were formed to influence elections. Subsequently so-called *527* organizations have formed that advocate for certain policies instead of specific candidates, although their media and other political tactics aim to influence election outcomes. Through *issue advocacy* advertising, or ads that discuss a political issue in a way that critiques a certain candidate, 527s play an increasingly influential role in elections.

Congress made sweeping changes to FECA in 2002 with passage of the Bipartisan Campaign Reform Act, also known as the McCain-Feingold Act. This legislation outlawed *soft money*, or money that is ostensibly donated to political parties for "party-building activities" but is often used to help candidates. It also restricted 527 organizations from running issue advocacy ads in the months leading up to an election. It is unclear whether this legislation will have the effect lawmakers intended or special interests will find loopholes enabling them to get around the new restrictions.

GOING NEGATIVE

Candidates have the option of running three different types of political advertisements: *issue, image,* and *negative.* Issue ads present the candidate's stance on policies, whereas image ads attempt to enhance the candidate's reputation in the eyes of voters. Candidates are increasingly *going negative,* that is, emphasizing their opponent's negative aspects instead of their own positive attributes. Most researchers agree that this approach can help candidates win elections, but there is debate as to its potential liabilities. Some argue that negative ads tend to be dishonest, can alienate more moderate voters, and might cause voters to tune out of politics and not vote at all on Election Day. Others argue that negative ads are more memorable than positive ads, increase voter awareness of candidates, and cause more people to turn out to vote. The jury is still out on the overall impact of going negative, suggesting perhaps that its effects vary from race to race.

SEE ALSO *Advertising; Computers: Science and Society; Democracy; Elections; Internet; Internet, Impact on Politics; Kennedy, John F.; Nixon, Richard M.;* *Persuasion; Political Parties; Primaries; Propaganda; Television; Voting*

BIBLIOGRAPHY

Ansolabehere, Stephen, and Shanto Iyengar. 1997. *Going Negative: How Attack Ads Shrink and Polarize the Electorate.* New York: Free Press.

Bimber, Bruce A., and Richard Davis. 2003. *Campaigning Online: The Internet in U.S. Elections.* New York: Oxford University Press.

Jacobson, Gary C. 2003. *The Politics of Congressional Elections.* 6th ed. New York: Longman.

Lau, Richard R., and Gerald M. Pomper. 2004. *Negative Campaigning: An Analysis of U.S. Senate Elections (Campaigning American Style).* New York: Rowman and Littlefield.

Shea, Daniel M., and Michael John Burton. 2006. *Campaign Craft: The Strategies, Tactics, and Art of Political Campaign Management.* 3rd ed. New York: Praeger.

Caroline Heldman

CAMPBELL, ANGUS
1910–1980

Angus Campbell was born in Indiana, but grew up in Portland, Oregon. He studied psychology at the University of Oregon, and completed his doctorate at Stanford University in 1936 under E. R. Hilgard. He taught at Northwestern University for six years, until World War II brought him to Washington, D.C., to study effects of the war on the public. He was introduced there to large sample surveys, as well as a group of like-minded social scientists headed by the psychologist Rensis Likert.

After the war Likert, Campbell, and colleagues moved to Ann Arbor, establishing the Institute for Social Research at the University of Michigan. Likert headed the institute, and Campbell became director of its largest component, the Survey Research Center (SRC). Here he enjoyed a field staff of interviewers spread over the country who produced valid national samples according to the strictest precepts of modern sampling theory. He also had access to the university's economists, sociologists, social psychologists, and public health experts who were excited by the new capability to represent the nation with a modest sample of one thousand or two thousand respondents.

While various scholars did studies through SRC every year, Campbell directed a few personally to address his own wide-ranging interests. He launched a national study of voters before and after the 1952 presidential election. This study has been repeated biennially (to include "off-year" congressional elections) ever since. This series yields an amazing panorama of trends in America's democratic processes for more than a half-century.

From the outset Campbell believed that party loyalties are a dominant force in the voting decision, but that voters defect from these loyalties occasionally, depending on the candidates and issues of the day. He wrote a central question to measure such underlying party identification, which remains a critical component of voting studies today.

Among the hundreds of publications from the election series over the years, Campbell and collaborators Philip Converse, Warren Miller, and Donald Stokes wrote a synthesis of early progress, *The American Voter* (1960), which achieved very wide circulation. Its impact was strong on political science as a discipline, which hitherto had focused mainly on historical and institutional studies. This "behavioral science revolution" brought quantification, hypothesis-testing, and estimation of causal flows to the discipline of political science, lending new weight to the "science" in its name. The international impact was also large: Foreign scholars visiting SRC were soon organizing parallel voting studies in their own democracies in Western Europe. By 2006 election studies had spread to nearly four dozen nations, and were intercommunicating to match measurements in order to maximize comparative studies of the voting process.

Campbell himself moved on to other topics. In the civil rights ferment of the 1960s he studied change in U.S. interracial attitudes. By the 1970s he turned to studies of the quality of life as perceived by the U.S. population. Once again, this subject rapidly became popular, and as before, the primary question Campbell wrote to measure a person's most global sense of well-being remains an essential item for replications of such studies here and abroad.

SEE ALSO *American National Election Studies (ANES); Attitudes, Racial; Behaviorism; Consumerism; Elections; Happiness; Likert Scale; Miller, Warren; Social Welfare Functions; Survey; Voting Patterns; Welfare*

BIBLIOGRAPHY

Campbell, Angus, Philip E. Converse, Warren E. Miller, and Donald E. Stokes. 1960. *The American Voter.* New York: John Wiley & Sons.

Campbell, Angus, Philip E. Converse, and Willard Rodgers. 1976. *The Quality of American Life.* New York: Russell Sage Foundation.

Philip E. Converse

CAMPBELL, DONALD
1916–1996

Donald Thomas Campbell was a master methodologist whose intellectual passions and scholarly achievements spanned the fields of social science research methodology, epistemology and philosophy of science, and the sociology and psychology of science.

Campbell's best-known works are on the methodology of social experimentation and quasi-experimentation (Campbell 1957; Campbell and Stanley 1963; Cook and Campbell 1979; Shadish et al. 2001). They are among the most influential contributions to the methodology of applied social science in the twentieth century. Although others had written about field experiments—for example, the preeminent statistician Ronald Fisher (1890–1962)— it was Campbell who introduced the methodology of *quasi-experimentation*, an inductive (but *non*statistical) methodology that seeks to understand the effects of the many unmanageable contingencies that lie beyond the control of experimenters. Although quasi-experimentation is "applied," especially in contexts involving the evaluation of social programs, it is nevertheless "theoretical." It is grounded in Campbell's philosophy of critical realism, his epistemology of pragmatic eliminative induction, his methodology of triangulation and the multitrait-multimethod matrix, his theory of pattern matching in science, and his sociology of science (Campbell 1988).

SOCIAL EXPERIMENTATION AND QUASI-EXPERIMENTATION

Experimentation and quasi-experimentation are extensions of *representative design*, a theory of inquiry developed by Campbell's two most influential teachers at Berkeley, Egon Brunswik (1903–1955) and Edward Tolman (1886–1959). Representative design requires that experiments be conducted in settings that are representative of an organism's typical ecology. Representative design is a fundamental departure from the classical experiment, in which one independent (treatment) variable is manipulated in order to determine its effect on a dependent (outcome) variable, with all other factors held constant through random selection and statistical controls. Representative design is appropriate when social experiments are carried out in uncertain, unstable, and causally complex environments.

The classical experiment, which involves an independent (treatment) variable that is manipulated in order to determine its effect on a dependent (outcome) variable, requires a treatment and control group, random selection of subjects, and random assignment of subjects to treatment and control groups. If any of these requirements are absent, it is not a classical ("true") experiment, but a *quasi-experiment.* Many of the most important social policy and program interventions are quasi-experiments because political, administrative, and ethical constraints rarely make it possible to satisfy the requirements of the classical experiment.

CRITICAL REALISM AND THE EPISTEMOLOGY OF PRAGMATIC ELIMINATIVE INDUCTION

Quasi-experimentation is expressly designed for research settings in which manifold contingencies are beyond the control of the experimenter. These contingencies give rise to many rival hypotheses (alternative explanations of the same outcome) that can threaten the validity of causal claims. Plausible rival hypotheses must be tested and, where possible, eliminated. This process of eliminative induction is an extension of John Stuart Mill's (1806–1873) *joint method of agreement and difference*; it also represents a (heavily qualified) version of Karl Popper's (1902–1994) *falsificationist* principle that hypotheses can be falsified but never proved.

Pragmatic (not logical-analytic) eliminative induction is part of Campbell's evolutionary critical-realist epistemology (Campbell 1974), according to which knowledge grows through processes of trial-and-error learning and selective retention. Quasi-experiments in education, welfare, health, and other social policy arenas embody such processes. When entire societies self-consciously and systematically engage in trial-and-error learning and selective retention, they are *experimenting societies* (see Campbell in Dunn 1998).

METHODOLOGICAL TRIANGULATION AND THE MULTITRAIT-MULTIMETHOD MATRIX

What we know as "truth" or objective knowledge is actually a product of theory interacting with data. Emblematic of Campbell's methodological work is its synthesis of subjective and objective, perception and reality, theory and data. He accomplished this synthesis through methodological triangulation—a process of comparing two or more perspectives toward the "same" object. His work with D. W. Fiske (1916–2003) on the multitrait-multimethod matrix (Campbell and Fiske 1959) represents a form of theory and method triangulation, where traits posited by a theory interact with methods of observation. The product is some level of convergent and discriminant validity. Underlying the multitrait-multimethod matrix is an epistemology usually referred to as a *coherence theory* of truth. Campbell and Fiske's 1959 paper is one of the most widely cited papers in the social and behavioral sciences.

PATTERN MATCHING IN SCIENCE

To the degree that products of the social and behavioral sciences merit the term *knowledge*, it is because they are grounded in representations of the social world achieved by matching observations of that world with abstract concepts of it. For Campbell, pattern matching is essential for attaining knowledge of everyday cultural objects and indispensable for achieving knowledge of inferred entities in science—the size and brightness of distant stars, the existence and magnitude of latent psychological variables such as alienation or intelligence, and the structure of complex social processes such as social mobility and economic growth. Campbell argued that these and other inferred entities are known indirectly and vicariously, through a process of pattern matching (Campbell 1966). He also contended that case studies can be a methodologically powerful form of pattern matching in the social sciences (Campbell 1975).

THE SOCIOLOGY OF SCIENTIFIC VALIDITY

Traditional sociology of knowledge, because it describes the social, political, and cultural conditions affecting science and other knowledge formations, is descriptive. Campbell's sociology of knowledge, which goes beyond description, sought to explain how differences in the social structures and processes of sciences affect the degree of validity achieved by those sciences. He called this normative sociology of science the *sociology of scientific validity* (Campbell 1986). Among the social factors that affect scientific validity are institutional incentive systems that reward quality research and punish those whose research is flawed by violating norms of science.

SEE ALSO *Experiments; Methodology; Natural Experiments; Philosophy of Science; Popper, Karl; Public Policy; Social Experiment; Sociology; Sociology, Knowledge in; Tolman, Edward*

BIBLIOGRAPHY

PRIMARY SOURCES

Campbell, Donald T. 1957. Factors Relevant to the Validity of Experiments in Social Settings. *Psychological Bulletin* 54: 297–312.

Campbell, Donald T. 1966. Pattern Matching as an Essential in Distal Knowing. In *The Psychology of Egon Brunswik*, ed. Kenneth R. Hammond, 81–106. New York: Holt, Rinehart, and Winston.

Campbell, Donald T. 1974. Evolutionary Epistemology. In *The Philosophy of Karl Popper*, ed. Paul A. Schilpp, 413–463. La Salle, IL: Open Court.

Campbell, Donald T. 1975. "Degrees of Freedom" and the Case Study. *Comparative Political Studies* 8: 178–193.

Campbell, Donald T. 1986. Science's Social System of Validity-Enhancing Collective Belief Change and the Problems of the Social Sciences. In *Metatheory in Social Science: Pluralisms and Subjectivities*, eds. D. W. Fiske and Richard A. Schweder, 108–135. Chicago: University of Chicago Press.

Campbell, Donald T. 1988. *Methodology and Epistemology for Social Science: Selected Papers*. Ed. E. Samuel Overman. Chicago: University of Chicago Press.

Campbell, Donald T., and Donald W. Fiske. 1959. Convergent and Discriminant Validation by the Multitrait-Multimethod Matrix. *Psychological Bulletin* 56: 81–105.

Campbell, Donald T., and Julian C. Stanley. 1963. *Experimental and Quasi-Experimental Designs for Research*. Chicago: Rand McNally.

Cook, Thomas D., and Donald T. Campbell. 1979. *Quasi-Experimentation: Design & Analysis Issues for Field Settings*. Boston: Houghton Mifflin.

Shadish, William R., Thomas D. Cook, and Donald T. Campbell. 2001. *Experimental and Quasi-Experimental Designs for Generalized Causal Inference*. Boston: Houghton Mifflin.

SECONDARY SOURCES

Brunswik, Egon. 1956. *Perception and the Representative Design of Psychological Experiments*. 2nd ed. Berkeley: University of California Press.

Dunn, William N. 1998. *The Experimenting Society: Essays in Honor of Donald T. Campbell*. New Brunswick, NJ: Transaction.

William N. Dunn

CANNIBALISM

The belief in the existence of man-eaters just beyond a culture's boundary is a time-honored and cherished notion for many parts of the world. In what we call advanced societies, such as our own, cannibals are thought to inhabit the remaining mysterious distant fringes of civilization such as the highlands of New Guinea and the rain forests of the Amazon. There, the inhabitants with a more limited view of the world suspect cannibals in the next valley or around the bend of the river. How and why this imagery came into existence and continues to be so compelling for both the lay public and academics alike is as debatable as it is apparent.

No better example of the longstanding Western proclivity to label distant people as cannibalistic can be found than in the work of the fifth century BCE Greek traveler Herodotus, the father of history and anthropology. Not far from the limits of Hellenic culture in an area we now recognize as central Asia, he noted (in *Herodotus: A New and Literal Version,* 1879) that "beyond the desert Anthropophagi dwell, … the only people that eat human flesh" (pp. 243, 273.) With these characteristic remarks, the author of the first account of exotic peoples set the paradigm generally employed over the succeeding centuries: First, those who did not share Western culture, those both different and inferior, are *the other*; and second, they were often labeled sight unseen as man-eaters.

This theme was repeated in some of the classic Roman texts and then later by medieval travel accounts of the then known world. Over time, many peoples, such as the Irish and the Scots, as well as the European Jews and North African Muslims, were cast by one or another obscure writer as consumers of human flesh. Eventually, the list of itinerant raconteurs included the famous Marco Polo, who in the late fourteenth century claimed to have traversed the Eurasian continent from Venice to China before residing there for a number of years.

Although the veracity of his account is now debated, what is significant is his report of unobserved cannibals on Jipangu (Japan) on the border of Kubla Khan's Mongol empire. A copy of this text, which even then was popular, was later in the library of Christopher Columbus and also occupied his imagination as he sailed into the New World while erroneously assuming he was on the eastern border of the Old World. Believing that he was in the vicinity of Jipangu, the admiral also recorded an encounter with cannibals in what was actually the Caribbean, probably in the vicinity of Cuba. Thus, for the first time contact with the rumored man-eaters was made, and the word *cannibal*, a Spanish derivation of Carib, entered the lexicon to replace Anthrophagi. Although the suspected cannibals were then seen, the act of cannibalism continued to go unobserved. This new context necessitated a revision of the ideological paradigm, which now assumed that the custom was repressed by conquest. There were also more profound practical implications, for at the time those degenerate enough to eat their own kind could be enslaved. In subsequent eras the label legitimized conquest and colonization as Western nations came into contact with a host of far-flung would-be cannibals.

This assumption and powerful image of the other as cannibal remained a feature of Western ideology for some centuries until it was eventually challenged in *The Man-Eating Myth* (Arens 1979). A review of some of the literature on the most infamous reputed man-eaters from North America, Africa, and New Guinea led to the book's conclusion that the idea of *gustatory cannibalism*—that is, an activity engaged in on a regular basis with social approval—could not be substantiated by the usual standards of academic inquiry.

The initial negative reaction to the conclusion, most explicit in a series of essays by cultural anthropologists (Brown and Tuzin 1983) has gradually lessened over time. Once the question whether it could be that so many, if not most, people of color were cannibals until contacted by white Europeans was explicitly framed for debate, it became intellectually and politically untenable in the postcolonial era to maintain what was formerly an implicit affirmative conclusion. There was also the eventual realization that the proposal did not rule out *survival and ritual cannibalism*. This new perspective, though, leads to related issues regarding how those implicated in this sort of activity are labeled, and then how to define *ritual* in a consistent manner.

As for the consumption of human flesh under dire conditions, it has been long recognized that this behavior is possible in any culture. This impression is substantiated by European shipwreck tales, as well as by the Donner Party incident when the party's members survived on the remains of their compatriots while stranded in California's Sierra Nevada Mountains in 1846. In no instance are those implicated—the French, the English, and Americans—subsequently labeled as *endo-cannibals*, eaters of their own kind. Similarly, this behavior may have been characteristic of, for example, the Inuit or other Native Americans, as deduced from historical sources or archeological evidence, such as that reported in Billman, Lambert, and Leonard's (2000) detailed article about the Mesa Verde region in the twelfth century. However, these groups are not stigmatized as cannibals by the general public. These contradictory impressions are objectively unacceptable.

The issue of *ritual* cannibalism is more complicated. Desiccated human body parts were sold as remedies for various human ailments by European and American apothecaries until the early twentieth century (Gordon-Grube 1988); some American food cultists advocate the consumption of the human placenta (Janszen 1980); and there is the use of human cadaver extracts in contemporary biomedicine, presumably to capture the strength of the deceased. These domestic customs may be considered bizarre, misguided, or even guided science, but they are never labeled ritual cannibalism. However, South American groups reported to consume the ashes of the dead for whatever reason are ipso facto deemed ritual cannibals. Again this situation is intellectually unacceptable and hints at cultural discrimination.

A recent consideration of the issue in Gananath Obeyesekere's *Cannibal Talk* (2005) recommends that we reserve the term *cannibalism* for the irrational fear that the other wants to eat us and use the term *anthropophagy* to refer to the actual practice in ritual and survival contexts. Perhaps it would be simpler to conclude that there are no cannibals in the sense of how the situation was once subjectively viewed; alternately, from a more objective contemporary perspective, we could all be cannibals. What is more obvious is that the cannibal epithet, as leveled by

one culture against another, is more common than the deed itself.

SEE ALSO *Anthropology; Religion; Rituals; Warfare, Nuclear*

BIBLIOGRAPHY

Arens, W. 1979. *The Man-Eating Myth: Anthropology and Anthropophagy.* New York: Oxford University Press.

Barker, Francis, Peter Hulme, and Margaret Iversen, eds. 1998. *Cannibalism and the Colonial World.* Cambridge, NJ: Cambridge University Press.

Billman, Brian R., Patricia M. Lambert, and L. B. Leonard. 2000. Cannibalism, Warfare, and Drought in the Mesa Verde Region During the Twelfth Century, A.D. *American Antiquity* 65: 145–178.

Brown, Paula, and Donald Tuzin, eds. 1983. *The Ethnography of Cannibalism.* Washington, DC: Society for Psychological Anthropology.

Gordon-Grube, Karen. 1988. Anthropophagy in Post-Renaissance Europe: The Tradition of Medicinal Cannibalism. *American Anthropologist* 90 (2): 405–409.

Janszen, Karen. 1980. Meat of Life. *Science Digest* (November–December): 78–81, 121.

Obeyesekere, Gananath. 2005. *Cannibal Talk: The Man-Eating Myth and Human Sacrifice in the South Seas.* Berkeley: University of California Press.

William Arens

CANTILLON, RICHARD
c. 1680–1734

Richard Cantillon was an Irish banker and economist who emigrated to Paris, where he profited from the financial scheme known as John Law's Mississippi bubble (1720). His lone surviving book, *Essai sur la nature du commerce en général* (Essay on the Nature of Commerce in General) was written around 1730 and circulated in manuscript form for a quarter century in France until it was published anonymously in 1755. Legend has it that Cantillon was murdered in London, although his biographer, Antoin Murphy, convincingly hypothesizes that he staged his murder and left the country to avoid impending legal battles.

Cantillon's *Essai* is often considered a product of his financial exploits because it contains a defense of usury that justifies charging illegally high rates of interest. It also contains an analysis and condemnation of what caused the Mississippi bubble. But it is much more than a mere position paper. Brevity notwithstanding, its scope and probity raise the *Essai* to the level of a theoretical treatise.

When the economist William Stanley Jevons (1835–1882) rediscovered Cantillon's *Essai* in 1880, he called it the "cradle of political economy" and "the first treatise on economics." The English translator of the *Essai*, Henry Higgs (1864–1940), wrote that Cantillon was "the economist's economist." Joseph Schumpeter (1883–1950) labeled the *Essai* the first "bird's-eye view of economic life" Schumpeter (1954, p. 222), and Murray Rothbard (1926–1995) dubbed Cantillon "the founding father of modern economics." Antoin Murphy concluded that the *Essai* has "stood the test of time and is of increasing interest to modern-day economists."

Cantillon's contributions to economics include critical aspects of methodology, such as the use of *ceteris paribus*, price and wage determination, the crucial role of the entrepreneur, the circular-flow nature of the economy, the price-specie flow mechanism, the function of money, and the problems of inflation. He showed that wealth was determined not by money but by the ability to consume, and that the source of wealth was land and productive labor. He demonstrated that saving and investment were critical to productivity and higher wages, and he maintained that in the absence of government intervention, markets—including the market for loans—would be regulated by competition. He also analyzed the forces that cause business cycles and stock market bubbles. It has been asserted that Cantillon's puzzling use of the term *intrinsic value* now represents the discovery, 140 years prior to its conventional dating, of the concept of opportunity cost, by means of which the economist analyzes not just the ticket price of a good, but the full cost to the decision maker, including his or her time.

Despite its relative obscurity, Cantillon's *Essai* was very influential. It provided a major stimulus to the founding of the physiocrat school in 1757. There is now strong evidence that it influenced David Hume's (1711–1776) economics. Adam Smith (1723–1790) referred to Cantillon in the *Wealth of Nations* (1776), where even the *invisible hand* is evocative of Cantillon. There are also strong parallels between Cantillon and Charles Louis Montesquieu (1689–1755), Étienne Bonnot de Condillac (1715–1780), Anne Robert Jacques Turgot (1721–1781), and Jean-Baptiste Say (1767–1832). Thus, Cantillon foreshadowed the physiocrat and classical schools of economics and the economics of the French Enlightenment.

SEE ALSO *Economics; Economics, Classical; Hume, David; Inflation; Laissez Faire; Law, John; Money; Physiocracy; Scottish Moralists; Smith, Adam; South Sea Bubble; Value*

BIBLIOGRAPHY

Cantillon, Richard. [1755] 1959. *Essai sur la nature du commerce en general*, ed. and trans. Henry Higgs. London: Cass.

Murphy, Antoin E. 1986. *Richard Cantillon: Entrepreneur and Economist*. New York: Oxford University Press.

Schumpeter, Joseph A. 1954. *History of Economic Analysis*. New York: Oxford University Press.

Mark Thornton

CAPACITY, FULL
SEE *Full Capacity.*

CAPITAL

Capital can mean many things, including a sum of money, an invested fund, a set of produced means of production, or human skills ("human capital"). In the theory of production, distribution, value, and growth, the term *capital* refers to capital goods or investment goods and skills. In this perspective, capital is an accumulable factor of production, as opposed to land and simple labor, which are not. The means of production encompass raw materials, tools, and instruments of production, and in the writings of some earlier authors also the means of subsistence enabling workers to perform their tasks. To the extent that natural resources, such as land, first have to be brought into a form that can be used productively, the investment in these resources and the resources themselves become amalgamated into what Karl Marx (1818–1883) referred to as "la terre-capital" (land-capital).

Capital in the sense of capital goods is typically grouped in broad categories, including the following. *Circulating* or *working* capital refers to capital goods advanced at the beginning of the period of production that contribute exclusively to the period's output: they "disappear" from the scene at the same time as their value is transferred to the product. *Fixed* capital, in contrast, refers to capital goods that are long-lived and cannot be traced on a given unit of output. In their case, the idea of a material-cum-value transmigration into the product seems to lose any foundation. However, as was suggested already at the time of the classical economists and was rigorously shown by the mathematician John von Neumann (1903–1957) and the economist Piero Sraffa (1898–1983), a coherent treatment is possible using a joint-products framework: a fixed capital item that enters production at the beginning of the production period is considered a different commodity from the item that exits at its end. In this way, fixed capital can be reduced to circulating capital.

In Marx we find the distinction between *constant* and *variable* capital: the latter refers to raw materials, tools, and instruments of production and represents *dead labor;* the former refers to wage goods spent in employing living labor, which, according to Marx, is the sole creator of value. American economist John Bates Clark (1847–1938) distinguished between *capital* and *capital goods*, the former being a fund of value earning its owner a return, interest, which equals the *marginal productivity of capital.*

As these examples show, a main issue in capital theory is whether capital is "productive" in the sense that it explains the existence of *profits* or *interest.* Critical reviews of early profit theories were put forward by Marx (1905–1910) and the Austrian economist Eugen von Böhm-Bawerk (1884). These authors developed their own approaches against the background of the earlier literature. At the cost of severe simplification, the various traditions in the theory of capital and distribution may be divided into two principal groups, one rooted in the surplus approach of the classical economists, the other in the demand and supply approach of the marginalist authors. Both traditions developed their arguments essentially within a long-period general framework of the analysis centered on the concept of a uniform rate of profit (or interest) and the corresponding set of normal prices.

The classical authors explained profits in terms of the *surplus product* left after the means of production used up in the course of production of given outputs in the system as a whole and the means of subsistence in the support of workers had been deducted from these outputs. Given wages are thus a characteristic feature of the early classical economists' approach. (The level of wages was then discussed in another part of the theory, typically by taking into account, for example, whether the society was "improving" or stagnant.) Production was conceived as a *circular flow* involving a strong degree of interconnectedness of the different industries of the economy. The rate of profits, expressed in material terms, is the ratio between the social surplus and social capital, that is, two aggregates of heterogeneous commodities. A comparison of these two vectors necessitated the development of a theory of value. The classical economists tried to tackle this problem typically by first identifying an "ultimate measure of value," which was designed to render heterogeneous commodities homogeneous. Several authors, including David Ricardo (1772–1823) and Marx, then reached the conclusion that "labor" was the sought standard and therefore advocated some version of the labor theory of value. By means of this theory, some of these authors, in a first step, determined the rate of profits and afterward, in a second

step, used their finding to determine normal competitive prices. Ladislaus von Bortkiewicz (1868–1931) aptly called this approach *successivist.*

Yet, as Sraffa showed, the successivist approach cannot generally be sustained: "the distribution of the surplus must be determined through the same mechanism and at the same time as are the prices of commodities" (1960, p. 6), that is, simultaneously. The classical authors did not have the instrument of simultaneous equations and the mathematics needed in order to solve them at their disposal. This helps to explain why they had recourse to the labor theory of value. This landed them, in the case of Marx, in the (in)famous problem of the "transformation" of labor values in prices of production. Commodities were produced by means of commodities and there was no way to circumnavigate simultaneous equations. Sraffa showed that a coherent formulation of the classical approach that was independent of the labor theory of value was possible: The rate of profits and competitive prices could be determined consistently in terms of the givens of the problem under consideration: (1) the system of production in use, characterized by the dominant methods of production employed to produce given gross outputs; and (2) the ruling real wage rate(s), or the share of wages.

The alternative marginalist explanation traced profits back to the productivity-enhancing effect of the use of capital goods. It consisted essentially of a generalization of the principle of intensive diminishing returns in agriculture indiscriminately to all industries and all factors of production alike. The older marginalist authors, with the exception of the French economist Léon Walras (1834–1910), were aware of the fact that in order to be consistent with the concept of a long-period equilibrium, the capital endowment of the economy could not be conceived as a set of given physical quantities of heterogeneous capital goods, but had to be expressed as a value magnitude: its commodity composition was seen to be a part and parcel of the equilibrium solution, determined by (1) preferences, (2) the technical alternatives from which cost-minimizing producers can choose, and (3) initial endowments of the economy of labor, land, and "value capital." The formidable problem for the marginalist approach consisted in the necessity of establishing the concept of a *quantity of capital*, which could be expressed independently of the *price of its service*, or the rate of profits, and whose relative scarcity then determined that rate. If such a concept could be shown to exist, profits could be explained analogously to intensive rent on homogeneous land, and a theoretical edifice could be erected on the universal applicability of the principle of demand and supply.

Doubts as to the sustainability of this concept had already surfaced at an early time, and had prompted some authors such as Friedrich August von Hayek (1899–

1992), Erik Lindahl (1891–1960), and John R. Hicks (1904–1989) in the late 1920s and early 1930s to abandon the long-period method and adopt instead temporary and intertemporal equilibrium methods (Garegnani 1976). Yet it was only during the so-called Cambridge controversies in the theory of capital in the 1960s and 1970s that the concept was conclusively shown to be untenable in general (see Garegnani 1970; Kurz and Salvadori 1995, chap. 14). The concept can only be used in exceedingly special cases, and it is ironic to see that these are precisely those cases in which the labor theory of value applies. Despite these findings, the concept is still widely employed, in much of macrotheory, for example, with its reliance on the (infamous) aggregate production function. In more recent times, temporary and intertemporal models have also come under attack (see the contributions by Pierangelo Garegnani and Bertram Schefold in Kurz [2000]).

With the process of globalization going on, there is a tendency toward an internationalization of capital and the worldwide equalization of the rate of profits. An analysis of the factors affecting this rate is an important task in contemporary accumulation and growth theory.

SEE ALSO *Cambridge Capital Controversy; Equity Markets; Hedging; Liquidity Premium; Marx, Karl; Physical Capital; Psychological Capital; Social Capital*

BIBLIOGRAPHY

Böhm-Bawerk, Eugen von. 1884. *Kapital und Kapitalzins.* Vol. 1: *Geschichte und Kritik der Kapitalzins-Theorien.* Innsbruck, Austria: Wagner. English translation: 1890. *Capital and Interest: A Critical History of Economical Theory.* Trans. William Smart. London: Macmillan.

Garegnani, Pierangelo. 1970. Heterogeneous Capital, the Production Function, and the Theory of Distribution. *Review of Economic Studies* 37: 291–325.

Garegnani, Pierangelo. 1976. On a Change in the Notion of Equilibrium in Recent Work on Value and Distribution. In *Essays in Modern Capital Theory*, eds. Murray Brown, Kazuo Sato, and Paul Zarembka, 25–45. Amsterdam: North-Holland.

Kurz, Heinz D., ed. 2000. *Critical Essays on Piero Sraffa's Legacy in Economics.* Cambridge, U.K.: Cambridge University Press.

Kurz, Heinz D., and Neri Salvadori. 1995. *Theory of Production: A Long-Period Analysis.* Cambridge, U.K., and New York: Cambridge University Press.

Marx, Karl. 1905–1910. *Theorien über den Mehrwert.* Ed. by Karl Kautsky. Stuttgart, Germany: J. H. W. Dietz. English translation: 1954. *Theories of Surplus Value.* 3 vols. Moscow: Progress Publishers.

Sraffa, Piero. 1960. *Production of Commodities by Means of Commodities: Prelude to a Critique of Economic Theory.* Cambridge, U.K.: Cambridge University Press.

Heinz D. Kurz

CAPITAL, HUMAN
SEE *Human Capital.*

CAPITAL, PHYSICAL
SEE *Physical Capital.*

CAPITAL, PSYCHOLOGICAL
SEE *Psychological Capital.*

CAPITAL, SOCIAL
SEE *Social Capital.*

CAPITAL ACCOUNT
SEE *Balance of Payments; Currency Appreciation and Depreciation.*

CAPITAL ACCUMULATION
SEE *Accumulation of Capital.*

CAPITAL ASSET PRICING MODEL
SEE *Finance.*

CAPITAL CONTROLS
Capital controls are the legal and quasi-legal regulations that govern the movement of capital (money, credit and

other financial assets; direct investment, and capital goods) across national borders, to restrict or stimulate out-flows or inflows, particularly speculative and abnormal flows, of capital. In short, capital controls are government practices that influence the volume, direction, character, and/or timing of short- and long-term capital transfers. The capital control regulations a government uses are categorized into four types: foreign exchange regulations (and exchange rate regimes); tax and revenue-generating policies (surcharges); investment and credit regulations; and trade or commercial restrictions. The status and enforceability of capital controls range from official/legal restrictions that are fully enforceable (if the administration desires), to bureaucratic restrictions left to the policies and discretion of regulatory agencies (and their resources), to social/customary restrictions that are enforced more through custom, cultural mores, and goodwill between the parties than any explicit law or policy.

PURPOSES, USES, AND FUNCTIONS

Although often maligned as counterproductive or ridiculed as ineffective, capital controls are used more than trade restrictions, and have been used throughout economic history by almost every country. Countries use capital controls for various purposes and for a wide variety of reasons, in particular to lessen the effects of volatile disequilibriating capital flows; to lessen capital flight; and to protect infant industries. Justifications for the use of capital controls include sheltering or isolating a country from volatile capital movements; saving foreign exchange and keeping domestic and foreign finances under national control; facilitating domestic full employment; forcing repatriation of nonreported capital; and generating government revenues.

In twentieth-century history the worldwide financial instability of the 1920s and 1930s led many economists and policy makers to advocate the use of capital controls. In the early 1930s, the English economist John Maynard Keynes was a strong proponent of capital controls and argued for their international institutionalization with the establishment of the International Monetary Fund (IMF) at the Bretton Woods conference in 1944. The IMF charter included a compromise, accepting the use of capital controls, particularly on capital account transactions, under specific conditions with a finite timetable, but promoting the principles of free trade.

Studies that have examined the use of capital controls find them to have helped countries control capital flight, maintain the desired exchange rate and desired level of international reserves, reduce exchange and interest rate volatility, retain domestic savings and protect labor's wage share, increase government revenues, and maintain the domestic tax base.

In her *Capital Control, Financial Regulation, and Industrial Policy in South Korea and Brazil* (1996) Jessica Gordon Nembhard explained that capital controls have a purpose within a country's development plan, in particular as the apex of a triad of complementary industrial development policies including credit controls and government entrepreneurship and economic planning. During the 1980s both the Republic of Korea (South Korea) and Brazil, for example, used similar financial strategies to encourage and support industrial development. These policies included capital controls, credit controls and preferential credit allocation, fiscal incentives, and trade restrictions to both control and reward the domestic public and private sectors for following the national development plans. There were structural differences, however, between the level of financial control, the types of restrictions used, and the two countries' abilities to effectively implement and maintain policies and planning efforts. The Republic of Korea was more successful than Brazil because of the specific types and configuration of controls used, the high level of financial control held by the state, the comprehensiveness of the coordination of government planning, and the administrative skills and consistency of implementation and enforcement exhibited by the Korean bureaucracy. South Korea had a more commercially open but financially closed economy. This combination worked well for many years.

CONTEMPORARY UTILIZATION OF CONTROLS AND TRENDS IN USE

Even with the international pressure for liberalization of capital controls coming mostly from the United States and the multilateral organizations such as the IMF and the World Bank, at the end of 2000 97.8 percent, or 182 of the 186 member countries of the IMF, maintained some level of restriction on capital account transactions (Monetary and Exchange Affairs Department [MEAD] 2003, p. 43). Most widely used restrictions were on transactions by commercial banks and other credit institutions, foreign direct investment, and real estate transactions. This was an increase in capital account restrictions from the 180 in 1997 and the 136 of 178, or 77.5 percent, of members in 1992. In addition, 133 countries, or 71.5 percent, continued to have controls on current account transactions in 2000 (MEAD 2003, p. 55), an increase from the 92 or 51.6 percent of countries in 1992. Most widely used were controls on import payments and on export proceeds, although few countries classified as "advanced" used current account restrictions. Among the group of countries categorized as "less developed" or "developing," use of controls actually increased between 1975 and 1989, when many European countries (members of the Organization for Economic Cooperation and Development [OECD]) were reducing their use of controls, and were maintained for the most part (with some fluctuation) throughout the 1990s.

According to the Monetary and Exchange Affairs Department of the IMF (2003), between 1997 and 2001 the "momentum of liberalization" slowed even though financial globalization continued and exchange rate regimes tended to move toward greater flexibility. MEAD found an increased use of certain types of capital controls on selected capital transactions such as those affecting institutional investors. MEAD suggested that countries become increasingly concerned with "risks associated with capital account liberalization following a series of crises in emerging market economics," which may explain the increased use of restrictions (MEAD 2003, p. 40).

LIBERALIZATION, ARGUMENTS AGAINST, AND THEORY OF THE SECOND BEST

Arguments against capital controls based on traditional economic theory assume that unrestricted capital movements and free trade are *Pareto optimal* (perfectly competitive) in a Walrasian economy. Restricted financial markets are assumed to be inefficient, to distort capital movements and to impede economic growth, because they misallocate resources, reduce investment opportunities, and hamper exchange rate flexibility and other automatic stabilizers. In addition, capital controls are considered ineffective because it is assumed that they cannot be enforced and only autarkic countries use them. Black markets, usury, and other illegal exchanges are presumed to be the evidence of inefficient markets and lack of enforceability. Governments, organizations, and scholars interested in promoting international economic integration, and the right of the owners of capital to take their resources and make their profits anywhere, support liberalization or easing of capital restrictions. Countries are supposed to use exchange rate and interest rate adjustment (flexible rates and devaluation) to address volatile capital movements and not use capital controls.

In traditional models capital controls are sometimes justified as a second-best solution in the face of temporary rigidities or distortions in the market, such as when it is necessary to defend an exchange rate disequilibrium, or when equalizing domestic with world interest rates limits the effectiveness of national monetary and fiscal policies. Some studies find that capital controls work well in the presence of other protectionist policies. Capital controls can, or should according to theory, be lifted or liberalized when the other distortions are removed, once a country's economy is more advanced, and/or in order for a country to join the world economy and open up its markets. Proponents of capital controls find that the distortions

and inequities are not temporary conditions, but perpetual market failures that require intervention. Empirical studies find that the use of controls continues. Restrictions on capital accounts can be rational and effective, evasion can be mitigated, and enforcement strengthened, especially when they are part of a set of strategic economic development policies.

SEE ALSO *Capital Flight; Dirigiste; Economic Growth; Financial Markets; Industrialization; Liberalization, Trade; Theory of Second Best*

BIBLIOGRAPHY

Alesina, Alberto, Vittorio Grilli, and Gian Maria Milesi-Ferretti. 1994. The Political Economy of Capital Controls. In *Capital Mobility: The Impact on Consumption, Investment, and Growth*, ed. Leonardo Leiderman and Assaf Razin, 289–321. Cambridge, U.K.: Cambridge University Press.

Ariyoshi, Akira, Karl Habermeier, Bernard Laurens, et al. 2000. Capital Controls: Country Experiences with Their Use and Liberalization. Occasional Paper 190. Washington, DC: International Monetary Fund, May 17. http://www.imf.org/external/pubs/ft/op/op190.

Bhagwati, Jagdish. 1978. *Anatomy and Consequences of Exchange Control Regimes*. Cambridge, MA: Ballinger Publishing Company.

Bloomfield, Arthur. 1946. Postwar Control of International Capital Movements. *The American Economic Review* 36: (2) (May): 687–716.

Caves, Richard E. 1976. The Welfare Economics of Controls on Capital Movements. In *Capital Movements and Their Control: Proceedings of the Second Conference of the International Center for Monetary and Banking Studies*, ed. Alexander K. Swoboda, 31–46. Geneva: A.W. Sijthoff-Leiden, Institut Universitaire de Hautes Etudes Internationales.

Cunningham, Thomas J. 1991. Liberal Discussion of Financial Liberalization. *Economic Review* 76: (6) (November/December): 1–8.

Edwards, Sebastian. 1986. The Order of Liberalization of the Current and Capital Accounts of the Balance of Payments. In *Economic Liberalization in Developing Countries*, eds. M. Choksi and D. Papgeorgiou, 185–223. Oxford: Basil Blackwell.

Gordon Nembhard, Jessica. 1996. *Capital Control, Financial Regulation, and Industrial Policy in South Korea and Brazil*. Westport, CT: Praeger Publishers.

Haaparanta, Pertti. 1988. Liberalization and Capital Flight. *The Economic and Social Review* 19: (4) (July): 237–248.

International Monetary Fund. 1993 (and various years including 2004). Summary Features of Exchange and Trade Systems in Member Countries. *Exchange Arrangements and Exchange Restrictions*, Annual Report, pp. 590–596.

Kaplan, Ethan, and Dani Rodrik. 2001. Did the Malaysian Capital Controls Work? Working Paper, Kennedy School of Government, Harvard University. http://ksghome.harvard.edu/~drodrik/Malaysia%20controlspdf.

Keynes, John Maynard. 1933. National Self-Sufficiency. *The Yale Review* 22: (4) (June): 755–769.

Krueger, Anne O. 1978. *Liberalization Attempts and Consequences.* Cambridge, MA: Ballinger Publishing Company.

Krugman, Paul. 1989. *Exchange Rate Instability.* Cambridge, MA: MIT Press.

Monetary and Exchange Affairs Department. 2003. *Exchange Arrangements and Foreign Exchange Markets: Developments and Issues.* Washington, DC: International Monetary Fund.

Neely, Christopher. 1999. An Introduction to Capital Controls. *Federal Reserve Bank of St. Louis Review* (November/December): 13–30. http://research.stlouisfed.org/publications/review/99/11/9911 cn.pdf.

Jessica Gordon Nembhard

CAPITAL FLIGHT

Capital flight is generally defined as an outflow of funds from a country motivated by an adverse change in the country's economic, political, or social environment. Some believe that this definition is too broad. They distinguish between outflows that reflect "normal" international diversification motivated by marginal changes in risk-adjusted returns and funds fleeing or propelled across national borders during a crisis. According to this view, only the latter category represents true capital flight. Related definitions restrict capital flight to short-term speculative outflows—"hot" money—or to an outflow of illegal transactions only. Some studies distinguish between the determinants of the outward flow of funds and those of the accumulated stock of capital flight over a period of time. To a great extent, the precise definition of capital flight used in any study is determined both by the purpose of the study and the available data.

Developmental economists tend to define capital flight broadly as the net unrecorded capital outflows for any reason from any capital-poor developing country. Other critics argue that this use of the term is more of a judgment than a definition—that *capital flight* is just a pejorative term for international diversification by a developing country. Defined in this way, capital flight presents developmental economics with a paradox. It is often observed that residents of a developing country engage in capital flight at the same time that entities in high-income countries are lending to or investing in the same developing country. How can both of these decisions be rational?

BURDEN OF CAPITAL FLIGHT

If the scale of capital flight is large enough, it will have both short-term and long-term adverse impacts. An example of the former is the sharp increase in capital flight during the Asian financial crisis of the late 1990s. The ability of countries in the region to deal with the bursting of domestic asset bubbles was severely constrained not only by a rapid and large outflow of capital but also by the necessity to immediately impose higher interest rates and capital controls in an attempt to slow the capital flight, even though these policies worsened the domestic situation.

In the long-term, capital flight tends to reduce gross domestic product (GDP) growth. Especially in developing countries, domestic savings diverted into foreign holdings will not result in domestic investment. This is especially harmful because the marginal social benefit of investment in such countries tends to be greater than the marginal private benefit. Capital flight is also generally associated with an increase in a country's foreign debt. Furthermore, the possibility of capital flight limits a government's policy choices, as some monetary and exchange-rate policies will lead to an acceleration of such flight.

In addition, capital flight tends to not only shrink a country's tax base but also make taxes less progressive. Wealthier families tend to have more opportunities to hide their funds abroad in order to conceal them from the tax collector. Capital flight facilitates corruption by providing concealment and sanctuary for ill-gotten gains. Finally, the possibility of large-scale capital flight discourages aid from international organizations and investment from other countries.

ESTIMATING CAPITAL FLIGHT

Capital flight involves a balancing of secrecy, expected returns, and risk. Attempts to increase the secrecy of capital flight, perhaps to avoid detection by a tax authority, tend to reduce return or increase risk. This necessary compromise increases the likelihood that capital flight will leave indirect evidence. While there are many methods of estimating capital flight, most are variations of either the balance of payments method or the residual method.

The balance of payments method assumes that the most important characteristic of flight capital is that it is "hot" money. Small changes in perceived returns or risks could result in a rapid discontinuous transfer or *wave* of funds moving out of the country. This wave will come to an end when investors have adjusted the share of each country's assets in their portfolios based on the new perceived return/risk profile. Based on this characteristic, the balance of payments estimate of capital flight is equal to the sum of (1) reported short-term capital exports by the nonbank sector and (2) the balancing entry, errors, and omissions. The inclusion of the latter reflects the belief that errors and omissions are largely composed of unrecorded short-term capital flows.

A more widely accepted method of estimating capital flight concentrates on capital flight as a residual. The current account balance, changes in international reserves, and the amount of net foreign direct investment determine a country's necessary amount of international borrowing. If actual foreign borrowing exceeds this necessary amount, then it is assumed that the difference (or residual) represents additional borrowing to offset capital flight. The balance of payments method and the residual measure tend to provide a similar rough guide to the pattern of a country's capital flight, but the residual method usually results in larger estimates of the size of these outflows.

Most studies of capital flight adjust their estimates to reflect the unique characteristics of each country both with respect to the treatment of foreign financial assets and liabilities, and the possibility of misinvoicing. Not all foreign financial assets are taken as evidence of capital flight; some may be necessary to facilitate foreign trade and finance and will have been reported to the developing country's government. These "legitimate" foreign financial assets are often subtracted from capital flight estimates. Another common adjustment is to use creditor data to fill gaps in a country's foreign debt statistics.

A more important adjustment is to correct for deliberate trade misinvoicing used to circumvent trade controls, avoid import tariffs, or facilitate capital flight. A resident may underinvoice his exports and then direct the unreported difference between the invoice amount and his actual receipts to some financial haven. Underinvoicing of exports (or overinvoicing of imports) widens the reported trade deficit and therefore reduces the residual estimate of capital flight. Counterpart data can be used to correct for misinvoicing. The export (or import) numbers of a country are replaced by the import (or export) numbers, adjusted for the cost of insurance and freight, of any of its trading partners that are believed to publish more reliable trade data.

DETERMINANTS OF CAPITAL FLIGHT

There is no consensus on the primary determinates of capital flight. The most widely held view is that capital flight results from attempts by portfolio holders to maximize risk-adjusted returns. The optimal portfolio will be based on the differential between domestic and foreign interest rates, beliefs about the relative over- or undervaluation of exchange rates, and expectations of monetary and credit policies at home and abroad as well as the rela-

tive risks that investors face in both countries. If one of these variables shifts in favor of another country, capital flight will occur. However, if the shift is in favor of the home country, there will be a repatriation of flight capital.

The simple portfolio model fails to explain the paradoxical situation in which portfolio holders in a developing country engage in capital flight at the same time that portfolio holders in high-income countries are investing in the country. One explanation is that domestic and foreign portfolio holders face discriminatory treatment— that is, they face different risks or returns. A developing country may provide tax benefits to foreign investors from high-income countries, or these investors may believe that they face less risk of an adverse change in regulation because of the implied protection of their home governments. As discussed below, this differential in benefits may lead to *round-tripping* or *revolving-door* transactions.

Transaction costs may provide another explanation of this paradox. Transaction costs include the costs of gathering accurate information about an asset or liability, finding and evaluating the other parties involved, negotiating an agreement, and possibly enforcing this agreement. In well-developed financial markets, transaction costs tend to account for only a small fraction of the value of a financial transaction, and the costs associated with international transactions tend to be higher than those associated with domestic ones.

However, in developing countries, neither of these assumptions is necessarily true. Developing countries tend to have a lower capital/labor ratio than high-income countries, and therefore the real return on capital in developing countries should be higher. However, the existence of large transaction costs may motivate portfolio managers in developing countries to split their holdings based on desired maturity. Short-term holdings will be invested internationally where transaction costs are lower (capital flight). However, long-term holdings, with a desired maturity long enough to amortize higher transaction costs, will take advantage of the higher real return and be invested at home. Therefore domestic and foreign investors with a long enough maturity preference may be willing to invest in a developing country experiencing capital flight.

Capital flight and external borrowing tend to be highly correlated for a variety of reasons. Both may simultaneously increase as a reaction to poor economic management. Foreign borrowing may cause capital flight by increasing the likelihood of a debt crisis and therefore increasing economic uncertainty. Capital flight may cause foreign borrowing in order to replace lost capital and foreign exchange. Foreign borrowing may occur to provide the funds for capital flight. Finally, round-tripping or revolving-door transactions may simultaneously increase both flight and debt. Round tripping occurs when portfolio holders in developing countries send funds to foreign banks with the understanding that these banks will lend these funds to entities in the less-developed countries controlled by the portfolio holders. The usual motivation for round tripping is to take advantage of government guarantees for foreign loans.

Corruption, the abuse of public power for private benefit, is often associated with capital flight because corruption increases the risk of investing in a country. Also individuals may send funds abroad to hide them from corrupt government officials, and these officials may illegally shift funds abroad to launder the bribes that they received. Foreign banks may also facilitate capital flight by either lending to corrupt governments in return for generous fees or providing special saving facilities to help corrupt officials hide their loot. In addition, studies have found that capital flight tends to be a function of past capital flight, the general macroeconomic environment, and political factors, such as political instability and poor governance.

CAPITAL CONTROLS AND OTHER MEANS OF REDUCING CAPITAL FLIGHT

Capital controls seek to reduce capital flight by reducing its risk-adjusted returns. When controls are enforced, financial or trade activities associated with capital flight may require additional documentation, permission, fees, or the posting of bonds. Despite the widespread use of capital controls, they appear to be more effective as a means of slowing capital flight rather than of preventing it entirely. The value of capital controls is that by acting as a speed bump they provide decision makers with time to decide on policies, coordinate their efforts with international organizations such as the International Monetary Fund, and execute policies effectively before uncontrolled capital flight brings about a financial collapse.

However, there are at least four reasons why capital controls may fail to reduce net capital flight—capital flight minus repatriation—in the long term. First, imposition of capital controls may be a signal that a government intends to adopt perverse fiscal or monetary policies. Second, before they will repatriate existing flight capital, portfolio holders will now require a higher degree of confidence in future relative risk-adjusted returns because new controls will make future capital flight more difficult. Third, reporting requirements, currency controls, enforcement procedures, and bureaucratic influence intended to prevent capital flight may significantly reduce the risk-adjusted return on domestic investments. Finally, imposition of a particular set of capital controls may simply encourage a search for new methods of capital flight.

This policy-avoidance response may be as simple as bribing a new official, or it may shift capital flight into an entirely different channel. The longer capital controls are in place, the less effective they become.

A long-term strategy for reducing capital flight should focus on getting the economic fundamentals right. In addition to achieving reasonable exchange and interest rates, the adoption of a pro-growth economic policy may be the most important way to reduce capital flight and encourage repatriation. In developing countries, an aggressive anticorruption effort should also be a part of any pro-growth policy.

SEE ALSO *Bribery; Capital; Capital Controls; Corruption; Crime and Criminology; Economic Crises; Finance; Hot Money; Loan Pushing; Political Instability, Indices of; Transaction Cost*

BIBLIOGRAPHY

Boyce, James K. 1992. The Revolving Door? External Debt and Capital Flight: A Philippine Case Study. *World Development* 20 (3): 335–349.

Cuddington, John T. 1986. *Capital Flight: Estimates, Issues, and Explanations.* Princeton Studies of International Finance 58. Princeton, NJ: Princeton University Press.

Darity, William, Jr. 1991. Banking on Capital Flight. In *Economic Problems of the 1990s: Europe, the Developing Countries, and the United States*, eds. Paul Davidson and J. A. Kregel, 31–40. Brookfield, VT: Edward Elgar Publishing.

Epstein, Gerald A., ed. 2005. *Capital Flight and Capital Controls in Developing Countries.* Northampton, MA: Edward Elgar Publishing.

Gunter, Frank R. 2004. Capital Flight from China: 1984–2001. *China Economic Review* 15 (1): 63–85.

Lessard, Donald R., and John Williamson. 1987. *Capital Flight and Third World Debt.* Washington, DC: Institute for International Economics.

Ndikumana, Léonce, and James K. Boyce. 2003. Public Debts and Private Assets: Explaining Capital Flight from Sub-Saharan African Countries. *World Development* 31 (1): 107–130.

Walter, Ingo. 1985. *Secret Money: The World of International Financial Secrecy.* Lexington, MA: Lexington Books.

Frank R. Gunter

CAPITAL MEASUREMENT

SEE *Cambridge Capital Controversy; Capital.*

CAPITAL PUNISHMENT

SEE *Punishment.*

CAPITAL THEORY

SEE *Capital.*

CAPITALISM

Capitalism, first used as a term by Werner Sombart around the beginning of the twentieth century, is a social system dominated by economic relations, particularly market relations. The institution of private property is elaborately developed and well secured, and property owners derive income from the sale of output made with labor hired for wages or salaries. The income of property owners can appear as profit, interest, or rent, depending mainly on the kind of property involved. Workers have little or no income-earning assets other than their capacity to labor, which they contract to sell to property owners (capitalists) for a definite period of time but not for a definite intensity. Property income may be increased by getting workers to increase the intensity of labor, that is, to work harder, faster, or smarter.

Although markets existed in a great variety of social systems, appearing back to the furthest extent of recorded history, capitalism is unique in the degree to which market relations affect every aspect of the social order. According to Karl Polanyi in *The Great Transformation* (1944), the rise of capitalism represents a major institutional reversal. Precapitalist societies often provided for markets within an elaborately structured cultural framework, in which social status and social roles were already established, such that markets played a decidedly subordinate role. Trade and traders had their place, often clearly delimited in time, space, and permitted function. Under capitalism, in contrast, the market itself increasingly provides the framework for the determination of social status and social roles; market relations increasingly determine the time, space, and function of every other aspect of the culture. Cultures are modified and subordinated to global markets, creating a world system beyond any single culture's design.

RESOURCE MARKETS: LAND AND LABOR

Specifically the rise of capitalism involves legal developments allowing for efficient markets for land and other natural resources. The sovereign rights of the state and the blood rights of family, clan, and tribe—whatever these may include—become limited and clearly distinguished from modern property rights, so that real estate and rental markets as well as more esoteric markets in mineral rights may thrive unencumbered by ambiguities and restrictions of tradition.

Similarly efficient labor markets are developed to accommodate wage labor on a massive scale that transcends or escapes human relationships based on tradition, intimate acquaintance, or direct coercion. In practically all precapitalist societies, there are some kinds of "subsistence" activity—perhaps in hunting, gathering, farming, fishing, or herding—to which almost anyone could turn for a living in default of any more exalted assignment or organized function. In developed capitalist societies, there is no default living. Access to requisite land or natural resources is not free and not otherwise institutionally guaranteed. Significant property ownership is neither universal nor necessarily even widespread in the population. In fact in the long actual history of the establishment of legal private property in its modern form in many countries, the bulk of property, through force and fraud, came into the hands of old elites and entrepreneurial upstarts, leaving most people without property and without legal access to resources or means of production. Hence involvement in market relations and in social networks becomes inevitable, and that presents a distinct set of challenges to the propertyless, more or less forcing many of them into the labor market and into a weak bargaining stance vis-à-vis the owners of property rights in the means of production.

An essential insight in Karl Marx's *Capital* (1867) is that the captive excess supply of labor, or in Marx's vivid terms the "reserve army of labor," creates a competitive environment in which workers can be expected to be compliant and wages are negotiated down to subsistence level. Specifically wages are not expected to bear any particular relation to the value of goods produced and sold by the employer-owners, and that provides a nonfleeting source of profitability. Thus Marx demonstrated that regular profit can come from property ownership in the means of production, even if those means of production are themselves produced entirely by workers.

Naturally the state of the capitalist labor market presents some glorious opportunities to employers, but it also presents challenges. Mere biological subsistence turns out to be quite distinct from maintenance of healthy, reliable, motivated, and skilled employees. To the extent that employers scan their labor supply for quality as well as quantity, they seek a labor market different in structure from that envisioned by classical and Marxist economists. As the experience of industrialists from Robert Owen in the 1820s to Henry Ford in the early 1900s repeatedly illustrated, it can be profitable under certain circumstances to invest more in the labor force, paying workers more than is customary or appears necessary in terms of current labor market conditions. This insight gave rise to the concept of human capital, according to which investment in workers can yield a return as readily as might investment in any other kind of productive equipment; to human resource management, including elaborate segmentation and structuring of the labor market; and finally to a variety of state-sponsored programs socializing the cost and standardizing the practice of basic education, sanitation, health care, and other basic investments in the population thought to improve the overall efficiency and productivity of labor. In short, actual labor markets fail to correspond to the classical vision to the extent that labor power cannot be merely "reproduced" in families outside the market, as in the Marxist model, but requires capitalist or socialized investment for its construction and maintenance.

Another challenge facing employers is to manage workers and the work environment so that the potential for profit is actually realized. Employees rarely work at peak productivity on their own initiative based on their own organizational efforts, so investment in human capital does not in itself suffice to maximize productivity and profits. Hence the need for management to organize and supervise on behalf of the enterprise owners, and hence the constant struggle at the work site between management and labor.

ENTREPRENEURSHIP AND THE BUSINESS FIRM

Unlike in precapitalist cultures, the organizing principles of capitalism are abstract and general. Law is highly formal, aspiring to universal reach, and markets involve stereotyped interactions among anonymous participants. It is no coincidence that capitalist processes are often comprehensible as games, as witnessed by the elaboration of game theory and its rapid extension beyond political science to economics and sociology. This creates an environment uniquely amenable to entrepreneurship.

Of course entrepreneurship even as currently understood is omnipresent in all social orders. History is full of accounts of military adventurers, poseurs, prophets, travelers, and merchants who preceded the arrival of the modern capitalist epoch. Presumably no society could be so structured, so rigid and predetermined, existing under circumstances so regular and predictable, as to provide no space for the restless and adventurous to innovate through that recognizable yet undeterminable combination of design and accident. Yet modern capitalist society was the first to recognize entrepreneurship as a regular rather than extraordinary function in a wide variety of fields of endeavor. It is even encouraged.

Two aspects of entrepreneurship deserve particular attention for purposes of understanding capitalism. The first is risk taking; the second is innovation. A certain amount of risk taking is encouraged under capitalism simply through the institution of property. Legally well-defined property rights allow an unprecedented expansion of the credit system by allowing enormous amounts of value to be put at its disposal in the form of collateral without the items constituting that collateral having been withdrawn from current productive use.

Even more space for purposeful investment in potentially risky ventures is provided by the modern corporate structure of business firms responsible for the large majority of the value of goods and services produced each year. This structure has evolved to spread and limit risk and thus to encourage voluntary contributions of funds. The spreading of risk is accomplished by selling shares, each of which is typically a miniscule fraction of the firm's total outstanding value and often fairly liquid—meaning that it can often be quickly sold if the need for cash arises. Limitation of risk is accomplished by the legal device of "limited liability." The maximum an investor can lose, unlike in a sole proprietorship or normal partnership, and the maximum an investor can be held legally liable for by virtue of that kind of participation is the total value of shares he or she holds. By allowing small, limited bets on the future, the corporation encourages risk taking and provides resources for entrepreneurship.

In most societies innovation—anything new that disrupts or undermines traditional ways of doing things—is vigorously rejected, and that rejection is overcome only by enormous endurance and determination or by forcible imposition. Under capitalism, this resistance is diminished. Property is protected, but its market value is not guaranteed. According to Joseph Schumpeter in *Theory of Economic Development* (1911) and *Business Cycles* (1939), economic growth comes in waves of innovations, often revolving around some central innovation, such as alternating current, the internal combustion engine, or the microchip. The initial innovation may be accompanied by a flurry of activity amid limitless hopes and give rise to a boom, but then follows disappointment and more importantly the destruction ("creative destruction"—another term first used by Sombart) of value in now obsolete goods, equipment, technologies, and skills; this tends to lead to depression. Eventually the further spread of economic activity based on the innovation helps lead to a recovery, but these innovation-led developments would perhaps never occur were the way not first cleared during the depression by "creative destruction."

THEORETICAL CURRENTS

Economists have come to view capitalism in three major ways. The classical and neoclassical schools emphasize the spread of market relations and describe efficiency gains expected as a consequence. Marxist and related schools (e.g., that inspired by Henry George's 1879 *Progress and Poverty*) focus on power relations and class structures implied by the prevailing system of property rights and emphasize how those hamper the achievement of many of the goals typically viewed as part of social progress, such as greater equality, more democracy, and more security. The Austrian school, including Schumpeter, deemphasizes efficiency and instead promotes the innovative potential of decentralized knowledge and action. Though property rights are formally protected, the value of actual property is freely created and destroyed in the course of progress.

SEE ALSO *Competition; Development Economics; Laissez Faire; Markets; Marx, Karl; Mode of Production; Primitive Accumulation; Profits; Rate of Profit*

BIBLIOGRAPHY

George, Henry. [1879] 1912. *Progress and Poverty: An Inquiry into the Cause of Industrial Depressions and of Increase of Want with Increase of Wealth: The Remedy.* Garden City, NY: Doubleday.

Marx, Karl. [1867] 1992. *Capital: A Critique of Political Economy.* Trans. Ben Fowkes. New York: Penguin.

Polanyi, Karl. [1944] 1957. *The Great Transformation: The Political and Economic Origins of Our Time.* Boston: Beacon.

Schumpeter, Joseph. [1911] 1949. *The Theory of Economic Development: An Inquiry into Profits, Capital, Credit, Interest, and the Business Cycle.* Cambridge, MA: Harvard University Press.

Schumpeter, Joseph. 1939. *Business Cycles: A Theoretical, Historical, and Statistical Analysis of the Capitalist Process.* New York: McGraw-Hill.

Schumpeter, Joseph. [1942] 2005. *Capitalism, Socialism, and Democracy.* London: Taylor and Francis.

Sombart, Werner. [1916] 1987. *Der moderne Kapitalismus. Historisch-systematische Darstellung des gesamteuropäischen Wirtschaftslebens von seinen Anfängen bis zur Gegenwart.* Munich: DTV.

Michael J. Brun

CAPITALISM, BLACK

The term *black capitalism*, which came into frequent use in the 1960s, refers to an increased interest in business, investment, entrepreneurship, and, broadly, economic development as a component of an overall strategy of black advancement. It built on several centuries of interest among African Americans in business ownership and participation, which had been opposed and stifled by overt white opposition. It was seldom espoused simply as a desirable "free market" principle in its own right.

EARLY APPROACHES

Black capitalism represented a change from the earlier stress on community-based development, citizen participation, community organizing, and collective strategies in the War on Poverty. In its late-twentieth-century form, it also was a Republican alternative to Democratic Party priorities that had emphasized broad-based spending on education, housing, training, and public works projects. Black capitalism eventually was embraced by many black activists who saw political potential in developing strong economic institutions, both for-profit and nonprofit. They considered businesses to be potential platforms for political action. Thus, black capitalism was warily and partially embraced by some black nationalists, some separatists, and by the Nation of Islam, as compatible with their distinct objectives.

Starting in the 1960s the federal government encouraged African Americans to develop businesses, and thousands were started, but their economic impact was small. Their slow growth led federal policy makers, politicians, activists, and business leaders to look for ways to accelerate the process by using direct government and private financing, and consulting assistance targeted to those businesses that had the greatest chance of growing into substantial companies. They also encouraged increased government and corporate purchasing as a stimulus to growth. By the 1980s success was judged by normal business criteria, rather than social criteria.

In the early phases of black capitalism (1965–1970), federal policy encouraged primarily retail and service businesses. The policy was implemented through direct government and guaranteed loans, government-sponsored management and technical assistance, and government purchasing, but results were small: The thousands of businesses started with the help of federal loans and technical and procurement assistance did not become a substantial factor in community development as was originally hoped. A new view emerged—that federal policy should emphasize the creation and development of businesses that stand the best chance of becoming large and competitive, and economically significant. The new approach promoted acquisitions of larger, going concerns, the creation of sizeable venture financing companies, and new, stronger banking relationships from mainstream credit sources. This approach helped individuals who had an idea but seldom the right experience, training, or capital to run a successful business. Later, a job creation rationale was added to give the policy broader appeal. But the idea of building truly strong competitive businesses continued to be resisted by policy makers and bureaucrats charged with making Federal programs work.

The policy was a hasty response to the political and social pressures of the poverty program era. But managerial inexperience, poor locations, faulty business planning, market inadequacies, and capital shortages led to business failures. Shoplifting, employee pilferage, and other crime also increased business costs and raised risks. Racially discriminatory lenders, investors, and purchasing officers in government and corporations also impeded progress. The policy was defective, and the results were poor. The small retail and local service businesses had lower than average revenues, high costs, inexperienced management, weak capital structures, and other competitive handicaps. They concentrated in low-growth and low-margin sectors, and provided little full-time employment. Typically, they had poor locations and limited access to the wider general market. Manufacturing companies were grossly underrepresented.

For gross comparison, "minority" business receipts in 1978 were $35 billion in a $2 trillion economy—2 percent of total receipts. The goal became to increase aggregate demand, with better federal government and corporate procurement policies, to lift "minority" receipts by 1982 to $75 billion in a $2.5 trillion economy, or 3 percent of total receipts.

THE SHIFT TO SUCCESS

By 1980 to 1985, several things changed. First, there emerged a pool of African American managers and entrepreneurs with MBAs from top business schools. Second, the federal government changed its practice on delivering technical consulting assistance. Previously, management and technical assistance had suffered because of political pressures to give contracts and grants for these services to inexperienced or ineffectual local consulting organizations; the government began to give fewer but larger grants to the best of the consulting groups, and this paid off in better assistance to clients with demonstrated capacity to make consistent profits. Finally, early skeptics among the trade unionists and community activists, as well as among political Republicans and Democrats, came to recognize the value of a stronger African American business sector.

Corporate Action The disappointing results from early efforts encouraged policy makers to look for better approaches. Federal practice moved upscale, to provide financing for larger businesses, including in manufacturing, and investment in firms with the potential to become publicly held. These operations sometimes became

African American–led through acquisition. This approach was implemented through expanded venture capital, investments in promising businesses, corporate spin-offs, strengthened African American banks, and the use of existing private and government programs to increase purchasing and subcontracting from minority companies.

This tactic of building on strengths helped more businesses to become significant and competitive. An additional effect was saved and new jobs when the companies were located in labor-surplus or distressed areas—primarily in northeastern and midwestern cities and rural areas—and might otherwise have closed or moved away. So this approach also served the interests of the Department of Housing and Urban Development, the Economic Development Administration, the Community Services Administration, and the Business and Industry Office of the Farmers Home Administration in the Department of Agriculture.

Venture Capital Another step that made black capitalism effective was the growth of venture-capital firms created by farsighted companies. Although they quickly evolved into private firms with no government funding, they began by using government funds provided by minority enterprise small business investment companies (MESBIC) programs.

In 1970 the government had initiated a venture-capital program, the MESBIC, which began as an outgrowth of the previously established small business investment company (SBIC) concept. MESBICs, like SBICs, ran into financial and operating problems during the early and mid-1970s, and many of their investments did poorly or failed, but they recovered and became increasingly important financing sources in major transactions.

The MESBIC program continued to evolve, and it became more attractive to corporate investors when legislation made it possible to leverage private participation up to four times with funds at less than market interest rates. Used imaginatively by corporate sponsors, the MESBIC program provided significant equity and debt to businesses that became reliable contractors, suppliers, customers, and partners. The new thinking was that private venture-capital firms, corporate venture groups, insurance companies, investment-banking firms, and commercial finance companies could, in the right circumstances, increase their participation in these business ventures as normal business practice.

The policy worked through a network of sources to find, screen, structure, and close substantial investments, especially in the acquisition of manufacturing businesses. In the early stages, companies acquired had annual sales averaging $3 million, and were purchased for an average of $1 million. In one case, a precision screw products company was bought for $1.4 million, and a few years later, in 1978 it had sales of $3 million. The African American purchasers raised $30,000, and the remaining $1,370,000 was financed privately. This model became a basis for moving upscale and into the mainstream.

These business deals were notable only because they involved African Americans—such financings were normal in everyday business. The criteria used in selecting businesses for acquisition were not limited to specific industries or types of companies, though manufacturing was preferred. Tests of risk, profitability, manageability, and return on investment were applied. The pool of African American investor-managers remained a constraint. The flow of ventures and the availability of finances were greater than the supply of appropriate investor-managers. But the discrepancy narrowed as well-trained MBAs reached the career points where moving into these situations was appropriate.

Several major corporations established MESBICs and then capitalized them at higher levels—up to $10 million. These larger MESBICs were often industry specific. In some cases, they financed businesses that the sponsors felt could become consistent suppliers. In the entertainment industry, MCA had a MESBIC that financed entertainment-related projects and companies in music and records. MCA New Ventures and three other MESBICs put together a package of $5.3 million in cash, loans, and services for the record company T-Elect. With $7.5 million capitalization, the National Association of Broadcasters established a MESBIC that will work with the National Telecommunications and Information Administration of the Commerce Department and with the Federal Communications Commission to help African Americans acquire radio and television stations.

Ironically, MESBIC staffs—African American professionals—tended to approach investments more pragmatically than many white senior managers from sponsoring corporations. They continued to think in terms of social responsibility, and thus preferred deals that were most risky and least attractive according to normal investment criteria. Such differences in viewpoint led to conflicts: What was the real point—businesses that can grow and become competitive and profitable, or social tokenism?

Spin-Offs In the late 1970s government representatives met with senior managers of General Motors, Eastman Kodak, Bankers Trust, First Pennsylvania Bank, Chase Manhattan, Hewlett-Packard, Levi Strauss, Kaiser Aluminum and Chemical, and others to discuss selling corporate units. No deals resulted, but the meetings served the purpose of raising expectations about black capitalism.

Corporations were encouraged to sell units that could operate independently. Spin-offs and independent acquisitions were carried out as straight business transactions at market prices and with normal fees to brokers and private financial participants. No subsidies or contributions from the corporate sellers or other private parties were sought. Applicable federal, state, and local loan and guarantee programs were used to augment private financing.

Commercial Banks Another policy change toward African American business development was an effort to upgrade the 100 commercial banks. The Federal Reserve System, the Office of the Comptroller of the Currency, the Federal Deposit Insurance Corporation, and the Commerce Department worked to improve the management, staff efficiency, marketing skills, and permanent capital base of these banks. These banks grew, some by acquiring branches of major banks, during the consolidation wave of the 1980s.

Corporate Purchasing Another dimension was the growing interest from major corporations. The government encouraged purchases by providing operating grants to and encouraging corporate participation in the National Minority Purchasing Council (NMPC), which included many "Fortune 1000" companies. Through the NMPC, African American companies received $1.8 billion in purchases from corporate businesses in 1978, and this volume grew steadily over the next twenty-five years.

Government regulations and programs also encouraged or required purchasing, contracting, and subcontracting. For example, the government required companies bidding on government work worth more than $500,000 to "minority" subcontract participation. Opposition to this practice led to reversals in the courts, but it became normal business practice for many large companies.

The 8a Program Federal procurement was a key element in accelerating black capitalism. The Small Business Administration's 8a program directed government contracts to "minority" businesses. In 1977, federal policy called for the rate of federal procurement from "minority" businesses to increase substantially, from $1.8 billion annually to $3 billion. Steady increases continued over the next twenty-five years, providing a substantial revenue base. Offices of Small and Disadvantaged Business Utilization (OSDBUs) in every federal agency institutionalized this policy and increased awareness of it among bureaucrats.

Black capitalism, and the policies that followed, were initially based on the mistaken assumption that the government could help cure poverty by transforming some of the poorest into entrepreneurs and managers, almost overnight. A sober assessment of these policies led to new insights—that building on strength was a more sensible route.

The managers and entrepreneurs in whom the government and private investors invested emerged as the kinds of people whom venture capitalists and other private financiers normally bet on. The approach, thus, called for specially designed government loans and other such financing only to the extent that these approaches were needed to reduce perceived risks stemming from businesses' locations or other unusual characteristics. Another tool that stimulated acquisition opportunities was tax incentives to sellers. These tax code provisions stimulated many sales of businesses in the 1980s and 1990s. Together, these evolving techniques, practices, and strategies made possible the phenomenon that came to be known as black capitalism.

SEE ALSO *Affirmative Action; African Americans; Black Conservatism; Black Liberalism; Black Nationalism; Business; Capitalism; Collectivism; Garvey, Marcus; Nation of Islam; Poverty; Separatism*

BIBLIOGRAPHY

America, Richard F. 1980. How Minority Business Can Build On Its Strength. *Harvard Business Review* 58: (May–June).

Bates, Timothy M. 2001. Financing the Development of Urban Minority Communities: Lessons from History. *Communities and Banking*, Federal Reserve Bank of Boston. Sum: 12–15. http://ideas.repec.org/a/fip/fedbcb/y2001isump12-15.html#provider.

Bradford, William D. 2003. The Wealth Dynamics of Entrepreneurship for Black and White Families in the U.S. *Review of Income and Wealth* 49 (1): 89–116.

Graves, Earl G. 1997. *How to Succeed in Business without Being White: Straight Talk on Making it in America.* New York: HarperBusiness.

Richard F. America

CAPITALISM, MANAGERIAL

Managerial capitalism emerged in the late nineteenth and early twentieth centuries in the United States, and challenged the traditional regime of personal capitalism, which was built on competitive interaction among small firms within industries. Managerial capitalism, dominated by big firms, prevailed during the 1950–1970 period.

As pointed out by Alfred Dupont Chandler Jr. (1984), despite differences in the pace, timing, and nature of change, large firms in the United States, Europe, and Japan tended to evolve according to a common pattern. They were characterized by what Adolph Berle and Gardiner Means (1932) identified as the separation between ownership and control. Dispersed ownership associated with the concentration of power in the hands of top management defines the managerial revolution (Chandler 1977). Managerial capitalism underscored the problem of controlling managers, who were shown to trade desire for growth against fear of mergers and takeovers. In this perspective, inspired by the institutionalist approach of Thorstein Veblen (in particular his 1921 work *The Engineers and the Price System*), John Kenneth Galbraith (1967) developed a vision of managerial capitalism as an economic system based on a logic of endless accumulation where firms are run by the real decision makers—the managers (who make up the technostructure)—and not by the capital owners. For Robin Lapthorn Marris (1964), the long-run growth rates of large-scale "managerial" corporations are determined by the financial and market environment, on the one hand, and by the interests of both managers and shareholders, on the other hand.

While large conglomerates and powerful industrial groups were emblematic of affluent economies, social problems were raised, particularly in the United States. William A. Darity Jr. explains that "the social dominance of the captains of industry has given way to the social dominance of … a professional-managerial elite" (1990, p. 247). Class divisions and economic inequalities are derived from the managerial age. In this context, Darity justifies government intervention on the basis of employment policy, including recommendations for work-sharing and early retirement.

In the last two decades of the twentieth century, competition increased, technological change began advancing at a stronger pace, and finance became more widely available. In this context, managerial capitalism was challenged by the emergence of patrimonial capitalism. Patrimonial capitalism arrived with financial globalization and the increased importance of small shareholders and pension funds, notably in the United States. Therefore, a new mode of corporate governance based on financial criteria has been imposed. The main objective is to protect external investors by limiting the obstacles that affect their control. Transparency, responsibility from top management, contestability of corporate control, and managerial compensation associated with the maximization of shareholder value are advocated. However, scandals in the early 2000s involving the management of public corporations such as Enron, Vivendi Universal, or WorldCom stress the contradictions of a growth system built on market finance. In parallel, new kinds of firms built around human capital have arisen (Rajan and Zingales 2000), and interfirm relationships have rapidly increased (Langlois 2003). As a result, forms of capitalism—managerial and financial capitalism—experienced so far are highly questioned. The coevolution of organizational forms and the economic system (Chandler 1990) suggests a renewed capitalism that would protect the interests of all corporate stakeholders and guarantee social equality.

SEE ALSO *Class, Rentier*

BIBLIOGRAPHY

Berle, Adolph A., and Gardiner C. Means. 1932. *The Modern Corporation and Private Property.* New York: Macmillan.

Chandler, Alfred Dupont, Jr. 1977. *The Visible Hand: The Managerial Revolution in American Business.* Cambridge, MA: Belknap.

Chandler, Alfred Dupont, Jr. 1984. The Emergence of Managerial Capitalism. *Business History Review* 58 (4): 473–503.

Chandler, Alfred Dupont, Jr. 1990. *Scale and Scope: The Dynamics of Industrial Capitalism.* Cambridge, MA: Belknap.

Darity, William A., Jr. 1990. Racial Inequality in the Managerial Age: An Alternative Vision to the NRC Report. *American Economic Review* 80 (2): 247–251.

Darity, William A., Jr. 1991. Underclass and Overclass: Race, Class, and Economic Inequality in the Managerial Age. In *Essays on the Economics of Discrimination*, ed. Emily P. Hoffman, 67–84. Kalamazoo, MI: Upjohn Institute for Employment Research.

Darity, William A., Jr. 1992. Financial Instability Hypothesis. In *The New Palgrave Dictionary of Money and Finance*, ed. John Eatwell, Murray Milgate, and Peter Newman, Vol. 2, 75–76. New York: Stockton.

Galbraith, John Kenneth. 1967. *The New Industrial State.* New York: Mentor.

Langlois, Richard N. 2003. The Vanishing Hand: The Changing Dynamics of Industrial Capitalism. *Industrial and Corporate Change* 12 (2): 351–385.

Marris, Robin Lapthorn. 1964. *The Economic Theory of "Managerial" Capitalism.* New York: Free Press.

Rajan, Raghuram G., and Luigi Zingales. 2000. The Governance of the New Enterprise. In *Corporate Governance: Theoretical and Empirical Perspectives*, ed. Xavier Vives, Chap. 6, 201–227. Cambridge, U.K.: Cambridge University Press.

Veblen, Thorstein. 1921. *The Engineers and the Price System.* New York: Huebsch.

Cécile Cézanne

CAPITALISM, STATE

Depending upon the evolution of social institutions, especially the state, capitalism assumes distinctive characteristics in different nations. The state—that is, government organizations of a nation and its territorial subdivisions and localities—protects and provides a legal framework for businesses operating through markets. In state capitalism, broadly defined, the state actively fosters, subsidizes, provides services to, regulates, and sometimes controls investor-owned business.

Many varieties of state capitalism can be found throughout the world. In formerly communist nations, for example, the state determines how the enterprises it previously owned can adopt features of capitalism, such as private ownership and buying and selling on open markets. State capitalism also includes established capitalist economies where authoritarian or fascist states direct the economy. In most democratic nations, state capitalism takes the form of welfare-state capitalism. For the market-oriented capitalism of the United States, strong military and international organizations are used to enforce a hierarchical economic order around the globe.

THE STATE AND THE TRANSITION TO CAPITALISM

Some communist regimes, like that of the People's Republic of China, have opted for a gradual transition to state capitalism. Despite the expansion of markets and private ownership, much state ownership and control remains. In contrast, Russia and Eastern Europe having attempted a rapid shift from communism to extensive private ownership and markets, can be characterized as transitional-state capitalism.

In the state capitalism of the People's Republic of China after 1993, markets and capitalism coexist with continuing state and collective ownership and government plans that determine the quantity of goods produced and the prices paid to enterprises for their products. Nevertheless, Chinese firms purchase materials and hire labor through markets. One-quarter of industrial goods were produced in 1999 by state-owned enterprises, one-third by collectively owned enterprises, and two-fifths by individually and family-owned enterprises and ventures with foreign corporations. In state enterprises one-third of the shares were privately owned. Top local government and party officials control collectively owned enterprises. In contrast, foreign joint ventures are freer from government interference and corruption and are judged by economists to be more efficient producers. However, much of China's economic growth stems from local government leaders who act as "bureaucratic entrepreneurs" (Gore 1998, p. 96), promoting growth in their communities.

"State capitalism" was initially a controversial concept that was coined and applied to the Soviet Union in 1950 by socialists sharply critical of the regime of Joseph Stalin. C. L. R. James used the term *state capitalism* to argue that the Soviet Union, far from being a worker's paradise as claimed by Stalinist communists, actually extracted surplus value from Soviet workers. Although there were practically no capitalist private enterprises in Stalin's Soviet Union, the Soviet state, according to James, exploited workers through bureaucratic regimentation just as capitalists did elsewhere.

At the end of the twentieth century in Russia, capitalism was not merely a conceptual label but rather a tangible reality of privately owned, profit-driven enterprises, operating in global markets. The capitalism in Russia could be considered state capitalism because the state, while somewhat less authoritarian than before, nonetheless has exercised tremendous power to create a new capitalist society. In Russia and Eastern Europe, the government has been a transitional state, setting policies for a very rapid adoption of capitalism. Russian and Eastern European leaders, in contrast to the Chinese, have pushed for a "shock therapy" transition through neo-liberal policies, opening their nations to global trade, attempting to stabilize their currency in relation to the dollar, and privatizing state-owned enterprises. Beginning in 1992, shares in Russian state-owned enterprises were purchased by employees of the enterprises (who held 40% of the shares in 1996), managers (held 18%), other Russian firms (11%), and individuals (6%). Although the government offered a voucher to each citizen to buy shares, most citizens sold or gave away their vouchers or placed them with investment funds. Enterprises whose shares had been largely sold accounted for more than 90 percent of Russian industrial output by 1998. The government then exchanged additional shares for loans from selected Russian private banks and investments from Western corporations. A small group of Russians received huge financial windfalls through their connections with government elites who directed the privatization process. Privatized enterprises were even more likely to show a loss than enterprises that remained in state hands. Privatization has not revived the ailing Russian economy, which lost one-half of its domestic production between 1989 and 1999.

In the transitional-state capitalism of the Czech Republic, compared to Russia, more shares of companies are held by the public, and fewer by workers in state enterprises. In the Czech Republic, shares amounting to one-half the value of state enterprises were privatized through vouchers distributed to citizens by 1995. Two-thirds of the vouchers were handed to investment privatization funds, run by state banks, which purchased shares of enterprises for individuals. In Poland, the state maintains an even larger role, maintaining more public enterprises and deciding which key enterprises are made available for foreign joint ownership.

STRONG STATES AND CAPITALISM, ORIENT AND OCCIDENT

The concept of state capitalism can also be applied to capitalist economies where an authoritarian, one-party government actively directs the economy. In South Korea, the military regime of Park Chung Hee (1917–1979) in the 1960s gave money to exporters, raised tariffs on imports, created industrial zones, controlled wages, and channeled capital to favored *chaebol* (coordinated industrial conglomerates), thereby producing rapid development of the steel, cement, shipbuilding, and machinery industries, followed by the chemical, auto, and electronics sectors in succeeding decades.

In the more established capitalist economy of Germany in 1933, the fascist regime that took power allowed cartels of large businesses to continue under the same ownership. Whereas the cartels preferred state policies to increase their exports, Führer Adolf Hitler developed an autarkic economy (independent from trade with rival industrial nations) to fight wars. Production increased because of new state-subsidized industries in motor vehicles, aviation, aluminum, and chemicals. After World War II, dictatorships in Spain, Portugal, and Greece supported the dominance of domestic banking and commercial establishments that played a junior rule to large U.S. and European firms.

In democratic nations with advanced economies, some national governments have brought together trade unions and big business associations into "corporatist" agreements on wages, prices, government budgets, welfare-state programs, investments, and economic growth. In Japan, the government Ministry of International Trade and Industry (MITI) brought business, labor, and government officials together and, between 1950 and 1980, successfully encouraged economic growth through an industrial policy that subsidized exports, developed technologies, and promoted new industries.

In Sweden, Norway, and Denmark, strong social-democratic political parties rooted in trade unions have produced relatively generous subsidies for children, paid leave for parenting, unemployment and medical insurance, and relatively egalitarian, government-provided retirement benefits. On the continent of Europe, welfare-state programs have been geared toward male breadwinners who have stable and well-paying jobs in unionized industries. As welfare-state spending has been cut throughout Europe, Anthony Giddens has advocated trimming subsidies for consumption and boosting investments in people, such as job training, education, and health care to make more productive workers.

Government programs providing pensions and health care in the United States, compared to other economically developed nations, have been less generous and comprehensive and have been adopted later in history or not at all. Presidents such as Ronald Reagan and George W. Bush attempted to cut welfare spending for the poor, reduce tax rates and business regulation, and increase spending for the military and foreign affairs.

Since the fifteenth century, dominant nations have developed strong states to gain a superior position in a world system of capitalism. By the beginning of the twenty-first century, national sovereignty had been eroded amid the rapid flow of goods, investments, and knowledge that spanned the globe. In their book *Empire* (2000), Michael Hardt and Antonio Negri argued that capitalism still requires state power; not in the form of a colonizing nation but rather in the form of international elites and institutions backed by the military power of the United States.

SEE ALSO *Capitalism*

BIBLIOGRAPHY

Adam, Jan. 1999. *Social Costs of Transformation to a Market Economy in Post-Socialist Countries: The Cases of Poland, the Czech Republic, and Hungary.* New York: St. Martin's Press.

Amsden, Alice H. 1989. *Asia's Next Giant: South Korea and Late Industrialization.* New York: Oxford University Press.

Blasi, Joseph R., Maya Kroumova, and Douglas Kruse. 1997. *Kremlin Capitalism: The Privatization of the Russian Economy.* Ithaca, NY: ILR Press.

Callon, Scott. 1995. *Divided Sun: MITI and the Breakdown of Japanese High-Tech Industrial Policy, 1975–1993.* Stanford, CA: Stanford University Press.

Esping-Andersen, Gosta. 1999. *Social Foundations of Postindustrial Economies.* Oxford: Oxford University Press.

Giddens, Anthony. 1998. *The Third Way and Its Critics.* Cambridge, U.K.: Polity Press.

Gold, David A., Clarence Y. H. Lo, and Erik O. Wright. 1975. Recent Developments in Marxist Theories of the Capitalist State. *Monthly Review* Part 1 in 27 (5): 29–43; Part 2 in 27 (6): 36–51.

Gore, Lance L. P. 1998. *Market Communism: The Institutional Foundation of China's Post-Mao Hyper-Growth.* Oxford: Oxford University Press.

Hardt, Michael, and Antonio Negri. 2000. *Empire.* Cambridge, MA: Harvard University Press.

James, Cyril Lionel Robert. 1986. *State Capitalism and World Revolution.* Chicago: Charles H. Kerr.

Lo, Clarence Y. H., and Michael Schwartz, eds. 1998. *Social Policy and the Conservative Agenda.* Malden, MA: Blackwell.

Overy, R. J. 1994. *War and Economy in the Third Reich.* New York: Oxford University Press.

Poulantzas, Nicos. 1976. *The Crisis of the Dictatorships: Portugal, Greece, Spain.* Trans. David Fernbach. Atlantic Highlands, NJ: Humanities Press.

Clarence Y. H. Lo

CAPITALISM AND SLAVERY

SEE *Williams, Eric.*

CAPITALIST MODE OF PRODUCTION

The concept of the capitalist mode of production (CMP) occupies a central place in Karl Marx's (1818–1883) view of productive relations, forms of exploitation, and conflict in modern society. The very notion of capitalism was used predominantly by Marxists well into the twentieth century, when it started to be thoroughly analyzed in a non-Marxist perspective by Max Weber (1864–1920) and Werner Sombart (1863–1941).

THE CAPITALIST MODE OF PRODUCTION IN THE THEORY OF KARL MARX

In his work, especially the *Grundrisse* (1857–1858) and the first volume of *Capital* (1867), Marx defined capitalism as a mode of production characterized by the separation of the direct producers, the working class, from the means of production or the productive assets, which are controlled by the bourgeoisie as private property. Ownership of the means of production enables the bourgeoisie to organize the industrial labor process, where individual workers are driven to seek employment by the needs of their own reproduction. Contrary to previous modes of production such as slavery and feudalism, the laborer is compelled to enter an employment relation not by external compulsion, but by economic necessity.

As a result, the employment relation is formally an individual contractual transaction between bourgeois capitalists and workers, who are juridically free. Once they enter the capitalist labor process, workers are remunerated with a wage, a monetary sum representing the "exchange value" with which the capitalist purchases the worker's labor power. The wage is expressed in terms of the duration of the working day, and is calculated on the basis of the goods that workers need to reproduce their ability to work. Therefore, the wage does not recognize specific forms of labor or skills, it only compensates "abstract" labor power.

In the productive process, workers operate machines and other means of production with which they create commodities whose values exceed workers' remunerations. When capitalists sell commodities on the market, "realizing" their value, they therefore appropriate the difference between the value of such goods and the value of the labor power used to produce them. Marx calls this difference "surplus value," which for him is the defining feature of the exploitative nature of capitalism. The money capitalists earn from realizing their surplus value contains a profit, which capitalists reinvest to restart the productive cycle in what Marx calls "extended reproduction" of capital. Marx saw the origins of profit and surplus extraction in the very process of production, not in market dynamics of supply and demand, as in the "bourgeois" political economy of Adam Smith (1723–1790) and David Ricardo (1772–1823). Nonetheless, Smith and Ricardo influenced Marx's concept of the division of labor and his "labor theory of value," respectively. Marx, however, regarded the market not as a realm of free individual initiative, but as an institution that materializes human exploitation and alienation.

For Marx, the CMP is a social process riddled with contradictions that originate from its own "laws of motion." The growing "concentration" of accumulated capital is what ultimately allows individual capitalists to increase their profits and drive competitors out of the market. The elimination of uncompetitive capitals produces a centralization of ownership in a smaller number of large companies. But successful competition also requires increasing investment in machinery ("constant capital"). As a result, the surplus value extracted from human labor is eroded and, in the long term, the rate of profit for the CMP as a whole tends to fall. In the process, masses of workers are expelled from the production process and end up swelling the unemployed "relative surplus population."

Marx described the laws of motion in the CMP far more precisely than in other modes of production. His aim was in fact to scientifically demonstrate how the demands of the working class are ultimately incompatible with capital's exploitative nature. As the contradictions of the CMP manifest themselves in periodic crises, workers become conscious of their own exploitation as a class. Therefore they organize to accelerate capitalism's eventual demise and establish a socialist society where class domination is abolished.

Marx tended to present the development of the CMP as a social dynamics whose general laws of motion could be scientifically ascertained. He was nonetheless quite aware that the process he described was historically specific and located largely in Western Europe. England had for him a prototypical CMP. There, the birth of a capitalist agriculture and the rise of mechanized manufacturing in the late eighteenth and early nineteenth centuries enabled the Industrial Revolution, which benefited from world trade and technological innovation. Marx associated the rise of capitalism with the establishment of a form of state whose laws and institutions protect private property, capital accumulation, and formal liberties that enable contractual relations between workers and capitalists. This stage of political development is represented by the liberal state, whose juridical and ideological "superstructure" is functional to reproduce the "base" of capitalist relations of exploitation.

CAPITALISM AND IMPERIALISM IN EARLY MARXIST DEBATES

Marx's awareness that the birth of capitalism was a historically and geographically specific process led him to recognize, as in his 1881 letter to Vera Zasulich, that Western Europe's "pure" transition to capitalism is not immutable and necessary for all societies. Many debates on the CMP in twentieth-century Marxism revolved around the different ways in which the economic structure of capitalism determines social and political relations, capitalist crises, the role of the state, and the significance of class struggles and workers' agency. Reformists in the Second International (1889–1916), especially Eduard Bernstein (1850–1932), argued that capitalism was not necessarily heading toward unsolvable crises, because governments' interventions in the economy could actually improve the conditions of the working class. In this view, therefore, socialism could be established through workers' participation in electoral politics, rather than revolution.

Vladimir Lenin's theory of imperialism, influenced by Rudolf Hilferding's *Finance Capital* (1910), argued that capitalism leads to a growing concentration of ownership in large monopolistic conglomerates. Antonio Gramsci (1891–1937) added to such trends the transition toward "Fordist" mass production. For Lenin (1870–1924) and Nikolai Bukharin (1888–1938), the growth of gigantic capitalist corporations, and their need for new markets, propelled Europe's colonial expansion and imperialist control of non-Western economies. In Rosa Luxemburg's *The Accumulation of Capital* (1913), colonialism and imperialism are responses to overproduction in metropolitan economies, and are coterminous with the ruthless destruction of precapitalist societies, what Marx referred to as "primitive accumulation" (1867). In contrast to reformist socialists, such views maintained that capitalism is shaped by crises and conflicts, and rejected the argument, held to some extent by Marx himself, that colonialism was a progressive force that destroyed pre-existing despotism and backwardness.

POSTWAR MARXIST PERSPECTIVES ON CAPITALISM, PRODUCTION, AND THE STATE

After World War II growing government intervention in the economy, and the rise of the welfare state, renewed interest in the relations between capitalism and the state among Marxist scholars. Important examples are the work of the "Frankfurt school" (especially Friedrich Pollock and

Herbert Marcuse) and Paul Sweezy's *Theory of Capitalist Development* (1942). In the 1970s and 1980s Ralph Miliband, James O'Connor, and the "regulation paradigm" (Michel Aglietta, Robert Boyer) underlined the important role of the state in stabilizing capitalism by financing the reproduction of the working class. Similarly, Nicos Poulantzas referred to the "relative autonomy" of the state as the manager of capital's "general interests." His reevaluation of the relevance of politics was linked to the work of "structuralist" Marxists, especially Louis Althusser (1918–1990), who viewed the economy as "determining" social relations without being necessarily "dominant."

Meanwhile, colonialism and imperialism led Marxist theorists of "dependency," especially André Gunder Frank (1929–2005), and of the "capitalist world economy," particularly Immanuel Wallerstein (b. 1930), to see capitalism as a global system articulated in "core" and "peripheral" societies. In both views, capitalist trade links the growth of industrialized countries to the continued underdevelopment of the world's peripheries. Critics, however, accuse such theories of making the periphery a passive object of domination, neglecting processes of production and the complexities of social relations in the global south. Structuralist analyses of the "articulation of modes of production" (by, for example, Althusser, Etienne Balibar, and Harold Wolpe) propose a view of capitalism as an "uneven" social formation that subordinates precapitalist societies, which nonetheless retain their specificities. "Uneven capitalist development" also features prominently in David Harvey's work, which also focuses on capitalism's negative environmental impacts.

Starting from the 1970s the concept of CMP also has been criticized by feminist Marxists (e.g., Mariarosa Dalla Costa, Leopoldina Fortunati, Maria Mies, Heidi Hartmann) who indicted its neglect of gender contradictions. In fact, they emphasized, capitalist production is made possible—also with the complicity of a working-class image of waged work as a manly occupation—by the confinement of women to the household role of unpaid workers.

Finally, "autonomist" Marxists—largely influenced by Italian "workerists" of the 1950s and 1960s (Raniero Panzieri, Mario Tronti, Antonio Negri) and by the work of Michel Foucault, Gilles Deleuze, and Felix Guattari—criticized traditional Marxist views of social relations as mechanically determined by economic dynamics. Instead, they considered class struggles and workers' subjectivity to be the main causes of capitalist crisis. In this view, as in Antonio Negri's and Michael Hardt's *Empire* (2000), capitalist responses to national class struggles ultimately opted for the economic liberalization policies that underpin the globalization of production and finance. Autonomists, in fact, see globalization as part of capital's broader strategy to establish its control beyond the workplace to the totality of the "social factory," human interactions, and everyday life.

BIBLIOGRAPHY

Alavi, Hamza, Doug McEachem, P. Burns, et al. 1982. *Capitalism and Colonial Production*. London: Croom Helm.

Brewer, Anthony. 1990. *Marxist Theories of Imperialism: A Critical Survey*. London: Routledge.

Cleaver, Harry. 2000. *Reading Capital Politically*. San Francisco: AK Press.

Harvey, David. 2006. *Spaces of Global Capitalism. A Theory of Uneven Geographical Development*. London: Verso.

Hilferding, Rudolf. [1910] 1985. *Finance Capital*. London: Routledge and Kegan Paul.

Jessop, Bob. *The Capitalist State: Marxist Theories and Methods*. New York: New York University Press.

Luxemburg, Rosa. [1913] 2003. *The Accumulation of Capital*. London: Routledge.

Milward, Bob. 2000. *Marxian Political Economy: Theory, History, and Contemporary Relevance*. Basingstoke, U.K.: Macmillan.

Negri, Antonio, and Michael Hardt. 2000. *Empire*. Cambridge, MA: Harvard University Press.

Read, Jason. 2003. *The Micropolitics of Capital: Marx and the Prehistory of the Present*. Albany: State University of New York Press.

Saad-Filho, Alberto. 2002. *The Value of Marx: Political Economy for Contemporary Capitalism*. London: Routledge.

Sweezy, Paul. 1942. *Theory of Capitalist Development*. New York: Oxford University Press.

Tucker, Robert C., ed. 1978. *The Marx-Engels Reader*. New York: Norton.

Wolpe, Harold. 1980. Introduction. In *The Articulation of Modes of Production: Essays from Economy and Society*, ed. Harold Wolpe, 1–43. London: Routledge and Kegan Paul.

Franco Barchiesi

CARDINALITY

SEE *Ordinality.*

CARIBBEAN, THE

The Caribbean lies at the heart of the Western hemisphere and was pivotal in Europe's rise to world predominance. Yet the islands that once marked the horizon of the West's self-perception, as well as the source of its wealth, have been spatially and temporally eviscerated from the imaginary geography of Western modernity. The physical incorporation and symbolic exclusion of the Caribbean from the imagined time-space of "modernity" has made certain ideas of "the West" viable, and they must therefore inform any effort to describe the Caribbean within the social sciences. Since their inception, the social sciences have used non-Western places as counterfoils for Western modernity—they have been viewed as "backward" or "traditional" places against which processes of modern progress, urbanization, industrialization, democratization, rationalization, individualization and so on could be gauged. Yet the Caribbean has never fit easily into such dichotomous visions of the world, for it was always a product of modernity and was in many ways postmodern *avant la lettre* (before it existed). The anthropologist Sidney Mintz has argued that the Caribbean was "the first part of the non-Western world to endure an era of intensive Westernizing activity." Thus, "the Caribbean *oikumenê* became 'modern' in some ways even before Europe itself; while the history of the region has lent to it a coherence not so much cultural as sociological" (Mintz 1996, p. 289).

Mintz supports a processual definition of the Caribbean as an *oikumenê* (ecumene, or "inhabited land"), a historic unit that is "an interwoven set of happenings and products" (Mintz 1996, p. 293). Franklin Knight likewise argues that "the sum of the common experiences and understandings of the Caribbean outweigh the territorial differences or peculiarities" (Knight 1990, p. xiv). The geographical region includes the islands of the Greater Antilles, the Lesser Antilles, and the Bahamas, as well as the coastal areas of Central and South America that have been politically and culturally linked to the Caribbean by processes of colonization, plantation development, and migration. It is also sometimes extended to include far-flung diasporas, especially in Europe and North America. While there are quite distinct traditions of study linked to areas such as the British West Indies, the French West Indies, or the Spanish Antilles, there has also been an increasing amount of comparative and cross-regional research. And while there are differences in the study of dependencies or colonies versus independent states, the Caribbean as a whole can be understood as being marked by complex and uneven processes of imperial decline, postcolonial nation-building, and regional integration.

Above all, the Caribbean was constituted by the global mobilities of colonization, slavery, and the transatlantic plantation system. With the rise of the sugar "plantation complex" the region was marked by the displacement of indigenous peoples by those arriving from northern and southern Europe, eastern and western Africa, and, later, the Indian subcontinent, China, and the Levant. Being more deeply and continuously affected by migration than any other world region, the essence of Caribbean life has always been movement. The very idea of this dispersed and fragmented region as a single place—and its naming and contemporary material existence—are constituted by mobilities of many different kinds, including flows of people, commodities, texts, images, capital, and knowledge. Thus, the Caribbean exists at the crossroads of multifaceted networks of mobility formed by the travels of both people and things, as well as by those people and things that do not move. Alongside the work of capitalist expansion and contraction associated with commodities such as tobacco, sugar, coffee, rum, salt, cotton, indigo, and, later, bananas and tropical fruit, the Caribbean has also been indelibly shaped by the work of imagination and culture-building over the past five hundred years.

Creolization is one of the crucial elements of Caribbean culture building, conceived as a process of indigenization, hybridization, and contested "creation and construction of culture out of fragmented, violent and disjunct pasts" (Mintz 1996, p. 302). Later, the arrival of Caribbean migrants in the metropoles such as London, New York, Toronto, and Miami allowed for the emergence of new kinds of pan-Caribbean identifications, arts movements, musical amalgams, and cultural events like Carnival. This region, more than any other, has long been at the forefront of transnational processes through its uprooted people, Creole cultures, and diasporas traveling across the world. It thus became central to the theorization of transnationality, diaspora, and postmodernity in the 1980s, and to the subsequent emergence of Black Atlantic studies and world history in the 1990s. Social scientists studying globalization turned to Caribbean theoretical concepts such as transculturation, creolization, and *marronage* to describe contemporary global cultural processes, even while they ignored some of the historical specificity and nuances of these concepts within Caribbean studies.

At the beginning of the twenty-first century, the region is enmeshed in complex mobilities, including circuitous migrations of people and diverse cultures; transnational flows of capital investment and financial services; technologically mediated flows of information, communication, and intellectual property; and unpredictable global risks and threats to security (e.g., drugs, diseases, criminals, hurricanes). These new mobilities and immobilities, both intra- and extra-Caribbean, are transforming the nature, scale, and temporalities of families, local communities, public spaces, governance structures, and individuals' commitments to a specific nation. Caribbean mobilities and moorings are paradigmatic of the complex rescaling of urban, national, and regional space. Daily practices of commuting, accessing goods for consumption, moving through public spaces, and communicating with the diaspora help to perform the presences and absences, the proximities and distances, that inform the

INTERNATIONAL ENCYCLOPEDIA OF THE SOCIAL SCIENCES, 2ND EDITION lived experience of spatiality in the Caribbean and its transnational diasporas.

Global risks associated with criminal activities, terrorism, environmental disasters, and other security issues are also producing new modes of surveillance and the governance of local mobilities within and outside of the region, with significant impact on forms of belonging and exclusion, of connection and disconnection. Thus, Caribbean societies—and the idea of the region as a whole—are being rescaled and respatialized by changes in the infrastructure of transportational and informational mobility, and cultural practices of travel and migration. Understanding exactly how the contemporary Caribbean is being both "demobilized" and "remobilized," and both deregulated and re-regulated, within the processes of urban, state, regional, and global restructuring can enable social scientists to move beyond the imagery of states as spatially fixed geographical containers for social processes, and to question scalar logics such as local-global. Thus, a rethinking of the processes that are remaking the Caribbean in the twenty-first century will be crucial to advancing the social sciences' approach to area studies and global studies in ways that finally move beyond its Eurocentric origins and assumed forms of territoriality.

SEE ALSO *Colonialism; Creolization; Economic Commission for Latin America and the Caribbean; Rastafari; Sociology, Latin American*

BIBLIOGRAPHY

Basch, Linda, Nina Glick Schiller, and Constance Szanton Blanc. 1994. *Nations Unbound: Trans-national Projects, Postcolonial Predicaments, and Deterritorialized Nation-States.* Amsterdam: Gordon and Breach.

Benitez Rojo, Antonio. 1996. *The Repeating Island: The Caribbean and the Postmodern Perspective*, 2nd ed. Trans. James E. Maraniss. Durham, NC: Duke University Press.

Kempadoo, Kamala. 2004. *Sexing the Caribbean: Gender, Race, and Sexual Labor.* New York: Routledge.

Klak, Thomas, ed. 1998. *Globalization and Neoliberalism: The Caribbean Context.* Lanham, MD: Rowman & Littlefield.

Knight, Franklin W. 1990. *The Caribbean: The Genesis of a Fragmented Nationalism*, 2nd ed. New York: Oxford University Press.

Mintz, Sidney. 1996. Enduring Substances, Trying Theories: The Caribbean Region as Oikumenê. *Journal of the Royal Anthropological Institute* 2 (2): 289–310.

Sheller, Mimi. 2003. *Consuming the Caribbean: From Arawaks to Zombies.* London: Routledge.

Mimi Sheller

CARMICHAEL, STOKELY (KWAME TURE)

SEE *Black Nationalism; Black Power.*

CARRYING COST

Carrying costs have played both a practical and a theoretical role in economics. From the practical standpoint, carrying costs are known as the costs of interest, warehousing, wastage, and possible decline in marketability, which holding for future use implies for marketable commodities. Thus those goods for which there has historically arisen a formal method of grading and of trading over time—forward or futures markets—are subject to such carrying costs and the existence of them is a well known fact for financial traders and commentators.

Theoretically, carrying costs entered the literature with Henry Crosby Emery's influential *Speculation on the Stock and Produce Exchanges of the United States* (1896). Emery noted that the level of carrying costs forms one determinant of future prices, along with expectations of price change, themselves dependent on expectations of future supplies and demand. In this way Emery put forward a doctrine of the social usefulness of commodity exchanges to end users, such as farmers and manufacturers, by virtue of the possible unburdening from these economic actors to traders of the risk of price fluctuations by the buying or selling futures contracts. Further, this explanation acquitted the commodity exchanges of the charge (frequently leveled in the nineteenth century) that they fostered antisocial speculation. Emery's view was given wide exposure in the works of Irving Fisher and Alfred Marshall, among many others.

The further development of the carrying cost concept was mostly due to the work of the English economist John Maynard Keynes. Keynes first suggested in his *A Tract on Monetary Reform* (1923) that a theory of the (then new) organized forward markets in different international currencies could be based on the short-term interest rates available to holders of currency in different money markets. This notion was to become carrying cost more generally in his later work, and his discussion centered on its role in the currency trade (in which he himself was actively engaged).

Keynes laid out a theory according to which such trading would be driven to a configuration of spot and future prices such as to ensure the traders could both pay the inevitable carrying cost of taking a long position and also make a (typically small) competitive profit. The premium or discount at which the future price stands in relation to the spot price is thus a barometer of expectations about the course of the price in the future. In normal times, under the expectation of steady or growing output the future price will be above the spot, and the traders can earn their "turn" and still pay their carrying costs (in currency in interest) out of this difference. In the parlance of his *A Treatise on Money* (1930), this is known as a "backwardation." In abnormal times, though, when there is a sudden onset of a "bear" position on any currency (as in the expectation of a recession or of political upheaval), it might be that the spot price prices are forced to fall below both the quoted and expected future price in order to induce traders to hold stocks of the good in question for the period of the contract. Such a "contango" on futures markets was evidence of the need to continue to pay mounting carrying costs (in the special case of easily stored and infinitely lived money, purely an interest charge) into an uncertain period of decline expected in its value.

In *A Treatise on Money* this theory of carrying costs and the economic role of futures trading was expanded to commodity markets (which Keynes also actively speculated in) and the term and concept was explicitly introduced. There it also played a part in a more systemic view of economic cycles. The main point made (in argument with Ralph G. Hawtrey) is that one should not look to futures trading to alleviate the severity and duration of downturns, because carrying costs severely limit the degree to which such markets may profitably carry over redundant stocks of liquid capital goods during the downturn. In consequence those stocks cannot be expected to be available to provide the working capital, and so ease the transition to, the next upturn (as Hawtrey had argued). In pursuing this line of reasoning, Keynes also suggested that the concept was of wider import, as even "less organized markets" (p. 128) were subject to carrying costs, but not in so formal and obvious a manner. This is the hint that was to be expanded into of full-blown theory of unemployment in his next book.

In *The General Theory of Money, Interest and Employment* (1936) Keynes suggested, particularly in chapter 17, that this theory of the forward market could be generalized to the whole economy, and, significantly, that it contained the clue to the answer of why economies might get "stuck" in unemployment equilibria (such as was then happening in Europe and North America). His generalization started from the notion that all outputs have carrying costs (often so high as to make their carrying over of them in inventory all but impossible). These costs formed a third element alongside the essential liquidity and productivity that all goods might possess in some degree. But some goods, considered as an asset, had the peculiar and socially defined quality of having the highest liquidity in excess of their carrying costs among all outlets for storing saved income. Such "money" goods

would be sought, for their superior ability to maintain their value through time. This quality, Keynes argued, was of particular importance in periods of economic downturns, since it provided harbors of safety for owners of wealth, who might therefore be reluctant to engage in alternative investments such as purchasing and using employment-generating "productive" assets. The lack of any social mechanism to discourage this individually rational, but perhaps socially dysfunctional, "flight to money," could explain the phenomena of high and persistent unemployment such as characterized the advanced capitalistic economies of the world in the 1930s and still often threatens them in the early twenty-first century.

SEE ALSO *Contango; Interest, Real Rate of; Keynes, John Maynard*

BIBLIOGRAPHY

Emery, Henry C. 1896. *Speculation on the Stock and Produce Exchanges of the United States.* New York: Columbia University Press.

Keynes, John M. 1923. *A Tract on Monetary Reform.* London: Macmillan.

Keynes, John M. 1930. *A Treatise on Money.* London: Macmillan.

Keynes, John M. 1936. *The General Theory of Employment, Interest and Money.* London: Macmillan.

Lawlor, Michael S. 2006. *The Economics of Keynes in Retrospect: An Intellectual History of the General Theory.* London: Palgrave Macmillan.

Michael S. Lawlor

CARTER, JIMMY
1924–

James Earl Carter, a U.S. naval officer, farmer, Georgia state senator and governor, and the thirty-ninth president of the United States, was the most inexperienced politician to serve as president in the latter half of the twentieth century. This inexperience contributed to President Carter's mixed legacy in foreign and domestic policies, despite having the largest majority of Democrats in the U.S. Congress since the Lyndon Baines Johnson (1908–1973) administration, as well as initial support from the American people to chart a new course in presidential politics.

Elected the first southern president since before the Civil War (1861–1865), Carter campaigned against corruption and dishonesty in Washington, maintaining that he would never lie to the American people. His honest character and an anti-Washington environment, including lingering public resentment over Gerald Ford's pardon of Richard Nixon (1913–1994), undoubtedly helped Carter build an early and commanding thirty-point lead in polls. But Carter needed the help of Ford's own gaffe in the second presidential debate, during which Ford stated that the Soviet Union did not dominate Eastern Europe, to narrowly defeat the incumbent and former vice president by only fifty-seven electoral votes. Carter would later understand the impact that the media could have on his presidency when they focused more on his cardigan sweaters (style) than his policy message about the oil shortage (substance) during his short-lived fireside chats.

In foreign policy, President Carter achieved significant victories and stunning defeats. Just as Nixon was the first U.S. president to visit China, Carter was the first to normalize relations with the Communist country. Carter also helped broker the Camp David Accords, which brought peace between Egypt and Israel in March 1979. He had earlier won a hard-fought victory in the Senate (however unpopular) when it ratified the Panama Canal Treaty in April 1978, turning control of the canal over to the Panamanian government partially in October 1979 and completely on December 31, 1999.

Despite receiving a bump in his job-approval ratings (from 31 to 52%, according to the Gallup Poll) following the seizure of hostages in Iran, Carter was criticized for his decision to admit the ailing shah of Iran into the United States for medical treatment. This action precipitated the taking of more than sixty American hostages from the U.S. embassy in Tehran on November 4, 1979. This crisis plagued the Carter presidency until his successor, Ronald Reagan (1911–2004), took the oath of office on January 20, 1981, when all the hostages were released. Previous diplomatic, economic, and military efforts to secure the release of the hostages had failed. Most politically damaging to the president and his reputation as chief diplomat and commander in chief was a failed rescue mission on April 24, 1980, in which three malfunctioning helicopters forced the operation to be aborted. Carter's inability to secure the hostages' release defined his presidency as a failure in foreign policy, despite its numerous diplomatic successes.

The relationship of the United States with the Soviet Union also proved mixed during the Carter presidency. Carter signed the SALT II arms control treaty with Soviet premier Leonid Brezhnev (1906–1982) in June 1979, but the U.S. Senate did not ratify it. The Soviet invasion of Afghanistan in December 1979 all but ended the administration's hope for ratification. The invasion also precipitated a U.S. grain embargo of the Soviet Union (ended by Reagan in 1981), a United Nations resolution calling for the withdrawal of Soviet troops from Afghanistan, and a boycott of the 1980 Summer Olympics in Moscow by the

United States and sixty-three other nations. It also led to the "Carter Doctrine," outlined in Carter's last State of the Union address in January 1980, which established that any attempt by the USSR "to gain control of the Persian Gulf region will be regarded as an assault on the vital interests of the United States."

Carter is often blamed for failing to deliver what all presidents must deliver to be politically successful and ensure their own reelection: a strong economy. His difficulties in convincing Congress and the American public to adopt his massive energy program are tantamount to the policy problems he faced. The final energy statute was much weaker than what he had requested, and the American people did not receive well his pleas for sacrifice and conservation, despite the intended benefits. Carter is often viewed as an unskilled legislative leader, in part because he proposed too many major legislative initiatives (Light 1999). Yet, his domestic victories have had a lasting impact on American society. Two major successes—founding the departments of Energy and Education—withstood calls for abolishment by the Reagan administration and remain influential and indicative of the legacy of the Carter presidency. Other successes, such as deregulation of the airlines (1978), natural gas prices (1978), and the trucking industry (1980) continue to affect American consumers, just as the Alaska Land Act (1980) set aside over 100 million acres of federal land for wilderness areas and national parks.

The failures of the Carter presidency clearly overshadowed his important policy successes. His opponent in the 1980 presidential election, the former Republican governor of California, Ronald Reagan, simplified voters' decisions to a retrospective evaluation of the current administration—are you better off now than you were four years ago? Carter lost by 10 percent in the popular vote, but won only six states and the District of Columbia—forty-nine electoral votes or 9 percent of the total—in his failed reelection bid on November 4, 1980.

As a former president, Carter has been involved in numerous humanitarian and diplomatic missions. Well known as a volunteer for Habitat for Humanity, Carter also led a diplomatic convoy to avert a crisis in Haiti (1994), lectured in political science at Emory University, and won the Nobel Peace Prize in 2002 "for his decades of untiring effort to find peaceful solutions to international conflicts, to advance democracy and human rights, and to promote economic and social development" (Nobel Committee 2002). Just as when he was president, Carter continued to foster human rights around the world. In these and other ways, Carter has been uniquely more respected and influential after 1980 than he was during his term as president.

SEE ALSO *Presidency, The*

BIBLIOGRAPHY

Carter, Jimmy. 1975. *Why Not the Best? The First Fifty Years.* Nashville, TN: Broadman.

Carter, Jimmy. 1980. State of the Union Address (January 23). http://www.jimmycarterlibrary.org/documents/speeches/su80jec.phtml.

Carter, Jimmy. 1982. *Keeping Faith: Memoirs of a President.* New York: Bantam.

Light, Paul C. 1999. *The President's Agenda: Domestic Policy Choice from Kennedy to Clinton.* 3rd ed. Baltimore, MD: Johns Hopkins University Press.

Nobel Committee. 2002. Press Release: The Nobel Peace Prize 2002. http://nobelprize.org/nobel_prizes/peace/laureates/2002/press.html.

Matthew Eshbaugh-Soha

CARTOONS, POLITICAL

Throughout world history, political cartoons have illustrated the age-old adage that a picture is worth a thousand words. Since the sixteenth century, illustrated caricatures have been used as satire, drawing attention to important political and social events of the day. But in 1843, the practice gained a new name when England's *Punch* magazine published a drawing parodying preliminary sketches of paintings commissioned for the houses of Parliament. "Cartoon No. 1," as the illustration was called, was the first use of the word *cartoon* to describe humorous, satirical, or witty drawings or caricatures. It used simple imagery to communicate a message aimed at influencing public debate and the political process.

A surprising forefather of the political cartoon is Martin Luther, the sixteenth-century religious reformer, who used illustrated booklets and posters in a campaign to reform the Catholic Church. In *Passional Christi und Antichristi* (1521), illustrated by the printmaker Lucas Cranach, Luther contrasted easily recognizable scenes from the Bible with scathing caricatures of the Catholic Church. One set of illustrations juxtaposed Christ driving the moneylenders out of the Temple with the Pope selling indulgences. The practice of using satirical drawings to make political commentary caught on in Europe, and the practice eventually spread around the world.

Political cartoons were very influential in early American political culture. In 1754, Benjamin Franklin became the first to publish a cartoon in an American newspaper. Franklin, a supporter of unifying the colonies for protective purposes, used a common superstition to get his message across. It was believed that a snake that had been severed would come to life again if its pieces were put back together before nightfall. Franklin drew a picture of a snake cut into eight pieces, with the caption "Join, or Die." Using easily recognizable symbols as shorthand for commentary remains a staple of modern political cartoons.

Even in the eighteenth century, political cartoons traveled around the world, crossing language and cultural barriers. One famous example is that of William "Boss" Tweed, the head of the political machine that had run New York City since 1789. Tweed was caricatured as a crook in a series of political cartoons by Thomas Nast in the American publication *Harper's Weekly*. "Stop them Damn Pictures," demanded Tweed, "I don't care so much what the papers write about me. My constituents can't read. But damn it, they can see pictures." When Tweed fled an American jail for Spain, a Spanish official recognized him from his cartoon likeness, leading to his arrest and return to America.

In the twenty-first century, cartoons are often used as a vehicle for disseminating political commentary around the world. Political cartoons now come in many forms, from the one-frame cartoons found on the editorial pages of newspapers to multipaneled cartoons commonly referred to as *comic strips*. Political content can also be found in other popular cartoon forms, such as comic books, graphic novels, and Japanese anime, and in different media venues, such as television, movie theaters, and the Internet. Recurring politically charged comic strips, or "funnies," are particularly well suited to using humor to deal with significant issues. Comic strips are able to address social and political issues by weaving them into the day-to-day lives of their characters. In America, the syndicated comic strips *Doonesbury* and *The Boondocks* are examples of daily comic strips that provide biting social commentary and critiques of the government.

SEE ALSO Nast, Thomas

BIBLIOGRAPHY

Hess, Stephen, and Sandy Northrup. 1996. *Drawn and Quartered: The History of American Political Cartoons.* Montgomery, AL: Elliott and Clark.

Luther, Martin. 1521. *Passional Christi und Antichristi.* Wittenberg, Germany: Johann Rhau Grunenberg. http://www.kb.dk/luther/passion/index.htm.

Katina Stapleton

CARVER, GEORGE WASHINGTON

SEE *Peanut Industry.*

CASE METHOD

The case method (or the case study) is a prolonged, intimate, and detailed investigation of a single case or a set of cases. The in-depth analysis of a case or small set of cases illuminates larger sociological processes and phenomena. The case method is used in urban and rural ethnographies, life histories, and social histories of a group of people or an event. Cases can be empirical, theoretical, or "discovered" during the research process. The case method requires an ongoing, engaged, and critical conversation between data collection and data analysis. Typically, the social scientist using the case method refines her definition of a case throughout the course of a study (Becker 1992). The case method is especially useful in illuminating social worlds that are not appreciated or understood by others.

The history of the ethnographic case study is grounded in a volume of works produced by the Chicago school during the early twentieth century. Early Chicago school scholars used the case method to illuminate people's understanding of urban culture (Zorbaugh [1929] 1976), race and ethnic relations, and social problems such as homelessness (Anderson and Council of Social Agencies of Chicago 1923), poverty and segregation (Wirth 1928), deviance, and delinquency (Thrasher 1927). The *naturalistic case study* grounds observations and concepts in everyday social interactions and processes, which are observed directly by the researcher. Social scientists using the *extended case method* seek to complicate or "extend" extant concepts and theory by explicitly linking the case under study to local, national, and global trends and histories (Burawoy 1998).

Today, the case method is valued for its utility in labeling previously undocumented or misunderstood activities and understanding complicated social or historical phenomena, including social problems such as poverty, homelessness, drug use, and inner-city violence. Like early Chicago school scholars, contemporary social scientists use participant observation and in-depth interviews to systematically examine a social group or social phenomenon, while also developing new and innovative ways to collect data (Emerson 2004). In addition to data collected from direct and participant observation, the case method also takes advantage of the available quantitative data, including public records, and, at times, archival data. The primary data source for ethnographic case studies is the field researcher's notebook. Throughout the research process, the social scientist takes copious field notes, which are essential to data analysis and to the final presentation of the study to outside audiences (Emerson 2004). A common analytical tool used in case studies is analytical induction; a working hypothesis is developed once the researcher begins to collect data on his first case

and then tests and refines his developing theory throughout the process of data collection and analysis (Becker 1998). Typically, the findings from a case study are presented in narrative form, as a story that conveys the lived experience of the social group, actor, organization, or historical event.

Large quantitative studies (such as a population census or a large-scale survey) emphasize researcher objectivity. In contrast, the case method uses a researcher's subjectivity (Ragin 1997) or reflexivity (Burawoy 1998) as a tool to deepen one's understanding of a social group or phenomenon. Field researchers who are concerned with limiting the influence of researcher bias may construct a team of field researchers that will effectively standardize the process of data collection and analysis (for example, Newman 1999). A noted strength of the case method approach is the validity of its findings. Typically, the researcher using the case method has a wealth of sources including field notes, interviews, media reports, and archived materials to "triangulate" or cross-check during the research process. Critics also argue that the case study method does not allow for the generalization of findings to a much larger population of cases. Some researchers identify this as a limitation of the case method in the presentation of their findings, while others argue that one can generalize from a single case study to others, if similar conditions exist (Becker 1967).

Social scientists who use the case method help to complicate our understanding of everyday life, social processes, and social phenomena in ways that are elusive or impossible for quantitative-based studies to accomplish. At times, the most rigorous case studies will form the foundation of larger quantitative studies. The deep insight generated from the case study illuminates the many problems that concern contemporary social scientists.

SEE ALSO *Anthropology; Case Method, Extended; Ethnography; Social Science*

BIBLIOGRAPHY

Anderson, E. 2001. Urban Ethnography. In *International Encyclopedia of the Social and Behavioral Sciences*, eds. Neil J. Smelser and Paul B. Baltes. Oxford: Pergamon Press.

Anderson, N., and Council of Social Agencies of Chicago. [1923] 1967. *The Hobo: The Sociology of the Homeless Man.* Chicago: University of Chicago Press.

Becker, H. S. 1967. Whose Side Are We On? *Social Problems* 14 (3): 239–247.

Becker, H. S. 1992. Cases, Causes, Conjunctures, Stories, and Imagery. In *What Is a Case?: Exploring the Foundations of Social Inquiry*, eds. Charles C. Ragin, Howard S. Becker, and Gideon Sjoberg, 205–215. Cambridge, U.K.: Cambridge University Press.

Burawoy, Michael. 1998. The Extended Case Method. *Sociological Theory* 16 (1): 4–33.

Emerson, Robert. 2004. Introduction. In *Being Here and Being There: Fieldwork Encounters and Ethnographic Discoveries*, Vol. 595 of *The ANNALS of the American Academy of Political and Social Science Series*, eds. Elijah Anderson, Scott Brooks, Raymond Gunn, and Nikki Jones. Thousand Oaks, CA: Sage.

Feagin, J. R., A. M. Orum, and G. Sjorberg, eds. 1991. *A Case for the Case Study*. Chapel Hill: University of North Carolina Press.

Newman, Katherine S. 1999. *No Shame in My Game: The Working Poor in the Inner-City*. New York: Knopf and the Russell Sage Foundation.

Ragin, Charles C. 1997. Turning the Tables: How Case-Oriented Research Challenges Variable-Oriented Research. *Comparative Social Research* 16: 27–42.

Ragin, Charles C., Howard. S. Becker, and Gideon Sjoberg, eds. 1992. *What Is a Case?: Exploring the Foundations of Social Inquiry*. Cambridge, U.K.: Cambridge University Press.

Thrasher, F. M. 1927. *The Gang: A Study of 1,313 Gangs in Chicago*. Chicago: University of Chicago Press.

Whyte, W. F. 1943. *Street Corner Society: The Social Structure of an Italian Slum*. Chicago: University of Chicago Press.

Wirth, L. 1928. *The Ghetto*. Chicago: University of Chicago Press.

Zorbaugh, H. W. [1929] 1976. *The Gold Coast and the Slum: A Sociological Study of Chicago's Near North Side*. Chicago: University of Chicago Press.

Nikki Jones

CASE METHOD, EXTENDED

The extended case method was initially developed by anthropologists Max Gluckman (1911–1975) and Jaap van Velsen (1921–1990) in the late 1950s and early 1960s. It was designed to confront the decontextualized abstractions of structural approaches with richly detailed accounts of the actions and choices of real individuals. As conceived by Gluckman, the method places less emphasis on identifying structural regularities and more on detailed analyses of social processes wherein individual strategies and choices reveal the context of everyday life. He placed particular emphasis on extending case studies temporally, as "the most fruitful use of cases consists in taking a series of specific incidents affecting the same persons or groups, through a long period of time, and showing … [the] change of social relations among these persons and groups, within the framework of their social system and culture" (1961, p. 10).

Gluckman distinguished extended cases from two more restricted uses of the case study, both of which tended to serve structuralism's concern with social morphology: *apt illustration* (describing a simple event or action in such a way that it serves as a persuasive illustration of some general normative principle), and the analysis of *social situations* (whereby more complex microsocial events are analyzed to reveal structural characteristics at the macro level). By contrast, the extended case method includes "analyzing the interrelation of structural ('universal') regularities, on the one hand, and the actual ('unique') behavior of individuals, on the other" (van Velsen 1967, p. 148).

Van Velsen, who preferred the term *situational analysis*, also noted that: "[Structural] analysis does not allow for the fact that individuals are often faced by a choice between alternative norms" (1967, p. 131). Moreover, for van Velsen, what ultimately recommends the method is its ability to illuminate the complex relationship between a social world of "norms in conflict" (1967, p. 146) and the strategies and choices of individuals. Van Velsen also suggests that extending case studies over a broad geographical area may help researchers clarify the problem of defining the appropriate unit of study (1967, pp. 145–146).

One of van Velsen's students, sociologist Michael Burawoy, further defined the extended case method by highlighting its reflexivity (i.e., applying its method to the investigation itself) and by advocating it as a means to reexamine the relationship between data and theory. Burawoy closely associates the extended case method with what he calls a *reflexive model of science* (1998). Like Gluckman and van Velsen, he emphasizes the importance of variations in the case through time and space, as these often help to delineate the forces shaping a particular society (1991).

Burawoy also proposes that field researchers use their observations of specific cases to challenge and reconstruct existing theory. On this line of thinking, cases are selected specifically for their theoretical relevance, and by using a case to challenge existing theory, generalization from a single case study becomes possible (1991). This is accomplished through identification and analysis of anomalous cases (i.e., cases not accounted for by the existing theory). According to Burawoy, careful attention to such anomalies "leads directly to an analysis of domination and resistance" (1991, p. 279), thereby qualifying the extended case method as "the most appropriate way of using participant observation to (re)construct theories of advanced capitalism" (1991, p. 271).

SEE ALSO *Case Method; Ethnography*

BIBLIOGRAPHY

Burawoy, Michael. 1991. The Extended Case Method. In *Ethnography Unbound: Power and Resistance in the Modern Metropolis*, ed. Michael Burawoy et al., 271–287. Berkeley: University of California Press.

Burawoy, Michael. 1998. The Extended Case Method. *Sociological Theory* 16 (1): 4–33.

Gluckman, Max. 1961. Ethnographic Data in British Social Anthropology. *Sociological Review* 9 (1): 5–17.

Van Velsen, Jaap. 1967. The Extended-case Method and Situational Analysis. In *The Craft of Social Anthropology*, ed. A. L. Epstein, 129–149. London: Tavistock.

Peter Hennen

CASE STUDIES

SEE *Case Method.*

CASINO CAPITALISM

In common parlance, the term *casino capitalism* refers to the unregulated excesses associated with the "boom and bust" cycles of large speculative ventures, such as Enron. Its origins in the literature probably lie with John Maynard Keynes (1883–1946) and his famous *General Theory of Employment, Interest, and Money*, first published in 1936. In this vigorous attack on the classical and neoclassical economics that was predominant at Cambridge in the 1930s, Keynes refers to the "casino capitalism" embodied in the winning and losing of fortunes on the stock market. Keynes had already spoken in the 1920s of the immoral and insidious influence of an economy freed from restraint, believing that unfettered greed would create a wave of social problems. In chapter 12 of the *General Theory*, Keynes refers to casinos twice, first when he comments:

> Speculators may do no harm as bubbles on a steady stream of enterprise. But the position is serious when enterprise becomes the bubble on a whirlpool of speculation. When the capital development of a country becomes a by-product of the activities of a casino, the job is likely to be ill-done. The measure of success attained by Wall Street, regarded as an institution of which the proper social purpose is to direct new investment into the most profitable channels in terms of future yield, cannot be claimed as one of the outstanding triumphs of *laissez-faire* capitalism. (Keynes 1936, p. 159)

Later in the same chapter, Keynes comments:

> It is usually agreed that casinos should, in the public interest, be inaccessible and expensive. And perhaps the same is true of Stock Exchanges. That the sins of the London Stock Exchange are less than those of Wall Street may be due, not so much to differences in national character, as to the fact that to the average Englishman Throgmorton Street is, compared with Wall Street to the average American, inaccessible and very expensive. (Keynes 1936, p. 159)

In her 1986 book *Casino Capitalism*, British economist Susan Strange (1923–1998) comments: "The Western financial system is rapidly coming to resemble nothing as much as a vast casino." Strange argues that, between about 1965 and 1985, considerable increases in risk and uncertainty in economic markets gave rise to substantial social and political disruptions in the global system. She links these changes to five major trends: (1) innovations in the way financial markets operate; (2) the increased scope of markets; (3) the shift from commercial to investment banking; (4) the rise of the Asian investment markets; and (5) the removal of government regulation from banking. Strange argues for increased regulation and more substantial American leadership, which she believes is required because of the predominant role of the United States in the world markets. Coming as it did during the period of Reaganomics, her advice fell on deaf ears.

The term *casino capitalism* also appears in the work of Irving Fisher (1867–1947) and Hyman Minsky (1919–1996). Fisher, along with others in the 1930s, was faced with the problem of explaining the tragedy of the Great Depression. The common view among economists of this era, of whom Keynes may be representative, was that financial markets were like casinos, rather than "markets" in the usual sense of the word, and that these speculations contributed mightily to the social ills of the day. Fisher, along with John Burr Williams (1900–1989) and Benjamin Graham (1894–1976), claimed that the casino metaphor was misplaced. Instead, they argued that the asset prices of financial assets reflected "intrinsic value," which in turn could be calculated by deciding the total value of dividends likely to be produced in the future.

As with the work of Strange, who found value in the ideas associated with the term *casino capitalism*, Minsky contributed to an analysis of uncertainty in markets. Minsky is famous for proposing the *financial instability hypothesis*, which argues that most forms of capitalism tend toward instability. He supported long-term large-scale economies with decided government intervention. Dimitri Papadimitriou and L. Randall Wray (1998) argue that Minsky's work, in this way, is best labeled *post-*

Keynesian because he attempted to set out the precise institutional means by which the casino system might be better regulated, whereas Keynes made only the most general of comments. In all these cases, the notion that capitalism is essentially speculative and little more than a system of big and small bets in a grand game of chance is at work, and most of the writings around this topic focus on ways to make this irrational system more susceptible to reason and stability.

SEE ALSO *Beauty Contest Metaphor; Business Cycles, Empirical Literature; Business Cycles, Political; Business Cycles, Real; Business Cycles, Theories; Economic Crises; Economics, Post Keynesian; Financial Instability Hypothesis; Financial Markets; Fisher, Irving; Keynes, John Maynard; Minsky, Hyman; Speculation; Stock Exchanges*

BIBLIOGRAPHY

Keynes, John Maynard. 1936. *The General Theory of Employment, Interest, and Money.* New York: Harcourt.

Papadimitriou, Dimitri B., and L. Randall Wray. 1998. The Economic Contributions of Hyman Minsky: Varieties of Capitalism and Institutional Reform. *Review of Political Economy* 10 (2): 199–225.

Strange, Susan. [1986] 1997. *Casino Capitalism.* Manchester, U.K.: Manchester University Press.

Christopher Wilkes

CASTANEDA, CARLOS
1925–1998

Born in Cajamarca, Peru, in 1925, Carlos Castaneda moved to Los Angeles in 1955. He completed creative writing classes before enrolling at the University of California, Los Angeles (UCLA), in 1959. Castaneda's third book was approved as his UCLA doctoral dissertation in anthropology in 1973, after he changed its title and added a dissertation abstract (Fikes 1993, pp. 46, 101). His ten books (now twelve) had sold some eight million copies in seventeen languages when he died in 1998.

From 1968 to 1976, Castaneda was America's most celebrated anthropologist. His fame was subsequently eclipsed as scholarly critiques exposed fraudulent elements in his ethnography. Debunking, however, has done little to diminish Castaneda's standing as a New Age icon. Within that distinctly antirational audience, he inspired shamanic tourism and a religious cult.

Most anthropologists assumed that Castaneda's first three or four books were ethnographically factual. The most compelling evidence of fraud in Castaneda's books is textual inconsistency, especially two mutually incompatible assertions made by him, or his fictional (composite) mentor, don Juan Matus, whom Castaneda called a "Yaqui Indian sorcerer." The ingestion of three species of sacred plants was, Castaneda claimed, integral to his apprenticeship with don Juan, who "related the use of *Datura stramonium* (jimsonweed) and *Psilocybe mexicana* (sacred mushrooms) to the acquisition of power he called an 'ally.' He related the use of *Lophophora williamsii* (peyote) to acquisition of wisdom, or knowledge of the right way to live" (Castaneda 1969, p. 9). In Castaneda's third book, don Juan revoked the value originally ascribed to acquiring allies, via jimsonweed and mushrooms, and learning righteousness with peyote, proclaiming instead that administration of those plants was merely a strategy to shatter Castaneda's "dogmatic certainty" about his worldview. By removing that obstacle, don Juan could implant his perspective on sorcery (Castaneda 1974, pp. xii–xiii; Fikes 1996, p. 140). Don Juan's new emphasis on his teaching of sorcery annuls the tutelary function he originally attributed to the spirits contained in peyote and the other plant allies.

Self-contradictory statements resulted when Castaneda addressed skeptics without reconciling those responses with his original statements. In 1968, shortly after Castaneda's first book appeared, R. Gordon Wasson (1898–1986), a renowned specialist on sacred mushrooms, wrote to Castaneda. Replying to Wasson, Castaneda, without justification, removed jimsonweed (*Datura*) from the category of plants possessing allies, as originally defined by don Juan (Castaneda 1969, p. 9). Castaneda's letter to Wasson asserted that, "unlike peyote and Jimson weed, the mushrooms contained don Juan's ally." Richard de Mille recognized another textual inconsistency in Castaneda's letter. Don Juan allegedly imposed a rule of "total secrecy" about revealing how he collected those mushrooms (de Mille 1980, p. 323). Castaneda violated that rule by divulging details: "Don Juan always picked the mushrooms with his left hand, transferred them to his right, and then put them through the neck of the gourd" (1980, p. 324). Another textual inconsistency documented by de Mille (1980, pp. 322–329) concerns Castaneda's "field notes," which put him in Sonora, Mexico, on September 6, 1968, the same day he dated his letter from Los Angeles to Wasson.

Disparities between Castaneda's claims and the reports of independent researchers also attest to fabrication. Castaneda's method of achieving ecstasy by smoking a mixture of plants—including psilocybin mushrooms— has never been corroborated by any other ethnographer. Actual verification is impossible because most of the plants in that mixture were never identified. His claim of becoming a crow after smoking those mushrooms, and being hypnotized by don Juan, is singular (Fikes 1996, p. 141).

Castaneda's textual inconsistencies and the numerous discrepancies between his books and at least one thousand reports of independent researchers render his portrait of peyotism an inane parody. Similarly, Weston La Barre (1911–1996), a specialist in peyote rituals performed in the Native American Church (NAC), condemned Castaneda's first two books as pseudo-ethnography (La Barre 1989, p. 272). Paradigmatic here is don Juan's momentous decision to accept Castaneda as his apprentice, because "Mescalito" (an erroneous name for the peyote spirit) had, in the form of a dog, caroused with Castaneda (1969, pp. 33–41). That assertion is aberrant (Fikes 1993, pp. 61–62) and was contradicted when don Juan usurped the tutelary function originally ascribed to peyote.

Castaneda failed to distinguish the most elementary aspects of peyote meetings, including the purpose of such meetings and the leader's identity (Fikes 1996, pp. 138–139; Fikes 2004). Don Juan declared that a light hovering above Castaneda in a peyote ritual was an omen. Castaneda never saw that light, and don Juan never clarified its meaning (Fikes 1996, p. 139). This unexplained "omen" contrasts with momentous experiences comprehended by recipients and validated by others, as illustrated by the light that led NAC leader Albert Hensley to read the biblical passage describing Jesus' baptism. Hensley's revelation set a precedent for baptism in the NAC (Fikes 1996, p. 139).

Castaneda's followers have sought shamans comparable to don Juan among the Yaqui (who do not venerate peyote) and Huichol (whose peyote pilgrimages are legendary). Recognizing peyote as the cornerstone of Castaneda's alleged apprenticeship, American tour operators have guided sightseers into the sacred land where Huichols venerate the peyote spirit. A steadily rising tide of tourists has stimulated Mexican authorities to incarcerate Huichol peyote hunters and has incited traditional Huichols to prohibit outsiders from entering their homeland without permits (Fikes 1999; Fikes and Weigand 2004). Castaneda's legacy survives in the Tensegrity cult based on his teachings.

BIBLIOGRAPHY

Castaneda, Carlos. [1968] 1969. *The Teachings of Don Juan: A Yaqui Way of Knowledge.* New York: Ballantine.

Castaneda, Carlos. [1972] 1974. *Journey to Ixtlan: The Lessons of Don Juan.* New York: Pocket Books.

de Mille, Richard, ed. 1980. *The Don Juan Papers: Further Castaneda Controversies.* Santa Barbara, CA: Ross-Erickson.

Fikes, Jay C. 1993. *Carlos Castaneda, Academic Opportunism, and the Psychedelic Sixties.* Victoria, BC: Millenia.

Fikes, Jay C. 1996. Carlos Castaneda and don Juan. In *The Encyclopedia of the Paranormal,* ed. Gordon Stein, 135–143. Amherst, NY: Prometheus.

Fikes, Jay C. 1999. Examining Ethics, Benefits, and Perils of Tours to Mexico. In *International Conference on Heritage, Multicultural Attractions, and Tourism,* Vol. 1, ed. Meral Korzay, 407–421. Istanbul, Turkey: Bosphorus University.

Fikes, Jay C. 2004. Peyote Ritual Use. In *Shamanism: An Encyclopedia of World Beliefs, Practices, and Culture,* eds. Mariko N. Walter and Eva J. N. Fridman, 336–339. Santa Barbara, CA: ABC-CLIO.

Fikes, Jay C., and Phil C. Weigand. 2004. Sensacionalismo y etnografia: El caso de los Huicholes de Jalisco. *Relaciones* 25 (98): 50–68.

La Barre, Weston. 1989. *The Peyote Cult.* 5th ed. Norman: University of Oklahoma Press.

Jay Courtney Fikes

CASTE

Nearly all societies have had some form of social stratification, whether ascriptive or achieved, based on race, class, religion, ethnicity, language, education, or occupation. The Hindu ascriptive caste system in India is perhaps the most complex and rigid. It is based on birth, which determines one's occupation (especially in contemporary rural India), and is maintained by endogamy, commensality, rituals, dietary practices, and norms of purity and pollution. The English term *caste* is derived from the Portuguese word *casta*, which refers to lineage, breed, or race.

THE HINDU CASTE SYSTEM

The Hindu caste system is interpreted in two ways. First is the standard *varna* description of the caste system as a fourfold division of Hindu society. Its origins are noted in the *Rig Veda,* one of the sacred texts of Hinduism, which dates back some 3,000 years. The term *varna,* which literally means color, does not reference the actual racial features of those who fall into the four *varnas,* as many scholars have established. *Brahmins* constitute the sacerdotal order, which has priestly duties including the interpretation of numerous complex religious texts in Sanskrit, a language that traditionally only they mastered. Below them are the *Kshatriyas,* the caste of warriors and rulers. They are followed by the *Vaisya,* who typically engage in trade and commerce. The bottom is the *Shudra,* or peasant and laborer caste, a large and diverse group that comprises artisans ranging from goldsmiths to washermen and peasants who may own sizeable tracts of land. Outside the fourfold system are the "untouchables," now commonly referred to as *Dalits* ("the oppressed"), who perform the most menial tasks. Normally, women in the top three *varnas* do not pursue the hereditary occupations, whereas Shudra and Dalit caste women do. The vast majority of India, which is rural, is caste-based as far as inheritance of occupations is concerned.

The hierarchy among various castes is further based on the notions of ritual purity and pollution. The higher the caste, the greater the purity of the group, while lower caste status is associated with pollution. Moreover, the nature of the occupation that one is born into also confers purity or pollution. For example those who dig graves, clean latrines, sweep streets, or work with leather are more polluting than those in "clean" occupations such as trade or priesthood. Those usually engaged in polluting occupations must maintain a prescribed distance from the castes deemed pure to avoid polluting them through contact. For this reason, it is not uncommon for lower caste groups to live in segregated colonies on the outskirts of Indian villages even today.

M. N. Srinivas (1962) and André Béteille (1996), among others, consider the *varna* description simplistic because it does not represent the empirical reality of caste in either ancient or modern India. Their interpretation of the caste system as a constellation of more than 3,500 *jatis* with internal and regional variations has gained validity among scholars. Whenever ordinary Indians refer to caste, they are referring to *jati*, not to *varna*. In the words of Béteille, "whereas *varna* refers primarily to order and classification, the primary reference of *jati* is to birth and the social identity ascribed by birth" (p. 22). In most sociological analyses (and here) the term *caste* is used to represent its *jati* dimension.

CASTE IN MODERN INDIA

Although the caste system has eroded to some extent, it still has a hold in contemporary Indian society. One factor in this has been the Indian constitution, which empowers the state to make special provisions for the advancement of low-caste citizens, including the more than 160 million Dalits (who are listed in a schedule attached to the constitution and thus called "Scheduled Castes"), the nearly 50 million tribals (also listed in a schedule and hence called the "Scheduled Tribes"), and the 500 million "Other Backward Classes." Under these provisions 15 percent of government jobs and university places have been reserved for members of the Scheduled Castes, 7 percent for Scheduled Tribes, and 27 percent for the Other Backward Classes. Initially, this affirmative action was to remain in place only until these marginalized castes caught up with the more privileged upper castes, but this has not yet happened, and there are strong pressures not only to extend indefinitely these policies but also to include caste groups that traditionally belong to

Shudra status. The constitution also provides for the reservation of electoral seats for Scheduled Castes in the parliament of India and all the state legislatures. Similar rules govern elections for village and district councils. Although these measures are necessary to create a level playing field for historically deprived caste groups, they also go against another constitutional objective—the elimination of discrimination based on caste.

The affirmative action measures have empowered Dalits to some extent. In 1997, a Dalit, K. R. Narayanan, became the president of India, and by 2001 more than 13 percent of senior bureaucrats in the government of India were Dalits (Gupta 2001, p. 13). However, such gains are overshadowed by the stubborn continuation of inequalities. Dalits and Scheduled Tribes, particularly women, are at the bottom of the economic ladder (Deshpande 2002). Dalits in rural India are still forced into indentured farm labor. In some parts of the country there is still strong opposition to them owning land and sharing public facilities such as temples and wells.

A second factor that has enabled the caste system to flourish is its function as a "vote bank." More often than not, elections are fought not so much over political ideologies and programs but on the caste identity of the contestants. Virtually all castes have well-organized and well-funded associations that mobilize voters for their caste's candidates. Although such mobilization enhances political awareness and participation by various castes, at the same time it also undermines efforts to create a casteless society.

A third factor is that at the individual level, caste identity is still hereditary. Unlike Christianity and Islam, Hinduism does not approve proselytization, and it has no ecclesiastical order. Effectively, then, caste functions as the church of Hinduism, operating with centuries-old customs, norms, and values. Given these conditions, there are no recognized means by which, for example, a Dalit can move up the *ritual* hierarchy, or a Brahmin move down. However, following India's independence in 1947 and adoption of a constitution that stipulated creation of a secular society, various mechanisms have evolved that have enabled members of lower castes, as a group, to claim superior *social status* when they emulate the customs, rituals, and way of life of upper castes (Srinivas 1962; Shah 2005). This process is called *Sanskritization*. For example, an individual (or a group) belonging to Shudra *jati* may become vegetarian, worship the gods that upper castes worship, and even recite Sanskritic hymns as part of its regular prayers, thus claiming status mobility (but not mobility in the ritual hierarchy). Sanskritization is an informal and voluntary process that does not involve participants' merging their identities with the caste whose way of life they imitate, nor will the higher *jati* welcome them to its fold just because they adopted their ways. Sanskritization is most effective when it occurs at the group level. However, the basic nature of ascription continues. For example, an African American can earn high status in terms of his accomplishments, but his ascriptive status remains unchanged—he is not white. Likewise, an untouchable in India can rise to the position of president of India, but he is still characterized in the media as first untouchable to become president: his caste identity precedes his accomplishment.

A fourth factor that facilitates the continuity of caste is endogamy. The vast majority of marriages in India are still arranged by elders who ensure that their children marry from their own caste. However, a recent report in a south Indian newspaper titled "An Arranged Love Marriage" refers to the flexibility that is emerging in arranged marriages (*Deccan Herald*). Such marriages are becoming common among the urban middle class when future partners who belong to same caste (and perhaps, class too) meet at work and go on "dates." When they find they are mutually suitable, the couple seek the consent of their parents who are more than willing to bless the union since it liberates them from the hassle of dowry negotiations, etc. And yet, this is still an urban phenomenon occurring only among a minority of those who are in the marriage market.

SOME VISIBLE CHANGES IN CASTE RELATIONS

Some aspects of the traditional caste system are changing, especially in urban areas. First, the inheritance of occupations by birth is no longer common except among the Dalits, especially in rural areas. More urban Dalits have succeeded in availing themselves of affirmative action measures. Furthermore, those of lower castes who live in urban areas have greater access to higher education, which makes them more competitive in the job market, especially in the private sector, where reservation policies are not applicable. At the time of this writing, the government of India has proposed to increase quotas for Old Backward Classes in all centrally funded institutions such as the Indian Institutes of Management, Indian Institutes of Technology, and others. This move has resulted in a public debate about the continuing centrality of caste in admission policies which in the end works against value of merit (for details see *India Today*).

Second, although restrictions based on purity and pollution continue to shape social distance and interactions between high and low castes in villages of India, where roughly 70 percent of India's population resides, they are becoming increasingly hard to observe or enforce in large towns and cities. Although it is easy to identify a Dalit in a small village, it is not that easy to identify a Brahmin or

a Dalit among, for example, public-transit passengers in a large city. As Indian society becomes increasingly modern, the norms of purity and pollution that are central to the traditional caste system are weakening.

Finally, traditionally caste-based dietary practices are eroding, especially in urban areas, due in part to the way in which nonvegetarian meals are packaged, especially in Western fast-food outlets. Many upper-caste Hindus may not cook meat in their homes, but they have few qualms about breaking dietary taboos in McDonald's, Pizza Hut, or similar fast-food outlets, which are becoming fashionable dining places for urban upwardly mobile Indians.

OTHER RELIGIONS AND CASTE

Many of the religions that entered India during the last five to ten centuries targeted poor and marginalized castes for conversion, but becoming a Christian or Muslim did not accord converts a status free of caste. Instead, for the vast majority, their caste identities stayed with them, and their children and grandchildren have been unable to shed them. At the same time, the converts have been denied by many legal jurisdictions the constitutional benefits of Scheduled Caste and Scheduled Tribe status. Recent attempts by those who converted to Christianity from the lowest castes of Hinduism (Scheduled Castes) to claim Scheduled Caste status and thus eligibility for constitutionally guaranteed benefits have not been successful. The same failure has greeted attempts by individuals in some regions of the country whose status is in proximity to Scheduled Castes, such as *dhobis* (washermen) and *chamars* (leather workers). In fact, conversion of a Dalit, who is Hindu by definition, to Christianity has not been advantageous to many. It might have given them a sense of hope and status but it also deprived them of some privileges that their old status as oppressed Hindus, entitled by the constitution to certain privileges, afforded.

Features of caste continue even in those religions such as Sikhism that emerged in protest against the rigidity of Hindu rites and rituals and, more importantly, against the ascriptive caste system. Over time, social divisions resembling caste hierarchy became part of Sikh society as Sikhs strongly protected and promoted their identities as Jat, Mazabi, and Ramgarhia Sikhs, with claims to superiority over each other and norms of endogamy.

Buddhism arose around the sixth century, partly in protest against the Hindu caste system. Although its founder was a Kshatriya, the most likely candidates for conversion have come from lower castes. While Buddhism extended its influence beyond the shores of India, it was not a great success in India until the 1950s, when Dr. Babasaheb Ambedkar, a Dalit who gave independent India its constitution, encouraged fellow Dalits to convert to Buddhism; millions did, and some still continue to do so. However, conversion to Buddhism (just as in the case of Christianity) did not amount to renunciation of one's caste identity. Although changing one's religion may be an act of protest against the caste system, Buddhist converts are reluctant to renounce their caste identity because they still want to obtain the benefits that the Dalit status entitles them to under the Indian constitution—a situation which is contradictory because converts to Christianity are not entitled to similar privileges.

CASTE OUTSIDE INDIA

In the late nineteenth and early twentieth centuries Britain, the colonial ruler of India, encouraged Indians to migrate to its other colonies in the Caribbean and Africa as indentured laborers in its bid to maintain its economic success. Most of the Indians who chose to migrate were members of lower castes who saw migration as an opportunity for upward mobility. Although the first generation of immigrants tended to retain their caste identities, particularly in matters of marriage and religious rites (Schwartz 1967), subsequent generations did not, because of the assimilative nature of economic, political, and juridical forces (Motwani, Gosine, and Barot-Motwani 1993; Gosine and Narine 1999). Caste cannot be easily transplanted to an environment where Hinduism is not the operative religion.

Systems of stratification comparable to the Indian caste system have been identified in other parts of the world. For example, in Nigeria the relations between the Ibo and Osu groups are similar to those of upper and lower castes. In Somalia a social group called Midgam or Madibhan suffers from all the impediments that Dalits experience: impurity, pollution, and social distance. The Burakumin of Japan have been compared with the Dalits, as they have faced similar restrictions. These restrictions were outlawed in 1871, but, as in the case of Dalits, discrimination continues, especially in matters of employment and marriage (Henshall 1999). These dichotomous divisions, however, do not come close to the intricate caste system. At best, they compare two opposite ends of caste system with another system similar to it, ignoring the middle, wherein lies the heart of caste system.

Even though there have been stout rejections of the claim that caste can be equated with race (see, among others, Gupta 2001) purely on the grounds of universal practices of discrimination based on ascription, scholars such as Gerald Berreman (1960; 1972) have attempted to compare American blacks to untouchable castes in India. However, the black-white dichotomous system in the United States differs from the fourfold caste system in India in that it is ordained not by religious considerations, but by economic and social ones (Cox 1948).

Nearly all societies are stratified in one way or another, and some groups will always be relegated to the margins. However, the Indian caste system is unique because of its complexity, its religious foundation, its hereditary occupational system, and its norms of endogamy. More important, caste has served to energize Indian polity because it has been a primary means of motivating and mobilizing citizens to take part in electoral politics. Perhaps that has been a positive aspect of caste in Indian society, but the time may come to look for other means of motivating the electorate in India.

SEE ALSO *Caste, Anthropology of; Hierarchy; Inequality, Political; Segregation; Stratification*

BIBLIOGRAPHY

Berreman, Gerald. 1960. Caste in India and the United States. *American Journal of Sociology* 66 (2): 120–127.

Berreman, Gerald. 1972. Race, Caste, and Other Invidious Distinctions in Social Stratification. *Race* 13 (4): 385–414.

Béteille, André. 1996. Varna and Jati. *Sociological Bulletin* 45 (1): 15–28.

Cox, Oliver C. 1948. *Caste, Class, and Race*. New York: Monthly Review Press.

Deccan Herald. 2006. An Arranged Love Marriage. June 26.

Deshpande, Ashwini. 2002. Assets versus Autonomy? The Changing Face of the Gender-Caste Overlap in India. *Feminist Economist* 8 (2): 19–35.

Gosine, Mahin, and Dhanpaul Narine, eds. 1999. *Sojourners to Settlers: Indian Migrants in the Caribbean and the Americas*. Windsor, NJ: Windsor Press.

Gupta, Dipankar. 2001. Caste, Race, Politics. http://www.india-seminar.com.

Henshall, Kenneth G. 1999. *Dimensions of Japanese Society: Gender, Margins, and Mainstream*. New York: Palgrave Macmillan.

India Today. 2006. Casting for Votes. May 15.

Motwani, Jagat K., Mahin Gosine, and Jyoti Barot-Motwani, eds. 1993. *Global Indian Diaspora: Yesterday, Today, and Tomorrow*. New York: Global Organization of People of Indian Origin.

Schwartz, Barton. 1967. *Caste in Overseas Indian Communities*. Chicago: Chandler Publishing.

Shah, A. M. 2005. Sanskritization Revisited. *Sociological Bulletin* 54 (2): 31–39.

Srinivas, M. N. 1962. Varna and Caste. In *Caste in Modern India and Other Essays*, 63–69. Bombay: Asia Publishing House.

Srinivas, M. N. 1966. Sanskritization. In *Social Change in Modern India*, 1–45. Berkeley: University of California Press.

G. N. Ramu

CASTE, ANTHROPOLOGY OF

The term *caste* refers, paradigmatically, to a social institution in India and elsewhere in South Asia in which endogamous descent groups, known as *castes* or *subcastes*, are hierarchically ranked. It has also been used to described hereditary forms of social stratification in non–South Asian contexts, such as Japan, the American South, and elsewhere. The validity of usage outside of South Asian contexts, however, ultimately turns on how we are to understand the paradigmatic Indian case—a matter of considerable and ongoing debate. This article therefore confines itself to the study of caste in India, from its emergence in the colonial period to today.

BEGINNINGS OF CASTE THEORY

Throughout South Asia individual castes and subcastes are referred to as *jāti*, an Indo-Aryan word meaning a category of related persons thought to be of the same physical and moral substance, though the word can also mean genus, species, or race and other allegedly natural types. *Caste*, meaning the systematic basis upon which individual *jātis* are organized, has never perfectly conformed to either popular or scholarly models; not only do the customs and practices of *jāti* hierarchies vary from region to region, they also are commonly interpreted in different ways even within a single village. All this has been well known since the colonial period. But while scholars had a growing appreciation of this empirical complexity, their basic interpretive framework remained, until recently, remarkably stable.

From the late eighteenth century, the colonial picture of caste society was shaped by Brahmin informants who regarded caste as a religious matter and who saw local *jāti* hierarchies as depending on the scriptural theory of *varṇa*—an idealized four-fold social division that proclaimed the spiritual authority of the *brahmana* (Brahmin) superior to the worldly power of the *kṣatriya* (warrior/king), who it enjoined to enforce brahminical law over the *vaiśya* (merchant) and *śūdra* (laborer). Colonial observers construed brahminical ideology as historical reality: The wily Brahmin had devised a hidebound social order that locked each caste into a particular occupation serving elite interests. Preoccupied with their own racial distinction, colonizers furthermore envisioned low-ranked laboring castes as conquered indigenes and high-ranked castes as the descendents of ancient Aryan colonizers. The guiding thread of colonial caste theory, however, was an orientalist notion of religious determinism—namely, that an elaborate ritual code had engendered universal respect for brahminical authority, enabling high-ranked castes to maintain unbroken control over the toiling masses for millennia.

THE RITUAL CONSENSUS

Speculative histories and detailed catalogues of caste-based customs dominated colonial anthropology until systematic village-based fieldwork in the 1950s looked at these customs' everyday context to see how caste actually worked. That more sophisticated approach, which the influential Indian anthropologist M. N. Srinivas exemplified, helped undermine stereotypes of caste society as static and passively determined by religious ideology. Srinivas showed that wealth and physical force often trumped mere ritual (1959), and that, although an individual's ritual status was indeed fixed by their *jāti*, whole *jātis* could sometimes increase their status by adopting the customs of higher-ranked castes (1956). Srinivas's important insights nevertheless remained within the received picture of the caste system as an essentially religious affair by treating the control of land and servile labor, merchant capital, the state, and sheer physical dominance—all of which were termed *secular*—as extrinsic factors that might interact with caste, but were not an inherent part of it.

The tendency to idealize caste as inherently distinct from these less exotic aspects of social reality was taken to a new extreme by French sociologist Louis Dumont, whose *Homo Hierarchicus* went so far as to attack empiricism itself as "Westernistic" and therefore incapable of grasping caste's true, Indian essence (1980 [1966], p. 32). For the closer anthropologists had looked, the more caste appeared to be but congeries of variable and even contradictory elements, its singular essence reduced to a vanishing point. If such an approach were "logically carried out," Dumont had observed in 1958, "we should have to pretend … that India is a mere geographical entity [i.e., lacking a singular cultural essence] similar to Africa" (p. 50). Dumont's solution was to redefine the object of inquiry itself as being, not the messy realities of everyday life, but the flexible ideological principle that rendered such realities coherent. He named this principle *hierarchy*, novelly defined as a universal consensus of values pervading all levels of society and cognition, subordinating the individual to the social whole, political and economic power to the spiritual authority of brahminical religion, and the substantial historical realities of *jāti* to the timeless ideal of *varṇa*—all of which he explained as the hierarchical "encompassment" of the impure by the pure. Those who saw caste as exploitive or as stifling individual freedom had simply failed to grasp the reality of a culture that simply does not accept the West's egalitarian and individualist ethic. Exploitation cannot exist in a caste society, Dumont reasoned, because "an economic phenomenon [like exploitation] presupposes an individual subject," whereas in caste society, "everything is directed to the whole … as part and parcel of the necessary order" (1980 [1966], p. 107).

Dumont's brilliant synthesis of the existing scholarship made *Homo Hierarchicus* a standard reference for all future discussions of caste, despite disagreement over its visionary epistemology. At one extreme, American anthropologist McKim Marriott (1976) embraced an all-determining cultural hiatus between India and the West even more absolute than Dumont's, for the secular factors Dumont had merely downgraded to a subordinate level were dissolved entirely in Marriott's *ethnosociology*—an account built completely on native categories, thereby consigning non–culturally recognized reality to theoretical oblivion. On the other side, many sober-minded anthropologists continued to regard both secular realities and caste ideology as a matter of empirical inquiry, while nevertheless accepting the culturalist definition of caste as ritual order.

POST-DUMONTIAN CRITIQUE

This picture, however, would soon be questioned by two distinct groups of researchers: ethnographers studying the lowest-ranked "untouchable" castes (today called *Dalits*), and historians investigating transformations of native society under colonial rule. Both questioned the social and political bases upon which official knowledge about caste had been produced; both ceased to assume that caste had some singular cultural essence, analyzing it instead as a composite phenomenon intrinsically and irreducibly involving relations of power.

Throughout India the panoply of local caste differences are overshadowed—especially in the traditional heartlands of deltaic civilization—by a singular social division today commonly identified with a ritual distinction between "touchable" *jātis* and "untouchable" ones. The latter, whose *jāti* names were once used interchangeably with terms for slave, remained largely beyond the pale of Hindu society until the early twentieth century. Quintessential outsiders, Dalits were paradoxically indispensable to the very existence, symbolic and material, of caste society: Compelled to remove polluting substances, their labor guaranteed that others remained pure; hereditarily tied to producing for others, they underwrote other castes' material privilege. Were "untouchables" consigned to a life of hard agricultural labor on account of their impurity, or was being coded impure and assigned polluting tasks simply part of what it meant to be under the total domination of others? One can abstract a noetic model of ritual purity from the complex social phenomenon of caste, à la Dumont, but it is unclear why caste itself should be defined by the result of this exercise. Not only would this seem to reduce the anthropological explanation of a society to that society's own self-understanding, it was also far from clear that what Dumont described was not simply the view of some Indians but not others. As

anthropologist Owen Lynch (1977) would argue, Dumont's claim to have accessed a civilizational truth encompassing all socially locatable and interested representations amounted to a form of theoretical solipsism. Specifically, Dumont's synthesis had ignored the testimony of the most dominated peoples, prompting Dalit specialist Gerald Berreman to dismiss it as merely the "rationale for a system of institutionalized inequality as advertised and endorsed by its … beneficiaries" (1971, p. 23), which only seemed plausible in the context of an anthropological tradition that had itself habitually privileged certain forms of representations and discounted others.

It would be wrong to assume, however, that anthropologists' neglect of the subaltern evidence meant they had simply reproduced the timeless ideology of elites. On the contrary, considerable evidence suggests that much of what anthropologists—as well as most Indians—have come to recognize as caste is a fallout of colonization and the practices by which colonizers sought to know and control the colonized. Research by historian Nicholas Dirks (1993), for instance, suggests that the subordination of kingly power to brahminical ritual, seen by Dumont as Hindu civilization's timeless truth, was in fact the handiwork of colonial power, which had reduced indigenous kings, for the first time in history, to a purely symbolic and genuinely inferior status. With the political authority of India's autonomous kingdoms no longer the legitimating framework for localized *jāti* arrangements, something quite new was born. As historical anthropologist Bernard Cohn (1984) showed, the novel idea that geographically and culturally distant *jātis* composed a single ritual order became an institutional reality, when, in the 1870s, census officials began to publicly rank all castes on this basis.

The claim is not, Dirks (2001) has stressed, that the British invented caste *ex nihilo*, but that they conceptually and administratively redefined it. Once formed and conceptualized within multiple, local logics—military, agrarian, mercantile, and (in the signal case of the Brahmin) religious—all of which were intrinsically political, caste was now subsumed under a single, allegedly apolitical, specifically Hindu, and pan-Indian social order. Defining caste religiously—as the ritual essence of a newly imagined Hindu community—made outsiders of Muslims and undermined real communities of allied Hindu and Muslim *jātis*. Dalits, conversely, were proclaimed (ritually disadvantaged) Hindus in the 1871 census, and were soon embraced as such by Hindu nationalists and reformers like Gandhi, who saw their inclusion within Hinduism as vital to national strength. Equally significant, however, was the fact that geographically disparate Dalit *jātis* had even been brought together into a single, officially recognized category. For in the 1920s they too would begin to assert an autonomous political identity, under the leadership of Dalit statesman B. R. Ambedkar, and to reject the Gandhian claim that their interests lay with the Hindu community and caste elites.

Liberated from foreign rule, the democratic Republic of India has introduced numerous policies to protect Dalits from abuse and to better their lot (as long as they do not renounce Hinduism for Islam or Christianity), and, in the arena of electoral politics, parties representing Dalits and other disadvantaged castes have begun to encroach on what was once the preserve of caste elites. Yet Dalits remain significantly below non-Dalit counterparts in all social and economic indicators, and as Smita Narula's well-corroborated Human Rights Watch report (1999) attests, in much of rural India dominant castes continue to stigmatize, exploit, and violently suppress Dalits. Even in more urbane settings, Dalits describe a pervasive climate of discrimination in housing, the workplace, and classrooms, and Dalit activists have sought international recognition for their plight—most prominently at the 2001 U.N. World Conference against Racism, Racial Discrimination, Xenophobia, and Related Intolerance. Indians from more privileged backgrounds, however, frequently lament Dalit antagonism as the "politicization of caste," a development they trace to colonial divide-and-rule policies. Indeed, in the latter decades of their rule, British officials had actively sought to undermine the nationalist movement by exploiting tensions between Dalits and the movement's overwhelmingly elite, high-caste Hindu leadership. The colonial roots of modern caste politics, however, go deeper and are more tangled than this observation implies. For claims about a "politicization of caste" are every bit as political and socially locatable as the Dalit activism they decry, and—by representing caste as formerly distinct from the political—are less a critique of colonial caste policy than the restatement of its fundamental premise.

SEE ALSO *Caste*

BIBLIOGRAPHY

Bayly, Susan. 1999. *Caste, Society and Politics in India from the Eighteenth Century to the Modern Age*. New York: Cambridge University Press.

Berreman, Gerald D. 1971. The Brahmannical View of Caste. *Contributions to Indian Sociology*, n.s., 5: 16–23. (Also in *Caste and Other Inequities: Essays on Inequality*, ed. Gerald D. Berreman, 155–163. Meerut, India: Folklore Institute, 1971.)

Cohn, Bernard. 1984. The Census, Social Structure, and Objectification in South Asia. *Folk* 26: 25–49. (Also in *An Anthropologist among the Historians and Other Essays*, ed. Bernard Cohn, 224–254. New York: Oxford University Press, 1987.)

Dirks, Nicholas B. 1993. *The Hollow Crown: Ethnohistory of an Indian Kingdom*. Ann Arbor: University of Michigan.

Dirks, Nicholas B. 2001. *Castes of Mind: Colonialism and the Making of Modern India*. Princeton, NJ: Princeton University Press.

Dumont, Louis. 1958. A. M. Hocart on Caste: Religion and Power. *Contributions to Indian Sociology* 2: 45–63.

Dumont, Louis. 1980. *Homo Hierarchicus: The Caste System and Its Implications*. Trans. Mark Sainsbury, Louis Dumont, and Basia Gulati. Chicago: University of Chicago Press. Originally published as *Homo hierarchicus: Le système des castes et ses implications* (Paris: Editions Gallimard, 1964).

Lynch, Owen M. 1977. Method and Theory in the Sociology of Louis Dumont. In *The New Wind: Changing Identities in South Asia*, ed. Kenneth David, 239–262. The Hague: Mouton.

Marriott, McKim. 1976. Hindu Transactions: Diversity without Dualism. In *Transaction and Meaning: Directions in the Anthropology of Exchange and Symbolic Behavior*, ed. Bruce Kapferer, 109–142. Philadelphia: Institute for the Study of Human Issues.

Narula, Smita. 1999. *Broken People: Caste Violence against India's "Untouchables"*. New York: Human Rights Watch.

Sharma, Ursula. 1999. *Caste*. Philadelphia: Open University Press.

Srinivas, M. N. 1956. A Note on Sanskritization and Westernization. *The Far Eastern Quarterly* 15 (4): 481–496.

Srinivas, M. N. 1959. The Dominant Caste in Rampura. *American Anthropologist*, n.s., 61 (1): 1–16.

Nathaniel P. Roberts

CASTE SYSTEM, INDIA
SEE *Caste*.

CASTRATION
SEE *Sterilization, Human*.

CASTRO, FIDEL
1926–

Fidel Castro, a first-generation Cuban, was born August 13, 1926, to a wealthy farming family in the eastern region of Oriente. Their 11,000 hectares produced wood, sugarcane, and cattle. His father had migrated from Galicia, Spain, while his religious peasant mother had been born in Cuba of Spanish parents. Both parents learned to read and write although neither went to school. Fidel Castro was one of six children.

When Castro was three years old, the worldwide economic depression hit rural Cuba. From 1929 to 1933 the island experienced widespread social and political upheaval, culminating when Fulgencio Batista (1901–1973), a sergeant, led a military revolt that put a radical government in power. Batista, at the behest of the American ambassador, then overthrew it and continued to dominate Cuban politics until 1959.

Castro initially went to a small rural school. At age six, in 1932, he left for a private Catholic elementary boarding school in Santiago de Cuba. Later he went to the leading elite Jesuit secondary school, Colegio Belén, in Cuba's capital city of Havana. From the Spanish priests he learned self-discipline. In 1943 he earned an award as the country's best secondary-school athlete. During school breaks, he visited the family farm and read newspaper reports about the Spanish Civil War (1936–1939) or World War II (1939–1945) to his parents and workers. In the Spanish conflict, his family supported Francisco Franco (1892–1975).

ENTERING POLITICS

In September 1945, at the age of nineteen, Castro entered the University of Havana. The campus was his springboard to national politics. Just the previous year, national elections had allowed the Partido Revolucionario Cubano (PRC), also known as the Auténtico Party, to set up a government. The PRC promised major social reforms and greater national independence. Castro immediately became involved in the tumultuous politics of the time. Students and professors transformed courses into discussions of Cuba's social, economic, and political problems.

In 1947 he participated in setting up a new populist political party, the Partido del Pueblo Cubano, or Ortodoxo Party, which had separated from the PRC. The Ortodoxos shared the same values as the PRC but claimed the Auténtico government had failed to deliver on its promised reforms and instead had become thoroughly corrupt.

Early in his life Castro had absorbed anticapitalist ideas based on Catholic counter-reformation conservative thought. While attending high school, he discovered the nationalist, anti-imperialist revolutionary writings and biography of the Cuban patriot José Martí (1853–1895). At the University of Havana he became acquainted with radical works, including those of the German political philosopher Karl Marx (1818–1883) and the Russian Communist leader Vladimir Lenin (1870–1924). He claims that in those days he became a utopian socialist and cites Martí as his primary influence.

During his university years, from 1945 to 1950, Castro was a political activist. In September 1947 he joined an armed expeditionary force composed of Cubans and exiles from the Dominican Republic intending to oust the government of the dictator Rafael Leónidas Trujillo (1891–1961). The invasion was never launched. The next year, in April 1948 as a representative of the Law Students Association of Cuba, Castro went to a Latin American University Students Congress in Bogotá, Colombia, which coincided with the United States' initiation of the Organization of American States and the advent of civil war in Colombia. The populist leader of the opposition was assassinated. For two days Castro participated in some of the early armed skirmishes, and then he returned home. Both incidents indicate that he, like many contemporaries in Cuba, identified with political struggles in the region. He was also involved in a political organization promoting the independence of Puerto Rico. By then he had acquired lifelong contacts with Latin American progressive political parties and leaders.

He graduated in 1950 with a law degree, having specialized in international law and social sciences. His main interests were politics, sociology, history, theory, and agriculture. As a student leader, radio commentator, and investigative political journalist, he developed a significant following among young people. The Ortodoxo Party recognized his oratorical and organizational skills and nominated him for the planned June 1952 national congressional election. However, on March 10, 1952, the military, led by Batista, carried out a second coup d'état, ending hopes that electoral politics could reform the island and throwing Cuba's constitutional system into a crisis.

ARMED REVOLUTIONARY

Like many other political reformists, the young Ortodoxos became committed revolutionaries, clandestinely organizing to oust the new military rulers. On July 26, 1953, civilians led by Castro attacked Santiago de Cuba's Moncada army barracks, the second largest in the country. It ended in failure. Some men were killed in the confrontation; others were captured and then assassinated. The survivors ended up in prison. From the summer of 1953 to May 1955, Castro was imprisoned at the Isle of Pines, but he continued to organize his associates inside and outside prison. He also read about political, economic, and social matters. In mid-May 1955, the Moncadistas were granted a political amnesty. Batista hoped such a move would earn him legitimacy. It did not. Meanwhile, by serving time, Castro had become one of the primary national opposition leaders in Cuba.

He spent May 1955 to November 1956 in exile in Mexico, where he organized and trained a guerrilla force. On December 2, 1956, eighty-two men who had embarked from the Mexican port of Tuxpan days earlier landed in Cuba in the southern portion of the Oriente.

The guerrilla insurgency had begun. The guerrillas gained control of significant portions of territory, launched an agrarian reform, recruited peasants, and created an alternative set of political institutions. Castro broadcast daily from a rebel shortwave radio station. From the Sierra Maestra Mountains, he coordinated the military and political struggle. From 1957 to 1958 the guerrillas were able to build a multi-class popular front against the dictatorship.

On December 31, 1958, the Batista military regime and political machine collapsed. This was a first in Latin America: a rural insurgency that defeated a regular military force supported by the U.S. government.

REVOLUTIONARY IN POWER

On January 1, 1959, less than six years after the initiation of open opposition to the Batista regime, Castro's revolutionary forces seized power. The Cuban revolution was about to begin. The fundamental questions of how the society's institutions would be organized and what the relationship would be with the United States and Latin America soon became paramount issues as the multi-class alliance that had supported the guerrillas fractured. Portions of the bourgeoisie and the middle classes wanted a return to a constitutional government without affecting social and economic institutions. However, landless peasants and the seasonally unemployed, among others, favored radical changes.

Moreover, the Cuban revolutionaries were aware of the political processes unfolding in Asia, Africa, and the Middle East. While the United States and the Soviet Union were engaged in the cold war, third-world countries were addressing the pressing problems of national independence, integration, decolonization, and socioeconomic development. Some of the same issues needed to be addressed in Cuba.

Even before the guerrillas left the Sierra Maestra, the U.S. government tried to prevent them from seizing power. Also, the United States gave political refuge to Batistianos, allowing them to plunder Cuba's national treasure. In January 1959, right-wing Batista forces in exile in the United States began hit-and-run attacks by air and sea, but the U.S. government turned a blind eye. Foreign relations between the two governments deteriorated rapidly.

Moderates and radicals within the new revolutionary regime immediately discovered the interconnection of domestic and foreign policy. Attempting to distribute land to the landless created confrontation with the United States because the best land was owned by American corporations. Increasing wages also affected American-owned corporations. Import-export policy impinged on the businesses that did precisely that, mostly American ones.

Moreover, the administration of President Dwight D. Eisenhower (1953–1961) had no intention of forfeiting American privileges enjoyed since 1898.

Nevertheless, the Cuban nationalists sought to bring about unprecedented independence. Any attempt to reform Cuba's social, economic, and political institutions would create confrontation between the two countries. American opposition only contributed to the radicalization of the revolutionary process.

Cuba had a mono-export economy, with one major buyer (the United States), yearly cyclical high unemployment, and much social inequality. Cuba was a poor and underdeveloped country, although different in one respect from other nation-states in the Caribbean. With Cuban capitalism so closely connected to American investments, nationalist efforts to control the country's resources easily became equated with anticapitalism. Cuban businesses did not come to the fore to defend their interests by differentiating themselves from U.S. interests. Rather, Cuban capital attached its politics and fate to the U.S. government.

RADICALIZATION OF THE REVOLUTION

The early Cuban revolutionary regime developed a three-fold strategy: a progressive redistribution of income, a radical change in the property system, and a lowering of major daily costs (such as food, rent, transportation, and public services) to benefit the lower classes. This resulted in broader political support among the lower classes and a reduction of the income and wealth of the upper classes, thus diminishing their available resources for counterrevolutionary activity.

As this radicalization advanced, the moderates within the revolutionary coalition joined the opposition or went into exile. Many members of the professions did the same. As the country lost skilled personnel, the state further centralized political, administrative, and economic resources. Facing a shortage of expertise, the revolutionary regime relied on the politically trustworthy, usually people who were radical, including Communists. Such trends further exacerbated the political climate and relations with the U.S. government.

By March 1960, the United States had begun formal covert programs to overthrow the government and kill its leaders. In April 1961, a Cuban exile invasion (Bay of Pigs) was organized, trained, financed, and directed by the Central Intelligence Agency. The fact that it was defeated by the Cubans reinforced the United States' commitment to oust the revolutionaries. The John F. Kennedy administration (1961–1963) further retaliated by organizing a second expeditionary force and imposing an economic embargo in February 1962.

NUCLEAR GAMBLE AND RELATIONS WITH SOVIETS

Havana and Moscow replied by surreptitiously installing tactical nuclear weapons on the island in 1962. Interestingly, Castro urged the Soviets to announce to the world that missiles were going to be installed as a matter of sovereign right on the part of Havana. The Soviet premier, however, did not listen to his advice.

Between April 1961 and March 1962, Castro removed key pro-Soviet Communists from critical positions in the government and the economy while negotiations with Moscow on missile installations were conducted. After October 1962, because of the way the Soviets handled the resolution of the Missile Crisis (Cubans were not informed of the negotiations), relations cooled. Havana made numerous moves to publicly assert its independence. The Soviets put up with Cuba questioning their position on the Sino-Soviet conflict, on the electoral politics of Communist parties in Latin America, the methods of building socialism, and the importance of politics based on moral rather than materialist perspectives. Havana, in other words, was to the left of Moscow. Such were the tense relations until 1972.

From 1972 to 1985, on domestic matters Cuba followed policies that were in accord with the Soviet model, but Castro constructed a foreign policy that challenged the Soviets. This was the case in Angola (1975), Ethiopia (1977), Nicaragua (1979), and an international organization called the Non-Aligned Movement (NAM; 1979). In 1980, Moscow informed Havana that it would not defend the island if U.S. military forces were to attack. Cuba had to develop its own military doctrine and structure from that point on. Thereafter, the political and ideological distance between the two countries grew, even though the island depended on Soviet economic subsidies.

From 1985 to 1990, Castro elaborated a critique of the old Soviet model while rejecting the reforms of Soviet leader Mikhail Gorbachev. The government in Moscow responded by further reducing assistance.

SPECIAL PERIOD

The demise of the Soviet bloc from 1989 to 1991 had major domestic implications in Cuba. It initiated the most difficult economic period in the history of the island—the so-called Special Period.

The United States took advantage of that juncture to increase Cuba's economic isolation. It was an extraordinary accomplishment that Castro's regime adapted its policies and survived. Moreover, by 2000 the island had slowly begun to regain the economic standards it had enjoyed in the early 1980s.

To break away from American-imposed isolation policies while distancing itself from the Soviets, Cuba developed a global foreign policy. Castro cultivated a personal relationship with key political, social, and cultural leaders from Africa, Asia, and Latin America. His close friends have included such nationalist progressives as Nelson Mandela (b. 1918; South Africa), Lázaro Cárdenas (1895–1970; Mexico), Omar Torrijos (1929–1981; Panama), Juan Bosch (1909–2001; Dominican Republic), Salvador Allende (1908–1973; Chile), Daniel Ortega (b. 1945; Nicaragua), Juan Domingo Perón (1895–1974; Argentina), Sékou Touré (1922–1984; Guinea), Ahmed Ben Bella (b. 1918; Algeria), Luiz Inácio Lula da Silva (b. 1945; Brazil), João Goulart (1918–1976; Brazil), Josip Broz Tito (1892–1980; Yugoslavia), Jawaharlal Nehru (1889–1964; India), and many others. The closest of all associations has been between Castro and Hugo Chávez (b. 1954), the president of Venezuela beginning in 1999. The older man recognized the revolutionary qualities of the Venezuelan as early as 1994. The two have similar national histories with a heavy reliance on mass mobilization. Chávez, however, attained and has maintained political power through electoral politics. Moreover, while the younger man respects the elder statesman, there is a unique reciprocity of respect and influence. Castro provides political and tactical advice, and Venezuela's economic resources have permitted Chávez to help Cuba surmount the economic crisis that began in 1991. Radical and revolutionary ideas and organization have been extended by their alliance beyond anything that Castro could have imagined.

In 1961 the Non-Aligned Movement was established in Belgrade, Serbia. Cuba was the only country from Latin America that was a founding member. In 2007 the NAM had 118 third-world countries. Twice Castro has been elected to lead the organization, an explicit mark of esteem for the political example and strategic perspectives of the Cuban revolutionary. Thus, Cuba has become identified with selfless internationalism, sending assistance, for example, to Angola, Mozambique, Nicaragua, Grenada, Venezuela, Algeria, North Vietnam, Ethiopia, Pakistan, and Haiti.

Once the Soviet Union and its Eastern European allies were gone, the government in Havana devised more activist policies toward the third-world nations, providing them with the human capital the island had been so successful in creating, particularly teachers, doctors, dentists, and technical people. In January 2007, Cuba had diplomatic relations with 183 countries.

Relations between the United States and Cuba have gone through different periods, but they have never been friendly. Full diplomatic relations were broken by the United States in January 1961. Thirteen months later, normal economic transactions were terminated by Washington. Only during the administration of President Jimmy Carter (1977–1981) was there a brief period during which some diplomatic ties were restored and travel between the two countries resumed. However, during the administration of George W. Bush (starting in 2001), travel to the island from the United States was highly restricted, including family and academic travel. Cuba cannot use the U.S. dollar in any international transaction, receive international credits, or use any banking institution tied to U.S. capital. Third parties outside the United States are also pressured not to engage in trade with the island. The degree of U.S. financial support to the opposition has increased, and the economic blockade/embargo has been heightened. Every year, the United Nations' General Assembly overwhelmingly votes against the U.S. policy, but the policy remains.

REVOLUTIONARY LEADER

Castro has been the paramount strategist, executive officer, ideologist, and macromanager of the revolutionary regime. He has been the revolution's main leader, spokesman, and coalition builder. Relying on historical reference, example, and metaphor, he has taught that action is the best educator. A radical nationalist, he integrated Martí and Marx. His political thought is rooted in ethical values rather than materialist theory. He has synchronized socialist European traditions with third-world customs while recognizing that each country must find its own way. He has dealt with development theory, nation building, internationalism, foreign debt, globalization, sustainable development, social justice, party building, and human psychology. Since the 1950s his political strategy has stressed unity among revolutionists. Mass mobilization has been a constant instrument and has included the literacy campaign, childhood vaccination, the creation of a territorial militia, and anticorruption campaigns.

Since 1959 resources have been concentrated in the rural areas and small towns, and the city of Havana has suffered. An ideology of inherent rights and entitlements has developed with a system that provides universal education, health and dental care, child care, and burial service free of charge. The state also assumes the responsibility of providing employment or giving the unemployed financial support. Cuba is one of the most educated countries in the third world, with a life expectancy of 77.5 years and an infant mortality rate of 6.5 per 1,000 live births (as of January 2007). Education and health claim 23 percent of the gross internal product. The number of libraries, schools, hospitals, and dams increased dramatically from1959 to the mid-1980s. Food has been subsidized since 1962, but it has been rationed as well. Just as libraries lend books, there are also centers that lend musi-

cal instruments at no cost. Every municipality has computer clubs where access is free. Thirteen percent of the population benefits from universal social security, and 4.2 percent receives social assistance checks.

The political system has changed from its original high dependence on charismatic leadership based on mass popular organizations (1959–1976) to a formal institutionalized political regime where officials are directly elected by the population, with no campaigning or Communist Party–proposed candidates. Still, charismatic authority continued to operate to balance and control the administrative state. Castro's contact with the population, which began in 1959 through mass rallies, has been preserved. He has been the unifying and integrating force among disparate factions in the revolutionary family.

Cuba does not permit alternative political parties or a political opposition to openly publish political materials. However, thirty-two Catholic publications do express positions that are opposed to the government, although in a subtle fashion. The political leadership maintains, based on Federalist Paper No. 8 by the U.S. founding father James Madison (1751–1836), that the external threat posed by the U.S. government's policies—including confrontation, isolation, invasion, financial assistance to opponents within the island, and an economic embargo that has lasted more than four decades—do not provide much space for a political opposition.

By the end of July 2006, Castro had transferred political power, in a provisional manner, to his brother and other individuals in what constitutes the establishment of a collective leadership. The question for most foreign observers is whether the Cuban revolution will survive the death of its leader. History will tell.

SEE ALSO *Authoritarianism; Bay of Pigs; Bush, George H. W.; Bush, George W.; Chavez, Hugo; Cuban Missile Crisis; Cuban Revolution; Franco, Francisco; Guerrilla Warfare; Khrushchev, Nikita; Leninism; Madison, James; Marx, Karl; Marxism; Reagan, Ronald; Revolution; Socialism; Spanish Civil War; Third World; Totalitarianism*

BIBLIOGRAPHY

Buch, Luis M., and Reinaldo Suáez. 2004. *Gobierno revolucionario cubano, primeros pasos.* Havana, Cuba: Editorial Ciencias Sociales.

Furiati, Claudia. 2003. *Fidel Castro: La historia me absolverá.* Barcelona, Spain: Plaza Janés.

Gott, Richard. 2004. *Cuba: A New History.* New Haven, CT: Yale University Press.

Guerra, Dolores, Margarita Concepción, and Amparo Hernández. 2004. *José Martí en el ideario de Fidel Castro.* Havana, Cuba: Centro de Estudios Martianos.

Liss, Sheldon B. 1994. *Fidel! Castro's Political and Social Thought.* Boulder, CO: Westview.

Lockwood, Lee. 1967. *Castro's Cuba, Cuba's Fidel: An American Journalist's Inside Look at Today's Cuba.* New York: Macmillan.

Martin, Lionel. 1978. *The Early Fidel: Roots of Castro's Communism.* Secaucus, NJ: Lyle Stuart.

Mencía, Mario. 1986. *Tiempos precursores.* Havana, Cuba: Editorial Ciencias Sociales.

Minà, Gianni. 1991. *An Encounter with Fidel.* Melbourne, Australia: Ocean Press.

Prada, Pedro. 2001. *La secretaria de la República.* Havana, Cuba: Editorial Ciencias Sociales.

Ramonet, Ignacio. 2006. *Fidel Castro: Biografía a dos voces.* Madrid, Spain: Debate.

Nelson P. Valdes

CATASTROPHE THEORY

Much of quantitative social science (such as principal factor analysis, linear regression, and least squares) seeks linear relationships among many variables. "Nonlinear" methods often seek to warp variables to bring them into linear relations, just as taking logarithms changes exponential growth into correlation with time, but allow more transforms. This approach fails for topologically nonlinear relationships such as (see Figure 1) the condition $x^2 + y^2 = 1$ between x and y. Knowing the value of x limits what is possible for y, but evenly scattered points (x,y) on the circle show no linear correlation between x and y, and no principal factor in any direction. No transformations of the variables improves this.

A mutual information test would reveal a link between x and y, but say little about its structure. Local analysis says more. The region D shows a strong linear relation between x and y, just as linearly testing temple attendance versus income on one Delhi suburb works better than on worldwide data. Around the points A or B, fitting a linear $y(x)$ reveals little: y is no function of x there (or at P and Q, vice versa). Nevertheless, x and y have a fold relation of a very common type. Just as "more equations than unknowns means no solutions," almost every failure of a $y(x)$ model for an (x,y) curve is a fold. With a smooth reparametrization it fits a piece of parabola. Globally there may be more than one fold: Figure 2 shows a more common relation between the two than the circle. This is more common partly because it can arise as part of the cusp (see Figure 3), which Hassler Whitney in the 1950s showed to be the almost-universal local relation between two surfaces where they cannot be adjusted to a linear or fold description.

René Thom in the 1960s developed a more general theory. This emphasizes the curves, surfaces, and so forth, arising as sets of minima, maxima, and other level points when changes in an external factor modify a function F of a multivariable internal x. Level points (energy-minimum equilibriums, etc.) represent simpler long-term behavior than limit cycles and chaotic attractors, and Thom thus referred to this as "elementary" catastrophe theory.

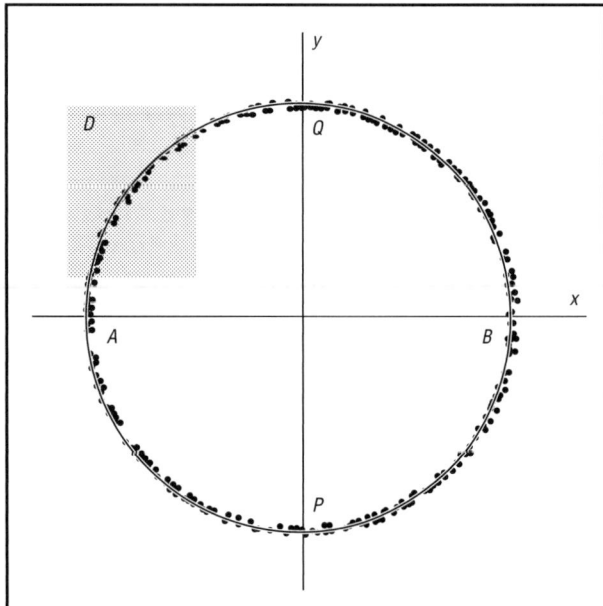

Figure 1

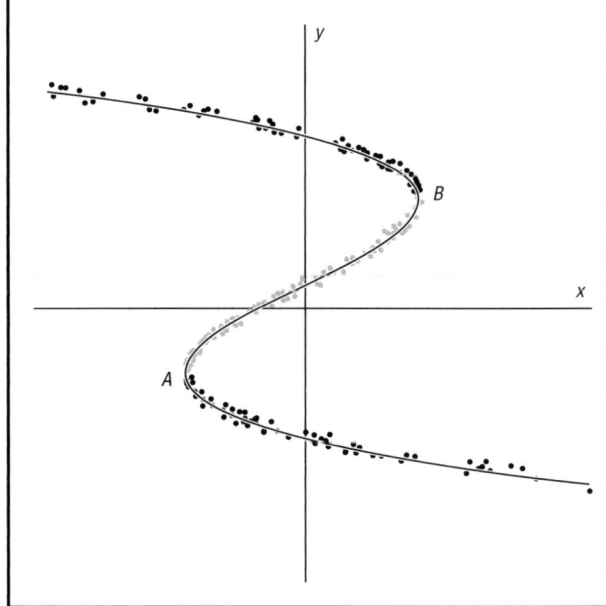

Figure 2

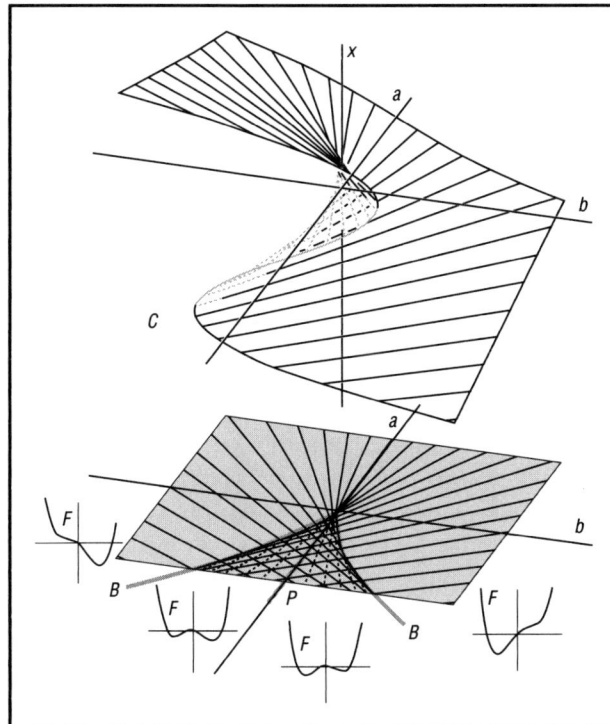

Figure 3

"General" catastrophe theory would include changes of chaotic regime, but the term has settled on the narrower use. The cusp, fold, and so on arise in both contexts. The (a,b) plane in Figure 2 generalizes the "phase diagram" of thermodynamics: crossing P changes which minimum is the deepest, while crossing B changes which minima even exist. Some systems always adopt the deepest minimum, others hold to a minimum until it vanishes, but in either case a smooth change in (a,b) can force a jump in x. The external factors might be, for example, gross economic indicators, while x represents all the alternatives of hiring, capital expenditure, shift timing, and so forth, over which a firm must maximize profit F—subject to the modifying external factors. (Figures 2 and 3 gray out states such as local minima of profit or maxima of pain, which a system actively avoids.)

Rigorous treatments of the mathematics include the work of V. I. Arnold, while Tim Poston and Ian Stewart aim at a wider scientific audience. Remarkably, the fold and cusp structures arise regardless of any (finite) number of variables needed to describe x. For 1-D and 2-D external factors, with scalar F and in the absence of special symmetries, any other structure falls apart into cusps and folds as easily as three planar lines through a common point fall into three crossings. They can occur in multiple places, such as the two folds in Figure 2, and in continua for n-D externals, such as the fold curve C (not isolated

fold points) in Figure 3, but 1-D and 2-D externals make them the universal local forms or "elementary catastrophes" (suggesting in French sudden discontinuity, as in departing "en catastrophe," but not necessarily disaster). Three external dimensions allow three more of these forms: 4-D gives another two, for the total of seven, which caught media attention. In higher dimensions they can still be classified, and have been applied in quantitative physics, but arise in continua of types rather than a small finite set. When the function F is replaced by vector dynamics, there are discontinuities (such as onset of oscillation or chaos, and self-organized criticality) not covered by this "elementary catastrophe" list.

Physics, engineering, and, increasingly, biology have successfully applied the methods by which the classification is reached, usually as part of the general "bifurcation theory" toolkit, to nonlinear models with precise data. Research in the social sciences has often attempted to use the classification theorem, not always appreciating the reparametrizations essential to it, or its local nature (folds and cusps are often multiple). Social complexity and noisy social data require multivariable models and statistical tools, even when a linear model is possible. A nonlinear model with few parameters can sometimes replace a linear one with many, as Johannes Kepler's (1571–1630) three laws replaced the hundreds of circles of Ptolemy (2nd century CE) and Nicolaus Copernicus (1473–1543). More often, essential nonlinearity in a few key directions must be combined with linearizability (differentiability) in many other directions: simply superposing the (b,x) folds around C in Figure 3, without adjusting for a, masks their structure. Bifurcation modeling for the social sciences must include tools such as principal factor analysis, not replace them. This extended theory is not yet in place, but the work of Courtney Brown represents important progress.

SEE ALSO *Chaos Theory; Phase Diagrams; Social Science; Statistics in the Social Sciences; Topology*

BIBLIOGRAPHY

Arnold, V. I. 1981. *Teoriya Katastrof.* Moscow: Znanie Publishers. Trans. G. S. Wassermann, based on a translation by R. K. Thomas, as *Catastrophe Theory.* 3rd rev. ed. (New York: Springer, 1992).

Brown, Courtney. 1995. *Chaos and Catastrophe Theories.* Thousand Oaks, CA: Sage Publications.

Poston, Tim, and Ian Stewart. 1996. *Catastrophe Theory and Its Applications.* Mineola, NY: Dover. (Originally published, San Francisco: Pitman, 1978.)

Thom, René. 1972. *Stabilité structurelle et Morphogénèse: Essai d'une théorie générale des modèles.* Reading, MA: W. A. Benjamin. Trans. D. H. Fowler as *Structural Stability and*

Morphogenesis: An Outline of a General Theory of Models (Reading, MA: Addison-Wesley Publishers, 1989).

Tim Poston

CATASTROPHIZING

SEE *Psychotherapy.*

CATHOLICISM

SEE *Christianity; Church, The; Roman Catholic Church.*

CATTLE INDUSTRY

The cattle industry is one of the world's most important agricultural enterprises. According to the United Nations, there were over 1.37 billion cattle worldwide in 2004. On a percentage basis, approximately 35 percent of these animals were in Asia, 23 percent in South America, 17 percent in Africa, 12 percent in North America, 10 percent in Europe, and 3 percent in Australia and Oceania. While this distribution is slanted toward Asia and South America, the livestock systems and uses of cattle vary substantially by location. For example, cattle often have dual purposes, particularly in Asia, where cattle are often used principally for traction and secondarily for meat and milk. In North and South America, however, cattle are used principally for meat and milk products.

According to William Lesser, a professor at Cornell University, cattle have been domesticated for several thousand years. He suggests that domesticated livestock provided early societies with four important functions: (1) a supply of high-quality protein, (2) the ability to store foodstuffs not directly consumable by humans, (3) hides for clothing and shoes, and (4) motive (traction) power (Lesser 1993, p. 31).

Lesser indicates that prior to the Industrial Revolution, cattle systems were relatively primitive. Cattle were kept without shelter, for example, and they had to forage for themselves. However, with the rise of the modern city during the Industrial Revolution, the cattle industry evolved from being a very local industry—where cattle generally provided traction, meat, leather, and livestock products for individual families—to an industry organized to produce cattle products that were transported from rural areas to urban centers.

Cattle primarily consume various types of forage, or fodder, and livestock systems have evolved in order for cattle and other livestock to harvest forages and convert the energy contained in forages into protein. This protein is then consumed by humans primarily in the form of milk and meat. Leather produced from cattle hides is also an important material used in making shoes, other clothing items, and clothing accessories.

In the United States, the evolution of the cattle industry may be best illustrated by the large cattle drives of the 1880s, where cattle were trailed (walked) from the south-central United States to rail centers such as Dodge City, Kansas. The cattle were then transported by rail to urban centers like Chicago, where they were slaughtered and processed. The beef was then shipped to urban consumers. The era of the cattle drive was the heyday of the American cowboy. Cowboys were necessary to control the cattle herds as they moved northward. This period of American history has been romanticized, as has the role of the cowboy as an independent free spirit who battles the elements to care for the cattle under his care. Today, of course, anyone who cares for cattle could be considered a cowboy, but the American cowboy remains an icon of the American West. The South American gaucho has also been romanticized in a similar fashion. Both the American cowboy and the gaucho are known for their distinctive clothing, equipment (such as a lariat), and their horsemanship.

Important technologies for shipping cattle carcasses and marketing cattle products were developed in the late 1800s by companies such as Cudahy, Wilson, and Swift. According to Lesser, this led to the rise of modern meatpacking, which was originally conceived on the same principles as the automobile industry. Henry Ford developed the idea of the modern assembly plant at the beginning of the twentieth century. Modern meatpacking plants have used the idea of product assembly in reverse, for they are essentially large disassembly plants. In meatpacking plants, cattle are slaughtered and their carcasses are disassembled and protected by plastic wrapping. The parts are then reassembled with like parts, referred to as "cuts," before being placed in a cardboard box for shipment. One of the most important innovations in meatpacking during the last decades of the twentieth century was the development of this boxing operation, which has largely replaced the traditional method of shipping whole cattle carcasses to butcher shops and retail outlets. Today, boxed beef is usually shipped directly to retailers, who are then required to provide only a minimal amount of additional preparation before the beef can be served or sold to the final consumer.

International trade in cattle and beef is now dominated by a few large exporting and importing countries. The United States is the world's largest beef and veal producer, though it holds a relatively small portion of the total international beef market. Other large beef-exporting countries include Brazil, Argentina, Uruguay, Canada, and Australia. Large beef-importing countries include Japan, South Korea, the United States, Canada, and Mexico. As the international trade in beef has increased, animal disease control and food safety have received increased attention. For example, concerns related to standardizing trade issues affected by bovine spongiform encephalopathy (BSE, or mad cow disease) and foot-and-mouth disease have become important issues in the international beef trade. Concerns regarding input use, such as growth-enhancing hormones, and the tracking of animals and meat have also resulted in trade frictions, especially between the United States and the European Union.

Systems for producing beef in the developed world are differentiated primarily by the types of feeds used during the final stages of growing the animal prior to slaughter. This final feeding stage is referred to as "finishing." In locations with abundant forage resources, cattle are primarily finished by grazing the animals. For instance, grass-fed beef is the primary type of beef produced in Argentina, Brazil, and Australia. In locations with abundant grain supplies, cattle are typically finished by feeding them grains. Grain-fed beef is common in North America, especially the United States and Canada.

The modern beef industry in the developed world faces a number of significant challenges. Some of these are related to the relatively small number of large firms involved in meatpacking and food retailing, which leads to fears on the part of farmers and consumers that these firms may have too much influence on prices and the variety and types of beef products that are available.

Other challenges involve building better connectivity and coordination in the marketing channel between the processes used to produce beef and the characteristics desired by consumers. For example, some consumers perceive that there are significant inconsistencies in the tenderness and flavor of beef, both of which are desirable characteristics, from one eating experience to the next. A growing number of consumers in developing countries are also demanding more information about the types of inputs and processes used to produce beef. This has led to more information being provided to consumers about beef products through labeling and certifications. For example, certifications such as "organic," assurances about the beef being produced under "natural" conditions, and assurances about the traceability of the beef are becoming more common. *Traceability* is defined as being able to track the beef product backward through all handlers and processors in the marketing chain to the original farm where the animal was born.

BIBLIOGRAPHY

Lesser, William. 1993. *Marketing Livestock and Meat.* Binghamton, NY: Food Products Press.

United Nations, Department of Economic and Social Affairs. 2005. *Statistical Yearbook.* New York: United Nations Publications.

DeeVon Bailey

CAUCASIANS

SEE *Race and Psychology.*

CAUSALITY

In economics and the social sciences the value of many variables (such as price of a product, crime rate, level of illiteracy, personal income, and consumption) is observed with great regularity. As a result, an empirical generating mechanism can be postulated that produces the observed values of the variable of interest. The investigation and understanding of this mechanism is one of the main tasks for social scientists and by doing so the issue of causation inevitably arises. Causation can be discussed in very general, abstract terms or the discussion can focus on the specific question of whether or not it is possible to test for causation using the data available.

The latter requires an operational procedure and definition (mechanisms and subsystems) and this formulation arises because of a lack of understanding of the working of a complex system. In this formulation, each mechanism, which might be represented by an equation, determines the value of a particular variable as a function of some others. The variable whose value is so determined (dependent or endogenous variable) is called the effect of the working of that particular mechanism, while the values of other variables entering into the mechanism (independent or exogenous variables) are the causes of that effect.

As a specific example, theoretical analysis may say that "y is a function of x," that is, changes in the independent variable x generate changes in the independent variable y. One might write this as $y = f(x)$. Empirical analysis then attempts to estimate the actual strength of the relationship between y and x. So, empirical seeks to uncover the data generating mechanism $y = \beta_0 + \beta_1 x$. Hence, if x increases by 1 unit y will increase by β_1 and if $x = 0$ then $y = \beta_0$.

Much of economics and social science is concerned with cause-and-effect propositions insofar as these disciplines pose causal relationships that postulate that a dependent variable's movements are causally determined by movements in a number of specific independent variables. However, one should not be deceived by the words *dependent* and *independent*. Although many theoretical economic relationships are causal by their nature, statistical analysis, for example linear regression, cannot prove causality. All regression analysis can do is test whether a significant quantitative relationship exists, measure the strength of this relationship, and postulate the direction of the quantitative relationships involved. Regression analysis cannot confirm causality. Judgments referring to causality are made through various causality tests.

The objective of any causal analysis is to try to influence the degree of belief held by an individual about the correctness of some causal theory. Hence, the task of the analysis is not to be complete in itself, but rather to have enough value to make one consider one's belief. There are basically two types of causal testing situations. In a cross-sectional causality analysis the question asked is why this variable behaves differently from the other. In a temporal causality analysis the question asked is why this variable changes behavior from period to period. Although many important economic questions can be phrased in the cross-section causal situation, they have received little causal testing in that context and many tests have been conducted for economic questions that can be stated as temporal causation. The definitions of causality and their interpretations may differ between cross-section and time-series cases. In all cases, however, the classification of variables into *exogenous* and *endogenous* and the causal structure of the mechanism (econometric model) are under scrutiny.

The relation between exogeneity and causality is the heart of any investigation into causal analysis. There are a number of definitions of exogeneity: weak, super, and strong exogeneity. A variable is said to be weakly exogenous for estimating a set of parameters if inference on the parameters conditional on this exogenous variable involves no loss of information. The concept of superexogeneity is related to the Lucas critique, which states that if a variable is weakly exogenous and the parameters in the equation remain invariant to changes in the marginal distribution of the variable, then the variable is said to be superexogenous. A variable is strongly exogenous if it is weakly exogenous and at the same time is not preceded by any of the endogenous variables of the model. The concept of strong exogeneity is linked to the concept of Granger causality, and should be considered as a test of precedence rather than causality as such. Hence, a variable is defined to be strongly exogenous if it is weakly exogenous and it is not caused by any of the endogenous variables in the Granger sense. However, in the usual simultaneous equations literature there is doubt as to what

extent the test for Granger noncausality is useful as a test for exogeneity. Nevertheless, some argue that Granger noncausality is useful as a descriptive device for time-series data.

The Granger causality test is based on two axioms, that the cause will occur before the effect and that the cause contains unique information about the effect. In practice, Granger causation tests whether A precedes B, or B precedes A, or they are contemporaneous. It is not a causality analysis as it is usually understood and in this limited sense Clive Granger (1969) devised some tests which proceed as follows: consider two time series, x_i and y_i. The series x_i fails to Granger cause y_i if in a regression of y_i on lagged y's and x's, the coefficients of the latter are zero. The lag length is, to some extent, arbitrary. An alternative test provided by Sims states that x_i fails to cause y_i in the Granger sense if in a regression of y_i on lagged, current, and future x's, the latter coefficients are zero. Although between the two tests there are some econometric differences, the two tests basically test the same hypothesis of precedence. This is the reason that many econometricians have suggested the use of the term *precedence* rather than Granger causality, since all one is testing is whether or not a certain variable precedes another and one is not testing causality as it is usually defined and understood.

The causality issue arises also in forecasting problems and techniques. Forecasting is the prediction of the behavior of future events and causal models are used to derive numerical forecasts. The causal models are regression and autoregression models used to produce numerical time series forecasts. The subject of a causal model is to identify one series as the main series of interest and to use another series as the predictor for the main series. It is argued that economic theory is necessary in order to provide the information needed to specify the causal relationships, because forecasts may not involve causal relationships.

In a general formulation of a causal time series model the predictor variable (exogenous) enters the equation at the same time as a contemporaneous variable and as a lagged independent variable. Even a simple causal model is fraught with difficulties. This is typically due to the problem of distinguishing the autocorrelation between dependent and independent variables from the cross-sectional correlation between the two. Cross-sectional correlations that appear significant but are induced by autocorrelations are called *spurious correlations*. The problem of spurious correlation arises because in many instances, the predictor variable is stochastic and thus we need to forecast its time series. Several causal models have been developed to cope with this problem and the most common is the regression model with autoregressive disturbances.

The estimation of the causal effect arises also in the case of random experimentation. The central idea of an ideal randomized experiment is that the causal effect can be measured by randomly selecting observations from a population and then randomly giving some of the observations a treatment, the causal effect of which researchers then investigate. If the treatment is assigned at random then the treatment level is distributed independently of any of the other determinants of the outcome, thereby eliminating the possibility of omitted variable bias. The causal effect on Y of treatment level X is a difference in expected values and thus is an unknown characteristic of a population. One way to measure the causal effect is to use data from a randomized control experiment. Because the treatment is randomly assigned, the causal effect can be estimated by the difference in the sample average outcomes between the treatment and control groups.

Despite the advantages of randomized controlled experiments, their application to economics faces severe hurdles, including ethical concerns and cost. The insights of experimental methods can, however, be applied to quasi experiments that provide ecometricians with a way to think about how to acquire new data sets, how to manipulate instrumental variables in their analysis, and how to evaluate the plausibility of the exogeneity assumptions that underlie Ordinary Least Squares (OLS) and instrumental variables estimation. In a quasi-experiment technique there are special circumstances that make it seem "as if" randomization has occurred. In quasi experiments, the causal effect can be estimated using a differences-in-differences estimator, possibly augmented with additional regressors; if the "as if" randomization only partly influences the treatment, then instrumental variables regression can be used instead. An important threat confronting quasi experiments is that sometimes the "as if" randomization is not really random, so the treatment (or the instrumental variable) is correlated with omitted variables and the resulting estimator of the causal effect is biased.

The issue of causality is very important in economic and social analysis but unfortunately not all analysts give the same meaning to this word. In discussing causal links, many economists emphasize the relevance of a sound economic theory in deriving causal propositions and they argue that caution should be applied in the inferences derived from the analysis.

SEE ALSO *Instrumental Variables Regression; Natural Experiments; Reflection Problem; Regression; Seemingly Unrelated Regressions; Selection Bias; Simultaneous Equation Bias*

BIBLIOGRAPHY

Frees, Edward W. 1996. *Data Analysis Using Regression Models: The Business Perspective.* Engelwood Cliffs, NJ: Prentice Hall.

Granger, Clive W. J. 1969. Investigating Causal Relations by Econometric Models and Cross-Spectral Methods. *Econometrica* 37: 424–438.

Maddala, G. S. 2001. *Introduction to Econometrics.* New York: Wiley.

Stock, James H., and Mark W. Watson. 2003. *Introduction to Econometrics.* New York: Addison-Wesley.

Persefoni Tsaliki

CAYTON, HORACE

SEE *Poverty, Urban.*

CENSORING, LEFT AND RIGHT

Censoring occurs when values of a variable within a certain range are unobserved, but it is known that the variable falls within this range. This differs from *truncation*, where values of a variable within a certain range are unobserved and it is unknown when the variable falls within this range. Both phenomena represent a loss of information, but the loss is less with censoring than with truncation. The two are sometimes confused in the literature; some examples are given in Léopold Simar and Paul Wilson (2007). George Maddala (1983) and Takeshi Amemiya (1984) list a number of empirical applications where censoring occurs.

Consider a sample of n draws Y_i, $i = 1 \ldots, n$ from a distribution function $F(y) = P(Y \leq y)$. If the sample is left-censored at c_1, then the values Y_i are not observed; instead, values Y_i^* are observed, where $Y_i^* = Y_i$ if $Y_i > c_1$ and $Y_i^* = c_1$ otherwise. For the cases where $Y_i^* = c_1$, all that is known about the underlying corresponding values Y_i is that they are less than or equal to c_1. Alternatively, if the sample is right-censored at c_2, then values Y_i^* are observed, where $Y_i^* = Y_i$ if $Y_i < c_2$, and $Y_i^* = c_2$ otherwise. In this scenario, for the cases where $Y_i^* = c_2$, all that is known about the Y_i is that they are greater than or equal to c_2. Samples can also be both left- and right-censored.

In models of duration, right-censoring often occurs, but left-censoring can also occur. For example, if agents are observed in some state (e.g., unemployment, in the case of individuals, or solvency, in the case of firms) until either they are observed to exit the state or until the period of observation ends, then some agents may still be in the given state at the end of the observation window. Observations on these agents will be right-censored. Similarly, at the beginning of the study, some (perhaps all) agents are observed to be already in the state of interest; for any agents whose time of entry into the state is unknown, their duration in the given state is left-censored (and perhaps also right-censored).

To illustrate censoring in a regression context, suppose

$$Y_i = \beta_1 + \beta_2 X_i + \varepsilon_i \qquad (1)$$

where $E(\varepsilon_i) = 0$. If Y_i is censored, then one must estimate the model

$$Y_i^* = \beta_1 + \beta_2 X_i + \varepsilon_i^* \qquad (2)$$

after replacing Y_i in (1) with Y_i^*, which necessarily results in a new error term in (2). Unless the censoring occurs in the extreme tails of the distribution of Y, ordinary least squares (OLS) estimation of the coefficients in (2) will yield biased and inconsistent estimates since OLS does not account for the censoring.

Censored regression models are typically estimated by the maximum likelihood method. If the errors in model (1) are assumed normally distributed with mean 0 and variance σ^2, then in the case of left-censoring at c_1 the likelihood function is given by

$$LF = \prod_{i\,|\,Yi^* = c1} \frac{1}{\sigma} \Phi\left(\sigma^{-1}(c_1 - \beta_1 - \beta_2 X_i)\right)$$

$$\prod_{i\,|\,Yi^* > c1} \frac{1}{\sigma} \varphi\left(\sigma^{-1}(Y_i^* - \beta_1 - \beta_2 X_i)\right) \qquad (3)$$

where ψ and Φ denote the standard normal density and distribution functions, respectively. This model was first proposed by James Tobin (1958), and is sometimes called the *tobit model*. The first product in (3) gives, for each observed value Y_i^* equal to c_1, the probability of obtaining a draw Y_i from $F(y)$ less than c_1.

The models presented above potentially suffer from several problems. Heteroskedasticity in the error terms can lead to inconsistent estimation. D. Petersen and Donald Waldman (1981) proposed modifications of the tobit-type models involving specification of particular models for the error variances. John Cragg (1971) proposed a generalized version of the tobit model that allows the probability of censoring to be independent of the regression model for the uncensored data. Perhaps the most vexing problem is the requirement of a distributional assumption for the errors in (2). It is straightforward to assume distributions other than the normal distribution and then work out the resulting likelihood

functions, but rather more difficult to avoid such assumptions altogether by using semi- or nonparametric methods. Adrian Pagan and Aman Ullah (1999) discuss several proposals, but these involve significant increases in computational burden or data requirements.

SEE ALSO *Censoring, Sample; Heckman Selection Correction Procedure; Heteroskedasticity; Logistic Regression; Probabilistic Regression; Properties of Estimators (Asymptotic and Exact)*

BIBLIOGRAPHY

Amemiya, Takeshi. 1984. Tobit Models: A Survey. *Journal of Econometrics* 24: 3–61.

Cragg, John G. 1971. Some Statistical Models for Limited Dependent Variables with Application to the Demand for Durable Goods. *Econometrica* 39 (5): 829–844.

Maddala, George S. 1983. *Limited-Dependent and Qualitative Variables in Econometrics.* Cambridge, U.K.: Cambridge University Press.

Pagan, Adrian, and Aman Ullah. 1999. *Nonparametric Econometrics.* Cambridge, U.K.: Cambridge University Press.

Petersen, D., and Donald Waldman. 1981. The Treatment of Heteroskedasticity in the Limited Dependent Variable Model. Unpublished working paper. Department of Economics. Chapel Hill: University of North Carolina.

Simar, Léopold, and Paul W. Wilson. 2007. Estimation and Inference in Two-stage, Semi-parametric Models of Productive Efficiency. *Journal of Econometrics* 136 (1): 31–64.

Tobin, James. 1958. Estimation of Relationships for Limited Dependent Variables. *Econometrica* 26 (1): 24–36.

Paul W. Wilson

CENSORING, SAMPLE

In order to define censoring in sample data, researchers first distinguish between latent data, the data that are hidden from the observer, and observed data, which are their measured counterparts. The latent data are modified between the original data creation and the observation by the analyst. Censoring occurs when certain values in the latent data are transformed so that their identities in the original data are masked or hidden from the observer.

A natural, familiar case is institutional censoring. Certain government statistics, such as income data on individuals and line of business data on firms, are censored to mask the identities of the persons or businesses. Thus income might be reported not as their original values, but only as being in a certain bracket. Censoring also occurs naturally in the way that certain data are observed. A leading example is the observations on durations in medical statistics. Observed data on the longevity after the surgery of heart transplant patients, or the length of survival after onset of a disease, are naturally censored if the individual leaves the observation setting before the transition takes place. Thus the hospital may at some point lose contact with the heart transplant patient. The observation consists of the knowledge that the patient was still alive at the time of his or her exit from the study, but not how long he or she survived. In another familiar case, the true levels of demand for sporting and entertainment events are not revealed by ticket sales because the venue may sell out. The observed reflection of the demand is only ticket sales, limited by the capacity of the venue. Some economic phenomena, known as corner solutions, also lead to censoring when the observed counterpart to a variable of interest has a boundary value. Thus the amount of insurance an individual desires may be censored at zero. The amount of investment that a business undertakes might be recorded as zero if the assets of the business are allowed to depreciate, such that the true investment is actually negative.

IMPLICATIONS FOR MODELING

Models of statistical phenomena usually describe relationships between, or co-movements of, variables. Censoring interferes with this sort of modeling. (See Greene 2003 and Maddala 1983 for analysis and extensions.) Suppose that the relationship occurs between the latent variables of interest. If a variable x^* is expected to explain the movement of variable y, and x^* is censored to reveal x, then the analyst will measure movements in y that are associated with movements in x^* when x does not change. In the opposite case, when it is y^* that is censored and x that is not, the analyst will observe movement in x that should be associated with movement in y, but is not. Either case leads to a distortion in the measured relationship between a censored variable and an uncensored one. Contemporary model builders accommodate this type of distortion by building specific models for the censoring process along with the relationship of interest. Controversy arises over the many assumptions that must be made in order to make reasonable analysis feasible. Ultimately, the estimated relationship, such as that between prices and ticket sales for sporting events, is also a function about what is assumed about the underlying process whereby true underlying data are translated into observed, censored data, for example, how true demand is translated into ticket sales.

SEE ALSO *Censoring, Left and Right*

BIBLIOGRAPHY

Greene, William H. 2003. *Econometric Analysis*. 5th ed. Upper Saddle River, NJ: Prentice Hall, 2003.

Maddala, G. S. 1983. *Limited-Dependent and Qualitative Variables in Econometrics*. Cambridge, U.K.: Cambridge University Press.

William Greene

CENSORSHIP

Censorship—or prior restraint—is the halting of a message by the government before the message is uttered. In the United States it has been called the "most serious, least tolerable" infringement of free speech because it halts speech before it can reach the marketplace of ideas (*Nebraska Press Association v. Stuart*, 1976). That is, the speech is not subject to discussion, debate, or rebuttal because it is stifled before such opportunities can be pursued. The word *censorship* has been applied to a wide variety of activities—including newspapers deciding not to publish controversial cartoons, department stores refusing to sell certain magazines, or private organizations firing newsletter editors because of the articles they published. None of these examples constitute censorship, however, because they do not involve government action.

Some governments defend control over expression on the grounds that full debate, particularly of governmental actions, is risky, in that it can undermine the government or be detrimental to national security. Even governments that adhere to doctrines prohibiting prior restraint, however, recognize that not all speech is allowed in all circumstances. Certain kinds of speech, such as that which might harm national security, cause a violent breach of the peace, or tempt a person into illegal conduct, can be restrained by the government. In the United States, recognition of the right to impose censorship in exceptional situations was established in the 1931 case of *Near v. Minnesota*, and has been reaffirmed in subsequent cases. For example, justices on the U.S. Supreme Court have noted that words that are likely to cause "direct, immediate and irreparable" harm to the country may be censored (*New York Times Co. v. United States*, 1971).

Governments that guarantee expressive rights without prior restraint do so generally on the basis that robust, open debate—even when expression is obnoxious or controversial—is the better avenue for decision-making.

Some confusion over the reach of the prior restraint doctrine has emerged because of governmental control over broadcasting, particularly in the United States and Canada. Broadcasting is regulated by the Federal Communications Commission in the United States, and by the Canadian Radio-Television and Telecommunications Commission in Canada. Neither agency has direct control over the content of broadcasting, but each provides a mechanism through which broadcasters make their messages available to listeners and viewers through a system of licensing. Such governmental regulation in both the United States and Canada has come to be known as the trusteeship model. The model is based on the rationale that the airwaves constitute a natural resource and, as such, belong to the citizenry. Because broadcasting's electronic spectrum is limited, there must be, therefore, some mechanism for picking and choosing among potential broadcasters. Broadcasters, then, are acting as trustees for the public in their use of the airwaves. Both Canada's Broadcasting Act of 1991 and the United States' Telecommunications Act of 1996, which amended the Communications Act of 1934, stipulate that individual broadcasters maintain control over the content of their broadcasts, but also prohibit certain kinds of communication, such as indecent or obscene speech.

SEE ALSO *Bill of Rights, U.S.; Civil Liberties; Freedom; Journalism; Liberty; McCarthyism; Media; Oppositionality, Schooling; Repression; Repressive Tolerance; Taboos; Tolerance, Political*

BIBLIOGRAPHY

Andre, Judith. 1992. 'Censorship': Some Distinctions. In *Philosophical Issues in Journalism*, ed. Elliot D. Cohen. New York: Oxford University Press.

Smolla, Rodney A. 1992. *Free Speech in an Open Society*. New York: Knopf.

Sunstein, Cass R. 1993. *Democracy and the Problem of Free Speech*. New York: Free Press.

W. Wat Hopkins

CENSUS

A census is a periodic, systematic enumeration of a population. Census-taking activities that counted at least certain segments of the population, such as those expected to be available for military service or to pay taxes, have been documented from ancient times. Modern censuses, broader in scope and content, are taken in many countries and gather statistical data that are used for myriad purposes.

Population counts were made in ancient Babylonia, Egypt, China, and India, some before 2000 or even 3000 BCE. Enumerations occurred in ancient Greece, and a comprehensive census was taken by the ancient Romans. Accounts of enumeration activities, largely to determine numbers of men available for military purposes, are included in the Old Testament. In the New Testament, the Roman census is central to the nativity story; it is said

to be occurring at the time of the birth of Jesus Christ, necessitating that people travel to be properly counted and taxed.

During the Middle Ages, censuses occurred periodically, including those in Japan, France, and Italy. The *Domesday Book*, compiled during the eleventh century for economic purposes under King William I (c. 1028–1087), provided a detailed "description of England." Later enumerations occurred after the plague swept through the population. During the eighteenth and nineteenth centuries, census efforts were undertaken in various countries around the globe. The first census in North America was conducted in 1666 in New France (Canada). Censuses were taken in Virginia and in most of the British territories before the Revolutionary War (1775–1783). Censuses are now routine in nations worldwide.

The U.S. decennial census, first taken in 1790, is the longest-running periodic census. It is required by Article 1, Section 2 of the Constitution for the primary purpose of reapportionment of the U.S. House of Representatives (i.e., determining the number of seats to which each state is entitled). Census data are also used in redistricting, the redrawing of political districts after reapportionment. More than five hundred other uses of census data have been mandated by federal laws.

Modern census data have numerous government, demographic, social, and economic uses. These uses include marketing research, strategic and capital planning, community advocacy, funding and resource allocation, and disaster relief. Census data are also widely used in academic, government, and genealogical research. Australian census data were even used to connect cases of maternal rubella (German measles) during pregnancy with deafness in children.

Census use, language, and content, however, have controversial implications. Censuses routinely track and quantify diversity by examining social demographics such as race and ethnicity, age, sex, class, disabilities, living arrangements, and family composition. Census "head of household" designations have been challenged as reflecting and perpetuating patriarchal patterns of power and authority implied in such terminology. Racial and ethnicity categorizations have proven contentious and continue to evolve, as do social constructions of those concepts. The analysis of same-sex couples has received increasing attention as well. When the 2001 census in England and Wales added a question on religion, 390,000 respondents recorded "Jedi" (the belief system featured in the popular *Star Wars* science fiction movies) as their religious preference, having been urged to do so by an Internet campaign. The campaign apparently had the unintended positive effect of encouraging people in their late teens and early twenties to complete their census forms. No census manages to count every member of the population. Certain categories of people, such as immigrants and the homeless, are the most likely to be missed and, therefore, undercounted and potentially underserved.

Some censuses, such as colonial censuses in Africa, have also raised concerns regarding motive, and some censuses have even involved human rights abuses of vulnerable subpopulations, such as the forced migrations of Native Americans in the nineteenth century. These abuses have been particularly evident during times of war. After the 1941 attack on Pearl Harbor, U.S. census data was used by the War Department (now the Department of Defense) in the identification and relocation of Japanese Americans to detention camps. Census data from Germany and occupied regions was central to furthering Nazi interests before and during World War II (1939–1945). It was used in propaganda, in the identification of Aryans and non-Aryans, in the extermination of Jews and others, and in advancing the regime's military goals.

The United Nations Statistics Division, through the World Population and Housing Census Program, has been active in supporting national census-taking worldwide, including the development of census methodology, the provision of technical assistance in conducting censuses, and the dissemination of census data. As census technology, techniques, procedures, research, and guidance become increasingly refined, awareness of various issues is heightened and they can be better addressed.

SEE ALSO *Aryans; Data; Data, Pseudopanel; Demography; Ethnicity; Human Rights; Measurement; Native Americans; Nazism; Population Growth; Population Studies; Public Health; Racial Classification; Religion; Survey*

BIBLIOGRAPHY

Alterman, Hyman. 1969. *Counting People: The Census in History.* New York: Harcourt, Brace.

Aly, Götz, and Karl Heinz Roth. 2004. *The Nazi Census: Identification and Control in the Third Reich.* Trans. Edwin Black and Assenka Oksiloff. Philadelphia: Temple University Press.

FPS Economy: Directorate-General, Statistics and Economic Information. 2007. Census in the World. http://statbel.fgov.be/census/links_en.asp.

Lancaster, Henry O. 1951. Deafness as an Epidemic Disease in Australia. *British Medical Journal* 2: 1429–1432.

Lavin, Michael R. 1996. *Understanding the Census: A Guide for Marketers, Planners, Grant Writers, and Other Data Users.* Kenmore, NY: Epoch.

National Statistics in the United Kingdom. 2003. 390,000 Jedis There Are: But Did Hoax Campaign Boost Response in Teens and 20s? http://www.statistics.gov.uk/cci/nugget.asp?id=297.

Rodriguez, Clara E. 2000. *Changing Race: Latinos, the Census, and the History of Ethnicity in the United States.* New York: New York University Press.

Seltzer, William. 2005. On the Use of Population Data Systems to Target Vulnerable Population Subgroups for Human Rights Abuses. *Coyuntura Social* 32: 31–44. http://www.uwm.edu/~margo/govstat/CoyunturaSocialpaper2005.pdf.

Seltzer, William, and Margo Anderson. 2000. After Pearl Harbor: The Proper Use of Population Data in Time of War. Paper presented at the Annual Meeting of the Population Association of America, Los Angeles, March 2000. http://www.amstat.org/about/statisticians/index.cfm?fuseaction=paperinfo&PaperID=1.

United Nations Statistics Division. http://unstats.un.org/unsd/default.htm.

U.S. Bureau of the Census. 1990. *Federal Legislative Use of Decennial Census Data.* 1990 Census Population and Housing Content Determination Report, CDR–14. Washington, DC: U.S. Government Printing Office.

U.S. Bureau of the Census. 2002. How the People Use the Census. http://www.census.gov/dmd/www/dropin4.htm.

U.S. Bureau of the Census. 2007. http://www.census.gov.

Kathy S. Stolley

CENTER FOR POLITICAL STUDIES

SEE *Pollsters.*

CENTER-PERIPHERY

SEE *Dependency Theory.*

CENTRAL BANKS

Central banks came into being in Europe in the late seventeenth century (Sweden in 1668, England in 1694) as government sponsored banks that were either state-owned (Swedish Riksbank) or privately owned (Bank of England). Their initial functions were basic in nature: giving financial support to the state in return for legislative advantages and monopoly power in the banking business. Central banks were also established to help centralize and standardize payments systems in countries such as Italy, Germany, and Switzerland, and, in Austria in 1816, to restore the value of the currency after government overspending during the Napoleonic wars. Regardless of the initial functions assigned to central banks, they slowly evolved into bankers' banks—in addition to being the government's bank—by becoming the main reserves depository institutions for the banking system.

Theories on central banking did not emerge until the late nineteenth century, when it was recognized that discretionary monetary policy had macroeconomic consequences for domestic economic activity as well as international trade balances, especially with regard to exchange rate policies under the gold standard, which was a commodity-money system since the currency was backed by gold reserves at the central bank (and the Bretton Woods system in the twentieth century, under which the U.S. dollar replaced gold as the international reserve currency). One of the early analysts of central banking, Walter Bagehot (1826–1877), founder of *The Economist* magazine, argued in his famous *Lombard Street* (1873) that central bankers are incapable of thinking theoretically about the daily transactions they engage in.

THEORY

Central banks play a crucial role in macroeconomic policy by acting as a lender of last resort to the banking system and by regulating and supervising the financial system. Policy priorities and the emphases of policies, however, differ depending on the theoretical framework from which central bank economists draw their policy inspiration.

Mainstream Approach The mainstream (neoclassical) approach argues that central banks should focus on price stability through money-supply targeting or inflation targeting. According to the logic of this argument, money is neutral in the long run; therefore any increase in the quantity of money would only lead to inflation in the long run. The mainstream approach recommends that the central bank be completely independent from the fiscal authority to prevent monetary expansions by irresponsible governments. Instead, the central bank is commissioned to expand the money supply steadily at a pre-announced rate (a monetary rule). This approach relies on the assumption that the central bank can actually control the quantity of money (verticalist or exogenous money approach) through the three traditional monetary tools: required reserve ration, discount rate, and open market operations. Hence the central bank can increase the quantity of money by decreasing the required reserve ratio, decreasing the discount rate, or buying bonds; and it can decrease the money supply by doing the opposite. The neoclassical view holds therefore that the quantity of money is exogenously determined by the central bank, whereas the interest rate is an endogenous variable determined by the interaction between money supply and money demand. This neoclassical model came under attack during the Great Depression by Cambridge University economist John Maynard Keynes, and later by the followers of the Keynesian revolution.

Post-Keynesian Approach The Post Keynesian approach, by contrast, argues that the money supply is an endogenous process over which the central bank has no control. The quantity of money is driven by the demand for credit by the private sector. The demand for credit is systematically accommodated by profit-seeking banks regardless of the required reserves available to them (horizontalist approach). In a fractional reserve banking system, financial innovation is the key to a successful banking operation. Banks usually extend credit to creditworthy customers, then worry about meeting their reserve requirements. Reserve requirements can be met by borrowing from domestic or foreign banks, by selling financial assets, signing repurchasing agreements with other financial institutions, shifting checking account balances to low-reserve requirement savings accounts, and, as a last resort, borrowing from the central bank (the lender of last resort). Post-Keynesian economists argue that the central bank has no control over an expanding economy, as it is the demand side that is pulling reserves from the central bank, with the latter being compelled to accommodate the market or else risk a financial crisis. For instance, a rapidly expanding economy requires a credit expansion by the entire banking system; the latter will face an inevitable shortage of reserves, thus driving up short-term interest rates above the central bank's target rate. The central bank must therefore intervene by providing liquidity to the market to prevent financial instability due to rising interest rates. The Post-Keynesian approach holds that the central bank's policy target cannot be the quantity of money, but rather the short-term interest rate that serves as a benchmark for the entire economy. Hence the interest rate is set exogenously while the quantity of money is an endogenous phenomenon.

Major financial crises have been prevented through central bank intervention as a lender of last resort, as for example after the September 11, 2001, attacks in the United States. In anticipation of a panic after the reopening of financial markets, the Federal Reserve Bank in an emergency meeting lowered its short-term interest rate target by fifty basis points; but most important, it snapped up all government securities offered by dealers, thus pumping up a record sum of $70.2 billion on September 13, 2001. As Paul Davidson notes in his 2002 book, the liquidity injection served not only to prevent a bond-market crash but also to reinstate positive expectations about the stability of the financial system.

Central bank leaders also play a crucial role in the formation of market expectations. Financial investors pay close attention to statements made by central bank officials because they know that central bankers have access to more accurate economic information and unpublished economic indicators, in addition to being in charge of key interest rates that act as benchmarks for the rest of the economy. If, for instance, investors detect a signal from the central bankers suggesting that the central bank is worried about inflation acceleration, and that the central bank is about to raise interest rates, then one would expect bond prices to go up, thus encouraging bond investors to buy more bonds and sell them at a later date; the reverse would ensue if investors were led to believe that the central bank was about to lower interest rates.

CENTRAL BANK INDEPENDENCE

The advocates of central bank independence argue that politicians cannot be trusted to make the tough political decisions as they tend to give in to political pressures, thus only an independent central bank can take action without fear of political retaliation. An independent central bank is expected to slow down the economy by raising interest rates when the unemployment rate drops low. This neoclassical argument rests on the idea that there is a trade off between unemployment and inflation, and that low unemployment rates will inevitably lead to accelerating inflation.

In addition to improved credibility and transparency, central bank independence favors the implementation of monetary rules. This is based on the New Classical view that money is neutral and that monetary policy is ineffective. The Lucas policy ineffectiveness argument states that any anticipated monetary policy will not affect output (thus will not affect employment). The policy ineffectiveness argument does not hold in the case of long-term labor contracts because policymakers in this case can change their behavior (for instance, the central bank can cheat on the announced rate of growth of the money supply). Thus a systematic monetary policy can have real effects. Finn Kydland and Edward Prescott (1977) argue that private agents are rational and thus expect the central bank to reoptimize its (previously announced) policy in the future. In game theory terms, this can be illustrated in a noncooperative Stackelberg game in which the central bank is the leader (it has private information and could change its policy at almost any time) and the private agents are the followers. This will lead the economy to a time-consistent suboptimal (Nash) equilibrium in which the social welfare function is not optimal, even though both the leader and the followers have tried their best to maximize their own respective utilities. It is noteworthy that the concept of the monetary authorities' credibility is

of critical importance to the dynamic game described above, if the central bank wishes to implement a monetary rule rather than discretionary monetary policy because of the repeated aspect of the game.

Between 1970 and 1982 New Classical economists demonstrated that anticipated monetary policy is ineffective because economic agents are rational. During that period they produced a substantial literature explaining business cycle fluctuations in terms of the rational expectations hypothesis and supply-side (mainly technological) shocks. The rational expectations hypothesis states that economic agents' subjective expectations concerning economic variables will coincide with the true or objective mathematical conditional expectations of those variables. This assumption should not, however, be considered as synonymous with perfect foresight. Rational expectations in the forward-looking approach (as opposed to the backward-looking approach of the adaptive expectations) imply that economic agents will use the publicly available information and will not systematically form wrong expectations. William Nordhaus used this approach to show that "a perfect democracy with retrospective evaluation of parties will make decisions against future generations" (1975, p. 187). Politicians can use an expansionist monetary policy during an electoral period in order to reduce unemployment and thereby collect more votes. Once reelected, the government can start fighting against the inflation caused by money expansion and therefore push unemployment probably above its initial level. Governments succeed in making use of this political business cycle because the public has a short memory and will not recognize the use of this policy during the next election. The political business cycle theory represents a major argument for central bank independence, meaning that an independent central bank is more likely to implement a noninflationary monetary policy that is consistent with the stability of the general level of prices. The empirical evidence, however, does not show any significant correlation between central bank independence and inflation. In fact, one of the key variables used to measure the central bank independence index is inflation. This approach tends to reduce inflation to expansionary monetary policy and does not take into account other factors such as price-setting power and external shocks in international commodity markets.

DEVELOPING COUNTRIES

Central banks in developing countries face considerable challenges. The conventional wisdom argues that developing countries must maintain a steady inflow of financial capital to finance their savings gap and to fuel the process of economic development. To ensure such conditions, the central bank has to keep inflation low and stable and the exchange rate pegged to a basket of hard currencies, and in some cases to a single hard currency such as the U.S. dollar or the euro. Such strategies entail keeping interest rates high and the value of the currency artificially overvalued—thus the need to accumulate hard currency reserves to defend the value of the currency. Most developing countries, however, run trade deficits that must be financed through borrowing in hard currencies, which accounts for most developing countries' recurring external debt problem. In order to prevent financial crisis, the central bank is then obliged to cater to the needs of financial markets by keeping interest rates artificially high, which helps create an inadequate climate for domestic investment. This neoliberal view has dominated central banking in developing countries since the 1980s. The primacy of the low-inflation goal over other macroeconomic goals has crippled many economies in the developing world. As Gerald Epstein (2005) argues, this approach stands in sharp contrast to what central banks have historically done in both developed and developing countries, namely financing government spending, promoting full employment, managing exchange rates, enforcing capital controls, and allocating credit to sectors of special social need such as health care, education, and housing.

WHAT CENTRAL BANKS CAN ACHIEVE

Post Keynesians argue that the central bank can help coordinate the achievement of full employment in both developed and developing countries. Because the government is the monopoly-issuer of its sovereign currency, it follows that there can be no financial constraint on government spending. Money is injected into the system through government spending, and is withdrawn from it through taxation or bond sales. Bonds are not issued to "finance" government deficits, but rather to give the private sector an interest-bearing alternative to cash. The government accepts its own money in payment of tax liabilities, hence creating a demand for the sovereign currency. The value of money then depends on the government's (and the central bank's) capability to manage the quantity of money and the level of interest rates in the economy. From this perspective, the government can finance a full employment program by offering to hire anyone at a fixed, socially established living wage to perform socially desirable tasks that the private sector would not otherwise perform. The role of the central bank becomes crucial in financing the program, managing the national debt, and adopting a flexible exchange rate regime. As L. Randall Wray (1998) observes, the central bank independence mantra becomes meaningless if one accepts the necessity of policy coordination between the treasury and the central bank in order to accommodate the economy.

SEE ALSO *Business Cycles, Real; Economic Crises; Economics, Keynesian; Economics, Neoclassical; Economics, New Classical; Economics, Post Keynesian; Expectations, Rational; Federal Reserve System, U.S.; Financial Markets; Full Employment; Game Theory; Inflation; Interest Rates; Macroeconomics; Monetarism; Monetary Base; Monetary Theory; Money; Nash Equilibrium; Policy, Monetary; Unemployment*

BIBLIOGRAPHY

Bagehot, Walter. 1873. *Lombard Street: A Description of the Money Market.* New York: Wiley, 1999.

Davidson, Paul. 2002. *Financial Markets, Money, and the Real World.* Cheltenham, U.K., and Northampton, MA: Edward Elgar.

Epstein, Gerald. 2005. Central Banks as Agents of Economic Development. Political Economy Research Institute, University of Massachusetts at Amherst. Working Paper Series no. 104 (September).

Goodhart, Charles. 1988. *The Evolution of Central Banks.* Cambridge, MA: MIT Press.

Kaldor, Nickolas. 1985. *The Scourge of Monetarism.* 2nd ed. Oxford and New York: Oxford University Press.

Keynes, John M. 1936. *The General Theory of Employment, Interest, and Money.* New York: Harcourt, Brace.

Kydland, Finn E., and Prescott, Edward C. 1977. Rules Rather than Discretion: The Inconsistency of Optimal Plans. *Journal of Political Economy* 85 (3): 473–492.

Lavoie, Marc, and Mario Seccareccia, eds. 2004. *Central Banking in the Modern World: Alternative Perspectives.* Cheltenham, U.K., and Northampton, MA: Edward Elgar.

Lucas, Robert E. 1975. An Equilibrium Model of Business Cycle. *Journal of Political Economy* 83: 1113–1144.

Moore, Basil J. 1982. *Horizontalists and Verticalists: The Macroeconomics of Credit Money.* Cambridge, U.K., and New York: Cambridge University Press.

Nordhaus, William D. 1975. The Political Business Cycle. *Review of Economic Studies* 42 (2): 169–190.

Wray, L. Randall. 1998. *Understanding Modern Money: The Key to Full Employment and Price Stability.* Cheltenham, U.K., and Northampton, MA: Edward Elgar.

Fadhel Kaboub

CENTRAL INTELLIGENCE AGENCY, U.S.

As a U.S. senator (D-MO), Harry S. Truman was well aware of the significant loss in lives and matériel that resulted from America's inadequate intelligence prior to the Japanese attack on Pearl Harbor in 1941. During his three-month tenure as vice president and, upon becoming president when Franklin D. Roosevelt died in April 1945, Truman experienced further dissatisfaction with the lack of coordination among U.S. intelligence units throughout the remaining months of World War II. After the war, the avoidance of a future Pearl Harbor—that is, achieving reliable warning, the premier objective of intelligence—became a high priority for the Truman administration as it pursued the establishment of a modern intelligence system. Lawmakers on Capitol Hill also evoked the memory of Pearl Harbor as they debated how to prevent surprise attacks against the United States.

The Truman administration soon faced another reason for making improvements in U.S. intelligence: a sense in 1946 that the Soviet Union had emerged on the world stage as a formidable and hostile adversary. War-weary American soldiers had barely returned home from Europe and Asia when Soviet-phobia began to grip Washington, D.C., stirred by Winston Churchill's "Iron Curtain" speech in 1946 and waves of vitriolic anti-West propaganda emanating from Moscow. As intelligence scholar Rhodri Jeffreys-Jones stated in *Eternal Vigilance* (1997), "past weaknesses" like Pearl Harbor served as part of the backdrop for the debate about reforming U.S. intelligence in 1946–1947, but more important were "present imperatives" (p. 23)—above all, the rise of Soviet power in the world. Just as the United States could have benefited greatly from having better indications and warning (I&W, in the intelligence acronym) about the movements of Japanese warships in 1941, so five years later did leaders in Washington seek reliable intelligence on the military capabilities and intentions of the Union of Soviet Socialist Republics (USSR).

THE CENTRAL INTELLIGENCE GROUP

One of Truman's top aides, Clark Clifford, recalled in his memoir *Counsel to the President* (1991): "By early 1946, President Truman was becoming increasingly annoyed by the flood of conflicting and uncoordinated intelligence reports flowing haphazardly across his desk" (p. 166). On January 22, 1946, he signed an executive order that created a Director of Central Intelligence (DCI) and a Central Intelligence Group (CIG), with the express purpose of achieving a "correlation and evaluation of intelligence relating to the national security." The order allowed the CIG to "centralize" research and analysis and "coordinate all foreign intelligence activities." Truman's original intent was, as he told biographer Merle Miller in the book *Plain Speaking* (1973), to avoid "having to look through a bunch of papers two feet high" and instead receive information that was "coordinated so that the President could arrive at the facts" (p. 420). In twenty-first-century termi-

nology, he longed for the "all-source fusion" of intelligence or, in a military term, intelligence jointness.

Yet the president never saw his hope fulfilled. From the beginning the CIG proved weak. One of its primary tasks was to put together the *Daily Summary*, the precursor to today's *President's Daily Brief*. Yet, intelligence units in the various departments balked at handing over information to the CIG. Secretary of State James F. Byrnes, for example, refused to pass along cables from his staff overseas, maintaining that he would tell the president directly what he needed to know. In response to this intransigence, Truman weighed in on behalf of the CIG and ordered Byrnes to cooperate in the preparation of the *Daily Summary*. Nevertheless, departments remained resentful and often resistant to the concept of intelligence sharing. White House support for the CIG notwithstanding, putting together the *Daily Summary* quickly became an exercise in futility.

The administration turned toward the idea of creating a stronger organization: a Central Intelligence Agency, or CIA. It soon became clear to President Truman, however, that the acquisition of a truly centralized intelligence system would come at too steep a price, in light of an even more urgent goal the White House sought to achieve: military consolidation. World War II had been rife with conflict between the services, often interrupting the pursuit of battlefield objectives. President aide Clark Clifford reflected in his memoir on how the administration had to play down intelligence reform in favor of settling the "first order of business—the war between the Army and the Navy." The "first priority," he continued, "was still to get the squabbling military services together behind a unification bill."

The creation of a Department of Defense, replacing the old Department of War, would provide a means for drawing the services closer together. The president did not wish to complicate the fight for unification by seeking, at the same time, intelligence consolidation that was bound to roil the military services as a threat to their own confederal and parochial approaches to intelligence. The one point that all the military services, as well as the Department of State and the Federal Bureau of Investigation (FBI), agreed on was that they did not want a strong central agency controlling their intelligence collection programs.

As a result, the Truman administration retreated from its goal of intelligence consolidation. The diluted language of the National Security Act of 1947 provided for only a weak DCI and a CIA that was little different from the failed CIG. As Clifford conceded, the effort fell "far short of our original intent" (p. 169). The landmark National Security Act of 1947 would mainly address the issue of military unification; intelligence was only a secondary consideration. The statute created a Central Intelligence Agency, but left the details vague on just how the new independent agency was supposed to carry out its charge to "correlate," "evaluate," and "disseminate" information to policymakers in light of the powerful grasp that the policy departments (like Defense and State) retained over their individual intelligence units. The law represented a delicate attempt to create a CIA that, as historian Michael Warner wrote in his study *Central Intelligence* (2001), would have to "steer between the two poles of centralization and departmental autonomy." As a result, the CIA "never quite became the integrator of U.S. intelligence that its Presidential and congressional parents had envisioned" (pp. 45, 47).

The rhetoric of "intelligence coordination" expressed in the law sounded good; but the reality of bringing coordination about was a different matter altogether. Genuine integration of America's intelligence agencies required a strong DCI, leading a truly central intelligence agency with budget and appointment powers over all the other secret agencies. In 1952 this cluster of secret agencies became known by the misnomer "the intelligence community." In reality, they remained separated organizations ("stovepiped," in intelligence slang) with their own powerful program directors ("gorillas") and allegiance to their own department secretaries. The DCI's authority as spelled out in the National Security Act of 1947 was feeble, leaving the nation's spymaster in a position of having to cajole, persuade, plead, even beg for coordination, rather than order it through the threat of budget and personnel retaliation against those "gorillas in the stovepipes" who failed to comply with the DCI's directives.

While the DCI more or less controlled the CIA and had a main office there, the other fourteen agencies (sixteen in the mid-2000s) enjoyed considerable autonomy. The Director was unable even to determine how the nation's intelligence budget of some $44 billion would be spent each year. In addition to the CIA, the other agencies include the National Security Agency (NSA); the National Geospatial-Intelligence Agency (NGA); the National Reconnaissance Organization (NRO); the Defense Intelligence Agency (DIA); the State Department's Intelligence and Research (INR); intelligence units in the Departments of Energy, Homeland Security, and Treasury; FBI intelligence; the Drug Enforcement Administration; the Coast Guard; and intelligence units within each of the military services (army, navy, air force, marines). Even twenty years after the creation of the CIA, one of its deputy directors, Adm. Rufus Taylor (who served from 1966 to 1969), referred to the various intelligence agencies as little more than a tribal federation.

An important part of the CIA's history since the Truman administration has been a series of efforts to overcome the flaw in its original design—that is, to strengthen the DCI and the CIA in their roles as collator and disseminator of information from throughout the broad intelligence community. The steam went out of each of these efforts after they confronted resistance from the various agency "gorillas" (the chiefs of each of the agencies) and the department secretaries, especially the secretary of defense in alliance with the congressional Armed Services Committees. "For the duration of the Cold War, the White House kept nudging successive Directors of Central Intelligence to do more to lead the Intelligence Community," Warner concluded. But a towering obstacle persisted: "Cabinet-level officials . . . saw no reason to cede power to a DCI" (p. 49).

THE PURPOSE OF THE CIA

The precursor to the CIA during World War II was the Office of Strategic Services (OSS). During that war, the OSS provided covert assistance to resistance movements in Europe and Asia, and became adept at providing research relevant to the war effort and on occasion carried out derring-do secret operations behind enemy lines. Its most long-lasting effect, though, was to serve as a training ground for individuals who would help create and lead the CIA once it was created in 1947. The OSS was disbanded after the war, but many of its experienced personnel soon entered the new CIA, including future directors Allen Dulles, Richard Helms, and William Colby.

The CIA, an independent organization situated neither within the organizational framework of the Pentagon nor in any of the other cabinet departments, continued the kind of operations employed by the OSS during World War II—only now with a much more prominent position in the government and a new adversary: the communist nations of the world. "The Agency," as the CIA is called by its own personnel, has three primary missions: the collection and interpretation ("analysis") of information gathered from every corner of the globe; the protection of U.S. government secrets against hostile intelligence services and other spies ("counterintelligence"); and the clandestine manipulation of events in foreign lands on behalf of America's interests, through the use of propaganda, political activities, economic disruption, and paramilitary operations (collectively known as "covert action" or "special activities").

Intelligence Collection and Analysis The collection of intelligence relies on machines (satellites and reconnaissance airplanes, for example; so-called technical intelligence or "techint," in the professional acronym); on human means (classic espionage or human intelligence;

"humint"); and on the sifting of information available in the open literature (newspapers, public speeches, and the like; sometimes referred to as open-source intelligence or "osint"). Each method has its drawbacks. Photographs taken by satellites can be useful, but Al Qaeda and other contemporary terrorist organizations have become adept at hiding in caves in Southwest Asia, out of sight from the cameras. Moreover, the CIA lacks sufficient spy handlers ("operations officers") abroad with good foreign language skills to recruit local agents ("assets"), especially in places where the United States has never had much of a presence (such as in China and nations in the Middle East and Southwest Asia). As a result, the human intelligence flowing back to the CIA is insufficient.

Even if this humint problem were solved, the community faces another, equally serious human deficiency: analytic brain power. The CIA does not have enough talented information interpreters ("analysts") to lend insight to the fire hose of data that streams into its offices each day from overseas. On the eve of the second Persian Gulf War, for instance, the agency had few analysts fluent in Arabic. It is deficient, too, in the number of analysts who understand the history and culture of places like Iran and Pakistan that the United States largely ignored during its concentration on the Communist part of the world during the cold war.

Counterintelligence The CIA's counterintelligence mission received its greatest setback in the period from 1984 to 1996. During that time, a CIA officer by the name of Aldrich H. Ames secretly spied on his own organization for the Soviet Union. He identified for the Soviets over 200 CIA operations against the USSR and revealed the names of nine CIA agents in Moscow, all of whom were then executed by Soviet officials. The CIA's top counterintelligence challenge is to protect the agency's computers and other facilities from foreign "moles"—penetration agents engaged in treason against the United States on behalf of terrorist groups or other American adversaries.

Covert Action Covert action has been the most controversial of the CIA's missions. It may be defined as those activities carried out by the agency to secretly influence and manipulate events abroad. This approach is often referred to as the "Third Option"—in between, on the one hand, sending in the marines and, on the other hand, relying on the diplomatic corps to achieve America's goals. The use of military force is "noisy" and likely to draw a quick reaction from adversaries, as well as stir widespread debate at home; and diplomacy can be notoriously slow and often ineffectual. Thus, covert action has had a special appeal to some policy officials: with this tool, they can move rapidly and in relative quiet, avoiding lengthy public discussions

over tactics and broader objectives (hence, the "quiet option" is another euphemism for covert action).

Covert action has often failed, as with the failed Bay of Pigs operation against Cuba in 1961 and the Iran-Contra scandal in 1986. The latter especially discredited covert action, because the Reagan administration carried out CIA paramilitary operations against Nicaragua despite vociferous congressional opposition. After the Iran-Contra episode, the budget for covert action plummeted to its lowest levels: less than 1 percent of the CIA's annual budget. It would take the terrorist attacks against the United States on September 11, 2001, to stimulate a renewed interest in this approach to foreign policy and funding for covert action began a rapid rise upward in the name of combating world terrorism. In 2001–2002, the use of CIA paramilitary operations against the Taliban regime in Afghanistan, in tandem with overt military operations by the indigenous Northern Alliance and U.S. bombing missions, opened a new chapter in America's reliance on covert action. Today the most lethal weapon of covert action is the Predator, a pilotless drone armed with Hellfire missiles.

While the CIA's secret propaganda operations against the Soviet Union and China during the cold war have been praised, the agency's operations in the developing world have been subjected to widespread criticism. The best known and most controversial example is Chile during the 1960s. In the Chilean presidential election of 1964, the CIA spent $3 million to blacken the reputation of Salvador Allende, the Socialist candidate with suspected ties to Moscow. On a per capita basis, this amount of money was equivalent to the secret expenditure of $60 million in a U.S. presidential election at the time, a staggering level of funding. The CIA managed to thwart Allende's election in 1964, but he persevered and in 1970 was elected president of Chile in a free and open election.

The CIA then turned to a range of propaganda and other covert actions designed to undermine his regime. The agency poured another $3 million worth of secret propaganda into the country between 1970 and 1973, in the form of press releases, radio commentary, films, pamphlets, posters, leaflets, direct mailings, paper streamers, and vivid wall paintings that conjured images of Communist tanks and firing squads that would supposedly soon become a part of life in Chile. Printing hundreds of thousands of copies, the CIA flooded the country (predominantly Catholic) with an anti-Communist pastoral letter written many years earlier by Pope Pius XI. The effect was to substantially weaken the Allende government.

Another well-known CIA covert action operation occurred in 1953, when the CIA joined British intelligence operatives in the overthrow of Mohammed

Mossadegh in Iran. In his place, the CIA installed a pro-West leader known as the shah of Iran, who provided the United States with loss-cost oil and a friendly government in the heart of the Middle East. The shah, though, lost the support of his people over time and was finally deposed by a revolution in 1979 that brought to power a fundamentalist Islamic regime in Iran.

The Special Case of Assassination Plots A special category within the domain of paramilitary operations is the assassination of foreign leaders. This option has gone by a number of euphemisms: "executive action," "terminate with extreme prejudice," and "neutralization." At one time during the cold war, proposals for assassination were screened by a special unit within the CIA called the "Health Alteration Committee."

Fidel Castro was America's prime target for assassination during the Kennedy administration. The agency emptied its medicine cabinet of drugs and poisons in various attempts to kill or debilitate the Cuban leader. Agency assets planned to dust his combat boots with depilatory powder, in hopes the chemical would enter his bloodstream through the soles of his feet and cause his charismatic beard to fall off. When this plot was abandoned (Castro's boots were not so accessible), other agents sought to inject his cigars with the hallucinogenic drug LSD, as well as with a deadly botulinum toxin. Again, the operations failed. Various other plots using guns failed as well, even though the CIA recruited the Mafia to assist in the assassination attempts inside Cuba. Another target of a CIA assassination plot was Patrice Lumumba of Congo, who was killed by a rival African faction just before the agency tried to poison him.

The most widely reported CIA operation to eliminate large numbers of lower-level officials from the scene arose in the context of the Vietnam War. Code-named the "Phoenix Program," the intention was to subdue the influence of the Communist Viet Cong (VC) in the South Vietnamese countryside. Some twenty thousand VC officials were killed as a result of this operation, though mostly in the context of military or paramilitary combat with South Vietnamese or U.S. troops.

In 1976 U.S. public revulsion toward the murder plots against foreign heads-of-state led to the signing of an executive order by President Gerald R. Ford prohibiting assassination as an instrument of U.S. foreign policy. The order, which states that "no person, employed by or acting on behalf of the United States Government, shall engage in, or conspire to engage in assassination," has been endorsed by every president since Ford. The executive order has been interpreted to have a wartime waiver, which allowed presidents to use assassination as an instrument of combat in Iraq and against Al Qaeda. Proponents of covert action argue that the defeat of such venal powers as the Communists during the cold war or terrorists today justifies the use of this method. Those taking a more ethical approach to foreign policy have objected, though, to the "anything goes" approach to a national security.

The Church Committee Inquiry The assassination plots were uncovered in 1975–1976 by the Church Committee in the U.S. Senate, named after its chairman Senator Frank Church (D-ID). This investigative panel formed after reporting in the *New York Times* in late 1974 indicated that the CIA may have used its secret powers to spy on American citizens, in an operation known as CHAOS. Investigators discovered the *Times* was correct about the illegal opening of mail sent or received by some 1.5 million American citizens, but this was only part of the story. The Committee discovered as well that the CIA had engaged in drug experiments against unsuspecting subjects, two of whom died from the side effects; had manipulated elections even in democratic regimes like Chile; and had infiltrated religious, media, and academic organizations inside the United States.

In the aftermath of this inquiry, Congress established permanent intelligence oversight committees in the Senate and the House, and passed legislation to provide closer supervision by lawmakers over the secret agencies. The purpose was to establish safeguards to ensure that Congress would be in a position to halt abuses by the CIA and America's other intelligence organizations. This is not to say that the Church Committee created a foolproof system of intelligence accountability. The Iran-Contra affair of 1986–1987 served as a reminder that even robust legislative safeguards are no guarantee against the misuse of power by determined conspirators in the executive branch. That scandal led to a further tightening of oversight procedures, including the creation of a CIA Office of Inspector General directly answerable to Congress.

The fear in 1975, when the Church Committee revealed the extent of intelligence abuses, was that the CIA and its companion agencies might begin to function as a secret government, subject to little review or restraint. Certainly, the Committee's findings suggested this had become the case. America had to relearn anew an old lesson well understood by the founding fathers, namely, that power can have a corrupting influence on those who hold it—the central idea that guided the writing of the Constitution in 1789. With the safeguards established by the members of the Church Committee and other key officeholders in 1976, citizens of the United States are far less likely to suffer abuse at the hands of the secret agencies than during the earlier years of benign neglect when the intelligence organizations were relatively free of supervision.

Some have faulted this increased accountability as an impediment to the conduct of swift and flexible intelligence operations necessary to defeat America's enemies abroad. The debate continues over the proper balance between accountability and efficiency—whether or not to have meaningful checks and balances in the domain of intelligence operations.

9/11 AND THE NEW INTELLIGENCE DEBATES

In the aftermath of the 9/11 terrorist attacks and mistakes about the existence of weapons of mass destruction (WMDs) in Iraq, official inquiries into the performance of the intelligence community pointed to the need for a strengthened DCI who could improve the sharing of information among the CIA and the other secret agencies. In July 2004, the 9/11 or Kean Commission (after its chair, Thomas H. Kean, a Republican former governor of New Jersey) advocated, along with a series of other reform proposals, the creation of a director of national intelligence, or DNI, with full budget and appointment powers over the intelligence community. In December 2004, Congress passed an intelligence reform bill, known as the Intelligence Reform and Terrorism Prevention Act, which established the DNI office. The Department of Defense and its allies in Congress managed, however, to dilute and obfuscate the authorities of the new intelligence director. As a result, the DNI—just like the DCI before—has ambiguous authority over budgets and hiring for all sixteen agencies. Not even the shock of the 9/11 and WMD intelligence failures have been enough to bring about the consolidation of the intelligence community.

Even a strong DNI with full authority over intelligence budgets and a mandate to bring about better information-sharing would not solve, in itself, America's intelligence weaknesses. Reformers agree that other necessary changes included the development of better human intelligence in places like the Middle East and Southwest Asia (so-called humint—old fashioned espionage); improved foreign language skills and knowledge of foreign countries among collectors and analysts; better data-sifting to sort through the flood of data that pours into Washington from collectors around the world, separating the important "signals" from the large mass of "noise"; and fully integrated information technology, both horizontally throughout the federal government and vertically from Washington, D.C., down to state and local counterterrorism officials.

THE FUTURE OF THE CIA

The 9/11 attacks and subsequent investigations failed to produce reforms that would have fulfilled President Truman's hopes for a strong national intelligence chief.

On the contrary, in a paradox the post-9/11 reforms have led to a diminution in the powers of the DNI and a decline in the coordinating role originally assigned to the CIA in 1947. The CIA is no longer the central focus in America's intelligence establishment; it has become just one of the nation's sixteen secret agencies. Even its authority over humint, once full, is now shared with the Department of Defense. Moreover, unlike the DCI, the DNI is not located at CIA headquarters, but rather in a building at Bolling Air Force Base, near National Airport, cut off from the CIA's experienced analytic and report-production facilities—indeed without any infrastructure beyond a small support staff. The DNI is in a weak position for trying to resolve the fissile tendencies of the intelligence "community." The CIA has been weakened, too, by its 9/11 and WMD failures.

During the second Bush administration, the United States found itself involved simultaneously in three wars: in Afghanistan and Iraq, as well as against global terrorism. Yet its intelligence agencies continued to display the same attributes that so troubled President Truman in 1947. They had yet to acquire firm leadership from a strong director of national intelligence, and they continued to be plagued by an inability to work together in a cohesive manner. Even the modest centralization of intelligence provided by the CIA in earlier years was on the wane as the agency found itself no longer at the core of the intelligence establishment.

SEE ALSO *Allende, Salvador; Bay of Pigs; Fahrenheit 9/11; Intelligence; Lumumba, Patrice*

BIBLIOGRAPHY

Barnet, Richard J. 1968. *Intervention and Revolution: The United States and the Third World.* New York: World Publishing.

Clifford, Clark, with Richard Holbrooke. 1991. *Counsel to the President: A Memoir.* New York: Random House.

Jeffreys-Jones, Rhodri, and Christopher Andrew, eds. 1997. *Eternal Vigilance? 50 Years of the CIA.* London: Cass.

Johnson, Loch K. 1996. *Secret Agencies.* New Haven, CT: Yale University Press.

Johnson, Loch K. 2004. Congressional Supervision of America's Secret Agencies: The Experience and Legacy of the Church Committee. *Public Administration Review* 64 (January–February): 3–14.

Miller, Merle. 1973. *Plain Speaking: An Oral Biography of Harry S. Truman.* New York: Berkeley.

Ranelagh, John. 1986. *The Agency.* New York: Simon & Schuster.

Treverton, Gregory F. 1987. *Covert Action.* New York: Basic Books.

Turner, Stansfield. 2005. *Burn before Reading.* New York: Hyperion.

U.S. Senate. 1975, 1976. Select Committee to Study Governmental Operations with Respect to Intelligence Activities (the Church Committee). *Interim and Final Reports.* Washington, DC: U.S. Government Printing Office.

Warner, Michael, ed. 2001. *Central Intelligence: Origin and Evolution.* Washington, DC: Center for the Study of Intelligence, Central Intelligence Agency.

Loch K. Johnson

CENTRAL LIMIT THEOREM

The central limit theorem (CLT) is a fundamental result from statistics. It states that the sum of a large number of independent identically distributed (iid) random variables will tend to be distributed according to the normal distribution. A first version of the CLT was proved by the English mathematician Abraham de Moivre (1667–1754). He showed how the normal distribution can be used to approximate the distribution of the number of heads that will result when a coin is tossed a large number of times.

The CLT is the cornerstone of most estimation and inference of statistical models, which in turn are widely used in empirical work in the social sciences. Statistical models involve unknown population parameters that are estimated from a sample. The estimators often take the form of sample averages. According to the CLT, the estimators will therefore be approximately normally distributed for a sufficiently large sample size. This result can be used to draw inference about the population parameters. One example of a statistical model used in social sciences is the linear regression model. Here, the CLT can be used to quantify whether a chosen set of variables explains the variation in a certain response variable.

THE THEOREM

Let $\{x_1, \ldots, x_n\}$ be a sample of n iid random variables with mean μ and variance σ^2. Consider the sum $S_n = x_1 + x_2 + \ldots + x_n$. One may easily check that the mean and standard deviation of S_n is $n\mu$ and $\sqrt{n}\sigma$. Normalize S_n as follows,

$$Z_n = \frac{S_n - n\mu}{\sqrt{n}\sigma}$$

such that Z_n has mean zero and standard deviation 1. The CLT then states that $Z_n \approx N(0,1)$ for n large enough. Formally, the above equation should be read as follows: For any $-\infty < z < +\infty$, $P(Z_n \leq z) \to \Phi(z)$ as $n \to \infty$, where $\Phi(\cdot)$ is the cumulative density function of the normal distribution.

A major drawback of the CLT is that it is silent about how large n should be before the quality of the approximation is good. This will depend on the distribution of the x_i's making up the sum.

APPLICATIONS

The CLT has a broad range of applications. Consider, for example, a binomial random variable S_n with parameters (n,p). This variable describes the number of heads in n tosses of a coin with probability $0 < p < 1$ of heads. Its distribution is given by

$$P(S_n = j) = \binom{n}{j} p^j (1 - p)^{n-j}, j = 0, 1, \ldots, n.$$

For n large, this distribution can be difficult to compute. Another way of representing S_n is as a sum of n iid Bernoulli random variables $\{x_1, \ldots, x_n\}$. That is, $S_n = x_1 + x_2 + \ldots + x_n$ where the distribution of x_i is $P(x_i = 1) = 1 - P(x_i = 0) = p$, $i = 1, \ldots, n$. So we can apply the CLT on S_n, which tells us that $S_n \approx N(np, np(1 - p))$ for n large enough since $\mu = E[x_i] = p$ and $\sigma^2 = Var(x_i) = p(1 - p)$. This result was first proved by de Moivre in 1733.

The most important use of the CLT is probably in drawing inference about population parameters in statistical models. Most estimators of parameters can be written as sums of the sample, and so the CLT can be used to obtain a measure of the precision of the estimator. In particular, it can be used to test hypotheses regarding the parameters. As a simple example, consider an iid sample $\{x_1, \ldots, x_n\}$ with unknown population mean μ and variance σ^2. A simple estimator of the parameter μ is the sample average,

$$\bar{x} = \frac{x_1 + \ldots + x_n}{n} = \frac{1}{n} S_n.$$

We can now use the CLT to conclude that

$$\frac{\bar{x} - \mu}{\sigma\sqrt{n}} = \frac{S_n - n\mu}{\sqrt{n}\sigma} \approx N(0,1)$$

Since the variance is unknown, it needs to be estimated. This can be done using the sample variance,

$$\hat{\sigma}^2 = \frac{1}{n} \sum_{i=1}^{n} (x_i - \bar{x})^2.$$

One can now use the normal approximation for inferential purposes. For example, we can estimate the standard error of $\bar{x}$ as $\hat{\sigma}/\sqrt{n}$. Also, we know that $\bar{x} - 1.96\sigma/\sqrt{n} \leq \mu \leq \bar{x} + 1.96\sigma/\sqrt{n}$ with approximately 95 percent probability, where 1.96 is the 97.5th percentile of the normal distribution; one normally refers to this as the *confidence interval.* The CLT can furthermore be used to test specific hypotheses regarding μ.

SEE ALSO *Descriptive Statistics; Distribution, Normal; Law of Large Numbers; Variables, Random*

BIBLIOGRAPHY

David, F. N. 1962. *Games, Gods, and Gambling: The Origins and History of Probability and Statistical Ideas from the Earliest Times to the Newtonian Era.* London: Griffin.

Grinstead, Charles M., and J. Laurie Snell. 1997. *Introduction to Probability.* 2nd rev. ed. Providence, RI: American Mathematical Society.

Dennis Kristensen

CENTRAL TENDENCIES, MEASURES OF

The *mean*, the *median*, and the *mode* are measures of central tendency, used singly or jointly, to summarize information about a variable. Percentage frequency distributions and graphs may also be used, but measures of central tendency are more concise and provide a single "typical" or "average" score for the variable under consideration. They are easy to calculate and are readily understood by the public. Each of the three measures of central tendency has assets and liabilities. The combined use of all three measures provides information about the degree of symmetry in the distribution of the variable because in a normal (i.e., Gaussian) distribution, the mean, median, and mode will all be the same.

The mean is generally assumed to be the arithmetic mean or the average; it is calculated by summing the individual scores of the variable and dividing these by the total number of scores. The formula for the population mean is $\mu = \Sigma X_i / N$, where μ is the population mean, X_i is the score on the variable for the ith subject, and N is the total number of subjects. The formula for the sample mean is $\bar{X} = \Sigma X_i / N$, where $\bar{X}$, sometimes referred to as *X-bar*, is the sample mean.

Although the problem of examining a set of observations and estimating an overall value was entertained as early as three centuries BCE by Babylonian astronomers (Plackett 1958), the arithmetic mean as a statistical concept did not appear until many centuries later. The term is first found in the mid-1690s in the writings of Edmund Halley (1656–1742), and it has been used to summarize observations of a variable since the time of Galileo (1564–1642). Carl Friedrich Gauss (1777–1855) may have been the first to show that lacking any other information about a variable's value for any one subject, the arithmetic mean represents the most probable value (Gauss [1809] 2004, p. 244).

The mean is an efficient description of the distribution of a variable's scores. For example, educators and students use the mean or grade point average (GPA) to describe academic achievement. Its primary limitation is that it works best when the variable it is describing is distributed normally. If there are outliers in the distribution—for example, one score or several scores lying outside the normal range—the mean will be skewed and may thus be misleading. The mean is heavily influenced by outlying values, and is thus not as robust as the median (see below). Second, the mean requires interval/ratio data, whereas the median can be used with both interval/ratio and ordinal data, and the mode can be used with nominal data.

The median, sometimes abbreviated *Md* or *Mdn*, is the halfway point or the midpoint score in a distribution of scores. Half of the scores are greater, and half the scores are less, than the median. The median is the score that divides the distribution exactly in half. If there is an odd number of scores, the median is the middle number; if there is an even number of scores, the median is the average of the two middle scores. The median is less likely to be influenced by extreme outliers, and is usually the preferred measure of central tendency for skewed data, such as income. The median has no special notation and is obtained in the same way for both a population and a sample.

The median gives a better description than the mean of a skewed variable. For example, if one is comparing the income in an area where there is only one person who is a billionaire and the bulk of the population lives in poverty, the median will more accurately reflect the central income of the population. The median can also be used when there are undetermined or infinite scores, making it impossible to determine a mean. The median also has limitations. It works best with small samples, or with large samples that are normally distributed. It is less efficient and more subject to sampling fluctuations than the mean. An early use in English of the statistical concept of median was Francis Galton's (1822–1911) observation that "the median … is the value which is exceeded by one-half of an infinitely large group, and which the other half falls short of" (1881, p. 245).

The mode is the score that occurs most frequently in a distribution. It has no special notation and is obtained in the same way for both a population and a sample. The mode has several advantages over the other measures of central tendency. First, it may be used with nominal data. Second, one can use the mode as a single number with discrete variables. Third, the mode is simple to calculate and present visually. Fourth, it provides a shape of the distribution as well as a measure of central tendency. Unlike the mean and the median, a distribution can have more than one mode. A single score that occurs most frequently is the modal score. If there are two scores that occur the most frequently, the distribution is referred to as *bimodal.* If there are multiple scores that occur at the same high frequency, then the distribution is labeled *multimodal.* The mode also has limitations, one of which is that it is inefficient in its use of data in that much of the data are not used. Although modal descriptions are easily understood, the mode is rarely used in research except as additional information or when included in the narrative. An early use of the statistical concept of the mode was by English mathematician Karl Pearson (1857–1936) in 1895 when he stated that "I have found it convenient to use the term mode for the abscissa corresponding to the ordinate of maximum frequency" (1895, p. 345).

Two limitations of all three measures of central tendency are that although they are commonly used as descriptive statistics, they do not provide sufficient statistical analysis to describe variation in a population or to elaborate the differences between cases or people. Therefore, they usually do not function in a stand-alone manner as a sole statistical description. Fortunately, the mean also functions as a basis for other statistical analyses that fill the gap, since what is most important in social research is not only the average but also the variation within the population. The mean is used in many statistical formulae. It is used as a basis for statistical analysis of variation, including the standard deviation (i.e., deviation from the mean), the coefficient of determination or R^2, covariance, analysis of variance, and regression. The mean is also used frequently in meta-analyses.

SEE ALSO *Mean, The; Mode, The; Regression Analysis*

BIBLIOGRAPHY

Galton, Francis. 1881. Range in Height, Weight, and Strength. In *Report of the British Association for the Advancement of Science*, 245–261. London: British Association for the Advancement of Science.

Gauss, Carl Friedrich. [1809] 2004. *Theory of Motion of the Heavenly Bodies Moving about the Sun in Conic Sections: A Translation of Theoria Motus.* Mineola, NY: Dover.

Gravetter, Frederick J., and Larry B. Wallnau. 2003. *Statistics for the Behavioral Sciences*, 6th ed. Belmont, CA: Wadsworth/Thomson.

Pearson, Karl. 1895. Contributions to the Theory of Evolution: II. Skew Variation in Homogeneous Material. *Philosophical Transactions of the Royal Society of London* 186: 343–414.

Plackett, R. L. 1958. Studies in the History of Probability and Statistics: VII. The Principle of the Arithmetic Mean. *Biometrica* 45: 130–135.

Mary Ann Davis
Dudley L. Poston Jr.

CENTRISM

In politics, *centrism* refers to the tendency to avoid political extremes by taking an ideologically intermediate position. A centrist promotes moderate policies by finding a middle ground between the left and the right and downplays ideological appeals in favor of a pragmatic or "catchall" party platform. Centrism can be seen as a means to maximize electoral support, especially among swing voters (those who will vote across party lines).

The left-right political spectrum is a traditional way of classifying ideologies, political positions, or political parties. The terms *left, right,* and *center* are believed to originate from the manner in which parliamentary factions were seated in the French Convention after the Revolution of 1789. Seated on the left were radicals such as the Montagnards and the Jacobins, who wanted to abolish the monarchy, the aristocracy, and even religion in France. Seated on the right were royalists and conservatives such as the Feuillants, who supported the king and the Catholic Church. Seated in the center were moderate republicans like the Girondins, who wanted to abolish the Bourbon monarchy but opposed radical demands for revolutionary terror and exporting the revolution to the rest of Europe.

In contrast to the center, both the left and the right are understood to represent well-defined political positions, or ideologies, that are polar opposites of each other. The left-right spectrum is linked to the rise of three main ideologies—conservatism, liberalism, and socialism. Conservatism is associated today with a right-wing stance; conservative ideology resists progressive social change and tries to conserve the status quo, or bring back the status quo ante of the *ancien regime.* Those to the right of conservatives are sometimes called ultraconservatives or the Far Right; These labels may refer to fascists, national socialists (Nazis), ultranationalists, religious extremists, and other reactionaries. Next to emerge was liberalism, which situates itself in the center of the political arena, claiming to be moderate, reformist, and thus centrist. The last of the three ideologies to arise, socialism is commonly seen as left-wing or radical, because socialists view themselves as the radical or militant heirs of the French Revolution. Unlike self-styled centrist liberals, socialists believe that social progress cannot always be achieved by gradualist liberal reforms alone and may require radical social change or even social revolution. Those to the left of socialists are typically labeled ultraleftists or the Far Left, often referring to anarchists, Communists, Trotskyists, Maoists, and other extreme leftists.

Center-leaning politicians or parties usually seek compromise between conflicting political extremes and often take middle-of-the-road stances designed to bridge opposite ideological camps. Political centrism is thus by definition a relational concept, because the positions considered centrist depend on the specific policies of the competing ideological poles that the moderates are trying to reconcile. Centrism is important in the early twenty-first century because it is believed to apply to a very large section of the politically active population. In many countries, most members of the voting public tend to identify themselves as independent rather than as either left-wing or right-wing. The *Economist* stated in April 2005, "Most Americans have fairly centrist views on everything from multiculturalism to abortion. They like to think of themselves as 'moderate' and 'non-judgmental.' More people identify themselves as independents (39%, according to the Pew Research Centre for the People & the Press) than as Democrats (31%) or Republicans (30%)."

Politicians of various parties thus try to appeal to this presumed majority in the center to reach beyond their traditional, narrow constituencies and win elections. Left-wing and right-wing parties dilute their more extreme positions, for both know that the bulk of voters are somewhere near the center. With ideological considerations toned down, centrism tends to make politics more tranquil and stable. The post–cold war decline of left-right divisions has hastened the spread of a new centrist ideology, which is more supportive of democracy and capitalism.

But this center-seeking or centripetal approach entails some risk. Candidates advocating centrist policies to gain wider voter appeal risk demobilizing potential voters and losing support from the more ideologically minded partisans of their own party. Calling itself "New Labour," the revamped British Labour Party won three successive general elections, but voter turnout declined from 71.29 percent in 1997 to 61.36 percent in 2005, as Prime Minister Tony Blair's policy of abandoning key socialist tenets and embracing the center ground alienated many Labour loyalists.

SEE ALSO *Cold War; Conservatism; Fascism; French Revolution; Left and Right; Left Wing; Liberalism; Moderates; Nazism; Right Wing; Socialism*

BIBLIOGRAPHY

Azmanova, Albena. 2004. Europe's Novel Political Cultures in the Early Twenty-First Century. *Contemporary Politics* 10 (2): 111–125.

Economist. 2005. Slumbering On. April 9: 28.

Hazan, Reuven Y. 1997. *Centre Parties: Polarisation and Competition in European Parliamentary Democracies*. London and Washington, DC: Pinter.

Sirota, David. 2005. Debunking "Centrism." *The Nation*, January 3. http://www.thenation.com/doc/20050103/sirota.

Rossen Vassilev

CHAMBERLAIN, NEVILLE
1869–1940

Although Arthur Neville Chamberlain entered Parliament in 1918 at the age of almost fifty, the election of a Conservative government in 1922 paved the way for his meteoric rise from postmaster-general, via the Ministry of Health to the Treasury and the second place in Stanley Baldwin's government within only ten months. Thereafter, a dynamic period of social reform between 1924 and 1929 and his leading role during the Conservative Party and financial crises of 1930–1931 ensured that he emerged swiftly as Baldwin's heir-apparent; claims powerfully reinforced by his success as chancellor of the exchequer between 1931 and 1937 when he presided over Britain's spectacular recovery from the Great Depression. Although there is much debate about the reasons for Britain's rapid return to prosperity, Chamberlain attributed it to a combination of a general tariff (introduced March 1932) and a "cheap money" policy designed to stimulate economic activity through low interest rates. Equally central to Chamberlain's strategy was an ostensibly rigid commitment to balanced budgets. Although condemned by critics as proof of an unimaginative passivity in face of mass unemployment, Chamberlain staunchly defended the policy as crucial to the maintenance of investor confidence that there would be no departure from "sound finance" into the hazardous realms of loan-financed public works.

From 1934 onward, Chamberlain was deeply preoccupied with the problems of defending a vast and vulnerable global empire from the cumulative threats posed by Japan, Italy, and Germany at a time when Britain could not afford to rearm sufficiently ever to contemplate the possibility of fighting three major powers in widely separated areas. After his succession to the premiership in May 1937, Chamberlain's response to this conundrum was to pursue with far greater vigor and determination his so-called double policy of rearmament and appeasement. The former was intended to repair defensive deficiencies at a pace the country could afford without jeopardizing long-term economic stability: Britain's so-called fourth arm of defense. The latter policy simultaneously attempted to achieve better diplomatic relations with the dictators by redressing their legitimate grievances, and in so doing either to remove the underlying causes of tension or to expose Germany's Adolf Hitler as an insatiable mentally unstable leader bent on world domination. Chamberlain thus described his strategy as one of hoping for the best while preparing for the worst.

In September 1938 this policy culminated in the Munich conference at which the largely German-speaking

Sudeten area of Czechoslovakia was ignominiously ceded to Hitler. Although Chamberlain's success in averting an imminent and probably unwinnable war was initially hailed as a great personal triumph, his ill-judged promise of "peace for our time" soon came back to haunt him when Hitler seized the remaining (non-German) part of Czechoslovakia in March 1939 and then invaded Poland six months later. Despite continuing as prime minister throughout the so-called Phoney War, increasing discontent with Chamberlain's leadership erupted in a parliamentary debate on May 7–8, 1940, when a substantial revolt of Members of Parliament inflicted a crushing moral (but not technical) defeat upon Chamberlain. He resigned as prime minister two days later but remained a key member of Winston Churchill's all-party coalition until shortly before his death from cancer on November 9, 1940.

SEE ALSO *Appeasement; Churchill, Winston; Conservative Party (Britain); Great Depression; Hitler, Adolf; Nazism; World War II*

BIBLIOGRAPHY

Dutton, David. 2001. *Neville Chamberlain*. London: Arnold.

Self, Robert. 2006. *Neville Chamberlain: A Biography*. Aldershot, U.K.: Ashgate.

Robert Self

CHANGE, TECHNOLOGICAL

Technological change refers to the process by which new products and processes are generated. When new technologies involve a new way of making existing products, the technological change is called *process innovation*. When they include entirely new products, the change is referred to as *product innovation*. The invention of assembly-line automobile production by the Ford Motor Company is a widely cited example of the former, while automated teller machines (ATMs) and facsimile machines can be seen as product innovations.

Broadly speaking, technological change spurs economic growth and general well-being by enabling better utilization of existing resources and by bringing about new and better products. Besides benefits to suppliers or inventors of new technologies via disproportionate profits, new technologies have benefits for consumers (e.g., innovations in health care) and for the society (e.g., better oil-drilling techniques enabling less wastage and a more effective utilization of the oil in the ground). Current technologies also make the development of future technologies easier by generating new ideas and possibilities.

Changing technologies, however, can have negative consequences for certain sectors or constituencies. Examples of negative aspects include pollution (including environmental, noise, and light pollution) associated with production processes, increased unemployment from labor-saving new technologies, and so forth. This suggests that society must consider the relative costs and benefits of new technologies.

The process of technological change can be seen to have three stages: invention, development, and diffusion. The invention stage involves the conception of a new idea. The idea might be about a new product or about a better technique for making existing products. The invention might be due to a latent demand (e.g., the cure for an existing illness); such inventions are referred to as *demand-pull inventions*. Inventions can alternately be supply driven, when they are by-products of the pursuit of other inventions. For instance, a number of products, such as the microwave oven, were by-products of the U.S. space program. Yet another possibility is that a new product or process might emerge as an unplanned by-product of the pursuit of another technology (serendipitous invention). In the development stage, the prototype of the invention or the idea is further developed and tested for possible side effects (as with pharmaceutical drugs) and reliability (as with vehicles and airplanes). The invention is also made user-friendly in this stage.

The final stage of the innovation process involves making it accessible to most users through market penetration. The benefits of an innovation, both to inventors and to society, are maximized only when the innovation is efficiently diffused. Some innovations are easy to adopt while others involve effort on the part of adopters. For instance, one must learn how to use a computer, a new type of software, or a new type of airplane. Thus, the diffusion of technologies takes time. A useful concept in this regard was provided by Zvi Griliches (1930–1999). Griliches examined the time path of diffusion for hybrid corn seeds. He found that the technology diffused like an S-curve over time, implying that initially diffusion occurred at an accelerated rate, then at a declining rate, and eventually the rate of diffusion tapered off. Various studies have examined the diffusion of other technologies (new airplanes, ATM machines, etc.), and generally the evidence seems to bear out the prevalence of the S-curve of diffusion.

There are different avenues of cooperation between the private and public sector in the three stages of innovation. For example, all three stages might take place in the same sector, or there might be cooperation in only some stages (e.g., government agriculture extension services subsidize the diffusion of many farming technologies).

Austrian economist Joseph Schumpeter (1883–1950) made significant contributions to the economics of technological change around the middle of the twentieth century. His best-known concept is referred to as the *Schumpeterian hypothesis*. According to this hypothesis, which linked market structure and innovation, monopolies (due to their large reserves) are perhaps better suited than competitive firms at bringing about new products and processes. This concept called into question the then widely held view that competitive markets were superior in all respects, and provided a redeeming feature of monopolies. Since its inception, the Schumpeterian hypothesis has been a matter of much debate and analysis in the economics literature.

The nature of technological change can vary across sector and products and over time. Broadly speaking, economists tend to classify technological change as *Hicks-neutral*, *Harrod-neutral*, or *labor-saving* (see, for example, Sato and Beckmann 1968). Under Hicks-neutral technological change, the rate of substitution of one input for another at the margin (think of substituting capital for one worker) remains unchanged if the factor proportions (i.e., capital-labor ratio) are constant. Harrod-neutral technological change refers to a constant capital-output ratio when the interest rate is unchanged. Finally, labor-saving technological change favors the capital input over labor. Numerous technologies involving increased computerization in recent years are examples of labor-saving technological change. Over time, researchers have conducted studies to test the nature of technological change for various sectors and countries.

A number of theories of technological change have been proposed by economists. Some of these theories have evolved over time by refinements of earlier theories, while others have benefited from new revelations. Adam Smith (1723–1790) recognized the role of changing technologies. According to him, improvements in production technology would emerge as a by-product of the division of labor, including the emergence of a profession of schedulers or organizers akin to modern-day engineers. A specialized worker doing the same job repetitively would tend to look for ways to save time and effort. In Smith's world, productivity could also increase indirectly via capital accumulation.

Karl Marx's (1818–1883) notion of the tendency of the rate of profit to fall stems from a recognition of technological change (process innovation) leading to more efficient production, and the replacement of labor with capital or machinery. Labor-saving innovation or mechanization occurs when Marx's capitalists are unable to further lengthen the working day and therefore are unable to extract further surplus value in absolute form from labor.

Kenneth Arrow introduced the notion that production processes may be refined over time as workers gain greater knowledge from repeat action. Thus, new process technologies might emerge; such change is formally described as *emerging* from learning-by-doing. The degree of appropriability of research benefits was considered by Arrow to be a strong incentive for firms to engage in research and development. Nathan Rosenberg postulated that the degree of innovation opportunities dictates the research effort that firms put forth. For instance, innovation opportunities expand with new developments in basic science. Richard Nelson and Sidney Winter proposed an alternative theory of technological change. This theory, referred to as the *evolutionary theory*, argues that technological change evolves over time as newer generations (or improvements) of existing technologies are developed. In other words, the evolutionary theory considers technological change to be less drastic.

The process of technological change is uncertain in that there is no guarantee of whether, when, and at what scale the innovation will occur. Four types of uncertainties are generally associated with the process of technological change. One, there is market uncertainty resulting from the lack of information about the winner of the innovation race. For example, of the many pharmaceutical firms pursuing a cure for an illness, none is certain about who will succeed, or when. This uncertainty sometimes results in excessive resources being devoted to the pursuit of a particular innovation as firms try to improve their odds of beating others. Two, there is technological uncertainty regarding a lack of knowledge about research resources sufficient to guarantee success. Will a doubling of the number of scientists employed by a drug company double its odds of inventing a successful cure? Third, there is diffusion uncertainty regarding the eventual users and market acceptance of the innovation. Finally, there is uncertainty about possible government regulatory action that the new product or process might face. These regulations might deal with safety, reliability, or the environment.

The pace of technological change can vary across industries, firms, and countries, depending upon the resources devoted to research and the nature of products or processes pursued. For instance, the electronics industry, by its nature, has more room for technological improvement than, say, the paper industry. Governments try to increase the rate of technological change by various means. These measures include directly engaging in research, providing research subsidies or tax breaks, inviting foreign investment (and consequently technology) in specific industries, and strengthening the laws for protecting intellectual property. Sometimes, however, governments have to monitor the introduction of new products and processes to ensure societal well-being. Examples of such cases include drug-testing regulation and testing for the environmental impacts of new technologies before they are introduced in the market.

In closing, our understanding of the process of technological change has improved over time. Technological change is an important input to a country's economic growth, and we owe a large part of our improving living standards to changing technologies. Some technologies, however, can have undesirable side effects. Another issue is that technological progress across nations is uneven, and the rapid diffusion of new technologies from developed nations to developing nations remains a challenge.

SEE ALSO *Growth Accounting; Physical Capital; Production; Schumpeter, Joseph; Solow Residual, The; Technology; Technology, Transfer of*

BIBLIOGRAPHY

Dasgupta, Partha, and Paul Stoneman, eds. 1987. *Economic Policy and Technological Performance* Cambridge, U.K.: Cambridge University Press.

Goel, Rajeev K. 1999. *Economic Models of Technological Change.* Westport, CT: Quorum.

Kamien, Morton I., and Nancy L. Schwartz. 1982. *Market Structure and Innovation.* Cambridge, U.K.: Cambridge University Press.

Nelson, Richard R., and Sidney G. Winter. 1982. *An Evolutionary Theory of Economic Change.* Cambridge, MA: Belknap.

Reinganum, Jennifer F. 1989. The Timing of Innovation: Research, Development, and Diffusion. In *Handbook of Industrial Organization*, ed. Richard Schmalensee and Robert Willig, 849–908. New York: Elsevier.

Sato, Ryuzo, and M. J. Beckmann. 1968. Neutral Inventions and Production Functions. *Review of Economic Studies* 35 (1): 57–66.

Schumpeter, Joseph. 1950. *Capitalism, Socialism, and Democracy.* 3rd ed. New York: Harper.

Rajeev K. Goel

CHAOS THEORY

Chaos theory is a theory of systems dynamics; that is, the analysis of the laws of motion of various systems over time. Complex dynamics investigates why certain systems, while evolving in a predictable fashion for some time, may display at other times a behavior, which looks erratic (random), hence unpredictable. In this context, the main thrust of chaos theory has been to demonstrate that behind this seemingly random behavior or disorder, there is, however, a deterministic underlying structure, which can be described and analyzed by means of differential equations that do not involve uncertainty.

Formally chaos is a nonlinear deterministic process that looks random, a case in which a dynamic mechanism yields a time path so erratic that it passes most standard statistical tests of randomness. Chaotic time paths often have the following features: (1) a trajectory that sometimes displays sharp qualitative changes, such as those associated with large random disturbances; (2) a time path that is extremely sensitive to microscopic changes in the values of its parameters; and (3) a time path that never returns to any point it had previously traversed, but which may, however, display an oscillatory pattern in a certain bounded region. The terms *chaos, strange attractors,* and *complex dynamics* have been used interchangeably in the literature to characterize these complex processes.

In linear dynamics, small causes give rise to small effects, and large causes produce large effects. Hence there is a certain sense of proportionality in linear thinking. Nonlinearity, on the other hand, connotes lack of proportionality: very small causes (small changes in the initial conditions, for instance) can give rise to very large effects. One implication of chaos theory, in this context, is to show that nonlinearities are not the exception but the rule of nature and life. Weather forecasting, for instance, is difficult because very small fluctuations in the environment give rise to very large-scale changes. Chaotic systems often possess fractal structures and time-dependent feedback mechanisms. A fractal structure consists of two major features: self-similarity (or scale-invariance) and lack of smoothness. Self-similarity refers to a system that always looks the same regardless of how many times the system is magnified. On the other hand, lack of smoothness relates to the disconnected appearance of fractals.

While the origins of chaos theory date back to the seminal work conducted in 1890 by the French mathematician Jules Henri Poincaré on the so-called three-body problem, it is Edward Lorenz's 1963 research on atmospheric dynamics and Benoit Mandelbrot's pathbreaking 1983 investigation of fractal geometry that have rekindled interest in chaos theory since the mid-twentieth century. Applications of complex dynamics have found fertile grounds in several fields such as fluid dynamics, plasma physics, chemistry, electrical engineering, signal processing, cardiology, finance, and time series econometrics and economics, some of which are surveyed in Julian Sprott's *Chaos and Time Series Analysis* (2003).

The roots of chaos analysis in economics can be traced back to the literature on business cycles, that is, the analysis of irregular fluctuations in the output level of an economy. While exogenous business cycle theories have become the orthodoxy during the last four decades, the emergence of chaos theory hinted at the possibility that erratic output fluctuations are due to the complex interaction of economic factors, and hence may be endogenously generated.

Chaos studies in theoretical economics have attempted to model economic systems in such a way that chaotic dynamics emerge during the adjustment period to equilibrium or in the evolution of the system itself over time. On the other hand, several empirical investigations have been done in order to identify chaotic behavior in financial and economic time-series data. While earlier empirical studies claimed to have found evidence of chaotic behavior in a number of economic time series, such as U.S. business cycle data, various monetary aggregates, and precious metal prices, subsequent research, such as that conducted by Aydin Cecen and Cahit Erkal in 1996, demonstrated that there is little evidence in favor of deterministic chaos in exchange rate returns.

SEE ALSO *Catastrophe Theory; Shocks*

BIBLIOGRAPHY

Cecen, Aydin A., and Cahit Erkal. 1996. Distinguishing Between Stochastic and Deterministic Behavior in Foreign Exchange Rate Returns: Further Evidence. *Economics Letters* 51: 323–329.

Lorenz, Edward. 1963. Deterministic Nonperiodic Flow. *Journal of the Atmospheric Sciences* 20: 130–141.

Mandelbrot, Benoit B. 1983. *Fractal Geometry of Nature*. New York: W. H. Freeman.

Poincaré, Jules Henri. 1890. Sur le Problème de Trois Corps et les Equations de la Dynamique. *Acta Mathematica* 13: 1–270.

Sprott, Julian C. 2003. *Chaos and Time Series Analysis*. New York: Oxford University Press.

Aydin A. Cecen

CHARITABLE FOUNDATIONS
SEE *Foundations, Charitable.*

CHAUVINISM
SEE *Jingoism.*

CHÁVEZ, CÉSAR
1927–1993

Of Mexican American ancestry, César Estrada Chávez was born in Yuma, Arizona, with deep roots in the American Southwest. He was the second-born child of Librado Chávez and Juana Estrada, whose families were displaced from their land, much like many other Mexicans who were tricked by attorneys, had their loans rejected because others coveted their land, or lost their land as a result of owing back taxes. On August 29, 1937, the Arizona state government took possession of the Chávez family's land, and later auctioned it off to the bank president who had refused the elder Chávez a loan to reclaim his property (La Botz 2006, p. 7; see also Montejano 1987 for a discussion of land displacement). The loss of their land forced the family to work in the agricultural fields of Arizona, and later in California's San Joaquin Valley, beginning when César was just a child of ten. As migrants, the family struggled under the most difficult of conditions, including grossly substandard pay. Despite having only an eighth-grade education, Chávez served in the Navy during World War II (1939–1945). After two years of service, he returned to grueling agricultural work; there was not much else available for a man who lacked a formal education and whose employment options were limited by racism.

Chávez's organizing career began as a result of a stint with the Community Services Organization (CSO), where he worked under the guidance of Fred Ross and Father Donald McDonnell in San José, California. After two years of struggle with CSO's board, who refused to support many of his proposals, Chávez set out on his own to organize the agricultural workers' union, using strategies he developed through his work with CSO, and guided by insights gained from personal experience of oppressive work conditions. Chávez patiently and systematically devised nonviolent strategies, such as the secondary boycott, which targeted specific businesses that bought goods from growers who refused to negotiate with or recognize the union. He also used fasting to highlight the shameful conditions under which farmworkers labored.

Chávez forged alliances with Filipinos and other workers of color and their families to organize the United Farm Workers Organizing Committee, which later became the United Farm Workers of America (UFWA). His ability to work in coalition with people of other faiths and political persuasions created lifelong partnerships, including with Gilbert Padilla and Dolores Huerta, who like him had been influenced by the pragmatic philosophy of Saul Alinsky's Industrial Areas Foundation. Together the three organized the first table boycott and negotiated a contract with the Schenely Corporation, signed on April 7, 1966. This agreement marked the success of a national campaign that was carried out by the farmworkers themselves. Their effort also pointed the way toward the formation of national alliances with Democratic and liberal politicians, and drew the support of the United Auto Worker's Union, as well as competition from the

Teamsters Union, after the Schenely Corporation brought Teamsters to the negotiating table. Later, the Teamsters would vie for contracts against the UFW.

Through his life work, Chávez created a revolution in agriculture and inspired the birth of the Chicano civil rights movement. His tireless support of American agricultural workers made him oppose governmental agreements such as the Bracero Program, which allowed Mexican workers to work in U.S. fields, and led him to fight against the use of undocumented workers, because they weakened unionization and adversely impacted the wages of Mexican Americans. Chávez was harshly criticized for these positions and lost the support of those who believe in workers' rights regardless of origin, especially when he later sided with conservatives who pushed for immigration restrictions in the 1980s. Still, Chávez maintained enough support to achieve the first agricultural workers law in a nation that had not allowed the unionization of farmworkers in the past. This was the California Agricultural Labor Relations Act, signed by Governor Jerry Brown in 1975, which established the Agricultural Labor Relations Board (ALRB) to oversee elections and to settle appeals.

Because of Chávez's willingness to confront racism and poverty in the agricultural fields, conditions for workers improved. The fruits of his labor included the eradication of the dreaded short hoe, the availability of portable toilets, the accessibility of drinking water, the creation of a hiring hall, the foundation of a service center and health clinic, and improvement of wages and benefits. A believer in nonviolence, Chávez continued to use legal means in his pursuit of social justice until the end. He passed away in Yuma, Arizona, working to fight a lawsuit against the UFW brought by Bruce Church Incorporated, the largest producer of lettuce and vegetables in Salinas, California. This was perceived as a move to destroy an already weak union; Church was suing the UFWA for millions of dollars in damages resulting from the 1980s lettuce boycott. In death, Chávez has become an icon, as a result of his activism and commitment to the struggle for farmworkers' rights and social justice, a commitment he selflessly carried out to the end as he sought to improve the lives of those who feed the nation. For his extraordinary efforts and to mark the legacy of his accomplishments and his service to humanity, President Bill Clinton awarded Chávez with a posthumous Medal of Freedom in 1994. As Paul Chávez remarked in the *San Jose Mercury News*, "when history writes its final chapter, [César Chávez] … will be remembered as a man who lived by his principles and who wasn't afraid of taking uncomfortable positions" (1993, p. 1A).

SEE ALSO *Agricultural Industry; Migrant Labor*

BIBLIOGRAPHY

Acuña, Rodolfo. 2004. *Occupied America: A History of Chicanos.* 5th ed. New York: Pearson Longman.

Chávez, Paul. 1993. A 'Warrior for Justice' Mourned Nationwide. *San Jose Mercury News* (April 24): 1A.

Griswold del Castillo, Richard, and Richard A. Garcia. 1995. *César Chávez: A Triumph of Spirit.* Norman: University of Oklahoma Press.

La Botz, Dan. 2006. *César Chávez and La Causa.* New York: Pearson Longman.

Levy, Jacques E. 1975. *César Chávez: Autobiography of La Causa.* New York: Norton.

Matthiessen, Peter. 1969. *Sal Si Puedes: César Chávez and the New American Revolution.* New York: Random House.

Méndez-Negrete, Josephine. 1994. We Remember César Chávez: A Catalyst for Change. *San José Studies* 20 (2): 71–83.

Montejano, David. 1987. *Mexicans and Anglos in the Making of Texas, 1937–1986.* Austin: University of Texas Press.

United Farm Workers Web site. The Story of Cesar Chavez. http://www.ufw.org/_page.php?menu=research&inc+history/07.html.

Josephine Méndez-Negrete

CHÁVEZ, HUGO
1954–

Venezuelan president Hugo Chávez and his policies have sparked controversy at home, throughout the Latin American region, and in the United States. Whereas Chávez's supporters value his social agenda, critics perceive him as ideological, intolerant, and impractical. Chávez, however, has stayed in power through democratic means and carries overwhelming support, despite large-scale attempts to remove him from office.

Hugo Rafael Chávez Frías was born in Sabaneta, Barinas, on July 28, 1954. He graduated from Venezuela's Academy of Military Sciences with a degree in engineering in 1975. Chávez first gained national attention in 1992 when he led an unsuccessful military coup to oust President Carlos Andrés Pérez. Chávez and a group of fellow military officers had founded the Revolutionary Bolivarian Movement ten years earlier; the group honored the nineteenth-century Venezuelan freedom fighter Simón Bolívar (1783–1830). Chávez sought to restore the Bolivarian ideas of national sovereignty, economic independence, and social services for the people. With these ideals, Chávez led the failed 1992 revolt, and was subsequently imprisoned for two years.

By 1994 Chávez had transformed from a "military rebel to a democratic player" (Canache 2002, p. 69). He founded the political party Movement of the Fifth

Republic leading up to the 1998 presidential elections. His platform emphasized his desire to end corruption, return oil to state control, and eliminate poverty (Marcano and Tyszka 2004, p. 31). This platform earned him political victory in 1998 with 56 percent of the vote, in 2000 with 60.3 percent, and in 2006 with 63 percent (Canache 2002, p. 69; Marcano and Tyszka 2004, p. 31; Political Database of the Americas). Chávez's popularity has grown since he shifted from the military to the political stage.

Chávez's mass appeal remains debatable. Scholars and journalists attribute his success to his emphasis on the country's poor through health and education programs (Canache 2002, p. 70; Fukuyama 2007, p. A18). Francis Fukuyama writes that Chávez maintains local appeal because of his social agenda, in which he "has opened clinics staffed with Cuban doctors in poor barrios throughout Venezuela" (2007, p. A18). The rise in oil prices on the world markets has allowed the government to increase social spending despite the country's external debt (Guevara 2005, p. 36).

However, critics argue that the statistics contradict the myth. Francisco Rodríguez argues that social spending in Venezuela decreased from 31.5 percent prior to Chávez's administration to 29.3 percent by 2004. The reduction of illiteracy dropped slightly, from 1.1 million before Chávez became president to 1.0 million illiterate Venezuelans over the age of fifteen during his tenure (Rodríguez 2007, p. 2). The percentage of poor families increased from 42 percent in 1999 to 60 percent in 2004, and unemployment levels reached 15 percent in both 1999 and 2004 (Marcano and Tyszka 2004, p. 390). Instead, Chávez's popularity is based on the country's double-digit economic growth, according to Rodriguez.

Chávez's opponents have threatened his grasp on power. In April 2002 rebel military officers staged a failed coup, which some Venezuelan officials believe was backed by the U.S. government (Morsbach 2006). Two years later, the opposition conducted a failed recall referendum, in which 59 percent of Venezuelans voted to allow Chávez to complete the remainder of his term (BBC News 2004).

As of 2007, Venezuela's economy remained stable while a large number of Venezuelans lived in deep poverty. Nevertheless, Chávez's support surpassed that of his critics.

SEE ALSO *Coup d'Etat; Left Wing; Nationalization; Petroleum Industry; Populism; Poverty; Social Movements; Socialism*

BIBLIOGRAPHY

BBC News. 2004. Venezuela Ratifies Chavez Victory. August 27. http://news.bbc.co.uk/2/hi/americas/3605772.stm.

Canache, Damarys. 2002. From Bullets to Ballots: The Emergence of Popular Support for Hugo Chávez. *Latin American Politics and Society* 44 (1): 69–90.

Fukuyama, Francis. 2007. Keeping Up With the Chávezes. *Wall Street Journal*, February 1: A17.

Guevara, Aleida. 2005. *Chávez, Venezuela, and the New Latin America: An Interview with Hugo Chávez*. New York: Ocean Press.

Marcano, Cristina, and Alberto Barrera Tyszka. 2004. *Hugo Chávez sin uniforme: Una historia personal*. Caracas, Venezuela: Grupo Editorial Random House Mondadori, S.A.

Morsbach, Greg. 2006. Venezuela Marks Coup Anniversary. BBC News, April 12. http://newsvote.bbc.co.uk/mpapps/pagetools/print/news.bbc.co.uk/2/hi/americas/4901718.stm.

Political Database of the Americas. Georgetown University, Center for Latin American Studies. http://pdba.georgetown.edu/.

Rodríguez, Francisco. 2007. Why Chávez Wins. *Foreign Policy*. http://www.foreignpolicy.com/story/cms.php?story_id=3685.

Sarita D. Jackson

CHECKS AND BALANCES

Although scholars dispute the precise origin of the phrase *checks and balances*, the basic idea of limiting political power through various institutional means is both ancient and modern. In the ancient worlds of the Greek city-state and the Roman Republic, a mixed constitution of the one, the few, and the many provided checks on governmental power, whether in the form of a monarchy (the rule of one), an aristocracy (the rule of the few), or a democracy (the rule of the many). This scheme of balancing and checking power, particularly as expressed in the works of Aristotle, Polybius, and Cicero, was a powerful influence in early modern Europe during the period of the Renaissance as expressed in the works of Niccolo Machiavelli, James Harrington, and Algernon Sydney. This ancient and Renaissance concept of a mixed constitution may also be found in the eighteenth-century works of Charles de Montesquieu, Francis Hutcheson, and William Blackstone. All of these works influenced the founders of the United States, notably John Adams, James Madison, and Thomas Jefferson. The classic literary study of the political dynamics in this scheme is William Shakespeare's play *Julius Caesar*.

The modern concept of checks and balances derives primarily from a mechanical view of the universe made popular in the seventeenth and eighteenth centuries by Galileo Galilei and Isaac Newton, among others. For Alexander Hamilton, in *Federalist* No. 9, a concept of "legislative balances and checks" was among the modern improvements in the science of politics. According to the modern view—as reflected in the United States Constitution—the legislative, executive, and judicial functions of government must check and balance each other in order to prevent any one branch of government from dominating the others. In the American scheme, for example, presidents may veto acts of Congress, but Congress has the power to override presidential vetoes by a two-thirds majority vote of both houses. Similarly, as established in the U.S. Supreme Court case of *Marbury v. Madison* (1803), federal judges may rule acts of Congress unconstitutional as occurred in the cases of *City of Boerne v. Flores* (1997) and *Clinton v. City of New York* (1998).

Checks and balances also refers often to issues of federalism, or the relationship between the national and state (or regional) governments. In the United States, for example, the Tenth Amendment to the United States Constitution grants "reserved" powers to the states. This has meant, according to the courts, the power of state governments in the United States to regulate health, safety, and morals. But the Fourteenth Amendment, ratified in 1868, checks this power by asserting that no state may deny any person "life, liberty, or property, without due process of law," nor may a state deny "equal protection of the laws." In a number of recent cases, the U.S. Supreme Court has interpreted these constitutional provisions so as to limit state prerogatives in such areas as capital punishment, affirmative action, privacy rights, and voting rights. For some, checks and balances also refers to modifications in American political practice outside of formal constitutional change or judicial interpretation. Among these modifications are the rise of national political parties, the expansion of presidential power, the creation by Congress of independent regulatory agencies (such as the Environmental Protection Agency), and changing technologies, particularly as these technologies make possible the more rapid exchange of information, such as through widespread access to the World Wide Web.

SEE ALSO *Aristocracy; Constitution, U.S.; Democracy; Machiavelli, Niccolò; Monarchy; Separation of Powers*

BIBLIOGRAPHY

Montesquieu, Charles de. 1989. *Montesquieu: The Spirit of the Laws.* Trans. and ed. Anne M. Cohler, Basia C. Miller, and Harold S. Stone. Cambridge, U.K.: Cambridge University Press. (Orig. pub. 1748).

Pocock, J. G. A. 1975. *Machiavellian Moment: Florentine Political Thought and the Atlantic Republican Tradition.* Princeton, NJ: Princeton University Press.

Timothy Hoye

CHERNOBYL

SEE *Disaster Management; Union of Soviet Socialist Republics*

CHEROKEES

The Cherokees have been one of the most historically significant indigenous cultural groups in the southeastern United States. There were three federally recognized Cherokee Indian nations at the beginning of the twenty-first century: the Eastern Band of Cherokee Indians (EBCI) in North Carolina, the Cherokee Nation of Oklahoma, and the United Keetoowah Band in Oklahoma. In addition, more than fifty other organizations in at least twelve states, as well as many individuals, claim Cherokee descent. The question of who is legitimately Cherokee and how many individual Cherokee Indians exist in America is a point of contention, and the distinction between individual claims to cultural or biological identity, on the one hand, and legal membership or citizenship in federally recognized tribes or sovereign tribal nations, on the other, is an important one.

Other issues facing Cherokee communities in the early twenty-first century include development and refinement of mechanisms for self-governance, political factionalism, increased economic development of tribal communities (including gaming, tourism, and natural resource management on tribal lands), cultural preservation, and the implementation of tribal programs and services for media, education, health, mental health, and social services. Like many other Native American communities, the Cherokees face high rates of drug and alcohol dependency, suicide, and health issues such as diabetes, and communities are particularly concerned about their at-risk youth.

Cherokees and their ancestral culture, believed to be related to the Iroquois, have lived in the southeastern region for at least 12,000 years. Lands once occupied by the Cherokees—before European contact in the 1500s and then forced removal in the 1830s to Oklahoma—encompassed parts of what are now nine states, including most of the Southern Appalachian mountain and foothill region. From original lands that covered 250,000 square miles, the Eastern Band maintained its culture on approximately 56,000 acres in western North Carolina as of 2007; the tribal assets of the Cherokee Nation of Oklahoma include about 66,000 acres.

SOCIAL ORGANIZATION, CULTURAL PRACTICES, AND LANGUAGE

Unlike many of the Plains tribes, the Cherokees were primarily agricultural rather than nomadic and called themselves *Ani'Yun'wiya*, the Principal People. They are matrilineal and matrilocal, meaning that they trace their descent through the women in their society and they live in the mother's or wife's household, since women traditionally owned all property. Traditional Cherokee social organization was structured around seven matrilineal clans, run by a Council of Grandmothers, reflecting the relationship of balance between the natural and spiritual worlds: *Anigilo(la)hi* (Long Hair); *Anisahoni* (Blue or Panther); *Aniwaya* (Wolf); *Anigatogewi* (Wild Potato); *Ani(k)awi* (Deer); *Anitsisqua* (Bird); *Aniwodi* (Paint). Each clan has traditional vocations, knowledges, and sacred ceremonial affiliations, and marriage within a clan is forbidden.

Throughout the Cherokee year, the communities have traditionally celebrated festivals or religious observances that reflected significant events related to the seasons, such as New Moon Festivals and Green Corn Ceremonies. Such events include feasting, dancing, purifications, sacred fires, and other ceremonies and rituals. The traditional Cherokee wedding is also a distinctive ceremony and a time for community celebration. Cherokees also actively participate in dances and ceremonies within the tribe as well as intertribal powwows to exhibit their traditional dance and music arts.

The arts have been a significant part of Cherokee culture and usually reflect the spiritual relationship between the Cherokees and the stone, wood, river cane, or clay from which various objects—baskets, pottery, carvings—are shaped. A revitalization of traditional arts is flourishing among the Cherokees through cooperatives and foundations such as the Qualla Arts and Crafts Mutual, Inc.

The Cherokee language, called *Tsalagi*, a member of the Southern Iroquoian language family, has a number of dialects and was spoken by about 22,000 Cherokees as of 2007 (only about 5 percent of the Cherokee population, due to nineteenth- and twentieth-century U.S. government policies punishing native speakers), although numbers are growing since it has become a required subject in many Cherokee schools and universities.

CHANGES WITH EUROPEAN CONTACT

Spanish explorer Hernando de Soto's entry into Cherokee territory in 1540, in his search for gold and silver, forever changed the way the Cherokees lived. DeSoto's party killed and enslaved many Cherokees, and the European invaders brought disease, death, and what would be permanent cultural dislocation to the Cherokees. Some estimate that as many as 95 percent of the Cherokee population died within the first two centuries of European contact.

By the eighteenth century, when waves of European settlers pushed westward into Cherokee territories, treaty lines were created but ultimately failed to protect the Cherokees from encroachment into their lands. Most of the remaining Cherokees reorganized and incorporated many aspects of European society into their dynamic culture to adapt to the changing demands of living near and among the new settlers. A more conservative faction, called the Old Settlers, voluntarily entered into a treaty with the U.S. government in 1817 to receive land in Arkansas in order to avoid assimilation; these were the ancestors of the United Keetoowah Band, the most conservative and traditional of the Cherokees.

A silversmith, Sequoyah, introduced a written form of the Cherokee language, called a syllabary, which was officially adopted by the Cherokee Nation in 1825. This led to widespread literacy and the publication of books, religious texts, almanacs, and newspapers. The tribe adopted a bicameral national government, a constitution, and a Supreme Court by 1827.

However, after white settlers discovered gold on Cherokee lands in north Georgia in the late 1820s, the state and federal government collaborated to confiscate Indian land and then offer this prized land to white settlers through land lotteries. President Andrew Jackson authorized the Indian Removal Act of 1830, beginning the tragic removal period when Cherokees were forced to leave behind their farms, homes, and land. However, the removal was not without opposition and a legal struggle.

Cherokee statesmen and leaders, such as Chief John Ross, and other Americans, including Daniel Webster, Henry Clay, and Samuel Worcester, passionately spoke out against removal and challenged Georgia's attempt to extinguish Indian title to land. These legal cases—especially *Worcester v. Georgia* (1832) and *Cherokee Nation v. Georgia* (1831)—became the two most influential decisions in Indian law. The U.S. Supreme Court ruled for Georgia in the 1831 case, but in the 1832 case affirmed Cherokee sovereignty. However, President Jackson defied the Court and ordered the Cherokee removal, using as justification the 1835 Treaty of New Echota, a treaty that had been signed by about 100 Cherokees who agreed to relinquish all lands east of the Mississippi River in exchange for land in Oklahoma and the promise of money, provisions, and other benefits.

The signing and the removal led to bitter factionalism among the Cherokees. However, the U.S. Army, under General Winfield Scott, enforced the Removal Act in

1838 and forced about 15,000 to 20,000 Cherokees from their homeland. An estimated 4,000 died from hunger, exposure, and disease along the "Trail of Tears" by boats and on foot to Indian Territory in Oklahoma.

THE EASTERN BAND OF CHEROKEE INDIANS

However, hundreds of Cherokees in the mountains of North Carolina had been able to escape from forced removal in 1838, and their descendants make up the Eastern Band today. After several years of legal limbo, in 1848 the U.S. Congress agreed to recognize their treaty rights if the state would accept them as permanent residents; it was not until 1866, following the Civil War, that North Carolina agreed, and in 1868, the tribal tripartite government reconstituted and held its first elections since the removal. In the 1870s, the federal government established the Qualla Boundary (a reservation) for about 1,200 Cherokees. By 2006, over 13,000 enrolled members of EBCI lived on the Eastern Cherokee lands held in trust by the federal government.

The EBCI, incorporated in 1889, is a sovereign nation whose members are not subject to county property taxes or state income tax. Enrollment in the EBCI requires 1/32 degree of Cherokee blood through descent from an enrollee on the 1924 Baker Roll, a census carried out the same year that Native Americans were granted U.S. citizenship. Tribal governance is carried out by an elected principal chief and vice chief, a Tribal Council representing the various communities and clan townships, and appointed judicial positions.

Tourism and gaming are the two primary sources of economic development of the modern Eastern Cherokee, with an active tribal Office of Economic Development. With tribal lands nestled in the Blue Ridge and Great Smoky Mountains and surrounded by national parks and forests—as well as the cultural appeal of the Indian heritage attractions such as living heritage museums and an outdoor historical drama—tourism has long been the major economic base of the EBCI. Harrah's Cherokee Casino opened in 1997 and became the largest tourist attraction in North Carolina. The introduction of gaming has radically affected living conditions in what was once one of North Carolina's most impoverished areas, because of the advent of the per-capita distribution of tribal and casino profits to all enrolled tribal members (an amount totaling nearly $100 million in fiscal year 2004). In addition to tribal agencies, the independent Cherokee Preservation Foundation works to preserve Cherokee culture, create jobs and other economic development opportunities, and renew the environment on tribal lands.

THE CHEROKEE NATION OF OKLAHOMA

In Oklahoma, the Trail of Tears survivors soon rebuilt a democratic form of government, churches, and educational system, newspapers, and businesses, with Tahlequah as their capital and center of cultural activity. In 1844, the *Cherokee Advocate*, printed in both Cherokee and English, became the first newspaper in a Native American language, and the literacy level among the Cherokees became higher than among their white counterparts. Prosperity flourished until the Civil War, when most Cherokees sided with the Confederacy. The government divided what remained of Cherokee tribal land into individual allotments given to Cherokees listed in the Dawes Roll in the late 1890s. Descendants of those original enrollees make up today's Cherokee Nation tribal citizenship.

The Cherokee Nation has the sovereign right, granted by treaty and law, to control and develop tribal assets. With about 280,000 enrolled tribal members as of mid-2007, the Cherokee Nation is the largest American Indian tribal nation (followed closely by the Navajo Nation with approximately 250,000 enrolled members). The land base remaining under federal trust relationship comprises more than 90,000 acres consisting of half tribal land and half allotment land belonging to individual tribal members.

The Cherokee Nation has a tripartite democratic government with a constitution, revised in 1976. Executive power is vested in the elected principal chief, legislative power in the elected Tribal Council, and judicial power in the Cherokee Nation Judicial Appeals Tribunal, comparable to a Supreme Court. It is the highest court of the Cherokee Nation, and it administers the Cherokee Nation Judicial Code as well as district courts and a law enforcement system.

The Cherokee Nation operates several enterprises, including Cherokee Nation Enterprises, which owns casino facilities, retail outlets, and Cherokee Nation Industries, Inc., a supplier to several major defense contractors. The Cherokee Nation also owns a landfill, golf course, ranch, and apartments for the elderly and disabled, and in total employs about 7,000 people, most of whom are tribal members.

SEE ALSO *Culture; Gambling; Gold, God, and Glory; Government; Identity; Iroquois; Land Claims; Mankiller, Wilma; Mental Health; Native Americans; Sequoyah; Sovereignty; Trail of Tears*

BIBLIOGRAPHY

Cherokee Nation of Oklahoma. http://www.cherokee.org.

Eastern Band of Cherokee Indians. http://www.nc-cherokee.com.

Ehle, John. 1988. *Trail of Tears: The Rise and Fall of the Cherokee Nation.* New York: Doubleday.

Finger, John R. 1984. *The Eastern Band of Cherokees, 1819–1900.* Knoxville: University of Tennessee Press.

Finger, John R. 1991. *Cherokee Americans: The Eastern Band of Cherokees in the Twentieth Century.* Lincoln: University of Nebraska Press.

Leeds, Georgia Rae. 1996. *The United Keetoowah Band of Cherokee Indians in Oklahoma.* New York: Peter Lang.

Mooney, James, and George Ellison. 1992. *James Mooney's History, Myths, and Sacred Formulas of the Cherokees.* Fairview, NC: Bright Mountain Books.

Perdue, Theda. 1998. *Cherokee Women: Gender and Culture Change, 1700–1835.* Lincoln: University of Nebraska Press.

Perdue, Theda. 2005. *The Cherokees.* Philadelphia: Chelsea House.

Perdue, Theda, and Michael D. Green, eds. 2004. *The Cherokee Removal: A Brief History with Documents,* 2nd ed. Boston: Bedford Books.

United Keetoowah Band. http://www.unitedkeetoowahband.org.

Williams, David. 1993. *The Georgia Gold Rush: Twenty-niners, Cherokees, and Gold Fever.* Columbia: University of South Carolina Press.

Pamela S. Wilson

CHIANG KAI-SHEK
1887–1975

Chiang Kai-shek was a Chinese political and military leader who took power after the death of Sun Yat-sen (1866–1925). Born into a salt-merchant family in Zhejiang province, Chiang's education included a military academy in Japan from 1908 to 1910, during which time he joined the anti-Manchu movement called the Revolutionary Alliance and became a disciple of Sun, the leader of Guomindang, the Nationalist Party.

In 1923 Sun took Russian advice to accept the Chinese Communist Party as an ally for his cause of national revolution and sent Chiang to the Soviet Union for military training. Upon his return Chiang was appointed head of the Whampoa Military Academy, which later became the most important political capital for Chiang, as many cadets had a personal allegiance to him. In 1925, upon Sun's death, Chiang became the new leader in the Guomindang and soon launched the Northern Expedition (1926–1928), the military campaign against the northern warlords, to unify the country. After a military success Chiang decided that he could not tolerate the Communists, who had been his ally during the expedition but who also began to encourage workers and peasants to launch a social revolution. He ordered a bloody suppression of Communists and labor activists in Shanghai, and his cooperation with the Communists was broken. Chiang established the Nationalist Government in Nanjing on April 28, 1927, six days after the Shanghai massacre.

Chiang's government made efforts to modernize the country, and his governing ideology was a mixture of Confucianism and European fascism. But Chiang faced challenges both at home and from abroad. In 1931 the Japanese occupied Manchuria by force and created a national crisis for Chiang, who decided to take issue with the Communists first before facing foreign invaders. The Communists, led by Mao Zedong, established rural bases through a policy of land redistribution. Despite continuous suppression from the government, the Communists survived and received popular support, first in Jiangxi in the southeast then, after the Long March, in Shaanxi in the northwest. In December 1936 Chiang was kidnapped in Xian by his military deputy, Zhang Xueliang (1898–2001), who resented Chiang's policy of not fighting the Japanese. The crisis ended peacefully as Chiang agreed to work with the Communists in fighting the common enemy. During the second Sino-Japanese War (1937–1945), Chiang remained China's national leader although the country was divided. The United States and China became allies during the war, but Chiang had a rocky relationship with his chief of allied staff, American general Joseph Stilwell (1883–1946), who was finally recalled by Washington in 1944. The American advisors were dismayed by the corruption of Chiang's government, as well as its ignorance and indifference.

Under Mao's leadership the Communists grew stronger during the war. Civil war broke out between Chiang's government and the Communists soon after World War II ended. Despite strong American financial and military support, Chiang lost the war, and his government was forced from the mainland to Taiwan. Chiang remained the president of the Guomindang Government, an authoritarian regime long supported by the United States, until his death in 1975.

SEE ALSO *Mao Zedong; Sun Yat-sen*

BIBLIOGRAPHY

Fairbank, John King, and Albert Feuerwerker, eds. 1986. *Republican China.* Vol. 13 of *The Cambridge History of China.* New York: Cambridge University Press.

Kan Liang

CHIAPAS

Chiapas is a land of stark contrasts: geographically, economically, and socially. One can find everything from frigid mountains to steaming jungles, from poor peasant farmers to wealthy oil executives, and deeply rooted ethnic differences between indigenous Maya and ladinos (those who trace at least part of their ancestry to Spain).

Chiapas is Mexico's southernmost and eighth most populous state (3.9 million in 2000). Most residents live in rural areas. Only three cities have more than 100,000 inhabitants: Tuxtla Gutiérrez, the political and economic center, Tapachula, a coastal port, and San Cristóbal de las Casas, a colonial city in the highlands. Chiapas's population is also the youngest in all Mexico with 50 percent at twenty years of age or younger. Many are indigenous; over 25 percent speak one (or more) of Chiapas's Mayan languages (Tzotzil, Tzeltal, Chol, Tojolobal, to name only the most common). Most are Catholic (64%), with a growing number of Protestants (14%), and a few Jewish, Muslim, and those without religious beliefs.

Agro-extractive industries dominate. Chiapas is one of Mexico's leading producers of coffee, corn, cattle, and cocoa. From Chiapas comes 54 percent of Mexico's hydroelectric power, 24 percent of its crude oil, and 47 percent of its natural gas. However, broad scale economic and social development was historically a low priority and not everyone has benefited equally. Twelve percent of homes lack electric power. Twenty-six percent of homes lack running water, and 43 percent adequate sewage. Fifty-three percent cook with wood. Chiapas also has the highest rate of illiteracy in Mexico (22%), the fewest doctors per person (1 per 17,856), and the second lowest life expectancy (sixty-seven years).

Inequities, exploitation, and ethnic distinctions began in the colonial period and continued after independence. In 1528 the Spanish conquistador Diego de Mazariegos subdued the indigenous populations of Chiapas. Chiapas had no mineral wealth, no gold, no silver. Its riches were agricultural products, including cochineal (red dye), cocoa, sugarcane, and tobacco, and forced indigenous labor, granted to Spaniards by the Crown, made their production possible. The conditions were so extreme and treatment so cruel that many died, others fled, and some rose in rebellion (the Tzeltal Rebellion of 1712, the Tzotzil Uprising of 1868). Independence in 1824 changed the form but not the nature of relations between indigenous and ladino. Liberal reforms privatized land held by the Catholic Church and indigenous communities. In Chiapas, ladinos used these reforms to obtain title to vacant lands, which often belonged, though not officially, to indigenous people. On these they established coffee and cattle ranches and obligated the very indigenous from whom the land had been taken to work for them, in forms often bordering on slavery. Thereby the general trend of wealthy landed ladino and poor landless indigenous continued.

Inequitable landholding was one of the causes of the Mexican Revolution in 1910 and land became a focal point for indigenous organizing in Chiapas. Article 27 of the Mexican Constitution of 1917 granted landless people the right to petition the government for land, which the government could expropriate from large landowners. The process was long and drawn out, pitted landless indigenous against landed ladino, and often required secretive organizing, land invasions, and armed confrontations. Indigenous organizing grew throughout the century, especially in the 1970s and 1980s, so that by 1992 over one-half the land in Chiapas was *ejido* (commonly held) and the indigenous had gained control of many local political offices and some commerce.

In 1992 the Mexican president Salinas de Gortari changed the constitution, abolished the *ejido,* and in so doing dashed the hopes of many landless poor and exacerbated political unrest. That unrest came to a head in 1994 with the Zapatista Rebellion. The day that the North American Free Trade Agreement (NAFTA) took effect poor, largely indigenous men and women—the EZLN, Zapatista Army of National Liberation—rose in rebellion. The Zapatistas had begun organizing in 1984 and voted to go to war in 1992. As their charismatic leader, *subcomandante* Marcos, put it, "If you don't have land, you're living dead, so why live. It is better to die fighting" (Russell 1995, p. 40). The Zapatistas demanded a wide range of social and political reforms. By 1996 the government and the Zapatistas had negotiated an uneasy truce. The Zapatistas refuse anything having to do with the "bad government," but receive important contributions from abroad. The government offers many forms of aid to those who reject *zapatismo* and acknowledge the government. In their intransigence both sides have polarized the countryside, pitting, to unprecedented degrees, indigenous against indigenous: the most devastating manifestation being the massacre in Acteal, during which more than fifty women and children, of a nonviolent Zapatista faction, were brutally murdered by a pro-government faction.

From the mid-1970s to the present, Chiapas has seen many changes: large-scale indigenous organizing, religious conversions, and rebellions. More so than ever before people migrate to cities in search of opportunity and, almost unheard of in the 1990s, residents, especially the young, leave Chiapas by the thousands bound for the United States.

SEE ALSO *Indigenous Rights; Liberation Movements*

BIBLIOGRAPHY

Benjamin, Thomas. 1996. *A Rich Land, a Poor People.* Albuquerque: University of New Mexico Press.

Collier, George. 1999. *Basta: Land and the Zapatista Rebellion.* Chicago: Food First Books.

Ponce de Leon, Juana, ed. 2001. *Our Weapon Is Our Word.* New York: Seven Stories Press.

Russell, Philip L. 1995. *The Chiapas Rebellion.* Austin, TX: Mexico Resource Center.

Pete Brown

CHICAGO *DEFENDER*

It can be argued that the most influential and radical voice for racial equality in the first quarter of the twentieth century was a Chicago-based newspaper, the Chicago *Defender.* Within the paper's first ten years of publication, its owner, Robert S. Abbott, had turned the one-time local black paper into the largest selling black newspaper in the United States. Scholars estimate that weekly circulation from 1915 to 1925 was as high as 250,000 a week, with the large majority of the copies distributed south of the Mason-Dixon Line.

With its sensationalistic and crusading editorial policy, the paper quickly gained the reputation of being the most radical and racially conscious black newspaper in America. This bold editorial philosophy was never more evident than during the turbulent period between 1916 and 1919, the epoch marked by America's involvement in World War I, the Great Black Migration out of the South, and the northern race riots of 1919.

The first of these events to grab the *Defender*'s attention was of the mistreatment of black soldiers in military training camps during the early years of World War I and the exclusion of prominent "race men" from the ranks of officers. The paper unflinchingly demanded safety, equal rights, and recognition for black soldiers who sacrificed their lives for freedom in Europe. Abbott was also diligent in underscoring the hypocrisy of the United States government, which asked men of color to die for the cause of liberty in Germany while it systematically denied them their basic civil rights at home.

While maintaining its concern for the black soldier in Europe, the *Defender* also began detailing both the atrocities inflicted on blacks in the American South and the burgeoning opportunities awaiting them in the industrialized North. By 1916, the recognition of this juxtaposition had evolved into a full-scale migration campaign. Abbott and his paper began encouraging a southern exodus away from the oppressive South and toward the "Promised Land" of the North. Black southerners read of the thou-sands who had already said, "FAREWELL TO THE SOUTH" (January 6, 1917) or of the "2 MILLION NEEDED" (October 4, 1916) to work in America's second city. They memorized Mr. Ward's poem, "Bound for the Promised Land," sang William Crosse's inspirational words to "The Land of Hope," and laughed at Fon Holly's political cartoons, "DESERTION" and "THE AWAKENING" (September 2, 1916, and August 19, 1916).

In the spring of 1919, however, the *Defender*'s "Promised Land" was undergoing a metamorphosis. As thousands of white soldiers returned home after the war, they found that the jobs, communities, and lifestyles they had left behind in Chicago were appropriated by thousands of black migrants.

This tension ultimately led to a three-day (July 27–30, 1919) race riot in Chicago—an event that forever changed the tenor of the *Defender*'s migration discourse. The bold headlines of the paper's August 2, 1919, issue summarized the situation: "RIOT SWEEPS CHICAGO," and "GHASTLY DEEDS ON RACE RIOTERS TOLD." When the dust settled, 23 blacks lay dead, with at least 537 others wounded. The call for southern migration ceased after the (blood) "Red Summer" of 1919. Abbott could no longer promise his readers a better life in his once-beloved city of Chicago.

In 1940 John H. Sengstacke, Abbott's nephew, assumed editorial control of the paper. Under his leadership, the *Defender* protested the treatment of African American servicemen fighting in World War II (1939–1945) and, once again, called for the integration of the U.S. armed forces. Facing the threat from the U.S. government of sedition charges, however, the *Defender* attenuated its traditionally radical editorial policy.

On February 6, 1956, the *Defender* became a daily newspaper. Nine years later, Sengstacke again expanded his influence as a voice for black equality by purchasing three additional black papers: the *Pittsburgh Courier*, the *Michigan Chronicle* in Detroit, and the *Tri-State Defender* in Memphis.

By the 1970s, however, the *Defender*, like many of the nation's other black newspapers, began to rapidly lose readership. At the time of Sengstacke's death in 1997, the *Defender*'s circulation declined to less than 20,000. In 2003 Abbott's heirs were forced to sell the legendary Chicago *Defender* to black-owned Real Times, Inc.

SEE ALSO *Politics, Black*

BIBLIOGRAPHY

DeSantis, Alan D. 1997. A Forgotten Leader: Robert S. Abbott and the *Chicago Defender* from 1910–1920. *Journalism History* 23 (2): 63–71.

DeSantis, Alan D. 1998. Selling the American Dream Myth to Black Southerners: The *Chicago Defender* and the Great Migration of 1915–1919. *Western Journal of Communication* 62 (4): 474–511.

Grossman, James R. 1989. *Land of Hope: Chicago, Black Southerners, and the Great Migration*. Chicago: University of Chicago Press.

Ottley, Roi. 1955. *The Lonely Warrior: The Life and Times of Robert S. Abbott*. Chicago: H. Regnery.

Alan D. DeSantis

CHICAGO SCHOOL

The post–World War II (1939–1945) period saw the emergence at the University of Chicago of a significant alternative in economics to both the tradition of American institutionalism and the emerging traditions of Keynesianism and general equilibrium theorizing. Usually associated with the work of Milton Friedman (monetarism) and George Stigler, and their students Gary Becker and Robert Emerson Lucas, the Chicago approach to economics is also present in the agricultural and development economics of Theodore W. Schultz, D. Gale Johnson, and Zvi Griliches; the labor economics of H. Gregg Lewis, Al Rees, and Sherwin Rosen; the industrial economics of Lester Telser, Harold Demsetz, and Sam Peltzman; the law and economics of Aaron Director, Ronald H. Coase, and Richard Posner; the economic history of Robert Fogel and Deidre McCloskey; the international economics of Harry Johnson and Arnold Harberger; and the social economics of Kevin Murphy and Steven Levitt. Two themes tie together these various manifestations of the Chicago approach: in each of them, Marshallian price theory is taken seriously, and economics is understood to be an applied science.

At a time when the economics discipline was moving toward both formalized general equilibrium models and refined econometric techniques, Chicago economists continued the interwar tradition of price theory taught by Jacob Viner and Frank H. Knight. From 1930 to the mid-1980s, graduate students read and reread a canon of books and essays by Viner, Knight, Henry Simons, Friedman, Stigler, Coase, and Becker to gain an intuitive appreciation for how economics could be applied to any social or economic problem. As Friedman's 1953 essay "The Methodology of Positive Economics" made clear, the Chicago approach applied a small set of simple tools to economic problems because they retained their predictive success despite their generality. Chicago's predilection for the application of price theoretic models to policy issues was also supported by the analytical egalitarianism of

Becker and Stigler's 1977 essay "De Gustibus Non Est Disputandum": look for explanations of economic change in the set of cost constraints individuals face, because people across time and place are assumed to hold similar values and tastes.

The methodological underpinnings of the Chicago approach were driven home to graduate students and faculty alike every week in the workshops that met regularly in the University of Chicago's Department of Economics, Graduate School of Business, and Law School. Starting in the mid-1940s, the workshops became the locus of most research and graduate training in economics at Chicago. After passing comprehensive examinations at the end of the first year, graduate students associated themselves with one or more workshops. Each workshop met weekly for critical examination of papers by faculty members, invited external guests, or senior graduate students. Most workshops functioned by "Chicago rules": papers were distributed prior to the meeting, which was devoted to discussion, rather than presentation, in order to uncover the methodological, theoretical, or empirical problems in the paper. The collective enterprise embodied in the workshop model encouraged faculty and graduate students to pursue interesting applications of price theory in settings where it was commonly understood to not be applicable: antitrust and anticompetition policy, economic development, crime and habitual behavior, law, religion, corporate finance, the family, history, and politics. In all these areas, Chicago economics extended the reach of the discipline by showing that useful, empirically based criticisms of policy frameworks could be built upon basic price-theoretic analytical foundations (Reder 1987).

Chicago economics has not shied away from controversy, either internal or external. The circle around Knight sparred with institutionalists and empirical economists within and outside the department during the 1930s and 1940s. From 1939 to 1955, the University of Chicago was the home of the Cowles Commission, a leader in formal modeling and hence at odds with the Chicago School approach. Alfred Cowles brought Oskar Lange, Jacob Marschak, and Tjalling Koopmans to Chicago, and played an important role in the development of both econometrics and Walrasian general equilibrium theory. The creation of the Shadow Open Market Committee in the early 1970s provided a public forum for the longstanding dispute between Chicago monetarists and the Federal Reserve System's general Keynesian orientation. Finally, the Chicago department's long-standing relation with Latin American students became the center of controversy when a group of Chicago-trained economists became the architects of economic transformation in Chile under General Augusto Pinochet. The impact of Chicago-inspired reforms there contributed to the spread of the Chicago approach across the developing world, and became the center of a global debate over privatization and market-based reforms.

SEE ALSO *Becker, Gary; Business Cycles, Real; Friedman, Milton; Harris, Abram L.; Laissez Faire; Law and Economics; Monetarism; Money Illusion; Permanent Income Hypothesis*

BIBLIOGRAPHY

Friedman, Milton. 1953. The Methodology of Positive Economics. In *Essays in Positive Economics*, 3–43. Chicago: University of Chicago Press.

Reder, Melvin W. 1987. Chicago School. In *The New Palgrave: A Dictionary of Economics*, ed. John Eatwell, Murray Milgate, and Peter Newman, vol. 1, 413–418. New York: Stockton.

Stigler, George J., and Gary S. Becker. 1977. De Gustibus Non Est Disputandum. *American Economic Review* 67 (2): 76–90.

Ross B. Emmett

CHICANO MOVEMENT
SEE *Mexican Americans.*

CHICANO/CHICANOS
SEE *Mexican Americans.*

CHIEF JOSEPH
c. 1840–1904

Chief Joseph, or *Hin-mut-too-yah-lat-kekht* (Thunder Rolling in the Mountains), was the outstanding leader from 1871 to 1904 of the largest and most influential band of nontreaty Nez Perce Indians. He was also one of several leaders who directed his people through the Nez Perce War of 1877 and the valiant but doomed effort to resist forced removal from their homeland in the Wallowa Mountains of northeastern Oregon.

Like many terms for American Indian people and places, *Nez Perce* is a misnomer. French traders first applied the term, attributing to the entire people an only occasional practice of nose piercing. The Nez Perce people refer to themselves as *Nimíipuu*, which translates roughly as "we people." Compared to their far more warlike east-

ern neighbors of the upper Plains, until the mid-nineteenth century the Nez Perce were mostly hospitable to American colonial agencies such as schools and missionaries. This relationship changed fairly dramatically shortly after the Treaty of 1855.

Joseph, born around 1840, was the son of Tuekakas, also known as Old Joseph, himself a powerful leader of the Nez Perce. Although some debate persists, Tuekakas was apparently a signatory to the Treaty of 1855 wherein a great deal of Nez Perce land was ceded to the United States in exchange for annuities. This treaty, which was abrogated by the U.S. government's failure to provide the promised annuities, began the process of Nez Perce expropriation that created a more or less permanent schism among the Nez Perce bands, and had a host of other penurious effects.

Joseph succeeded his ailing father as leader of the Wallowa Valley band of Nez Perce in 1871. He inherited a complex and finally insurmountable set of cultural and political problems that can be traced most directly to the Treaty of 1863, which came to replace the abrogated Treaty of 1855. The Treaty of 1863 formalized the division of the Nez Perce into "treaty" and "nontreaty" factions. The "upper" Nez Perce, represented by a man named (ironically) Lawyer, agreed to a massive sale of territory that included the Wallowa Valley. Critically, however, four Nez Perce bands, including Joseph's, did not sign and flatly refused the terms of the treaty. U.S. officials nevertheless asserted Lawyer's authority to cede, effectively, his neighbor's land. The U.S. government thus asserted that Joseph's homeland was federal territory, an assertion emphatically not shared by Joseph, his father, and the Wallowa Valley Nez Perce. Federal claims to the Wallowa Valley did much to precipitate the momentous Nez Perce War of 1877 and brought national attention to the Nez Perce and Chief Joseph.

Joseph made his first appearance as the principal representative of his people at a meeting with U.S. agents in March 1873. The U.S. position was that Joseph's band must leave Wallowa and move onto the Lapwai Reservation. Joseph responded to the demand unequivocally:

> The white man has no right to come here and take our country.... Neither Lawyer nor any other chief had authority to sell this land. It has always belonged to my people. It came unclouded to them from our fathers, and we will defend this land as long as a drop of Indian blood warms the hearts of our men. (Howard 1978, p. 92)

Joseph impressed the U.S. representatives with both the quality of his character and his legal arguments. Consequently, an executive order from President Ulysses S. Grant withdrew the Wallowa Valley from settlement;

however, this order, hotly contested by settlers, was reversed in 1875. In 1877 the U.S. Department of the Interior made the decision to compel Joseph and his band, by force if necessary, to remove to the Lapwai Reservation.

U.S. agents and representatives of Nez Perce non-treaty bands held a final council at Lapwai in 1877. The council went very badly for the Nez Perce, and their extraordinary record of peacefully tolerating a host of injustices came to an end. Although it appears that Joseph, with the utmost reluctance, agreed to remove to Lapwai, he and the other nontreaty bands were overtaken by events when a few young Nez Perce warriors exacted revenge killings on several settlers. Thus the Nez Perce war of 1877, the final significant conflict of the era of Indian wars, began.

The Nez Perce fought a brilliant running battle, complete with narrow escapes and decisive victories, against U.S. forces for several months and over 1,700 miles. In October 1877, after the Battle of the Bearpaw Mountains, they were finally surrounded and forced to surrender, a day's march short of refuge in Canada. Joseph was the only principal Nez Perce leader to survive the hostilities, so the surrender agreement fell to him, and he responded with one of the most powerful examples of American Indian oration that we have on reliable record. The oration famously concludes: "Hear me, my chiefs. I am tired; my heart is sick and sad. From where the sun now stands I will fight no more forever" (Howard 1978, p. 330). The sun stood at 2:20 P.M. on October 5, 1877.

In violation of the assurances made to Joseph by Colonel Nelson Miles at the surrender, Joseph and the remaining Nez Perce were interred on reservations in Kansas and then Oklahoma for the next twelve years. In 1885 they were moved to the Colville Indian Reservation in eastern Washington. Chief Joseph died September 21, 1904.

SEE ALSO *Annexation; Colonialism; Land Claims; Native Americans*

BIBLIOGRAPHY

Beal, Merrill, D. 1966. *I Will Fight No More Forever: Chief Joseph and the Nez Perce War*. Seattle: University of Washington Press.

Howard, Helen Addison. 1978. *Saga of Chief Joseph*. Lincoln: University of Nebraska Press.

Nurburn, Kent. 2006. *Chief Joseph and the Flight of the Nez Perce: The Untold Story of an American Tragedy*. San Francisco: HarperSanFrancisco.

Stephen A. Germic

CHILD BEHAVIOR CHECKLIST

The Child Behavior Checklist for Ages 6 to 18 (CBCL/6–18) is a standardized questionnaire for assessing children's behavioral, emotional, and social problems and competencies. It can be self-administered by parent figures or administered by interviewers. A version for ages one-and-a-half to five years (CBCL/1.5–5) assesses language development as well as problems. These questionnaires are components of the Achenbach System of Empirically Based Assessment (ASEBA). The ASEBA also includes questionnaires completed by preschool teachers and daycare providers (for ages one-and-a-half to five), school teachers (for ages six to eighteen), youths (ages eleven to eighteen), clinical interviewers, observers, and psychological test administrators. Additional ASEBA questionnaires are available for assessing adults (ages eighteen to fifty-nine and sixty to ninety-plus). Because behavior may vary from one situation to another, the different questionnaires are designed to capture both the similarities and differences in behavior across different situations, as seen by different people.

Starting in the 1960s, psychologist Thomas Achenbach began developing the ASEBA to provide practical, low-cost measures of problems and competencies for clinical and research purposes. Statistical analyses of ASEBA questionnaires have identified syndromes of problems that are scored on profiles. The profiles display an individual's scores on syndrome scales in relation to norms for peers of the same age and gender. Examples of syndromes include attention problems, aggressive behavior, anxiety/depression, and social problems. Additional scales are provided for scoring broad groupings of problems designated as *internalizing* (problems within the self) and *externalizing* (conflicts with others and with social mores).

ASEBA forms are also scored on *DSM*-oriented scales that consist of problems identified by international panels of experts as being consistent with diagnostic categories of the American Psychiatric Association's *Diagnostic and Statistical Manual of Mental Disorders* (*DSM*-IV, 1994). Examples of *DSM*-oriented scales scored for ages six to eighteen include anxiety problems, attention-deficit/hyperactivity problems, oppositional defiant problems, and conduct problems.

ASEBA questionnaires have been translated into over seventy-five languages. Their use has been reported in some six thousand publications from sixty-seven countries. The publications span hundreds of topics, such as child abuse, adoption, aggression, bullying, anxiety, asthma, autism, cancer, cross-cultural findings, delinquency, depression, diabetes, stress, substance abuse, suicidal behavior, and treatment. ASEBA questionnaires, lists of translations, research summaries, and other information can be obtained at the ASEBA Web site. Computer programs are available for scoring all ASEBA questionnaires. The programs compare reports by different people (e.g., mother, father, youth, teachers) via side-by-side displays of scores obtained from each form that was completed for the individual who is being assessed.

A multicultural computer program provides norms based on parent, teacher, and self-reports obtained for tens of thousands of children and youth from over thirty countries. This program enables users to compare individuals' scores with norms for various groups of countries. It is valuable for assessing children residing in their own countries and also for assessing immigrant children living in host countries. A Web-based application enables users to transmit questionnaires electronically and respondents to complete questionnaires on the Web. The ASEBA is widely used in mental health services, schools, medical practices, child and family service agencies, health maintenance organizations, public health agencies, child guidance, training programs, and research.

No assessment instrument can tap every characteristic that might be potentially relevant to every individual in every culture. Consequently, people completing ASEBA questionnaires are invited to add problems and strengths not already listed and to provide open-ended descriptive information. Because no single source of data is sufficient for comprehensive assessment, users are urged to obtain data from multiple informants and multiple assessment procedures. Users are also advised that no scores on ASEBA scales should be automatically equated with particular diagnoses or disorders. Instead, users should integrate ASEBA data with other types of data to provide comprehensive evaluations of functioning.

Most ASEBA forms are designed to be self-administered by people having at least fifth-grade reading skills. However, for people who are unable to complete the self-administered forms independently, interviewers without specialized training can read the questions aloud and record the respondent's answers. The Test Observation Form (TOF) and Semistructured Clinical Interview for Children and Adolescents (SCICA) require training in direct assessment of children. The Direct Observation Form (DOF) requires training in observation of children in group settings, such as classrooms. Interpretation of data from all ASEBA instruments requires training in standardized assessment equivalent to the master's degree level in psychology, education, or related fields, or two years of residency in medical specialties such as psychiatry or pediatrics.

Critiques of ASEBA questionnaires have been published by Amanda Doss (2005), Robert McMahon and Paul Frick (2005), and Robert Spies and Barbara Plake (2005).

BIBLIOGRAPHY

Achenbach, Thomas M., and Leslie A. Rescorla. 2001. *Manual for the ASEBA School-Age Forms & Profiles: Child Behavior Checklist for Ages 6–18, Teacher's Report Form, Youth Self-Report, An Integrated System of Multi-informant Assessment.* Burlington: University of Vermont, Research Center for Children, Youth, and Families.

Achenbach, Thomas M., and Leslie A. Rescorla. 2007. *Multicultural Supplement to the Manual for the ASEBA School-Age Forms & Profiles.* Burlington: University of Vermont, Research Center for Children, Youth, and Families.

Achenbach, Thomas M., and Leslie A. Rescorla. 2007. *Multicultural Understanding of Child and Adolescent Psychopathology: Implications for Mental Health Assessment.* New York: Guilford.

ASEBA: Achenbach System of Empirically Based Assessment. http://www.aseba.org/.

Buros Institute of Mental Measurements. 2005. Review of the Achenbach System of Empirically Based Assessment. In *Texts in Print VII*, eds. Robert A. Spies and Barbara S. Plake. Lincoln, NE: Author. http://www.unl.edu/buros.

Doss, Amanda J. 2005. Evidence-Based Diagnosis: Incorporating Diagnostic Instruments into Clinical Practice. *Journal of the American Academy of Child and Adolescent Psychiatry* 44: 947–952.

McMahon, Robert J., and Paul J. Frick. 2005. Evidence-Based Assessment of Conduct Problems in Children and Adolescents. *Journal of Clinical Child and Adolescent Psychology* 34: 477–505.

Thomas M. Achenbach

CHILD DEVELOPMENT

Child development is the study of the different processes assumed to influence human growth and development from birth through adolescence. Development takes place within multiple domains (e.g., cognitive, physical, socioemotional). Yet the processes underlying development can be common across the different domains of development.

TYPES OF PROCESSES THAT INFLUENCE DEVELOPMENT

In-wired Development Although human beings grow and develop at different paces, there are some aspects of development that are consistent for most, if not all, human beings. This consistency suggests that human bodies are designed to grow and develop in a relatively sequential and orderly fashion because the mechanisms responsible for these changes are *in-wired*. That is, these mechanisms are present at birth and are essentially time-released through adolescence and beyond. For example, an infant will exhibit a grasping reflex when his or her palm is touched. At a later stage, that same infant will develop greater strength and more finely tuned motor skills, such as the ability to intentionally pick up and manipulate an interesting toy.

Development Through Acting Upon the Environment
Children are born with sense systems (i.e., vision, smell, hearing, taste, and touch) that allow them to explore and act upon people and objects in their environments. Children may throw different things to see if they bounce or make interesting sounds (e.g., balls, cups, keys). They may place different things in their mouths (e.g., their mother's fingers, rattles) to see if they are hard or soft or can fit inside their mouths. Children may perceive certain smells and associate them with different experiences. It is through active exploration that children begin to learn the properties of different things and relate them to other things that they "know."

Development Through Passive Reactions to the Environment
Children's development can also be stimulated by their exposure to the activities that take place in the contexts in which they live and function. For instance, language development is stimulated by immersion within specific language environments. Researchers have found critical periods in early infant development whereby simple exposure to everyday conversation helps children develop the ability to produce certain phonemes (speech sounds) specific to a language. If immersion within specific language environments occurs after a certain period—approximately six to nine months of age—then the child will not be able to make some speech sounds in the same manner as a native speaker.

DIFFERENT DOMAINS OF CHILD DEVELOPMENT

Child development researchers seek to identify and understand age-related developmental changes and abilities and how outside influences such as context (e.g., Urie Bronfenbrenner's ecological systems theory) and culture (e.g., A. Wade Boykin's triarchic theory of minority child development) affect developmental outcomes. Below are brief descriptions of the different domains in which development can take place.

Biological Domain *Physical development* refers to the development of the entire human body, including changes in physical stature and strength, pubertal changes in adolescence, the development of perceptual and motor skills, and brain development. Arnold Gesell's (1880–1961) maturational theory proposed that children's growth and development is biologically driven and unfolds in a series of fixed sequences or milestones in physical, motor, and

perceptual domains. Although children vary in their rates of development (e.g., they don't all start to crawl or talk at exactly the same age), they all progress through the same sequences.

Sensory and perceptual development. Perception is the organization and interpretation of information received through our *senses*. Although sensory systems are functional at birth, they are not yet mature. In *The Construction of Reality in the Child* (1954), Jean Piaget (1896–1980) asserted the belief—also held by other theorists—that senses function independently at birth, and with development and experience become more interconnected. By interacting with the environment, children actively construct an understanding of the world, gradually making connections between different types of sensory information.

Other theorists, such as Eleanor Gibson (1910–2002) in *Principles of Perceptual Learning and Development* (1969), argue that the main task of perceptual development is for children to discover the function or permanent properties of objects. Gibson developed the first *visual cliff* method to assess depth perception. The visual cliff strategy helped demonstrate that most infants refused to crawl over the edge of a small cliff with a drop-off covered by glass. Their refusal to crawl over the "edge" was assumed to indicate that they could perceive depth and that depth perception is not learned. Rather, the environment is learned in that it contains information necessary for individuals to make decisions about how to navigate it (e.g., where to walk and not walk). These experiences demonstrate the interconnections between the child's physical world and cognitive development.

Cognitive Domain Piaget's theory of cognitive development describes how children construct an understanding of the world by interacting with their physical and social environments. Children adapt to their environments by developing mental organizations, or *schemes,* to organize their understanding of the world. Adaptation consists of two processes—assimilation and accommodation. Assimilation involves fitting new information into existing schemes (e.g., a child calling a cat "doggy" because it has four legs and fur). Accommodation involves altering existing schemes to accept new information (e.g., a child altering his or her scheme for "doggy" to include barking so that the scheme can no longer include cats).

Lev Vygotsky's (1896–1934) sociocultural theory stresses the importance of social interactions to cognitive development. Vygotsky asserted that learning is a socially mediated, cultural activity that takes place within the *zone of proximal development* (ZPD). Specifically, the ZPD denotes the difference between what children can do on their own and what they can accomplish with the support of more knowledgeable individuals from their culture.

It is important to note that what and how children learn is influenced by their cognitive developmental status. For example, children might be able to learn and repeat complex words and phrases in middle childhood, yet not be able to understand them conceptually—in abstract terms—until adolescence.

Psychosocial Domain *Socioemotional development.* There are critical precursors of social and psychological development. For instance, *attachment* refers to the development of an emotional bond between infant and mother or primary caregiver. Mary Ainsworth (1913–1999) developed the *Strange Situation* to determine the quality of the attachment between caregiver and child. This strategy assesses children's reactions to their mothers after their mothers leave them alone in a room that is later entered by a stranger. The strategy assumes that if a child reacts in negative ways to the mother upon return, there is a poor relationship between caregiver and child. The importance of attachment to socioemotional and cognitive development was recognized by studies of infants in orphanages during the 1950s and 1960s. In the absence of an attachment relationship, these infants experienced severe developmental delays.

Ego-identity development. Sigmund Freud (1856–1939) believed that personality is formed in the first years of life as children deal with inner conflicts. Erik Erikson (1902–1994) extended Freud's theory, proposing that development unfolds in a series of stages spanning infancy to old age. Each developmental stage involves a challenge and corresponding consequence if that challenge is not met. For example, during infancy the challenge is for infants to develop a sense of trust in the world based on responsive caregiving. If the infant's needs are not consistently met, the infant does not trust that the world is a safe place. This sense of mistrust affects children as they get older and face the developmental challenge of becoming more independent from their parents during adolescence.

While Erikson would characterize adolescence as the period in which identity development is the primary challenge to be resolved, the precursors of identity development can be recognized much earlier. Identity develops along a number of dimensions (e.g., gender, race, ethnicity, social class, physical ability, etc.). Often, different aspects of identity will only become salient for individuals when they become aware of specific differences between themselves and others (e.g., skin color, socioeconomic status, abilities, etc.). Children become aware of differences in treatment and the presence of stereotypes.

Mamie Phipps Clark (1917–1983) and Kenneth Clark (1914–2005) used doll studies to demonstrate the early awareness of social devaluation and negative racial stereotypes. The Clarks posited that black children become aware of racial stereotypes and develop personal racial preferences early in childhood. Doll studies are experimental strategies using dolls that do and do not share characteristics of a child (e.g., gender, skin color, clothing) in order to determine what and with whom a child identifies and the characteristics a child attributes to himself or herself. This strategy assumes that what children believe about the dolls can be indicative of their beliefs about themselves and their sense of identity and self-esteem. In 1954 the Clarks' research was used in a landmark U.S. Supreme Court case, *Brown v. Board of Education,* to demonstrate that segregation—which limited black American's access to high-quality educational institutions and other resources readily available to white Americans—resulted in low self-esteem among African American children. Specifically, the children in the Clarks' studies associated being black (or having dark skin) with negative connotations (i.e., bad, dirty, not smart).

About twenty years later, Margaret Beale Spencer revisited the Clarks' work, demonstrating how *cognitive egocentrism*—a normative, cognitive developmental process—can protect the identity development of young black children, allowing them to maintain high self-esteem despite their awareness of negative racial stereotypes. That is, when they are still cognitively egocentric, children can be aware of color connotations yet not apply their "knowledge" of color connotations to themselves. Spencer's subsequent research demonstrates how improvements in the ability to assume the perspectives of others and how becoming less cognitively egocentric in later developmental stages—another normative cognitive developmental process—results in cognitive dissonance. That is, in the absence of positive racial socialization, young people face the difficult task of reconciling their perceptions of societal stereotypes with their perceptions of themselves and others who share their physical characteristics (i.e., phenotype). In contrast to the Clarks' research, Spencer demonstrates both the complexity of identity formation processes and the multiple influences on identity development. While normative processes of cognitive development can influence how children perceive and make meaning of their daily experiences in terms of differences in race and varied indicators of social class, other external factors, such as racial socialization by parents, serve a protective function and mitigate the potentially detrimental effects of negative racial stereotypes on identity development.

More recent studies using similar methods to assess children's awareness of negative stereotypes and color connotations have yielded similar findings. Yet, if the differences in interpretations asserted by the Clarks and Spencer are any indication, such findings must be interpreted within the specific social and historical contexts in which they are conducted. That is, in addition to cognitive developmental status, current social norms and socialization experiences must also be taken into account.

CHANGING METHODOLOGIES IN THE STUDY OF CHILD DEVELOPMENT

Given the diverse theories of development, there are different methodologies for determining the existing and emergent abilities of children and young people (e.g., the Strange Situation, mirror studies, puppet interviews, habituation studies, doll studies, etc). These strategies are based on assumptions about development, the meaning and function of observable behaviors, and similarities among the contexts in which children live and function. Some of these assumptions may be problematic, at best, when considering the experiences of diverse youth of color, immigrants, and youngsters from families that experience intergenerational poverty. As social scientists come up with improved theories, greater cultural competence, and better strategies for studying child behavior, increasingly articulated and nuanced understandings of child development are formulated.

SEE ALSO *Adolescent Psychology; Ainsworth, Mary; Attachment Theory; Child Behavior Checklist; Children; Clark, Kenneth B.; Developmental Psychology; Erikson, Erik; Freud, Sigmund; Piaget, Jean; Research, Longitudinal*

BIBLIOGRAPHY

Crain, William. 2000. *Theories of Development: Concepts and Applications.* 4th ed. Upper Saddle River, NJ: Prentice Hall.

Dupree, Davido, Margaret Beale Spencer, and Sonya Bell. 1997. African-American Children. In *Transcultural Child Development: Psychological Assessment and Treatment*, eds. Gloria Johnson-Powell and Joe Yamamoto, 237–268. New York: Wiley.

Muuss, Rolf E. 1996. *Theories of Adolescence.* 6th ed. New York: McGraw-Hill.

Rogoff, Barbara. 2003. *The Cultural Nature of Human Development.* New York: Oxford University Press.

Spencer, Margaret Beale. 2006. Phenomenology and Ecological Systems Theory: Development of Diverse Groups. In *Handbook of Child Psychology*, 6th ed., eds. William Damon and Richard Lerner, vol. 1, chap. 15, 829–893. Hoboken, NJ: Wiley.

Spencer, Margaret Beale, and Sanford Dornbusch. 1990. Challenges in Studying Minority Youth. In *At the Threshold: The Developing Adolescent*, eds. S. Shirley Feldman and Glenn Elliot, 123–146. Cambridge, MA: Harvard University Press.

Spencer, Margaret Beale, and Carol Markstrom-Adams. 1990. Identity Processes Among Racial and Ethnic Minority Children in America. *Child Development* 61 (2): 290–310.

Thomas, Alexander, and Stella Chess. 1977. *Temperament and Development.* New York: Bruner/Mazel.

Suzanne Fegley
Davido Dupree
Margaret Beale Spencer

CHILD LABOR

Child labor is work done by persons under age eighteen (or younger, depending on applicable national law) that is harmful to them for being abusive, exploitive, hazardous, or otherwise contrary to their best interests. It is a subset of a larger class of children's work, some of which may be compatible with children's best interests (variously expressed as beneficial, benign, or harmless children's work). Broadly defined, *child labor* recognizes that childhood is a culturally specific concept and that the particular contexts within which children's work is assigned and organized tend to determine both its costs and its benefits (Ennew, Myers, and Plateau 2005). While in most cultures some work by children is viewed as healthy for maturation and socialization, child labor is not. It is understood to violate human rights law and policy.

The number of children who are engaged in child labor globally is uncertain. The answer to this question varies according to activity, place, society, and other factors. It is estimated that in 2007 there exist some 250 million child workers worldwide (predominantly in developing countries), with perhaps as many as 75 percent of them working in agriculture and related activities, most of the remainder in the nonagricultural informal sector, and only a small portion in the formal sector. Yet unknown is the exact percentage of these working children who experience child labor specifically.

It nevertheless is widely accepted that large numbers of the world's working children toil in appalling conditions, are ruthlessly exploited to perform dangerous jobs with little or no pay, and are thus often made to suffer severe physical and emotional abuse—in brick factories, carpet-weaving centers, fishing platforms, leather tanning shops, mines, and other hazardous places, often as cogs in the global economy; in domestic service, vulnerable to sexual and other indignities that escape public scrutiny and accountability; on the streets as prostitutes, forced to trade in sex against their will; and as soldiers in life-threatening conflict situations. Working long hours, often beaten or otherwise abused, and commonly trafficked from one country to another, their health is severely threatened, their very lives endangered. Many, if they survive, are deformed and disabled before they can mature physically, mentally, or emotionally. Typically, they are unable to obtain the education that can liberate and improve their lives, a condition that is deemed generally to constitute child abuse in and of itself (Bissell 2005; Bissell and Shiefelbein 2003).

The causes of child labor, while steeped in culture, are linked to economics—primarily poverty, necessitating that children contribute to family income. Likewise, the reduction and eradication of child labor is tied fundamentally to economics. In North America and western Europe, for example, major economically based trends (e.g., industrial development, higher wages, technological innovation, more accessible and prolonged education, lower birth rates, the entry of women into the workforce) best explain, along with state regulation and changing popular ideas about childhood, most of the long-term declines in child labor. Labor movements and other forms of social action also have played an important role, shaping public perceptions and values about children and child rearing.

Because of this variety and complexity, economists and other experts point out that effective policies to combat child labor require flexibility to accommodate the many and diverse factors involved in its reduction and eradication. They especially emphasize the critical importance of presenting poor families and children with economic opportunities and incentives that can free them from having to rely on child labor for survival (Basu 1999; Basu and Tzannatos 2003; Anker 2000, 2001; Grootaert and Patrinos 1999).

Human rights discourse and activism—especially since the 1989 United Nations Convention on the Rights of the Child—have likewise become influential in combating child labor, advancing the case for at least minimal standards of socioeconomic and political justice to hasten its elimination. Increasingly child labor is understood to be a multidimensional human rights problem in violation of a broad panoply of entitlements with which all members of the human family are endowed (Weston and Teerink 2005a, 2005b). The Convention on the Rights of the Child ensures that children specifically, including working children, are not overlooked in this regard. Thus does Article 3(1) stipulate that "in all actions concerning children … the best interests of the child shall be a primary consideration"; and thus, to this end, does Article 32(1) recognize "the right of the child to be protected from economic exploitation and from performing any work that is likely to be hazardous or to interfere with the child's education, or to be harmful to the child's health or physical, mental, spiritual, moral, or social development."

While poverty and other economic factors will continue as driving forces behind child labor, a human rights approach to the individual child and society—holistic and multifaceted—is indispensable to holding the world community and its member states accountable in eradicating the phenomenon (Weston and Teerink 2005a, 2005b). Recognizing child labor as a human rights problem signals that notions of human dignity are central to all aspects of a working child's life and to the means by which child labor is reduced or eliminated. In this setting, states, multilateral international organizations, nongovernmental organizations, and business enterprises are expected to act affirmatively to guarantee that children's rights are not violated within either the work in which they are engaged or the means by which that work is controlled. In addition, children must be informed of their rights so as to be able to engage their full participation in the realization of their rights. To assert a *right* of a child to be free from abusive, exploitative, and hazardous work bespeaks duty, not optional—often capricious—benevolence.

SEE ALSO *Children's Rights; Human Rights*

BIBLIOGRAPHY

Anker, Richard. 2000. The Economics of Child Labour: A Framework for Measurement. *International Labour Review* 139 (3): 257–280.

Anker, Richard. 2001. Child Labour and Its Elimination: Actors and Institutions. In *Child Labour: Policy Options*, eds. Kristoffel Lieten and Ben White, 85–102. Amsterdam: Askant.

Basu, Kaushik. 1999. International Labor Standards and Child labor. *Challenge* 42 (5): 82–93.

Basu, Kaushik, and Zafiris Tzannatos. 2003. The Global Child Labor Problem: What Do We Know and What Can We Do? *The World Bank Economic Review* 17 (2): 147–173.

Bissell, Susan L. 2005. Earning and Learning: Tensions and Compatibility. In *Child Labor and Human Rights: Making Children Matter*, ed. Burns H. Weston, 377–399. London and Boulder, CO: Lynne Rienner.

Bissell, Susan, and Ernesto Shiefelbein. 2003. *Education to Combat Abusive Child Labor*. Washington, DC: USAID Bureau for Economic Growth, Culture, Agriculture, and Trade.

Ennew, Judith, William E. Myers, and Dominique Pierre Plateau. 2005. Defining Child Labor as if Human Rights Really Matter. In *Child Labor and Human Rights: Making Children Matter*, ed. Burns H. Weston, 27–54. London and Boulder, CO: Lynne Rienner.

Grootaert, Christiaan, and Henry Anthony Patrinos, eds. 1999. *The Policy Analysis of Child Labor: A Comparative Study*. New York: St. Martin's Press.

United Nations. Convention on the Rights of the Child. 1989. http://www.ohchr.org/english/law/pdf/crc.pdf.

Weston, Burns H., and Mark B. Teerink. 2005a. Rethinking Child Labor: A Multidimensional Problem. In *Child Labor and Human Rights: Making Children Matter*, ed. Burns H. Weston, 3–25. London and Boulder, CO: Lynne Rienner.

Weston, Burns H., and Mark B. Teerink. 2005b. Rethinking Child Labor: A Multifaceted Human Rights Solution. In

Child Labor and Human Rights: Making Children Matter, ed. Burns H. Weston, 235–266. London and Boulder, CO: Lynne Rienner.

Burns H. Weston
William E. Myers

CHILD STUDY MOVEMENT

SEE *Maturation.*

CHILD SUPPORT

SEE *Divorce and Separation.*

CHILD CARE

SEE *Day Care.*

CHILDLESSNESS

The term *childlessness* refers to a lifetime of being childless and can be applied both to couples that have never borne a child and to single women or men. Most research, and hence most available data, focuses on women. In some populations the proportion of women experiencing childlessness has been as low as 2 or 3 percent, and in others it has been ten times this minimum level. In the twentieth-century United States, for instance, the level of childlessness for women born in the first decade of the century (and bearing children during the depression of the 1930s) and for those born in the 1950s (and bearing children during the century's last three decades) was approximately 20 percent. By contrast, it was approximately 10 percent for U.S. women born in the 1930s (and bearing children during the baby boom of the 1950s).

There are four dominant paths to childlessness. First, persons can decide at a young age that they want no children and maintain this position over their lifetimes. Second, persons can intend to have children but postpone childbearing to an age when they are unable to have children, because of subfecundity or infecundity (i.e., limited ability or inability, for biological reasons, to conceive and carry a birth to term). Third, persons who desire and expect children but who are willing to have them only if they are married or in a stable union may become childless as a result of failing to establish such unions. Finally, persons can be unable to bear children due to infecundity present from a young age. The prevalence of each of these reasons for childlessness varies across time and place. In the United States and Europe in the early twenty-first century, the second and third reasons are most prevalent.

There have been many attempts to distinguish voluntary from involuntary childlessness, but this distinction is problematic. Voluntariness is ascribed to those who deliberately choose childlessness and involuntariness to those who are infecund due to congenital abnormalities, malnutrition, or disease. Note that only the first and fourth pathways described above neatly conform to this distinction. The second pathway (postponement followed by infecundity) combines a period of voluntary childlessness with an involuntary period. The third pathway (childlessness due to non-marriage) is in some sense involuntary but is due to a social constraint (the pressure to establish an appropriate union) rather than something biological.

Subfecundity and infecundity, both major contributors to childlessness, have two sources. First, reduced fecundity can occur at any age due to a large number of diseases. For instance, many sexually transmitted infections can lead to pelvic inflammatory disease that results in scarring of the fallopian tubes, thus inhibiting the release of ovum in females. This particular problem may be solved by assisted reproductive technology (ART), which encompasses techniques such as in vitro fertilization. In the United States in 2005, 1 percent of all births resulted from in vitro fertilization. The second cause of infertility is senescence-related (i.e., due to aging). From the time women are in their mid- to late twenties, fecundity declines at an increasing rate with increasing age. ART can overcome some of these senescence-related problems, but technologies still cannot overcome many of them.

Childless adults face a stigma, although its degree varies by time and place. Stigma is greatest in contexts where there are few or no life-course alternatives to marriage and parenthood. In these contexts being unmarried or childless places one outside acceptable adult statuses. The consequences for women are often more severe than for men. Childlessness can lead the husband to take another wife or can provide justification for divorce or abandonment of the wife. In the late twentieth century many societies experienced feminist social movements and assertions that parenthood and childlessness are equally legitimate lifestyle choices.

While childbirth is the dominant pathway to parenthood, the permanently childless may become parents through adoption. Like childless adults, adopted children face a stigma that varies across time and place.

SEE ALSO *Family; Feminism; Fertility, Human; Infertility Drugs, Psychosocial Issues; Stigma*

BIBLIOGRAPHY

McFalls, Joseph A., Jr. 1990. The Risks of Reproductive Impairment in the Later Years of Childbearing. *Annual Review of Sociology* 16: 491–519.

Rindfuss, Ronald R., S. Philip Morgan, and Gray Swicegood. 1989. *First Births in America: Changes in the Timing of Parenthood.* Berkeley: University of California Press.

Sobotka, Tomáš. 2004. *Postponement of Childbearing and Low Fertility in Europe.* Amsterdam: Dutch University Press.

S. Philip Morgan

CHILDREN

Although seemingly intuitive, the meaning of the term *children* depends on the context. From a strict biological perspective, the term *children* refers to the offspring of a female and male who have mated. However, the term need not refer only to biological offspring, as it also applies to socially defined categories of children including stepchildren, adopted children, and foster children. By law, one is considered a *minor* until the age of eighteen. However, the law distinguishes children from minors in general. According to the law, a child under the age of fourteen is a "*child of tender age.*" The term *juvenile* is used to categorize individuals between fourteen and seventeen years of age, thus distinguishing juveniles from children.

The United Nations' *Convention on the Rights of the Child* (1989) sets forth the universal human rights of children: "the right to survival; the right to develop to the fullest; the right to protection from harmful influences, abuse and exploitation; and the right to participate fully in family, cultural and social life." The four core principles of the convention are: "non-discrimination; devotion to the best interests of the child; the right to life, survival and development; and the right to participation."

Although these meanings are valid, the meaning of the term *children* extends beyond the concrete terms imposed by legal and biological reality. From a developmental standpoint, the term can be used to describe individuals from infancy through preadolescence (before puberty), thus including the following periods of human development: infancy, early childhood, and middle childhood. Children undergo significant biological, cognitive, and social changes during each of these stages.

Growth during infancy is characterized by rapid changes in height and weight. Children are born with reflexes such as those that enable them to suck and turn their heads. They are also sensitive and responsive to the facial features and vocalizations of others, particularly their primary caregivers. By twelve to eighteen months of age, children are able to share attention between a person and an object, known as "joint attention," and they use words and gestures such as pointing to communicate. Children also transition through the stages of locomotion, from crawling to independent upright walking and their early fine motor skills develop. Social interactions initially emerge in dyadic turn-taking bouts between caregiver and child and features of temperament (personality) also emerge. By age two, children are able to recognize their reflections (self) in a mirror, combine words to communicate, search for hidden objects, and manipulate objects during play. Early experiences in infancy set the stage for children's later growth and development. Developmental outcomes during this period are strongly influenced by both nature (genetic influences) and nurture (environmental influences) and risk susceptibility.

Ages two to five mark the early childhood/preschool age period of children's development. By age three, although children's body weight is only 20 percent of its adult size, children's brain size is 80 percent of its adult size. By age five, children's lexicon contains approximately 5,000 to 10,000 words and the syntactic complexity of their language increases significantly. Further developments in children's self-concept and increased narrative skills facilitate children's ability to form and share information about past events (autobiographical memory). Problem-solving skills involving planning and the use of strategies also emerge. Between ages three and five, children's ability to distinguish their thoughts and beliefs from others, known as "theory of mind," develops. Young children's egocentrism affects their view of the world, themselves, and others and is reflected in their inability to effectively coordinate their actions with their peers in play contexts. Play during the early childhood years is "parallel" in nature, defined as two or more children engaged in related activities in close physical proximity to each other. Although parents actively structure and facilitate the social lives and experiences of their children during this period, peers also serve as influential forces.

The hallmark of the middle childhood period is the transition to formal schooling. Although many children attend daycare and/or preschool during the early childhood period, the first day of school marks a cultural passage around the world. Children's physical growth is slow, yet consistent during this period. Between ages five and seven, children's thought shifts from egocentric to concrete operational thought—children are now capable of abstract thinking and understanding and interpreting the thoughts and beliefs of others. Executive functioning capacities, including their conscious ability to control and inhibit their actions, as well as problem-solving, reasoning, working memory, and attention further develop. The peer group becomes increasingly important, as children spend more than 40 percent of their day with peers. Children are labeled by their peers; categories such as "popular" and "rejected" emerge, as well as the consequences of such social status labels. The development of the self-concept in relation to self-esteem and self-competence as well as moral understanding and beliefs also play integral roles during this period. From a developmental perspective, childhood ends with the onset of puberty.

In addition to legal, biological, social, and developmental definitions of children, one must also consider the impact of the sociohistorical and sociocultural context in which children develop. Children learn by actively participating in cultural activities that promote their growth. Opportunities to learn are embedded in activities at play, school, and work contexts. However, the opportunities afforded to children vary as a function of their cultural upbringing, including the social and economic status of their community and the belief systems regarding their participation in cultural activities.

Children are the product of complex interactions between their genes and the environments in which their development is nested, including, but not limited to, family, school, and community contexts, and the broader cultural belief systems espoused by their nation. Children's experiences and outcomes set the stage for their future development and adjustment in the next stages of human development: adolescence and adulthood.

SEE ALSO *Attachment Theory; Child Behavior Checklist; Child Development; Development; Developmental Psychology; Family; Family Structure; Parent-Child Relationships; Self-Awareness Theory; Stages of Development*

BIBLIOGRAPHY

Berk, L. E. 2006. *Child Development.* 7th ed. Boston: Allyn & Bacon.

Cole, M., S. R. Cole, and C. Lightfoot. 2005. *The Development of Children.* 5th ed. New York: Worth Publishers.

UNICEF. 1989. Convention on the Rights of the Child. http://www.unicef.org/crc/.

Vasta, R., S. A. Miller, and S. Ellis. 2003. *Child Psychology.* 4th ed. New York: Wiley.

Joann P. Benigno

CHILDREN'S RIGHTS

Children's rights involve a double claim. First, they reaffirm children as full members of the human family and assert that children have an equal right to the protection of their fundamental human rights without discrimination based on age. Second, children's rights acknowledge children's developing capacity as well as their vulnerability and encompass additional, special rights for children.

The concept of children's rights has gradually evolved and has not always included both equal and special human rights. Children's rights emerged at the end of the nineteenth century in the context of uncontrolled industrialization and its dire consequences for the living conditions of poor working-class children. The child protection movement considered it a moral duty to alleviate the plight of vulnerable children, who were seen as passive victims and mere objects of intervention. These concerns gave rise to the development of child protection legislation and policies regarding child labor, compulsory education, and juvenile justice, and also led to the adoption of the *1924 Declaration of the Rights of the Child* (Geneva Declaration) containing a list of protections that ought to be granted to children.

With the advent and development of the welfare state, throughout the twentieth century, children's rights became increasingly framed within social welfare discourse. In addition to protection against all forms of neglect, cruelty, and exploitation, children's rights now also included the right to special provisions, such as education, health care, family support, and social welfare services. This welfarist view is reflected in the *1959 United Nations Declaration of the Rights of the Child*, which builds upon children's dependency on both their family and the state. During the 1970s, in step with other civil rights and antiauthoritarian emancipation movements, the children's liberation movement began to challenge the exclusive attention being paid to children's protection and welfare rights. The movement argued in favor of children's right to autonomy, including the right to freedom of speech, freedom of assembly, and due process guarantees in judicial proceedings. The child liberationist's claim for children's equal rights was directed against both family and state, whose paternalistic approaches to children were viewed as an impediment to young people's pursuit of autonomy and full participation in society.

The protectionist, welfarist, and liberationist approaches to children's rights converged in the *1989 United Nations Convention on the Rights of the Child*, a legally binding international instrument that has been ratified by all UN member states, except for Somalia and the United States. This convention contains a broad range of rights, including civil and political rights as well as social, economic, and cultural rights, and can be summarized by the so-called "three Ps," which include protection rights (e.g., against violence or exploitation), provision rights (e.g., education or health care provisions), and participation rights (e.g., freedom of expression or right to information). The convention's core message is that children are no longer to be seen as mere passive objects of intervention, but should be recognized as bearers of rights. Children therefore have the right, in accordance with their evolving capacities, to actively take part in shaping their own lives and environments. Since its adoption, various interest groups have made intensive use of the convention as an advocacy tool in a vast array of fields directly and indirectly relating to children's lives and promoting both children's equal and special rights.

SEE ALSO *Child Labor; Children; Civil Rights; Human Rights*

BIBLIOGRAPHY

Archard, David. 2004. *Children: Rights and Childhood.* 2nd ed. London: Routledge.

Verhellen, Eugeen. 2000. *Convention on the Rights of the Child: Background, Motivation, Strategies, Main Themes.* 3rd ed. Louvain, Belgium: Garant.

Karl Hanson

CHINESE AMERICANS

Chinese Americans can trace their roots to the mid-nineteenth century. Although it is not known when the first Chinese ventured into North America, Harry H. L. Kitano and Roger Daniels (2001) suggest that the first major wave of Chinese immigration to the United States occurred just before the California gold rush of 1849. Although Chinese Americans do not have the long history of African Americans and Latino Americans, they are also not a new immigrant group. Rather, Chinese Americans are a well-established U.S. ethnic group that has faced long-standing social, political, and economic discrimination as well as outright government exclusion (e.g., via immigration laws and policies). Chinese people immigrated to the United States during a variety of periods, and they differed demographically from one another: some were professional elites, while others were cheap labor. Initially most were men.

HISTORY OF CHINESE IMMIGRATION TO THE UNITED STATES

The United States has a long history of immigration and naturalization laws and policies that excluded Chinese from entering the country. In the mid- to late nineteenth century there were no formal policies to prevent immigrants from coming to the United States. As a result Chinese laborers, fleeing from what Sucheng Chan (1991) refers to as a time of natural disasters and extreme political turmoil in China, sought work in the United States, a

place that many Chinese believed offered unlimited wealth, resources, and opportunities for success. Unlike other minority groups, such as Africans, who were forced to come to America against their wills, most Chinese immigrants were sojourners who intended to work in the United States for a short time and eventually return to their homes in China. However, similar to other racial minorities in the United States, Chinese workers were relegated to second-class citizenship and often treated as inferior or subhuman compared to whites. Large numbers of Chinese laborers were coerced and even physically forced to work on plantations, in mines, and on the railroads. When their labor was no longer needed, exclusionary immigration laws based on race and nationality were instituted, preventing new Chinese workers from entering the United States. The Chinese Exclusion Act, passed in 1882, prevented Chinese laborers from immigrating to the United States for ten years and prohibited naturalization. In 1888 the Scott Act barred all Chinese laborers legally residing in America reentry into the United States after visiting China. The Geary Act (1892) extended the Chinese Exclusion Act for another ten years. Chinese laborers were barred from entering the United States indefinitely in 1902. In 1917 the U.S. Congress prohibited the entry of natives from China, South and Southeast Asia, Afghanistan, and parts of what is now known as the Middle East.

The anti-immigration movement of the early twentieth century was coupled with violence and racism against all Asian immigrants but in particular the Chinese. The anti-immigrant sentiments prevalent during this time were based on numerous fears, particularly a fear of "foreignness," or the idea of difference, usually based on ethnocentric notions of biological and cultural inferiority. White Americans also feared that immigrants would take their jobs, jobs that in many instances were not sought by whites.

In 1943 the Chinese Exclusion Act of 1882 was repealed, and a quota of 105 Chinese immigrants per year was established. The War Brides Act of 1945 allowed veterans of World War II (1939–1945) to bring their foreign-born wives and children to the United States, increasing the number of Chinese women who were allowed to immigrate to the United States. Until then the Page Act of 1875, implemented in an effort to reduce the number of Asian prostitutes in the United States, limited the immigration attempts of most Chinese women. The McCarran-Walter Immigration and Nationality Act of 1952 eliminated racial and ethnic restrictions from the country's immigration and naturalization policies and opened the door for many Chinese women wanting to immigrate to the United States. Likewise the Immigration and Naturalization Act of 1965 removed quotas for immigrants from the Eastern Hemisphere, resulting in high levels of immigration from China, Japan, and various Southeast Asian countries. The new immigration guidelines allowed 170,000 immigrants from the Eastern Hemisphere to enter the United States, with no more than 20,000 per country, along with 120,000 immigrants from the Western Hemisphere. The law also prioritized reunification of families and made it easier for Chinese immigrants to become naturalized. Additionally children of immigrants were granted citizenship, a privilege that was typically denied in the past.

As a result of the Immigration and Naturalization Act of 1965, the rate of immigration to the United States increased, and the nature of immigration changed as more people of color were allowed entry to the United States, creating a substantial shift in the racial and ethnic composition of the population. The number of Chinese immigrants and Chinese Americans in the United States increased from around 125,000 in the early 1900s to well over 1.6 million by 1990.

CHINESE AMERICANS AND THE MODEL MINORITY MYTH

Some researchers argue that American-born Chinese began to outnumber immigrants from China residing in the United States starting in the 1940s, and that trend has continued into the twenty-first century. Chinese Americans are not a monolithic group but rather a diverse population. Some have enjoyed the economic success that comes with higher education and a professional career, but many Chinese Americans are low-skilled laborers with little education and low socioeconomic status. Stereotypes of Chinese Americans often misrepresent their experiences, and according to Frank Wu (2002), racial prejudice and discrimination directed at Chinese Americans often result from such stereotypes. For example, the *model minority* myth, which arose in the mid-1960s, holds that the success of Asian Americans, including Chinese Americans, is due to their hard work and diligence, ignoring how race, class, and reasons for migration can influence the experiences of different immigrant groups.

The model minority myth also exacerbates conflict between Asian Americans and other U.S. minority groups by setting Asian Americans on a pedestal as a "model" group that has "made it" because of dedication and a positive work ethic that other minority groups may lack. Furthermore the model minority myth ignores the fact that many Chinese Americans are not highly educated professionals but are low-skilled laborers who do not experience economic success. Thus the model minority myth obscures the contextual situation of each immigrant group. Chinese immigrants who migrated shortly after the Immigration Act of 1965, for example, were predominantly educated professionals, giving them and their chil-

dren an economic advantage that many earlier Chinese immigrants lacked.

The model minority myth deflects attention from racist structural factors that have impeded the success of many immigrants and people of color in the United States. It promotes the ideology of individuality as a way to achieve success in America and ignores the barriers (such as racist immigration laws and policies) facing many immigrant groups and their children in achieving success.

CHINESE AMERICANS AND CITIZENSHIP

Although Chinese Americans have fared better in the United States than some other Asian groups (e.g., Filipinos, Vietnamese, Hmong), they have been far from immune to the effects of racism. Numerous studies have documented incidents of overt racism experienced by Chinese Americans, ranging from verbal insults and differential treatment to hate crimes and violence. The murder of Vincent Chin, a young Chinese American man, exemplifies the type of racially motivated violence that Asian Americans may experience. Chin was severely beaten on June 19, 1982, outside a bar in Detroit. He died four days later, five days before his wedding. The perpetrators, two out-of-work autoworkers, claimed they had mistaken Chin for Japanese, a group they blamed for problems within Detroit's automobile industry.

Chinese Americans have also had their citizenship questioned. Citizenship was once legally denied to both Chinese immigrants and their American-born descendants because of their race. In the early twenty-first century, although Chinese Americans are legal citizens, they are often not culturally viewed as citizens because they are not white. Scholars argue that racialized ethnics, such as Chinese Americans, are often assumed to be foreign rather than American. Mia Tuan's 1998 study of the Asian Americans' experience revealed that many Asian Americans, including Chinese Americans, are often asked where they are from. When "America" is the response, most whites, unsatisfied that Asians can be Americans, will continue by asking, "no, where are you *really* from." Thus as Frank Wu (2002) pointed out, Asian Americans are seen as "perpetual foreigners" in the United States. The perpetual foreigner syndrome was evident in some media coverage of the 1998 Winter Olympics. During the figure skating competition, Michelle Kwan, a Chinese American skater, lost the gold medal to Tara Lipinski, a white American. A subsequent MSNBC headline read, "American Beats Out Kwan," suggesting that Kwan was not as American as Lipinski. Four years later, in the *Seattle Times*, a similar headline appeared when Kwan lost to another white American, Sarah Hughes, in the 2002 winter Olympics: "Hughes Good as Gold: American

Outshines Kwan, Slutskaya in Skating Surprise." Both headlines are examples of how a sense of belonging, a privilege associated with citizenship, is denied to Chinese Americans because of their race and how racialized ethnics are not able to fully assimilate into the mainstream.

While Chinese cultural centers and Chinatowns reflect one of the many impacts Chinese Americans have had on American culture, Chinese American laborers represent another major contribution to American culture and history. In 1869 the Union Pacific Railroad and the Eastern Pacific Railroad were joined together by the Transcontinental Railroad, connecting the eastern part of the United States to the western. Chinese laborers provided a substantial number of workers to complete the project and were paid less than their white counterparts. The completion of this railroad aided in the economic development of the western part of the United States. Thus while Chinese American laborers have historically been exploited financially and faced racial discrimination, they were integral in the economic development of the United States through their hard work on the railroads.

Chinese Americans have lived in the United States for more than a century, but their history has been plagued with racism. Racist immigration and naturalization laws and policies excluded Chinese from migrating to the United States and denied them rights and privileges associated with citizenship. Although these laws and policies have been dismantled, Chinese Americans still face stereotypes, such as the model minority myth, that minimize the breadth of their experiences. The history of Chinese immigrants provides a contextual framework with which to understand the situation of Chinese Americans.

SEE ALSO *Assimilation; Citizenship; Immigrants, Asian; Immigration; Model Minority; Nativism; Naturalization; Racism*

BIBLIOGRAPHY

Alvarez, Alvin. Asian Americans and Racism: When Bad Things Happen to "Model Minorities." *Cultural Diversity and Ethnic Minority Psychology* (12) 3: 477–492.

Chan, Sucheng. 1991. *Asian Americans: An Interpretive History.* Boston: Twayne.

Fong, Timothy. 1994. *The First Suburban Chinatown: The Remaking of Monterey Park, California.* Philadelphia: Temple University Press.

Fong, Timothy, and Larry H. Shinagawa, eds. 2000. *Asian Americans: Experiences and Perspectives.* Upper Saddle River, NJ: Prentice Hall.

Kitano, Harry H. L., and Roger Daniels. 2001. *Asian Americans: Emerging Minorities.* 3rd ed. Upper Saddle River, NJ: Prentice Hall.

Tuan, Mia. 1998. *Forever Foreigners or Honorary Whites? The Asian Ethnic Experience Today.* New Brunswick, NJ: Rutgers University Press.

Tuan, Mia. 1999. Neither Real Americans nor Real Asians? Multigeneration Asian Ethnics Navigating the Terrain of Authenticity. *Qualitative Sociology* (22) 2: 105–125.

Wu, Frank H. 2002. *Yellow: Race in America beyond Black and White.* New York: Basic Books.

Saher Selod
David G. Embrick

CHINESE DIASPORA

Diaspora is a Greek term, meaning the widespread scattering of seeds. Its biblical use refers to the dispersal of the Jews around the Roman Empire. Until the 1990s it was rarely found in the social sciences, and is also absent from previous editions of this Encyclopedia and from the 1994 *Dictionary of Sociology*. The international distribution of middlemen minorities during premodern times was long considered of only historical interest, with little relevance to the modern world of capitalist corporations and nation-state societies. Members of various diasporas were conceptualized as *ethnic groups*, *minorities*, and *immigrant communities*, with a focus on their place within individual host societies, rather than on their transnational connections.

Only in the last decades of the twentieth century, with increasing globalization, did the need for a collective term become apparent. Daniel Chirot and Anthony Reid proposed the term *essential outsiders*; Joel Kotkin used *global tribes*. Neither term caught on, however. Khachig Tololyan launched the journal *Diaspora*, in December 1991, with the claim that transnational diasporas were "the exemplary communities of the trans-national moment," and new diaspora studies (of Africans, Chechens, Indians, Irish, Italians, Palestinians, and Filipinos) have multiplied.

Diaspora is a collective noun, referring to people who have (themselves or their ancestors) been scattered from a place of origin, and to elements of their common identity and culture. If a diaspora is only constituted by shared memories and common attributes, these are likely, with the passage of generations, to fade through assimilation. Long-term survival for diasporic communities generally depends on continuing transnational communication and flows. Thus, historically, the most tenacious diasporas have often been those interconnected by long-distance trade.

THE CHINESE OUTSIDE
MAINLAND CHINA

China has for over two thousand years been a great power in the East, yet it has nearly always seen itself as a land-based empire, indifferent or hostile to the traders and emigrants who left its shores, fleeing poverty or conflict or seeking economic opportunities. Chinese have been important traders around the South China Sea since before the twelfth century. They were predominant middlemen in precolonial and colonial times in Southeast Asia and Vietnam, and served as intermediaries between local producers and colonizers. Like other such groups, they suffered periodic persecutions and expulsions. Chinese trading communities around the region and the world thus largely established themselves and their transnational relations with each other as self-regulating entities, with limited state support or protection and with their own associations and welfare provision.

Wang Gungwu (in *China and the Chinese Overseas,* 1991) argues that these Chinese established a *peripheral capitalism,* on the fringes or outside the reach of the imperial (and later the Communist) state. Only here was Chinese merchant culture able to flourish, away from a repressive and contemptuous mandarinate, whose Confucianism emphasized ritual and hierarchy and disapproved of trade, risk, and profit. Wang describes how the Chinese overseas created their own distinctive institutions, by reshaping and developing the traditions they had brought with them and combining them with influences from the lands where they settled and the local women they married. These traditions included the Taoist and Zen Buddhist beliefs common in southern China, the sophisticated monetary and lending practices of Chinese peasants, and a facility in forming cooperative organizations. Another resource, described by Gary Hamilton (in *Business Networks and Economic Development in East and Southeast Asia,* 1991), was the experience some brought of imperial China's urban guilds, which had set their own standards for weights and measures and had enforced contracts without relying (as had the guilds of medieval Europe) on state enforcement.

Most diasporic Chinese came from the outer parts of the empire, from its southern coastal provinces of Guangdong and Fujian, where state control was looser, or via treaty ports or the ceded territories of Hong Kong or Macao. One concentration of emigrants from the mainland was based in Taiwan, which was only attached to China late and insecurely. Settled from China from the sixteenth century—often by merchants and pirates from Fujian, who were seeking a base for maritime activities, and by rebels against the Manchu dynasty—Taiwan only came under central control after 1684, and was always lightly administered and notoriously lawless thereafter.

From 1895 until 1945 it was a colony of Japan and after 1949 it was ruled by Kuomintang exiles from the Communist mainland.

In time, many diasporic Chinese assimilated completely, yet continuity was assured by new waves of emigrants, who worked for, learnt from, and then replaced their predecessors. In Chinese business culture today there are some direct continuities with features of merchant culture and institutions in the China of five hundred years ago. Yet most of the members of modern diasporic communities can trace their own family's origins to villages in China left at most only a couple of generations ago. For a majority in Southeast Asia, the migration of their family occurred in the period preceding the last world war. For most in Hong Kong it is even more recent—until 1981 those born in China were a majority. Thus a persisting feature of these often-ancient communities is their intense social mobility and constant self-rejuvenation.

In the mid-nineteenth century, gold rushes attracted significant numbers of Chinese to California and Australia, where many remained. By the end of the century, however, restrictions on immigration and widespread discrimination led to a decline in numbers, the demise of associations, and ghettoization within narrow economic niches. Ivan Light, in *Ethnic Enterprise in America* (1972, p.7), comments that the "classic small businesses of prewar Chinese were … monuments to the discrimination that had created them." In contrast, the 1920s saw large-scale movements, including of women, into flourishing Chinese settlements in Southeast Asia.

In the decades after World War II the situation reversed. Postcolonial nationalist or Communist regimes in Southeast Asia and Vietnam restricted, persecuted, or expelled the Chinese in their midst, whereas racially based barriers to entry were lifted in the United States in 1965 and the White Australia policy was terminated in 1973.

Chirot and Reid (1997) explore the analogies between diasporic Chinese in Southeast Asia and Jews, viewing both as "essential," but periodically scapegoated, "outsiders." In Malaysia, discriminatory rules favored *bumiputras* (indigenous Malays) but failed to halt the rise of Chinese business. In Thailand, Chinese de-sinified their names. Many were expelled from Vietnam after the Communist victory. In Indonesia, Chinese cultural expression was banned until recently, and widespread anti-Chinese riots and rapes followed the Asian Crisis and the fall of Suharto in 1998.

In the last decades of the twentieth century, new waves of secondary immigration increasingly moved from Asian countries of settlement to North America and Australia and fresh flows came from Mainland China. Today, at the start of the twenty-first century, Chinese communities are to be found everywhere in the world, including throughout the Americas and Europe, as well as in Russia. There is, for example, an active Chinese Association in Johannesburg.

A CHINESE DIASPORA?

Can the some twenty-five million Chinese outside China (double that number if we include those in Hong Kong and Taiwan), sometimes called the *ethnic Chinese* or the *overseas Chinese* or the *Chinese overseas*, be called a *diaspora*? The suggestion has been academically controversial, and not only among those who wish to reserve the concept for the Jewish people.

An academic divide long carved up Chinese studies into segments, placing in separate compartments the China specialists, the East Asianists, the Southeast Asianists, and the experts on ethnic Chinese in Western countries. Those who speak of a diaspora have been accused of oversimplifying and blundering into areas beyond their competence. Reality is indeed varied and complex, but these particular divides result from the staking out of academic and political territories, rather than from insurmountable barriers in lived experience. If questions about linkages are not posed, however, the answers are unlikely to obtrude on our vision because there are also statistical divides, created by the political units for which data are collected and presented. Also a factor are the ideological preferences of those who wished to focus on national loyalties and assimilationist hopes, and to deny any transnational attachment, especially one that might involve a Cold War opponent. To justify the concept of a Chinese diaspora, two arguments need to be made, showing both similarities and interrelationships between and among diasporic communities.

First, it must be demonstrated that despite the multiplicity of national, political, and class loyalties and the diversity of cultural and historical trajectories, there exist significant similarities and elements of a shared identity. Evidence for such commonalities is particularly to be found in studies of the economic activities of Chinese around the world, which demonstrate clearly a strong tendency to establish mainly small family businesses, with important elements of a distinctive and shared business culture and mode of operating.

John T. Omohundro (1981) describes the Chinese of Iloilo in the Philippines in 1970 as a one-class community, without gentry, in which the vast majority were self-employed descendants of penniless immigrants. In this community, young employees saw themselves as the rich businessmen of the future and old employees were seen as ex-apprentices who had bungled their chances. The status of women and junior members within the family rose as the family business grew and their role within it expanded. Similar accounts from many other times and

places (including America and Australia) demonstrate how both opportunities (including their own effective business traditions and skills) and legal and discriminatory barriers (which often excluded them from agriculture and the military, and from managerial and bureaucratic positions in the state or big business) pushed every person with any ambition into self-employment.

Even education was more likely to lead back into business, or at least into an independent profession, than into high-status employment. Within the Chinese business community, managerial and bureaucratic positions were rare and these tended to be subject to owners' mistrust, while access to top positions was reserved for family members. Independent business activities have provided the predominant role model, the community leadership, and often the most common activity for mature adults in diaspora communities.

In most Chinese diasporic communities, one of the central and continuing attributes of business is a persistence of family control over entrepreneurial decision-making, even in the largest companies, where professional management and public flotation may be well-established. The tendency, with a few noteworthy exceptions, has been toward a multiplication of relatively small units in a conglomerate structure under the family's control, rather than the expansion of size and market share of large bureaucratically organized firms. This too has reduced the visibility of the concentrations of capital involved. Western and Japanese systems of capitalism have tended to present a duality of large corporations and small and medium firms, with major differences between them and limited opportunities to move back and forth. In Chinese capitalism, many features are common to both large and small operators, leading to greater similarities and continuities and opportunities for mobility up and down. Small firms, with large entrepreneurial ambitions and transnational networks, and with a leading role for highly educated family members, can grow fast by multiplication. Tycoons may own hundreds of such small firms and retain the personalistic style of small operators; they may also be weakened or have their wealth split up if key managers leave to set up independently or if inheritance is divided.

In their external relations (with lenders, borrowers, suppliers, customers, contractors, and subcontractors), Chinese capitalists tend to minimize reliance on legal protection. Chinese capitalism is distinguished by a preference for long-term, personalized, but opportunistically extensible networks, based on trust and upheld by the indispensability of reputation.

Another feature, at least in recent times, has been a preference for a strategy of diversification, in the interests of maximizing flexibility, not "putting all your eggs in one basket," and taking advantage of novel and unpredictable opportunities that open-ended networks may present. This allows individual family members to carve out a territory of their own, promoting harmony, and is facilitated by the freedom of owner-managers to make rapid decisions.

The temporary usefulness of this Chinese business culture was rarely contested. It used to be claimed, however, that these distinctive features were transitional, doomed to decline as they adjusted to modernity and the mainstream or were driven out by competition with modern capitalism. By the 1980s, however, "modernity" itself had been changed by processes of globalization, including cheap and rapid communications, growth in the flows of people, goods, money, and information, the spread of deregulation, the opening of the frontiers of previously largely autarkic Communist regimes, the weakening of economic control by national governments, increasing worldwide subcontracting, and direct foreign investment in globally integrated production. The balance of advantage shifted to the flexible, entrepreneurial businesses of the diaspora, whose previously largely redundant transnational "sleeper" networks now sprang into life.

THE CHINESE DIASPORA IN THE ERA OF GLOBALIZATION

The second requirement for justifying the term *diaspora* is to show that the similarities between separate communities create the conditions for actual transnational linkages and interrelationship. Through much of the twentieth century, such linkages and interrelationships were at best incipient and potential, blocked as they were through a long period of nationalism and stagnant world trade. Only in the last decades of the century, in the period of globalization, have constant and increasing transnational diasporic activities and movements across various divides become apparent. Experts within particular fields of Chinese studies have tended, however, to be blind to these newly growing linkages, constructed by the movement of goods and capital and by people (business people, refugees, students, visitors) investing and trading, remigrating, or returning to their place of origin, all weaving far-flung networks of kinship and friendship. Widely noticed or not, such linkages and the similarities that facilitate them are likely to persist, insofar as they are an asset in an age of globalization.

From the 1980s, locally initiated and funded manufacturing, finance, and markets were developing faster within East and Southeast Asia, along with a progressive integration of regional trade and investment flows. The previously discrete Chinese trading or manufacturing communities around the region now had the motive and opportunity to start diversifying, upgrading, and linking up, using their transnational networks to benefit from and contribute to the export-led economic growth of the region.

The volume of trade of the countries in which Chinese diaspora networks were active (including China, Hong Kong, and Taiwan and the countries of Southeast Asia—the Philippines, Indonesia, Singapore, Thailand, Malaysia, and Vietnam) grew slowly between 1980 and 1985 and then more than doubled by 1990. By 1996 it had increased by another 126 percent, over a period during which total world trade increased by only 56 percent. Intraregional trade, between these countries, increased even faster, up by nearly 160 percent from 1990 to 1996. All parts of the region experienced accelerated growth. Trade between the two great Chinese entrepôts of Hong Kong and Singapore (including the re-exports they channeled in both directions between China and Southeast Asia) increased at rates similar to those of intraregional trade as a whole.

In the 1990s the countries in which diasporic Chinese were prominent economic actors emerged as major international investors. Already by the late 1980s their combined outward investments were jointly on a par with those of Japan. After 1991, as Japan substantially reduced its global foreign investment, they clearly overtook her. By 1996 these countries provided around 14 percent of total world flows of realized foreign direct investment, most of it directed to the countries of their own region. There can be no doubt that most of this investment came from Chinese diaspora sources within these countries. In contrast, Japan was by then providing only about half that proportion of the world total, most of it directed outside the region.

Turn-of-the-century studies of Chinese ethnic business concentrations in America and Australia—in California, Vancouver, and Brisbane, for example—have also found a trend for traders and investors to start using their transnational networks to develop a role as bridges to Asia, adding their weight to the diaspora's global flows.

The most significant opportunity for the diaspora, both the small businesses and the tycoons, was the economic opening of, first, China's Pearl River Delta after 1985, and then of all of the coastal provinces (from which most in the diaspora had originated) and the rest of the country. Diasporic Chinese were responsible for some 80 percent of the massive foreign investment in China up to the end of the twentieth century and were still accounting for over 50 percent in the middle of the first decade of the twenty-first. They served as a bridge between China and the world economy, helping to transform China into one of the great exporting nations of the world, and a rising economic superpower. Their role, and the crucial importance of the transnational networks that made it possible, is documented in some detail in Lever-Tracy et al (1996).

CONCLUSION

Before the turn of the century, the multiplication of successful contacts with other parts of the diaspora and with the mainland was promoting re-sinification. Children were now often encouraged to learn Chinese, new Chinese associations proliferated, and dormant Chinese identities and knowledge were resurfacing. Economic success has bred a new ethnic pride and a cultural flowering, and diasporic Chinese are now even able to influence the Chinese government.

SEE ALSO *East Indian Diaspora; Jewish Diaspora; Palestinian Diaspora*

BIBLIOGRAPHY

Chirot, Daniel, and Anthony Reid, eds. 1997. *Essential Outsiders: Chinese and Jews in the Modern Transformation of Southeast Asia and Central Europe.* Seattle and London: University of Washington Press.

Cushman, Jennifer W., and Wang Gungwu, eds. 1988. *Changing Identities of the Southeast Asian Chinese since World War II.* Hong Kong: Hong Kong University Press.

Hamilton, Gary, ed. 1991. *Business Networks and Economic Development in East and Southeast Asia.* Hong Kong: Centre for Asian Studies, University of Hong Kong.

Lever-Tracy, Constance, David Ip, and Noel Tracy. 1996. *The Chinese Diaspora and Mainland China: An Emerging Economic Synergy.* Houndmills, U.K.: Macmillan.

Light, Ivan H. 1972. *Ethnic Enterprise in America: Business and Welfare among Chinese, Japanese, and Blacks.* Berkeley: University of California Press.

Lim, Linda Y. C., and L. A. Peter Gosling, eds. 1983. *Ethnicity and Economic Activity.* Vol. 1 of *The Chinese in Southeast Asia.* Singapore: Maruzen Asia.

McKeown, Adam. 1999. Conceptualising Chinese Diasporas, 1842–1949. *Journal of Asian Studies* 58 (2): 306–337.

Omohundro, John T. 1981. *Chinese Merchant Families in Iloilo: Commerce and Kin in a Central Philippine City.* Quezon City: Ateneo de Manila University Press.

Pan, Lynn. 1990. *Sons of the Yellow Emperor: The Story of the Overseas Chinese.* London: Secker & Warburg.

Pan, Lynn, ed. 1999. *The Encyclopedia of the Chinese Overseas.* Cambridge, MA: Harvard University Press.

Pieke, Frank N., Pál Nyíri, Mette Thunø, and Antonella Ceccagno. 2004. *Transnational Chinese: Fujianese Migrants in Europe.* Stanford, CA: Stanford University Press.

Wang, Gungwu. 1991. *China and the Chinese Overseas.* Singapore: Times Academic Press.

Wong Siu-Lun. 1988. The Applicability of Asian Family Values to Other Socio-Cultural Settings. In *In Search of an East Asian Development Model*, ed. Peter L. Berger and Hsin-Huang Michael Hsiao, 134–152. New Brunswick, NJ: Transaction Books.

Constance Lever-Tracy

CHINESE EXCLUSION ACT

SEE *Chinese Americans; Immigrants to North America*

CHINESE REVOLUTION

The term *Chinese Revolution* refers to a series of great political upheavals in China between 1911 and 1949 that brought the classical, Confucian, imperial era to an end and eventually led to Communist rule and the establishment of the People's Republic of China. The first phase of the Chinese Revolution started with the republican revolution of 1911, which came about as a result of growing social unrest, the disruptive and humiliating presence of Western and Japanese troops on Chinese soil, and the inability of the imperial government to launch the process of China's belated modernization or even to defend national sovereignty and dignity. The Manchu-descended Qing dynasty (1644–1912) was easily overthrown by a popular rebellion led by nationalist leader Sun Yat-sen (1866–1925), his National People's Party (Guomindang), and other revolutionary groups. The last Qing monarch, child emperor Pu Yi (1906–1967), was forced to abdicate on February 12, 1912. A republic was proclaimed under the provisional Nanjing Constitution of 1912, which was supposed to translate into practice Sun Yat-sen's three principles for the revolution: democracy, nationalism, and socialism.

A republican government headed by General Yuan Shikai (1859–1916), the military leader of the most powerful revolutionary faction, was established in the ancient capital, Beijing. In spite of his greater popularity, Sun Yat-sen, who briefly became nominal president in 1913, had to step aside in Yuan's favor in order to avoid a civil war. Having initially committed himself to a constitutional order in China, General Yuan proved to be more interested in imposing a centralized personal dictatorship. He suspended the republican constitution, dispersed the fledgling national assembly in Nanjing, proclaimed himself president for life, and even tried to bring back the abolished monarchy with himself as emperor. Yuan Shikai was deposed in 1916 and replaced by another military warlord in Beijing. This political crisis only deepened the power vacuum in Chinese politics, which persisted until the ultimate triumph in 1949 of Communist leader Mao Zedong (1893–1976).

The Paris Peace Conference of 1919 after World War I (1914–1918) sparked great nationalist turmoil in the young Chinese Republic. Having participated in the war on the side of the victorious Entente allies, the Chinese hoped to see an end to the imposed and unequal foreign treaties under which China had been coerced to grant

Western powers and Japan "extraterritorial" rule over the main Chinese seaports, as well as unfair and predatory trade privileges. They felt betrayed when the so-called treaty port system was left in place, frustrating Chinese hopes for territorial integrity and national self-determination. To add insult to injury, defeated Germany's land "concessions" in China were turned over to Japan as a result of a secret treaty signed in 1917 by Britain, France, and the warlord government in Beijing. The ensuing sense of national outrage and betrayal ignited a storm of popular unrest in Beijing, in which angry Chinese from all walks of life participated in a student-led demonstration held at the famous Tiananmen Square on May 4, 1919. The Tiananmen protesters were later joined by many other patriotic-minded Chinese in a nationwide wave of demonstrations, marches, strikes, and boycotts of Japanese goods that became known as the "May Fourth movement" and which contributed immensely to the explosive growth and radicalization of Chinese nationalism.

The second phase of the Chinese Revolution was the Nationalist revolution, which began in the early 1920s. By 1923 Sun Yat-sen had formed a military-political alliance with the recently formed Chinese Communist Party (CCP) in an attempt to restore national unity and prevent a civil war. Inspired by the example of Vladimir I. Lenin (1870–1924) and his Bolshevik revolution in Russia, Sun Yat-sen also established close ties with Moscow, receiving Soviet advisers, weapons, military training, and economic assistance. With Soviet help, Sun Yat-sen and his associates set up a Nationalist government in Guangzhou, which modified Sun's "Three Principles of the People" to stress a more radical, anti-imperialist, and anticapitalist ideological agenda. The Guomindang's National Liberation Army, led by General Chiang Kai-shek (Jiang Jieshi, 1887–1975), Sun's brother-in-law, fanned out of Guangzhou to challenge the power of local warlords, who had sprung up across China in the absence of a strong central authority. But Sun's death in 1925 left the Chinese Republic without a unifying figure, and it soon fell into the internecine conflict and bloodshed that he had feared.

By 1927 Chiang Kai-shek had emerged as the Guomindang's new leader, trying to extend the authority of the Guangzhou government and meet the serious challenge posed by local warlords and their separatist ambitions, as well as by growing Communist influence throughout the country. In a military effort to reunify China, he and his Communist allies waged a successful military campaign against the powerful northern warlords, overrunning half of China's provinces and many important cities. But a new civil war broke out when Chiang moved to destroy his alliance with the Communists and also severed most ties with the Soviet Union. Under pressure from wealthier and more conservative members of the Guomindang, he turned on his erstwhile Communist allies, starting with the so-called Shanghai massacre of 1927, in which tens of thousands of Communist Party members were brutally executed by the Nationalists in Shanghai and many other Chinese cities in what came to be known as the Nationalist "White Terror."

With the Communists temporarily crushed and driven out of the cities, Chiang resumed his northern expedition against the local warlords and their private armies. By 1928 most of China, including Beijing, was finally brought under Nationalist control, thereby ending the period of warlordism (even though some northern warlords continued to defy the central government's authority until 1937). The new Guomindang government established at Nanjing, however, was weakened by the stubborn opposition of the Communists and especially by imperial Japan's invasion and occupation of Manchuria in 1931. Even after the Japanese attack, Chiang pressed the fight against the Communists, whom he regarded as the more dangerous enemy. His decision not to fight Japan's aggression in Manchuria cost him and his party a loss of support among the more nationalistic sectors of Chinese society, who began to view the Communists, rather than the Nationalists, as leading the struggle for national sovereignty and unification.

Chiang launched a series of military offensives that surrounded the Communist troops in southeast China in 1930, but legendary Communist military commander Zhu De (1886–1976) managed to break out of the encirclement and resorted to rural guerrilla warfare to harrass his Nationalist opponents. Zhu De had created a well-trained, disciplined, and highly mobile professional military corps, the Red Army, which was based on the peasantry as the main revolutionary force in a country that was predominantly rural, agrarian, and agricultural. Under constant attack by the numerically superior Guomindang troops, the Communists retreated to the southeastern province of Jiangxi, where they proclaimed the short-lived Chinese Soviet Republic (1931–1933). They introduced radical land reforms, which attracted significant support among the poor peasants. After more Nationalist assaults, the Communists were forced to flee Jiangxi, which led to their famous Long March to escape total rout. The 6,000-mile Long March to the northwest, which took place from October 1934 to October 1935, depleted the Communist ranks from over 100,000 to little more than 20,000 survivors, mainly as a result of skirmishes with the pursuing Guomindang soldiers, as well as the harsh weather and terrain conditions. But it also resulted in the emergence of Mao Zedong as the ablest and most charismatic Communist leader. The exhausted Red Army troops finally settled around Yenan in Shanxi Province, where they remained until 1946.

Chiang Kai-shek ordered the Manchurian units of his army to move against Mao's weakened forces in 1936, but his plan to finish off the Communists backfired. Determined to liberate their home region from Japanese occupation and encouraged by the Communists, mutinous Manchurian officers arrested Chiang and held him captive for two weeks, demanding an end to the civil war and the formation of a united front against Japan. Their patriotic revolt eventually led to an uneasy alliance between the Guomindang and the Communists to expel the foreign invader. For a while, most of China rallied behind the Guomindang government for an all-out resistance against the Japanese. In 1937 full-scale fighting broke out between the Chinese and the Japanese Imperial Army in the so-called Second Sino-Japanese War, which later merged with World War II (1939–1945). The Japanese armies overran most of eastern China and the main coastal cities, which forced the Guomindang government to relocate its capital far inland to Chongqing. Japan's brutal occupation and wanton disregard for Chinese lives was symbolized by the infamous "rape of Nanjing," in which Japanese soldiers pillaged and burned the city, while systematically massacring nearly three hundred thousand men, women, and children. With logistical and air support from the United States and Britain, the Chinese troops—especially the militarily more effective Communist guerrilla units—managed to tie down the bulk of the Japanese Imperial Army inside mainland China. Abandoned by the Guomindang government, millions of poor peasants in eastern China turned away from the Nationalists, relying instead on the Red Army for protection from the Japanese occupation forces. The national mass mobilization in the struggle against Japan only reinforced the existing bonds of unity and cooperation between the peasantry and the Communists that had originated in the years of their Yenan retreat. Animosity between the Nationalists and the Communists persisted, however, as Chiang's army continued to blockade the areas under Mao's control.

The last phase of the Chinese Revolution was the Communist revolution, which began with the resumption of the civil war, temporarily interrupted by the Sino-Japanese War of 1937 to 1945, and culminated with Communist Party rule being established throughout China in 1949. While all Chinese had pooled military resources against the Japanese during World War II, open civil war flared up again in 1946, when the Red Army (now renamed the People's Liberation Army) and the ruling Nationalists resumed fighting each other. Dominated by the conservative landlord class, which was determined to preserve the traditional semifeudal order, the Guomindang was losing the support of urban-based middle-class professionals and businessmen, who demanded wide-ranging social and economic reforms. Using skillful

propaganda and moderating their radical land redistribution program, the Communists mobilized millions of disaffected Chinese, especially in the impoverished countryside. By 1945 the Communist Party had more than 1.2 million members and the People's Liberation Army numbered about 1 million soldiers ready to fight to the death for the proclaimed Communist ideals of economic equality, social justice, and national independence. With strong support from Moscow, the Communists had acquired the numbers, organizational resources, and military strength necessary to successfully challenge Guomindang rule. Diplomatic efforts, spearheaded by U.S. general George Catlett Marshall (1880–1959), to mediate a negotiated agreement between the warring parties failed to prevent the renewal of all-out conflict.

At first the strategic initiative was in the hands of the Nationalists, who were receiving substantial U.S. military and financial assistance. American ships and planes helped transport Chiang's troops, who captured all principal cities, including Yenan, the coastal areas, and most of northern China, but failed to weaken the Communist stranglehold on the countryside. Communist military leader Zhu De used aggressive guerrilla tactics, launching hard-hitting counterattacks against the enemy's overstretched overland lines of communications and supply. Throughout 1948 the Communist "war of the villages against the cities" proved to be so effective in encircling enemy-held areas and urban centers that the Nationalist troops in Manchuria were completely cut off and had to be resupplied by air. By the end of the year, all of China north of the Yangtze River was under Mao's control. In 1949 the demoralized Nationalist forces were decisively defeated, compelling Chiang Kai-shek to resign the presidency and seek a negotiated peace with his adversaries. But it was too late for any compromise settlement with the victorious Communists. Meeting only token resistance, the People's Liberation Army began its final push to capture the remainder of China south of the Yangtze, including the major cities of Nanjing, Guangzhou, and Shanghai. On January 31, Beijing fell to the advancing Communist forces. Following their total defeat, Chiang, his government, and fifty thousand surviving Nationalist soldiers were evacuated to the island of Formosa (now Taiwan), where the Guomindang was the dominant political party into the 1990s. With the civil war finally over, on October 1, 1949, Mao Zedong proclaimed the People's Republic of China before huge cheering crowds in Beijing's Tiananmen Square.

SEE ALSO *Communism; Guerrilla Warfare; Mao Zedong; Mobilization; Nationalism and Nationality; Revolution; Sun Yat-sen; Union of Soviet Socialist Republics*

BIBLIOGRAPHY

Bianco, Lucien. 1971. *Origins of the Chinese Revolution, 1915–1949*. Trans. Muriel Bell. Stanford, CA: Stanford University Press.

Eastman, Lloyd E. 1984. *Seeds of Destruction: Nationalist China in War and Revolution, 1937–1949*. Stanford, CA: Stanford University Press.

Leutner, Mechthild, ed. 2002. *The Chinese Revolution in the 1920s: Between Triumph and Disaster*. London and New York: Routledge Curzon.

Saich, Tony, ed. 1996. *The Rise to Power of the Chinese Communist Party: Documents and Analysis*. Armonk, NY: Sharpe.

Saich, Tony, and Hans J. van de Ven, eds. 1995. *New Perspectives on the Chinese Communist Revolution*. Armonk, NY: Sharpe.

Schiffrin, Harold Z. 1968. *Sun Yat-sen and the Origins of the Chinese Revolution*. Berkeley: University of California Press.

Schrecker, John E. 2004. *The Chinese Revolution in Historical Perspective*. 2nd ed. Westport, CT: Praeger.

Sheridan, James E. 1975. *China in Disintegration: The Republican Era in Chinese History, 1912–1949*. New York: Free Press.

Snow, Edgar. 1968. *Red Star over China*. Rev. and enlarged ed. New York: Grove.

Weston, Anthony. 1980. *The Chinese Revolution*. Saint Paul, MN: Greenhaven.

Rossen Vassilev

CHISHOLM, SHIRLEY
1924–2005

Shirley Anita St. Hill Chisholm, the first black woman elected to the U.S. Congress, was born in Brooklyn, New York, on November 30, 1924. Chisholm graduated from Brooklyn College in 1946 and began her career as an educator. Her belief in the power and necessity of education motivated her to earn her master's degree in early childhood education from Columbia University in New York in 1952 and eventually launched the political career for which she is revered. Working with the New York City Bureau of Child Welfare, along with her involvement in local organizations, Chisholm solidified many of the relationships that led to her election to the New York State Assembly in 1964. Only four years after assuming that position, Chisholm made the transition from state politics to national politics with her election to the U.S. House of Representatives in 1968, becoming the first black woman elected to Congress.

In Congress, Chisholm continued to live up to her campaign slogan of "Unbought and Unbossed." She routinely spoke against politics and policies that she viewed as unfavorable to the American people. Moreover, Chisholm did not let the exigencies of reelection rule her actions in Congress. She did what she thought was right, proper, and best. This frequently made her unpopular both with her mostly male colleagues and her constituents. As a result, much of Chisholm's career was spent on the margins. She was conscious of how both her race and gender excluded her from the male dominated social network that ran Congress. Her commitment never waned, despite this opposition, and as a result she was elected to seven terms in the House of Representatives before retiring in 1982. She was also one of the founding members of the Congressional Black Caucus in 1971.

Despite her historical importance as a congresswoman, Chisholm is best known for her run for the U.S. presidency in 1972. Chisholm ran in the Democratic primary against several male contenders, but not to win in a conventional sense. Chisholm felt that her candidacy served primarily a reform function by keeping her male counterparts focused on the issues. Despite her intentions in entering the race, she faced discrimination from the mostly male political establishment. Many felt that Chisholm should have allowed a black man to run for president before a women tried to do so. Furthermore, her presence in the race was unwelcome, as evidenced by the lack of media coverage of her candidacy. Well aware of these dynamics, Chisholm was undaunted and entered the primary. Though she would lose, she was able to make a notable showing in the primary. After her foray into presidential politics, Chisholm returned to the House of Representatives, where she served until 1982. Upon retiring, Chisholm settled into a quiet life with her husband, Arthur Hardwick. In 1991 Chisholm, now a widow, relocated to Florida where she lived until her death in January 2005.

Chisholm's success came from her commitment to humanistic, people-centered leadership. She wanted to inspire individuals, especially women, to believe in their abilities to effect change in their world. Her goals transcended color as she worked tirelessly for a responsive government that would act for the sake of all people, not for special interests. Though it cost her at times, Chisholm remained faithful to the principles of democracy. She was a reflective leader at a tumultuous time, and this is the legacy her leadership leaves behind.

SEE ALSO *National Organization of Women; Women and Politics*

BIBLIOGRAPHY

Brownmiller, Susan. 1970. *Shirley Chisholm: A Biography*. Garden City, NY: Doubleday.

Chisholm, Shirley. 1970. *Unbought and Unbossed*. Boston: Houghton Mifflin.

Chisholm, Shirley. 1973. *The Good Fight*. New York: Harper.

Duffy, Susan, ed. 1988. *Shirley Chisholm: A Bibliography of Writings by and about Her*. Metuchen, NJ: Scarecrow.

Niambi Carter

CHI-SQUARE

The term *chi-square* (χ^2) refers to a distribution, a variable that is χ^2-distributed, or a statistical test employing the χ^2 distribution. A χ^2 distribution with k degrees of freedom (*df*) has mean k, variance $2k$, and mode $k - 2$ (if $k > 2$), and is denoted χ^2_{df}. Much of its usefulness in statistical inference derives from the fact that the sample variance of a normally distributed variable is χ^2-distributed with $df = N - 1$. All χ^2 distributions are asymmetrical, right-skewed, and non-negative. Owing to the broad utility of the χ^2 distribution, tabled χ^2 probability values can be found in virtually every introductory statistics text.

X^2 TEST FOR POPULATION VARIANCES

A test of the null hypothesis that $\sigma^2 = \sigma^2_0$ (e.g., $H_0: \sigma^2 = 1.8$) is conducted by obtaining the sample variance s^2, computing the test statistic

$$G = \frac{(N - 1)s^2}{\sigma^2_0} \qquad (1)$$

and consulting values of the χ^2_{N-1} distribution. For a two-tailed test, G is compared to the critical values associated with the lower and upper $(50 \times \alpha)\%$ of the χ^2_{N-1} distribution. Rejection implies, with confidence $1 - \alpha$, that the sample is not drawn from a normally distributed population with variance σ^2_0.

X^2 TESTS OF GOODNESS OF FIT AND INDEPENDENCE

The χ^2 goodness of fit test compares two finite frequency distributions—one a set of observed frequency counts in C categories, the other a set of counts expected on the basis of theory or chance. The statistic

$$G = \sum_{i=1}^{C} \frac{(O_i - E_i)^2}{E_i} \qquad (2)$$

is computed, where O_i and E_i are, respectively, the observed and expected frequencies for category i given a fixed total sample size N. G is approximately χ^2-distributed with $df = C - 1$. If the null hypothesis of equality is rejected, the test implies a statistically significant departure from expectations.

This test can be extended to test the null hypothesis that several frequency distributions are independent. For example, given a 3×4 contingency table of frequencies, where $R = 3$ rows (conditions) and $C = 4$ columns (categories), G may be computed as

$$G = \sum_{j=1}^{R} \sum_{i=1}^{C} \frac{(O_{ij} - E_{ij})^2}{E_{ij}} \qquad (3)$$

and compared against a $\chi^2_{(R-1)(C-1)}$ distribution. Expected frequencies are computed as the product of the marginal totals for column i and row j divided by N. Rejection of the null hypothesis implies that not all rows (or columns) were sampled from independent populations. This test may be extended to any number of dimensions.

These χ^2 tests have been found to work well with average expected frequencies as low as 2. However, these tests are inappropriate if the assumption of independent observations is violated.

COMPARISON OF DISTRIBUTIONS

A common application of χ^2 is to test the hypothesis that a sample's parent population follows a particular continuous probability density function. The test is conducted by first dividing the hypothetical distribution into C "bins" of equal width. The frequencies expected for each bin (E_j) are approximated by computing the probability of randomly selecting a case from that bin and multiplying by N. Observed frequencies (O_j) are obtained by using the same bin limits in the observed distribution. The one-tailed test is conducted by using equation 2 and comparing the result to the critical value drawn from a χ^2_{C-1} distribution. Note that the number of bins, and points of division between bins, must be chosen arbitrarily, yet these decisions can have a large impact on conclusions.

The χ^2 distribution has many other applications in the social sciences, including Bartlett's test of homogeneity of variance, Friedman's test for median differences, tests for heteroscedasticity, nonparametric measures of association, and likelihood ratios. In addition, χ^2 statistics form the basis for many model fit and selection indices used in latent variable analyses, item response theory, logistic regression, and other advanced techniques. All of these methods involve the evaluation of the discrepancy between a model's implications and observed data.

SEE ALSO *Distribution, Normal*

BIBLIOGRAPHY

Howell, David C. 2006. *Statistical Methods for Psychology*. 6th ed. Belmont, CA: Wadsworth Publishing.

Pearson, Karl. 1900. On the Criterion That a Given System of Deviations From the Probable in the Case of a Correlated System of Variables Is Such That It Can Be Reasonably

Supposed To Have Arisen From Random Sampling. *Philosophical Magazine* 50: 157–175.

Kristopher J. Preacher

CHOICE IN ECONOMICS

The theory of choice, individual and social, was mainly developed by economists, with crucial contributions from psychologists, political scientists, sociologists, mathematicians, and philosophers.

Individual choice concerns the selection by an individual of alternatives from a set. In standard microeconomic theory, the individual is supposed to have a preference over a set (or a utility function, that is, a numerical representation of the preference). A standard behavioral assumption asserts that the individual selects the best alternatives according to his or her preference. This implies that the preference and the set of alternatives have appropriate mathematical properties. This is the case, for instance, if the set of alternatives is *finite* (the number of alternatives is a positive integer) and the preference is a *weak ordering* (a ranking of the alternatives from the most preferred to the least preferred with possible ties). When the set of alternatives is the standard budget set of microeconomics, the selection is still possible when appropriate topological assumptions are made on the weak ordering and the space of goods. The selected alternatives are the *demand set*. If there is a single alternative, it is the *individual demand*. It will depend, given a preference, on the budget set that is defined by the individual's wealth and the prices. For a given wealth, as a consequence, demand depends on prices. The behavioral maximization assumption is illuminatingly discussed by Amartya Sen (2002).

Although in microeconomics the standard direction is from preference (or utility) to choice (or demand), *revealed preference theory* reverses this direction. It is alleged that choice is observable, but preference is not. In revealed preference theory, choice is supposed to reveal preference. More precisely, if choice satisfies suitable consistency properties, one can retrieve preference. As an example of such a consistency condition, imagine that you are making a choice in a department store that includes a food department. Your choice in the entire store that happens to be food must be identical to the selection of food you would make if you visited only the food department. Given this kind of consistency condition, it is possible to retrieve a preference that is a weak ordering.

Uncertainty in individual choice differs whether it is *objective uncertainty*, à la John von Neumann (1903–1957) and Oskar Morgenstern (1902–1977), or *subjective uncertainty*, à la Leonard Savage (1917–1971). This entry will discuss only objective uncertainty. In this case, the recourse to utility functions is imperative. The set of alternatives is the set of probabilities over prospects—say, lotteries if the prospects are prizes. The individual has a preference given, for instance, by a weak ordering over the set of lotteries. With a utility function representing a weak ordering (which is possible given appropriate conditions), the only property of the real numbers one can use is the ordering property ("greater than or equal to"). The utility functions are said to be ordinal. They are unique up to a strictly increasing transformation. Over lotteries (with further assumptions), one obtains a utility function (called the *von Neumann-Morgenstern utility function*) that satisfies the expected utility hypothesis: The utility of a lottery is equal to the sum of the utilities of the prizes weighted by the probabilities. For instance, in a lottery with two prizes, a bicycle and a car, if the probability to win the bicycle is .99 and the probability to win the car is .01, the utility of the lottery is equal to .99 times the utility of the bicycle plus .01 times the utility of the car. When the expected utility hypothesis is satisfied, the utility function is unique up to an affine positive transformation, and differences of utility become meaningful because these differences can be compared according to the "greater than or equal to" relation. Such utility functions are called *cardinal*. They are used as the basic element of decision theory under risk, where some further assumptions are made on the utility function (concavity, derivability and properties of derivatives).

Social choice is about the selection of alternatives made by a group of individuals. There are obviously two aspects of social choice corresponding to its double origin: voting and social ethics. Although there were precursors in antiquity and medieval times, the birth of social choice theory is generally attributed to the Marquis de Condorcet (1743–1794) and Jean-Charles Borda (1733–1799), two French scholars, at the end of the eighteenth century. The tremendous modern development of this theory stems from the works of Kenneth Arrow and Duncan Black (1908–1991). Individuals are supposed to have preferences over a set of alternatives. Since these preferences are generally conflicting, one must construct rules to obtain a synthetic (or social) preference or a social choice. Arrow's (im)possibility theorem asserts that there does not exist any rule satisfying specified properties. On the other hand, Black's analysis demonstrates that majority rule generates a social preference provided that some homogeneity of individual preferences (single-peakedness) is assumed.

Arrow's book ([1951] 1963) established the formalism in which social choice theory has developed since then. Two major results are due to Sen and to Allan Gibbard and Mark Satterthwaite. Sen showed the impossibility of having a rule that admits a minimal level of liberty in the society (the group of individuals) and a principle of unanimity (according to which the social preference or the social choice must respect the unanimous preferences of the individuals). Gibbard and Satterthwaite proved independently that there was no rule that was immune to the strategic behavior of individuals—that is, there are situations in which it is advantageous for an individual to reveal a preference that is not his or her sincere preference.

When individual preferences are over uncertain prospects and are represented by von Neumann-Morgenstern utility functions, John Harsanyi (1920–2000) showed that the utilitarianism doctrine could be revived. In a rather caricatural way, the utilitarianism doctrine asserts that social utility is the sum of individual utilities and that social utility has to be maximized. In some of his works, Harsanyi provided a scientific foundation for a kind of weighted utilitarianism. Harsanyi's utilitarianism is often opposed to the liberal egalitarianism of John Rawls (1921–2002).

A major trend of recent research on voting theory is about scoring systems (e.g., the plurality rule used in the United States and Great Britain or Borda's rule). Donald Saari's contributions to scoring rules are a major advance in social choice and voting theory, with important possible applications.

SEE ALSO *Arrow, Kenneth J.; Condorcet, Marquis de; Constrained Choice; Expected Utility Theory; Maximization; Paradox of Voting; Rationality; Rawls, John; Risk; Trade-offs; Uncertainty; Utilitarianism; Utility Function; Utility, Von Neumann-Morgenstern; Von Neumann, John; Voting Schemes; Welfare Economics*

BIBLIOGRAPHY

Arrow, Kenneth J. [1951] 1963. *Social Choice and Individual Values.* 2nd ed. New York: Wiley.

Arrow Kenneth J. 1984. *Collected Papers,* Vol. 1: *Social Choice and Justice.* Oxford: Blackwell.

Arrow Kenneth J. 1984. *Collected Papers,* Vol. 3: *Individual Choice under Certainty and Uncertainty.* Oxford: Blackwell.

Black, Duncan. 1958. *The Theory of Committees and Elections.* Cambridge, U.K.: Cambridge University Press.

Gaertner, Wulf. 2006. *A Primer in Social Choice Theory.* Oxford: Oxford University Press.

Harsanyi, John C. 1976. *Essays on Ethics, Social Behavior, and Scientific Explanation.* Dordrecht, Netherlands: Reidel.

Kahneman Daniel, and Amos Tversky, eds. 2000. *Choices, Values, and Frames.* Cambridge, U.K.: Cambridge University Press.

Kreps, David M. 1988. *Notes on the Theory of Choice.* Boulder, CO: Westview.

Saari, Donald. 1995. *Basic Geometry of Voting.* Berlin: Springer.

Sen, Amartya K. 1970. *Collective Choice and Social Welfare.* San Francisco, CA: Holden-Day.

Sen, Amartya K. 2002. *Rationality and Freedom.* Cambridge, MA: Harvard University Press.

Taylor, Alan D. 2005. *Social Choice and the Mathematics of Manipulation.* Cambridge, U.K.: Cambridge University Press.

von Neumann, John, and Oskar Morgenstern. 1953. *The Theory of Games and Economic Behavior.* 3rd ed. Princeton, NJ: Princeton University Press.

Maurice Salles

CHOICE IN PSYCHOLOGY

Since the mid-twentieth century the term choice has been operationally defined in a variety of different ways in psychology. Consequently, the study of choice in psychology reflects this variability. Choice has often been studied as the outcome of a decision-making process. Economic theories of rational choice assume both that the decisions individuals make will determine their behavior and that decisions will be made based on a general set of rational laws. In particular, it is assumed that (1) the decision maker is able to compare all of the alternatives; (2) all comparisons will be consistent (i.e., if A is preferred to B, and B to C, C may not be preferred to A), and (3) the decision maker will engage in utility maximization; that is, will always choose the most preferred option to achieve desired ends.

Aware of the reality that the decisions people make do not always conform to conventional economic assumptions of rational choice, the psychologist Herbert Simon proposed the notion of bounded rationality. That is, rational choice is limited by the cognitive capability of the individual and the complexity of the environment in which a decision is made. Simon proposed that agents will, therefore, engage in satisficing, or accept a choice that is good enough but not necessarily perfect. Simon's assertions pointed to a notable difference between economic and psychological views of rationality. Namely, traditional economic theories assume that the world is perceived as it really is and that there are no limits on the decision maker's cognitive capabilities. Consequently, economics takes a substantive view of rationality. That is, choices can be predicted based entirely on knowledge about the real world because decision makers always reach a decision that is objectively optimal. In contrast, a strength of the psychological view of rationality is that it is assumed that the decision maker has limited knowledge and cognitive capacity and does not necessarily perceive the world the way it really is. Consequently, psychological theories focus on the process by which decisions are made.

Building on Simon's contributions, cognitive psychologists Amos Tversky and Daniel Kahneman originated prospect theory to explain irrational human economic choices. In empirical studies on framing, Tversky and Kahneman demonstrated systematic reversals of preference when the same problem is presented in different ways. For example, when decisions are framed in terms of a potential gain, individuals are more likely to engage in risk aversion. Whereas when decisions are framed in terms of a loss, individuals will be more likely to choose the risky option. Tversky and Kahneman documented a number of judgment heuristics and biases that influence the way people assess probabilities under uncertain conditions and thus influence the decisions they make. Notable heuristics and biases include the availability heuristic, base-rate fallacy, anchoring and adjustment, conjunction fallacy, clustering illusion, and representativeness heuristic.

Psychologists have also studied choice as an experience that has consequences for an individual's sense of personal control, motivation, and self-regulation. According to Edward Deci and other theorists, it is theorized that autonomy and competence are fundamental human needs that underlie intrinsic motivation, the drive to engage in a task for its own sake. Social contexts that satisfy these needs will enhance intrinsic motivation and related outcomes. Consequently, research on the topic has suggested that the provision of choice may be one contextual factor linked to adaptive motivational and achievement outcomes. Even the perception of choice, as opposed to true choices, has been demonstrated to have beneficial effects on motivation-related constructs.

However, late-twentieth-century research has suggested that choice is not ubiquitously beneficial. In particular, although Caucasian Americans seem to benefit from making personal choices, individuals from Asian cultures seem to benefit more when choices are made by significant others. Further, proponents of self-regulatory perspectives of choice have shown that choice may actually have detrimental effects to the extent that making a choice is effortful, resulting in decreased energy needed for future tasks. In fact, research has shown that having fewer choices is more motivating than having an extensive, and potentially overwhelming, array of choices. Potential explanations for contradictory findings have been offered.

In particular, the nature of the choice experience may be influential moderator of the effect.

SEE ALSO *Choice in Economics; Decision-making; Rational Choice Theory; Rationality*

BIBLIOGRAPHY

Iyengar, Sheena S., and Mark Lepper. 2002. Choice and Its Consequences: On the Costs and Benefits of Self-Determination. In *Self and Motivation: Emerging Psychological Perspectives*. Eds. Abraham Tesser, Diederik A. Stapel, and Joanne V. Wood, 71–96. Washington, DC: American Psychological Association.

Simon, Herbert A. [1982] 1997. *Models of Bounded Rationality*. Vols. 1–3. Cambridge, MA: MIT Press.

Simon, Herbert A. 1987. Rationality in Psychology and Economics. In *Rational Choice: The Contrast between Economics and Psychology*. Eds. Robin M. Hogarth and Melvin W. Reder, 25–40. Chicago: University of Chicago Press.

Tversky, Amos, and Daniel Kahneman. 1974. Judgment under Uncertainty: Heuristics and Biases. *Science* 185 (4157): 1124–1131.

Tversky, Amos, and Daniel Kahneman. 1981. The Framing of Decisions and the Psychology of Choice. *Science* 211 (4481): 453–458.

Erika A. Patall

CHOLESKY DECOMPOSITION

The Cholesky decomposition factorizes a positive definite matrix A into a lower triangular matrix L and its transpose, L':

$$A = LL'$$

This decomposition is named after André-Louis Cholesky (1875–1918), a French artillery officer who invented the method in the context of his work in the Geodesic Section of the Army Geographic Service.

The $k \times k$ real symmetric matrix A is positive definite if and only if $x'Ax > 0$ for any nonzero k-vector. For such matrices, the corresponding Cholesky factor L (sometimes called the *matrix square root*) always exists and is unique. Matrices of this sort arise in many econometric contexts, making the Cholesky decomposition a very useful computational tool. For example, it can be used to solve the normal equations of least squares to produce coefficient estimates in multiple regression analysis. In this case, the place of A is occupied by the matrix of squares and cross-products of the regressors, $X'X$.

Given the Cholesky decomposition of *A*, the set of linear equations *Ax = b* in the unknown vector *x* may be written as *LL′x = b*. Writing *y* for *L′x*, we get *Ly = b*, which may be solved for *y*, then *y = L′x* is solved for *x*. It is trivial to solve equations on the pattern *Mx = b* for triangular *M*.

Algorithms for computing the decomposition are based on the following relationships between the elements a_{ij} of *A* and the elements l_{ij} of *L*:

$$l_{i,j} = \frac{1}{l_{j,j}} \left(a_{i,j} - \sum_{k=1}^{j-1} l_{i,k} l_{j,k} \right), \quad i > j \quad (1)$$

$$l_{i,i} = \sqrt{a_{i,i} - \sum_{k=1}^{i-1} l_{i,k}^2} \quad (2)$$

Element l_{ij} can be computed if we know the elements to the left and above. The Cholesky-Crout algorithm starts from the upper left corner of *L* and calculates the matrix column by column.

The beauty of the Cholesky method is that it is numerically stable and accurate (as noted by Turing 1948) while requiring fewer floating-point operations and less workspace (computer memory) than alternative methods. It does, however, have a problem if the matrix *A* is very ill-conditioned. (In the econometric context mentioned above, this occurs if there is a high degree of collinearity among the variables in the data matrix *X*.) Computing the decomposition requires that we calculate a sequence of square roots. The values under the square root sign in equation (2) are always positive in exact arithmetic, but for ill-conditioned *A* they may be very small. Given the rounding error inherent in finite-precision computer arithmetic, these values may go negative—in which case the algorithm cannot continue—or they may simply fall below the magnitude at which rounding error is an acceptable proportion of the computed value. A practical implementation of the Cholesky algorithm for a digital computer must check for this condition and terminate if need be. If the Cholesky method fails, one can resort to the computationally more expensive QR or SVD decomposition methods.

Besides solving sets of linear equations, the Cholesky decomposition has a further use in econometrics that deserves mention, namely, decomposing the covariance matrix for a set of residuals in the context of a vector autoregression. This sort of analysis was pioneered by Christopher Sims (1980) and quickly became popular. The role of the decomposition is to permit the simulation of the response of a system to a disturbance in any one of the variables, and also to perform an accounting of the proportions of the forecast error variance attributable to disturbances in each of the variables.

SEE ALSO *Matrix Algebra*

BIBLIOGRAPHY

Golub, Gene H., and Charles F. Van Loan. 1996. *Matrix Computations*. 3rd ed. Baltimore, MD: Johns Hopkins University Press.

O'Connor, John J., and Edmund F. Robertson. 2005. André-Louis Cholesky. School of Mathematics and Statistics, University of St. Andrews: MacTutor History of Mathematics archive. http://www-history.mcs.st-andrews.ac.uk/Biographies/Cholesky.html.

Sims, Christopher. 1980. Macroeconomics and Reality. *Econometrica* 48 (1): 1–48.

Turing, Alan M. 1948. Rounding-Off Errors in Matrix Processes. *Quarterly Journal of Mechanics and Applied Mathematics* 1 (1): 287–308.

Allin Cottrell

CHOMSKY, NOAM
1928–

In the field of linguistics, Noam Chomsky occupies a position close to that held by Isaac Newton in physics during the eighteenth century. Because language is central to being human, Chomsky has also long occupied a foundational role in the cognitive sciences that have burgeoned since the middle of the twentieth century. While Newton had an equally intense and ambitious career as an alchemist and a doomsday Biblical scholar, the politic Sir Isaac kept these careers, largely successfully, a dark secret. Chomsky, however, has published dozens of books and countless articles throughout his life expressing leftist, egalitarian, anarchist views with almost unimpeachable moral authority and meticulous scholarship. Yet Chomsky has insisted that his scientific work in no way supports or "proves" his political views, other than his insistence that humans, in having cognitive command of a discrete infinity of linguistic structures, are beyond the comprehension of the empiricist behaviorism dominant in mid-twentieth-century American academic circles.

Born in Philadelphia in 1928, Chomsky pursued his undergraduate studies at the University of Pennsylvania, where he studied with Zellig Harris, a structural linguist who saw linguistics as the compact description of a community's time-bound finite corpus of utterances (literally, sonic sequences of supposed phonetic atoms). Chomsky completed his graduate work while a Junior Fellow at Harvard University between 1951 and 1954, and he became a professor at MIT in 1955, rapidly advancing to a series of distinguished professorships. His books *Syntactic Structures* (1957) and *Aspects of the Theory of*

Syntax (1965), which have made him the most cited living author, soon revolutionized linguistics.

The opening three sentences of *Syntactic Structures* tersely render his formalized, mentalist, and nativist view:

> Syntactical investigation of a given language has as its goal the construction of a device for producing the sentences of the language under investigation…. The ultimate outcome of [such] investigations should be a theory of linguistic structures in which the descriptive devices utilized in particular grammars are presented and studied abstractly…. One function of this theory is to provide a general method for selecting a grammar for each language, given a corpus of this language. (Chomsky 1957, p. x)

Formally speaking, one cannot describe a human language by listing its sentences, simply because there are an infinite number of them. One must therefore describe a device that would generate these, and only these, sentences. This "device" would display the knowledge that a competent human speaker of this language has. Language is the device, the internal brain/mind device, not the finite behavioral outputs that this device, coupled with others, produces. Linguistics is thus a branch of psychology.

Behaviorists such as B. F. Skinner thought that knowledge of language consisted of associations between particular words (heard sound sequences). Through repetition, humans learn the sound sequences "How are you," "I would like a red apple," and "I am fine," but not "Are you how," "Red a like would I apple," "Am fine I," and so on. An associative grammar like this is called *finite state* grammar; it fits well with the empiricist notion that humans learn everything through (sequences of) sensory experience, and it makes no use of "dubious" abstractions such as noun, pronoun, verb, auxiliary verb, or adjective.

Yet there is massive evidence that people routinely produce new sentences that they have never heard before and that have never been produced in the history of their language. Even if sentences are limited to fifteen words or less, there are literally trillions of different but perfectly grammatical sentences of English. In fact, Chomsky gave a decisive formal proof that no human language could be generated by a finite-state grammar. We simply have to internalize at least a *phrase structure* grammar that makes use of rules that deal in abstract categories such as noun phrase, verb phrase, noun, pronoun, verb, auxiliary verb, adjective, and so on. Indeed, Chomsky proved that even a phrase-structure grammar is not all that is needed, and that the surface structure of a sentence is not a reliable guide to its deeper features.

Human languages have in common many principles and processes, word forms and structures, and rules and features. What the linguist describes, therefore, belongs to human language as much as to a particular language (abstracting, of course, from the peculiarities of particular idiolects and dialects toward humanly universal cognition). Indeed, every one of the hundreds of human language that has been described makes use of the same phrase-structural concepts of noun phrase, verb phrase, pronoun, verb, adjective, and so on. In the linguistic theory of the last two decades, it appears that a small number of principles and initial parameter settings determine every aspect of grammar that makes a human language and differentiates it from other human languages (a good thing, too, because the human baby seems equally prepared to take on any human language to which it is exposed). Chomsky has speculated that a Martian anthropologist would regard all human languages as essentially the same language.

"A general method for selecting a grammar for each language," given a sample corpus, would also be the knowledge a human child brings to the samples of a language to which the child is exposed. A vast body of evidence about child language development has persuaded nearly all linguists and cognitive scientists that the human child is preprogrammed with a "language acquisition device." To give an example from personal experience that is familiar to investigators of language learning, the two-year-old daughter of this author, Casey, exploded into using auxiliary verbs and tag negations over the space of two weeks, saying "I am going," "I can't," "Susan isn't here." All of the auxiliary verbs came in at virtually the same time, and Casey tag-negated only those verbs, no others: She never said "I eatn't," "I gon't," "Susan walkn't," or "The cat grabn't the bird." She also said "I amn't" and "I am going, amn't I." No one around Casey ever said "amn't," but she went on happily using the construction, and it wasn't until she started school two years later that she realized no one else talked that way. Of course, Casey was doing what comes naturally. In some sense, she (or some part of her brain/mind) knew what auxiliary verbs and regular verbs were, and she knew that you could tag-negate (put "n't" after) auxiliaries but not after other verbs. She also never said "I am going, aren't I," because she knew that "am" is a singular verb, that "are" is a plural verb, and that "I," being a singular pronoun, could not take a plural verb ("are").

Now, of course, Casey had never heard the English words "noun," "verb," "auxiliary verb," "tag-negate," "pronoun," "plural," or "singular." Nonetheless, she (or some part of her brain) knew perfectly well the word kinds that these English words name, just as a monolingual speaker of Urdu knows what nouns, pronouns, and verbs are, although he may have no idea what spoken label (in Urdu or English) to use for these perfectly familiar word kinds. It is this sense of knowing, of linguistic competence, that linguistics now clearly emphasizes.

But how did Casey know about these things when no one around her ever tried to explain them to her? The linguist's answer is that hearing something is an auxiliary verb or a pronoun is just like seeing that something is a red ball or a small animal. So Casey, just like any other human child whether in a literate or tribal community, identified the different word kinds present in her environment, although no one was explicitly coaching her to do this. She recognized that auxiliary verbs, but not other verbs, could be tag-negated, so she said "I amn't," just as she said "I can't" or "He isn't," because she saw that "am" was an auxiliary verb, and so could be tagged with "n't." Speaking and hearing a natural language is a competence acquired naturally (in the first several years of life), while reading and writing requires—unfortunately—years of effort and explicit instruction. Similarly, our basic visual/motor competencies come to us naturally in our first years. Our recently burgeoning "cognitive sciences" attend to this central aspect of being human, the characteristic competencies or faculties that make us *homo sapiens*.

Chomsky maintains that his work in linguistics, and cognitive science generally, have virtually no connection with his political and moral views—views for which he claims no expertise, although he has published countless articles, books, interviews, and commentaries on political and moral matters. He claims no professional expertise in such matters because he believes that no one really has such expertise. To Chomsky, political and moral matters can and must be understood by all citizens, not just by elites or would-be professional apologists for elites (or, more particularly, corporate wealth and power). Chomsky rose to public attention (and the Nixon White House's "enemies" list) for his opposition to the Vietnam War, although his subsequent opposition to U.S. imperialism more generally, particularly in the Middle East, and his criticism of the U.S. media bias have muted his ability to address the U.S. public. Hence, Chomsky and his political and moral views are better known outside of the United States. It should be said that Chomsky has consistently maintained that U.S. behavior, as a dominant world power, is no worse than previous dominant world powers, such as Britain in the eighteenth and nineteenth centuries and Imperial Rome.

BIBLIOGRAPHY

Barsky, Robert. 1997. *Noam Chomsky: A Life of Dissent.* Cambridge, MA: MIT Press.

Chomsky, Noam. 1957. *Syntactic Structures.* The Hague: Mouton.

Chomsky, Noam. 1965. *Aspects of the Theory of Syntax.* Cambridge, MA: MIT Press.

Leiber, Justin. 1975. *Noam Chomsky: A Philosophic Overview.* New York: St. Martin's Press.

Justin Leiber

CHOW TEST

The term *Chow test* refers to a family of statistical tests used mainly, but not exclusively, in econometrics. The aim of all the tests in the family is to test for parameter constancy across all the observations of the sample of data under analysis. In econometric modeling, parameters usually have some economic interpretation, such as the responsiveness, or elasticity, of some variable to changes in another. If a model is to have any predictive power, it is important to check the assumption of parameter constancy. A Chow test is a way to perform such a check.

Economic data frequently take the form of time series. A time series constitutes a record of the history of an economic variable, such as the unemployment rate. Each individual observation of a time series is associated with a given period of time, which may be a year, a quarter, or even, in the case of financial data, a few minutes. In time series modeling, one looks for patterns in the dynamic evolution of a set of series. Such patterns can take various general forms, but all of them depend on parameters, the values of which are usually unknown.

From time to time the economic environment undergoes structural changes. A classic example is the Great Depression of the 1930s, a later one the abandonment in the 1990s of many European national currencies in favor of a single currency, the euro. Changes of this importance can be expected to lead to changes in the values of at least some of the parameters of economic models, and these changes often can be detected by a Chow test.

The term *cross-section data* is used to designate data sets that record aspects of economic units, such as firms, households, or governments, at a particular point in time. Failure of parameter constancy can arise in cross-section models if the observed units display too much heterogeneity so that, for instance, men may be described by parameters different from those suitable for women, rich countries may differ from poor ones, and small firms from large ones.

In 1960 Gregory Chow, then an associate professor at Cornell University (and from 1970 to 2001 a professor of economics at Princeton University, where the Econometric Research Program is now named in his honor), published a paper in *Econometrica* in which he laid out various versions of the Chow test. Chow's main research interest at that time was the demand for automobiles in the United States. In earlier work he had proposed an econometric model based on data for the years 1921 to 1953, and as data had become available for the period 1954 to 1957, Chow wanted to see whether his old model could explain the new data. He used the tests he had developed in his earlier paper for this purpose, and concluded that the old model was still good.

Students of econometrics in the 1960s found Chow's paper hard to understand. Consequently, in 1970 Franklin Fisher, a professor of economics at the Massachusetts Institute of Technology, published an article in *Econometrica* in which he set Chow's tests in the context of the statistical literature, and showed how they all could be viewed as F tests, that is, standard tests used to check whether a parameter or parameters are significantly different from zero. As a result of Fisher's exposition, the Chow test became a very widely used tool of applied econometrics, implemented in all standard software.

SEE ALSO *Test Statistics*

BIBLIOGRAPHY

Chow, Gregory C. 1960. Tests of Equality Between Sets of Coefficients in Two Linear Regressions. *Econometrica* 28: 591–605.

Fisher, Franklin M. 1970. Tests of Equality Between Sets of Coefficients in Two Linear Regressions: An Expository Note. *Econometrica* 38: 361–366.

Russell Davidson

CHRISTIANITY

Christianity, as its name suggests, is a religion practiced worldwide devoted to the worship and example of Jesus Christ. Jesus was a preacher who lived and taught in Israel two thousand years ago. The word *Christ* means "anointed" and refers to the fact that his followers believed he was anointed by God, whom many Christians believe to be his father, to redeem Israel. These disciples considered the work of Jesus to be the fulfillment of prophesies in the Hebrew scriptures, which they came to call the Old Testament. For a New Testament they added gospels (stories of his life) and epistles, which were letters to early Christian communities. These focus on the account of Jesus' death by crucifixion, their belief that he was raised from the dead, and the idea that his disciples were commissioned to carry his message to the entire world.

THE JEWISH HERITAGE AND CHRISTIAN EXPANSION

Despite the common roots of Judaism and Christianity, almost at once Christians and Jews went separate ways and sometimes fell into conflict, which led to Christian anti-Semitism and frequent persecutions of Jews. In the twenty-first century serious efforts are bringing the two communities into conversation and often common action, but relations remain tense in some communities.

From their original home in Jerusalem, believers in Jesus quickly moved north and east, where at Antioch in Syria they were first named "Christians." During the next four centuries this faith born in Asia also became a vigorous presence in North Africa, which was part of the Roman Empire, and in Europe, with which it came to be most identified until the twentieth century. In the fourth century Christianity, once harassed or forbidden, became the favorite of emperors and the established religion of the Roman Empire. In and after the sixteenth century missionaries and colonialists took the faith into South and North America, and in the early twenty-first century its churches prosper most in the Americas, sub-Saharan Africa, and Asia. About two billion followers, almost one-third of the human race, consider themselves Christian.

CENTURIES OF CONFLICT AND ENTERPRISE

Though Roman emperors were some of the first enemies of Christianity, the sudden rise of Islam in the seventh century led to Muslim conquests of most of North Africa, where Christianity eventually all but disappeared. Muslims also conquered Palestine—the "Holy Land" to Christians, Jews, and Muslims—and advanced in Europe. During the eleventh, twelfth, and thirteenth centuries Christian leaders called for crusades to retake the holy places, especially in Jerusalem, and undertook many military ventures against then-Islamic territories.

Internal conflicts also beset Christianity. In the eleventh century the Eastern and Western churches, long in tension over doctrine and practice, separated. At issue in the separation was both the refusal of the Eastern Christians to regard the pope as the supreme authority and a doctrinal point about how Jesus Christ related to God the Father. Many political and cultural issues also led to the break. Within Western, or Roman Catholic, realms there was also conflict, some of it marked by the Inquisition, a name given to severe efforts by official Catholicism to purge itself of individuals and groups that were suspected of heresy against the church (which generally included anyone who was not a practicing Catholic or who refused to convert). The Protestant Reformation, beginning in the early sixteenth century, permanently divided the Western church. That Reformation was fought over, among other things, the authority of the church and the Bible, with Protestants claiming that they relied only on the divinely inspired scriptures and not on human authority, such as that of the pope (the leader of the Roman Catholic Church). In more recent times Protestants have argued among themselves over biblical authority: was the Bible the "inerrant" word of God, or might it be interpreted in such ways that its human elements also stand out?

Through it all the same zeal that produced crusades, inquisitions, schisms, and reformations inspired clerics and laypeople alike to create distinctive cultures marked by the invention of the university in the late Middle Ages, cathedrals, great art, and institutions for providing health care. Such energies also led to diversity in teaching and governance. Roman Catholics remained loyal to the pope. Lutheranism, inspired by the German religious reformer Martin Luther (1483–1546), eventually became recognized worldwide as another denomination of Christianity. Similarly the Church of England (Anglicanism), or in the United States the Episcopal Church, rejected papal authority. A third tradition, often called Reformed—informed by the writings of the French theologian and reformer John Calvin (1509–1564) in Switzerland, parts of Germany, and the Netherlands along with John Knox (1513–1572) in Scotland—stressed divine sovereignty. Still another cluster, sometimes called Radical or Anabaptist because its adherents "rebaptized" those who had been received into the church through infant baptism, spread, though its members were often persecuted by other Christians.

STORIES, DOCTRINE, AND ORGANIZATION

While Christian teaching draws most deeply on the Bible, its leaders found it necessary to advance from telling informal stories to engaging in more formal expression in doctrines—official teachings that define the tenets of the faith. At a series of ecumenical (worldwide) councils during and after the fourth century, theologians, emperors, and bishops wrestled with basic questions. Christianity is strongly monotheistic, professing faith in one God (as is Judaism and Islam). But Christians also believe in a complex doctrine called the Holy Trinity, by which God is considered as existing in three persons: the Father (God), the Son (Jesus), and the Holy Spirit. They also wrestle with the ways to affirm and proclaim that the human Jesus also has divine status. Later councils dealt with the workings and effects of Christ in the church and in the greater community. According to Christian doctrine, Jesus is regarded as the "savior" of believers from their sin, which has distanced them from God, as well as the one who brings them salvation and inspires them to acts of love and justice.

Christians have worked with many forms of organization, usually stressing either episcopal government—which means rule by bishops, as in Roman Catholicism,

Eastern Orthodoxy, and Anglicanism—or more "democratic" patterns, such as rule by elders or congregants themselves in the millions of local Protestant congregations or parishes. Referring to Christianity as a community may seem strained, because it is broken into around thirty thousand subcommunities called church bodies or in some places denominations. In the third millennium the most rapid new growth is in Pentecostalism, a movement of believers who profess the power of the third person of the Trinity, the Holy Spirit. Pentecostalism stresses the immediate experience of God through "signs," such as healing or speaking in indecipherable spirit-guided vocalizations (speaking in tongues).

The central act of Christians everywhere is worship, usually guided by an ordained or specially appointed leader, named a priest, pastor, or preacher. Christian worship can be formal in cathedrals or informal in home and outdoor settings. Most Christians stress preaching at worship, meaning pronouncing judgment on erring believers and verbally offering forgiveness or grace to those who repent and set out to change their ways.

The other feature in most Christian assemblies is the sacramental life. Most Christians baptize new members with water and offer followers a sacrament, or Eucharist, which was instituted at Jesus' Last Supper, where bread and wine are consecrated and consumed in remembrance of Jesus' death (also called the Communion). Through this sacrament it is believed that members receive forgiveness, deepen their community life, and are empowered to serve God, especially by serving their neighbors and people in need.

SOCIAL AND CULTURAL CONTEXTS

Throughout its history Christianity has been influenced by the societies in which it thrives. After opposition within the Roman Empire early on, Christianity became the religion established and protected by law. The spectrum of attitudes within the Christian community includes everything from ascetic monasticism to artistic creations. In early Christianity church and regime were separate, and in modern free societies "church and state" remain legally distinct. At the same time Christian faith is very much a public affair, promoting movements of social reform and charity. Furthermore while Jesus' own teaching inspires pacifists and other peacemakers, faith in a powerful and judgmental God has also authorized arbitrary rule and wars.

Devoted as Christians have been to social, cultural, and often political expressions, their creeds or statements of faith also teach that the world as it is now will someday end. While many Christians may agree that the future and the end are determined by God, they differ widely on the questions of how the end will come, though somehow most associate it with the "Second Coming" of Jesus Christ.

SEE ALSO *Church, The; Church and State; Coptic Christian Church; Greek Orthodox Church; Heaven; Hell; Jesus Christ; Judaism; Martyrdom; Orthodoxy; Protestant Ethic; Protestantism; Rastafari; Religion; Roman Catholic Church; Santería*

BIBLIOGRAPHY

Bowden, John, ed. 2005. *Christianity: The Complete Guide*. London: Continuum.

Edwards, David Lawrence. 1997. *Christianity: The First Two Thousand Years*. Maryknoll, NY: Orbis Books.

Littell, Franklin H. 2001. *Historical Atlas of Christianity*. 2nd ed. New York: Continuum.

McManners, John, ed. 1990. *The Oxford Illustrated History of Christianity*. New York: Oxford University Press.

Martin E. Marty

CHURCH, THE

The English word *church* and the German *Kirche* derive from the Greek *Kyriake*, which means "that which belongs to the Lord." The Romance languages derive their words for church (*iglesia, chiesa, église*, etc.) from the Latin word *ecclesia*, which derives from the Greek, *ekklesia*, which means "convocation" or "assembly." In the Greek Septuagint translation of the Hebrew Bible, *ekklesia* is used about 100 times to render Hebrew words like *qahal* that refer to the "assembly" of the Lord. In the New Testament the term *ekklesia* occurs 114 times and is used either for the whole Christian community (Gal. 1:13; 1 Cor. 15:9; Matt. 16:8) or for local or particular churches (1 Cor. 1:2; Rev. 1:4, 2:1, etc.).

Only one of the four Gospels, Matthew, uses the word *ekklesia* (Matt. 16:8; 18:17), but the term is used twenty-three times in Acts, sixty-five times in Paul, and twenty times in Revelation. This absence of *ekklesia* in three of the Gospels is probably the result of the Christian belief that the church only replaces Israel as the "People of God" following Jesus' death, resurrection, and ascension and the outpouring of the Holy Spirit on the day of Pentecost (Acts 2). Christians, however, see the words and actions of Jesus during his earthly ministry as foundational for the church, and they look upon the history of Israel from the time of Abraham to Jesus as the "preparation" or "prefiguring" of the Christian Church.

THE EARLY CHURCH

The New Testament relates the spread of the Christian Church through the preaching of Jesus' disciples (followers) and apostles (those commissioned by Jesus to preach his message). The Acts of the Apostles, written by Luke, tells the story of the spread of the church from "Jerusalem, throughout Judea and Samaria, and to the ends of the earth," namely, Rome (Acts 1:8).

In the early church, leadership seems to have been both charismatic (some were "prophets"; 1 Cor. 12:48) and hierarchical (with overseers/bishops; elders/presbyters, and ministers/deacons; Phil. 1:1; 1 Tim. 3:1–13, 5:17–20; Titus 1:7–9). In the early second century Ignatius the Martyr (d. c. 107) testifies to three distinct ministries or orders in the universal ("catholic") church: bishop (*episkopos*), presbyter (*presbyteros*), and deacon (*diakonos*). By the end of the second century Irenaeus (c. 130–200), the bishop of Lyons, points to the Church of Rome as having a "more powerful principality" because it is the church of the apostles Peter and Paul.

The "rule of faith" in the early church was the teaching of Jesus and the apostles. By the late second century, however, Bishop Irenaeus upholds the normative value of the four written testimonies to Jesus' life and mission known as the Gospels of Matthew, Mark, Luke, and John (written c. 65–90 CE). The letters attributed to Paul also achieve scriptural status, and by the late fourth century (367) Bishop Athanasius of Alexandria, Egypt, specifies the definitive list, or "canon," of the twenty-seven writings of the New Testament as they remain in the early twenty-first century. The African Councils of Hippo (393) and Carthage (397) endorse the longer list of forty-six Old Testament books as canonical (a list later upheld by the Catholic Council of Trent in 1546, although the Protestant Reformers favored the shorter Old Testament of thirty-nine books).

The Christian Church spread throughout the Near East and the Mediterranean basin during the first three centuries of the Common Era in spite of periodic persecutions from Roman emperors, such as Nero (64–68), Domitian (95–96), Trajan (106–117), Marcus Aurelius (161–180), Decius (249–251), and Diocletian and Galerius (303–311). The spread of the faith amid such persecutions prompted the Christian writer Tertullian (c. 150–220) to remark that "the blood of the martyrs is the seed of Christians."

In 313 the Roman emperor Constantine (later baptized a Christian) granted legal recognition and religious freedom to Christianity by the Edict of Milan. In 330 he moved the capital of the empire from Rome to Byzantium in Asia Minor (later renamed Constantinople). This move led to the recognition of Constantinople as the "New Rome" and a leading center of Christian culture. By the fifth century there were five major centers or "sees" of the Christian Church: Rome in Italy, Constantinople in Asia Minor, Alexandria in Egypt, Antioch in Syria, and Jerusalem.

THE DEVELOPMENT OF CHURCH DOCTRINE

Between 325 and 787 seven major (ecumenical) church councils were held to clarify points of doctrine in resistance to various teachings considered to be false or heretical. A profession of faith linked to the first two ecumenical councils of Nicea I (325) and Constantinople I (381) summarized the basic points of Christian faith, especially the belief in the Trinity (three persons in one God: the Father, the Son, and the Holy Spirit) and Jesus Christ as consubstantial or "one in essence" with the Father. This profession of faith, known as the Nicene-Constantinopolitan Creed (or simply the Nicene Creed) also describes the Christian Church as "one, holy, Catholic and apostolic."

Other doctrinal proclamations followed. The Council of Ephesus in 431 affirmed Mary as the "God-bearer" or "Mother of God." The Council of Chalcedon in 451 described Jesus as one person with two natures (human and divine). The Second Council of Nicea in 787 condemned iconoclasm (opposition to the use of sacred images or icons) and reaffirmed the right to give veneration (though not worship) to icons of Jesus, Mary, the angels, and the saints. This council also reaffirmed the condemnation of forced conversions to the Christian faith.

Although these councils sought unity in the church, various groups of Christians resisted their teachings and formed separate ecclesial bodies. The Arian churches (named after the Egyptian Christian priest Arius) denied the full divinity of Christ and rejected Nicea I and Constantinople I. The Church of the East, or "Nestorian Church," rejected the teaching of Ephesus (431) on Mary as the Mother of God. It found refuge in the Persian Empire and spread to parts of India and China. Large numbers of Christians in Armenia, Egypt, Ethiopia, and East Syria resisted the doctrine of Chalcedon (451) and formed the "Monophysite" (one-nature) churches, also known as the Oriental Orthodox churches.

THE CHURCH IN THE MIDDLE AGES

In the 600s Islam rose under Muhammad (570–632), beginning in Arabia. The Muslims, or followers of Islam, denied the Trinity and understood Jesus as a prophet/messenger of God rather than the divine Son of God. They claimed that their holy book, the Qur'an, corrected the mistakes of the Jewish and Christian scriptures. The Muslims became a military power and conquered Jerusalem in 638; Alexandria, Egypt, in 642; Carthage, North Africa, in 698; and Spain in 712. The Muslims were set to conquer the rest of Europe but were defeated by Charles Martel in 732 in France.

Because of the threat of Islamic expansion, the popes in the West formed an alliance with the Franks for military protection. The crowning of the Frankish king Charlemagne as the Holy Roman Emperor by Pope Leo III in 800 can be understood as the beginning of the Middle Ages in the West. The Byzantine Christians resented the recognition of another "Roman" emperor because they saw themselves in continuity with the empire of Constantine. This resentment contributed to the 1054 schism (split) between the churches of Rome and Constantinople, which led to an enduring separation of the Eastern Orthodox Churches from the Catholic Church under the pope. The split was mostly over the Orthodox rejection of the pope's primacy of jurisdiction over the churches in the East and the addition of the phrase "and the Son" (*filioque*) to the creed. Later attempts at reunion in 1274 and 1439 were not successful.

In spite of the split between Rome and Constantinople, the perceived threat of Islam, now under the rule of the Turks, led to the Byzantine emperor appealing to the pope for military aid. The result was the Crusades, a series of military ventures authorized by the popes and other Christian leaders to recapture the Holy Land from the Muslims. These Crusades began in 1095 and ended in 1291. Jerusalem was captured by the crusaders in 1099 and a Latin kingdom established. The Muslims, however, regained control of the holy city in 1187, and the other Crusades were mostly failures. Some tragedies also took place, such as the sack of Constantinople in 1204 by the Western crusaders, which deepened the split between Rome and Constantinople.

The church, as a cultural and political entity, played a major role in the history of western and eastern Europe during the Middle Ages (c. 800–1400), and it provided inspiration and support for education and the arts. Though elements of pre-Christian classicism revived during the Renaissance (c. 1400s–1500s), Europe remained essentially Christian, and the secular rulers defended the church (though tensions did exist). Non-Christians, such as the Jews, also lived in Christian Europe during this time, but their situation was sometimes precarious.

THE RISE OF PROTESTANTISM

The Reform or Protestant movements of the 1500s resulted in new Christian churches distinct from the Catholic Church under the pope. The Protestant movements—identified traditionally as Anglican, Lutheran, Calvinist/Reformed, Anabaptist, and Spiritualist—tended to accept only the Bible as the normative Christian authority. When Protestant groups differed in their interpretations of the Bible, multiple Protestant groups were formed.

The Protestant movements resulted in wars of religion when nations and rulers sided with either the Protestants or the pope. By the time of the Treaty of Westphalia of 1648, the landscape of Europe was broken up into various Catholic and Protestant regions, with the prevailing policy of following the religion of the local region's ruler (*cuius regio, huius religio*). Beginning in the 1500s Catholic and Protestant explorers began to bring their church structures with them to Asia, Africa, and the Americas.

THE CHURCH IN THE MODERN WORLD

Christianity in the early twenty-first century comprises three main groups, Catholic, Orthodox, and Protestant, with Anglicans claiming aspects of both Catholicism and Protestantism. For Catholics (often called "Roman Catholics") the church is held in communion by the three visible bonds: unity of faith, unity of seven sacraments, and unity of ecclesial government (bishops in communion with and under the pope, the bishop of Rome). Catholics also conceive of the church as visible and invisible, consisting of three states: the faithful on earth, those undergoing postmortem purification, and the saints in heaven.

Orthodox Christians (those of right worship and doctrine) see themselves as the "one, holy, apostolic and Catholic Church" of the Nicene Creed. This one church is a communion of self-governing (autocephalous) churches bound together by the apostolic succession of true bishops, divine worship and the seven sacraments (or mysteries), and the apostolic faith of the first seven ecumenical councils (Catholics, though, accept twenty-one councils as ecumenical).

Except for the Anglicans/Episcopalians (who see themselves in continuity with the apostolic succession of bishops), Protestant Christians tend to understand the church as "the congregation of the saints" (Lutheran Confession of Augsburg, 1530) or as "the universal Church, which is invisible," consisting of "the whole number of the elect" (Calvinist Westminster Confession of Faith, 1643). While the visible church is important for the teaching of correct doctrine and the rightful administration of the sacraments (reduced from seven to baptism and the Lord's Supper), Protestants tend to understand the church more as an invisible communion of those chosen by God for justification in Christ. Especially among contemporary "evangelical" Christians, the denomination of one's Christian community does not matter as much as one's faith and commitment to Jesus Christ as Lord and Savior.

Since the rise of modern secular states (late 1700s–1900s), the Christian churches generally no longer enjoy the patronage of state support. They do, however, play an important role in various works of charity, education, and involvement with causes of peace and social justice. The witness of the church has grown to be more moral than political, although a political dimension is clearly present in many cases.

SEE ALSO *Christianity; Church and State; Coptic Christian Church; Greek Orthodox Church; Islam, Shia and Sunni; Jesus Christ; Militarism; Muhammad; Protestantism; Religion; Roman Catholic Church; Vatican, The; War*

BIBLIOGRAPHY

Auer, Johann. 1993. *The Church: The Universal Sacrament of Salvation*. Trans. Michael Waldstein. Washington, DC: Catholic University of America Press.

Bettenson, Henry, and Chris Maunder, eds. 1999. *Documents of the Christian Church*. 3rd ed. Oxford and New York: Oxford University Press.

McManners, John, ed. 1993. *The Oxford History of Christianity*. Oxford and New York: Oxford University Press.

O'Collins, Gerald, and Mario Farrugia. 2003. *Catholicism: The Story of Catholic Christianity*. Oxford and New York: Oxford University Press.

Ware, Timothy. 1993. *The Orthodox Church*. 2nd ed. New York: Penguin Books.

Robert Fastiggi

CHURCH AND STATE

Relations between the sacred and the secular have long been important issues in Western democracies. In particular, legal questions surrounding the relationship between church and state in the United States have frequently animated American politics since World War II (1939–1945). The 1940 Supreme Court decision in *Cantwell v. Connecticut* had the effect of incorporating the religion clauses of the First Amendment of the U.S. Constitution, and applied these provisions to the acts of state governments. The incorporation of the First Amendment clauses dealing with religion has resulted in a large outpouring of case law during the final third of the twentieth century, as well as the first decade of the twenty-first.

THE ESTABLISHMENT CLAUSE

The First Amendment of the U.S. Constitution begins with the phrase, "Congress shall make no law respecting an establishment of religion." This phrase, usually termed the *establishment clause*, has, in recent decades, defined the limits under which government (and, by extension, popular majorities) can provide symbolic support for religious values or material support for religious organizations.

There are two general theories by which the establishment clause can be interpreted. According to advocates of *accommodationism*, the establishment clause simply prohibits government from designating an official church, or providing preferential treatment to one church or religious tradition. Neutral, nonpreferential assistance to religion is considered permissible by accommodationists. By contrast, adherents of *separationism* believe that any assistance for religion by government is unconstitutional and that there must exist a "high wall" of separation between church and state.

The operative legal precedent with respect to establishment-clause jurisprudence is the 1971 case of *Lemon v. Kurtzman*. In *Lemon*, the court held that government assistance to religion was not constitutional unless such assistance: (1) had a primarily secular purpose; (2) had a primarily secular effect; and (3) did not result in "excessive entanglement" between church and state. The *Lemon* test is considered to represent a generally separationist precedent, since it limits general assistance to religion, as well as assistance to particular religions.

In general, the Supreme Court has employed the *Lemon* test in cases posing establishment clause issues, but the Court has begun to relax its application of the criteria under which government assistance to religion can be rejected as unconstitutional. To illustrate, in *Agostini v. Felton* (1997), the Court ruled that state governments could provide (and fund) remedial instructors in parochial schools. Similarly, by a five-to-four margin, the Court held in *Zelman v. Simmons-Harris* (2002) that a program of government-financed tuition vouchers for students at private schools did not violate the "effects" prong of *Lemon*, despite the fact that a large majority of private schools in Ohio were religiously affiliated. Thus, the U.S. Supreme Court is gradually moving in a more accommodationist direction from a generally separationist precedent.

Of course, many governmental accommodations to religion are politically popular, and are therefore frequently enacted by elected officials. Most conspicuously, the policy of government-supported "faith-based initiatives" was proposed by President Bill Clinton and enacted with the support of President George W. Bush. The constitutionality of such initiatives had not been subjected to court tests as of 2006, and recipients of such grants had to conform to certain standards to ensure that government funds were only used for "secular" purposes. This trend is clearly moving in the direction of a looser interpretation of the establishment clause, although the actual amount of government assistance to religious bodies is uncertain.

THE FREE EXERCISE CLAUSE

The second First Amendment clause that deals with religion—"or prohibiting the free exercise thereof"—is generally termed the *free exercise clause*. The free exercise clause has usually defined the limits of governmental power to control religiously motivated activities.

There are two general theories of the free exercise clause. *Libertarianism* entails a belief that religious obligations often supersede the requirements of citizenship and that government should be very deferential to religious beliefs. Proponents of *communalism* believe that religion is accorded no special protection under the free exercise clause and that the clause simply prohibits government from singling out religious practices for specific regulation. However, communalists believe that generally neutral laws that happen to restrict religious liberty pose no constitutional difficulty.

In the 1990s the Supreme Court's free exercise jurisprudence took a drastic shift in the direction of communalism. Prior to 1990, the Court's reading of the free exercise clause could generally be characterized as libertarian. Based on precedents such as *Sherbert v. Verner* (1963) and *Wisconsin v. Yoder* (1972), the Court held that government could only interfere with religious free exercise if the restriction on religious freedom served an "essential" government purpose, and if the means of achieving that purpose were the least restrictive available. The *Sherbert-Yoder* test was thus quite deferential to the free exercise claims of religious minorities.

In 1990 the Court held in *Employment Division v. Smith* that otherwise valid laws that had the effect of restricting religious freedom were constitutionally permissible, unless religious practice was singled out for specific regulation, or unless the legislature had made an explicit exception. In *City of Boerne v. Flores* (1997), the Supreme Court reaffirmed this ruling and struck down a congressional statute intended to restore the *Sherbert-Yoder* standard. Thus, the *Smith* ruling signaled an important change in the manner in which the Court interprets the free exercise clause.

Some critics have charged that the *Smith* ruling was intended to make it easier for government to regulate religions that lie outside of the theological or cultural mainstream. Indeed, one effect of *Smith* has been to permit government at all levels to be less deferential to unconventional religious traditions. However, the Court's reaffirmation of the *Smith* ruling in *Boerne* (which limited the free exercise prerogatives of the Roman Catholic Church in a predominantly Catholic area) suggests that the Court is willing to limit the scope of the free exercise clause in a relatively uniform manner. Of course, elected officials are more likely to regulate the activities of unpopular religious groups, and Americans have been shown to be less tolerant of practitioners of faith traditions outside of the Judeo-Christian tradition.

TENSION BETWEEN THE RELIGION CLAUSES

In general, courts in the United States have tended to treat establishment clause issues separately from issues involving the free exercise clause. However, many actual controversies have seemed to involve both considerations, and supporters of different policies have typically invoked both clauses in support of their positions. For example, the U.S. Supreme Court has, in a long string of decisions, restricted state-sponsored religious expression in public schools on establishment clause grounds. These decisions have proscribed organized classroom prayer, a moment of silence for "prayer or meditation," ceremonial prayers at high school sporting events or graduations, and restrictions on the teaching of evolution in biology classes. In such cases, opponents of these decisions have criticized these court rulings on free exercise grounds.

Parties to these decisions, as well as members of Congress and state legislators, have argued that the right of religious free exercise entails the right to express one's religious beliefs publicly, and government policies that limit such expression violate the free exercise clause. Such arguments typically emphasize the "voluntary" nature of school prayer or an "even-handed approach" to the creation-evolution controversy, and suggest that the courts are restricting constitutionally protected religious expression with an overly broad interpretation of the establishment clause.

Arguably, it matters a great deal whether a particular controversy is characterized as an issue of religious establishment or a question of religious free exercise. While many legal scholars have attempted to provide a general solution to the tension between the Constitution's two religion clauses, such arguments typically involve the assertion that one of the religion clauses has priority over the other. However, neither the text of the Constitution nor recent Supreme Court rulings provide meaningful guidance as to how apparent conflicts between the establishment and free exercise clauses should be resolved.

CHURCH-STATE RELATIONS IN COMPARATIVE PERSPECTIVE

Although the tension between the religion clauses of the First Amendment of the U.S. Constitution is a frequent source of confusion (as well as litigation), comparison with other Western democracies suggests that the combi-

nation of establishment and free exercise concerns may be fortuitous for the practice of American politics. Religion is a visible but hardly dominant force in political discourse in the United States, which provides multiple sources of transcendent values for political life.

By contrast, several other democracies provide government support for religious bodies (such as subsidies for schools or clergy salaries), which would be considered a violation of the establishment clause in the United States. Indeed, several European nations have legally established churches. Some analysts have suggested that this sort of governmental support results in a decline in religious membership and practice, since government support reduces the need for churches to attract support from members or potential members.

In other nations, such as France and Turkey, a policy of *laicite* constitutes attempts by the government to reduce or eliminate the presence of religion in the public life of the nation. In such settings, some religious adherents (especially those who identify with minority faith traditions) appear to experience divided loyalties between the demands of citizenship and discipleship. Religious behaviors (including such matters as clothing or the display of religious symbols) are frequent sources of social and political conflict in such nations.

SEE ALSO *Church, The; Religion; State, The; Theocracy; Tolerance, Political*

BIBLIOGRAPHY

Black, Amy E., Douglas L. Koopman, and David Ryden. 2004. *Of Little Faith: The Politics of George W. Bush's Faith-Based Initiatives.* Washington, DC: Georgetown University Press.

Davis, Derek H. 1996. Resolving Not to Resolve the Tension Between the Establishment and Free Exercise Clauses. *Journal of Church and State* 38: 245–259.

Jelen, Ted G. 2000. *To Serve God and Mammon: Church-State Relations in American Politics.* Boulder, CO: Westview.

Jelen, Ted G., and Clyde Wilcox. 1994. *Public Attitudes Toward Church and State.* Armonk, NY: Sharpe.

Levy, Leonard. 1994. *The Establishment Clause: Religion and the First Amendment.* 2nd ed. Chapel Hill: University of North Carolina Press.

Monsma, Stephen V. 1993. *Positive Neutrality: Letting Religious Freedom Ring.* Westport, CT: Praeger.

Monsma, Stephen V., and J. Christopher Soper. 1997. *The Challenge of Pluralism: Church and State in Five Democracies.* Lanham, MD: Rowman and Littlefield.

Stark, Rodney, and Roger Finke. 2000. *Acts of Faith: Explaining the Human Side of Religion.* Berkeley: University of California Press.

Wald, Kenneth D. 2003. *Religion and Politics in the United States.* 4th ed. Lanham, MD: Rowman and Littlefield.

Ted G. Jelen

CHURCHILL, WINSTON
1874–1965

Winston Churchill was a British politician, writer, and orator. He is best remembered for his opposition to the appeasement of Nazi Germany in the 1930s, for his inspirational leadership of the United Kingdom from 1940 to 1945, and for his warnings about the dangers of Soviet expansionism in 1946.

CHILDHOOD AND EARLY EXPERIENCE

Winston Leonard Spencer Churchill was born at Blenheim Palace in Oxfordshire on November 30, 1874, the eldest son of the Conservative politician Lord Randolph Churchill and his American wife, Jennie. His grandfather was the Seventh Duke of Marlborough and, despite his half American parentage, he had a very traditional British aristocratic upbringing, attending boarding schools from the age of seven at Ascot, Brighton, and Harrow. His behavior was often willful and rebellious and although his academic performance was not exceptional, when engaged he could show considerable ability. His passion was for the army, and in 1893 he was admitted to the officer training school at Sandhurst. The death of Lord Randolph in January 1895 had an enormous effect on the young Churchill, motivating him to prove himself as a worthy son.

Between 1895 and 1899 Churchill saw active military service in Cuba, India, and the Sudan. He used the periods between campaigns to improve his general education, and wrote up his military experiences as newspaper articles and books in order to earn fame and fortune. He was determined to enter politics and left the army to unsuccessfully contest the seat of Oldham in 1899. A few months later he became a war correspondent, covering the conflict between the British and the Boer republics in South Africa. He was captured, but managed to escape. This adventure made him an international celebrity and ensured his election to Parliament in 1900.

POLITICAL LIFE

Churchill began his political life as a Conservative. Yet when the Conservative Party began to move away from the policy of free trade toward one of tariff protection, Churchill refused to move with them and dramatically crossed the floor of the House of Commons to become a Liberal. He rose rapidly within his new party, becoming a government minister in 1908. The Liberal government introduced social change at home, while wrestling with increasing international tension abroad. Churchill was responsible for basic unemployment insurance and over-

saw improvements in prison conditions. There were always clear limits to his radicalism. He was a strong opponent of socialism, took a tough line against industrial unrest, and opposed the campaign of the female suffrage movement.

By the outbreak of World War I in 1914 Churchill was the minister with responsibility for the British navy, a role he clearly relished. Unfortunately, his determination to bring the fleet into action led to his support for the disastrous Dardanelles campaign, during which attempts were made by British submarines to pass through the Dardanelles and disrupt Ottoman Empire shipping in the Sea of Marmara. Churchill lost his job, but after a brief spell in the trenches on the western front, was brought back as a member of Lloyd George's national government, serving in a succession of government posts until the fall of the administration in 1921.

Churchill became increasingly concerned with the spread of communism abroad and socialism at home. He broke with the Liberal Party and rejoined the Conservatives, serving as chancellor of the Exchequer from 1924 until 1929. He was undoubtedly a great public figure but many regarded him as past his prime. A lifelong defender of the British Empire, Churchill was out of sympathy with mainstream political thinking over his opposition to greater independence for India. He found himself excluded from the national governments of the 1930s and was forced to spend time at Chartwell, his beloved home, writing history. From 1933 onward he became increasingly concerned by the threat posed to Europe by a revived militaristic Germany under Adolf Hitler's national socialist regime, and was a vocal opponent of the Western powers' policy of appeasement toward the fascist dictator. In the aftermath of the dismemberment of Czechoslovakia, public opinion shifted decisively behind Churchill and when Britain declared war on Germany in September 1939, Prime Minister Neville Chamberlain had no choice but to bring him back into the government as First Lord of the Admiralty.

POST AS PRIME MINISTER

Churchill became prime minister of a national government on May 10, 1940, the day that Hitler launched his blitzkrieg offensive against France and the Low Countries. The next few months saw him lead Britain during a period of crisis, when, following the collapse of France, Britain faced the threat of invasion and was subjected to the full onslaught of the German air force. Churchill's great achievement was to imbue his administration and, through the power of his oratory, the wider British public with the will to resist. He turned himself into an iconic figure, with his trademark cigar, bow tie, and two-fingered "Victory" salute. Behind the scenes, he worked hard to win increasing support from the United States. Following the German invasion of the Soviet Union and the Japanese attack on Pearl Harbor, he engaged in difficult shuttle diplomacy to build and sustain the Grand Alliance with Soviet political leader Joseph Stalin and President Franklin D. Roosevelt. His stature remained high, even as Britain's war contribution paled beside that of the United States and Soviet Union. Put simply, his policy was to take the offensive and to strive for victory.

There is no doubt that Churchill expected to win the general election of 1945, but the Conservatives were defeated by the Labour Party, and he found himself out of office. He remained a major figure on the international stage, and in March 1946 he used his stature to warn of the dangers of Soviet expansionism in his famous "Iron Curtain" speech delivered at Fulton, Missouri. He also called for European reconciliation and spoke in support of the nascent United Europe movement. Not yet ready to retire from public life, he published his account of *The Second World War* (1948–1954) before winning a further term as prime minister in 1951. His policy was to call for summit discussions with the Soviet Union while building up Britain's nuclear force and strengthening relations with the United States. Ill health finally forced his retirement in 1955. His reputation now secure, he published his *A History of the English-Speaking Peoples* (1956–1958). In the last two decades of his life he received many honors, including knighthood, the Nobel Prize in Literature, and honorary American citizenship.

Sir Winston Churchill died on January 24, 1965, seventy years to the day after the death of his father. He was given a state funeral and is buried in Bladon parish churchyard, within sight of his birthplace at Blenheim.

SEE ALSO *Chamberlain, Neville; Conservative Party (Britain); Hitler, Adolf; Iron Curtain; Stalin, Joseph; Union of Soviet Socialist Republics; World War I; World War II*

BIBLIOGRAPHY

Brendon, Piers. 1984. *Winston Churchill: A Brief Life.* New York: Harper and Row.

Churchill, Randolph S., and Sir Martin Gilbert. 1966–88. *Winston S. Churchill.* 8 vols. Boston: Houghton Mifflin.

Jenkins, Roy. 2001. *Churchill: A Biography.* New York: Farrar, Straus, and Giroux.

Reynolds, David. 2004. *In Command of History.* London: Allen Lane.

Allen Packwood

CIA

SEE *Central Intelligence Agency, U.S..*

CIRCULAR FLOW

SEE *Quesnay, Francois.*

CIRCUMPLEX MODEL

SEE *Leary, Timothy.*

CITATIONS

A citation is a reference to any published work as well as any form of communication with sufficient details to uniquely identify the item. When academics, scientists, and other professionals refer to any published work in their own published work, they *cite* it, giving the author, year, title, and locus of publication (journal, book, working paper, etc.).

In academia, according to the principle of meritocracy, scholars, departments, and institutions are evaluated through objective criteria. One of the main instruments used to measure the quantity and quality of academic output is *citation analysis*. A citation count is used as a proxy of impact, signaling quality, because it informs how often a given published work, author, or journal is cited in the literature. It allows us to build rankings of scholars, departments, institutions, and journals. These rankings are subjected to significant variations over time. For instance, in economics, only three journals—*American Economic Review, Econometrica,* and the *Journal of Political Economy*—appear consistently in the list of top ten journals of the profession during the 1970–1995 period (e.g., Laband and Piette 1994; Hodgson and Rothman 1999).

According to David Laband and J. P. Sophocleus (1985), citations are the scientific community's version of dollar voting by consumers for consumption goods. Holding prices constant, consumers decide to buy goods from certain producers because of the quality of their merchandise. Whether the purchase decision is influenced by the buyer's friendship or family relationship with the seller does not matter. The relevant point is the volume of sales in which market shares are based. The same holds true for the consumption of scientific literature. What matters is the volume of citations, not the motivation behind each specific citation.

Any citation count has several dimensions. Among them, the sample of authors and journals, the time period in consideration, and self citations play an important role in defining the relative importance of an author, article, and journal.

In two papers in the journal *Science*, David Hamilton (1990, 1991) showed that about half of all science papers were never cited within five years after publication. David Pendlebury (1991) corrected the figures to show that "uncitedness" figures were 22 percent in the physical sciences, 48 percent in the social sciences, and 93 percent in humanities. Based on these figures, *Newsweek* concluded that "nearly half the scientific work in this country is worthless" (p. 44), suggesting that resources invested in science are wasted.

According to Arjo Klamer and Hendrik van Dalen (2002, 2005), the skewed distribution of citations is part and parcel of what they call the *attention game* in science. Because there are too many articles for any scholar to pay attention to, she has to make a selection and usually follows others in doing so. There is a snowball effect in the sense that one scholar reads an article because others cite it; by citing it in her work, others may turn to the article as well. This is consistent with the reward system of science and in particular with the Matthew effects of science (Merton 1968) in which a few scientists get most of the credit and recognition for ideas and discoveries made by many other scientists. For instance, Diana Crane (1965) found that highly productive scientists at a major university gained recognition more often than equally productive scientists at a less prestigious university.

Besides the leadership effect described above, the number of citations may also be influenced by academic networks because of their positive externalities. Any scholar with a wide academic network can more easily communicate her work through seminar presentations, workshops, and conferences, and publish it in influential books, monographs, and professional journals. Another important source of citations related to academic networks is the relative importance of the scholar's network. A scholar working in any given field who has access to leading professionals, departments, associations, and their respective publication venues may find it easier to be influential and therefore to be widely cited.

The number of citations increases with the number of publications or the type of journals in which a scholar publishes. João Ricardo Faria (2003) presented a model in which the scholar is assumed to maximize the success of her career as measured by the number of citations of her work. The scholar may choose to publish in top journals, which have a higher rate of rejection, therefore making the expected number of publications low; a scholar with these preferences is called a *K*-strategist. If the scholar chooses to publish in lesser-known journals with lower rejection rates, she ends up having many papers accepted for publication; in this case, she is an *r*-strategist. Faria showed that any scholar following either an *r*- or *K*-strategy may achieve the same final amount of citations, and he conjectured that the most successful strategy is the one that combines both approaches to quantity and quality, a strategy called *Samuelson ray*. Samuelson ray is named after Paul A. Samuelson, because he has been one of the most productive and influential economists to date.

The number of citations to a scholar's publications may vary over time with the quality of her work, the reputation of the journals where she has published, and the number of papers the scholar has published. Faria (2005) studied a Stackelberg differential game with scholars and editors. Journal editors are leaders who maximize the quality of the papers they publish, while the scholar is the follower willing to maximize the number of papers published, constrained by the way her work is cited. Faria showed that the number of citations increases with rules aimed at increasing a scholar's productivity (i.e., tenure requirements) and with a journal's reputation.

BIBLIOGRAPHY

Crane, Diana. 1965. Scientists at Major and Minor Universities: A Study of Productivity and Recognition. *American Sociological Review* 30: 699–714.

Faria, João R. 2003. What Type of Economist Are You: *r*-Strategist or *K*-Strategist? *Journal of Economic Studies* 30: 144–154.

Faria, João R. 2005. The Game Academics Play: Editors Versus Authors. *Bulletin of Economic Research* 57: 1–12.

Hamilton, David P. 1990. Publishing by—or for?—The Numbers. *Science* 250: 1331–1332.

Hamilton, David P. 1991. Research Papers: Who's Uncited Now? *Science* 251: 25.

Hodgson, G., and H. Rothman. 1999. The Editors and Authors of Economics Journals: A Case of Institutional Oligopoly? *Economic Journal* 109 (453): 165–186.

Klamer, Arjo, and Hendrik P. van Dalen. 2002. Attention and the Art of Scientific Publishing. *Journal of Economic Methodology* 9: 289–315.

Klamer, Arjo, and Hendrik P. van Dalen. 2005. Is Science a Case of Wasteful Competition? *Kyklos* 58: 395–414.

Laband, David N., and M. J. Piette. 1994. The Relative Impacts of Economics Journals: 1970–1990. *Journal of Economic Literature* 32: 640–666.

Laband, David N., and J. P. Sophocleus. 1985. Revealed Preference for Economics Journals: Citations as Dollar Votes. *Public Choice* 46: 317–324.

Merton, Robert K. 1968. The Matthew Effect in Science. *Science* 159: 56–63.

Pendlebury, David. 1991. Gridlock in the Labs: Does the Country Really Need All Those Scientists? *Newsweek* 117, no. 2: 44.

Pendlebury, David. 1991. Letters to the Editor: Science, Citation, and Funding. *Science* 251: 1410–1411.

João Ricardo Faria

CITIES

The earliest cities were created more than 5,500 years ago in Mesopotamia. Those and other ancient cities were few in number and by twenty-first-century standards had small populations, primitive housing, and simple technology. However, cities brought enormous changes in human society. Over the years cities have existed, only a minority of the human population has lived in them; nevertheless, cities have been the locus of political, economic, cultural, and environmental changes that have transformed life on Earth.

URBAN TRANSFORMATION THEORIES

Scholars studying cities identify many significant transformations in them. This section summarizes five perspectives on these changes.

One perspective contends that city characteristics (i.e., high population density, diversity) cause city people to behave as they do. For example, increased occupational division of labor is associated with the shift from village to city. This important element of the urban transformation is usually explained by the French sociologist Emile Durkheim's "dynamic density" principle: when many people try to survive in a concentrated area they specialize and refine the work they do to avoid direct competition with others, avoid redundancy, and improve the quality of their products or services. Similarly, cities are filled with strangers who have few preexisting bonds of loyalty, trust, or obligation. To enable them to better deal with each other, city life relies extensively on written contracts, laws, and courts to enforce them.

Likewise, Georg Simmel explained city-dwellers' social behavior with inherent qualities of cities. He observed that compared to people from small towns, urbanites are reserved, blasé, aloof, calculating, more attuned to fashion, and engaged in "extravagances of mannerism and caprice" (Simmel 1969 p. 57). This, he argued, is because large cities are filled with people and things that generate a plethora of cacophonous, threatening, and contradictory images and messages. Urbanites' traits previously mentioned are useful screening and coping devices they use to avoid those disconcerting stimuli and maintain a semblance of sanity and individuality.

Louis Wirth's 1938 article "Urbanism as a Way of Life" epitomizes the notion that city characteristics produce a particular urban pattern of social life. He defined a city as "a relatively large, dense, and permanent settlement of socially heterogeneous individuals" (Wirth 1969, p. 148), and derived numerous social interaction patterns as consequences of population size, density, and diversity. Wirth proposed that in cities bonds of kinship and neighborliness weaken; tradition and familial authority attenuate and are only partially replaced by formal control mechanisms. Although individuals gain greater personal freedom and both social and spatial mobility are common, city residents' social relations are segmented, impersonal, anomic, and imbued with "a spirit of competition, aggrandizement, and mutual exploitation" (Wirth 1969, p. 156). Wirth also indicated that as cities dominate their hinterlands, business corporations in them become more cut-throat and soulless, and cities' subareas become "a mosaic of social worlds" (Wirth 1969, p. 155) with stark contrasts between nearby neighborhoods' socioeconomic level, ethnic composition, housing, businesses, and land uses. Finally, Wirth suggested that in cities individual people count for little, have difficulty knowing how they fit in or what is really in their own best interests, and therefore they become susceptible to mass movements or charismatic leaders. Wirth's portrait of urban life suggests that social problems and alienation are inherent elements of large modern cities.

Other perspectives, including Herbert Gans' *Urban Villagers* (1962), contradict Wirth's. One counter-response is a "rediscovery of community" perspective arising from many empirical studies in cities and suburbs. Together these studies suggest that the depersonalized, alienated, contract-driven urban world of attenuated local and familial bonds described above is an overgeneralization and is contradicted by the continued existence of close-knit neighborhoods and strong group ties in parts of many cities.

This rediscovered community perspective claims Wirth's "urbanism as a way of life" has not swept community from every corner of the metropolis. It contends that the kinds of people (i.e., their socio-economic level, life-cycle stage, ethnicity, sexual orientation, and socio-political values) living in a neighborhood has a greater effect on social life in it than does the place's population size, density, and heterogeneity. Depending upon the kinds of people in an area (i.e., their needs and interests) they may work to create or maintain an active local community life, or they may let it languish and disappear. Also, community institutions preserve or build strong personal relations in city or suburban neighborhoods. Certain stores, religious institutions, "third places" (e.g., bars, coffee shops), or social clubs become the ground from which community ties grow. These are supplemented by personal networks such as those established in chain migrations to cities or by local community activists.

Another perspective on city life emphasizes underlying economic processes, inequalities, and the distribution of power. The key contention here is that the most powerful causal forces in a city are not inherent qualities of cities, but instead are conflicts of interests among the city's economic classes, land ownership laws, and land use decisions that serve certain groups' interests. The first analysis of urban poverty, Friedrich Engels' mid-1840s study of working-class sections of England's industrial cities, illustrates this perspective. Engels argued that neither of these cities' two salient features—(1) huge differences in living conditions between a small upper class and a huge impoverished class of factory workers; and (2) disintegration of society into isolated individuals—is caused by anything inherent in large cities. Instead, he contended that these are produced by the capitalist economy, which causes brutal competition, exploitation, lowered wages, and unstable employment in these cities. Engels also said that the upper class controlled decisions regarding land use. This enabled them to arrange that cheap low-quality housing for workers is far from the better neighborhoods of the rich, guaranteeing the affluent would not have to see or be threatened by the squalor, unhealthy conditions, and misery of factory workers' slums.

For much of the twentieth century the Engels/ Marxian perspective was eclipsed in urban studies by the influence of Wirth and an urban ecological perspective embodied in Ernest Burgess's concentric zone model (and revisions by geographers' sector and multiple nuclei models). It contended that in any era cities develop a characteristic socio-spatial structure produced by the era's primary mode of transportation, construction technology, local topography, and, most importantly, economic competition for prime urban locations among individuals, groups, and businesses with unequal purchasing power. Segregation of immigrants and racial-ethnic minorities was attributed to a desire for living near others with similar culture and low economic standing, which prevents them from living in cities' better neighborhoods.

By the 1970s the ecological perspective received criticism for the meager attention it gave to racism as causing urban racial ghettos and underestimation of the role of powerful government and private interest groups in making urban transportation and land use decisions. Researchers with critical perspectives developed explanations showing how cities are influenced by globalization, "growth machines," "place entrepreneurs," public-private partnerships, and institutionalized norms regarding gendered and racialized space. The city, in Mark Gottdiener and Ray Hutchison's "sociospatial" perspective, no longer is the large dense dominant heart of the metropolitan

area, where the skyscrapers, theaters, and museums are located; instead the city is a vast "multinucleated metropolitan region" containing dispersed centers and realms (e.g., "edge cities") that perform most economic and cultural functions the central city once performed. In this perspective the strongest creators and modifiers of the new metropolis are government programs that subsidize suburbanization, real estate industries' land use decisions, and cultural innovators (in architecture, design, advertising, or arts) who craft new forms, symbols, and desires for the metropolitan public.

MODERN CITIES AND THEIR PROBLEMS

Today's largest metropolitan areas are in Asia and Latin America. Of the twenty with the highest populations, only New York, Los Angeles, Moscow, and London are in Europe or the United States. Since 1970 Asian and Latin American cities (Seoul, Shanghai, Mexico City, Sao Paulo) and African cities (Cairo, Lagos) have grown tremendously due to internal migration. Migrants pour in largely because governments' and large corporations' attempts at economic development disrupt local subsistence patterns in the countryside (e.g., conversion to capital-intensive agriculture, resource extraction). With insufficient housing and sanitation to absorb so many migrants, overcrowding and pollution are serious problems. Newcomers in rapidly growing Latin American and African cities have taken over land and created impoverished squatter settlements. Urban population growth outpaces these cities' supply of jobs. This oversupply of workers causes low wages and results in enormous informal economies, with their attendant problems. Cities in Asia's newly industrialized countries (e.g., Korea, Singapore) are marked by the development of global corporations engaged in manufacture, commerce, financial services, and technology. These businesses' profitability and power enhance cities' standing among world cities and turn sections of them into cosmopolitan centers. Moreover, their executives and white-collar workers expand the ranks of the cities' upper and middle class and generate demand for goods and services provided by lower paid workers. Nevertheless, these mega-cities, like those of Latin America, remain places with a small middle class; huge gaps exist between the living conditions of the small privileged class and the poor population.

Cities in the United States face problems so severe that many observers believe they will never regain the prominence they had from 1900 to 1970. Due to suburbanization, initially by affluent whites and later by middle-class blacks and immigrants, only 30 percent of the U.S. population lives in cities. In many large cities most residents are African American or Latino, and often neighborhoods have highly concentrated poverty. With this demographic shift, political clout in legislatures moved from cities to more conservative suburbs. Old cities in the Northeast and Midwest deteriorated. With deindustrialization many cities lost well-paying manufacturing jobs, which were not replaced with sufficient well-paying service industry jobs. City residents experienced high unemployment, cuts in city services, poor schools, and high crime rates. Older neighborhoods saw disinvestment by federal housing policy, which funneled money and new construction into white suburban areas, and by private lending and insurance companies, which "red-lined" city areas, making it more costly for families and businesses to move into or upgrade city neighborhoods. Ironically, federal programs that did make large investments (highway construction, public housing, urban renewal) in cities from 1950 to 1970 have been criticized as doing more to destroy than improve city neighborhoods.

Since 1990, many cities experienced some revitalization, population increase, and reduction in poverty concentration. Federal policy closing large public housing projects and creating mixed-income areas (HOPE VI) is partly responsible for this. Additionally, efforts by community development corporations (assisted by private foundations and city government) have improved housing and safety in some city neighborhoods. Revitalization also occurs with gentrification, as affluent people buy and renovate cheap housing close to the center of a city and then move in or sell to other affluent residents. While this process enlarges cities' middle class and brings new businesses (improving the tax base), it can displace the less affluent. Where gentrification is extensive it reduces low-cost housing and can put the poor at greater risk of homelessness. Although the cities' situation may not be as bleak as in the late 1980s, the problems are by no means resolved. In fact, many are appearing elsewhere, especially the older ring of suburbs near cities' boundaries.

SEE ALSO *Sociology, Urban; Suburban Sprawl; Towns; Urban Renewal; Urban Sprawl; Urban Studies; Urbanity; Urbanization*

BIBLIOGRAPHY

Engels, Friedrich. [1845] 1958. *The Condition of the Working Class in England.* Palo Alto, CA: Stanford University Press.

Gans, Herbert. 1962. *The Urban Villagers.* New York: Free Press.

Gottdiener, Mark, and Ray Hutchison. 2000. *The New Urban Sociology.* 2nd ed. Boston: McGraw Hill.

Logan, John R., and Harvey L. Molotch. 1987. *Urban Fortunes.* Berkeley: University of California Press.

Simmel, Georg. [1905] 1969. The Metropolis and Mental Life. In *Classic Essays on the Culture of Cities*, ed. Richard Sennett, 47–60. New York: Appleton-Century-Crofts.

Wellman, Barry, and Barry Leighton. 1979. Networks, Neighborhoods, and Communities: Approaches to the Community Question. *Urban Affairs Quarterly* 14 (3): 363–390.

Wirth, Louis. [1905] 1969. Urbanism as a Way of Life. In *Classic Essays on the Culture of Cities*, ed. Richard Sennett, 143–164. New York: Appleton-Century-Crofts.

Charles Jaret

CITIZENSHIP

Citizenship can be succinctly defined in terms of two component features. First, it constitutes membership in a polity, and as such it inevitably involves a tension between inclusion and exclusion, between those deemed eligible for citizenship and those who are denied the right to become members. In its earliest form in ancient Greece, the polity in question was the city-state. In the modern world, it was transformed during the era of democratic revolutions into the nation-state. Second, membership brings with it a reciprocal set of duties and rights, both of which vary by place and time, though some are universal. Thus paying taxes and obeying the law are among the duties expected of citizens in all nations, while the right to participate in the political process in various ways—by voting, running for office, debating, petitioning, and so forth—is an inherent feature of democratic citizenship. This leads to a final point: citizenship exists only in democratic regimes, for in nondemocratic ones people are subjects rather than citizens. In this regard, there are three crucial features that characterize the democratic political system: (1) the right to participate in the public sphere; (2) limitations on the power of government over the individual; and (3) a system based on the rule of law, not the arbitrary rule of rulers.

The principal fault lines used to define the boundaries of inclusion versus exclusion have historically been based on three major social divisions: class, gender, and race. And, indeed, though much has changed, these divisions remain significant—and in fact tend to be intersecting. During the formative period of all the modern democratic regimes, beginning in the eighteenth century, the privileged white, property-owning male citizens were intent on disqualifying a majority of their nation's residents from citizenship rights. Confronted with a disjunction between the egalitarian ideals of democratic theory and the desire to exclude from full societal membership certain categories of persons who did not share their class, gender, or racial identities, they responded by creating justifications for social exclusion. For their part, the white working class, women, and nonwhites responded, always in difficult circumstances and with varying degrees of success, by creating social movements aimed at acquiring the political voice that had been denied them. The white working class had, by the late nineteenth century, succeeded in being included, though not as genuine equals. A similar inclusion would come slower for women and racial and ethnic minorities, where in many cases this did not occur until the later part of the twentieth century. Thus, American blacks did not overcome the barriers created by Jim Crow until the 1960s, Australia's Aboriginal population did not receive the right to vote until the same time, and in some Swiss cantons women did not acquire the right to vote until 1990.

As with inclusion, the development of the rights of citizens entails a dynamic process. Analyses of this process are generally framed in terms of the thesis advanced by the British social theorist T. H. Marshall, who distinguished between three types of rights: civil, political, and social. In his view, these types are distinct not only analytically, but also historically. Civil rights refer to such aspects of individual freedom as free speech, freedom of religious expression, and the right to engage in economic and civic life. Political rights involve those rights that ensure the ability to actively participate in the realm of politics. Finally, social rights involve the rights to various welfare provisions designed to guarantee to all a minimum standard of living necessary for the other two rights to be meaningful. Included are guarantees of educational opportunities, health care, decent and affordable housing, pensions, and so forth. Marshall thought that civil rights emerged in the eighteenth century, political rights in the nineteenth, and social rights in the twentieth, with the birth of modern welfare states. The historical record calls into question the unilateral depiction of the evolution of rights, but it is the case that all of the world's liberal democracies did develop welfare states guaranteeing various forms of social rights. In his view, whereas the other types of rights do not challenge capitalism's production of unacceptable levels of inequality, social rights are intended to do so. Inequality does not cease to exist, but it becomes less consequential in shaping the life chances of individuals and impeding the goal of the equality of people qua citizens. The historical record indicates that welfare states have not actually managed to achieve this goal, and moreover, the neoliberal assault on the welfare state has resulted in an increase in levels of inequality.

Debates over the duties of citizens have pitted republican (and communitarian) theory versus liberal theory. The former position calls for an involved citizenry, while the latter is less inclined to ask or require citizens to be too actively engaged in politics. For example, republicans would be inclined to support universal conscription into military service or some alternative form of public service while liberals would not. Nevertheless, both positions believe that for democracies to succeed they need an informed and active citizenry. The distinction between the two traditions has much to do with differing perspectives on the levels of activity required. By the latter part of the twentieth century, a lively discourse emerged about the presumed tendency on the part of citizens in the United States, and to a somewhat lesser degree elsewhere, to withdraw from civic and political involvement, as evidenced, for instance, in the widespread interest in the Harvard political scientist Robert Putnam's "bowling alone" thesis.

If in the past citizenship has been construed in terms of the individual, multiculturalism has raised the specter of the emergence of group rights. Although many, but not all, of the world's liberal democracies have developed a multicultural sensibility, only two to date have implemented official state policies designed to promote multiculturalism: Canada and Australia. While some observers contend that the multicultural moment has ended, they fail to appreciate its novelty, specifically, as the scholar Jeffrey Alexander has argued, insofar as it signals a new form of civil society. Moreover, even without explicit multicultural agendas, there is evidence of a growing appreciation that difference and integration are not necessarily antithetical.

Finally, there is evidence of a growing interest in developments that suggest the world is entering a new era in which the nation-state's monopoly on defining citizenship is being challenged. In part, this is due to the rapid expansion of people with dual or multiple citizenships and the growing willingness by governments to legalize or tolerate this situation. This increase is largely attributable to transnational immigration, which though not entirely new is more significant today due to new communications technologies and improved transportation networks. Whether or not transnationalism is largely a phenomenon of the immigrant generation, or will persist into the generations of their children and grandchildren, is an unanswered question in the early twenty-first century. Likewise, it is also unclear whether dual citizenship becomes merely formal, in which the citizenship of primary residence is the only salient one, or whether active involvements in two nations' political systems persist.

Second, as exponents of postnationalist thought contend, supra-state entities such as the United Nations and the European Union (EU) are increasingly coming to assume some of the roles traditionally located solely with the nation-state. This is particularly the case with the issue of human rights, where there is evidence of the embryonic form of a global human rights regime. It is also relevant to environmental concerns, as the Kyoto Protocol makes clear, for these are matters that transcend existing political borders. Although the EU is unique, the fact that citizens of its member states can treat their social rights as applying outside of their national boundaries signals yet a new development of interest. In such a situation, social rights are portable within the EU, thus for example allowing German retirees to move to Portugal while collecting their German pensions, while at the same time permitting Portuguese workers free access to German labor markets. Much remains uncertain about where these developments might lead, but given the pace of change since the mid-twentieth century many social scientists predict that the twenty-first century will see changes in the location of citizenship brought about by globalization. At the same time, some of the earlier enthusiasm about the prospects for the decline of the nation-state has been unrealized, and in fact in the so-called age of terrorism nation-states have reasserted themselves and in the process raised concerns about the erosion of some rights.

SEE ALSO *Civil Rights; Civil Society; Immigrants to North America*

BIBLIOGRAPHY

Alexander, Jeffrey C. 2006. *The Civil Sphere.* New York: Oxford University Press.

Kivisto, Peter. 2002. *Multiculturalism in a Global Society.* Malden, MA: Blackwell Publishing.

Kivisto, Peter, and Thomas Faist. 2007. *Citizenship: Discourse, Theory, and Transnational Prospects.* Malden, MA: Blackwell Publishing.

Marshall, T. H. 1964. *Class, Citizenship, and Social Development.* Garden City, NY: Doubleday and Company.

Putnam, Robert. 2000. *Bowling Alone: The Collapse and Revival of American Community.* New York: Simon & Schuster.

Turner, Bryan S. 1986. *Citizenship and Capitalism.* London: Allen & Unwin.

Peter Kivisto

CITY-STATE

City-state refers to a sovereign political entity composed of an urban area and its surrounding territory. It can be usefully contrasted with *country*, which typically has a greater geographical expanse and larger population. Politically, city-states have been governed by a variety of regimes ranging from authoritarian to democratic. In many cases, they enter into formal or informal alliances with others because of economic or military interests, but they usually maintain their basic political autonomy. Culturally, city-states are often homogeneous. Their relatively small size limits diversity and facilitates a sense of commonality among citizens.

The history of the city-state extends back to the ancient world and includes several ages in which it played particularly significant political roles. The first city-states developed among the ancient Sumerians in the lower part of Mesopotamia. Later, they became the fundamental political unit for the classical Greek civilization in the southern-most region of the Balkan Peninsula. During the medieval and early modern periods they were prominent in Italy and areas of Germany. However, with the rise of the modern nation-state, many city-states lost or gave up their political autonomy. Today, city-states continue to exist, but usually as isolated enclaves in a world of larger political entities.

Perhaps the best-known examples of the city-state are the ancient Greek *poleis* of Athens and Sparta. These two city-states were bitter military and political rivals, although there were instances of cooperation to repel Persian invaders. The political and cultural differences between the two are quite striking. Sparta was a militaristic state ruled by a mixed government combining monarchical, aristocratic, and democratic elements. Its citizens lived very austere, disciplined lives. Little attention was given to the arts. In contrast, Athens was the center of Greek culture, producing great works of architecture, art, literature, and philosophy. Among its citizens there was an appreciation of leisure and intellectual activities. The Athenian city-state is especially known for its development of a direct form of democratic government. All male citizens were allowed to participate in the assembly, and older (male) citizens were eligible to sit on the council.

Contemporary examples of city-states include Monaco, Singapore, and Vatican City. Monaco is a very small constitutional monarchy that borders the Mediterranean Sea on the southern coast of France near the Italian border. Even though it relies on France for military protection, Monaco continues to be a politically autonomous state. Singapore is an island state located between Malaysia and Indonesia. It was founded as a British trading colony in 1819 and became an independent city-state in 1965. Singapore is currently governed by a parliamentary republic. Vatican City is a tiny enclave located in the city of Rome. It gained political autonomy in 1929 and has maintained an ecclesiastical form of government, with the Pope serving as the chief of state. Italy is responsible for the defense of Vatican City, with the Pontifical Swiss Guard providing limited security within the city.

The city-state's political significance has certainly waned in the contemporary world—it may even seem like an anachronism in the age of the large modern state. Nonetheless, the idea of a small, politically autonomous community can still have power over the political imagination; it can provide valuable inspiration for communitarians and advocates of direct democracy.

SEE ALSO *Vatican, The*

BIBLIOGRAPHY

Parker, Geoffrey. 2005. *Sovereign City: The City-State Ancient and Modern.* London: Reaktion Books.

Sealey, Raphael. 1977. *A History of the Greek City State, 700–338 B.C.* Berkeley: University of California Press.

Johnny Goldfinger

CIVIC ENGAGEMENT

SEE *Volunteerism.*

CIVIL AERONAUTICS AUTHORITY 1938

SEE *Aviation Industry.*

CIVIL DISOBEDIENCE

Civil disobedience is a form of sociopolitical protest consisting of the deliberate and intentional breaking of a law that is believed to be unjust. As John Rawls defines it in *A Theory of Justice* ([1971] 1991), civil disobedience is "a public, nonviolent, conscientious yet political act contrary to law usually done with the aim of bringing about a change in the law or policies of the government" (p. 320). It is marked by several distinctive and defining features. Firstly, to qualify as civil disobedience, such lawbreaking must be undertaken only after other legal and political avenues have been exhausted (or blocked repeatedly by civil authorities). Secondly, it must be done openly and in plain view of a wider public. Thirdly, the protesters' reasons for breaking the law must be articulated and explained to that public. (Taken together, the second and third criteria are sometimes called the *publicity requirement.*) Fourthly, such disobedience must be nonviolent and cause no harm or injury to anyone other than the protesters (in the event that the authorities use physical force). And fifthly, the protesters must accept whatever punishment is meted out to them by civil authorities.

The term *civil disobedience* was coined by the editors of Henry David Thoreau's posthumously published works. Apparently believing that Thoreau's "Resistance to Civil Government" (1849) had a title that sounded too militant, they renamed his now classic essay "Civil Disobedience." In that brief essay, Thoreau articulates and defends the idea that passive resistance is a right and duty of democratic citizens. To act in ways that cause "friction" in the "machinery" of injustice is not itself unjust; quite the contrary, Thoreau contends. In Thoreau's own case, resistance took the form of refusing to pay taxes that would help support the extension of slavery into Mexican territory by means of the Mexican War. This led to his arrest and brief imprisonment.

Thoreau's token act of resistance had little effect, but it led him to write the brief essay that has since been read, reread, and translated into dozens of different languages. "Civil Disobedience" has inspired dissidents and dissenters as varied as Leo Tolstoy in czarist Russia, Mohandas K. Gandhi in British-ruled India, Nelson Mandela and Steve Biko in South Africa, Andrei Sakharov in the Soviet Union, and Martin Luther King Jr. in the United States as well as Wei Jingsheng and the student protesters in China's Tiananmen Square. In short, Thoreau's little acorn of an essay has sprouted a forest of oaks.

Civil disobedience has both moral and practical aspects. The fundamental moral principles upon which civil disobedience rests are that it is unjust to accept or to turn a blind eye to injustice, that it is categorically wrong for one human being to harm another, that it is wrong to return harm for harm, and that it is better to suffer injustice than to act unjustly. To critics who claim that breaking the law is ipso facto unjust, defenders of civil disobedience reply that to obey an egregiously unjust law constitutes a "crime of obedience" (Kelman and Hamilton 1989). Moreover laws are made by human beings who are fallible and are capable of acting (or legislating) in unjust ways. If the law in question cannot be changed legally, it may be challenged extralegally and in nonviolent ways. As Rawls notes, in a perfectly just democracy, civil disobedience would be out of place, but that is not the sort of society in which we actually live. Therefore an almost just or imperfectly just democratic society that aspires to be just must make provision for civil disobedience (Rawls 1999, p. 319). By contrast, in an unjust and undemocratic society, more covert and clandestine forms of resistance may be undertaken and justified, as was the case with the pre–Civil War Underground Railroad that smuggled escaped slaves to freedom or the actions of those who during the Holocaust hid and protected Jews in defiance of Nazi law. Because such covert actions violate the publicity requirement, they do not count as acts of civil disobedience but fall instead under the heading of "conscientious refusal" (Rawls 1999, pp. 323–326).

Moving from the moral to the practical side of civil disobedience, its defenders maintain that to counter violence with violence only begets more violence, producing an ever-wider spiral of attack and counterattack. To intervene nonviolently might initially provoke more violence, but over the longer haul, it helps break the spiral of violent action and reaction. On an equally practical note, bystanders who witness the suffering of civilly disobedient protesters may be moved to sympathize and side with their cause (as happened, for example, when fire hoses and fierce dogs were turned on peaceful civil rights protesters in the American South).

The theory and practice of civil disobedience holds that an individual or group should counter violence with nonviolence, hatred with love, injustice with justice. This is a most demanding doctrine and typically requires training in the tactics and techniques of nonviolence. It also requires, as King (1963) and others have pointed out, that we look for and appeal to the best in our adversaries. Civil disobedience requires not only that resisters rely on their own consciences but also that they act in ways that appeal to the consciences of those they act against as well as to the consciences of bystanders or witnesses. Because of this, acts of civil disobedience may, at least potentially, perform important and perhaps indispensable mobilizing and corrective functions for flawed and sometimes dysfunctional democratic societies (Power 1972; Ball 1972, chap. 4; Rawls 1999, p. 336).

SEE ALSO *Democracy; Ethics; Gandhi, Mohandas K.; Justice; King, Martin Luther, Jr.; Law; Mandela, Nelson; Morality; Passive Resistance; Protest; Rawls, John; State, The; Thoreau, Henry David; Violence*

BIBLIOGRAPHY

Ball, Terence. 1972. *Civil Disobedience and Civil Deviance.* Beverly Hills, CA, and London: Sage Publications.

Bedau, Hugo Adam. 1961. On Civil Disobedience. *Journal of Philosophy* 58 (21): 653–661.

Bedau, Hugo Adam, ed. 1969. *Civil Disobedience: Theory and Practice.* New York: Pegasus.

Kelman, Herbert C., and V. Lee Hamilton. 1989. *Crimes of Obedience: Toward a Social Psychology of Authority and Responsibility.* New Haven, CT: Yale University Press.

King, Martin Luther, Jr. [1963] 1969. Letter from Birmingham City Jail. In *Civil Disobedience*, ed. Hugo Adam Bedau, 72–89. New York: Pegasus.

Power, Paul F. 1972. Civil Disobedience as Functional Opposition. *Journal of Politics* 34 (1): 37–55.

Rawls, John. [1971] 1999. *A Theory of Justice.* Rev. ed. Cambridge, MA: Harvard University Press.

Sibley, Mulford Q. 1970. *The Obligation to Disobey: Conscience and the Law.* New York: Council on Religion and International Affairs.

Singer, Peter. 1973. *Democracy and Disobedience.* Oxford: Oxford University Press.

Thoreau, Henry David. [1849] 1996. Civil Disobedience. In *Thoreau: Political Writings*, ed. Nancy L. Rosenblum, 1–21.

Cambridge, U.K.: Cambridge University Press. (Originally published as "Resistance to Civil Government.")

Wei Jingsheng. 1998. *The Courage to Stand Alone: Letters from Prison and Other Writings.* New York: Penguin Books.

Zashin, Elliot M. 1972. *Civil Disobedience and Democracy.* New York: Free Press.

Terence Ball

CIVIL LIBERTIES

Civil liberties are individual freedoms intended to protect citizens from government. These freedoms include, but are not limited to, equal protection under the law, freedom of speech and association, religious freedom, and the right to a fair hearing or trial when accused of committing a crime. While many tend to use the terms *civil liberties* and *civil rights* interchangeably, civil liberties can be distinguished from civil rights in some fundamental ways. The primary distinction is that civil rights are protections by government against discrimination on the basis of individual characteristics like race, ethnicity, gender, or disability status, whereas civil liberties are most appropriately thought of as protections from government encroachment. Thus civil rights tend to require government action, while civil liberties are typically best served by government inaction.

Civil liberties are typically enumerated and guaranteed via the constitution of a nation-state but can also be guaranteed by other legal documents and conventions. One example of an enumeration of civil liberties that is not contained in a state's constitution is the International Covenant on Civil and Political Rights (ICCPR), a United Nations treaty created in 1966 and designed to protect civil rights and liberties globally. The ICCPR obliges nations who ratified it to protect individual liberties like freedom of speech, the right to a fair trial, and equal protection under the law via appropriate legislative, judicial, and administrative measures. Another example is the European Convention on Human Rights (ECHR), adopted by the Council of Europe in 1950. In addition to enumerating civil liberties and many civil and human rights, the ECHR established the European Court of Human Rights to adjudicate cases brought by individuals and groups who feel their rights under the ECHR were violated.

The United States is an example of a nation with constitutionally guaranteed civil liberties. In the U.S. Constitution, the most important protections for citizens against government imposition are set forth in the Bill of Rights, which are the first ten amendments to the Constitution. Additionally, in its capacity as the arbiter of disputes between government and the citizenry, the federal judiciary of the United States has slowly expanded the coverage of the Bill of Rights to include protections from state and local governments. This process is generally referred to as the *nationalization* or *incorporation* of the Bill of Rights, and occurred via expanded interpretation of the due process clause and the equal protection clause of the Fourteenth Amendment of the U.S. Constitution.

Though many governments profess civil liberties protections through various legal documents and conventions, it is not uncommon for these same governments to violate these protections and infringe upon the individual freedoms of their citizens, especially in times of crisis. For example, when national security concerns conflict with an individual's right to privacy or protection from unlawful imprisonment, many governments privilege national security over civil liberties and are thus more inclined to commit violations. Because of some governments' proclivity to infringe upon individual liberties, nonprofit organizations, such as Amnesty International, Human Rights Watch, and the American Civil Liberties Union, have been established with the missions of protecting and extending individuals' rights and liberties and holding governments accountable for their encroachments.

SEE ALSO *Bill of Rights, U.S.; Citizenship; Civil Rights; Constitution, U.S.; Constitutions; Due Process; Equal Protection; Freedom; Government; Human Rights; Individualism; Liberty; National Security; Nation-State; Public Rights; United Nations*

BIBLIOGRAPHY

Carlson, Scott N., and Gregory Gisvold. 2003. *Practical Guide to the International Covenant on Civil and Political Rights.* Ardsley, NY: Transnational.

Feldman, David. 2002. *Civil Liberties and Human Rights in England and Wales.* 2nd ed. Oxford and New York: Oxford University Press.

Foster, Steven. 2006. *The Judiciary, Civil Liberties, and Human Rights.* Edinburgh, U.K.: Edinburgh University Press.

Irons, Peter H. 2005. *Cases and Controversies: Civil Rights and Liberties in Context.* Upper Saddle River, NJ: Pearson Prentice Hall.

Kernell, Samuel, and Gary C. Jacobson. 2006. *The Logic of American Politics.* 3rd ed. Washington, DC: CQ.

Monique L. Lyle

CIVIL-MILITARY RELATION

The term *civil-military relations* denotes the field of social science inquiry that analyzes the relationship between the armed forces and society and/or the state. Since the state is often defined, following Max Weber, as the organ of society that holds the monopoly on the legitimate use of force, the relationship between formally constituted bodies of force and the state or society is a major indicator of the nature of that state. Indeed, in our own time the presence of independent military organizations or paramilitaries organized along political, sectarian, or ethnic lines and not answering to the command of a legitimate state testifies to the presence of the phenomenon of state failure in such countries as Iraq, the former Yugoslavia, Lebanon, and several sub-Saharan African states. Where all political power literally grows out of the barrel of a gun, the state and a legitimate political order are absent and anarchy, if not a war of all against all, reigns.

Alternatively, although the method by which the armed forces are subordinated to the executive and accountable to the legislative body varies in democratic states, the depoliticization of armed forces (including the police), their inability to take part in partisan politics, and their enforced accountability to legitimately elected organizations and heads of state testify to the democratic tendencies of the state. In these states, the use of force is under legal control, and ideally force can be employed only with legislative approval. In such a state the military similarly regulates itself by means of the internal rule of law (military law codes), which ensures that officers and soldiers are accountable for their acts. In the twentieth century and beyond, efforts have been made, beginning with the Nuremberg and other anti-Nazi trials, to extend that accountability to the international sphere, making commanding officers and even soldiers responsible to properly organized international tribunals for their acts.

Likewise in antidemocratic—that is, authoritarian—states, a critical signifier of the nature of the state lies in the sphere of civil-military relations. If the armed forces and police are divided into multiple overlapping forces with overlapping jurisdictions and the authority to monitor each other, this indicates that the legislature is weak and has been bypassed in its role of enforcing accountability. It entails as well the supremacy of the executive, which is above accountability to the legislature and its ability to exercise direct control over the armed forces through such multiple overlapping militaries. In such a state the military is politicized, a player in partisan politics, or else the means by which ambitious politicians seize power. Alternatively, a general or generals may decide to use the forces under their command, whether regular army, secret police, or some other force, to seize power for themselves. Here again the forms of such relationships among the executive, legislative, and military may vary widely among states. Nevertheless, these symptoms of authoritarianism and lack of legal accountability lead to the presumption of the existence of an authoritarian if not totalitarian state. And in totalitarian states, if not authoritarian ones, the primary function of the state is to prepare for war. Such states are frequently, if not always, organized for military action against either internal or external adversaries. In this case, not only are democratic controls over the armed forces absent but also war and a military ethos for the state administration are glorified. Even if a state is not militaristic in the sense of glorifying war, such regimes often promulgate a cult of so-called military virtues and discipline that should characterize the state administration.

This leads to the question of the relationship of the military to society. Crucial questions here are whether the soldiery is organized as a professional volunteer force or conscripted, the ethnic and religious composition of the armed forces, and the relationships among different armed forces, the police, and the military—or what in Europe is increasingly called the security sector. It also is critical to determine if the military and its commanders, as well as the police, can break criminal laws with impunity or whether they are truly subordinate and accountable to their country's laws. This consideration obviously includes the extent of economic corruption and the ability simply to seize property by force, the latter being a sign of a demoralized military and a failing state. In this connection the field of civil-military relations also embraces the question of public support for the armed force and the image society holds of its members.

The public standing of the armed forces in any society is a good indicator of the nature of the relationship between that society and its armed forces. For all that the armed forces are trained specialists in the use and control of violence, they are recruited from society and cannot be artificially isolated from a society's values or pathologies. Thus a society undergoing stress will find that stress translated into its armed forces, even if there is a lag between them.

The field of civil-military relations encompasses the entire range of relationships between the various forms and missions that armed forces take and the society and state that empowers them to act. It is an inherently comparative field because all states and societies have armed forces with which they interact. Indeed, the absence of either the state or the armed forces in the equation underscores the severity of a crisis for the community in question. Yet despite this inherent bias toward a comparative approach, each state and society relates uniquely to its own armed forces. The topicality of this relationship remains crucial to the understanding not only of our own state and government but to the broader world of international relations.

SEE ALSO *Authoritarianism; Civil Society; Democracy; Ideal Type; Janowitz, Morris; Militarism; Military; Military Regimes; Nazism; Selective Service; State,* *The; Totalitarianism; War; War and Peace; War Crimes; Weber, Max*

BIBLIOGRAPHY

Desch, Michael C. 1999. *Civilian Control of the Military: The Changing Security Environment.* Baltimore, MD: Johns Hopkins University Press.

Feaver, Peter D., and Richard H. Kohn, eds. 2001. *Soldiers and Civilians: The Civil-Military Gap and American National Security.* Cambridge, MA: MIT Press.

Finer, Samuel E. 1988. *The Man on Horseback: The Role of the Military in Politics,* 2nd ed. Boulder, CO: Westview Press.

Herspring, Dale R. 2005. *The Pentagon and the Presidency: Civil-Military Relations from FDR to George W. Bush.* Lawrence: University Press of Kansas.

Huntington, Samuel P. 1957. *The Soldier and the State: The Theory and Politics of Civil-Military Relations.* Cambridge, MA: Harvard University Press.

Janowitz, Morris. 1960. *The Professional Soldier: A Social and Political Portrait.* Glencoe, IL: The Free Press.

Stephen Blank

CIVIL RIGHTS

The term *civil rights* refers to equal treatment for individuals under the law. Political scientists Morris Fiorina, Paul Peterson, D. Stephen Voss, and Bertram Johnson define civil rights as "embody[ing] the American guarantee to equal treatment under the law—not just for racial groups, as people often assume, but more generally" (2007, p. 381). Civil rights are related to, but distinct from, civil liberties and human rights. In the American context, *civil liberties* are the freedoms granted to citizens in the Bill of Rights, the first ten amendments to the U.S. Constitution. These include, among other things, the freedoms of speech, peaceable assembly, and religion; protections against unreasonable searches and seizures, forced self-incrimination, and cruel and unusual punishment; and, for criminal suspects, the rights to a trial by jury and to representation by an attorney. These protections derive largely from the First, Fourth, Fifth, Sixth, and Eighth Amendments, all part of the Bill of Rights. Many other nations also grant both civil rights and civil liberties to their citizens through their constitutions or legislation.

Human rights are those rights that most scholars believe all human beings should have, regardless of which nation they live in. In 1948 the United Nations adopted the Universal Declaration of Human Rights, which declares that human rights include, among other things, rights to life, liberty, security, travel, property ownership, education, free thought and religion, work, rest, leisure, and an adequate standard of living. The declaration also prohibits governments from certain practices, including torture and arbitrary arrest and detention. Human rights, then, are conferred not by individual nations, but by virtue of being human. Human rights may also be more broadly defined to include some rights outside the reach of both civil rights and civil liberties.

CIVIL RIGHTS AND DIFFERENT TREATMENT OF INDIVIDUALS

Civil rights derive from the U.S. Constitution, specifically the Fourteenth Amendment's equal protection clause, which states that government cannot "deny to any person within its jurisdiction the equal protection of the laws." In practice, government often draws distinctions between individuals, and the Fourteenth Amendment prohibits some, but not all, of these distinctions. When governments can treat people differently is a question often resolved by the courts. Some distinctions, such as race, are automatically suspect; the courts apply "strict scrutiny," where government must demonstrate a "compelling state interest" and show there is no other way to pursue that interest. This test is very difficult to meet. In 1978 the Supreme Court prohibited a strictly race-based quota system for admitting students to the medical school at the University of California at Davis. In 1995 the Court prohibited a program that awarded municipal contracts to minority-owned firms on the basis of race.

Other distinctions, such as gender, receive "heightened scrutiny," which is somewhat less demanding. Still, the courts often overturn government actions that treat men and women differently. In 1976 the Supreme Court overturned an Oklahoma law that established a drinking age of twenty-one for men but eighteen for women. And in 1996 the Court prohibited the state-run Virginia Military Institute's policy of admitting only male students. Still other distinctions, such as age, are evaluated by the courts based on whether the government can show a "rational basis" for its action. For example, states seeking to place special restrictions on issuing driver's licenses to people over seventy-five years old must only show that the state's actions are reasonably related to promoting a legitimate government purpose. In short, the answer to the question "when can government treat individuals differently?" depends on the basis for classifying people.

CONSEQUENCES OF THE ABSENCE OF CIVIL RIGHTS

Civil rights are widely regarded as essential in democratic societies. The absence of civil rights would mean governments have few limits against enacting laws that enshrine unequal treatment by declaring some groups superior to others. American history provides many examples. The extreme racial segregation and discrimination against southern blacks between 1880 and 1965 resulted from the conviction among most southern whites that civil rights did not exist for blacks. Without civil rights, government could pass laws prohibiting blacks from holding certain kinds of jobs or requiring black and white schoolchildren to attend segregated schools, as many, mostly southern, states did before the Supreme Court prohibited segregated public schools in 1954. Without civil rights, government could not require that women be admitted to state-supported military academies, be allowed to practice the occupation of their choice, or even be allowed to hold checking accounts in their own name. Without civil rights, public buildings would not necessarily be accessible to the physically disabled, as the 1990 Americans with Disabilities Act requires. Without civil rights, governments would be free to declare same-sex sodomy (but not opposite-sex sodomy) illegal—as Texas and several other states did before the Supreme Court overturned such laws in 2003. Without civil rights, governments could pass restrictive immigration laws targeting people of certain national origins, denying them entry.

Guarantees of civil rights, then, protect people based on race and ethnicity, but also other factors, including nationality, gender, disability status, and sexual orientation. The presence of civil rights protects citizens against discrimination by their government, and often, by private action. The absence of civil rights opens the door to group-based domination, discrimination, and oppression, and would raise serious doubts about any society's claim of upholding "liberty and justice for all."

SEE ALSO *Black Power; Citizenship; Civil Disobedience; Civil Liberties; Civil Rights Movement, U.S.; Constitution, U.S.; Disability; Due Process; Equal Protection; Human Rights; Public Rights; Sexual Orientation, Social and Economic Consequences*

BIBLIOGRAPHY

Fiorina, Morris P., Paul E. Peterson, D. Stephen Voss, and Bertram Johnson. 2007. *America's New Democracy*. 3rd ed., 2006 election update. New York: Pearson Longman.

United Nations. 1948. *The Universal Declaration of Human Rights*. http://www.un.org/Overview/rights.html.

U.S. Supreme Court. 1954. *Brown v. Board of Education*. http://caselaw.lp.findlaw.com/scripts/getcase.pl?court=US&vol=347&invol=483.

U.S. Supreme Court. 1978. *Regents of the University of California v. Bakke*. http://caselaw.lp.findlaw.com/scripts/getcase.pl?court=US&vol=438&invol=265.

U.S. Supreme Court. 1995. *Adarand Contractors v. Pena*. http://caselaw.lp.findlaw.com/scripts/getcase.pl?court=US&vol=000&invol=u10252.

U.S. Supreme Court. 1996. *United States v. Virginia.* http://caselaw.lp.findlaw.com/scripts/getcase.pl?court=US&vol=000&invol=u20026.

U.S. Supreme Court. 2003. *Lawrence et al. v. Texas.* http://caselaw.lp.findlaw.com/scripts/getcase.pl?court=US&vol=000&invol=02-102.

Fred Slocum

CIVIL RIGHTS, COLD WAR

During the cold war, civil rights violations within the United States captured the interest of the world, causing many to wonder whether race discrimination undermined the nation's global leadership. How could American democracy be a model for the world to follow, peoples of other nations asked, when within the United States citizens were disenfranchised, segregated, and sometimes lynched because of their race? Discrimination was widely seen as the nation's Achilles' heel.

In 1947, after violent attacks on African American World War II veterans in the South raised concern at home and abroad, President Harry S. Truman's Committee on Civil Rights issued a report which argued that the United States needed to improve its civil rights record, in part because race discrimination harmed U.S. foreign relations. By the late 1940s, the Soviet Union used racial discrimination in America as a principal anti-U.S. propaganda theme. Soviet propaganda was often exaggerated, but propaganda on race was particularly effective, simply because there was so much truth to it.

Global interest gave the civil rights movement international allies. In 1947 W. E. B. Du Bois wrote a petition for the National Association for the Advancement of Colored People (NAACP) to the new United Nations, "An Appeal to the World," to enlist U.N. support for the rights of African Americans. Du Bois, Paul Robeson, and others who criticized American race discrimination in an international context, lost their passports during the 1950s. Meanwhile, through the Voice of America and overseas information programs, the U.S. government tried to rehabilitate the image of American race relations, casting it as a story of enlightened progress under democracy. Some civil rights leaders, such as NAACP Executive Secretary Walter White, were staunchly anti-Communist and tried to aid the effort to convince peoples of other nations that African Americans could flourish in the United States, and that democracy was a better system of government than communism. Ultimately, however, American leaders believed that only civil rights progress would dampen the negative effect of racial problems on U.S. foreign relations.

In 1952 the Justice Department filed an Amicus Curiae brief in support of school desegregation in *Brown v. Board of Education* (1954), citing Secretary of State Dean Acheson as authority, and arguing that a crucial national interest was at stake in the case: foreign relations. When the Supreme Court ruled that segregation was unconstitutional, the decision was celebrated around the world. A challenge soon arose when Arkansas governor Orval Faubus blocked nine African American students from attending Little Rock's Central High School (1957). The Little Rock Crisis generated global criticism, and led jazz artist Louis Armstrong to cancel a State Department–sponsored trip to the Soviet Union; if "people over there ask me what's wrong with my country," Armstrong asked, "what am I supposed to say?" (Giddins 2001, p. 127). President Dwight D. Eisenhower, concerned with damage to U.S. foreign relations and other factors, sent in federal troops to escort the students into school. The world press lauded the president for putting the force of the U.S. government behind civil rights.

International interest gave the civil rights movement important leverage in the 1960s. The Nobel Peace Prize awarded to Martin Luther King Jr. in 1964 was one sign of global support. When Police Commissioner Eugene "Bull" Connor ordered fire fighters and police to use high-powered fire-hoses and police dogs on civil rights demonstrators marching in Birmingham, Alabama, in 1963, images of these violent tactics filled the world press. Domestic and international pressure led President John F. Kennedy to call for a strong civil rights bill. Passage of the Civil Rights Act of 1964 was celebrated around the world as a sign that the U.S. government was firmly behind civil rights reform. Formal legal change helped restore the image of America, even though inequities in American communities remained.

SEE ALSO Brown v. Board of Education, *1954; Civil Rights; Civil Rights Movement, U.S.; Discrimination; Discrimination, Racial; Du Bois, W. E. B.; Eisenhower, Dwight D.; Kennedy, John F.; McCarthyism; National Association for the Advancement of Colored People (NAACP); Nobel Peace Prize; Robeson, Paul; Roosevelt, Franklin D.; Truman, Harry S.; Union of Soviet Socialist Republics; White, Walter*

BIBLIOGRAPHY

Borstelmann, Thomas. 2001. *The Cold War and the Color Line: American Race Relations in the Global Arena.* Cambridge, MA: Harvard University Press.

Dudziak, Mary L. 2000. *Cold War Civil Rights: Race and the Image of American Democracy*. Princeton, NJ: Princeton University Press.

Giddins, Gary. 2001. *Satchmo: The Genius of Louis Armstrong*. 2nd ed. Cambridge, MA: Da Capo Press.

Plummer, Brenda Gayle. 1996. *Rising Wind: Black Americans and U.S. Foreign Affairs, 1935–1960*. Chapel Hill: University of North Carolina Press.

Mary L. Dudziak

CIVIL RIGHTS MOVEMENT, U.S.

The civil rights movement in the United States is most commonly identified as the long-term effort to achieve legal, political, social, economic, and educational equality and justice for African Americans, especially the interval from 1954 to 1968.

ORIGINS OF THE CIVIL RIGHTS MOVEMENT

After Reconstruction ended in 1877, state and local governments in the South quickly enacted and enforced laws that required or allowed private racial discrimination and the racial segregation of public institutions and services. Other state laws circumvented the Fifteenth Amendment by using poll taxes, literacy tests, grandfather clauses, and white primaries to prevent blacks from voting. Collectively known as Jim Crow, these laws were unofficially enforced by the Ku Klux Klan, a white terrorist organization.

U.S. Supreme Court decisions also helped to legitimize Jim Crow laws and discourage renewed federal intervention. In the "Civil Rights Cases" of 1883, the Supreme Court struck down the Civil Rights Act of 1875. Congress did not pass another civil rights bill until 1957. In the *Plessy v. Ferguson* decision of 1896, the Supreme Court upheld a Louisiana law that required the segregation of railroad passengers. The court ruled that such segregation laws were constitutionally allowed under its "separate but equal" interpretation of the Tenth and Fourteenth Amendments.

LEGAL AND POLITICAL ACTIVISM OF THE CIVIL RIGHTS MOVEMENT: 1910–1968

In 1910 W. E. B. Du Bois (1868–1963), a black educator and writer, established the National Association for the Advancement of Colored People (NAACP). The NAACP Legal Defense and Educational Fund's initial purpose was to promote civil rights for African Americans through court cases. This organization's most famous legal victory was the Supreme Court's unanimous decision in *Brown v. Board of Education* (1954). The *Brown* decision overturned *Plessy* and ordered the end of de jure racial segregation in public education. Thurgood Marshall (1908–1993), the association's chief legal counsel in this case, became the first black Supreme Court justice in 1967.

Racial segregation and the disfranchisement of southern blacks continued during the 1950s and early 1960s. Most southern states refused to effectively implement the *Brown* decision. Southern governors such as George C. Wallace (1919–1998) of Alabama, Ross Barnett of Mississippi, and Orville Faubus of Arkansas exploited racial issues by dramatically resisting federal court orders to integrate public schools and state universities. Senator J. Strom Thurmond of South Carolina, who ran for president in 1948 as the nominee of the anti–civil rights "Dixiecrat" Party, tried to prevent passage of the Civil Rights Act of 1957 through a record-breaking filibuster. In major nonsouthern cities with growing black populations, African Americans experienced de facto segregation in public schools, as well as racial discrimination in housing, jobs, and customer service.

The civil rights movement became better known to Americans nationally because of televised news coverage of civil rights demonstrations in the South, especially those led by Martin Luther King Jr. (1929–1968), a black minister in Alabama. There was also national media coverage of President Dwight D. Eisenhower's (1890–1969) use of the U.S. Army to enforce racial integration at a high school in Little Rock, Arkansas, and the racially motivated murders of fourteen-year-old Emmett Till in Mississippi in 1955 for allegedly whistling at a white woman, and of three civil rights activists in Mississippi in 1964.

Organized as the Southern Christian Leadership Conference (SCLC), King's movement attracted white legal, financial, and political support from throughout the nation. Influenced by the nonviolent civil disobedience of Mohandas K. Gandhi (1869–1948), King's first success in defying and ending racial segregation was the Montgomery, Alabama, bus boycott of 1955 to 1956. After Rosa Parks (1913–2005), a black seamstress, was arrested for violating the segregated seating of bus passengers, King led a boycott of local buses, which forced the end of segregated bus seating in Montgomery. The Montgomery bus boycott inspired similar peaceful protests elsewhere in the South, such as the sit-in protests by black college students seeking service at lunch counters and the Freedom Riders seeking to racially integrate Greyhound buses and passenger facilities on an interstate basis.

Many of the participants in the Freedom Rides and the voter registration project in Mississippi during the summer of 1964 were members of the Student Nonviolent Coordinating Committee (SNCC) and the Congress of Racial Equality (CORE). SNCC and CORE were also prominent in organizing King's August 1963 March on Washington. Earlier, in his "Letter from a Birmingham Jail," King expressed his exasperation with people who urged caution and patience in his incessant yet peaceful quest for civil rights and justice for African Americans.

Malcolm X (1925–1965) was the most militant and prominent critic of King's pacifism. Malcolm X, a black Muslim religious and political leader based in New York City, asserted that African Americans should reject pacifism and arm themselves for protection against whites. He also rejected racial integration in a white-dominated society and urged the development of black separatism in order to promote economic independence and an African-based cultural identity among blacks. Although Malcolm X was murdered by rival black Muslims in 1965, his influence on the civil rights movement persisted in the formation of the Black Panthers and King's later opposition to the Vietnam War (1957–1975), his linkage between racial justice and economic justice, and his increased activism on racial issues in northern cities, especially Chicago.

The most significant national legislative accomplishments of the civil rights movement were the Civil Rights Acts of 1964 and 1968 and the Voting Rights Act of 1965. The Civil Rights Act of 1964 prohibited racial discrimination in public accommodations, public facilities, employment, and the use of federal funds. The Voting Rights Act of 1965 authorized the federal government to register voters and supervise elections, prohibited literacy tests, and expressed opposition to poll taxes. The most controversial provision of the Civil Rights Act of 1968 prohibited racial discrimination in the sale and rental of housing.

THE LEGACY OF THE CIVIL RIGHTS MOVEMENT

After the assassination of King in 1968, the further advancement of civil rights for African Americans became more controversial among whites as they associated the civil rights movement with black militancy, affirmative action, and court-ordered busing to racially integrate non-southern schools. Nevertheless, the black civil rights movement inspired other civil rights movements in the United States, especially those for women, gays, opponents of the Vietnam War, and Latinos, the latter led by César Chávez (1927–1993) and the United Farm Workers of America.

SEE ALSO Brown v. Board of Education, *1954; African Americans; Black Power; Civil Disobedience; Civil Liberties; Civil Rights; Congress of Racial Equality; Du Bois, W. E. B.; Eisenhower, Dwight D.; Gandhi, Mohandas K.; Human Rights; Integration; Jim Crow; King, Martin Luther, Jr.; Marshall, Thurgood; Militants; National Association for the Advancement of Colored People (NAACP); Passive Resistance; Public Rights; Reconstruction Era (U.S.); Segregation; Social Movements; Student Nonviolent Coordinating Committee; Supreme Court, U.S.; Vietnam War; Voting Rights Act*

BIBLIOGRAPHY

Branch, Taylor. 1988. *Parting the Waters: America in the King Years, 1954–63.* New York: Simon and Schuster.

Oates, Stephen B. 1982. *Let the Trumpet Sound: The Life of Martin Luther King, Jr.* New York: New American Library.

Sitkoff, Harvard. 1981. *The Struggle for Black Equality, 1954–1980.* New York: Hill and Wang.

Sean J. Savage

CIVIL SOCIETY

Civil society (from the Latin *civilis societas*) is the realm of independent activity and voluntary association that is not organized by the state. The origin of the term is often traced to the Scottish Enlightenment philosopher Adam Ferguson (1723–1816) and his *Essay on the History of Civil Society* (1767). Ferguson saw the new commercial civilization then displacing the older clan-based feudal order of the Scottish Highlands as enhancing individual liberty through the introduction of "civil society," "civil life," and "economic society." In the same intellectual tradition, another Scottish Enlightenment philosopher and social theorist, Adam Smith (1723–1790), referred to the notion of civil society as the capacity of human communities for autonomous self-organization. For both Ferguson and Smith, the example of the free, self-regulating economic market demonstrated the possibility of social organization without the heavy-handed supervision of the state.

But it was the German idealist philosopher Georg Wilhelm Friedrich Hegel (1770–1831) who first drew the boundary between the spheres of state and society in his *Elements of the Philosophy of Right* (1820). For Hegel, civil society (*bürgerliche Gesellschaft*) was the realm of the particular counterposed to the state. It occupied the mesolevel (or intermediate stage) between the dialectical opposites of the macrocommunity of the state and the microcommunity of the family. In his view, civil society was a temporary mode of relations interposed between the individual (or the family) and the state, which was to be transcended when particular and common interests combined.

There are several competing definitions of what the concept of civil society involves. For some writers, like the French Enlightenment philosopher Charles Louis de Montesquieu (1689–1755) and the French social commentator Alexis de Tocqueville (1805–1859), civil society was the realm of intermediate associations that stood between the individual and the state. It includes social and economic arrangements, ethical and legal codes, contractual obligations, and institutions apart from the state, but its key attribute is that it refers to public life rather than private or household-based activities. Civil society is juxtaposed to the family and the state and exists within the framework of the rule of law, accepting a certain commitment to the political community and the rules of the game established by the state. Most writers in this tradition seem to have in mind the domain of public participation in voluntary organizations, the mass media, professional associations, labor unions, social movements, and the like. In their writings, civil society becomes a description for all nonstate aspects of society, including the economy, culture, social structures, and even politics.

Other thinkers, like the Swiss-born Enlightenment philosopher Jean-Jacques Rousseau (1712–1778) and the German social theorist and revolutionary Karl Marx (1818–1883), tended to be more critical of civil society, which they saw as an economic and social order, developing in accordance with its own rules and independently of the state. In this conceptualization, civil society meant the social, economic, legal, and ethical arrangements of modern, industrial-capitalist society considered apart from the state. The concept generally referred to the specific mode of relations between the state and self-organized social groups which was first attained by the modern European nations, although its seeds can be found in earlier periods. While praising civil society, which is voluntarily formed by the citizens as a sphere of social self-organization between the private realm of the domestic and the state, Rousseau (1762) recognized that civil society can be plagued by evils such as social injustice, elitism, and economic inequality that contradicted his idea of the "general will" of the entire citizenry (*volonté générale*). While Marx stressed the economic character of civil society in the fashion of Ferguson and Smith, he viewed it as an expression of crass materialism, brutal exploitation, anarchic competition, and economic inefficiency (Marx 1843). According to him, civil society was a morally decadent, oligarchic society rife with greed, egoism, individualism, and alienation that benefited only the privileged class of the "bourgeoisie" (that is, the wealthy owners of productive capital) who lived off the labor of the rest of society, especially the industrial working class (the "proletariat").

For the prominent Italian Marxist theorist Antonio Gramsci (1891–1937), civil society was the bastion of "hegemony" by the economically dominant "bourgeois" class. In contrast to Marx, he defined civil society as a predominantly cultural and ideological sphere rather than an exclusively economic domain. He argued that in the developed capitalist countries, the state has close institutional and ideological links with civil society, in which the "active consent" of the mass public is manufactured on a daily basis. Public consent is not achieved through political democracy but through ideological hegemony—that is, propaganda, indoctrination, public education, and the inculcation of a worldview biased in favor of the socially and politically dominant class. Therefore, civil society is ultimately supportive of the "bourgeois" state, which uses it to shape popular beliefs and aspirations in its own ideological image (Gramsci 2001).

Today the study of civil society focuses on the causal link between democratization and the nonpolitical aspects of the contemporary social order, leaving open to debate the question of whether or not there is incongruence and conflict between civil society and the state. The existence of a self-organized, vibrant, and fully developed civil society that is free of the state and has numerous autonomous public arenas within which various voluntary associations regulate their own activities and govern their own members is a necessary, but not sufficient, condition for a viable democracy and the transition from an authoritarian or totalitarian regime to a democratic one. Civil society discourse has more recently drawn on the experience of the collapse of communism in Eastern Europe, where the anticommunist opposition embraced the revival of civil society as its raison d'être during the years leading up to the revolutions of 1989. In fact the downfall of communism has often been linked theoretically to the revolt of residual or nascent civil society against the political intolerance and ideological rigidity of the communist state.

SEE ALSO *Associations, Voluntary; Authoritarianism; Capitalism; Communism; Democratization; Gramsci, Antonio; Hegel, Georg Wilhelm Friedrich; Hegemony; Ideology; Marx, Karl; Rousseau, Jean-Jacques; Smith, Adam; Society; State, The; Tocqueville, Alexis de*

BIBLIOGRAPHY

Baker, Gideon. 2002. *Civil Society and Democratic Theory: Alternative Voices.* London and New York: Routledge.

Cohen, Jean L., and Andrew Arato. 1994. *Civil Society and Political Theory.* Cambridge, MA: MIT Press.

Dahrendorf, Ralf. 1997. *After 1989: Morals, Revolution, and Civil Society.* New York: St. Martin's Press.

Gramsci, Antonio. 2001. *Selections from the Prison Notebooks.* Trans. and ed. Quintin Hoare and Geoffrey N. Smith. London: Electric Book.

Keane, John. 1998. *Civil Society: Old Images, New Visions.* Stanford, CA: Stanford University Press.

Marx, Karl. [1843] 1958. *On the Jewish Question.* Trans. Helen Lederer. Cincinnati, OH: Hebrew Union College. (Orig. pub. as *Zur Judenfrage,* 1843.)

Rosenblum, Nancy L., and Robert C. Post, eds. 2002. *Civil Society and Government.* Princeton, NJ: Princeton University Press.

Rousseau, Jean-Jacques. [1762] 1987. *On the Social Contract.* Trans. and ed. Donald A. Cress. Indianapolis: Hackett. (Orig. pub. as *Du Contrat Social,* 1762.)

Seligman, Adam B. 1995. *The Idea of Civil Society.* Princeton, NJ: Princeton University Press.

Rossen Vassilev

CIVIL WAR, MEXICAN

SEE *Mexican Revolution (1910–1920).*

CIVIL WARS

Since the end of World War II (1939–1945), civil wars (wars within nations) have surpassed interstate wars (wars between nations) as the most frequent and destructive forms of organized armed conflict in the world. The Correlates of War Project, a major data archive on armed conflict, reports that there were only twenty-three interstate wars between 1945 and 1997, resulting in 3.3 million battle deaths. By contrast, there were more than four times as many civil wars (108), resulting in almost four times as many casualties (11.4 million; Sarkees 2000).

A second shift in the patterns of conflict is that until the breakup of the Soviet Union in 1991, almost all of the civil wars that occurred since 1945 took place in third world nations of Asia, Africa, and Latin America. By contrast, the interstate wars that punctuated the historical record of the three centuries prior to World War II took place primarily in Europe among the major powers of the international system (Holsti 1996). Yet from 1945 until 1991, Europe was almost completely free of armed conflict on its soil (Holsti 1992, p. 37; 1996).

A third salient pattern in the recent wave of civil wars is that once a nation experienced one civil war, it was very likely to experience a second one. The 108 civil wars in the Correlates of War data set occurred in only fifty-four nations. Only twenty-six of those nations had one and only one civil war, while the remaining twenty-eight

nations had at least two and as many as five separate civil wars. Thus, for a certain subset of nations, civil war is a chronically recurrent condition.

One encouraging trend to emerge since the end of the Cold War is the willingness of the international community to broker negotiated settlements to civil wars and to support those settlements with peacekeeping forces. Nineteen of the twenty-six civil wars that ended in negotiated settlements were resolved after 1988, including United Nations (UN)–mediated settlements to protracted civil wars in Cambodia, Mozambique, and El Salvador, to name but a few. Not all of these peace settlements have lasted: the peace established by settlement agreements in Angola, Colombia, and Lebanon, for example, later broke down into renewed civil war. However, when negotiated settlements are supported by UN peacekeeping forces, the resulting peace has proven to be rather durable (Fortna 2004; Doyle and Sambanis 2000).

FORMS OF CIVIL WAR

The term *civil war* is used to describe organized armed conflict between the armed forces of a sovereign state and one or more rebel organizations drawn from the population of that nation. Two subtypes of civil war can be distinguished: *revolutions* and *secessionist revolts.* In a revolution, the rebels seek to overthrow the existing government and assume control of the state themselves. Civil wars in Nicaragua (1978–1979), El Salvador (1979–1992), and Cambodia (1970–1975, 1979–1991) are examples of revolutionary civil wars. In a secessionist revolt, the rebels seek not to take over the existing state but to gain independence from it by creating a second sovereign nation-state out of a portion of the territory of the original nation. The Tamil revolt in Sri Lanka that began in 1983, the Eritrean revolt against Ethiopia (1974–1990), and the Biafra revolt in Nigeria (1967–1970) are examples of secessionist revolts.

A further distinction among civil wars concerns whether they are *ethnic conflicts* or not. Among revolutionary civil wars, those that are nonethnic or *ideological* typically involved peasant-based insurgencies in nations where the agricultural sector dominates the economy. Where land ownership is concentrated in the hands of a small landed elite, the large peasant majority is often relegated to a life of poverty as landless or land-poor cultivators. When an authoritarian state employs repression to preserve the prerogatives of the landed elite against peasant-based dissident movements, revolutionary insurgencies can arise by drawing support from landless and land-poor peasants. The civil wars in El Salvador, Peru, Colombia, and Guatemala followed this pattern.

In ethnic conflicts, the same issues of inequality and repression generate the grievances that motivate rebels and their supporters. However, ethnicity adds another dimension to the conflict between state and society. In ethnic revolutions, ethnicity and inequality often coincide: those who are victims of various forms of inequality are from one ethnic group, while those who enjoy a disproportionate share of the advantages available in the nation are from a different ethnic group. Ethnic divisions add cultural and identity issues to the fuel of conflict. Members of one ethnic group fear the suppression of their culture, language, religion, and heritage at the hands of a regime dominated by a rival ethnic group. Where ethnic groups out of power are concentrated in geographic enclaves, their response to this *ethnic security dilemma* is often to launch a secessionist war aimed at establishing their homeland as a separate sovereign nation. The Eritrean secession from Ethiopia fits this pattern. Where ethnic groups are more intermixed geographically, groups out of power often resort to revolutionary violence in an attempt to overthrow a state dominated by their ethnic rivals and to establish themselves in power. The ethnic revolutions in Angola and Rwanda fit this pattern.

CAUSES OF CIVIL WAR

The observable patterns of conflict discussed earlier provide some clues as to the factors that make a nation more or less susceptible to the outbreak of civil war. The fact that until 1991 almost all civil wars occurred in third world nations suggests that factors common to third world nations but not postindustrial democracies or former Leninist regimes might be implicated in the causal process leading to civil war. One such feature is that almost all of these nations were at one time colonies of European powers. Colonial powers harnessed the economies of these regions to serve the demands of markets in Europe and North America. In so doing, they disrupted existing patterns of agricultural production for local markets, as well as the patterns of community organization that supported that production and provided indigenous communities with reliable survival strategies (Migdal 1988).

Decolonization may have conferred formal sovereignty on former colonies, but rarely did the departing colonial power endow the postcolonial state with the institutional capacity or economic wherewithal to develop a strong and effective state capable of providing its constituents with civil order and a reasonable level of material well-being. Lacking legitimacy based on effective performance, weak states came to perceive any dissident challenge—peaceful or otherwise—as a threat to the state itself. The weak state responded with the one policy instrument at its disposal: military repression. Repression forced challengers to resort to violence of their own in order to advance their claims and defend themselves

against the state. This cycle of violence begetting violence often escalated to civil war.

Empirical research on predictors of civil war onset provides support for the proposition that the *weak state syndrome* described above is associated with susceptibility to civil war. A number of correlates of the weak state syndrome consistently distinguish nations that experience civil war from those that do not. Not surprisingly, civil wars are more likely to occur among nations that have lower levels of economic development (Fearon and Laitin 2003; Collier and Hoeffler 1998). Where poverty is widespread, the opportunity costs of participating in armed rebellion are lower: participants have less to lose by joining an armed rebellion than would be the case were they more prosperous. Rebel recruiting is facilitated by low levels of economic well-being (Collier and Hoeffler 1998). Economic underdevelopment also constrains the capacity of the state to respond to dissident movements with accommodative reforms that might defuse tensions short of armed conflict.

Other dimensions of state strength affect a nation's susceptibility to civil war as well. Although the evidence is mixed, there is some support for the proposition that both democracies and autocracies are less likely to experience civil war than weak authoritarian regimes (Henderson and Singer 2000; Auvinen 1997; Hegre et al. 2001). The institutions of democracy provide aggrieved groups with an alternative to violence as a means to seek redress of their grievances. Elected leaders have an electoral incentive to address those grievances with accommodative policies, and they risk electoral costs if they respond with repression. Highly autocratic regimes are also relatively immune to civil war because the overwhelming coercive capacity of such states precludes armed uprisings by repressing dissent preemptively.

It is the weak authoritarian regimes (anocracies) or nations undergoing the transition to democracy that are the most susceptible to civil war (Hegre et al. 2001). They lack both the institutional capacity to resolve popular grievances through accommodative policies and the coercive capacity to repress dissent preemptively. When faced with a dissident challenge, such regimes attempt to repress it but fail, confronting dissidents with the choice of withdrawing from politics and suffering in silence or adopting violent tactics of their own to overthrow the incumbent regime.

HOW CIVIL WARS END

One feature of civil wars that has drawn considerable attention recently has been the question of their duration (how long they last) and their outcome (whether they end in a government victory, a rebel victory, or some sort of negotiated settlement). Civil wars do tend to last longer than interstate wars: the 108 civil wars described in the Correlates of War lasted an average of 1,665 days, whereas the twenty-three interstate wars lasted only 480 days on average. Because civil wars have lasted so long, new civil wars began at a faster rate than ongoing wars ended (until about 1994), with the result being a relentless accumulation of ongoing civil wars (Fearon 2004). The long duration of civil wars also accounts for their destructiveness. The rate at which casualties occur is usually lower in civil wars than in interstate wars; interstate wars are, on average, more intensely destructive. However, because civil wars last so much longer than interstate wars, their cumulative death toll usually exceeds that of interstate wars.

The duration of civil wars also affects their outcome. There is evidence that military victories by either the government or the rebels usually occur fairly early in the conflict if they occur at all. For rebel movements especially, the evidence suggests that if they are going to win, victory will occur within the first two or three years of the conflict. Governments, too, tend to win early if they win at all (Mason et al. 1999). Past some point (about eight to ten years into the civil war), neither side is likely to achieve military victory, and they settle into what William Zartman has termed a *mutually hurting stalemate* (1993, p. 24), whereby neither side has the capacity to defeat the other, but both sides have the capacity to deny victory to their rival.

It is at this point that civil wars become ripe for resolution. Third-party mediation—usually by the United Nations—can bring about a negotiated settlement to the conflict. While negotiated settlements are more likely than military victories to be followed by renewed conflict (Licklider 1995), negotiated settlements supported by UN peacekeeping forces are more likely to last (Fortna 2004; Doyle and Sambanis 2000). Peacekeepers provide both sides with credible guarantees that they can disarm and demobilize without fear of their rival violating the agreement and achieving through deception what they could not achieve on the battlefield (Walter 2002). Data from the UN's Department of Peacekeeping Operations indicate that forty-seven of the sixty peacekeeping operations established since 1945 have been deployed in civil wars, and forty-three of those were deployed after the cold war ended. Thus, UN brokering of peace agreements and deployment of peacekeeping forces have brought about a decline in the frequency, duration, and deadliness of civil wars, developments that offer some hope for future trends in the frequency, duration, and destructiveness of civil war.

SEE ALSO *Coup d'Etat; Destabilization; Diplomacy; Dissidents; Genocide; Guerilla Warfare; Lebanese Civil War; Peace; Spanish Civil War; U.S. Civil War; United Nations; Yugoslavian Civil War*

BIBLIOGRAPHY

Auvinen, Juha. 1997. Political Conflict in Less Developed Countries, 1981–89. *Journal of Peace Research* 34: 177–195.

Collier, Paul, and Anke Hoeffler. 1998. On the Economic Causes of Civil War. *Oxford Economic Papers* 50 (4): 563–573.

Correlates of War Project. http://www.correlatesofwar.org/.

Doyle, Michael, and Nicholas Sambanis. 2000. International Peacebuilding: A Theoretical and Quantitative Analysis. *American Political Science Review* 94: 779–801.

Fearon, James D. 2004. Why Do Some Civil Wars Last So Much Longer Than Others. *Journal of Peace Research* 41 (3): 275–301.

Fearon, James D., and David D. Laitin. 2003. Ethnicity, Insurgency, and Civil War. *American Political Science Review* 97 (1): 75–90.

Fortna, Paige. 2004. Does Peacekeeping Keep the Peace? International Intervention and the Duration of Peace After Civil War. *International Studies Quarterly* 48 (2): 269–292.

Hegre, Håvard, Tanja Ellingsen, Nils Petter Gleditsch, and Scott Gates. 2001. Toward a Democratic Civil Peace? Democracy, Political Change, and Civil War, 1816–1992. *American Political Science Review* 95 (1): 34–48.

Henderson, Errol A., and J. David Singer. 2000. Civil War in the Post-Colonial World, 1946–92. *Journal of Peace Research* 37: 275–299.

Holsti, K. J. 1992. International Theory and War in the Third World. In *The Insecurity Dilemma: National Security of Third World States*, ed. Brian L. Job, 37–60. Boulder, CO: Lynne Rienner.

Holsti, K. J. 1996. *The State, War, and the State of War.* Cambridge, U.K.: Cambridge University Press.

Horowitz, Donald L. 1985. *Ethnic Groups in Conflict.* Berkeley: University of California Press.

Licklider, Roy. 1995. The Consequences of Negotiated Settlements in Civil Wars, 1945–1993. *American Political Science Review* 89 (3): 681–690

Mason, T. David. 2004. *Caught in the Crossfire: Revolutions, Repression, and the Rational Peasant.* Boulder, CO: Rowman & Littlefield.

Mason, T. David, Joseph P. Weingarten, and Patrick J. Fett. 1999. Win, Lose, or Draw: Predicting the Outcome of Civil Wars. *Political Research Quarterly* 52 (2): 239–268.

Migdal, Joel S. 1988. *Strong Societies and Weak States: State-Society Relations and State Capabilities in the Third World.* Princeton, NJ: Princeton University Press.

Sarkees, Meredith Reid. 2000. The Correlates of War Data on War: An Update to 1997. *Conflict Management and Peace Science* 18 (1): 123–144.

United Nations Department of Peacekeeping Operations. http://www.un.org/Depts/dpko/dpko/index.asp.

Walter, Barbara. 2002. *Committing to Peace: The Successful Settlement of Civil Wars.* Princeton, NJ: Princeton University Press.

Zartman, I. William. 1993. The Unfinished Agenda: Negotiating Internal Conflicts. In *Stopping the Killing: How*

Civil Wars End, ed. Roy Licklider, 20–34. New York: New York University Press.

T. David Mason

CIVILIZATION

A Latinate word *civilization* ranks among the master concepts in the history of modernity. As such, it bears enormous semantic and historical density and has important relations with other master concepts of the modern, such as *history* (in the modern sense of a collective singular totality), *progress, development, culture* (in both the high and low senses), and *modernity* itself. The earliest recorded use of the term *civilization* in English dates from the first decade of the eighteenth century, though it appeared in a strictly legal context, referring to the conversion of a criminal matter to a civil one; this meaning is now obsolete (even as a juridical dimension extends into present usage). In its relevant modern sense, *civilization* was established in the second half of the eighteenth century—especially in the wake of the French Revolution (1789–1799)—and was further consolidated through the nineteenth century as a comparative and hierarchizing metahistorical, meta-anthropological concept. The term has since experienced a complex trajectory, shot through with ethico-political moment, always with the Euro-American world (especially the habits and ideologies of its elite classes) as the critical reference point.

The noun *civilization* built on the seventeenth-century verb *civilize* to indicate both the process of uplifting to a higher state of humanity and of subjection to law, as well as the denouement of such development. Civilization was thus understood to be simultaneously the process and the end state of progress. This process was further understood to be stadial, progressing from savagery through barbarism to civilization, a schema that was variously rearticulated and nuanced over the course of the nineteenth century. Though other civilizations were recognized (e.g., ancient Egypt)—typically state-based and stratified societies of imperial reach, with major cities, monumental architectural features, and significant written literatures—these were found to be lacking in some aspect of leading contemporary Western societies and were considered to that extent barbaric.

The semantic elements of *civilization* correspond closely with features of the European historical horizon in which the term emerged and matured. This horizon, extending from circa 1500 onward, includes: colonialism (co-emergent with the Renaissance, but accelerating from the second half of the eighteenth century through the nineteenth); the intensification of urbanization and the

eventual emergence of major European capitals; the interrelated processes of the marginalization of the Catholic church in the European state system, the emergence of Protestant sects, and the spiritualization of strands of Christian theology; the monopolization of violence by the absolutist state, and the related development of courtly manners; the achievement of a law-governed European inter-state system (first through the 1648 Treaty of Westphalia, and then the 1815 Congress of Vienna); the spread of disciplinary institutions and technologies of the self; the global rise of European capital, and the correlative emergence and consolidation of European bourgeois classes and consumerism; the development of private property from the late seventeenth century and accelerating from the second half of the century (e.g., in England with the enclosures movement); the interrelated development of parliaments, national polities/states, and electoral democracy (beginning in the seventeenth century in England for the propertied classes and extending both horizontally and vertically throughout the eighteenth, nineteenth, and twentieth centuries to universal adult franchise, excluding the non-European colonies); and of course the development of the arts, sciences, and technology, especially at an accelerated pace since the Enlightenment (i.e., roughly the eighteenth century).

Thus, the significations accruing to *civilization* have been the following: European/Western; urban and urbane; secular and spiritual; law-abiding and nonviolent (i.e., limited to legalized violence, both within and between states); polished, courteous, and polite; disciplined, orderly, and productive; laissez faire, bourgeois, and comfortable; respectful of private property; fraternal and free; cultured, knowledgeable, and the master of nature. The uncivilized conversely are: non-Western; rural, or worse, savage; idolatrous, fanatical, literalist, and theocratic; unlawful and violent (i.e., given to violence outside juridical procedure); crude or rude; lazy, anarchic, and unproductive; communistic, poor, and inconvenienced or beleaguered; piratical and thievish; fratricidal (or, indeed, cannibalistic) and unfree; uncultured, ignorant, illiterate, superstitious, and at nature's mercy. Given this stark set of binaries, it is not surprising that the *civilizing mission* (a related concept that emerged in the nineteenth century) has often been the ideological counterpart of projects of colonial domination and genocide, especially in the non-Western world, but also in the European hinterland and vis-à-vis European minorities and subaltern classes.

Marginal to the main thrust of the concept's history, critiques of civilization have accompanied it throughout, from Jean-Jacques Rousseau (1712–1778) in the mid-eighteenth century through Romanticism to anarcho-primitivist strands in the contemporary antiglobalization movement (Zerzan 2005). These critiques, especially in

German lands in the nineteenth century (Elias 2000), have often relied on the concept of *culture* as a more local, authentic, egalitarian, and communitarian alternative, though just as often culture has been co-opted by nationalist projects. There is ultimately much slippage between culture and civilization. This slippage is evidenced in Samuel Huntington's much discussed book, *The Clash of Civilizations and the Remaking of World Order* (1996), where the concept of civilization appears to be just culture on a grand scale—which is moreover decoupled from the now largely archaic concept of civility: Would it be possible to imagine a "clash of civilities"?

The first recorded use of the word *civilization* in its relevant, modern, as opposed to the archaic juridical sense, points toward another semantic element that has received remarkably little attention given its extraordinary significance. It is now accepted that the term was first used in 1756 in *L'ami des hommes* (The Friend of Man) by Victor de Riqueti (1715–1789), the marquis de Mirabeau, an important physiocrat. In this work, Mirabeau asserts: "Religion is without doubt humanity's first and most useful constraint; it is the mainspring of civilization" (cited in Mazlish 2004, p. 5). The close association in Mirabeau between religion and civilization (at a time when the term *religion* was all but synonymous with Christianity, non-Christian peoples being found to be either lacking religion, or possessing more or less pale approximations or deviations of Christianity) surprises only because of the inherited dogma that the civilizational process coincides with the vanishing of religion (in which direction the first step is the avowed rationalization of religion, that is, the emergence of the Protestant sect). In fact, civilization has been coupled with Christianity and (Western) Christendom throughout its career (Perkins 2004), and missionaries have been key and continuing agents of the civilizing mission. Even today, a measure of merely the iceberg's tip in this regard is the character of debates on the accession of Turkey to the European Union, as well as the statements of prominent Western opinion makers and leaders in the wake of the events of September 11, 2001 (most explicitly U.S. president George W. Bush and Italian prime minister Silvio Berlusconi). Even in high scholarship, an important sociologist of religion, Rodney Stark, published a book in 2005 under the title *The Victory of Reason: How Christianity Led to Freedom, Capitalism, and Western Success.*

Given the historicist character of civilization, this coupling is inevitable: If civilization arose, or developed its standard form, in Christendom, how can the latter not continue to be credited and effectively associated with its achievement? Relatedly, if secularism (an important constituent of civilization) emerged out of the Protestant Reformation—as is frequently avowed, especially in the

United States—how can the latter not be so accredited and effectively linked? The same can be said for the originary relationship between capitalism and civilization, a view registered in the cold war perception of the Soviet Union as an example of barbarism and "Asiatic despotism." This view is no doubt also indebted to the shifting cartography of the "uncivilized" Orient, which has often extended into eastern Europe (or even central Europe, as during the Third Reich), not to mention the enduring if older legacy of the secession of the Eastern Church from Rome.

In charting the trajectory of civilization, contemporary scholars often index and discuss attitudes of superiority in premodern and non-Western contexts (e.g., the old Chinese binary of "*kaihua/wenming* versus *fan*," which roughly corresponds to "civilized versus barbarian"). But it is important to keep the following in mind: It is no doubt the case that all human collectivities have ways of distinguishing themselves from others, and this process takes on an increasingly hierarchical accent in large stratified collectivities. With stratification, moreover, come concepts that discriminate between members of various levels and groups within. However, both the flexibility and form of the inside-outside distinction, as well as the forms of internal hierarchy, vary widely, and are in each case specific, even if dynamic. For the exercise to have any meaning, therefore, it is critical that analysis stays with this specificity. The surest guide in this regard is the material language of the concept in its discursive trajectory, that is, the Latinity of *civilization*. Furthermore, the non-Latinate analogs that have emerged since the mid-1800s (e.g., the Japanese *bunmeikaika*, coined circa 1880) are translations carried out in a highly asymmetrical historical context dominated by the Latinate, and are thus both defensive and derivative. Indeed, the force of Eurocentric civilizational discourse has been such that anticolonial ideologies have attempted to claim the origins of "civilization" for themselves, as in the Afrocentric scholarship of Cheikh Anta Diop. However, if other conceptions of civilization did hold out some hope in the first half of the twentieth century, as anticolonial movements highlighted the inconsistencies between the theory and practice of European civilization, and attempted to imagine alternatives—exemplified by Mohandas Gandhi's (1869–1948) famous quip about Western civilization that "it would be a good idea"—at the beginning of the twenty-first century, civilization appears to function as the master concept for the legitimation of elites everywhere.

SEE ALSO *Culture; Diop, Cheikh Anta*

BIBLIOGRAPHY

Diamond, Stanley. 1974. *In Search of the Primitive: A Critique of Civilization.* New Brunswick, NJ: Transaction.

Diop, Cheikh Anta. 1991. *Civilization or Barbarism: An Authentic Anthropology*. Trans. Yaa-Lengi Meema Ngemi. Eds. Harold J. Salemson and Marjolijn de Jager. New York: Lawrence Hill.

Elias, Norbert. [1939] 2000. *The Civilizing Process: Sociogenetic and Psychogenetic Investigations*. Rev. ed. Trans. Edmund Jephcott. Oxford, U.K.: Blackwell.

Febvre, Lucien. [1930] 1973. Civilisation: Evolution of a Word and a Group of Ideas. In *A New Kind of History: From the Writings of Febvre*, ed. Peter Burke, trans. K. Folca, 289–296. London: Routledge and Kegan Paul.

Huntington, Samuel. 1996. *The Clash of Civilizations and the Remaking of World Order*. New York: Simon and Schuster.

Mazlish, Bruce. 2004. *Civilization and Its Contents*. Stanford, CA: Stanford University Press.

Perkins, Mary Anne. 2004. *Christendom and European Identity: The Legacy of a Grand Narrative Since 1789*. New York: de Gruyter.

Starobinski, Jean. 1993. The Word *Civilization*. In *Blessings in Disguise, or, The Morality of Evil*, 1–35. Trans. Arthur Goldhammer. Cambridge, U.K.: Polity.

Williams, Raymond. 1983. *Keywords: A Vocabulary of Culture and Society*. Rev. ed. London: Fontana.

Zerzan, John, ed. 2005. *Against Civilization: Readings and Reflections*. 2nd ed. Los Angeles: Feral House.

Nauman Naqvi

CIVILIZATIONS, CLASH OF

The "clash of civilizations" is a thesis that guides contemporary social science research in a comparative and global perspective. It is also a concept frequently used in political and public discourse, especially regarding the relationship between the "West" and Islam. This entry is intended to provide readers with an understanding of the origins and meaning of the clash of civilizations, selected research pertinent to this thesis, and a critical examination of this thesis and research.

Although historian Bernard Lewis had used the term earlier, the political scientist Samuel P. Huntington popularized the "clash of civilizations" in a highly influential 1993 article in the journal *Foreign Affairs* and in a best-selling book, *The Clash of Civilizations and the Remaking of World Order* (1996). In these works, Huntington puts forth the clash of civilizations thesis in an attempt to explain the causes, character, and consequences of divisions among people and between states after the collapse of Eastern European Communism in the late twentieth century. The thesis combines historical insights with contemporary developments, such as the increasing importance of religion and the rise of religious fundamentalism.

Huntington writes, "the most important distinctions among people [today] are not ideological, political, or economic. They are cultural" (1996, p. 21). "The most important groupings of states are no longer the three blocs of the Cold War," Huntington further asserts, "but rather the world's seven or eight civilizations" (1996, p. 21). These civilizations contain all of the elements of culture, such as language, history, identity, customs, institutions, and religion, but the clash of civilizations thesis holds that religion is the major fault line. Accordingly, the world's people and states are classified into the following civilizations, largely on the basis of their religious traditions: Sinic (Chinese), Japanese, Hindu, Islamic, Orthodox, Western (Christian), Latin American, and "possibly," African. As evidence in support of this thesis, Huntington points in his 1993 article to fighting among (Western Christian) Croats, (Muslim) Bosnians, and (Orthodox) Serbs in the former Yugoslavia, U.S. bombing of Baghdad, and the subsequent negative Muslim reaction. Furthermore, Huntington predicts, "the next world war, if there is one, will be a war between civilizations" (1993, p. 39). The most dangerous civilizational conflicts, from Huntington's perspective, will arise from Western arrogance, Muslim intolerance, and Sinic assertiveness.

In the wake of the September 11, 2001, attacks, the global "war on terror," and the U.S.-led invasion of Iraq in 2003, social scientists increasingly turned their attention to Huntington's claims of an Islamic-Western clash of civilizations. The main controversy centers on whether religious traditions, such as Islam, are impediments to democracy. In fact, Muslim countries (e.g., Saudi Arabia, Iran, and Pakistan) are more likely than Western countries (e.g., the United States, most of the countries in the European Union, and Australia) to have authoritarian regimes in which citizens have little or no say in government. From Huntington's perspective (1996), this is because Western Christianity emphasizes democratic pluralism, separation of religion and state, rule of law, and individual rights to a greater extent than Islam: Islamic tenets hold that God rules the universe; there is no separation of religion and state in Islam; Islamic law reflects God's, not humans', desire; and Muslims are treated as unitary, without regard to any social divisions. However, Huntington (1993) recognizes that the West attempts to impose its liberal-democratic values on other civilizations through its control of international governmental organizations, such as the United Nations.

Social scientists have challenged the general propositions of the clash of civilizations thesis, including the perception that Islam and democracy are incompatible. To begin, the thesis ignores variation within civilizations, as people may identify with their nation, race/ethnicity, or even their religious denomination or sect to a greater extent than they identify with their civilization. More specifically, social scientists point out that there is nothing inherently antidemocratic about Islam. To the contrary, Mansoor Moaddel notes a correspondence between concepts in Islamic scripture and democratic political arrangements: "Such concepts as *shura* (consultative body), *ijma* (consensus), and *masliha* (unity) pointed to an affinity between Islam and democracy" (2002, p. 365). Still other social scientists have collected survey data from people in Muslim countries and found that their values are not as monolithic as the clash of civilizations thesis suggests, except on issues regarding secularism. People in Muslim countries also hold evaluations of democracy that are similar to those of their counterparts in Western countries. Yet, people in Muslim countries are more likely to favor religious political leaders and are less supportive of gender equality and homosexuality than people in Western countries (Inglehart and Norris 2003; Norris and Inglehart 2004), a finding seemingly supporting the clash of civilizations thesis.

While it is clear that there are institutional and value differences between countries, including between countries that form Islamic and Western civilizations, it is unclear if these differences are due to the nature of religious traditions. An alternative explanation that Huntington rejects is that these differences may instead be the consequence of countries' different levels of "modernization" and economic development. Economic development is positively related to the institutionalization of democracy and a political culture emphasizing democratic values (Geddes 1999; Norris and Inglehart 2004). From this perspective, it thus makes sense that Western countries, which tend to be substantially more wealthy than countries in the Islamic or African civilizations, are more likely to be democratic.

In sum, social science research indicates that some of the patterns that the clash of civilizations thesis posits are real. Although contemporary events might seem to lend further credence to this thesis, there is limited systematic evidence on the extent to which civilizations clash with one another. Finally, social scientists are divided on whether these patterns and conflicts are due to religious traditions, economic development, or other factors.

SEE ALSO *Civilization; Huntington, Samuel P.*

BIBLIOGRAPHY

Geddes, Barbara. 1999. What Do We Know about Democratization after Twenty Years? *Annual Review of Political Science* 2: 115–144.

Huntington, Samuel P. 1993. The Clash of Civilizations? *Foreign Affairs* 72 (3): 22–49.

Huntington, Samuel P. 1996. *The Clash of Civilizations and the Remaking of World Order*. New York: Simon and Schuster.

Inglehart, Ronald, and Pippa Norris. 2003. *Rising Tide: Gender Equality and Cultural Change around the World*. Cambridge U.K.: Cambridge University Press.

Moaddel, Mansoor. 2002. The Study of Islamic Culture and Politics: An Overview and Assessment. *Annual Review of Sociology* 28: 359–386.

Norris, Pippa, and Ronald Inglehart. 2004. *Sacred and Secular: Religion and Politics Worldwide*. Cambridge, U.K.: Cambridge University Press.

Jeffrey C. Dixon

CLARK, KENNETH B.
1914–2005

Kenneth Bancroft Clark and his wife, Mamie Phipps Clark (1917–1983), were arguably the most famous African American psychologist couple of the twentieth century. Their research was cited in the U.S. Supreme Court's 1954 *Brown v. Board of Education* decision that declared segregated schools unconstitutional. During the 1940s and early 1950s, they conducted tests that were designed to identify racial identification and racial preference in young children. One of these experiments came to be known famously as the *doll test*. The Clarks concluded that racial segregation created psychological damage in African American and white children, although the Court neglected to address the latter issue. However, many scholars, teachers, and social welfare professionals since the 1960s have contended that this research was flawed, particularly the methodology used in the doll tests. They argued that the tests were too limited in their capacity to lead to the conclusion that African American children in particular were psychologically damaged. They maintained that the Clarks posed African Americans as damaged for political purposes in order to gain white support for racial integration.

Clark was born in Panama, the son of Jamaican migrant workers. When he was five, his mother moved to Harlem in New York City with him and his younger sister. He graduated from Howard University with B.A. and M.A. degrees in psychology in 1935 and 1936. His professors included political scientist Ralph Bunche (1904–1971) and Francis Cecil Sumner (1895–1954), the first African American to earn a PhD in psychology. In 1940 Clark became the first African American to receive a PhD in psychology from Columbia University; his wife became the second two years later (they had married in 1938). During graduate school, he worked on Gunnar Myrdal's (1898–1987) famous study, *An American Dilemma* (1944). After teaching at Hampton University, Clark became in 1942 the first African American psychology professor at City College in New York. He remained there until his retirement in 1975.

Clark is best known for his involvement in the *Brown* case; much of his research was included in his first book, *Prejudice and Your Child* (1955). To his supporters, his career exemplified a steadfast dedication to integration; his detractors on the other hand ridiculed his integrationist positions. Yet Clark was far more complicated intellectually. He viewed racism as part of a larger problem involving what he called the "dilemma of power." Because humanity had never resolved "the issue of power versus ideals," human beings could rationalize conflicts between abstract concepts of justice and equality on the one hand, while maintaining privilege and status on the other. In other words, he pushed further W. E. B. Du Bois's (1868–1963) contention that the problem of the twentieth century was the color line. Clark also disagreed with Myrdal's position that racism contradicted the American creed; instead, he argued that beliefs in equality and white supremacy were not contradictory but compatible.

This intellectual framework shaped Clark's research and activism during the 1960s and 1970s, especially his second and third books, *Dark Ghetto, Dilemmas of Social Power* (1965) and *Pathos of Power* (1974). The former work used Harlem as a prism to present a bleak and pessimistic view of the impact of ghettoization on the daily lives of its citizens. Many readers interpreted his work as an endorsement of the "culture-of-poverty" thesis that was in vogue at the time among many scholars in fields such as anthropology, sociology, and education, but Clark presented a much more complex analysis of African American life in the ghetto than he has generally been credited for. He was highly critical of the cultural approach, charging that such analyses substituted for discredited biological theories to explain and justify racial differences. Instead, he argued, for instance, that "educational deprivation" was a more accurate term to describe what was actually happening in schools once they became predominately poor and black; because of their powerlessness, they no longer received the basic services—good teachers, competent administrators, decent buildings— that wealthier and whiter communities received. In that sense, *Dark Ghetto* was more of an indictment of American society, rather than solely a critique of African American community life.

In addition to his writings, Clark was influential in both activist and policymaking circles. In 1946 he and his wife founded the Northside Center for Child Development, the first interracial institution of its kind in New York City. His research led to his participation in the 1950 White House Conference on Children and Youth. Aware that the problems of education and poverty were linked, he designed the ambitious Harlem Youth

Opportunities Unlimited (HARYOU) program in the early 1960s as a model for the "war on poverty." He was named in 1966 to the board of regents of the New York State Department of Education and in 1968 to the board of the New York State Urban Development Corporation. In 1967 Clark founded the Metropolitan Applied Research Center (MARC), which led a concerted effort to reject the culture-of-poverty thesis through publications and applied programs. MARC also worked to close the educational achievement gap through such efforts as its program (known as the Clark Plan) to reform the Washington, D.C., school system. Finally, in 1971, Clark became the first African American elected president of the American Psychological Association.

Despite his accomplishments, Clark grew pessimistic about the state of racial progress. He thought that he had failed at his most important work—HARYOU, the Clark Plan, and his efforts on school desegregation—to empower the black poor and close the educational achievement gap. Ironically, the man who wrote so eloquently about the lack of power in African American life concluded that he too lacked power.

SEE ALSO *Achievement Gap, Racial;* Brown v. Board of Education, *1954*

BIBLIOGRAPHY

Clark, Kenneth B. 1965. *Dark Ghetto, Dilemmas of Social Power.* New York: Harper and Row.

Freeman, Damon. 2004. Not So Simple Justice: Kenneth B. Clark, Civil Rights, and the Dilemma of Power, 1940–1980. PhD diss., Indiana University, Bloomington.

Markowitz, Gerald, and David Rosner. 1996. *Children, Race, and Power: Kenneth and Mamie Clark's Northside Center.* Charlottesville: University Press of Virginia.

Damon Freeman

CLASS

Much has been written on class in the years since Seymour Martin Lipset wrote his entry in the first edition of this encyclopedia, published in 1968. Lipset viewed the literature on class in terms of "social stratification," which he believed was divided into two approaches, the functionalist and the "social change" perspectives. Nevertheless, the bulk of his piece was centered not on contemporary studies, but on Karl Marx (1818–1883), Max Weber (1864–1920), and Émile Durkheim (1858–1917), who, Lipset argued, continued to animate the central debates of his time. The classics are no less important today, but this essay will aim to balance them with the now canonical debates of the mid-twentieth century and the vast and multifaceted literature that has amassed since then.

MARX, WEBER, AND DURKHEIM

Any discussion of class must begin with Karl Marx. As Lipset once noted, while David Ricardo (1772–1823), Adam Smith (1723–1790), and others may have written about class before Marx, it was Marx who set the terms of debate for later sociological thinkers (Lipset 1968). For Marx, classes do not exist in societies where production for the group results in an equitable distribution of resources and requires that each member or unit contribute to the collective requirements of life. Classes emerge only when one subset of a community seizes private control of the means of production (e.g., land, factories) and coercively extracts *surplus labor* from another subset of the community, that is, labor that neither the first group needs nor the second group must give in order to survive.

Marx viewed the extraction of surplus labor as a fundamentally exploitative act, since the real exchange value of any given commodity is only ever equal to the labor time socially necessary to make it. This is called the *labor theory of value*. Any effort to squeeze out *surplus value* requires that human beings be forced to work for free beyond the labor time socially necessary both to maintain their labor power (e.g., through food and raiment) and to produce its equivalent in commodities. Thus, one's class is determined by one's relationship to the means of production: those who own the means of production and therefore forcibly extract surplus value comprise one class, while those who do not own the means of production and are therefore coerced to generate surplus value form another class. Like master and bondsman under slavery and lord and serf under feudalism, capitalism is predicated on two classes: the factory owners or *bourgeoisie* and the factory workers or *proletariat*. All of these, however, only form "objective" classes, meaning that they are classes determined merely by their proprietary relationship to the means of production. The subjective form of class, by contrast, is a class that is conscious of itself as a collectivity of similarly positioned individuals and is therefore capable of class action. The distinction between objective and subjective forms of class is infamously that of the class-in-itself (*an sich*) and the class-for-itself (*für sich*).

According to some interpretations of Marx's work, particularly those of the *Communist Manifesto* (1848), the transition from a merely existing working class to a conscious and therefore revolutionary working class is inevitable, as is the classless communist society that workers will eventually found. Because of its revolutionary and progressive potential in every epoch of production, class is said to be the very motor of history (Marx and Engels

[1848] 1998; Marx [1852] 1996; Marx [1867] 1906). Hence, the oft-quoted claim, "The history of all hitherto existing society is the history of class struggles" (Marx and Engels [1848] 1998, p. 34).

Max Weber did not doubt the existence of exploitative class relations in modern society. Rather, he questioned Marx's definition of class, its centrality in modern life compared to other forms of domination, and the apparent inevitability of class action in Marx's work. In Weber's foundational piece on this subject, "Class, Status, Party" (1922), class is conceived of not as a group but as a sea of unconnected individuals who share the same "life chances," of which ownership of the means of production is just one example. Life chances comprise the bargaining power that one brings to the market for the purpose of maximizing income and includes professional authority, skills, and education. Just because one shares a similar set of life chances with others, however, does not mean that one will join with similarly positioned individuals in class action. Shared life chances are a necessary condition of class action, but they are by no means a guarantee, for there are other forms of domination apart from the economic that have the capacity to contravene class action. Societies that are organized according to "status" are less susceptible to class action, because they are stratified according to noneconomic concerns such as family, ethnic, or religious heritage. Partisan allegiances may also be an impediment to class solidarity (Weber 1946).

Émile Durkheim's foremost contribution to class analysis was to conceive of it in terms of occupational specialization in a modern and largely peaceful division of labor. Durkheim sought to explain the transition from the "mechanical solidarity" of primitive societies, whose coherence was based on the resemblance of actors and the dominance of a collective consciousness, to the "organic solidarity" characteristic of modern societies, whose coherence was based on the complementarity of highly specialized individuals. Organic solidarity breaks down only when individuals are coerced into tasks that they do not want to perform. Thus, the central challenge of modern societies is to match individuals with tasks that suit their natural talents. This is why organic solidarity may be achieved by contracts or exchange, which bind individuals through a system of rights and duties, and in turn give rise to rules that guarantee regular cooperation between the divided functions (Durkheim [1893] 1960).

STRATIFICATION

Kingsley Davis (1908–1997) and Wilbert Moore's (1914–1987) now-foundational piece, "Some Principles of Stratification" (1945), marked the translation of Durkheimian sociology into contemporary debates on class. Davis and Moore took as their challenge the question of how modern societies so successfully channeled their members into an elaborate and specialized division of labor. Infusing Durkheim with Weber's emphasis on skills as life chances on the market, they reasoned that this monumental undertaking would require nothing less than a mechanism that could motivate the most qualified people to train for, seek, and perform the duties of the most important positions. Famously they hypothesized that an unequal system of occupational rewards was necessary to track the talented to their rightful place in the division of labor. Thus, professionals earn more than manual laborers, because the former positions must have greater built-in economic incentives to motivate the most highly talented to undertake the costly educational sacrifice necessary for those jobs. Social inequality, in other words, was not the result of the exploitation of one part of society by another and therefore a thing to be abhorred, but merely the system through which society unconsciously placed its most talented members into the most functionally important roles, without which society would be imperiled.

Among the more prominent early responses to Davis and Moore was that of Melvin Tumin (1919–1994), who argued that "functional importance" is an ideological construct. Power, he insisted, is a better measure of who gets ahead, such that the result of stratification, far from tracking the most talented people to the top, actually strangles talent at the bottom, making stratification deeply dysfunctional. Later Lipset and Reinhard Bendix (1916–1991) showed conclusively that the belief in upward mobility far exceeded the actual rate in the United States, while Peter Blau (1918–2002) and Otis Duncan (1921–2004) introduced path analysis to demonstrate the enduring effects of parental background and schooling on occupational attainment (Tumin 1953; Lipset and Bendix 1959; Blau and Duncan 1967).

But if Davis and Moore marked the introduction of Durkheim and Weber into the functionalist approach to class, then Ralf Dahrendorf (1957), the founder of modern conflict theory, did so for Marx and Weber. Dahrendorf sought to create an alternative to Talcott Parsons's (1902–1979) functionalist social system that could better account for internal conflict. A "Left Weberian" who saw class as fundamentally exploitative, Dahrendorf argued that Marx's focus on property as the ultimate marker of class was limited, especially in light of the control exercised by nonowner managers. Property and the coercive extraction of surplus value were for him subordinate forms of a more general social relation, authority, which served as the basis of binary "class conflict" in a variety of social settings including, but not limited to, industrial production. Dahrendorf, however, was criticized for expanding the meaning of class so far beyond the economic realm as to make the term meaningless (see, for example, Coser 1960).

Responding to Nicos Poulantzas (1936–1979), whose *Political Power and Social Classes* (1973) identified a "new petty bourgeoisie," Erik Olin Wright (1978, 1997) argued that a new class of white-collar workers had emerged as a result of elaborate organizational hierarchies and the separation of ownership from directive control of large industrial corporations (Giddens and Held 1982). Workers and owners continued to occupy diametrically opposed class positions, but white-collar workers had come to occupy "contradictory class locations" in which the latter enjoyed some degree or combination of autonomy, skill, and authority on the job. Though critics have argued that Wright smuggled Weber into his Marxist framework by expanding the basis of class location beyond exploitation and production, Wright nevertheless found a dividing line between white-collar employees who identify more with labor and those who identify more with capital, thus articulating a bourgeois-proletarian divide for a new age.

TWO CHALLENGES

In the aftermath of the Soviets' repression of democratic movements in Hungary (1956–1957) and Czechoslovakia (1968–1969), class analysis and in particular Marxism were assailed on several fronts both for what was seen as the perversion of Marx's humanist vision by state-sponsored socialism and for the exclusion of non-class-based identities, inequalities, and movements from public discourse. With respect to the latter, Frank Parkin (1979), another Left Weberian like Dahrendorf, criticized structural Marxism's assumption of internally homogeneous classes, as well as its inability to account for the enforcement of social boundaries between elites and workers. As an alternative, Parkin advanced the concept of "social closure," the process by which social collectivities, whether by class, race, gender, or a combination of these, seek either to maximize rewards by restricting access to resources and opportunities (in the case of elites) or to usurp rewards previously denied to them (in the case of nonelites).

Alberto Melucci (1980) likewise criticized the social-movement literature for emphasizing the political realm of movement activity while neglecting its nonpolitical or "social" dimensions. This, he noted, made sense in the study of working-class movements, which often have an institutionalized political arm, but did not square with women's movements, for instance, which, in addition to struggling for political rights, also seek to address social concerns of difference and recognition and do not vie for state power. More recently, Sonya Rose (1992) has argued that gender is not a secondary by-product of class relations as Friedrich Engels (1820–1895) and some Marxist feminists have suggested, but rather a central component thereof. Thus, in late nineteenth-century England, factory wages were adjusted by gender not only to the benefit of capital, but also to the benefit of men, as it reinforced a discourse of female respectability tied to the subordination of women in the household and society at large.

E. P. Thompson's (1924–1993) critique of structural Marxism in the *Making of the English Working Class* (1963) was a lightning rod for emerging controversies within Marxism itself. The main point of this critique is that workers do not constitute a class because they share a similar structural position, but because they forge themselves into a class through their own language, culture, and struggle. The working class on this account is always already a conspirator in its own creation, thereby negating the analytical necessity for the in-itself/for-itself dichotomy. This challenge to the structural Marxism of Poulantzas, Perry Anderson (1980), and Louis Althusser (1971), among others, was led initially by the British cultural studies school of Thompson, Raymond Williams (1977), and sociologist Stuart Hall (1983).

Subsequent research, not all Marxist, has celebrated the agency of class actors, as in James Scott's account of subversive everyday behavior in *Weapons of the Weak* (1985); the indigenous culture of workers, such as Craig Calhoun's "reactionary revolutionaries"; and the processual, as opposed to the positional, dimensions of class formation exemplified by Anthony Giddens's concept of "structuration" and Pierre Bourdieu's (1930–2002) "habitus" (Bourdieu 1977; Przeworski 1978; Sewell 1980; Calhoun 1983; Bourdieu 1984; Giddens 1984; Katznelson and Zolberg 1985; Fantasia 1988; Bourdieu 1990; Steinmetz 1992; Somers 1997).

For Bourdieu, as an example, class typically functions at the level of shared dispositions or *habitus* (e.g., tastes, bodily carriage, language), which, though stemming from certain shared material conditions, manifests itself more as a "feel for the game" than as a primarily economic relationship. One is, without the effort of reflection, a "virtuoso" in negotiating the social terrain of one's class, very much as a professional soccer player, to use Bourdieu's analogy, knows precisely when and with what force and curvature to kick the ball in a breakaway situation. These dispositions only emerge recognizably as "class" when crises drag the material and dispositional differences among groups from the field of the unspoken (referred to as *doxa*) to the field of public opinion. Habitus, it is important to note, is not a fixed set of dispositions, but rather given to improvisation and thus to transforming the terms of class belonging. The analytical result is that class, through habitus, is neither structure nor agency, but structuring or both simultaneously.

THE FUTURE

One possible implication of this constant reworking of class is that it is no longer a workable analytical concept.

Paul Kingston's *The Classless Society* (2000) is among the latest in a long line of studies that question the predictive power of class in shaping mobility, culture, voting, and consciousness, among other outcomes. On the other hand, there is a movement afoot to rebuild class analysis. David Grusky and Jesper Sørensen (1998), for example, contend that class models can be made more plausible if analysts radically disaggregate occupational categories to the unit occupational level. Moreover, the eclipse of the Soviet Union in 1991 and the attendant rise of neoliberalism have put the question of class back on the table if there had ever been any doubt. Noting the deepening class polarization since the late 1970s, David Harvey (2006) has argued that neoliberalism is a failed utopian rhetoric masking a far more successful project to restore economic power to the ruling classes. Future lines of inquiry include new forms of international class formation, the evolving relationship of party to class as the institutionalized Left goes into decline, and the disappearance of wage-based employment and thus of the very basis of social citizenship and welfare.

SEE ALSO *Bahro, Rudolf; Bourdieu, Pierre; Bureaucracy; Capitalism; Class Conflict; Durkheim, Émile; Elites; False Consciousness; Feudal Mode of Production; Feudalism; Habitus; Hierarchy; Labor; Labor Theory of Value; Left and Right; Marx, Karl; Mode of Production; New Class, The; Oligarchy; Poulantzas, Nicos; Power Elite; Ricardo, David; Slave Mode of Production; Smith, Adam; Stratification; Surplus; Thompson, Edward P.; Weber, Max; Working Class*

BIBLIOGRAPHY

Althusser, Louis. 1971. *Lenin and Philosophy, and Other Essays.* Trans. Ben Brewster. London: New Left.

Anderson, Perry. 1980. *Arguments within English Marxism.* London: New Left.

Blau, Peter M., and Otis Dudley Duncan. 1967. *The American Occupational Structure.* New York: Wiley.

Bourdieu, Pierre. 1977. *Outline of a Theory of Practice.* Trans. Richard Nice. Cambridge, U.K., and New York: Cambridge University Press.

Bourdieu, Pierre. 1984. *Distinction: A Social Critique of the Judgement of Taste.* Trans. Richard Nice. Cambridge, MA: Harvard University Press.

Bourdieu, Pierre. 1990. *Logic of Practice.* Trans. Richard Nice. Cambridge, U.K.: Polity.

Calhoun, Craig Jackson. 1983. The Radicalism of Tradition: Community Strength or Venerable Disguise and Borrowed Language? *American Journal of Sociology* 88: 886–914.

Coser, Lewis A. 1960. Review of *Class and Class Conflict in Industrial Society* by Ralf Dahrendorf. *American Journal of Sociology* 65: 520–521.

Dahrendorf, Ralf. [1957] 1959. *Class and Class Conflict in Industrial Society.* Stanford, CA: Stanford University Press.

Davis, Kingsley, and Wilbert E. Moore. 1945. Some Principles of Stratification. *American Sociological Review* 10: 242–249.

Durkheim, Émile. [1893] 1960. *The Division of Labor in Society.* Trans. George Simpson. Glencoe, IL: Free Press.

Engels, Friedrich. [1884] 1972. *The Origin of the Family, Private Property, and the State, in the Light of the Researches of Lewis H. Morgan.* New York: International Publishers.

Fantasia, Rick. 1988. *Cultures of Solidarity: Consciousness, Action, and Contemporary American Workers.* Berkeley: University of California Press.

Giddens, Anthony. 1984. *The Constitution of Society: Outline of the Theory of Structuration.* Berkeley: University of California Press.

Giddens, Anthony, and David Held. 1982. *Classes, Power, and Conflict: Classical and Contemporary Debates.* Berkeley: University of California Press.

Grusky, David B., and Jesper B. Sørensen. 1998. Can Class Analysis Be Salvaged? *American Journal of Sociology* 103: 1187–1234.

Hall, Stuart. 1983. The Problem of Ideology: Marxism without Guarantees. In *Marx: A Hundred Years On,* ed. Betty Matthews, 56–85. London: Lawrence and Wishart.

Harvey, David. 2006. *Spaces of Global Capitalism: Towards a Theory of Uneven Geographical Development.* London and New York: Verso.

Katznelson, Ira, and Aristide Zolberg. 1985. *Working-Class Formation: Nineteenth-century Patterns in Western Europe and the United States.* Princeton, NJ: Princeton University Press.

Kingston, Paul W. 2000. *The Classless Society.* Stanford, CA: Stanford University Press.

Lipset, Seymour Martin. 1968. Social Class. In *International Encyclopedia of the Social Sciences,* ed. David L. Sills, vol. 15, 296–316. New York: Macmillan.

Lipset, Seymour Martin, and Reinhard Bendix. 1959. *Social Mobility in Industrial Society.* Berkeley: University of California Press.

Marx, Karl. [1852] 1996. The Eighteenth Brumaire of Louis Bonaparte. In *Marx: Later Political Writings,* ed. Terrell Carver, 31–127. Cambridge, U.K., and New York: Cambridge University Press.

Marx, Karl. [1867] 1906. *Capital: A Critique of Political Economy.* New York: Modern Library.

Marx, Karl, and Friedrich Engels. [1848] 1998. *The Communist Manifesto: A Modern Edition.* London and New York: Verso.

Melucci, Alberto. 1980. The New Social Movements: A Theoretical Approach. *Social Science Information* 19: 199–226.

Parkin, Frank. 1979. *Marxism and Class Theory: A Bourgeois Critique.* New York: Columbia University Press.

Poulantzas, Nicos. 1973. *Political Power and Social Classes.* Trans. Timothy O'Hagan. London: New Left.

Przeworski, Adam. 1978. Proletariat into a Class: The Process of Class Formation from Kautsky's *The Class Struggle* to Recent Debates. *Politics and Society* 7: 343–401.

Rose, Sonya. 1992. *Limited Livelihoods: Gender and Class in Nineteenth-Century England.* Berkeley: University of California Press.

Scott, James. 1985. *Weapons of the Weak: Everyday Forms of Peasant Resistance.* New Haven, CT: Yale University Press.

Sewell, William H., Jr. 1980. *Work and Revolution in France: The Language of Labor from the Old Regime to 1848.* Cambridge, U.K., and New York: Cambridge University Press.

Somers, Margaret. 1997. Deconstructing and Reconstructing Class Formation Theory: Narrativity, Relational Analysis, and Social Theory. In *Reworking Class,* ed. John R. Hall, 73–106. Ithaca, NY: Cornell University Press.

Steinmetz, George. 1992. Reflections on the Role of Social Narratives in Working-Class Formation: Narrative Theory in the Social Sciences. *Social Science History* 16: 489–516.

Thompson, E. P. 1963. *The Making of the English Working Class.* London: Gollancz.

Tumin, Melvin M. 1953. Some Principles of Stratification: A Critical Analysis. *American Sociological Review* 18: 387–394.

Weber, Max. [1922] 1946. Class, Status, Party. In *From Max Weber: Essays in Sociology,* eds. H. H. Gerth and C. Wright Mills, 180–195. New York: Oxford University Press.

Williams, Raymond. 1977. *Marxism and Literature.* Oxford, U.K.: Oxford University Press.

Wright, Erik Olin. 1978. *Class, Crisis, and the State.* London: New Left.

Wright, Erik Olin. 1997. *Class Counts: Comparative Studies in Class Analysis.* Cambridge, U.K., and New York: Cambridge University Press.

Cedric de Leon

CLASS, LEISURE

In *The Theory of the Leisure Class* (1899), American economist Thorstein Veblen (1857–1929) distinguishes between two classes of individuals, the class that is focused on productive labor and the *leisure class*, a division that developed during the barbarian/feudal stage of society. These groups can be understood as similar to Karl Marx's (1818–1883) notion of classes within capitalism, in which the proletariat and the capitalist (bourgeoisie) class are in conflict over the distribution of society's wealth, power, and the division of labor. However, Veblen incorporates culture into this division with an understanding of production and consumption, material life, status, and economic stratification. According to Veblen, modern economic behavior was based on the struggle for competitive economic standing, as the aristocratic consumption of luxuries served as a litmus test for elite status during the peak of capitalist industrialization. The leisure class itself consists of social elites, businesspeople, and captains of industry (those at the top of the social-class pyramid), who engage in pecuniary activities that detract from the productive aspect of society.

Members of the leisure class attempt to garner status and competitive social advantage through their patterns of consumption (of goods and symbols) and their conduct, thereby driving economic life around status rather than utility. Social status is symbolized by the leisure class through *conspicuous waste, conspicuous consumption,* and *conspicuous leisure,* which are used to communicate and enhance social position and social standing and to obtain heightened self-evaluation. Conspicuous waste is evidence that one can afford to be frivolous with items as well as time (no need to work); conspicuous consumption is the socially visible display of expensive goods that signify class status. Both of these activities indicate wealth and the ability to afford leisure, meaning the lack of a need to perform manual and useful labor.

Conspicuous leisure is the benchmark for determining elite status and serves as a symbolic statement that one is above laboring. In this way, it functions similarly to what Pierre Bourdieu (1930–2002) referred to as *cultural capital* in that it is a description of class compounded with status. Lower-status groups emulate the leisure class in an attempt to increase their own status. Veblen discusses how women are exploited by men through vicarious conspicuous consumption, waste, and leisure, where women perform the conspicuous activity of leisure, and men benefit in terms of status from these activities. For example, ideals of feminine beauty (frailty, weakness, paleness—indicating that the woman is not able to labor), certain restrictive fashions that incapacitate labor, and the removal of women from socially visible productive labor all contribute to the good name of the household and its master.

SEE ALSO *Capitalism; Conspicuous Consumption; Stratification; Veblen, Thorstein*

BIBLIOGRAPHY

Bourdieu, Pierre. 1979. *Distinctions: A Social Critique of the Judgment of Taste.* Trans. Richard Nice. Cambridge, MA: Harvard University Press.

Tucker, Robert, ed. 1978. *The Marx-Engels Reader.* New York: Norton.

Veblen, Thorstein. [1899] 1994. *Theory of the Leisure Class.* New York: Penguin.

Ryan Ashley Caldwell

CLASS, MANAGERIAL

SEE *Managerial Class.*

CLASS, RENTIER

Rentier is a class of people who derive their incomes from financial titles to property. Though the term makes an analogy with the old rent-earning class of great landowners, rentiers are characterized by their more distant relationship to the property they own. Rather than living in an estate in the midst of their property, they own a variety of anonymous income-earning assets, most typically shares and instruments of debt. From the rentiers, all vestiges of the paternalism, noblesse oblige, and personal dependence that once characterized the landowning aristocracy have vanished, leaving them as pure consumers of financial revenues.

While with industrialization a portion of the landowning class transformed itself into rentiers—particularly those, like the duke of Westminster, whose lands became urban—the existence of a rentier class can be seen as an inevitable consequence of the development of capitalist financial institutions. The term *rentier* came to prominence in the early twentieth century and remained influential in economic discourse during the 1920s and 1930s. In the early twenty-first century it is again attracting attention as the financial sector comes to be dominant in mature capitalist economies.

What causes the financial sector to replace manufacturing as the bedrock of the economy? Its supposed role is to fund investment. Savings are meant to be channeled through the banks, investment trusts, and the stock market into firms that want to carry out investment in new capital stock. This process obviously does occur, but in many capitalist countries the financial accounts show that industrial and commercial companies are net suppliers rather than users of funds. It is by no means obvious why, in the face of continuing improvements in information-processing technology, the sector that carries out this channeling of funds should over time absorb a larger and larger portion of national resources and appear to contribute an increasing share of national income.

Channeling funds is manipulation of information. The "funds" are records kept by the banking system, and their channeling is a sequence of transfers between records. The records long ago moved from paper to computer databases. The power of computers has improved by leaps and bounds. One would have thought that the labor required to manage this system would have declined. The mechanization of agriculture eliminated the peasantry, but computers have not laid waste to the City of London. Why?

The key to this paradox is to realize that, despite the modern jargon of a financial services "industry" that offers financial "products" to customers, the financial sector is not a productive industry in the normal sense. Its structural position in capitalistic information flows ensures its

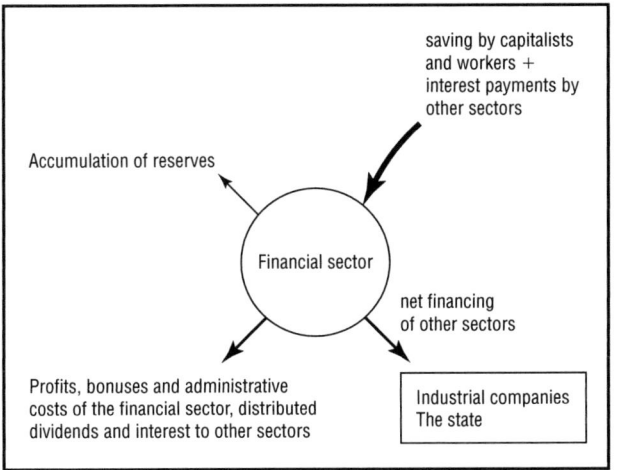

Figure 1

continued command over resources despite changes in technology that would decimate any other industry.

Figure 1 shows in summary form the flows of funds into and out of the financial sector. Savings by individual capitalists, by firms, and from the pension schemes of employees enter the system. Funding flows out to firms carrying out capital investment and also typically to the state to fund the public debt. However, money also flows out as costs: the income of the financial sector itself. This comprises wages of its employees, the bonuses it pays, the distributed dividends of financial companies, and the costs of buildings and equipment that the sector uses. Let us denote savings by σ, bonuses and costs by β, and funding of investment by φ.

The residual, which we will denote by δ, is made up by the change in the money balances of the financial sector itself: $\delta = \sigma - \beta - \varphi$. We need to explain why β, the costs/income of the financial sector, rises as a share of national income over time.

It has been argued that the real rate of return on capital tends to decline over the course of capitalist development (Marx [1894] 1971; Lebowitz 1976; Moseley 1990; Michaelson, Cockshott, and Cottrell 1995; Duménil 2002; Edvinsson 2003, 2005). If the rate of interest does not fall at a corresponding rate, then the level of voluntary fundraising by firms will decline, because a diminishing portion of firms will be making enough profits to cover the rate of interest. However, the level of savings will not necessarily decline at a corresponding rate.

The distribution of income in capitalist societies will be highly uneven (Levy and Solomon 1997, 1998; Reed 2001, 2003). A large proportion of income goes to a small part of the population. People with high incomes tend to save most of it. A decline in the rate of profit on capital

will not alter this. It just means that the book value of the assets of those with high incomes rises. So savings going into the financial system will not decline. The disproportion between share issues and savings tends to make share prices rise; this in turn will induce a rise in the costs of the financial sector β through bonuses and so on.

A feedback mechanism is at play here. The average price of shares rises until the extra bonuses earned by the financial sector absorbs any excess of savings over investment. The argument above takes certain things as given—in particular, the separation of the capitalist class into a set of rentiers and a set of firms engaged in direct production. While this is a realistic portrayal of mature capitalism, it is not capitalism's aboriginal condition. In an earlier phase of capitalism, the rich did not save through financial intermediaries; they saved by investing in their own businesses. One has to ask what mechanism caused an initial population of capitalist masters to polarize into these two subgroups: functioning businesspeople and rentiers who invest only indirectly.

The transition process can be understood as a consequence of the dispersion of profit rates in an initial population of capitalists. Capitalists whose profit rates are above average find it beneficial to borrow funds to invest in their own business; those whose profit rates are below the interest rate gain more by depositing their profits with financial institutions than they would by reinvesting. Borrowing raises what is called the *gearing ratio* of borrowing firms and lowers that of lenders. Industrial capitalists initially earning a low rate of return in industry come, by lending, to acquire negative gearing ratios. In the process they transform themselves from entrepreneurs into rentiers.

The designation rentier was initially applied to individual people, but it applies equally well to any legal entity in the same situation. Limited companies, with respect to their fellow companies, have begun to function as rentiers: that is, they derive their income primarily from their financial rather than their industrial assets. As the demand for funds in the industrial and commercial sector dries up in the face of high interest rates, lending comes to be directed increasingly toward the funding of state debt and consumer credit. With a growing portion of capital depending on interest rather than industrial profit, there develops an increased political pressure to maintain high interest rates. This baneful effect of the rentier interest, which was already lambasted by J. A. Hobson (1902) and John Maynard Keynes (1925, 1936) for its role in consuming capital and hindering investment, looks set to grow. Early twentieth-century critics of the rentier class like Hobson, Keynes, Thorstein Veblen, and even V. I. Lenin identified another trait—its predatory character. To this trait they attributed the disaster of World War I and the deferred disaster of the Versailles treaty.

The rentier interest stood ultimately on moral grounds quite alien to those of natural right. Speaking of the absentee ownership of natural resources, Veblen remarked, "The owners own them not by virtue of having produced or earned them. … These owners own them because they own them, … title is traceable to an act of seizure, legalized by statue or confirmed by long undisturbed possession" (1923, p. 51). This trait is best exemplified today by Russian rentiers like Roman Abramovich, whose billions derive from the greatest undisguised seizure of natural resources within living memory.

SEE ALSO *Capitalism, Managerial*

BIBLIOGRAPHY

Duménil, Gérard. 2002. The Profit Rate: Where and How Much Did It Fall? Did It Recover? (USA 1948–2000). *Review of Radical Political Economy* 34 (4): 437–461.

Edvinsson, Rodney. 2003. A Tendency for the Rate of Profit to Fall? Theoretical Considerations and Empirical Evidence for Sweden, 1800–2000. Paper presented at the Economic-Historical Meeting in Lund, Sweden, October 17–19, 2003. http://www.countdownnet.info/archivio/analisi/Europa/402.pdf.

Edvinsson, Rodney. 2005. Growth, Accumulation, Crisis: With New Macroeconomic Data for Sweden, 1800–2000. PhD diss., Stockholm University.

Hobson, J. A. 1902. *Imperialism: A Study*. London: Unwin Hyman.

Keynes, John Maynard. 1925. *The Economic Consequences of Mr. Churchill*. London: Hogarth.

Keynes, John Maynard. 1936. *The General Theory of Employment, Interest, and Money*. London: Macmillan.

Lebowitz, Michael A. 1976. Marx's Falling Rate of Profit: A Dialectical View. *Canadian Journal of Economics* 9 (2): 232–254.

Levy, Moshe, and Sorin Solomon. 1997. New Evidence for the Power-Law Distribution of Wealth. *Physica A* 242 (1–2): 90–94.

Levy, Moshe, and Sorin Solomon. 1998. Of Wealth, Power, and Law: The Origin of Scaling in Economics. CiteSeer digital publication. http://citeseer.ist.psu.edu/63648.html.

Marx, Karl. [1894] 1971. *Capital*. Vol. 3. Moscow: Progress Publishers.

Michaelson, Greg, W. Paul Cockshott, and Allin F. Cottrell. 1995. Testing Marx: Some New Results from U.K. Data. *Capital and Class* 55 (Spring): 103–129.

Moseley, Fred. 1990. The Decline of the Rate of Profit in the Postwar U.S. Economy: An Alternative Marxian Explanation. *Review of Radical Political Economics* 22 (2–3): 17–37.

Reed, William J. 2001. The Pareto, Zipf, and Other Power Laws. *Economics Letters* 74 (1): 15–19.

Reed, William J. 2003. The Pareto Law of Incomes: An Explanation and an Extension. *Physica A* 319: 469–486.

Veblen, Thorstein. 1923. *Absentee Ownership and Business Enterprise in Recent Times: The Case of America*. London: Allen and Unwin.

Paul Cockshott

CLASS, SOCIAL
SEE *Class.*

CLASS CONFLICT

Class conflicts are a crucial determinant of historical change, for "history … is the history of class struggles" (Marx and Engels [1848] 1998, p. 2); they are endemic because class interests are contradictory, and irresolvable as long as the mode of production remains unchanged. Class conflicts are inherent in the relationship between owners of means of production, who appropriate most of the surplus value created through production, and the direct producers whose share allows them, at best, only to reproduce themselves as workers. Non-Marxist theories of class, based on functionalist or Weberian perspectives, tend to underemphasize the collective dimension of class and its foundation in the objective relationship of people to the means of production. They define class, instead, as an attribute of individuals constructed on the basis of their education, occupation, income, ownership of resources, place in the occupational hierarchy, and so on. Consequently, they conflate class with socioeconomic status, thus obscuring the qualitative differences between class structure and social stratification.

In precapitalist social formations, class struggles assumed different forms, depending on the level of development of the productive forces, and the forms of appropriation of the surplus. Land was the main means of production and complex patterns of land ownership were reflected in complex networks of class relations and struggles between masters and slaves, "patricians and plebeians, lords and serfs, guild-master and journeyman" (Marx and Engels [1848] 1998, p. 2), landowners and tenant farmers, and so forth. The Roman and Greek economies, for example, were "slave economies," despite the presence of free, independent peasants and small producers, because "the main way in which the dominant propertied classes of the ancient world derived their surplus … was due to unfree labor" (de Ste. Croix 1981, p. 52). And the process of "primitive accumulation" through which money and commodities became capital, and serfs, independent peasants, and small producers became wageworkers, entailed the expropriation of direct producers from the land through unrelenting class struggles; its history "is written in the annals of mankind in letters of blood and fire" (Marx [1867] 1967, pp. 713–716).

In capitalist social formations today, where labor is formally free, the struggle centers around wage levels and the length of the working day, for capitalists seek to keep wages low, working hours long, and profits high. In the market, where workers and capitalists meet as equal commodity owners, capitalists purchase the only commodity workers can sell: labor power. The use value of labor power is the production of value far greater than its own (i.e., the value of the wages capitalists pay); this value is embodied in the product. In the context of production, there is no equality: Capitalists control working conditions, the labor process, the length of the working day, and they own the product (Marx [1867] 1967, chs. VI and VII). Workers' demands for the eight-hour day led to violent class struggles in the nineteenth and early twentieth centuries (Foner 1986). Conflicts about the length of the working day persist today; some employers impose overtime rather than hire more workers and low wages force many workers to hold more than one job or work more than eight hours a day.

The revolutionary worldwide confrontation between capital and labor predicted in the *Communist Manifesto* (Marx and Engels [1848] 1998) has yet to happen, however, and localized attempts in Eastern Europe, China, and Latin America have failed. Workers today do not have class consciousness in the classic sense; they do not share a sense of themselves as a class with common anticapitalist grievances and, consequently, they are not a "class for itself" united and with clarity of purpose (Marx [1846] 1947). They are only concerned with economic survival, not with the overthrow of capitalism: They are merely a "class in itself," objectively identifiable by social scientists, but lacking self-awareness. Workers' spontaneous consciousness is largely individualistic and "economistic," a phenomenon that Marxist theorists have addressed in different ways.

V. I. Lenin argued that "the working class, exclusively by its own effort, is able to develop only trade union consciousness" ([1902] 1967, p. 122), hence his support for the role of a "vanguard party" and the bourgeois intelligentsia in politically educating the working class. Adhering to the principle of historical materialism, that social existence determines consciousness (Marx and Engels [1846] 1947, pp. 13–14), Georg Lukacs emphasized the role of *praxis* or human activity in the formation of class consciousness. It is through working-class praxis that society can become conscious of itself, for the proletariat is both the subject and object of history (Lukacs 1971, pp. 18–19). Only from the class standpoint of the proletariat is it possible to comprehend social reality as a totality, a crucial prerequisite to acting as a self-conscious class (p. 20). It is unclear, however, how this comprehension will emerge, because the forces of history unfold independently of individuals' intentions and consciousness. Consciousness, Lukacs states, is "*subjectively* justified" in its historical context, though it "*objectively* ... appears as 'false consciousness' ... [because] it by-passes the essence of the evolution of society ... [and] fails to express it adequately" (pp. 47–50; italics in original). Whatever the intended motives and goals of this "false consciousness" may be, however, they further "the *objective* aims of society" (p. 50; italics in original).

Class consciousness, consequently, is something different from the ordinary thoughts individuals develop through praxis; it is neither "the sum nor the average of what is thought or felt by the single individuals who make up the class" (p. 51). Rather, it is "the appropriate and rational reactions 'imputed' ... to a particular typical position in the process of production" (p. 51). Using Weber's methodology (Kalberg 2005, pp. 14–22), Lukacs constructs an ideal type of class consciousness, by relating it to society as a whole and then inferring the thoughts and feelings that individuals in different class positions would have if they had access to knowledge of the totality (i.e., the mode of production) and of their place in it (p. 51). Impeding the development of "true" proletarian class consciousness are commodity fetishism and other reifications characteristic of capitalist culture. Lukacs's arguments imply, however, that as capitalism develops, workers will eventually discern their place and objectives in the totality and will therefore consciously further the "aims of history."

Whether social reality will eventually become "transparent" or ideology will always cloud class consciousness and, more generally, people's spontaneous understanding of their conditions of existence, remains an unresolved issue. Louis Althusser's view is that ideology as such, unlike specific ideologies, "has no history"; it is, like Freud's unconscious, omnipresent and eternal (Althusser 2001, p. 109). To say that ideology is eternal is to point out that individuals, spontaneously, cannot penetrate the logic of history and thus acquire knowledge of the unintended consequences of their actions. The opacity of social reality is a transhistorical aspect of the human condition, unlikely to change even after capitalism has been superseded by a society in which the direct producers are in control of the mode of production. And to say that ideology has no history is to recognize that all forms of consciousness and all systematic products of intellectual labor (morality, religion, philosophy, and politics) are the outcome of human material practices under historically specific conditions of existence (Marx and Engels [1846] 1947, pp 14–15).

The capitalist state rules through repressive (e.g., army, police, prisons) and ideological (e.g., family, schools, media, religion) state apparatuses. Through the latter, individuals are transformed into subjects, uncritically accepting their subjection to the Subject (i.e., God, Race, Nation, and Capital) whose power is exerted through the subjectification process. Ideologies have a material existence in practices, rituals, and institutions; they interpellate individuals as particular subjects (e.g., male, female, black, white, worker, capitalist, criminal), eliciting immediate recognition because individuals, whose social existence is embedded in ideological and material practices and rituals, are "always-already subjects" (Althusser 2001, pp. 112–119). In a society in which class is part of the common sense understanding of the world and of political discourse, class would enter into the formation of subjectivities. In the United States, however, where people are "afflicted with a serious case of social amnesia" (Aronowitz 1992, p. 72), it is the interpellation of cultural identities that structures people's subjectivities. It is through identities, rather than class, that people understand their lives and this is why the power of ideology stems from "the degree to which, in Althusser's terms, it becomes … lived experience" (Aronowitz 1992, p. 36). Thus conceived, ideology precludes the spontaneous emergence of class consciousness, without the intervention of political parties and intellectuals bringing to the working classes an analysis of their lives that may tear away the ideological veils.

In the *Communist Manifesto*, Marx and Engels confidently predicted that class conflicts would eventually result in the overthrow of capitalism. Their argument rests upon the notion of a dialectical relationship between the active and the reserve armies of labor, which assumed that the same workers would, because of the ebbs and flows of capital accumulation, experience both periods of poverty and unemployment and of economic well being. These experiences would, presumably, be the material condition for the rise of a class-conscious working class, the "grave diggers" of the bourgeoisie, self-consciously engaging in anticapitalist class struggles (Marx and Engels [1848] 1998, pp. 23–24; Arrighi 1990, pp. 29–30). But while that was the case in the nineteenth and early twentieth centuries, as capitalism spread throughout the world it divided the global working classes, with most of the active armies located in the advanced capitalist countries and most of the reserve armies located in the poorer countries. Within countries, the gap between the active and the reserve armies grew large, and the ideological effects that emerged from workers' sharing common conditions of existence largely disappeared after World War II. Today, globalization has produced a "reshuffling" of the global working classes; most of the active army is now in the poorer countries, whereas workers in the wealthy countries face declining wages and competition from immigrant labor willing to work for less (Arrighi 1990, p. 53).

As these changes accelerate, class conflicts might become more widespread, but this does not necessarily mean that class consciousness will eventually replace other forms of workers' consciousness, such as, for example, identity politics, racism, or xenophobia. In any case, class conflicts will continue for as long as capitalism remains the dominant mode of production. Such conflicts have been and will continue to be fought under a variety of ideological banners because people, as "ensembles of social relations" (Marx 1947, p. 198), live their lives at the crossroads of multiple experiences. Marx pointed the way toward an understanding of the relationship between social change, conflicts, and consciousness. In the process of studying change, "it is always necessary to distinguish between the material transformation of the economic conditions of production, which can be determined with the precision of natural science, and the legal, political, religious, artistic or philosophic—in short, ideological forms in which men become conscious of this conflict and fight it out" ([1859] 1970, p. 21). From Marx's standpoint, class consciousness should not be understood in purely economic terms, but in all its complexity. It emerges from changes in people's experiences and participation in class conflicts, which together pose challenges to the ideologies that have shaped their representations of those conflicts and experiences. Common experiences, the basis for the emergence of class consciousness, are "determined" by the productive relations into which men are born—or enter involuntarily. Class consciousness is the way in which these experiences are handled in cultural terms (Thompson 1966, pp. 9–10). These insights from Marx and E. P. Thompson indicate that it is necessary to examine the underlying class basis of contemporary processes of political mobilization and of struggles such as those happening in Bolivia, Mexico, and Venezuela. Underlying populist and indigenous movements for social justice and national independence from imperialist and corporate domination are material class interests, which fuel the rise of political leaders like Evo Morales (Bolivia), Lopez Obrador (Mexico), and Hugo Chavez (Venezuela), as well as the national and transnational opposition to them.

While class conflicts are inherent in class societies, this does not mean that if classless societies become possible in the future, conflicts will end. Class conflicts are grounded in struggles around the production and appropriation of the surplus. Under capitalism, they presuppose the existence of the capitalist and working classes. Were these classes to be abolished and some form of collective ownership of the means of production to replace capitalism, social conflicts would not end, however; the division of labor would continue to divide the population according to occupation, skills, and economic rewards. Struggles over redistribution of income would replace class conflicts focused on the abolition of the mode of production. And because racial, ethnic, gender, and other differences irreducible to class would continue to exist, struggles about recognition (Fraser 1995) would continue as well. Conflicts based on social stratification would continue for as long as the subjective and material conditions inherited from capitalism persisted and competed with new forms of consciousness, practices, institutions, and so forth. The interconnections between experience and consciousness suggests, however, that as class conflict disappeared, the material conditions for social antagonisms at the level of social stratification would likely be eroded as well. In any case, as long as capitalism is the dominant mode of production, class conflict will continue to shape national and transnational political struggles.

SEE ALSO *Class; Marx, Karl; Middle Class; Surplus Value*

BIBLIOGRAPHY

Althusser, Louis. [1971] 2001. *Lenin and Philosophy, and Other Essays.* Trans. Ben Brewster. New York: Monthly Review Press.

Aronowitz, Stanley. 1992. *The Politics of Identity: Class, Culture, Social Movements.* New York: Routledge.

Arrighi, Giovanni. 1990. Marxist Century, American Century: The Making and Remaking of the World Labour Movement. *New Left Review* 179 (January–February): 29–63.

de Ste. Croix, G. E. M. 1981. *The Class Struggle in the Ancient Greek World: From the Archaic Age to the Arab Conquests.* Ithaca, NY: Cornell University Press.

Foner, Philip S. 1986. *May Day: A Short History of the International Worker's Holiday, 1886–1986.* New York: International Publishers.

Kalberg, Stephen, ed. 2005. *Max Weber: Readings and Commentary on Modernity.* Malden, MA: Blackwell Publishing.

Lenin, V. I. [1902] 1967. What Is To Be Done? In *Lenin: 1897 to January 1917*, 97–248. Vol. 1 of *Selected Works in Three Volumes.* New York: International Publishers.

Lukacs, Georg. 1971. *History and Class Consciousness: Studies in Marxist Dialectics.* Trans. Rodney Livingstone. Cambridge, MA: MIT Press.

Marx, Karl, and Frederick Engels. [1846] 1947. *The German Ideology.* Ed. R. Pascal; trans. W. Lough and C. P. Magill. New York: International Publishers.

Marx, Karl, and Friedrich Engels. [1848] 1998. *The Communist Manifesto.* Ed. Christopher Phelps. New York: Monthly Review Press.

Marx, Karl. [1859] 1970. *A Contribution to the Critique of Political Economy.* Ed. Maurice Dobb; trans. S. W. Ryazanskaya. New York: International Publishers.

Marx, Karl. [1867] 1967. *The Process of Capitalist Production.* Vol. 1 of *Capital: A Critique of Political Economy.* Ed. Frederick Engels; trans. S. Moore and E. Aveling. New York: International Publishers.

Thompson, E. P. 1966. *The Making of the English Working Class.* New York: Vintage Books.

Martha E. Gimenez

CLASS CONSCIOUSNESS

The concept of class consciousness emerged in nineteenth-century socialist theories of social emancipation, mainly in the work of Karl Marx (1818–1883). Marx's critique of the idealist philosophy of Georg W. F. Hegel (1770–1831) led him to state, in his *German Ideology* (1845), that human consciousness is determined by material experiences and conditions, and not the reverse. As Marx argued in the *Eighteenth Brumaire of Louis Bonaparte* (1852), class consciousness entails both the common interests of a social class as arising from its material situation ("class in itself") and the solidarity articulated from such interests in the struggle against another class ("class for itself").

The protagonist of Marx's idea of class consciousness is mainly the proletariat in the capitalist mode of production. Working-class consciousness is in this view the highest and truest form of consciousness ever expressed by a subaltern social group. In fact, for the first time in history, the consciousness of the oppressed can directly confront the economic mechanisms of exploitation. It does not, therefore, have to deal with the religious ideas, customs, and traditions that, in the words of the *Communist Manifesto* (1848), had "veiled" social relations in earlier epochs.

Marx's analysis of class consciousness remained, however, unfinished as part of his general discussion on classes in the third volume of *Capital* (1894), a project that was interrupted when Marx died. Twentieth-century Marxists developed the concept in debates that to a large extent revolved around the relations between class consciousness and the organization of workers. Georg Lukács's (1885–1971) *History and Class Consciousness* (1971) saw "true" class consciousness as the proletariat's awareness of its revolutionary goal and, at the same time, as the most adequate set of reactions that could be "imputed" to particular positions in the production process. The revolutionary party is for Lukács the personification of the collective consciousness of the working class. Vladimir I. Lenin (1870–1924) and Karl Kautsky (1854–1938) emphasized the role of organization by arguing that real class consciousness can only be brought to the working class from outside, a task that for Lenin required a party of professional revolutionaries. Below this level, Lenin saw a realm of merely "economist" consciousness, symbolized by trade unions' struggles for their immediate demands.

The views of Lenin, Kautsky, and Lukács have been widely debated and criticized by various Marxist activists and scholars. In contrast to Lenin's theory of the party, Rosa Luxemburg (1870–1919) argued that class consciousness arises spontaneously from workers' experiences of struggle, especially mass strikes. Karl Korsch's (1886–1961) *Marxism and Philosophy* (1923) asserted that class consciousness is not the mere subjective reflection of economic conditions because ideology and politics can also independently shape social power relations. The autonomous role of ideology was further discussed in the structuralist tradition, especially in the work of Louis Althusser (1918–1990). It was, however, Antonio Gramsci (1891–1937) who placed this aspect at the center of his analysis. He argued that class struggle involves a contestation over "hegemony," whereby the working class needs "organic intellectuals," of which the party is an expression, who must be able to engage and shape the "common sense" of society.

Marxist analyses have since departed from earlier views of class consciousness as merely determined by economic conditions and ultimately represented by formal organizations. Social historians Edward P. Thompson and Eric J. Hobsbawm underline the complexity of workers' consciousness, and the fact that their everyday experiences do not necessarily progress toward revolutionary ideas, being indeed often influenced by precapitalist notions of justice or collective identities. The view of human subjectivity in the work of members of the Frankfurt school, especially Herbert Marcuse (1898–1979), is influenced by psychoanalysis, and argues that consumerism has largely subdued the radicalism of a working class that is increasingly co-opted by capitalism. In Jean-Paul Sartre's (1905–1980) "political economy of everyday life," and in Wilhelm Reich's (1897–1957) theory of psychic oppression, class consciousness is replaced by a theory of "serialized" and alienated human nature.

Such analyses tend to agree that as capitalism is able to extend middle-class consumption patterns, workers in industrialized countries lose their revolutionary potential. Conversely, class consciousness is replaced by a multiplicity of oppositional identities in the work of feminist scholars and in currents influenced by postmodernism, such as "autonomist Marxism." Workers' centrality in anticapitalist politics gives way to the development of social movements that express the specific demands of women, the unemployed, students, and indigenous people. At the same time, critics of the Leninist idea of the party stress the importance of horizontality and consensus as conditions for a shared awareness to emerge among diverse social actors. Moreover, production is no longer seen as the principal terrain where collective consciousness is developed. For Henri Lefebvre (1901–1991), the broader social space and everyday life become battlefields for the advancement of projects of social emancipation. After the 1970s, "cultural studies" scholars like Dick Hebdige and Stuart Hall, strongly influenced by Gramsci, emphasized contestation over symbolic practices, subcultures, and the media as autonomous terrains of analysis.

SEE ALSO *Alienation; Marxism*

BIBLIOGRAPHY

Gottlieb, Roger S. 1987. *History and Subjectivity. The Transformation of Marxist Theory.* Philadelphia: Temple University Press.

Lukács, Georg. 1971. *History and Class Consciousness. Studies in Marxist Dialectics.* Trans. Rodney Livingstone. Cambridge, MA: MIT Press.

Mészaros, István, ed. 1971. *Aspects of History and Class Consciousness.* London: Routledge and Kegan Paul.

Wright, Erik Olin. 1997. *Class Counts: Comparative Studies in Class Analysis.* Cambridge, U.K.: Cambridge University Press.

Franco Barchiesi

CLASSICAL CONDITIONING

The formation of connections or associations between related sensations, emotions, or thoughts is the basis for an evolutionarily old and important form of learning known as *classical conditioning*. Since the late nineteenth century, a collection of standardized conditioning (training) procedures have been used to study associative learning and, more recently, its neurobiological underpinnings.

IVAN PAVLOV

The Russian physiologist Ivan Pavlov (1849–1936) is customarily credited with discovering classical conditioning. In fact, the idea that associations develop between stimuli that are close together (contiguous) in space or time was first articulated by the Greek philosopher Aristotle (384–322 BCE). Pavlov did discover (i.e., identify and develop) an empirical approach for studying classical conditioning, codifying the procedures and terminology that remain the standard (Pavlov 1927).

Pavlov's interest in classical conditioning emerged out of his research on the physiology of digestion, for which he was awarded the Nobel Prize in medicine in 1904. Pavlov and his technicians realized that a dog's stomach secretions could be triggered not only by food reaching the stomach, but also by seeing or chewing the food, and even by the environment in which the food is delivered. The secretion of saliva was also found to be associable, with dogs salivating to stimuli that regularly preceded the presentation of food, including novel stimuli, such as a bell, that had never before induced salivation.

CLASSICAL CONDITIONING

With classical or Pavlovian conditioning, the neutral *conditioned stimulus* (CS) is paired with a biologically significant *unconditioned stimulus* (US), until such time that the CS comes to elicit a learned or *conditioned response* (CR). Returning to Pavlov's dogs, after experiencing repeated pairings of the bell (CS) and food (US), the previously neutral bell began to elicit salivation. In this example, both the CR and the *unconditioned response* (UR) happen to be a salivatory response. This need not always be the case—the CR can also oppose or be entirely unrelated to the UR.

Two aspects of the CS-US temporal relationship impact the strength of Pavlovian conditioning: (1) the amount of time that elapses between the onset of the first and second stimulus (i.e., the *interstimulus interval*, or ISI); and (2) the order in which the CS and US are presented. In short- and long-*delay conditioning*, the CS precedes the US with a shorter or longer ISI, respectively. The addition of a break between the offset of the CS and the onset of the US results in *trace conditioning*. *Simultaneous conditioning*, as its name implies, requires that the CS and US be presented at the same time. Finally, with *backward conditioning*, the CS is presented after the onset of the US. As a general rule, the rate of learning in classical conditioning accelerates as the CS grows progressively more accurate in predicting the US. Delay conditioning is normally acquired fastest, followed by trace conditioning. Simultaneous and backward conditioning typically produce little or no learning.

APPETITIVE/AVERSIVE CONDITIONING

Appetitive conditioning utilizes a positive reinforcing stimulus—for example, access to food, water, or sex. Interestingly, animals conditioned with an appetitive stimulus, such as food, will often approach and contact the stimulus signaling its availability. If a localized visual stimulus (CS) repeatedly signals the delivery of food (US), pigeons will often peck at the CS before approaching the food cup, although pecking is not required for food access. Interestingly, the tracking of a food signal appears to be modality-specific. When trained with an auditory CS, which is presumably less localized in space, pigeons do not peck at the CS but instead advance toward the food cup directly (Brown and Jenkins 1968).

Aversive conditioning is accomplished with a mildly painful or otherwise unpleasant US. The two-process model of aversive conditioning posits that emotional (i.e., fear) CRs emerge first, followed by more specialized and adaptive motor CRs (Konorski 1967). Fear and motor conditioning are normally studied independently of one another—each utilizing distinct experimental procedures.

In a typical fear-conditioning experiment, the tone or light CS is paired with a mild electrical shock or loud noise US. Fear conditioning, which engenders a variety of autonomic and behavioral responses, is a very rapid form of learning—requiring only a single CS-US pairing under the right conditions (LeDoux 2000).

The most commonly studied motor CR is the anticipatory eyeblink. After being paired with an air puff or a mild shock to the eye (US), the tone or light CS comes to elicit a blink CR. Hundreds of trials are often required to properly time the response, but subjects eventually learn to execute the CR just before US onset (Christian and Thompson 2003).

The amygdala, in the brain's medial temporal lobe, is critical for acquiring conditioned fear. The anticipatory eyeblink, on the other hand, is reliant on circuitry in the brain stem and cerebellum. In both cases, the repeated pairing of the CS and US allows the neural signals initiated by each stimulus to converge and interact. CS-US associative synaptic plasticity in the amygdala and cerebellum enables changes in CS neural activation patterns, bringing emotional and motor-conditioned responses, respectively, under control of the CS.

EXTINCTION

To this point, classical conditioning has been discussed in terms of nascent or established associations among stimuli. In the real world, such relationships rarely remain static—the CS may over time lose its ability to accurately predict the US. In a procedure called *extinction*, the CS is presented alone, once conditioning is complete, in order to weaken or extinguish the CS-US association and, by extension, the behavioral CR. The reduction in conditioned responding is not due to simple forgetting, however, which may occur following a prolonged absence of the CS. Extinction requires new learning on the part of the organism—learning that the CS is no longer predictive of the US.

Results from several behavioral phenomena make clear that extinction is not the result of unlearning the CS-US association. First, relearning the CS-US association is significantly faster following extinction then during the original acquisition. Second, an extinguished CR can temporarily reappear if an arousing or sensitizing stimulus is presented just before the CS. Third, over time an extinguished CR can spontaneously recover if the CS is represented. All three findings support the idea that the original CS-US association remains intact—though inhibited—once extinguished.

THERAPEUTIC/CLINICAL APPROACHES

Classical conditioning principles underlie many therapeutic techniques. *Exposure therapy*, for instance, is designed to aid patients who respond to particular objects or situations with unrealistic or excessive fear. For instance, *Counterconditioning* requires that the triggering stimulus be paired with a positive event or object. A patient might be shown a spider and then given a teddy bear—associating the spider with the comfort afforded by the bear. With *desensitization*, a patient's irrational fears are rendered incompatible by slowly introducing progressively stronger versions of the triggering stimulus—for example, a picture of a spider, a plastic spider, and then a real spider.

Classical conditioning can also be applied to clinical studies that focus on human behavioral and cognitive processing. The brain regions engaged by classical eyeblink conditioning—including the brain stem, cerebellum, and limbic system—are the same brain regions affected by numerous clinical disorders. Discerning differences in the acquisition and timing of eyeblink CRs for patients, relative to control subjects, is an effective diagnostic tool for studying the brain-behavior correlates of clinical pathology. Autistic subjects, for instance, acquire eyeblink CRs at a faster rate and with an earlier onset time than age-matched controls (see Steinmetz et al. [2001] for a review).

PSYCHOLOGICAL PHENOMENA

Classical conditioning plays a role in many psychological phenomena. Emotions, as already noted, condition rapidly and easily, especially when the emotion is intensely felt. A traumatic experience can elicit strong emotions that become associated with other aspects of the situation, including the location, other people involved, and even the time of day. Attitudes and preferences are equally susceptible to modification by association. Attitudes toward people of other races, nationalities, or religions can be influenced by how they are portrayed in the news or entertainment media. Similarly, advertisers have long recognized the benefits of linking a consumer product, be it beer, jeans, or a car—with a positive reinforcer, such as an attractive model.

DRUG ADDICTION

Drug use is typically associated with a specific environment and a specific administration ritual (e.g., injection). These cues can be conditioned to predict the onset of the drug's effect and, in turn, generate compensatory responses to counteract those effects—helping the body maintain homeostasis. A drug that decreases a user's heartbeat would eventually, if taken in the same place and way, be offset by a compensatory heart rate increase. The activation of compensatory CRs also coincides and contributes to drug tolerance, necessitating more drug be taken for the same effect. Inasmuch, the chance of an overdose increases—due to a limited compensatory CR—

if the drug is taken in a new environment or administered in a novel fashion (Siegel 1999).

OPERANT/INSTRUMENTAL CONDITIONING

Another form of associative learning, termed *operant* or *instrumental conditioning*, depends on association formation between the stimulus and response (S-R learning), unlike classical conditioning, which relies on S-S learning. Edward Thorndike (1874–1949) pioneered much of the early research on operant conditioning. He famously observed that a cat placed inside a latched cage would, through trial and error, learn how to unlatch the cage if rewarded with a piece of fish on the outside. From these observations and others, Thorndike formulated the *law of effect*, which states: the S-R association is strengthened or weakened depending on whether the consequent effect (US) is reinforcing or punishing.

By the mid-twentieth century, the premiere researcher on operant conditioning was B. F. Skinner (1904–1990). Skinner found that an animal's behavior could be shaped by progressively narrowing the range of reinforced behaviors, a process called *successive approximation*. He also developed free-operant procedures for studying S-R learning. The typical Skinner box contained one or more stimulus lights, one or more levers that an animal could press, and one or more places in which reinforcers, like food, could be delivered. With hundreds to thousands of potential lever-press responses per session, Skinner focused his analyses on how rapidly the animal repeated the response.

SEE ALSO *Operant Conditioning; Pavlov, Ivan; Reinforcement Theories*

BIBLIOGRAPHY

Brown, Paul L., and Herbert M. Jenkins. 1968. Auto-shaping of the Pigeon's Key Peck. *Journal of Experimental Analysis of Behavior* 11: 1–8.

Christian, Kimberly M., and Richard F. Thompson. 2003. Neural Substrates of Eyeblink Conditioning: Acquisition and Retention. *Learning and Memory* 10: 427–455.

Konorski, Jerzy. 1967. *Integrative Activity of the Brain: An Interdisciplinary Approach.* Chicago: University of Chicago Press.

LeDoux, Joseph E. 2000. Emotion Circuits in the Brain. *Annual Review of Neuroscience* 23: 155–184.

Pavlov, Ivan P. 1927. *Conditioned Reflexes: An Investigation of the Physiological Activity of the Cerebral Cortex.* Trans. G. V. Anrep. London: Oxford University Press.

Siegel, Shephard. 1999. Drug Anticipation and Drug Addiction: The 1998 H. David Archibald Lecture. *Addiction* 94 (8): 1113–1124.

Steinmetz, Joseph E., Jo-Anne Tracy, and John T. Green. 2001. Classical Eyeblink Conditioning: Clinical Models and Applications. *Integrative Physiological and Behavioral Science* 36 (3): 220–238.

Derick H. Lindquist
Joseph E. Steinmetz

CLASSICAL MUSIC

European classical music is both a topic of research and a source of ideas for social science. It can be studied as a set of specialized professions, an economic system, or an example of small-group interaction processes. As a source of ideas it helps social scientists reconsider classical social-science theories of culture types and the rise and fall of civilizations that have fallen out of favor but have much to contribute.

As Europe developed, technologically and socially, to become the dominant civilization in the world, its music also developed, embodying many of the same cultural tendencies that led to the spectacular success of this small region. One can chart the developments in complex vocal and orchestral music from roughly 1600, when a late–Italian Renaissance attempt to revive ancient Greek music drama led to the creation of grand opera, or starting as early as 1200, when music began to express European nationalism. An example is the 1228 "Palestina Song" by Walther von der Vogelweide, celebrating the Sixth Crusade's capture of Jerusalem.

For centuries, among the most complex machines were European musical instruments: church organs, harpsichords, and pianos. Among the most complex civilian activities on earth were performances of major European musical works, such as Claudio Monteverdi's 1607 opera *L'Orfeo*, Johann Sebastian Bach's Mass in B-minor completed in 1749, and Ludwig van Beethoven's 1824 Ninth Symphony. Coordination of such complex social activities required a system of musical notation far more advanced than possessed by any other civilization, division of labor among many highly skilled professionals, development of musical theory tied to mathematics and aesthetics, and strict discipline within a social system that rewarded individual achievements by composers, conductors, and soloists.

From the Crusades until World War I, European music evolved in a rather linear direction, for example, first gradually rationalizing musical scales until the time of Bach, and then progressively exploiting the chromatic possibilities of the well-tempered scale, notably in Richard Wagner's 1859 *Tristan and Isolde*. These were made possible by technological developments, such as from increasingly complex harpsichords to the powerful eighty-eight-key modern piano and the addition of valves to brass instruments. Serious music had reached the limits of progress in this direction in Arnold Schoenberg's ponderous oratorio *Gurre-Lieder*, first performed in 1913, the same year that Igor Stravinsky's dynamic *Rite of Spring* sought to revive the European spirit through an influx of primitivism. To a very real extent, war brought an end to the European dream in 1914. Schoenberg's response was to develop a system of atonal composition that was either a rejection of the European sense of melody or the fulfillment of the European evolution toward chromaticism in harmony. His mathematical *twelve-tone method* based a piece on a *tone row*, a series of the twelve tones of the octave, not repeating one until the other eleven had been played. He attempted to compose an entire religious opera, *Moses und Aron*, based on a single tone row representing God's law. Schoenberg was unable to finish this work, and although many composers adopted his system, Stravinsky among them, it marked the effective end of European classical music rather than a new beginning.

European classical music illustrates the theory of Oswald Spengler, who argued that each great civilization begins with a unified set of ideas, builds on them, and attains their logical conclusion, at which point the civilization collapses. Pitirim Sorokin described this cycle of birth and death as a gradual shift from the original set of ideas that flourish in the civilization's *ideational* or growth phase, to the gradual loss of faith that comes in the *sensate* or decline phase, which could be followed by another ideational phase.

Crosscutting these cyclical theories was Friedrich Nietzsche's explicitly music-based theory of competition between *Apollonian* and *Dionysian* styles—roughly intellectual versus intuitive, or what Curt Sachs called *ethos* and *pathos*—as in the difference between Bach and Wagner. Following an information-theory approach, Leonard Meyer has argued that listeners develop expectations about what is to come next in music, both in a single work and within a broad tradition, and creativity violates these expectations. Thus, novelty gradually expanded the scope of European music, often by alternating between Apollonian and Dionysian extremes, leading in the twentieth century either to collapse or to a fluctuating stasis. The fact that every feature of European music differs from other traditions, such as the Arabic or Chinese, dovetails with Samuel Huntington's theory that the world is not converging on one "modern" culture but faces a clash of civilizations.

SEE ALSO *Civilization; Civilizations, Clash of; Culture, Low and High; Distinctions, Social and Cultural; Division of Labor; Music; Music, Psychology of; Nationalism and Nationality; Professionalization*

BIBLIOGRAPHY

Bainbridge, William Sims. 1985. Cultural Genetics. In *Religious Movements*, ed. Rodney Stark, 157–198. New York: Paragon.

Brindle, Reginald Smith. 1966. *Serial Composition.* London and New York: Oxford University Press.

Grout, Donald Jay, and Claude V. Palisca. 2006. *A History of Western Music,* 7th ed. New York: Norton.

Hubbard, Frank. 1965. *Three Centuries of Harpsichord Making.* Cambridge, MA: Harvard University Press.

Huntington, Samuel P. 1996. *The Clash of Civilizations and the Remaking of World Order.* New York: Simon and Schuster.

Lorraine, Renee Cox. 2001. *Music, Tendencies, and Inhibitions: Reflections on a Theory of Leonard Meyer.* Lanham, MD: Scarecrow Press.

Meyer, Leonard B. 1994. *Music, the Arts, and Ideas.* Chicago: University of Chicago Press.

Nietzsche, Friedrich Wilhelm. 1872. *The Birth of Tragedy and The Case of Wagner.* New York: Vintage, 1967.

Pollens, Stewart. 1995. *The Early Pianoforte.* Cambridge, U.K.: Cambridge University Press.

Sachs, Curt. 1946. *The Commonwealth of Art: Style in the Fine Arts, Music, and the Dance.* New York: Norton.

Sorokin, Pitirim A. 1941. *Social and Cultural Dynamics.* New York: American Book Company.

Spengler, Oswald. 1918. *The Decline of the West.* 2 vols. New York: Knopf, 1945.

William Sims Bainbridge

CLASSICAL STATISTICAL ANALYSIS

Classical statistical analysis seeks to describe the distribution of a measurable property (descriptive statistics) and to determine the reliability of a sample drawn from a population (inferential statistics). Classical statistical analysis is based on repeatedly measuring properties of objects and aims at predicting the frequency with which certain results will occur when the measuring operation is repeated at random or stochastically.

Properties can be measured repeatedly of the same object or only once per object. However, in the latter case, one must measure a number of sufficiently similar objects. Typical examples are measuring the outcome of tossing a coin or rolling a die repeatedly and count the occurrences of the possible outcomes as well as measuring the chemical composition of the next hundred or thousand pills produced in the production line of a pharmaceutical plant. In the former case the same object (one and the same die cast) is "measured" several times (with respect to the question which number it shows); in the latter case many distinguishable, but similar objects are measured

with respect to their composition which in the case of pills is expected to be more or less identical, such that the repetition is not with the same object, but with the next available similar object.

One of the central concepts of classical statistical analysis is to determine the empirical frequency distribution that yields the absolute or relative frequency of the occurrence of each of the possible results of the repeated measurement of a property of an object or a class of objects when only a finite number of different outcomes is possible (discrete case). If one thinks of an infinitely repeated and arbitrarily precise measurement where every outcome is (or can be) different (as would be the case if the range of the property is the set of real numbers), then the relative frequency of a single outcome would not be very instructive; instead one uses the distribution function in this (continuous) case which, for every numerical value x of the measured property, yields the absolute or relative frequency of the occurrence of all values smaller than x. This function is usually noted as $F(x)$, and its derivative $F'(x) = f(x)$ is called frequency density function.

If one wants to describe an empirical distribution, the complete function table is seldom instructive. This is why the empirical frequency or distribution functions are often represented by a few parameters that describe the essential features of the distribution. The so-called moments of the distribution represent the distribution completely, and the lower-order moments represent the distribution at least in a satisfactory manner. Moments are defined as follows:

$$m_k = 1/n \sum_{i=1}^{n} (x_i - c)^k,$$

where k is the order of the moment, n is the number of repetitions or objects measured, and c is a constant that is usually either 0 (moment about the origin) or the arithmetic mean (moment about the mean), the first-order mean about the origin being the arithmetic mean.

In the frequentist interpretation of probability, frequency can be seen as the realization of the concept of probability: It is quite intuitive to believe that if the probability of a certain outcome is some number between 0 and 1, then the expected relative frequency of this outcome would be the same number, at least in the long run. From this, one of the concepts of probability is derived, yielding probability distribution and density functions as models for their empirical correlates. These functions are usually also noted as $f(x)$ and $F(x)$, respectively, and their moments are also defined much like in the above formula, but with a difference that takes into account that there is no finite number n of measurement repetitions:

$$m_k = \sum_{x=0}^{\infty} (x - c)^k f(x)$$
$$m_k = \int_{-\infty}^{\infty} (x - c)^k f(x)\, dx,$$

where the first equation can be applied to discrete numerical variables (e.g., the results of counting), while the second equation can be applied to continuous variables.

Again, the first-order moment about 0 is the mean, and the other moments are usually calculated about this mean. In many important cases one would be satisfied to know the mean (as an indicator for the central tendency of the distribution) and the second-order moment about the mean, namely the variance (as the most prominent indicator for the variation). For the important case of the normal or Gaussian distribution, these two parameters are sufficient to describe the distribution completely.

If one models an empirical distribution with a theoretical distribution (any non-negative function for which the zero-order moment evaluates to 1, as this is the probability for the variable to have any arbitrary value within its domain), one can estimate its parameters from the moments of the empirical distributions calculated from the finite number of repeated measurements taken in a sample, especially in the case where the normal distribution is a satisfactory model of the empirical distribution, as in this case mean and variance allow the calculation of all interesting values of the probability density function $f(x)$ and of the distribution function $F(x)$.

Empirical and theoretical distributions need not be restricted to the case of a single property or variable, they are also defined for the multivariate case. Given that empirical moments can always be calculated from the measurements taken in a sample, these moments are also results of a random process, just like the original measurements. In this respect, the mean, variance, correlation coefficient or any other statistical parameter calculated from the finite number of objects in a sample is also the outcome of a random experiment (measurement taken from a randomly selected set of objects instead of exactly one object). And for these derived measurements theoretical distributions are also available, and these models of the empirical moments allow the estimation with which probability one could expect the respective parameter to fall into a specified interval in the next sample to be taken.

If, for instance, one has a sample of 1,000 interviewees of whom 520 answered they were going to vote for party A in the upcoming election, and 480 announced they were going to vote for party B, then the parameter π_A—the proportion of A-voters in the overall population—could be estimated to be 0.52, but this estimate would be a stochastic variable, which approximately obeys a normal distribution with mean 0.52 and variance 0.0002496 (or standard deviation 0.0158), and from this result one can conclude that another sample of another 1,000 interviewees from the same overall population would lead to another estimate whose value would lie within the interval [0.489, 0.551] (between 0.52 ± 1.96 0.0158) with a probability of 95 percent (the so-called 95 percent confidence interval, which in the case of the normal distribution is centered about the mean with a width

of 3.92 standard deviations). Or, to put it in other words, the probability of finding more than 551 A-voters in another sample of 1,000 interviewees from the same population is 0.025. Bayesian statistics, as opposed to classical statistics, would argue from the same numbers that the probability is 0.95 that the population parameter falls within the interval [0.489, 0.551].

SEE ALSO *Bayesian Statistics; Descriptive Statistics; Inference, Bayesian; Inference, Statistical; Sampling; Variables, Random*

BIBLIOGRAPHY

Hoel, Paul G. 1984. *Introduction to Mathematical Statistics.* 5th ed. Hoboken, NJ: Wiley.

Iversen, Gudmund. 1984. *Bayesian Statistical Inference.* Beverly Hills, CA: Sage.

Klaus G. Troitzsch

CLASSICAL TEST THEORY
SEE *Psychometrics.*

CLASSIFICATION, RACIAL
SEE *Racial Classification.*

CLAY-CLAY MODELS
SEE *Vintage Models.*

CLEAVAGES

In political science, cleavages explain the underlying dimensions of contestation in countries as well as the formation and persistence of political party systems. But cleavages are more than just political divisions. In their seminal article "Cleavage Structures, Party Systems, and Voter Alignments" (1967), Seymour Martin Lipset and Stein Rokkan defined cleavages as having three main characteristics. First, a cleavage involves a social division that separates people by sociocultural or socioeconomic characteristics. Second, people involved in the division must be aware of their collective identity and must be willing to act on the basis of that identity. Finally, a cleavage must be expressed in organizational terms, such as political parties or interest groups. These characteristics not only distinguish a cleavage from a temporary issue-based conflict but also allow researchers to consider the persistence or decay of cleavages.

In Western Europe, four main cleavages defined the party systems of the post–World War II period (Lipset and Rokkan 1967). The national revolution yielded two potential cleavages: the religious and the center/periphery. Historians and political scientists alike recognize the significance of religious conflict in the formation of party systems. It pitted state builders against the church, especially in Catholic countries. The religious cleavage is unevenly distributed across Europe, being especially significant in those countries with a substantial Catholic minority or majority, such as Belgium, Germany, Italy, and the Netherlands (Lijphart 1999). In political terms, this cleavage contributes to the social left-right dimension in many countries on contested issues such as divorce, abortion, and gay rights. In the early twenty-first century a new religious cleavage may be emerging in European countries with significant Muslim minorities.

The center/periphery cleavage also arose during nation-building times, between centralizing forces and the peripheral peoples who sought to retain independence or autonomy. In almost all countries in Western Europe, there are organizational manifestations of regionalist or ethnic groups. The social characteristics that define this cleavage can be linguistic or ethnic differences. The center/periphery or cultural-ethnic cleavage is contested in all the societies that Arend Lijphart, in *Patterns of Democracy* (1999), considers plural, that is, having substantial cultural or ethnic diversity.

In plural societies, especially beyond the developed world, contestation over this cleavage may be associated with ethnic violence. But, as Robert Dahl, in *Preface to Democratic Theory* (1956), argues, plural societies, like the United States, can achieve a level of democratic success if cleavages are cross-cutting rather than reinforcing. In other words, most individuals belong to more than one group and, so long as the memberships do not overlap, a coherent and tyrannical majority is unlikely to form.

In addition to the national revolution, the industrial revolution created or strengthened two additional cleavages. First, the national revolutions in Europe often pitted rural and agrarian interests against industrial entrepreneurs. Second, the industrial revolution crystallized the class conflict between workers and owners in many European countries. Politically, this cleavage manifests itself as the political-economic left-right dimension. As Lipset and Rokkan note (1967), the worker/owner cleavage is "the expression of the democratic class struggle."

This cleavage remains the main dimension of political contestation in almost all advanced industrial democracies (Lijphart 1999).

In retrospect, party systems institutionalized the existing cleavages in European society. Thus, the Conservative party in Britain represented the owners against Labour, while elsewhere in Europe, Christian Democratic parties represented Catholic social doctrine. In the late twentieth century, many political scientists considered whether European party systems remained frozen around these underlying cleavages, or whether new cleavages had emerged, such as a postindustrial or postmaterialist cleavage. The concept of cleavage thus retains its significance in both theoretical and empirical research.

SEE ALSO *Dahl, Robert Alan; Pluralism; Politics*

BIBLIOGRAPHY

Dahl, Robert. 1956. *A Preface to Democratic Theory.* Chicago: University of Chicago Press.

Lijphart, Arend. 1999. *Patterns of Democracy: Government Forms and Performance in Thirty-Six Countries.* New Haven, CT: Yale University Press.

Lipset, Seymour Martin, and Stein Rokkan. 1967. Cleavage Structures, Party Systems, and Voter Alignments. In *Party Systems and Voter Alignments: Cross-National Perspectives,* ed. Seymour Martin Lipset and Stein Rokkan, 1–64. New York: Free Press.

Seth Jolly

CLIENTELISM

Political scientists, sociologists, and anthropologists use clientelism to describe a certain type of relationship between individuals and larger groups of people that is not based on other types of relationships such as common class, ethnicity, or religion. In this sense, clientelism is a residual concept that can be used to explain strong patterns of allegiance and loyalty within larger groups in situations where they cannot be explained by other more traditional means.

Although definitions of clientelism vary, most suggest that at the level of individuals it involves a direct relationship between two people that is based on personal and intense feelings of comradeship and loyalty. From this starting point, larger clusters of such interpersonal relationships can form that result in the construction of collectivities such as labor unions and political parties. Regardless of the type of collectivity that is being studied, social scientists that use clientelism as a concept for explaining behavior share the view that the collectivity is based upon a complex and sophisticated set of interpersonal relationships.

In the social sciences, this concept has been most extensively used by political scientists attempting to explain patterns of allegiance and loyalty either in urban settings or in rural areas where there are high concentrations of poor people. For example, there is a large body of literature that attempts to explain the nineteenth- and early-twentieth-century politics in cities such as New York, Chicago, and Boston in terms of the existence of personal networks in urban slums that connected individual workers and their families to ward healers, and eventually to the bosses who ran these cities. It is argued that this system of so-called machine politics was the result of a tacit bargain between leaders and followers. In exchange for jobs and favors from the bosses and their local representatives, the bosses were able to maintain loyal cadres of supporters who served as the basis for the establishment of modern political parties.

Because such machine politics in large U.S. cities came to be viewed by social scientists and citizens alike as a breeding ground for patronage and corruption, clientelism came to have a highly negative connotation. In fact, it came to be associated with the so-called primitive form of democratic politics practiced in developing regions of the world. During the 1960s and 1970s, a good amount was written concerning the specific nature of the pathology of clientelism in Asia, the Middle East, Africa, and Latin America. Perhaps because of its combination of emerging democratic politics, rapid industrialization, and feudal patterns of landholding, Latin America received more attention than any other developing region.

In Latin America clientelism was frequently referred to in terms of patron-client relationships. Historically, the patron was a large landowner who was able to offer his peasant "clients" physical protection and job security in exchange for his labor and political support. Given the largely feudal nature of many Latin American societies, the patron-client relationship was hierarchical (vertical) in nature. Such patron-client patterns have been used by political scientists to explain the history and evolution of parties and party systems in countries such as Mexico and Colombia.

Although the concept of clientelism is not used as extensively as it was during the 1960s and 1970s to explain political phenomena, it continues to prove beneficial for assessing developments in certain regions of the world. For example, it has been used to explain how Hizbollah (the Party of God) has been able to create a loyal following among Palestinian refugees living in Lebanon despite the fact that these refugees are not permitted to vote in Lebanese elections.

SEE ALSO *Corruption; Crony Capitalism; Hierarchy; Patronage*

BIBLIOGRAPHY

Kawata, Junichi. 2006. *Comparing Political Corruption and Clientelism.* Burlington, VT: Ashgate Publishing.

Schmidt, Steffan W., James C. Scott, Carl Lande, and Laura Guasti, eds. 1977. *Friends, Followers, and Factions: A Reader in Political Clientelism.* Berkeley: University of California Press.

Steve C. Ropp

CLINTON, BILL
1946–

Bill Clinton was the forty-second president of the United States, serving from 1993 to 2001. He was born William Jefferson Blythe III on August 19, 1946, in Hope, Arkansas. His father, William Jefferson Blythe Jr. (1918–1946), was a salesman who died in an auto accident before Clinton was born. When Bill Clinton was fourteen, he legally adopted the surname of his stepfather, Roger C. Clinton Sr. (1908–1967).

While attending Georgetown University, Clinton interned with Senator J. William Fulbright (1905–1995) of Arkansas, a prominent critic of the Vietnam War (1957–1975). Avoiding military service, Clinton was awarded a Rhodes Scholarship to study at Oxford University in 1968 and earned a law degree from Yale University in 1973. While at Yale, Clinton met and later married fellow law student Hillary Rodham.

In addition to opposing the Vietnam War, Clinton worked in the 1972 Democratic presidential campaign and unsuccessfully ran for a congressional seat in Arkansas in 1974. In 1976 Clinton was elected attorney general of Arkansas. He was elected governor of Arkansas in 1978, but was defeated for reelection in 1980. In 1982 Clinton was again elected governor of Arkansas and served in this position until December 12, 1992. During his second stint as governor, Clinton projected a more moderate, populist image to Arkansas voters. His policies emphasized public school reforms, economic development, and tax relief for the elderly.

THE 1992 PRESIDENTIAL ELECTION

Bill Clinton formally announced his candidacy for the 1992 Democratic presidential nomination in Little Rock on October 31, 1991. After securing an impressive, second-place finish in the New Hampshire primary and winning southern primaries, Clinton's victories in the New York and California primaries assured him of the Democratic presidential nomination. Meanwhile, Republican president George H. W. Bush's reelection campaign was weakened by the lingering effects of the 1990–1991 recession, Bush's violation of his 1988 promise not to raise taxes, dwindling public concern with foreign policy, and the independent presidential candidacy of Ross Perot, a Texas billionaire.

The Democratic national convention of 1992 highlighted the need for generational change in the White House by nominating baby boomers Bill Clinton for president and Senator Al Gore Jr. of Tennessee for vice president. Clinton won the election with 43 percent of the popular votes. Perot's receipt of 18.9 percent of the popular votes enabled Clinton to carry most states in the Electoral College.

CLINTON'S FIRST TERM

With a Democratic Congress, Clinton signed into law the Family and Medical Leave Act of 1993, the Omnibus Budget Reconciliation Act of 1993, the Brady Handgun Violence Prevention Act of 1993, the AmeriCorps Act of 1993, and the North American Free Trade Agreement (NAFTA) in 1994. Clinton's inexperience in dealing with Congress was evident in his withdrawal of Lani Guinier's nomination as assistant attorney general for civil rights following criticism of her writings on affirmative action. The most controversial and unsuccessful domestic policy initiative of Clinton's presidency was his proposed Health Security Act, that is, a universal health-care plan. He appointed Hillary Clinton as the chair of the Task Force on National Health Care Reform and announced this task force's proposal in a speech to Congress on September 22, 1993. Public and congressional opposition to Clinton's plan increased as its complex, confusing details were criticized as socialized medicine by Republicans, conservative media commentators, and interest groups. The rejection of Clinton's health-care plan contributed to the Republican landslide in the 1994 congressional elections.

After the Republicans won control of Congress in 1994, Clinton repositioned himself as a moderate seeking bipartisan cooperation and compromise. His poll ratings steadily improved in 1995 and 1996 as the public perceived Republicans in Congress, especially Speaker of the House Newt Gingrich, as excessively conservative and unreasonable in their policy relationship with Clinton. Clinton, however, waited until after the 1996 Democratic national convention to sign the Welfare Reform Act of 1996, which most House Democrats opposed. With a prosperous economy and no major foreign policy crises, Clinton was easily reelected president in 1996.

CLINTON'S FOREIGN POLICY

Bill Clinton perceived the post–cold war era as an opportunity for the United States to improve and expand multilateral efforts to promote democracy, free trade, environmental protection, humanitarian relief, and the resolution of political and military conflicts in Northern Ireland, Bosnia, Somalia, and Palestine. Clinton ordered brief, unsuccessful U.S. military interventions in Somalia and Haiti. The United States also joined NATO allies in aerial bombings to end Serbia's "ethnic cleansing" and force an end to the war in Bosnia. Responding to Iraqi president Saddam Hussein's (1937–2006) expulsion of UN weapons inspectors and other violations of international law, Clinton publicly supported "regime change" in Iraq but limited his military response to launching cruise missiles.

Clinton wanted to avoid a stronger military response toward Iraq that might alienate European and Middle Eastern allies, the United Nations, and the American public. Following the 1993 terrorist bombing of the World Trade Center in New York City, however, Clinton signed into law tougher antiterrorism legislation. Nonetheless, George W. Bush's Republican presidential campaign in 2000 criticized Clinton for failing to effectively address Iraqi and other threats to national security.

SCANDALS, CONTROVERSIES, AND IMPEACHMENT

Before his sexual affair with White House intern Monica Lewinsky became a public issue in 1998, Clinton had experienced media, congressional, and judicial investigations into his sexual behavior in the lawsuit of Paula Jones, Hillary Clinton's involvement in the failed Whitewater investment, and his firing of employees in the White House travel office. Some conservative critics also accused Clinton of ordering the murders of Vincent Foster (1945–1993), the deputy White House counsel, and Secretary of Commerce Ron Brown (1941–1996). Foster's death was officially ruled to be a suicide, and Brown died in a plane crash in Croatia.

Independent counsel Kenneth Starr began to investigate Lewinsky's affair with Clinton because of contradictions between her testimony and Clinton's in the Jones case. At a January 1998 press conference, Clinton firmly denied having "sexual relations" with Lewinsky. Clinton continued to receive high job approval ratings, and the Democrats gained five House seats in the 1998 elections. Newt Gingrich soon resigned from the speakership and the House. Nonetheless, the House of Representatives impeached Clinton on charges of perjury and obstruction of justice on December 19, 1998. After a trial in the Senate, the Senate acquitted Clinton on February 12, 1999. Throughout these proceedings, polls indicated that most Americans opposed Clinton's impeachment, trial, and removal from office.

Bill Clinton devoted the remainder of his term to improving race relations, achieving a budget surplus, and negotiating a new trade agreement with China. In order to benefit Al Gore's presidential campaign and Hillary Clinton's Senate campaign in New York, he frequently reminded audiences of his administration's domestic policy successes and the country's prosperous economy. Wanting to avoid association with Clinton's scandals, especially in fund-raising for the 1996 election, Gore carefully limited Clinton's role in his unsuccessful 2000 presidential campaign. Some political analysts have argued that had Clinton been more involved in the campaign, Gore might have carried Clinton's home state of Arkansas and his own home state of Tennessee. Winning these two states would have won the election for Gore, regardless of the outcome of the disputed electoral votes in Florida.

As Bill Clinton prepared to leave office in 2001, he attracted controversy when he pardoned Marc Rich. Rich was a billionaire who fled to Switzerland because of charges of tax evasion and violations of oil embargoes against Iran and Libya. Denise Rich, his wife, had previously made large contributions to the Democratic Party and Clinton's presidential library and foundation.

PUBLIC PERCEPTION OF CLINTON DURING HIS PRESIDENCY

Americans generally expressed an ambivalent, complex perception of Bill Clinton. During his second term, most Americans gave Clinton high job approval ratings, especially on the economy, and opposed his impeachment while simultaneously perceiving him to be dishonest, politically expedient, and detrimental to the moral character of the presidency. Among specific demographic groups, Clinton attracted consistent, loyal support from African Americans, Jews, unmarried women, and young adults, along with consistent, staunch opposition from married white men, white Christian fundamentalists, and gun owners. Criticism of Clinton's policies and personal character was hardened and intensified by the rise of conservative talk radio programs, the Fox news network, and the Internet.

POSTPRESIDENCY ACTIVITIES

Besides supervising his presidential library and foundation, Bill Clinton regularly traveled nationally and internationally as a well-paid public speaker. Clinton raised funds for his foundation, the Democratic Party, and philanthropy, especially AIDS research and treatment, environmental protection, and relief for victims of Hurricane Katrina and the 2004 Asian tsunami. In some of these charitable efforts, Clinton teamed with former president

George H. W. Bush. After Senator Hillary Clinton became a candidate for the Democratic presidential nomination of 2008, Bill Clinton became more publicly prominent in his relationship with her when he and she performed a parody of the television show, *The Sopranos.*

SEE ALSO *Baby Boomers; Bush, George H. W.; Democratic Party, U.S.; Elections; Hussein, Saddam; North American Free Trade Agreement; Presidency, The; Terrorism; Welfare; Welfare State*

BIBLIOGRAPHY

Berman, William C. 2001. *From the Center to the Edge: The Politics and Policies of the Clinton Presidency.* Lanham, MD: Rowman and Littlefield.

Clinton, Bill. 2004. *My Life.* New York: Knopf.

Hamilton, Nigel. 2003. *Bill Clinton: An American Journey.* New York: Random House.

Sean J. Savage

CLIOMETRICS

From a purely etymological standpoint, the term *cliometrics* should have a very broad meaning. After all, Clio was the muse of history in ancient Greek mythology, and *metrics* comes from the Greek and Latin word for measurement. Hence, cliometrics could encompass any application of measurement to history, placing it in the same inclusive inventory of methods as biometrics, psychometrics, and econometrics. That is, it would represent a quantitative method that does for history what the others do for biology, psychology, and economics, respectively. Yet the term is most often applied to a very specific form of economic history, namely, that in which historical data are analyzed using modern economic theory and econometric methods. By this restricted application, it may be said to constitute a specialized branch of economics rather than a method in history.

HISTORICAL ORIGINS

Although it is always difficult to assign a precise date to any intellectual movement, cliometrics is often said to have begun with the 1958 article "The Economics of Slavery in the Ante-Bellum South," which Alfred Conrad and John Meyer published in the *Journal of Political Economy.* Whether this was truly the genesis or not, a full-fledged cliometric revolution definitely took off sometime in the 1960s. In that decade it became apparent that the practitioners of standard economic history—many of whom were strictly historians rather than economists—had to confront those who advocated what was called the "new economic history." In 1960 Douglass North, an early champion of this innovative approach, became coeditor of the *Journal of Economic History*, the official publication of the Economic History Association. Just a few years later the journal *Explorations in Entrepreneurial History* (soon renamed *Explorations in Economic History*) emerged as a major outlet for cliometric research. Also in the early 1960s Purdue University in Indiana became the site for annual cliometrics meetings where the new economic historians could present and discuss applications of the discipline's theory and methods to history.

Once cliometrics began to enjoy a conspicuous presence in the research on economic history, the next step was for the practice to become institutionalized as a formal subdiscipline within economics. As noted on their Web site, this step was taken in 1983 with the founding of the Cliometric Society, which was explicitly identified as "an academic organization of individuals interested in using economic theory and statistical techniques to study economic history." Although the cliometrics revolution began in the United States, the movement gradually spread to other countries that featured active scholarship in economic history, such as France and Germany.

CENTRAL CONTRIBUTIONS

The single most important sign that cliometrics had come of age occurred in 1993. In that year the Nobel Prize in economics was bestowed upon Robert Fogel and Douglass North, the two most prominent researchers in the field. Fogel and North were honored specifically "for having renewed research in economic history by applying economic theory and quantitative methods in order to explain economic and institutional change." This was the first time that any economic historian had received this prestigious award. North's contributions to cliometrics went well beyond his role as coeditor of the *Journal of Economic History*; he also wrote a series of now-classic volumes in the new economic history that illustrated the assets of the technique. Among these is the 1973 *The Rise of the Western World: A New Economic History* (with Robert Thomas).

Yet, in some respects, Fogel's place in the history of cliometrics is even more striking. Indeed, he is sometimes described as the founder of econometric history as well as the person who actually coined the term *cliometrics* for the new methodology. These claims aside, it is his name that has been most strongly associated with the movement, and his involvement was apparent from the very outset of his career: His doctoral dissertation applied the innovative approach to the impact of the railroads on economic growth in the United States prior to the Civil War. This cliometric research was later published in *Railroads and*

American Economic Growth: Essays in Econometric History (1964). One central feature of Fogel's analysis was the use of "counterfactual" arguments. By a detailed cost-benefit analysis he investigated how the early U.S. economy would have been affected had the railroads not been built, an assumption clearly contrary to historical reality.

Another basis for Fogel's prominence is the highly controversial nature of the research he conducted with Stanley Engerman on the economic profitability of slavery in the antebellum United States. Their conclusions were published in *Time on the Cross: The Economics of American Negro Slavery* (1974). This book consisted of two volumes, the first devoted to scrutiny of the basic substantive issue, the second assigned to a detailed discussion of their data sources and statistical analyses. Because Fogel and Engerman showed that slavery was indeed profitable and that black slaves were in certain ways better off than white industrial laborers in northern cities, some critics accused them as composing an apology for slavery, that "peculiar institution." Yet that accusation was unjustified. The authors were simply arguing that slavery constituted an efficient means of production—however morally repugnant.

GENERAL CRITIQUE

The cliometric revolution of the 1960s and 1970s was supremely successful. It began as a movement led by a few "young turks" against an "old guard" who dominated the leadership positions of the profession. Still, in less than twenty years the new economic history emerged as the prevailing approach in the discipline. Moreover, because cliometrics applied macroeconomic models and econometric methods, its proponents had much more in common with economists than with historians. As a result, departments of economics at major U.S. research universities became increasingly inclined to hire cliometricians rather than conventional economic historians. In a sense, economic historians had been replaced by historical economists, that is, by scholars who differ from their colleagues mostly in that they use older rather than newer data.

Despite this apparent success, the victory was not absolute. Although cliometrics dominates economic history in its country of origin, it has had somewhat less success abroad. For instance, at the beginning of the twenty-first century a bona fide cliometric revolution had yet to take place in German economic history. Moreover, the procedure still has its vocal critics. Some observers believe that cliometrics has relied too heavily on standard macroeconomic models that cannot capture the complexities of the economic systems being analyzed. Other critics doubt whether the available historical data can bear the weight of econometric inferences, particularly when they entail strong counterfactual arguments. Even so, it seems likely that cliometrics will continue to consolidate its presence within economic history. This prognosis is supported by the founding of the French Cliometric Association in 2001. Furthermore, in 2007 this association, in collaboration with the Cliometric Society, began publishing *Cliometrica: Journal of Historical Economics and Econometric History*. Hence, the growth curve for cliometrics still exhibits an upward trajectory.

At least this conclusion holds for cliometrics in its narrow meaning. If the term is used according to its broader etymology, quantitative history has made much less progress outside of economics. For instance, research devoted to the quantitative but psychological analysis of historic creators and leaders—more often called *historiometrics*—remains a peripheral enterprise within psychology. Cliometrics may have had a more intrinsic connection with economics than it did with other disciplines that occasionally analyzed historical data. More specifically, economics is not only highly quantitative but also strongly historical insofar as change and growth are crucial components of economic theory and analysis. Hence, the supremacy of cliometrics may remain confined to economics, thereby justifying a restricted conception of the term.

BIBLIOGRAPHY

Cliometric Society Web site. http://eh.net/Clio/.

Conrad, Alfred H., and John R. Meyer. 1958. The Economics of Slavery in the Ante-Bellum South. *Journal of Political Economy* 66: 95–130.

Fogel, Robert W. 1964. *Railroads and American Economic Growth: Essays in Econometric History*. Baltimore: Johns Hopkins Press.

Fogel, Robert W., and Stanley L. Engerman. 1974. *Time on the Cross: The Economics of American Negro Slavery*. Boston: Little, Brown.

Golden, Claudia. 1995. Cliometrics and the Nobel. *Journal of Economic Perspectives* 9 (2): 191–208.

Greif, Avner. 1997. Cliometrics after 40 Years. *American Economic Review* 87 (2): 400–403.

Haskins, Loren, and Kirk Jeffrey. 1990. *Understanding Quantitative History*. Cambridge, MA: MIT Press.

North, Douglass C., and Robert Paul Thomas. 1973. *The Rise of the Western World: A New Economic History*. Cambridge, U.K.: Cambridge University Press.

Simonton, Dean Keith. 2003. Qualitative and Quantitative Analyses of Historical Data. *Annual Review of Psychology* 54: 617–640.

Williamson, Samuel H., John S. Lyons, and Louis P. Cain, eds. 2006. *Reflections on the Cliometrics Revolution: Conversations with Economic Historians*. New York: Routledge.

Dean Keith Simonton

CLIQUES, PEER

SEE *Peer Cliques.*

CLOCK TIME

Throughout most of history, the passage of time was registered by familiar regularities such as day and night and the phases of the moon, or more accurately by the apparent motions of certain stars. The second was defined by the ancient Babylonians to be 1/84,600 of a day. Modern calendars are still based on *astronomical time* using the Gregorian calendar, introduced in 1582, in which the year is defined as 365.2425 days.

Until the scientific revolution and the ages of exploration and industrialization that followed, most people had no need for accurate clocks. Farmers and fishermen measured time in relation to familiar processes in the cycle of work and domestic chores. Labor took place in the natural period from dawn to dusk. The sundial was widely used to tell time during the day. The great advance in the accuracy of household clocks came about in the mid-seventeenth century with the application of the pendulum, which had been introduced into scientific experiments by Galileo in 1602. English clock- and watchmaking became dominant in 1680 and remained so until competition from the French and Swiss caught up about a century later.

In 1759 John Harrison produced a clock that could keep exact Greenwich Mean Time (the mean solar time of the meridian of the Royal Observatory in Greenwich, England, used as the prime basis of standard time) at sea, enabling mariners to determine their longitude on the globe and making accurate marine navigation possible for the first time. Today the primary time standard is provided by a Cesium Fountain atomic clock at the National Institute for Standards and Technology laboratory in Boulder, Colorado, which will not gain or lose a second in more than 60 million years.

With the rise of science, the second has undergone several redefinitions to make it more useful in the laboratory. The most recent change occurred in 1967, when the second was redefined by international agreement as the duration of 9,192,631,770 periods of the radiation corresponding to the transition between the two hyperfine energy levels of the ground state of the Cesium[133] atom at rest at absolute zero. The minute remains 60 seconds, the hour remains 60 minutes, and the day remains 24 hours, following ancient traditions. The day is still taken to be 84,600 seconds, as in ancient Babylonia. Modern calendars need to be corrected occasionally to keep them in harmony with the seasons because of the lack of complete synchronization between atomic time and the motions of astronomical bodies.

Nothing seems so ubiquitous—so absolute and universal—as time. Yet, in his 1905 "special theory of relativity" Albert Einstein showed that the times measured on clocks are different for clocks that are moving with respect to one another—an effect called "time dilation." This called into question some of the deepest intuitions of time. No moment in time can be labeled a universal "present." There is no past or future that applies to every point in space. Two events separated in space can never be judged to be objectively simultaneous. The whole notion of cause and effect has to be carefully rethought.

Unless one is making highly precise measurements with atomic clocks, time dilation is important only when the relative speeds of clocks are near the speed of light, so there are not noticeable effects in everyday life. However, Einstein's theory has been confirmed by a century of experiments involving high-energy particles that move near the speed of light, as well as low-speed measurements with atomic clocks. Although it is not necessary to take into account the relativity of time in the social sphere, it is important not to draw universal, philosophical, or metaphysical conclusions based on notions related to time that are inferred from normal human experience.

Philosophers and theologians have introduced alternate "metaphysical times" more along the lines of common experience, but these have no connection with scientific observations. Scientific models uniformly assume that time is, by definition, what is measured on a clock and that time is relative.

SEE ALSO *Capitalism; Industrialization; Industry; Modernization; Productivity; Revolutions, Scientific; Science; Thompson, Edward P.; Work; Work Day*

BIBLIOGRAPHY

Davies, Paul. 1995. *About Time: Einstein's Unfinished Revolution.* New York: Simon and Schuster.

Price, Huw. 1996. *Time's Arrow and Archimedes' Point.* New York and Oxford: Oxford University Press.

Sobel, Dava. 1995. *Longitude: The True Story of a Lone Genius Who Solved the Greatest Scientific Problem of His Time.* New York: Walker.

Stenger, Victor J. 2000. *Timeless Reality: Symmetry, Simplicity, and Multiple Universes.* Amherst, NY: Prometheus Books.

Stenger, Victor J. 2006. *The Comprehensible Cosmos: Where Do the Laws of Physics Come From?* Amherst, NY: Prometheus Books.

Thompson, E. P. 1967. Time, Work-Discipline, and Industrial Capitalism. *Past and Present* 38 (December): 56–97.

Victor J. Stenger

CLOSED SHOP
SEE *Labor Law.*

CLOWER, ROBERT
SEE *Barro-Grossman Model; Walras' Law.*

CLUB OF ROME

Founded in Rome in early 1968 by a group of European businesspeople and scientists, the Club of Rome is a nonprofit nongovernmental organization (NGO) that serves as an international think tank on global issues. The Club of Rome is run by an Executive Committee of eleven members that appoints a president, vice presidents, a secretary-general, and a treasurer. The president of the club represents the organization to the outside world; HRH Prince El Hassan bin Talal of Jordan became president of the Club of Rome in 1999.

Individual membership in the Club of Rome is restricted to those who are elected by the Executive Committee. There are three levels of individual membership. (1) Active members are persons of established reputation whose work is international in scope and whose views on global issues are congruent with the Club of Rome. Serving terms of five years, the number of active members is limited to one hundred. The Club of Rome's professed aim is to balance membership in this category by regions, cultures, professions, age, and gender. The public listing of active members reveals men and women from such fields as banking, private industry, academe, government (both elective office and bureaus), and other NGOs. (2) Associate members are individuals who are involved with the work of the club or wish to cooperate in the future. They may apply for membership or be recommended by a member of the club and are elected by the Executive Committee for five-year terms. Again, associate members are drawn from those who have attained distinction in a variety of fields, though those from academe and research institutes dominate this category. (3) Honorary members are persons of high reputation or office whose work can support the mission of the club. Honorary members must be proposed by a member of the club and are elected by the Executive Committee. The membership of this group is dominated by former high government officials, though there are a few academics as well.

The professed mission of the Club of Rome is to "act as a global catalyst of change" by sponsoring studies and conferences and issuing reports and news releases that focus on long-term global problems and their interrelationships. The club is committed to an interdisciplinary perspective that highlights both the increasing interdependence of and problems among nation-states. From its first report in 1972, titled *The Limits to Growth*, the Club of Rome has dedicated itself to identifying the most critical problems facing humanity; analyzing the interrelationships of these problems on the basis of an interdisciplinary, holistic, and global perspective; and positing future scenarios based on humanity's response to these problems. The club has identified a number of significant global issues, referred to as *world problematique*, facing humanity, including: depletion and pollution of the environment; demographic problems of both growth and aging; uneven development within and between nations; the decline of traditional values; dysfunctional governments; the quality and distribution of work; the sociocultural impact of new technologies; dysfunctional educational systems; the globalization of the economy; and international financial disorder.

The best-known report sponsored by the Club of Rome was its first, *The Limits to Growth*. The book was based on multiple simulations of a "systems dynamics" computer model of five major human activities: industrial production, population, agricultural production, resource use, and pollution. The basis of systems dynamics is the assumption that the often complex and intricate interrelationships between components of a system are essential in determining the behavior of the components as well as of the overall system itself. Accordingly, levels and rates of change in each of the sectors were interrelated through mathematical formulae that sought to simulate the impact of growth in one sector (for example, a growth in agricultural production) on levels and rates of change in the other four sectors. The model was then run under differing assumptions regarding physical limits to growth (supposing the known reserves of resources versus doubling those known reserves). The results of the simulations lent support to the idea of physical limits to continued growth consisting of resource depletion and pollution, with the authors arguing that if present growth trends continue, these limits will probably be reached within the next century; the typical mode of hitting these limits was one of "overshoot and collapse." Rather than a simple prediction of doom, however, the report argues that the world can move quickly to establish a condition of economic and population stability that is sustainable and a state of global equilibrium that more equitably distributes resources to each person on earth.

The Club of Rome's main focus is upon global problems associated with population and economic growth. It espouses a neo-Malthusian agenda of limiting population growth and promoting sustainable economic development in order to address perceived problems of environmental degradation.

SEE ALSO *Birth Control; Elites; Limits of Growth; Malthus, Thomas Robert; Malthusian Trap; Natural Resources, Nonrenewable; Overpopulation; Population Control*

BIBLIOGRAPHY

Club of Rome. http://www.clubofrome.org.

Meadows, Donella, Dennis Meadows, Jørgen Randers, and William H. Behren III. 1972. *The Limits to Growth: A Report for the Club of Rome's Project on the Predicament of Mankind.* New York: Universe.

Frank W. Elwell

CLUSTER ANALYSIS

Quantitative social science often involves measurements of several variables for a number of cases (individuals or subjects). Searching for groupings, or *clusters*, is an important exploratory technique. Grouping can provide a means for summarizing data, identifying outliers, or suggesting questions to study.

A well-known clustering is that of stars into a main sequence, white giants, and red dwarfs, according to temperature and luminosity. The military has used cluster analysis of anthropometric data to reduce the number of different uniform sizes kept in inventory. Cluster analysis in marketing is called *market segmentation;* consumers are clustered according to psychographic, demographic, and purchasing behavior variables. The United States has been divided into a number of clusters according to lifestyle and buying habits.

Establishing the *profile* of a case, an observational unit, is the first step in cluster analysis. The profile of a case is its pattern of scores across a set of correlated variables. Cases with similar profiles should be in the same cluster; cases with disparate profiles, in different clusters. The mean profile of a cluster is the *centroid*, the set of means of the variables, for the individuals in that cluster. Cluster profiles provide a good summary of the data. Examining them provides insight as to what the clusters mean. A cluster's profile can suggest an interpretation and a name for it.

There are two broad types of clustering algorithms: hierarchical clustering and nonhierarchical clustering (partitioning). Hierarchical clustering follows one of two approaches. *Agglomerative clustering* starts with each case as a unique cluster, and with each step combines cases to form larger clusters until there is only one or a few larger clusters. *Divisive clustering* begins with one large cluster and splits it into smaller clusters.

There are several ways to define intercluster distance. This can be done by forming all pairs of objects, with one object in one cluster and one in the other, and computing the distances between the members of these pairs. *Single linkage* is based on the shortest of these; *complete linkage* on the longest; and *average linkage* on their mean. Joe Ward's method (1963) is based on the sum of squares between the two clusters, summed over all variables. The centroid method is based on the distance between cluster centroids.

Nonhierarchical clustering is partitioning of the sample. The *K*-means algorithm assigns each case to the cluster having the nearest centroid. The process begins by partitioning the cases into *K* initial clusters and assigning each case to the cluster whose centroid is nearest. The centroids of the cluster receiving the new case and the cluster losing the case are updated. This is repeated until no more reassignments take place. The ISODATA algorithm is similar to *K*-means, except one loops through all cases before the centroids are updated. An alternative to starting with an initial clustering is to start with an initialization of the centroids—for example, as the first *K* cases in the dataset or as *K* cases randomly chosen from it.

The notion of *nearest* requires a notion of *distance*. Often, rightly or wrongly, researchers use *Euclidean distance*, which is the length of the hypotenuse of a right triangle formed between the points. Euclidean distance is appropriate for variables that are uncorrelated and have equal variances. Standardization of the data is needed if the range or scale of one variable is much larger than that of others. *Mahalanobis distance* (statistical distance), which adjusts for different variances and for the correlations among the variables, is preferred.

It is sometimes suggested that researchers start with hierarchical clustering to generate initial centroids, and then use nonhierarchical clustering. A conceptual model for clustering is that the sample comes from a mixture of several populations. This leads to a mathematical probability model called the *finite mixture model*. If the within-cluster type of distribution is specified (such as multivariate normal), then the *method of maximum likelihood* can be used to estimate the parameters. This is done with an iterative algorithm.

There are several procedures for determining the number of clusters. This task should be guided by substantive theory and the practicality of the results. A criterion such as between-groups sum of squares or likelihood can be plotted against the number of clusters in a *scree plot*. When a normal mixture model is used, model selection criteria such as Akaike information criterion (AIC) and Bayesian information criterion (BIC) can be used.

Once the clusters are formed, researchers can use *discriminant analysis* to determine which variables account for the clustering and to classify new cases into the clusters. Some cluster techniques operate on distances or similarities rather than raw data. Variables can be clustered using their correlations as similarities. Simultaneous clustering of cases and variables is called *block clustering*. If a subset of the cases has similar values on a subset of the variables, these cases and variables form a block.

James MacQueen's development of his *K*-means algorithm (1967) was a milestone in the development of cluster analysis. John Wolfe (1970) was the first to program maximum likelihood clustering for the finite normal mixture model. John Hartigan's *Clustering Algorithms* (1975) did much to stimulate interest in cluster analysis. Geoff McLachlan and David Peel's *Finite Mixture Models* (2000) is a comprehensive presentation of model-based clustering.

BIBLIOGRAPHY

Hartigan, John A. 1975. *Clustering Algorithms*. New York: Wiley.

MacQueen, James B. 1967. Some Methods for Classification and Analysis of Multivariate Observations. In *Proceedings of the Fifth Berkeley Symposium on Mathematical Statistics and Probability*. Vol. 1: *Theory of Statistics*, ed. Lucien M. LeCam and Jerzy Neyman, 281–297. Berkeley: University of California Press.

McLachlan, Geoffrey, and David Peel. 2000. *Finite Mixture Models*. New York: Wiley.

Ward, Joe H., Jr. 1963. Hierarchical Grouping to Optimize an Objective Function. *Journal of the American Statistical Association* 58: 236–244.

Wolfe, John H. 1970. Pattern Clustering by Multivariate Mixture Analysis. *Multivariate Behavioral Research* 5: 329–350.

Stanley L. Sclove

COALITION

The term *coalition* encompasses a wide range of political activities and outcomes. At the most basic level, a coalition is said to exist when two or more political groups or actors agree to pursue some common objective(s), pool resources in pursuit of such common objective(s), and actively communicate during joint action to achieve such common objective(s). In contrast to the competitive, majoritarian, "winner-take-all" approach to politics, coalitions emphasize collaboration and group coordination. Understanding coalitions helps scholars and practitioners answer one of the immutable questions of politics: Why do avowed adversaries sometimes cooperate? If politics is largely about bargaining and compromise, then the transformation of political competitors into allies is of the utmost importance, whatever the situation, setting, or scope.

Researchers and theorists ask three classes of questions about coalitions: those concerning coalition *formation*, those concerning coalition *maintenance*, and those concerning coalition *termination*. Observers of coalition formation attempt to explain, and purport to predict, the outcomes and payoffs to political actors engaged in bargaining over the composition of a coalition. Much less studied but no less important is coalition maintenance—the concerns of coalition maintenance shift analysis from outcomes to processes, asking questions about communication among partners, joint decision making, policy output, and the efficacy of an alliance. A more recent scholarly concern with coalition termination seeks to identify the sources and consequences of coalition breakup.

As a basic unit of analysis in political science, coalitions are scrutinized as they occur among such actors as interest groups in society, political parties in the electorate, legislative factions in representative assemblies, and states in the international arena. There are, for example, constellations of small grassroots groups that coalesce as *social coalitions* to advance a shared agenda (as illustrated by the Rainbow/PUSH Coalition for advancing civil rights in the United States). There are *electoral coalitions* in which cooperating political parties agree to transfer voter support to one another in districts where doing so enhances the likelihood of victory (as in France's double-ballot system for parliamentary elections). There are ad hoc *legislative* or *voting coalitions* in which members of political parties agree to join forces in support of specific policy or legislation (as in the U.S. Congress).

Perhaps most prominent in the political science literature on coalitions is the scrutiny given to *power sharing* or *governing coalitions*, in which political parties agree to collaborate in the joint distribution of cabinet posts and government ministries. Often, small minority parties located strategically in between major party blocs become "kingmakers," holding disproportionate power to make or break a winning coalition. Outside the Anglo-American democracies, from Italy to Israel and Belgium to Germany, such governing coalitions are typically the norm in parliamentary systems. In international politics, strategic alliances linking two or more states in pursuit of some commonly shared objective may be referred to as coalitions (as in the case of the United States' "coalition of the willing" designed to oust Saddam Hussein's regime in Iraq). A rich body of literature seeking to develop and test coalition theories has focused on the motivations that lead political actors to pursue coalitions of different sizes (*minimum-winning coalitions* or *oversized coalitions*), ideological complexions, and novelty.

SEE ALSO *Alliances; Coalition Theory; Congress, U.S.; Cooperation; Democracy; Government, Coalition;*

Hussein, Saddam; Minorities; Parliaments and Parliamentary Systems; Political Parties; Politics

BIBLIOGRAPHY

Baylis, Thomas A. 1989. *Governing by Committee: Collegial Leadership in Advanced Societies.* Albany: State University of New York Press.

Cook, Terrence E. 2002. *Nested Political Coalitions: Nation, Regime, Program, Cabinet.* Westport, CT: Praeger.

Groennings, Sven, E. W. Kelley, and Michael Leiserson, eds. 1970. *The Study of Coalition Behavior: Theoretical Perspectives and Cases from Four Continents.* New York: Holt, Rinehart, and Winston.

Hinckley, Barbara. 1981. *Coalitions & Politics.* New York: Harcourt Brace Jovanovich.

William M. Downs

COALITION THEORY

Political scientists, along with counterparts in other social science disciplines, have sought a number of theoretical approaches to describing, explaining, and predicting coalitional behavior. Coalitions arise in situations with at least three actors (individuals, groups, countries), wherein no single actor can achieve an optimal outcome on its own; rather, cooperation with one or more other actors is necessary. Coalition theories purport to shed light on why alliances emerge, why they take the forms they do, how they endure, and why they collapse.

Much of coalition theory embraces the basic assumptions of rational political behavior. Faced with dilemmas about how to maximize gains through cooperation with one or more other parties, rational political actors will weigh preferentially ordered alternative strategies and consistently pursue coalition options connected with more preferred outcomes. The game-theoretic tradition, which has dominated coalition research, flows directly from this foundational assumption of rationality. Game theorists view the process of coalition formation as a social interaction in which bargaining behaviors can be modeled by a priori assumptions and deductive propositions about what the negotiators value most.

Conventional coalition theory generally makes four assumptions: relevant players in the coalition game are unified parties, each of which can be considered a single bargaining entity with indivisible motives; the coalition game is zero-sum, with gains by one party constituting losses for another; the universe of possible coalitions is formed by all "winning" combinations of actors; and the game of coalition formation is a single-shot event, independent of previous or future bargaining between the parties to the game. From these baseline assumptions, formal coalition theory has advanced at least two major strands of research: size-criterion studies (the "office-seeking" tradition) and ideological/policy distance (the "policy-seeking" tradition).

In his 1962 book William Riker deduced a "size principle" by which in *n*-person "games" coalitions of minimum size would be expected to form. Hoping to craft a minimum-winning coalition large enough to win but no larger, rational actors in Riker's model would, for example, consistently decide to form coalitions of no more than 201 members in a 400-seat parliament. Similarly, in the hypothetical 400-member parliament a coalition of two equally powerful parties combining for 60 percent of the seats would be preferred to a coalition of four equally powerful parties with 60 percent of the seats. The clear assumption is that the overwhelming motivation of rational political actors in coalitional situations is the zero-sum maximization of a fixed prize to be shared among the fewest actors possible. Self-interested actors driven by garnering for themselves the largest share of a fixed-sum prize tend to see the virtues of compromising principles or policies if doing so increases the likelihood of winning.

Advocates of a rival policy-seeking theoretical approach to understanding coalitions countered that actors seek to build alliances with those partners closest to them ideologically and do not simply jump to form alliances with any constellation of "strange bedfellows" that produces victory. In this theoretical camp, articulated most clearly by Abram De Swaan in his seminal 1973 book, the argument is that players in the coalition game seek to minimize the range of policy disagreement and ideological heterogeneity among members of a potential winning coalition. In a legislative context, this anticipates that the most frequent type of coalition found would be those in which members of the winning government would be adjacent or "connected" if placed on an ordinal, single-dimension left-right ideological scale.

Coalition theory has developed considerably since the pioneering works of Riker, De Swaan, and others. Scholars now seek to replace the traditional office-seeking versus policy-seeking dichotomy by borrowing from spatial theories of party competition to model bargaining on the basis of multiple policy dimensions. Still, criticisms of traditional coalition theory abound. Detractors contend that formal theories based on rational choice/game theoretic propositions fail to capture the practice and reality of coalition politics. Models of unconstrained minimalist rationality operating within the context of laboratory-pure "games," say the critics, cannot account for the frequent departures from minimum-winning coalitions (namely, the occurrence of oversized "surplus majority" coalitions or undersized "minority" coalitions). Further, it

may be wrong to assume that all coalition actors pursue the same goals, behave as monolithic unitary actors, and engage in the same kind of complex calculus of mathematical alternatives. Whereas some political scientists see the way forward as a choice between formal coalition theory (based on deductive assumptions about rational behavior) and rich description (detailing cases and actor characteristics), others claim such a choice to be a false dichotomy. Advancing knowledge about political coalitions, this latter group contends, will come through systematic and meaningful measurement of structural features that constrain rational behavior.

SEE ALSO *Coalition; Game Theory; Government; Left and Right; Majorities; Minorities; Parliaments and Parliamentary Systems; Political Science; Politics; Rational Choice Theory; Zero-sum Game*

BIBLIOGRAPHY

Baron, David P., and John A. Ferejohn. 1989. Bargaining in Legislatures. *American Political Science Review* 83 (4): 1181–1206.

De Swaan, Abram. 1973. *Coalition Theories and Cabinet Formations: A Study of Formal Theories of Coalition Formation Applied to Nine European Parliaments After 1918.* San Francisco: Jossey-Bass.

Gamson, William A. 1961. A Theory of Coalition Formation. *American Sociological Review* 26 (3): 373–382.

Laver, Michael, and Norman Schofield. 1990. *Multiparty Government: The Politics of Coalition in Europe.* Oxford and New York: Oxford University Press. (Repr., Ann Arbor: University of Michigan Press, 1998.)

Pridham, Geoffrey, ed. 1986. *Coalitional Behaviour in Theory and Practice: An Inductive Model for Western Europe.* Cambridge, U.K., and New York: Cambridge University Press.

Riker, William H. 1962. *The Theory of Political Coalitions.* New Haven, CT: Yale University Press. (Repr., Westport, CT: Greenwood Press, 1984.)

Tsebelis, George. 1990. *Nested Games: Rational Choice in Comparative Politics.* Berkeley: University of California Press.

William M. Downs

COAL MINING
SEE *Appalachia; Mining Industry.*

COARD, BERNARD
SEE *Grenadian Revolution.*

COASE, RONALD
1910–

Economist Ronald Harry Coase was born in Middlesex, Great Britain, in 1910. At the age of eighteen, Coase enrolled at the London School of Economics, studying for a bachelor of commerce degree. He passed his degree examinations in 1931, and "knew a little about economics as well as a little about law, accounting, and statistics" (Coase 1991a, p. 37). After graduating, he was awarded a traveling scholarship, which brought him to the United States to study the structure of American industry. In 1932 Coase started his academic career in Great Britain as an assistant lecturer at the Dundee School of Economics and Commerce, where he was a colleague of Duncan Black (1908–1991). Subsequently, Coase worked at the University of Liverpool (1934–1935) and the London School of Economics (1935–1951). In 1951 he moved to the United States, where he taught at the University of Buffalo (1951–1958) and the University of Virginia (1958–1964) before joining the economics faculty at the University of Chicago in 1964. He remained there until his retirement in 1981. While in Chicago, he also served as editor of the *Journal of Law and Economics* (1964–1982).

In 1991 Coase was awarded the Nobel Memorial Prize in Economics, primarily on the basis of his paper "The Nature of the Firm," published in *Economica* in 1937. In this paper, Coase asks why there should be a coordinating organization "in view of the fact that it is usually argued that co-ordination will be done by the price mechanism?" (Coase 1937, p. 388). In addressing this question, Coase strikes gold when he introduces the concept of *transaction cost*: "The main reason why it is profitable to establish a firm would seem to be that there is a cost of using the price mechanism" (p. 390). This explanation brings the firm and any other organization or institution within the economic domain. It creates neoinstitutional economics. Rereading his own paper years later, Coase claims to have been struck by its extreme simplicity (Coase 1991b, p. 52).

Another paper cited by the Swedish Academy when awarding Coase the Nobel Prize was "The Problem of Social Cost" (1960). This paper elaborates on a question posed in Coase's earlier article "The Federal Communications Commission" (1959), a question similar to that posed in "The Nature of the Firm": Why does etheric scarcity require government regulation, whereas for other scarce means, such as capital and labor, the price mechanism is used? Coase argues that the absence of property rights blocks the use of the price mechanism to allocate the etheric scarcity to its highest bidder. At the same time, in a zero-transaction-cost world, all welfare effects, side effects included, will be traded efficiently. This idea is what economist George Stigler (1911–1991)

termed the *Coase theorem* (Stigler 1966, p. 113). Assignment of property rights may reduce transaction cost and induce trade, for example, in externalities.

Coase's position is that a transaction cost is positive, underlining that this cost profiles economic transactions and their accompanying social arrangements. Otherwise, economic theory may result in "blackboard economics," that is, formulating economic theory without taking account of information problems. Coase has a coherent view of the economic system, which he owes to his London School of Economics master Arnold Plant (1898–1978), who he claims "introduced me to Adam Smith's 'invisible hand.'" (Coase 1991d, p. 229). This view enabled Coase to formulate his seminal 1937 paper as "a young man who knew virtually no economics" (Coase 1991c, p. 62). Coase shows the normal working of the economic system in the light of transaction cost. The winning of the Nobel Prize induced Coase to remark: "It is a strange experience to be praised in my eighties for work I did in my twenties" (Coase 1991d, p. 231).

SEE ALSO *Coase Theorem; Economics, Institutional; Economics, Nobel Prize in; Social Cost; Transaction Cost*

BIBLIOGRAPHY

Coase, Ronald H. 1937. The Nature of the Firm. *Economica* 4 (n.s.): 386–405.

Coase, Ronald H. 1959. The Federal Communications Commission. *Journal of Law and Economics* 2: 1–40.

Coase, Ronald H. 1960. The Problem of Social Cost. *Journal of Law and Economics* 3: 1–44.

Coase, Ronald H. 1988. *The Firm, the Market, and the Law.* Chicago: University of Chicago Press.

Coase, Ronald H. 1991a. The Nature of the Firm: Origin. In *The Nature of the Firm: Origins, Evolution, and Development,* ed. Oliver E. Williamson and Sidney G. Winter, 34–47. New York: Oxford University Press.

Coase, Ronald H. 1991b. The Nature of the Firm: Meaning. In *The Nature of the Firm: Origins, Evolution, and Development,* ed. Oliver E. Williamson and Sidney G. Winter, 48–60. New York: Oxford University Press.

Coase, Ronald H. 1991c. The Nature of the Firm: Influence. In *The Nature of the Firm: Origins, Evolution, and Development,* ed. Oliver E. Williamson and Sidney G. Winter, 61–74. New York: Oxford University Press.

Coase, Ronald H. 1991d. 1991 Nobel Lecture: The Institutional Structure of Production. In *The Nature of the Firm: Origins, Evolution, and Development,* ed. Oliver E. Williamson and Sidney G. Winter, 227–235. New York: Oxford University Press.

Stigler, George J. 1966. *The Theory of Price.* 3rd ed. New York: Macmillan.

Williamson, Oliver E., and Sidney G. Winter, eds. 1991. *The Nature of the Firm: Origins, Evolution, and Development*. New York: Oxford University Press.

Piet de Vries

COASE THEOREM

In 1960 Ronald H. Coase, who won the Nobel Prize in Economics in 1991, published his paper *The Problem of Social Cost*. It presents the Coase Theorem as a new perspective on external effects, particularly harmful effects. Coase formulated his theorem as follows: "With costless market transactions, the decision of the courts concerning liability for damage would be without effect on the allocation of resources" (1960, p. 10). This theorem floors Arthur Pigou's welfare-economic approach of externalities. Since the publication of Pigou's *The Economics of Welfare* (1920) economists were used to seeing externalities (side effects) as divergences between private and social net products. In this respect, the conventional thought is that if A inflicts harm on B, A should be restrained. The harm is a (social) cost to B, not having been taken account of in A's private-cost-benefit calculation. Governmental interventions such as taxes remedy this private-social-product divergence, as a prerequisite for economically efficient decisions in the market place. This is the Pigovian approach.

The case of *Sturges v. Bridgman*, used by Coase, may illustrate the Pigovian approach, and shows that the Pigovian route runs into serious problems: For many years, a confectioner has had some machinery in operation on his premises. A doctor then occupies neighboring premises. After some years, the doctor builds a consulting room right next to the room containing the confectioner's machinery. The vibration and noise produced by the confectioner's machinery makes the doctor's use of the consulting room impossible, resulting in an income loss of, say, $100. The doctor goes to court and the court orders the confectioner to refrain from using his machinery. This judgment matches the Pigovian line of thought. The confectioner's production decision did not take the doctor's (social) costs into account. At the same time, the sentence makes clear that considering the problem in terms of private and social products ignores the reciprocal nature. Suppression of the confectioner's harm to the doctor inevitably harms the confectioner. It might be that the sentence harms the confectioner for more than $100. In that case, it is inefficient to ban the confectioner's business. The social net product is less than it might be.

Coase's perspective on the problem of social cost is "to avoid the more serious harm" (Coase 1959, p. 26).

Coase formulated this starting point of his theorem in a paper preceding the "Social Cost" paper. In his paper, "The Federal Communications Commission" (1959), Coase wondered why etheric scarcity requires government regulation, whereas for other scarce means such as capital, labor, and land the American economic system uses the price mechanism. Coase identified that it is the absence of property rights in radio frequencies that blocks the use of the pricing system. Well-defined property rights for frequencies will lead to wave trade, allocating a frequency to the highest bidder. "Chaos disappears; and so does the government except that a legal system to define property rights and to arbitrate disputes is, of course, necessary" (p. 14).

In his "Social Cost" paper Coase elaborated this property-rights perspective. Referring to the *Sturges v. Bridgman* case, the liability sentence affects the property rights concerning the neighboring premises, and foremost defines these property rights. The confectioner's liability will induce him to indemnify the doctor if his business brings him an income higher than the doctor's harm of $100. Similarly, the confectioner will move his machinery if this option costs less than $100. On the other hand, if the sentence had been that the doctor had no right to stop the confectioner's business, the doctor might pay the removal option, if priced at less than $100. Property rights bring about trade when mutual benefits are present. It must be said that the cost of transaction may hinder a beneficial deal. However, the Coase Theorem claims that market transactions allocate property rights to the highest bidder provided that transaction cost is zero.

Coase regretted that the zero-transaction-cost-world assumption of the theorem, in which "people can negotiate their way to efficiency" (Farrell 1987, p. 113), has received so much emphasis in the economics literature. People certainly do not live in such a world. Therefore, the most compelling message of the Coase Theorem is to take into account positive transaction cost in fashioning social arrangements. Key variable transaction cost should urge lawyers and legislators to identify in what manner the social net products might be increased. An elaboration of the Coase Theorem is the creation of air-polluting-emission rights. These rights induce polluters to seek emission-reduction alternatives, opening options to sell the rights profitably to the highest bidder.

SEE ALSO *Externality; Overfishing; Pollution; Property Rights; Tragedy of the Commons; Transaction Cost*

BIBLIOGRAPHY

Coase, Ronald. 1959. The Federal Communications Commission. *Journal of Law and Economics* 2: 1–40.

Coase, Ronald. 1960. The Problem of Social Cost. *Journal of Law and Economics* 3: 1–44.

Coase, Ronald. 1988. *The Firm, the Market, and the Law.* Chicago: University of Chicago Press.

Farrell, Joseph. 1987. Information and the Coase Theorem. *The Journal of Economic Perspectives* 1: 113–129.

Pigou, Arthur C. [1920] 1978. *The Economics of Welfare.* New York: AMS Press.

Piet de Vries

COBWEB CYCLES

Cobweb cycles are the result of lagged response of commodity production to price changes, due to the intrinsic delay between production decisions and actual supply of goods. The typical example is agricultural production, where gestation lags can vary from one season (as with corn) to a few seasons (livestock) to some years (fruit trees).

The idea is rather old: It was applied to agricultural cycles in the 1820s, and it provided the basis for a non-agricultural cycle model by John Wade in 1833. In more recent times, Albert Aftalion's business cycle theory also relied on prices sending wrong signals to entrepreneurs because of a lag between production and supply preventing the system from settling into equilibrium (1913). The first analytical treatment, however, came in 1930, when

the independent researches of Jan Tinbergen, Umberto Ricci, and Henry Schultz (all published in German) looked at such cycles as examples of the introduction of time lags in the adjustment process after a disturbance to equilibrium in the commodity market occurs. These authors, elaborating on Arthur Hanau's finding that hog production in Germany was influenced by past hog prices, showed that lags generate two-phase discontinuous cycles, of a period twice the lag and of constant, increasing, or decreasing amplitude depending on the relative elasticities of the supply and demand curves. Figure 1, which represents the diverging case, is self-explanatory as to the origin of the term *cobweb cycle* (apparently coined by Kaldor 1934 in English and by Leontief 1934 in German).

In 1934 Wassily Leontief examined the case of non-linear supply and demand curves, and showed that certain conditions can give rise to persistent limit cycles, to which the system would converge.

The analysis was further generalized in two directions. The simplest treatment assumed that production decisions react on the market price prevailing at the time, thus implying specific rules about the formation of expectations. A first generalization considered distributed lags, either by treating the expected price as a weighted average of past prices, or by supposing that producers react not to

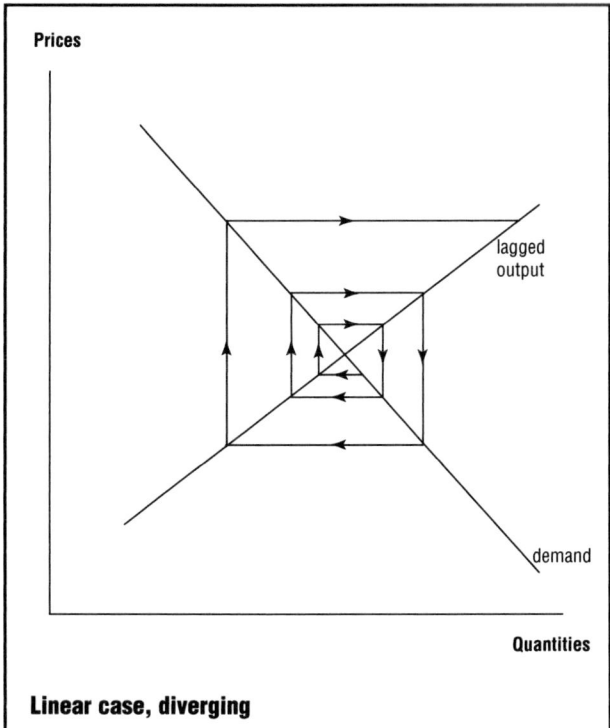

Linear case, diverging

Figure 1

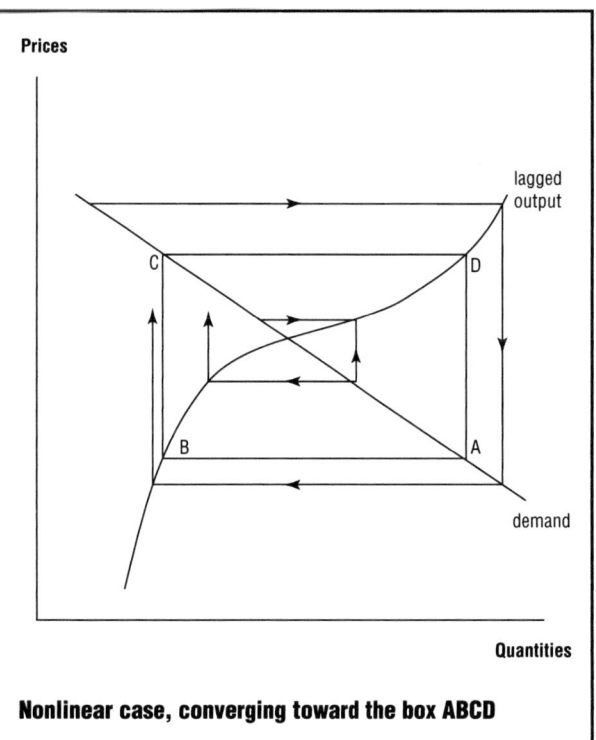

Nonlinear case, converging toward the box ABCD

Figure 2

immediate price variations but to their expectation as to the "normal" price level; the latter is revised period after period, adapting it to the movement of actual prices (Nerlove 1958). This stabilizes the model to some extent, the more so the less the weight of recent events with respect to past ones.

A second generalization disposed of the determinism of the model by introducing an error term. The corresponding modelling develops the suggestion derived from John Muth's observation that "farmers' expectations and the prediction of the model have the opposite sign" (Muth 1961, p. 331; similarly, pp. 333–334): Stochastic models have been elaborated assuming instead that expectations are rational, thus postulating that they are unbiased with respect to the theory's prediction—that is, not systematically wrong in an easily predictable way (see, for example, Pashigian 1970).

As these developments of the simplest model occurred, the reflection on the epistemic implications of the cobweb phenomenon was turned on its head. Its first formulation immediately suggested that the instability potentially caused by the lag could offer an escape to the contradiction, widely perceived in the 1920s and 1930s, between the persistence of cycles and the dominant static economic theory, which postulated that a disturbed system would gravitate toward its equilibrium position so that persistent fluctuations could only be explained in terms of systematic exogenous shocks (Ezekiel 1938, pp. 255 and 278–280; Kaldor 1934, pp. 132–136; Rosenstein-Rodan 1934, pp. 91–92). The limit cycles of the nonlinear cobweb led to the interpretation of the cycle as a "generalized equilibrium state" (Samuelson 1948, pp. 371–373), that is, of a possible state of periodic or quasi-periodic motion as "natural" as the stationary state was for static economics.

The reflections on expectations brought the discussion about how to explain the cycle back to its starting place. The assumption of adaptive expectations itself implied an increased stability of the system by electing the long-run normal price as the determinant of output (Mills 1961, p. 334). Finally, the postulate that expectations are rational assumes the cycle away, except as the consequence of the summation of random exogenous shocks on which the burden of the explanation is shifted (Muth 1961, p. 333; Pashigian 1970, p. 352).

SEE ALSO *Adaptive Expectations; Business Cycles, Theories; Expectations; Expectations, Rational*

BIBLIOGRAPHY

Aftalion, Albert. 1913. *Les crises périodiques de surproduction* [trans. Periodic crises of overproduction]. Paris: Marcel Rivière.

Ezekiel, Mordecai. 1938. The Cobweb Theorem. *Quarterly Journal of Economics* 52 (2): 255–280.

Hanau, Arthur. 1928. Die Prognose der Schweinepreise. [trans. Forecasting pork prices.] *Vierteljahrhefte zur Konjunkturforschung.* Sonderheft 7: 4–41.

Kaldor, Nicholas. 1934. A Classificatory Note on the Determinateness of Equilibrium. *Review of Economic Studies* 1 (2): 121–136.

Leontief, Wassily. 1934. Verzoegerte Angebotsanpassung und partielles Gleichgewicht. [trans. Delayed supply adjustment and partial equilibrium.] *Zeitschrift fuer Nationaloekomie* 5 (December): 670–676.

Mills, Edwin S. 1961. The Use of Adaptive Expectations in Stability Analysis: A Comment. *Quarterly Journal of Economics* 75 (2): 330–335.

Muth, John F. 1961. Rational Expectations and the Theory of Price Movements. *Econometrica* 29 (3): 315–335.

Nerlove, Marc. 1958. Adaptive Expectations and Cobweb Phenomena. *Quarterly Journal of Economics* 72 (2): 227–240.

Pashigian, Peter B. 1970. Rational Expectations and the Cobweb Theory. *Journal of Political Economy* 78 (2): 338–352.

Ricci, Umberto. Die 'synthetische Oekonomie' von Henry Ludwell Moore. [trans. *Synthetic economics* by Henry Ludwell Moore.] *Zeitschrift fuer Nationaloekonomie* I:5 649–668.

Rosenstein-Rodan, P. N. 1934. The Rôle of Time in Economic Theory. *Economica* N.S. 1 (1): 77–97.

Samuelson, Paul Anthony. 1948. Dynamic Process Analysis. In *A Survey of Contemporary Economics*, ed. E. H. Ellis, 352–387. Philadelphia: Blakiston.

Schultz, Henry. 1930. *Der Sinn der statistischen Nachfragekurven.* [trans. The Significance of Statistical Demand Curves.] Bonn: Schroeder Verlag.

Tinbergen, Jan. [1930] 1997. Determination and Interpretation of Supply Curves: An Example. In *The Foundations of Econometric Analysis*, ed. David F. Hendry and Mary S. Morgan, 233–245. Cambridge, U.K.: Cambridge University Press.

Wade, John. 1833. *History of the Middle and Working Classes.* London: Effingham Wilson. Reprinted 1966, New York: Kelley.

Waugh, Frederick V. 1964. Cobweb Models. *Journal of Farm Economics* 46 (4): 732–750.

Daniele Besomi

COCAINE

SEE *Drugs of Abuse.*

CODE NAPOLÉON

SEE *Napoléon Bonaparte.*

CODETERMINATION

Codetermination guarantees worker representation in the management of a firm. It is commonly found in coordinated market economies such as Germany. Liberal market economies, such as the United States, typically do not legislate mandatory worker representation in firms.

Germany introduced codetermination in 1951, establishing employee participation at two levels of corporate governance: the firm level, with works councils, and a higher level, with employee representatives on the supervisory board. Employee representation is most extensive in the coal, iron, and steel industries, where near parity is legislated, nominally giving equal representation to employees and employers. In 1976 the German government extended codetermination to other industries, but without full parity (European Foundation 2005c). Under these rules, worker representation is extensive but not uniform across issue areas. Most significantly, workers have a voice on issues that concern health and safety at work, personnel matters, training, and renumeration (European Foundation 2005d).

In Austria codetermination allows employees to influence firm decisions that affect their employment conditions, but it is limited to disciplinary procedures and some renumeration matters where firms must receive the works council's approval before making changes (European Foundation 2005a). Codetermination reinforces norms of trust between firms and employees, yielding an environment of relatively peaceful industrial relations.

Sweden established rules in 1976 that promoted employee participation in firm decision making, but the laws pertain only to firms that have collective bargaining agreements with their unions (European Foundation 2005e). Similarly, the 1978 Co-operation Act in Finland regulates industrial relations, allowing employees to participate in decision making on limited matters, including training and worker welfare (European Foundation 2005b). Although the policies in Sweden and Finland are often called codetermination, the policies are neither as extensive nor as broadly applicable as in Germany. Thus, the institution of codetermination varies across countries, industries, and issue areas.

As the barriers to trade and labor mobility are lowered in the European Union, analyzing the costs and benefits of codetermination is critical. In the case of full parity, as in the coal and steel industries in Germany, board members perceive slower decision making due to worker inclusion as a significant disadvantage (Hopt 1984). This cost must be balanced against the advantages of trust and information sharing. In a more recent survey in Sweden, for instance, a majority of directors had a "rather positive" or "very positive" view of worker representation on employee boards. And in fact, the Swedish survey demonstrated that codetermination actually increased efficiency (Levinson 2001, pp. 265–266).

Further, increased worker representation should result in better working conditions for employees and for greater industrial peace; otherwise, either workers or employers would oppose the policy. Analysis of hourly earnings confirms that codetermination does increase hourly earnings (Svejnar 1981, p. 194). Codetermination also seems to have a positive effect on cooperation between firms and their employees (Levinson 2001, p. 266).

Nevertheless, codetermination may not be suitable for every country or firm. Legislating codetermination in multinational corporations is complicated by legal and economic factors, as the Netherlands implicitly acknowledges by granting multinational corporations exemptions from codetermination (Hopt 1984, p. 1363). Also, codetermination is a characteristic of coordinated market economies, where coordination by nonmarket mechanisms is critical to economic success (Hall and Soskice 2001). Mandating codetermination in liberal market economies may be counterproductive because the market itself provides the critical source of coordination, providing comparative advantages.

SEE ALSO *Diplomacy; International Relations*

BIBLIOGRAPHY

European Foundation for the Improvement of Living and Working Conditions. 2005a. EMIRE: Austria—Co-Determination. http://www.eurofound.europa.eu/emire/AUSTRIA/ANCHOR-MITBESTIMMUNG-AT.html.

European Foundation for the Improvement of Living and Working Conditions. 2005b. EMIRE: Finland—Co-Determination Agreement. http://www.eurofound.europa.eu/emire/FINLAND/ANCHOR-MY-Ouml-T-Auml-M-Auml—Auml-R-Auml—Auml-MISSOPIMUSMEDBEST-Auml-MMANDEAVTAL-FI.html.

European Foundation for the Improvement of Living and Working Conditions. 2005c. EMIRE: Germany—Co-Determination. http://www.eurofound.europa.eu/emire/GERMANY/CODETERMINATION-DE.html.

European Foundation for the Improvement of Living and Working Conditions. 2005d. EMIRE: Germany—Co-Determination Rights of the Works Council. http://www.eurofound.europa.eu/emire/GERMANY/CODETERMINATIONRIGHTSOFTHEWORKSCOUNCIL-DE.html.

European Foundation for the Improvement of Living and Working Conditions. 2005e. EMIRE: Sweden—Co-Determination. http://www.eurofound.europa.eu/emire/SWEDEN/ANCHOR-MEDBEST-Auml-MMANDELAGEN-SE.html.

Hall, Peter A., and David Soskice. 2001. *Varieties of Capitalism: The Institutional Foundations of Comparative Advantage.* New York: Oxford University Press.

Hopt, Klaus J. 1984. New Ways in Corporate Governance: European Experiments with Labor Representation on Corporate Boards. *Michigan Law Review* 82 (April–May): 1338–1363.

Levinson, Klas. 2001. Employee Representatives in Company Boards in Sweden. *Industrial Relations Journal* 32 (September): 264–274.

Svejnar, Jan. 1981. Relative Wage Effects of Unions, Dictatorship, and Codetermination: Econometric Evidence from Germany. *Review of Economics and Statistics* 63 (May): 188–197.

Seth Jolly

COFFEE INDUSTRY

The coffee plant is a woody perennial evergreen belonging to the Rubiaceae family. There are two types of coffee, arabica (*Coffea arabica*) and robusta (*Coffea canephora*). Arabica, which accounts for about two-thirds of global output, is grown at high altitudes in Latin America and northeastern Africa. It has more aroma and less caffeine than robusta, which is grown in humid areas at low altitudes in Asia and western and southern sub-Saharan Africa. The coffee plant can grow up to 10 meters high, but it is usually kept at about 3 meters. It takes two to three years for the coffee plant to produce cherries. Scientific evidence indicates that arabica is indigenous to Ethiopia, while robusta is indigenous to Uganda. It appears that coffee was produced in Ethiopia at a larger scale and then spread to other parts of Africa. Coffee cultivation was introduced to Java by Dutch traders in 1699. A few years later the French introduced coffee to Martinique. Coffee was first cultivated in Brazil in 1727.

Although the origins of the coffee drink are unknown, the usefulness of coffee beans was probably recognized as early as 1000 CE by Arab traders who chewed coffee beans in order to suppress their appetite and stay awake, thus helping them cross large distances in the desert. The world's first coffee shop reportedly opened five centuries later in Constantinople (now Istanbul, Turkey). Coffee was introduced to the West by Italian traders in the early seventeenth century, with the first coffee shops opening in London and Paris later in that century.

The processing of coffee involves several steps. After harvesting, the skin of the cherry is removed, and the bean is cleaned to become a green bean, the internationally traded commodity. The green beans are roasted, giving them a dark brown color. Following the grinding of roasted beans, consumers use various brewing techniques to convert the ground beans into a beverage. In Europe, most coffee is consumed in espresso-like form, whereas in North America coffee is mostly consumed in drip form (although that practice has been changing since the beginning of the "Starbucks revolution" during the 1990s). In Asia, most people drink instant coffee. Scandinavian countries lead the world with per capita consumption of almost 10 kilograms of coffee per year from 2000 to 2005. The European Union average during this period was 5.0 kilograms, followed by the United States (4.1 kilograms), and Japan (3.2 kilograms), according to U.S. Department of Agriculture estimates (USDA 2006).

PRODUCTION, TRADE, AND PRICES

Most tropical countries produce coffee. Latin America accounts for 60 percent of global output, followed by Asia (24%) and Africa (16%). From 2001 to 2006, more than half of world output was produced in three countries: Brazil (35%), Vietnam (11%), and Colombia (10%). Other significant producers were Indonesia (5%) and Ethiopia, India, and Mexico (4% each). Coffee in some countries, notably Brazil, is produced on large farms with modern equipment, including irrigation, tractors, and even coffee harvesters. In other regions, especially Central America, Africa, and Asia, coffee is produced by smallholders. In some Africa countries, smallholders own as little as one-quarter of a hectare of land. In this setting, the key input is labor and, to a limited extent, chemicals. In some East African countries there are also coffee estates that use large numbers of permanent workers.

More than 80 percent of coffee is traded internationally and consumed mainly by high-income countries. In some years, coffee is the second most-traded commodity after crude oil, generating about $15 billion in export revenue. The United States accounts for about 18 percent of global consumption, followed by Brazil (13%), Germany (9%), Japan (6%), and France and Italy (5% each).

Coffee is traded in green bean form. Although there are numerous coffee trading companies, most coffee trade is handled by five or six large multinationals. Coffee prices are determined in futures exchanges. Highly-liquid coffee futures contracts are traded at the New York Board of Trade for arabica and at the London International Financial Futures and Options Exchange for robusta. Less-liquid contracts are traded at the Commodity Exchanges of São Paulo, Singapore, and Bangalore.

Coffee prices are generally highly volatile (much more so than other commodity prices). This volatility reflects the fact that Brazil, the dominant supplier, suffers occasional frosts, thus subjecting its coffee output to considerable fluctuations. Hedge funds also play a role in price volatility, especially in the short term. Beginning in

2000, coffee experienced one of the most dramatic price declines in the history of the industry (an episode referred to as the *coffee crisis*). In October 2001 arabica averaged $1.24 per kilogram, a nine-year low, while in January 2002 robusta dropped to $0.50 per kilogram (the lowest nominal level since the price of $0.49 per kilogram set in May 1965). The main factor behind the price collapse was oversupply, especially in Brazil, which averaged a record output of thirty-three million bags of coffee during the previous four seasons, and in Vietnam, which emerged as the dominant robusta producer, overtaking Colombia as the world's second-largest coffee producer. The oversupply, caused by lower-cost producers, led some to argue, convincingly, that the coffee crisis was a market-driven outcome of the coffee industry adjusting to new global market realities (Lindsey 2003).

THE POLICY ENVIRONMENT

The coffee market has been subject to considerable policy interventions both at national and international levels. Takamasa Akiyama (2001) reported that only fifteen of the world's fifty-one coffee-producing countries had private marketing systems in 1985. Twenty-five countries sold coffee through state-owned enterprises, while another eleven had mixed state- and private-sector marketing bodies. By 2007 the coffee sectors of most countries were operating with private-sector marketing arrangements.

The coffee market has also been subject to a series of coffee agreements administered by the International Coffee Organization (ICO), which was established in 1962 to stabilize coffee prices by dictating how much coffee each producer could export. Research has shown that coffee prices were higher under the ICO than they would have been otherwise (Gilbert 1995). There were likely political reasons behind the ICO's supply measures. According to Robert Bates (1997), the United States, a powerful ICO member, used the organization during the 1960s and 1970s to increase the income of Central American coffee-producing countries in the hope that this action would contain the spread of communism in the region. Similarly, western European countries viewed ICO-induced high coffee prices as a way to provide aid to their former African colonies.

Most coffee-producing countries (accounting for 90 percent of global output) and almost all developed coffee-consuming countries were members of the ICO (interestingly, communist countries, which were not members of the ICO, bought coffee under free trading arrangements). The last international coffee agreement was effective from September 1980 to July 1989, after which the ICO was abandoned. A more recent attempt to regulate supplies through another organization, the Association of Coffee Producing Countries, failed.

FACTORS INFLUENCING THE INDUSTRY'S LONG-TERM OUTLOOK

In the absence of new international initiatives or domestic policies by dominant producers, the outlook for the coffee market depends entirely on supply-and-demand forces. Vietnam's emergence as a major robusta producer is likely to influence robusta prices for many years. In 1980 Vietnam produced 140,000 60-kilogram bags of coffee—less than 0.2 percent of world production. In 2001 Vietnam exceeded 13.3 million bags—more than 11.4 percent of world production. Vietnam is a low-cost producer, and as of 2007 its coffee trees were very young and had yet to reach maximum yields. Brazil has been able to maintain unprecedented output levels, averaging more than 39 million bags during 2003–2006. Extensive mechanization of coffee harvesting has lowered production costs, while better varieties with higher yields have been developed and adopted. Shifting production north, away from frost-prone areas in the south, has reduced the likelihood of weather-related supply disruptions. And the extensive use of irrigation has stabilized and sustained yields.

On the demand side, the coffee industry faces growing competition from the soft drink industry. For example, the 1970 annual per capita consumption of soft drinks in the United States was 86 liters; by 1999, annual per capita consumption had exceeded 200 liters, according to U.S. Department of Agriculture data.

Numerous other factors are likely to influence the coffee industry's long-term outlook. First, new technologies enable roasters to eliminate the harsh taste of some coffees, essentially achieving a higher level of quality from lower-quality beans. Second, roasters have been more flexible in their ability to make short-term switches between coffee types, implying that the premia of certain types of coffee cannot be retained for long. Third, a small segment of the market has emerged that focuses on product differentiation, such as organic, gourmet, and shade coffee. The implication of these developments is that the demand outlook is likely to differ from one coffee producer to another. Specifically, any expansion in coffee demand is likely to occur at the two ends of the spectrum: lower-quality beans (reflecting improved technology) and specialty coffees (reflecting expansion to niche markets).

Several new patterns have emerged in coffee promotion and distribution as well. Coffee promotion used to take the form of national brands, represented by the familiar Juan Valdez campaign of the National Federation of Coffee Growers of Colombia. Other types of promotions were undertaken by coffee-trading companies, such as Maxwell House's "Good to the Last Drop" campaign. The market and trade setting has shifted considerably since the mid-1980s.

In 2007 as much as 10 percent of coffee is branded according to such characteristics as subnational origin (e.g., Kilimanjaro coffee rather than Tanzanian coffee, or Harare coffee rather than Ethiopian coffee); social aspects (e.g., fair trade coffee, which ensures a minimum price to growers); and organic, shade, or bird-friendly production (which ensures compliance with certain environmental criteria).

A second emerging pattern is the development of direct relationships between major coffee retailers, such as Starbucks, and producer organizations that can ensure that the coffee these retailers sell adheres to certain social criteria. Initially, it was believed that, in addition to offering more choices to consumers, these new marketing and branding mechanisms would provide a boost to the income of small coffee growers. While this was the case initially, research has shown that the premia received by coffee growers have declined and are likely to shrink even more as increasing numbers of producers join the specialty coffee marketing channels (Kilian et al. 2006).

SEE ALSO *Addiction; Agricultural Industry; Colonialism*

BIBLIOGRAPHY

Akiyama, Takamasa. 2001. Coffee Market Liberalization since 1990. In *Commodity Market Reforms: Lessons of Two Decades*, eds. Takamasa Akiyama, John Baffes, Donald Larson, and Panos Varangis, 83–120. Washington, DC: World Bank.

Baffes, John, Bryan Lewin, and Panos Varangis. 2005. Coffee: Market Setting and Policies. In *Global Agricultural Trade and Developing Countries*, eds. M. Ataman Aksoy and John C. Beghin, 297–310. Washington, DC: World Bank.

Bates, Robert H. 1997. *Open-Economy Politics: The Political Economy of the World Coffee Trade*. Princeton, NJ: Princeton University Press.

Gilbert, Christopher L. 1995. International Commodity Control: Retrospect and Prospect. Policy Research Working Paper 1545. Washington, DC: World Bank, International Economics Dept., Commodity Policy and Analysis Unit.

Kilian, Bernard, Connie Jones, Lawrence Pratt, and Andrès Villalobos. 2006. Is Sustainable Agriculture a Viable Strategy to Improve Farm Income in Central America? A Case Study on Coffee. *Journal of Business Research* 59 (3): 322–330.

Lindsey, Brink. 2003. Grounds for Complaint? Understanding the "Coffee Crisis." Trade Briefing Paper no. 16. Washington, DC: Cato Institute Center for Trade Policy Studies. http://www.freetrade.org/pubs/briefs/tbp-016.pdf.

United States Department of Agriculture. 2006. Tropical Products: World Markets and Trade. Foreign Agricultural Service, Circular Series, FTROP 4-06. http://www.fas.usda.gov/psdonline/circulars/tropical.pdf.

John Baffes

COGNITION

Cognitive psychology is the scientific study of the mental processes that underlie behavior. These mental processes comprise a number of areas, including attention, memory, perception, thinking, reasoning, problem solving, decision making, language, knowledge representation, mental imagery, and motivation and concept formation. This focus on mental processes contrasts with behaviorism, which studied only behaviors that could be directly observed. Cognitive psychology is flourishing at the beginning of the twenty-first century, and its principles have been applied to clinical and counseling psychology, personality theory, developmental psychology, social psychology, comparative psychology, forensics and legal psychology, and education, among other disciplines. Other independent schools of thought have developed from cognitive psychology, including cognitive science and cognitive neuroscience.

HISTORY

Some historians have argued that cognitive psychology represents a shift in the psychological paradigm away from the limits of behaviorism (Gardner 1985; Sperry 1993). Others suggest that cognitive psychology simply represents a return to the same topics that existed prior to the founding of behaviorism (Hergenhahn 1994, p. 555). Extensive evidence indicates that cognitive psychology does not represent the study of a novel topic but a return to a focus on mental events that behaviorism failed to allow. Throughout the history of psychology, some form of cognitive psychology always existed (Hergenhahn 1997, p. 551). The questions raised by cognitive psychologists also occupied early thinkers. The ancient Greek philosopher Aristotle (384–322 BCE), for example, wrote on various topics in cognitive psychology. However, during the 1930s to 1950s, when radical behaviorism was experiencing its strongest period, it was generally accepted that cognitive events either did not exist or should be ignored by psychologists because they could not be studied objectively (Hergenhahn 1997, p. 551). However, as psychologists became less captivated by behaviorism, they began to shift toward a cognitive approach that was broader in scope than behaviorism.

The Downfall of Behaviorism Several findings led to the downfall of behaviorism and the eventual rise of cognitive psychology. According to strict behaviorism, two things must occur if an organism is to learn: (1) the organism must actually perform the behavior, and (2) the behavior must lead to some type of a consequence (i.e., reinforcement or punishment). The continuation of behaviorism's control of psychology rested on these basic premises. However, three major findings showed these premises to be unnecessary: cognitive maps, latent learning, and observational learning (or modeling).

Cognitive Maps and Latent Learning The American psychologist Edward Chace Tolman (1886–1959) is best known for his research on cognitive maps and latent learning. His work with cognitive maps showed that an organism could possess a mental representation of a physical space that would allow the organism to follow alternate routes to a food reward even if the organism was never reinforced for that route in the past (Tolman et al. 1946). Tolman's work with latent learning showed that rats were able to learn their way through a maze even if they never received reinforcement while they explored the maze (Tolman and Honzik 1930). In Tolman's study, the number of errors made by rats that were regularly rewarded gradually decreased as they learned their way through a maze. Other rats in a no-reward condition received no reinforcement for the first ten days of training but were simply placed in the maze for the same amount of time as the regularly rewarded rats. On the eleventh day, these rats were given a food reward. Much to the behaviorists' surprise, these rats made the same number of errors as the regularly rewarded rats on the twelfth day of training, rather than showing the gradual learning curve predicted by behaviorists. This research showed that the rats learned the maze, even without reinforcement.

Observational Learning and Modeling Psychologist Albert Bandura is probably best known for his work demonstrating observational learning. Bandura showed that organisms can learn by watching another organism receive reinforcement or punishment (Bandura et al. 1966). Thus, it is not necessary that the learner actually perform the behavior, nor must the learner receive reinforcement or punishment in order to learn.

Each of these findings failed to validate the most basic behaviorist premises. Additionally, many psychologists began to become less enchanted with behaviorism because of the limitations concerning what could be studied. For example, behaviorists felt that psychology should study only topics or phenomena that could be studied objectively and directly observed. Although cognitive psychology retained the practice of studying topics in an objective, scientific manner, the inclusion of only those topics that were based on direct observation was eliminated. While many research topics of interest to psychologists (thinking, perception, attention, motivation, emotion, decision processes, problem solving, language, etc.) stood outside the realm of psychological study under behaviorism, many of these topics became central to the cognitive psychology movement and are still studied today.

The Rise of Cognitive Psychology Richard Robins, Samuel Gosling, and Kenneth Craik (1999) have presented an analysis of the gradual decline in the behaviorist approach and the eventual rise of cognitive psychology. Cognitive psychology became more and more influential as it overtook the behaviorist approach by 1970 based on the number of articles published in the most prominent psychology journals. There were, however, several important earlier publications and studies that led to the resurgence of cognitive psychology.

The German psychologist Hermann Ebbinghaus (1850–1909) demonstrated in 1885 that complex mental processes, such as memory, could be studied using an objective, experimental approach. He studied nonsense syllables (or letter strings that did not make up words, such as YHB) and recorded the number of trials it took to learn the list to perfection. He then measured the *savings score* (i.e., how much time was saved as one learned the list to perfection again) as a measure of memory.

The Principles of Psychology (1890) by William James (1842–1910) cited numerous studies investigating cognitive phenomena and discussed many topics that currently interest cognitive psychologists, such as attention, perception, memory, and reasoning. James also argued that the human mind does not simply react to stimuli in the environment (a common behaviorist idea) but instead is dynamic and interactive.

Remembering: A Study in Experimental and Social Psychology (1932), by British psychologist Frederic Charles Bartlett (1886–1969), showed that memory was predictable and subject to systematic errors. In particular, Bartlett noted that memory errors were influenced by the rememberer's attitudes, beliefs, schemas, and preconceptions. He proposed that memory is a constructive process such that our own interpretations and biases have a huge impact on what we remember, rather than remembering strictly verbatim information.

American psychologist George A. Miller is probably the one scientist who has had the largest impact in the formation of cognitive psychology as a formal school of thought. In fact, many historians have suggested that his article "The Magical Number Seven, Plus or Minus Two: Some Limits on our Capacity for Processing Information" (1956) was the official beginning of cognitive psychology. This article essentially defined the capacity limits of short-term memory.

Several additional events were also critical for the development of cognitive psychology as a formal school of thought. World War II (1939–1945) led to the development of cognitive psychology and human factors engineering (Proctor and Van Zandt 1994, p. 5). As more complex instruments were developed, the U.S. military became increasingly interested in how humans interacted with such instruments. These questions involved such topics as attention, memory, perception, and decision making. On September 11, 1956, many important researchers attended a symposium at the Massachusetts Institute of Technology and become excited about the direction of this new approach (Matlin 2005, p. 7). So important was this symposium that some historians have argued that this date marks the official beginning of cognitive psychology.

German-born psychologist Ulric Neisser coined the term *cognitive psychology* with the publication of his book *Cognitive Psychology* in 1967. The journal *Cognitive Psychology* was founded in 1969, providing an outlet for researchers specifically interested in cognitive topics. Fifteen additional journals focusing on cognitive psychology were established during the next twenty years, indicating a rise in interest in cognitive topics and the rise of cognitive psychology.

AREAS OF INTEREST IN COGNITIVE PSYCHOLOGY

Attention. This area of research looks at an array of topics that focus on our ability to pay attention to specific stimuli while excluding other stimuli (selective attention) or to pay attention to two stimuli at the same time (divided attention). Topics include pattern recognition, object recognition, selective attention, divided attention, and subliminal perception.

Perception. Perception is the use of previous knowledge to gather and interpret stimuli registered by the senses (Matlin 2005). This process actively organizes and interprets sensory information in order to make it meaningful. Perception is usually discussed in conjunction with sensory processes with simple stimuli, but it is also studied in terms of how it functions in more complex social situations. For example, if someone bumped into you while walking down the street, your perception of the incident might be dependent upon the characteristics of the other individual. You might interpret it as an accident if an elderly woman bumped into you, but your interpretation might be different if the other person was a member of a group of boisterous teenagers.

Memory. This broad area of research focuses on the encoding, storage, and retrieval processes involved when one remembers information at a later time. Experts generally agree that memories are a result of not only the specific event that is being remembered but also the specific thoughts, emotions, and knowledge that the rememberer possesses. Furthermore, events or thoughts that occur after the encoded event also have an impact on what is remembered.

Language. This area of research focuses on how humans (and nonhumans) acquire and use language. There is also a major focus on the specific language rules (or grammar) that accompany language processing.

Thinking. This broad area of research includes various topics such as problem solving, decision making, mental imagery, and logic. The general focus is on the internal thought processes. Such thought processes may occur prior to overt behavior or during overt behavior, or they may occur as a result of external stimuli. Cognitive neuroscience may use brain-imaging techniques to provide objective measurements of when thinking occurs and which part of the brain is active during specific tasks.

Knowledge Representation. This area of research investigates how information is stored and accessed by the brain. Much of the research in this area focuses on mental models that explain how knowledge is stored in the brain. The two main codes that have been proposed for knowledge representation are based upon analog or propositional codes. Other major areas of research include categorization and how people utilize schemas and scripts in everyday life.

Artificial Intelligence. The information-processing approach to cognitive psychology uses the computer as a model for the human mind. This branch of cognitive psychology led to connectionist frameworks and the parallel distributed processing approach to studying cognition. The analogy that is the basis for the study of artificial intelligence is that computer connections between stored knowledge or idea units are similar to the physical, neural networks present in the brain (McClelland and Rumelhart 1985).

OTHER DISCIPLINES THAT EVOLVED FROM COGNITIVE PSYCHOLOGY

Cognitive Neuroscience. This area combines the basic research techniques and issues from cognitive psychology with various methods (e.g., brain scanning, event-related potential, and single-cell recording) to evaluate the physiological functioning of the brain. Cognitive neuroscience has helped scientists better understand how the brain works and what each part of the brain does, and it provides insight into brain abnormalities or damage.

Cognitive Science. Cognitive science is a multidisciplinary field that studies the workings of the mind by combining the approaches of cognitive psychology, neuroscience, and computer science. It may include other fields, such as philosophy, sociology, linguistics, and anthropology (Sobel 2001). Cognitive science takes a more holistic approach, since it utilizes techniques and theories from many different fields of study.

SEE ALSO *Memory; Social Cognition*

BIBLIOGRAPHY

Bandura, Albert, Joan E. Grusec, and Frances L. Menlove. 1966. Observational Learning as a Function of Symbolization and Incentive Set. *Child Development* 37: 499–506.

Bartlett, Frederic C. 1932. *Remembering: A Study in Experimental and Social Psychology*. New York: Macmillan.

Ebbinghaus, Hermann. [1885] 1913. *Memory: A Contribution to Experimental Psychology*. Trans. Henry A. Ruger and Clara E. Bussenues. New York: Teachers College, Columbia University.

Gardner, Howard. 1985. *The Mind's New Science: A History of the Cognitive Revolution*. New York: Basic Books.

Hergenhahn, B. R. 1994. *An Introduction to the History of Psychology*. 3rd ed. Pacific Grove, CA: Brooks/Cole. (5th ed. 2005. Belmont, CA: Wadsworth).

James, William. 1890. *The Principles of Psychology*. New York: Holt.

Matlin, Margaret W. 2005. *Cognition*. 6th ed. New York: Wiley.

McClelland, James L., and David E. Rumelhart. 1985. Distributed Memory and the Representation of General and Specific Information. *Journal of Experimental Psychology: General* 114: 159–188.

Miller, George A. 1956. The Magical Number Seven, Plus or Minus Two: Some Limits on our Capacity for Processing Information. *Psychological Review* 63: 81–97.

Neisser, Ulric. 1967. *Cognitive Psychology*. New York: Appleton-Century-Crofts.

Proctor, Robert W., and Trisha Van Zandt. 1994. *Human Factors in Simple and Complex Systems*. Needham Heights, MA: Allyn and Bacon.

Robins, Richard W., Samuel D. Gosling, and Kenneth H. Craik. 1999. An Empirical Analysis of Trends in Psychology. *American Psychologist* 54: 117–128.

Sobel, Carolyn P. 2001. *The Cognitive Sciences: An Interdisciplinary Approach*. Mountain View, CA: Mayfield.

Sperry, Roger W. 1993. The Impact and Promise of the Cognitive Revolution. *American Psychologist* 48: 878–885.

Tolman, Edward C., and Charles H. Honzik. 1930. Introduction and Removal of Reward, and Maze Performance in Rats. *University of California Publications in Psychology* 4: 257–273.

Tolman, Edward C., B. F. Ritchie, and D. Kalish. 1946. Studies in Spatial Learning: II. Place Learning vs. Response Learning. *Journal of Experimental Psychology* 36: 221–229.

Jeffrey S. Anastasi

COGNITIVE BALANCE

SEE *Cognitive Dissonance; Equilibrium in Psychology.*

COGNITIVE-BEHAVIOR THERAPY

SEE *Learned Helplessness.*

COGNITIVE-DEVELOPMENTAL PERSPECTIVE

SEE *Developmental Psychology.*

COGNITIVE DISSONANCE

Cognitive dissonance is a social psychological theory introduced by Leon Festinger (1957), describing the way in which people cope with and rationalize inconsistencies in their experience, such as holding incompatible beliefs, acting in ways that violate their values, being forced to choose one of two equally attractive alternatives, or discovering that their efforts were not worth the result obtained. The term refers both to a lack of harmony among one's thoughts and to the discomfort that results from this, which individuals are motivated to reduce by changing their mind or their behavior in the service of greater cognitive consonance. From its initial focus on discordant thoughts, the theory has evolved over the years to stress that the ultimate motivation for reducing dissonance is to preserve the belief that one is a good and rational person, and the theory is now primarily used to understand processes by which individuals justify past behavior to themselves. The concept has also been fruitfully borrowed by other social sciences: Sociologists, for example, use the theory to study the experience of individuals with conflicting identities, to analyze the maintenance of myths, and to explore aspects of religious life. Economists have used it to understand investment decisions, happiness with allocation decisions, or satisfaction with welfare policies.

EXPERIMENTAL DEMONSTRATIONS OF THE POWER OF DISSONANCE

In the first experimental demonstration of how people reduce dissonance, Festinger showed that when students agreed to lie to a peer for a token reward of one dollar (by saying that a boring task was in fact interesting), they came to like the task more than if they were compensated with twenty dollars. The discomfort of having lied with no obvious justification was alleviated by deciding that it was not such a lie after all. Unable to change the memory of their past behavior, they addressed the dissonance by altering the other incompatible cognition, and pronounced the task more interesting. This finding was inconsistent with learning theories prevalent at the time, which predicted that organisms would prefer those behaviors for which they are rewarded most. It was also a striking demonstration of how, contrary to the common perception that attitudes always govern behavior, behavior can also influence attitudes.

Later dissonance research relied heavily on two experimental procedures capturing the discomfort that lingers after difficult decisions. Most inspired by the original Festinger demonstration, the *induced compliance* paradigm requires that participants write an essay on a topic that they care about, but in support of a position opposite to their own. When the experimenter emphasizes that participants are free to refuse to write the essay, they still write it, but eventually change their stance from their original position toward the position in the essay. No such change happens when participants are simply instructed to write the essay with no room for choice. As before, the discomfort caused by misrepresenting their attitude without sufficient justification led high-choice participants to bring their attitudes more in line with their actions.

A second widely used procedure, the *forced choice* paradigm, introduced by Jack Brehm (1956), illustrates how people cope after they have had to pick one of two options when they had no clear-cut initial preference. After making such a choice (in Brehm's study, housewives had to pick one of two moderately but equally attractive household appliances to take home as a gift), a typical reaction is to immediately start liking the chosen option more, and the rejected option less. This spread of alternatives prevents postdecisional regret and increases comfort with one's decision. Difficult choices in everyday life are followed by similar mental work aimed at reducing dissonance by bringing to mind thoughts that support one's choice, such as benefits of the chosen option or flaws of the rejected one.

A noteworthy feature of the theory is its proposal that a "cold" incompatibility between pieces of information in the mind would lead to a "hot" motivational state, a discomfort that individuals would feel a strong urge to reduce. What does this discomfort feel like? In the induced compliance paradigm, individuals report psychological discomfort just after agreeing to write the essay, but less so after they have been given a chance to express their revised attitude. Stress measures such as skin conductance have also been used to show that individuals experiencing dissonance are more physiologically aroused. Dissonance researchers have also relied on *misattribution* instructions to show the role of discomfort more indirectly: When participants in an induced compliance paradigm were told that a pill they just took might make them feel tense, the discomfort arising from writing the essay was ascribed (misattributed) to the pill, and participants changed their attitude less than when the pill was revealed to be just a placebo. This again demonstrates that attitude change results from discomfort with the inconsistent cognitions, because cognitions are left alone when discomfort is attributed elsewhere.

Besides these powerful experimental demonstrations, social psychologists have also used the theory to understand, for example, why new members disappointed by a group still appreciate it more if they went through harsh initiation practices to get admitted (effort justification), how individuals come to terms with doing things that they know are bad for them (e.g., smoking), or how, more encouraging, people who are reminded that their habits do not fit their values sometimes start practicing what they preach. And while the bulk of the research has focused on attitude change as the means to reduce dissonance, psychologists have shown that discomfort can also be reduced by trivializing the inconsistency, denying responsibility for the problematic behavior, looking for social support for a disconfirmed belief, or by taking substances such as alcohol that directly alter one's psychological state.

CONTROVERSIES AND ALTERNATIVE MODELS

Cognitive dissonance is the theory that has inspired the most debate and reinterpretation in social psychology. One early attempt at reappraisal was Daryl Bem's *self-perception* theory (1972), which argued that what looks like attitude change does not result from inconsistent cognitions, but rather from the fact that individuals first learn about their own preferences and attitudes by observing their own behavior. As they would if observing others, individuals who saw themselves agree to write an essay for little reward inferred that they must be sympathetic with the position defended—and discomfort need not be involved. Similarly, individuals choosing one option over another in the forced-choice paradigm inferred that they must like the chosen option more. After much debate, psychologists now believe that self-perception explains the effects observed in unimportant domains, where people do not hold strong preformed attitudes, but that in important domains where individuals have strong attitudes, dissonance (and its accompanying discomfort) is a

11

Hiding

The color and stick-like shape of a praying mantis help it hide.

Green mantises may hide on plant leaves.

Brown mantises may hide on the bark of trees.

They blend in well, so the insects they hunt can't see them easily.

Animals that want to eat praying mantises, such as birds and snakes, can't see them either.

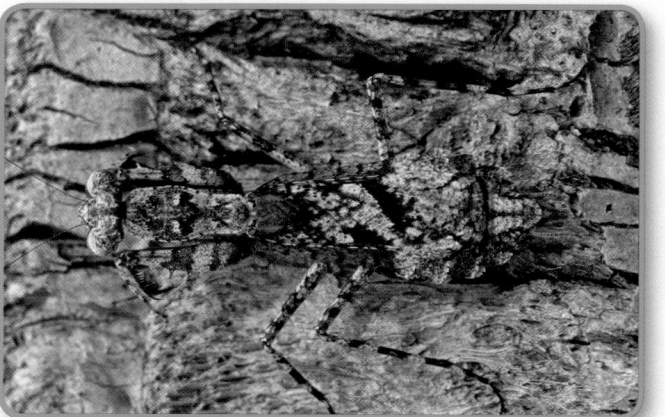

There are about 1,800 kinds of praying mantises. Some are white, pink, or purple. They can hide among beautiful flowers.

13

Eggs in a Case

In the fall, a female praying mantis is ready to lay her eggs.

She makes an **egg case** with white foam from her body.

She lays 100 to 400 eggs in the foam.

The case turns hard and brown and keeps the eggs safe all winter long.

egg case

A female makes several egg cases during the fall. She makes them on plant stems and branches.

Coming Out

When summer comes, tiny baby mantises wiggle out of their egg case.

The babies, called **nymphs**, hang upside down from the case by thin silk threads.

Then they drop to the ground.

egg case

nymphs

nymphs

Praying mantis nymphs are shaped like adults, but they are smaller and have no wings.

Old and New Exoskeletons

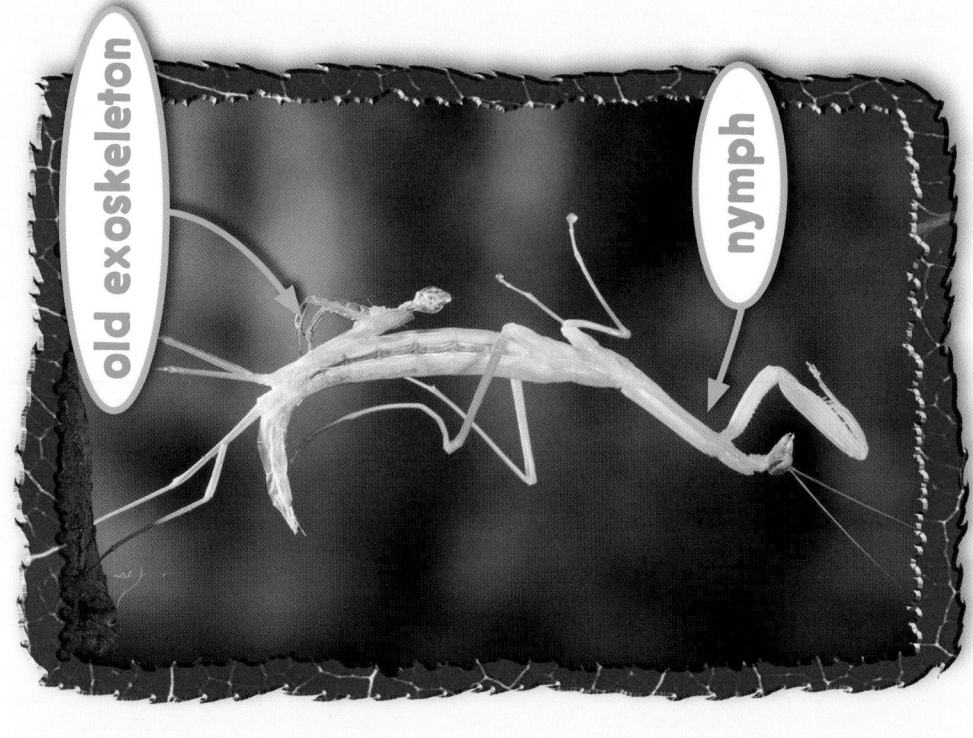

old exoskeleton

nymph

When a nymph comes out of its egg case, it has an exoskeleton.

The hard covering cannot grow, however, and soon becomes too tight.

As the nymph gets bigger, it sheds its old exoskeleton so that a new one can form.

This change is called molting.

After molting six to nine times, a nymph becomes an adult.

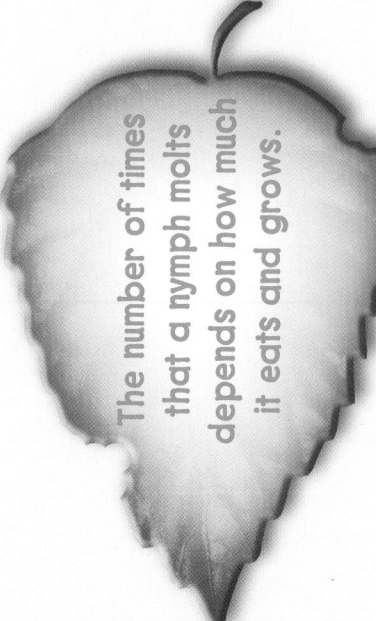

The number of times that a nymph molts depends on how much it eats and grows.

Insects, Beware!

Adult praying mantises are fierce and hungry creatures.

They are always hunting, day and night.

Other insects need to be careful.

They never know when a deadly mantis will strike!

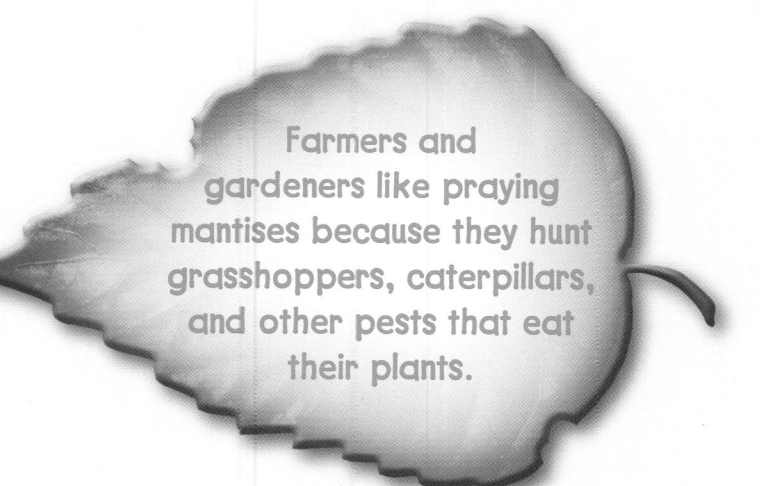

Farmers and gardeners like praying mantises because they hunt grasshoppers, caterpillars, and other pests that eat their plants.

bee

grasshopper

A World of Invertebrates

An animal that has a skeleton with a **backbone** inside its body is a *vertebrate* (VUR-tuh-brit). Mammals, birds, fish, reptiles, and amphibians are all vertebrates.

An animal that does not have a skeleton with a backbone inside its body is an *invertebrate* (in-VUR-tuh-brit). More than 95 percent of all kinds of animals on Earth are invertebrates.

Some invertebrates, such as insects and spiders, have hard skeletons—called exoskeletons—outside their bodies. Other invertebrates, such as worms and jellyfish, have soft, squishy bodies with no exoskeletons to protect them.

Here are four insects that are closely related to praying mantises. Like all insects, they are invertebrates.

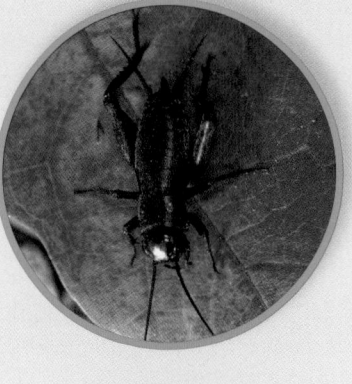
Cricket

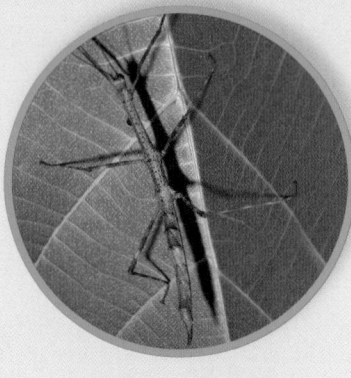
Walkingstick

Cockroach

Grasshopper

Glossary

backbone
(BAK-*bohn*)
a group of
connected bones
that run along
the backs of some
animals, such as
dogs, cats, and fish;
also called a spine

egg case
(EG KAYSS)
the container
that a female
mantis makes to
protect her eggs
until they hatch

insects (IN-sekts)
small animals that
have six legs, three
main body parts,
two antennas, and
a hard covering called
an exoskeleton

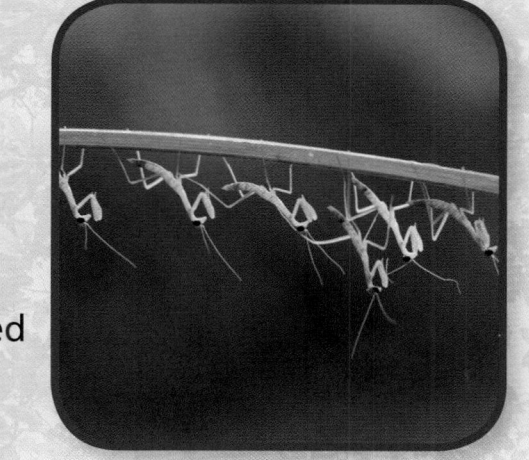

nymphs
(NIMFS) young
insects that
change into adults
by growing and
shedding their
exoskeleton again
and again

Index

antennas 6, 10

backbone 22

cleaning 10–11

cockroach 22

cricket 22

egg case 14–15, 16, 18

eggs 14

enemies 12

exoskeleton 6, 18–19, 22

eyes 10

food 4, 7, 10, 20

grasshoppers 4, 9, 20–21, 22

hiding 12–13

hunting 4, 7, 8, 20

legs 6, 8, 10

life cycle 14–15, 16–17, 18–19

molting 18

nymphs 16–17, 18

walkingstick 22

Read More

Brimner, Larry Dane. *Praying Mantises.* Danbury, CT: Children's Press (1999).

Stefoff, Rebecca. *Praying Mantis.* New York: Benchmark Books (1997).

Stone, Tanya. *Mantises (Wild Wild World).* Farmington Hills, MI: Blackbirch Press (2003).

Learn More Online

To learn more about praying mantises, visit
www.bearportpublishing.com/NoBackbone-Insects

About the Author

Meish Goldish has written more than 100 books
for children. He lives in Brooklyn, New York.